ANTHONY TROLLOPE

GREAT CLASSIC LIBRARY

ANTHONY TROLLOPE

BARCHESTER TOWERS

MISS MACKENZIE

COUSIN HENRY

LONGMEADOW

Barchester Towers was first published in 1857
Miss Mackenzie was first published in 1865
Cousin Henry was first published in 1879

This collected volume published in 1995 by Longmeadow Press,
201 High Ridge Road, Stamford, CT 06904

Cover design by Les Needham
Interior design by Gwyn Lewis
ISBN 0-681-10348-5
Printed in Great Britain
First Longmeadow Press Edition
0 9 8 7 6 5 4 3 2 1

Contents

BARCHESTER TOWERS

ONE

Who will be the New Bishop?

IN THE LATTER DAYS OF JULY in the year 185–, a most important question was for ten days hourly asked in the cathedral city of Barchester, and answered every hour in various ways – Who was to be the new Bishop?

The death of old Dr Grantly, who had for many years filled that chair with meek authority, took place exactly as the ministry of Lord —— was going to give place to that of Lord ——. The illness of the good old man was long and lingering, and it became at last a matter of intense interest to those concerned whether the new appointment should be made by a conservative or liberal government.

It was pretty well understood that the out-going premier had made his selection, and that if the question rested with him, the mitre would descend on the head of Archdeacon Grantly, the old bishop's son. The archdeacon had long managed the affairs of the diocese; and for some months previous to the demise of his father, rumour had confidently assigned to him the reversion of his father's honours.

Bishop Grantly died as he had lived, peaceably, slowly, without pain and without excitement. The breath ebbed from him almost imperceptibly, and for a month before his death, it was a question whether he were alive or dead.

A trying time was this for the archdeacon, for whom was designed the reversion of his father's see by those who then had the giving away of espiscopal thrones. I would not be understood to say that the prime minister had in so many words promised the bishopric to Dr Grantly. He was too discreet a man for that. There is a proverb with reference to the killing of cats, and those who know anything either of high or low government places, will be well aware that a promise may be made without positive words, and that an expectant may be put into the highest state of encouragement, though the great man on whose breath he hangs may have done no more than whisper that 'Mr So-and-so is certainly a rising man.'

Such a whisper had been made, and was known by those who heard it to signify that the cures of the diocese of Barchester should not be taken out of the hands of the archdeacon. The then prime minister was all in all at Oxford, and had lately passed a night at the house of the master of Lazarus. Now the master of Lazarus – which is, by the bye, in many respects the most comfortable, as well as the richest college at Oxford – was the archdeacon's most intimate friend and most trusted counsellor. On the occasion of the prime minister's visit, Dr Grantly was of course present, and the meeting was very gracious. On the following morning

Dr Gwynne, the master, told the archdeacon that in his opinion the thing was settled.

At this time the bishop was quite on his last legs; but the ministry also were tottering. Dr Grantly returned from Oxford happy and elated, to resume his place in the palace, and to continue to perform for the father the last duties of a son; which, to give him his due, he performed with more tender care than was to be expected from his usual somewhat worldly manners.

A month since the physicians had named four weeks as the outside period during which breath could be supported within the body of the dying man. At the end of the month the physicians wondered, and named another fortnight. The old man lived on wine alone, but at the end of the fortnight he still lived; and the tidings of the fall of the ministry became more frequent. Sir Lamda Mewnew and Sir Omicron Pie, the two great London doctors, now came down for the fifth time, and declared, shaking their learned heads, that another week of life was impossible; and as they sat down to lunch in the episcopal dining-room, whispered to the archdeacon their own private knowledge that the ministry must fall within five days. The son returned to his father's room, and after administering with his own hands the sustaining modicum of madeira, sat down by the bedside to calculate his chances.

The ministry were to be out within five days: his father was to be dead within – No, he rejected that view of the subject. The ministry were to be out, and the diocese might probably be vacant at the same period. There was much doubt as to the names of the men who were to succeed to power, and a week must elapse before a Cabinet was formed. Would not vacancies be filled by the out-going men during this week? Dr Grantly had a kind of idea that such would be the case, but did not know; and then he wondered at his own ignorance on such a question.

He tried to keep his mind away from the subject, but he could not. The race was so very close, and the stakes were so very high. He then looked at the dying man's impassive, placid face. There was no sign there of death or disease; it was something thinner than of yore, somewhat grayer, and the deep lines of age more marked; but, as far as he could judge, life might yet hang there for weeks to come. Sir Lamda Mewnew and Sir Omicron Pie had thrice been wrong, and might yet be wrong thrice again. The old bishop slept during twenty of the twenty-four hours, but during the short periods of his waking moments, he knew both his son and his dear old friend, Mr Harding, the archdeacon's father-in-law, and would thank them tenderly for their care and love. Now he lay sleeping like a baby, resting easily on his back, his mouth just open, and his few gray hairs straggling from beneath his cap; his breath was perfectly noiseless, and his thin, wan hand, which lay above the coverlid, never moved. Nothing could be easier than the old man's passage from this world to the next.

But by no means easy were the emotions of him who sat there watching.

He knew it must be now or never. He was already over fifty, and there was little chance that his friends who were now leaving office would soon return to it. No probable British prime minister but he who was now in, he who was so soon to be out, would think of making a bishop of Dr Grantly. Thus he thought long and sadly, in deep silence, and then gazed at that still living face, and then at last dared to ask himself whether he really longed for his father's death.

The effort was a salutary one, and the question was answered in a moment. The proud, wishful, worldly man, sank on his knees by the bedside, and taking the bishop's hand within his own, prayed eagerly that his sins might be forgiven him.

His face was still buried in the clothes when the door of the bed-room opened noiselessly, and Mr Harding entered with a velvet step. Mr Harding's attendance at that bedside had been nearly as constant as that of the archdeacon, and his ingress and egress was as much a matter of course as that of his son-in-law. He was standing close beside the archdeacon before he was perceived, and would also have knelt in prayer had he not feared that his doing so might have caused some sudden start, and have disturbed the dying man. Dr Grantly, however, instantly perceived him, and rose from his knees. As he did so Mr Harding took both his hands, and pressed them warmly. There was more fellowship between them at that moment than there had ever been before, and it so happened that after circumstances greatly preserved the feeling. As they stood there pressing each other's hands, the tears rolled freely down their cheeks.

'God bless you, my dears,' – said the bishop with feeble voice as he woke – 'God bless you – may God bless you both, my dear children:' and so he died.

There was no loud rattle in the throat, no dreadful struggle, no palpable sign of death; but the lower jaw fell a little from its place, and the eyes, which had been so constantly closed in sleep, now remained fixed and open. Neither Mr Harding nor Dr Grantly knew that life was gone, though both suspected it.

'I believe it's all over,' said Mr Harding, still pressing the other's hands. 'I think – nay, I hope it is.'

'I will ring the bell,' said the other, speaking all but in a whisper. 'Mrs Phillips should be here.'

Mrs Phillips, the nurse, was soon in the room, and immediately, with practiced hand, closed those staring eyes.

'It's all over, Mrs Phillips?' asked Mr Harding.

'My lord's no more,' said Mrs Phillips, turning round and curtseying low with solemn face; 'his lordship's gone more like a sleeping babby than any that I ever saw.'

'It's a great relief, archdeacon,' said Mr Harding, 'a great relief – dear, good, excellent old man. Oh that our last moments may be as innocent and as peaceful as his!'

'Surely,' said Mrs Phillips. 'The Lord be praised for all his mercies; but, for a meek, mild, gentle-spoken Christian, his lordship was –' and Mrs Phillips, with unaffected but easy grief, put up her white apron to her flowing eyes.

'You cannot but rejoice that it is over,' said Mr Harding, still consoling his friend. The archdeacon's mind, however, had already travelled from the death chamber to the closet of the prime minister. He had brought himself to pray for his father's life, but now that that life was done, minutes were too precious to be lost. It was now useless to dally with the fact of the bishop's death – useless to lose perhaps everything for the pretence of a foolish sentiment.

But how was he to act while his father-in-law stood there holding his hand? how, without appearing unfeeling, was he to forget his father in the bishop – to overlook what he had lost, and think only of what he might possibly gain?

'No; I suppose not,' said he, at last, in answer to Mr Harding. 'We have all expected it so long.'

Mr Harding took him by the arm and led him from the room. 'We will see him again to-morrow morning,' said he; 'we had better leave the room now to the women.' And so they went down stairs.

It was already evening and nearly dark. It was most important that the prime minister should know that night that the diocese was vacant. Everything might depend on it; and so, in answer to Mr Harding's further consolation, the archdeacon suggested that a telegraph message should be immediately sent off to London. Mr Harding who had really been somewhat surprised to find Dr Grantly, as he thought, so much affected, was rather taken aback; but he made no objection. He knew that the archdeacon had some hope of succeeding to his father's place, though he by no means knew how highly raised that hope had been.

'Yes,' said Dr Grantly, collecting himself and shaking off his weakness, 'we must send a message at once; we don't know what might be the consequence of delay. Will you do it?'

'I! oh yes; certainly: I'll do anything, only I don't know exactly what it is you want.'

Dr Grantly sat down before a writing table, and taking pen and ink, wrote on a slip of paper as follows:–

'By Electric Telegraph.
'For the Earl of ——, Downing Street, or elsewhere.
' "The Bishop of Barchester is dead."
'Message sent by the Rev. Septimus Harding.'

'There,' said he, 'just take that to the telegraph office at the railway station, and give it in as it is; they'll probably make you copy it on to one of their own slips; that's all you'll have to do: then you'll have to pay them half-a-crown;' and the archdeacon put his hand in his pocket and pulled out the necessary sum.

Mr Harding felt very much like an errand-boy, and also felt that he was called on to perform his duties as such at rather an unseemly time; but he said nothing, and took the slip of paper and the proffered coin.

'But you've put my name into it, archdeacon.'

'Yes,' said the other, 'there should be the name of some clergyman you know, and what name so proper as that of so old a friend as yourself? The Earl won't look at the name, you may be sure of that; but my dear Mr Harding, pray don't lose any time.'

Mr Harding got as far as the library door on his way to the station, when he suddenly remembered the news with which he was fraught when he entered the poor bishop's bed-room. He had found the moment so inopportune for any mundane tidings, that he had repressed the words which were on his tongue, and immediately afterwards all recollection of the circumstance was for the time banished by the scene which had occurred.

'But, archdeacon,' said he, turning back, 'I forgot to tell you – The ministry are out.'

'Out!' ejaculated the archdeacon, in a tone which too plainly showed his anxiety and dismay, although under the circumstances of the moment he endeavoured to control himself: 'Out! who told you so?'

Mr Harding explained that news to this effect had come down by electric telegraph, and that the tidings had been left at the palace door by Mr Chadwick.

The archdeacon sat silent for awhile meditating, and Mr Harding stood looking at him. 'Never mind,' said the archdeacon at last; 'send the message all the same. The news must be sent to some one, and there is at present no one else in a position to receive it. Do it at once, my dear friend; you know I would not trouble you, were I in a state to do it myself. A few minutes' time is of the greatest importance.'

Mr Harding went out and sent the message, and it may be as well that we should follow it to its destination. Within thirty minutes of its leaving Barchester it reached the Earl of —— in his inner library. What elaborate letters, what eloquent appeals, what indignant remonstrances, he might there have to frame, at such a moment, may be conceived, but not described! How he was preparing his thunder for successful rivals, standing like a British peer with his back to the sea-coal fire, and his hands in his breeches pockets – how his fine eye was lit up with anger, and his forehead gleamed with patriotism – how he stamped his foot as he thought of his heavy associates – how he all but swore as he remembered how much too clever one of them had been – my creative readers may imagine. But was he so engaged? No: history and truth compel me to deny it. He was sitting easily in a lounging chair, conning over a Newmarket list, and by his elbow on the table was lying open an uncut French novel on which he was engaged.

He opened the cover in which the message was enclosed, and having read it, he took his pen and wrote on the back of it –

> 'For the Earl of ——,
> 'With the Earl of ——'s compliments,'

and sent it off again on its journey.

Thus terminated our unfortunate friend's chance of possessing the glories of a bishopric.

The names of many divines were given in the papers as that of the bishop elect. 'The British Grandmother' declared that Dr Gwynne was to be the man, in compliment to the late ministry. This was a heavy blow to Dr Grantly, but he was not doomed to see himself superseded by his friend. 'The Anglican Devotee' put forward confidently the claims of a great London preacher of austere doctrines; and 'The Eastern Hemisphere,' an evening paper supposed to possess much official knowledge, declared in favour of an eminent naturalist, a gentleman most completely versed in the knowledge of rocks and minerals, but supposed by many to hold on religious subjects no special doctrines whatever. 'The Jupiter,' that daily paper, which, as we all know, is the only true source of infallibly correct information on all subjects, for a while was silent, but at last spoke out. The merits of all these candidates were discussed and somewhat irreverently disposed of, and then 'The Jupiter' declared that Dr Proudie was to be the man.

Dr Proudie was the man. Just a month after the demise of the late bishop, Dr Proudie kissed the Queen's hand as his successor elect.

We must beg to be allowed to draw a curtain over the sorrows of the archdeacon as he sat, sombre and sad at heart, in the study of his parsonage at Plumstead Episcopi. On the day subsequent to the despatch of the message he heard that the Earl of —— had consented to undertake the formation of a ministry, and from that moment he knew that his chance was over. Many will think that he was wicked to grieve for the loss of episcopal power, wicked to have coveted it, nay, wicked even to have thought about it, in the way and at the moments he had done so.

With such censures I cannot profess that I completely agree. The *nolo episcopari*, though still in use, is so directly at variance with the tendency of all human wishes, that it cannot be thought to express the true aspirations of rising priests in the Church of England. A lawyer does not sin in seeking to be a judge, or in compassing his wishes by all honest means. A young diplomate entertains a fair ambition when he looks forward to be the lord of a first-rate embassy; and a poor novelist when he attempts to rival Dickens or rise above Fitzjeames, commits no fault, though he may be foolish. Sydney Smith truly said that in these recreant days we cannot expect to find the majesty of St Paul beneath the cassock of a curate. If we look to our clergymen to be more than men, we shall probably teach ourselves to think that they are less, and can hardly hope to raise the character of the pastor by denying to him the right to entertain the aspirations of a man.

Our archdeacon was worldly – who among us is not so? He was ambitious – who among us is ashamed to own that 'last infirmity of noble minds!' He was avaricious, my readers will say. 'No – it was for no love of lucre that he wished to be bishop of Barchester. He was his father's only child, and his father had left him great wealth. His preferment brought him in nearly three thousand a year. The bishopric, as cut down by the Ecclesiastical Commission, was only five. He would be a richer man as archdeacon than he could be as bishop. But he certainly did desire to play first fiddle; he did desire to sit in full lawn sleeves among the peers of the realm; and he did desire, if the truth must out, to be called 'My Lord' by his reverend brethren.

His hopes, however, were they innocent or sinful, were not fated to be realistic; and Dr Proudie was consecrated Bishop of Barchester.

※ TWO ※

Hiram's Hospital according to Act of Parliament

IT IS HARDLY NECESSARY THAT I SHOULD here give to the public any lengthened biography of Mr Harding, up to the period of the commencement of this tale. The public cannot have forgotten how ill that sensitive gentleman bore the attack that was made on him in the columns of the Jupiter, with reference to the income which he received as warden of Hiram's Hospital, in the city of Barchester. Nor can it yet be forgotten that a law-suit was instituted against him on the matter of that charity by Mr John Bold, who afterwards married his, Mr Harding's, younger and then only unmarried daughter. Under pressure of these attacks, Mr Harding had resigned his wardenship, though strongly recommended to abstain from doing so, both by his friends and by his lawyers. He did, however, resign it, and betook himself manfully to the duties of the small parish of St Cuthbert's, in the city, of which he was vicar, continuing also to perform those of precentor of the cathedral, a situation of small emolument which had hitherto been supposed to be joined, as a matter of course, to the wardenship of the Hospital above spoken of.

When he left the hospital from which he had been so ruthlessly driven, and settled himself down in his own modest manner in the High Street of Barchester, he had not expected that others would make more fuss about it than he was inclined to do himself; and the extent of his hope was, that the movement might have been made in time to prevent any further paragraphs in the Jupiter. His affairs, however, were not allowed to subside thus quietly, and people were quite as much inclined to talk about the disinterested sacrifice he had made, as they had before been to upbraid him for his cupidity.

The most remarkable thing that occurred, was the receipt of an autograph letter from the Archbishop of Canterbury, in which the primate very warmly praised his conduct, and begged to know what his intentions were for the future. Mr Harding replied that he intended to be rector of St Cuthbert's, in Barchester: and so that matter dropped. Then the newspapers took up his case, the Jupiter among the rest, and wafted his name in eulogistic strains through every reading-room in the nation. It was discovered also, that he was the author of that great musical work, Harding's Church music, – and a new edition was spoken of, though, I believe, never printed. It is, however, certain that the work was introduced into the Royal Chapel at St James's, and that a long criticism appeared in the Musical Scrutator, declaring that in no previous work of the kind had so much research been joined with such exalted musical ability, and asserting that the name of Harding would henceforward be known wherever the Arts were cultivated, or Religion valued.

This was high praise, and I will not deny that Mr Harding was gratified by such flattery; for if Mr Harding was vain on any subject, it was on that of music. But here the matter rested. The second edition, if printed, was never purchased; the copies which had been introduced into the Royal Chapel disappeared again, and were laid by in peace, with a load of similar literature. Mr Towers, of the Jupiter, and his brethren, occupied themselves with other names, and the undying fame promised to our friend was clearly intended to be posthumous.

Mr Harding had spent much of his time with his friend the bishop, much with his daughter Mrs Bold, now, alas, a widow; and had almost daily visited the wretched remnant of his former subjects, the few surviving bedesmen now left at Hiram's Hospital. Six of them were still living. The number, according to old Hiram's will, should always have been twelve. But after the abdication of their warden, the bishop had appointed no successor to him, no new occupants of the charity had been nominated, and it appeared as though the hospital at Barchester would fall into abeyance, unless the powers that be should take some steps towards putting it once more into working order.

During the past five years, the powers that be had not overlooked Barchester Hospital, and sundry political doctors had taken the matter in hand. Shortly after Mr Harding's resignation, the Jupiter had very clearly shown what ought to be done. In about half a column it had distributed the income, rebuilt the building, put an end to all bickerings, regenerated kindly feeling, provided for Mr Harding, and placed the whole thing on a footing which could not but be satisfactory to the city and Bishop of Barchester, and to the nation at large. The wisdom of this scheme was testified by the number of letters which 'Common Sense,' 'Veritas,' and 'One that loves fair play' sent to the Jupiter, all expressing admiration, and amplifying on the details given. It is singular enough that no adverse letter appeared at all, and, therefore, none of course was written.

But Cassandra was not believed, and even the wisdom of the Jupiter sometimes falls on deaf ears. Though other plans did not put themselves forward in the columns of the Jupiter, reformers of church charities were not slack to make known in various places their different nostrums for setting Hiram's Hospital on its feet again. A learned bishop took occasion, in the Upper House, to allude to the matter, intimating that he had communicated on the subject with his right reverend brother of Barchester. The radical member for Staleybridge had suggested that the funds should be alienated for the education of the agricultural poor of the country, and he amused the house by some anecdotes touching the superstition and habits of the agriculturists in question. A political pamphleteer had produced a few dozen pages, which he called 'Who are John Hiram's heirs?' intending to give an infallible rule for the governance of all such establishments; and, at last, a member of the government promised that in the next session a short bill should be introduced for regulating the affairs of Barchester, and other kindred concerns.

The next session came, and, contrary to custom, the bill came also. Men's minds were then intent on other things. The first threatenings of a huge war hung heavily over the nation, and the question as to Hiram's heirs did not appear to interest very many people either in or out of the house. The bill, however, was read and re-read, and in some undistinguished manner passed through its eleven stages without appeal or dissent. What would John Hiram have said in the matter, could he have predicted that some forty-five gentlemen would take on themselves to make a law altering the whole purport of his will, without in the least knowing at the moment of their making it, what it was that they were doing? It is however to be hoped that the under-secretary for the Home Office knew, for to him had the matter been confided.

The bill, however, did pass, and at the time at which this history is supposed to commence, it had been ordained that there should be, as heretofore, twelve old men in Barchester Hospital, each with 1s. 4d. a day; that there should also be twelve old women to be located in a house to be built, each with 1s. 2d. a day; that there should be a matron, with a house and 70l. a year; a steward with 150l. a year; and latterly, a warden with 450l. a year, who should have the spiritual guidance of both establishments, and the temporal guidance of that appertaining to the male sex. The bishop, dean, and warden were, as formerly, to appoint in turn the recipients of the charity, and the bishop was to appoint the officers. There was nothing said as to the wardenship being held by the precentor of the cathedral, nor a word as to Mr Harding's right to the situation.

It was not, however, till some months after the death of the old bishop, and almost immediately consequent on the installation of his successor, that notice was given that the reform was about to be carried out. The new law and the new bishop were among the earliest works of a new ministry, or rather of a ministry who, having for a while given place to their opponents, had then returned to power; and the death of Dr Grantly occurred, as we have seen, exactly at the period of the change.

Poor Eleanor Bold! How well does that widow's cap become her, and the solemn gravity with which she devotes herself to her new duties. Poor Eleanor!

Poor Eleanor! I cannot say that with me John Bold was ever a favorite. I never thought him worthy of the wife he had won. But in her estimation he was most worthy. Hers was one of those feminine hearts which cling to a husband, not with idolatry, for worship can admit of no defect in its idol, but with the perfect tenacity of ivy. As the parasite plant will follow even the defects of the trunk which it embraces, so did Eleanor cling to and love the very faults of her husband. She had once declared that whatever her father did should in her eyes be right. She then transferred her allegiance, and became ever ready to defend the worst failings of her lord and master.

And John Bold was a man to be loved by a woman; he was himself affectionate, he was confiding and manly; and that arrogance of thought, unsustained by first-rate abilities, that attempt at being better than his neighbours which jarred so painfully on the feelings of his acquaintance, did not injure him in the estimation of his wife.

Could she even have admitted that he had a fault, his early death would have blotted out the memory of it. She wept as for the loss of the most perfect treasure with which mortal woman had ever been endowed; for weeks after he was gone the idea of future happiness in this world was hateful to her; consolation, as it is called, was insupportable, and tears and sleep were her only relief.

But God tempers the wind to the shorn lamb. She knew that she had within her the living source of other cares. She knew that there was to be created for her another subject of weal or woe, of unutterable joy or despairing sorrow, as God in his mercy might vouchsafe to her. At first this did but augment her grief! To be the mother of a poor infant, orphaned before it was born, brought forth to the sorrows of an ever desolate hearth, nurtured amidst tears and wailing, and then turned adrift into the world without the aid of a father's care! There was at first no joy in this.

By degrees, however, her heart became anxious for another object, and, before its birth, the stranger was expected with all the eagerness of a longing mother. Just eight months after the father's death a second John Bold was born, and if the worship of one creature can be innocent in another, let us hope that the adoration offered over the cradle of the fatherless infant may not be imputed as a sin.

It will not be worth our while to define the character of the child, or to

10

point out in how far the faults of the father were redeemed within that little breast by the virtues of the mother. The baby, as a baby, was all that was delightful, and I cannot foresee that it will be necessary for us to inquire into the facts of his after life. Our present business at Barchester will not occupy us above a year or two at the furthest, and I will leave it to some other pen to produce, if necessary, the biography of John Bold the Younger.

But, as a baby, this baby was all that could be desired. This fact no one attempted to deny. 'Is he not delightful?' she would say to her father, looking up into his face from her knees, her lustrous eyes overflowing with soft tears, her young face encircled by her close widow's cap and her hands on each side of the cradle in which her treasure was sleeping. The grandfather would gladly admit that the treasure was delightful, and the uncle archdeacon himself would agree, and Mrs Grantly, Eleanor's sister, would re-echo the word with true sisterly energy; and Mary Bold – but Mary Bold was a second worshipper at the same shrine.

The baby was really delightful; he took his food with a will, struck out his toes merrily whenever his legs were uncovered, and did not have fits. These are supposed to be the strongest points of baby perfection, and in all these our baby excelled.

And thus the widow's deep grief was softened, and a sweet balm was poured into the wound which she had thought nothing but death could heal. How much kinder is God to us than we are willing to be to ourselves! At the loss of every dear face, at the last going of every well beloved one, we all doom ourselves to an eternity of sorrow, and look to waste ourselves away in an ever-running fountain of tears. How seldom does such grief endure! how blessed is the goodness which forbids it to do so! 'Let me ever remember my living friends, but forget them as soon as dead,' was the prayer of a wise man who understood the mercy of God. Few perhaps would have the courage to express such a wish, and yet to do so would only be to ask for that release from sorrow, which a kind Creator almost always extends to us.

I would not, however, have it imagined that Mrs Bold forgot her husband. She daily thought of him with all conjugal love, and enshrined his memory in the innermost centre of her heart. But yet she was happy in her baby. It was so sweet to press the living toy to her breast, and feel that a human being existed who did owe, and was to owe everything to her; whose daily food was drawn from herself; whose little wants could all be satisfied by her; whose little heart would first love her and her only; whose infant tongue would make its first effort in calling her by the sweetest name a woman can hear. And so Eleanor's bosom became tranquil, and she set about her new duties eagerly and gratefully.

As regards the concerns of the world, John Bold had left his widow in prosperous circumstances. He had bequeathed to her all that he possessed, and that comprised an income much exceeding what she or her friends

11

thought necessary for her. It amounted to nearly a thousand a year; and when she reflected on its extent, her dearest hope was to hand it over, not only unimpaired but increased, to her husband's son, to her own darling, to the little man who now lay sleeping on her knee, happily ignorant of the cares which were to be accumulated in his behalf.

When John Bold died she earnestly implored her father to come and live with her, but this Mr Harding declined, though for some weeks he remained with her as a visitor. He could not be prevailed upon to forego the possession of some small home of his own, and so remained in the lodgings he had first selected over a chemist's shop in the High Street of Barchester.

✂ THREE ✂

Dr and Mrs Proudie

THIS NARRATIVE IS SUPPOSED TO COMMENCE IMMEDIATELY after the installation of Dr Proudie. I will not describe the ceremony, as I do not precisely understand its nature. I am ignorant whether a bishop be chaired like a member of parliament, or carried in a gilt coach like a lord mayor, or sworn in like a justice of peace, or introduced like a peer to the upper house, or led between two brethren like a knight of the garter; but I do know that everything was properly done, and that nothing fit or becoming to a young bishop was omitted on the occasion.

Dr Proudie was not the man to allow anything to be omitted that might be becoming to his new dignity. He understood well the value of forms, and knew that the due observance of rank could not be maintained unless the exterior trappings belonging to it were held in proper esteem. He was a man born to move in high circles; at least so he thought himself, and circumstances had certainly sustained him in this view. He was the nephew of an Irish baron by his mother's side, and his wife was the niece of a Scotch earl. He had for years held some clerical office appertaining to courtly matters, which had enabled him to live in London, and to entrust his parish to his curate. He had been preacher to the royal beefeaters, curator of theological manuscripts in the Ecclesiastical Courts, chaplain to the Queen's yeomanry guard, and almoner to his Royal Highness the Prince of Rappe-Blankenburg.

His residence in the metropolis, rendered necessary by the duties thus entrusted to him, his high connections, and the peculiar talents and nature of the man, recommended him to persons in power; and Dr Proudie became known as a useful and rising clergyman.

Some few years since, even within the memory of many who are not yet willing to call themselves old, a liberal clergyman was a person not frequently to be met. Sydney Smith was such, and was looked on as little better than an infidel: a few others also might be named, but they were 'raræ aves,' and were regarded with doubt and distrust by their brethren. No man was so surely a tory as a country rector – nowhere were the powers that be so cherished as at Oxford.

When, however, Dr Whately was made an archbishop, and Dr Hampden some years afterwards regius professor, many wise divines saw that a change was taking place in men's minds, and that more liberal ideas would henceforward be suitable to the priests as well as to the laity. Clergymen began to be heard of who had ceased to anathematise papists on the one hand, or vilify dissenters on the other. It appeared clear that high church principles, as they are called, were no longer to be surest claims to promotion with at any rate one section of statesmen, and Dr Proudie was one among those who early in life adapted himself to the views held by the whigs on most theological and religious subjects. He bore with the idolatry of Rome, tolerated even the infidelity of Socinianism, and was hand and glove with the Presbyterian Synods of Scotland and Ulster.

Such a man at such a time was found to be useful, and Dr Proudie's name began to appear in the newpapers. He was made one of a commission who went over to Ireland to arrange matters preparative to the working of the national board; he became honorary secretary to another commission nominated to inquire into the revenues of cathedral chapters; and had had something to do with both the regium donum and the Maynooth grant.

It must not on this account be taken as proved that Dr Proudie was a man of great mental powers, or even of much capacity for business, for such qualities had not been required in him. In the arrangement of those church reforms with which he was connected, the ideas and original conception of the work to be done were generally furnished by the liberal statesmen of the day, and the labour of the details was borne by officials of a lower rank. It was, however, thought expedient that the name of some clergyman should appear in such matters, and as Dr Proudie had become known as a tolerating divine, great use of this sort was made of his name. If he did not do much active good, he never did any harm; he was amenable to those who were really in authority, and at the sittings of the various boards to which he belonged maintained a kind of dignity which had its value.

He was certainly possessed of sufficient tact to answer the purpose for which he was required without making himself troublesome; but it must not therefore be surmised that he doubted his own power, or failed to believe that he could himself take a high part in high affairs when his own turn came. He was biding his time, and patiently looking forward to the days when he himself would sit authoritative at some board, and talk and direct, and rule the roost, while lesser stars sat round and obeyed, as he had so well accustomed himself to do.

His reward and his time had now come. He was selected for the vacant bishopric, and on the next vacancy which might occur in any diocese would take his place in the House of Lords, prepared to give not a silent vote in all matters concerning the weal of the church establishment. Toleration was to be the basis on which he was to fight his battles, and in the honest courage of his heart he thought no evil would come to him in encountering even such foes as his brethren of Exeter and Oxford.

Dr Proudie was an ambitious man, and before he was well consecrated Bishop of Barchester, he had begun to look up to archiepiscopal splendour, and the glories of Lambeth, or at any rate of Bishopsthorpe. He was comparatively young, and had, as he fondly flattered himself, been selected as possessing such gifts, natural and acquired, as must be sure to recommend him to a yet higher notice, now that a higher sphere was opened to him. Dr Proudie was, therefore, quite prepared to take a conspicuous part in all theological affairs appertaining to these realms: and having such views, by no means intended to bury himself at Barchester as his predecessor had done. No: London should still be his ground: a comfortable mansion in a provincial city might be well enough for the dead months of the year. Indeed Dr Proudie had always felt it necessary to his position to retire from London when other great and fashionable people did so; but London should still be his fixed residence, and it was in London that he resolved to exercise that hospitality so peculiarly recommended to all bishops by St Paul. How otherwise could he keep himself before the world? how else give to the government, in matters theological, the full benefit of his weight and talents?

This resolution was no doubts a salutary one as regarded the world at large, but was not likely to make him popular either with the clergy or people of Barchester. Dr Grantly had always lived there; and in truth it was hard for a bishop to be popular after Dr Grantly. His income had averaged 9000*l.* a year; his successor was to be rigidly limited to 5000*l.* He had but one child on whom to spend his money; Dr Proudie had seven or eight. He had been a man of few personal expenses, and they had been confined to the tastes of a moderate gentleman; but Dr Proudie had to maintain a position in fashionable society, and had that to do with comparatively small means. Dr Grantly had certainly kept his carriage, as became a bishop; but his carriage, horses, and coachman, though they did very well for Barchester, would have been almost ridiculous at Westminster. Dr Proudie determined that her husband's equipage should not shame her, and things on which Mrs Proudie resolved, were generally accomplished.

From all this it was likely to result that Dr Proudie would not spend much money at Barchester; whereas his predecessor had dealt with the tradesmen of the city in a manner very much to their satisfaction. The Grantlys, father and son, had spent their money like gentlemen; but it soon became whispered in Barchester that Dr Proudie was not unacquainted with those prudent devices by which the utmost show of wealth is produced from limited means.

In person Dr Proudie is a good-looking man; spruce and dapper, and very tidy. He is somewhat below middle height, being about five feet four; but he makes up for the inches which he wants by the dignity with which he carries those which he has. It is no fault of his own if he has not a commanding eye, for he studies hard to assume it. His features are well formed, though perhaps the sharpness of his nose may give to his face in the eyes of some people an air of insignificance. If so, it is greatly redeemed by his mouth and chin, of which he is justly proud.

Dr Proudie may well be said to have been a fortunate man, for he was not born to wealth, and he is now bishop of Barchester; but nevertheless he has his cares. He has a large family, of whom the three eldest are daughters, now all grown up and fit for fashionable life; and he has a wife. It is not my intention to breathe a word against the character of Mrs Proudie, but still I cannot think that with all her virtues she adds much to her husband's happiness. The truth is that in matters domestic she rules supreme over her titular lord, and rules with a rod of iron. Nor is this all. Things domestic Dr Proudie might have abandoned to her, if not voluntarily, yet willingly. But Mrs Proudie is not satisfied with such home dominion, and stretches her power over all his movements, and will not even abstain from things spiritual. In fact, the bishop is henpecked.

The archdeacon's wife, in her happy home at Plumstead, knows how to assume the full privileges of her rank, and express her own mind in becoming tone and place. But Mrs Grantly's sway, if sway she has, is easy and beneficent. She never shames her husband; before the world she is a pattern of obedience; her voice is never loud, nor her looks sharp; doubtless she values power, and has not unsuccessfully striven to acquire it; but she knows what should be the limits of a woman's rule.

Not so Mrs Proudie. This lady is habitually authoritative to all, but to her poor husband she is despotic. Successful as has been his career in the eyes of the world, it would seem that in the eyes of his wife he is never right. All hope of defending himself has long passed from him; indeed he rarely even attempts self-justification; and is aware that submission produces the nearest approach to peace which his own house can ever attain.

Mrs Proudie has not been able to sit at the boards and committees to which her husband has been called by the state; nor, as he often reflects, can she make her voice heard in the House of Lords. It may be that she will refuse to him permission to attend to this branch of a bishop's duties; it may be that she will insist on his close attendance to his own closet. He has never whispered a word on the subject to living ears, but he has already made his fixed resolve. Should such an attempt be made he will rebel. Dogs have turned against their masters, and even Neapolitans against their rulers, when oppression has been too severe. And Dr Proudie feels within himself that if the cord be drawn too tight, he also can muster courage and resist.

The state of vassalage in which our bishop has been kept by his wife has not tended to exalt his character in the eyes of his daughters, who assume in addressing their father too much of that authority which is not properly belonging, at any rate, to them. They are, on the whole, fine engaging young ladies. They are tall and robust like their mother, whose high cheekbones, and – we may say auburn hair, they all inherit. They think somewhat too much of their grand uncles, who have not hitherto returned the compliment by thinking much of them. But now that their father is a bishop, it is probable that family ties will be drawn closer. Considering their connection with the church, they entertain but few prejudices against the pleasures of the world; and have certainly not distressed their parents, as too many English girls have lately done, by any enthusiastic wish to devote themselves to the seclusion of a protestant nunnery. Dr Proudie's sons are still at school.

One other marked peculiarity in the character of the bishop's wife must be mentioned. Though not averse to the society and manners of the world, she is in her own way a religious woman; and the form in which this tendency shows itself in her is by a strict observance of Sabbatarian rule. Dissipation and low dresses during the week are, under her control, attoned for by three services, an evening sermon read by herself, and a perfect abstinence from any cheering employment on the Sunday. Unfortunately for those under her roof to whom the dissipation and low dresses are not extended, her servants namely and her husband, the compensating strictness of the Sabbath includes all. Woe betide the recreant housemaid who is found to have been listening to the honey of a sweetheart in the Regent's park, instead of the soul-stirring evening discourse of Mr Slope. Not only is she sent adrift, but she is so sent with a character which leaves her little hope of a decent place. Woe betide the six-foot hero who escorts Mrs Proudie to her pew in red plush breeches, if he slips away to the neighbouring beer-shop, instead of falling into the back seat appropriated to his use. Mrs Proudie has the eyes of Argus for such offenders. Occasional drunkenness in the week may be overlooked, for six feet on low wages are hardly to be procured if the morals are always kept at a high pitch; but not even for grandeur or economy will Mrs Proudie forgive a desecration of the Sabbath.

In such matters Mrs Proudie allows herself to be often guided by their eloquent preacher, the Rev. Mr Slope, and as Dr Proudie is guided by his wife, it necessarily follows that the eminent man we have named has obtained a good deal of control over Dr Proudie in matters concerning religion. Mr Slope's only preferment has hitherto been that of reader and preacher in a London district church: and on the consecration of his friend the new bishop, he readily gave this up to undertake the onerous but congenial duties of domestic chaplain to his lordship.

Mr Slope, however, on his first introduction must not be brought before the public at the tail of a chapter.

✂ FOUR ✂

The Bishop's Chaplain

OF THE REV. MR SLOPE'S PERSONAGE I am not able to say much. I have heard it asserted that he is lineally descended from that eminent physician who assisted at the birth of Mr T. Shandy, and that in early years he added an 'e' to his name, for the sake of euphony, as other great men have done before him. If this be so, I presume he was christened Obadiah, for that is his name, in commemoration of the conflict in which his ancestor so distinguished himself. All my researches on the subject have, however, failed in enabling me to fix the date on which the family changed its religion.

He had been a sizar at Cambridge, and had there conducted himself at any rate successfully, for in due process of time he was an M.A., having university pupils under his care. From thence he was transferred to London, and became preacher at a new district church built on the confines of Baker Street. He was in this position when congenial ideas on religious subjects recommended him to Mrs Proudie, and the intercourse had become close and confidential.

Having been thus familiarly thrown among the Misses Proudie, it was no more than natural that some softer feeling than friendship should be engendered. There have been some passages of love between him and the eldest hope, Olivia; but they have hitherto resulted in no favourable arrangement. In truth, Mr Slope having made a declaration of affection, afterwards withdrew it on finding that the doctor had no immediate worldly funds with which to endow his child; and it may easily be conceived that Miss Proudie, after such an announcement on his part, was not readily disposed to receive any further show of affection. On the appointment of Dr Proudie to the bishopric of Barchester, Mr Slope's views were in truth somewhat altered. Bishops, even though they be poor, can provide for clerical children, and Mr Slope began to regret that he had not been more disinterested. He no sooner heard the tidings of the doctor's elevation, than he recommenced his siege, not violently, indeed, but respectfully, and at a distance. Olivia Proudie, however, was a girl of spirit: she had the blood of two peers in her veins, and, better still, she had another lover on her books; so Mr Slope sighed in vain; and the pair soon found it convenient to establish a mutual bond of inveterate hatred.

It may be thought singular that Mrs Proudie's friendship for the young clergyman should remain firm after such an affair; but, to tell the truth, she had known nothing of it. Though very fond of Mr Slope herself, she had never conceived the idea that either of her daughters would become so, and remembering their high birth and social advantages, expected for

17

them matches of a different sort. Neither the gentleman nor the lady found it necessary to enlighten her. Olivia's two sisters had each known of the affair, so had all the servants, so had all the people living in the adjoining houses on either side; but Mrs Proudie had been kept in the dark.

Mr Slope soon comforted himself with the reflection, that as he had been selected as chaplain to the bishop, it would probably be in his power to get the good things in the bishop's gift, without troubling himself with the bishop's daughter; and he found himself able to endure the pangs of rejected love. As he sat himself down in the railway carriage, confronting the bishop and Mrs Proudie, as they started on their first journey to Barchester, he began to form in his own mind a plan of his future life. He knew well his patron's strong points, but he knew the weak ones as well. He understood correctly enough to what attempts the new bishop's high spirit would soar, and he rightly guessed that public life would better suit the great man's taste, than the small details of diocesan duty.

He, therefore, he, Mr Slope, would in effect be bishop of Barchester. Such was his resolve; and to give Mr Slope his due, he had both courage and spirit to bear him out in his resolution. He knew that he should have a hard battle to fight, for the power and patronage of the see would be equally coveted by another great mind – Mrs Proudie would also choose to be bishop of Barchester. Mr Slope, however, flattered himself that he could out-manoœvre the lady. She must live much in London, while he would always be on the spot. She would necessarily remain ignorant of much, while he would know everything belonging to the diocese. At first, doubtless, he must flatter and cajole, perhaps yield, in some things; but he did not doubt of ultimate triumph. If all other means failed, he could join the bishop against his wife, inspire courage into the unhappy man, lay an axe to the root of the woman's power, and emancipate the husband.

Such were his thoughts as he sat looking at the sleeping pair in the railway carriage, and Mr Slope is not the man to trouble himself with such thoughts for nothing. He is possessed of more than average abilities, and is of good courage. Though he can stoop to fawn, and stoop low indeed, if need be, he has still within him the power to assume the tyrant; and with the power he has certainly the wish. His acquirements are not of the highest order, but such as they are they are completely under control, and he knows the use of them. He is gifted with a certain kind of pulpit eloquence, not likely indeed to be persuasive with men, but powerful with the softer sex. In hi sermons he deals greatly in denunciations, excites the minds of his weaker hearers with a not unpleasant terror, and leaves an impression on their minds that all mankind are in a perilous state, and all womankind too, except those who attend regularly to the evening lectures in Baker Street. His looks and tones are extremely severe, so much so that one cannot but fancy that he regards the greater part of the world as being infinitely too bad for his care. As he walks through the streets, his very face denotes his horror of the world's wickedness; and there is always an anathema lurking in the corner of his eye.

In doctrine, he, like his patron, is tolerant of dissent, if so strict a mind can be called tolerant of anything. With Wesleyan-Methodists he has something in common, but his soul trembles in agony at the iniquities of the Puseyites. His aversion is carried to things outward as well as inward. His gall rises at a new church with a high pitched roof; and full-breasted black silk waistcoat is with him a symbol of Satan; and a profane jest-book would not, in his view, more foully desecrate the church seat of a Christian, than a book of prayer printed with red letters, and ornamented with a cross on the back. Most active clergymen have their hobby, and Sunday observances are his. Sunday, however, is a word which never pollutes his mouth – it is always 'the Sabbath.' The 'desecration of the Sabbath,' as he delights to call it, is to him meat and drink – he thrives upon that as policemen do on the general evil habits of the community. It is the loved subject of all his evening discourses, the source of all his eloquence, the secret of all his power over the female heart. To him the revelation of God appears only in that one law given for Jewish observance. To him the mercies of our Saviour speak in vain, to him in vain has been preached that sermon which fell from divine lips on the mountain – 'Blessed are the meek, for they shall inherit the earth' – 'Blessed are the merciful, for they shall obtain mercy.' To him the New Testament is comparatively of little moment, for from it can he draw no fresh authority for that dominion which he loves to exercise over at least a seventh part of man's allotted time here below.

Mr Slope is tall, and not ill made. His feet and hands are large, as has ever been the case with all his family, but he has a broad chest and wide shoulders to carry off these excrescences, and on the whole his figure is good. His countenance, however, is not specially prepossessing. His hair is lank, and of a dull pale reddish hue. It is always formed into three straight lumpy masses, each brushed with admirable precision, and cemented with much grease; two of them adhere closely to the sides of his face, and the other lies at right angles above them. He wears no whiskers, and is always punctiliously shaven. His face is nearly of the same colour as his hair, though perhaps a little redder: it is not unlike beef – beef, however, one would say, of a bad quality. His forehead is capacious and high, but square and heavy, and unpleasantly shining. His mouth is large, though his lips are thin and bloodless; and his big, prominent, pale brown eyes inspire anything but confidence. His nose, however, is his redeeming feature: it is pronounced straight and well-formed; though I myself should have liked it better did it not possess a somewhat spongy, porous appearance, as though it had been cleverly formed out of a red coloured cork.

I never could endure to shake hands with Mr Slope. A cold, clammy perspiration always exudes from him, the small drops are ever to be seen standing on his brow, and his friendly grasp is unpleasant.

Such is Mr Slope – such is the man who has suddenly fallen into the midst of Barchester Close, and is destined there to assume the station which has heretofore been filled by the son of the late bishop. Think, oh, my meditative reader, what an associate we have here for those comfortable prebendaries, those gentlemanlike clerical doctors, those happy well-used well-fed minor canons, who have grown into existence at Barchester under the kindly wings of Bishop Grantly!

But not as a mere associate for these does Mr Slope travel down to Barchester with the bishop and his wife. He intends to be, if not their master, at least the chief among them. He intends to lead, and to have followers; he intends to hold the purse strings of the diocese, and draw round him an obedient herd of his poor and hungry brethren.

And here we can hardly fail to draw a comparison between the archdeacon and our new private chaplain; and despite the manifold faults of the former, one can hardly fail to make it much to his advantage.

Both men are eager, much too eager, to support and increase the power of their order. Both are anxious that the world should be priest-governed, though they have probably never confessed so much, even to themselves. Both begrudge any other kind of dominion held by man over man. Dr Grantly, if he admits the Queen's supremacy in things spiritual, only admits it as being due to the *quasi* priesthood conveyed in the consecrating qualities of her coronation; and he regards things temporal as being by their nature subject to those which are spiritual. Mr Slope's ideas of sacerdotal rule are of quite a different class. He cares nothing, one way or the other, for the Queen's supremacy; these to his ears are empty words, meaning nothing. Forms he regards but little, and such titular expressions as supremacy, consecration, ordination, and the like, convey of themselves no significance to him. Let him be supreme who can. The temporal king, judge, or gaoler, can work but on the body. The spiritual master, if he have the necessary gifts, and can duly use them, has a wider field of empire. He works upon the soul. If he can make himself he believed, he can be all powerful over those who listen. If he be careful to meddle with none who are too strong in intellect, or too weak in flesh, he may indeed be supreme. And such was the ambition of Mr Slope.

Dr Grantly interfered very little with the worldly doings of those who were in any way subject to him. I do not mean to say that he omitted to notice misconduct among his clergy, immortality in his parish, or omissions in his family; but he was not anxious to do so where the necessity could be avoided. He was not troubled with a propensity to be curious, and as long as those around him were tainted with no heretical leaning towards dissent, as long as they fully and freely admitted the efficacy of Mother church, he was willing that that mother should be merciful and affectionate, prone to indulgence, and unwilling to chastise. He himself enjoyed the good things of this world, and liked to let it be known that he did so. He cordially despised any brother rector who thought harm of dinner-parties, or dreaded the dangers of a moderate claret-jug; consequently dinner-parties and claret-jugs were common in the diocese. He liked to give laws and to be obeyed in them implicitly, but he endeavoured that his ordinance should be within the compass of the man, and not unpalatable to the gentleman. He had ruled among his clerical neighbours now for sundry years, and as he had maintained his power without becoming unpopular, it may be presumed that he had exercised some wisdom.

Of Mr Slope's conduct much cannot be said, as his grand career is yet to commence; but it may be premised that his tastes will be very different from those of the archdeacon. He conceives it to be his duty to know all the private doings and desires of the flock entrusted to his care. From the poorer classes he exacts an unconditional obedience to set rules of conduct, and if disobeyed he has recourse, like his great ancestor, to the fulminations of an Ernulfus: 'Thou shalt be damned in thy going in and in thy coming out – in thy eating and thy drinking,' &c. &c. &c. With the rich, experience has already taught him that a different line of action is necessary. Men in the upper walks of life do not mind being cursed, and the women, presuming that it be done in delicate phrase, rather like it. But he has not, therefore, given up so important a portion of believing Christians. With the men, indeed, he is generally at variance; they are hardened sinners, on whom the voice of the priestly charmer too often falls in vain; but with the ladies, old and young, firm and frail, devout and dissipated, he is, as he conceives, all powerful. He can reprove faults with so much flattery, and utter censure in so caressing a manner, that the female heart, if it glow with a spark of low church susceptibility, cannot withstand him. In many houses he is thus an admired guest: the husbands, for their wives' sake, are fain to admit him; and when once admitted it is not easy to shake him off. He has, however, a pawing, greasy way with him, which does not endear him to those who do not value him for their souls' sake, and he is not a man to make himself at once popular in a large circle such as is now likely to surround him at Barchester.

⌘ FIVE ⌘

A Morning Visit

It was known that Dr Proudie would immediately have to reappoint to the wardenship of the hospital under the act of Parliament to which allusion has been made; but no one imagined that any choice was left to him – no one for a moment thought that he could appoint any other than Mr Harding. Mr Harding himself, when he heard how the matter had been settled, without troubling himself much on the subject, considered it as certain that he would go back to his pleasant house and garden. And though there would be much that was melancholy, nay, almost heartrending, in such a return, he still was glad that it was to be so. His daughter might probably be persuaded to return there with him. She had, indeed, all but promised to do so, though she still entertained an idea that that greatest of mortals, that important atom of humanity, that little god upon earth, Johnny Bold her baby, ought to have a house of his own over his head.

Such being the state of Mr Harding's mind in the matter, he did not feel any peculiar personal interest in the appointment of Dr Proudie to the bishopric. He, as well as others at Barchester, regretted that a man should be sent among them who, they were aware, was not of their way of thinking; but Mr Harding himself was not a bigoted man on points of church doctrine, and he was quite prepared to welcome Dr Proudie to Barchester in a graceful and becoming manner. He had nothing to seek and nothing to fear; he felt that it behoved him to be on good terms with this bishop, and he did not anticipate any obstacle that would prevent it.

In such a frame of mind he proceeded to pay his respects at the palace the second day after the arrival of the bishop and his chaplain. But he did not go alone. Dr Grantly proposed to accompany him, and Mr Harding was not sorry to have a companion, who would remove from his shoulders the burden of the conversation in such an interview. In the affair of the consecration Dr Grantly had been introduced to the bishop, and Mr Harding had also been there. He had, however, kept himself in the background, and he was now to be presented to the great man for the first time.

The archdeacon's feelings were of a much stronger nature. He was not exactly the man to overlook his own slighted claims, or to forgive the preference shown to another. Dr Proudie was playing Venus to his Juno, and he was prepared to wage an internecine war against the owner of the wished-for apple, and all his satellites, private chaplains, and others.

Nevertheless, it behoved him also to conduct himself towards the intruder as an old archdeacon should conduct himself to an incoming bishop; and though he was well aware of all Dr Proudie's abominable opinions as regarded dissenters, church reform, the hebdomadal council, and such like; though he disliked the man, and hated the doctrines, still he was prepared to show respect to the station of the bishop. So he and Mr Harding called together at the palace.

His lordship was at home, and the two visitors were shown through the accustomed hall into the well-known room, where the good old bishop used to sit. The furniture had been bought at a valuation, and every chair and table, every bookshelf against the wall, and every square in the carpet, was as well known to each of them as their own bedrooms. Nevertheless they at once felt that they were strangers there. The furniture was for the most part the same, yet the place had been metamorphosed. A new sofa had been introduced, a horrid chintz affair, most unprelatical and almost irreligious: such a sofa as never yet stood in the study of any decent high church clergyman of the Church of England. The old curtains had also given away. They had, to be sure, become dingy, and that which had been originally a rich and goodly ruby had degenerated into a reddish brown. Mr Harding, however, thought the old reddish brown much preferable to the gaudy buff-coloured trumpery moreen which Mrs Proudie had deemed good enough for her husband's own room in the provincial city of Barchester.

Our friends found Dr Proudie sitting on the old bishop's chair, looking very nice in his new apron; they found, too, Mr Slope standing on the hearthrug, persuasive and eager, just as the archdeacon used to stand; but on the sofa they also found Mrs Proudie, an innovation for which a precedent might in vain be sought in all the annals of the Barchester bishopric!

There she was, however, and they could only make the best of her. The introductions were gone through in much form. The archdeacon shook hands with the bishop, and named Mr Harding, who received such an amount of greeting as was due from a bishop to a precentor. His lordship then presented them to his lady wife; the archdeacon first, with archi-diaconal honours, and then the precentor with diminished parade. After this Mr Slope presented himself. The bishop, it is true, did mention his name, and so did Mrs Proudie too, in a louder tone; but Mr Slope took upon himself the chief burden of his own introduction. He had great pleasure in making himself acquainted with Dr Grantly; he had heard much of the archdeacon's good works in that part of the diocese in which his duties as archdeacon had been exercised (thus purposely ignoring the archdeacon's hitherto unlimited dominion over the diocese at large). He was aware that his lordship depended greatly on the assistance which Dr Grantly would be able to give him in that portion of his diocese. He then thrust out his hand, and grasping that of his new foe, bedewed it unmercifully. Dr Grantly in return bowed, looked stiff, contracted his eyebrows, and wiped his hand with his pocket-handkerchief. Nothing abashed, Mr Slope then noticed the precentor, and descended to the grade of the lower clergy. He gave him a squeeze of the hand, damp indeed, but affectionate, and was very glad to make the acquaintance of Mr ——; oh yes, Mr Harding; he had not exactly caught the name – 'Precentor in the cathedral,' surmised Mr Slope. Mr Harding confessed that such was the humble sphere of his work. 'Some parish duty as well,' suggested Mr Slope. Mr Harding acknowledged the diminutive incumbency of St Cuthbert's. Mr Slope then left him alone, having condescended sufficiently, and joined the conversation among the higher powers.

There were four persons there, each of whom considered himself the most important personage to the diocese; himself, indeed, or herself, as Mrs Proudie was one of them; and with such a difference of opinion it was not probable that they would get on pleasantly together. The bishop himself actually wore the visible apron, and trusted mainly to that – to that and his title, both being facts which could not be overlooked. The archdeacon knew his subject, and really understood the business of bishoping, which the others did not; and this was his strong ground. Mrs Proudie had her sex to back her, and her habit of command, and was nothing daunted by the high tone of Dr Grantly's face and figure. Mr Slope had only himself and his own courage and tact to depend on, but he nevertheless was perfectly self-assured, and did not doubt but that he should soon get the better of weak men who trusted so much to externals, as both bishop and archdeacon appeared to do.

'Do you reside in Barchester, Dr Grantly?' asked the lady with her sweetest smile.

Dr Grantly explained that he lived in his own parish of Plumstead Episcopi, a few miles out of the city. Whereupon the lady hoped that the distance was not too great for country visiting, as she would be so glad to make the acquaintance of Mrs Grantly. She would take the earliest opportunity, after the arrival of her horses at Barchester; their horses were at present in London; their horses were not immediately coming down, as the bishop would be obliged, in a few days, to return to town. Dr Grantly was no doubt aware that the bishop was at present much called upon by the 'University Improvement Committee:' indeed, the Committee could not well proceed without him, as their final report had now to be drawn up. The bishop had also to prepare a scheme for the 'Manufacturing Towns Morning and Evening Sunday School Society,' of which he was a patron, or president, or director, and therefore the horses would not come down to Barchester at present; but whenever the horses did come down, she would take the earliest opportunity of calling at Plumstead Episcopi, providing the distance was not too great for country visiting.

The archdeacon made his fifth bow: he had made one at each mention of the horses; and promised that Mrs Grantly would do herself the honour of calling at the palace on an early day. Mrs Proudie declared that she would be delighted: she hadn't liked to ask, not being quite sure whether Mrs Grantly had horses; besides, the distance might have been, &c. &c.

Dr Grantly again bowed, but said nothing. He could have brought every individual possession of the whole family of the Proudies, and have restored them as a gift, without much feeling the loss; and had kept a separate pair of horses for the exclusive use of his wife since the day of his marriage; whereas Mrs Proudie had been hitherto jobbed about the streets of London at so much a month during the season; and at other times had managed to walk, or hire a smart fly from the livery stables.

'Are the arrangements with reference to the Sabbath-day schools generally pretty good in your archdeaconry?' asked Mr Slope.

'Sabbath-day schools!' repeated the archdeacon with an affectation of surprise. 'Upon my word, I can't tell; it depends mainly on the parson's wife and daughters. There is none at Plumstead.'

This was almost a fib on the part of the archdeacon, for Mrs Grantly has a very nice school. To be sure it is not a Sunday school exclusively, and is not so designated; but that exemplary lady always attends there an hour before church, and hears the children say their catechism, and sees that they are clean and tidy for church, with their hands washed, and their shoes tied; and Grisel and Florinda, her daughters, carry thither a basket of large buns, baked on the Saturday afternoon, and distribute them to all the children not especially under disgrace, which buns are carried home after church with considerable content, and eaten hot at tea, being then split and toasted. The children of Plumstead would indeed open their eyes if they heard their venerated pastor declare that there was no Sunday school at his parish.

Mr Slope merely opened his eyes wider, and slightly shrugged his shoulders. He was not, however, prepared to give up his darling project.

'I fear there is a great deal of Sabbath travelling here,' said he. 'On looking at the "Bradshaw," I see that there are three trains in and three out every Sabbath. Could nothing be done to induce the company to withdraw them? Don't you think, Dr Grantly, that a little energy might diminish the evil?'

'Not being a director, I really can't say. But if you can withdraw the passengers, the company, I dare say, will withdraw the trains,' said the doctor. 'It's merely a question of dividends.'

'But surely, Dr Grantly.' said the lady, 'surely we should look at it differently. You and I, for instance, in our position: surely we should do all that we can to control so grievous a sin. Don't you think so, Mr Harding?' and she turned to the precentor, who was sitting mute and unhappy.

Mr Harding thought that all porters and stokers, guards, breaksmen, and pointsmen ought to have an opportunity of going to church, and he hoped that they all had.

'But surely, surely,' continued Mrs Proudie, 'surely that is not enough. Surely that will not secure such an observance of the Sabbath as we are taught to conceive is not only exedient but indispensable; surely –'

Come what come might, Dr Grantly was not to be forced into a dissertation on a point of doctrine with Mrs Proudie, nor yet with Mr Slope; so without much ceremony he turned his back upon the sofa, and began to hope that Dr Proudie had found that the palace repairs had been such as to meet his wishes.

'Yes, yes,' said his lordship; upon the whole he thought so – upon the whole, he didn't know that there was much ground for complaint; the architect, perhaps, might have – but his double, Mr Slope, who had sidled over to the bishop's chair, would not allow his lordship to finish his ambiguous speech.

'There is one point I would like to mention, Mr Archdeacon. His lordship asked me to step through the premises, and I see that the stalls in the second stable are not perfect.'

'Why – there's standing there for a dozen horses,' said the archdeacon.

'Perhaps so,' said the other; 'indeed, I've no doubt of it; but visitors, you know, often require so much accommodation. There are so many of the bishop's relatives who always bring their own horses.'

Dr Grantly promised that due provision for the relatives' horses should be made, as far at least as the extent of the original stable building would allow. He would himself communicate with the architect.

'And the coach-house, Dr Grantly,' continued Mr Slope; 'there is really hardly room for a second carriage in the large coach-house, and the smaller one, of course, holds only one.'

'And the gas,' chimed in the lady; 'there is no gas through the house, none whatever, but in the kitchen and passages. Surely the palace should have been fitted through with pipes for gas, and hot water too. There is no hot water laid on anywhere above the ground-floor; surely there should be the means of getting hot water in the bed-rooms without having it brought in jugs from the kitchen.'

The bishop had a decided opinion that there should be pipes for hot water. Hot water was very essential for the comfort of the palace. It was, indeed, a requisite in any decent gentleman's house.

Mr Slope had remarked that the coping on the garden wall was in many places imperfect.

Mrs Proudie had discovered a large hole, evidently the work of rats, in the servants' hall.

The bishop expressed an utter detestation of rats. There was nothing, he believed, in this world, that he so much hated as a rat.

Mr Slope had, moreover, observed that the locks of the out-houses were very imperfect: he might specify the coal-cellar, and the woodhouse.

Mrs Proudie had also seen that those on the doors of the servants' bedrooms were in an equally bad condition; indeed the locks all through the house were old-fashioned and unserviceable.

The bishop thought that a great deal depended on a good lock, and quite as much on the key. He had observed that the fault very often lay with the key, especially if the wards were in any way twisted.

Mr Slope was going on with his catalogue of grievances, when he was somewhat loudly interrupted by the archdeacon, who succeeded in explaining that the diocesan architect, or rather his foreman, was the person to be addressed on such subjects; and that he, Dr Grantly, had inquired as to the comfort of the palace, merely as a point of compliment. He was sorry, however, that so many things had been found amiss: and then he rose from his chair to escape.

Mrs Proudie, though she had contrived to lend her assistance in recapitulating the palatial dilapidations, had not on that account given up her hold of Mr Harding, nor ceased from her cross-examinations as to the iniquity of Sabbatical amusements. Over and over again had she thrown out her 'Surely, surely,' at Mr Harding's devoted head, and ill had that gentleman been able to parry the attack.

He had never before found himself subjected to such a nuisance. Ladies hitherto, when they had consulted him on religious subjects, had listened to what he might choose to say and with some deference, and had differed, if they differed, in silence. But Mrs Proudie interrogated him, and then lectured. 'Neither thou, nor thy son, nor thy daughter, nor thy man servant, nor thy maid servant,' said she, impressively, and more than once, as though Mr Harding had forgotten the words. She shook her finger at him as she quoted the favourite law, as though menacing him with punishment; and then called upon him categorically to state whether he did not think that travelling on the Sabbath was an abomination and a desecration.

Mr Harding had never been so hard pressed in his life. He felt that he ought to rebuke the lady for presuming so to talk to a gentleman and a clergyman many years her senior; but he recoiled from the idea of scolding the bishop's wife, in the bishop's presence, on his first visit to the palace; moreover, to tell the truth, he was somewhat afraid of her. She, seeing him sit silent and absorbed, by no means refrained from the attack.

'I hope, Mr Harding,' said she, shaking her head slowly and solemnly, 'I hope you will not leave me to think that you approve of Sabbath travelling,' and she looked a look of unutterable meaning into his eyes.

There was no standing this, for Mr Slope was now looking at him, and so was the bishop, and so was the archdeacon, who had completed his adieux on that side of the room. Mr Harding therefore got up also, and putting out his hand to Mrs Proudie said: 'If you will come to St Cuthbert's some Sunday, I will preach you a sermon on that subject.'

And so the archdeacon and the precentor took their departure, bowing low to the lady, shaking hands with the lord, and escaping from Mr Slope in the best manner each could. Mr Harding was again maltreated; but Dr Grantly swore deeply in the bottom of his heart, that no earthly consideration should ever again induce him to touch the paw of that impure and filthy animal.

And now, had I the pen of a mighty poet, would I sing in epic verse the noble wrath of the archdeacon. The palace steps descend to a broad gravel sweep, from whence a small gate opens out into the street, very near the covered gateway leading into the close. The road from the palace door turns to the left, through the spacious gardens, and terminates on the London-road, half a mile from the cathedral.

Till they had both passed this small gate and entered the close, neither of them spoke a word; but the precentor clearly saw from his companion's face that a tornado was to be expected, nor was he himself inclined to stop it.

Though by nature far less irritable than the archdeacon, even he was angry: he even – that mild and courteous man – was inclined to express himself in anything but courteous terms.

✖ SIX ✖

War

'GOOD HEAVENS!' EXCLAIMED THE ARCHDEACON, AS HE placed his foot on the gravel walk of the close, and raising his hat with one hand, passed the other somewhat violently over his now grizzled locks; smoke issued forth from the uplifted beaver as it were a cloud of wrath, and the safety-valve of his anger opened, and emitted a visible steam, preventing positive explosion and probable apoplexy. 'Good heavens!' – and the archdeacon looked up to the gray pinnacles of the cathedral tower, making a mute appeal to that still living witness which had looked down on the doings of so many bishops of Barchester.

'I don't think I shall ever like that Mr Slope,' said Mr Harding.

'Like him!' roared the archdeacon, standing still for a moment to give more force to his voice; 'like him!' All the ravens of the close cawed their assent. The old bells of the tower, in chiming the hour, echoed the words; and the swallows flying out from their nests mutely expressed a similar opinion. Like Mr Slope! Why no, it was not very probable that any Barchester-bred living thing should like Mr Slope!

'Nor Mrs Proudie either,' said Mr Harding.

The archdeacon hereupon forgot himself. I will not follow his example, nor shock my readers by transcribing the term in which he expressed his feeling as to the lady who had been named. The ravens and the last lingering notes of the clock bells were less scrupulous, and repeated in corresponding echoes the very improper exclamation. The archdeacon again raised his hat, and another salutary escape of steam was effected.

There was a pause, during which the precentor tried to realise the fact that the wife of a bishop of Barchester had been thus designated, in the close of the cathedral, by the lips of its own archdeacon: but he could not do it.

'The bishop seems to be a quiet man enough,' suggested Mr Harding, having acknowledged to himself his own failure.

'Idiot!' exclaimed the doctor, who for the nonce was not capable of more than such spasmodic attempts at utterance.

'Well, he did not seem very bright,' said Mr Harding, 'and yet he has always had the reputation of a clever man. I suppose he's cautious and not inclined to express himself very freely.'

The new bishop of Barchester was already so contemptible a creature in

28

Dr Grantly's eyes, that he could not condescend to discuss his character. He was a puppet to be played by others; a mere wax doll, done up in an apron and a shovel hat, to be stuck on a throne or elsewhere, and pulled about by wires as others chose. Dr Grantly did not choose to let himself down low enough to talk about Dr Proudie; but he saw that he would have to talk about the other members of his household, the coadjutor bishops, who had brought his lordship down, as it were, in a box, and were about to handle the wires as they willed. This in itself was a terrible vexation to the archdeacon. Could he have ignored the chaplain, and have fought the bishop, there would have been, at any rate, nothing degrading in such a contest. Let the Queen make whom she would bishop of Barchester; a man, or even an ape, when once a bishop, would be a respectable adversary, if he would but fight, himself. But what was such a person as Dr Grantly to do, when such another person as Mr Slope was put forward as his antagonist?

If he, our archdeacon, refused the combat, Mr Slope would walk triumphant over the field, and have the diocese of Barchester under his heel.

If, on the other hand, the archdeacon accepted as his enemy the man whom the new puppet bishop put before him as such, he would have to talk about Mr Slope, and write about Mr Slope, and in all matters treat with Mr Slope, as a being standing, in some degree, on ground similar to his own. He would have to meet Mr Slope; to – Bah! the idea was sickening. He could not bring himself to have to do with Mr Slope.

'He is the most thoroughly bestial creature that ever I set my eyes upon,' said the archdeacon.

'Who – the bishop?' asked the other, innocently.

'Bishop! no – I'm not talking about the bishop. How on earth such a creature got ordained! – they'll ordain anybody now, I know; but he's been in the church these ten years; and they used to be a little careful ten years ago.'

'Oh! you mean Mr Slope.'

'Did you ever see any animal less like a gentleman?' asked Dr Grantly.

'I can't say I felt myself much disposed to like him.'

'Like him!' again shouted the doctor, and the assenting ravens again cawed an echo; 'of course, you don't like him: it's not a question of liking. But what are we to do with him?'

'Do with him?' asked Mr Harding.

'Yes – what are we to do with him? How are we to treat him? There he is, and there he'll stay. He has put his foot in that palace, and he will never take it out again till he's driven. How are we to get rid of him?'

'I don't suppose he can do us much harm.'

'Not do harm! – Well, I think you'll find yourself of a different opinion before a month is gone. What would you say now, if he got himself put into the hospital? Would that be harm?'

Mr Harding mused awhile, and then said he didn't think the new bishop would put Mr Slope into the hospital.

'If he doesn't put him there, he'll put him somewhere else where he'll be as bad. I tell you that that man, to all intents and purposes, will be Bishop of Barchester;' and again Dr Grantly raised his hat, and rubbed his hand thoughtfully and sadly over his head.

'Impudent scoundrel!' he continued after a while. 'To dare to cross-examine me about the Sunday schools in the diocese, and Sunday travelling too: I never in my life met his equal for sheer impudence. Why, he must have thought we were two candidates for ordination!'

'I declare I thought Mrs Proudie was the worst of the two,' said Mr Harding.

'When a woman is impertinent, one must only put up with it, and keep out of her way in future; but I am not inclined to put up with Mr Slope. "Sabbath travelling!" ' and the doctor attempted to imitate the peculiar drawl of the man he so much disliked: ' "Sabbath travelling!" Those are the sort of men who will ruin the Church of England, and make the profession of a clergyman disreputable. It is not the dissenters or the papists that we should fear, but the set of canting, low-bred hypocrites who are wriggling their way in among us; men who have no fixed principle, no standard ideas of religion or doctrine, but who take up some popular cry, as this fellow has done about "Sabbath travelling." '

Dr Grantly did not again repeat the question aloud, but he did so constantly to himself, 'What were they to do with Mr Slope?' How was he openly, before the world, to show that he utterly disapproved of and abhorred such a man?

Hitherto Barchester had escaped the taint of any extreme rigour of church doctrine. The clergyman of the city and neighbourhood, though very well inclined to promote high-church principles, privileges, and prerogatives, had never committed themselves to tendencies, which are somewhat too loosely called Puseyite practices. They all preached in their black gowns, as their fathers had done before them; they wore ordinary black cloth waistcoats; they had no candles on their altars, either lighted or unlighted; they made no private genuflexions, and were contented to confine themselves to such ceremonial observances as had been in vogue for the last hundred years. The services were decently and demurely read in their parish churches, chanting was confined to the cathedral, and the science of intoning was unknown. One young man who had come direct from Oxford as a curate to Plumstead had, after the lapse of two or three Sundays, made a faint attempt, much to the bewilderment of the poorer part of the congregation. Dr Grantly had not been present on the occasion; but Mrs Grantly, who had her own opinion on the subject, immediately after the service expressed a hope that the young gentleman had not been taken ill, and offered to send him all kinds of condiments supposed to be good for a sore throat. After that there had been no more intoning at Plumstead Episcopi.

But now the archdeacon began to meditate on some strong measures of absolute opposition. Dr Proudie and his crew were of the lowest possible order of Church of England clergymen, and therefore it behoved him, Dr Grantly, to be of the very highest. Dr Proudie would abolish all forms and ceremonies, and therefore Dr Grantly felt the sudden necessity of multiplying them. Dr Proudie would consent to deprive the church of all collective authority and rule, and therefore Dr Grantly would stand up for the full power of convocation, and the renewal of all its ancient privileges.

It was true that he could not himself intone the service, but he could procure the co-operation of any number of gentlemanlike curates well trained in the mystery of doing so. He would not willingly alter his own fashion of dress, but he could people Barchester with young clergyman dressed in the longest frocks, and in the highest-breasted silk waistcoats. He certainly was not prepared to cross himself, or to advocate the real presence; but, without going this length, there was various observances, by adopting which he could plainly show his antipathy to such men as Dr Proudie and Mr Slope.

All these things passed through his mind as he paced up and down the close with Mr Harding. War, war, internecine war was in his heart. He felt that, as regarded himself and Mr Slope, one of the two must be annihilated as far as the city of Barchester was concerned; and he did not intend to give way until there was not left to him an inch of ground on which he could stand. He still flattered himself that he could make Barchester too hot to hold Mr Slope, and he had no weakness of spirit to prevent his bringing about such a consummation if it were in his power.

'I suppose Susan must call at the palace,' said Mr Harding.

'Yes, she shall call there; but it shall be once and once only. I dare say "the horses" won't find it convenient to come out to Plumstead very soon, and when that once is done the matter may drop.'

'I don't suppose Eleanor need call. I don't think Eleanor would get on at all well with Mrs Proudie.'

'Not the least necessity in life,' replied the archdeacon, not without the reflection that a ceremony which was necessary for his wife, might not be at all binding on the widow of John Bold. 'Not the slightest reason on earth why she should do so, if she doesn't like it. For myself, I don't think that any decent young woman should be subjected to the nuisance of being in the same room with that man.'

And so the two clergymen parted, Mr Harding going to his daughter's house, and the archdeacon seeking the seclusion of his brougham.

The new inhabitants of the palace did not express any higher opinion of their visitors than their visitors had expressed of them. Though they did not use quite such strong language as Dr Grantly had done, they felt as much personal aversion, and were quite as well aware as he was that there would be a battle to be fought, and that there was hardly room for Proudieism in Barchester as long as Grantlyism was predominant.

Indeed, it may be doubted whether Mr Slope had not already within its breast a better prepared system of strategy, a more accurately-defined line of hostile conduct than the archdeacon. Dr Grantly was going to fight because he found that he hated the man. Mr Slope had predetermined to hate the man, because he foresaw the necessity of fighting him. When he had first reviewed the *carte du pays*, previous to his entry into Barchester, the idea had occurred to him of conciliating the archdeacon, of cajoling and flattering him into submission, and of obtaining the upper hand by cunning instead of courage. A little inquiry, however, sufficed to convince him that all his cunning would fail to win over such a man as Dr Grantly to such a mode of action as that to be adopted by Mr Slope; and then he determined to fall back upon his courage. He at once saw that open battle against Dr Grantly and all Dr Grantly's adherents was a necessity of his position, and he deliberately planned the most expedient methods of giving offence.

Soon after his arrival the bishop had intimated to the dean that, with the permission of the canon then in residence, his chaplain would preach in the cathedral on the next Sunday. The canon in residence happened to be the Hon. and Rev. Dr Vesey Stanhope, who at this time was very busy on the shores of the Lake of Como, adding to that unique collection of butterflies for which he is so famous. Or, rather, he would have been in residence but for the butterflies and other such summer-day considerations; and the vicar-choral, who was to take his place in the pulpit, by no means objected to having his work done for him by Mr Slope.

Mr Slope accordingly preached, and if a preacher can have satisfaction in being listened to, Mr Slope ought to have been gratified. I have reason to think that he was gratified, and that he left the pulpit with the conviction that he had done what he intended to do when he entered it.

On this occasion the new bishop took his seat for the first time in the throne allotted to him. New scarlet cushions and drapery had been prepared, with new gilt binding and new fringe. The old carved oak-wood of the throne, ascending with its numerous grotesque pinnacles half-way up to the roof of the choir, had been washed and dusted, and rubbed, and it all looked very smart. Ah! how often sitting there, in happy early days, on those lowly benches in front of the altar, have I whiled away the tedium of a sermon in considering how best I might thread my way up amidst those wooden towers, and climb safely to the topmost pinnacle!

All Barchester went to hear Mr Slope; either for that or to gaze at the new bishop. All the best bonnets of the city were there, and moreover all the best glossy clerical hats. Not a stall but had its fitting occupant; for though some of the prebendaries might be away in Italy or elsewhere, their places were filled by brethren, who flocked into Barchester on the occasion. The dean was there, a heavy old man, now too old, indeed, to attend frequently in his place; and so was the archdeacon. So also were the chancellor, the treasurer, the precentor, sundry canons and minor canons, and every lay member of the choir, prepared to sing the new bishop in with due melody and harmonious expression of sacred welcome.

The service was certainly very well performed. Such was always the case at Barchester, as the musical education of the choir had been good, and the voice had been carefully selected. The psalms were beautifully chanted; the Te Deum was magnificently sung; and the litany was given in a manner, which is still to be found at Barchester, but, if my taste be correct, is to be found nowhere else. The litany in Barchester cathedral has long been the special task to which Mr Harding's skill and voice have been devoted. Crowded audiences generally make good performers, and though Mr Harding was not aware of any extraordinary exertion on his part, yet probably he rather exceeded his usual mark. Others were doing their best, and it was natural that he should emulate his brethren. So the service went on, and at last Mr Slope got into the pulpit.

He chose for his text a verse from the precepts addressed by St Paul to Timothy, as to the conduct necessary in a spiritual pastor and guide, and it was immediately evident that the good clergy of Barchester were to have a lesson.

'Study to show thyself approved unto God, a workman that needeth not to be ashamed, rightly dividing the word of truth.' These were the words of his text, and with such a subject in such a place, it may be supposed that such a preacher would be listened to by such an audience. He was listened to with breathless attention, and not without considerable surprise. Whatever opinion of Mr Slope might have been held in Barchester before he commenced his discourse, none of his hearers, when it was over, could mistake him either for a fool or a coward.

It would not be becoming were I to travestie a sermon, or even to repeat the language of it in the pages of a novel. In endeavouring to depict the characters of the persons of whom I write, I am to a certain extent forced to speak of sacred things. I trust, however, that I shall not be thought to scoff at the pulpit, though some may imagine that I do not feel all the reverence that is due to the cloth. I may question the infallibility of the teachers, but I hope that I shall not therefore be accused of doubt as to the thing to be taught.

Mr Slope, in commencing his sermon, showed no slight tact in his ambiguous manner of hinting that, humble as he was himself, he stood there as the mouthpiece of the illustrious divine who sat opposite to him; and having premised so much, he gave forth a very accurate definition of the conduct which that prelate would rejoice to see in the clergymen now brought under his jurisdiction. It is only necessary to say, that the peculiar points insisted upon were exactly those which were most distasteful to the clergy of the diocese, and most averse to their practice and opinions; and that all those peculiar habits and privileges which have always been dear to high-church priests, to that party which is now scandalously called the high-and-dry church, were ridiculed, abused, and anathematised. Now, the clergymen of the diocese of Barchester are all of the high-and-dry church.

Having thus, according to his own opinion, explained how a clergyman should show himself approved unto God, as a workman that needeth not to be ashamed, he went on to explain how the word of truth should be divided; and here he took a rather narrow view of the question, and fetched his arguments from afar. His object was to express his abomination of all ceremonious modes of utterance, to cry down any religious feeling which might be excited, not by the sense, but by the sound of words, and in fact to insult cathedral practices. Had St Paul spoken of rightly pronouncing instead of rightly dividing the word of truth, this part of his sermon would have been more to the purpose; but the preacher's immediate object was to preach Mr Slope's doctrine, and not St Paul's, and he contrived to give the necessary twist to the text with some skill.

He could not exactly say, preaching from a cathedral pulpit, that chanting should be abandoned in cathedral services. By such an assertion, he would have overshot his mark and rendered himself absurd, to the delight of his hearers. He could, however, and did, allude with heavy denunciations to the practice of intoning in parish churches, although the practice was all but unknown in the diocese; and from thence he came round to the undue preponderance, which he asserted, music had over meaning in the beautiful service which they had just heard. He was aware, he said, that the practices of our ancestors could not be abandoned at a moment's notice; the feelings of the aged would be outraged, and the minds of respectable men would be shocked. There were many, he was aware, of not sufficient calibre of thought to perceive, of not sufficient education to know, that a mode of service, which was effective when outward ceremonies were of more moment than inward feelings, had become all but barbarous at a time when inward conviction was everything, when each word of the minister's lips should fall intelligibly into the listener's heart. Formerly the religion of the multitude had been an affair of the imagination: now, in these latter days, it had become necessary that a Christian should have a reason for his faith – should not only believe, but digest – not only hear, but understand. The words of our morning service, how beautiful, how apposite, how intelligible they were, when read with simple and distinct decorum! but how much of the meaning of the words was lost when they were produced with all the meretricious charms of melody ! &c. &c.

Here was a sermon to be preached before Mr Archdeacon Grantly, Mr Precentor Harding, and the rest of them! before a whole dean and chapter assembled in their own cathedral! before men who had grown old in the exercise of their peculiar services, with a full conviction of their excellence for all intended purposes! This too from such a man, a clerical *parvenu*, a man without a cure, a mere chaplain, an intruder among them; a fellow raked up, so said Dr Grantly, from the gutters of Marylebone! They had to sit through it! None of them, not even Dr Grantly, could close his ears, nor leave the house of God during the hours of service. They were under an obligation of listening, and that too, without any immediate power of reply.

There is, perhaps, no greater hardship at present inflicted on mankind in civilised and free countries, than the necessity of listening to sermons. No one but a preaching clergyman has, in these realms, the power of compelling an audience to sit silent, and be tormented. No one but a preaching clergyman can revel in platitudes, truisms, and untruisms, and yet receive, as his undisputed privilege, the same respectful demeanor as though words of impassioned eloquence, or persuasive logic, fell from his lips. Let a professor of law or physic find his place in a lecture-room, and there pour forth jejune words and useless empty phrases, and he will pour them forth to empty benches. Let a barrister attempt to talk without talking well, and he will talk but seldom. A judge's charge need be listened to per force by none but the jury, prisoner, and gaoler. A member of Parliament can be coughed down or counted out. Town-councillors can be tabooed. But no one can rid himself of the preaching clergyman. He is the bore of the age, the old man whom we Sindbads cannot shake off, the nightmare that disturbs our Sunday's rest, the incubus that overloads our religion and makes God's service distasteful. We are not forced into church! No: but we desire more than that. We desire not to be forced to stay away. We desire, nay, we are resolute, to enjoy the comfort of public worship; but we desire also that we may do so without an amount of tedium which ordinary human nature cannot endure with patience; that we may be able to leave the house of God, without that anxious longing for escape, which is the common consequence of common sermons.

With what complacency will a young parson deduce false conclusions from misunderstood texts, and then theaten us with all the penalties of Hades if we neglect to comply with the injunctions he has given us! Yes, my too self-confident juvenile friend, I do believe in those mysteries, which are so common in your mouth; I do believe in the unadulterated word which you hold there in your hand; but you must pardon me if, in some things, I doubt your interpretation. The bible is good, the prayer-book is good, nay, you yourself would be acceptable, if you would read to me some portion of those time-honored discourses which our great divines have elaborated in the full maturity of their powers. But you must excuse me, my insufficient young lecturer, if I yawn over your imperfect sentences, your repeated phrases, your false pathos, your drawlings and denouncings, your humming and hawing, your oh-ing and ah-ing, your black gloves and your white handkerchief. To me, it all means nothing; and hours are too precious to be so wasted – if one could only avoid it.

And here I must make a protest against the pretence, so often put forward by the working clergy, that they are overburdened by the multitude of sermons to be preached. We are all too fond of our own voices, and a preacher is encouraged in the vanity of making his heard by the privilege of a compelled audience. His sermon is the pleasant morsel of his life, his delicious moment of self-exaltation. 'I have preached nine sermons this week,' said a young friend to me the other day, with hand languidly raised to his brow, the picture of an over-burdened martyr. 'Nine this week, seven last week, four the week before. I have preached twenty-three sermons this month. It is really too much.' 'Too much, indeed,' said I, shuddering; 'too much for the strength of any one.' 'Yes,' he answered meekly, 'indeed it is; I am beginning to feel it painfully.' 'Would,' said I, 'you could feel it – would that you could be made to feel it.' But he never guessed that my heart was wrung for the poor listeners.

There was, at any rate, no tedium felt in listening to Mr Slope on the occasion in question. His subject came too home to his audience to be dull; and, to tell the truth, Mr Slope had the gift of using words forcibly. He was heard through his thirty minutes of eloquence with mute attention and open ears; but with angry eyes, which glared round from one enraged parson to another, with wide-spread nostrils from which already burst forth fumes of indignation, and with many shufflings of the feet and uneasy motions of the body, which betokened minds disturbed, and hearts not at peace with all the world.

At last the bishop, who, of all the congregation, had been most surprised, and whose hair almost stood on end with terror, gave the blessing in a manner not at all equal to that in which he had long been practicing it in his own study, and the congregation was free to go their way.

✖ SEVEN ✖

The Dean and Chapter take Counsel

ALL BARCHESTER WAS IN A TUMULT. Dr Grantly could hardly get himself out of the cathedral porch before he exploded in his wrath. The old dean betook himself silently to his deanery, afraid to speak; and there sat, half stupefied, pondering many things in vain. Mr Harding crept forth solitary and unhappy; and, slowly passing beneath the elms of the close, could scarcely bring himself to believe that the words which he had heard had proceeded from the pulpit of Barchester cathedral. Was he again to be disturbed? was his whole life to be shown up as a useless sham a second time? would he have to abdicate his precentorship, as he had his wardenship, and to give up chanting, as he had given up his twelve old bedesmen? And what if he did! Some other Jupiter, some other Mr Slope, would come and turn him out of St Cuthbert's. Surely he could not have been wrong all his life in chanting the litany as he had done! He began, however, to have his doubts. Doubting himself was Mr Harding's weakness. It is not, however, the usual fault of his order.

Yes! all Barchester was in a tumult. It was not only the clergy who were affected. The laity also had listened to Mr Slope's new doctrine, all with surprise, some with indignation, and some with a mixed feeling, in which dislike of the preacher was not so strongly blended. The old bishop and his chaplains, the dean and his canons and minor canons, the old choir, and especially Mr Harding who was at the head of it, had all been popular in Barchester. They had spent their money and done good; the poor had not been ground down; the clergy in society had neither been overbearing nor austere; and the whole repute of the city was due to its ecclesiastical importance. Yet there were those who had heard Mr Slope with satisfaction.

It is so pleasant to receive a fillip of excitement when suffering from the dull routine of every-day life! The anthems and Te Deums were in themselves delightful, but they had been heard so often! Mr Slope was certainly not delightful, but he was new, and, moreover, clever. They had long thought it slow, so said now many of the Barchesterians, to go on as they had done in their old humdrum way, giving ear to none of the religious changes which were moving the world without. People in advance of the age now had new ideas, and it was quite time that Barchester should go in advance. Mr Slope might be right. Sunday certainly had not been strictly kept in Barchester, except as regarded the cathedral services. Indeed the two hours between services had long been appropriated to morning calls and hot luncheons. Then Sunday schools! really more ought to have been done as to Sunday schools; Sabbath-day schools Mr Slope had called them. The late bishop had really not thought of Sunday schools as he should have done. (These people probably did not reflect that catechisms and collects are quite as hard work to the young mind as book-keeping is to the elderly; and that quite as little feeling of worship enters into the one task as the other.) And then, as regarded that great question of musical services, there might be much to be said on Mr Slope's side of the question. It certainly was the fact, that people went to the cathedral to hear the music, &c. &c.

And so a party absolutely formed itself in Barchester on Mr Slope's side of the question! This consisted, among the upper classes, chiefly of ladies. No man – that is, no gentleman – could possibly be attracted by Mr Slope, or consent to sit at the feet of so abhorrent a Gamaliel. Ladies are sometimes less nice in their appreciation of physical disqualification; and, provided that a man speak to them well, they will listen, though he speak from a mouth never so deformed and hideous. Wilkes was most fortunate as a lover; and the damp, sandy-haired, saucer-eyed, red-fisted Mr Slope was powerful only over the female breast.

There were, however, one or two of the neighbouring clergy who thought it not quite safe to neglect the baskets in which for the nonce were stored the loaves and fishes of the diocese of Barchester. They, and they only, came to call on Mr Slope after his performance in the cathedral pulpit. Among these Mr Quiverful, the rector of Puddingdale, whose wife still continued to present him from year to year with fresh pledges of her love, and so to increase his cares and, it is to be hoped, his happiness equally. Who can wonder that a gentleman, with fourteen living children and a bare income of 400*l*. a year, should look after the loaves and fishes, even when they are under the thumb of a Mr Slope?

Very soon after the Sunday on which the sermon was preached, the leading clergy of the neighbourhood held high debate together as to how Mr Slope should be put down. In the first place he should never again preach from the pulpits of Barchester cathedral. This was Dr Grantly's earliest dictum; and they all agreed, providing only that they had the power to exclude him. Dr Grantly declared that the power rested with the dean and chapter, observing that no clergyman out of the chapter had a claim to preach there, saving only the bishop himself. To this the dean assented, but alleged that contests on such a subject would be unseemly; to which rejoined a meagre little doctor, one of the cathedral prebendaries, that the contest must be all on the side of Mr Slope if every prebendary were always there ready to take his own place in the pulpit. Cunning little meagre doctor, whom it suits well to live in his own cosy house within Barchester close, and who is well content to have his little fling at Dr Vesey Stanhope and other absentees, whose Italian villas, or enticing London homes, are more tempting than cathedral stalls and residences!

To this answered the burly chancellor, a man rather silent indeed, but very sensible, that absent prebendaries had their vicars, and that in such case the vicar's right to the pulpit was the same as that of the higher order. To which the dean assented, groaning deeply at these truths. Thereupon, however, the meager doctor remarked that they would be in the hands of their minor canons, one of whom might at any hour betray his trust. Whereon was heard from the burly chancellor an ejaculation sounding somewhat like 'Pooh, pooh, pooh!' but it might be that the worthy man was but blowing out the heavy breath from his windpipe. Why silence him at all? suggested Mr Harding. Let them not be ashamed to hear what any man might have to preach to them, unless he preached false doctrine; in which case, let the bishop silence him. So spoke our friend; vainly; for human ends must be attained by human means. But the death saw a ray of hope out of those purblind old eyes of his. Yes, let them tell the bishop how distasteful to them was this Mr Slope: a new bishop just come to his seat could not wish to insult his clergy while the gloss was yet fresh on his first apron.

Then up rose Dr Grantly; and, having thus collected the scattered wisdom of his associates, spoke forth with words of deep authority. When I say up rose the archdeacon, I speak of the inner man, which then sprang up to more immediate action, for the doctor had, bodily, been standing all along with his back to the dean's empty fire-grate, and the tails of his frock coat supported over his two arms. His hands were in his breeches pockets.

'It is quite clear that this man must not be allowed to preach again in this cathedral. We all see that, except our dear friend here, the milk of whose nature runs so softly, that he would not have the heart to refuse the Pope the loan of his pulpit, if the Pope would come and ask it. We must not, however, allow the man to preach again here. It is not because his opinion on church matters may be different from ours – with that one would not quarrel. It is because he has purposely insulted us. When he went up into the pulpit last Sunday, his studied object was to give offense to men who had grown old in reverence of those things of which he dared to speak so slightingly. What! to come here a stranger, a young, unknown, and unfriended stranger, and tell us, in the name of the bishop his master, that we are ignorant of our duties, old-fashioned, and useless! I don't know whether most to admire his courage or his impudence! And one thing I will tell you: that sermon originated solely with the man himself. The bishop was no more a party to it than was the dean here. You all know how grieved I am to see a bishop in this diocese holding the latitudinarian ideas by which Dr Proudie has made himself conspicuous. You all know how greatly I should distrust the opinions of such a man. But in this matter I hold him to be blameless. I believe Dr Proudie has lived too long among gentlemen to be guilty, or to instigate another to be guilty, of so gross an outrage. No! that man uttered what was untrue when he hinted that he was speaking as the mouthpiece of the bishop. It suited his ambitious views at once to throw down the gauntlet to us – at once to defy us here in the quiet of our own religious duties – here within the walls of our own loved cathedral – here where we have for so many years exercised our ministry without schism and with good repute. Such an attack upon us, coming from such a quarter, is abominable.'

'Abominable,' groaned the dean. 'Abominable,' muttered the meagre doctor. 'Abominable,' re-echoed the chancellor, uttering the sound from the bottom of his deep chest. 'I really think it was,' said Mr Harding.

'Most abominable and most unjustifiable,' continued the archdeacon. 'But, Mr Dean, thank God, that pulpit is still our own: your own, I should say. That pulpit belongs solely to the dean and chapter of Barchester Cathedral, and, as yet, Mr Slope is no part of that chapter. You, Mr Dean, have suggested that we should appeal to the bishop to abstain from forcing this man on us; but what if the bishop allow himself to be ruled by his chaplain? In my opinion, the matter is in our own hands. Mr Slope cannot preach there without permission asked and obtained, and let that permission be invariably refused. Let all participation in the ministry of the cathedral service be refused to him. Then, if the bishop choose to interfere, we shall know what answer to make to the bishop. My friend here has suggested that this man may again find his way into the pulpit by undertaking the duty of some of your minor canons; but I am sure that we may fully trust to these gentlemen to support us, when it is known that the dean objects to any such transfer.'

'Of course you may,' said the chancellor.

There was much more discussion among the learned conclave, all of which, of course, ended in obedience to the archdeacon's commands. They had too long been accustomed to his rule to shake it off so soon; and in this particular case they had none of them a wish to abet the man whom he was so anxious to put down.

Such a meeting as that we have just recorded is not held in such a city as Barchester unknown and untold of. Not only was the fact of the meeting talked of in every respectable house, including the palace, but the very speeches of the dean, the archdeacon, and chancellor were repeated; not without many additions and imaginary circumstances, according to the tastes and opinions of the relaters.

All, however, agreed in saying that Mr Slope was to be debarred from opening his mouth in the cathedral of Barchester; many believed that the vergers were to be ordered to refuse him even the accommodation of a seat; and some of the most far-going advocates for strong measures, declared that his sermon was looked upon as an indictable offence, and that proceedings were to be taken against him for brawling.

The party who were inclined to defend him – the enthusiastically religious young ladies, and the middle-aged spinsters desirous of a move – of course took up his defence the more warmly on account of this attack. If they could not hear Mr Slope in the cathedral, they would hear him elsewhere; they would leave the dull dean, the dull old prebendaries, and the scarcely less dull young minor canons, to preach to each other; they would work slippers and cushions, and hem bands for Mr Slope, make him a happy martyr, and stick him up in some new Sion or Bethesda, and put the cathedral quite out of fashion.

Dr and Mrs Proudie at once returned to London. They thought it expedient not to have to encounter any personal application from the dean and chapter respecting the sermon, till the violence of the storm had expanded itself; but they left Mr Slope behind them nothing daunted, and he went about his work zealously, flattering such as would listen to his flattery, whispering religious twaddle into the ears of foolish women, ingratiating himself with the few clergy who would receive him, visiting the houses of the poor, inquiring into all people, prying into everything, and searching with his minutest eye into all palatial dilapidations. He did

not, however, make any immediate attempt to preach again in the cathedral.
And so all Barchester was by the ears.

✕ EIGHT ✕

The Ex-Warden Rejoices in his Probable
Return to the Hospital

AMONG THE LADIES IN BARCHESTER WHO HAVE hitherto acknowledged
Mr Slope as their spiritual director, must not be reckoned either the
widow Bold, or her sister-in-law. On the first outbreak of the wrath of the
denizens of the close, none had been more animated against the intruder
than these two ladies. And this was natural. Who could be so proud of the
musical distinction of their own cathedral as the favourite daughter of the
precentor? Who would be so likely to resent an insult offered to the old
choir? And in such matters Miss Bold and her sister-in-law had but one
opinion.

This wrath, however, has in some degree been mitigated, and I regret
to say that these ladies allowed Mr Slope to be his own apologist. About a
fortnight after the sermon had been preached, they were both of them not
a little surprised by hearing Mr Slope announced, as the page in buttons
opened Mrs Bold's drawing-room door. Indeed, what living man could,
by a mere morning visit, have surprised them more? Here was the great
enemy of all that was good in Barchester coming into their own drawing-
room, and they had no strong arm, no ready tongue, near at hand for
their protection. The widow snatched her baby out of its cradle into her
lap, and Mary Bold stood up ready to die manfully in that baby's behalf,
should, under any circumstances, such a sacrifice become necessary.

In this manner was Mr Slope received. But when he left, he was
allowed by each lady to take her hand, and to make his adieux as
gentlemen do who have been graciously entertained! Yes; he shook
hands with them, and was curtseyed out courteously, the buttoned page
opening the door, as he would have done for the best canon of them all.
He had touched the baby's little hand and blessed him with a fervid
blessing; he had spoken to the widow of her early sorrows, and Eleanor's
silent tears had not rebuked him; he had told Mary Bold that her devotion
would be rewarded, and Mary Bold had heard the praise without disgust.
And how had he done all this? how had he so quickly turned aversion
into, at any rate, acquaintance? how had he overcome the enmity with
which these ladies had been ready to receive him, and made his peace
with them so easily?

My readers will guess from what I have written that I myself do not like

41

Mr Slope; but I am constrained to admit that he is a man of parts. He knows how to say a soft word in the proper place; he knows how to adapt his flattery to the ears of his hearers; he knows the wiles of the serpent, and he uses them. Could Mr Slope have adapted his manners to men as well as to women, could he ever have learnt the ways of a gentleman, he might have risen to great things.

He commenced his acquaintance with Eleanor by praising her father. He had, he said, become aware that he had unfortunately offended the feelings of a man of whom he could not speak too highly; he would not now allude to a subject which was probably too serious for drawing-room conversation, but he would say, that it had been very far from him to utter a word in disparagement of a man, of whom all the world, at least the clerical world, spoke so highly as it did of Mr Harding. And so he went on, unsaying a great deal of his sermon, expressing his highest admiration for the precentor's musical talents, eulogising the father and the daughter and the sister-in-law, speaking in that low silky whisper which he always had specially prepared for feminine ears, and, ultimately, gaining his object. When he left, he expressed a hope that he might again be allowed to call; and though Eleanor gave no verbal assent to this, she did not express dissent: and so Mr Slope's right to visit at the widow's house was established.

The day after this visit Eleanor told her father of it, and expressed an opinion that Mr Slope was not quite so black as he had been painted. Mr Harding opened his eyes rather wider than usual when he heard what had occurred, but he said little; he could not agree in any praise of Mr Slope, and it was not his practice to say much evil of any one. He did not, however, like the visit, and simple-minded as he was, he felt sure that Mr Slope had some deeper motive than the mere pleasure of making soft speeches to two ladies.

Mr Harding, however, had come to see his daughter with other purpose than that of speaking either good or evil of Mr Slope. He had come to tell her that the place of warden in Hiram's hospital was again to be filled up, and that in all probability he would once more return to his old home and his twelve bedesmen.

'But,' said he, laughing. 'I shall be greatly shorn of my ancient glory.'

'Why so, papa?'

'This new act of parliament, that is to put us all on our feet again,' continued he, 'settles my income at four hundred and fifty pounds per annum.'

'Four hundred and fifty,' said she, 'instead of eight hundred! Well; that is rather shabby. But still, papa, you'll have the dear old house and the garden?'

'My dear,' said he, 'it's worth twice the money;' and as he spoke he showed a jaunty kind of satisfaction in the tone and manner, and in the quick, pleasant way in which he paced Eleanor's drawing-room. 'It's worth twice the money. I shall have the house and the garden, and a larger income than I can possibly want.'

'At any rate, you'll have no extravagant daughter to provide for;' and as she spoke, the young widow put her arm within his, and made him sit on the sofa beside her; 'at any rate you'll not have that expense.'

'No, my dear; and I shall be rather lonely without her; but we won't think of that now. As regards income I shall have plenty for all I want. I shall have my old house; and I don't mind owning now that I have felt sometimes the inconvenience of living in a lodging. Lodgings are very nice for young men, but at my time of life there is a want of – I hardly know what to call it, perhaps not respectability –'

'Oh, papa! I'm sure there's been nothing like that. Nobody has thought it; nobody in all Barchester has been more respected than you have been since you took those rooms in High Street. Nobody! Not the dean in his deanery, or the archdeacon out at Plumstead.'

'The archdeacon would not be much obliged to you if he heard you,' said he, smiling somewhat at the exclusive manner in which his daughter confined her illustration to the church dignitaries of the chapter of Barchester; 'but at any rate I shall be glad to get back to the old house. Since I heard that it was all settled, I have begun to fancy that I can't be comfortable without my two sitting-rooms.'

'Come and stay with me, papa, till it is settled – there's a dear papa.'

'Thank ye, Nelly. But no; I won't do that. It would make two movings. I shall be very glad to get back to my old men again. Alas! alas! There have six of them gone in these few last years. Six out of twelve! And the others I fear have had but a sorry life of it there. Poor Bunce, poor old Bunce!'

Bunce was one of the surviving recipients of Hiram's charity; an old man, now over ninety, who had long been a favourite of Mr Harding's.

'How happy old Bunce will be,' said Mrs Bold, clapping her soft hands softly. 'How happy they all will be to have you back again. You may be sure there will soon be friendship among them again when you are there.'

'But,' said he, half laughing, 'I am to have new troubles, which will be terrible to me. There are to be twelve old women, and a matron. How shall I manage twelve women and a matron!'

'The matron will manage the women of course.'

'And who'll manage the matron?' said he.

'She won't want to be managed. She'll be a great lady herself, I suppose. But, papa, where will the matron live? she is not to live in the warden's house with you, is she?'

'Well, I hope not, my dear.'

'Oh, papa, I tell you fairly, I won't have a matron for a new stepmother.'

'You shan't, my dear; that is, if I can help it. But they are going to build another house for the matron and the women; and I believe they haven't even fixed yet on the site of the building.'

'And have they appointed the matron?' said Eleanor.

'They haven't appointed the warden yet,' replied he.

'But there's no doubt about that, I suppose,' said his daughter.

Mr Harding explained that he thought there was no doubt; that the archdeacon had declared as much, saying that the bishop and his chaplain between them had not the power to appoint any one else, even if they had the will to do so, and sufficient impudence to carry out such a will. The archdeacon was of opinion, that though Mr Harding had resigned his wardenship, and had done so unconditionally, he had done so under circumstances which left the bishop no choice as to his reappointment, now that the affair of the hospital had been settled on a new basis by act of parliament. Such was the archdeacon's opinion, and his father-in-law received it without a shadow of doubt.

Dr Grantly had always been strongly opposed to Mr Harding's resignation of the place. He had done all in his power to dissuade him from it. He had considered that Mr Harding was bound to withstand the popular clamour with which he was attacked for receiving so large an income as eight hundred a year from such a charity, and was not even yet satisfied that his father-in-law's conduct had not been pusillanimous and undignified. He looked also on this reduction of the warden's income as a shabby, paltry scheme on the part of government for escaping from a difficulty into which it had been brought by the public press. Dr Grantly observed that the government had no more right to dispose of a sum of four hundred and fifty pounds a year out of the income of Hiram's legacy, than of nine hundred; whereas, as he said, the bishop, dean, and chapter clearly had a right to settle what sum should be paid. He also declared that the government had no more right to saddle the charity with twelve old women than with twelve hundred; and he was, therefore, very indignant on the matter. He probably forgot when so talking that government had done nothing of the kind, and had never assumed any such might or any such right. He made the common mistake of attributing to the government, which in such matters is powerless, the doings of parliament, which in such matters is omnipotent.

But though he felt that the glory and honour of the situation of warden of Barchester hospital were indeed curtailed by the new arrangement; that the whole establishment had to a certain degree been made vile by the touch of Whig commissioners; that the place with its lessened income, its old women, and other innovations, was very different from the hospital of former days; still the archdeacon was too practical a man of the world to wish that his father-in-law, who had at present little more than 200*l.* per annum for all his wants, should refuse the situation, defiled, undignified, and commission-ridden as it was.

Mr Harding had, accordingly, made up his mind that he would return to his old home at the hospital, and to tell the truth, had experienced almost a childish pleasure in the idea of doing so. The diminished income was to him not even the source of momentary regret. The matron and the old women did rather go against the grain; but he was able to console himself with the reflection, that, after all, such an arrangement might be of real service to the poor of the city. The thought that he must receive his re-appointment as the gift of the new bishop, and probably through the hands of Mr Slope, annoyed him a little; but his mind was set at rest by the assurance of the archdeacon that there would be no favour in such a presentation. The re-appointment of the old warden would be regarded by all the world as a matter of course. Mr Harding, therefore, felt no hesitation in telling his daughter that they might look upon his return to his old quarters as a settled matter.

'And you won't have to ask for it, papa.'

'Certainly not, my dear. There is no ground on which I could ask for any favour from the bishop, whom, indeed, I hardly know. Nor would I ask a favour, the granting of which might possibly be made a question to be settled by Mr Slope. No,' said he, moved for a moment by a spirit very unlike his own. 'I certainly shall be very glad to go back to the hospital; but I would never go there, if it were necessary that my doing so should be the subject of a request to Mr Slope.'

This little outbreak of her father's anger jarred on the present tone of Eleanor's mind. She had not learnt to like Mr Slope, but she had learnt to think that he had much respect for her father; and she would, therefore, willingly use her efforts to induce something like good feeling between them.

'Papa,' said she, 'I think you somewhat mistake Mr Slope's character.'

'Do I?' said he, placidly.

'I think you do, papa. I think he intended no personal disrespect to you when he preached the sermon which made the archdeacon and the dean so angry!'

'I never supposed he did, my dear. I hope I never inquired within myself whether he did or no. Such a matter would be unworthy of any inquiry, and very unworthy of the consideration of the chapter. But I fear he intended disrespect to the ministration of God's services, as conducted in conformity with the rules of the Church of England.'

'But might it not be that he thought it his duty to express his dissent from that which you, and the dean, and all of us here so much approve?'

'It can hardly be the duty of a young man rudely to assail the religious convictions of his elders in the church. Courtesy should have kept him silent, even if neither charity nor modesty could do so.'

'But Mr Slope would say that on such a subject the commands of his heavenly Master do not admit of his being silent.'

'Nor of his being courteous, Eleanor?'

'He did not say that, papa.'

'Believe me, my child, that Christian ministers are never called on by God's word to insult the convictions, or even the prejudices of their brethren: and that religion is at any rate not less susceptible of urbane and courteous conduct among men, than any other study which men may take up. I am sorry to say that I cannot defend Mr Slope's sermon in the cathedral. But come, my dear, put on your bonnet, and let us walk round the dear old gardens at the hospital. I have never yet had the heart to go beyond the court-yard since we left the place. Now I think I can venture to enter.'

Eleanor rang the bell, and gave a variety of imperative charges as to the welfare of the precious baby, whom, all but unwillingly, she was about to leave for an hour or so, and then sauntered forth with her father to revisit the old hospital. It had been forbidden ground to her as well as to him since the day on which they had walked forth together from its walls.

✼ NINE ✼

The Stanhope Family

IT IS NOW THREE MONTHS SINCE Dr Proudie began his reign, and changes have already been effected in the diocese which show at least the energy of an active mind. Among other things absentee clergymen have been favoured with hints much too strong to be overlooked. Poor dear old Bishop Grantly had on this matter been too lenient, and the archdeacon had never been inclined to be severe with those who were absent on reputable pretences, and who provided for their duties in a liberal way.

Among the greatest of the diocesan sinners in this respect was Dr Vesey Stanhope. Years had now passed since he had done a day's duty; and yet there was no reason against his doing duty except a want of inclination on his own part. He held a prebendal stall in the diocese; one of the best residences in the close; and the two large rectories of Crabtree Canonicorum, and Stogpingum. Indeed, he had the cure of three parishes, for that of Eiderdown was joined to Stogpingum. He had resided in Italy for twelve years. His first going there had been attributed to a sore throat; and that sore throat, though never repeated in any violent manner, had stood him in such stead, that it had enabled him to live in easy idleness ever since.

He had now been summoned home – not, indeed, with rough violence, or by any peremptory command, but by a mandate which he found himself unable to disregard. Mr Slope had written to him by the bishop's desire. In the first place, the bishop much wanted the valuable co-operation of Dr Vesey Stanhope in the diocese; in the next, the bishop thought it his imperative duty to become personally acquainted with the most conspicuous of his diocesan clergy; then the bishop thought it essentially necessary for Dr Stanhope's own interests, that Dr Stanhope should, at any rate for a time, return to Barchester; and lastly, it was said that so strong a feeling was at the present moment evinced by the hierarchs of the church with reference to the absence of its clerical members, that it behoved Dr Vesey Stanhope not to allow his name to stand among those which would probably in a few months be submitted to the councils of the nation.

There was something so ambiguously frightful in this last threat that Dr Stanhope determined to spend two or three summer months at his residence in Barchester. His rectories were inhabited by his curates, and he felt himself from disuse to be unfit for parochial duty; but his prebendal home was kept empty for him, and he thought it probable that he might be able now and again to preach a prebendal sermon. He arrived, therefore, with all his family at Barchester, and he and they must be introduced to my readers.

The great family characteristic of the Stanhopes might probably be said to be heartlessness; but this want of feeling was, in most of them, accompanied by so great an amount of good nature as to make itself but little noticeable to the world. They were so prone to oblige their neighbours that their neighbours failed to perceive how indifferent to them was the happiness and well-being of those around them. The Stanhopes would visit you in your sickness (provided it were not contagious), would bring you oranges, French novels, and the last new bit of scandal, and then hear of your death or your recovery with an equally indifferent composure. Their conduct to each other was the same as to the world; they bore and forebore: and there was sometimes, as will be seen, much necessity for forbearing: but their love among themselves rarely reached above this. It is astonishing how much each of the family was able to do, and how much each did, to prevent the well-being of the other four.

For there were five in all; the doctor, namely, and Mrs Stanhope, two daughters, and one son. The doctor, perhaps, was the least singular and most estimable of them all, and yet such good qualities as he possessed were all negative. He was a good looking rather plethoric gentleman of about sixty years of age. His hair was snow white, very plentiful, and somewhat like wool of the finest description. His whiskers were very large and very white, and gave to his face the appearance of a benevolent sleepy old lion. His dress was always unexceptionable. Although he had lived so many years in Italy it was invariably of a decent clerical hue, but it never was hyperclerical. He was a man not given to much talking, but what little he did say was generally well said. His reading seldom went beyond romances and poetry of the lightest and not always most moral description. He was thoroughly a *bon vivant*; an accomplished judge of wine, though he never drank to excess; and a most inexorable critic in all affairs touching the kitchen. He had had much to forgive in his own family, since a family had grown up around him, and had forgiven everything – except inattention to his dinner. His weakness in that respect was now fully understood, and his temper but seldom tried. As Dr Stanhope was a clergyman, it may be supposed that his religious convictions made up a considerable part of his character; but this was not so. That he had religious convictions must be believed; but he rarely obtruded them, even on his children. This abstinence on his part was not systematic, but very characteristic of the man. It was not that he had predetermined never to influence their thoughts; but he was so habitually idle that his time for doing so had never come till the opportunity for doing so was gone forever. Whatever conviction the father may have had, the children were at any rate but indifferent members of the church from which he drew his income.

Such was Dr Stanhope. The features of Mrs Stanhope's character were even less plainly marked than those of her lord. The *far niente* of her Italian life had entered into her very soul, and brought her to regard a state of inactivity as the only earthly good. In manner and appearance she was exceedingly prepossessing. She had been a beauty, and even now, at fifty-five, she was a handsome woman. Her dress was always perfect: she never dressed but once in the day, and never appeared till between three and four; but when she did appear, she appeared at her best. Whether the toil rested partly with her, or wholly with her handmaid, it is not for such a one as the author even to imagine. The structure of her attire was always elaborate, and yet never over laboured. She was rich in apparel, but not bedizened with finery; her ornaments were costly, rare, and such as could not fail to attract notice, but they did not look as though worn with that purpose. She well knew the great architectural secret of decorating her constructions, and never descended to construct a decoration. But when we have said that Mrs Stanhope knew how to dress, and used her knowledge daily, we have said all. Other purpose in life she had none. It was something, indeed, that she did not interfere with the purposes of others. In early life she had undergone great trials with reference to the doctor's dinners; but for the last ten or twelve years her eldest daughter Charlotte had taken that labour off her hands, and she had had little to trouble her – little, that is, till the edict for this terrible English journey had gone forth: since, then, indeed, her life had been laborious enough. For such a one, the toil of being carried from the shores of Como to the city of Barchester is more than labour enough, let the care of the carriers be ever so vigilant. Mrs Stanhope had been obliged to have every one of her dresses taken in from the effects of the journey.

Charlotte Stanhope was at this time about thirty-five years old; and, whatever may have been her faults, she had none of those which belong particularly to old young ladies. She neither dressed young, nor talked young, nor indeed looked young. She appeared to be perfectly content with her time of life, and in no way affected the graces of youth. She was a fine young woman; and had she been a man, would have been a very fine young man. All that was done in the house, and that was not done by servants, was done by her. She gave the orders, paid the bills, hired and dismissed the domestics, made the tea, carved the meat, and managed everything in the Stanhope household. She, and she alone, could ever induce her father to look into the state of his worldly concerns. She, and she alone, could in any degree control the absurdities of her sister. She, and she alone, prevented the whole family from falling into utter disrepute and beggary. It was by her advice that they now found themselves very unpleasantly situated in Barchester.

So far, the character of Charlotte Stanhope is not unprepossessing. But it remains to be said, that the influence which she had in her family, though it had been used to a certain extent for their worldly well-being, had not been used to their real benefit, as it might have been. She had aided her father in his indifference to his professional duties, counselling him that his livings were as much his individual property as the estates of his elder brother were the property of that worthy peer. She had for years past stifled every little rising wish for a return to England which the doctor had from time to time expressed. She had encouraged her mother in her idleness in order that she herself might be mistress and manager of the Stanhope household. She had encouraged and fostered the follies of her sister, though she was always willing, and often able, to protect her from their probable result. She had done her best, and had thoroughly succeeded in spoiling her brother, and turning him loose upon the world an idle man without a profession, and without a shilling that he could call his own.

Miss Stanhope was a clever woman, able to talk on most subjects, and quite indifferent as to what the subject was. She prided herself on her freedom from English prejudice, and she might have added, from feminine delicacy. On religion she was a pure freethinker, and with much want of true affection, delighted to throw out her own views before the troubled mind of her father. To have shaken what remained of his Church of England faith would have gratified her much; but the idea of his abandoning his preferment in the church had never once presented itself to her mind. How could he indeed, when he had no income from any other source?

But the two most prominent members of the family still remain to be described. The second child had been christened Madeline, and had been a great beauty. We need not say had been, for she was never more beautiful than at the time of which we write, though her person for many years had been disfigured by an accident. It is unnecessary that we should give in detail the early history of Madeline Stanhope. She had gone to Italy when about seventeen years of age, and had been allowed to make the most of her surpassing beauty in the saloons of Milan, and among the crowded villas along the shores of the Lake of Como. She had become famous for adventures in which her character was just not lost, and had destroyed the hearts of a dozen cavaliers without once being touched in her own. Blood had flowed in quarrels about her charms, and she heard of these encounters with pleasurable excitement. It had been told of her that on one occasion she had stood by in the disguise of a page, and had seen her lover fall.

As is so often the case, she had married the very worst of those who sought her hand. Why she had chosen Paulo Neroni, a man of no birth and no property, a mere captain in the pope's guard, one who had come up to Milan either simply as an adventurer or else as a spy, a man of harsh temper and oily manners, mean in figure, swarthy in face, and so false in words as to be hourly detected, need not now be told. When the moment for doing so came, she had probably no alternative. He at any rate, had become her husband; and after a prolonged honeymoon among the lakes, they had gone together to Rome, the papal captain having vainly endeavoured to induce his wife to remain behind him.

Six months afterwards she arrived at her father's house a cripple, and a mother. She had arrived without even notice, with hardly clothes to cover her, and without one of those many ornaments which had graced her bridal *trousseau*. Her baby was in the arms of a poor girl from Milan, whom she had taken in exchange for the Roman maid who had accompanied her thus far, and who had then, as her mistress said, become homesick and had returned. It was clear that the lady had determined that there should be no witness to tell stories of her life in Rome.

She had fallen, she said, in ascending a ruin, and had fatally injured the sinews of her knee; so fatally, that when she stood she lost eight inches of her accustomed height; so fatally, that when she essayed to move, she could only drag herself painfully along, with protruded hip and extended foot in a manner less graceful than that of a hunchback. She had consequently made up her mind, once and for ever, that she would never stand, and never attempt to move herself.

Stories were not slow to follow her, averring that she had been cruelly ill used by Neroni, and that to his violence had she owed her accident. Be that as it may, little had been said about her husband, but that little had made it clearly intelligible to the family that Signor Neroni was to be seen and heard of no more. There was no question as to re-admitting the poor ill used beauty to her old family rights, no question as to adopting her infant daughter beneath the Stanhope roof tree. Though heartless, the Stanhopes were not selfish. The two were taken in, petted, made much of, for a time all but adored, and then felt by the two parents to be great nuisances in the house. But in the house the lady was, and there she remained, having her own way, though that way was not very comfortable with the customary usages of an English clergyman.

Madame Neroni, though forced to give up all motion in the world, had no intention whatever of giving up the world itself. The beauty of her face was uninjured, and that beauty was of a peculiar kind. Her copious rich brown hair was worn in Grecian *bandeaux* round her head, displaying as much as possible of her forehead and cheeks. Her forehead, though rather low, was very beautiful from its perfect contour and pearly whiteness. Her eyes were long and large, and marvellously bright; might I venture to say, bright as Lucifer's, I should perhaps best express the depth of their brilliancy. They were dreadful eyes to look at, such as would absolutely deter any man of quiet mind and easy spirit from attempting a passage of arms with such foes. There was talent in them, and the fire of passion and the play of wit, but there was no love. Cruelty was there instead, and courage, a desire of masterhood, cunning, and a wish for mischief. And yet, as eyes, they were very beautiful. The eyelashes were long and perfect, and the long steady unabashed gaze, with which she would look into the face of her admirer, fascinated while it frightened him. She was a basilisk from whom an ardent lover of beauty could make no escape. Her nose and mouth and teeth and chin and neck and bust were perfect, much more so at twenty-eight than they had been at eighteen. What wonder that with such charms still glowing in her face, and with such deformity destroying her figure, she should resolve to be seen, but only to be seen reclining on a sofa.

Her resolve had not been carried out without difficulty. She had still frequented the opera at Milan; she had still been seen occasionally in the saloons of the *noblesse*; she had caused herself to be carried in and out from her carriage, and that in such a manner as in no wise to disturb her charms, disarrange her dress, or expose her deformities. Her sister always accompanied her and a maid, a manservant also, and on state occasions, two. It was impossible that her purpose could have been achieved with less: and yet, poor as she was, she had achieved her purpose. And then again the more dissolute Italian youths of Milan frequented the Stanhope villa and surrounded her couch, not greatly to her father's satisfaction. Sometimes his spirit would rise, a dark spot would show itself on his cheek, and he would rebel; but Charlotte would assuage him with some peculiar triumph of her culinary art, and all again would be smooth for a while.

Madeline affected all manner of rich and quaint devices in the garniture of her room, her person, and her feminine belongings. In nothing was this more apparent than in the visiting card which she had prepared for her use. For such an article one would say that she, in her present state, could have but small need, seeing how improbable it was that she should make a morning call: but not such was her own opinion. Her card was surrounded by a deep border of gilding; on this she had imprinted, in three lines –

> 'La Signora Madeline
> 'Vesey Neroni.
> – Nata Stanhope.'

And over the name she had a bright gilt coronet, which certainly looked very magnificent. How she had come to concoct such a name for herself it would be difficult to explain. Her father had been christened Vesey, as another man is christened Thomas; and she had no more right to assume it than would have the daughter of a Mr Josiah Jones to call herself Mrs Josiah Smith, on marrying a man of the latter name. The gold coronet was equally out of place, and perhaps inserted with even less excuse. Paulo Neroni had had not the faintest title to call himself a scion of even Italian nobility. Had the pair met in England Neroni would probably have been a count; but they had met in Italy, and any such pretence on his part would have been simply ridiculous. A coronet, however, was a pretty ornament, and if it could solace a poor cripple to have such on her card, who would begrudge it to her?

Of her husband, or of his individual family, she never spoke; but with her admirers she would often allude in a mysterious way to her married life and isolated state, and, pointing to her daughter, would call her the last of the blood of the emperors, thus referring Neroni's extraction to the old Roman family from which the worst of the Cæsars sprang.

The 'Signora' was not without talent, and not without a certain sort of industry; she was an indomitable letter writer, and her letters were worth the postage: they were full of wit, mischief, satire, love, latitudinarian philosophy, free religion, and, sometimes, alas! loose ribaldry. The subject, however, depended entirely on the recipient, and she was prepared to correspond with any one but moral young ladies or stiff old women. She wrote also a kind of poetry, generally in Italian, and short romances, generally in French. She read much of a desultory sort of literature, and as a modern linguist had really made great proficiency. Such was the lady who had now come to wound the hearts of the men of Barchester.

Ethelbert Stanhope was in some respects like his younger sister, but he was less inestimable as a man than she as a woman. His great fault was an entire absence of that principle which should have induced him, as the son of a man without fortune, to earn his own bread. Many attempts had been made to get him to do so, but these had all been frustrated, not so much by idleness on his part, as by a disinclination to exert himself in any way not to his taste. He had been educated at Eton, and had been intended for the Church, but had left Cambridge in disgust after a single term, and notified to his father his intention to study for the bar. Preparatory to that, he thought it well that he should attend a German university, and consequently went to Leipsic. There he remained two years, and brought away a knowledge of German and a taste for the fine arts. He still, however, intended himself for the bar, took chambers, engaged himself to sit at the feet of a learned pundit, and spent a season in London. He there found that all his aptitudes inclined him to the life of an artist, and he determined to live by painting. With this object he returned to Milan, and had himself rigged out for Rome. As a painter he might have earned his bread, for he wanted only diligence to excel; but when at Rome his mind was carried away by other things: he soon wrote home for money, saying that he had been converted to the Mother Church, that he was already an acolyte of the Jesuits, and that he was about to start with others to Palestine on a mission for converting Jews. He did go to Judea, but being unable to convert the Jews, was converted by them. He again wrote home, to say that Moses was the only giver of perfect laws to the world, that the coming of the true Messiah was at hand, that great things were doing in Palestine, and that he had met one of the family of Sidonia, a most remarkable man, who was now on his way to Western Europe, and whom he had induced to deviate from his route with the object of calling at the Stanhope villa. Ethelbert then expressed his hope that his mother and sisters would listen to this wonderful prophet. His father he knew could not do so from pecuniary considerations. This Sidonia, however, did not take so strong a fancy to him as another of that family once did a young English nobleman. At least he provided him with no heaps of gold as large as lions; so that the Judaised Ethelbert was again obliged to draw on the revenues of the Christian Church.

It is needless to tell how the father swore that he would send no more money and receive no Jew; nor how Charlotte declared that Ethelbert could not be left penniless in Jerusalem, and how 'La Signora Neroni' resolved to have Sidonia at her feet. The money was sent, and the Jew did come. The Jew did come, but he was not at all to the taste of 'La Signora.' He was a dirty little old man, and though he had provided no golden lions, he had, it seems, relieved young Stanhope's necessities. He positively refused to leave the villa till he had got a bill from the doctor on his London bankers.

Ethelbert did not long remain a Jew. He soon reappeared at the villa without prejudices on the subject of his religion, and with a firm resolve to achieve fame and fortune as a sculptor. He brought with him some models which he had originated at Rome, and which really gave such fair promise that his father was induced to go to further expense in furthering these views. Ethelbert opened an establishment, or rather took lodgings and a workshop, at Carrara, and there spoilt much marble, and made some few pretty images. Since that period, now four years ago, he had alternated between Carrara and the villa, but his sojourns at the workshop became shorter and shorter, and those at the villa longer and longer. 'Twas no wonder; for Carrara is not a spot in which an Englishman would like to dwell.

When the family started for England he had resolved not to be left behind, and with the assistance of his elder sister had carried his point against his father's wishes. It was necessary, he said, that he should come to England for orders. How otherwise was he to bring his profession to account?

In personal appearance Ethelbert Stanhope was the most singular of beings. He was certainly very handsome. He had his sister Madeline's eyes without their stare, and without their hard cunning cruel firmness. They were also very much lighter, and of so light and clear a blue as to make his face remarkable, if nothing else did so. On entering a room with him, Ethelbert's blue eyes would be the first thing you would see, and on leaving it almost the last you would forget. His light hair was very long and silky, coming down over his coat. His beard had been prepared in holy land, and was patriarchal. He never shaved, and rarely trimmed it. It was glossy, soft, clean, and altogether not unprepossessing. It was such, that ladies might desire to reel it off and work it into their patterns in lieu of floss silk. His complexion was fair and almost pink, he was small in height, and slender in limb, but well-made, and his voice was of peculiar sweetness.

In manner and dress he was equally remarkable. He had none of the *mauvaise honte* of an Englishman. He required no introduction to make himself agreeable to any person. He habitually addressed strangers, ladies as well as men, without any such formality, and in doing so never seemed to meet with rebuke. His costume cannot be described, because it was so various; but it was always totally opposed in every principle of colour and construction to the dress of those with whom he for the time consorted.

He was habitually addicted to making love to ladies, and did so without any scruple of conscience, or any idea that such a practice was amiss. He had no heart to touch himself, and was literally unaware that humanity was subject to such an infliction. He had not thought much about it; but, had he been asked, would have said, that ill-treating a lady's heart meant injuring her promotion in the world. His principles therefore forbade him to pay attention to a girl, if he thought any man was present whom it might suit her to marry. In this manner, his good nature frequently interfered with his amusement; but he had no other motive in abstaining from the fullest declarations of love to every girl that pleased his eye.

Bertie Stanhope, as he was generally called, was, however, popular with both sexes; and with Italians as well as English. His circle of acquaintance was very large, and embraced people of all sorts. He had no respect for rank, and no aversion to those below him. He had lived on familar terms with English peers, German shopkeepers, and Roman priests. All people were nearly alike to him. He was above, or rather below, all prejudices. No virtue could charm him, no vice shock him. He had about him a natural good manner, which seemed to qualify him for the highest circles, and yet he was never out of place in the lowest. He had no principle, no regard for others, no self-respect, no desire to be other than a drone in the hive, if only he could, as a drone, get what honey was sufficient for him. Of honey, in his latter days, it may probably be presaged, that he will have but short allowance.

Such was the family of the Stanhopes, who, at this period, suddenly joined themselves to the ecclesiastical circle of Barchester close. Any stranger union, it would be impossible perhaps to conceive. And it was not as though they all fell down into the cathedral precincts hitherto unknown and untalked of. In such case no amalgamation would have been at all probable between the new comers and either the Proudie set or the Grantly set. But such was far from being the case. The Stanhopes were all known by name in

Barchester, and Barchester was prepared to receive them with open arms. The doctor was one of her prebendaries, one of her rectors, one of her pillars of strength; and was, moreover, counted on, as a sure ally, both by Proudies and Grantlys.

He himself was the brother of one peer, and his wife was the sister of another – and both these peers were lords of whiggish tendency, with whom the new bishop had some sort of alliance. This was sufficient to give to Mr Slope high hope that he might enlist Dr Stanhope on his side, before his enemies could out-manœuver him. On the other hand, the old dean had many many years ago, in the days of the doctor's clerical energies, been instrumental in assisting him in his views as to preferment; and many many years ago also, the two doctors, Stanhope and Grantly, had, as young parsons, been joyous together in the common rooms of Oxford. Dr Grantly, consequently, did not doubt but that the new comer would range himself under his banners.

Little did any of them dream of what ingredients the Stanhope family was now composed.

✖ TEN ✖

Mrs Proudie's Reception – Commenced

THE BISHOP AND HIS WIFE HAD ONLY spent three or four days in Barchester on the occasion of their first visit. His lordship had, as we have seen, taken his seat on his throne; but his demeanour there, into which it had been his intention to infuse much hierarchal dignity, had been a good deal disarranged by the audacity of his chaplain's sermon. He had hardly dared to look his clergy in the face, and to declare by the severity of his countenance that in truth he meant all that his factotum was saying on his behalf; nor yet did he dare to throw Mr Slope over, and show to those around him that he was no party to the sermon, and would resent it.

He had accordingly blessed his people in a shambling manner, not at all to his own satisfaction, and had walked back to his palace with his mind very doubtful as to what he would say to his chaplain on the subject. He did not remain long in doubt. He had hardly doffed his lawn when the partner of all his toils entered his study, and exclaimed even before she had seated herself –

'Bishop, did you ever hear a more sublime, more spirit-moving, more appropriate discourse than that?'

'Well, my love; ha – hum – he!' The bishop did not know what to say.

'I hope, my lord, you don't mean to say you disapprove?'

There was a look about the lady's eye which did not admit of my lord's disapproving at that moment. He felt that if he intended to disapprove, it must be now or never; but he also felt that it could not be now. It was not in him to say to the wife of his bosom that Mr Slope's sermon was ill-timed, impertinent and vexatious.

'No, no,' replied the bishop. 'No, I can't say I disapprove – a very clever sermon and very well intended, and I dare say will do a great deal of good.' This last praise was added, seeing that what he had already said by no means satisfied Mrs Proudie.

'I hope it will,' said she. 'I am sure it was well deserved. Did you ever in your life, bishop, hear anything so like play-acting as the way in which Mr Harding sings the litany? I shall beg Mr Slope to continue a course of sermons on the subject till all that is altered. We will have at any rate, in our cathedral, a decent, godly, modest morning service. There must be no more play-acting here now;' and so the lady rang for lunch.

The bishop knew more about cathedrals and deans, and precentors and church services than his wife did, and also more of a bishop's powers. But he thought it better at present to let the subject drop.

'My dear,' said he, 'I think we must go back to London on Tuesday. I find my staying here will be very inconvenient to the Government.'

The bishop knew that to this proposal his wife would not object; and he also felt that by thus retreating from the ground of battle, the heat of the fight might be got over in his absence.

'Mr Slope will remain here, of course?' said the lady.

'Oh, of course,' said the bishop.

Thus, after less than a week's sojourn in his palace, did the bishop fly from Barchester; nor did he return to it for two months, the London season being then over. During that time Mr Slope was not idle, but he did not again essay to preach in the cathedral. In answer to Mrs Proudie's letters, advising a course of sermons, he had pleaded that he would at any rate wish to put off such an undertaking till she was there to hear them.

He had employed his time in consolidating a Proudie and Slope party – or rather a Slope and Proudie party, and he had not employed his time in vain. He did not meddle with the dean and chapter, except by giving them little teasing intimations of the bishop's wishes about this and the bishop's feelings about that, in a manner which was to them sufficiently annoying, but which they could not resent. He preached once or twice in a distant church in the suburbs of the city, but made no allusion to the cathedral service. He commenced the establishment of two 'Bishop's Barchester Sabbath-day Schools,' gave notice of a proposed 'Bishop's Barchester Young Men's Sabbath Evening Lecture Room' – and wrote three or four letters to the manager of the Barchester branch railway, informing him how anxious the bishop was that the Sunday trains should be discontinued.

At the end of two months, however, the bishop and the lady reappeared; and as a happy harbinger of their return, heralded their advent by the promise of an evening party on the largest scale. The tickets of invitation were sent out from London – they were dated from Bruton Street, and were despatched by the odious Sabbath breaking railway, in a huge brown paper parcel to Mr Slope. Everybody calling himself a gentleman, or herself a lady, within the city of Barchester, and a circle of two miles round it, was included. Tickets were sent to all the diocesan clergy, and also to many other persons of priestly note, of whose absence the bishop, or at least the bishop's wife, felt tolerably confident. It was intended, however, to be a thronged and noticeable affair, and preparations were made for receiving some hundreds.

And now there arose considerable agitation among the Grantlyites whether or no they would attend the episcopal bidding. The first feeling with them all was to send the briefest excuses both for themselves and their wives and daughters. But by degrees policy prevailed over passion. The archdeacon perceived that he would be making a false step if he allowed the cathedral clergy to give the bishop just ground of umbrage. They all met in conclave and agreed to go. They would show that they were willing to respect the office, much as they might dislike the man. They agreed to go. The old dean would crawl in, if it were but for half an hour. The chancellor, treasurer, archdeacon, prebendaries, and minor canons would all go, and would all take their wives. Mr Harding was especially bidden to do so, resolving in his heart to keep himself far removed from Mrs Proudie. And Mrs Bold was determined to go, though assured by her father that there was no necessity for such a sacrifice on her part. When all Barchester was to be there, neither Eleanor nor Mary Bold understood why they should stay away. Had they not been invited separately? and had not a separate little note from the chaplain, couched in the most respectful language, been enclosed with the huge episcopal card?

And the Stanhopes would be there, one and all. Even the lethargic mother would so far bestir herself on such an occasion. They had only just arrived. The card was at the residence waiting for them. No one in Barchester had seen them; and what better opportunity could they have of showing themselves to the Barchester world? Some few old friends, such as the archdeacon and his wife, had called, and had found the doctor and his eldest daughter; but the *élite* of the family were not yet known.

The doctor indeed wished in his heart to prevent the signora from accepting the bishop's invitation; but she herself had fully determined that she would accept it. If her father was ashamed of having his daughter carried into a bishop's palace, she had no such feeling.

'Indeed, I shall,' she had said to her sister who had gently endeavoured to dissuade her, by saying that the company would consist wholly of parsons and parsons' wives. 'Parsons, I suppose, are much the same as other men, if you strip them of their black coats; and as to their wives, I dare say they won't trouble me. You may tell papa I don't at all mean to be left at home.'

Papa was told, and felt that he could do nothing but yield. He also felt that it was useless for him now to be ashamed of his children. Such as they were, they had become such under his auspices; as he had made his bed, so he must lie upon it; as he had sown his seed, so must he reap his corn. He did not indeed utter such reflections in such language, but such was the gist of his thoughts. It was not because Madeline was a cripple that he shrank from seeing her make one of the bishop's guests; but because he knew that she would practise her accustomed lures, and behave herself in a way that could not fail of being distasteful to the propriety of Englishwomen. These things had annoyed but not shocked him in Italy. There they had shocked no one; but here in Barchester, here among his fellow parsons, he was ashamed that they should be seen. Such had been his feelings, but he repressed them. What if his brother clergymen were shocked! They could not take from him his preferment because the manners of his married daughter were too free.

La Signora Neroni had, at any rate, no fear that she would shock anybody. Her ambition was to create a sensation, to have parsons at her feet, seeing that the manhood of Barchester consisted mainly of parsons, and to send, if possible, every parson's wife home with a green fit of jealousy. None could be too old for her, and hardly any too young. None too sanctified, and none too worldly. She was quite prepared to entrap the bishop himself, and then to turn up her nose at the bishop's wife. She did not doubt of success, for she had always succeeded; but one thing was absolutely necessary, she must secure the entire use of a sofa.

The card sent to Dr and Mrs Stanhope and family, had been so sent in an envelope, having on the cover Mr Slope's name. The signora soon learnt that Mrs Proudie was not yet at the palace, and that the chaplain was managing everything. It was much more in her line to apply to him than to the lady, and she accordingly wrote him the prettiest little billet in the world. In five lines she explained everything, declared how impossible it was for her not to be desirous to make the acquaintance of such persons as the Bishop of Barchester and his wife, and she might add also of Mr Slope, depicted her own grievous state, and concluded by being assured that Mrs Proudie would forgive her extreme hardihood in petitioning to be allowed to be carried to a sofa. She then enclosed one of her beautiful cards. In return she received as polite an answer from Mr Slope – a sofa should be kept in the large drawing-room, immediately at the top of the grand stairs, especially for her use.

And now the day of the party had arrived. The bishop and his wife came down from town, only on the morning of the eventful day, as behoved such great people to do; but Mr Slope had toiled day and might to see that everything should be in right order. There had been much to do. No company had been seen in the palace since heaven knows when. New furniture had been required, new pots and pans, new cups and saucers, new dishes and plates. Mrs Proudie had at first declared that she would condescend to nothing so vulgar as eating and drinking; but Mr Slope had talked, or rather written her out of economy! Bishops should be given to hospitality, and hospitality meant eating and drinking. So the supper was conceded; the guests, however, were to stand as they consumed it.

There were four rooms opening into each other on the first floor of the house, which were denominated the drawing-rooms, the reception-room, and Mrs Proudie's boudoir. In olden days one of these had been Bishop Grantly's bed-room, and another his common sitting-room and study. The present bishop, however, had been moved down into a back parlour, and had been given to understand, that he could very well receive his clergy in the dining-room, should they arrive in too large a flock to be admitted into his small sanctum. He had been unwilling to yield, but after a short debate had yielded.

Mrs Proudie's heart beat high as she inspected her suite of rooms. They were really very magnificent, or at least would be so by candlelight; and they had nevertheless been got up with commendable economy. Large rooms when full of people and full of light look well, because they are large, and are full, and are light. Small rooms are those which require costly fittings and rich furniture. Mrs Proudie knew this, and made the most of it; she had therefore a huge gas lamp with a dozen burners hanging from each of the ceilings.

People were to arrive at ten, supper was to last from twelve till one, and at half-past one everybody was to be gone. Carriages were to come in at the gate in the town and depart at the gate outside. They were desired to take up at a quarter before one. It was managed excellently, and Mr Slope was invaluable.

At half-past nine the bishop and his wife and their three daughters entered the great reception-room, and very grand and very solemn they were. Mr Slope was down-stairs giving the last orders about the wine. He well understood that curates and country vicars with their belongings did not require so generous an article as the dignitaries of the close. There is a useful gradation in such things, and Marsala at 20s. a dozen did very well for the exterior supplementary tables in the corner.

'Bishop,' said the lady, as his lordship sat himself down, 'don't sit on that sofa, if you please; it is to be kept separate for a lady.'

The bishop jumped up and seated himself on a cane-bottomed chair. '*A* lady?' he inquired meekly; 'do you mean one particular lady, my dear?'

'Yes, Bishop, one particular lady,' said his wife, disdaining to explain.

'She has got no legs, papa,' said the youngest daughter, tittering.

'No legs!' said the bishop, opening his eyes.

'Nonsense, Netta, what stuff you talk,' said Olivia. 'She has got legs, but she can't use them. She has always to be kept lying down, and three or four men carry her about everywhere.'

'Laws, how odd!' said Augusta. 'Always carried about by four men! I'm sure I shouldn't like it. Am I right behind, mamma? I feel as if I was open;' and she turned her back to her anxious parent.

'Open! to be sure you are,' said she, 'and a yard of petticoat strings hanging out. I don't know why I pay such high wages to Mrs Richards, if she can't take the trouble to see whether or no you are fit to be looked at,' and Mrs Proudie poked the strings here, and twitched the dress there, and gave her daughter a shove and a shake, and then pronounced it all right.

'But,' rejoined the bishop, who was dying with curiosity about the mysterious lady and her legs, 'who is it that is to have the sofa? What's her name, Netta?'

A thundering rap at the front door interrupted the conversation. Mrs Proudie stood up and shook herself gently, and touched her cap on each side as she looked in the mirror. Each of the girls stood on tiptoe, and rearranged the bows on their bosoms; and Mr Slope rushed up stairs three steps at a time.

'But who is it, Netta?' whispered the bishop to his youngest daughter.

'La Signora Madeline Vesey Neroni,' whispered back the daughter; 'and mind you don't let any one sit upon the sofa.'

'La Signora Madeline Vicinironi!' muttered, to himself, the bewildered prelate. Had he been told that the Begum of Oude was to be there, or Queen Pomara of the Western Isles, he could not have been more astonished. La Signora Madeline Vicinironi, who, having no legs to stand on, had bespoken a sofa in his drawing-room! – who could she be? He however could now make no further inquiry, as Dr and Mrs Stanhope were announced. They had been sent on out of the way a little before the time, in order that the signora might have plenty of time to get herself conveniently packed into the carriage.

The bishop was all smiles for the prebendary's wife, and the bishop's wife was all smiles for the prebendary. Mr Slope was presented, and was delighted to make the acquaintance of one of whom he had heard so much. The doctor bowed very low, and then looked as though he could not return the compliment as regarded Mr Slope, of whom, indeed, he had heard nothing. The doctor, in spite of his long absence, knew an English gentleman when he saw him.

And then the guests came in shoals: Mr and Mrs Quiverful and their three grown daughters. Mr and Mrs Chadwick and their three daughters. The burly chancellor and his wife and clerical son from Oxford. The meagre little doctor without incumbrance. Mr Harding with Eleanor and Miss Bold. The dean leaning on a gaunt spinster, his only child now living with him, a lady very learned in stones, ferns, plants, and vermin, and who had written a book about petals. A wonderful woman in her way was Miss Trefoil. Mr Finnie, the attorney, with his wife, was to be seen, much to the dismay of many who had never met him in a drawing-room before. The five Barchester doctors were all there, and old Scalpen, the retired apothecary and toothdrawer, who was first taught to consider himself as belonging to the higher orders by the receipt of the bishop's card. Then came the archdeacon and his wife, with their elder daughter Griselda, a slim pale retiring girl of seventeen, who kept close to her mother, and looked out on the world with quiet watchful eyes, one who gave promise of much beauty when time should have ripened it.

And so the rooms became full, and knots were formed, and every new comer paid his respects to my lord and passed on, not presuming to occupy too much of the great man's attention. The archdeacon shook hands very heartily with Doctor Stanhope, and Mrs Grantly seated herself by the doctor's wife. And Mrs Proudie moved about with well regulated grace, measuring out the quantity of her favours to the quality of her guests, just as Mr Slope had been doing with the wine. But the sofa was still empty, and five-and-twenty ladies and five gentlemen had been courteously warned off it by the mindful chaplain.

'Why doesn't she come?' said the bishop to himself. His mind was so preoccupied with the signora, that he hardly remembered how to behave himself *en bishop*.

At last a carriage dashed up to the hall steps with a very different manner of approach from that of any other vehicle that had been there that evening. A perfect commotion took place. The doctor, who heard it as he was standing in the drawing-room, knew that his daughter was coming, and retired into the furthest corner, where he might not see her entrance. Mrs Proudie perked herself up, feeling that some important piece of business was in hand. The bishop was instinctively aware that La Signora Vicinironi was come at last, and Mr Slope hurried into the hall to give his assistance.

He was, however, nearly knocked down and trampled on by the cortège that he encountered on the hall steps. He got himself picked up as well as he could, and followed the cortège up stairs. The signora was carried head foremost, her head being the care of her brother and an Italian man-servant who was accustomed to the work; her feet were in the care of the lady's maid and the lady's Italian page; and Charlotte Stanhope followed to see that all was done with due grace and decorum. In this manner they climbed easily into the drawing-room, and a broad way through the crowd having been opened, the signora rested safely on her couch. She had sent a servant beforehand to learn whether it was a right or a left hand sofa, for it required that she should dress accordingly, particularly as regarded her bracelets.

And very becoming her dress was. It was white velvet, without any other garniture than rich white lace worked with pearls across her bosom, and the same round the armlets of her dress. Across her brow she wore a band of red velvet, on the centre of which shone a magnificent Cupid in mosaic, the tints of whose wings were of the most lovely azure, and the colour of his chubby cheeks the clearest pink. On the one arm which her position required her to expose she wore three magnificent bracelets, each of different stones. Beneath her on the sofa, and over the cushion and head of it, was spread a crimson silk mantle or shawl, which went under her whole body and concealed her feet. Dressed as she was and looking as she did, so beautiful and yet so motionless, with the pure brilliancy of her white dress brought out and strengthened by the colour beneath it, with that lovely head, and those large bold bright staring eyes, it was impossible that either man or woman should do other than look at her.

Neither man nor woman for some minutes did do other.

Her bearers too were worthy of note. The three servants were Italian, and though perhaps not peculiar in their own country, were very much so in the palace at Barchester. The man especially attracted notice, and created a doubt in the mind of some whether he were a friend or a domestic. The same doubt was felt as to Ethelbert. The man was attired in a loose-fitting common black cloth morning coat. He had a jaunty fat well-pleased clean face, on which no atom of beard appeared, and he wore round his neck a loose black silk neckhandkerchief. The bishop essayed to make him a bow, but the man, who was well-trained, took no notice of him, and walked out of the room quite at his ease, followed by the woman and the boy.

Ethelbert Stanhope was dressed in light blue from head to foot. He had on the loosest possible blue coat, cut square like a shooting coat, and very short. It was lined with silk of azure blue. He had on a blue satin waistcoat, a blue neckhandkerchief which was fastened beneath his throat with a coral ring, and very loose blue trowsers which almost concealed his feet. His soft glossy beard was softer and more glossy than ever.

The bishop, who had made one mistake, thought that he also was a servant, and therefore tried to make way for him to pass. But Ethelbert soon corrected the error.

✂ ELEVEN ✂

Mrs Proudie's Reception – Concluded

'BISHOP OF BARCHESTER, I PRESUME?' SAID BERTIE Stanhope, putting out his hand, frankly; 'I am delighted to make your acquaintance. We are in rather close quarters here, a'nt we?'

In truth they were. They had been crowded up behind the head of the sofa: the bishop in waiting to receive his guest, and the other in carrying her; and they now had hardly room to move themselves.

The bishop gave his hand quickly, and made his little studied bow, and was delighted to make – He couldn't go on, for he did not know whether his friend was a signor, or a count, or a prince.

'My sister really puts you all to great trouble,' said Bertie.

'Not at all!' The bishop was delighted to have the opportunity of welcoming the Signora Vicinironi – so at least he said – and attempted to force his way round to the front of the sofa. He had, at any rate, learnt that his strange guests were brother and sister. The man, he presumed, must be Signor Vicinironi – or count, or prince, as it might be. It was wonderful what good English he spoke. There was just a twang of foreign accent, and no more.

'Do you like Barchester on the whole?' asked Bertie.

The bishop, looking dignified, said that he did like Barchester.

'You've not been here very long, I believe,' said Bertie.

'No – not long,' said the bishop, and tried again to make his way between the back of the sofa and a heavy rector, who was staring over it at the grimaces of the signora.

'You weren't a bishop before, were you?'

Dr Proudie explained that this was the first diocese he had held.

'Ah – I thought so,' said Bertie; 'but you are changed about sometimes, a'nt you?'

'Translations are occasionally made,' said Dr Proudie; 'but not so frequently as in former days.'

'They've cut them all down to pretty nearly the same figure, haven't they?' said Bertie.

To this the bishop could not bring himself to make any answer, but again attempted to move the rector.

'But the work, I suppose, is different?' continued Bertie. 'Is there much to do here, at Barchester?' This was said exactly in the tone that a young Admiralty clerk might use in asking the same question of a brother acolyte at the Treasury.

'The work of a bishop of the Church of England,' said Dr Proudie, with considerable dignity, 'is not easy. The responsibility which he has to bear is very great indeed.'

'Is it?' said Bertie, opening wide his wonderful blue eyes. 'Well; I never was afraid of responsibility. I once had thoughts of being a bishop, myself.'

'Had thoughts of being a bishop!' said Dr Proudie, much amazed.

'That is, a parson – a parson first, you know, and a bishop afterwards. If I had once begun, I'd have stuck to it. But, on the whole, I like the Church of Rome the best.'

The bishop could not discuss the point, so he remained silent.

'Now, there's my father,' continued Bertie; 'he hasn't stuck to it. I fancy he didn't like saying the same thing over so often. By the bye, Bishop, have you seen my father?'

The bishop was more amazed than ever. Had he seen his father? 'No,' he replied; 'he had not yet had the pleasure: he hoped he might;' and, as he said so, he resolved to bear heavy on that fat, immovable rector, if ever he had the power of doing do.

'He's in the room somewhere,' said Bertie, 'and he'll turn up soon. By the bye, do you know much about the Jews?'

At last the bishop saw a way out. 'I beg your pardon,' said he; 'but I'm forced to go round the room.'

'Well – I believe I'll follow in your wake,' said Bertie. 'Terribly hot – isn't it?' This he addressed to the fat rector with whom he had brought himself into the closest contact. 'They've got this sofa into the worst possible part of the room; suppose we move it. Take care, Madeline.'

The sofa had certainly been so placed that those who were behind it found great difficulty in getting out; – there was but a narrow gangway, which one person could stop. This was a bad arrangement, and one which Bertie thought it might be well to improve.

'Take care, Madeline,' said he; and turning to the fat rector, added, 'Just help me with a slight push.'

The rector's weight was resting on the sofa, and unwittingly lent all its impetus to accelerate and increase the motion which Bertie intentionally originated. The sofa rushed from its moorings, and ran half-way into the middle of the room. Dr Proudie was standing with Mr Slope in front of the signora, and had been trying to be condescending and sociable; but she was not in the very best of tempers; for she found that, whenever she spoke to the lady, the lady replied by speaking to Mr Slope. Mr Slope was a favourite, no doubt; but Mrs Proudie had no idea of being less thought of than the chaplain. She was beginning to be stately, stiff, and offended, when unfortunately the castor of the sofa caught itself in her lace train, and carried away there is no saying how much of her garniture. Gathers were heard to go, stitches to crack, plaits to fly open, flounces were seen to fall, and breadths to expose themselves – a long ruin of rent lace disfigured the carpet, and still clung to the vile wheel on which the sofa moved.

So, when a granite battery is raised, excellent to the eyes of warfaring men, is its strength and symmetry admired. It is the work of years. Its neat embrasures, its finished parapets, its casemated stories, show all the skills of modern science. But, anon, a small spark is applied to the treacherous fusee – a cloud of dust arises to the heavens – and then nothing is to be seen but dirt and dust and ugly fragments.

We know what was the wrath of Juno when her beauty was despised. We know too what storms of passion even celestial minds can yield. As Juno may have looked at Paris on Mount Ida, so did Mrs Proudie look on Ethelbert Stanhope when he pushed the leg of the sofa into her lace train.

'Oh, you idiot, Bertie!' said the signora, seeing what had been done, and what were to be the conseqences.

'Idiot!' re-echoed Mrs Proudie, as though the word were not half strong enough to express the required meaning; 'I'll let him know –' and then looking round to learn, at a glance, the worst, she saw that at present it behoved her to collect the scattered *débris* of her dress.

Bertie, when he saw what he had done, rushed over the sofa, and threw himself on one knee before the offended lady. His object, doubtless, was to liberate the torn lace from the castor; but he looked as though he were imploring pardon from a goddess.

'Unhand it, sir!' said Mrs Proudie. From what scrap of dramatic poetry she had extracted the word cannot be said; but it must have rested on her memory, and now seemed opportunely dignified for the occasion.

'I'll fly to the looms of the fairies to repair the damage, if you'll only forgive me,' said Ethelbert, still on his knees.

'Unhand it, sir!' said Mrs Proudie, with redoubled emphasis, and all but furious wrath. This allusion to the fairies was a direct mockery, and intended to turn her into ridicule. So at least it seemed to her. 'Unhand it, sir!' she almost screamed.

'It's not me; it's the cursed sofa,' said Bertie, looking imploringly in her face, and holding up both his hands to show that he was not touching her belongings, but still remaining on his knees.

Hereupon the signora laughed; not loud, indeed, but yet audibly. And as the tigress bereft of her young will turn with equal anger on any within reach, so did Mrs Proudie turn upon her female guest.

'Madam!' she said – and it is beyond the power of prose to tell of the fire which flashed from her eyes.

The signora stared her full in the face for a moment, and then turning to her brother said, playfully, 'Bertie, you idiot, get up.'

By this time the bishop, and Mr Slope, and her three daughters were around her, and had collected together the wide runs of her magnificence. The girls fell into circular rank behind their mother, and thus following her and carrying out the fragments, they left the reception-rooms in a manner not altogether devoid of dignity. Dr Proudie had to retire and re-array herself.

As soon as the constellation had swept by, Ethelbert rose from his knees, and turning with anger to the fat rector, said: 'After all it was your doing, sir – not mine. But perhaps you are waiting for preferment, and so I bore it.'

Whereupon there was a laugh against the fat rector, in which both the bishop and the chaplain joined; and thus things got themselves again into order.

'Oh! my lord, I am so sorry for this accident,' said the signora, putting out her hand so as to force the bishop to take it. 'My brother is so thoughtless. Pray sit down, and let me have the pleasure of making your acquaintance. Though I am so poor a creature as to want a sofa, I am not so selfish as to require it all.' Madeline could always dispose herself so as to make room for a gentleman, though, as she declared, the crinoline of her lady friends was much too bulky to be so accommodated.

'It was solely for the pleasure of meeting you that I have had myself dragged here,' she continued. 'Of course, with your occupation, one cannot even hope that you should have time to come to us, that is, in the way of calling. And at your English dinner-parties all is so dull and so stately. Do you know, my lord, that in coming to England my only consolation has been the thought that I should know you;' and she looked at him with the look of a she-devil.

The bishop, however, thought that she looked very like an angel, and accepting the proffered seat, sat down beside her. He uttered some platitude as to his deep obligation for the trouble she had taken, and wondered more and more who she was.

'Of course you know my sad story?' she continued.

The bishop didn't know a word of it. He knew, however, or thought he knew, that she couldn't walk into a room like other people, and so made the most of that. He put on a look of ineffable distress, and said that he was aware how God had afflicted her.

The signora just touched the corner of her eyes with the most lovely of pocket-handkerchiefs. Yes, she said – she had been sorely tried – tried, she thought, beyond the common endurance of humanity; but while her child was left to her, everything was left. 'Oh! my lord,' she exclaimed, 'you must see that infant – the last bud of a wondrous tree: you must let a mother hope that you will lay your holy hands on her innocent head, and consecrate her for female virtues. May I hope it?' said she, looking into the bishop's eye, and touching the bishop's arm with her hand.

The bishop was but a man, and said she might. After all, what was it but a request that he would confirm her daughter? – a request, indeed, very unnecessary to make, as he should do so as a matter of course, if the young lady came forward in the usual way.

'The blood of Tiberius,' said the signora, in all but a whisper; 'the blood of Tiberius flows in her veins. She is the last of the Neros!'

The bishop had heard of the last of the Visigoths, and had floating in his brain some indistinct idea of the last of the Mohicans, but to have the last of the Neros thus brought before him for a blessing was very staggering. Still he liked the lady: she had a proper way of thinking, and talked with more propriety than her brother. But who were they? It was now quite clear that that blue madman with the silky beard was not a Prince Vicinironi. The lady was married, and was of course one of the Vicinironis by right of the husband. So the bishop went on learning.

'When will you see her?' said the signora with a start.

'See whom?' said the bishop.

'My child,' said the mother.

'What is the young lady's age?' asked the bishop.

'She is just seven,' said the signora.

'Oh,' said the bishop, shaking his head; 'she is much too young – very much too young.'

'But in sunny Italy you know, we do not count by years,' and the signora gave the bishop one of her very sweetest smiles.

'But indeed, she is a great deal too young,' persisted the bishop; 'we never confirm before –'

'But you might speak to her; you might let her hear from your consecrated lips, that she is not a castaway because she is a Roman; that she may be a Nero and yet a Christian; that she may owe her black locks and dark cheeks to the blood of the pagan Caesars, and yet herself be a child of grace; you will tell her this, won't you, my friend?'

The friend said he would, and asked if the child could say her catechism.

'No,' said the signora, 'I would not allow her to learn lessons such as those in a land ridden over by priests, and polluted by the idolatry of Rome. It is here, here in Barchester, that she must first be taught to lisp those holy words. Oh, that you could be her instructor!'

Now, Dr Proudie certainly liked the lady, but, seeing that he was a bishop, it was not probable that he was going to instruct a little girl in the first rudiments of her catechism; so he said he'd send a teacher.

'But you'll see her, yourself, my lord?'

The bishop said he would, but where should he call.

'At papa's house,' said the signora, with an air of some little surprise at the question.

The bishop actually wanted the courage to ask her who was her papa; so he was forced at last to leave her without fathoming the mystery. Mrs Proudie, in her second best, had now returned to the rooms, and her husband thought it as well that he should not remain in too close conversation with the lady whom his wife appeared to hold in such slight esteem. Presently he came across his youngest daughter.

'Netta,' said he, 'do you know who is the father of that Signora Vicinironi?'

'It isn't Vicinironi, papa,' said Netta; 'but Vesey Neroni, and she's Doctor Stanhope's daughter. But I must go and do the civil to Griselda Grantly; I declare nobody has spoken a word to the poor girl this evening.'

Dr Stanhope! Dr Vesey Stanhope! Dr Vesey Stanhope's daughter, of whose marriage with a dissolute Italian scamp he now remembered to have heard something! And that impertinent blue cub who had examined him as to his episcopal bearings was old Stanhope's son, and the lady who had entreated him to come and teach her child the catechism was old Stanhope's daughter! the daughter of one of his own prebendaries! As these things flashed across his mind, he was nearly as angry as his wife had been. Nevertheless, he could not but own that the mother of the last of the Neros was an agreeable woman.

Dr Proudie tripped out into the adjoining room, in which were congregated a crowd of Grantlyite clergymen, among whom the archdeacon was standing pre-eminent, while the old dean was sitting nearly buried in a huge arm-chair by the fire-place. The bishop was very anxious to be gracious, and, if possible, to diminish the bitterness which his chaplain had occasioned. Let Mr Slope do the *fortiter in re*, he himself would pour in the *suaviter in modo*.

'Pray don't stir, Mr Dean, pray don't stir,' he said, as the old man essayed to get up; 'I take it as a great kindness, your coming to such an *omnium gatherum* as this. But we have hardly got settled yet, and Mrs Proudie has not been able to see her friends as she would wish to do. Well, Mr Archdeacon, after all, we have not been so hard upon you at Oxford.'

'No,' said the archdeacon; 'you've only drawn our teeth and cut out our tongues; you've allowed us still to breathe and swallow.'

'Ha, ha, ha!' laughed the bishop; 'it's not quite so easy to cut out the tongue of an Oxford magnate – and as for teeth – ha, ha, ha! Why, in the way we've left the matter, it's very odd if the heads of colleges don't have their own way quite as fully as when the hebdomadal board was in all its glory; what do you say, Mr Dean?'

'An old man, my lord, never likes changes,' said the dean.

'You must have been sad bunglers if it is so,' said the archdeacon; 'and indeed, to tell the truth, I think you have bungled it. At any rate, you must own this; you have not done the half what you boasted you would do.'

'Now, as regards your system of professors –' began the chancellor slowly. He was never destined to get beyond such beginning.

'Talking of professors,' said a soft clear voice, close behind the chancellor's elbow; 'how much you Englishmen might learn from Germany; only you are all too proud.'

The bishop looking round, perceived that that abominable young Stanhope had pursued him. The dean stared at him, as though he were some unearthly apparition; so also did two or three prebendaries and minor canons. The archdeacon laughed.

'The German professors are men of learning,' said Mr Harding, 'but –'

'German professors!' groaned out the chancellor, as though his nervous system had received a shock which nothing but a week of Oxford air could cure.

'Yes,' continued Ethelbert; not at all understanding why a German professor should be contemptible in the eyes of an Oxford don. 'Not but what the name is best earned at Oxford. In Germany the professors do teach; at Oxford, I believe they only profess to do so, and sometimes not even that. You'll have those universities of yours about your ears soon, if you don't consent to take a lesson from Germany.'

There was no answering this. Dignified clergymen of sixty years of age could not condescend to discuss such a matter with a young man with such clothes and such a beard.

'Have you got good water out at Plumstead, Mr Archdeacon?' said the bishop by way of changing the conversation.

'Pretty good,' said Dr Grantly.

'But by no means so good as his wine, my lord,' said a witty minor canon.

'Nor so generally used,' said another; 'that is for inward application.'

'Ha, ha, ha!' laughed the bishop, 'a good cellar of wine is a very comfortable thing in a house.'

'Your German professors, sir, prefer beer, I believe,' said the sarcastic little meagre prebendary.

'They don't think much of either,' said Ethelbert; 'and that perhaps accounts for their superiority. Now the Jewish professor –'

The insult was becoming too deep for the spirit of Oxford to endure, so the archdeacon walked off one way and the chancellor another, followed by their disciples, and the bishop and the young reformer were left together on the hearth-rug.

'I was a Jew once myself,' began Bertie.

The bishop was determined not to stand another examination, or be led on any terms into Palestine; so he again remembered that he had to do something very particular, and left young Stanhope with the dean. The dean did not get the worst of it, for Ethelbert gave him a true account of his remarkable doings in the Holy Land.

'Oh, Mr Harding,' said the bishop, overtaking the *ci-devant* warden; 'I wanted to say one word about the hospital. You know, of course, that it is to be filled up.'

Mr Harding's heart beat a little, and he said that he had heard so.

'Of course,' continued the bishop; 'there can be only one man whom I could wish to see in that situation. I don't know what your own views may be, Mr Harding –'

'They are very simply told, my lord,' said the other; 'to take the place if it be offered me, and to put up with the want of it should another man get it.'

The bishop professed himself delighted to hear it; Mr Harding might be quite sure that no other man would get it. There were some few circumstances which would in a slight degree change the nature of the duties. Mr Harding was probably aware of this, and would, perhaps, not object to discuss the matter with Mr Slope. It was a subject to which Mr Slope had given a good deal of attention.

Mr Harding felt, he knew not why, oppressed and annoyed. What could Mr Slope do to him? He knew that there were to be changes. The nature of them must be communicated to the warden through somebody, and through whom so naturally as the bishop's chaplain. 'Twas thus he tried to argue himself back to an easy mind, but in vain.

Mr Slope in the mean time had taken the seat which the bishop had vacated on the signora's sofa, and remained with that lady till it was time to marshal the folk to supper. Not with contented eyes had Mrs Proudie seen this. Had not this woman laughed at her distress, and had not Mr Slope heard it? Was she not an intriguing Italian woman, half wife and half not, full of affectation, airs, and impudence? Was she not horribly bedizened with velvet and pearls, with velvet and pearls, too, which had not been torn off her back? Above all, did she not pretend to be more beautiful than her neighbours? To say that Mrs Proudie was jealous would give a wrong idea of her feelings. She had not the slightest desire that Mr Slope should be in love with herself. But she desired the incense of Mr Slope's spiritual and temporal services, and did not choose that they should be turned out of their course to such an object as Signora Neroni. She considered also that Mr Slope ought in duty to hate the signora; and it appeared from his manner that he was very far from hating her.

'Come, Mr Slope,' she said, sweeping by, and looking all that she felt; 'can't you make yourself useful? Do pray take Mrs Grantly down to supper.'

Mrs Grantly heard and escaped. The words were hardly out of Mrs Proudie's mouth, before the intended victim had stuck her hand through the arm of one of her husband's curates, and saved herself. What would the archdeacon have said had he seen her walking down stairs with Mr Slope?

Mr Slope heard also, but was by no means so obedient as was expected. Indeed, the period of Mr Slope's obedience to Mrs Proudie was drawing to a close. He did not wish yet to break with her, nor to break with her at all, if it could be avoided. But he intended to be master in that palace, and as she had made the same resolution it was not improbable that they might come to blows.

Before leaving the signora he arranged a little table before her, and begged to know what he should bring her. She was quite indifferent, she said – nothing – anything. It was now she felt the misery of her position, now that she must be left alone. Well, a little chicken, some ham, and a glass of champagne.

Mr Slope had to explain, not without blushing for his patron, that there was no champagne.

Sherry would do just as well. And then Mr Slope descended with the learned Miss Trefoil on his arm. Could she tell him, he asked, whether the ferns of Barsetshire were equal to those of Cumberland? His strongest worldly passion was for ferns – and before she could answer him he left her wedged between the door and the sideboard. It was fifty minutes before she escaped, and even then unfed.

'You are not leaving us, Mr Slope,' said the watchful lady of the house, seeing her slave escaping towards the door, with stores of provisions held high above the heads of the guests.

Mr Slope explained that the Signora Neroni was in want of her supper.

'Pray, Mr Slope, let her brother take it to her,' said Mrs Proudie, quite out loud. 'It is out of the question that you should be so employed. Pray, Mr Slope, oblige me; I am sure Mr Stanhope will wait upon his sister.'

Ethelbert was most agreeably occupied in the furthest corner of the room, making himself both useful and agreeable to Mrs Proudie's youngest daughter.

'I couldn't get out, madam, if Madeline were starving for her supper,' said he; 'I'm physically fixed, unless I could fly.'

The lady's anger was increased by seeing that her daughter also had gone over to the enemy; and when she saw, that in spite of her remonstrances, in the teeth of her positive orders, Mr Slope went off to the drawing-room, the cup of her indignation ran over, and she could not restrain herself. 'Such manners I never saw,' she said, muttering. 'I cannot, and will not permit it;' and then, after fussing and fuming for a few minutes, she pushed her way through the crowd, and followed Mr Slope.

When she reached the room above, she found it absolutely deserted, except by the guilty pair. The signora was sitting very comfortably up to her supper, and Mr Slope was leaning over her and administering to her wants. They had been discussing the merits of Sabbath-day schools, and the lady had suggested that as she could not possibly go to the children, she might be indulged in the wish of her heart by having the children brought to her.

'And when shall it be, Mr Slope?' said she.

Mr Slope was saved the necessity of committing himself to a promise by the entry of Mrs Proudie. She swept close up to the sofa so as to confront the guilty pair, stared full at them for a moment, and then said as she passed on to the next room, 'Mr Slope, his lordship is especially desirous of your attendance below; you will greatly oblige me if you will join him.' And so she stalked on.

Mr Slope muttered something in reply, and prepared to go down stairs. As for the bishop's wanting him, he knew his lady patroness well enough to take that assertion at what it was worth; but he did not wish to make himself the hero of a scene, or to become conspicuous for more gallantry than the occasion required.

'Is she always like this?' said the signora.

'Yes – always – madam,' said Mrs Proudie, returning; 'always the same – always equally adverse to impropriety of conduct of every description;' and she stalked back through the room again, following Mr Slope out of the door.

The signora couldn't follow her, or she certainly would have done so. But she laughed loud, and sent the sound of it ringing through the lobby and down the stairs after Mrs Proudie's feet. Had she been as active as Grimaldi, she could probably have taken no better revenge.

'Mr Slope,' said Mrs Proudie, catching the delinquent at the door, 'I am surprised that you should leave my company to attend on such a painted Jezebel as that.'

'But she's lame, Mrs Proudie, and cannot move. Somebody must have waited upon her.'

'Lame,' said Mrs Proudie; 'I'd lame her if she belonged to me. What business had she here at all? – such impertinence – such affectation.'

In the hall and adjacent rooms all manner of cloaking and shawling was going on, and the Barchester folk were getting themselves gone. Mrs Proudie did her best to smirk at each and every one, as they made their adieux, but she was hardly successful. Her temper had been tried fearfully. By slow degrees, the guests went.

'Send back the carriage quick,' said Ethelbert, as Dr and Mrs Stanhope took their departure.

The younger Stanhopes were left to the very last, and an uncomfortable party they made with the bishop's family. They all went into the dining room, and then the bishop observing that 'the lady' was alone in the drawing-room, they followed him up. Mrs Proudie kept Mr Slope and her daughters in close conversation, resolving that he should not be indulged, nor they polluted. The bishop, in mortal dread of Bertie and the Jews, tried to converse with Charlotte Stanhope about the climate of Italy. Bertie and the signora had no resource but in each other.

'Did you get your supper, at last, Madeline?' said the impudent or else mischievous young man.

'Oh, yes,' said Madeline; 'Mr Slope was so very kind as to bring it me. I fear, however, he put himself to more inconvenience than I wished.'

Mrs Proudie looked at her, but said nothing. The meaning of her look might have been thus translated: 'If ever you find yourself within these walls again, I'll give you leave to be as impudent and affected, and as mischievous as you please.'

At last the carriage returned with the three Italian servants, and La Signora Madeline Vesey Neroni was carried out, as she had been carried in.

The lady of the palace retired to her chamber by no means contented with the result of her first grand party at Barchester.

✂ TWELVE ✂

Slope versus Harding

TWO OR THREE DAYS AFTER THE PARTY, Mr Harding received a note, begging him to call on Mr Slope, at the palace, at an early hour the following morning. There was nothing uncivil in the communication, and yet the tone of it was thoroughly displeasing. It was as follows:

MY DEAR MR HARDING,

Will you favour me by calling on me at the palace to-morrow morning at 9.30 A.M. The bishop wishes me to speak to you touching the hospital. I hope you will excuse my naming so early an hour. I do so as my time is greatly occupied. If, however, it is positively inconvenient to you, I will change it to 10. You will, perhaps, be kind enough to let me have a note in reply.

> 'Believe me to be,
> 'My dear Mr Harding,
> 'Your assured friend,
>
> 'OBH. SLOPE.

'The Palace, Monday morning,
  '20th August, 185 –.'

Mr Harding neither could nor would believe anything of the sort; and he thought, moreover, that Mr Slope was rather impertinent to call himself by such a name. His assured friend, indeed! How many assured friends generally fall to the lot of a man in this world? And by what process are they made? and how much of such process had taken place as yet between Mr Harding and Mr Slope? Mr Harding could not help asking himself these questions as he read and re-read the note before him. He answered it, however, as follows:

DEAR SIR,
I will call at the palace to-morrow at 9.30 A.M. as you desire.
> 'Truly yours,
>
> 'S. HARDING.

'High Street, Barchester, Monday.'

And on the following morning, punctually at half-past nine, he knocked at the palace door, and asked for Mr Slope.

The bishop had one small room allotted to him on the ground-floor, and Mr Slope had another. Into this latter Mr Harding was shown, and asked to sit down. Mr Slope was not yet there. The ex-warden stood up at the window looking into the garden, and could not help thinking how very short a time had passed since the whole of that house had been open to him, as though he had been a child of the family, born and bred in it. He remembered how the old servants used to smile as they opened the door to him; how the familiar butler would say, when he had been absent a few hours longer than usual,' A sight of you, Mr Harding, is good for sore eyes;' how the fussy housekeeper would swear that he couldn't have dined, or couldn't have breakfasted, or couldn't have lunched. And then, above all, he remembered the pleasant gleam of inward satisfaction which always spread itself over the old bishop's face, whenever his friend entered his room.

A tear came into each eye as he reflected that all this was gone. What use would the hospital be to him now? He was alone in the world, and getting old; he would soon, very soon have to go, and leave it all, as his dear old friend had gone – go, and leave the hospital, and his accustomed place in the cathedral, and his haunts and pleasures, to younger and perhaps wiser men. That chanting of his! perhaps, in truth, the time for it had gone by. He felt as though the world were sinking from his feet; as though this, this was the time for him to turn with confidence to those hopes which he had preached with confidence to others. 'What,' said he to himself, 'can a man's religion be worth, if it does not support him against the natural melancholy of declining years?' And, as he looked out through his dimmed eyes into the bright parterres of the bishop's garden, he felt that he had the support which he wanted.

Nevertheless, he did not like to be thus kept waiting. If Mr Slope did not really wish to see him at half-past nine o'clock, why force him to come away from his lodgings with his breakfast in his throat? To tell the truth, it was policy on the part of Mr Slope. Mr Slope had made up his mind that Mr Harding should either accept the hospital and abject submission, or else refuse it altogether; and had calculated that he would probably be more quick to do the latter, if he could be got to enter upon the subject in an ill-humour. Perhaps Mr Slope was not altogether wrong in his calculation.

It was nearly ten when Mr Slope hurried into the room, and, muttering something about the bishop and diocesan duties, shook Mr Harding's hand ruthlessly, and begged him to be seated.

Now the air of superiority which this man assumed, did go against the grain of Mr Harding; and yet he did not know how to resent it. The whole tendency of his mind and disposition was opposed to any contra-assumption of grandeur on his own part, and he hadn't the worldly spirit or quickness necessary to put down insolent pretensions by downright and open rebuke, as the archdeacon would have done. There was nothing for Mr Harding but to submit, and he accordingly did so.

'About the hospital, Mr Harding?' began Mr Slope, speaking of it as the head of a college at Cambridge might speak of some sizarship which had to be disposed of.

Mr Harding crossed one leg over another, and then one hand over the other on the top of them, and looked Mr Slope in the face; but he said nothing.

'It's to be filled up again,' said Mr Slope. Mr Harding said that he had understood so.

'Of course, you know, the income will be very much reduced,' continued Mr Slope. 'The bishop wished to be liberal, and he therefore told the government that he thought it ought to be put at not less than £450. I think on the whole the bishop was right; for though the services required will not be of a very onerous nature, they will be more so than they were before. And it is, perhaps, well that the clergy immediately attached to the cathedral town should be made as comfortable as the extent of the ecclesiastical means at our disposal will allow. Those are the bishop's ideas, and I must say mine also.'

Mr Harding sat rubbing one hand on the other, but said not a word.

'So much for the income, Mr Harding. The house will, of course, remain to the warden, as before. It should, however, I think, be stipulated that he should paint inside every seven years, and outside every three years, and be subject to dilapidations, in the event of vacating, either by death or otherwise. But this is a matter on which the bishop must yet be consulted.'

Mr Harding still rubbed his hands, and still sat silent, gazing up into Mr Slope's unprepossessing face.

'Then, as to the duties,' continued he, 'I believe, if I am rightly informed, there can hardly be said to have been any duties hitherto,' and he gave a sort of half laugh, as though to pass off the accusation in the guise of a pleasantry.

Mr Harding thought of the happy, easy years he had passed in his old home; of the worn-out, aged men whom he had succoured; of his good intentions; and of his work, which had certainly been of the lightest. He thought of these things, doubting for a moment whether he did or did not deserve the sarcasm. He gave his enemy the benefit of the doubt, and did not rebuke him. He merely observed, very tranquilly, and perhaps with too much humility, that the duties of the situation, such as they were, had, he believed, been done to the satisfaction of the late bishop.

Mr Slope again smiled, and this time the smile was intended to operate against the memory of the late bishop, rather than against the energy of the ex-warden; and so it was understood by Mr Harding. The colour rose to his cheeks, and he began to feel very angry.

'You must be aware, Mr Harding, that things are a good deal changed in Barchester,' said Mr Slope.

Mr Harding said that he was aware of it. 'And not only in Barchester, Mr Harding, but in the world at large. It is not only in Barchester that a new man is carrying out new measures and casting away the useless rubbish of past centuries. The same thing is going on throughout the country. Work is now required from every man who receives wages; and they who have to superintend the doing of work, and the paying of wages, are bound to see that this rule is carried out. New men, Mr Harding, are now needed, and are now forthcoming in the church, as well as in other professions.'

All this was wormwood to our old friend. He had never rated very high his own abilities or activity; but all the feelings of his heart were with the old clergy, and any antipathies of which his heart was susceptible, were directed against those new, busy, uncharitable, self-lauding men, of whom Mr Slope was so good an example.

'Perhaps,' said he, 'the bishop will prefer a new man at the hospital?'

'By no means,' said Mr Slope. 'The bishop is very anxious that you should accept the appointment; but he wishes you should understand beforehand what will be the required duties. In the first place, a Sabbath-day school will be attached to the hospital.'

'What! for the old men?' asked Mr Harding.

'No, Mr Harding, not for the old men, but for the benefit of the children of such of the poor of Barchester as it may suit. The bishop will expect that you shall attend this school, and the teachers shall be under your inspection and care.'

Mr Harding slipped his topmost hand off the other, and began to rub the calf of the leg which was supported.

'As to the old men,' continued Mr Slope, 'and the old women who are to form a part of the hospital, the bishop is desirous that you shall have morning and evening service on the premises every Sabbath, and one week-day service; that you shall preach to them once at least on Sundays; and that the whole hospital be always collected for morning and evening prayer. The bishop thinks that this will render it unnecessary that any separate seats in the cathedral should be reserved for the hospital inmates.'

Mr Slope paused, but Mr Harding still said nothing.

'Indeed, it would be difficult to find seats for the women; and, on the whole, Mr Harding, I may as well say at once, that for the people of that class the cathedral service does not appear to me the most useful – even if it be so for any class of people.'

'We will not discuss that, if you please,' said Mr Harding.

'I am not desirous of doing so; at least, not at the present moment. I hope, however, you fully understand the bishop's wishes about the new establishment of the hospital; and if, as I do not doubt, I shall receive from you an assurance that you accord with his lordship's views, it will give me very great pleasure to be the bearer from his lordship to you of the presentation to the appointment.'

'But if I disagree with his lordship's views?' asked Mr Harding.

'But I hope you do not,' said Mr Slope.

'But if I do?' again asked the other.

'If such unfortunately should be the case, which I can hardly conceive, I presume your own feelings will dictate to you the propriety of declining the appointment.'

'But if I accept the appointment, and yet disagree with the bishop, what then?'

This question rather bothered Mr Slope. It was true that he had talked the matter over with the bishop, and had received a sort of authority for suggesting to Mr Harding the propriety of a Sunday school, and certain hospital services; but he had no authority for saying that these propositions were to be made peremptory conditions attached to the appointment. The bishop's idea had been that Mr Harding would of course consent, and that the school would become, like the rest of those new establishments in the city, under the control of his wife and his chaplain. Mr Slope's idea had been more correct. He intended that Mr Harding should refuse the situation, and that an ally of his own should get it; but he had not conceived the possibility of Mr Harding openly accepting the appointment, and as openly rejecting the conditions.

'It is not, I presume, probable,' said he, 'that you will accept from the hands of the bishop a piece of preferment, with a fixed predetermination to disacknowledge the duties attached to it.'

'If I become warden,' said Mr Harding, 'and neglect my duty, the bishop has means by which he can remedy the grievance.'

'I hardly expected such an argument from you, or I may say the suggestion of such a line of conduct,' said Mr Slope, with a great look of injured virtue.

'Nor did I expect such a proposition.'

'I shall be glad at any rate to know what answer I am to make to his lordship,' said Mr Slope.

'I will take an early opportunity of seeing his lordship myself,' said Mr Harding.

'Such an arrangement,' said Mr Slope, 'will hardly give his lordship satisfaction. Indeed, it is impossible that the bishop should himself see every clergyman in the diocese on every subject of patronage that may rise. The bishop, I believe, did see you on the matter, and I really cannot see why he should be troubled to do so again.'

'Do you know, Mr Slope, how long I have been officiating as a clergyman in this city?' Mr Slope's wish was now nearly fulfilled. Mr Harding had become angry, and it was probable that he might commit himself.

'I really do not see what that has to do with the question. You cannot think the bishop would be justified in allowing you to regard as a sinecure a situation that requires an active man, merely because you have been employed for many years in the cathedral.'

'But it might induce the bishop to see me, if I asked him to do so. I shall consult my friends in this matter, Mr Slope; but I mean to be guilty of no subterfuge – you may tell the bishop that as I altogether disagree with his views about the hospital, I shall decline the situation if I find that any such conditions are attached to it as those you have suggested;' and so saying, Mr Harding took his hat and went his way.

Mr Slope was contented. He considered himself at liberty to accept Mr Harding's last speech as an absolute refusal of the appointment. At least, he so represented it to the bishop and to Mrs Proudie.

'That is very surprising,' said the bishop.

'Not at all,' said Mrs Proudie; 'you little know how determined the whole set of them are to withstand your authority.'

'But Mr Harding was so anxious for it,' said the bishop.

'Yes,' said Mr Slope, 'if he can hold it without the slightest ackowledgement of your lordship's jurisdiction.'

'That is out of the question,' said the bishop.

'I should imagine it to be quite so,' said the chaplain.

'Indeed, I should think so,' said the lady.

'I really am sorry for it,' said the bishop.

'I don't know that there is much cause for sorrow,' said the lady. 'Mr Quiverful is a much more deserving man, more in need of it, and one who will make himself much more useful in the close neighbourhood of the palace.'

'I suppose I had better see Quiverful?' said the chaplain.

'I suppose you had,' said the bishop.

⌘ THIRTEEN ⌘

The Rubbish Cart

MR HARDING WAS NOT A HAPPY MAN as he walked down the palace pathway, and stepped out into the close. His preferment and pleasant house were a second time gone from him; but that he could endure. He had been schooled and insulted by a man young enough to be his son; but that he could put up with. He could even draw from the very injuries, which had been inflicted on him, some of that consolation, which we may believe martyrs always receive from the injustice of their own sufferings, and which is generally proportioned in its strength to the extent of cruelty with which martyrs are treated. He had admitted to his daughter that he wanted the comfort of his old home, and yet he could have returned to his lodgings in the High Street, if not with exultation, at least with satisfaction, had that been all. But the venom of the chaplain's harangue had worked into his blood, and sapped the life of his sweet contentment.

'New men are carrying out new measures, and are carting away the useless rubbish of past centuries!' What cruel words these had been; and how often are they now used with all the heartless cruelty of a Slope! A man is sufficiently condemned if it can only be shown that either in politics or religion he does not belong to some new school established within the last score of years. He may then regard himself as rubbish and expect to be carted away. A man is nothing now unless he has within him a full appreciation of the new era; an era in which it would seem that neither honesty nor truth is very desirable, but in which success is the only touchstone of merit. We must laugh at every thing that is established. Let the joke be ever so bad, ever so untrue to the real principles of joking; nevertheless we must laugh – or else beware the cart. We must talk, think, and live up to the spirit of the times, and write up to it too, if that cacoethes be upon us, or else we are nought. New men and new measures, long credit and few scruples, great success or wonderful ruin, such are now the tastes of Englishmen who know how to live. Alas, alas! under such circumstances Mr Harding could not but feel that he was an Englishman who did not know how to live. This new doctrine of Mr Slope and the rubbish cart, new at least at Barchester, sadly disturbed his equanimity.

'The same thing is going on throughout the whole country!' 'Work is now required from every man who receives wages!' And had he been living all his life receiving wages, and doing no work? Had he in truth so lived as to be now in his old age justly reckoned as rubbish fit only to be hidden away in some huge dust hole? The school of men to whom he professes to belong, the Grantlys, the Gwynnes, and the old high set of Oxford divines, are afflicted with no such self-accusations as these which troubled Mr Harding. They, as a rule, are as satisfied with the wisdom and propriety of their own conduct as can be any Mr Slope, or any Dr Proudie, with his own. But unfortunately for himself Mr Harding had little of this self-reliance. When he heard himself designated as rubbish by the Slopes of the world, he had no other resource than to make inquiry within his own bosom as to the truth of the designation. Alas, alas! the evidence seemed generally to go against him.

He had professed to himself in the bishop's parlour that in these coming sources of the sorrow of age, in these fits of sad regret from which the latter years of few reflecting men can be free, religion would suffice to comfort him. Yes, religion could console him for the loss of any worldly good; but was his religion of that active sort which would enable him so to repent of misspent years as to pass those that were left to him in a spirit of hope for the future? And such repentance itself, is it not a work of agony and of tears? It is very easy to talk of repentance; but a man has to walk over hot ploughshares before he can complete it; to be skinned alive as was St Bartholomew; to be stuck full of arrows as was St Sebastian; to lie broiling on a gridiron like St Lorenzo! How if his past life required such repentance as this? had he the energy to go through with it?

Mr Harding after leaving the palace, walked slowly for an hour or so beneath the shady elms of the close, and then betook himself to his daughter's house. He had at any rate made up his mind that he would go out to Plumstead to consult Dr Grantly, and that he would in the first instance tell Eleanor what had occurred.

And now he was doomed to undergo another misery. Mr Slope had forestalled him at the widow's house. He had called there on the preceding afternoon. He could not, he had said, deny himself the pleasure of telling Mrs Bold that her father was about to return to the pretty house at Hiram's hospital. He had been instructed by the bishop to inform Mr Harding that the appointment would now be made at once. The bishop was of course only too happy to be able to be the means of restoring to Mr Harding the preferment which he had so long adorned. And then by degrees Mr Slope had introduced the subject of the pretty school which he hoped before long to see attached to the hospital. He had quite fascinated Mrs Bold by his description of this picturesque, useful, and charitable appendage, and she had gone so far as to say that she had no doubt her father would approve, and that she herself would gladly undertake a class.

Any one who had heard the entirely different tone, and seen the entirely different manner in which Mr Slope had spoken of this projected institution to the daughter and to the father, could not have failed to own that Mr Slope was a man of genius. He said nothing to Mrs Bold about the hospital sermons and services, nothing about the exclusion of the old men from the cathedral, nothing about dilapidation and painting, nothing about carting away the rubbish. Eleanor had said to herself that certainly she did not like Mr Slope personally, but that he was a very active, zealous clergyman, and would no doubt be useful in Barchester. All this paved the way for much additional misery to Mr Harding.

Eleanor put on her happiest face as she heard her father on the stairs, for she thought she had only to congratulate him; but directly she saw his face, she knew that there was but little matter for congratulation. She had seen him with the same weary look of sorrow on one or two occasions before, and remembered it well. She had seen him when he first read that attack upon himself in the Jupiter which had ultimately caused him to resign the hospital; and she had seen him also when the archdeacon had persuaded him to remain there against his own sense of propriety and honour. She knew at a glance that his spirit was in deep trouble.

'Oh, papa, what is it?' said she, putting down her boy to crawl upon the floor.

'I came to tell you, my dear,' said he, 'that I am going out to Plumstead: you won't come with me, I suppose?'

'To Plumstead, papa? Shall you stay there?'

'I suppose I shall, to night: I must consult the archdeacon about this weary hospital. Ah me! I wish I had never thought of it again.'

'Why, papa, what is the matter?'

'I've been with Mr Slope, my dear, and he isn't the pleasantest companion in the world, at least not to me.' Eleanor gave a sort of half blush; but she was wrong if she imagined that her father in any way alluded to her acquaintance with Mr Slope.

'Well, papa.'

'He wants to turn the hospital into a Sunday school and a preaching house; and I suppose he will have his way. I do not feel myself adapted for such an establishment, and therefore, I suppose, I must refuse the appointment.'

'What would be the harm of the school, papa?'

'The want of a proper schoolmaster, my dear.'

'But that would of course be supplied.'

'Mr Slope wishes to supply it by making me his school-master. But as I am hardly fit for such work, I intend to decline.'

'Oh, papa! Mr Slope doesn't intend that. He was here yesterday, and what he intends –'

'He was here yesterday, was he?' asked Mr Harding.

'Yes, papa.'

'And talking about the hospital?'

'He was saying how glad he would be, and the bishop too, to see you back there again. And then he spoke about the Sunday school; and to tell the truth I agreed with him; and I thought you would have done so too. Mr Slope spoke of a school, not inside the hospital, but just connected with it, of which you would be the patron and visitor; and I thought you would have liked such a school as that; and I promised to look after it and to take a class – and it all seemed so very – But, oh, papa! I shall be so miserable if I find I have done wrong.'

'Nothing wrong at all, my dear,' said he, gently, very gently rejecting his daughter's caress. 'There can be nothing wrong in your wishing to make yourself useful; indeed, you ought to do so by all means. Every one must now exert himself who would not choose to go to the wall.' Poor Mr Harding thus attempted in his misery to preach the new doctrine to his child. 'Himself or herself, it's all the same,' he continued; 'you will be quite right, my dear, to do something of this sort; but –'

'Well, papa.'

'I am not quite sure that if I were you I would select Mr Slope for my guide.'

'But I never have done so, and never shall.'

'It would be very wicked of me to speak evil of him, for to tell the truth I know no evil of him; but I am not quite sure that he is honest. That he is not gentleman-like in his manners, of that I am quite sure.'

'I never thought of taking him for my guide, papa.'

'As for myself, my dear,' continued he, 'we know the old proverb – "It's bad teaching an old dog tricks." I must decline the Sunday school, and shall therefore probably decline the hospital also. But I will first see your brother-in-law.' So he took up his hat, kissed the baby, and withdrew, leaving Eleanor in as low spirits as himself.

All this was a great aggravation to his misery. He had so few with whom to sympathise, that he could not afford to be cut off from the one whose sympathy was of the most value to him. And yet it seemed probable that this would be the case. He did not own to himself that he wished his daughter to hate Mr Slope; yet had she expressed such a feeling there would have been very little bitterness in the rebuke he would have given her for so uncharitable a state of mind. The fact, however, was that she was on friendly terms with Mr Slope, that she coincided with his views, adhered at once to his plans, and listened with delight to his teaching. Mr Harding hardly wished his daughter to hate the man, but he would have preferred that to her loving him.

He walked away to the inn to order a fly, went home to put up his carpet bag, and then started for Plumstead. There was, at any rate, no danger that the archdeacon would fraternise with Mr Slope; but then he would recommend internecine war, public appeals, loud reproaches, and all the paraphernalia of open battle. Now that alternative was hardly more to Mr Harding's taste than the other.

When Mr Harding reached the parsonage he found that the archdeacon was out, and would not be home till dinner-time, so he began his complaint to his elder daughter. Mrs Grantly entertained quite as strong an antagonism to Mr Slope as did her husband; she was also quite as alive to the necessity of combating the Proudie faction, of supporting the old church interest of the close, of keeping in her own set such of the loaves and fishes as duly belonged to it; and was quite as well prepared as her lord to carry on the battle without giving or taking quarter. Not that she was a woman prone to quarreling, or ill inclined to live at peace with her clerical neighbors; but she felt, as did the archdeacon, that the presence of Mr Slope in Barchester was an insult to every one connected with the late bishop, and that his assumed dominion in the diocese was a spiritual injury to her husband. Hitherto people had little guessed how bitter Mrs Grantly could be. She lived on the best of terms with all the rectors' wives around her. She had been popular with all the ladies connected with the close. Though much the wealthiest of the ecclesiastical matrons of the county, she had so managed her affairs that her carriage and horses had given umbrage to none. She had never thrown herself among the county grandees so as to excite the envy of other clergymen's wives. She had never talked too loudly of earls and countesses, or boasted that she gave her governess sixty pounds a year, or her cook seventy. Mrs Grantly had lived the life of a wise, discreet, peace-making woman; and the people of Barchester were surprised at the amount of military vigour she displayed as general of the feminine Grantlyite forces.

Mrs Grantly soon learnt that her sister Eleanor had promised to assist Mr Slope in the affairs of the hospital; and it was on this point that her attention soon fixed itself.

'How can Eleanor endure him!' said she.

'He is a very crafty man,' said her father, 'and his craft has been successful in making Eleanor think that he is a meek, charitable, good clergyman. God forgive me, if I wrong him, but such is not his true character in my opinion.'

'His true character, indeed!' said she, with something approaching to scorn for her father's moderation. 'I only hope he won't have craft enough to make Eleanor forget herself and her position.'

'Do you mean marry him?' said he, startled out of his usual demeanour by the abruptness and horror of so dreadful a proportion.

'What is there so improbable in it? Of course that would be his own object if he thought he had any chance of success. Eleanor has a thousand a year entirely at her own disposal, and what better fortune could fall to Mr Slope's lot than the transferring of the disposal of such a fortune to himself?'

'But you can't think she likes him, Susan?'

'Why not?' said Susan. 'Why shouldn't she like him? He's just the sort of man to get on with a woman left as she is, with no one to look after her.'

'Look after her!' said the unhappy father; 'don't we look after her?'

'Ah, papa, how innocent you are! Of course it was to be expected that Eleanor should marry again. I should be the last to advise her against it, if she would only wait the proper time, and then marry at least a gentleman.'

'But you don't really mean to say that you suppose Eleanor has ever thought of marrying Mr Slope? Why, Mr Bold has only been dead a year.'

'Eighteen months,' said his daughter. 'But I don't suppose Eleanor has ever thought about it. It is very probable, though, that he has, and that he will try and make her do so; and that he will succeed too, if we don't take care what we are about.'

This was quite a new phase of the affair to poor Mr Harding. To have thrust upon him as his son-in-law, as the husband of his favourite child, the only man in the world whom he really positively disliked, would be a misfortune which he felt he would not know how to endure patiently. But then, could there be any ground for so dreadful a surmise? In all worldly matters he was apt to look upon the opinion of his eldest daughter, as one generally sound and trustworthy. In her appreciation of character, of motives, and the probable conduct both of men and women, she was usually not far wrong. She had early foreseen the marriage of Eleanor and John Bold; she had at a glance deciphered the character of the new bishop and his chaplain; could it possibly be that her present surmise should ever come forth as true?

'But you don't think that she likes him?' said Mr Harding again.

'Well, papa, I can't say that I think she dislikes him as she ought to do. Why is he visiting there as a confidential friend, when he never ought to have been admitted inside the house? Why is it that she speaks to him about your welfare and your position, as she clearly has done? At the bishop's party the other night, I saw her talking to him for half an hour at the stretch.'

'I thought Mr Slope seemed to talk to nobody there but that daughter of Stanhope's,' said Mr Harding, wishing to defend his child.

'Oh, Mr Slope is a cleverer man than you think of, papa, and keeps more than one iron in the fire.'

To give Eleanor her due, any suspicion as to the slightest inclination on her part towards Mr Slope was a wrong to her. She had no more idea of marrying Mr Slope than she had of marrying the bishop; and the idea that Mr Slope would present himself as a suitor had never occurred to her. Indeed, to give her her due again, she had never thought about suitors since her husband's death. But nevertheless it was true that she had overcome all that repugnance to the man which was so strongly felt for him by the rest of the Grantly faction. She had forgiven him his sermon. She had forgiven him his low church tendencies, his Sabbath schools, and puritanical observances. She had forgiven his pharisaical arrogance, and even his greasy face and oily vulgar manners. Having agreed to overlook such offenses as these, why should she not in time be taught to regard Mr Slope as a suitor?

And as to him, it must also be affirmed that he was hitherto equally innocent of the crime imputed to him. How it had come to pass that a man whose eyes were generally so widely open to everything around him had not perceived that this young widow was rich as well as beautiful, cannot probably now be explained. But such was the fact. Mr Slope had ingratiated himself with Mrs Bold, merely as he had done with other ladies, in order to strengthen his party in the city. He subsequently amended his error; but it was not till after the interview between him and Mr Harding.

✂ FOURTEEN ✂

The New Champion

THE ARCHDEACON DID NOT RETURN TO THE parsonage till close upon the hour of dinner, and there was therefore no time to discuss matters before that important ceremony. He seemed to be in an especial good humour, and welcomed his father-in-law with a sort of jovial earnestness that was usual with him when things on which he was intent were going on as he would have them.

'It's all settled, my dear,' said he to his wife as he washed his hands in his dressing-room, while she, according to her wont, sat listening in the bedroom; 'Arabin has agreed to accept the living. He'll be here next week.' And the archdeacon scrubbed his hands and rubbed his face with a violent alacrity, which showed that Arabin's coming was a great point gained.

'Will he come here to Plumstead?' said the wife.

'He has promised to stay a month with us,' said the archdeacon, 'so that he may see what his parish is like. You'll like Arabin very much. He's a gentleman in every respect, and full of humour.'

'He's very queer, isn't he?' asked the lady.

'Well – he is a little odd in some of his fancies; but there's nothing about him you won't like. He is as staunch a churchman as there is at Oxford. I really don't know what we should do without Arabin. It's a great thing for me to have him so near me; and if anything can put Slope down, Arabin will do it.'

The Reverend Francis Arabin was a fellow of Lazarus, the favoured disciple of the great Dr Gwynne, a high churchman at all points; so high, indeed, that at one period of his career he had all but toppled over into the cesspool of Rome; a poet and also a polemical writer, a great pet in the common rooms at Oxford, an eloquent clergyman, a droll, odd, humorous, energetic, conscientious man, and, as the archdeacon had boasted of him, a thorough gentleman. As he will hereafter be brought more closely to our notice, it is now only necessary to add, that he had just been presented to the vicarage of St Ewold by Dr Grantly, in whose gift as archdeacon the living lay. St Ewold is a parish lying just without the city of Barchester. The suburbs of the new town, indeed, are partly within its precincts, and the pretty church and parsonage are not much above a mile distant from the city gate.

St Ewold is not a rich piece of preferment – it is worth some three or four hundred a year at most, and has generally been held by a clergyman attached to the cathedral choir. The archdeacon, however, felt, when the living on this occasion became vacant, that it imperatively behoved him to aid the force of his party with some tower of strength, if any such tower could be got to occupy St Ewold's. He had discussed the matter with his brethren in Barchester; not in any weak spirit as the holder of patronage to be used for his own or his family's benefit, but as one to whom was committed a trust, on the due administration of which much of the church's welfare might depend. He had submitted to them the name of Mr Arabin, as though the choice had rested with them all in conclave, and they had unanimously admitted that, if Mr Arabin would accept St Ewold's no better choice could possibly be made.

If Mr Arabin would accept St Ewold's! There lay the difficulty. Mr Arabin was a man standing somewhat prominently before the world, that is, before the Church of England world. He was not a rich man, it is true, for he held no preferment but his fellowship; but he was a man not over anxious for riches, not married of course, and one whose time was greatly taken up in discussing, both in print and on platforms, the privileges and practices of the church to which he belonged. As the archdeacon had done battle for its temporalities, so did Mr Arabin do battle for its spiritualities; and both had done so conscientiously; that is, not so much each for his own benefit as for that of others.

Holding such a position as Mr Arabin did, there was much reason to doubt whether he would consent to become the parson of St Ewold's, and Dr Grantly had taken the trouble to go himself to Oxford on the matter. Dr Gwynne and Dr Grantly together had succeeded in persuading this eminent divine that duty required him to go to Barchester. There were wheels within wheels in this affair. For some time past Mr Arabin had been engaged in a tremendous controversy with no less a person than Mr Slope, respecting the apostolic succession. These two gentlemen had never seen each other, but they had been extremely bitter in print. Mr Slope had endeavoured to strengthen his cause by calling Mr Arabin an owl, and Mr Arabin had retaliated by hinting that Mr Slope was an infidel. This battle had been commenced in the columns of the daily Jupiter, a powerful newspaper, the manager of which was very friendly to Mr Slope's view of the case. The matter, however, had become too tedious for the readers of the Jupiter, and a little note had therefore been appended to one of Mr Slope's most telling rejoinders, in which it had been stated that no further letters from the reverend gentleman could be inserted except as advertisements.

Other methods of publication were, however, found less expensive than advertisements in the Jupiter; and the war went on merrily. Mr Slope declared that the main part of the consecration of a clergyman was the self-devotion of the inner man to the duties of the ministry. Mr Arabin contended that a man was not consecrated at all, had, indeed, no single attribute of a clergyman, unless he became so through the imposition of some bishop's hands, who had become a bishop through the imposition of other hands, and so on in a direct line to one of the apostles. Each had repeatedly hung the other on the horns of a dilemma; but neither seemed to be a whit the worse for the hanging; and so the war went on merrily.

Whether or no the near neighbourhood of the foe may have acted in any way as an inducement to Mr Arabin to accept the living of St Ewold, we will not pretend to say; but it had at any rate been settled in Dr Gwynne's library, at Lazarus, that he would accept it, and that he would lend his assistance towards driving the enemy out of Barchester, or, at any rate, silencing him while he remained there. Mr Arabin intended to keep his rooms at Oxford, and to have the assistance of a curate at St Ewold; but he promised to give as much time as possible to the neighbourhood of Barchester, and from so great a man Dr Grantly was quite satisfied with such a promise. It was no small part of the satisfaction derivable from such an arrangement that Bishop Proudie would be forced to institute into a living, immediately under his own nose, the enemy of his favourite chaplain.

All through dinner the archdeacon's good humour shone brightly in his face. He ate the good things heartily, he drank wine with his wife and daughter, he talked pleasantly of his doings at Oxford, told his father-in-law that he ought to visit Dr Gwynne at Lazarus, and launched out again in praise of Mr Arabin.

'Is Mr Arabin married, papa?' asked Griselda.

'No, my dear; the fellow of a college is never married.'

'Is he a young man, papa?'

'About forty, I believe,' said the archdeacon.

'Oh!' said Griselda. Had her father said eighty, Mr Arabin would not have appeared to her to be very much older.

When the two gentlemen were left alone over their wine, Mr Harding told his tale of woe. But even this, sad as it was, did not much diminish the archdeacon's good humour, though it greatly added to his pugnacity.

'He can't do it,' said Dr Grantly over and over again, as his father-in-law explained to him the terms on which the new warden of the hospital was to be appointed; 'he can't do it. What he says is not worth the trouble of listening to. He can't alter the duties of the place.'

'Who can't?' asked the ex-warden.

'Neither the bishop nor the chaplain, nor yet the bishop's wife, who, I take it, has really more to say to such matters than either of the other two. The whole body corporate of the palace together have no power to turn the warden of the hospital into a Sunday schoolmaster.'

'But the bishop has the power to appoint whom he pleases, and –'

'I don't know that; I rather think he'll find he has no such power. Let him try it, and see what the press will say. For once we shall have the popular cry on our side. But Proudie, ass as he is, knows the world too well to get such a hornet's nest about his ears.'

Mr Harding winced at the idea of the press. He had had enough of that sort of publicity, and was unwilling to be shown up a second time either as a monster or as a martyr. He gently remarked that he hoped the newspapers would not get hold of his name again, and then suggested that perhaps it would be better that he should abandon his object. 'I am getting old,' said he; 'and after all I doubt whether I am fit to undertake new duties.'

'New duties!' said the archdeacon: 'don't I tell you there shall be no new duties?'

'Or, perhaps, old duties either,' said Mr Harding; 'I think I will remain content as I am.' The picture of Mr Slope carting away the rubbish was still present to his mind.

The archdeacon drank off his glass of claret, and prepared himself to be energetic. 'I do hope,' said he, 'that you are not going to be so weak as to allow such a man as Mr Slope to deter you from doing what you know it is your duty to do. You know it is your duty to resume your place at the hospital now that parliament has so settled the stipend as to remove those difficulties which induced you to resign it. You cannot deny this; and should your timidity now prevent you from doing so, your conscience will hereafter never forgive you;' and as he finished this clause of his speech, he pushed over the bottle to his companion.

'Your conscience will never forgive you,' he continued. 'You resigned the place from conscientious scruples, scruples which I greatly respected, though I did not share them. All your friends respected them, and you left your old house as rich in reputation as you were ruined in fortune. It is now expected that you will return. Dr Gwynne was saying only the other day –'

'Dr Gwynne does not reflect how much older a man I am now than when he last saw me.'

'Old – nonsense!' said the archdeacon; 'you never thought yourself old till you listened to the impudent trash of that coxcomb at the palace.'

'I shall by sixty-five if I live till November,' said Mr Harding.

'And seventy-five, if you live till November ten years,' said the archdeacon. 'And you bid fair to be as efficient then as you were ten years ago. But for heaven's sake let us have no pretence in this matter. Your plea of old age is only a pretence. But you're not drinking your wine. It is only a pretence. The fact is, you are half afraid of this Slope, and would rather subject yourself to comparative poverty and discomfort, than come to blows with a man who will trample on you, if you let him.'

'I certainly don't like coming to blows, if I can help it.'

'Nor I neither – but sometimes we can't help it. This man's object is to induce you to refuse the hospital, that he may put some creature of his own into it; that he may show his power, and insult us all by insulting you, whose cause and character are so intimately bound up with that of the chapter. You owe it to us all to resist him in this, even if you have no solicitude for yourself. But surely, for your own sake, you will not be so lily-livered as to fall into this trap which he has baited for you, and let him take the very bread out of your mouth without a struggle.'

Mr Harding did not like being called lily-livered, and was rather inclined to resent it. 'I doubt there is any true courage,' said he, 'in squabbling for money.'

'If honest men did not squabble for money, in this wicked world of ours, the dishonest men would get it all; and I do not see that the cause of virtue would be much improved. No – we must use the means which we have. If we were to carry your argument home, we might give away every shilling of revenue which the church has; and I presume you are not prepared to say that the church would be strengthened by such a sacrifice.' The archdeacon filled his glass and then emptied it, drinking with much reverence a silent toast to the well-being and permanent security of those temporalities which were so dear to his soul.

'I think all quarrels between a clergyman and his bishop should be avoided,' said Mr Harding.

'I think so too; but it is quite as much the duty of the bishop to look to that as of his inferior. I tell you what, my friend; I'll see the bishop in this matter, that is, if you will allow me; and you may be sure I will not compromise you. My opinion is, that all this trash about the Sunday-schools and the sermons has originated wholly with Slope and Mrs Proudie, and that the bishop knows nothing about it. The bishop can't very well refuse to see me, and I'll come upon him when he has neither his wife nor his chaplain by him. I think you'll find that it will end in his sending you the appointment without any condition whatever. And as to the seats in the cathedral, we may safely leave that to Mr Dean. I believe the fool positively thinks that the bishop could walk away with the cathedral if he pleased.'

And so the matter was arranged between them. Mr Harding had come expressly for advice, and therefore felt himself bound to take the advice given him. He had known, moreover, beforehand, that the archdeacon would not hear of his giving the matter up, and accordingly though he had in perfect good faith put forward his own views, he was prepared to yield.

They therefore went into the drawing-room in good humour with each other, and the evening passed pleasantly in prophetic discussions on the future wars of Arabin and Slope. The frogs and the mice would be nothing to them, nor the angers of Agamemnon and Achilles. How the archdeacon rubbed his hands, and plumed himself on the success of his last move. He could not himself descend into the arena with Slope, but Arabin would have no such scruples. Arabin was exactly the man for such work, and the only man whom he knew that was fit for it.

The archdeacon's good humour and high buoyancy continued till, when reclining on his pillow, Mrs Grantly commenced to give him her view of the state of affairs at Barchester. And then certainly he was startled. The last words he said that might were as follows:–

'If she does, by heaven I'll never speak to her again. She dragged me into the mire once, but I'll not pollute myself with such filth as that –' And the archdeacon gave a shudder which shook the whole room, so violently was he convulsed with the thought which then agitated his mind.

Now in this matter, the widow Bold was scandalously ill-treated by her relatives. She had spoken to the man three or four times, and had expressed her willingness to teach in a Sunday-school. Such was the full extent of her sins in the matter of Mr Slope. Poor Eleanor! But time will show.

The next morning Mr Harding returned to Barchester, no further word having been spoken in his hearing respecting Mr Slope's acquaintance with his younger daughter. But he observed that the archdeacon at breakfast was less cordial than he had been on the preceding evening.

✂ FIFTEEN ✂

The Widow's Suitors

MR SLOPE LOST NO TIME IN AVAILING himself of the bishop's permission to see Mr Quiverful, and it was in his interview with this worthy pastor that he first learned that Mrs Bold was worth the wooing. He rode out to Puddingdale to communicate to the embryo warden the good will of the bishop in his favour, and during the discussion on the matter it was not unnatural that the pecuniary resources of Mr Harding and his family should become the subject of remark.

Mr Quiverful, with his fourteen children and his four hundred a year, was a very poor man, and the prospect of this new preferment, which was to be held together with his living, was very grateful to him. To what clergyman so circumstanced would not such a prospect be very grateful? But Mr Quiverful had long been acquainted with Mr Harding, and had received kindness at his hands, so that his heart misgave him as he thought of supplanting a friend at the hospital. Nevertheless, he was extremely civil, cringingly civil, to Mr Slope; treated him quite as the great man; entreated this great man to do him the honour to drink a glass of sherry, at which, as it was very poor Marsala, the now pampered Slope turned up his nose; and ended by declaring his extreme obligation to the bishop and Mr Slope, and his great desire to accept the hospital, if – if it were certainly the case that Mr Harding had refused it.

What man, as needy as Mr Quiverful, would have been more disinterested?

'Mr Harding did positively refuse it,' said Mr Slope, with a certain air of offended dignity, 'when he heard of the conditions to which the appointment is now subjected. Of course, you understand, Mr Quiverful, that the same conditions will be imposed on yourself.'

Mr Quiverful cared nothing for the conditions. He would have undertaken to preach any number of sermons Mr Slope might have chosen to dictate, and to pass every remaining hour of his Sundays within the walls of a Sunday-school. What sacrifices, or, at any rate, what promises, would have been too much to make for such an addition to his income, and for such a house! But his mind still recurred to Mr Harding.

'To be sure,' said he; 'Mr Harding's daughter is very rich, and why should he trouble himself with the hospital?'

'You mean Mrs Grantly,' said Slope.

'I meant his widowed daughter,' said the other. 'Mrs Bold has twelve hundred a year of her own, and I suppose Mr Harding means to live with her.'

'Twelve hundred a year of her own!' said Slope, and very shortly afterwards took his leave, avoiding, as far as it was possible for him to do, any further allusion to the hospital. Twelve hundred a year, said he to himself, as he rode slowly home. If it were the fact that Mrs Bold had twelve hundred a year of her own, what a fool would he be to oppose her father's return to his old place. The train of Mr Slope's ideas will probably be plain to all my readers. Why should he not make the twelve hundred a year his own? and if he did so, would it not be well for him to have a father-in-law comfortably provided with the good things of this world? would it not, moreover, be much more easy for him to gain the daughter, if he did all in his power to forward the father's views?

These questions presented themselves to him in a very forcible way, and yet there were many points of doubt. If he resolved the restore to Mr Harding his former place, he must take the necessary steps for doing so at once; he must immediately talk over the bishop, quarrel on the matter with Mrs Proudie whom he knew he could not talk over, and let Mr Quiverful know that he had been a little too precipitate as to Mr Harding's positive refusal. That he could effect all this, he did not doubt; but he did not wish to effect it for nothing. He did not wish to give way to Mr Harding, and then be rejected by the daughter. He did not wish to lose one influential friend before he had gained another.

And thus he rode home, meditating many things in his mind. It occurred to him that Mrs Bold was sister-in-law to the archdeacon; and that not even for twelve hundred a year would he submit to that imperious man. A rich wife was a great desideratum to him, but success in his profession was still greater; there were, moreover, other rich women who might be willing to become wives; and after all, this twelve hundred a year might, when inquired into, melt away into some small sum utterly beneath his notice. Then also he remembered that Mrs Bold had a son.

Another circumstance also much influenced him, though it was one which may almost be said to have influenced him against his will. The vision of the Signora Neroni was perpetually before his eyes. It would be too much to say that Mr Slope was lost in love, but yet he thought, and kept continually thinking, that he had never seen so beautiful a woman. He was a man whose nature was open to such impulses, and the wiles of the Italianised charmer had been thoroughly successful in imposing upon his thoughts. We will not talk about his heart: not that he had no heart, but because his heart had little to do with his present feelings. His taste had been pleased, his eyes charmed, and his vanity gratified. He had been dazzled by a sort of loveliness which he had never before seen, and had been caught by an easy, free, voluptuous manner which was perfectly new to him. He had never been so tempted before, and the temptation was now irresistible. He had not owned to himself that he cared for this woman more than for others around him; but yet he thought often of the time when he might see her next, and made, almost unconsciously, little cunning plans for seeing her frequently.

He had called at Dr Stanhope's house the day after the bishop's party, and then the warmth of his admiration had been fed with fresh fuel. If the signora had been kind in her manner and flattering in her speech when lying upon the bishop's sofa, with the eyes of so many on her, she had been much more so in her mother's drawing-room, with no one present but her sister to repress either her nature or her art. Mr Slope had thus left her quite bewildered, and could not willingly admit into his brain any scheme, a part of which would be the necessity of his abandoning all further special friendship with this lady.

And so he slowly rode along very meditative.

And here the author must beg it to be remembered that Mr Slope was not in all things a bad man. His motives, like those of most men, were mixed; and though his conduct was generally very different from that which we would wish to praise, it was actuated perhaps as often as that of the majority of the world by a desire to do his duty. He believed in the religion which he taught, harsh, unpalatable, uncharitable as that religion was. He believed those whom he wished to get under his hoof, the Grantlys and Gwynnes of the church, to be the enemies of that religion. He believed himself to be a pillar of strength, destined to do great things; and with that subtle, selfish, ambiguous sophistry to which the minds of all men are so subject, he had taught himself to think that in doing much for the promotion of his own interests he was doing much also for the promotion of religion. But Mr Slope had never been an immoral man. Indeed, he had resisted temptations to immorality with a strength of purpose that was creditable to him. He had early in life devoted himself to works which were not compatible with the ordinary pleasures of youth, and he had abandoned such pleasures not without a struggle. It must therefore be conceived that he did not admit to himself that he warmly admired the beauty of a married woman without heartfelt stings of conscience; and to pacify that conscience, he had to teach himself that the nature of his admiration was innocent.

And thus he rode along meditative and ill at ease. His conscience had not a word to say against his choosing the widow and her fortune. That he looked upon as a godly work rather than otherwise; as a deed which, if carried through, would redound to his credit as a Christian. On that side lay no future remorse, no conduct which he might probably have to forget, no inward stings. If it should turn out to be really the fact that Mrs Bold had twelve hundred a year at her own disposal, Mr Slope would rather look upon it as a duty which he owed his religion to make himself the master of the wife and the money; as a duty too, in which some amount of self-sacrifice would be necessary. He would have to give up his friendship with the signora, his resistance to Mr Harding, his antipathy – no, he found on mature self-examination, that he could not bring himself to give up his antipathy to Dr Grantly. He would marry the lady as the enemy of her brother-in-law if such an arrangement suited her; if not, she must look elsewhere for a husband.

It was with such resolve as this that he reached Barchester. He would at once ascertain what the truth might be as to the lady's wealth, and having done this, he would be ruled by circumstances in his conduct respecting the hospital. If he found that he could turn round and secure the place for Mr Harding without much self-sacrifice, he would do so; but if not, he would woo the daughter in opposition to the father. But in no case would he succumb to the archdeacon.

He saw his horse taken round to the stable, and immediately went forth to commence his inquiries. To give Mr Slope his due, he was not a man who ever let much grass grow under his feet.

Poor Eleanor! She was doomed to be the intended victim of more schemes than one.

About the time that Mr Slope was visiting the vicar of Puddingdale, a discussion took place respecting her charms and wealth at Dr Stanhope's house in the close. There had been morning callers there, and people had told some truth and also some falsehood respecting the property which John Bold had left behind him. By degrees the visitors went, and as the doctor went with them, and as the doctor's wife had not made her appearance, Charlotte Stanhope and her brother were left together. He was sitting idly at the table, scrawling caricatures of Barchester notables, then yawning, then turning over a book or two, and evidently at a loss how to kill his time without much labor.

'You haven't done much, Bertie, about getting any orders,' said his sister.

'Orders!' said he; 'who on earth is there at Barchester to give one orders? Who among the people here could possibly think it worth his while to have his head done into marble?'

'Then you mean to give up our profession,' said she.

'No, I don't,' said he, going on with some absurd portrait of the bishop. 'Look at that, Lotte; isn't it the little man all over, apron and all? I'd go on with my profession at once, as you call it, if the governor would set me up with a studio in London; but as to sculpture at Barchester – I suppose half the people here don't know what a torso means.'

'The government will not give you a shilling to start you in London,' said Lotte. 'Indeed, he can't give you what would be sufficient, for he has not got it. But you might start yourself very well, if you pleased.'

'How the deuce am I do to it?' said he.

'To tell you the truth, Bertie, you'll never make a penny by any profession.'

'That's what I often think myself,' said he, not in the least offended. 'Some men have a great gift of making money, but they can't spend it. Others can't put two shillings together, but they have a great talent for all sorts of outlay. I begin to think that my genius is wholly in the latter line.'

'How do you mean to live then?' asked the sister.

'I suppose I must regard myself as a young raven, and look for heavenly manna; besides, we have all got something when the governor goes.'

'Yes – you'll have enough to supply yourself with gloves and boots; that is, if the Jews have not got the possession of it all. I believe they have the most of it already. I wonder, Bertie, at your indifference; that you, with your talents and personal advantages, should never try to settle yourself in life. I look forward with dread to the time when the governor must go. Mother, and Madeline, and I – we shall be poor enough, but you will have absolutely nothing.'

'Sufficient for the day is the evil thereof,' said Bertie.

'Will you take my advice?' said his sister.

'*Cela dépend*,' said the brother.

'Will you marry a wife with money?'

'At any rate,' said he, 'I won't marry one without: wives with money a'nt so easy to get now-a-days; the parsons pick them all up.'

'And a parson will pick up the wife I mean for you, if you do not look quickly about it; the wife I mean is Mrs Bold.'

'Whew-w-w-w!' whistled Bertie, 'a widow!'

'She is very beautiful,' said Charlotte.

'With a son and heir all ready to my hand,' said Bertie.

'A baby that will very likely die,' said Charlotte.

'I don't see that,' said Bertie. 'But however, he may live for me – I don't wish to kill him; only, it must be owned that a ready-made family is a drawback.'

'There is only one after all,' pleaded Charlotte.

'And that a very little one, as the maid-servant said,' rejoined Bertie.

'Beggars mustn't be choosers, Bertie; you can't have everything.'

'God knows I am not unreasonable,' said he, 'nor yet opinionated; and if you'll arrange it all for me, Lotte, I'll marry the lady. Only mark this; the money must be sure, and the income at my own disposal, at any rate for the lady's life.'

Charlotte was explaining to her brother that he must make love for himself if he meant to carry on the matter, and was encouraging him to do so, by warm eulogiums on Eleanor's beauty, when the signora was brought into the drawing-room. When at home, and subject to the gaze of none but her own family, she allowed herself to be dragged about by two persons, and her two bearers now deposited her on her sofa. She was not quite so grand in her apparel as she had been at the bishop's party, but yet she was dressed with much care, and though there was a look of care and pain about her eyes, she was, even by daylight, extremely beautiful.

'Well, Madeline; so I'm going to be married,' Bertie began, as soon as the servants had withdrawn.

'There's no other foolish thing left, that you haven't done,' said Madeline, 'and therfore you are quite right to try that.'

'Oh, you think it's a foolish thing, do you?' said he. 'There's Lotte advising me to marry by all means. But on such a subject your opinion ought to be the best; you have experience to guide you.'

'Yes, I have,' said Madeline, with a sort of harsh sadness in her tone, which seemed to say – What is it to you if I am sad? I have never asked your sympathy.

Bertie was sorry when he saw that she was hurt by what he said, and he came and squatted on the floor close before her face to make his peace with her.

'Come, Mad, I was only joking; you know that. But in sober earnest, Lotte is advising me to marry. She wants me to marry this Mrs Bold. She's a widow with lots of tin, a fine baby, a beautiful complexion, and the *George and Dragon* hotel up in the High Street. By Jove, Lotte, if I marry her, I'll keep the public house myself – it's just the life to suit me.'

'What?' said Madeline, 'that vapid swarthy creature in the widow's cap, who looked as though her clothes had been stuck on her back with a pitchfork!' The signora never allowed any woman to be beautiful.

'Instead of being vapid,' said Lotte, 'I call her a very lovely woman. She was by far the loveliest woman in the rooms the other night; that is, excepting you, Madeline.'

Even the compliment did not soften the asperity of the maimed beauty. 'Every woman is charming according to Lotte,' she said; 'I never knew an eye with so little true appreciation. In the first place, what woman on earth could look well in such a thing as that she had on her head?'

'Of course she wears a widow's cap; but she'll put that off when Bertie marries her.'

'I don't see any of course in it,' said Madeline. 'The death of twenty husbands should not make me undergo such a penance. It is as much a relic of paganism as the sacrifice of a Hindoo woman at the burning of her husband's body. If not so bloody, it is quite as barbarous, and quite as useless.'

'But you don't blame her for that,' said Bertie. 'She does it because it's the custom of the country. People would think ill of her if she didn't do it.'

'Exactly,' said Madeline. 'She is just one of those English nonentities who would tie her head up in a bag for three months every summer, if her mother and her grandmother had tied up their heads before her. It would never occur to her, to think whether there was any use in submitting to such a nuisance.'

'It's very hard, in a country like England, for a young woman to set herself in opposition to prejudices of that sort,' said the prudent Charlotte.

'What you mean is, that it's very hard for a fool not to be a fool,' said Madeline.

Bertie Stanhope had been so much knocked about the world from his earliest years, that he had not retained much respect for the gravity of English customs; but even to his mind an idea presented itself, that, perhaps in a wife, true British prejudice would not in the long run be less agreeable than Anglo-Italian freedom from restraint. He did not exactly say so, but he expressed the idea in another way.

'I fancy,' said he, 'that if I were do die, and then walk, I should think that my widow looked better in one of those caps than any other kind of head-dress.'

'Yes – and you'd fancy also that she could do nothing better than shut herself up and cry for you, or else burn herself. But she would think differently. She'd probably wear one of those horrid she-helmets, because she'd want the courage not to do so; but she'd wear it with a heart longing for the time when she might be allowed to throw it off. I hate such shallow false pretences. For my part, I would let the world say what it pleased, and show no grief if I felt none – and perhaps not, if I did.'

'But wearing a widow's cap won't lessen her fortune,' said Charlotte.

'Or increase it,' said Madeline. 'Then why on earth does she do it?'

'But Lotte's object is to make her put it off,' said Bertie.

'If it be true that she has got twelve hundred a year quite at her own disposal, and she be not utterly vulgar in her manners, I would advise you to marry her. I dare say she is to be had for the asking: and as you are not going to marry her for love, it doesn't much matter whether she is good-looking or not. As to your really marrying a woman for love, I don't believe *you* are fool enough for that.'

'Oh, Madeline!' exclaimed her sister.

'And oh, Charlotte!' said the other.

'You don't mean to say that no man can love a woman unless he be a fool?'

'I mean very much the same thing – that any man who is willing to sacrifice his interest to get possession of a pretty face is a fool. Pretty faces are to be had cheaper than that. I hate your mawkish sentimentality, Lotte. You know as well as I do in what way husbands and wives generally live together; you know how far the warmth of conjugal affection can withstand the trial of a bad dinner, of a rainy day, or of the least privation which poverty brings with it; you know what freedom a man claims for himself, what slavery he would exact from his wife if he could! And you know also how wives generally obey. Marriage means tyranny on one side and deceit on the other. I say that a man is a fool to sacrifice his interests for such a bargain. A woman, too generally, has no other way of living.'

'But Bertie has no other way of living,' said Charlotte.

'Then, in God's name, let him marry Mrs Bold,' said Madeline. And so it was settled between them.

But let the gentle-hearted reader be under no apprehension whatsoever. It is not destined that Eleanor shall marry Mr Slope or Bertie Stanhope. And here, perhaps, it may be allowed to the novelist to explain his views on a very important point in the art of telling tales. He ventures to reprobate that system which goes so far to violate all proper confidences between the author and his readers, by maintaining nearly to the end of the third volume a mystery as to the fate of their favourite personage. Nay, more, and worse than this, is too frequently done. Have not often the profoundest efforts of genius been used to baffle the aspirations of the reader, to raise false hopes and false fears, and to give rise to expectations which are never to be realised? Are not promises all but made of delightful horrors, in lieu of which the writer produces nothing but most common-place realities in his final chapter? And is there not a species of deceit in this to which the honesty of the present age should lend no countenance?

And what can be the worth of that solicitude which a peep into the third volume can utterly dissipate? What the value of those literary charms which are absolutely destroyed by their enjoyment? When we have once learnt what was that picture before which was hung Mrs Radcliffe's solemn curtain, we feel no further interest about either the frame or the veil. They are to us, merely a receptacle for old bones, an inappropriate coffin, which we would wish to have decently buried out of our sight.

And then, how grievous a thing it is to have the pleasure of your novel destroyed by the ill-considered triumph of a previous reader. 'Oh, you needn't be alarmed for Augusta, of course she accepts Gustavus in the end.' 'How very ill-natured you are, Susan,' says Kitty, with tears in her eyes; 'I don't care a bit about it now.' Dear Kitty, if you will read my book, you may defy the ill-nature of your sister. There shall be no secret that she can tell you. Nay, take the last chapter if you please – learn from its pages all the results of our troubled story, and the story shall have lost none of its interest, if indeed there be any interest in it to lose.

Our doctrine is, that the author and the reader should move along together in full confidence with each other. Let the personages of the drama undergo ever so complete a comedy of errors among themselves, but let the spectator never mistake the Syracusan for the Ephesian; otherwise he is one of the dupes, and the part of a dupe is never dignified.

I would not for the value of this chapter have it believed by a single reader that my Eleanor could bring herself to marry Mr Slope, or that she should be sacrificed to a Bertie Stanhope. But among the good folk of Barchester many believed both the one and the other.

❉ SIXTEEN ❉

Baby Worship

'DIDDLE, DIDDLE, DIDDLE, DIDDLE, DUM, DUM, DUM,' said or sung Eleanor Bold.

'Diddle, diddle, diddle, diddle, dum, dum, dum,' continued Mary Bold, taking up the second part in this concerted piece.

The only audience at the concert was the baby, who however gave such vociferous applause, that the performers presuming it to amount to an encore, commenced again.

'Diddle, diddle, diddle, diddle, dum, dum, dum: hasn't he got lovely legs?' said the rapturous mother.

'H'm 'm 'm 'm 'm,' simmered Mary, burying her lips in the little fellow's fat neck, by way of kissing him.

'H'm 'm 'm 'm 'm,' simmered the mamma, burying her lips also in his fat round short legs. 'He's a dawty little bold darling, so he is; and he has the nicest little pink legs in all the world, so he has;' and the simmering and the kissing went on over again, and as though the ladies were very hungry, and determined to eat him.

'Well, then, he's his own mother's own darling: well, he shall – oh, oh – Mary, Mary – did you ever see? What am I to do? My naughty, naughty,

naughty, naughty little Johnny.' All these energetic exclamations were elicited by the delight of the mother in finding that her son was strong enough, and mischievous enough, to pull all her hair out from under her cap. 'He's been and pulled down all mamma's hair, and he's the naughtiest, naughtiest, naughtiest little man that ever, ever, ever, ever, ever –'

A regular service of baby worship was going on. Mary Bold was sitting on a low easy chair, with the boy in her lap, and Eleanor was kneeling before the object of her idolatry. As she tried to cover up the little fellow's face with her long, glossy, dark brown locks, and permitted him to pull them hither and thither, as he would, she looked very beautiful in spite of the widow's cap which she still wore. There was a quiet, enduring, grateful sweetness about her face, which grew so strongly upon those who knew her, as to make the great praise of her beauty which came from her old friends, appear marvellously exaggerated to those who were only slightly acquainted with her. Her loveliness was like that of many landscapes, which require to be often seen to be fully enjoyed. There was a depth of dark clear brightness in her eyes which was lost upon a quick observer, a character about her mouth which only showed itself to those with whom she familiarly conversed, a glorious form of head the perfect symmetry of which required the eye of an artist for its appreciation. She had none of that dazzling brilliancy, of that voluptuous Rubens beauty, of that pearly whiteness, and those vermilion tints, which immediately entranced with the power of a basilisk men who came within reach of Madeline Neroni. It was all but impossible to resist the signora, but no one was called upon for any resistance towards Eleanor. You might begin to talk to her as though she were your sister, and it would not be till your head was on your pillow, that the truth and intensity of her beauty would flash upon you; that the sweetness of her voice would come upon your ear. A sudden half-hour with the Neroni, was like falling into a pit; an evening spent with Eleanor like an unexpected ramble in some quiet fields of asphodel.

'We'll cover him up till there sha'n't be a morsel of his little 'ittle 'ittle 'ittle nose to be seen,' said the mother, stretching her streaming locks over the infant's face. The child screamed with delight, and kicked till Mary Bold was hardly able to hold him.

At this moment the door opened, and Mr Slope was announced. Up jumped Eleanor, and with a sudden quick motion of her hands pushed back her hair over her shoulders. It would have been perhaps better for her that she had not, for she thus showed more of her confusion than she would have done had she remained as she was. Mr Slope, however, immediately recognised her loveliness, and thought to himself, that irrespective of her fortune, she would be an inmate that a man might well desire for his house, a partner for his bosom's care very well qualified to make care lie easy. Eleanor hurried out of the room to re-adjust her cap, muttering some unnecessary apology about her baby. And while she is gone, we will briefly go back and state what had been hitherto the results of Mr Slope's meditations on his scheme of matrimony.

His inquiries as to the widow's income had at any rate been so far successful as to induce him to determine to go on with the speculation. As regarded Mr Harding, he had also resolved to do what he could without injury to himself. To Mrs Proudie he determined not to speak on the matter, at least not at present. His object was to instigate a little rebellion on the part of the bishop. He thought that such a state of things would be advisable not only in respect to Messrs Harding and Quiverful, but also in the affairs of the diocese generally. Mr Slope was by no means of opinion that Dr Proudie was fit to rule, but he conscientiously thought it wrong that his brother clergy should be subjected to petticoat government. He therefore made up his mind to infuse a little of his spirit into the bishop, sufficient to induce him to oppose his wife, though not enough to make him altogether insubordinate.

He had therefore taken an opportunity of again speaking to his lordship about the hospital, and had endeavoured to make it appear that after all it would be unwise to exclude Mr Harding from the appointment. Mr Slope, however, had a harder task than he had imagined. Mrs Proudie, anxious to assume to herself as much as possible of the merit of patronage, had written to Mrs Quiverful, requesting her to call at the palace; and had then explained to that matron, with much mystery, condescension, and dignity, the good that was in store for her and her progeny. Indeed Mrs Proudie had been so engaged at the very time that Mr Slope had been doing the same with the husband at Puddingdale Vicarage, and had thus in a measure committed herself. The thanks, the humility, the gratitude, the surprise of Mrs Quiverful had been very overpowering; she had all but embraced the knees of her patroness, and had promised that the prayers of fourteen unprovided babes (so Mrs Quiverful had described her own family, the eldest of which was a stout young woman of three-and-twenty) should be put up to heaven morning and evening for the munificent friend whom God had sent to them. Such incense as this was not unpleasing to Mrs Proudie, and she made the most of it. She offered her general assistance to the fourteen unprovided babes, if, as she had no doubt, she should find them worthy; expressed a hope that the eldest of them would be fit to undertake tuition in her Sabbath schools, and altogether made herself a very great lady in the estimation of Mrs Quiverful.

Having done this, she thought it prudent to drop a few words before the bishop, letting him know that she had acquainted the Puddingdale family with their good fortune; so that he might perceive that he stood committed to the appointment. The husband well understood the *ruse* of his wife, but he did not resent it. He knew that she was taking the patronage out of his hands; he was resolved to put an end to her interference, and re-assume his powers. But then he thought this was not the best time to do it. He put off the evil hour, as many a man in similar circumstances has done before him.

Such having been the case, Mr Slope naturally encountered a difficulty in talking over the bishop, a difficulty indeed which he found could not be overcome except at the cost of a general outbreak at the palace. A general outbreak at the present moment might be good policy, but it also might not. It was at any rate not a step to be lightly taken. He began by whispering to the bishop that he feared that public opinion would be against him if Mr Harding did not reappear at the hospital. The bishop answered with some warmth that Mr Quiverful had been promised the appointment on Mr Slope's advice. 'Not promised!' said Mr Slope. 'Yes, promised,' replied the bishop, 'and Mrs Proudie has seen Mrs Quiverful on the subject.' This was quite unexpected on the part of Mr Slope, but his presence of mind did not fail him, and he turned the statement to his own account.

'Ah, my lord,' said he, 'we shall all be in scrapes if the ladies interfere.'

This was too much in unison with my lord's feelings to be altogether unpalatable, and yet such an allusion to interference demanded a rebuke. My lord was somewhat astounded also, though not altogether made miserable, by finding that there was a point of difference between his wife and his chaplain.

'I don't know what you mean by interference,' said the bishop mildly. 'When Mrs Proudie heard that Mr Quiverful was to be appointed, it was not unnatural that she should wish to see Mrs Quiverful about the schools. I really cannot say that I see any interference.'

'I only speak, my lord, for your own comfort,' said Slope; 'for your own comfort and dignity in the diocese. I can have no other motive. As far as personal feelings go, Mrs Proudie is the best friend I have. I must always remember that. But still, in my present position, my first duty is to your lordship.'

'I'm sure of that, Mr Slope, I am quite sure of that;' said the bishop mollified: 'and you really think that Mr Harding should have the hospital?'

'Upon my word, I'm inclined to think so. I am quite prepared to take upon myself the blame of first suggesting Mr Quiverful's name. But since doing so, I have found that there is so strong a feeling in the diocese in favour of Mr Harding, that I think your lordship should give way. I hear also that Mr Harding has modified the objections he first felt to your lordship's propositions. And as to what has passed between Mrs Proudie and Mrs Quiverful, the circumstances may be a little inconvenient, but I really do not think that that should weigh in a matter of so much moment.'

And thus the poor bishop was left in a dreadfully undecided state as to what he should do. His mind, however, slightly inclined itself to the appointment of Mr Harding, seeing that by such a step, he should have the assistance of Mr Slope in opposing Mrs Proudie.

Such was the state of affairs at the palace, when Mr Slope called at Mrs Bold's house, and found her playing with her baby. When she ran out of the room, Mr Slope began praising the weather to Mary Bold, then he praised the baby and kissed him, and then he praised the mother, and then he praised Miss Bold herself. Mrs Bold, however, was not long before she came back.

'I have to apologise for calling at so very early an hour,' began Mr Slope, 'but I was really so anxious to speak to you that I hope you and Miss Bold will excuse me.'

Eleanor muttered something in which the words 'certainly,' and 'of course,' and 'not early at all,' were just audible, and then apologised for her own appearance, declaring with a smile, that her baby was becoming such a big boy that he was quite unmanageable.

'He's a great big naughty boy,' said she to the child; 'and we must send him away to a great big rough romping school, where they have great big rods, and do terrible things to naughty boys who don't do what their own mammas tell them;' and she then commenced another course of kissing, being actuated thereto by the terrible idea of sending her child away which her own imagination had depicted.

'And where the masters don't have such beautiful long hair to be dishevelled,' said Mr Slope, taking up the joke and paying a compliment at the same time.

Eleanor thought he might as well have left the compliment alone; but she said nothing and looked nothing, being occupied as she was with the baby.

'Let me take him,' said Mary. 'His clothes are nearly off his back with his romping,' and so saying she left the room with the child. Miss Bold had heard Mr Slope say he had something pressing to say to Eleanor, and thinking that she might be *de trop* took this opportunity of getting herself out of the room.

'Don't be long, Mary,' said Eleanor, as Miss Bold shut the door.

'I am glad, Mrs Bold, to have the opportunity of having ten minutes' conversation with you alone,' began Mr Slope. 'Will you let me openly ask you a plain question?'

'Certainly,' said she.

'And I am sure you will give me a plain and open answer.'

'Either that or none at all,' said she, laughing.

'My question is this, Mrs Bold; is your father really anxious to go back to the hospital?'

'Why do you ask me?' said she. 'Why don't you ask himself?'

'My dear Mrs Bold, I'll tell you why. There are wheels within wheels, all of which I would explain to you, only I fear that there is not time. It is essentially necessary that I should have an answer to this question, otherwise I cannot know how to advance your father's wishes; and it is quite impossible that I should ask himself. No one can esteem your father more than I do, but I doubt if this feeling is reciprocal.' It certainly was not. 'I must be candid with you as the only means of avoiding ultimate consequences, which may be most injurious to Mr Harding. I fear there is a feeling, I will not even call it a prejudice, with regard to myself in Barchester, which is not in my favour. You remember that sermon –'

'Oh! Mr Slope, we need not go back to that,' said Eleanor.

'For one moment, Mrs Bold. It is not that I may talk of myself, but because it is so essential that you should understand how matters stand. That sermon may have been ill-judged – it was certainy misunderstood; but I will say nothing about that now; only this, that it did give rise to a feeling against myself which your father shares with others. It may be that he has proper cause, but the result is that he is not inclined to meet me on friendly terms. I put it to yourself whether you do not know this to be the case.'

Eleanor made no answer, and Mr Slope, in the eagerness of his address, edged his chair a little nearer to the widow's seat, unperceived by her.

'Such being so,' continued Mr Slope, 'I cannot ask him this question as I can ask it of you. In spite of my delinquencies since I came to Barchester you have allowed me to regard you as a friend.' Eleanor made a little motion with her head which was hardly confirmatory, but Mr Slope if he noticed it, did not appear to do so. 'To you I can speak openly, and explain the feelings of my heart. This your father would not allow. Unfortunately the bishop has thought it right that this matter of the hospital should pass through my hands. There have been some details to get up with which he would not trouble himself, and thus it has come to pass that I was forced to have an interview with your father on the matter.'

'I am aware of that,' said Eleanor.

'Of course,' said he. 'In that interview Mr Harding left the impression on my mind that he did not wish to return to the hospital.'

'How could that be?' said Eleanor, at last stirred up to forget the cold propriety of demeanour which she had determined to maintain.

'My dear Mrs Bold, I give you my word that such was the case,' said he, again getting a little nearer to her. 'And what is more than that, before my interview with Mr Harding, certain persons at the palace, I do not mean the bishop, had told me that such was the fact. I own, I hardly believed it; I own, I thought that your father would wish on every account, for conscience' sake, for the sake of those old men, for old association, and the memory of dear days long gone by, on every account I thought that he would wish to resume his duties. But I was told that such was not his wish; and he certainly left me with the impression that I had been told the truth.'

'Well!' said Eleanor, now sufficiently roused on the matter.

'I hear Miss Bold's step,' said Mr Slope; 'would it be asking too great a favour to beg you to – I know you can manage anything with Miss Bold.'

Eleanor did not like the word manage, but still she went out, and asked Mary to leave them alone for another quarter of an hour.

'Thank you, Mrs Bold – I am so very grateful for this confidence. Well, I left your father with this impression. Indeed, I may say that he made me understand that he declined the appointment.'

'Not the appointment,' said Eleanor. 'I am sure he did not decline the appointment. But he said that he would not agree – that is, that he did not like the scheme about the schools and the services, and all that. I am quite sure he never said that he wished to refuse the place.'

'Oh, Mrs Bold!' said Mr Slope, in a manner almost impassioned. 'I would not, for the world, say to so good a daughter a word against so good a father. But you must, for his sake, let me show you exactly how the matter stands at present. Mr Harding was a little flurried when I told him of the bishop's wishes about the school. I did so, perhaps, with the less caution because you yourself had so perfectly agreed with me on the same subject. He was a little put out and spoke warmly. "Tell the bishop," said he," that I quite disagree with him – and shall not return to the hospital as such conditions are attached to it." What he said was to that effect; indeed, his words were, if anything, stronger than those. I had no alternative but to repeat them to his lordship, who said that he could look on them in no other light than a refusal. He also had heard the report that your father did not wish for the appointment, and putting all these things together, he thought he had no choice but to look for some one else. He has consequently offered the place to Mr Quiverful.'

'Offered the place to Mr Quiverful!' repeated Eleanor, her eyes suffused with tears. 'Then, Mr Slope, there is an end of it.'

'No, my friend – not so,' said he. 'It is to prevent such being the end of it that I am now here. I may at any rate presume that I have got an answer to my question, and that Mr Harding is desirous of returning.'

'Desirous of returning – of course he is,' said Eleanor; 'of course he wishes to have back his house and his income, and his place in the world; to have back what he gave up with such self-denying honesty, if he can have them without restraints on his conduct to which at his age it would be impossible that he should submit. How can the bishop ask a man of his age to turn schoolmaster to a pack of children?'

'Out of the question,' said Mr Slope, laughing slightly; 'of course no such demand shall be made on your father. I can at any rate promise you that I will not be the medium of any so absurd a requisition. We wished your father to preach in the hospital, as the inmates may naturally be too old to leave it; but even that shall not be insisted on. We wished also it attach a Sabbath-day school to the hospital, thinking that such an establishment could not but be useful under the surveillance of so good a clergyman as Mr Harding, and also under your own. But, dear Mrs Bold; we won't talk of these things now. One thing is clear; we must do what we can to annul this rash offer the bishop has made to Mr Quiverful. Your father wouldn't see Quiverful, would be? Quiverful is an honorable man, and would not, for a moment, stand in your father's way.'

'What?' said Eleanor; 'ask a man with fourteen children to give up his preferment! I am quite sure he will do no such thing.'

'I suppose not,' said Slope; and he again drew near to Mrs Bold, so that now they were very close to each other. Eleanor did not think much about it, but instinctively moved away a little. How greatly would she have increased the distance could she have guessed what had been said about her at Plumstead! 'I suppose not. But it is out of the question that Quiverful should supersede your father – quite out of the question. The bishop has been too rash. An idea occurs to me, which may, perhaps, with God's blessing, put us right. My dear Mrs Bold, would you object to seeing the bishop yourself?'

'Why should not my father see him?' said Eleanor. She had once before in her life interfered in her father's affairs, and then not to much advantage. She was older now, and felt that she should take no step in a matter so vital to him without his consent.

'Why, to tell the truth,' said Mr Slope, with a look of sorrow, as though he greatly bewailed the want of charity in his patron, 'the bishop fancies that he has cause of anger against your father. I fear an interview would lead to further ill will.'

'Why,' said Eleanor, 'my father is the mildest, the gentlest man living.'

'I only know,' said Slope, 'that he has the best of daughters. So you would not see the bishop? As to getting an interview, I could manage that for you without the slightest annoyance to yourself.'

'I could do nothing, Mr Slope, without consulting my father.'

'Ah!' said he, 'that would be useless; you would then only be your father's messenger. Does anything occur to yourself? Something must be done. Your father shall not be ruined by so ridiculous a misunderstanding.'

Eleanor said that nothing occurred to her, but that it was very hard; and the tears came to her eyes and rolled down her cheeks. Mr Slope would have given much to have had the privilege of drying them; but he had tact enough to know that he had still a great deal to do before he could even hope for any privilege with Mrs Bold.

'It cuts me to the heart to see you so grieved,' said he. 'But pray let me assure you that your father's interests shall not be sacrificed if it be possible for me to protect them. I will tell the bishop openly what are the facts. I will explain to him that he has hardly the right to appoint any other than your father, and will show him that if he does so he will be guilty of great injustice – and you, Mrs Bold, you will have the charity at any rate to believe this of me, that I am truly anxious for your father's welfare – for his and for your own.'

The widow hardly knew what answer to make. She was quite aware that her father would not be at all thankful to Mr Slope; she had a strong wish to share her father's feelings; and yet she could not but acknowledge that Mr Slope was very kind. Her father, who was generally so charitable to all men, who seldom spoke ill of any one, had warned her against Mr Slope, and yet she did not know how to abstain from thanking him. What interest could he have in the matter but that which he professed? Nevertheless there was that in his manner which even she distrusted. She felt, she did not know why, that there was something about him which ought to put her on her guard.

Mr Slope read all this in her hesitating manner just as plainly as though she had opened her heart to him. It was the talent of the man that he could so read the inward feelings of women with whom he conversed. He knew that Eleanor was doubting him, and that if she thanked him she would only do so because she could not help it; but yet this did not make him angry or even annoy him. Rome was not built in a day.

'I did not come for thanks,' continued he, seeing her hesitation; 'and do not want them – at any rate before they are merited. But this I do want, Mrs Bold, that I may make to myself friends in this fold to which it has pleased God to call me as one of the humblest of his shepherds. If I cannot do so, my task here must indeed be a sad one. I will at any rate endeavour to deserve them.'

'I'm sure,' said she, 'You will soon make plenty of friends.' She felt herself obliged to say something.

'That will be nothing unless they are such as will sympathise with my feelings; unless they are such as I can reverence and admire – and love. If the best and purest turn away from me, I cannot bring myself to be satisfied with the friendship of the less estimable. In such case I must live alone.'

'Oh! I'm sure you will not do that, Mr Slope.' Eleanor meant nothing, but it suited him to appear to think some special allusion had been intended.

'Indeed, Mrs Bold, I shall live alone, quite alone as far as the heart is concerned, if those with whom I yearn to ally myself turn away from me. But enough of this; I have called you my friend, and I hope you will not contradict me. I trust the time may come when I may also call your father so. May god bless you, Mrs Bold, you and your darling boy. And tell your father from me that what can be done for his interest shall be done.'

And so he took his leave, pressing the widow's hand rather more closely than usual. Circumstances, however, seemed just then to make this intelligible, and the lady did not feel called on to resent it.

'I cannot understand him,' said Eleanor to Mary Bold, a few minutes afterwards. 'I do not know whether he is a good man or a bad man –whether he is true or false.'

'Then give him the benefit of the doubt,' said Mary, 'and believe the best.'

'On the whole, I think I do,' said Eleanor. 'I think I do believe that he means well – and if so, it is a shame that we should revile him, and make him miserable while he is among us. But, oh, Mary, I fear papa will be disappointed in the hospital.'

SEVENTEEN

Who Shall be Cock of the Walk?

ALL THIS TIME THINGS WERE GOING ON somewhat uneasily at the palace. The hint or two which Mr Slope had given was by no means thrown away upon the bishop. He had a feeling that if he ever meant to oppose the now almost unendurable despotism of his wife, he must lose no further time in doing so; that if he ever meant to be himself master in his own diocese, let alone his own house, he should begin at once. It would have been easier to have done so from the day of his consecration than now, but easier now than when Mrs Proudie should have succeeded in thoroughly mastering the diocesan details. Then the proffered assistance of Mr Slope was a great thing for him, a most unexpected and invaluable aid. Hitherto he had looked on the two as allied forces; and had considered that as allies they were impregnable. He had begun to believe that his only chance of escape would be by the advancement of Mr Slope to some distant and rich preferment. But now it seemed that one of his enemies, certainly the least potent of them, but nevertheless one very important, was willing to desert his own camp. Assisted by Mr Slope what might he not do? He walked up and down his little study, almost thinking that the time might come when he would be able to appropriate to his own use the big room up stairs, in which his predecessor had always sat.

As he revolved these things in his mind a note was brought to him from Archdeacon Grantly, in which that divine begged his lordship to do him the honour of seeing him on the morrow – would his lordship have the kindness to name an hour? Dr Grantly's proposed visit would have reference to the reappointment of Mr Harding to the wardenship of Barchester hospital. The bishop having read his note was informed that the archdeacon's servant was waiting for an answer.

Here at once a great opportunity offered itself to the bishop of acting on his own responsibility. He bethought himself however of his new ally, and rang the bell for Mr Slope. It turned out that Mr Slope was not in the house; and then, greatly daring, the bishop with his own unassisted spirit wrote a note to the archdeacon saying that he would see him, and naming an hour for doing so. Having watched from his study-window that the messenger got safely off from the premises with this despatch, he began to turn over in his mind what step he should next take.

To-morrow he would have to declare to the archdeacon either that Mr Harding should have the appointment, or that he should not have it. The bishop felt that he could not honestly throw over the Quiverfuls without informing Mrs Proudie, and he resolved at last to brave the lioness in her den and tell her that circumstances were such that it behoved him to reappoint Mr Harding. He did not feel that he should at all derogate from his new courage by promising Mrs Proudie that the very first piece of available preferment at his disposal should be given to Quiverful to atone for the injury done to him. If he could mollify the lioness with such a sop, how happy would he think his first efforts to have been!

Not without many misgivings did he find himself in Mrs Proudie's boudoir. He had at first thought of sending for her. But it was not at all impossible that she might chose to take such a message amiss, and then also it might be some protection to him to have his daughters present at the interview. He found her sitting with her account books before her nibbling the end of her pencil evidently mersed in pecuniary difficulties, and harassed in mind by the multiplicity of palatial expenses, and the heavy cost of episcopal grandeur. Her daughters were around her. Olivia was reading a novel, Augusta was crossing a note to her bosom friend in Baker Street, and Netta was working diminutive coach wheels for the bottom of a petticoat. If the bishop could get the better of his wife in her present mood, he would be a man indeed. He might then consider the victory his own for ever. After all, in such cases the matter between husband and wife stands much the same as it does between two boys at the same school, two cocks in the same yard, or two armies on the same continent. The conqueror once is generally the conqueror for ever after. The prestige of victory is every thing.

'Ahem – my dear,' began the bishop, 'if you are disengaged, I wished to speak to you.' Mrs Proudie put her pencil down carefully at the point to which she had dotted her figure, marked down in her memory the sum she had arrived at, and then looked up, sourly enough, into her helpmate's face. 'If you are busy, another time will do as well,' continued the bishop, whose courage like Bob Acres' had oozed out, now that he found himself on the ground of battle.

'What is it about, Bishop?' asked the lady.

'Well – it was about those Quiverfuls – but I see you are engaged. Another time will do just as well for me.'

'What about the Quiverfuls? It is quite understood I believe, that they are to come to the hospital. There is to be no doubt about that, is there?' and as she spoke she kept her pencil sternly and vigorously fixed on the column of figures before her.

'Why, my dear, there is a difficulty,' said the bishop.

'A difficulty!' said Mrs Proudie, 'what difficulty? The place has been promised to Mr Quiverful, and of course he must have it. He has made all his arrangements. He has written for a curate for Puddingdale, he has spoken to the auctioneer about selling his farm, horses, and cows, and in all respects considers the place as his own. Of course he must have it.'

Now, bishop, look well to thyself, and call up all the manhood that is in thee. Think how much is at stake. If now thou art not true to thy guns, no

Slope can hereafter aid thee. How can he who deserts his own colours at the first smell of gunpowder expect faith in any ally. Thou thyself hast sought the battle-field; fight out the battle manfully now thou art there. Courage, bishop, courage! Frowns cannot kill, nor can sharp words break any bones. After all the apron is thine own. she can appoint no wardens, give away no benefices, nominate no chaplains, an' thou art but true to thyself. Up, man, and at her with a constant heart.

Some little monitor within the bishop's breast so addressed him. But then there was another monitor there which advised him differently, and as follows. Remember, bishop, she is a woman, and such a woman too as thou well knowest: a battle of words with such a woman is the very mischief. Were it not better for thee to carry on this war, if it must be waged, from behind thine own table in thine own study? Does not every cock fight best on his own dunghill? Thy daughters also are here, the pledges of thy love, the fruits of thy loins; is it well that they should see thee in the hour of thy victory over their mother? nay, is it well that they should see thee in the possible hour of thy defeat? Besides, hast thou not chosen thy opportunity with wonderful little skill, indeed with no touch of that sagacity for which thou art famous? Will it not turn out that thou art wrong in this matter, and thine enemy right; that thou hast actually pledged thyself in this matter of the hospital, and that now thou wouldest turn upon thy wife because she requires from thee but the fulfilment of thy promise? Art thou not a Christian bishop, and is not thy word to be held sacred whatever be the result? Return, bishop, to thy sanctum on the lower floor, and postpone thy combative propensities for some occasion in which at least thou mayest fight the battle against odds less tremendously against thee.

All this passed within the bishop's bosom while Mrs Proudie still sat with her fixed pencil, and the figure of her sum still enduring on the tablets of her memory. '£4 17s. 7d.' she said to herself. 'Of course Mr Quiverful must have the hospital,' she said out loud to her lord.

'Well, my dear, I merely wanted to suggest to you that Mr Slope seems to think that if Mr Harding be not appointed, public feeling in the matter would be against us, and that the press might perhaps take it up.'

'Mr Slope seems to think!' said Mrs Proudie, in a tone of voice which plainly showed the bishop that he was right in looking for a breach in that quarter. 'And what has Mr Slope to do with it? I hope, my lord, you are not going to allow yourself to be governed by a chaplain.' And now in her eagerness the lady lost her place in her account.

'Certainly not, my dear. Nothing I can assure you is less probable. But still Mr Slope may be useful in finding how the wind blows, and I really thought that if we could give something else as good to the Quiverfuls –'

'Nonsense,' said Mrs Proudie; 'it would be years before you could give them anything else that could suit them half as well, and as for the press and the public, and all that, remember there are two ways of telling a story. If Mr

Harding is fool enough to tell his tale, we can also tell ours. The place was offered to him, and he refused it. It has now been given to some one else, and there's an end of it. At least, I should think so.'

'Well, my dear, I rather believe you are right;' said the bishop, and sneaking out of the room, he went down stairs, troubled in his mind as to how he should receive the archdeacon on the morrow. He felt himself not very well just at present; and began to consider that he might, not improbably, be detained in his room the next morning by an attack of bile. He was, unfortunately, very subject to bilious annoyances.

'Mr Slope, indeed! I'll Slope him,' said the indignant matron to her listening progeny. 'I don't know what has come to Mr Slope. I believe he thinks he is to be Bishop of Barchester himself, because I've taken him by the hand, and got your father to make him his domestic chaplain.'

'He was always full of impudence,' said Olivia; 'I told you so once before, mamma.' Olivia, however, had not thought him too impudent when once before he had proposed to make her Mrs Slope.

'Well, Olivia, I always thought you liked him,' said Augusta, who at that moment had some grudge against her sister. 'I always disliked the man, because I think him thoroughly vulgar.'

'There you're wrong,' said Mrs Proudie; 'he's not vulgar at all; and what is more, he is a soul-stirring, eloquent preacher; but he must be taught to know his place if he is to remain in this house.'

'He has the horridest eyes I ever saw in a man's head,' said Netta; 'and I tell you what, he's terribly greedy; did you see all the currant pie he ate yesterday?'

When Mr Slope got home he soon learnt from the bishop, as much from his manner as his words, that Mrs Proudie's behests in the matter of the hospital were to be obeyed. Dr Proudie let fall something as to 'this occasion only,' and 'keeping all affairs about patronage exclusively in his own hands.' But he was quite decided about Mr Harding; and as Mr Slope did not wish to have both the prelate and the priestess against him, he did not at present see that he could do anything but yield.

He merely remarked that he would of course carry out the bishop's views, and that he was quite sure that if the bishop trusted to his own judgment things in the diocese would certainly be well ordered. Mr Slope knew that if you hit a nail on the head often enough, it will penetrate at last.

He was sitting alone in his room on the same evening when a light knock was made on his door, and before he could answer it the door was opened, and his patroness appeared. He was all smiles in a moment, but so was not she also. She took, however, the chair that was offered to her, and thus began her expostulation –

'Mr Slope, I did not at all approve your conduct the other night with that Italian woman. Any one would have thought that you were her lover.'

'Good gracious, my dear madam,' said Mr Slope, with a look of horror. 'Why, she is a married woman.'

That's more than I know,' said Mrs Proudie; 'however she chooses to pass for such. But married or not married, such attention as you paid to her was improper. I cannot believe that you would wish to give offence in my drawing-room, Mr Slope; but I owe it to myself and my daughters to tell you that I disapprove your conduct.'

Mr Slope opened wide his huge protruding eyes, and stared out of them with a look of well-feigned surprise. 'Why, Mrs Proudie,' said he, 'I did but fetch her something to eat when she said she was hungry.'

'And you have called on her since,' continued she, looking at the culprit with the stern look of a detective policeman in the act of declaring himself.

Mr Slope turned over in his mind whether it would be well for him to tell his termagant at once that he should call on whom he liked, and do what he liked; but he remembered that his footing in Barchester was not yet sufficiently firm, and that it would be better for him to pacify her.

'I certainly called since at Dr Stanhope's house, and certainly saw Madame Neroni.'

'Yes, and you saw her alone,' said the episcopal Argus.

'Undoubtedly, I did,' said Mr Slope, 'but that was because nobody else happened to be in the room. Surely it was no fault of mine if the rest of the family were out.'

'Perhaps not; but I assure you, Mr Slope, you will fall greatly in my estimation if I find that you allow yourself to be caught by the lures of that woman. I know women better than you do, Mr Slope, and you may believe me that that signora, as she calls herself, is not a fitting companion for a strict evangelical, unmarried young clergyman.'

How Mr Slope would have liked to laugh at her, had he dared! But he did not dare. So he merely said, 'I can assure you, Mrs Proudie, the lady in question is nothing to me.'

'Well, I hope not, Mr Slope. But I have considered it my duty to give you this caution; and now there is another thing I feel myself called on to speak about; it is your conduct to the bishop, Mr Slope.'

'My conduct to the bishop,' said he, now truly surprised and ignorant what the lady alluded to.

'Yes, Mr Slope; your conduct to the bishop. It is by no means what I would wish to see it.'

'Has the bishop said anything, Mrs Proudie?'

'No, the bishop has said nothing. He probably thinks that any remarks on the matter will come better from me, who first introduced you to his lordship's notice. The fact is, Mr Slope, you are a little inclined to take too much upon yourself.'

An angry spot showed itself on Mr Slope's cheeks, and it was with difficulty that he controlled himself. But he did do so, and sat quite silent while the lady went on.

'It is the fault of many young men in your position, and therefore the bishop is not inclined at present to resent it. You will, no doubt, soon learn what is required from you, and what is not. If you will take my advice, however, you will be careful not to obtrude advice upon the bishop in any matter touching patronage. If his lordship wants advice, he knows where to look for it.' And then having added to her counsel a string of platitudes as to what was desirable and what not desirable in the conduct of a strictly evangelical, unmarried young clergyman, Mrs Proudie retreated, leaving the chaplain to his thoughts.

The upshot of his thoughts was this, that there certainly was not room in the diocese for the energies of both himself and Mrs Proudie, and that it behoved him quickly to ascertain whether his energies or hers were to prevail.

⚹ EIGHTEEN ⚹

The Widow's Persecution

EARLY ON THE FOLLOWING MORNING MR SLOPE was summoned to the bishop's dressing-room, and went there fully expecting that he should find his lordship very indignant, and spirited up by his wife to repeat the rebuke which she had administered on the previous day. Mr Slope had resolved that at any rate from him he would not stand it, and entered the dressing-room in rather a combative disposition; but he found the bishop in the most placid and gentlest of humours. His lordship complained of being rather unwell, had a slight headache, and was not quite the thing in his stomach; but there was nothing the matter with his temper.

'Oh, Slope,' said he, taking the chaplain's proffered hand, 'Archdeacon Grantly is to call on me this morning, and I really am not fit to see him. I fear I must trouble you, to see him for me;' and then Dr Proudie proceeded to explain what it was that must be said to Dr Grantly. He was to be told in fact in the civilest words in which the tidings could be conveyed, that Mr Harding having refused the wardenship, the appointment had been offered to Mr Quiverful and accepted by him.

Mr Slope again pointed out to his patron that he thought he was perhaps not quite wise in his decision, and this he did *sotto voce*. But even with this precaution it was not safe to say much, and during the little that he did say, the bishop made a very slight, but still a very ominous gesture with his thumb towards the door which opened from his dressing-room to some inner sanctuary. Mr Slope at once took the hint, and said no more; but he perceived that there was to be confidence between him and his patron, that the league desired by him was to be made, and that this appointment of Mr Quiverful was to be the last sacrifice offered on the altar of conjugal obedience. All this Mr Slope read in the slight motion of the bishop's thumb, and he read it correctly. There was no need of parchments and seals, of attestations, explanations, and professions. The bargain was understood between them, and Mr Slope gave the bishop his hand upon it. The bishop understood the little extra squeeze, and an intelligible gleam of assent twinkled in his eye.

'Pray be civil to the archdeacon, Mr Slope,' said he out loud; 'but make him quite understand that in this matter Mr Harding has put it out of my power to oblige him.'

It would be a calumny on Mrs Proudie to suggest that she was sitting in her bed-room with her ear at the keyhole during this interview. She had within her a spirit of decorum which prevented her from descending to such baseness. To put her ear to a key-hole or to listen at a chink, was a trick for a housemaid.

Mrs Proudie knew this, and therefore she did not do it; but she stationed herself as near to the door as she well could, that she might, if possible, get the advantage which the housemaid would have had, without descending to the housemaid's artifice.

It was little, however, that she heard, and that little was only sufficient to deceive her. She saw nothing of that friendly pressure, perceived nothing of that concluded bargain; she did not even dream of the treacherous resolves which those two false men had made together to upset her in the pride of her station, to dash the cup from her lip before she had drank of it, to sweep away all her power before she had tasted its sweets! Traitors that they were; the husband of her bosom, and the outcast whom she had fostered and brought to the warmth of the world's brightest fireside! But neither of them had the magnanimity of this woman. Though two men have thus leagued themselves together against her, even yet the battle is not lost.

Mr Slope felt pretty sure that Dr Grantly would decline the honour of seeing him, and such turned out to be the case. The archdeacon, when the palace door was opened to him, was greeted by a note. Mr Slope presented his compliments, &c. &c. The bishop was ill in his room, and very greatly regretted, &c. &c. Mr Slope had been charged with the bishop's views, and if agreeable to the archdeacon, would do himself the honour, &c. &c. The archdeacon, however, was not agreeable, and having read his note in the hall, crumpled it up in his hand, and muttering something about sorrow for his lordship's illness, took his leave, without sending as much as a verbal message in answer to Mr Slope's note.

'Ill!' said the archdeacon to himself as he flung himself into his brougham. 'The man is absolutely a coward. He is afraid to see me. Ill, indeed!' The archdeacon was never ill himself, and did not therefore understand that any one else could in truth be prevented by illness from keeping an appointment. He regarded all such excuses as subterfuges, and in the present instance he was not far wrong.

Dr Grantly desired to be driven to his father-in-law's lodgings in the High Street, and hearing from the servant that Mr Harding was at his daughter's, followed him to Mrs Bold's house, and there found him. The archdeacon was fuming with rage when he got into the drawing-room, and had by this time nearly forgotten the pusillanimity of the bishop in the villany of the chaplain.

'Look at that,' said he, throwing Mr Slope's crumpled note to Mr Harding. 'I am to be told that if I choose I may have the honour of seeing Mr Slope, and that too, after a positive engagement with the bishop.'

'But he says the bishop is ill,' said Mr Harding.

'Pshaw! You don't mean to say that you are deceived by such an excuse as that. He was well enough yesterday. Now I tell you what, I will see the bishop; and I will tell him also very plainly what I think of his conduct. I will see him, or else Barchester will soon be too hot to hold him.'

Eleanor was sitting in the room, but Dr Grantly had hardly noticed her in his anger. Eleanor now said to him, with the greatest innocence, 'I wish you had seen Mr Slope, Dr Grantly, because I think perhaps it might have done good.'

The archdeacon turned on her with almost brutal wrath. Had she at once owned that she had accepted Mr Slope for her second husband, he could hardly have felt more convinced of her belonging body and soul to the Slope and Proudie party than he now did on hearing her express such a wish as this. Poor Eleanor!

'See him!' said the archdeacon glaring at her; 'and why am I to be called on to lower myself in the world's esteem and my own by coming in contact with such a man as that? I have hitherto lived among gentlemen, and do not mean to be dragged into other company by anybody.'

Poor Mr Harding well knew what the archdeacon meant, but Eleanor was as innocent as her own baby. She could not understand how the archdeacon could consider himself to be dragged into bad company by condescending to speak to Mr Slope for a few minutes when the interests of her father might be served by his doing so.

'I was talking for a full hour yesterday to Mr Slope,' said she, with some little assumption of dignity, 'and I did not find myself lowered by it.'

'Perhaps not,' said he. 'But if you'll be good enough to allow me, I shall judge for myself in such matters. And I tell you what, Eleanor; it will be much better for you if you will allow yourself to be guided also by the advice of those who are your friends. If you do not you will be apt to find that you have no friends left who can advise you.'

Eleanor blushed up to the roots for her hair. But even now she had not the slightest idea of what was passing in the archdeacon's mind. No thought of love-making or love-receiving had yet found its way to her heart since the death of poor John Bold; and if it were possible that such a thought should spring there, the man must be far different from Mr Slope that could give it birth.

Nevertheless Eleanor blushed deeply, for she felt she was charged with improper conduct, and she did so with the more inward pain because her father did not instantly rally to her side; that father for whose sake and love she had submitted to be the receptacle of Mr Slope's confidence. She had given a detailed account of all that had passed to her father; and though he had not absolutely agreed with her about Mr Slope's views touching the hospital, yet he had said nothing to make her think that she had been wrong in talking to him.

She was far too angry to humble herself before her brother-in-law. Indeed, she had never accustomed herself to be very abject before him, and they had never been confidential allies. 'I do not the least understand what you mean, Dr Grantly,' said she. 'I do not know that I can accuse myself of doing anything that my friends should disapprove. Mr Slope called here expressly to ask what papa's wishes were about the hospital; and as I believe he called with friendly intentions I told him.'

'Friendly intentions!' sneered the archdeacon.

'I believe you greatly wrong Mr Slope,' continued Eleanor; 'but I have explained this to papa already; and as you do not seem to approve of what I say, Dr Grantly, I will with your permission leave you and papa together,' and so saying she walked slowly out of the room.

All this made Mr Harding very unhappy. It was quite clear that the archdeacon and his wife had made up their minds that Eleanor was going to marry Mr Slope. Mr Harding could not really bring himself to think that she would do so, but yet he could not deny that circumstances made it appear that the man's company was not disagreeable to her. She was now constantly seeing him, and yet she received visits from no other unmarried gentleman. She always took his part when his conduct was canvassed, although she was aware how personally objectionable he was to her friends. Then, again, Mr Harding felt that if she should choose to become Mrs Slope, he had nothing that he could justly urge against her doing so. She had full right to please herself, and he, as a father, could not say that she would disgrace herself by marrying a clergyman who stood so well before the world as Mr Slope did. As for quarrelling with his daughter on account of such a marriage, and separating himself from her as the archdeacon had threatened to do, that, with Mr Harding, would be out of the question. If she should determine to marry this man, he must get over his aversion as best he could. His Eleanor, his own old companion in their old happy home, must still be the friend of his bosom, the child of his heart. Let who would cast her off, he would not. If it were fated that he should have to sit in his old age at the same table with that man whom of all men he disliked the most, he would meet his fate as best he might. Anything to him would be preferable to the loss of his daughter.

Such being his feelings, he hardly knew how to take part with Eleanor against the archdeacon, or with the archdeacon against Eleanor. It will be said that he should never have suspected her. Alas! he never should have done so. But Mr Harding was by no means a perfect character. In his indecision, his weakness, his proneness to be led by others, his want of self-confidence, he was very far from being perfect. And then it must be remembered that such a marriage as that which the archdeacon contemplated with disgust, which we who know Mr Slope so well would regard with equal disgust, did not appear so monstrous to Mr Harding, because in his charity he did not hate the chaplain as the archdeacon did, and as we do.

He was, however, very unhappy when his daughter left the room, and he had recourse to an old trick of his that was customary to him in his times of sadness. He began playing some slow tune upon an imaginary violoncello, drawing one hand slowly backwards and forwards as though he held a bow in it, and modulating the unreal cords with the other.

'She'll marry that man as sure as two and two make four,' said the practical archdeacon.

'I hope not, I hope not,' said the father. 'But if she does, what can I say to her? I have no right to object to him.'

'No right!' exclaimed Dr Grantly.

'No right as her father. He is in my own profession, and for aught we know a good man.'

To this the archdeacon would by no means assent. It was not well, however, to argue the case against Eleanor in her own drawing-room, and so they both walked forth and discussed the matter in all its bearings under the elm trees of the close. Mr Harding also explained to his son-in-law what had been the purport, at any rate the alleged purport, of Mr Slope's last visit to the widow. He, however, stated that he could not bring himself to believe that Mr Slope had any real anxiety such as that he had pretended. 'I cannot forget his demeanour to myself,' said Mr Harding, 'and it is not possible that his ideas should have changed so soon.'

'I see it all,' said the archdeacon. 'The sly *tartufe*! He thinks to buy the daughter by providing for the father. He means to show how powerful he is, how good he is, and how much he is willing to do for her *beaux yeux*; yes, I see it now. But we'll be too many for him yet, Mr Harding;' he said, turning to his companion with some gravity, and pressing his hand upon the other's arm. 'It would, perhaps, be better for you to lose the hospital than get it on such terms.'

'Lose it!' said Mr Harding; 'why I've lost it already. I don't want it. I've made up my mind to do without it. I'll withdraw altogether. I'll just go and write a line to the bishop and tell him that I withdraw my claim altogether.'

Nothing would have pleased him better than to be allowed to escape from the trouble and difficulty in such a manner. But he was now going too fast for the archdeacon.

'No – no – no! we'll do no such thing,' said Dr Grantly; 'we'll still have the hospital. I hardly doubt but that we'll have it. But not by Mr Slope's assistance. If that be necessary we'll lose it; but we'll have it, spite of his teeth, if we can. Arabin will be at Plumstead to-morrow; you must come over and talk to him.'

The two now turned into the cathedral library, which was used by the clergymen of the close as a sort of ecclesiastical club-room, for writing sermons and sometimes letters; also for reading theological works, and sometimes magazines and newspapers. The theological works were not disturbed, perhaps, quite as often as from the appearance of the building the outside public might have been led to expect. Here the two allies settled on their course of action. The archdeacon wrote a letter to the bishop, strongly worded, but still respectful, in which he put forward his father-in-law's claim to the appointment, and expressed his own regret that he had not been able to see his lordship when he called. Of Mr Slope he made no mention whatsoever. It was then settled that Mr Harding should go out to Plumstead on the following day; and after considerable discussion on the matter, the archdeacon proposed to ask Eleanor there also, so as to withdraw her, if possible, from Mr Slope's attentions. 'A week or two,' said he, 'may teach her what he is, and while she is there she will be out of harm's way. Mr Slope won't come there after her.'

Eleanor was not a little surprised when her brother-in-law came back and very civilly pressed her to go out to Plumstead with her father. She instantly perceived that her father had been fighting her battles for her behind her back. She felt thankful to him, and for his sake she would not show her resentment to the archdeacon by refusing his invitation. But she could not, she said, go on the morrow; she had an invitation to drink tea at the Stanhopes which she had promised to accept. She would, she added, go with her father on the next day, if he would wait; or she would follow him.

'The Stanhopes!' said Dr Grantly; 'I did not know you were so intimate with them.'

'I did not know it myself,' said she, 'till Miss Stanhope called yesterday. However, I like her very much, and I have promised to go and play chess with some of them.'

'Have they a party there?' said the archdeacon, still fearful of Mr Slope.

'Oh, no,' said Eleanor; 'Miss Stanhope said there was to be nobody at all. But she had heard that Mary had left me for a few weeks, and she had learnt from some one that I play chess, and so she came over on purpose to ask me to go in.'

'Well, that's very friendly,' said the ex-warden. 'They certainly do look more like foreigners than English people, but I dare say they are none the worse for that.'

The archdeacon was inclined to look upon the Stanhopes with favourable eyes, and had nothing to object on the matter. It was therefore arranged that Mr Harding should postpone his visit to Plumstead for one day, and then take with him Eleanor, the baby, and the nurse.

Mr Slope is certainly becoming of some importance in Barchester.

✜ NINETEEN ✜

Barchester by Moonlight

THERE WAS MUCH CAUSE FOR GRIEF AND occasional perturbation of spirits in the Stanhope family, but yet they rarely seemed to be grieved or to be disturbed. It was the peculiar gift of each of them that each was able to bear his or her own burden without complaint, and perhaps without sympathy. They habitually looked on the sunny side of the wall, if there was a gleam on either side for them to look at; and, if there was none, they endured the shade with an indifference which, if not stoical, answered the end at which the Stoics aimed. Old Stanhope could not but feel that he had ill-performed his duties as a father and a clergyman; and could hardly look forward to his own death without grief at the position in which he would leave his family. His income for many years had been as high as 3000*l*. a year, and yet they had among them no other provision than their mother's fortune of 10,000*l*. He had not only spent his income, but was in debt. Yet with all this, he seldom showed much outward sign of trouble.

It was the same with the mother. If she added little to the pleasures of her children she detracted still less: she neither grumbled at her lot, nor spoke much of her past or future sufferings; as long as she had a maid to adjust her dress, and had those dresses well made, nature with her was satisfied. It was the same with the children. Charlotte never rebuked her father with the prospect of their future poverty, nor did it seem to grieve her that she was becoming an old maid so quickly; her temper was rarely ruffled, and, if we might judge by her appearance, she was always happy. The signora was not so sweet-tempered, but she possessed much enduring courage; she seldom complained – never, indeed, to her family. Though she had a cause for affliction which would have utterly broken down the heart of most women as beautiful as she and as devoid of all religious support, yet, she bore her suffering in silence, or alluded to it only to elicit the sympathy and stimulate the admiration of the men with whom she flirted. As to Bertie, one would have imagined from the sound of his voice and the gleam of his eye that he had not a sorrow not a care in the world. Nor had he. He was incapable of anticipating to-morrow's griefs. The prospect of future want no more disturbed his appetite than does that of the butcher's knife disturb the appetite of the sheep.

Such was the usual tenour of their way; but there were rare exceptions. Occasionally the father would allow an angry glance to fall from his eye, and the lion would send forth a low dangerous roar as though he meditated some deed of blood. Occasionally also Madame Neroni would become bitter against mankind, more than usually antagonistic to the world's decencies, and would seem as though she was about to break from her moorings and allow herself to be carried forth by the tide of her feelings to utter ruin and shipwreck. She, however, like the rest of them, had no real feelings, could feel no true passion. In that was her security. Before she resolved on any contemplated escapade she would make a small calculation, and generally summed up that the Stanhope villa or even Barchester close was better than the world at large.

They were most irregular in their hours. The father was generally the earliest in the breakfast-parlour, and Charlotte would soon follow and give him his coffee; but the others breakfasted anywhere, anyhow, and at any time. On the morning after the archdeacon's futile visit to the palace, Dr Stanhope came down stairs with an ominously dark look about his eyebrows; his white locks were rougher than usual, and he breathed thickly and loudly as he took his seat in his arm-chair. He had open letters in his hand, and when Charlotte came into the room he was still reading them. She went up and kissed him as was her wont, but he hardly noticed her as she did so, and she knew at once that something was the matter.

'What's the meaning of that?' said he, throwing over the table a letter with a Milan post-mark. Charlotte was a little frightened as she took it up, but her mind was relieved when she saw that it was merely the bill of their Italian milliner. The sum total was certainly large, but not so large as to create an important row.

'It's for our clothes, papa, for six months before we came here. The three of us can't dress for nothing you know.'

'Nothing, indeed!' said he, looking at the figures, which in Milanese denominations were certainly monstrous.

'The man should have sent it to me,' said Charlotte.

'I wish he had with all my heart – if you would have paid it. I see enough in it, to know that three quarters of it are for Madeline.'

'She has little else to amuse her, sir,' said Charlotte with true good nature.

'And I suppose he has nothing else to amuse him,' said the doctor, throwing over another letter to his daughter. It was from some member of the family of Sidonia, and politely requested the father to pay a small trifle of 700l., being the amount of a bill discounted in favour of Mr Ethelbert Stanhope, and now overdue for a period of nine months.

Charlotte read the letter, slowly folded it up, and put it under the edge of the tea-tray.

'I suppose he has nothing to amuse him but discounting bills with Jews. Does he think I'll pay that?'

'I am sure he thinks no such thing,' said she.

'And who does he think will pay it?'

'As far as honesty goes I suppose it won't much matter if it is never paid,' said she. 'I dare say he got very little of it.'

'I suppose it won't much matter either,' said the father, 'if he goes to prison and rots there. It seems to me that that's the other alternative.'

Dr Stanhope spoke of the custom of his youth. But his daughter, though she had lived so long abroad, was much more completely versed in the ways of the English world. 'If the man arrests him,' said she, 'he must go through the court.'

It is thus, thou great family of Sidonia – it is thus that we Gentiles treat thee, when, in our extremest need, thou and thine have aided us with mountains of gold as big as lions – and occasionally with wine-warrants and orders for dozens of dressing-cases.

'What, and become an insolvent?' said the doctor.

'He's that already,' said Charlotte, wishing always to get over a difficulty.

'What a condition,' said the doctor, 'for the son of a clergyman of the Church of England.'

'I don't see why clergymen's sons should pay their debts more than other young men,' said Charlotte.

'He's had as much from me since he left school as is held sufficient for the eldest son of many a nobleman,' said the angry father.

'Well, sir,' said Charlotte, 'give him another chance.'

'What!' said the doctor, 'do you mean that I am to pay that Jew?'

'Oh no! I wouldn't pay him, he must take his chance; and if the worst comes to the worst, Bertie must go abroad. But I want you to be civil to Bertie, and let him remain here as long as we stop. He has a plan in his head, that may put him on his feet after all.'

'Has he any plan for following up his profession?'

'Oh, he'll do that too; but that must follow. He's thinking of getting married.'

Just at that moment the door opened, and Bertie came in whistling. The doctor immediately devoted himself to his egg, and allowed Bertie to whistle himself round to his sister's side without noticing him.

Charlotte gave a sign to him with her eye, first glancing at her father, and then at the letter, the corner of which peeped out from under the tea-tray. Bertie saw and understood, and with the quiet motion of a cat abstracted the letter, and made himself acquainted with its contents. The doctor, however, had seen him, deep as he appeared to be mersed in his egg-shell, and said in his harshest voice, 'Well, sir, do you know that gentleman?'

'Yes, sir,' said Bertie. 'I have a sort of acquaintance with him, but none that can justify him in troubling you. If you will allow me, sir, I will answer this.'

'At any rate I sha'n't,' said the father, and then he added, after a pause, 'Is it true, sir, that you owe the man 700*l.*?'

'Well,' said Bertie, 'I think I should be inclined to dispute the amount, if I were in a condition to pay him such of it as I really do owe him.'

'Has he your bill for 700*l.*?' said the father, speaking very loudly and very angrily.

'Well, I believe he has,' said Bertie; 'but all the money I ever got from him was 150*l.*'

'And what became of the 500*l.*?'

'Why, sir; the commission was 100*l.* or so, and I took the remainder in paving-stones and rocking horses.'

'Paving stones and rocking-horses!' said the doctor, 'where are they?'

'Oh, sir, I suppose they are in London somewhere – but I'll inquire if you wish for them.'

'He's an idiot,' said the doctor, 'and it's sheer folly to waste more money on him. Nothing can save him from ruin,' and so saying, the unhappy father walked out of the room.

'Would the governor like to have the paving-stones?' said Bertie to his sister.

'I'll tell you what,' said she. 'If you don't take care, you will find yourself loosed upon the world without even a house over your head; you don't know him as well as I do. He's very angry.'

Bertie stroked his big beard, sipped his tea, chatted over his misfortunes in a half comic, half serious tone, and ended by promising his sister that he would do his very best to make himself agreeable to the widow Bold. Then Charlotte followed her father to his own room and softened down his wrath, and persuaded him to say nothing more about the Jew bill discounter, at any rate for a few weeks. He even went so far as to say he would pay the 700*l.*, or at any rate settle the bill, if he saw a certainty of his son's securing for himself anything like a decent provision in life. Nothing was said openly between them about poor Eleanor: but the father and the daughter understood each other.

They all met together in the drawing-room at nine o'clock, in perfect good humour with each other; and about that hour Mrs Bold was announced. She had never been in the house before, though she had of course called; and now she felt it strange to find herself there in her usual evening dress, entering the drawing-room of these strangers in this friendly unceremonious way, as though she had known them all her life. But in three minutes they made her at home. Charlotte tripped down the stairs and took her bonnet from her, and Bertie came to relieve her from her shawl, and the signora smiled on her as she could smile when she chose to be gracious, and the old doctor shook hands with her in a kind benedictory manner that went to her heart at once, and made her feel that he must be a good man.

She had not been seated for about five minutes when the doors again opened, and Mr Slope was announced. She felt rather surprised, because she was told that nobody was to be there, and it was very evident from the manner of some of them, that Mr Slope was unexpected. But still there was not much in it. In such invitations a bachelor or two more or less are always spoken of as nobodies, and there was no reason why Mr Slope should not drink tea at Dr Stanhope's as well as Eleanor herself. He, however, was very much surprised and not very much gratified at finding that his own embryo spouse made one of the party. He had come there to gratify himself by gazing on Madame Neroni's beauty, and listening to and returning her flattery: and though he had not owned as much to himself, he still felt that if he spent the evening as he had intended to do, he might probably not thereby advance his suit with Mrs Bold.

The signora, who had no idea of a rival, received Mr Slope with her usual marks of distinction. As he took her hand, she made some confidential communication to him in a low voice, declaring that she had a plan to communicate with him after tea, and was evidently prepared to go on with her work of reducing the chaplain to a state of captivity. Poor Mr Slope was rather beside himself. He thought that Eleanor could not but have learnt from his demeanour that he was an admirer of her own, and he had also flattered himself that the idea was not unacceptable to her. What would she think of him if he now devoted himself to a married woman!

But Eleanor was not inclined to be severe in her criticisms on him in this respect, and felt no annoyance of any kind, when she found herself seated between Bertie and Charlotte Stanhope. She had no suspicion of Mr Slope's intentions; she had no suspicion even of the suspicion of other people; but still she felt well pleased not to have Mr Slope too near to her.

And she was not ill-pleased to have Bertie Stanhope near her. It was rarely indeed that he failed to make an agreeable impression on strangers. With a bishop indeed who thought much of his own dignity it was possible that he might fail, but hardly with a young and pretty woman. He possessed the tact of becoming instantly intimate with women without giving rise to any fear of impertinence. He had about him somewhat of the propensities of a tame cat. It seemed quite natural that he should have be petted, caressed, and treated with familiar good nature, and that in return he should purr, and be sleek and graceful, and above all never show his claws. Like other tame cats, however, he had his claws, and sometimes made them dangerous.

When tea was over Charlotte went to the open window and declared loudly that the full harvest moon was much too beautiful to be disregarded, and called them all to look at it. To tell the truth, there was but one there who cared much about the moon's beauty, and that one was not Charlotte; but she knew how valuable an aid to her purpose the chaste goddess might become, and could easily create a little enthusiasm for the purpose of the moment. Eleanor and Bertie were soon with her. The doctor was now quiet in his arm-chair, and Mrs Stanhope in hers, both prepared for slumber.

'Are you a Whewellite or a Brewsterite, or a t'othermanite, Mrs Bold?' said Charlotte, who knew a little about everything, and had read about a third of each of the books to which she alluded.

'Oh!' said Eleanor; 'I have not read any of the books, but I feel sure that there is one man in the moon at least, if not more.'

'You don't believe in the pulpy gelatinous matter?' said Bertie.

'I heard about that,' said Eleanor; 'and I really think it's almost wicked to talk in such a manner. How can we argue about God's power in the other stars from the laws which he has given for our rule in this one?'

'How indeed!' said Bertie. 'Why shouldn't there be a race of salamanders in Venus? and even if there be nothing but fish in Jupiter, why shouldn't the fish there be as wide awake as the men and women here?'

'That would be saying very little for them,' said Charlotte. 'I am for Dr Whewell myself; for I do not think that men and women are worth being repeated in such countless worlds. There may be souls in other stars, but I doubt their having any bodies attached to them. But come, Mrs Bold, let us put our bonnets on and walk round the close. If we are to discuss sidereal questions, we shall do so much better under the towers of the cathedral, than stuck in this narrow window.'

Mrs Bold made no objection, and a party was made to walk out. Charlotte Stanhope well knew the rule as to three being not company, and she had therefore to induce her sister to allow Mr Slope to accompany them.

'Come, Mr Slope,' she said; 'I'm sure you'll join us. We shall be in again in a quarter of an hour, Madeline.'

Madeline read in her eye all that she had to say, knew her object, and as she had to depend on her sister for so many of her amusements, she felt that she must yield. It was hard to be left alone while others of her own age walked out to feel the soft influence of the bright night, but it would be harder still to be without the sort of sanction which Charlotte gave to all her flirtations and intrigues. Charlotte's eye told her that she must give up just at present for the good of the family, and so Madeline obeyed.

But Charlotte's eyes said nothing of the sort to Mr Slope. He had no objection at all to the *tête-à-tête* with the signora, which the departure of the other three would allow him, and gently whispered to her, 'I shall not leave you alone.'

'Oh, yes,' said she; 'go – pray go, pray go, for my sake. Do not think that I am so selfish. It is understood that nobody is kept within for me. You will understand this too when you know me better. Pray join them, Mr Slope, but when you come in speak to me for five minutes before you leave us.'

Mr Slope understood that he was to go, and he therefore joined the party in the hall. He would have had no objection at all to this arrangement, if he could have secured Mrs Bold's arm; but this of course was out of the question. Indeed, his fate was all very soon settled, for no sooner had he reached the hall-door than Miss Stanhope put her hand within his arm, and Bertie walked off with Eleanor just as naturally as though she were already his own property.

And so they sauntered forth: first they walked round the close, according to their avowed intent; then they went under the old arched gateway below St Cuthbert's little church, and then they turned behind the grounds of the bishop's palace, and so on till they came to the bridge just at the edge of the town, from which passers-by can look down into the gardens of Hiram's Hospital; and here Charlotte and Mr Slope, who were in advance, stopped till the other two came up to them. Mr Slope knew that the gable ends in the moonlight, were those of Mr Harding's late abode, and would not have stopped on such a spot, in such company, if he could have avoided it; but Miss Stanhope would not take the hint which he tried to give.

'This is a very pretty place, Mrs Bold,' said Charlotte; 'by far the prettiest place near Barchester. I wonder your father gave it up.'

It was a very pretty placce, and now by the deceitful light of the moon looked twice larger, twice prettier, twice more antiquely picturesque than it would have done in truth-telling daylight. Who does not know the air of complex multiplicity and the mysterious interesting grace which the moon always lends to old gabled buildings half surrounded, as was the hospital, by fine trees! As seen from the bridge on the night of which we are speaking, Mr Harding's late abode did look very lovely; and though Eleanor did not grieve at her father's having left it, she felt at the moment an intense wish that he might be allowed to return.

'He is going to return to it almost immediately, is he not?' asked Bertie.

Eleanor made no immediately reply. Many such a question passes unanswered, without the notice of the questioner; but such was not now the case. They all remained silent as though expecting her to reply, and after a moment or two, Charlotte said, 'I believe it is settled that Mr Harding returns to the hospital, is it not?'

'I don't think anything about it is settled yet,' said Eleanor.

'But it must be a matter of course,' said Bertie; 'that is, if your father wishes it; who else on earth could hold it after what has occurred?'

Eleanor quietly made her companion understand that the matter was one which she could not discuss in the present company; and then they passed on; Charlotte said she would go a short way up the hill out of the town so as to look back upon the towers of the cathedral, and as Eleanor leant upon Bertie's arm for assistance in the walk, she told him how the matter stood between her father and the bishop.

'And, he,' said Bertie, pointing on to Mr Slope, 'what part does he take in it?'

Eleanor explained how Mr Slope had at first endeavoured to tyrannise over her father, but how he had latterly come round, and done all he could to talk the bishop over in Mr Harding's favour. 'But my father,' said she, 'is hardly inclined to trust him; they all say he is so arrogant to the old clergymen of the city.'

'Take my word for it,' said Bertie, 'your father is right. If I am not very much mistaken, that man is both arrogant and false.'

They strolled up to the top of the hill, and then returned through the fields by a footpath which leads by a small wooden bridge, or rather a plank with a rustic rail to it, over the river to the other side of the cathedral from that at which they had started. They had thus walked round the bishop's grounds, through which the river runs, and round the cathedral and adjacent fields, and it was past eleven before they reached the doctor's door.

'It is very late,' said Eleanor, 'it will be a shame to disturb your mother again at such an hour.'

'Oh,' said Charlotte, laughing, 'you won't disturb mamma; I dare say she is in bed by this time, and Madeline would be furious if you did not come in and see her. Come, Bertie, take Mrs Bold's bonnet from her.'

They went up the stairs, and found the signora alone, reading. She looked somewhat sad and melancholy, but not more so perhaps than was sufficient to excite additional interest in the bosom of Mr Slope; and she was soon deep in whispered intercourse with that happy gentleman, who was allowed to find a resting-place on her sofa. The signora had a way of whispering that was peculiarly her own, and was exactly the reverse of that which prevails among great tragedians. The great tragedian hisses out a positive whisper, made with bated breath, and produced by inarticulated tongue-formed sounds, but yet he is audible through the whole house. The signora however used no hisses, and produced all her words in a clear silver tone, but they could only be heard by the ear into which they were poured.

Charlotte hurried and skurried about the room hither and thither, doing, or pretending to do many things; and then saying something about seeing her mother, ran up stairs. Eleanor was thus left alone with Bertie, and she hardly felt an hour fly by her. To give Bertie his due credit, he could not have played his cards better. He did not make love to her, nor sigh, nor look languishing; but he was amusing and familiar, yet respectful; and when he left Eleanor at her own door at one o'clock, which he did by the bye with the assistance of the now jealous Slope, she thought that he was one of the most agreeable men, and the Stanhopes decidedly the most agreeable family, that she had ever met.

Mr Arabin

THE REV. FRANCIS ARABIN, FELLOW OF LAZARUS, late professor of poetry at Oxford, and present vicar of St Ewold, in the diocese of Barchester, must now be introduced personally to the reader. And as he will fill a conspicuous place in the volume, it is desirable that he should be made to stand before the reader's eye by the aid of such protraiture as the author is able to produce.

It is to be regretted that no mental method of daguerreotype or photography has yet been discovered, by which the characters of men can be reduced to writing and put into grammatical language with an unerring precision of truthful description. How often does the novelist feel, ay, and the historian also and the biographer, that he has conceived within his mind and accurately depicted on the tablet of his brain the full character and personage of a man, and that nevertheless, when he flies to pen and ink to perpetuate the portrait, his words forsake, elude, disappoint, and play the deuce with him, till at the end of a dozen pages the man described has no more resemblance to the man conceived than the sign board at the corner of the street has to the Duke of Cambridge?

And yet such mechanical descriptive skill would hardly give more satisfaction to the reader than the skill of the photographer does to the anxious mother desirous to possess an absolute duplicate of her beloved child. The likeness is indeed true; but it is a dull, dead, unfeeling, inauspicious likeness. The face is indeed there, and those looking at it will know at once whose image it is; but the owner of the face will not be proud of the resemblance.

There is no royal road to learning; no short cut to the acquirement of any valuable art. Let photographers and daguerreotypers do what they will, and improve as they may with further skill on that which skill has already done, they will never achieve a portrait of the human face divine. Let biographers, novelists, and the rest of us groan as we may under the burdens which we so often feel too heavy for our shoulders; we must either bear them up like men, or own ourselves too weak for the work we have undertaken. There is no way of writing well and also of writing easily.

Labor omnia vincit improbus. Such should be the chosen motto of every labourer, and it may be that labour if adequately enduring, may suffice at last to produce even some not untrue resemblance of the Rev. Francis Arabin.

Of his doings in the world, and of the sort of fame which he has achieved, enough has been already said. It has also been said that he is forty years of age, and still unmarried. He was the younger son of a country gentleman of a small fortune in the north of England. At an early age he went to Winchester, and was intended by his father for New College; but though studious as a boy, he was not studious within the prescribed limits; and at the age of eighteen he left school with a character for talent, but without a scholarship. All that he had obtained, over and above the advantage of his character, was a gold medal for English verse, and hence was derived a strong presumption on the part of his friends that he was destined to add another name to the imperishable list of English poets.

From Winchester he went to Oxford, and was entered as a commoner at Balliol. Here his special career very soon commenced. He utterly eschewed the society of fast men, gave no wine parties, kept no horses, rowed no boats, joined no rows, and was the pride of his college tutor. Such at least was his career till he had taken his little go; and then he commenced a course of action which, though not less creditable to himself as a man, was hardly so much to the taste of the tutor. He became a member of a vigorous debating society, and rendered himself remarkable there for humorous energy. Though always in earnest, yet his earnestness was always droll. To be true in his ideas, unanswerable in his syllogisms, and just in his aspirations was not enough for him. He had failed, failed in his own opinion as well as that of others when others came to know him, if he could not reduce the arguments of his opponents to an absurdity, and conquer both by wit and reason. To say that his object was ever to raise a laugh, would be most untrue. He hated such common and unnecessary evidence of satisfaction on the part of his hearers. A joke that required to be laughed at was, with him, not worth uttering. He could appreciate by a keener sense than that of his ears the success of his wit, and would see in the eyes of his auditory whether or no he was understood and appreciated.

He had been a religious lad before he left school. That is, he had addicted himself to a party in religion, and having done so had received that benefit which most men do who become partisans in such a cause. We are much too apt to look at schism in our church as an unmitigated evil. Moderate schism, if there may be such a thing, at any rate calls attention to the subject, draws in supporters who would otherwise have been inattentive to the matter, and teaches men to think upon religion. How great an amount of good of this description has followed that movement in the Church of England which commenced with the publication of Froude's Remains!

As a boy young Arabin took up the cudgels on the side of the Tractarians, and at Oxford he sat for a while at the feet of the great Newman. To this cause he lent all his faculties. For it he concocted verses, for it he made speeches, for it he scintillated the brightest sparks of his quiet wit. For it he ate and drank and dressed, and had his being. In due process of time he took his degree, and wrote himself B.A., but he did not do so with any remarkable amount of academical éclat. He had occupied himself too much with high church matters, and the polemics, politics, and outward demonstrations usually concurrent with high churchmanship, to devote himself with sufficient vigour to the acquisition of a double first. He was not a double first, nor even a first class man; but he revenged himself on the university by putting firsts and double firsts out of fashion for the year, and laughing down a species of pedantry which at the age of twenty-three leaves no room in a man's mind for graver subjects than conic sections or Greek accents.

Greek accents, however, and conic sections were esteemed necessaries at Balliol, and there was no admittance there for Mr Arabin within the list of its fellows. Lazarus, however, the richest and most comfortable abode of Oxford dons, opened its bosom to the young champion of a church militant. Mr Arabin was ordained, and became a fellow soon after taking his degree, and shortly after that was chosen professor of poetry.

And now came the moment of his great danger. After many mental struggles, and an agony of doubt which may be well surmised, the great prophet of the Tractarians confessed himself a Roman Catholic. Mr Newman left the Church of England, and with him carried many a waverer. He did not carry off Mr Arabin, but the escape which that gentleman had was a very narrow one. He left Oxford for a while that he might meditate in complete peace on the step which appeared to him to be all but unavoidable, and shut himself up in a little village on the sea-shore of one of our remotest counties, that he might learn by communing with his own soul whether or no he could with a safe conscience remain within the pale of his mother church.

Things would have gone badly with him there had he been left entirely to himself. Every thing was against him: all his worldly interests required him to remain a Protestant; and he looked on his worldly interests as a legion of foes, to get the better of whom was a point of extremist honour. In his then state of ecstatic agony such a conquest would have cost him little; he could easily have thrown away all his livelihood; but it cost him much to get over the idea that by choosing the Church of England he should be open in his own mind to the charge that he had been led to such a choice by unworthy motives. Then his heart was against him: he loved with a strong and eager love the man who had hitherto been his guide, and yearned to follow his footsteps. His tastes were against him: the ceremonies and pomps of the Church of Rome, their august feasts and solemn fasts, invited his imagination and pleased his eye. His flesh was against him: how great an aid would it be to be a poor, weak, wavering man to be constrained to high moral duties, self-denial, obedience, and chastity by laws which were certain in their enactments, and not to be broken without loud, palpable, unmistakable sin! Then his faith was against him: he required to believe so much; panted so eagerly to give signs of his belief; deemed it so insufficient to wash himself simply in the waters of Jordan; that some great deed, such as that of forsaking everything for a true church, had for him allurements almost past withstanding.

Mr Arabin was at this time a very young man, and when he left Oxford for his far retreat was much too confident in his powers of fence, and too apt to look down on the ordinary sense of ordinary people, to expect aid in the battle that he had to fight from any chance inhabitants of the spot which he had selected. But Providence was good to him; and there, in that all but desolate place, on the storm-beat shore of that distant sea, he met one who gradually calmed his mind, quieted his imagination, and taught him something of a Christian's duty. When Mr Arabin left Oxford, he was inclined to look upon the rural clergymen of most English parishes almost with contempt. It was his ambition, should he remain within the fold of their church, to do somewhat towards redeeming and rectifying their inferiority, and to assist in infusing energy and faith into the hearts of Christian ministers, who were, as he thought, too often satisfied to go through life without much show of either.

And yet it was from such a one that Mr Arabin in his extremest need received that aid which he so much required. It was from the poor curate of a small Cornish parish, that he first learnt to know that the highest laws for the governance of a Christian's duty must act from within and not from without; that no man can become a serviceable servant solely by obedience to written edicts; and that the safety which he was about to seek within the gates of Rome was no other than the selfish freedom from personal danger which the bad soldier attempts to gain who counterfeits illness on the eve of a battle.

Mr Arabin returned to Oxford a humbler but a better and happier man; and from that time forth he put his shoulder to the wheel as a clergyman of the Church for which he had been educated. The intercourse of those among whom he familiarly lived kept him staunch to the principles of that system of the Church to which he had always belonged. Since his severance from Mr Newman, no one had had so strong an influence over him as the head of his college. During the time of his expected apostacy, Dr Gwynne had not felt much predisposition in favour of the young fellow. Though a High Churchman himself within moderate limits, Dr Gwynne felt no sympathy with men who could not satisfy their faiths with the Thirty-nine Articles. He regarded the enthusiasm of such as Newman as a state of mind more nearly allied to madness than to religion; and when he saw it evinced by very young men, was inclined to attribute a good deal of it to vanity. Dr Gwynne himself, though a religious man, was also a thoroughly practical man of the world, and he regarded with no favourable eye the tenets of any one who looked on the two things as incompatible. When he found that Mr Arabin was a half Roman, he began to regret all he had done towards bestowing a fellowship on so unworthy a recipient; and when again he learnt that Mr Arabin would probably complete his journey to Rome, he regarded with some satisfaction the fact that in such case the fellowship would be again vacant.

When, however, Mr Arabin returned and professed himself a confirmed Protestant, the master of Lazarus again opened his arms to him, and gradually he became the pet of the college. For some little time he was saturnine, silent, and unwilling to take any prominent part in university broils; but gradually his mind recovered, or rather made its tone, and he became known as a man always ready at a moment's notice to take up the cudgels in opposition to anything that savoured of an evangelical bearing. He was great in sermons, great on platforms, great after dinner conversations, and always pleasant as well as great. He took delight in elections, served on committees, opposed tooth and nail all projects of university reform, and talked jovially over his glass of port of the ruin to be anticipated by the Church, and of the sacrilege daily committed by the Whigs. The ordeal through which he had gone, in resisting the blandishments of the lady of Rome, had certainly done much towards the strengthening of his character. Although in small and outward matters he was self-confident enough, nevertheless in things affecting the inner man he aimed at a humility of spirit which would never have been attractive to him but for that visit to the coast of Cornwall. This visit he now repeated every year.

Such is an interior view of Mr Arabin at the time when he accepted the living of St Ewold. Exteriorly, he was not a remarkable person. He was above the middle height, well made, and very active. His hair which had been jet black, was now tinged with gray, but his face bore no sign of years. It would perhaps be wrong to say that he was handsome, but his face was, nevertheless, pleasant to look upon. The cheek bones were rather too high for beauty, and the formation of the forehead too massive and heavy: but the eyes, nose, and mouth were perfect. There was a continual play of lambent fire about his eyes, which gave promise of either pathos or humour whenever he essayed to speak, and that promise was rarely broken. There was a gentle play about his mouth which declared that his wit never descended to sarcasm, and that there was no ill-nature in his repartee.

Mr Arabin was a popular man among women, but more so as a general than a special favourite. Living as a fellow at Oxford, marriage with him had been out of the question, and it may be doubted whether he had ever allowed his heart to be touched. Though belonging to a Church in which celibacy is not the required lot of his ministers, he had come to regard himself as one of those clergymen to whom to be a bachelor is almost a necessity. He had never looked for parochial duty, and his career at Oxford was utterly incompatible with such domestic joys as a wife and nursery. He looked on women, therefore, in the same light that one sees them regarded by many Romish priests. He liked to have near him that which was pretty and amusing, but women generally were little more to him than children. He talked to them without putting out all his powers, and listened to them without any idea that what he should hear from them could either actuate his conduct or influence his opinion.

Such was Mr Arabin, the new vicar of St Ewold, who is going to stay with the Grantlys at Plumstead Episcopi.

Mr Arabin reached Plumstead the day before Mr Harding and Eleanor, and the Grantly family were thus enabled to make his acquaintance and discuss his qualifications before the arrival of the other guests. Griselda told Florinda her younger sister, when they had retired for the night, that he did not talk at all like a young man: and she decided with the authority that seventeen has over sixteen, that he was not at all nice, although his eyes were lovely. As usual, sixteen implicitly acceded to the dictum of seventeen in such a matter, and said that he certainly was not nice. They then branched off on the relative merits of other clerical bachelors in the vicinity, and both determined without any feeling of jealousy between them that a certain Rev. Augustus Green was by many degrees the most estimable of the lot. The gentleman in question had certainly much in his favour, as, having a comfortable allowance from his father, he could devote the whole proceeds of his curacy to violet gloves and unexceptionable neck ties. Having thus fixedly resolved that the new comer had nothing about him to shake the pre-eminence of the exalted Green, the two girls went to sleep in each other's arms, contented with themselves and the world.

Mrs Grantly at first sight came to much the same conclusion about her husband's favourite as her daughters had done, though, in seeking to measure his relative value, she did not compare him to Mr Green; indeed, she made no comparison by name between him and any one else; but she remarked to her husband that one person's swans were very often another person's geese, thereby clearly showing that Mr Arabin had not yet proved his qualifications in swanhood to her satisfaction.

'Well, Susan,' said he, rather offended at hearing his friend spoken of so disrespectfully, 'if you take Mr Arabin for a goose, I cannot say that I think very highly of your discrimination.'

'A goose! No of course, he's not a goose. I've no doubt he's a very clever man. But you're so matter-of-fact, archdeacon, when it suits your purpose, that one can't trust oneself to any *façon de parler*. I've no doubt Mr Arabin is a very valuable man – at Oxford, and that he'll be a good vicar at St Ewold. All I mean is, that having passed one evening with him, I don't find him to be absolutely a paragon. In the first place, if I am not mistaken, he is a little inclined to be conceited.'

'Of all the men that I know intimately,' said the archdeacon, 'Arabin is, in my opinion the most free from any taint of self-conceit. His fault is that he's too diffident.'

'Perhaps so,' said the lady; 'only I must own I did not find it out this evening.'

Nothing further was said about him. Dr Grantly thought that his wife was abusing Mr Arabin merely because he had praised him; and Mrs Grantly knew that it was useless arguing for or against any person in favour of or in opposition to whom the archdeacon had already pronounced a strong opinion.

In truth they were both right. Mr Arabin was a diffident man in social intercourse with those whom he did not intimately know; when placed in situations which it was his business to fill, and discussing matters with which it was his duty to be conversant, Mr Arabin was from habit brazen-faced enough. When standing on a platform in Exeter Hall, no man would be less mazed than he by the eyes of the crowd before him; for such was the work which his profession had called on him to perform; but he shrank from a strong expression of opinion in general society, and his doing so not uncommonly made it appear that he considered the company not worth the trouble of his energy. He was averse to dictate when the place did not seem to him to justify dictation; and as those subjects on which people wished to hear him speak were such as he was accustomed to treat with decision, he generally shunned the traps there were laid to allure him into discussion, and, by doing so, not unfrequently subjected himself to such charges as those brought against him by Mrs Grantly.

Mr Arabin, as he sat at his open window, enjoying the delicious moonlight and gazing at the gray towers of the church, which stood almost within the rectory grounds, little dreamed that he was the subject of so many friendly or unfriendly criticisms. Considering how much we are all given to discuss the characters of others, and discuss them often not in the strictest spirit of charity; it is singular how little we are inclined to think that others can speak ill-naturedly of us, and how angry and hurt we are when proof reaches us that they have done so. It is hardly too much to say, that we all of us occasionally speak of our dearest friends in a manner in which those dearest friends would very little like to hear themselves mentioned; and that we nevertheless expect that our dearest friends shall invariably speak of us as though they were blind to all our faults, but keenly alive to every shade of our virtues.

It did not occur to Mr Arabin that he was spoken of at all. It seemed to him, when he compared himself with his host, that he was a person of so little consequence to any, that he was worth no one's words or thoughts. He was utterly alone in the world as regarded domestic ties and those inner familiar relations which are hardly possible between others than husbands and wives, parents and children, or brothers and sisters. He had often discussed with himself the necessity of such bonds for a man's happiness in this world, and had generally satisfied himself with the answer that happiness in this world is not a necessity. Herein he deceived himself, or rather tried to do so. He, like others, yearned for the enjoyment of whatever he saw enjoyable; and though he attempted, with the modern stoicism of so many Christians, to make himself believe that joy and sorrow were matters which here should be held as perfectly indifferent, these things were not indifferent to him. He was tired of his Oxford rooms and his college life. He regarded the wife and children of his friend with something like envy; he all but coveted the pleasant drawing-room, with its pretty windows opening on to lawns and flowerbeds, the apparel of the comfortable house, and – above all – the air of home which encompassed it all.

It will be said that no time can have been so fitted for such desires on his part as this, when he had just possessed himself of a country parish, of a living among fields and gardens, of a house which a wife would grace. It is true there was a difference between the opulence of Plumstead and the modest economy of St Ewold; but surely Mr Arabin was not a man to sigh after wealth! Of all men, his friends would have unanimously declared he was the last to do so. But how little our friends know us! In his period of stoical rejection of this world's happiness, he had cast from him as utter dross all anxiety as to fortune. He had, as it were, proclaimed himself to be indifferent to promotion, and those who chiefly admired his talents, and would mainly have exerted themselves to secure to them their deserved reward, had taken him at his word. And now, if the truth must out, he felt himself disappointed – disappointed not by them but by himself. The daydream of his youth was over, and at the age of forty he felt that he was not fit to work in the spirit of an apostle. He had mistaken himself, and learned his mistake when it was past remedy. He had professed himself indifferent to mitres and diaconal residences, to rich livings and pleasant glebes, and now he had to own to himself that he was sighing for the good things of other men, on whom in his pride he had ventured to look down.

Not for wealth, in its vulgar sense, had he ever sighed; not for the enjoyment of rich things had he ever longed; but for the allotted share of wordly bliss, which a wife, and children, and happy home could give him, for that usual amount of comfort which he had ventured to reject as unnecessary for him, he did now feel that he would have been wiser to have searched.

He knew that his talents, his position, and his friends would have won for him promotion, had he put himself in the way of winning it. Instead of doing so, he had allowed himself to be persuaded to accept a living which would give him an income of some 300*l*. a year, should he, by marrying, throw up his fellowship. Such, at the age of forty, was the worldly result of labour, which the world had chosen to regard as successful. The world also thought that Mr Arabin was, in his own estimation, sufficiently paid. Alas! alas! the world was mistaken; and Mr Arabin was beginning to ascertain that such was the case.

And here, may I beg the reader not to be hard in his judgment upon this man. Is not the state at which he has arrived, the natural result of efforts to reach that which is not the condition of humanity? Is not modern stoicism, built though it be on Christianity, as great an outrage on human nature as was the stoicism of the ancients? The philosophy of Zeno was built on true laws, but on true laws misunderstood, and therefore misapplied. It is the same with our Stoics here, who would teach us that wealth and worldly comfort and happiness on earth are not worth the search. Alas, for a doctrine which can find no believing pupils and no true teachers!

The case of Mr Arabin was the more singular, as he belonged to a branch of the Church of England well inclined to regard its temporalities with avowed favour, and had habitually lived with men who were accustomed to much worldly comfort. But such was his idiosyncrasy, that these very facts had produced within him, in early life, a state of mind that was not natural to him. He was content to be a High Churchman, if he could be so on principles of his own, and could strike out a course showing a marked difference from those with whom he consorted. He was ready to be a partisan as long as he was allowed to have a course of action and of thought unlike that of his party. His party had indulged him, and he began to feel that his party was right and himself wrong, just when such a conviction was too late to be of service to him. He discovered, when such discovery was no longer serviceable, that it *would* have been worth his while to have worked for the usual pay assigned to work in this world, and have earned a wife and children, with a carriage for them to sit in; to have earned a pleasant dining-room, in which his friends could drink his wine, and the power of walking up the high street of his country town, with the knowledge that all its tradesmen would have gladly welcomed him within their doors. Other men arrived at those convictions in their start in life, and so worked up to them. To him they had come when they were too late to be of use.

It has been said that Mr Arabin was a man of pleasantry and it may be thought that such a state of mind as that described, would be antagonistic to humour. But surely such is not the case. Wit is the outward mental casing of the man, and has no more to do with the inner mind of thoughts and feelings than have the rich brocaded garments of the priest at the altar with the asceticism of the anchorite below them, whose skin is tormented with sackcloth, and whose body is half flayed with rods. Nay, will not such a one often rejoice more than any other in the rich show of his outer apparel? Will it not be food for his pride to feel that he groans inwardly, while he shines outwardly? So it is with the mental efforts which men make. Those which they show forth daily to the world are often the opposites of the inner workings of the spirit.

In the archdeacon's drawing-room, Mr Arabin had sparkled with his usual unaffected brilliancy, but when he retired to his bed-room, he sat there sad, at his open window, repining within himself that he also had no wife, no bairns, no soft sward of lawn duly mown for him to lie on, no herd of attendant curates, no bowings from the banker's clerks, no rich rectory. That apostleship that he had thought of had evaded his grasp, and he was now only vicar of St Ewold's, with a taste for a mitre. Truly he had fallen between two stools.

✖ TWENTY-ONE ✖

St Ewold's Parsonage

WHEN MR HARDING AND MRS BOLD REACHED the rectory on the following morning, the archdeacon and his friend were at St Ewold's. They had gone over that the new vicar might inspect his church, and be introduced to the squire, and were not expected back before dinner. Mr Harding rambled out by himself, and strolled, as was his wont at Plumstead, about the lawn and round the church; and as he did so, the two sisters naturally fell into conversation about Barchester.

There was not much sisterly confidence between them. Mrs Grantly was ten years older than Eleanor, and had been married while Eleanor was yet a child. They had never, therefore, poured into each other's ears their hopes and loves; and now that one was a wife and the other a widow, it was not probable that they would begin to do so. They lived too much asunder to be able to fall into that kind of intercourse which makes confidence between sisters almost a necessity; and, moreover, that which is so easy at eighteen is often very difficult at twenty-eight. Mrs Grantly knew this, and did not, therefore, expect confidence from her sister; and yet she longed to ask her whether in real truth Mr Slope was agreeable to her.

It was by no means difficult to turn the conversation to Mr Slope. That gentleman had become so famous at Barchester, had so much to do with all clergymen connected with the city, and was so specially concerned in the affairs of Mr Harding, that it would have been odd if Mr Harding's daughters had not talked about him. Mrs Grantly was soon abusing him, which she did with her whole heart; and Mrs Bold was nearly as eager to defend him. She positively disliked the man, would have been delighted to learn that he had taken himself off so that she should never see him again, had indeed almost a fear of him, and yet she constantly found herself taking his part. The abuse of other people, and abuse of a nature that she felt to be unjust, imposed this necessity on her, and at last made Mr Slope's defence an habitual course of argument with her.

From Mr Slope the conversation turned to the Stanhopes, and Mrs Grantly was listening with some interest to Eleanor's account of the family, when it dropped out that Mr Slope made one of the party.

'What!' said the lady of the rectory, 'was Mr Slope there too?'

Eleanor merely replied that such had been the case.

'Why, Eleanor, he must be very fond of you, I think; he seems to follow you everywhere.'

Even this did not open Eleanor's eyes. She merely laughed, and said that she imagined Mr Slope found other attraction at Dr Stanhope's. And so they parted. Mrs Grantly felt quite convinced that the odious match would take place; and Mrs Bold as convinced that that unfortunate chaplain, disagreeable as he must be allowed to be, was more sinned against than sinning.

The archdeacon of course heard before dinner that Eleanor had remained the day before in Barchester with the view of meeting Mr Slope, and that she had so met him. He remembered how she had positively stated that there were to be no guests at the Stanhopes, and he did not hesitate to accuse her of deceit. Moreover, the fact, or rather presumed fact, of her being deceitful on such a matter, spoke but too plainly in evidence against her as to her imputed crime of receiving Mr Slope as a lover.

'I am afraid that anything we can do will be too late,' said the archdeacon. 'I own I am fairly surprised. I never liked your sister's taste with regard to men; but still I did not give her credit for – ugh!'

'And so soon, too,' said Mrs Grantly, who thought more, perhaps, of her sister's indecorum in having a lover before she had put off her weeds, than her bad taste in having such a lover as Mr Slope.

'Well, my dear, I shall be sorry to be harsh, or to do anything that can hurt your father; but, positively, neither that man nor his wife shall come within my doors.'

Mrs Grantly sighed, and then attempted to console herself and her lord by remarking that, after all, the thing was not accomplished yet. Now that Eleanor was at Plumstead, much might be done to wean her from her fatal passion. Poor Eleanor!

The evening passed off without anything to make it remarkable. Mr Arabin discussed the parish of St Ewold with the archdeacon, and Mrs Grantly and Mr Harding, who knew the personages of the parish, joined in. Eleanor also knew them, but she said little. Mr Arabin did not apparently take much notice of her, and she was not in a humour to receive at that time with any special grace any special favourite of her brother-in-law. Her first idea on reaching her bed-room was that a much pleasanter family party might be met at Dr Stanhope's than at the rectory. She began to think that she was getting tired of clergymen and their respectable humdrum wearisome mode of living, and that after all, people in the outer world, who had lived in Italy, London, or elsewhere, need not necessarily be regarded as atrocious and abominable. The Stanhopes, she had thought, were a giddy, thoughtless, extravagant set of people; but she had seen nothing wrong about them, and had, on the other hand, found that they thoroughly knew how to make their house agreeable. It was a thousand pities, she thought, that the archdeacon should not have a little of the same *savoir vivre*. Mr Arabin, as we have said, did not apparently take much notice of her; but yet he did not go to bed without feeling that he had been in company with a very pretty woman; and as is the case with most bachelors, and some married men, regarded the prospect of his month's visit at Plumstead in a pleasanter light, when he learnt that a very pretty woman was to share it with him.

Before they all retired it was settled that the whole party should drive over on the following day to inspect the parsonage at St Ewold. The three clergymen were to discuss dilapidations, and the two ladies were to lend their assistance in suggesting such changes as might be necessary for a bachelor's abode. Accordingly, soon after breakfast, the carriage was at the door. There was only room for four inside, and the archdeacon got upon the box. Eleanor found herself opposite to Mr Arabin, and was, therefore, in a manner forced into conversation with him. They were soon on comfortable terms together; and had she thought about it, she would have thought that, in spite of his black cloth, Mr Arabin would not have been a bad addition to the Stanhope family party.

Now that the archdeacon was away, they could all trifle. Mr Harding began by telling them in the most innocent manner imaginable an old legend about Mr Arabin's new parish. There was, he said, in days of yore, an illustrious priestess of St Ewold, famed through the whole country for curing all manner of diseases. She had a well, as all priestesses have ever had, which well was extant to this day, and shared in the minds of many of the people the sanctity which belonged to the consecrated ground of the parish church. Mr Arabin declared that he should look on such tenets on the part of his parishioners as anything but orthodox. And Mrs Grantly replied that she so entirely disagreed with him as to think that no parish was in a proper state that had not its priestess as well as its priest. 'The duties are never well done,' said she, 'unless they are so divided.'

'I suppose, papa,' said Eleanor, 'that in the olden times the priestess bore all the sway herself. Mr Arabin, perhaps, thinks that such might be too much the case now if a sacred lady were admitted within the parish.'

'I think, at any rate,' said he, 'that it is safer to run no such risk. No priestly pride has ever exceeded that of sacerdotal females. A very lowly curate I might, perhaps, essay to rule; but a curatess would be sure to get the better of me.'

'There are certainly examples of such accidents happening,' said Mrs Grantly. 'They do say that there is a priestess at Barchester who is very imperious to all things touching the altar. Perhaps the fear of such a fate as that is before your eyes.'

When they were joined by the archdeacon on the gravel before the vicarage, they descended again to grave dullness. Not that Archdeacon Grantly was a dull man; but his frolic humours were of a cumbrous kind; and his wit, when he was witty, did not generally extend itself to his auditory. On the present occasion he was soon making speeches about wounded roofs and walls, which he declared to be in want of some surgeon's art.

There was not a partition that he did not tap, nor a block of chimneys that he did not narrowly examine; all water-pipes, flues, cisterns, and sewers underwent an investigation; and he even descended, in the care of his friend, so far as to bore sundry boards in the floors with a bradawl.

Mr Arabin accompanied him through the rooms, trying to look wise in such domestic matters, and the other three also followed. Mrs Grantly showed that she had not herself been priestess of a parish twenty years for nothing, and examined the bells and window panes in a very knowing way.

'You will, at any rate, have a beautiful prospect out of your own window, if this is to be your private sanctum,' said Eleanor. She was standing at the lattice of a little room up stairs, from which the view certainly was very lovely. It was from the back of the vicarage, and there was nothing to interrupt the eye between the house and the glorious gray pile of the cathedral. The intermediate ground, however, was beautifully studded with timber. In the immediate foreground ran the little river which afterwards skirted the city; and, just to the right of the cathedral, the pointed gables and chimneys of Hiram's Hospital peeped out of the elms which encompass it.

'Yes,' said he, joining her. 'I shall have a beautifully complete view of my adversaries. I shall sit down before the hostile town, and fire away at them at a very pleasant distance. I shall just be able to lodge a shot in the hospital, should the enemy ever get possession of it; and as for the palace, I have it within full range.'

'I never saw anything like you clergymen,' said Eleanor; 'you are always thinking of fighting each other.'

'Either that,' said he, 'or else supporting each other. The pity is that we cannot do the one without the other. But are we not here to fight? Is not ours a church militant? What is all our work but fighting, and hard fighting, if it be well done?'

'But not with each other.'

'That's as it may be. The same complaint which you make of me for battling with another clergyman of our own church, the Mohammedan would make against me for battling with the error of a priest of Rome. Yet, surely, you would not be inclined to say that I should be wrong to do battle with such as him. A pagan, too, with his multiplicity of gods, would think it equally odd that the Christian and the Mohammedan should disagree.'

'Ah! but you wage your wars about trifles so bitterly.'

'Wars about trifles,' said he, 'are always bitter, especially among neighbours. When the differences are great, and the parties comparative strangers, men quarrel with courtesy. What combatants are ever so eager as two brothers?'

'But do not such contentions bring scandal on the church?'

'More scandal would fall on the church if there were no such contentions. We have but one way to avoid them – that of acknowledging a common head of our church, whose word on all points of doctrine shall be authoritative. Such a termination of our difficulties is alluring enough. It has charms which are irresistible to many, and all but irresistible, I own, to me.'

'You speak now of the Church of Rome?' said Eleanor.

'No,' said he, 'not necessarily of the Church of Rome; but of *a* church with *a* head. Had it pleased God to vouchsafe to us such a church our path would have been easy. But easy paths have not been thought good for us.'

He paused and stood silent for a while, thinking of the time when he had so nearly sacrificed all he had, his powers of mind, his free agency, the fresh running waters of his mind's fountain, his very inner self, for an easy path in which no fighting would be needed; and then he continued: – 'What you say is partly true; our contentions do bring on us some scandal. The outer world, though it constantly reviles us for our human infirmities, and throws in our teeth the fact that being clergymen we are still no more than men, demands of us that we should do our work with godlike perfection. There is nothing godlike about us; we differ from each other with the acerbity common to man – we triumph over each other with human frailty – we allow differences on subjects of divine origin to produce among us antipathies and enmities which are anything but divine. This is all true. But what would you have in place of it? There is no infallible head for a church on earth. This dream of believing man has been tried, and we see in Italy and in Spain what has come of it. Grant that there are and have been no bickerings within the pale of the Pope's Church. Such an assumption would be utterly untrue; but let us grant it, and then let us say which church has incurred the heavier scandals.'

There was a quiet earnestness about Mr Arabin, as he half acknowledged and half defended himself from the charge brought against him, which surprised Eleanor. She had been used all her life to listen to clerical discussion; but the points at issue between the disputants had so seldom been of more than temporal significance as to have left on her mind no feeling of reverence for such subjects. There had always been a hard worldly leaven of the love either of income or of power in the strains she had heard; there had been no panting for the truth; no aspirations after religious purity. It had always been taken for granted by those around her that they were undubitably right, that there was no ground for doubt, that the hard uphill work of ascertaining what the duty of a clergyman should be had been already accomplished in full; and that what remained for an active militant parson to do, was to hold his own against all comers. Her father, it is true, was an exception to this; but then he was so essentially anti-militant in all things, that she classed him in her own mind apart from all others. She had never argued the matter within herself, or considered whether this common tone was or was not faulty; but she was sick of it without knowing that she was so. And now she found to her surprise and not without a certain pleasurable excitement, that this new comer among them spoke in a manner very different from that to which she was accustomed.

'It is so easy to condemn,' said he, continuing the thread of his thoughts. 'I know no life that must be so delicious as that of a writer for newspapers, or a leading member of the opposition – to thunder forth accusations against men in power; show up the worst side of everything that is produced; to pick holes in every coat; to be indignant, sarcastic, jocose, moral, or supercilious; to damn what faint praise, or crush with open calumny! What can be so easy as this when the critic has to be responsible for nothing? You condemn what I do; but put yourself in my position and do the reverse, and then see if I cannot condemn you.'

'Oh! Mr Arabin, I do not condemn you.'

'Pardon me, you do, Mrs Bold – you as one of the world; you are now the opposition member; you are now composing your leading article, and well and bitterly you do it. "Let dogs delight to bark and bite;" you fitly begin with an elegant quotation; "but if we are to have a church at all, in heaven's name let the pastors who preside over it keep their hands from each other's throats. Lawyers can live without befouling each other's names; doctors do not fight duels. Why is it that clergymen alone should indulge themselves in such unrestrained liberty of abuse against each other?" and so you go on reviling us for our ungodly quarrels, our sectarian propensities, and scandalous differences. It will, however, give you no trouble to write another article next week in which we, or some of us, shall be twitted with an unseemly apathy in matters of our vocation. It will not fall on you to reconcile the discrepancy; your readers will never ask you how the poor parson is to be urgent in season and out of season, and yet never come in contact with men who think widely differently from him. You, when you condemn this foreign treaty, or that official arrangement, will have to incur no blame for the graver faults of any different measure. It is so easy to condemn; and so pleasant too; for eulogy charms no listeners as detraction does.'

Eleanor only half followed in his raillery, but she caught his meaning. 'I know I ought to apologise for presuming to criticise you,' she said; 'but I was thinking with sorrow of the ill-will that has lately come among us at Barchester, and I spoke more freely than I should have done.'

'Peace on earth and good-will among men, are, like heaven, promises for the future;' said he, following rather his own thoughts than hers. 'When that prophecy is accomplished, there will no longer be any need for clergymen.'

Here they were interrupted by the archdeacon, whose voice was heard from the cellar shouting the vicar.

'Arabin, Arabin,' – and then turning to his wife, who was apparently at his elbow – 'where has he gone to? This cellar is perfectly abominable. It would be murder to put a bottle of wine into it till it has been roofed, walled, and floored. How on earth old Goodenough ever got on with it, I cannot guess. But then Goodenough never had a glass of wine that any man could drink.'

'What is it, archdeacon?' said the vicar, running down stairs, and leaving Eleanor above to her meditations.

'This cellar must be roofed, walled, and floored,' repeated the archdeacon. 'Now mind what I say, and don't let the architect persuade you that it will do; half of these fellows know nothing about wine. This place as it is now would be damp and cold in winter, and hot and muggy in summer. I wouldn't give a straw for the best wine that ever was vinted, after it had lain here a couple of years.'

Mr Arabin assented, and promised that the cellar should be reconstructed according to the archdeacon's receipt.

'And, Arabin, look here; was such an attempt at a kitchen grate ever seen?'

'The grate is really very bad,' said Mrs Grantly; 'I am sure the priestess won't approve of it, when she is brought home to the scene of her future duties. Really, Mr Arabin, no priestess accustomed to such an excellent well as that above could put up with such a grate as this.'

'If there must be a priestess at St Ewold's at all, Mrs Grantly, I think we will leave her to her well, and not call down her divine wrath on any of the imperfections rising from our human poverty. However, I own I am amenable to the attractions of a well-cooked dinner, and the grate shall certainly be changed.'

By this time the archdeacon had again ascended, and was now in the dining-room. 'Arabin,' said he, speaking in his usual loud clear voice, and with that tone of dictation which was so common to him; 'you must positively alter this dining-room of such proportions!' and the archdeacon stepped the room long-ways and crossways with ponderous steps, as though a certain amount of ecclesiastical dignity could be imparted even to such an occupation as that by the manner of doing it. 'Barely sixteen; you may call it a square.'

'It would do very well for a round table,' suggested the ex-warden.

Now there was something peculiarly unorthodox in the archdeacon's estimation in the idea of a round table. He had always been accustomed to a goodly board of decent length, comfortably elongating itself according to the number of the guests, nearly black with perpetual rubbing, and as bright as a mirror. Now round dinner tables are generally of oak, or else of such new construction as not to have acquired the peculiar hue which was so pleasing to him. He connected them with what he called the nasty new fangled method of leaving a cloth on the table, as though to warn people that they were not to sit long. In his eyes there was something democratic and parvenue in a round table. He imagined that dissenters and calico-printers chiefly used them, and perhaps a few literary lions more conspicuous for their wit than their gentility. He was a little flurried at the idea of such an article being introduced into the diocese by a protégé of his own, and at the instigation of his father-in-law.

'A round dinner-table,' said he, with some heat, 'is the most abominable article of furniture that ever was invented. I hope that Arabin has more taste than to allow such a thing in his house.'

Poor Mr Harding felt himself completely snubbed, and of course said nothing further; but Mr Arabin, who had yielded submissively in the small matters of the cellar and kitchen grate, found himself obliged to oppose reforms which might be of a nature too expensive for his pocket.

'But it seems to me, archdeacon, that I can very well lengthen the room without pulling down the wall, and if I pull down the wall, I must build it up again; then if I throw out a bow on this side, I must do the same on the other, then if I do it for the ground floor, I must carry it up to the floor above. That will be putting a new front to the house, and will cost, I suppose, a couple of hundred pounds. The ecclesiastical commissioners will hardly assist me when they hear that my grievance consists in having a dining-room only sixteen feet long.'

The archdeacon proceeded to explain that nothing would be easier than adding six feet to the front of the dining-room, without touching any other in the house. Such irregularities of construction in small country houses were, he said, rather graceful than otherwise, and he offered to pay for the whole thing out of his own pocket if it cost more than forty pounds. Mr Arabin, however, was firm, and, although the archdeacon fussed and fumed about it, would not give way.

Forty pounds, he said, was a matter of serious moment to him, and his friends, if under such circumstances they would be good-natured enough to come to him at all, must put up with the misery of a square room. He was willing to compromise matters by disclaiming any intention of having a round table.

'But,' said Mrs Grantly, 'what if the priestess insists on having both the rooms enlarged?'

'The priestess in that case must do it for herself, Mrs Grantly.'

'I have no doubt she will be well able to do so,' replied the lady; 'to do that and many more wonderful things. I am quite sure that the priestess of St Ewold, when she does come, won't come empty-handed.'

Mr Arabin, however, did not appear well inclined to enter into speculative expenses on such a chance as this, and therefore, any material alterations in the house, the cost of which could not fairly be made to lie at the door either of the ecclesiastical commissioners or of the estate of the late incumbent, were tabooed. With this essential exception, the archdeacon ordered, suggested, and carried all points before him in a manner very much to his own satisfaction. A close observer, had there been one there, might have seen that his wife had been quite as useful in the matter as himself. No one knew better than Mrs Grantly the appurtenances necessary to a comfortable house. She did not, however, think it necessary to lay claim to any of the glory which her lord and master was so ready to appropriate as his own.

Having gone through their work effectually and systematically, the party returned to Plumstead well satisfied with their expedition.

※ TWENTY-TWO ※

The Thornes of Ullathorne

ON THE FOLLOWING SUNDAY MR ARABIN WAS to read himself in at his new church. It was agreed at the rectory that the archdeacon should go over with him and assist at the reading-desk, and that Mr Harding should take the archdeacon's duty at Plumstead Church. Mrs Grantly had her school and her buns to attend to, and professed that she could not be spared; but Mrs Bold was to accompany them. It was further agreed also, that they would lunch at the squire's house, and return home after the afternoon service.

Wilfred Thorne, Esq., of Ullathorne, was the squire of St Ewold's; or rather the squire of Ullathorne; for the domain of the modern landlord was of wider notoriety than the fame of the ancient saint. He was a fair specimen of what that race has come to in our days, which a century ago was, as we are told, fairly represented by Squire Western. If that representation be a true one, few classes of men can have made faster strides in improvement. Mr Thorne, however, was a man possessed of quite a sufficient number of foibles to lay him open to much ridicule. He was still a bachelor, being about fifty, and was not a little proud of his person. When living at home at Ullathorne there was not much room for such pride, and there therefore he always looked like a gentleman, and like that which he certainly was, the first man in his parish. But during the month or six weeks which he annually spent in London, he tried so hard to look like a great man there also, which he certainly was not, that he was put down as a fool by many at his club. He was a man of considerable literary attainment in a certain way and on certain subjects. His favourite authors were Montaigne and Burton, and he knew more perhaps than any other man in his own county, and the next to it, of the English essayists of the two last centuries. He possessed complete sets of the 'Idler,' the 'Spectator,' the 'Tatler,' the 'Guardian,' and the 'Rambler;' and would discourse by hours together on the superiority of such publications to anything which has since been produced in our Edinburghs and Quarterlies. He was a great proficient in all questions of genealogy, and knew enough of almost every gentleman's family in England to say of what blood and lineage were descended all those who had any claim to be considered as possessors of any such luxuries. For blood and lineage he himself had a more profound respect. He counted back his own ancestors to some period long antecedent to the Conquest; and could tell you if you would listen to him, how it had come to pass that they, like Cedric the Saxon, had been permitted to hold their own among the Norman barons. It was not, according to his showing, on account of any weak complaisance on the part of his family towards their Norman neighbours. Some Ealfreid of Ullathorne once fortified his own castle, and held out, not only that, but the then existing cathedral of Barchester also, against one Geoffrey De Burgh, in the time of King John; and Mr Thorne possessed the whole history of the siege written on vellum, and illuminated in a most costly manner. It little signified that no one could read the writing, as, had that been possible, no one could have understood the language. Mr Thorne could, however, give you all the particulars in good English, and had no objection to do so.

It would be unjust to say that he looked down on men whose families were of recent date. He did not do so. He frequently consorted with such, and had chosen many of his friends from among them. But he looked on them as great millionaires are apt to look on those who have small incomes; as men who have Sophocles at their fingers' ends regard those who know nothing of Greek. They might doubtless be good sort of people, entitled to much praise for virtue, very admirable for talent, highly respectable in every way; but they were without the one great good gift. Such was Mr Thorne's way of thinking on this matter; nothing could atone for the loss of good blood; nothing could neutralise its good effects. Few indeed were now possessed of it, but the possession was on that account the more precious. It was very pleasant to hear Mr Thorne descant on this matter. Were you in your ignorance to surmise that such a one was of a good family because the head of his family was a baronet of an old date, he would open his eyes with a delightful look of affected surprise, and modestly remind you that baronetcies only dated from James I. He would gently sigh if you spoke of the blood of the Fitzgeralds and De Burghs; would hardly allow the claims of the Howards and Lowthers; and has before now alluded to the Talbots as a family who had hardly yet achieved the full honours of a pedigree.

In speaking once of a wide spread race whose name had received the honours of three coronets, scions from which sat for various constituencies, some one of whose members had been in almost every cabinet formed during the present century, a brilliant race such as there are few in England, Mr Thorne had called them all 'dirt.' He had not intended any disrespect to these men. He admired them in many senses, and allowed them their privileges without envy. He had merely meant to express his feeling that the streams which ran through their veins were not yet purified by time to that perfection, had not become so genuine an ichor, as to be worthy of being called blood in the geanealogical sense.

When Mr Arabin was first introduced to him, Mr Thorne had immediately suggested that he was one of the Arabins of Uphill Stanton. Mr Arabin replied that he was a very distant relative of the family alluded. To this Mr Thorne surmised that the relationship could not be very distant. Mr Arabin assured him that it was so distant that the families knew nothing of each other. Mr Thorne laughed that there was now existing no branch of his family separated from the parent stock at an earlier date than the reign of Elizabeth; and that therefore Mr Arabin could not call himself distant. Mr Arabin himself was quite clearly an Arabin of Uphill Stanton.

'But,' said the vicar, 'Uphill Stanton has been sold to the De Greys, and has been in their hands for the last fifty years.'

'And when it has been there one hundred and fifty, if it unluckily remain there so long,' said Mr Thorne, 'your descendants will not be a whit the less entitled to describe themselves as being of the family of Uphill Stanton. Thank God, no De Grey can buy that – and, thank God – no Arabin, and no Thorne, can sell it.'

In politics, Mr Thorne was an unflinching conservative. He looked on those fifty-three Trojans, who, as Mr Dod tells us, censured free trade in November, 1852, as the only patriots left among the public men of England. When that terrible crisis of free trade had arrived, when the repeal of the corn laws was carried by those very men whom Mr Thorne had hitherto regarded as the only possible saviours of his country, he was for a time paralysed. His country was lost; but that was comparatively a small thing. Other countries had flourished and fallen, and the human race still went on improving under God's providence. But now all trust in human faith must for ever be at an end. Not only must ruin come, but it must come through the apostasy of those who had been regarded as the truest of true believers. Politics in England, as a pursuit for gentlemen, must be at an end. Had Mr Thorne been trodden under foot by a Whig, he could have borne it as a Tory and a martyr; but to be so utterly thrown over and deceived by those he had so earnestly supported, so thoroughly trusted, was more than he could endure and live. He therefore ceased to live as a politician, and refused to hold any converse with the world at large on the state of the country.

Such were Mr Thorne's impressions for the first two or three years after Sir Robert Peel's apostasy; but by degrees his temper, as did that of the others, cooled down. He began once more to move about, to frequent the bench and the market, and to be seen at dinners, shoulder to shoulder with some of those who had so cruelly betrayed him. It was a necessity for him to live, and that plan of his for avoiding the world did not answer. He, however, and others around him who still maintained the same staunch principles of protection – men like himself, who were too true to flinch at the cry of a mob – had their own way of consoling themselves. They were, and felt themselves to be, the only true depositaries left of certain Eleusinian mysteries, of certain deep and wondrous services of worship by which alone the gods could be rightly approached. To them and them only was it now given to know these things, and to perpetuate them, if that might still be done, by the careful and secret education of their children.

We have read how private and peculiar forms of worship have been carried on from age to age in families, which to the outer world have apparently adhered to the services of some ordinary church. And so by degrees it was with Mr Thorne. He learnt at length to listen calmly while protection was talked of as a thing dead, although he knew within himself that it was still quick with a mystic life. Nor was he without a certain pleasure that such knowledge though given to him should be debarred from the multitude. He became accustomed to hear, even among country gentlemen, that free trade was after all not so bad, and to hear this without dispute, although conscious within himself that everything good in England had gone with his old palladium. He had within him something of the feeling of Cato, who gloried that he could kill himself because Romans were no longer worthy of their name. Mr Thorne had no thought of killing himself, being a Christian, and still possessing his 4000l. a year; but the feeling was not on that account the less comfortable.

Mr Thorne was a sportsman, and had been active though not outrageous in his sports. Previous to the great downfall of politics in his country, he had supported the hunt by every means in his power. He had preserved game till no goose or turkey could show a tail in the parish of St Ewold's. He had planted gorse covers with more care than oaks and larches. He had been more anxious for the comfort of his foxes than of his ewes and lambs. No meet had been more popular than Ullathorne; no man's stables had been more liberally open to the horses of distant men than Mr Thorne's; no man had said more, written more, or done more to keep the club up. The theory of protection could expand itself so thoroughly in the practices of a country hunt! But when the great ruin came; when the noble master of the Barsetshire hounds supported the recreant minister in the House of Lords, and basely surrendered his truth, his manhood, his friends, and his honour for the hope of a garter, then Mr Thorne gave up his hunt. He did not cut his covers, for that would not have been the act of a gentleman. He did not kill his foxes, for that according to his light would have been murder. He did not say that his covers should not be drawn, or his earths stopped, for that would have been illegal according to the by-laws prevailing among country gentlemen. But he absented himself from home on the occasion of every meet at Ullathorne, left the covers to their fate, and could not be persuaded to take his pink coat out of the press, or his hunters out of his stable. This lasted for two years, and then by degrees he came round. He first appeared at a neighbouring meet on a pony, dressed in his shooting coat, as though he had trotted in by accident; then he walked up one morning on foot to see his favourite gorse drawn, and when his groom brought his mare out by chance, he did not refuse to mount her. He was next persuaded, by one of the immortal fifty-three, to bring his hunting materials over to the other side of the county, and take a fortnight with the hounds there; and so gradually he returned to his old life. But in hunting as in other things he was only supported by an inward feeling of mystic superiority to those with whom he shared the common breath of outer life.

Mr Thorne did not live in solitude at Ullathorne. He had a sister, who was ten years older than himself, and who participated in his prejudices and feelings so strongly, that she was a living caricature of all his foibles. She would not open a modern quarterly, did not choose to see a magazine in her drawing-room, and would not have polluted her fingers with a shred of the 'Times' for any consideration. She spoke of Addison, Swift, and Steele, as though they were still living, regarded De Foe as the best known novelist of his country, and thought of Fielding as a young but meritorious novice in the fields of romance. In poetry, she was familiar with names as late as Dryden, and had once been seduced into reading the 'Rape of the Lock;' but she regarded Spenser as the purest type of her country's literature in this line. Genealogy was her favourite insanity. Those things which are the pride of most genealogists were to her contemptible. Arms and mottoes set her beside herself. Ealfried of Ullathorne had wanted no motto to assist him in cleaving to the brisket Geoffrey De Burgh; and Ealfried's great grandfather, the gigantic Ullafrid, had required no other arms than those which nature gave him to hurl from the top of his own castle a cousin of the base invading Norman. To her all modern English names were equally insignificant: Hengist, Horsa, and such like, had for her ears the only true savour of nobility. She was not contented unless she could go beyond the Saxons; and would certainly have christened her children, had she had children, by the names of the ancient Britons. In some respects she was not unlike Scott's Ulrica, and had she been given to cursing, she would certainly have done so in the names of Mista, Skogula, and Zernebock. Not having submitted to the embraces of any polluting Norman, as poor Ulrica had done, and having assisted no parricide, the milk of human kindness was not curdled in her bosom. She never cursed, therefore, but blessed rather. This, however, she did in a strange uncouth Saxon manner that would have been unintelligible to any peasants but her own.

As a politician, Miss Thorne had been so thoroughly disgusted with public life by base deeds long antecedent to the Corn Law question, that that had but little moved her. In her estimation her brother had been a fast young man, hurried away by a too ardent temperament into democratic tendencies. Now happily he was brought to sounder views by seeing the iniquity of the world. She had not yet reconciled herself to the Reform Bill, and still groaned in spirit over the defalcations of the Duke as touching the Catholic Emancipation. If asked whom she thought the Queen should take as her counsellor, she would probably have named Lord Eldon; and when reminded that that venerable man was no longer present in the flesh to assist us, she would probably have answered with a sigh that none now could help us but the dead.

In religion, Miss Thorne was a pure Druidess. We would not have it understood by that, that she did actually in these latter days assist at any human sacrifices, or that she was in fact hostile to the Church of Christ. She had adopted the Christian religion as a milder form of the worship of her ancestors, and always appealed to her doing so as evidence that she had no prejudices against reform, when it could be shown that reform was salutary. This reform was the most modern of any to which she had as yet acceded, it being presumed that British ladies had given up their paint and taken to some sort of petticoats before the days of St Augustine. That further feminine step in advance which combines paint and petticoats together, had not found a votary in Miss Thorne.

But she was a Druidess in this, that she regretted she knew not what in the usages and practices of her Church. She sometimes talked and constantly thought of good things gone by, though she had but the faintest idea of what those good things had been. She imagined that a purity had existed which was now gone; that a piety had adorned our pastors and a simple docility our people, for which it may be feared history gave her but little true warrant. She was accustomed to speak of Cranmer as though he had been the firmest and most simple-minded of martyrs, and of Elizabeth as though the pure Protestant faith of her people had been the one anxiety of her life. It would have been cruel to undeceive her, had it been possible; but it would have been impossible to make her believe that the one was a time-serving priest, willing to go any length to keep his place, and that the other was in heart a papist, with this sole proviso, that she should be her own pope.

And so Miss Thorne went on sighing and regretting, looking back to the divine right of kings as the ruling axiom of a golden age, and cherishing, low down in the bottom of her heart of hearts, a dear unmentioned wish for the restoration of some exiled Stuart. Who would deny her the luxury of her sighs, or the sweetness of her soft regrets!

In her person and her dress she was perfect, and well she knew her own perfection. She was a small elegantly made old woman, with a face from which the glow of her youth had not departed without leaving some streaks of a roseate hue. She was proud of her colour, proud of her grey hair which she wore in short crisp curls peering out all around her face from the dainty white lace cap. To think of all the money that she spent in lace used to break the heart of poor Mrs Quiverful with her seven daughters. She was proud of her teeth, which were still white and numerous, proud of her bright cheery eye, proud of her short jaunty step, and very proud of the neat, precise, small feet with which those steps were taken. She was proud also, ay, very proud, of the rich brocaded silk in which it was her custom to ruffle through her drawing-room.

We know what was the custom of the lady of Branksome –

> Nine-and-twenty knights of fame
> Hung their shields in Branksome Hall.

The lady of Ullathorne was not so martial in her habits, but hardly less costly. She might have boasted that nine-and-twenty silken skirts might have been produced in her chamber, each fit to stand alone. The nine-and-twenty shields of the Scottish heroes were less independent, and hardly more potent to withstand any attack that might be made on them. Miss Thorne when fully dressed might be said to have been armed cap-a-pie, and she was always fully dressed, as far as was ever known to mortal man.

For all this rich attire Miss Thorne was not indebted to the generosity of her brother. She had a very comfortable independence of her own, which she divided among juvenile relatives, the milliners, and the poor, giving much the largest share to the latter. It may be imagined, therefore, that with all her little follies she was not unpopular. All her follies have, we believe, been told. Her virtues were too numerous to describe, and not sufficiently interesting to deserve description.

While we are on the subject of the Thornes, one word must be said of the house they lived in. It was not a large house, nor a fine house, nor perhaps to modern ideas a very commodious house; but by those who love the peculiar colour and peculiar ornaments of genuine Tudor architecture it was considered a perfect gem. We beg to own ourselves among the number, and therefore take this opportunity to express our surprise that so little is known by English men and women of the beauties of English architecture. The ruins of the Colosseum, the Campanile at Florence, St Mark's, Cologne, the Bourse and Notre Dame, are with our tourists as familiar as household words; but they know nothing of the glories of Wiltshire, Dorsetshire, and Somersetshire. Nay, we much question whether many noted travellers, men who have pitched their tents perhaps under Mount Sinai, are not still ignorant that there are glories in Wiltshire, Dorsetshire, and Somersetshire. We beg that they will go and see.

Mr Thorne's house was called Ullathorne Court, and was properly so called; for the house itself formed two sides of a quadrangle, which was completed on the other two sides by a wall about twenty feet high. This wall was built of cut stone, rudely cut indeed, and now much worn, but of a beautiful rich tawny yellow colour, the effect of that stonecrop of minute growth, which it had taken three centuries to produce. The top of this wall was ornamented by huge round stone balls of the same colour as the wall itself. Entrance into the court was had through a pair of iron gates, so massive that no one could comfortably open them, consequently they were rarely disturbed. From the gateway two paths led obliquely across the court; that to the left reaching the hall-door, which was in the corner made by the angle of the house, and that to the right leading to the back entrance, which was at the further end of the longer portion of the building.

With those who are now adepts in contriving house accommodation, it will militate much against Ullathorne Court, that no carriage could be brought to the hall-door. If you enter Ullathorne at all, you must do so, fair reader, on foot, or at least in a bath-chair. No vehicle drawn by horses ever comes within that iron gate. But this is nothing to the next horror that will encounter you. On entering the front door, which you do by no very grand portal, you find yourself immediately in the dining-room. What – no hall? exclaims my luxurious friend, accustomed to all the comfortable appurtenances of modern life. Yes, kind sir; a noble hall, if you will but observe it; a true old English hall of excellent dimensions for a country gentleman's family; but, if you please, no dining-parlour.

Both Mr and Miss Thorne were proud of this peculiarity of their dwelling, though the brother was once all but tempted by his friends to alter it. They delighted in the knowledge that they, like Cedric, positively dined in their true hall, even though they so dined tête-à-tête. But though they had never owned, they had felt and endeavoured to remedy the discomfort of such an arrangement. A huge screen partitioned off the front door and a portion of the hall, and from the angle so screened off a second door led into a passage, which ran along the larger side of the house next to the courtyard. Either my reader or I must be a bad hand at topography, if it be not clear that the great hall forms the ground-floor of the smaller portion of the mansion, that which was to your left as you entered the iron gate, and that it occupies the whole of this wing of the building. It must be equally clear that it looks out on a trim mown lawn, through three quadrangular windows with stone mullions, each window divided into a larger portion at the bottom, and a smaller portion at the top, and each portion again divided into five by perpendicular stone supporters. There may be windows which give a better light than such as these, and it may be, as my utilitarian friend observes, that the giving of light is the desired object of a window. I will not argue the point with him. Indeed I cannot. But I shall not the less die in the assured conviction that no sort of description of window is capable of imparting half so much happiness to mankind as that which had been adopted at Ullathorne Court. What – not an oriel? says Miss Diana de Midellage. No, Miss Diana; not even an oriel, beautiful as is an oriel window. It has not about it so perfect a feeling of quiet English homely comfort. Let oriel windows grace a college, or the half public mansion of a potent peer; but for the sitting room of quiet country ladies, of ordinary homely folk, nothing can equal the square mullioned windows of the Tudor architects.

The hall was hung round with family female insipidities by Lely, and unprepossessing male Thornes in red coats by Kneller; each Thorne having been let into a panel in the wainscoting, in the proper manner. At the further end of the room was a huge fire-place, which afforded much ground of difference between the brother and sister. An antiquated grate that would hold about a hundred weight of coal, had been stuck on to the hearth, by Mr

Thorne's father. This hearth had of course been intended for the consumption of wood fagots, and the iron dogs for the purpose were still
standing, though half buried in the masonry of the grate. Miss Thorne was
very anxious to revert to the dogs. The dear good old creature was always
glad to revert to anything, and had she been systematically indulged, would
doubtless in time have reflected that fingers were made before forks, and
have reverted accordingly. But in the affairs of the fireplace, Mr Thorne
would not revert. Country gentlemen around him, all had comfortable
grates in their dining-rooms. He was not exactly the man to have suggested
a modern usage; but he was not so far prejudiced as to banish those which
his father had prepared for his use. Mr Thorne had, indeed, once suggested
that with very little contrivance the front door might have been so altered, as
to open at least into the passage; but on hearing this, his sister Monica, such
was Miss Thorne's name, had been taken ill, and had remained so for a
week. Before she came down stairs she received a pledge from her brother
that the entrance should never be changed in her lifetime.

At the end of the hall opposite to the fire-place a door led into the
drawing-room, which was of equal size, and lighted with precisely similar
windows. But yet the aspect of the room was very different. It was papered,
and the ceiling, which in the hall showed the old rafters, was whitened and
finished with a modern cornice. Miss Thorne's drawing-room, or, as she
always called it, withdrawing-room, was a beautiful apartment. The
windows opened on to the full extent of the lovely trim garden; immediately
before the windows were plots of flowers in stiff, stately, stubborn little
beds, each bed surrounded by a stone coping of its own; beyond, there was a
low parapet wall, on which stood urns and images, fawns, nymphs, satyrs,
and a whole tribe of Pan's followers; and then again, beyond that, a beautiful
lawn sloped away to a sunk fence which divided the garden from the park.
Mr Thorne's study was at the end of the drawing-room, and beyond that
were the kitchen and the offices. Doors opened into both Miss Thorne's
withdrawing-room and Mr Thorne's sanctum from the passage above
alluded to; which, as it came to the latter room, widened itself so as to make
space for the huge black oak stairs, which led to the upper regions.

Such was the interior of Ullathorne Court. But having thus described it,
perhaps somewhat too tediously, we beg to say that it is not the interior to
which we wish to call the English tourist's attention, though we advise him
to lose no legitimate opportunity of becoming acquainted with it in a friendly
manner. It is the outside of Ullathorne that is so lovely. Let the tourist get
admission at least into the garden, and fling himself on that soft sward just
opposite to the exterior angle of the house. He will there get the double
frontage, and enjoy that which is so lovely – the expanse of architectural
beauty without the formal dullness of one long line.

It is the colour of Ullathorne that is so remarkable. It is all of that delicious
tawny hue which no stone can give, unless it has on it the vegetable richness

of centuries. Strike the wall with your hand, and you will think that the stone has on it no covering, but rub it carefully, and you will find that the colour comes off upon your finger. No colourist that ever yet worked from a palette has been able to come up to this rich colouring of years crowding themselves on years.

Ullathorne is a high building for a country house, for it possesses three stories; and in each story, the windows are of the same sort as that described, though varying in size, and varying also in their lines athwart the house. Those of the ground floor are all uniform in size and position. But those above are irregular both in size and place, and this irregularity gives a bizarre and not unpicturesque appearance to the building. Along the top, on every side, runs a low parapet, which nearly hides the roof, and at the corners are more figures of fawns and satyrs.

Such as Ullathorne House. But we must say one word of the approach to it, which shall include all the description which we mean to give of the church also. The picturesque old church of St Ewold's stands immediately opposite to the iron gates which open into the court, and is all but surrounded by the branches of the lime trees, which form the avenue leading up to the house from both sides. This avenue is magnificent, but it would lose much of its value in the eyes of many proprietors, by the fact that the road through it is not private property. It is a public lane between hedge rows, with a broad grass margin on each side of the road, from which the lime trees spring. Ullathorne Court, therefore, does not stand absolutely surrounded by its own grounds, though Mr Thorne is owner of all the adjacent land. This, however, is the source of very little annoyance to him. Men, when they are acquiring property, think much of such things, but they who live where their ancestors have lived for years, do not feel the misfortune. It never occurred either to Mr or Miss Thorne that they were not sufficiently private, because the world at large might, if it so wished, walk or drive by their iron gates. That part of the world which availed itself of the privilege was however very small.

Such a year or two since were the Thornes of Ullathorne. Such, we believe, are the inhabitants of many an English country home. May it be long before their number diminishes.

TWENTY-THREE

Mr Arabin Reads himself in at St Ewold's

ON THE SUNDAY MORNING THE ARCHDEACON WITH his sister-in-law and Mr Arabin drove over to Ullathorne, as had been arranged. On their way thither the new vicar declared himself to be considerably disturbed in his mind at the idea of thus facing his parishioners for the first time. He had, he said, been always subject to *mauvaise honte* and an annoying degree of bashfulness, which often unfitted him for any work of a novel description; and now he felt this so strongly that he feared he should acquit himself badly in St Ewold's reading-desk. He knew, he said, that those sharp little eyes of Miss Thorne would be on him, and that they greatly ridiculed. He himself knew not, and had never known, what it was to be shy. He could not conceive that Miss Thorne, surrounded as she would be by the peasants of Ullathorne, and a few of the poorer inhabitants of the suburbs of Barchester, could in any way affect the composure of a man well accustomed to address the learned congregation of St Mary's at Oxford, and he laughed accordingly at the idea of Mr Arabin's modesty.

Thereupon Mr Arabin commenced to subtilise. The change, he said, from St Mary's to St Ewold's was quite as powerful on the spirits as would be that from St Ewold's to St Mary's. Would not a peer who, by chance of fortune, might suddenly be driven to herd among navvies be as afraid of the jeers of his companions, as would any navvy suddenly exalted to a seat among peers? Whereupon the archdeacon declared with a loud laugh that he would tell Miss Throne that her new minister had likened her to a navvy. Eleanor, however, pronounced such a conclusion to be unfair; a comparison might be very just in its proportions which did not at all assimilate the things compared. But Mr Arabin went on subtilising, regarding neither the archdeacon's raillery nor Eleanor's defence. A young lady, he said, would execute with most perfect self-possession a difficult piece of music in a room crowded with strangers, who would not be able to express herself in intelligible language, even on any ordinary subject and among her most intimate friends, if she were required to do so standing on a box somewhat elevated among them. It was all an affair of education, and he at forty found it difficult to education himself anew.

Eleanor dissented on the matter of the box; and averred she could speak very well about dresses, or babies, or legs of mutton from any box, provided it were big enough for her to stand upon without fear, even though all her friends were listening to her. The archdeacon was sure she would not be able to say a word; but this proved nothing in favour of Mr Arabin. Mr Arabin said that he would try the question out with Mrs Bold, and get her on a box some day when the rectory might be full of visitors. To this Eleanor assented, making condition that the visitors should be of their own set, and the archdeacon cogitated in his mind, whether by such a condition it was intended that Mr Slope should be included, resolving also that, if so, the trial would certainly never take place in the rectory drawing-room at Plumstead.

And so arguing, they drove up to the iron gates of Ullathorne Court.

Mr and Miss Thorne were standing ready dressed for church in the hall, and greeted their clerical visitors with cordiality. The archdeacon was an old favourite. He was a clergyman of the old school, and this recommended him to the lady. He had always been an opponent of free trade as long as free trade was an open question; and now that it was no longer so, he, being a clergyman, had not been obliged, like most of his lay Tory companions, to read his recantation. He could therefore be regarded as a supporter of the immaculate fifty-three, and was on this account a favourite with Mr Thorne. The little bell was tinkling, and the rural population of the parish were standing about the lane, leaning on the church stile, and against the walls of the old court, anxious to get a look at their new minister as he passed from the house to the rectory. The archdeacon's servant had already preceded them thither with the vestments.

They all went forth together; and when the ladies passed into the church the three gentlemen tarried a moment in the lane, that Mr Thorne might name to the vicar with some kind of one-sided introduction, the most leading among his parishioners.

'Here are our churchwardens, Mr Arabin; Farmer Greenacre and Mr Stiles. Mr Stiles has the mill as you go into Barchester; and very good churchwardens they are.'

'Not very severe, I hope,' said Mr Arabin: the two ecclesiastical officers touched their hats, and each made a leg in the approved rural fashion, assuring the vicar that they were very glad to have the honour of seeing him, and adding that the weather was very good for the harvest. Mr Stiles being a man somewhat versed in town life, had an impression of his own dignity, and did not quite like leaving his pastor under the erroneous idea that he being a churchwarden kept the children in order during church time. 'Twas thus he understood Mr Arabin's allusion to his severity, and hastened to put matters right by observing that 'Sexton Clodheve looked to the younguns, and perhaps sometimes there may be a thought too much stick going on during sermon.' Mr Arabin's bright eye twinkled as he caught that of the archdeacon; and he smiled to himself as he observed how ignorant his officers were of the nature of their authority, and of the surveillance which it was their duty to keep even over himself.

Mr Arabin read the lessons and preached. It was enough to put a man a little out, let him have been ever so used to pulpit reading, to see the knowing way in which the farmers cocked their ears, and set about a mental criticism as to whether their new minister did or did not fall short of the excellence of him who had lately departed from them. A mental and silent criticism it was for the existing moment, but soon to be made public among the elders of St Ewold's over the green graves of their poor children and forefathers. The excellence, however, of poor old Mr Goddenough had not been wonderful, and there were few there who did not deem that Mr Arabin did his work sufficiently well, in spite of the slightly nervous affection which at first impeded him, and which nearly drove the archdeacon beside himself.

But the sermon was the thing to try the man. It often surprises us that very young men can muster courage to preach for the first time to a strange congregation. Men who are as yet but little more than boys, who have but just left, what indeed we may not call a school, but a seminary intended for their tuition as scholars, whose thoughts have been mostly of boating, cricketing, and wine parties, ascend a rostrum high above the heads of the submissive crowd, not that they may read God's word to those below, but that they may preach their own word for the edification of their hearers. It seems strange to us that they are not stricken dumb by the new and awful solemnity of their position. How am I, just turned twenty-three, who have never yet passed ten thoughtful days since the power of thought first came to me, how am I to instruct these greybeards, who with the weary thinking of so many years have approached so near the grave? Can I teach them their duty? Can I explain to them that which I so imperfectly understand, that which years of study may have made so plain to them? Has my newly acquired privilege, as one of God's ministers, imparted to me as yet any fitness for the wonderful work of a preacher?

It must be supposed that such ideas do occur to young clergymen, and yet they overcome, apparently with ease, this difficulty which to us appears to be all but insurmountable. We have never been subjected in the way of ordination to the power of a bishop's hands. It may be that there is in them something that sustains the spirit and banishes the natural modesty of youth. But for ourselves we must own that the deep affection which Dominie Sampson felt for his young pupils has not more endeared him to us than the bashful spirit which sent him mute and inglorious from the pulpit when he rose there with the futile attempt to preach God's gospel.

There is a rule in our church which forbids the younger order of our clergymen to perform a certain portion of the service. The absolution must be read by a minister in priest's orders. If there be no such minister present, the congregation can have the benefit of no absolution but that which each may succeed in administering to himself. The rule may be a good one, though the necessity for it hardly comes home to the general understanding. But this forbearance on the part of youth would be much more appreciated if it were extended likewise to sermons. The only danger would be that congregations would be too anxious to prevent their young clergymen from advancing themselves in the ranks of the ministry. Clergymen who could not preach would be such blessings that they would be bribed to adhere to their incompetence.

Mr Arabin, however, had not the modesty of youth to impede him, and he succeeded with his sermon even better than with the lessons. He took for his text two verses out of the second epistle of St John, 'Whosoever transgresseth, and abideth not in the doctrine of Christ hath not God. He that abideth in the doctrine of Christ he hath both the Father and Son. If there come any unto you and bring not this doctrine, receive him not into your house, neither bid him God speed.' He told them that the house of theirs to which he alluded was this their church in which he now addressed them for the first time; that their most welcome and proper manner of bidding him God speed would be their patient obedience to his teaching of the gospel; but that he could put forward no claim to such conduct on their part unless he taught them the great Christian doctrine of works and faith combined. On this he enlarged, but not very amply, and after twenty minutes succeeded in sending his new friends home to their baked mutton and pudding well pleased with their new minister.

Then came the lunch at Ullathorne. As soon as they were in the hall Miss Thorne took Mr Arabin's hand, and assured him that she received him into her house, into the temple, she said, in which she worshipped, and bade him God speed with all her heart. Mr Arabin was touched, and squeezed the spinster's hand without uttering a word in reply. Then Mr Thorne expressed a hope that Mr Arabin found the church easy to fill, and Mr Arabin having replied that he had no doubt he should do so as soon as he had learnt to pitch his voice to the building, they all sat down to the good things before them.

Miss Thorne took special care of Mrs Bold. Eleanor still wore her widow's weeds, and therefore had about her that air of grave and sad maternity which is the lot of recent widows. This opened the soft heart of Miss Throne, and made her look on her young guest as though too much could not be done for her. She heaped chicken and ham upon her plate, and poured out for her a full bumper of port wine. When Eleanor, who was not sorry to get it, had drunk a little of it, Miss Thorne at once essayed to fill it again. To this Eleanor objected, but in vain. Miss Thorne winked and nodded and whispered, saying that it was the proper thing and must be done, and that she knew all about it; and so she desired Mrs Bold to drink it up, and not mind any body.

'It is your duty, you know, to support yourself,' she said into the ear of the young mother; 'there's more than yourself depending on it;' and thus she coshered up Eleanor with cold fowl and port wine. How it is that poor men's wives, who have no cold fowl and port wine on which to be coshered up, nurse their children without difficulty, whereas the wives of rich men, who eat and drink everything that is good, cannot do so, we will for the present leave to the doctors and the mothers to settle between them.

And then Miss Thorne was great about teeth. Little Johnny Bold had been troubled for the last few days with his first incipient masticator, and with that freemasonry which exists among ladies, Miss Thorne became aware of the fact before Eleanor had half finished her wing. The old lady prescribed at once a receipt which had been much in vogue in the young days of her grandmother, and warned Eleanor with solemn voice against the fallacies of modern medicine.'

'Take his coral, my dear,' said she, 'and rub it well with carrot-juice; rub it till the juice dries on it, and then give it him to play with –'

'But he hasn't got a coral,' said Eleanor.

'Not got a coral!' said Miss Thorne, with almost angry vehemence. 'Not got a coral – how could you expect that he should cut his teeth? Have you got Daffy's Elixir?'

Eleanor explained that she had not. It had not been ordered by Mr Rerechild, the Barchester doctor whom she employed; and then the young mother mentioned some shockingly modern succedaneum, which Mr Rerechild's new lights had taught him to recommend.

Miss Thorne look awfully severe. 'Take care, my dear,' said she, 'that the man knows what he's about; take care he doesn't destroy your little boy. But' – and she softened into sorrow as she said it, and spoke more in pity than in anger – 'but I don't know who there is in Barchester now that you can trust. Poor dear old Doctor Bumpwell, indeed –'

'Why, Miss Thorne, he died when I was a little girl.'

'Yes, my dear, he did, and an unfortunate day it was for Barchester. As to those young men that have come up since' (Mr Rerechild, by the bye, was quite as old as Miss Thorne herself), 'one doesn't know where they came from or who they are, or whether they know anything about their business or not.'

'I think there are very clever men in Barchester,' said Eleanor.

'Perhaps there may be; only I don't know them; and it's admitted on all sides that medical men aren't now what they used to be. They used to be talented, observing, educated men. But now any whipper-snapper out of an apothecary's shop can call himself a doctor. I believe no kind of education is now thought necessary.'

Eleanor was herself the widow of a medical man, and felt a little inclined to resent all these hard sayings. But Miss Thorne was so essentially good-natured that it was impossible to resent anything she said. She therefore sipped her wine and finished her chicken.

'At any rate, my dear, don't forget the carrot-juice, and by all means get him a coral at once. My grandmother Thorne had the best teeth in the county, and carried them to the grave with her at eighty. I have heard her say it was all the carrot-juice. She couldn't bear the Barchester doctors. Even poor old Dr Bumpwell didn't please her.' It clearly never occurred to Miss Thorne that some fifty years ago Dr Bumpwell was only a rising man, and therefore as much in need of character in the eyes of the then ladies of Ullathorne, as the present doctors were in her own.

The archdeacon made a very good lunch, and talked to his host about turnip-drillers and new machines for reaping; while the host, thinking it only polite to attend to a stranger, and fearing that perhaps he might not care about turnip crops on a Sunday, mooted all manner of ecclesiastical subjects.

'I never saw a heavier lot of wheat, Thorne, than you've got there in that field beyond the copse. I suppose that's guano,' said the archdeacon.

'Yes, guano. I get it from Bristol myself. You'll find you often have a tolerable congregation of Barchester people out here, Mr Arabin. They are very fond of St Ewold's, particularly of an afternoon, when the weather is not too hot for the walk.'

'I am under an obligation to them for staying away to-day, at any rate,' said the vicar. 'The congregation can never be too small for a maiden sermon.'

'I got a ton and a half at Bradley's in High Street,' said the archdeacon, 'and it was a complete take in. I don't believe there was five hundred-weight of guano in it.'

'That Bradley never has anything good,' said Miss Thorne, who had just caught the name during her whisperings with Eleanor. 'And such a nice shop as there used to be in that very house before he came. Wilfred, don't you remember what good things old Ambleoff used to have?'

'There have been three men since Ambleoff's time,' said the archdeacon, 'and each as bad as the other. But who gets it for you at Bristol, Thorne?'

'I ran up myself this year and bought it out of the ship. I am afraid as the evenings get short, Mr Arabin, you'll find the reading desk too dark. I must send a fellow with an axe and make him lop off some of those branches.'

Mr Arabin declared that the morning light at any rate was perfect, and deprecated any interference with the lime trees. And then they took a stroll out among the trim parterres, and Mr Arabin explained to Mrs Bold the difference between a naiad and a dryad, and dilated on vases and the shapes of urns. Miss Thorne busied herself among her pansies; and her brother, finding it quite impracticable to give anything of a peculiarly Sunday tone to the conversation, abandoned the attempt, and had it out with the archdeacon about the Bristol guano.

At three o'clock they again went into church; and now Mr Arabin read the service and the archdeacon preached. Nearly the same congregation was present, with some adventurous pedestrians from the city, who had not thought the heat of the mid-day August sun too great to deter them. The archdeacon took his text from the Epistle of Philemon. 'I beseech thee for my son Onesimus, whom I have begotten in my bonds.' From such a text it may be imagined the kind of sermon which Dr Grantly preached, and on the whole it was neither dull, nor bad, nor out of place.

He told them that it had become his duty to look about for a pastor for them, to supply the place of one who had been long among them; and that in this manner he regarded as a son him whom he had selected, as St Paul had regarded the young disciple whom he sent forth. Then he took a little merit to himself for having studiously provided the best man he could without reference to patronage or favour; but he did not say that the best man according to his views was he who was best able to subdue Mr Slope, and make that gentleman's situation in Barchester too hot to be comfortable. As to the bonds, they had consisted in the exceeding struggle which he had made to get a good clergyman for them. He deprecated any comparison between himself and St Paul, but said that he was entitled to beseech them for their good will towards Mr Arabin, in the same manner that the apostle had besought Philemon and his household with regard to Onesimus.

The archdeacon's sermon, text, blessing and all, was concluded within the half hour. Then they shook hands with their Ullathorne friends, and returned to Plumstead. 'Twas thus that Mr Arabin read himself in at St Ewold's.

❊ TWENTY-FOUR ❊

Mr Slope Manages Matters Very Cleverly at Puddingdale

THE NEXT TWO WEEKS PASSED PLEASANTLY ENOUGH at Plumstead. The whole party there assembled seemed to get on well together. Eleanor made the house agreeable, and the archdeacon and Mrs Grantly seemed to have forgotten their iniquity as regarded Mr Slope. Mr Harding had his violoncello, and played to them while his daughters accompanied him. Johnny Bold, by the help either of Mr Rerechild or else by that of his coral and carrot-juice, got through his teething troubles. There had been gaieties too of all sorts. They had dined at Ullathorne, and the Thornes had dined at the Rectory. Eleanor had been duly put to stand on her box, and in that position had found herself quite unable to express her opinion on the merits of flounces, such having been the subject given to try her elocution. Mr Arabin had of course been much in his own parish, looking to the doings at his vicarage, calling on his parishioners, and taking on himself the duties of his new calling. But still he had been every evening at Plumstead, and Mrs Grantly was partly willing to agree with her husband that he was a pleasant inmate in a house.

They had also been at a dinner party at Dr Stanhope's, of which Mr Arabin had made one. He also, moth-like, burnt his wings in the flames of the signora's candle. Mrs Bold, too, had been there, and had felt somewhat displeased with the taste, want of taste she called it, shown by Mr Arabin in paying so much attention to Madame Neroni. It was as infallible that Madeline should displease and irritate the women, as that she should charm and captivate the men. The one result followed naturally on the other. It was quite true that Mr Arabin had been charmed. He thought her a very clever and a very handsome woman; he thought also that her peculiar affliction entitled her to the sympathy of all. He had never, he said, met so much suffering joined to such perfect beauty and so clear a mind. 'Twas thus he spoke of the signora coming home in the archdeacon's carriage; and Eleanor by no means liked to hear the praise. It was, however, exceedingly unjust of her to be angry with Mr

Arabin, as she had herself spent a very pleasant evening with Bertie Stanhope, who had taken her down to dinner, and had not left her side for one moment after the gentlemen came out of the dining-room. It was unfair that she should amuse herself with Bertie and yet begrudge her new friend his license of amusing himself with Bertie's sister. And yet she did so. She was half angry with him in the carriage, and said something about meretricious manners. Mr Arabin did not understand the ways of women very well, or else he might have flattered himself that Eleanor was in love with him.

But Eleanor was not in love with him. How many shades are there between love and indifference, and how little the graduated scale is understood! She had now been nearly three weeks in the same house with Mr Arabin, and had received much of his attention, and listened daily to his conversation. He had usually devoted at least some portion of his evening to her exclusively. At Dr Stanhope's he had devoted himself exclusively to another. It does not require that a woman should be in love to be irritated at this; it does not require that she should even acknowledge to herself that it is unpleasant to her. Eleanor had no such self-knowledge. She thought in her own heart that it was only on Mr Arabin's account that she regretted that he could condescend to be amused by the signora. 'I thought he had more mind,' she said to herself, as she sat watching her baby's cradle on her return from the party. 'After all, I believe Mr Stanhope is the pleasanter man of the two.' Alas for the memory of poor John Bold! Eleanor was not in love with Bertie Stanhope, nor was she in love with Mr Arabin. But her devotion to her late husband was fast fading, when she could revolve in her mind, over the cradle of his infant, the faults and failings of other aspirants to her favour.

Will any one blame my heroine for this? Let him or her rather thank God for all His goodness – for His mercy endureth for ever.

Eleanor in truth, was not in love; neither was Mr Arabin. Neither indeed was Bertie Stanhope, though he had already found occasion to say nearly as much as that he was. The widow's cap had prevented him from making a positive declaration, when otherwise he would have considered himself entitled to do so on a third or fourth interview. It was, after all, but a small cap now, and had but little of the weeping-willow left in its construction. It is singular how these emblems of grief fade away by unseen gradations. Each pretends to be the counterpart of the forerunner, and yet the last little bit of crimped white crape that sits so jauntily on the back of the head, is as dissimilar to the first huge mountain of woe which disfigured the face of the weeper, as the state of the Hindoo is to the jointure of the English dowager.

But let it be clearly understood that Eleanor was in love with no one, and that no one was in love with Eleanor. Under these circumstances her anger against Mr Arabin did not last long, and before two days were over they were both as good friends as ever. She could not but like him, for every hour spent in his company was spent pleasantly. And yet she could not quite like him, for there was always apparent in his conversation a certain feeling on his part that he hardly thought it worth his while to be in earnest. It was almost as though he were playing with a child. She knew well enough that he was in truth a sober thoughtful man, who in some matters and on some occasions could endure an agony of earnestness. And yet to her he was always gently playful. Could she have seen his brow once clouded she might have learnt to love him.

So things went on at Plumstead, and on the whole not unpleasantly, till a huge storm darkened the horizon, and came down upon the inhabitants of the rectory with all the fury of a water-spout. It was astonishing how in a few minutes the whole face of the heavens was changed. The party broke up from breakfast in perfect harmony; but fierce passions had arisen before the evening, which did not admit of their sitting at the same board for dinner. To explain this, it will be necessary to go back a little.

It will be remembered that the bishop expressed to Mr Slope in his dressing-room, his determination that Mr Quiverful should be confirmed in his appointment to the hospital, and that his lordship requested Mr Slope to communicate this decision to the archdeacon. It will also be remembered that the archdeacon had indignantly declined seeing Mr Slope, and had, instead, written a strong letter to the bishop, in which he all but demanded the situation of warden for Mr Harding. To this letter the archdeacon received an immediate formal reply from Mr Slope, in which it was stated, that the bishop had received and would give his best consideration to the archdeacon's letter.

The archdeacon felt himself somewhat checkmated by this reply. What could he do with a man who would neither see him, nor argue with him by letter, and who had undoubtedly the power of appointing any clergyman he pleased? He had consulted with Mr Arabin, who had suggested the propriety of calling in the aid of the master of Lazarus. 'If,' said he, 'you and Dr Gwynne formally declare your intention of waiting upon the bishop, the bishop will not dare to refuse to see you; and if two such men as you are see him together, you will probably not leave him without carrying your point.'

The archdeacon did not quite like admitting the necessity of his being backed by the master of Lazarus before he could obtain admission into the episcopal palace of Barchester; but still he felt that the advice was good, and he resolved to take it. He wrote again to the bishop, expressing a hope that nothing further would be done in the matter of the hospital, till the consideration promised by his lordship had been given, and then sent off a warm appeal to his friend the master, imploring him to come to Plumstead and assist in driving the bishop into compliance. The master had rejoined, raising some difficulty, but not declining; and the archdeacon had again pressed his point, insisting on the necessity for immediate action. Dr Gwynne unfortunately had the gout, and could therefore name no immediate day, but still agreed to come, if it should be finally found necessary. So the matter stood, as regarded the party at Plumstead.

But Mr Harding had another friend fighting his battle for him, quite as powerful as the master of Lazarus, and this was Mr Slope. Though the bishop had so pertinaciously insisted on giving way to his wife in the matter of the hospital, Mr Slope did not think it necessary to abandon his object. He had, he thought, daily more and more reason to imagine that the widow would receive his overtures favourably, and he could not but feel that Mr Harding at the hospital, and placed there by his means, would be more likely to receive him as son-in-law, than Mr Harding growling in opposition and disappointment under the archdeacon's wing at Plumstead. Moreover, to give Mr Slope due credit, he was actuated by greater motives even than these. He wanted a wife, and he wanted money, but he wanted power more than either. He had fully realised the fact that he must come to blows with Mrs Proudie. He had no desire to remain in Barchester as her chaplain. Sooner than do so, he would risk the loss of his whole connection with the diocese. What! was he to feel within him the possession of no ordinary talents; was he to know himself to be courageous, firm, and, in matters where his conscience did not interfere, unscrupulous; and yet be contented to be the working factotum of a woman-prelate? Mr Slope had higher ideas of his own destiny. Either he or Mrs Proudie must go to the wall; and now had come the time when he would try which it should be.

The bishop had declared that Mr Quiverful should be the new warden. As Mr Slope went down stairs prepared to see the archdeacon if necessary, but fully satisfied that no such necessity would arise, he declared to himself that Mr Harding should be warden. With the object of carrying this point, he rode over to Puddingdale, and had a further interview with the worthy expectant of clerical good things. Mr Quiverful was on the whole a worthy man. The impossible task of bringing up as ladies and gentlemen fourteen children on an income which was insufficient to give them with decency the common necessaries in life, had had an effect upon him not beneficial either to his spirit, or his keen sense of honour. Who can boast that he would have supported such a burden with a different result? Mr Quiverful was an honest, pains-taking, drudging man; anxious, indeed, for bread and meat, anxious for means to quiet his butcher and cover with returning smiles the now sour countenance of the baker's wife, but anxious also to be right with his own conscience. He was not careful, as another might be who sat on an easier worldly seat, to stand well with those around him, to shun a breath which might sully his name, or a rumour which might affect his honour. He could not afford such niceties of conduct, such moral luxuries. It must suffice for him to be ordinarily honest according to the ordinary honesty of the world's ways, and to let men's tongues wag as they would.

He had felt that his brother clergymen, men whom he had known for the last twenty years, looked coldly on him from the first moment that he had shown himself willing to sit at the feet of Mr Slope; he had seen that their looks grew colder still, when it became bruited about that he was about to be the bishop's new warden at Hiram's hospital. This was painful enough; but it was the cross which he was doomed to bear. He thought of his wife, whose last new silk dress was six years in wear. He thought of all his young flock, whom he could hardly take to church with him on Sundays, for there were not decent shoes and stockings for them all to wear. He thought of the well-worn sleeves of his own black coat, and of the stern face of the draper from whom he would fain ask for cloth to make another, did he not know that the credit would be refused him. Then he thought of the comfortable house in Barchester, of the comfortable income, of his boys sent to school, of his girls with books in their hands instead of darning needles, of his wife's face again covered with smiles, and of his daily board again covered with plenty. He thought of these things; and do thou also, reader, think of them, and then wonder, if thou canst, that Mr Slope had appeared to him to possess all those good gifts which could grace a bishop's chaplain. 'How beautiful upon the mountains are the feet of him that bringeth good tidings.'

Why, moreover, should the Barchester clergy have looked coldly on Mr Quiverful? Had they not all shown that they regarded with complacency the loaves and fishes of their mother church? Had they not all, by some hook or crook, done better for themselves than he had done? They were not burdened as he was burdened. Dr Grantly had five children, and nearly as many thousands a year on which to feed them. It was very well for him to turn up his nose at a new bishop who could do nothing for him, and a chaplain who was beneath his notice; but it was cruel in a man so circumstanced to set the world against the father of fourteen children because he was anxious to obtain for them an honourable support! He, Mr Quiverful, had not asked for the wardenship; he had not even accepted it till he had been assured that Mr Harding had refused it. How hard then that he should be blamed for doing that which not to have done would have argued a most insane imprudence?

Thus in this matter of the hospital poor Mr Quiverful had his trials; and he had also his consolations. On the whole the consolations were the more vivid of the two. The stern draper heard of the coming promotion, and the wealth of his warehouse was at Mr Quiverful's disposal. Coming events cast their shadows before, and the coming event of Mr Quiverful's transference to Barchester produced a delicious shadow in the shape of a new outfit for Mrs Quiverful and her three elder daughters. Such consolations come home to the heart of a man, and quite home to the heart of a woman. Whatever the husband might feel, the wife cared nothing for frowns of dean, archdeacon, or prebendary. To her the outsides and insides of her husband and fourteen children were everything. In her bosom every other ambition had been swallowed up in that maternal ambition of seeing them and him and herself duly clad and properly fed. It had come to that with her that life had now no other purpose. She recked nothing of the imaginary rights of others. She had no patience with her husband when he declared to her that he could not accept the hospital unless he knew that Mr Harding had refused it. Her husband had no right to be Quixotic at the expense of fourteen children. The narrow escape of throwing away his good fortune which her lord had had, almost paralysed her. Now, indeed, they had received the full promise not only from Mr Slope, but also from Mrs Proudie. Now, indeed, they might reckon with safety on their good fortune. But what if all had been lost? What if her fourteen bairns had been resteeped to the hips in poverty by the morbid sentimentality of their father? Mrs Quiverful was just at present a happy woman, but yet it nearly took her breath away when she thought of the risk they had run.

'I don't know what your father means when he talks so much of what is due to Mr Harding,' she said to her eldest daughter. 'Does he think that Mr Harding would give him 450*l*. a year out of fine feeling? And what signifies it whom he offends, as long as he gets the place? He does not expect anything better. It passes me to think how your father can be so soft, while everybody around him is so griping.'

Thus, while the outer world was accusing Mr Quiverful of rapacity for promotion and of disregard to his honour, the inner world of his own household was falling foul of him, with equal vehemence, for his willingness to sacrifice their interest to a false feeling of sentimental pride. It is astonishing how much difference the point of view makes in the aspect of all that we look at!

Such were the feelings of the different members of the family at Puddingdale on the occasion of Mr Slope's second visit. Mrs Quiverful, as soon as she saw his horse coming up the avenue from the vicarage gate, hastily packed up her huge basket of needlework, and hurried herself and her daughter out of the room in which she was sitting with her husband. 'It's Mr Slope,' she said. 'He's come to settle with you about the hospital. I do hope we shall now be able to move at once.' And she hastened to bid the maid of all work to go to the door, so that the welcome great man might not be kept waiting.

Mr Slope thus found Mr Quiverful alone. Mrs Quiverful went off to her kitchen and back settlements with anxious beating heart, almost dreading that there might be some slip between the cup of her happiness and the lip of her fruition, but yet comforting herself with the reflection that after what had taken place, any such slip could hardly be possible.

Mr Slope was all smiles as he shook his brother clergyman's hand, and said that he had ridden over because he thought it right at once to put Mr Quiverful in possession of the facts of the matter regarding the warden-ship of the hospital. As he spoke, the poor expectant husband and father saw at a glance that his brilliant hopes were to be dashed to the ground, and that his visitor was now there for the purpose of unsaying what on his former visit he had said. There was something in the tone of his voice, something in the glance of his eye, which told the tale. Mr Quiverful knew it all at once. He maintained his self-possession, however, smiled with a slight unmeaning smile, and merely said that he was obliged to Mr Slope for the trouble he was taking.

'It has been a troublesome matter from first to last,' said Mr Slope; 'and the bishop has hardly known how to act. Between ourselves – but mind this of course must go no further, Mr Quiverful.'

Mr Quiverful said that of course it should not. 'the truth is, that poor Mr Harding has hardly known his own mind. You remember our last conversation, no doubt.'

Mr Quiverful assured him that he remembered it very well indeed.

'You will remember that I told you that Mr Harding had refused to return to the hospital.'

Mr Quiverful declared that nothing could be more distinct on his memory.

'And acting on this refusal, I suggested that you should take the hospital,' continued Mr Slope.

'I understood you to say that the bishop had authorised you to offer it to me.'

'Did I? did I go so far as that? Well, perhaps it may be, that in my anxiety on your behalf I did commit myself further than I should have done. So far as my own memory serves me, I don't think I did go quite so far as that. But I own I was very anxious that you should get it; and I may have said more than was quite prudent.'

'But,' said Mr Quiverful, in his deep anxiety to prove his case, 'my wife received as distinct a promise from Mrs Proudie as one human being could give to another.'

Mr Slope smiled, and gently shook his head. He meant that smile for a pleasant smile, but it was diabolical in the eyes of the man he was speaking to. 'Mrs Proudie!' he said. 'If we are to go to what passes between the ladies in these matters, we shall really be in a nest of troubles from which we shall never extricate ourselves. Mrs Proudie is a most excellent lady, kind-hearted, charitable, pious, and in every way estimable. But, my dear Mr Quiverful, the patronage of the diocese is not in their hands.'

Mr Quiverful for a moment sat panic-stricken and silent. 'Am I to understand, then, that I have received no promise?' he said, as soon as he had sufficiently collected his thoughts.

'If you will allow me, I will tell you exactly how the matter rests. You certainly did receive a promise conditional on Mr Harding's refusal. I am sure you will do me the justice to remember that you yourself declared that you could accept the appointment on no other condition than the knowledge that Mr Harding had declined it.'

'Yes,' said Mr Quiverful; 'I did say that, certainly.'

'Well; it now appears that he did not refuse it.'

'But surely you told me, and repeated it more than once, that he had done so in your own hearing.'

'So I understood him. But it seems I was in error. But don't for a moment, Mr Quiverful, suppose that I mean to throw you over. No. Having held out my hand to a man in your position, with your large family and pressing claims, I am not now going to draw it back again. I only want you to act with me fairly and honestly.'

'Whatever I do, I shall endeavour at any rate to act fairly,' said the poor man, feeling that he had to fall back for support on the spirit of martyrdom within him.

'I am sure you will,' said the other. 'I am sure you have no wish to obtain possession of an income which belongs by all right to another. No man knows better than you do Mr Harding's history, or can better appreciate his character. Mr Harding is very desirous of returning to his old position, and the bishop feels that he is at the present moment somewhat hampered, though of course he is not bound, by the conversation which took place on the matter between you and me.'

'Well,' said Mr Quiverful, dreadfully doubtful as to what his conduct under such circumstances should be, and fruitlessly striving to harden his nerves with some of that instinct of self-preservation which made his wife so bold.

'The wardenship of this little hospital is not the only thing in the bishop's gift, Mr Quiverful, nor is it by many degrees the best. And his lordship is not the man to forget any one whom he has once marked with approval. If you would allow me to advise you as a friend –'

'Indeed I shall be most grateful to you,' said the poor vicar of Puddingdale –

'I should advise you to withdraw from any opposition to Mr Harding's claims. If you persist in your demand, I do not think you will ultimately succeed. Mr Harding has all but a positive right to the place. But if you will allow me to inform the bishop that you decline to stand in Mr Harding's way, I think I may promise you – though, by the bye, it must not be taken as a formal promise – that the bishop will not allow you to be a poorer man than you would have been had you become warden.'

Mr Quiverful sat in his arm chair silent, gazing at vacancy. What was he to say? All this that came from Mr Slope was so true. Mr Harding had a right to the hospital. The bishop had a great many good things to give away. Both the bishop and Mr Slope would be excellent friends and terrible enemies to a man in his position. And then he had no proof of any promise; he could not force the bishop to appoint him.

'Well, Mr Quiverful, what do you say about it?'

'Oh, of course, whatever you think fit, Mr Slope. It's a great disappointment, a very great disappointment. I won't deny that I am a very poor man, Mr Slope.'

'In the end, Mr Quiverful, you will find that it will have been better for you.'

The interview ended in Mr Slope receiving a full renunciation from Mr Quiverful of any claim he might have to the appointment in question. It was only given verbally and without witnesses; but then the original promise was made in the same way.

Mr Slope again assured him that he should not be forgotten, and then rode back to Barchester, satisfied that he would now be able to mould the bishop to his wishes.

✺ TWENTY-FIVE ✺

Fourteen Arguments in Favour of Mr Quiverful's Claims

WE HAVE MOST OF US HEARD OF the terrible anger of a lioness when, surrounded by her cubs, she guards her prey. Few of us wish to disturb the mother of a litter of puppies when mouthing a bone in the midst of her young family. Medea and her children are familiar to us, and so is the grief of Constance. Mrs Quiverful, when she first heard from her husband the news which he had to impart, felt within her bosom all the rage of a lioness, the rapacity of the hound, the fury of the tragic queen, and the deep despair of the bereaved mother.

Doubting, but yet hardly fearing, what might have been the tenor of Mr Slope's discourse, she rushed back to her husband as soon as the front door was closed behind the visitor. It was well for Mr Slope that he so escaped – the anger of such a woman, at such a moment, would have cowed even him. As a general rule, it is highly desirable that ladies should keep their temper; a woman when she storms always makes herself ugly, and usually ridiculous also. There is nothing so odious to man as a virago. Though Theseus loved an Amazon, he showed his love but roughly; and from the time of Theseus downward, no man ever wished to have his wife remarkable rather for forward prowess than retiring gentleness. A low voice 'is an excellent thing in woman.'

Such may be laid down as a very general rule; and few women should allow themselves to deviate from it, and then only on rare occasions. But if there be a time when a woman may let her hair to the winds, when she may loose her arms, and scream out trumpet-tongued to the ears of men, it is when nature calls out within her not for her own wants, but for the wants of those whom her womb has borne, whom her breasts have suckled, for those who look to her for their daily bread as naturally as man looks to his Creator.

There was nothing poetic in the nature of Mrs Quiverful. She was neither a Medea nor a Constance. When angry, she spoke out her anger in plain words, and in a tone which might have been modulated with advantage; but she did so, at any rate, without affectation. Now, without knowing it, she rose to a tragic vein.

'Well, my dear; we are not to have it.' Such were the words with which her ears were greeted when she entered the parlour, still hot from the kitchen fire. And the face of her husband spoke even more plainly than his words:–

> E'en such a man, so faint, so spiritless,
> So dull, so dead in look, so woe-begone,
> Drew Priam's curtain in the dead of night.

'What!' said she – and Mrs Siddons could not have put more passion into a single syllable – 'What! not have it? who says so?' And she sat opposite to her husband, with her elbows on the table, her hands clasped together, and her coarse, solid, but once handsome face stretched over it towards him.

She sat as silent as death while he told his story, and very dreadful to him her silence was. He told it very lamely and badly, but still in such a manner that she soon understood the whole of it.

'And so you have resigned it?' said she.

'I have had no opportunity of accepting it,' he replied. 'I had no witnesses to Mr Slope's offer, even if that offer would bind the bishop. It was better for me, on the whole, to keep on good terms with such men than to fight for what I should never get!'

'Witnesses!' she screamed, rising quickly to her feet, and walking up and down the room. 'Do clergymen require witnesses to their words? He made the promise in the bishop's name, and if it is to be broken I'll know the reason why. Did he not positively say that the bishop had sent him to offer you the place?'

'He did, my dear. But that is now nothing to the purpose.'

'It is everything to the purpose, Mr Quiverful. Witnesses indeed! and then to talk of *your* honour being questioned, because you wish to provide for fourteen children. It is everything to the purpose; and so they shall know, if I scream it into their ears from the town cross of Barchester.'

'You forget, Letitia, that the bishop has so many things in his gift. We must wait a little longer. That is all.'

'Wait! Shall we feed the children by waiting? Will waiting put George, and Tom, and Sam, out into the world? Will it enable my poor girls to give up some of their drudgery? Will waiting make Bessy and Jane fit even to be governesses? Will waiting pay for the things we got in Barchester last week?'

'It is all we can do, my dear. The disappointment is as much to me as to you; and yet, God knows, I feel it more for your sake than my own.'

Mrs Quiverful was looking full into her husband's face, and saw a small hot tear appear on each of those furrowed cheeks. This was too much for her woman's heart. He also had risen, and was standing with his back to the empty grate. She rushed towards him, and, seizing him in her arms, sobbed aloud upon his bosom.

'You are too good, too soft, too yielding,' she said at last. 'These men, when they want you, they use you like a cat's-paw; and when they want you no longer, they throw you aside like an old shoe. This is twice they have treated you so.'

'In one way this will be all for the better,' argued he. 'It will make the bishop feel that he is bound to do something for me.'

'At any rate, he shall hear of it,' said the lady, again reverting to her more angry mood. 'At any rate he shall hear of it, and that loudly; and so shall she. She little knows Letitia Quiverful, if she thinks I will sit down quietly with the loss after all that passed between us at the palace. If there's any feeling within her, I'll make her ashamed of herself,' – and she paced the room again, stamping the floor as she went with her fat heavy foot. 'Good heavens! what a heart she must have within her to treat in such a way as this the father of fourteen unprovided children!'

Mr Quiverful proceeded to explain that he didn't think that Mrs Proudie had had anything to do with it.

'Don't tell me,' said Mrs Quiverful; 'I know more about it than that. Doesn't all the world know that Mrs Proudie is bishop of Barchester, and that Mr Slope is merely her creature? Wasn't it she that made me the promise, just as though the thing was in her own particular gift? I tell you, it was that woman who sent him over here to-day, because, for some reason of her own, she wants to go back from her word.'

'My dear, you're wrong –'

'Now, Q., don't be so soft,' she continued. 'Take my word for it, the bishop knows no more about it than Jemima does.' Jemima was the two-year-old. 'And if you'll take my advice, you'll lose no time in going over and seeing him yourself.'

Soft, however, as Mr Quiverful might be, he would not allow himself to be talked out of his opinion on this occasion; and proceeded with much minuteness to explain to his wife the tone in which Mr Slope had spoken of Mrs Proudie's interference in diocesan matters. As he did so, a new idea gradually instilled itself into the matron's head, and a new course of conduct presented itself to her judgment. What if, after all, Mrs Proudie knew nothing of this visit of Mr Slope's? In that case, might it not be possible that that lady would still be staunch to her in this matter, still stand her friend, and, perhaps, possibly carry her through in opposition to Mr Slope? Mrs Quiverful said nothing as this vague hope occurred to her, but listened with more than ordinary patience to what her husband had to say. While he was still explaining that in all probability the world was wrong in its estimation of

Mrs Proudie's power and authority, she had fully made up her mind as to her course of action. She did not, however, proclaim her intention. She shook her head ominously as he continued his narration; and when he had completed she rose to go, merely observing that it was cruel, cruel treatment. She then asked him if he would mind waiting for a late dinner instead of dining at their usual hour of three, and, having received from him a concession on this point, she proceeded to carry her purpose into execution.

She determined that she would at once go to the palace; that she would do so, if possible, before Mrs Proudie could have had an interview with Mr Slope; and that she would be either submissive piteous and pathetic, or else indignant violent and exacting, according to the manner in which she was received.

She was quite confident in her own power. Strengthened as she was by the pressing wants of fourteen children, she felt that she could make her way through legions of episcopal servants, and force herself, if need be, into the presence of the lady who had so wronged her. She had no shame about it, no *mauvaise honte*, no dread of archdeacons. She would, as she declared to her husband, make her wail heard in the market-place if she did not get redress and justice. It might be very well for an unmarried young curate to be shamefaced in such matters; it might be all right that a snug rector, really in want of nothing, but still looking for better preferment, should carry on his affairs decently under the rose. But Mrs Quiverful, with fourteen children, had given over being shamefaced, and, in some things, had given over being decent. If it were intended that she should be ill used in the manner proposed by Mr Slope, it should not be done under the rose. All the world should know of it.

In her present mood, Mrs Quiverful was not over careful about her attire. She tied her bonnet under her chin, threw her shawl over her shoulders, armed herself with the old family cotton umbrella, and started for Barchester. A journey to the palace was not quite so easy a thing for Mrs Quiverful as for our friend at Plumstead. Plumstead is nine miles from Barchester, and Puddingdale is but four. But the archdeacon could order round his brougham, and his high-trotting fast bay gelding would take him into the city within the hour. There was no brougham in the coach-house of Puddingdale Vicarage, no bay horse in the stables. There was no method of locomotion for its inhabitants but that which nature has assigned to a man.

Mrs Quiverful was a broad heavy woman, not young, nor given to walking. In her kitchen, and in the family dormitories, she was active enough; but her pace and gait were not adapted for the road. A walk into Barchester and back in the middle of an August day would be to her a terrible task, if not altogether impracticable. There was living in the parish, about half a mile from the vicarage on the road to the city, a decent, kindly farmer, well to do as regards this world, and so far mindful of the next that he attended his parish church with decent regularity. To him Mrs Quiverful had before now appealed in some of her more pressing family troubles, and had not appealed in vain. At his door she now presented herself, and, having explained to his wife that most urgent business required her to go at once to Barchester, begged that Farmer Subsoil would take her thither in his tax-cart. The farmer did not reject her plan; and, as soon as Prince could be got into his collar, they started on their journey.

Mrs Quiverful did not mention the purpose of her business, nor did the farmer alloy his kindness by any unseemly questions. She merely begged to be put down at the bridge going into the city, and to be taken up again at the same place in the course of two hours. The farmer promised to be punctual to his appointment, and the lady, supported by her umbrella, took the short cut to the close, and in a few minutes was at the bishop's door.

Hitherto she had felt no dread with regard to the coming interview. She had felt nothing but an indignant longing to pour forth her claims, and declare her wrongs, if those claims were not fully admitted. But now the difficulty of her situation touched her a little. She had been at the palace once before, but then she went to give grateful thanks. Those who have thanks to return for favours received find easy admittance to the halls of the great. Such is not always the case with men, or even with women, who have favours to beg. Still less easy is access for those who demand the fulfilment of promises already made.

Mrs Quiverful had not been slow to learn the ways of the world. She knew all this, and she knew also that her cotton umbrella and all but ragged shawl would not command respect in the eyes of the palatial servants. If she were too humble, she knew well that she would never succeed. To overcome by imperious overbearing with such a shawl as hers upon her shoulders, and such a bonnet on her head, would have required a personal bearing very superior to that with which nature had endowed her. Of this also Mrs Quiverful was aware. She must make it known that she was the wife of a gentleman and a clergyman, and must yet condescend to conciliate.

The poor lady knew but one way to overcome these difficulties at the very threshold of her enterprise, and to this she resorted. Low as were the domestic funds at Puddingdale, she still retained possession of half-a-crown, and this she sacrificed to the avarice of Mrs Proudie's metropolitan sesquipedalian serving-man. She was, she said, Mrs Quiverful of Puddingdale, the wife of the Rev. Mr Quiverful. She wished to see Mrs Proudie. It was indeed quite indispensable that she should see Mrs Proudie. James Fitzplush looked worse than dubious, did not know whether his lady were out, or engaged, or in her bed-room; thought it most probable she was subject to one of these or to some other cause that would make her invisible; but Mrs Quiverful could sit down in the waiting-room while inquiry was being made of Mrs Proudie's maid.

'Look here, my man,' said Mrs Quiverful; 'I must see her;' and she put her card and half-a-crown – think of it, my reader, think of it; her last half-crown – into the man's hand, and sat herself down on a chair in the waiting-room.

Whether the bribe carried the day, or whether the bishop's wife really chose to see the vicar's wife, it boots not now to inquire. The man returned, and begging Mrs Quiverful to follow him, ushered her into the presence of the mistress of the diocese.

Mrs Quiverful at once saw that her patroness was in a smiling humour. Triumph sat throned upon her brow, and all the joys of dominion hovered about her curls. Her lord had that morning contested with her a great point. He had received an invitation to spend a couple of days with the archbishop. His soul longed for the gratification. Not a word, however, in his grace's note alluded to the fact of his being a married man; and, if he went at all, he must go alone. This necessity would have presented no insurmountable bar to the visit, or have mutilated much against the pleasure, had he been able to go without any reference to Mrs Proudie. But this he could not do. He could not order his portmanteau to be packed, and start with his own man, merely telling the lady of his heart that he would probably be back on Saturday. There are men – may we not rather say monsters? who do such things; and there are wives – may we not rather say slaves? – who put up with such usage. But Doctor and Mrs Proudie were not among the number.

The bishop, with some beating about the bush, made the lady understand that he very much wished to go. The lady, without any beating about the bush, made the bishop understand that she wouldn't hear of it. It would be useless here to repeat the arguments that were used on each side, and needless to record the result. Those who are married will understand very well how the battle was lost and won; and those who are single will never understand it till they learn the lesson which experience alone can give. When Mrs Quiverful was shown into Mrs Proudie's room, that lady had only returned a few minutes from her lord. But before she left him she had seen the answer to the archbishop's note written and sealed. No wonder that her face was wreathed with smiles as she received Mrs Quiverful.

She instantly spoke of the subject which was so near the heart of her visitor. 'Well, Mrs Quiverful,' said she, 'is it decided yet when you are to move into Barchester?'

'That woman,' as she had an hour or two since been called, became instantly re-endowed with all the graces that can adorn a bishop's wife. Mrs Quiverful immediately saw that her business was to be piteous, and that nothing was to be gained by indignation; nothing, indeed, unless she could be indignant in company with her patroness.

'Oh, Mrs Proudie,' she began, 'I fear we are not to move to Barchester at all.'

'Why not?' said that lady sharply, dropping at a moment's notice her smiles and condescension, and turning with her sharp quick way to business which she saw at a glance was important.

And then Mrs Quiverful told her tale. As she progressed in the history of her wrongs she perceived that the heavier she leant upon Mr Slope the blacker became Mrs Proudie's brow, but that such blackness was not injurious to her own cause. When Mr Slope was at Puddingdale vicarage that morning she had regarded him as the creature of the lady-bishop; now she perceived that they were enemies. She admitted her mistake to herself without any pain or humiliation. She had but one feeling, and that was confined to her family. She cared little how she twisted and turned among these new comers at the bishop's palace so long as she could twist her husband into the warden's house. She cared not which was her friend or which was her enemy, if only she could get this preferment which she so sorely wanted.

She told her tale, and Mrs Proudie listened to it almost in silence. She told how Mr Slope had cozened her husband into resigning his claim, and had declared that it was the bishop's will that none but Mr Harding should be warden. Mrs Proudie's brow became blacker and blacker. At last she started from her chair, and begging Mrs Quiverful to sit and wait for her return, marched out of the room.

'Oh, Mrs Proudie, it's for fourteen children – for fourteen children.' Such was the burden that fell on her ear as she closed the door behind her.

TWENTY-SIX

Mrs Proudie Wrestles and Gets a Fall

IT WAS HARDLY AN HOUR SINCE MRS Proudie had left her husband's apartment victorious, and yet so indomitable was her courage that she now returned thither panting for another combat. She was greatly angry with what she thought was his duplicity. He had so clearly given her a promise on this matter of the hospital. He had been already so absolutely vanquished on that point. Mrs Proudie began to feel that if every affair was to be thus discussed and battled about twice and even thrice, the work of the diocese would be too much even for her.

Without knocking at the door she walked quickly into her husband's room, and found him seated at his office table, with Mr Slope opposite to him. Between his fingers was the very note which he had written to the archbishop in her presence – and it was open! Yes, he had absolutely violated the seal which had been made sacred by her approval. They were sitting in deep conclave, and it was too clear that the purport of the archbishop's invitation had been absolutely canvassed again, after it had been already debated and decided on in obedience to her behests! Mr Slope rose from his chair, and bowed slightly. The two opposing spirits looked each other fully in the face, and they knew that they were looking each at an enemy.

'What is this, bishop, about Mr Quiverful?' said she, coming to the end of the table and standing there.

Mr Slope did not allow the bishop to answer, but replied himself. 'I have been out to Puddingdale this morning, ma'am, and have seen Mr Quiverful. Mr Quiverful has abandoned his claim to the hospital, because he is now aware that Mr Harding is desirous to fill his own place. Under these circumstances I have strongly advised his lordship to nominate Mr Harding.'

'Mr Quiverful has not abandoned anything,' said the lady, with a very imperious voice. 'His lordship's word has been pledged to him, and it must be respected.'

The bishop still remained silent. He was anxiously desirous of making his old enemy bite the dust beneath his feet. His new ally had told him that nothing was more easy for him than to do so. The ally was there now at his elbow to help him, and yet his courage failed him. It is so hard to conquer when the prestige of former victories is all against one. It is so hard for the cock who has once been beaten out of his yard to resume his courage and again take a proud place upon a dunghill.

'Perhaps I ought not to interfere,' said Mr Slope, 'but yet –'

'Certainly you ought not,' said the infuriated dame.

'But yet,' continued Mr Slope, not regarding the interruption, 'I have thought it my imperative duty to recommend the bishop not to slight Mr Harding's claims.'

'Mr Harding should have known his own mind,' said the lady.

'If Mr Harding be not replaced at the hospital, his lordship will have to encounter much ill will, not only in the diocese, but in the world at large. Besides, taking a higher ground, his lordship, as I understood, feels it to be his duty to gratify, in this matter, so very worthy a man and so good a clergyman as Mr Harding.'

'And what is to become of the Sabbath-day school, and of the Sunday services in the hospital?' said Mrs Proudie, with something very nearly approaching to a sneer on her face.

'I understand that Mr Harding makes no objection to the Sabbath-day school,' said Mr Slope. 'And as to the hospital services, that matter will be best discussed after his appointment. If he has any permanent objection, then, I fear, the matter must rest.'

'You have a very easy conscience in such matters, Mr Slope,' said she.

'I should not have an easy conscience,' he rejoined, 'but a conscience very far from being easy, if anything said or done by me should lead the bishop to act unadvisedly in this matter. It is clear that in the interview I had with Mr Harding, I misunderstood him –'

'And it is equally clear that you have misunderstood Mr Quiverful,' said she, now at the top of her wrath. 'What business have you at all with these interviews? Who desired you to go to Mr Quiverful this morning? Who commissioned you to manage this affair? Will you answer me, sir? – who sent you to Mr Quiverful this morning?'

There was a dead pause in the room. Mr Slope had risen from his chair, and was standing with his hand on the back of it, looking at first very solemn and now very black. Mrs Proudie was standing as she had at first placed herself, at the end of the table, and as she interrogated her foe she struck her hand upon it with almost more than feminine vigour. The bishop was sitting in his easy chair twiddling his thumbs, turning his eyes now to his wife, and now to his chaplain, as each took up the cudgels. How comfortable it would be if they could fight it out between them without the necessity of any interference on his part; fight it out so that one should kill the other utterly, as far as diocesan life was concerned, so that he, the bishop, might know clearly by whom it behoved him to be led. There would be the comfort of quiet in either case; but if the bishop had a wish as to which might prove the victor, that wish was certainly not antagonistic to Mr Slope.

'Better the d —— you know than the d —— you don't know,' is an old saying, and perhaps a true one; but the bishop had not realised the truth of it.

'Will you answer me, sir?' she repeated. 'Who instructed you to call on Mr Quiverful this morning?' There was another pause. 'Do you intend to answer me, sir?'

'I think, Mrs Proudie, that under all circumstances it will be better for me not to answer such a question,' said Mr Slope. Mr Slope had many tones in his voice, all duly under his command; among them was a sanctified low tone, and a sanctified loud tone; and he now used the former.

'Did any one send you, sir?'

'Mrs Proudie,' said Mr Slope. 'I am quite aware how much I owe to your kindness. I am aware also what is due by courtesy from a gentleman to a lady. But there are higher considerations than either of those, and I hope I shall be forgiven if I now allow myself to be actuated solely by them. My duty in this matter is to his lordship, and I can admit of no questioning but from him. He has approved of what I have done, and you must excuse me if I say, that having that approval and my own, I want none other.'

What horrid words were these which greeted the ear of Mrs Proudie? The matter was indeed too clear. There was premeditated mutiny in the camp. Not only had ill-conditioned minds become insubordinate by the fruition of a little power, but sedition had been overtly taught and preached. The bishop had not yet been twelve months in his chair, and rebellion had already reared her hideous head within the palace. Anarchy and misrule would quickly follow, unless she took immediate and strong measures to put down the conspiracy which she had detected.

'Mr Slope,' she said, with slow and dignified voice, differing much from that which she had hitherto used, 'Mr Slope, I will trouble you, if you please, to leave the apartment. I wish to speak to my lord alone.'

Mr Slope also felt that everything depended on the present interview. Should the bishop now be repetticoated, his thraldom would be complete and for ever. The present moment was peculiarly propitious for rebellion. The bishop had clearly committed himself by breaking the seal of the answer to the archbishop; he had therefore fear to influence him. Mr Slope had told him that no consideration ought to induce him to refuse the archbishop's invitation; he had therefore hope to influence him. He had accepted Mr Quiverful's resignation, and therefore dreaded having to renew that matter with his wife. He had been screwed up to the pitch of asserting a will of his own, and might possibly be carried on till by an absolute success he should have been taught how possible it was to succeed. Now was the moment for victory or rout. It was now that Mr Slope must make himself master of the diocese, or else resign his place and begin his search for fortune again. He saw all this plainly. After what had taken place any compromise between him and the lady was impossible. Let him once leave the room at her bidding, and leave the bishop in her hands, and he might at once pack up his portmanteau and bid adieu to episcopal honours, Mrs Bold, and the Signora Neroni.

And yet it was not so easy to keep his ground when he was bidden by a lady to go; or to continue to make a third in a party between a husband and wife when the wife expressed a wish for a *tête-à-tête* with her husband.

'Mr Slope,' she repeated, 'I wish to be alone with my lord.'

'His lordship has summoned me on most important diocesan business,' said Mr Slope, glancing with uneasy eye at Dr Proudie. He felt that he must trust something to the bishop, and yet that trust was so woefully ill-placed. 'My leaving him at the present moment is, I fear, impossible.'

'Do you bandy words with me, you ungrateful man?' said she. 'My lord, will you do me the favour to beg Mr Slope to leave the room?'

My lord scratched his head, but for the moment said nothing. This was as much as Mr Slope expected from him, and was on the whole, for him, an active exercise of marital rights.

'My lord,' said the lady, 'is Mr Slope to leave this room, or am I?'

Here Mrs Proudie made a false step. She should not have alluded to the possibility of retreat on her part. She should not have expressed the idea that her order for Mr Slope's expulsion could be treated otherwise than by immediate obedience. In answer to such a question the bishop naturally said in his own mind, that as it was necessary that one should leave the room, perhaps it might be as well that Mrs Proudie did so. He did say so in his own right mind, but externally he again scratched his head and again twiddled his thumbs.

Mrs Proudie was boiling over with wrath. Alas, alas! could she but have kept her temper as her enemy did, she would have conquered as she had ever conquered. But divine anger got the better of her, as it has done of other heroines, and she fell.

'My lord,' said she, 'am I to be vouchsafed an answer or am I not?'

At last he broke his deep silence and proclaimed himself a Slopeite. 'Why, my dear,' said he, 'Mr Slope and I are very busy.'

That was all. There was nothing more necessary. He had gone to the battle-field, stood the dust and heat of the day, encountered the fury of the foe, and won the victory. How easy is success to those who will only be true to themselves!

Mr Slope saw at once the full amount of his gain, and turned on the vanquished lady a look of triumph which she never forgot and never forgave. Here he was wrong. He should have looked humbly at her, and with meek entreating eye have deprecated her anger. He should have said by his glance that he asked pardon for his success, and that he hoped forgiveness for the stand which he had been forced to make in the cause of duty. So might he perchance have somewhat mollified that imperious bosom, and prepared the way for future terms. But Mr Slope meant to rule without terms. Ah, forgetful, inexperienced man! Can you cause that little trembling victim to be divorced from the woman that possesses him? Can you provide that they shall be separated at bed and board? Is he not flesh of her flesh and bone of her bone, and must he not so continue? It is very well now for you to stand your ground, and triumph as she is driven ignominiously from the room; but can you be present when those curtains are drawn, when that awful helmet of proof has been tied beneath the chin, when the small remnants of the bishop's prowess shall be cowed by the tassel above his head? Can you then intrude yourself when the wife wishes 'to speak to my lord alone'?

But for the moment Mr Slope's triumph was complete; for Mrs Proudie without further parley left the room, and did not forget to shut the door after her. Then followed a close conference between the new allies, in which was said much which it astonished Mr Slope to say and the bishop to hear. And yet the one said it and the other heard it without ill will. There was no mincing of matters now. The chaplain plainly told the bishop that the world gave him credit for being under the governance of his wife; that his credit and character in the diocese were suffering; that he would surely get himself into hot water if he allowed Mrs Proudie to interfere in matters which were not suitable for a woman's powers; and in fact that he would become contemptible if he did not throw off the yoke under which he groaned. The bishop at first hummed and hawed, and affected to deny the truth of what was said. But his denial was not stout and quickly broke down. He soon admitted by silence his state of vassalage, and pledged himself, with Mr Slope's assistance, to change his courses. Mr Slope also did not make out a bad case for himself. He explained how it grieved him to run counter to a lady who had always been his patroness, who had befriended him in so many ways, who had, in fact, recommended him to the bishop's notice; but, as he stated, his duty was now imperative; he held a situation of peculiar confidence, and was immediately and especially attached to the bishop's person. In such a situation his conscience required that he should regard solely the bishop's interests, and therefore he had ventured to speak out.

The bishop took this for what it was worth, and Mr Slope only intended that he should do so. It gilded the pill which Mr Slope had to administer, and which the bishop thought would be less bitter than the other pill which he had so long been taking.

'My lord,' had his immediate reward, like a good child. He was instructed to write and at once did write another note to the archbishop accepting his grace's invitation. This note Mr Slope, more prudent than the lady, himself took away and posted with his own hands. Thus he made sure that this act of self-jurisdiction should be as nearly as possible a *fait accompli*. He begged, and coaxed, and threatened the bishop with a view of making him also write at once to Mr Harding; but the bishop, though temporarily emancipated from his wife, was not yet enthralled to Mr Slope. He said, and probably said truly, that such an offer must be made in some official form; that he was not yet prepared to sign the form; and that he should prefer seeing Mr Harding before he did so. Mr Slope might, however, beg Mr Harding to call upon him. Not disappointed with his achievement Mr Slope went his way. He first posted the precious note which he had in his pocket, and then pursued other enterprises in which we must follow him in other chapters.

Mrs Proudie, having received such satisfaction as was to be derived from slamming her husband's door, did not at once betake herself to Mrs Quiverful. Indeed for the first few moments after her repulse she felt that she could not again see that lady. She would have to own that she had been beaten, to confess that the diadem had passed from her brow, and the sceptre from her hand! No, she would send a message to her with the promise of a letter on the next day or the day after. Thus resolving, she betook herself to her bed-room; but here she again changed her mind. The air of that sacred enclosure somewhat restored her courage, and gave her more heart. As Achilles warmed at the sight of his armour, as Don Quixote's heart grew strong when he grasped his lance, so did Mrs Proudie look forward to fresh laurels, as her eye fell on her husband's pillow. She would not despair. Having so resolved, she descended with dignified mien and refreshed countenance to Mrs Quiverful.

This scene in the bishop's study took longer in the acting than in the telling. We have not, perhaps, had the whole of the conversation. At any rate Mrs Quiverful was beginning to be very impatient, and was thinking that farmer Subsoil would be tired of waiting for her, when Mrs Proudie returned. Oh! who can tell the palpitations of that maternal heart, as the suppliant looked into the face of the great lady to see written there either a promise of house, income, comfort and future competence, or else the doom of continued and ever increasing poverty. Poor mother! poor wife! there was little there to comfort you!

'Mrs Quiverful,' thus spoke the lady with considerable austerity, and without sitting down herself, 'I find that your husband has behaved in this matter in a very weak and foolish manner.'

Mrs Quiverful immediately rose upon her feet, thinking it disrespectful to remain sitting while the wife of the bishop stood. But she was desired to sit down again, and made to do so, so that Mrs Proudie might stand and preach over her. It is generally considered an offensive thing for a gentleman to keep his seat while another is kept standing before him, and we presume the same law holds with regard to ladies. It often is so felt; but we are inclined to say that it never produces half the discomfort or half the feeling of implied inferiority that is shown by a great man who desires his visitor to be seated while he himself speaks from his legs. Such a solecism in good breeding, when construed into English, means this: 'The accepted rules of courtesy in the world require that I should offer you a seat; if I did not do so, you would bring a charge against me in the world of being arrogant and ill-mannered; I will obey the world; but, nevertheless, I will not put myself on an equality with you. You may sit down, but I won't sit with you. Sit, therefore, at my bidding, and I'll stand and talk at you!'

This was just what Mrs Proudie meant to say; and Mrs Quiverful, though she was too anxious and too flurried thus to translate the full meaning of the manœuver, did not fail to feel its effect. She was cowed and uncomfortable, and a second time essayed to rise from her chair.

'Pray be seated. Mrs Quiverful, pray keep you seat. Your husband, I say, has been most weak and most foolish. It is impossible, Mrs Quiverful, to help people who will not help themselves. I much fear that I can now do nothing for you in this matter.'

'Oh! Mrs Proudie – don't say so,' said the poor woman again jumping up.

'*Pray* be seated Mrs Quiverful. I much fear that I can do nothing further for you in this matter. Your husband has, in a most unaccountable manner, taken upon himself to resign that which I was empowered to offer him. As a matter of course, the bishop expects that his clergy shall know their own minds. What he may ultimately do – what we may finally decide on doing – I cannot now say. Knowing the extent of your family –'

'Fourteen children, Mrs Proudie, fourteen of them! and barely bread – barely, bread! It's hard for the children of a clergyman, it's hard for one who has always done his duty respectably!' Not a word fell from her about herself; but the tears came streaming down her big coarse cheeks, on which the dust of the August road had left its traces.

Mrs Proudie has not been portrayed in these pages as an agreeable or an amiable lady. There has been no intention to impress the reader much in her favour. It is ordained that all novels should have a male and a female angel, and a male and a female devil. If it be considered that this rule is obeyed in these pages, the latter character must be supposed to have fallen to the lot of Mrs Proudie. But she was not all devil. There was a heart inside that stiff-ribbed bodice, though not, perhaps, of large dimensions, and certainly not easily accessible. Mrs Quiverful, however, did gain access, and Mrs Proudie proved herself a woman. Whether it was the fourteen children with their probable bare bread and their possible bare backs, or the respectability of the father's work, or the mingled dust and tears on the mother's face, we will not pretend to say. But Mrs Proudie was touched.

She did not show it as other women might have done. She did not give Mrs Quiverful eau-de-Cologne, or order her a glass of wine. She did not take her to her toilet table, and offer her the use of brushes and combs, towels and water. She did not say soft little speeches and coax her kindly back to equanimity. Mrs Quiverful, despite her rough appearance, would have been as amenable to such little tender cares as any lady in the land. But none such were forthcoming. Instead of this, Mrs Proudie slapped one hand upon the other, and declared – not with an oath; for as a lady and a Sabbatarian and a she-bishop, she could not swear – but with an adjuration, that 'she wouldn't have it done.'

The meaning of this was that she wouldn't have Mr Quiverful's promised appointment cozened away by the treachery of Mr Slope and the weakness of her husband. This meaning she very soon explained to Mrs Quiverful.

'Why was your husband such a fool,' said she, now dismounted from her high horse and sitting confidentially down close to her visitor, 'as to take the bait which that man threw to him? If he had not been so utterly foolish, nothing could have prevented your going to the hospital.'

Poor Mrs Quiverful was ready enough with her own tongue in accusing her husband to his face of being soft, and perhaps did not always speak of him to her children quite so respectfully as she might have done. But she did not at all like to hear him abused by others, and began to vindicate him, and to explain that of course he had taken Mr Slope to be an emissary from Mrs Proudie herself: that Mr Slope was thought to be peculiarly her friend; and that, therefore, Mr Quiverful would have been failing in respect to her had he assumed to doubt what Mr Slope had said.

Thus mollified Mrs Proudie again declared that 'she would not have it done,' and at last sent Mrs Quiverful home with an assurance that, to the furthest stretch of her power and influence in the palace, the appointment of Mr Quiverful should be insisted on. As she repeated the word 'insisted,' she thought of the bishop in his night-cap, and with compressed lips slightly shook her head. Oh! my aspiring pastors, divines to whose ears *nolo episcopari* are the sweetest of words, which of you would be a bishop on such terms as these?

Mrs Quiverful got home in the farmer's cart, not indeed with a light heart, but satisfied that she had done right in making her visit.

TWENTY-SEVEN

A Love Scene

MR SLOPE, AS WE HAVE SAID, LEFT the palace with a feeling of considerable triumph. Not that he thought that his difficulties were all over; he did not so deceive himself; but he felt that he had played his first move well, as well as the pieces on the board would allow; and that he had nothing with which to reproach himself. He first of all posted the letter to the archbishop, and having made that sure he proceeded to push the advantage which he had gained. Had Mrs Bold been at home, he would have called on her; but he knew that she was at Plumstead, so he wrote the following note. It was the beginning of what, he trusted, might be a long and tender series of epistles.

'MY DEAR MRS BOLD,

You will understand perfectly that I cannot at present correspond with your father. I heartily wish that I could, and hope the day may be not long distant when mists shall have cleared away, and we may know each other. But I cannot preclude myself from the pleasure of sending you these few lines to say that Mr Q has to-day, in my presence, resigned any title that he ever had to the wardenship of the hospital, and that the bishop has assured me that it is his intention to offer it to your esteemed father.

'Will you, with my respectful compliments, ask him, who I believe is now a fellow-visitor with you, to call on the bishop either on Wednesday or Thursday, between ten and one. *This is by the bishop's desire*. If you will so far oblige me as to let me have a line naming either day, and the hour which will suit Mr Harding, I will take care that the servants shall have orders to show him in without delay. Perhaps I should say no more – but still I wish you could make your father understand that no subject will be mooted between his lordship and him, which will refer at all to the method in which he may choose to perform his duty. I for one, am persuaded that no clergyman could perform it more satisfactorily than he did, or than he will do again.

'On a former occasion I was indiscreet and much too impatient, considering your father's age and my own. I hope he will not now refuse my apology. I still hope also that with your aid and sweet pious labours, we may live to attach such a Sabbath school to the old endowment, as may, by God's grace and furtherance, be a blessing to the poor of this city.

'You will see at once that this letter is confidential. The subject, of course, makes it so. But, equally of course, it is for your parent's eye as well as for your own, should you think proper to show it to him.

'I hope my darling little friend Johnny is as strong as ever – dear little fellow. Does he still continue his rude assaults on those beautiful long silken tresses?

'I can assure you your friends miss you from Barchester sorely; but it would be cruel to begrudge you your sojourn among flowers and fields during this truly sultry weather.

'Pray believe me, my dear Mrs Bold,
'Yours most sincerely,
'OBADIAH SLOPE.

'Barchester, Friday.'

Now this letter, taken as a whole, and with the consideration that Mr Slope wished to assume a great degree of intimacy with Eleanor, would not have been bad, but for the allusion to the tresses. Gentlemen do not write to ladies about their tresses, unless they are on very intimate terms indeed. But Mr Slope could not be expected to be aware of this. He longed to put a little affection into his epistle, and yet he thought it injudicious, as the letter would, he knew, be shown to Mr Harding. He would have insisted that the letter should be strictly private and seen by no eyes but Eleanor's own, had he not felt that such an injunction would have been disobeyed. He therefore restrained his passion, did not sign himself 'yours affectionately,' and contented himself instead with the compliment to the tresses.

Having finished his letter, he took it to Mrs Bold's house, and learning there, from the servant, that things were to be sent out to Plumstead, that afternoon, left it, with many injunctions, in her hands.

We will now follow Mr Slope so as to complete the day with him, and then return to his letter and its momentous fate in the next chapter.

There is an old song which gives us some very good advice about courting:–

> It's gude to be off with the auld luve
> Before ye be on wi' the new.

Of the wisdom of this maxim Mr Slope was ignorant, and accordingly, having written his letter to Mrs Bold, he proceeded to call upon the Signora Neroni. Indeed it was hard to say which was the old love and which the new, Mr Slope having been smitten with both so nearly at the same time. Perhaps he thought it not amiss to have two strings to his bow. But two strings to Cupid's bow are always dangerous to him on whose behalf they are to be used. A man should remember that between two stools he may fall to the ground.

But in sooth Mr Slope was pursuing Mrs Bold in obedience to his better instincts, and the signora in obedience to his worser. Had he won the widow and worn her, no one could have blamed him. You, O reader, and I, and Eleanor's other friends would have received the story of such a winning with much disgust and disappointment; but we should have been angry with Eleanor, not with Mr Slope. Bishop, male and female, dean and chapter and diocesan clergy in full congress, could have found nothing to disapprove of in such an alliance. Convocation itself, that mysterious and mighty synod, could in no wise have fallen foul of it. The possession of 1000*l.* a year and a beautiful wife would not at all have hurt the voice of the pulpit charmer, or lessened the grace and piety of the exemplary clergyman.

But not of such a nature were likely to be his dealings with the Signora Neroni. In the first place he knew that her husband was living, and therefore he could not woo her honestly. Then again she had nothing to recommend her to his honest wooing had such been possible. She was not only portionless, but also from misfortune unfitted to be chosen as the wife of any man who wanted a useful mate. Mr Slope was aware that she was a helpless hopeless cripple.

But Mr Slope could not help himself. He knew that he was wrong in devoting his time to the back drawing-room in Dr Stanhope's house. He knew that what took place there would if divulged utterly ruin him with Mrs Bold. He knew that scandal would soon come upon his heels and spread abroad among the black coats of Barchester some tidings, exaggerated tidings, of the sighs which he poured into the lady's ears. He knew that he was acting against the recognised principles of his life, against those laws of conduct by which he hoped to achieve much higher success. But as we have said, he could not help himself. Passion, for the first time in his life, passion was too strong for him.

As for the signora, no such plea can be put forward for her, for in truth she cared no more for Mr Slope than she did for twenty others who had been at her feet before him. She willingly, nay greedily, accepted his homage. He was the finest fly that Barchester had hitherto afforded to her web; and the signora was a powerful spider that made wondrous webs, and could in no way live without catching flies. Her taste in this respect was abominable, for she had no use for the victims when caught. She could not eat them matrimonially, as young lady-flies do whose webs are most frequently of their mother's weaving. Nor could she devour them by any escapade of a less legitimate description. Her unfortunate affliction precluded her from all hope of levanting with a lover. It would be impossible to run away with a lady who required three servants to move her from a sofa.

The signora was subdued by no passion. Her time for love was gone. She had lived out her heart, such heart as she had ever had, in her early years, at an age when Mr Slope was thinking of the second book of Euclid and his unpaid bill at the buttery hatch. In age the lady was younger than the gentleman; but in feelings, in knowledge of the affairs of love, in intrigue, he was immeasurably her junior. It was necessary to her to have some man at her feet. It was the one customary excitement of her life. She delighted in the exercise of power which this gave her; it was now nearly the only food for her ambition; she would boast to her sister that she could make a fool of any man, and the sister, as little imbued with feminine delicacy as herself, good naturedly thought it but fair that such amusement should be afforded to a poor invalid who was debarred from the ordinary pleasures of life.

Mr Slope was madly in love, but hardly knew it. The signora spitted him, as a boy does a cockchafer on a cork, that she might enjoy the energetic agony of his gyrations. And she knew very well what she was doing.

Mr Slope having added to his person all such adornments as are possible to a clergyman making a morning visit, such as a clean neck tie, clean handkerchief, new gloves, and a *soupçon* of not unnecessary scent called about three o'clock at the doctor's door. At about this hour the signora was almost always alone in the back drawing-room. The mother had not come down. The doctor was out or in his own room. Bertie was out, and Charlotte at any rate left the room if any one called whose object was specially with her sister. Such was her idea of being charitable and sisterly.

Mr Slope, as was his custom, asked for Mr Stanhope, and was told, as was the servant's custom, that the signora was in the drawing-room. Upstairs he accordingly went. He found her, as he always did, lying on her sofa with a French volume before her, and a beautiful little inlaid writing case open on her table. At the moment of his entrance she was in the act of writing.

'Ah my friend,' said she, putting out her left hand to him across her desk, 'I did not expect you to-day and was this very instant, writing to you –'

Mr Slope, taking the soft fair delicate hand in his, and very soft and fair and delicate it was, bowed over it his huge red head and kissed it. It was a sight to see, a deed to record if the author could fitly do it, a picture to put on canvass. Mr Slope was big, awkward, cumbrous, and having his heart in his pursuit was ill at ease. The lady was fair, as we have said, and delicate; every thing about her was fine and refined; her hand in his looked like a rose lying among carrots, and when he kissed it he looked as a cow might do on finding such a flower among her food. She was graceful as a couchant goddess, and, moreover, as self-possessed as Venus must have been when courting Adonis.

Oh, that such grace and such beauty should have condescended to waste itself on such a pursuit!

'I was in the act of writing to you,' said she, 'but now my scrawl may go into the basket;' and she raised the sheet of gilded note paper from off her desk as though to tear it.

'Indeed it shall not,' said he, laying the embargo of half a stone weight of human flesh and blood upon the devoted paper. 'Nothing that you write for my eyes, signora, shall be so desecrated,' and he took up the letter, put that also among the carrots and fed on it, and then proceeded to read it.

'Gracious me! Mr Slope,' said she, 'I hope you don't mean to say that you keep all the trash I write to you. Half my time I don't know what I write, and when I do, I know it is only fit for the back of the fire. I hope you have not that ugly trick of keeping letters.'

'At any rate, I don't throw them into a waste-paper basket. If destruction is their doomed lot, they perish worthily, and are burnt on a pyre, as Dido was of old.'

'With a steel pen struck through them, of course,' said she, 'to make the simile more complete. Of all the ladies of my acquaintance I think Lady Dido was the most absurd. Why did she not do as Cleopatra did? Why did she not take out her ships and insist on going with him? She could not bear to lose the land she had got by a swindle; and then she could not bear the loss of her lover. So she fell between two stools. Mr Slope, whatever you do, never mingle love and business.'

Mr Slope blushed up to his eyes, and over his mottled forehead to the very roots of his hair. He felt sure that the signora knew all about his intentions with reference to Mrs Bold. His conscience told him that he was detected. His doom was to be spoken; he was to be punished for his duplicity, and rejected by the beautiful creature before him. Poor man. He little dreamt that had all his intentions with reference to Mrs Bold been known to the signora, it would only have added zest to that lady's amusement. It was all very well to have Mr Slope at her feet, to show her power by making an utter fool of a clergyman, to gratify her own fidelity by thus proving the little strength which religion had in controlling the passions even of a religious man; but it would be an increased gratification if she could be made to understand that she was at the same time alluring her victim away from another, whose love if secured would be in every way beneficent and salutary.

The signora had indeed discovered with the keen instinct of such a woman, that Mr Slope was bent on matrimony with Mrs Bold, but in alluding to Dido she had not thought of it. She instantly perceived, however, from her lover's blushes, what was on his mind, and was not slow in taking advantage of it.

She looked him full in the face, not angrily, nor yet with a smile, but with an intense, and overpowering gaze; and then holding up her forefinger, and slightly shaking her head she said:–

'Whatever you do, my friend, do not mingle love and business. Either stick to your treasure and your city of wealth, or else follow your love like a true man. But never attempt both. If you do, you'll have to die with a broken heart as did poor Dido. Which is it to be with you, Mr Slope, love or money?'

Mr Slope was not so ready with a pathetic answer as he usually was with touching episodes in his extempore sermons. He felt that he ought to say something pretty, something also that should remove the impression on the mind of his lady love. But he was rather put about how to do it.

'Love,' said he, 'true overpowering love, must be the strongest passion a man can feel; it must control every other wish, and put aside every other pursuit. But with me love will never act in that way unless it be returned;' and he threw upon a signora a look of tenderness which was intended to make up for all the deficiencies of his speech.

'Take my advice,' said she. 'Never mind love. After all, what is it? The dream of a few weeks. That is all its joy. The disappointment of a life is its Nemesis. Who was ever successful in true love? Success in love argues that the love is false. True love is always despondent or tragical. Juliet loved, Haidee loved, Dido loved, and what came of it? Troilus loved and ceased to be a man.'

'Troilus loved and was fooled,' said the more manly chaplain. 'A man may love and yet not be a Troilus. All women are not Cressids.'

'No; all women are not Cressids. The falsehood is not always on the woman's side. Imogen was true, but how was she rewarded? Her lord believed her to be the paramour of the first he who came near her in his absence. Desdemona was true and was smothered. Ophelia was true and went mad. There is no happiness in love, except at the end of an English novel. But in wealth, money, houses, lands, goods and chattels, in the good things of this world, yes, in them there is something tangible, something that can be retained and enjoyed.'

'Oh no,' said Mr Slope, feeling himself bound to enter some protest against so very unorthodox a doctrine, 'this world's wealth will make no one happy.'

'And what will make you happy – you – you?' said she, raising herself up, and speaking to him with energy across the table. 'From what source do you look for happiness? Do not say that you look for none? I shall not believe you. It is a search in which every human being spends an existence.'

'And the search is always in vain,' said Mr Slope. 'We look for happiness on earth, while we ought to be content to hope for it in heaven.'

'Pshaw! you preach a doctrine which you know you don't believe. It is the way with you all. If you know that there is no earthly happiness, why do you long to be a bishop or a man? Why do you want lands and income?'

'I have the natural ambition of a man,' said he.

'Of course you have, and the natural passions; and therefore I say that you don't believe the doctrine you preach. St Paul was an enthusiast. He believed so that his ambition and passions did not war against his creed. So does the Eastern fanatic who passes half his life erect upon a pillar. As for me, I will believe in no belief that does not make itself manifest by outward signs. I will think no preaching sincere that is not recommended by the practice of the preacher.'

Mr Slope was startled and horrified, but he felt that he could not answer.

How could he stand up and preach the lessons of his Master, being there as he was, on the devil's business? He was a true believer, otherwise this would have been nothing to him. He had audacity for most things, but he had not audacity to make a plaything of the Lord's word. All this the signora understood, and felt much interest as she saw her cockchafer whirl round upon her pin.

'Your wit delights in such arguments,' said he, 'but your heart and your reason do not go along with them.'

'My heart!' said she; 'you quite mistake the principles of my composition if you imagine that there is such a thing about me.' After all, there was very little that was false in anything that the signora said. If Mr Slope allowed himself to be deceived it was his own fault. Nothing could have been more open than her declarations about herself.

The little writing table with her desk was still standing before her, a barrier, as it were, against the enemy. She was sitting as nearly upright as she ever did, and he had brought a chair close to the sofa, so that there was only the corner of the table between him and her. It so happened that as she spoke her hand lay upon the table, and as Mr Slope answered her he put his hand upon hers.

'No heart!' said he. 'That is a heavy charge which you bring against yourself, and one of which I cannot find you guilty –'

She withdrew her hand, not quickly and angrily, as though insulted by his touch, but gently and slowly.

'You are in no condition to give a verdict on the matter,' said she, 'as you have not tried me. No; don't say that you intend doing so, for you know you have no intention of the kind; nor indeed have I either. As for you, you will take your vows where they will result in something more substantial than the pursuit of such a ghostlike, ghastly love as mine –'

'Your love should be sufficient to satisfy the dream of a monarch,' said Mr Slope, not quite clear as to the meaning of his words.

'Say an archbishop, Mr Slope,' said she. Poor fellow! she was very cruel to him. He went round again upon his cork on this allusion to his profession. He tried, however, to smile, and gently accused her of joking on a matter, which was, he said, to him of such vital moment.

'Why – what gulls do you men make of us,' she replied. 'How do you fool us to the top of our bent; and of all men you clergymen are the most fluent of your honeyed caressing words. Now look me in the face, Mr Slope, boldly and openly.'

Mr Slope did look at her with a languishing loving eye, and as he did so, he again put forth his hand to get hold of hers.

'I told you to look at me boldly, Mr Slope; but confine your boldness to your eyes.'

'Oh, Madeline!' he sighed.

'Well, my name is Madeline,' said she; 'but none except my own family usually call me so. Now look me in the face, Mr Slope. Am I to understand that you say you love me?'

Mr Slope never had said so. If he had come there with any formed plan at all, his intention was to make love to the lady without uttering any such declaration. It was, however, quite impossible that he should now deny his love. He had, therefore, nothing for it, but to go down on his knees distractedly against the sofa, and swear that he did love her with a love passing the love of man.

The signora received the assurance with very little palpitation or appearance of surprise. 'And now answer me another question,' said she; 'when are you to be married to my dear friend Eleanor Bold?'

Poor Mr Slope went round and round in mortal agony. In such a condition as his it was really very hard for him to know what answer to give. And yet no answer would be his surest condemnation. He might as well at once plead guilty to the charge brought against him.

'And why do you accuse me of such dissimulation?' said he.

'Dissimulation! I said nothing of dissimulation. I made no charge against you, and make none. Pray don't defend yourself to me. You swear that you are devoted to my beauty, and yet you are on the eve of matrimony with another. I feel this is to be rather a compliment. It is to Mrs Bold that you must defend yourself. That you may find difficult; unless, indeed, you can keep her in the dark. You clergymen are cleverer than other men.'

'Signora, I have told you that I loved you, and now you rail at me?'

'Rail at you. God bless the man; what would he have? Come, answer me this at your leisure – not without thinking now, but leisurely and with consideration – Are you not going to be married to Mrs Bold?'

'I am not,' said he. And as he said it, he almost hated, with an exquisite hatred, the woman whom he could not help loving with an exquisite love.

'But surely you are a worshipper of hers?'

'I am not,' said Mr Slope, to whom the word worshipper was peculiarly distasteful. The signora had conceived that it would be so.

'I wonder at that,' said she. 'Do you not admire her? To my eye she is the perfection of English beauty. And then she is rich too. I should have thought she was just the person to attract you. Come, Mr Slope, let me give you advice on this matter. Marry the charming widow! she will be a good mother to your children, and an excellent mistress of a clergyman's household.'

'Oh, signora, how can you be so cruel?'

'Cruel,' said she, changing the voice of banter which she had been using for one which was expressively earnest in its tone; 'is that cruelty?'

'How can I love another, while my heart is entirely your own?'

'If that were cruelty, Mr Slope, what might you say of me if I were to declare that I returned your passion? What would you think if I bound you even by a lover's oath to do daily penance at this couch of mine? What can I give in return for a man's love? Ah, dear friend, you have not realised the conditions of my fate.'

Mr Slope was not on his knees all this time. After his declaration of love he had risen from them as quickly as he thought consistent with the new position which he now filled, and as he stood was leaning on the back of his chair. This outburst of tenderness on the Signora's part quite overcame him, and made him feel for the moment that he could sacrifice everything to be assured of the love of the beautiful creature before him, maimed, lame, and already married as she was,

'And can I not sympathise with your lot,' said he, now seating himself on her sofa, and pushing away the table with his foot.

'Sympathy is so near to pity!' said she. 'If you pity me, cripple as I am, I shall spurn you from me.'

'Oh, Madeline, I will only love you,' and again he caught her hand and devoured it with kisses. Now she did not draw it from him, but sat there as he kissed it, looking at him with her great eyes, just as a great spider would look at a great fly that was quite securely caught.

'Suppose Signor Neroni were to come to Barchester,' said she,' would you make his acquaintance?'

'Signor Neroni!' said he.

'Would you introduce him to the bishop, and Mrs Proudie, and the young ladies?' said she, again having recourse to that horrid quizzing voice which Mr Slope so particularly hated.

'Why do you ask such a question?' said he.

'Because it is necessary that you should know that there is a Signor Neroni. I think you had forgotten it.'

'If I thought that you retained for that wretch one particle of the love of which he was never worthy, I would die before I would distract you by telling you what I feel. No! were your husband the master of your heart, I might perhaps love you; but you should never know it.'

'My heart again! how you talk. And you consider then, that if a husband be not master of his wife's heart, he has no right to her fealty; if a wife ceases to love, she may cease to be true. Is that your doctrine on this matter, as a minister of the Church of England?'

Mr Slope tried hard within himself to cast off the pollution with which he felt that he was defiling his soul. He strove to tear himself away from the noxious siren that had bewitched him. But he could not do it. He could not be again heart free. He had looked for rapturous joy in loving this lovely creature, and he already found that he met with little but disappointment and self-rebuke. He had come across the fruit of the Dead Sea, so sweet and delicious to the eye, so bitter and nauseous to the taste. He had put the apple to his mouth, and it had turned to ashes between his teeth. Yet he could not tear himself away. He knew, he could not but know, that she jeered at him, ridiculed his love, and insulted the weakness of his religion. But she half permitted his adoration, and that half permission added such fuel to his fire that all the fountain of his piety could not quench it. He began to feel savage, irritated, and revengeful. He meditated some severity of speech, some taunt that should cut her, as her taunts cut him. He reflected as he stood there for a moment, silent before her, that if he desired to quell her proud spirit, he should do so by being prouder even than herself; that if he wished to have her at his feet suppliant for his love it behoved him to conquer her by indifference. All this passed through his mind. As far as dead knowledge went, he knew, or thought he knew, how a woman should be tamed. But when he essayed to bring his tactics to bear, he failed like a child. What chance has dead knowledge with experience in any of the transactions between man and man? What possible chance between man and woman? Mr Slope loved furiously, insanely, and truly; but he had never played the game of love. The signora did not love at all, but she was up to every move of the board. It was Philidor pitted against a school-boy.

And so she continued to insult him, and he continued to bear it.

'Sacrifice the world for love!' said she, in answer to some renewed vapid declaration of his passion, 'how often has the same thing been said, and how invariably with the same falsehood!'

'Falsehood,' said he. 'Do you say that I am false to you? do you say that my love is not real?'

'False? of course it is false, false as the father of falsehood – if indeed falsehoods need a sire and are not self-begotten since the world began. You are ready to sacrifice the world for love? Come let us see what you will sacrifice. I care nothing for nuptial vows. The wretch, I think you were kind enough to call him so, whom I swore to love and obey, is so base that he can only be thought of with repulsive disgust. In the council chamber of my heart I have divorced him. To me that is as good as though aged lords had gloated for months over the details of his licentious life. I care nothing for what the world can say. Will you be as frank? Will you take me to your home as your wife? Will you call me Mrs Slope before bishop, dean, and prebendaries?' The poor tortured wretch stood silent, not knowing what to say. 'What! you won't do that. Tell me, what part of the world is it that you will sacrifice for my charms?'

'Were you free to marry, I would take you to my house to-morrow and wish no higher privilege.'

'I am free;' said she, almost starting up in her energy. For though there was no truth in her pretended regard for her clerical admirer, there was a mixture of real feeling in the scorn and satire with which she spoke of love and marriage generally. 'I am free; free as the winds. Come; will you take me as I am? Have your wish sacrifice the world, and prove yourself a true man.'

Mr Slope should have taken her at her word. She would have drawn back, and he would have had the full advantage of the offer. But he did not.

Instead of doing so, he stood wrapt in astonishment, passing his fingers through his lank red hair, and thinking as he stared upon her animated countenance that her wondrous beauty grew more and more wonderful as he gazed on it. 'Ha! ha! ha!' she laughed out loud. 'Come Mr Slope; don't talk of sacrificing the world again. People beyond one-and-twenty should never dream of such a thing. You and I, if we have the dregs of any love left in us, if we have the remnants of a passion remaining in our hearts, should husband our resources better. We are not in our *première jeunesse*. The world is a very nice place. Your world, at any rate, is so. You have all manner of fat rectories to get, and possible bishoprics to enjoy. Come, confess; on second thoughts you would not sacrifice such things for the smiles of a lame lady?'

It was impossible for him to answer this. In order to be in any way dignified, he felt that he must be silent.

'Come,' said she – 'don't boody with me: don't be angry because I speak out some home truths. Alas, the world, as I have found it, has taught me bitter truths. Come, tell me that I am forgiven. Are we not to be friends?' and she again put out her hand to him.

He sat himself down in the chair beside her, and took her proffered hand and leant over her.

'There,' said she, with her sweetest softest smile – a smile to withstand which a man should be cased in triple steel, 'there; seal your forgiveness on it,' and she raised it towards his face. He kissed it again and again, and stretched over her as though desirous of extending the charity of his pardon beyond the hand that was offered to him. She managed, however, to check his ardour. For one so easily allured as this poor chaplain, her hand was surely enough.

'Oh, Madeline!' said he, 'tell me that you love me – do you – do you love me?'

'Hush,' said she. 'There is my mother's step. Our *tête-à-tête* has been of monstrous length. Now you had better go. But we shall see you soon again, shall we not?'

Mr Slope promised that he would call again on the following day.

'And, Mr Slope,' she continued, 'pray answer my note. You have it in your hand, though I declare during these two hours you have not been gracious enough to read it. It is about the Sabbath school and the children. You know how anxious I am to have them here. I have been learning the catechism myself, on purpose. You must manage it for me next week. I will teach them, at any rate, to submit themselves to their spiritual pastors and masters.'

Mr Slope said but little on the subject of Sabbath schools, but he made his adieu, and betook himself home with a sad heart, troubled mind, and uneasy conscience.

✖ TWENTY-EIGHT ✖

Mrs Bold is Entertained by Dr and Mrs Grantly at Plumstead

IT WILL BE REMEMBERED THAT MR SLOPE, when leaving his *billet doux* at the house of Mrs Bold, had been informed that it would be sent out to her at Plumstead that afternoon. The archdeacon and Mr Harding had in fact come into town together in the brougham, and it had been arranged that they should call for Eleanor's parcels as they left on their way home. Accordingly they did so call, and the maid, as she handed to the coachman a small basket and large bundle carefully and neatly packed, gave in at the carriage window Mr Slope's epistle. The archdeacon, who was sitting next to the window, took it, and immediately recognised the hand-writing of his enemy.

'Who left this?' said he.

'Mr Slope called with it himself, your reverence,' said the girl; 'and was very anxious that missus should have it to-day.'

So the brougham drove off, and the letter was left in the archdeacon's hand. He looked at it as though he held a basket of adders. He could not have thought worse of the document had he read it and discovered it to be licentious and atheistical. He did, moreover, what so many wise people are accustomed to do in similar circumstances; he immediately condemned the person to whom the letter was written, as though she were necessarily a *particeps criminis*.

Poor Mr Harding, though by no means inclined to forward Mr Slope's intimacy with his daughter, would have given anything to have kept the letter from his son-in-law. But that was now impossible. There it was in his hand; and he looked as thoroughly disgusted as though he were quite sure that it contained all the rhapsodies of a favoured lover.

'It's very hard on me,' said he, after awhile, 'that this should go on under my roof.'

Now here the archdeacon was certainly most unreasonablable. Having invited his sister-in-law to his house, it was a natural consequence that she should receive her letters there. And if Mr Slope chose to write to her, his letter would, as a matter of course, be sent after her. Moreover, the very fact of an invitation to one's house implies confidence on the part of the inviter. He had shown that he thought Mrs Bold to be a fit person to stay with him by his asking her to do so, and it was most cruel to her that he should complain of her violating the sanctity of his roof-tree, when the laches committed were none of her committing.

Mr Harding felt this; and felt also that when the archdeacon talked thus about his roof, what he said was most offensive to himself as Eleanor's father. If Eleanor did receive a letter from Mr Slope, what was there in that to pollute the purity of Dr Grantly's household? He was indignant that his daughter should be so judged and so spoken of; and he made up his mind that even as Mrs Slope she must be dearer to him than any other creature on God's earth. He almost broke out, and said as much; but for the moment he restrained himself.

'Here,' said the archdeacon, handing the offensive missile to his father-in-law; 'I am not going to be the bearer of his love letters. You are her father, and may do as you think fit with it.'

By doing as he thought fit with it, the archdeacon certainly meant that Mr Harding would be justified in opening and reading the letter, and taking any steps which might in consequence be necessary. To tell the truth, Dr Grantly did feel rather a stronger curiosity than was justified by his outraged virtue, to see the contents of the letter. Of course he could not open it himself, but he wished to make Mr Harding understand that he, as Eleanor's father, would be fully justified in doing so. The idea of such a proceeding never occurred to Mr Harding. His authority over Eleanor ceased when she became the wife of John Bold. He had not the slightest wish to pry into her correspondence. He consequently put the letter into his pocket, and only wished that he had been able to do so without the archdeacon's knowledge. They both sat silent during half the journey home, and then Dr Grantly said, 'Perhaps Susan had better give it to her. She can explain to her sister, better than either you or I can do, how deep is the disgrace of such an acquaintance.'

'I think you are very hard upon Eleanor,' replied Mr Harding. 'I will not allow that she has disgraced herself, nor do I think it likely that she will do so. She has a right to correspond with whom she pleases, and I shall not take upon myself to blame her because she gets a letter from Slope.'

'I suppose,' said Dr Grantly, 'you don't wish her to marry the man. I suppose you'll admit that she would disgrace herself if she did do so.'

'I do not wish her to marry him,' said the perplexed father; 'I do not like him, and do not think he would make a good husband. But if Eleanor chooses to do so, I shall certainly not think that she disgraces herself.'

'Good heavens!' exclaimed Dr Grantly, and threw himself back into the corner of his brougham. Mr Harding said nothing more, but commenced playing a dirge, with an imaginary fiddle bow upon an imaginary violoncello, for which there did not appear to be quite room enough in the carriage; and he continued the tune, with sundry variations, till he arrived at the rectory door.

The archdeacon had been meditating sad things in his mind. Hitherto he had always looked on his father-in-law as a true partisan, though he knew him to be a man devoid of all the combative qualifications for that character. He had felt no fear that Mr Harding would go over to the enemy, though he had never counted much on the ex-warden's prowess in breaking the hostile ranks. Now, however, it seemed that Eleanor, with her wiles, had completely trepanned and bewildered her father, cheated him out of his judgment, robbed him of the predilections and tastes of his life, and caused him to be tolerant of a man whose arrogance and vulgarity would, a few years since, have been unendurable to him. That the whole thing was as good as arranged between Eleanor and Mr Slope there was no longer any room to doubt. That Mr Harding knew that such was the case, even this could hardly be doubted. It was too manifest that he at any rate suspected it, and was prepared to sanction it.

And to tell the truth, such was the case. Mr Harding disliked Mr Slope as much as it was in his nature to dislike any man. Had his daughter wished to do her worst to displease him by a second marriage, she could hardly have succeeded better than by marrying Mr Slope. But, as he said to himself now very often, what right had he to condemn her if she did nothing that was really wrong? If she liked Mr Slope it was her affair. It was indeed miraculous to him that a woman with such a mind, so educated, so refined, so nice in her tastes, should like such a man. Then he asked himself whether it was possible that she did so?

Ah, thou weak man; most charitable, most Christian, but weakest of men! Why couldst thou not have asked herself? Was she not the daughter of thy loins, the child of thy heart, the best beloved to thee of all humanity? Had she not proved to thee, by years of closest affection, her truth and goodness and filial obedience? And yet, knowing and feeling all this, thou couldst endure to go groping in darkness, hearing her named in strains which wounded thy loving heart, and being unable to defend her as thou shouldst have done!

Mr Harding had not believed, did not believe, that his daughter meant to marry this man; but he feared to commit himself to such an opinion. If she did do it there would be then no means of retreat. The wishes of his heart were – First, that there should be no truth in the archdeacon's surmises; and in this wish he would have fain trusted entirely, had he dared so to do; Secondly, that the match might be prevented, if unfortunately, it had been contemplated by Eleanor; Thirdly, that should she be so infatuated as to marry this man, he might justify his conduct, and declare that no cause existed for his separating himself from her.

He wanted to believe her incapable of such a marriage; he wanted to show that he so believed of her; but he wanted also to be able to say hereafter, that she had done nothing amiss, if she should unfortunately prove herself to be different from what he thought her to be.

Nothing but affection could justify such fickleness; but affection did justify it. There was but little of the Roman about Mr Harding. He could not sacrifice his Lucretia even though she should be polluted by the accepted addresses of the clerical Tarquin at the palace. If Tarquin could be prevented, well and good; but if not, the father would still open his heart to his daughter, and accept her as she presented herself, Tarquin and all.

Dr Grantly's mind was of a stronger calibre, and he was by no means deficient in heart. He loved with an honest genuine love his wife and children and friends. He loved his father-in-law; and was quite prepared to love Eleanor too, if she would be one of his party, if she would be on his side, if she would regard the Slopes and the Proudies as the enemies of mankind, and acknowledge and feel the comfortable merits of the Gwynnes and Arabins. He wished to be what he called 'safe' with all those whom he had admitted to the penetralia of his house and heart. He could luxuriate in no society that was deficient in a certain feeling of a faithful staunch high-churchism, which to him was tantamount to freemasonry. He was not strict in his lines of definition. He endured without impatience many different shades of Anglo-church conservatism; but with the Slopes and Proudies he could not go on all fours.

He was wanting in, moreover, or perhaps it would be more correct to say, he was not troubled by that womanly tenderness which was so peculiar to Mr Harding. His feelings towards his friends were, that while they stuck to him he would stick to them; that he would work with them shoulder and shoulder; that he would be faithful to the faithful. He knew nothing of that beautiful love which can be true to a false friend.

And thus these two men, each miserable enough in his own way, returned to Plumstead.

It was getting late when they arrived there, and the ladies had already gone up to dress. Nothing more was said as the two parted in the hall. As Mr Harding passed to his own room he knocked at Eleanor's door and handed in the letter. The archdeacon hurried to his own territory, there to unburden his heart to his faithful partner.

What colloquy took place between the marital chamber and the adjoining dressing-room shall not be detailed. The reader, now intimate with the persons concerned, can well imagine it. The whole tenor of it also might be read in Mrs Grantly's brow as she came down to dinner.

Eleanor, when she received the letter from her father's hand, had no idea from whom it came. She had never seen Mr Slope's hand-writing, or if so had forgotten it; and did not think of him as she twisted the letter as people do twist letters when they do not immediately recognise their correspondents either by the writing or the seal. She was sitting at her glass brushing her hair, and rising every other minute to play with her boy who was sprawling on the bed, and who engaged pretty nearly the whole attention of the maid as well as of his mother.

At last, sitting before her toilet table, she broke the seal, and turning over the leaf saw Mr Slope's name. She first felt surprised, and then annoyed, and then anxious. As she read it she became interested. She was so delighted to find that all obstacles to her father's return to the hospital were apparently removed that she did not observe the fulsome language in which the tidings were conveyed. She merely perceived that she was commissioned to tell her father that such was the case, and she did not realise the fact that such a communication should not have been made, in the first instance, to her by an unmarried young clergyman. She felt, on the whole, grateful to Mr Slope, and anxious to get on her dress that she might run with the news to her father. Then she came to the allusion to her own pious labours, and she said in her heart that Mr Slope was an affected ass. Then she went on again and was offended by her boy being called Mr Slope's darling – he was nobody's darling but her own; or at any rate not the darling of a disagreeable stranger like Mr Slope. Lastly she arrived at the tresses and felt a qualm of disgust. She looked up in the glass, and there they were before long her, long and silken, certainly, and very beautiful. I will not say but that she knew them to be so, but she felt angry with them and brushed them roughly and carelessly. She crumpled the letter up with angry violence, and resolved, almost without thinking of it, that she would not show it to her father. She would merely tell him the contents of it. She then comforted herself again with her boy, had her dress fastened, and went down to dinner.

As she tripped down the stairs she began to ascertain that there was some difficulty in her situation. She could not keep from her father the news about the hospital, nor could she comfortably confess the letter from Mr Slope before the Grantlys. Her father had already gone down. She had heard his step upon the lobby. She resolved therefore to take him aside, and tell him her little bit of news. Poor girl! she had no idea how severely the unfortunate letter had already been discussed.

When she entered the drawing-room the whole party were there, including Mr Arabin, and the whole party looked glum and sour. The two girls sat silent and apart as though they were aware that something was wrong. Even Mr Arabin was solemn and silent. Eleanor had not seen him since breakfast. He had been the whole day at St Ewold's, and such having been the case it was natural that he should tell how matters were going on there. He did nothing of the kind, however, but remained solemn and silent. They were all solemn and silent. Eleanor knew in her heart that they had been talking about her, and her heart misgave her as she thought of Mr Slope and his letter. At any rate she felt it to be quite impossible to speak to her father alone while matters were in this state.

Dinner was soon announced, and Dr Grantly, as was his wont, gave Eleanor his arm. But he did so as though the doing it were an outrage on his feelings rendered necessary by sternest necessity. With quick sympathy Eleanor felt this, and hardly put her fingers on his coat sleeve. It may be guessed in what way the dinner-hour was passed. Dr Grantly said a few words to Mr Arabin, Mr Arabin said a few words to her father, and he tried to say a few words to Eleanor. She felt that she had been tried and found guilty of something, though she knew not what. She longed to say out to them all, 'Well, what is it that I have done; out with it, and let me know my crime; for heaven's sake let me hear the worst of it;' but she could not. She could say nothing, but sat there silent, half feeling that she was guilty, and trying in vain to pretend even to eat her dinner.

At last the cloth was drawn, and the ladies were not long following it. When they were gone the gentlemen were somewhat more sociable but not much so. They could not of course talk over Eleanor's sins. The archdeacon had indeed so far betrayed his sister-in-law as to whisper into Mr Arabin's ear in the study, as they met there before dinner, a hint of what he feared. He did so with the gravest and saddest of fears, and Mr Arabin became grave and apparently sad enough as he heard it. He opened his eyes and his mouth and said in a sort of whisper 'Mr Slope!' in the same way as he might have said 'The Cholera!' had his friend told him that that horrid disease was in his nursery. 'I fear so, I fear so,' said the archdeacon, and then together they left the room.

We will not accurately analyse Mr Arabin's feelings on receipt of such astounding tidings. It will suffice to say that he was surprised, vexed, sorrowful, and ill at ease. He had not perhaps thought very much about Eleanor, but he had appreciated her influence, and had felt that close intimacy with her in a country house was pleasant to him, and also beneficial. He had spoken highly of her intelligence to the archdeacon, and had walked about the shrubberies with her, carrying her boy on his back. When Mr Arabin had called Johnny his darling, Eleanor was not angry.

Thus the three men sat over their wine, all thinking of the same subject, but unable to speak of it to each other. So we will leave them, and follow the ladies into the drawing-room.

Mrs Grantly had received a commission from her husband, and had undertaken it with some unwillingness. He had desired her to speak gravely to Eleanor, and to tell her that, if she persisted in her adherence to Mr Slope, she could no longer look for the countenance of her present friends. Mrs Grantly probably knew her sister better than the doctor did, and assured him that it would be in vain to talk to her. The only course likely to be of any service in her opinion was to keep Eleanor away from Barchester. Perhaps she might have added, for she had a very keen eye in such things, that there might also be ground for hope in keeping Eleanor near Mr Arabin. Of this, however, she said nothing. But the archdeacon would not be talked over; he spoke much of his conscience, and declared that if Mrs Grantly would not do it he would. So instigated, the lady undertook the task, stating, however, her full conviction that her interference would be worse than useless. And so it proved.

As soon as they were in the drawing-room Mrs Grantly found some excuse for sending her girls away, and then began her task. She knew well that she could exercise but very slight authority over her sister. Their various modes of life, and the distance between their residences, had prevented any very close confidence. They had hardly lived together since Eleanor was a child. Eleanor had moreover, especially in latter years, resented in a quiet sort of way the dictatorial authority which the archdeacon seemed to exercise over her father, and on this account had been unwilling to allow the archdeacon's wife to exercise authority over herself.

'You got a note just before dinner, I believe,' began the eldest sister.

Eleanor acknowledged that she had done so, and felt that she turned red as she acknowledged it. She would have given anything to have kept her colour, but the more she tried to do so the more signally she failed.

'Was it not from Mr Slope?'

Eleanor said that the letter was from Mr Slope.

'Is he a regular correspondent of yours, Eleanor?'

'Not exactly,' said she, already beginning to feel angry at the cross-examination. She determined, and why it would be difficult to say, that nothing should induce her to tell her sister Susan what was the subject of the letter. Mrs Grantly, she knew, was intimidated by the archdeacon, and she would not plead to any arraignment made against her by him.

'But, Eleanor dear, why do you get letters from Mr Slope at all, knowing, as you do, he is a person so distasteful to papa, and to the archdeacon, and indeed to all your friends?'

'In the first place, Susan, I don't get letters from him; and in the next place, as Mr Slope wrote the one letter which I have got, and as I only received it, which I could not very well help doing, as papa handed it to me, I think you had better ask Mr Slope instead of me.'

'What was his letter about, Eleanor?'

'I cannot tell you,' said she, 'because it was confidential. It was on business respecting a third person.'

'It was in no way personal to yourself, then?'

'I won't exactly say that, Susan,' said she, getting more and more angry at her sister's questions.

'Well, I must say it's rather singular,' said Mrs Grantly, affecting to laugh, 'that a young lady in your position should receive a letter from an unmarried gentleman of which she will not tell the contents, and which she is ashamed to show to her sister.'

'I am not ashamed,' said Eleanor blazing up; 'I am not ashamed of anything in the matter; only I do not choose to be cross-examined as to my letters by any one.'

'Well, dear,' said the other, 'I cannot but tell you that I do not think Mr Slope a proper correspondent for you.'

'If he be ever so improper, how can I help his having written to me? But you are all prejudiced against him to such an extent, that that which would be kind and generous in another man is odious and impudent in him. I hate a religion that teaches one to be so onesided in one's charity.'

'I am sorry, Eleanor, that you hate the religion you find here; but surely you should remember that in such matters the archdeacon must know more of the world than you do. I don't ask you to respect or comply with me, although I am, unfortunately, so many years your senior; but surely, in such a matter as this, you might consent to be guided by the archdeacon. He is most anxious to be your friend if you will let him.'

'In such a matter as what?' said Eleanor very testily. 'Upon my word I don't know what this is all about.'

'We all want you to drop Mr Slope.'

'You all want me to be as illiberal as yourselves. That I shall never be. I see no harm in Mr Slope's acquaintance, and I shall not insult the man by telling him that I do. He has thought it necessary to write to me, and I do not want the archdeacon's advice about the letter. If I did I would ask it.'

'Then, Eleanor, it is my duty to tell you,' and now she spoke with a tremendous gravity, 'that the archdeacon thinks that such a correspondence is disgraceful, and that he cannot allow it to go on in his house.'

Eleanor's eyes flashed fire as she answered her sister, jumping up from her seat as she did so. 'You may tell the archdeacon that wherever I am I shall receive what letters I please and from whom I please. And as for the word disgraceful, if Dr Grantly has used it of me he has been unmanly and inhospitable,' and she walked off to the door. 'When papa comes from the dining-room I will thank you to ask him to step up to my bed-room. I will show him Mr Slope's letter, but I will show it to no one else.' And so saying she retreated to her baby.

She had no conception of the crime with which she was charged. The idea that she could be thought by her friends to regard Mr Slope as a lover, had never flashed upon her. She conceived that they were all prejudiced and illiberal in their persecution of him, and therefore she would not join in the persecution, even though she greatly disliked the man.

Eleanor was very angry as she seated herself in a low chair by her open window at the foot of her child's bed. 'To dare to say I have disgraced myself,' she repeated to herself more than once. 'How papa can put up with that man's arrogance! I will certainly not sit down to dinner in his house again unless he begs my pardon for that word.' And then a thought struck her that Mr Arabin might perchance hear of her 'disgraceful' correspondence with Mr Slope, and she turned crimson with pure vexation. Oh, if she had known the truth? If she could have conceived that Mr Arabin had been informed as a fact that she was going to marry Mr Slope!

She had not been long in her room before her father joined her. As he left the drawing-room Mrs Grantly took her husband into the recess of the window, and told him how signally she had failed.

'I will speak to her myself before I go to bed,' said the archdeacon.

'Pray do no such thing,' said she; 'you can do no good and will only make an unseemly quarrel in the house. You have no idea how headstrong she can be.'

The archdeacon declared that as to that he was quite indifferent. He knew his duty and would do it. Mr Harding was weak in the extreme in such matters. He would not have it hereafter on his conscience that he had not done all that in him lay to prevent so disgraceful an alliance. It was in vain that Mrs Grantly assured him that speaking to Eleanor angrily would only hasten such a crisis, and render it certain if at present there were any doubt. He was angry, self-willed, and sore. The fact that a lady of his household had received a letter from Mr Slope had wounded his pride in the sorest place, and nothing could control him.

Mr Harding looked worn and woebegone as he entered his daughter's room. These sorrows worried him sadly. He felt that if they were continued he must go to the wall in the manner so kindly prophesied to him by the chaplain. He knocked gently at his daughter's door, waited till he was distinctly bade to enter, and then appeared as though he and not she were the suspected criminal.

Eleanor's arm was soon within his, and she had soon kissed his forehead and caressed him, not with joyous but with eager love. 'Oh, papa,' she said, 'I do so want to speak to you. They have been talking about me down stairs to-night; don't you know they have, papa?'

Mr Harding confessed with a sort of murmur that the archdeacon had been speaking of her.

'I shall hate Dr Grantly soon –'

'Oh my dear!'

'Well; I shall. I cannot help it. He is so uncharitable, so unkind, so suspicious of every one that does not worship himself: and then he is so monstrously arrogant to other people who have a right to their opinions as well as he has to his own.'

'He is an earnest eager man, my dear: but he never means to be unkind.'

'He is unkind, papa, most unkind. There, I got that letter from Mr Slope before dinner. It was you yourself who gave it to me. There; pray read it. It is all for you. It should have been addressed to you. You know how they have been talking about it down stairs. You know how they behaved to me at dinner. And since dinner Susan has been preaching to me, till I could not remain in the room with her. Read it, papa; and then say whether that is a letter that need make Mr Grantly so outrageous.'

Mr Harding took his arm from his daughter's waist, and slowly read the letter. She expected to see his countenance lit with joy as he learnt that his path back to the hospital was made so smooth; but she was doomed to disappointment, as had once been the case before on a somewhat similar occasion. His first feeling was one of unmitigated disgust that Mr Slope should have chosen to interfere in his behalf. He had been anxious to get back to the hospital, but he would have infinitely sooner resigned all pretensions to the place, than have owed it in any manner to Mr Slope's influence in his favour. Then he thoroughly disliked the tone of Mr Slope's letter; it was unctuous, false, and unwholesome, like the man. He saw, which Eleanor had failed to see, that much more had been intended than was expressed. The appeal to Eleanor's pious labours as separate from his own grated sadly against his feelings as a father. And then when he came to the 'darling boy' and the 'silken tresses,' he slowly closed and folded the letter in despair. It was impossible that Mr Slope should so write unless he had been encouraged. It was impossible Eleanor should have received such a letter, and have received it without annoyance, unless she were willing to encourage him. So at least Mr Harding argued to himself.

How hard it is to judge accurately of the feelings of others. Mr Harding, as he came to the close of the letter, in his heart condemned his daughter for indelicacy, and it made him miserable to do so. She was not responsible for what Mr Slope might write. True. But then she expressed no disgust at it. She had rather expressed approval of the letter as a whole. She had given it to him to read, as a vindication for herself and also for him. The father's spirits sank within him as he felt that he could not acquit her.

And yet it was the true feminine delicacy of Eleanor's mind which brought her on this condemnation. Listen to me, ladies, and I beseech *you* to acquit her. She thought of this man, this lover of whom she was so unconscious, exactly as her father did, exactly as the Grantlys did. At least she esteemed him personally as they did. But she believed him to be in the main an honest man, and one truly inclined to assist her father. She felt herself bound, after what had passed, to show this letter to Mr Harding. She thought it necessary that he should know what Mr Slope had to say. But she did not think it necessary to apologise for, or condemn, or even allude to the vulgarity of the man's tone, which arose, as does all vulgarity, from ignorance. It was nauseous to her to have a man like Mr Slope commenting on her personal attractions; and she did not think it necessary to dilate with her father upon what was nauseous. She never supposed they could disagree on such a subject. It would have been painful for her to point it out, painful for her to speak strongly against a man of whom, on the whole, she was anxious to think and speak well. In encountering such a man she had encountered what was disagreeable, as she might do in walking the streets. But in such encounters she never thought it necessary to dwell on what disgusted her.

And he, foolish weak loving man, would not say one word, though one word would have cleared up everything. There would have been a deluge of tears, and in ten minutes every one in the house would have understood how matters really were. The father would have been delighted. The sister would have kissed her sister and begged a thousand pardons. The archdeacon would have apologised and wondered, and raised his eyebrows, and gone to bed a happy man. And Mr Arabin – Mr Arabin would have dreamt of Eleanor, have awoke in the morning with ideas of love, and retired to rest the next evening with schemes of marriage. But, alas! all this was not to be.

Mr Harding slowly folded the letter, handed it back to her, kissed her forehead and bade God bless her. He then crept slowly away to his own room.

As soon as he had left the passage another knock was given at Eleanor's door, and Mrs Grantly's very demure own maid, entering on tiptoe, wanted to know would Mrs Bold be so kind as to speak to the archdeacon for two minutes, in the archdeacon's study, if not disagreeable. The archdeacon's compliments, and he wouldn't detain her two minutes.

Eleanor thought it was very disagreeable; she was tired and fagged and sick at heart; her present feelings towards Dr Grantly were anything but those of affection. She was, however, no coward, and therefore promised to be in the study in five minutes. So she arranged her hair, tied on her cap, and went down with a palpitating heart.

❋ TWENTY-NINE ❋

A Serious Interview

THERE ARE PEOPLE WHO DELIGHT IN SERIOUS interviews, especially when to them appertains the part of offering advice or administering rebuke, and perhaps the archdeacon was one of these. Yet on this occasion he did not prepare himself for the coming conversation with much anticipation of pleasure. Whatever might be his faults he was not an inhospitable man, and he almost felt that he was sinning against hospitality in upbraiding Eleanor in his own house. Then, also he was not quite sure that he would get the best of it. His wife had told him that he decidedly would not, and he usually gave credit to what his wife said. He was, however, so convinced of what he considered to be the impropriety of Eleanor's conduct, and so assured also of his own duty in trying to check it, that his conscience would not allow him to take his wife's advice and go to bed quietly.

Eleanor's face as she entered the room was not such as to reassure him. As a rule she was always mild in manner and gentle in conduct; but there was that in her eye which made it not an easy task to scold her. In truth she had been little used to scolding. No one since her childhood had tried it but the archdeacon, and he had generally failed when he did try it. He had never done so since her marriage; and now, when he saw her quiet easy step, as she entered his room, he almost wished that he had taken his wife's advice.

He began by apologising for the trouble he was giving her. She begged him not to mention it, assured him that walking down stairs was no trouble to her at all, and then took a seat and waited impatiently for him to begin his attack.

'My dear Eleanor,' he said, 'I hope you believe me when I assure you that you have no sincerer friend than I am.' To this Eleanor answered nothing, and therefore he proceeded. 'If you had a brother of your own I should not probably trouble you with what I am going to say. But as it is I cannot but think that it must be a comfort to you to know that you have near you one who is as anxious for your welfare as any brother of your own could be.'

'I never had a brother,' said she.

'I know you never had, and it is therefore that I speak to you.'

'I never had a brother,' she repeated; 'but I have hardly felt the want. Papa has been to me both father and brother.'

'Your father is the fondest and most affectionate of men. But –'

'He is – the fondest and most affectionate of men, and the best of counsellors. While he lives I can never want advice.'

This rather put the archdeacon out. He could not exactly contradict what his sister-in-law said about her father; and yet he did not at all agree with her. He wanted her to understand that he tendered his assistance because her father was a soft good-natured gentleman, not sufficiently knowing in the ways of the world; but he could not say this to her. So he had to rush into the subject-matter of his proffered counsel without any acknowledgement on her part that she could need it, or would be grateful for it.

'Susan tells me that you received a letter this evening from Mr Slope.'

'Yes; papa brought it in the brougham. Did he not tell you?'

'And Susan says that you objected to let her know what it was about.'

'I don't think she asked me. But had she done so I should not have told her. I don't think it nice to be asked about one's letters. If one wishes to show them one does so without being asked.'

'True. Quite so. What you say is quite true. But is not the fact of your receiving letters from Mr Slope, which you do not wish to show to your friends, a circumstance which must excite some – some surprise – some suspicion –'

'Suspicion!' said she, not speaking above her usual voice, speaking still in a soft womanly tone, but yet with indignation; 'suspicion! and who suspects me, and of what?' And then there was a pause, for the archdeacon was not quite ready to explain the ground of his suspicion. 'No, Dr Grantly, I did not choose to show Mr Slope's letter to Susan. I could not show it to any one till papa had seen it. If you have any wish to read it now, you can do so,' and she handed the letter to him over the table.

This was an amount of compliance which he had not at all expected, and which rather upset him in his tactics. However, he took the letter, perused it carefully, and then refolding it, kept it on the table under his hand. To him it appeared to be in almost every respect the letter of a declared lover; it seemed to corroborate his worst suspicions; and the fact of Eleanor's showing it to him was all but tantamount to a declaration on her part, that it was her pleasure to receive love-letters from Mr Slope. He almost entirely overlooked the real subject-matter of the epistle; so intent was he on the forthcoming courtship and marriage.

'I'll thank you to give it me back, if you please, Dr Grantly.'

He took it in his hand and held it up, but made no immediate overture to return it. 'And Mr Harding has seen this?' said he.

'Of course he has,' said she; 'it was written that he might see it. It refers solely to his business – of course I showed it to him.'

'And, Eleanor, do you think that that is a proper letter for you – for a person in your condition – to receive from Mr Slope?'

'Quite a proper letter,' said she, speaking, perhaps, a little out of obstinacy; probably forgetting at the moment the objectionable mention of her silken curls.

'Then, Eleanor, it is my duty to tell you that I wholly differ from you.'

'So I suppose,' said she, instigated now by sheer opposition and determination not to succumb. 'You think Mr Slope is a messenger direct from Satan. I think he is an industrious, well meaning clergyman. It's a pity that we differ as we do. But, as we do differ, we had probably better not talk about it.'

Here Eleanor undoubtedly put herself in the wrong. She might probably have refused to talk to Dr Grantly on the matter in dispute without any impropriety; but having consented to listen to him, she had no business to tell him that he regarded Mr Slope as an emissary from the evil one; nor was she justified in praising Mr Slope, seeing that in her heart of hearts she did not think well of him. She was, however, wounded in spirit, and angry and bitter. She had been subjected to contumely and cross-questioning and ill-usage through the whole evening. No one, not even Mr Arabin, not even her father, had been kind to her. All this she attributed to the prejudice and conceit of the archdeacon, and therefore she resolved to set no bounds to her antagonism to him. She would neither give nor take quarter. He had greatly presumed in daring to question her about her correspondence, and she was determined to show that she thought so.

'Eleanor, you are forgetting yourself,' said he, looking very sternly at her. 'Otherwise you would never tell me that I conceive any man to be a messenger from Satan.'

'But you do,' said she. 'Nothing is too bad for him. Give me that letter, if you please;' and she stretched out her hand and took it from him. 'He has been doing his best to serve papa, doing more than any of papa's friends could do; and yet, because he is the chaplain of a bishop whom you don't like, you speak of him as though he had no right to the usage of a gentleman.'

'He has done nothing for your father.'

'I believe that he has done a great deal; and, as far as I am concerned, I am grateful to him. Nothing that you can say can prevent my being so. I judge people by their acts, and his, as far as I can see them, are good.' She then paused for a moment. 'If you have nothing further to say, I shall be obliged by being permitted to say good night – I am very tired.'

Dr Grantly had, as he thought, done his best to be gracious to his sister-in-law. He had endeavoured not to be harsh to her, and had striven to pluck the sting from his rebuke. But he did not intend that she should leave him without hearing him.

'I have something to say, Eleanor; and I fear I must trouble you to hear it. You profess that it is quite proper that you should receive from Mr Slope such letters as that you have in your hand. Susan and I think very differently. You are, of course, your own mistress, and much as we both must grieve should anything separate you from us, we have no power to prevent you from taking steps which may lead to such a separation. If you are so wilful as to reject the counsel of your friends, you must be allowed to cater for yourself. But Eleanor, I may at any rate ask you this. Is it worth your while to break away from all those you have loved – from all who love you – for the sake of Mr Slope?'

'I don't know what you mean, Dr Grantly; I don't know what you're talking about. I don't want to break away from anybody.'

'But you will do so if you connect yourself with Mr Slope. Eleanor, I must speak out to you. You must choose between your sister and myself and our friends, and Mr Slope and his friends. I say nothing of your father, as you may probably understand his feelings better than I do.'

'What do you mean, Dr Grantly? What am I to understand? I never heard such wicked prejudice in my life.'

'It is no prejudice, Eleanor. I have known the world longer than you have done. Mr Slope is altogether beneath you. You ought to know and feel that he is so. Pray – pray think of this before it is too late.'

'Too late!'

'Or if you will not believe me, ask Susan; you cannot think she is prejudiced against you. Or even consult your father, he is not prejudiced against you. Ask Mr Arabin –'

'You haven't spoken to Mr Arabin about this!' said she, jumping up and standing before him.

'Eleanor, all the world in and about Barchester will be speaking of it soon.'

'But have you spoken to Mr Arabin about me and Mr Slope?'

'Certainly I have, and he quite agrees with me.'

'Agrees with what?' said she. 'I think you are trying to drive me mad.'

'He agrees with me and Susan that it is quite impossible you should be received at Plumstead as Mrs Slope.'

Not being favourites with the tragic muse we do not dare to attempt any description of Eleanor's face when she first heard the name of Mrs Slope pronounced as that which would or should or might at some time appertain to herself. The look, such as it was, Dr Grantly did not soon forget. For a moment or two she could find no words to express her deep anger and deep disgust; and, indeed, at this conjuncture, words did not come to her very freely.

'How dare you be so impertinent?' at last she said; and then hurried out of the room, without giving the archdeacon the opportunity of uttering another word. It was with difficulty she contained herself till she reached her own room; and then locking the door, she threw herself on her bed and sobbed as though her heart would break.

But even yet she had no conception of the truth. She had no idea that her father and her sister had for days past conceived in sober earnest the idea that she was going to marry this man. She did not even then believe that the archdeacon thought that she would do so. By some manœuvre of her brain, she attributed the origin of the accusation to Mr Arabin, and as she did so her anger against him was excessive, and the vexation of her spirit almost unendurable. She could not bring herself to think that the charge was made seriously. It appeared to her most probable that the archdeacon and Mr Arabin had talked over her objectionable acquaintance with Mr Slope; that Mr Arabin, in his jeering, sarcastic way, had suggested the odious match as being the severest way of treating with contumely her acquaintance with his enemy; and that the archdeacon, taking the idea from him, thought proper to punish her by the allusion. The whole night she lay awake thinking of what had been said, and this appeared to be the most probable solution.

But the reflection that Mr Arabin should have in any way mentioned her name in connection with that of Mr Slope was overpowering; and the spiteful ill-nature of the archdeacon, in repeating the charge to her, made her wish to leave his house almost before the day had broken. One thing was certain: nothing should make her stay there beyond the following morning, and nothing should make her sit down to breakfast in company with Dr Grantly. When she thought of the man whose name had been linked with her own, she cried from sheer disgust. It was only because she would be thus disgusted, thus pained and shocked and cut to the quick, that the archdeacon had spoken the horrid word. He wanted to make her quarrel with Mr Slope, and therefore he had outraged her by his abominable vulgarity. She determined that at any rate he should know that she appreciated it.

Nor was the archdeacon a bit better satisfied with the result of his serious interview than was Eleanor. He gathered from it, as indeed he could hardly fail to do, that she was very angry with him; but he thought that she was thus angry, not because she was suspected of an intention to marry Mr Slope, but because such an intention was imputed to her as a crime. Dr Grantly regarded this supposed union with disgust; but it never occurred to him that Eleanor was outraged, because she looked at it exactly in the same light.

He returned to his wife vexed and somewhat disconsolate, but, neverthe-less, confirmed in his wrath against his sister-in-law. 'Her whole behaviour,' said he, 'has been most objectionable. She handed me his love letter to read as though she were proud of it. And she is proud of it. She is proud of having this slavering, greedy man at her feet. She will throw herself and John Bold's money into his lap; she will ruin her boy, disgrace her father and you, and be a wretched miserable woman.'

His spouse who was sitting at her toilet table, continued her avocations, making no answer to all this. She had known that the archdeacon would gain nothing by interfering; but she was too charitable to provoke him by saying so while he was in such deep sorrow.

'This comes of a man making such a will as that of Bold's,' he continued. 'Eleanor is no more fitted to be trusted with such an amount of money in her own hands than is a charity-school girl.' Still Mrs Grantly made no reply. 'But I have done my duty; I can do nothing further. I have told her plainly that she cannot be allowed to form a link of connection between me and that man. From henceforward it will not be in my power to make her welcome at Plumstead. I cannot have Mr Slope's love letters coming here. Susan, I think you had better let her understand that as her mind on this subject seems to be irrevocably fixed, it will be better for all parties that she should return to Barchester.'

Now Mrs Grantly was angry with Eleanor, nearly as angry as her husband; but she had no idea of turning her sister out of the house. She, therefore, at length spoke out, and explained to the archdeacon in her own mild seducing way, that he was fuming and fussing and fretting himself very unnecessarily. She declared that things, if left alone, would arrange themselves much better than he could arrange them; and at last succeeded in inducing him to go to bed in a somewhat less inhospitable state of mind.

On the following morning Eleanor's maid was commissioned to send word into the dining-room that her mistress was not well enough to attend prayers, and that she would breakfast in her own room. Here she was visited by her father and declared to him her intention of returning immediately to Barchester. He was hardly surprised by the announcement. All the household seemed to be aware that something had gone wrong. Every one walked about with subdued feet, and people's shoes seemed to creak more than usual. There was a look of conscious intelligence on the faces of the women: and the men attempted, but in vain, to converse as though nothing were the matter. All this had weighed heavily on the heart of Mr Harding; and when Eleanor told him that her immediate return to Barchester was a necessity, he merely sighed piteously, and said that he would be ready to accompany her.

But here she objected strenuously. She had a great wish, she said, to go alone; a great desire that it might be seen that her father was not implicated in her quarrel with Dr Grantly. To this at last he gave way; but not a word passed between them about Mr Slope – not a word was said, not a question asked as to the serious interview on the preceding evening. There was, indeed, very little confidence between them, though neither of them knew why it should be so. Eleanor once asked him whether he would not call upon the bishop; but he answered rather tartly that he did not know – he did not think he should, but he could not say just at present. And so they parted. Each was miserably anxious for some show of affection, for some return of confidence, for some sign of the feeling that usually bound them together. But none was given. The father could not bring himself to question his daughter about her supposed lover; and the daughter would not sully her mouth by repeating the odious word with which Dr Grantly had roused her wrath. And so they parted.

There was some trouble in arranging the method of Eleanor's return. She begged her father to send for a postchaise; but when Mrs Grantly heard of this, she objected strongly. If Eleanor would go away in dudgeon with the archdeacon, why should she let all the servants and all the neighbourhood know that she had done so? So at last Eleanor consented to make use of the Plumstead carriage; and as the archdeacon had gone out immediately after breakfast and was not to return till dinner-time, she also consented to postpone her journey till after lunch, and to join the family at that time. As to the subject of the quarrel not a word was said by any one. The affair of the carriage was arranged by Mr Harding, who acted as Mercury between the two ladies; they, when they met, kissed each other very lovingly, and then sat down each to her crochet work as though nothing was amiss in all the world.

❋ THIRTY ❋

❋ Another Love Scene ❋

BUT THERE WAS ANOTHER VISITOR AT THE rectory whose feelings in this unfortunate matter must be somewhat strictly analysed. Mr Arabin had heard from his friend of the probability of Eleanor's marriage with Mr Slope with amazement, but not with incredulity. It has been said that he was not in love with Eleanor, and up to this period this certainly had been true. But as soon as he heard that she loved some one else, he began to be very fond of her himself. He did not make up his mind that he wished to have her for his wife; he had never thought of her, and did not now think of her, in connection with himself; but he experienced an inward indefinable feeling of deep regret, a gnawing sorrow, an unconquerable depression of spirits, and also a species of self-abasement that he – he Mr Arabin – had not done something to prevent that other he, that vile he, whom he so thoroughly despised, from carrying off this sweet prize.

Whatever man may have reached the age of forty unmarried without knowing something of such feelings must have been very successful or else very cold hearted.

Mr Arabin had never thought of trimming the sails of his bark so that he might sail as convoy to this rich argosy. He had seen that Mrs Bold was beautiful, but he had not dreamt of making her beauty his own. He knew that Mrs Bold was rich, but he had had no more idea of appropriating her wealth than that of Dr Grantly. He had discovered that Mrs Bold was intelligent, warm-hearted, agreeable, sensible, all, in fact, that a man could wish his wife to be; but the higher were her attractions, the greater her claims to consideration, the less had he imagined that he might possibly become the possessor of them. Such had been his instinct rather than his thoughts, so humble and so diffident. Now his diffidence was to be rewarded by his seeing this woman, whose beauty was to his eyes perfect, whose wealth was such as to have deterred him from thinking of her, whose widowhood would have silenced him had he not been so deterred, by his seeing her become the prey of – Obadiah Slope!

On the morning of Mrs Bold's departure he got on his horse to ride over to St Ewold's. As he rode he kept muttering to himself a line from Van Artevelde,

> How little flattering is woman's love.

And then he strove to recall his mind and to think of other affairs, his parish, his college, his creed – but his thoughts would revert to Mr Slope and the Flemish chieftain –

> When we think upon it,
> How little flattering is woman's love,
> Given commonly to whosoe'er is nearest
> And propped with most advantage.

It was not that Mrs Bold should marry any one but him; he had not put himself forward as a suitor; but that she should marry Mr Slope – and so he repeated over again –

> Outward grace
> Nor inward light is needful – day by day
> Men wanting both are mated with the best
> And loftiest of God's feminine creation,
> Whose love takes no distinction but of gender,
> And ridicules the very name of choice.

And so he went on, troubled much in his mind.

He had but an uneasy ride of it that morning, and little good did he do at St Ewold's.

The necessary alterations in his house were being fast completed, and he walked through the rooms, and went up and down the stairs and rambled through the garden; but he could not wake himself to much interest about them. He stood still at every window to look out and think upon Mr Slope. At almost every window he had before stood and chatted with Eleanor. She and Mrs Grantly had been there continually, and while Mrs Grantly had been giving orders, and seeing that orders had been complied with, he and Eleanor had conversed on all things appertaining to a clergyman's profession. He thought how often he had laid down the law to her, and how sweetly she had borne with his somewhat dictatorial decrees. He remembered her listening intelligence, her gentle but quick replies, her interest in all that concerned the church, in all that concerned him; and then he struck his riding whip against the window sill, and declared to himself that it was impossible that Eleanor Bold should marry Mr Slope.

And yet he did not really believe, as he should have done, that it was impossible. He should have known her well enough to feel that it was truly impossible. He should have been aware that Eleanor had that within her which would surely protect her from such degradation. But he, like so many others, was deficient in confidence in woman. He said to himself over and over again that it was impossible that Eleanor Bold should become Mrs Slope, and yet he believed that she would do so. And so he rambled about, and could do and think of nothing. He was thoroughly uncomfortable, thoroughly ill at ease, cross with himself and every body else, and feeding in his heart on animosity towards Mr Slope. This was not as it should be, as he knew and felt; but he could not help himself. In truth Mr Arabin was now in love with Mrs Bold, though ignorant of the fact himself. He was in love, and, though forty years old, was in love without being aware of it. He fumed and fretted, and did not know what was the matter, as a youth might do at one-and-twenty. And so having done no good at St Ewold's, he rode back much earlier than was usual with him, instigated by some inward unacknowledged hope that he might see Mrs Bold before she left.

Eleanor had not passed a pleasant morning. She was irritated with every one, and not least with herself. She felt that she had been hardly used, but she felt also that she had not played her own cards well. She should have held herself so far above suspicions as to have received her sister's innuendoes and the archdeacon's lecture with indifference. She had not done this, but had shown herself angry and sore, and was now ashamed of her own petulance, and yet unable to discontinue it.

The greater part of the morning she had spent alone; but after a while her father joined her. He had fully made up his mind that, come what come might, nothing should separate him from his younger daughter. It was a hard task for him to reconcile himself to the idea of seeing her at the head of Mr Slope's table; but he got through it. Mr Slope, as he argued to himself, was a respectable man and a clergyman; and he, as Eleanor's father, had no right even to endeavour to prevent her from marrying such a one. He longed to tell her now he had determined to prefer her to all the world, how he was prepared to admit that she was not wrong, how thoroughly he differed from Dr Grantly; but he could not bring himself to mention Mr Slope's name. There was yet a chance that they were all wrong in their surmise! and, being thus in doubt, he could not bring himself to speak openly to her on the subject.

He was sitting with her in the drawing-room, with his arm round her waist, saying every now and then some little soft words of affection, and working hard with his imaginary fiddle-bow, when Mr Arabin entered the room. He immediately got up, and the two made some trite remarks to each other, neither thinking of what he was saying, while Eleanor kept her seat on the sofa mute and moody. Mr Arabin was included in the list of those against whom her anger was excited. He, too, had dared to talk about her acquaintance with Mr Slope; he, too, had dared to blame her for not making an enemy of his enemy. She had not intended to see him before her departure, and was now but little inclined to be gracious.

There was a feeling through the whole house that something was wrong. Mr Arabin, when he saw Eleanor, could not succeed in looking or in speaking as though he knew nothing of all this. He could not be cheerful and positive and contradictory with her, as was his wont. He had not been two minutes in the room before he felt that he had done wrong to return; and the moment he heard her voice, he thoroughly wished himself back at St Ewold's. Why, indeed, should he have wished to have aught further to say to the future wife of Mr Slope?

'I am sorry to hear that you are to leave us so soon,' said he, striving in vain to use his ordinary voice. In answer to this she muttered something about the necessity of her being in Barchester, and betook herself most industriously to her crochet work.

Then there was a little more trite conversation between Mr Arabin and Mr Harding; trite, and hard, and vapid, and senseless. Neither of them had anything to say to the other, and yet neither at such a moment liked to remain silent. At last Mr Harding, taking advantage of a pause, escaped out of the room, and Eleanor and Mr Arabin were left together.

'Your going will be a great break-up to our party,' said he.

She again muttered something which was all but inaudible; but kept her eyes fixed upon her work.

'We have had a very pleasant month here,' said he; 'at least I have; and I am sorry it should be so soon over.'

'I have already been from home longer than I intended,' said she; 'and it is time that I should return.'

'Well, pleasant hours and pleasant days must come to an end. It is a pity that so few of them are pleasant; or perhaps, rather' –

'It is a pity, certainly, that men and women do so much to destroy the pleasantness of their days,' said she, interrupting him. 'It is a pity that there should be so little charity abroad.'

'Charity should begin at home,' said he; and he was proceeding to explain that he as a clergyman could not be what she would call charitable at the expense of those principles which he considered it his duty to teach, when he remembered that it would be worse than vain to argue on such a matter with the future wife of Mr Slope. 'But you are just leaving us,' he continued, 'and I will not weary your last hour with another lecture. As it is, I fear I have given you too many.'

'You should practise as well as preach, Mr Arabin?'

'Undoubtedly I should. So should we all. All of us who presume to teach are bound to do our utmost towards fulfilling our own lessons. I thoroughly allow my deficiency in doing so: but I do not quite know now to what you allude. Have you any special reason for telling me now that I should practise as well as preach?'

Eleanor made no answer. She longed to let him know the cause of her anger, to upbraid him for speaking of her disrespectfully, and then at last to forgive him, and so part friends. She felt that she would be unhappy to leave him in her present frame of mind; but yet she could hardly bring herself to speak of Mr Slope. And how could she allude to the innuendo thrown out by the archdeacon, and thrown out, as she believed, at the instigation of Mr Arabin? She wanted to make him know that he was wrong, to make him aware that he had ill-treated her, in order that the sweetness of her forgiveness might be enhanced. She felt that she liked him too well to be contented to part with him in displeasure; and yet she could not get over her deep displeasure without some explanation, some acknowledgment on his part, some assurance that he would never again so sin against her.

'Why do you tell me that I should practise what I preach?' continued he.

'All men should do so.'

'Certainly. That is as it were understood and acknowledged. But you do not say so to all men, or to all clergymen. The advice, good as it is, is not given except in allusion to some special deficiency. If you will tell me my special deficiency, I will endeavour to profit by the advice.'

She paused for a while, and then looking full in his face, she said, 'You are not bold enough, Mr Arabin, to speak out to me openly and plainly, and yet you expect me, a woman, to speak openly to you. Why did you speak calumny of me to Dr Grantly behind my back?'

'Calumny!' said he, and his whole face became suffused with blood; 'what calumny? If I have spoken calumny of you, I will beg your pardon, and his to whom I spoke it, and God's pardon also. But what calumny have I spoken of you to Dr Grantly?'

She also blushed deeply. She could not bring herself to ask him whether he had not spoken of her as another man's wife. 'You know that best yourself,' said she; 'but I ask you as a man of honour, if you have not spoken of me as you would not have spoken of your own sister; or rather I will not ask you,' she continued, finding that he did not immediately answer her. 'I will not put you to the necessity of answering such a question. Dr Grantly has told me what you said.'

'Dr Grantly certainly asked me for my advice, and I gave it. He asked me' –

'I know he did, Mr Arabin. He asked you whether he would be doing right to receive me at Plumstead, if I continued my acquaintance with a gentleman who happens to be personally disagreeable to yourself and to him?'

'You are mistaken, Mrs Bold. I have no personal knowledge of Mr Slope; I never met him in my life.'

'You are not the less individually hostile to him. It is not for me to question the propriety of your enmity; but I had a right to expect that my name should not have been mixed up in your hostilities. This has been done, and been done by you in a manner the most injurious and the most distressing to me as a woman. I must confess, Mr Arabin, that from you I expected a different sort of usage.'

As she spoke she with difficulty restrained her tears; but she did restrain them. Had she given way and sobbed aloud, as in such cases a woman should do, he would have melted at once, implored her pardon, perhaps knelt at her feet and declared his love. Everything would have been explained, and Eleanor would have gone back to Barchester with a contented mind. How easily would she have forgiven and forgotten the archdeacon's suspicions had she but heard the whole truth from Mr Arabin. But then where would have been my novel? She did not cry, and Mr Arabin did not melt.

'You do me an injustice,' said he. 'My advice was asked by Dr Grantly, and I was obliged to give it.'

'Dr Grantly has been most officious, most impertinent. I have as complete a right to form my acquaintance as he has to form his. What would you have said, had I consulted you as to the propriety of my banishing Dr Grantly from my house because he knows Lord Tattenham Corner? I am sure Lord Tattenham is quite as objectionable an acquaintance for a clergyman as Mr Slope is for a clergy-man's daughter.'

'I don't know Lord Tattenham Corner.'

'No; but Dr Grantly does. It is nothing to me if he knows all the lords on every racecourse in England. I shall not interfere with him; nor shall he with me.'

'I am sorry to differ with you, Mrs Bold; but as you have spoken to me on this matter, and especially as you blame me for what little I said on the subject, I must tell you that I do differ from you. Dr Grantly's position as a man in the world gives him a right to choose his own acquaintances, subject to certain influences. If he chooses them badly, those influences will be used. If he consorts with persons unsuitable to him, his bishop will interfere. What the bishop is to Dr Grantly, Dr Grantly is to you.'

'I deny it. I utterly deny it,' said Eleanor, jumping from her seat, and literally flashing before Mr Arabin, as she stood on the drawing-room floor. He had never seen her so excited, he had never seen her look half so beautiful.

'I utterly deny it,' said she. 'Dr Grantly has no sort of jurisdiction over me whatsoever. Do you and he forget that I am not altogether alone in the word? Do you forget that I have a father? Dr Grantly, I believe, always has forgotten it.'

'From you, Mr Arabin,' she continued, 'I would have listened to advice because I should have expected it to have been given as one friend may advise another; not as a schoolmaster gives an order to a pupil. I might have differed from you; on this matter I should have done so; but had you spoken to me in your usual manner and with your usual freedom I should not have been angry. But now – was it manly of you, Mr Arabin, to speak of me in this way – so disrespectful – so – ? I cannot bring myself to repeat what you said. You must understand what I feel. Was it just of you to speak of me in such a way, and to advise my sister's husband to turn me out of my sister's house, because I chose to know a man of whose doctrine you disapprove?'

'I have no alternative left to me, Mrs Bold,' said he, standing with his back to the fire-place, looking down intently at the carpet pattern, and speaking with a slow measured voice, 'but to tell you plainly what did take place between me and Dr Grantly.'

'Well,' said she, finding that he paused for a moment.

'I am afraid that what I may say may pain you.'

'It cannot well do so more than what you have already done,' said she.

'Dr Grantly asked me whether I thought it would be prudent for him to receive you in his house as the wife of Mr Slope, and I told him that I thought it would be imprudent. Believing it to be utterly impossible that Mr Slope and –'

'Thank you, Mr Arabin, that is sufficient. I do not want to know your reasons,' said she, speaking with a terribly calm voice. 'I have shown to this gentleman the common-place civility of a neighbour; and because I have done so, because I have not indulged against him in all the rancour and hatred which you and Dr Grantly consider due to all clergyman who do not agree with yourselves, you conclude that I am to marry him; – or rather you do not conclude so – no rational man could really come to such an outrageous conclusion without better ground; – you have not thought so – but, as I am in a position in which such an accusation must be peculiarly painful, it is made in order that I may be terrified into hostility against this enemy of yours.'

As she finished speaking, she walked to the drawing-room window and stepped out into the garden. Mr Arabin was left in the room, still occupied in counting the pattern on the carpet. He had, however, distinctly heard and accurately marked every word that she had spoken. Was it not clear from what she had said, that the archdeacon had been wrong in imputing to her any attachment to Mr Slope? Was it not clear that Eleanor was still free to make another choice? It may seem strange that he should for a moment have had a doubt; and yet he did doubt. She had not absolutely denied the charge; she had not expressly said that it was untrue. Mr Arabin understood little of the nature of a woman's feelings, or he would have known how improbable it was that she should make any clearer declaration than she had done. Few men do understand the nature of a woman's heart, till years have robbed such understanding of its value. And it is well that it should be so, or men would triumph too easily.

Mr Arabin stood counting the carpet, unhappy, wretchedly unhappy, at the hard words that had been spoken to him; and yet happy, exquisitely happy, as he thought that after all the woman whom he so regarded was not to become the wife of the man whom he so much disliked. As he stood there he began to be aware that he was himself in love. Forty years had passed over his head, and as yet woman's beauty had never given him an uneasy hour. His present hour was very uneasy.

Not that he remained there for half or a quarter of that time. In spite of what Eleanor had said, Mr Arabin was, in truth, a manly man. Having ascertained that he loved this woman, and having now reason to believe that she was free to receive his love, at least if she pleased to do so, he followed her into the garden to make such wooing as he could.

He was not long in finding her. She was walking to and fro beneath the avenue of elms that stood in the archdeacon's grounds, skirting the churchyard. What had passed between her and Mr Arabin, had not, alas, tended to lessen the acerbity of her spirit. She was very angry; more angry with him than with any one. How could he have so misunderstood her? She had been so intimate with him, had allowed him such latitude in what he had chosen to say to her, had complied with his ideas, cherished his views, fostered his precepts, cared for his comforts, made much of him in every way in which a pretty woman can make much of an unmarried man without committing herself or her feelings! She had been doing this, and while she had been doing it he had regarded her as the affianced wife of another man.

As she passed along the avenue, every now and then an unbidden tear would force itself on her cheek, and as she raised her hand to brush it away she stamped with her little foot upon the sward with very spite to think that she had been so treated.

Mr Arabin was very near to her when she first saw him, and she turned short round and retraced her steps down the avenue, trying to rid her cheeks of all trace of the tell-tale tears. It was a needless endeavour, for Mr Arabin was in a state of mind that hardly allowed him to observe such trifles. He followed her down the walk, and overtook her just as she reached the end of it.

He had not considered how he would address her; he had not thought what he would say. He had only felt that it was wretchedness to him to quarrel with her, and that it would be happiness to be allowed to love her. And yet he could not lower himself by asking her pardon. He had done her no wrong. He had not calumniated her, not injured her, as she had accused him of doing. He could not confess sins of which he had not been guilty. He could only let the past be past, and ask her as to her and his hopes for the future.

'I hope we are not to part as enemies?' said he.

'There shall be no enmity on my part,' said Eleanor; 'I endeavour to avoid all enmities. It would be a hollow pretence were I to say that there can be true friendship between us after what has just passed. People cannot make their friends of those whom they despise.'

'And am I despised?'

'I must have been so before you could have spoken of me as you did. And I was deceived, cruelly deceived. I believed that you thought well of me; I believed that you esteemed me.'

'Thought well of you and esteemed you!' said he. 'In justifying myself before you, I must use stronger words than those.' He paused for a moment, and Eleanor's heart beat with painful violence within her bosom as she waited for him to go on. 'I have esteemed, do esteem you, as I never yet esteemed any woman. Think well of you! I never thought to think so well, so much of any human creature. Speak calumny of you! Insult you! Wilfully injure you! I wish it were my privilege to shield you from calumny, insult, and injury. Calumny! ah, me. 'Twere almost better that it were so. Better than to worship with a sinful worship; sinful and vain also.' And then he walked along beside her, with his hands clasped behind his back, looking down on the grass beneath his feet, and utterly at a loss how to express his meaning. And Eleanor walked beside him determined at least to give him no assistance.

'Ah me!' he uttered at last, speaking rather to himself than to her. 'Ah me! these Plumstead walks were pleasant enough, if one could have but heart's ease; but without that the dull dead stones of Oxford were far preferable; and St Ewold's too; Mrs Bold, I am beginning to think that I mistook myself when I came hither. A Romish priest now would have escaped all this. Oh, Father of heaven! how good for us would it be, if thou couldest vouchsafe to us a certain rule.'

'And have we not a certain rule, Mr Arabin?'

'Yes – yes, surely; "Lead us not into temptation but deliver us from evil." But what is temptation? what is evil? Is this evil – is this temptation?'

Poor Mr Arabin! It would not come out of him, that deep true love of his. He could not bring himself to utter it in plain language that would require and demand an answer. He knew not how to say to the woman by his side, 'Since the fact is that you do not love that other man, that you are not to be his wife, can you love me, will you be my wife?' These were the words which were in his heart, but with all his sighs he could not draw them to his lips. He would have given anything, everything for power to ask this simple question; but glib as was his tongue in pulpits and on platforms, now he could not find a word wherewith to express the plain wish of his heart.

And yet Eleanor understood him as thoroughly as though he had declared his passion with all the elegant fluency of a practiced Lothario. With a woman's instinct she followed every bend of his mind, as he spoke of the pleasantness of Plumstead and the stones of Oxford, as he alluded to the safety of the Romish priest and the hidden perils of temptation. She knew that it all meant love. She knew that this man at her side, this accomplished scholar, this practised orator, this great polemical combatant, was striving and striving in vain to tell her that his heart was no longer his own.

She knew this, and felt a sort of joy in knowing it; and yet she would not come to his aid. He had offended her deeply, had treated her unworthily, the more unworthily seeing that he had learnt to love her, and Eleanor could not bring herself to abandon her revenge. She did not ask herself whether or no she would ultimately accept his love. She did not even acknowledge to herself that she now perceived it with pleasure. At the present moment it did not touch her heart; it merely appeased her pride and flattered her vanity. Mr Arabin had dared to associate her name with that of Mr Slope, and now her spirit was soothed by finding that he would fain associate it with his own. And so she walked on beside him inhaling incense, but giving out no sweetness in return.

'Answer me this,' said Mr Arabin, stopping suddenly in his walk, and stepping forward so that he faced his companion. 'Answer me this one question. You do not love Mr Slope? you do not intend to be his wife?'

Mr Arabin certainly did not go the right way to win such a woman as Eleanor Bold. Just as her wrath was evaporating, as it was disappearing before the true warmth of his untold love, he re-kindled it by a most useless repetition of his original sin. Had he known what he was about he should never have mentioned Mr Slope's name before Eleanor Bold, till he had made her all his own. Then, and not till then, he might have talked of Mr Slope with as much triumph as he chose.

'I shall answer no such question,' said she; 'and what is more, I must tell you that nothing can justify your asking it. Good morning!'

And so saying she stepped proudly across the lawn, and passing through the drawing-room window joined her father and sister at lunch in the dining-room. Half an hour afterwards she was in the carriage, and so she left Plumstead without again seeing Mr Arabin.

His walk was long and sad among the sombre trees that overshadowed the churchyard. He left the archdeacon's grounds that he might escape attention, and sauntered among the green hillocks under which lay at rest so many of the once loving swains and forgotten beauties of Plumstead. To his ears Eleanor's last words sounded like a knell never to be reversed. He could not comprehend that she might be angry with him, indignant with him, remorseless with him, and yet love him. He could not make up his mind whether or no Mr Slope was in truth a favoured rival. If not, why should she not have answered his question?

Poor Mr Arabin – untaught, illiterate, boorish, ignorant man! That at forty years of age you should know so little of the workings of a woman's heart!

✖ THIRTY-ONE ✖

The Bishop's Library

AND THUS THE PLEASANT PARTY AT PLUMSTEAD was broken up. It had been a very pleasant party as long as they had all remained in good humour with one another. Mrs Grantly had felt her house to be gayer and brighter than it had been for many a long day, and the archdeacon had been aware that the month had passed pleasantly without attributing the pleasure to any other special merits than those of his own hospitality. Within three or four days of Eleanor's departure Mr Harding had also returned, and Mr Arabin had gone to Oxford to spend one week there previous to his settling at the vicarage of St Ewold's. He had gone laden with many messages to Dr Gwynne touching the iniquity of the doings in Barchester palace, and the peril in which it was believed the hospital still stood in spite of the assurances contained in Mr Slope's inauspicious letter.

During Eleanor's drive into Barchester she had not much opportunity of reflecting on Mr Arabin. She had been constrained to divert her mind both from his sins and his love by the necessity of conversing with her sister, and maintaining the appearance of parting with her on good terms. When the carriage reached her own door, and while she was in the act of giving her last kiss to her sister and nieces, Mary Bold ran out and exclaimed,

'Oh! Eleanor – have you heard? – oh! Mrs Grantly, have you heard what has happened? The poor dean!'

'Good heavens!' said Mrs Grantly; 'what – what has happened?'

'This morning at nine he had a fit of apoplexy, and he has not spoken since. I very much fear that by this time he is no more.'

Mrs Grantly had been very intimate with the dean, and was therefore much shocked. Eleanor had not known him so well; nevertheless she was sufficiently acquainted with his person and manners to feel startled and grieved also at the tidings she now received. 'I will go at once to the deanery,' said Mrs Grantly; 'the archdeacon, I am sure, will be there. If there is any news to send you I will let Thomas call before he leaves town.'

And so the carriage drove off, leaving Eleanor and her baby with Mary Bold.

Mrs Grantly had been quite right. The archdeacon was at the deanery. He had come into Barchester that morning by himself, not caring to intrude himself upon Eleanor, and he also immediately on his arrival had heard of the dean's fit. There was, as we have before said, a library or reading room connecting the cathedral with the dean's house. This was generally called the bishop's library, because a certain bishop of Barchester was supposed to have added it to the cathedral. It was built immediately over a portion of the cloisters, and a flight of stairs descended from it into the room in which the cathedral clergymen put their surplices on and off. As it also opened directly into the dean's house, it was the passage through which that dignitary usually went to his public devotions. Who had or had not the right of entry into it, it might be difficult to say; but the people of Barchester believed that it belonged to the dean, and the clergymen of Barchester believed it belonged to the chapter.

On the morning in question most of the resident clergymen who constituted the chapter, and some few others, were here assembled, and among them as usual the archdeacon towered with high authority. He had heard of the dean's fit before he was over the bridge which led into the town, and had at once come to the well known clerical trysting place. He had been there by eleven o'clock, and had remained ever since. From time to time the medical men who had been called in came through from the deanery into the liberary, uttered little bulletins, and then returned. There was it appears very little hope of the old man's rallying, indeed no hope of any thing like a final recovery. The only question was whether he must die at once speechless, unconscious, stricken to death by his first heavy fit; or whether by due aid of medical skill he might not be so far brought back to this world as to become conscious of his state, and enabled to address one prayer to his Maker before he was called to meet Him face to face at the judgment seat.

Sir Omicron Pie had been sent for from London. That great man had shown himself a wonderful adept at keeping life still moving within an old man's heart in the case of good old Bishop Grantly, and it might be reasonably expected that he would be equally successful with a dean. In the mean time Dr Fillgrave and Mr Rerechild were doing their best; and poor Miss Trefoil sat at the head of her father's bed, longing, as in such cases daughters do long, to be allowed to do something to show her love; if it were only to chafe his feet with her hands, or wait in menial offices on those autocratic doctors; anything so that now in the time of need she might be of use.

The archdeacon alone of the attendant clergy had been admitted for a moment into the sick man's chamber. He had crept in with creaking shoes, had said with smothered voice a word of consolation to the sorrowing daughter, had looked on the distorted face of his old friend with solemn but yet eager scrutinising eye, as though he said in his heart 'and so some day it

218

will probably be with me;' and then having whispered an unmeaning word or two to the doctors, had creaked his way back again into the library.

'He'll never speak again, I fear,' said the archdeacon as he noiselessly closed the door, as though the unconscious dying man, from whom all sense had fled, would have heard in his distant chamber the spring of the lock which was now so carefully handled.

'Indeed! indeed! is he so bad?' said the meagre little prebendary, turning over in his own mind all the probable candidates for the deanery, and wondering whether the archdeacon would think it worth his while to accept it. 'The fit must have been very violent.'

'When a man over seventy has a stroke of apoplexy, it seldom comes very lightly,' said the burly chancellor.

'He was an excellent sweet-tempered man,' said one of the vicars choral. 'Heaven knows how we shall repair his loss.'

'He was indeed,' said a minor canon; 'and a great blessing to all those privileged to take a share of the services of our cathedral. I suppose the government will appoint, Mr Archdeacon. I trust we may have no stranger.'

'We will not talk about his successor,' said the archdeacon, 'while there is yet hope.'

'Oh no, of course not,' said the minor canon. 'It would be exceedingly indecorous? but –'

'I know of no man,' said the meagre little prebendary, 'who has better interest with the present government than Mr Slope.'

'Mr Slope,' said two or three at once almost sotto voce. 'Mr, Slope dean of Barchester!'

'Pooh!' exclaimed the burly chancellor.

'The bishop would do anything for him,' said the little prebendary.

'And so would Mrs Proudie,' said the vicar choral.

'Pooh!' said the chancellor.

The archdeacon had almost turned pale at the idea. What if Mr Slope should become dean of Barchester? To be sure there was no adequate ground, indeed no ground at all, for presuming that such a desecration could even be contemplated. But nevertheless it was on the cards. Dr Proudie had interest with the government, and the man carried as it were Dr Proudie in his pocket. How should they all conduct themselves if Mr Slope were to become dean of Barchester? The bare idea for a moment struck even Dr Grantly dumb.

'It would certainly not be very pleasant for us to have Mr Slope at the deanery,' said the little prebendary, chuckling inwardly at the evident consternation which his surmise had created.

'About as pleasant and as probable as having you in the palace,' said the chancellor.

'I should think such an appointment highly improbable,' said the minor canon, 'and, moreover, extremely injudicious. Should not you, Mr Archdeacon?'

'I should presume such a thing to be quite of the question,' said the archdeacon; 'but at the present moment I am thinking rather of our poor friend who is lying so near us than of Mr Slope.'

'Of course, of course,' said the vicar choral with a very solemn air; 'of course you are. So are we all. Poor Dr Trefoil; the best of men, but –'

'It's the most comfortable dean's residence in England,' said a second prebendary. 'Fifteen acres in the grounds. It is better than many of the bishop's palaces.'

'And full two thousand a year,' said the meagre doctor.

'It is cut down to 1200*l.* said the chancellor.

'No,' said the second prebendary. 'It is to be fifteen. A special case was made.'

'No such thing,' said the chancellor.

'You'll find I'm right,' said the prebendary.

'I'm sure I read it in the report,' said the minor canon.

'Nonsense,' said the chancellor. 'They couldn't do it. There were to be no exceptions but London and Durham.'

'And Canterbury and York,' said the vicar choral, modestly.

'What do you say, Grantly?' said the meagre little doctor.

'Say about what?' said the archdeacon, who had been looking as though he were thinking about his friend the dean, but who had in reality been thinking about Mr Slope.

'What is the next dean to have, twelve or fifteen?'

'Twelve,' said the archdeacon authoritatively, thereby putting an end at once to all doubt and dispute among his subordinates as far as that subject was concerned.

'Well, I certainly thought it was fifteen,' said the minor canon.

'Pooh!' said the burly chancellor. At this moment the door opened, and in came Dr Fillgrave.

'How is he?' 'Is he conscious?' 'Can he speak?' 'I hope not dead?' 'No worse news, doctor, I trust?' 'I hope, I trust, something better, doctor?' said half a dozen voices all at once, each in a tone of extremest anxiety. It was pleasant to see how popular the good old dean was among his clergy.

'No change, gentlemen; not the slightest change – but a telegraphic message has arrived – Sir Omicron Pie will be here by the 9.15 P.M. train. If any man can do anything Sir Omicron Pie will do it. But all that skill can do has been done.'

'We are sure of that Dr Fillgrave,' said the archdeacon; 'we are quite sure of that. But yet you know –'

'Oh! quite right,' said the doctor, 'quite right – I should have done just the same – I advised it at once. I said to Rerechild at once that with such a life and such a man, Sir Omicron should be summoned – of course I knew the expense was nothing – so distinguished, you know, and so popular. Nevertheless, all that human skill can do has been done.'

Just at this period Mrs Grantly's carriage drove into the close, and the archdeacon went down to confirm the news which she had heard before.

By the 9.15 P.M. train Sir Omicron Pie did arrive. And in the course of the night a sort of consciousness returned to the poor old dean. Whether this was due to Sir Omicron Pie is a question on which it may be well not to offer an opinion. Dr Fillgrave was very clear in his own mind, but Sir Omicron himself is thought to have differed from that learned doctor. At any rate Sir Omicron expressed an opinion that the dean had yet some days to live.

For the eight or ten next days, accordingly, the poor dean remained in the same state, half conscious and half comatose, and the attendant clergy began to think that no new appointment would be necessary for some few months to come.

✳ THIRTY-TWO ✳

A New Candidate for Ecclesiastical Honours

THE DEAN'S ILLNESS OCCASIONED MUCH MENTAL TURMOIL in other places besides the deanery and adjoining library; and the idea which occurred to the meagre little prebendary about Mr Slope did not occur to him alone.

The bishop was sitting listlessly in his study when the news reached him of the dean's illness. It was brought to him by Mr Slope, who of course was not the last person in Barchester to hear it. It was also not slow in finding its way to Mrs Proudie's ears. It may be presumed that there was not just then much friendly intercourse between these two rival claimants for his lordship's obedience. Indeed, though living in the same house, they had not met since the stormy interview between them in the bishop's study on the preceding day.

On that occasion Mrs Proudie had been defeated. That the prestige of continual victory should have been torn from her standards was a subject of great sorrow to that militant lady; but though defeated, she was not overcome. She felt that she might yet recover her lost ground, that she might yet hurl Mr Slope down to the dust from which she had picked him, and force her sinning lord to sue for pardon in sackcloth and ashes.

On that memorable day, memorable for his mutiny and rebellion against her high behests, he had carried his way with a high hand, and had really begun to think it possible that the days of his slavery were counted. He had begun to hope that he was now about to enter into a free land, a land delicious with milk which he himself might quaff, and honey which would not tantalise him by being only honey to the eye. When Mrs

Proudie banged the door, as she left his room, he felt himself every inch a bishop. To be sure his spirit had been a little cowed by his chaplain's subsequent lecture; but on the whole he was highly pleased with himself, and flattered himself that the worst was over. 'Ce n'est que le premier pas qui coûte,' he reflected; and now that the first step had been so magnanimously taken, all the rest would follow easily.

He met his wife as a matter of course at dinner, where little or nothing was said that could ruffle the bishop's happiness. His daughters and the servants were present and protected him.

He made one or two trifling remarks on the subject of his projected visit to the archbishop, in order to show to all concerned that he intended to have his own way; and the very servants perceiving the change transferred a little of their reverence from their mistress to their master. All which the master perceived; and so also did the mistress. But Mrs Proudie bided her time.

After dinner he returned to his study where Mr Slope soon found him, and there they had tea together and planned many things. For some few minutes the bishop was really happy; but as the clock on the chimney piece warned him that the stilly hours of night were drawing on, as he looked at his chamber candlestick and knew that he must use it, his heart sank within him again. He was as a ghost, all whose power of wandering free through these upper regions ceases at cock-crow; or rather he was the opposite of the ghost, for till cock-crow he must again be a serf. And would that be all? Could he trust himself to come down to breakfast a free man in the morning.

He was nearly an hour later than usual, when he betook himself to his rest. Rest! what rest! However, he took a couple of glasses of sherry, and mounted the stairs. Far be it from us to follow him thither. There are some things which no novelist, no historian, should attempt; some few scenes in life's drama which even no poet should dare to paint. Let that which passed between Dr Proudie and his wife on this night be understood to be among them.

He came down the following morning a sad and thoughtful man. He was attenuated in appearance; one might almost say emaciated. I doubt whether his now grizzled locks had not palpably become more gray than on the preceding evening. At any rate he had aged materially. Years do not make a man old gradually and at an even pace. Look through the world and see if this is not so always, except in those rare cases in which the human being lives and dies without joys and without sorrows, like a vegetable. A man shall be possessed of florid youthful blooming health till, it matters not what age. Thirty – forty – fifty, then comes some nipping frost, some period of agony, that robs the fibres of the body of their succulence, and the hale and hearty man is counted among the old.

He came down and breakfasted alone; Mrs Proudie being indisposed took her coffee in her bed-room, and her daughters waited upon her there. He ate his breakfast alone, and then, hardly knowing what he did, he betook himself to his usual seat in his study. He tried to solace himself with his coming visit to the archbishop. That effort of his own free will at any rate remained to him as an enduring triumph. But somehow, now that he had achieved it, he did not seem to care so much about it. It was his ambition that had prompted him to take his place at the archi-episcopal table, and his ambition was now quite dead within him.

He was ths seated when Mr Slope made his appearance, with breathless impatience.

'My lord, the dean is dead.'

'Good heavens!' exclaimed the bishop, startled out of his apathy by an announcement so sad and so sudden.

'He is either dead or now dying. He has had an apoplectic fit, and I am told that there is not the slightest hope; indeed, I do not doubt that by this time he is no more.'

Bells were rung, and servants were immediately sent to inquire. In the course of the morning, the bishop, leaning on his chaplain's arm, himself called at the deanery door. Mrs Proudie sent to Miss Trefoil all manner of offers of assistance. The Miss Proudies sent also, and there was immense sympathy between the palace and the deanery. The answer to all inquiries was unvaried. The dean was just the same; and Sir Omicron Pie was expected down by the 9.15 P.M. train.

And then Mr Slope began to meditate, as others also had done, as to who might possibly be the new dean; and it occurred to him, as it had also occurred to others, that it might be possible that he should be the new dean himself. And then the question as to the twelve hundred, or fifteen hundred, or two thousand, ran in his mind, as it had run through those of the other clergymen in the cathedral library.

Whether it might be two thousand, or fifteen or twelve hundred, it would in any case undoubtedly be a great thing for him, if he could get it. The gratification to his ambition would be greater even than that of his covetousness. How glorious to out-top the archdeacon in his own cathedral city; to sit above prebendaries and canons, and have the cathedral pulpit and all the cathedral services altogether at his own disposal!

But it might be easier to wish for this than to obtain it. Mr Slope, however, was not without some means of forwarding his views, and he at any rate did not let the grass grow under his feet. In the first place he thought – and not vainly – that he could count upon what assistance the bishop could give him. He immediately changed his views with regard to his patron; he made up his mind that if he became dean, he would hand his lordship back again to his wife's vassalage; and he thought it possible that his lordship might not be sorry to rid himself of one of his mentors. Mr Slope had also taken some steps towards making his name known to other men in power. There was a certain chief-commissioner of national schools who at the present moment was presumed to stand especially high in the good graces of the government big wigs, and with him Mr Slope had contrived to establish a sort of epistolary intimacy. He thought that he might safely apply to Sir Nicholas Fitzwhiggin; and he felt sure that if Sir Nicholas chose to exert himself, the promise of such a piece of preferment would be had for the asking for.

Then he also had the press at his building, or flattered himself that he had so. The daily Jupiter had taken his part in a very thorough manner in those polemical contests of his with Mr Arabin; he had on more than one occasion absolutely had an interview with a gentleman on the staff of that paper, who, if not the editor, was as good as the editor; and had long been in the habit of writing telling letters on all manner of ecclesiastical abuses, which he signed with his initials, and sent to his editorial friend with private notes signed in his own name. Indeed, he and Mr Towers – such was the name of the powerful gentleman of the press with whom he was connected – were generally very amiable with each other. Mr Slope's little productions were always printed and occasionally commented upon; and thus, in a small sort of way, he had become a literary celebrity. This public life had great charms for him, though it certainly also had its drawbacks. On one occasion, when speaking in the presence of reporters, he had failed to uphold and praise and swear by that special line of conduct which had been upheld and praised and sworn by in the Jupiter, and then he had been much surprised and at the moment not a little irritated to find himself lacerated most unmercifully by his old ally. He was quizzed and bespattered and made a fool of, just as though, or rather worse than if, he had been a constant enemy instead of a constant friend. He had hitherto not learnt that a man who aspires to be on the staff of the Jupiter must surrender all individuality. But ultimately this little castigation had broken no bones between him and his friend Mr Towers. Mr Slope was one of those who understood the world too well to show himself angry with such a potentate as the Jupiter. He had kissed the rod that scourged him, and now thought that he might fairly look for his reward. He determined that he would at once let Mr Towers know that he was a candidate for the place which was about to become vacant. More than one piece of preferment had lately been given away much in accordance with advice tendered to the government in the columns of the Jupiter.

But it was incumbent on Mr Slope first to secure the bishop. He specially felt that it behoved him to do this before the visit to the archbishop was made. It was really quite providential that the dean should have fallen ill just at the very nick of time. If Dr Proudie could be instigated to take the matter up warmly, he might manage a good deal while staying at the archbishop's palace. Feeling this very strongly Mr Slope determined to sound the bishop that very afternoon. He was to start on the following morning to London, and therefore not a moment could be lost with safety.

He went into the bishop study about five o'clock, and found him still sitting alone. It might have been supposed that he had hardly moved since the little excitement occasioned by his walk to the dean's door. He still wore on his face that dull dead look of half unconscious suffering. He was doing nothing, reading nothing, thinking of nothing, but simply gazing on vacancy when Mr Slope for the second time that day entered his room.

'Well, Slope,' said he, somewhat impatiently; for, to tell the truth, he was not anxious just at present to have much conversation with Mr Slope.

'Your lordship will be sorry to hear that as yet the poor dean has shown no sign of amendment.'

'Oh – ah – hasn't he? Poor man! I'm sure I'm very sorry. I suppose Sir Omicron has not arrived yet?'

'No; not till the 9.15 P.M. train.'

'I wonder they didn't have a special. They say Dr Trefoil is very rich.'

'Very rich, I believe,' said Mr Slope. 'But the truth is, all the doctors in London can do no good; no other good than to show that every possible care has been taken. Poor Dr Trefoil is not long for this world; my lord.'

'I suppose not – I suppose not.'

'Oh no; indeed, his best friends could not wish that he should outlive such a shock, for his intellects cannot possibly survive it.'

'Poor man! poor man!' said the bishop.

'It will naturally be a matter of much moment to your lordship who is to succeed him,' said Mr Slope. 'It would be a great thing if you could secure the appointment for some person of your own way of thinking on important points. The party hostile to us are very strong here in Barchester – much too strong.'

'Yes, yes. If poor Dr Trefoil is to go, it will be a great thing to get a good man in his place.'

'It will be everything to your lordship to get a man on whose co-operation you can reckon. Only think what trouble we might have if Dr Grantly, or Dr Hyandry, or any of that way of thinking, were to get it.'

'It is not very probable that Lord —— will give it to any of that school; why should he?'

'No. Not probable; certainly not; but it's possible. Great interest will probably be made. If I might venture to advise your lordship, I would suggest that you should discuss the matter with his grace next week. I have no doubt that your wishes, if made known and backed by his grace, would be paramount with Lord ——'

'Well, I don't know that; Lord —— has always been very kind to me, very kind. But I am unwilling to interfere in such matters unless asked. And indeed if asked, I don't know whom, at this moment, I should recommend.'

Mr Slope, even Mr Slope, felt at the present rather abashed. He hardly knew how to frame his little request in language sufficiently modest. He had recognised and acknowledged to himself the necessity of shocking the bishop in the first instance by the temerity of his application, and his difficulty was how best to remedy that by his adroitness and eloquence. 'I doubted myself,' said he, 'whether your lordship would have any one immediately in your eye, and it is on this account that I venture to submit to you an idea that I have been turning over in my own mind. If poor Dr Trefoil must go, I really do not see why, with your lordship's assistance, I should not hold the preferment myself.'

'You!' exclaimed the bishop, in a manner that Mr Slope could hardly have considered complimentary.

The ice was now broken, and Mr Slope became fluent enough. 'I have been thinking of looking for it. If your lordship will press the matter on the archbishop, I do not doubt but I shall succeed. You see I shall be the first to move, which is a great matter. Then I can count upon assistance from the public press: my name is known, I may say, somewhat favourably known to that portion of the press which is now most influential with the government, and I have friends also in the government. But, nevertheless, it is to you, my lord, that I look for assistance. It is from your hands that I would most willingly receive the benefit. And, which should ever be the chief consideration in such matters, you must know better than any other person whatsoever what qualifications I possess.'

The bishop sat for a while dumbfounded. Mr Slope dean of Barchester! The idea of such a transformation of character would never have occurred to his own unaided intellect. At first he went on thinking why, for what reasons, on what account, Mr Slope should be dean of Barchester. But by degrees the direction of his thoughts changed, and he began to think why, for what reasons, on what account, Mr Slope should not be dean of Barchester. As far as he himself, the bishop, was concerned, he could well spare the services of his chaplain. That little idea of using Mr Slope as a counterpoise to his wife had well nigh evaporated. He had all but acknowledged the futility of the scheme. If indeed he could have slept in his chaplain's bed-room instead of his wife's there might have been something in it. But ——. And thus as Mr Slope was speaking, the bishop began to recognise the idea that that gentleman might become dean of Barchester without impropriety; not moved, indeed, by Mr Slope's eloquence, for he did not follow the tenor of his speech; but led thereto by his own cogitations.

'I need not say,' continued Mr Slope, 'that it would be my chief desire to act in all matters connected with the cathedral as far as possible in accordance with your views. I know your lordship so well (and I hope you know me well enough to have the same feelings), that I am satisfied that my being in that position would add materially to your own comfort, and enable you to extend the sphere of your useful influence. As I said before, it is most desirable that there should be but one opinion among the dignitaries of the same diocese. I doubt much whether I would accept such an appointment in any diocese in which I should be constrained to differ much from the bishop. In this case there would be a delightful uniformity of opinion.'

Mr Slope perfectly well perceived that the bishop did not follow a word that he said, but nevertheless he went on talking. He knew it was necessary that Dr Proudie should recover from his surprise, and he knew also that he must give him the opportunity of appearing to have been persuaded by argument. So he went on, and produced a multitude of fitting reasons all tending to show that no one on earth could make so good a dean of Barchester as himself, that the government and the public would assuredly coincide in desiring that he, Mr Slope, should be dean of Barchester; but that for high considerations of ecclesiastical polity it would be especially desirable that this piece of preferment should be so bestowed through the instrumentality of the bishop of the diocese.

'But I really don't know what I could do in the matter,' said the bishop.

'If you would mention it to the archbishop; if you could tell his grace that you consider such an appointment very desirable, that you have it much at heart with a view to putting an end to schism in the diocese; if you did this with your usual energy, you would probably find no difficulty in inducing his grace to promise that he would mention it to Lord ——. Of course you would let the archbishop know that I am not looking for the preferment solely through his intervention; that you do not exactly require him to ask it as a favour; that you expect that I shall get it through other sources, as is indeed the case; but that you are very anxious that his grace should express his approval of such an arrangement to Lord ——'

It ended in the bishop promising to do as he was bid. Not that he so promised without a stipulation. 'About that hospital,' he said, in the middle of the conference. 'I was never so troubled in my life;' which was about the truth. 'You haven't spoken to Mr Harding since I saw you?'

Mr Slope assured his patron that he had not.

'Ah well, then – I think upon the whole it will be better to let Quiverful have it. It has been half promised to him, and he has a large family and is very poor. I think on the whole it will be better to make out the nomination for Mr Quiverful.'

'But, my lord,' said Mr Slope, still thinking that he was bound to make a fight for his own view on this matter, and remembering that it still behoved him to maintain his lately acquired supremacy over Mrs Proudie, lest he should fail in his views regarding the deanery – 'but my lord, I am really much afraid ——'

'Remember, Mr Slope,' said the bishop, 'I can hold out no sort of hope to you in this matter of succeeding poor Dr Trefoil. I will certainly speak to the archbishop, as you wish it, but I cannot think ——'

'Well, my lord,' said Mr Slope, fully understanding the bishop, and in his turn interrupting him, 'perhaps your lordship is right about Mr Quiverful. I have no doubt I can easily arrange matters with Mr Harding, and I will make out the nomination for your signature as you direct.'

'Yes, Slope, I think that will be best; and you may be sure that any little that I can do to forward your views shall be done.'

And so they parted.

Mr Slope had now much business on his hands. He had to make his daily visit to the signora. This common prudence should have now induced him to omit, but he was infatuated; and could not bring himself to be commonly prudent. He determined therefore that he would drink tea at the Stanhopes'; and he determined also, or thought that he determined, that having done so he would go thither no more. He had also to arrange his matters with Mrs Bold. He was of opinion that Eleanor would grace the deanery as perfectly as she would the chaplain's cottage; and he thought, moreover, that Eleanor's fortune would excellently repair any dilapidations and curtailments in the dean's stipend which might have been made by that ruthless ecclesiastical commission.

Touching Mrs Bold his hopes now soared high. Mr Slope was one of that numerous multitude of swains who think that all is fair in love, and he had accordingly not refrained from using the services of Mrs Bold's own maid. From her he had learnt much of what had taken place at Plumstead; not exactly with truth, for 'the own maid' had not been able to divine the exact truth, but with some sort of similitude to it. He had been told that the archdeacon and Mrs Grantly and Mr Harding and Mr Arabin had all quarrelled with 'missus' for having received a letter from Mr Slope; that 'missus' had positively refused to give the letter up; that she had received from the archdeacon the option of giving up either Mr Slope and his letter, or else the society of Plumstead rectory; and that 'missus' had declared with much indignation, that 'she didn't care a straw for the society of Plumstead rectory,' and that she wouldn't give up Mr Slope for any of them.

Considering the source from whence this came, it was not quite so untrue as might have been expected. It showed pretty plainly what had been the nature of the conversation in the servants' hall; and coupled as it was with the certainty of Eleanor's sudden return, it appeared to Mr Slope to be so far worthy of credit as to justify him in thinking that the fair widow would in all human probability accept his offer.

All this work was therefore to be done. It was desirable he thought that he should make his offer before it was known that Mr Quiverful was finally appointed to the hospital. In his letter to Eleanor he had plainly declared that Mr Harding was to have the appointment. It would be very difficult to explain this away; and were he to write another letter to Eleanor, telling the truth and throwing the blame on the bishop, it would naturally injure him in her estimation. He determined therefore to let that matter disclose itself as it would, and to lose no time in throwing himself at her feet.

Then he had to solicit the assistance of Sir Nicholas Fitzwhiggin and Mr Towers, and he went directly from the bishop's presence to compose his letters to those gentlemen. As Mr Slope was esteemed an adept at letter writing, they shall be given in full.

'(Private.)   'Palace, Barchester, Sept. 185–.

'MY DEAR SIR NICHOLAS

I hope that the intercourse which has been between us will preclude you from regarding my present application as an intrusion. You cannot I imagine have yet heard that poor dear old Dr Trefoil has been seized with apoplexy. It is a subject of profound grief to every one in Barchester, for he has always been an excellent man – excellent as a man and as a clergyman. He is, however, full of years, and his life could not under any circumstances have been much longer spared. You may probably have known him.

'There is, it appears, no probable chance of his recovery. Sir Omicron Pie is, I believe, at present with him. At any rate the medical men here have declared that one or two days more must limit the tether of his mortal coil, I sincerely trust that his soul may wing its flight to that haven where it may for ever be at rest and for ever be happy.

'The bishop has been speaking to me about the preferment, and he is anxious that it should be conferred on me. I confess that I can hardly venture, at my age, to look for such advancement; but I am so far encouraged by his lordship, that I believe I shall be induced to do so. His lordship goes to ── to-morrow, and is intent on mentioning the subject to the archbishop.

'I know well how deservedly great is your weight with the present government. In any matter touching church preferment you would of course be listened to. Now that the matter has been put into my head, I am of course anxious to be successful. If you can assist me by your good word, you will confer on me one additional favour.

'I had better add, that Lord ── cannot as yet know of this piece of preferment having fallen in, or rather of its certainty of falling (for poor dear Dr Trefoil is past hope). Should Lord ── first hear it from you, that might probably be thought to give you a fair claim to express your opinion.

'Of course our grand object is, that we should all be of one opinion in church matters. This is most desirable at Barchester; it is this that makes our good bishop so anxious about it. You may probably think it expedient to point this out to Lord ── if it shall be in your power to oblige me by mentioning the subject to his lordship.

                    'Believe me, my dear Sir Nicholas,
                              'Your most faithful servant,
                                        'OBADIAH SLOPE.'

His letter to Mr Towers was written in quite a different strain. Mr Slope conceived that he completely understood the difference in character and position of the two men whom he addressed. He knew that for such a man as Sir Nicholas Fitzwhiggin a little flummery was necessary, and that it might be of the easy everyday description. Accordingly his letter to Sir Nicholas was written *currente calamo*, with very little trouble. But to such a man as Mr Towers it was not so easy to write a letter that should be effective and yet not offensive, that should carry its point without undue interference. It was not difficult to flatter Dr Proudie or Sir Nicholas Fitzwhiggin, but very difficult to flatter Mr Towers without letting the flattery declare itself. This, however, had to be done. Moreover, this letter must, in appearance at least, be written without effort, and be fluent, unconstrained, and demonstrative of no doubt or fear on the part of the writer. Therefore the epistle to Mr Towers was studied, and recopied, and elaborated at the cost of so many minutes, that Mr Slope had hardly time to dress himself and reach Dr Stanhope's that evening.

When despatched it ran as follows:–

'(Private.)   'Barchester. Sept. 185–'

(He purposely omitted any allusion to the 'palace,' thinking that Mr Towers might not like it. A great man, he remembered, had been once much condemned for dating a letter from Windsor Castle.)

'MY DEAR SIR'

We were all a good deal shocked here this morning by hearing that poor old Dean Trefoil had been stricken with apoplexy. The fit took him about 9 A.M. I am writing now to save the post, and he is still alive, but past all hope, or possibility I believe, of living. Sir Omicron Pie is here, or will be very shortly; but all that even Sir Omicron can do, is to ratify the sentence of his less distinguished brethren that nothing can be done. Poor Dr Trefoil's race on this side the grave is run. I do not know whether you knew him. He was a good, quiet, charitable man, of the old school of course, as any clergyman over seventy years of age must necessarily be.

'But I do not write merely with the object of sending you such news as this: doubtless some one of your Mercuries will have seen and heard and reported so much; I write as you usually do yourself, rather with a view to the future than to the past.

'Rumour is already rife here as to Dr Trefoil's successor, and among those named as possible future deans your humble servant is, I believe, not the least frequently spoken of; in short I am looking for the preferment. You may probably know that since Bishop Proudie came to this diocese I have exerted myself here a good deal; and I may certainly say not without some success. He and I are nearly always of the same opinion on points of doctorine as well as church discipline, and therefore I have had, as his confidential chaplain, very much in my own hands; but I confess to you that I have a higher ambition than to remain the chaplain of any bishop.

'There are no positions in which more energy is now needed than those of our deans. The whole of our enormous cathedral establishments have been allowed to go to sleep – nay, they are all but dead and ready for the sepulchre! And yet of what prodigious moment they might be made, if, as was intended, they were so managed as to lead the way and show an example for all our parochial clergy!

'The bishop here is most anxious for my success; indeed, he goes tomorrow to press the matter on the archbishop. I believe also I may count on the support of at least one most effective member of the government. But I confess that the support of the Jupiter, if I be thought worthy of it, would be more gratifying to me than any other; more gratifying if by it I should be successful; and more gratifying also, if, although so supported, I should be unsuccessful.

'The time has, in fact, come in which no government can venture to fill up the high places of the Church in defiance of the public press. The age of honourable bishops and noble deans has gone by; and any clergyman however humbly born can now hope for success, if his industry, talent, and character be sufficient to call forth the manifest opinion of the public in his favour.

'At the present moment we all feel that any counsel given in such matters by the Jupiter has the greatest weight – is, indeed, generally followed; and we feel also – I am speaking of clergymen of my own age and standing – that it should be so. There can be no patron less interested than the Jupiter, and none that more thoroughly understands the wants of the people.

'I am sure you will not suspect me of asking from you any support which the paper with which you are connected cannot conscientiously give me. My object in writing is to let you know that I am a candidate for the appointment. It is for you to judge whether or no you can assist my views. I should not, of course, have written to you on such a matter had I not believed (and I have had good reason so to believe) that the Jupiter approves of my views on ecclesiastical polity.

'The bishop expresses a fear that I may be considered too young for such a station, my age being thirty-six. I cannot think that at the present day any hesitation need to be felt on such a point. The public has lost its love for antiquated servants. If a man will ever be fit to do good work he will be fit at thirty-six years of age.

'Believe me very faithfully yours,

'OBADIAH SLOPE.

'T. TOWERS, ESQ
'—— Court,
 'Middle Temple.'

Having thus exerted himself, Mr Slope posted his letters, and passed the remainder of the evening at the feet of his mistress.

Mr Slope will be accused of deceit in his mode of canvassing. It will be said that he lied in the application he made to each of his three patrons. I believe it must be owned that he did so. He could not hesitate on account of his youth, and yet be quite assured that he was not too young. He could not count chiefly on the bishop's support, and chiefly also on that of the newspaper. He did not think that the bishop was going to —— to press the matter on the archbishop. It must be owned that in his canvassing Mr Slope was as false as he well could be.

Let it, however, be asked of those who are conversant with such matters, whether he was more false than men usually are on such occasions. We English gentlemen hate the name of a lie; but how often do we find public men who believe each other's words?

※ THIRTY-THREE ※

Mrs Proudie Victrix

THE NEXT WEEK PASSED OVER AT BARCHESTER with much apparent tranquillity. The hearts, however, of some of the inhabitants were not so tranquil as the streets of the city. The poor old dean still continued to live, just as Sir Omicron Pie had prophesied that he would do, much to the amazement, and some thought disgust, of Dr Fillgrave. The bishop still remained away. He had stayed a day or two in town, and had also remained longer at the archbishop's than he had intended. Mr Slope had as yet received no line in answer to either of his letters; but he had learnt the cause of this. Sir Nicholas was stalking a deer, or attending the Queen, in the Highlands; and even the indefatigable Mr Towers had stolen an autumn holiday, and had made one of the yearly tribe who now ascend Mont Blanc. Mr Slope learnt that he was not expected back till the last day of September.

Mrs Bold was thrown much with the Stanhopes, of whom she became fonder and fonder. If asked, she would have said that Charlotte Stanhope was her especial friend, and so she would have thought. But, to tell the truth, she liked Bertie nearly as well; she had no more idea of regarding him as a lover than she would have had of looking at a big tame dog in such a light. Bertie had become very intimate with her, and made little speeches to her, and said little things of a sort very different from the speeches and sayings of other men. But then this was almost always done before his sisters; and he, with his long silken beard, his light blue eyes and strange dress, was so unlike other men. She admitted him to a kind of familiarity which she had never known with any one else, and of which she by no means understood the danger. She blushed once at finding that she had called him Bertie, and on the same day only barely remembered her position in time to check herself from playing upon him some personal practical joke to which she was instigated by Charlotte.

In all this Eleanor was perfectly innocent, and Bertie Stanhope could hardly be called guilty. But every familiarity into which Eleanor was entrapped was deliberately planned by his sister. She knew well how to play her game, and played it without mercy; she knew, none so well, what was her brother's character, and she would have handed over to him the young widow, and the young widow's money, and the money of the widow's child, without remorse. With her pretended friendship and warm cordiality, she strove to connect Eleanor so closely with her brother as to make it impossible that she should go back even if she wished it. But Charlotte Stanhope knew really nothing of Eleanor's character; did not even understand that there were such characters. She did not comprehend that a young and pretty woman could be playful and familiar with a man such as Bertie Stanhope, and yet have no idea in her head, no feeling in her heart that she would have been ashamed to own to all the world. Charlotte Stanhope did not in the least conceive that her new friend was a woman whom nothing could entrap into an inconsiderate marriage, whose mind would have revolted from the slightest impropriety had· she been aware that any impropriety existed.

Miss Stanhope, however, had tact enough to make herself and her father's house very agreeable to Mrs Bold. There was with them all an absence of stiffness and formality which was peculiarly agreeable to Eleanor after the great dose of clerical arrogance which she had lately been constrained to take. She played chess with them, walked with them, and drank tea with them; studied or pretended to study astronomy; assisted them in writing stories in rhyme, in turning prose tragedy into comic verse, or comic stories into would-be tragic poetry. She had not conceived the possibility of her doing such things as she now did. She found with the Stanhopes new amusements and employments, new pursuits, which in themselves could not be wrong, and which were exceedingly alluring.

Is it not a pity that people who are bright and clever should so often be exceedingly improper? and that those who are never improper should so often be dull and heavy? Now Charlotte Stanhope was always bright, and never heavy: but her propriety was doubtful.

But during all this time Eleanor by no means forgot Mr Arabin, nor did she forget Mr Slope. She had parted from Mr Arabin in her anger. She was still angry at what she regarded as his impertinent interference; but nevertheless she looked forward to meeting him again, and also looked forward to forgiving him. The words that Mr Arabin had uttered still sounded in her ears. She knew that if not intended for a declaration of love, they did signify that he loved her; and she felt also that if he ever did make such a declaration, it might be that she should not receive it unkindly. She was still angry with him, very angry with him; so angry that she would bite her lip and stamp her foot as she thought of what he had said and done. But nevertheless she yearned to let him know that he was forgiven; all that she required was that he should own that he had sinned.

She was to meet him at Ullathorne on the last day of the present month. Miss Thorne had invited all the country round to a breakfast on the lawn. There were to be tents, and archery, and dancing for the ladies on the lawn, and for the swains and girls in the paddock. There were to be fiddlers and fifers, races for the boys, poles to be climbed, ditches full of water to be jumped over, horse-collars to be grinned through (this latter amusement was an addition of the stewards, and not arranged by Miss Thorne in the original programme), and every game to be played which, in a long course of reading, Miss Thorne could ascertain to have been played in the good days of Queen Elizabeth. Everything of more modern growth was to be tabooed, if possible. On one subject Miss Thorne was very unhappy. She had been turning in her mind the matter of a bull-ring, but could not succeed in making anything of it. She would not for the world have done, or allowed to be done, anything that was cruel; as to the promoting the torture of a bull for the amusement of her young neighbours, it need hardly be said that Miss Thorne would be the last to think of it.

And yet there was something so charming in the name. A bull-ring, however, without a bull would only be a memento of the decadence of the times, and she felt herself constrained to abandon the idea. Quintains, however, she was determined to have, and had poles and swivels and bags of flour prepared accordingly. She would no doubt have been anxious for something small in the way of a tournament; but, as she said to her brother, that had been tried, and the age had proved itself too decidedly inferior to its fore-runners to admit of such a pastime. Mr Thorne did not seem to participate much in her regret, feeling perhaps that a full suit of chain-armour would have added but little to his own personal comfort.

This party at Ullathorne had been planned in the first place as a sort of welcoming to Mr Arabin on his entrance into St Ewold's parsonage; an intended harvest-home gala for the labourers and their wives and children had subsequently been amalgamated with it, and thus it had grown to its present dimensions. All the Plumstead party had of course been asked, and at the time of the invitation Eleanor had intended to have gone with her sister. Now her plans were altered, and she was going with the Stanhopes. The Proudies were also to be there; and as Mr Slope had not been included in the invitation to the palace, the signora, whose impudence never deserted her, asked permission of Miss Thorne to bring him.

This permission Miss Thorne gave, having no other alternative; but she did so with a trembling heart, fearing Mr Arabin would be offended. Immediately on his return she apologised, almost with tears, so dire an enmity was presumed to rage between the two gentlemen. But Mr Arabin comforted her by an assurance that he should meet Mr Slope with the greatest pleasure imaginable and made her promise that she would introduce them to each other.

But this triumph of Mr Slope's was not so agreeable to Eleanor, who since her return to Barchester had done her best to avoid him. She would not give way to the Plumstead folk when they so ungenerously accused her of being in love with this odious man; but, nevertheless, knowing that she was so accused, she was fully alive to the expediency of keeping out of his way and dropping him by degrees. She had seen very little of him since her return. Her servant had been instructed to say to all visitors that she was out. She could not bring herself to specify Mr Slope particularly, and in order to avoid him she had thus debarred herself from all her friends. She had excepted Charlotte Stanhope, and by degrees a few others also. Once she had met him at the Stanhopes'; but, as a rule, Mr Slope's visits there were made in the morning, and hers in the evening. On that one occasion Charlotte had managed to preserve her from any annoyance. This was very good-natured on the part of Charlotte, as Eleanor thought, and also very sharp-witted, as Eleanor had told her friend nothing of her reasons for wishing to avoid that gentleman. The fact, however, was, that Charlotte had learnt from her sister that Mr Slope would probably put himself forward as a suitor for the widow's hand, and she was consequently sufficiently alive to the expediency of guarding Bertie's future wife from any danger in that quarter.

Nevertheless the Stanhopes were pledged to take Mr Slope with them to Ullathorne. An arrangement was therefore necessarily made, which was very disagreeable to Eleanor. Dr Stanhope, with herself, Charlotte, and Mr Slope, were to go together, and Bertie was to follow with his sister Madeline. It was clearly visible by Eleanor's face that this assortment was very disagreeable to her; and Charlotte, who was much encouraged thereby in her own little plan, made a thousand apologies.

'I see you don't like it, my dear,' said she, 'but we could not manage otherwise. Bertie would give his eyes to go with you, but Madeline cannot possibly go without him. Nor could we possibly put Mr Slope and Madeline in the same carriage without any one else. They'd both be ruined for ever, you know, and not admitted inside Ullathorne gates, I should imagine, after such an impropriety.'

'Of course that wouldn't do,' said Eleanor; 'but couldn't I go in the carriage with the signora and your brother?'

'Impossible!' said Charlotte. 'When she is there, there is only room for two.' The signora, in truth, did not care to do her travelling in the presence of strangers.

'Well then,' said Eleanor, 'you are all so kind, Charlotte, and so good to me, that I am sure you won't be offended; but I think I'll not go at all.'

'Not go at all! what nonsense! indeed you shall.' It had been absolutely determined in family council that Bertie should propose on that very occasion.

'Or I can take a fly,' said Eleanor. 'You know I am not embarrassed by so many difficulties as you young ladies; I can go alone.'

'Nonsense! my dear. Don't think of such a thing; after all it is only for an hour or so; and, to tell the truth, I don't know what it is you dislike so. I thought you and Mr Slope were great friends. What is it you dislike?'

'Oh! nothing particular,' said Eleanor; 'only I thought it would be a family party.'

'Of course it would be much nicer, much more snug, if Bertie could go with us. It is he that is badly treated. I can assure you he is much more afraid of Mr Slope than you are. But you see Madeline cannot go without him – and she, poor creature, goes out so seldom! I am sure you don't begrudge her this, though her vagary does knock about our own party a little.'

Of course Eleanor made a thousand protestations, and uttered a thousand hopes that Madeline would enjoy herself. And of course she had to give way, and undertake to go in the carriage with Mr Slope. In fact, she was driven either to do this, or to explain why she would not do so. Now she could not bring herself to explain to Charlotte Stanhope all that had passed at Plumstead.

But it was to her a sore necessity. She thought of a thousand little schemes for avoiding it; she would plead illness, and not go at all; she would persuade Mary Bold to go although not asked, and then make a necessity of having a carriage of her own to take her sister-in-law; anything, in fact, she could do rather than be seen by Mr Arabin getting out of the same carriage with Mr Slope. However, when the momentous morning came she had no scheme matured, and then Mr Slope handed her into Dr Stanhope's carriage, and following her steps, sat opposite to her.

The bishop returned on the eve of the Ullathorne party, and was received at home with radiant smiles by the partner of all his cares. On his arrival he crept up to his dressing-room with somewhat of a palpitating heart; he had overstayed his allotted time by three days, and was not without much fear of penalties. Nothing, however, could be more affectionately cordial than the greeting he received: the girls came out and kissed him in a manner that was quite soothing to his spirit; and Mrs Proudie, 'albeit, unused to the melting mood,' squeezed him in her arms, and almost in words called him her dear, darling, good, pet, little bishop. All this was a very pleasant surprise.

Mrs Proudie had somewhat changed her tactics; not that she had seen any cause to disapprove of her former line of conduct, but she had now brought matters to such a point that she calculated that she might safely do so. She had got the better of Mr Slope, and she now thought well to show her husband that when allowed to get the better of everybody, when obeyed by him and permitted to rule over others, she would take care that he should have his reward. Mr Slope had not a chance against her; not only could she stun the poor bishop by her midnight anger, but she could assuage and soothe him, if she so willed, by daily indulgences. She could furnish his room for him, turn him out as smart a bishop as any on the bench, give him good dinners, warm fires, and an easy life; all this she would do if he would but be quietly obedient. But if not – ! To speak sooth, however, his sufferings on that dreadful night had been so poignant, as to leave him little spirit for further rebellion.

As soon as he had dressed himself she returned to his room. 'I hope you enjoyed yourself at —— ' said she, seating herself on one side of the fire while he remained in his arm-chair on the other, stroking the calves of his legs. It was the first time he had had a fire in his room since the summer, and it pleased him; for the good bishop loved to be warm and cozy. Yes, he said, he had enjoyed himself very much. Nothing could be more polite than the archbishop; and Mrs Archbishop had been equally charming.

Mrs Proudie was delighted to hear it; nothing, she declared, pleased her so much as to think

Her bairn respectit like the lave.

She did not put it precisely in these words, but what she said came to the same thing; and then, having petted and fondled her little man sufficiently, she proceeded to business.

'The poor dean is still alive,' said she.

'So I hear, so I hear,' said the bishop. 'I'll go to the deanery directly after breakfast to-morrow.'

'We are going to this party at Ullathorne to-morrow morning, my dear; we must be there early, you know – by twelve o'clock I suppose.'

'Oh – ah!' said the bishop; 'then I'll certainly call the next day.'

'Was much said about it at, —— ?' asked Mrs Proudie.

'About what?' said the bishop.

'Filling up the dean's place,' said Mrs Proudie. As she spoke a spark of the wonted fire returned to her eye, and the bishop felt himself to be a little less comfortable than before.

'Filling up the dean's place; that is, if the dean dies? —— very little, my dear. It was mentioned, just mentioned.'

'And what did you say about it, bishop?'

'Why, I said that I thought that if, that is, should – should the dean die, that is, I said I thought – ' As he went on stammering and floundering, he saw that his wife's eye was fixed sternly on him. Why should he encounter such evil for a man whom he loved so slightly as Mr Slope? Why should he give up his enjoyments and his ease, and such dignity as might be allowed to him, to fight a losing battle for a chaplain? The chaplain after all, if successful, would be as great a tyrant as his wife. Why fight at all? why contend? why be uneasy? From that moment he determined to fling Mr Slope to the winds, and take the goods the gods provided.

'I am told,' said Mrs Proudie, speaking very slowly, 'that Mr Slope is looking to be the new dean.'

'Yes – certainly, I believe he is,' said the bishop.

'And what does the archbishop say about that?' asked Mrs Proudie.

'Well, my dear, to tell the truth, I promised Mr Slope to speak to the archbishop. Mr Slope spoke to me about it. It is very arrogant of him, I must say – but that is nothing to me.'

'Arrogant!' said Mrs Proudie; 'it is the most impudent piece of pretension I ever heard of in my life. Mr Slope dean of Barchester, indeed! And what did you do in the matter, bishop?'

'Why, my dear, I did speak to the archbishop.'

'You don't mean to tell me,' said Mrs Proudie, 'that you are going to make yourself ridiculous by lending your name to such a preposterous attempt as this? Mr Slope dean of Barchester, indeed!' And she tossed her head, and put her arms a-kimbo, with an air of confident defiance that made her husband quite sure that Mr Slope never would be dean of Barchester. In truth, Mrs Proudie was all but invincible; had she married Petruchio, it may be doubted whether that arch wife-tamer would have been able to keep her legs out of those garments which are presumed by men to be peculiarly unfitted for feminine use.

'It is preposterous, my dear.'

'Then why have you endeavoured to assist him?'

'Why – my dear, I haven't assisted him – much.'

'But why have you done it at all? why have you mixed your name up in any thing so ridiculous? What was it you did say to the archbishop?'

'Why, I just did mention it; I just did say that – that in the event of the poor dean's death, Mr Slope would – would –'

'Would what?'

'I forget how I put it – would take it if he could get it; something of that sort. I didn't say much more than that.'

'You shouldn't have said anything at all. And what did the archbishop say?'

'He didn't say anything; he just bowed and rubbed his hands. Somebody else came up at the moment, and as we were discussing the new parochial universal school committee, the matter of the new dean dropped; after that I didn't think it wise to renew it.'

'Renew it! I am very sorry you ever mentioned it. What will the archbishop think of you?'

'You may be sure, my dear, the archbishop thought very little about it.'

'But why did you think about it, bishop? how could you think of making such a creature as that Dean of Barchester? Dean of Barchester! I suppose he'll be looking for a bishopric some of these days – a man that hardly knows who his own father was; a man that I found without bread to his mouth, or a coat to his back. Dean of Barchester, indeed! I'll dean him.'

Mrs Proudie considered herself to be in politics a pure Whig; all her family belonged to the Whig party. Now among all ranks of Englishmen and

Englishwomen (Mrs Proudie should, I think, be ranked among the former, on the score of her great strength of mind), no one is so hostile to lowly born pretenders to high station as the pure Whig.

The bishop thought it necessary to exculpate himself. 'Why, my dear,' said he, 'it appeared to me that you and Mr Slope did not get on quite so well as you used to.'

'Get on!' said Mrs Proudie, moving her foot uneasily on the hearth-rug, and compressing her lips in a manner that betokened much danger to the subject of their discourse.

'I began to find that he was objectionable to you,' – Mrs Proudie's foot worked on the hearth-rug with great rapidity – 'and that you would be more comfortable if he was out of the palace,' – Mrs Proudie smiled, as a hyena may probably smile before he begins his laugh – 'and therefore I thought that if he got this place, and so ceased to be my chaplain, you might be pleased at such an arrangement.'

And then the hyena laughed out. Pleased at such an arrangement! pleased at having her enemy converted into a dean with twelve hundred a year! Medea, when she describes the customs of her native country (I am quoting from Robson's edition), assures her astonished auditor that in her land captives, when taken, are eaten. 'You pardon them?' says Medea. 'We do indeed,' says the mild Grecian. 'We eat them!' says she of Colchis, with terrific energy. Mrs Proudie was the Medea of Barchester; she had no idea of not eating Mr Slope. Pardon him! merely get rid of him! make a dean of him! It was not so they did with their captives in her country, among people of her sort! Mr Slope had no such mercy to expect, she would pick him to the very last bone.

'Oh, yes, my dear, of course he'll cease to be your chaplain,' said she. 'After what has passed, that must be a matter of course. I couldn't for a moment think of living in the same house with such a man. Besides, he has shown himself quite unfit for such a situation; making broils and quarrels among the clergy, getting you, my dear, into scrapes, and taking upon himself as though he were as good as bishop himself. Of course he'll go. But because he leaves the palace, that is no reason why he should get into the deanery.'

'Oh, of course not!' said the bishop; 'but to save appearances you know, my dear –'

'I don't want to save appearances; I want Mr Slope to appear just what he is – a false, designing, mean, intriguing man. I have my eye on him; he little knows what I see. He is misconducting himself in the most disgraceful way with that lame Italian woman. That family is a disgrace to Barchester, and Mr Slope is a disgrace to Barchester! If he doesn't look well to it, he'll have his gown stripped off his back instead of having a dean's hat on his head. Dean, indeed! The man has gone mad with arrogance.'

The bishop said nothing further to excuse either himself or his chaplain, and having shown himself passive and docile was again taken into favour. They soon went to dinner, and he spent the pleasantest evening he had had in his own house for a long time. His daughter played and sang to him as he sipped his coffee and read his newspaper, and Mrs Proudie asked good-natured little questions about the archbishop; and then he went happily to bed, and slept as quietly as though Mrs Proudie had been Griselda herself. While shaving himself in the morning and preparing for the festivities of Ullathorne, he fully resolved to run no more tilts against a warrior so fully armed at all points as was Mrs Proudie.

✄ THIRTY-FOUR ✄

Oxford – the Master and Tutor of Lazarus

MR ARABIN, AS WE HAVE SAID, HAD but a sad walk of it under the trees of Plumstead churchyard. He did not appear to any of the family till dinner time, and then he seemed, as far as their judgment went, to be quite himself. He had, as was his wont, asked himself a great many questions, and given himself a great many answers; and the upshot of this was that he had set himself down for an ass. He had determined that he was much too old and much too rusty to commence the manœuvres of love-making; that he had let the time slip through his hands which should have been used for such purposes; and that now he must lie on his bed as he had made it. Then he asked himself whether in truth he did love this woman; and he answered himself, not without a long struggle, but at last honestly, that he certainly did love her. He then asked himself whether he did not also love her money; and he again answered himself that he did so. But here he did not answer honestly. It was and ever had been his weakness to look for impure motives for his own conduct. No doubt, circumstanced as he was, with a small living and a fellowship, accustomed as he had been to collegiate luxuries and expensive comforts, he might have hesitated to marry a penniless woman had he felt ever so strong a predilection for the woman herself; no doubt Eleanor's fortune put all such difficulties out of the question; but it was equally without doubt that his love for her had crept upon him without the slightest idea on his part that he could ever benefit his own condition by sharing her wealth.

When he had stood on the hearth-rug, counting the pattern, and counting also the future chances of his own life, the remembrances of Mrs Bold's comfortable income had not certainly damped his first assured feeling of love for her. And why should it have done so? Need it have done so with the purest of men? Be that as it may, Mr Arabin decided against himself; he decided that it had done so in his case, and that he was not the purest of men.

He also decided, which was more to his purpose, that Eleanor did not care a straw for him, and that very probably she did care a straw for his rival. Then he made up his mind not to think of her any more, and went on thinking of her till he was almost in a state to drown himself in the little brook which ran at the bottom of the archdeacon's grounds.

And ever and again his mind would revert to the Signora Neroni, and he would make comparisons between her and Eleanor Bold, not always in favour of the latter. The signora had listened to him, and flattered him, and believed in him; at least she had told him so. Mrs Bold had also listened to him, but had never flattered him; had not always believed in him: and now had broken from him in violent rage. The signora, too, was the more lovely woman of the two, and had also the additional attraction of her affliction; for to him it was an attraction.

But he never could have loved the Signora Neroni as he felt that he now loved Eleanor! and so he flung stones into the brook, instead of flinging in himself, and sat down on its margin as sad a gentleman as you shall meet in a summer's day.

He heard the dinner-bell ring from the churchyard, and he knew that it was time to recover his self-possession. He felt that he was disgracing himself in his own eyes, that he had been idling his time and neglecting the high duties which he had taken upon himself to perform. He should have spent this afternoon among the poor at St Ewold's, instead of wandering about at Plumstead, an ancient love-lorn swain, dejected and sighing, full of imaginary sorrows and Wertherian grief. He was thoroughly ashamed of himself, and determined to lose no time in retrieving his character, so damaged in his own eyes. Thus when he appeared at dinner he was as animated as ever, and was the author of most of the conversation which graced the archdeacon's board on that evening. Mr Harding was ill at ease and sick at heart, and did not care to appear more comfortable than he really was; what little he did say was said to his daughter. He thought that the archdeacon and Mr Arabin had leagued together against Eleanor's comfort; and his wish now was to break away from the pair, and undergo in his Barchester lodgings whatever Fate had in store for him. He hated the name of the hospital; his attempt to regain his lost inheritance there had brought upon him so much suffering. As far as he was concerned, Mr Quiverful was now welcome to the place.

And the archdeacon was not very lively. The poor dean's illness was of course discussed in the first place. Dr Grantly did not mention Mr Slope's name in connexion with the expected event of Dr Trefoil's death; he did not wish to say anything about Mr Slope just at present, nor did he wish to make known his sad surmises; but the idea that his enemy might possibly become Dean of Barchester made him very gloomy. Should such an event take place, such a dire catastrophe come about, there would be an end to his life as far as his life was connected with the city of Barchester. He must give up all his old haunts, all his old habits, and live quietly as a retired rector at Plumstead. It had been a severe trial for him to have Dr Proudie in the palace; but with Mr Slope also in the deanery, he felt that he should be unable to draw his breath in Barchester close.

Thus it came to pass that in spite of the sorrow at his heart, Mr Arabin was apparently the gayest of the party. Both Mr Harding and Mrs Grantly were in a slight degree angry with him on account of his want of gloom. To the one it appeared as though he were triumphing at Eleanor's banishment, and to the other that he was not affected as he should have been by all the sad circumstances of the day, Eleanor's obstinacy, Mr Slope's success, and the poor dean's apoplexy. And so they were all at cross purposes.

Mr Harding left the room almost together with the ladies, and then the archdeacon opened his heart to Mr Arabin. He still harped upon the hospital. 'What did that fellow mean,' said he, 'by saying in his letter to Mrs Bold, that if Mr Harding would call on the bishop it would be all right? Of course I would not be guided by anything he might say; but still it may be well that Mr Harding should see the bishop. It would be foolish to let the thing slip through our fingers because Mrs Bold is determined to make a fool of herself.'

Mr Arabin hinted that he was not quite so sure that Mrs Bold would make a fool of herself. He said that he was not convinced that she did regard Mr Slope so warmly as she was supposed to do. The archdeacon questioned and cross-questioned him about this, but elicited nothing; and at last remained firm in his own conviction that he was destined, *malgré lui*, to be the brother-in-law of Mr Slope. Mr Arabin strongly advised that Mr Harding should take no step regarding the hospital in connexion with, or in consequence of, Mr Slope's letter. 'If the bishop really means to confer the appointment on Mr Harding,' argued Mr Arabin, 'he will take care to let him have some other intimation than a message conveyed through a letter to a lady. Were Mr Harding to present himself at the palace he might merely be playing Mr Slope's game;' and thus it was settled that nothing should be done till the great Dr Gwynne's arrival, or at any rate without that potentate's sanction.

It was droll to observe how these men talked of Mr Harding as though he were a puppet, and planned their intrigues and small ecclesiastical manœuvres in reference to Mr Harding's future position, without dreaming of taking him into their confidence. There was a comfortable house and income in question, and it was very desirable, and certainly very just, that Mr Harding should have them; but that, at present, was not the main point; it was expedient to beat the bishop, and if possible to smash Mr Slope. Mr Slope had set up, or was supposed to have set up, a rival candidate. Of all things the most desirable would have been to have had Mr Quiverful's appointment published to the public, and then annulled by the clamour of an indignant world, loud in the defence of Mr Harding's rights. But of such an event the chance was small; a slight fraction only of the world would be indignant, and that fraction would be one not accustomed to loud speaking. And then the preferment had in a sort of way been offered to Mr Harding, and had in a sort of way been refused by him.

Mr Slope's wicked, cunning hand had been peculiarly conspicuous in the way in which this had been brought to pass, and it was the success of Mr Slope's cunning which was so painfully grating to the feelings of the archdeacon. That which of all things he most dreaded was that he should be out-generalled by Mr Slope: and just at present it appeared probable that Mr Slope would turn his flank, steal a march on him, cut off his provisions, carry his strong town by a *coup de main*, and at last beat him thoroughly in a regular pitched battle. The archdeacon felt that his flank had been turned when desired to wait on Mr Slope instead of the bishop, that a march had been stolen when Mr Harding was induced to refuse the bishop's offer, that his provisions would be cut off when Mr Quiverful got the hospital, that Eleanor was the strong town doomed to be taken, and that Mr Slope, as Dean of Barchester, would be regarded by all the world as the conqueror in the final conflict.

Dr Gwynne was the *Deus ex machinâ* who was to come down upon the Barchester stage, and bring about deliverance from these terrible evils. But how can melodramatic *dénouements* be properly brought about, how can vice and Mr Slope be punished, and virtue and the archdeacon be rewarded, while the avenging god is laid up with the gout? In the mean time evil may be triumphant, and poor innocence, transfixed to the earth by an arrow from Dr Proudie's quiver, may lie dead upon the ground, not to be resuscitated even by Dr Gwynne.

Two or three days after Eleanor's departure, Mr Arabin went to Oxford, and soon found himself closeted with the august head of his college. It was quite clear that Dr Gwynne was not very sanguine as to the effects of his journey to Barchester, and not over anxious to interfere with the bishop. He had had the gout but was very nearly convalescent, and Mr Arabin at once saw that had the mission been one of which the master thoroughly approved, he would before this have been at Plumstead.

As it was, Dr Gwynne was resolved on visiting his friend, and willingly promised to return to Barchester with Mr Arabin. He could not bring himself to believe that there was any probability that Mr Slope would be made Dean of Barchester. Rumour, he said, had reached even his ears, not at all favourable to that gentleman's character, and he expressed himself strongly of opinion that any such appointment was quite out of the question. At this stage of the proceedings, the master's right-hand man, Tom Staple, was called in to assist at the conference. Tom Staple was the Tutor of Lazarus, and moreover a great man at Oxford. Though universally known by a species of nomenclature so very undignified, Tom Staple was one who maintained a high dignity in the University. He was, as it were, the leader of the Oxford tutors, a body of men who consider themselves collectively as being by very little, if at all, second in importance to the heads themselves. It is not always the case that the master, or warden, or provost, or principal can hit it off exactly with his tutor. A tutor is by no means indisposed to have a will of his own. But at Lazarus they were great friends and firm allies at the time of which we are writing.

Tom Staple was a hale strong man of about forty-five; short in stature, swarthy in face, with strong sturdy black hair, and crisp black beard, of which very little was allowed to show itself in shape of whiskers. He always wore a white neckcloth, clean indeed, but not tied with that scrupulous care which now distinguishes some of our younger clergy. He was, of course, always clothed in a seemly suit of solemn black. Mr Staple was a decent cleanly liver, not over addicted to any sensuality; but nevertheless a somewhat warmish hue was beginning to adorn his nose, the peculiar effect, as his friends averred, of a certain pipe of port introduced into the cellars of Lazarus the very same year in which the tutor entered it as a freshman. There was also, perhaps, a little redolence of port wine, as it were the slightest possible twang, in Mr Staple's voice.

In these latter days Tom Staple was not a happy man; University reform had long been his bugbear, and now was his bane. It was not with him as with most others, an affair of politics, respecting which, when the need existed, he could, for parties' sake or on behalf of principle, maintain a certain amount of necessary zeal; it was not with him a subject for dilettante warfare, and courteous common-place opposition. To him it was life and death. The *statu quo* of the University was his only idea of life, and any reformation was as bad to him as death. He would willingly have been a martyr in the cause, had the cause admitted of martyrdom.

At the present day, unfortunately, public affairs will allow of no martyrs, and therefore it is that there is such a deficiency of zeal. Could gentlemen of 10,000l. a year have died on their own door-steps in defence of protection, no doubt some half-dozen glorious old baronets would have so fallen, and the school of protection would at this day have been crowded with scholars. Who can fight strenuously in any combat in which there is no danger? Tom Staple would have willingly been impaled before a Committee of the House, could he by such self-sacrifice have infused his own spirit into the component members of the hebdomadal board.

Tom Staple was one of those who in his heart approved of the credit system which had of old been in vogue between the students and tradesmen of the University. He knew and acknowledged to himself that it was useless in these degenerate days publicly to contend with the Jupiter on such a subject. The Jupiter had undertaken to rule the University, and Tom Staple was well aware that the Jupiter was too powerful for him. But in secret, and among his safe companions, he would argue that the system of credit was an ordeal good for young men to undergo.

The bad men, said he, the weak and worthless, blunder into danger and burn their feet; but the good men, they who have any character, they who have that within them which can reflect credit on their Alma Mater, they come through scatheless. What merit will there be to a young man to get through safely, if he be guarded and protected and restrained like a schoolboy? By so doing, the period of the ordeal is only postponed, and the manhood of the man will be deferred from the age of twenty to that of twenty-four. If you bind him with leading-strings at college, he will break loose while eating for the bar in London; bind him there, and he will break loose afterwards, when he is a married man. The wild oats must be sown somewhere. 'Twas thus that Tom Staple would argue of young men; not, indeed, with much consistency, but still with some practical knowledge of the subject gathered from long experience.

And now Tom Staple proffered such wisdom as he had for the assistance of Dr Gwynne and Mr Arabin.

'Quite out of the question,' said he, arguing that Mr Slope could not possibly be made the new Dean of Barchester.

'So I think,' said the master. 'He has no standing, and, if all I hear be true, very little character.'

'As to character,' said Tom Staple, 'I don't think much of that. They rather like loose parsons for deans; a little fast living, or a dash of infidelity, is no bad recommendation to a cathedral close. But they couldn't make Mr Slope; the last two deans have been Cambridge men; you'll not show me an instance of their making three men running from the same University. We don't get our share, and never shall, I suppose; but we must at least have one out of three.'

'Those sort of rules are all gone by now,' said Mr Arabin.

'Everything has gone by, I believe,' said Tom Staple. 'The cigar has been smoked out, and we are the ashes.'

'Speak for yourself, Staple,' said the master.

'I speak for all,' said the tutor, stoutly. 'It is coming to that, that there will be no life left anywhere in the country. No one is any longer fit to rule himself, or those belonging to him. The Government is to find us all in everything, and the press is to find the Government. Nevertheless, Mr Slope won't be Dean of Barchester.'

'And who will be warden of the hospital?' said Mr Arabin.

'I hear that Mr Quiverful is already appointed,' said Tom Staple.

'I think not,' said the master. 'And I think, moreover, that Dr Proudie will not be so short-sighted as to run against such a rock: Mr Slope should himself have sense enough to prevent it.'

'But perhaps Mr Slope may have no objection to see his patron on a rock,' said the suspicious tutor.

'What could he get by that?' asked Mr Arabin.

'It is impossible to see the doubles of such a man,' said Mr Staple. 'It seems quite clear that Bishop Proudie is altogether in his hands, and it is equally clear that he has been moving heaven and earth to get this Mr Quiverful into the hospital, although he must know that such an appointment would be most damaging to the bishop. It is impossible to understand such a man, and dreadful to think,' added Tom Staple, sighing deeply, 'that the welfare and fortunes of good men may depend on his intrigues.'

Dr Gwynne or Mr Staple were not in the least aware, nor even was Mr Arabin, that this Mr Slope, of whom they were talking, had been using his utmost efforts to put their own candidate into the hospital; and that in lieu of being permanent in the palace, his own expulsion therefrom had been already decided on by the high powers of the diocese.

'I'll tell you what,' said the tutor, 'if this Quiverful is thrust into the hospital and Dr Trefoil does die, I should not wonder if the Government were to make Mr Harding Dean of Barchester. They would feel bound to do something for him after all that was said when he resigned.'

Dr Gwynne at the moment made no reply to this suggestion; but it did not the less impress itself on his mind. If Mr Harding could not be warden of the hospital, why should he not be Dean of Barchester?

And so the conference ended without any very fixed resolution, and Dr Gwynne and Mr Arabin prepared for their journey to Plumstead on the morrow.

✖ THIRTY-FIVE ✖

Miss Thorne's Fête Champêtre

THE DAY OF THE ULLATHORNE PARTY ARRIVED, and all the world were there; or at least so much of the world as had been included in Miss Thorne's invitation. As we have said, the bishop returned home on the previous evening, and on the same evening, and by the same train, came Dr Gwynne and Mr Arabin from Oxford. The archdeacon with his brougham was in waiting for the Master of Lazarus, so that there was a goodly show of church dignitaries on the platform of the railway.

The Stanhope party was finally arranged in the odious manner already described, and Eleanor got into the doctor's carriage full of apprehension and presentiment of further misfortune, whereas Mr Slope entered the vehicle elate with triumph.

He had received that morning a very civil note from Sir Nicholas Fitzwhiggin; not promising much indeed; but then Mr Slope knew, or fancied that he knew, that it was not etiquette for government officers to make promises. Though Sir Nicholas promised nothing he implied a good deal; declared his conviction that Mr Slope would make an excellent dean, and wished him every kind of success. To be sure he added that, not being in the cabinet, he was never consulted on such matters, and that even if he spoke on the subject his voice would go for nothing. But all this Mr Slope took for the prudent reserve of official life. To complete his anticipated triumphs, another letter was brought to him just as he was about to start to Ullathorne.

Mr Slope also enjoyed the idea of handing Mrs Bold out of Dr Stanhope's carriage before the multitude at Ullathorne gate, as much as Eleanor dreaded the same ceremony. He had fully made up his mind to throw himself and his fortune at the widow's feet, and had almost determined to select the present propitious morning for doing so. The signora had of late been less than civil to him. She had indeed admitted his visits, and listened, at any rate without anger, to his love; but she had tortured him and reviled him, jeered at him and ridiculed him, while she allowed him to call her the most beautiful of living women, to kiss her hand, and to proclaim himself with reiterated oaths her adorer, her slave, and worshipper.

Miss Thorne was in great perturbation, yet in great glory, on the morning of the gala day. Mr Thorne also, though the party was none of his giving, had much heavy work on his hands. But perhaps the most overtasked, the most anxious, and the most effective of all the Ullathorne household was Mr Plomacy, the steward. This last personage had, in the time of Mr Thorne's father, when the Directory held dominion in France, gone over to Paris with letters in his boot heel for some of the royal party; and such had been his good luck that he had returned safe. He had then been very young and was now very old, but the exploit gave him a character for political enterprise and secret discretion which still availed him as thoroughly as it had done in its freshest gloss. Mr Plomacy had been steward of Ullathorne for more than fifty years, and a very easy life he had had of it. Who could require much absolute work from a man who had carried safely at his heel that which if discovered would have cost him his head? Consequently Mr Plomacy had never worked hard, and of latter years had never worked at all. He had a taste for timber, and therefore he marked the trees that were to be cut down; he had a taste for gardening, and would therefore allow no shrub to be planted or bed to be made without his express sanction. In these matters he was sometimes driven to run counter to his mistress, but he rarely allowed his mistress to carry the point against him.

But on occasions such as the present Mr Plomacy came out strong. He had the honour of the family at heart; he thoroughly appreciated the duties of hospitality; and therefore, when gala doings were going on, always took the management into his own hands and reigned supreme over master and mistress.

To give Mr Plomacy his due, old as he was, he thoroughly understood such work as he had in hand, and did it well.

The order of the day was to be as follows. The quality, as the upper classes in rural districts are designated by the lower with so much true discrimination, were to eat a breakfast, and the non-quality were to eat a dinner. Two marquees had been erected for these two banquets, that for the quality on the esoteric or garden side of a certain deep ha-ha; and that for the non-quality on the exoteric or paddock side of the same. Both were of huge dimensions; that on the outer side was, one may say, on an egregious scale; but Mr Plomacy declared that neither would be sufficient. To remedy this, an auxiliary banquet was prepared in the dining-room, and a subsidiary board was to be spread *sub dio* for the accommodation of the lower class of yokels on the Ullathorne property.

No one who has not had a hand in the preparation of such an affair can understand the manifold difficulties which Miss Thorne encountered in her project. Had she not been made throughout of the very finest whale-bone, riveted with the best Yorkshire steel, she must have sunk under them. Had not Mr Plomacy felt how much was justly expected from a man who at one time carried the destinies of Europe in his boot, he would have given way; and his mistress, so deserted, must have perished among her poles and canvass.

In the first place there was a dreadful line to be drawn. Who were to dispose themselves within the ha-ha, and who without? To this the unthinking will give an off-hand answer, as they will to every ponderous question. Oh, the bishop and such like within the ha-ha; and Farmer Greenacre and such like without. True, my unthinking friend; but who shall define these such-likes? It is in such definitions that the whole difficulty of society consists. To seat the bishop on an arm chair on the lawn and place Farmer Greenacre at the end of a long table in the paddock is easy enough; but where will you put Mrs Lookaloft, whose husband, though a tenant on the estate, hunts in a red coat, whose daughters go to a fashionable seminary in Barchester, who calls her farm house Rosebank, and who has a pianoforte in her drawing-room? The Misses Lookaloft, as they call themseves, won't sit contented among the bumpkins. Mrs Lookaloft won't squeeze her fine clothes on a bench and talk familiarly about cream and ducklings to good Mrs Greenacre. And yet Mrs Lookaloft is no fit companion and never has been the associate of the Thornes and the Grantlys. And if Mrs Lookaloft be admitted within the sanctum of fashionable life, if she be allowed with her three daughters to leap the ha-ha, why not the wives and daughters of other families also? Mrs Greenacre is at present well contented with the paddock, but she might cease to be so if she saw Mrs Lookaloft on the lawn. And thus poor Miss Thorne had a hard time of it.

And how was she to divide her guests between the marquee and the parlour? She had a countess coming, an Honourable John and an Honourable George, and a whole bevy of Ladies Amelia, Rosina, Margaretta, &c.; she had a leash of baronets with their baronnettes; and, as we all know, she had a bishop. If she put them on the lawn, no one would go into the parlour; if she put them into the parlour, no one would go into the tent. She thought of keeping the old people in the house, and leaving the lawn to the lovers. She might as well have seated herself at once in a hornet's nest. Mr Plomacy knew better than this. 'Bless your soul, Ma'am,' said he, 'there won't be no old ladies; not one, barring yourself and old Mrs Clantantram.'

Personally Miss Thorne accepted this distinction in her favour as a compliment to her good sense; but nevertheless she had no desire to be closeted on the coming occasion with Mrs Clantantram. She gave up all idea of any arbitrary division of her guests, and determined if possible to put the bishop on the lawn and the countess in the house, to sprinkle the baronets, and thus divide the attractions. What to do with the Lookalofts even Mr Plomacy could not decide. They must take their chance. They had been invited; and they might probably have the good sense to stay away if they objected to mix with the rest of the tenantry.

Then Mr Plomacy declared his apprehension that the Honourable Johns and Honourable Georges would come in a sort of amphibious costume, half morning half evening, satin neckhandkerchiefs, frock coats, primrose gloves, and polished boots; and that, being so dressed, they would decline riding at the quintain, or taking part in any of the athletic games which Miss Thorne had prepared with so much fond care. If the Lord Johns and Lord Georges didn't ride at the quintain, Miss Thorne might be sure that nobody else would.

'But,' said she in dolorous voice, all but overcome by her cares; 'it was specially signified that there were to be sports.'

'And so there will be, of course,' said Mr Plomacy. 'They'll all be sporting with the young ladies in the laurel walks. Them's the sports they care most about now-a-days. If you gets the young men at the quintain, you'll have all the young women in the pouts.'

'Can't they look on, as their great grandmothers did before them?' said Miss Thorne.

'It seems to me that the ladies ain't contented with looking now-a-days. Whatever the men do they'll do. If you'll have side saddles on the nags, and let them go at the quintain too, it'll answer capital, no doubt.'

Miss Thorne made no reply. She felt that she had no good ground on which to defend her sex of the present generation from the sarcasm of Mr Plomacy. She had once declared, in one of her warmer moments, 'that now-a-days the gentlemen were all women, and the ladies all men.' She could not alter the debased character of the age. But, such being the case, why should she take on herself to cater for the amusement of people of such degraded tastes? This question she asked herself more than once, and she could only answer herself with a sigh. There was her own brother Wilfred, on whose shoulders rested all the ancient honours of Ullathorne house; it was very doubtful whether even he would consent to 'go at the quintain,' as Mr Plomacy not injudiciously expressed it.

And now the morning arrived. The Ullathorne household was early on the move. Cooks were cooking in the kitchen long before daylight, and men were dragging out tables and hammering red baize on to benches at the earliest dawn. With what dread eagerness did Miss Thorne look out at the weather as soon as the parting veil of night permitted her to look at all! In this respect at any rate there was nothing to grieve her. The glass had been rising for the last three days, and the morning broke with that dull chill steady grey haze which in autumn generally presages a clear and dry day. By seven she was dressed and down. Miss Thorne knew nothing of the modern luxury of *déshabilles*. She would as soon have thought of appearing before her brother without her stockings as without her stays; and Miss Thorne's stays were no trifle.

And yet there was nothing for her to do when down. She fidgeted out to the lawn, and then back into the kitchen. She put on her high-heeled clogs, and fidgeted out into the paddock. Then she went into the small home park where the quintain was erected. The pole and cross bar and the swivel, and the target and the bag of flour were all complete. She got up on a carpenter's bench and touched the target with her hand; it went round with beautiful ease; the swivel had been oiled to perfection. She almost wished to take old Plomacy at his word, to get on a side saddle and have a tilt at it herself. What must a young man be, thought she, who could prefer maundering among laurel trees with a wishy-washy school girl to such fun as this? 'Well,' said she aloud to herself, 'one man can take a horse to water, but a thousand can't make him drink. There it is. If they haven't the spirit to enjoy it, the fault shan't be mine;' and so she returned to the house.

At a little after eight her brother came down, and they had a sort of scrap breakfast in his study. The tea was made without the customary urn, and they dispensed with the usual rolls and toast. Eggs also were missing, for every egg in the parish had been whipped into custards, baked into pies, or boiled into lobster salad. The allowance of fresh butter was short, and Mr Thorne was obliged to eat the leg of a fowl without having it devilled in the manner he loved.

'I have been looking at the quintain, Wilfred,' said she, 'and it appears to be quite right.'

'Oh – ah; yes;' said he. 'It seemed to be so yesterday when I saw it.' Mr Thorne was beginning to be rather bored by his sister's love of sports, and had especially no affection for this quintain post.

'I wish you'd just try it after breakfast,' said she. 'You could have the saddle put on Mark Antony, and the pole is there all handy. You can take the flour bag off, you know, if you think Mark Antony won't be quick enough,' added Miss Thorne, seeing that her brother's countenance was not indicative of complete accordance with her little proposition.

Now Mark Antony was a valuable old hunter, excellently suited to Mr Thorne's usual requirements, steady indeed at his fences, but extremely sure, very good in deep ground, and safe on the roads. But he had never yet been ridden at a quintain, and Mr Thorne was not inclined to put him to the trial, either with or without the bag of flour. He hummed and hawed, and finally declared that he was afraid Mark Antony would shy.

'Then try the cob,' said the indefatigable Miss Thorne.

'He's in physic,' said Wilfred.

'There's the Beelzebub colt,' said his sister; 'I know he's in the stable, because I saw Peter exercising him just now.'

'My dear Monica, he's so wild, that it's as much as I can do to manage him at all. He'd destroy himself and me too, if I attempted to ride him at such a rattletrap as that.'

A rattletrap! The quintain that she had put up with so much anxious care; the game that she had prepared for the amusement of the stalwart yeoman of the country; the sport that had been honoured by the affection of so many of their ancestors! It cut her to the heart to hear it so denominated by her own brother. There were but the two of them left together in the world; and it had ever been one of the rules by which Miss Thorne had regulated her conduct through life, to say nothing that could provoke her brother. She had often had to suffer from his indifference to time-honoured British customs; but she had always suffered in silence. It was part of her creed that the head of the family should never be upbraided in his own house; and Miss Thorne had lived up to her creed. Now, however, she was greatly tried. The colour mounted to her ancient cheek, and the fire blazed in her still bright eye; but yet she said nothing. She resolved that at any rate, to him nothing more should be said about the quintain that day.

She sipped her tea in silent sorrow, and thought with painful regret of the glorious days when her great ancestor Ealfried had successfully held Ullathorne against a Norman invader. There was no such spirit now left in her family except that small useless spark which burnt in her own bosom. And she herself, was not she at this moment intent on entertaining a descendant of those very Normans, a vain proud countess with a frenchified name, who would only think that she graced Ullathorne too highly by entering its portals? Was it likely that an honourable John, the son of an Earl De Courcy, should ride at a quintain in company with Saxon yeomen? And why should she expect her brother to do that which her brother's guests would decline to do?

Some dim faint idea of the impracticability of her own views flitted across her brain. Perhaps it was necessary that races doomed to live on the same soil should give way to each other, and adopt each other's pursuits. Perhaps it was impossible that after more than five centuries of close intercourse, Normans should remain Normans, and Saxons, Saxons. Perhaps after all her neighbours were wiser than herself. Such ideas did occasionally present themselves to Miss Thorne's mind, and make her sad enough. But it never occurred to her that her favourite quintain was but a modern copy of a Norman knight's amusement, an adaptation of the noble tourney to the tastes and habits of the Saxon yeoman. Of this she was ignorant, and it would have been cruelty to instruct her.

When Mr Thorne saw the tear in her eye, he repented himself of his contemptuous expression. By him also it was recognised as a binding law that every whim of his sister was to be respected. He was not perhaps so firm in his observances to her, as she was in hers to him. But his intentions were equally good, and whenever he found that he had forgotten them it was matter of grief to him.

'My dear Monica,' said he, 'I beg your pardon; I don't in the least mean to speak ill of the game. When I called it a rattletrap, I merely meant that it was so for a man of my age. You know you always forget that I ain't a young man.'

'I am quite sure you are not an old man, Wilfred,' said she, accepting the apology in her heart, and smiling at him with the tear still on her cheek.

'If I was five-and-twenty, or thirty,' continued he, 'I should like nothing better than riding at the quintain all day.'

'But you are not too old to hunt or to shoot,' said she. 'If you can jump over a ditch and hedge I am sure you could turn the quintain round.'

'But when I ride over the hedges, my dear – and it isn't very often I do that – but when I do ride over the hedges there isn't any bag of flour coming after me. Think how I'd look taking the countess out to breakfast with the back of my head all covered with meal.'

Miss Thorne said nothing further. She didn't like the allusion to the countess. She couldn't be satisfied with the reflection that the sports of Ullathorne should be interfered with by the personal attentions necessary for a Lady De Courcy. But she saw that it was useless for her to push the matter further. It was conceded that Mr Thorne was to be spared the quintain; and Miss Thorne determined to trust wholly to a youthful knight of hers, an immense favourite, who, as she often declared, was a pattern to the young men of the age, and an excellent sample of an English yeoman.

This was Farmer Greenacre's eldest son; who, to tell the truth, had from his earliest years taken the exact measure of Miss Thorne's foot. In his boyhood he had never failed to obtain from her, apples, pocket money, and forgiveness for his numerous trespasses; and now in his early manhood he got privileges and immunities which were equally valuable. He was allowed a day or two's shooting in September; he schooled the squire's horses; got slips of trees out of the orchard, and roots of flowers out of the garden; and had the fishing of the little river altogether in his own hands. He had undertaken to come mounted on a nag of his father's, and show the way at the quintain post. Whatever young Greenacre did the others would do after him. The juvenile Lookalofts might stand aloof, but the rest of the youth of Ullathorne would be sure to venture if Harry

Greenacre showed the way. And so Miss Thorne made up her mind to dispense with the noble Johns and Georges, and trust, as her ancestors had done before her, to the thews and sinews of native Ullathorne growth.

At about nine the lower orders began to congregate in the paddock and park, under the surveillance of Mr Plomacy and the head gardener and head groom, who were sworn in as his deputies, and were to assist him in keeping the peace and promoting the sports. Many of the younger inhabitants of the neighbourhood, thinking that they could not have too much of a good thing, had come at a very early hour, and the road between the house and the church had been thronged for some time before the gates were thrown open.

And then another difficulty of huge dimensions arose, a difficulty which Mr Plomacy had indeed foreseen and, for which he was in some sort provided. Some of those who wished to share Miss Thorne's hospitality were not so particular as they should have been as to the preliminary ceremony of an invitation. They doubtless conceived that they had been overlooked by accident; and instead of taking this in dudgeon, as their betters would have done, they good-naturedly put up with the slight, and showed that they did so by presenting themselves at the gate in their Sunday best.

Mr Plomacy, however, well knew who were welcome and who were not. To some, even though uninvited, he allowed ingress. 'Don't be too particular, Plomacy,' his mistress had said; 'especially with the children. If they live anywhere near, let them in.'

Acting on this hint, Mr Plomacy did let in many an eager urchin, and a few tidily dressed girls with their swains, who in no way belonged to the property. But to the denizens of the city he was inexorable. Many a Barchester apprentice made his appearance there that day, and urged with piteous supplication that he had been working all the week in making saddles and boots for the use of Ullathorne, in compounding doses for the horses, or cutting up carcases for the kitchen. No such claim was allowed. Mr Plomacy knew nothing about the city apprentices; he was to admit the tenants and labourers on the estate; Miss Thorne wasn't going to take in the whole city of Barchester; and so on.

Nevertheless, before the day was half over, all this was found to be useless. Almost anybody who chose to come made his way into the park, and the care of the guardians was transferred to the tables on which the banquet was spread. Even here there was many an unauthorised claimant for a place, of whom it was impossible to get quit without more commotion than the place and food were worth.

THIRTY-SIX

Ullathorne Sports – Act I

THE TROUBLE IN CIVILISED LIFE OF ENTERTAINING company, as it is called too generally without much regard to strict veracity, is so great that it cannot but be matter of wonder that people are so fond of attempting it. It is difficult to ascertain what is the *quid pro quo*. If they who give such laborious parties, and who endure such toil and turmoil in the vain hope of giving them successfully, really enjoyed the parties given by others, the matter could be understood. A sense of justice would induce men and women to undergo, in behalf of others, those miseries which others had undergone in their behalf. But they all profess that going out is as great a bore as receiving; and to look at them when they are out, one cannot but believe them.

Entertain! Who shall have sufficient self-assurance, who shall feel sufficient confidence in his own powers to dare to boast that he can entertain his company? A clown can sometimes do so, and sometimes a dancer in short petticoats and stuffed pink legs; occasionally, perhaps, a singer. But beyond these, success in this art of entertaining is not often achieved. Young men and girls linking themselves kind with kind, pairing like birds in spring because nature wills it, they, after a simple fashion, do entertain each other. Few others even try.

Ladies, when they open their houses, modestly confessing, it may be presumed, their own incapacity, mainly trust to wax candles and upholstery. Gentlemen seem to rely on their white waistcoats. To these are added for the delight of the more sensual, champagne and such good things of the table as fashion allows to be still considered as comestible. Even in this respect the world is deteriorating. All the good soups are now tabooed; and at the houses of one's accustomed friends, small barristers, doctors, government clerks, and such like, (for we cannot all of us always live as grandees, surrounded by an elysium of livery servants), one gets a cold potato handed to one as a sort of finale to one's slice of mutton. Alas! for those happy days when one could say to one's neighbourhood, 'Jones, shall I give you some mashed turnip? may I trouble you for a little cabbage?' And then the pleasure of drinking wine with Mrs Jones and Miss Smith; with all the Joneses and all the Smiths! These latter-day habits are certainly more economical.

Miss Thorne, however, boldly attempted to leave the modern beaten track, and made a positive effort to entertain her guests. Alas! she did so with but moderate success. They had all their own way of going, and would not go her way. She piped to them, but they would not dance. She offered to them good honest household cake, made of currants and flour and eggs and sweatmeat; but they would feed themselves on trashy wafers from the shop of the Barchester pastry-cook, on chalk and gum and adulterated sugar. Poor Miss Thorne! yours is not the first honest soul that has vainly striven to recall the glories of happy days gone by! If fashion suggests to a Lady De Courcy that when invited to a *déjeûner* at twelve she ought to come at three, no eloquence of thine will teach her the advantage of a nearer approach to punctuality.

She had fondly thought that when she called on her friends to come at twelve, and specially begged them to believe that she meant it, she would be able to see them comfortably seated in their tents at two. Vain woman – or rather ignorant woman – ignorant of the advances of that civilisation which the world had witnessed while she was growing old. At twelve she found herself alone, dressed in all the glory of the newest of her many suits of raiment; with strong shoes however, and a serviceable bonnet on her head, and a warm rich shawl on her shoulders. Thus clad she peered out into the tent, went to the ha-ha, and satisfied herself that at any rate the youngsters were amusing themselves, spoke a word to Mrs Greenacre over the ditch, and took one look at the quintain. Three or four young farmers were turning the machine round and round, and poking at the bag of flour in a manner not at all intended by the inventor of the game; but no mounted sportsmen were there. Miss Thorne looked at her watch. It was only fifteen minutes past twelve, and it was understood that Harry Greenacre was not to begin till the half hour.

Miss Thorne returned to her drawing-room rather quicker than was her wont, fearing that the countess might come and find none to welcome her. She need not have hurried, for no one was there. At half-past twelve she peeped into the kitchen; at a quarter to one she was joined by her brother; and just then the first fashionable arrival took place. Mrs Clantantram was announced.

No announcement was necessary, indeed; for the good lady's voice was heard as she walked across the court-yard to the house scolding the unfortunate postilion who had driven her from Barchester. At the moment, Miss Thorne could not but be thankful that the other guests were more fashionable, and were thus spared the fury of Mrs Clantantram's indignation.

'Oh Miss Thorne, look here!' said she, as soon as she found herself in the drawing-room; 'do look at my roquelaure! It's clean spoilt, and for ever. I wouldn't but wear it because I knew you wished us all to be grand to-day; and yet I had my misgivings. Oh dear, oh dear! It was five-and-twenty shillings a yard.'

The Barchester post horses had misbehaved in some unfortunate manner just as Mrs Clantantram was getting out of the chaise and had nearly thrown her under the wheel.

Mrs Clantantram belonged to other days, and therefore, though she had but little else to recommend her, Miss Thorne was to a certain extent fond of her. She sent the roquelaure away to be cleaned, and lent her one of her best shawls out of her own wardrobe.

The next comer was Mr Arabin, who was immediately informed of Mrs Clantantram's misfortune, and of her determination to pay neither master nor post-boy; although, as she remarked, she intended to get her lift home before she made known her mind upon that matter. Then a good deal of rustling was heard in the sort of lobby that was used for the ladies' outside cloaks; and the door having been thrown wide open, the servant announced, not in the most confident of voices, Mrs Lookaloft, and the Miss Lookalofts, and Mr Augustus Lookaloft.

Poor man! we mean the footman. He knew, none better, that Mrs Lookaloft had no business there, that she was not wanted there, and would not be welcome. But he had not the courage to tell a stout lady with a low dress, short sleeves, and satin at eight shillings a yard, that she had come to the wrong tent; he had not dared to hint to young ladies with white dancing shoes and long gloves, that there was a place ready for them in the paddock. And thus Mrs Lookaloft carried her point, broke through the guards, and made her way into the citadel. That she would have to pass an uncomfortable time there, she had surmised before. But nothing now could rob her of the power of boasting that she had consorted on the lawn with the squire and Miss Thorne, with a countess, a bishop, and the country grandees, while Mrs Greenacre and such like were walking about with the ploughboys in the park. It was a great point gained by Mrs Lookaloft, and it might be fairly expected that from this time forward the tradesmen of Barchester would, with undoubting pens, address her husband as T. Lookaloft, Esquire.

Mrs Lookaloft's pluck carried her through everything, and she walked triumphant into the Ullathorne drawing-room; but her children did feel a little abashed at the sort of reception they met with. It was not in Miss Thorne's heart to insult her own guests; but neither was it in her disposition to overlook such effrontery.

'Oh, Mrs Lookaloft, is this you,' said she; 'and your daughters and son? Well, we're very glad to see you; but I'm sorry you've come in such low dresses, as we are all going out of doors. Could we lend you something?'

'Oh dear no! thank ye, Miss Thorne,' said the mother; 'the girls and myself are quite used to low dresses, when we're out.'

'Are you, indeed?' said Miss Thorne shuddering; but the shudder was lost on Mrs Lookaloft.

'And where's Lookaloft?' said the master of the house, coming up to welcome his tenant's wife. Let the faults of the family be what they would, he could not but remember that their rent was well paid; he was therefore not willing to give them a cold shoulder.

'Such a headache, Mr Thorne!' said Mrs Lookaloft. 'In fact he couldn't stir, or you may be certain on such a day he would not have absented hisself.'

'Dear me,' said Miss Thorne. 'If he is so ill, I'm sure you'd wish to be with him.'

'Not at all!' said Mrs Lookaloft. 'Not at all, Miss Thorne. It is only bilious you know, and when he's that way he can bear nobody nigh him.'

The fact however was that Mr Lookaloft, having either more sense or less courage than his wife, had not chosen to intrude on Miss Thorne's drawing-room; and as he could not very well have gone among the plebeians while his wife was with the patricians, he thought it most expedient to remain at Rosebank.

Mrs Lookaloft soon found herself on a sofa, and the Miss Lookalofts on two chairs, while Mr Augustus stood near the door; and here they remained till in due time they were seated all four together at the bottom of the dining-room table.

Then the Grantlys came; the archdeacon and Mrs Grantly and the two girls, and Dr Gwynne and Mr Harding; and as ill luck would have it, they were closely followed by Dr Stanhope's carriage. As Eleanor looked out of the carriage window, she saw her brother-in-law helping the ladies out, and threw herself back into her seat, dreading to be discovered. She had had an odious journey. Mr Slope's civility had been more than ordinarily greasy; and now, though he had not in fact said anything which she could notice, she had for the first time entertained a suspicion that he was intending to make love to her. Was it after all true that she had been conducting herself in a way that justified the world in thinking that she liked the man? After all, could it be possible that the archdeacon and Mr Arabin were right, and that she was wrong? Charlotte Stanhope had also been watching Mr Slope, and had come to the conclusion that it behoved her brother to lose no further time, if he meant to gain the widow. She almost regretted that it had not been contrived that Bertie should be at Ullathorne before them.

Dr Grantly did not see his sister-in-law in company with Mr Slope, but Mr Arabin did. Mr Arabin came out with Mr Thorne to the front door to welcome Mrs Grantly, and he remained in the courtyard till all their party had passed on. Eleanor hung back in the carriage as long as she well could, but she was nearest to the door, and when Mr Slope, having alighted, offered her his hand, she had no alternative but to take it. Mr Arabin standing at the open door, while Mrs Grantly was shaking hands with some one within, saw a clergyman alight from the carriage whom he at once knew to be Mr Slope, and then he saw this clergyman hand out Mrs Bold. Having seen so much, Mr Arabin, rather sick at heart, followed Mrs Grantly into the house.

Eleanor was, however, spared any further immediate degradation, for Dr Stanhope gave her his arm across the courtyard, and Mr Slope was fain to throw away his attention upon Charlotte.

They had hardly passed into the house, and from the house to the lawn, when, with a loud rattle and such noise as great men and great women are entitled to make in their passage through the world, the Proudies drove up. It was soon apparent that no every day comer was at the door. One servant whispered to another that it was the bishop, and the word soon ran through all the hangers-on and strange grooms and coachmen about the place. There was quite a little cortége to see the bishop and his 'lady' walk across the courtyard, and the good man was pleased to see that the church was held in such respect in the parish of St Ewold's.

And now the guests came fast and thick, and the lawn began to be crowded, and the room to be full. Voices buzzed, silk rustled against silk, and muslin crumpled against muslin. Miss Thorne became more happy than she had been, and again bethought her of sports. There were targets and bows and arrows prepared at the further end of the lawn. Here the gardens of the place encroached with a somewhat wide sweep upon the paddock, and gave ample room for the doings of the toxophilites. Miss Thorne got together such daughters of Diana as could bend a bow, and marshalled them to the targets. There were the Grantly girls and the Proudie girls and the Chadwick girls, and the two daughters of the burly chancellor, and Miss Knowle; and with them went Frederick and Augustus Chadwick and young Knowle of Knowle park, and Frank Foster of the Elms, and Mr Vellem Deeds the dashing attorney of the High Street, and the Rev. Mr White, all of whom, as in duty bound, attended the steps of the three Miss Proudies.

'Did you ever ride at the quintain, Mr Foster?' said Miss Thorne, as she walked with her party, across the lawn.

'The quintain?' said young Foster, who considered himself a dab at horsemanship. 'Is it a sort of gate, Miss Thorne?'

Miss Thorne had to explain the noble game she spoke of, and Frank Foster had to own that he never had ridden at the quintain.

'Would you like to come and see?' said Miss Thorne. 'There'll be plenty here without you, if you like it.'

'Well, I don't mind,' said Frank; 'I suppose the ladies can come too.'

'Oh yes,' said Miss Thorne; 'those who like it; I have no doubt they'll go to see your prowess, if you'll ride, Mr Foster.'

Mr Foster looked down at a most unexceptionable pair of pantaloons, which had arrived from London only the day before. They were the very things, at least he thought so, for a picnic or fête champêtre; but he was not prepared to ride in them. Nor was he more encouraged than had been Mr Thorne, by the idea of being attacked from behind by the bag of flour which Miss Thorne had graphically described to him.

'Well, I don't know about riding, Miss Thorne,' said he; 'I fear I'm not quite prepared.'

Miss Thorne sighed, but said nothing further. She left the toxophilites to their bows and arrows, and returned towards the house. But as she passed by the entrance to the small park, she thought that she might at any rate encourage the yeomen by her presence, as she could not induce her more fashionable guests to mix with them in their manly amusements. Accordingly she once more betook herself to the quintain post.

Here to her great delight she found Harry Greenacre ready mounted, with his pole in his hand, and a lot of comrades standing round him, encouraging him to the assault. She stood at a little distance and nodded to him in token of her good pleasure.

'Shall I begin, ma'am?' said Harry fingering his long staff in a rather awkward way, while his horse moved uneasily beneath him, not accustomed to a rider armed with such a weapon.

'Yes, yes,' said Miss Thorne, standing triumphant as the queen of beauty, on an inverted tub which some chance had brought thither from the farm-yard.

'Here goes then,' said Harry as he wheeled his horse round to get the necessary momentum of a sharp gallop. The quintain post stood right before him, and the square board at which he was to tilt was fairly in his way. If he hit that duly in the middle, and maintained his pace as he did so, it was calculated that he would be carried out of reach of the flour bag, which, suspended at the other end of the cross-bar on the post, would swing round when the board was struck. It was also calculated that if the rider did not maintain his pace, he would get a blow from the flour bag just at the back of his head, and bear about him the signs of his awkwardness to the great amusement of the lookers-on.

Harry Greenacre did not object to being powdered with flour in the service of his mistress, and therefore gallantly touched his steed with his spur, having laid his lance in rest to the best of his ability. But his ability in this respect was not great, and his appurtenances probably not very good; consequently, he struck his horse with his pole unintentionally on the side of the head as he started. The animal swerved and shied, and galloped off wide of the quintain. Harry well accustomed to manage a horse, but not to do so with a twelve-foot rod on his arm, lowered his right hand to the bridle and thus the end of the lance came to the ground, and got between the legs of the steed. Down came rider and steed and staff. Young Greenacre was thrown some six feet over the horse's head, and poor Miss Thorne almost fell off her tub in a swoon.

'Oh gracious, he's killed,' shrieked a woman who was near him when he fell.

'The Lord be good to him! his poor mother, his poor mother!' said another.

'Well, drat them dangerous plays all the world over,' said an old crone.

'He has broke his neck sure enough, if ever man did,' said a fourth.

Poor Miss Thorne. She heard all this and yet did not quite swoon. She made her way through the crowd as best she could, sick herself almost to death. Oh, his mother – his poor mother! how could she ever forgive herself. The agony of that moment was terrific. She could hardly get to the place where the poor lad was lying, as three or four men in front were about the horse which had risen with some difficulty; but at last she found herself close to the young farmer.

'Has he marked himself? for heaven's sake tell me that; has he marked his knees?' said Harry, slowly rising and rubbing his left shoulder with his right hand, and thinking only of his horse's legs. Miss Thorne soon found that he had not broken his neck, nor any of his bones, nor been injured in any essential way. But from that time forth she never instigated any one to ride at a quintain.

Eleanor left Dr Stanhope as soon as she could do so civilly, and went in quest of her father whom she found on the lawn in company with Mr Arabin. She was not sorry to find them together. She was anxious to disabuse at any rate her father's mind as to this report which had got abroad respecting her, and would have been well pleased to have been able to do the same with regard to Mr Arabin. She put her own through her father's arm, coming up behind his back, and then tendered her hand also to the vicar of St Ewold's.

'And how did you come?' said Mr Harding, when the first greeting was over.

'The Stanhopes brought me,' said she; 'their carriage was obliged to come twice, and has now gone back for the signora.' As she spoke she caught Mr Arabin's eye, and saw that he was looking pointedly at her with a severe expression. She understood at once the accusation contained in his glance. It said as plainly as an eye could speak, 'Yes, you came with the Stanhopes, but you did so in order that you might be in company with Mr Slope.'

'Our party,' said she, still addressing her father 'consisted of the doctor and Charlotte Stanhope, myself, and Mr Slope.' As she mentioned the last name she felt her father's arm quiver slightly beneath her touch. At the same moment Mr Arabin turned away from them, and joining his hands behind his back strolled away by one of the paths.

'Papa,' said she, 'it was impossible to help coming in the same carriage with Mr Slope; it was quite impossible. I had promised to come with them before I dreamt of his coming, and afterwards I could not get out of it without explaining and giving rise to talk. You weren't at home, you know, I couldn't possibly help it.' She said all this so quickly that by the time her apology was spoken she was quite out of breath.

'I don't know why you should have wished to help it, my dear,' said her father.

'Yes, papa, you do; you must know, you do know all the things they said at Plumstead. I am sure you do. You know all the archdeacon said.

How unjust he was; and Mr Arabin too. He's a horrid man, a horrid odious man, but –'

'Who is an odious man, my dear? Mr Arabin?'

'No; but Mr Slope. You know I mean Mr Slope. He's the most odious man I ever met in my life, and it was most unfortunate my having to come here in the same carriage with him. But how could I help it?'

A great weight began to move itself off Mr Harding's mind. So, after all, the archdeacon with all his wisdom, and Mrs Grantly with all her tact, and Mr Arabin with all his talent, were in the wrong. His own child, his Eleanor, the daughter of whom he was so proud was not to become the wife of a Mr Slope. He had been about to give his sanction to the marriage, so certified had he been of the fact; and now he learnt that this imputed lover of Eleanor's was at any rate as much disliked by her as by any one of the family. Mr Harding, however, was by no means sufficiently a man of the world to conceal the blunder he had made. He could not pretend that he had entertained no suspicion; he could not make believe that he had never joined the archdeacon in his surmises. He was greatly surprised, and gratified beyond measure, and he could not help showing that such was the case.

'My darling girl,' said he, 'I am so delighted, so overjoyed. My own child; you have taken such a weight off my mind.'

'But surely, papa, *you* didn't think –'

'I didn't know what to think, my dear. The archdeacon told me that –'

'The archdeacon!' said Eleanor, her face lighting up with passion. 'A man like the archdeacon might, one would think, be better employed than in traducing his sister-in-law, and creating bitterness between a father and his daughter!'

'He didn't mean to do that, Eleanor.'

'What did he mean then? Why did he interfere with me, and fill your mind with such falsehood?'

'Never mind it now, my child; never mind it now. We shall all know you better now.'

'Oh, papa, that you should have thought it! that you should have suspected me!'

'I don't know what you mean by suspicion, Eleanor. There would be nothing disgraceful, you know; nothing wrong in such a marriage. Nothing that could have justified my interfering as your father.' And Mr Harding would have proceeded in his own defence to make out that Mr Slope after all was a very good sort of man, and a very fitting second husband for a young widow, had he not been interrupted by Eleanor's greater energy.

'It would be disgraceful,' said she; 'it would be wrong; it would be abominable. Could I do such a horrid thing, I should expect no one to speak to me. Ugh –' and she shuddered as she thought of the matrimonial torch which her friends had been so ready to light on her behalf. 'I don't wonder at Dr Grantly; I don't wonder at Susan; but, oh, papa, I do wonder at you. How could you, how could you believe it?' Poor Eleanor, as she thought of her father's defalcation, could resist her tears no longer, and was forced to cover her face with her handkerchief.

The place was not very opportune for her grief. They were walking through the shrubberies, and there were many people near them. Poor Mr Harding stammered out his excuse as best he could, and Eleanor with an effort controlled her tears, and returned her handkerchief to her pocket. She did not find it difficult to forgive her father, nor could she altogether refuse to join him in the returning gaiety of spirit to which her present avowal gave rise. It was such a load off his heart to think that he should not be called on to welcome Mr Slope as his son-in-law. It was such a relief to him to find that his daughter's feelings and his own were now, as they ever had been, in unison. He had been so unhappy for the last six weeks about this wretched Mr Slope! He was so indifferent as to the loss of the hospital, so thankful for the recovery of his daughter, that, strong as was the ground for Eleanor's anger, she could not find it in her heart to be long angry with him.

'Dear papa,' she said, hanging closely to his arm, 'never suspect me again: promise me that you never will. Whatever I do, you may be sure I shall tell you first; you may be sure I shall consult you.'

And Mr Harding did promise, and owned his sin, and promised again. And so, while he promised amendment and she uttered forgiveness, they returned together to the drawing-room windows.

And what had Eleanor meant when she declared that *whatever she did*, she would tell her father first? What was she thinking of doing?

So ended the first act of the melodrama which Eleanor was called on to perform this day at Ullathorne.

❀ THIRTY-SEVEN ❀

The Signora Neroni, the Countess De Courcy, and Mrs Proudie meet each other at Ullathorne

AND NOW THERE WERE NEW ARRIVALS. JUST as Eleanor reached the drawing-room the signora was being wheeled into it. She had been brought out of the carriage into the dining-room and there placed on a sofa, and was now in the act of entering the other room, by the joint aid of her brother and sister, Mr Arabin, and two servants in livery. She was all in her glory, and looked so pathetically happy, so full of affliction and grace, was so beautiful, so pitiable, and so charming, that it was almost impossible not to be glad she was there.

Miss Thorne was unaffectedly glad to welcome her. In fact, the signora was a sort of lion; and though there was no drop of the Leohunter blood in

Miss Thorne's veins, she nevertheless did like to see attractive people at her house. The signora was attractive, and on her first settlement in the dining-room she had whispered two or three soft feminine words into Miss Thorne's ear, which, at the moment, had quite touched that lady's heart.

'Oh, Miss Thorne; where is Miss Thorne:' she said, as soon as her attendants had placed her in her position just before one of the windows, from whence she could see all that was going on upon the lawn; 'How am I to thank you for permitting a creature like me to be here? But if you knew the pleasure you give me, I am sure you would excuse the trouble I bring with me.' And as she spoke she squeezed the spinster's little hand between her own.

'We are delighted to see you here,' said Miss Thorne; 'you give us no trouble at all, and we think it a great favour conferred by you to come and see us; don't we, Wilfred?'

'A very great favour indeed,' said Mr Thorne, with a gallant bow, but of a somewhat less cordial welcome than that conceded by his sister. Mr Thorne had heard perhaps more of the antecedents of his guest than his sister had done, and had not as yet undergone the power of the signora's charms.

But while the mother of the last of the Neros was thus in her full splendour, with crowds of people gazing at her and the *élite* of the company standing round her couch, her glory was paled by the arrival of the Countess De Courcy. Miss Thorne had now been waiting three hours for the countess, and could not therefore but show very evident gratification when the arrival at last took place. She and her brother of course went off to welcome the tilted grandees, and with them, alas, went many of the signora's admirers.

'Oh, Mr Thorne,' said the countess, while in the act of being disrobed of her fur cloaks, and re-robed in her gauze shawls, 'what dreadful roads you have; perfectly frightful.'

It happened that Mr Thorne was way-warden for the district, and not liking the attack, began to excuse his roads.

'Oh yes, indeed they are,' said the countess, not minding him in the least, 'perfectly dreadful; are they not, Margaretta? Why, my dear Miss Thorne, we left Courcy Castle just at eleven; it was only just past eleven, was it not, John? and –'

'Just past one, I think you mean,' said the Honourable John, turning from the group and eyeing the signora through his glass. The signora gave him back his own, as the saying is, and more with it; so that the young nobleman was forced to avert his glance, and drop his glass.

'I say Thorne,' whispered he, 'who the deuce is that on the sofa?'

'Dr Stanhope's daughter,' whispered back Mr Thorne. 'Signora Neroni, she calls herself.'

'Whew-ew-ew!' whistled the Honourable John. 'The devil she is! I have heard no end of stories about that filly. You must positively introduce me, Thorne; you positively must.'

Mr Thorne, who was respectability itself, did not quite like having a guest about whom the Honourable John De Courcy had heard no end of stories; but he couldn't help himself. He merely resolved that before he went to bed he would let his sister know somewhat of the history of the lady she was so willing to welcome. The innocence of Miss Thorne, at her time of life was perfectly charming; but even innocence may be dangerous.

'John may say what he likes,' continued the countess, urging her excuses to Miss Thorne; 'I am sure we were past the castle gate before twelve, weren't we, Margaretta?'

'Upon my word I don't know,' said the Lady Margaretta, 'for I was half asleep. But I do know that I was called sometime in the middle of the night, and was dressing myself before daylight.'

Wise people, when they are in the wrong, always put themselves right by finding fault with the people against whom they have sinned. Lady De Courcy was a wise woman; and therefore, having treated Miss Thorne very badly by staying away till three o'clock, she assumed the offensive and attacked Mr Thorne's roads. Her daughter, not less wise, attacked Miss Thorne's early hours. The art of doing this is among the most precious of those usually cultivated by persons who know how to live. There is no withstanding it. Who can go systematically to work, and having done battle with the primary accusation and settled that, then bring forward a counter-charge and support that also? Life is not long enough for such labours. A man in the right relies easily on his rectitude, and therefore goes about unarmed. His very strength is his weakness. A man in the wrong knows that he must look to his weapons; his very weakness is his strength. The one is never prepared for combat, the other is always ready. Therefore it is that in this world the man that is in the wrong almost invariably conquers the man that is in the right, and invariably despises him.

A man must be an idiot or else an angel, who after the age of forty shall attempt to be just to his neighbours. Many like the Lady Margaretta have learnt their lesson at a much earlier age. But this of course depends on the school in which they have been taught.

Poor Miss Thorne was altogether overcome. She knew very well that she had been ill treated, and yet she found herself making apologies to Lady De Courcy. To do her ladyship justice, she received them very graciously, and allowed herself with her train of daughters to be led towards the lawn.

There were two windows in the drawing-room wide open for the countess to pass through; but she saw that there was a woman on a sofa, at the third window, and that that woman had, as it were, a following attached to her. Her ladyship therefore determined to investigate the woman. The De Courcys were hereditarily short sighted, and had been so for thirty centuries at least. So Lady De Courcy, who when she entered the family had adopted the family habits, did as her son had done before her, and taking her glass to investigate the Signora Neroni, pressed in among the gentlemen who surrounded the couch, and bowed slightly to those whom she chose to honour by her acquaintance.

In order to get to the window she had to pass close to the front of the couch, and as she did so she stared hard at the occupant. The occupant in return stared hard at the countess. The countess who since her countess-ship commenced had been accustomed to see all eyes, not royal, ducal or marquesal, fall before her own, paused as she went on, raised her eyebrows, and stared even harder than before. But she had now to do with one who cared little for countesses. It was, one may say, impossible for mortal man or woman to abash Madeline Neroni. She opened her large bright lustrous eyes wider and wider, till she seemed to be all eyes. She gazed up into the lady's face, not as though she did it with an effort, but as if she delighted in doing it. She used no glass to assist her effrontery, and needed none. The faintest possible smile of derision played round her mouth, and her nostrils were slightly dilated, as if in sure anticipation of her triumph. And it was sure. The Countess De Courcy, in spite of her thirty centuries and De Courcy castle, and the fact that Lord De Courcy was grand master of the ponies to the Prince of Wales, had not a chance with her. At first the little circlet of gold wavered in the countess's hand, then the hand shook, then the circlet fell, the countess's head tossed itself into the air, and the countess's feet shambled out to the lawn. She did not however go so fast but what she heard the signora's voice, asking –

'Who on earth is that woman, Mr Slope?'

'That is Lady De Courcy.'

'Oh, ah. I might have supposed so. Ha, ha, ha. Well, that's as good as a play.'

It was as good as a play to any there who had eyes to observe it, and wit to comment on what they observed.

But the Lady De Courcy soon found a congenial spirit on the lawn. There she encountered Mrs Proudie, and as Mrs Proudie was not only the wife of a bishop, but was also the cousin of an earl, Lady De Courcy considered her to be the fittest companion she was likely to meet in that assemblage. They were accordingly delighted to see each other. Mrs Proudie by no means despised a countess, and as this countess lived in the county and within a sort of extensive visiting distance of Barchester, she was glad to have this opportunity of ingratiating herself.

'My dear Lady De Courcy, I am so delighted,' said she, looking as little grim as it was in her nature to do. 'I hardly expected to see you here. It is such a distance, and then you know, such a crowd.'

'And such roads, Mrs Proudie! I really wonder how the people ever get about. But I don't suppose they ever do.'

'Well, I really don't know; but I suppose not. The Thornes don't, I know,' said Mrs Proudie. 'Very nice person, Miss Thorne, isn't she?'

'Oh, delightful, and so queer; I've known her these twenty years. A great pet of mine is dear Miss Thorne. She is so very strange, you know. She always makes me think of the Esquimaux and the Indians. Isn't her dress quite delightful?'

'Delightful,' said Mrs Proudie; 'I wonder now whether she paints. Did you ever see such colour?'

'Oh, of course,' said Lady De Courcy; 'that is, I have no doubt she does. But, Mrs Proudie, who is that woman on the sofa by the window? just step this way and you'll see her, there –' and the countess led her to a spot where she could plainly see the signora's well-remembered face and figure.

She did not however do so without being equally well seen by the signora. 'Look, look,' said that lady to Mr Slope, who was still standing near to her; 'see the high spiritualities and temporalities of the land in league together, and all against poor me. I'll wager my bracelet, Mr Slope, against your next sermon, that they've taken up their position there on purpose to pull me to pieces. Well, I can't rush to the combat, but I know how to protect myself if the enemy come near me.'

But the enemy knew better. They could gain nothing by contact with the Signora Neroni, and they could abuse her as they pleased at a distance from her on the lawn.

'She's that horrid Italian woman, Lady De Courcy; you must have heard of her.'

'What Italian woman?' said her ladyship, quite alive to the coming story; 'I don't think I've heard of any Italian woman coming into the country. She doesn't look Italian either.'

'Oh, you must have heard of her,' said Mrs Proudie. 'No, she's not absolutely Italian. She is Dr Stanhope's daughter – Dr Stanhope the prebendary; and she calls herself the Signora Neroni.'

'Oh-h-h-h!' exclaimed the countess.

'I was sure you had heard of her,' continued Mrs Proudie. 'I don't know anything about her husband. They do say that some man named Neroni is still alive. I believe she did marry such a man abroad, but I do not at all know who or what he was.'

'Ah-h-h-h!' said the countess, shaking her head with much intelligence, as every additional 'h' fell from her lips. 'I know all about it now. I have heard George mention her. George knows all about her. George heard about her in Rome.'

'She's an abominable woman, at any rate,' said Mrs Proudie.

'Insufferable,' said the countess.

'She made her way into the palace once, before I knew anything about her; and I cannot tell you how dreadfully indecent her conduct was.'

'Was it?' said the delighted countess.

'Insufferable,' said the prelatess.

'But why does she lie on a sofa?' asked Lady De Courcy.

'She has only one leg,' replied Mrs Proudie.

'Only one leg!' said Lady De Courcy, who felt to a certain degree dissatisfied that the signora was thus incapacitated. 'Was she born so?'

'Oh, no,' said Mrs Proudie – and her ladyship felt somewhat recomforted by the assurance – 'she had two. But that Signor Neroni beat her, I believe, till she was obliged to have one amputated. At any rate, she entirely lost the use of it.'

'Unfortunate creature!' said the countess, who herself knew something of matrimonial trials.

'Yes,' said Mrs Proudie; 'one would pity her, in spite of her past bad conduct, if she now knew how to behave herself. But she does not. She is the most insolent creature I ever put my eyes on.'

'Indeed she is,' said Lady De Courcy.

'And her conduct with men is so abominable, that she is not fit to be admitted into any lady's drawing-room.'

'Dear me!' said the countess, becoming again excited, happy, and merciless.

'You saw that man standing near her – the clergyman with the red hair?'
'Yes, yes.'

'She has absolutely ruined that man. The bishop, or I should rather take the blame on myself, for it was I – I brought him down from London to Barchester. He is a tolerable preacher, an active young man, and I therefore introduced him to the bishop. That woman, Lady De Courcy, has got hold of him, and has so disgraced him, that I am forced to require that he shall leave the palace; and I doubt very much whether he won't lose his gown!'

'Why what an idiot the man must be!' said the countess.

'You don't know the intriguing villainy of that woman,' said Mrs Proudie, remembering her torn flounces.

'But you say she has only got one leg!'

'She is as full of mischief as tho' she had ten. Look at her eyes, Lady De Courcy. Did you ever see such eyes in a decent woman's head?'

'Indeed I never did, Mrs Proudie.'

'And her effrontery, and her voice; I quite pity her poor father, who is really a good sort of man.'

'Dr Stanhope, isn't he?'

'Yes, Dr Stanhope. He is one of our prebendaries – a good quiet sort of man himself. But I am surprised that he should let his daughter conduct herself as she does.'

'I suppose he can't help it,' said the countess.

'But a clergyman, you know, Lady De Courcy! He should at any rate prevent her from exhibiting in public, if he cannot induce her to behave at home. But he is to be pitied. I believe he has a desperate life of it with the lot of them. That apish-looking man there, with the long beard and the loose trousers – he is the woman's brother. He is nearly as bad as she is. They are both of them infidels.'

'Infidels!' said Lady De Courcy, 'and their father a prebendary!'

'Yes, and likely to be the new dean too,' said Mrs Proudie.

'Oh, yes, poor dear Dr Trefoil!' said the countess, who had once in her life spoken to that gentleman; 'I was so distressed to hear it, Mrs Proudie. And so Dr Stanhope is to be the new dean! He comes of an excellent family, and I wish him success in spite of his daughter. Perhaps, Mrs Proudie, when he is dean they'll be better able to see the error of their ways.'

To this Mrs Proudie said nothing. Her dislike of the Signora Neroni was too deep to admit of her even hoping that that lady should see the error of her ways. Mrs Proudie looked on the signora as one of the lost – one of those beyond the reach of Christian charity, and was therefore able to enjoy the luxury of hating her, without the drawback of wishing her eventually well out of her sins.

Any further conversation between these congenial souls was prevented by the advent of Mr Thorne, who came to lead the countess to the tent. Indeed, he had been desired to do so some ten minutes since; but he had been delayed in the drawing-room by the signora. She had contrived to detain him, to get him near to her sofa, and at last to make him seat himself on a chair close to her beautiful arm. The fish took the bait, was hooked, and caught, and landed. Within that ten minutes he had heard the whole of the signora's history in such strains as she chose to use in telling it. He learnt from the lady's own lips the whole of that mysterious tale to which the Honourable George had merely alluded. He discovered that the beautiful creature lying before him had been more sinned against than sinning. She had owned to him that she had been weak, confiding and indifferent to the world's opinion, and that she had therefore been ill-used, deceived and evil spoken of. She had spoken to him of her mutilated limb, her youth destroyed in its fullest bloom, her beauty robbed of its every charm, her life blighted, her hopes withered; and as she did so, a tear dropped from her eye to her cheek. She had told him of these things, and asked for his sympathy.

What could a good-natured genial Anglo-Saxon Squire Thorne do but promise to sympathise with her? Mr Thorne did promise to sympathise; promised also to come and see the last of the Neros, to hear more of those fearful Roman days, of those light and innocent but dangerous hours which flitted by so fast on the shores of Como, and to make himself the confidant of the signora's sorrows.

We need hardly say that he dropped all idea of warning his sister against the dangerous lady. He had been mistaken; never so much mistaken in his life. He had always regarded that Honourable George as a coarse brutal-minded young man; now he was more convinced than ever that he was so. It was by such men as the Honourable George that the reputations of such women as Madeline Neroni were imperilled and damaged. He would go and see the lady in her own house; he was fully sure in his own mind of the soundness of his own judgment; if he found her, as he believed he should do, an injured well-disposed warm-hearted woman, he would get his sister Monica to invite her out to Ullathorne.

'No,' said she, as at her instance he got up to leave her, and declared that he himself would attend upon her wants; 'no, no, my friend; I positively put a veto upon your doing so. What, in your own house, with an assemblage round you such as there is here! Do you wish to make every woman hate me and every man stare at me? I lay a positive order on you not to come near me again to-day. Come and see me at home. It is only at home that I can talk; it is only at home that I really can live and enjoy myself. My days of going out, days such as these, are rare indeed. Come and see me at home, Mr Thorne, and then I will not bid you to leave me.'

It is, we believe, common with young men of five and twenty to look on their seniors – on men of, say, double their own age – as so many stocks and stones – stocks and stones, that is, in regard to feminine beauty. There never was a greater mistake. Women, indeed, generally know better; but on this subject men of one age are thoroughly ignorant of what is the very nature of mankind of other ages. No experience of what goes on in the world, no reading of history, no observation of life, has any effect in teaching the truth. Men of fifty don't dance mazurkas, being generally too fat and wheezy; nor do they sit for the hour together on river banks at their mistresses' feet, being somewhat afraid of rheumatism. But for real true love, love at first sight, love to devotion, love that robs a man of his sleep, love that 'will gaze an eagle blind,' love that 'will hear the lowest sound when the suspicious tread of theft is stopped,' love that is, 'like a Hercules, still climbing trees in the Hesperides,' – we believe the best age is from forty-five to seventy; up to that, men are generally given to mere flirting.

At the present moment Mr Thorne, _ætat_. fifty, was over head and ears in love at first sight with the Signora Madeline Vesey Neroni, _nata_ Stanhope.

Nevertheless he was sufficiently master of himself to offer his arm with all propriety to Lady De Courcy, and the countess graciously permitted herself to be led to the tent. Such had been Miss Thorne's orders, as she had succeeded in inducing the bishop to lead old Lady Knowle to the top of the dining-room. One of the baronets was sent off in quest of Mrs Proudie, and found that lady on the lawn not in the best of humours. Mr Thorne and the countess had left her too abruptly; she had in vain looked about for an attendant chaplain, or even a stray curate; they were all drawing long bows with the young ladies at the bottom of the lawn, or finding places for their graceful co-toxophilites in some snug corner of the tent. In such position Mrs Proudie had been wont in earlier days to fall back upon Mr Slope; but now she could never fall back upon him again. She gave her head one shake as she thought of her lone position, and that shake was as good as a week deducted from Mr Slope's longer sojourn in Barchester. Sir Harkaway Gorse, however, relieved her present misery, though his doing so by no means mitigated the sinning chaplain's doom.

And now the eating and drinking began in earnest. Dr Grantly, to his great horror, found himself leagued to Mrs Clantantram. Mrs Clantantram had a great regard for the archdeacon, which was not cordially returned; and when she, coming up to him, whispered in his ear, 'Come, archdeacon, I'm sure you won't begrudge an old friend the favour of your arm,' and then proceeded to tell him the whole history of her roquelaure, he resolved that he would shake her off before he was fifteen minutes older. But latterly the archdeacon had not been successful in his resolutions; and on the present occasion Mrs Clantantram stuck to him till the banquet was over.

Dr Gwynne got a baronet's wife, and Mrs Grantly fell to the lot of a baronet. Charlotte Stanhope attached herself to Mr Harding in order to make room for Bertie, who succeeded in sitting down in the dining-room next to Mrs Bold. To speak sooth, now that he had love in earnest to make, his heart almost failed him.

Eleanor had been right glad to avail herself of his arm, seeing that Mr Slope was hovering nigh her. In striving to avoid that terrible Charybdis of Slope she was in great danger of falling into an unseen Scylla on the other hand, that Scylla being Bertie Stanhope. Nothing could be more gracious than she was to Bertie. She almost jumped at his proffered arm. Charlotte perceived this from a distance, and triumphed in her heart; Bertie felt it, and was encouraged; Mr Slope saw it, and glowered with jealousy. Eleanor and Bertie sat down to table in the dining-room; and as she took her seat at his right hand, she found that Mr Slope was already in possession of the chair at her own.

As these things were going on in the dining-room, Mr Arabin was hanging enraptured and alone over the signora's sofa; and Eleanor from her seat could look through the open door and see that he was doing so.

❊ THIRTY-EIGHT ❊

The Bishop Sits Down to Breakfast,
and the Dean Dies

THE BISHOP OF BARCHESTER SAID GRACE OVER the well-spread board in the Ullathorne dining-room; and while he did so the last breath was flying from the dean of Barchester as he lay in his sick room in the deanery. When the bishop of Barchester raised his first glass of champagne to his lips, the deanship of Barchester was a good thing in the gift of the prime minister. Before the bishop of Barchester had left the table, the minister of the day was made aware of the fact at his country seat in Hampshire, and had already turned over in his mind the names of five very respectable aspirants for the preferment. It is at present only necessary to say that Mr Slope's name was not among the five.

' 'Twas merry in the hall when the beards wagged all;' and the clerical beards wagged merrily in the hall of Ullathorne that day. It was not till after the last cork had been drawn, the last speech made, the last nut cracked, that tidings reached and were whispered about that the poor dean was no more. It was well for the happiness of the clerical beards that this little delay took place, as otherwise decency would have forbidden them to wag at all.

But there was one sad man among them that day. Mr Arabin's beard did not wag as it should have done. He had come there hoping the best, striving to think the best, about Eleanor; turning over in his mind all the words he remembered to have fallen from her about Mr Slope, and trying to gather from them a conviction unfavourable to his rival. He had not exactly resolved to come that day to some decisive proof as to the widow's intention; but he had meant, if possible, to re-cultivate his friendship with Eleanor; and in his present frame of mind any such re-cultivation must have ended in a declaration of love.

He had passed the previous night alone at his new parsonage, and it was the first night that he had so passed. It had been dull and sombre enough. Mrs Grantly had been right in saying that a priestess would be wanting at St Ewold's. He had sat there alone with his glass before him, and then with his teapot, thinking about Eleanor Bold. As is usual in such meditations, he did little but blame her; blame her for liking Mr Slope, and blame her for not liking him; blame her for her cordiality to himself, and blame her for her want of cordiality; blame her for being stubborn, headstrong, and passionate; and yet the more he thought of her the higher she rose in his affection. If only it should turn out, if only it could be made to turn out, that she had defended Mr Slope, not from love, but on principle, all would be right. Such principle in itself would be admirable, loveable, womanly; he felt that he could be pleased to allow Mr Slope just so much favour as that. But if – And then Mr Arabin poked his fire most unnecessarily, spoke crossly to his new parlour-maid who came in for the tea-things, and threw himself back in his chair determined to go to sleep. Why had she been so stiffnecked when asked a plain question? She could not but have known in what light he regarded her. Why had she not answered a plain question, and so put an end to his misery? Then, instead of going to sleep in his arm-chair, Mr Arabin walked about the room as though he had been possessed.

On the following morning, when he attended Miss Thorne's behests, he was still in a somewhat confused state. His first duty had been to converse with Mrs Clantantram, and that lady had found it impossible to elicit the slightest sympathy from him on the subject of her roquelaure. Miss Thorne had asked him whether Mrs Bold was coming with the Grantlys; and the two names of Bold and Grantly together had nearly made him jump from his seat.

He was in this state of confused uncertainty, hope, and doubt, when he saw Mr Slope, with his most polished smile, handing Eleanor out of her carriage. He thought of nothing more. He never considered whether the carriage belonged to her or to Mr Slope, or to any one else to whom they might both be mutually obliged without any concert between themselves. This sight in his present state of mind was quite enough to upset him and his resolves. It was clear as noonday. Had he seen her handed into a carriage by Mr Slope at a church door with a white veil over her head, the truth could not be more manifest. He went into the house, and, as we have seen, soon found himself walking with Mr Harding. Shortly afterwards Eleanor came up; and then he had to leave his companion, and either go about alone or find another. While in this state he was encountered by the archdeacon.

'I wonder,' said Dr Grantly, 'if it be true that Mr Slope and Mrs Bold came here together. Susan says she is almost sure she saw their faces in the same carriage as she got out of her own.'

Mr Arabin had nothing for it but to bear his testimony to the correctness of Mrs Grantly's eyesight.

'It is perfectly shameful,' said the archdeacon; 'or I should rather say, shameless. She was asked here as my guest; and if she be determined to disgrace herself, she should have feeling enough not to do so before my immediate friends. I wonder how that man got himself invited. I wonder whether she had the face to bring him.'

To this Mr Arabin could answer nothing, nor did he wish to answer anything. Though he abused Eleanor to himself, he did not choose to abuse her to any one else, nor was he well pleased to hear any one else speak ill of her. Dr Grantly, however, was very angry, and did not spare his sister-in-law. Mr Arabin therefore left him as soon as he could, and wandered back into the house.

He had not been there long, when the signora was brought in. For some time he kept himself out of temptation, and merely hovered round her at a distance; but as soon as Mr Thorne had left her, he yielded himself up to the basilisk, and allowed himself to be made prey of.

It is impossible to say how the knowledge had been acquired, but the signora had a sort of instinctive knowledge that Mr Arabin was an admirer of Mrs Bold. Men hunt foxes by the aid of dogs, and are aware that they do so by the strong organ of smell with which the dog is endowed. They do not, however, in the least comprehend how such a sense can work with such acuteness. The organ by which women instinctively, as it were, know and feel how other women are regarded by men, and how also men are regarded by other women, is equally strong, and equally incomprehensible. A glance, a word, a motion, suffices: by some such acute exercise of her feminine senses the signora was aware that Mr Arabin loved Eleanor Bold; and therefore, by a further exercise of her peculiar feminine propensities, it was quite natural for her to entrap Mr Arabin into her net.

The work was half done before she came to Ullathorne, and when could she have a better opportunity of completing it? She had had almost enough of Mr Slope, though she could not quite resist the fun of driving a very sanctimonious clergyman to madness by a desperate and ruinous passion. Mr Thorne had fallen too easily to give much pleasure in the chase. His position as a man of wealth might make his alliance of value, but as a lover he was very second-rate. We may say that she regarded him somewhat as a sportsman does a pheasant. The bird is so easily shot, that he would not be worth the shooting were it not for the very respectable appearance that he makes in a larder. The signora would not waste much time in shooting Mr Thorne, but still he was worth bagging for family uses.

But Mr Arabin was game of another sort. The signora was herself possessed of quite sufficient intelligence to know that Mr Arabin was a man more than usually intellectual. She knew also, that as a clergyman he was of a much higher stamp than Mr Slope, and that as a gentleman he was better educated than Mr Thorne. She would never have attempted to drive Mr Arabin into ridiculous misery as she did Mr Slope, nor would she think it possible to dispose of him in ten minutes as she had done with Mr Thorne.

Such were her reflections about Mr Arabin. As to Mr Arabin, it cannot be said that he reflected at all about the signora. He knew that she was beautiful, and he felt that she was able to charm him. He required charming in his present misery, and therefore he went and stood at the head of her couch. She knew all about it. Such were her peculiar gifts. It was her nature to see that he required charming, and it was her province to charm him. As the Eastern idler swallows his dose of opium, as the London reprobate swallows his dose of gin, so with similiar desires and for similar reasons did Mr Arabin prepare to swallow the charms of the Signora Neroni.

'Why an't you shooting with bows and arrows, Mr Arabin?' said she, when they were nearly alone together in the drawing-room; 'or talking with young ladies in shady bowers, or turning your talents to account in some way? What was a bachelor like you asked here for? Don't you mean to earn your cold chicken and champagne? Were I you, I should be ashamed to be so idle.'

Mr Arabin murmured some sort of answer. Though he wished to be charmed, he was hardly yet in a mood to be playful in return.

'Why, what ails you, Mr Arabin?' said she, 'here you are in your own parish; Miss Thorne tells me that her party is given expressly in your honour; and yet you are the only dull man at it. Your friend Mr Slope was with me a few minutes since, full of life and spirits; why don't you rival him?'

It was not difficult for so acute an observer as Madeline Neroni to see that she had hit the nail on the head and driven the bolt home. Mr Arabin winced visibly before her attack, and she knew at once that he was jealous of Mr Slope.

'But I look on you and Mr Slope as the very antipodes of men,' said she.

'There is nothing in which you are not each the reverse of the other, except in belonging to the same profession; and even in that you are so unlike as perfectly to maintain the rule. He is gregarious, you are given to solitude. He is active, you are passive. He works, you think. He likes women, you despise them. He is fond of position and power, and so are you, but for directly different reasons. He loves to be praised, you very foolishly abhor it. He will gain his rewards, which will be an insipid useful wife, a comfortable income, and a reputation for sanctimony. You will also gain yours.'

'Well, and what will they be?' said Mr Arabin, who knew that he was being flattered, and yet suffered himself to put up with it. 'What will be my rewards?'

'The heart of some woman whom you will be too austere to own that you love, and the respect of some few friends which you will be too proud to own that you value.'

'Rich rewards,' said he; 'but of little worth if they are to be so treated.'

'Oh, you are not to look for such success as awaits Mr Slope. He is born to be a successful man. He suggests to himself an object, and then starts for it with eager intention. Nothing will deter him from his pursuit. He will have no scruples, no fears, no hesitation. His desire is to be a bishop with a rising family, the wife will come first, and in due time the apron. You will see all this, and then –'

'Well, and what then?'

'Then you will begin to wish that you had done the same.'

Mr Arabin looked placidly out at the lawn, and resting his shoulder on the head of the sofa, rubbed his chin with his hand. It was a trick he had when he was thinking deeply; and what the signora said made him think. Was it not all true? Would he not hereafter look back, if not at Mr Slope, at some others, perhaps not equally gifted with himself, who had risen in the world while he had lagged behind, and then wish that he had done the same?

'Is not such the doom of all speculative men of talent?' said she. 'Do they not all sit rapt as you now are, cutting imaginary silken cords with their fine edges, while those not so highly tempered sever the every-day Gordian knots of the world's struggle, and win wealth and renown? Steel too highly polished, edges too sharp, do not do for this world's work, Mr Arabin.'

Who was this woman that thus read the secrets of his heart, and re-uttered to him the unwelcome bodings of his own soul? He looked full into her face when she had done speaking, and said, 'Am I one of those foolish blades, too sharp and too fine to do a useful day's work?'

'Why do you let the Slopes of the world out-distance you?' said she. 'Is not the blood in your veins as warm as his? does not your pulse beat as fast? Has not God made you a man, and intended you to do a man's work here, ay, and to take a man's wages also?'

Mr Arabin sat ruminating and rubbing his face, and wondering why these things were said to him; but he replied nothing. The signora went on –

'The greatest mistake any man ever made is to suppose that the good things of the world are not worth the winning. And it is a mistake so opposed to the religion which you preach! Why does God permit his bishops one after another to have their five thousands and ten thousands a year if such wealth be bad and not worth having? Why are beautiful things given to us, and luxuries and pleasant enjoyments, if they be not intended to be used? They must be meant for some one, and what is good for a layman cannot surely be bad for a clerk. You try to despise these good things, but you only try; you don't succeed.'

'Don't I?' said Mr Arabin, still musing, and not knowing what he said.

'I ask you the question; do you succeed?'

'Mr Arabin looked at her piteously. It seemed to him as though he were being interrogated by some inner spirit of his own, to whom he could not refuse an answer, and to whom he did not dare to give a false reply.

'Come, Mr Arabin, confess; do you succeed? Is money so contemptible? Is worldly power so worthless? Is feminine beauty a trifle to be so slightly regarded by a wise man?'

'Feminine beauty!' said he, gazing into her face, as though all the feminine beauty in the world were concentrated there. 'Why do you say I do not regard it?'

'If you look at me like that, Mr Arabin, I shall alter my opinion – or should do so, were I not of course aware that I have no beauty of my own worth regarding.'

The gentleman blushed crimson, but the lady did not blush at all. A slightly increased colour animated her face, just so much so as to give her an air of special interest. She expected a compliment from her admirer, but she was rather grateful than otherwise by finding that he did not pay it to her. Messrs Slope and Thorne, Messrs Brown, Jones and Robinson, they all paid her compliments. She was rather in hopes that she would ultimately succeed in inducing Mr Arabin to abuse her.

'But your gaze,' said she, 'is one of wonder, and not of admiration. You wonder at my audacity in asking you such questions about yourself.'

'Well, I do rather,' said he.

'Nevertheless I expect an answer, Mr Arabin. Why were women made beautiful if men are not to regard them?'

'But men do regard them,' he replied.

'And why not you?'

'You are begging the question, Madame Neroni.'

'I am sure I shall beg nothing, Mr Arabin, which you will not grant, and I do beg for an answer. Do you not as a rule think women below your notice as companions? Let us see. There is the widow Bold looking round at you from her chair this minute. What would you say to her as a companion for life?'

Mr Arabin, rising from his position, leaned over the sofa and looked through the drawing-room door to the place where Eleanor was seated between Bertie Stanhope and Mr Slope. She at once caught his glance, and averted her own. She was not pleasantly placed in her present position. Mr Slope was doing his best to attract her attention; and she was striving to prevent his doing so by talking to Mr Stanhope, while her mind was intently fixed on Mr Arabin and Madame Neroni. Bertie Stanhope endeavoured to take advantage of her favours, but he was thinking more of the manner in which he would by-and-by throw himself at her feet, than of amusing her at the present moment.

'There,' said the signora. 'She was stretching her beautiful neck to look at you, and now you have disturbed her. Well I declare, I believe I am wrong about you; I believe that you do think Mrs Bold a charming woman. Your looks seem to say so; and by her looks I should say that she is jealous of me. Come, Mr Arabin, confide in me, and if it is so, I'll do all in my power to make up the match.'

It is needless to say that the signora was not very sincere in her offer. She was never sincere on such subjects. She never expected others to be so, nor did she expect others to think her so. Such matters were her playthings, her billiard table, her hounds and hunters, her waltzes and polkas, her picnics and summer-day excursions. She had little else to amuse her, and therefore played at love-making in all its forms. She was now playing at it with Mr Arabin, and did not at all expect the earnestness and truth of his answer.

'All in your power would be nothing,' said he; 'for Mrs Bold is, I imagine, already engaged to another.'

'Then you own the impeachment yourself.'

'You cross-question me rather unfairly,' he replied, 'and I do not know why I answer you at all. Mrs Bold is a very beautiful woman, and as intelligent as beautiful. It is impossible to know her without admiring her.'

'So you think the widow a very beautiful woman?'

'Indeed I do.'

'And one that would grace the parsonage of St Ewold's.'

'One that would well grace any man's house.'

'And you really have the effrontery to tell me this,' said she; 'to tell me, who, as you very well know, set up to be a beauty myself, and who am at this very moment taking such an interest in your affairs, you really have the effrontery to tell me that Mrs Bold is the most beautiful woman you know.'

'I did not say so,' said Mr Arabin; 'you are more beautiful –'

'Ah, come now, that is something like. I thought you could not be so unfeeling.'

'You are more beautiful, perhaps more clever.'

'Thank you, thank you, Mr Arabin. I knew that you and I should be friends.'

'But –'

'Not a word further. I will not hear a word further. If you talk till midnight, you cannot improve what you have said.'

'But Madame Neroni, Mrs Bold –'

'I will not hear a word about Mrs Bold. Dread thoughts of strychnine did pass across my brain, but she is welcome to the second place.'

'Her place –'

'I won't hear anything about her or her place. I am satisfied, and that is enough. But, Mr Arabin, I am dying with hunger; beautiful and clever as I am, you know I cannot go to my food, and yet you do not bring it to me.'

This at any rate was so true as to make it necessary that Mr Arabin should act upon it, and he accordingly went into the dining-room and supplied the signora's wants.

'And yourself?' said she.

'Oh,' said he, 'I am not hungry; I never eat at this hour.'

'Come, come Mr Arabin, don't let love interfere with your appetite. It never does with mine. Give me half a glass more champagne, and then go to the table. Mrs Bold will do me an injury if you stay talking to me any longer.'

Mr Arabin did as he was bid. He took her plate and glass from her, and going into the dining-room, helped himself to a sandwich from the crowded table and began munching it in a corner.

As he was doing so, Miss Thorne, who had hardly sat down for a moment, came into the room, and seeing him standing, was greatly distressed.

'Oh, my dear Mr Arabin,' said she, 'have you never sat down yet? I am so distressed. You of all men too.'

Mr Arabin assured her that he had only just come into the room.

'That is the very reason why you should lose no more time. Come, I'll make room for you. Thank'ee, my dear,' she said, seeing that Mrs Bold was making an attempt to move from her chair, 'but I would not for worlds see you stir, for all the ladies would think it necessary to follow. But, perhaps, if Mr Stanhope has done – just for a minute, Mr Stanhope – till I can get another chair.'

And so Bertie had to rise to make way for his rival. This he did, as he did everything, with an air of good-humoured pleasantry which made it impossible for Mr Arabin to refuse the proffered seat.

'His bishopric let another take,' said Bertie; the quotation being certainly not very appropriate, either for the occasion or the person spoken to. 'I have eaten and am satisfied; Mr Arabin, pray take my chair. I wish for your sake that it really was a bishop's seat.'

Mr Arabin did sit down, and as he did so, Mrs Bold got up as though to follow her neighbour.

'Pray, pray don't move,' said Mrs Thorne, almost forcing Eleanor back into her chair. 'Mr Stanhope is not going to leave us. He will stand behind you like a true knight as he is. And now I think of it, Mr Arabin, let me introduce you to Mr Slope. Mr Slope, Mr Arabin.' And the two gentlemen bowed stiffly to each other across the lady whom they both intended to marry, while the other gentleman who also intended to marry her stood behind, watching them.

The two had never met each other before, and the present was certainly not a good opportunity for much cordial conversation, even if cordial conversation between them had been possible. As it was, the whole four who formed the party seemed as though their tongues were tied. Mr Slope, who was wide awake to what he hoped was his coming opportunity, was not much concerned in the interest of the moment. His wish was to see Eleanor move, that he might pursue her. Bertie was not exactly in the same frame of mind; the evil day was near enough; there was no reason why he should precipitate it. He had made up his mind to marry Eleanor Bold if he could, and was resolved to-day to take the first preliminary step towards doing so. But there was time enough before him. He was not going to make an offer of marriage over the table-cloth. Having thus good-naturedly made way for Mr Arabin, he was willing also to let him talk to the future Mrs Stanhope as long as they remained in their present position.

Mr Arabin having bowed to Mr Slope, began eating his food without saying a word further. He was full of thought, and though he ate he did so unconsciously.

But poor Eleanor was the most to be pitied. The only friend on whom she thought she could rely, was Bertie Stanhope, and he, it seemed, was determined to desert her. Mr Arabin did not attempt to address her. She said a few words in reply to some remarks from Mr Slope, and then feeling the situation too much for her, started from her chair in spite of Miss Thorne, and hurried from the room. Mr Slope followed her, and young Stanhope lost the occasion.

Madeline Neroni, when she was left alone, could not help pondering much on the singular interview she had had with this singular man. Not a word that she had spoken to him had been intended by her to be received as true, and yet he had answered her in the very spirit of truth. He had done so, and she had been aware that he had done so. She had wormed from him his secret; and he, debarred as it would seem from man's usual privilege of lying, had innocently laid bare his whole soul to her. He loved Eleanor Bold, but Eleanor was not in his eye so beautiful as herself. He would fain have Eleanor for his wife, but yet he had acknowledged that she was the less gifted of the two. The man had literally been unable to falsify his thoughts when questioned, and had been compelled to be true *malgrè lui*, even when truth must have been so disagreeable to him.

This teacher of men, this Oxford pundit, this double-distilled quintessence of university perfection, this writer of religious treatises, this speaker of ecclesiastical speeches, had been like a little child in her hands; she had turned him inside out, and read his very heart as she might have done that of a young girl. She could not but despise him for his facile openness, and yet she liked him for it too. It was a novelty to her, a new trait in a man's character. She felt also that she could never so completely make a fool of him as she did of the Slopes and Thornes. She felt that she never could induce Mr Arabin to make protestations to her that were not true, or to listen to nonsense that was mere nonsense.

It was quite clear that Mr Arabin was heartily in love with Mrs Bold, and the signora, with very unwonted good nature, began to turn it over in her mind whether she could not do him a good turn. Of course Bertie was to have the first chance. It was an understood family arrangement that her brother was, if possible, to marry the widow Bold. Madeline knew too well his necessities and what was due to her sister to interfere with so excellent a plan, as long as it might be feasible. But she had strong suspicion that it was not feasible. She did not think it likely that Mrs Bold would accept a man in her brother's position, and she had frequently said so to Charlotte. She was inclined to believe that Mr Slope had more chance of success; and with her it would be a labour of love to rob Mr Slope of his wife.

And so the signora resolved, should Bertie fail, to do a good-natured act for once in her life, and give up Mr Arabin to the woman whom he loved.

❈ THIRTY-NINE ❈

The Lookalofts and the Greenacres

ON THE WHOLE, MISS THORNE'S PROVISION FOR the amusement and feeding of the outer classes in the exoteric paddock was not unsuccessful.

Two little drawbacks to the general happiness did take place, but they were of a temporary nature, and apparent rather than real. The first was the downfall of young Harry Greenacre, and the other the uprise of Mrs Lookaloft and her family.

As to the quintain, it became more popular among the boys on foot, than it would ever have been among the men on horseback, even had young Greenacre been more successful. It was twirled round and round till it was nearly twirled out of the ground; and the bag of flour was used with great gusto in powdering the backs and heads of all who could be coaxed within its vicinity.

Of course it was reported all through the assemblage that Harry was dead, and there was a pathetic scene between him and his mother when it was found that he had escaped scatheless from the fall. A good deal of beer was drunk on the occasion, and the quintain was 'dratted' and 'bothered,' and very generally anathematised by all the mothers who had young sons likely to be placed in similar jeopardy. But the affair of Mrs Lookaloft was of a more serious nature.

'I do tell 'ee plainly – face to face – she be there in madam's drawing-room; herself and Gussy, and them two walloping gals, dressed up to their very eyeses.' This was said by a very positive, very indignant, and very fat farmer's wife, who was sitting on the end of a bench leaning on the handle of a huge cotton umbrella.

'But you didn't zee her, Dame Guffern?' said Mrs Greenacre, whom this information, joined to the recent peril undergone by her son, almost overpowered. Mr Greenacre held just as much land as Mr Lookaloft, paid his rent quite as punctually, and his opinion in the vestry-room was reckoned to be every whit as good. Mrs Lookaloft's rise in the world had been wormwood to Mrs Greenacre. She had no taste herself for the sort of finery which had converted Barleystubb farm into Rosebank, and which had occasionally graced Mr Lookaloft's letters with the dignity of esquirehood. She had no wish to convert her own homestead into Violet Villa, or to see her goodman go about with a new-fangled handle to his name. But it was a mortal injury to her that Mrs Lookaloft should be successful in her hunt after such honours. She had abused and ridiculed Mrs Lookaloft to the extent of her little power. She had pushed against her going out of church, and had excused herself with all the easiness of equality. 'Ah, dame, I axes pardon; but you be grown so mortal stout these times.' She had inquired with apparent cordiality of Mr Lookaloft, after 'the woman that owned him,' and had, as she thought, been on the whole able to hold her own pretty well against her aspiring neighbour. Now, however, she found herself distinctly put into a separate and inferior class. Mrs Lookaloft was asked into the Ullathorne drawing-room merely because she called her house Rosebank, and had talked over her husband into buying pianos and silk dresses instead of putting his money by to stock farms for his sons.

Mrs Greenacre, much as she reverenced Miss Thorne, and highly as she respected her husband's landlord, could not but look on this as an act of injustice done to her and hers. Hitherto the Lookalofts had never been recognised as being of a different class from the Greenacres. Their pretensions were all self-pretensions, their finery was all paid for by themselves and not granted to them by others. The local sovereigns of the vicinity, the district fountains of honour, had hitherto conferred on them the stamp of no rank. Hitherto their crinoline petticoats, late hours, and mincing gait had been a fair subject of Mrs Greenacre's raillery, and this raillery had been a safety valve for her envy. Now, however, and from henceforward, the case would be very different. Now the Lookalofts would boast that their aspirations had been sanctioned by the gentry of the country; now they would declare with some show of truth that their claims to peculiar consideration had been recognised. They had sat as equal guests in the presence of bishops and baronets; they had been curtseyed to by Miss Thorne on her own drawing-room carpet; they were about to sit down to table in company with a live countess! Bab Lookaloft, as she had always been called by the young Greenacres in the days of their juvenile equality, might possibly sit next to the Honourable George, and that wretched Gussy might be permitted to hand a custard to the Lady Margaretta De Courcy.

The fruition of those honours, or such of them as fell to the lot of the envied family, was not such as should have caused much envy. The attention paid to the Lookalofts by the De Courcys was very limited, and the amount of entertainment which they received from the bishop's society was hardly in itself a recompense for the dull monotony of their day. But of what they endured Mrs Greenacre took no account; she thought only of what she considered they must enjoy, and of the dreadfully exalted tone of living which would be manifested by the Rosebank family, as the consequence of their present distinction.

'But did 'ee zee 'em there, dame, did 'ee zee 'em there with your own eyes?' asked poor Mrs Greenacre; still hoping that there might be some ground for doubt.

'And how could I do that, unless so be I was there myself?' asked Mrs Guffern. 'I didn't zet eyes on none of them this blessed morning, but I zee'd them as did. You know our John; well, he will be for keeping company with Betsey Rusk, madam's own maid, you know. And Betsey isn't none of your common kitchen wenches. So Betsey, she came out to our John, you know, and she's always vastly polite to me, is Betsey Rusk, I must say. So before she took so much as one turn with John, she told me every ha'porth that was going on up in the house.'

'Did she now?' said Mrs Greenacre.

'Indeed she did,' said Mrs Guffern.

'And she told you them people was up there in the drawing-room?'

'She told me she zee'd them come in – that they was dressed finer by half nor any of the family, with all their neckses and buzoms stark naked as a born babby.'

'The minxes!' exclaimed Mrs Greenacre, who felt herself more put about by this than any other mark of aristocratic distinction which her enemies had assumed.

'Yes, indeed,' continued Mrs Guffern, 'as naked as you please, while all the quality was dressed just as you and I be, Mrs Greenacre.'

'Drat their impudence,' said Mrs Greenacre, from whose well-covered bosom all milk of human kindness was receding, as far as the family of the Lookalofts were concerned.

'So says I,' said Mrs Guffern; 'and so says my goodman, Thomas Guffern, when he hear'd it. "Molly," says he to me. "if ever you takes to going about o' mornings with yourself all naked in them ways, I begs you won't come back no more to the old house." So says I, "Thomas, no more I wull." "But," says he, "drat it, how the deuce does she manage with her rheumatiz, and she not a rag on her:" ' and Mrs Guffern laughed loudly as she thought of Mrs Lookaloft's probable sufferings from rheumatic attacks.

'But to liken herself that way to folk that ha' blood in their veins,' said Mrs Greenacre.

'Well, but that warn't all neither that Betsey told. There they all swelled into madam's drawing-room, like so many turkey cocks, as much as to say, "and who dare say no to us?" and Gregory was thinking of telling of 'em to come down here, only his heart failed him 'cause of the grand way they were dressed. So in they went; but madam looked at them as glum as death.'

'Well now,' said Mrs Greenacre, greatly relieved, 'so they wasn't axed different from us at all then?'

'Betsey says that Gregory says that madam wasn't a bit too well pleased to see them where they was, and that, to his believing, they were expected to come here just like the rest of us.'

There was great consolation in this. Not that Mrs Greenacre was altogether satisfied. She felt that justice to herself demanded that Mrs Lookaloft should not only not be encouraged, but that she should also be absolutely punished. What had been done at that scriptural banquet, of which Mrs Greenacre so often read the account to her family? Why had not Miss Thorne boldly gone to the intruder and said, 'Friend, thou hast come up hither to high places not fitted to thee. Go down lower, and thou wilt find thy mates.' Let the Lookalofts be treated at the present moment with ever so cold a shoulder, they would still be enabled to boast hereafter of their position, their aspirations, and their honour.

'Well, with all her grandeur, I do wonder that she be so mean,' continued Mrs Greenacre, unable to dismiss the subject. 'Did you hear, goodman?' she went on, about to repeat the whole story to her husband who then came up. 'There's dame Lookaloft and Bab and Gussy and the lot of 'em all sitting as grand as fivepence in madam's drawing-room, and they not axed no more nor you nor me. Did you ever hear tell the like o' that?'

'Well, and what for shouldn't they?' said Farmer Greenacre.

'Likening theyselves to the quality, as though they was estated folk, or the like o' that!' said Mrs Guffern.

'Well, if they likes it and madam likes it, they's welcome for me,' said the farmer. 'Now I likes this place better, cause I be more at home like, and don't have to pay for them fine clothes for the missus. Every one to his taste, Mrs Guffern, and if neighbour Lookaloft thinks that he has the best of it, he's welcome.'

Mrs Greenacres sat down by her husband's side to begin the heavy work of the banquet, and she did so in some measure with restored tranquility, but nevertheless she shook her head at her gossip to show that in this instance she did not quite approve of her husband's doctrine.

'And I'll tell 'ee what, dames,' continued he; 'if so be that we cannot enjoy the dinner that madam gives us because Mother Lookaloft is sitting up there on a grand sofa, I think we ought all to go home. If we greet at that, what'll we do when true sorrow comes across us? How would you be now, dame, if the boy there had broke his neck when he got the tumble?'

Mrs Greenacre was humbled and said nothing further on the matter. But let prudent men, such as Mr Greenacre, preach as they will, the family of the Lookalofts certainly does occasion a good deal of heart-burning in the world at large.

It was pleasant to see Mr Plomacy, as leaning on his stout stick he went about among the rural guests, acting as a sort of head constable as well as master of the revels. 'Now, young 'un, if you can't manage to get along without that screeching, you'd better go to the other side of the twelve-acre field, and take your dinner with you. Come girls, what do you stand there for, twirling of your thumbs? come out, and let the lads see you; you've no need to be so ashamed of your faces. Hollo! there, who are you? how did you make your way in here?'

This last disagreeable question was put to a young man of about twenty-four, who did not, in Mr Plomacy's eye, bear sufficient vestiges of a rural education and residence.

'If you please, your worship, Master Barrell the coachman let me in at the church wicket, 'cause I do be working mostly al'ays for the family.'

'Then Mister Barrell the coachman may let you out again,' said Mr Plomacy, not even conciliated by the magisterial dignity which had been conceded to him. 'What's your name? and what trade are you, and who do you work for?'

'I'm Stubbs, your worship, Bob Stubbs; and – and – and –'

'And what's your trade, Stubbs?'

'Plaisterer, please your worship.'

'I'll plaister you, and Barrell too; you'll just walk out of this 'ere field as quick as you walked in. We don't want no plaisterers; when we do, we'll send for 'em. Come, my buck, walk.'

Stubbs the plasterer was much downcast at this dreadful edict. He was a sprightly fellow, and had contrived since his egress into the Ullathorne elysium to attract to himself a forest nymph, to whom he was whispering a plasterer's usual soft nothings, when he was encountered by the great Mr Plomacy. It was dreadful to be thus dissevered from his dryad, and sent howling back to a Barchester pandemonium just as the nectar and ambrosia were about to descend on the fields of asphodel. He began to try what prayers would do, but city prayers were vain against the great rural potentate. Not only did Mr Plomacy order his exit, but raising his stick to show the way which led to the gate that had been left in the custody of that false Cerberus Barrell, proceeded himself to see the edict of banishment carried out.

The goddess Mercy, however, the sweetest goddess that ever sat upon a cloud, and the dearest to poor frail erring man, appeared on the field in the person of Mr Greenacre. Never was interceding goddess more welcome.

'Come, man,' said Mr Greenacre, 'never stick at trifles such a day as this. I know the lad well. Let him bide at my axing. Madam won't miss what he can eat and drink, I know.'

Now Mr Plomacy and Mr Greenacre were sworn friends. Mr Plomacy had at his own disposal as comfortable a room as there was in Ullathorne House; but he was a bachelor, and alone there; and, moreover, smoking in the house was not allowed even to Mr Plomacy. His moments of truest happiness were spent in a huge arm-chair in the warmest corner of Mrs Greenacre's beautifully clean front kitchen. 'Twas there that the inner man dissolved itself, and poured itself out in streams of pleasant chat; 'twas there that he was respected and yet at his ease; 'twas there, and perhaps there only, that he could unburden himself from the ceremonies of life without offending the dignity of those above him, or incurring the familiarity of those below. 'Twas there that his long pipe was always to be found on the accustomed chimney board, not only permitted but encouraged.

Such being the state of the case, it was not to be supposed that Mr Plomacy could refuse such a favour to Mr Greenacre; but nevertheless he did not grant it without some further show of austere authority.

'Eat and drink, Mr Greenacre! No. It's not what he eats and drinks; but the example such a chap shows, coming in where he's not invited – a chap of his age too. He too that never did a day's work about Ullathorne since he was born. Plaisterer! I'll plaister him!'

'He worked long enough for me, then, Mr Plomacy. And a good hand he is at setting tiles as any in Barchester,' said the other, not sticking quite to veracity, as indeed mercy never should. 'Come, come, let him alone to-day, and quarrel with him to-morrow. You wouldn't shame him before his lass there?'

'It goes against the grain with me, then,' said Mr Plomacy. 'And take care, you Stubbs, and behave yourself. If I hear a row I shall know where it comes from. I'm up to you Barchester journeymen; I know what suff you're made of.'

And so Stubbs went off happy, pulling at the forelock of his shock head of hair in honour of the steward's clemency, and giving another double pull at it in honour of the farmer's kindness. And as he went he swore within his grateful heart, that if ever Farmer Greenacre wanted a day's work done for nothing, he was the lad to do it for him. Which promise it was not probable that he would ever be called on to perform.

But Mr Plomacy was not quite happy in his mind, for he thought of the unjust steward, and began to reflect whether he had not made for himself friends of the mammon of unrighteousness. This, however, did not interfere with the manner in which he performed his duties at the bottom of the long board; nor did Mr Greenacre perform his the worse at the top on account of the good wishes of Stubbs the plasterer. Moreover, the guests did not think it anything amiss when Mr Plomacy, rising to say grace, prayed that God would make them all truly thankful for the good things which Madam Thorne in her great liberality had set before them!

All this time the quality in the tent on the lawn were getting on swimmingly; that is, if champagne without restriction can enable quality folk to swim. Sir Harkaway Gorse proposed the health of Miss Thorne, and likened her to a blood race-horse, always in condition, and not to be tired down by any amount of work. Mr Thorne returned thanks, saying he hoped his sister would always be found able to run when called upon, and then gave the health and prosperity of the De Courcy family. His sister was very much honoured by seeing so many of them at her poor board. They were all aware that important avocations made the absence of the earl necessary. As his duty to his prince had called him from his family hearth, he, Mr Thorne, could not venture to regret that he did not see him at Ullathorne; but nevertheless he would venture to say – that was to express a wish – an opinion he meant to say – And so Mr Thorne became somewhat gravelled, as country gentlemen in similar circumstances usually do; but he ultimately sat down, declaring that he had much satisfaction in drinking the noble earl's health, together with that of the countess, and all the family of De Courcy castle.

And then the Honourable George returned thanks. We will not follow him through the different periods of his somewhat irregular eloquence. Those immediately in his neighbourhood found it at first rather difficult to get him on his legs, but much greater difficulty was soon experienced in inducing him to resume his seat. One of two arrangements should certainly be made in these days: either let all speech-making on festive occasions be utterly tabooed and made as it were impossible; or else let those who are to exercise the privilege be first subjected to a competing examination before the civil service examining commissioners. As it is now, the Honourable Georges do but little honour to our exertions in favour of British education.

In the dining-room the bishop went through the honours of the day with much more neatness and propriety. He also drank Miss Thorne's health, and did it in a manner becoming the bench which he adorned. The party there, was perhaps a little more dull, a shade less lively than that in the tent. But what was lost in mirth, was fully made up in decorum.

And so the banquets passed off at the various tables with great eclat and universal delight.

✖ FORTY ✖

Ullathorne Sports – Act II

'THAT WHICH HAS MADE THEM DRUNK, HAS made me bold.' 'Twas thus that Mr Slope encouraged himself, as he left the dining-room in pursuit of

Eleanor. He had not indeed seen in that room any person really intoxicated; but there had been a good deal of wine drunk, and Mr Slope had not hesitated to take his share, in order to screw himself up to the undertaking which he had in hand. He is not the first man who has thought it expedient to call in the assistance of Bacchus on such an occasion.

Eleanor was out through the window, and on the grass before she perceived that she was followed. Just at that moment the guests were nearly all occupied at the tables. Here and there were to be seen a constant couple or two, who preferred their own sweet discourse to the jingle of glasses, or the charms of rhetoric which fell from the mouths of the Honourable George and the bishop of Barchester; but the grounds were as nearly vacant as Mr Slope could wish them to be.

Eleanor saw that she was pursued, and as a deer, when escape is no longer possible, will turn to bay and attack the hounds, so did she turn upon Mr Slope.

'Pray don't let me take you from the room,' said she, speaking with all the stiffness which she knew how to use. 'I have come out to look for a friend. I must beg of you, Mr Slope, to go back.'

But Mr Slope would not be thus entreated. He had observed all day that Mrs Bold was not cordial to him, and this had to a certain extent oppressed him. But he did not deduce from this any assurance that his aspirations were in vain. He saw that she was angry with him. Might she not be so because he had so long tampered with her feelings – might it not arise from his having, as he knew was the case, caused her name to be bruited about in conjunction with his own, without having given her the opportunity of confessing to the world that henceforth their names were to be one and the same? Poor lady! He had within him a certain Christian conscience-stricken feeling of remorse on this head. It might be that he had wronged her by his tardiness. He had, however, at the present moment imbibed too much of Mr Thorne's champagne to have any inward misgivings. He was right in repeating the boast of Lady Macbeth: he was not drunk; but he was bold enough for anything. It was a pity that in such a state he could not have encountered Mrs Proudie.

'You must permit me to attend you,' said he; 'I could not think of allowing you to go alone.'

'Indeed you must, Mr Slope,' said Eleanor still very stiffly; 'for it is my special wish to be alone.'

The time for letting the great secret escape him had already come. Mr Slope saw that it must be now or never, and he was determined that it should be now. This was not his first attempt at winning a fair lady. He had been on his knees, looked unutterable things with his eyes, and whispered honeyed words before this. Indeed he was somewhat an adept at these things, and had only to adapt to the perhaps different taste of Mrs Bold the well-remembered rhapsodies which had once so much gratified Olivia Proudie.

'Do not ask me to leave you, Mrs Bold,' said he with an impassioned look, impassioned and sanctified as well, with that sort of look which is not uncommon with gentlemen of Mr Slope's school, and which may perhaps be called the tender-pious. 'Do not ask me to leave you, till I have spoken a few words with which my heart is full; which I have come hither purposely to say.'

Eleanor saw how it was now. She knew directly what it was she was about to go through, and very miserable the knowledge made her. Of course she could refuse Mr Slope, and there would be an end of that, one might say. But there would not be an end of it as far as Eleanor was concerned. The very fact of Mr Slope's making an offer to her would be a triumph to the archdeacon, and in a great measure a vindication of Mr Arabin's conduct. The widow could not bring herself to endure with patience the idea that she had been in the wrong. She had defended Mr Slope, she had declared herself quite justified in admitting him among her acquaintance, had ridiculed the ideas of his considering himself as more than an acquaintance, and had resented the archdeacon's caution in her behalf: now it was about to be proved to her in a manner sufficiently disagreeable that the archdeacon had been right, and she herself had been entirely wrong.

'I don't know what you can have to say to me, Mr Slope, that you could not have said when we were sitting at table just now;' and she closed her lips, and steadied her eyeballs, and looked at him in a manner that ought to have frozen him.

But gentlemen are not easily frozen when they are full of champagne, and it would not at any time have been easy to freeze Mr Slope.

'There are things, Mrs Bold, which a man cannot well say before a crowd; which perhaps he cannot well say at any time; which indeed he may most fervently desire to get spoken, and which he may yet find it almost impossible to utter. It is such things as these, that I now wish to say to you;' and then the tender-pious look was repeated, with a little more emphasis even than before.

Eleanor had not found it practicable to stand stock still before the dining-room window, and there receive his offer in full view of Miss Thorne's guests. She had therefore in self-defence walked on, and thus Mr Slope had gained his object of walking with her. He now offered her his arm.

'Thank you, Mr Slope, I am much obliged to you; but for the very short time that I shall remain with you I shall prefer walking alone.'

'And must it be so short?' said he; 'must it be –'

'Yes,' said Eleanor, interrupting him; 'as short as possible, if you please, sir.'

'I had hoped, Mrs Bold – I had hoped –'

'Pray hope nothing, Mr Slope, as far as I am concerned; pray do not; I do not know, and need not know what hope you mean. Our acquaintance is very slight, and will probably remain so. Pray, pray let that be enough; there is at any rate no necessity for us to quarrel.'

Mrs Bold was certainly treating Mr Slope rather cavalierly, and he felt it so. She was rejecting him before he had offered himself, and informed him at the same time that he was taking a great deal too much on himself to be so familiar. She did not even make an attempt

> From such a sharp and waspish word as 'no'
> To pluck the sting.

He was still determined to be very tender and very pious, seeing that in spite of all Mrs Bold had said to him, he not yet abandoned hope; but he was inclined also to be somewhat angry. The widow was bearing herself, as he thought, with too high a hand, was speaking of herself in much too imperious a tone. She had clearly no idea that an honour was being conferred on her. Mr Slope would be tender as long as he could, but he began to think, if that failed, it would not be amiss if he also mounted himself for a while on his high horse. Mr Slope could undoubtedly be very tender, but he could be very savage also, and he knew his own abilities.

'That is cruel,' said he, 'and unchristian too. The worst of us are all still bidden to hope. What have I done that you should pass on me so severe a sentence?' and then he paused a moment, during which the widow walked steadily on with measured step, saying nothing further.

'Beautiful woman,' at last he burst forth; 'beautiful woman, you cannot pretend to be ignorant that I adore you. Yes, Eleanor, yes, I love you. I love you with the truest affection which man can bear to woman. Next to my hopes of heaven are my hopes of possessing you.' (Mr Slope's memory here played him false, or he would not have omitted the deanery.) 'How sweet to walk to heaven with you by my side, with you for my guide, mutual guides. Say, Eleanor, dearest Eleanor, shall we walk that sweet path together?'

Eleanor had no intention of ever walking together with Mr Slope on any other path than that special one of Miss Thorne's which they now occupied; but as she had been unable to prevent the expression of Mr Slope's wishes and aspirations, she resolved to hear him out to the end, before she answered him.

'Ah! Eleanor,' he continued, and it seemed to be his idea that as he had once found courage to pronounce her Christian name, he could not utter it often enough. 'Ah! Eleanor, will it not be sweet, with the Lord's assistance, to travel hand in hand through this mortal valley which his mercies will make pleasant to us, till hereafter we shall dwell together at the foot of his throne?' And then a more tenderly pious glance than ever beamed from the lover's eyes. 'Ah! Eleanor –'

'My name, Mr Slope, is Mrs Bold,' said Eleanor, who, though

determined to hear out the tale of his love, was too much disgusted by his blasphemy to be able to bear much more of it.

'Sweetest angel, be not so cold,' said he, and as he said it the champagne broke forth, and he contrived to pass his arm round her waist. He did this with considerable cleverness, for up to this point Eleanor had contrived with tolerable success to keep her distance from him. They had got into a walk nearly enveloped by shrubs, and Mr Slope therefore no doubt considered that as they were now alone it was fitting that he should give her some outward demonstration of that affection of which he talked so much. It may perhaps be presumed that the same stamp of measures had been found to succeed with Olivia Proudie. Be this as it may, it was not successful with Eleanor Bold.

She sprang from him as she would have jumped from an adder, but she did not spring far; not, indeed, beyond arm's length; and then, quick as thought, she raised her little hand and dealt him a box on the ear with such right good will, that it sounded among the trees like a miniature thunder-clap.

And now it is to be feared that every well-bred reader of these pages will lay down the book with disgust, feeling that, after all, the heroine is unworthy of sympathy. She is a hoyden, one will say. At any rate she is not a lady, another will exclaim. I have suspected her all through, a third will declare; she has no idea of the dignity of a matron; or of the peculiar propriety which her position demands. At one moment she is romping with young Stanhope; then she is making eyes at Mr Arabin; anon she comes to fisty-cuffs with a third lover; and all before she is yet a widow of two years' standing.

She cannot altogether be defended; and yet it may be averred that she is not a hoyden, not given to romping, nor prone to boxing. It were to be wished devoutly that she had not struck Mr Slope in the face. In doing so she derogated from her dignity and committed herself. Had she been educated in Belgravia, had she been brought up by any sterner mentor than that fond father, had she lived longer under the rule of a husband, she might, perhaps, have saved herself from this great fault. As it was, the provocation was too much for her, the temptation to instant resentment of the insult too strong. She was too keen in the feeling of independence, a feeling dangerous for a young woman, but one in which her position peculiarly tempted her to indulge. And then Mr Slope's face, tinted with a deeper dye than usual by the wine he had drunk, simpering and puckering itself with pseudo piety and tender grimaces, seemed specially to call for such punishment. She had, too, a true instinct as to the man; he was capable of rebuke in this way and in no other. To him the blow from her little hand was as much an insult as a blow from a man would have been to another. It went direct to his pride. He conceived himself lowered in his dignity, and personally outraged. He could almost have struck at her again in his rage. Even the pain was a great annoyance to him, and the feeling that his clerical character had been wholly disregarded, sorely vexed him.

There are such men; men who can endure no taint on their personal self-respect, even from a woman – men whose bodies are to themselves such sacred temples, that a joke against them is desecration, and a rough touch downright sacrilege. Mr Slope was such a man; and, therefore, the slap on the face that he got from Eleanor was, as far as he was concerned, the fittest rebuke which could have been administered to him.

But, nevertheless, she should not have raised her hand against the man. Ladies' hands, so soft, so sweet, so delicious to the touch, so grateful to the eye, so gracious in their gentle doings, were not made to belabour men's faces. The moment the deed was done Eleanor felt that she had sinned against all propriety, and would have given little worlds to recall the blow. In her first agony of sorrow she all but begged the man's pardon. Her next impulse, however, and the one which she obeyed, was to run away.

'I never, never will speak another word to you,' she said, gasping with emotion and the loss of breath which her exertion and violent feelings occasioned her, and so saying she put foot to the ground and ran quickly back along the path to the house.

But how shall I sing the divine wrath of Mr Slope, or how invoke the tragic muse to describe the rage which swelled the celestial bosom of the bishop's chaplain? Such an undertaking by no means befits the low-heeled buskin of modern fiction. The painter put a veil over Agamemnon's face when called on to depict the father's grief at the early doom of his devoted daughter. The god, when he resolved to punish the rebellious winds, abstained from mouthing empty threats. We will not attempt to tell with what mighty surgings of the inner heart Mr Slope swore to revenge himself on the woman who had disgraced him, nor will we vainly strive to depict his deep agony of soul.

There he is, however, alone in the garden walk, and we must contrive to bring him out of it. He was not willing to come forth quite at once. His cheek was stinging with the weight of Eleanor's fingers, and he fancied that every one who looked at him would be able to see on his face the traces of what he had endured. He stood awhile, becoming redder and redder with rage. He stood motionless, undecided, glaring with his eyes, thinking of the pains and penalties of Hades, and meditating how he might best devote his enemy to the infernal gods with all the passion of his accustomed eloquence. He longed in his heart to be preaching at her. 'Twas thus that he was ordinarily avenged of sinning mortal men and women. Could he at once have ascended his Sunday rostrum and fulminated at her such denunciations as his spirit delighted in, his bosom would have been greatly eased.

But how preach to Mr Thorne's laurels, or how preach indeed at all in such a vanity fair as this now going on at Ullathorne? And then he began to feel a righteous disgust at the wickedness of the doings around him. He had been justly chastised for lending, by his presence, a sanction to such worldly lures. The gaiety of society, the mirth of banquets, the laughter of the young, and the eating and drinking of the elders were, for awhile, without excuse in his sight. What had he now brought down upon himself by sojourning thus in the tents of the heathen? He had consorted with idolaters round the altars of Baal; and therefore a sore punishment had come upon him. He then thought of the Signora Neroni, and his soul within him was full of sorrow. He had an inkling – a true inkling – that he was a wicked, sinful man; but it led him in no right direction; he could admit no charity in his heart. He felt debasement coming on him, and he longed to shake it off, to rise up in his stirrup, to mount to high places and great power, that he might get up into a mighty pulpit and preach to the world a loud sermon against Mrs Bold.

There he stood fixed to the gravel for about ten minutes. Fortune favoured him so far that no prying eyes came to look upon him in his misery. Then a shudder passed over his whole frame; he collected himself, and slowly wound his way round to the lawn, advancing along the path and not returning in the direction which Eleanor had taken. When he reached the tent he found the bishop standing there in conversation with the master of Lazarus. His lordship had come out to air himself after the exertion of his speech.

'This is very pleasant – very pleasant, my lord, is it not?' said Mr Slope with his most gracious smile, and pointing to the tent; 'very pleasant. It is delightful to see so many persons enjoying themselves so thoroughly.'

Mr Slope thought he might force the bishop to introduce him to Dr Gwynne. A very great example had declared and practised the wisdom of being everything to everybody, and Mr Slope was desirous of following it. His maxim was never to lose a chance. The bishop, however, at the present moment was not very anxious to increase Mr Slope's circle of acquaintance among his clerical brethren. He had his own reasons for dropping any marked allusion to his domestic chaplain, and he therefore made his shoulder rather cold for the occasion.

'Very, very,' said he without turning round, or even deigning to look at Mr Slope. 'And therefore, Dr Gwynne, I really think you will find that the hebdomadal board will exercise as wide and as general an authority as at the present moment. I, for one, Dr Gwynne –'

'Dr Gwynne,' said Mr Slope, raising his hat, and resolving not to be outwitted by such an insignificant little goose as the bishop of Barchester.

The master of Lazarus also raised his hat and bowed very politely to Mr Slope. There is not a more courteous gentleman in the queen's dominions than the master of Lazarus.

'My lord,' said Mr Slope; 'pray do me the honour of introducing me to Dr Gwynne. The opportunity is too much in my favour to be lost.'

The bishop had no help for it. 'My chaplain, Dr Gwynne,' said he; 'my present chaplain, Mr Slope.' He certainly made the introduction as unsatisfactory to the chaplain as possible, and by the use of the word present, seemed to indicate that Mr Slope might probably not long enjoy the honour which he now held. But Mr Slope cared nothing for this. He understood the innuendo, and disregarded it. It might probably come to pass that he would be in a situation to resign his chaplaincy before the bishop was in a situation to dismiss him from it. What need the future dean of Barchester care for the bishop, or for the bishop's wife? Had not Mr Slope, just as he was entering Dr Stanhope's carriage, received an all important note from Tom Towers of the Jupiter? had he not that note this moment in his pocket?

So disregarding the bishop, he began to open out a conversation with the master of Lazarus.

But suddenly an interruption came, not altogether unwelcome to Mr Slope. One of the bishop's servants came up to his master's shoulders with a long, grave face, and whispered into the bishop's ear.

'What is it, John?' said the bishop.

'The dean, my lord; he is dead.'

Mr Slope had no further desire to converse with the master of Lazarus, and was very soon on his road back to Barchester.

Eleanor, as we have said, having declared her intention of never holding further communication with Mr Slope, ran hurriedly back towards the house. The thought, however, of what she had done grieved her greatly, and she could not abstain from bursting into tears. 'Twas thus she played the second act in that day's melodrame.

✖ FORTY-ONE ✖

Mrs Bold Confides her Sorrow to her Friend Miss Stanhope

WHEN MRS BOLD CAME TO THE END of the walk and faced the lawn, she began to bethink herself what she should do. Was she to wait there till Mr Slope caught her, or was she to go in among the crowd with tears in her eyes and passion in her face? She might in truth have stood there long enough without any reasonable fear of further immediate persecution from Mr Slope; but we are all inclined to magnify the bugbears which frighten us. In her present state of dread she did not know of what atrocity he might venture to be guilty. Had any one told her a week ago that he would have put his arm round her waist at this party of Miss Thorne's, she would have been utterly incredulous. Had she been informed that he would be seen on the following Sunday walking down the High-street in a scarlet coat and top-boots, she would not have thought such a phenomenon more improbable.

But this improbable iniquity he had committed; and now there was nothing she could not believe of him. In the first place it was quite manifest that he was tipsy; in the next place, it was to be taken as proved that all his religion was sheer hypocrisy; and finally the man was utterly shameless. She therefore stood watching for the sound of his footfall, not without some fear that he might creep out at her suddenly from among the bushes.

As she thus stood, she saw Charlotte Stanhope at a little distance from her walking quickly across the grass. Eleanor's handkerchief was in her hand, and putting it to her face so as to conceal her tears, she ran across the lawn and joined her friend.

'Oh, Charlotte,' she said, almost too much out of breath to speak very plainly; 'I am so glad I have found you.'

'Glad you have found me!' said Charlotte, laughing: 'that's a good joke. Why Bertie and I have been looking for you everywhere. He swears that you have gone off with Mr Slope, and is now on the point of hanging himself.'

'Oh, Charlotte, don't,' said Mrs Bold.

'Why, my child, what on earth is the matter with you!' said Miss Stanhope, perceiving that Eleanor's hand trembled on her own arm, and finding also that her companion was still half choked by tears. 'Goodness heaven! something has distressed you. What is it? What can I do for you?'

Eleanor answered her only by a sort of spasmodic gurgle in her throat. She was a good deal upset, as people say, and could not at the moment collect herself.

'Come here, this way, Mrs Bold; come this way, and we shall not be seen. What has happened to vex you so? What can I do for you? Can Bertie do anything?'

'Oh, no, no, no, no,' said Eleanor. 'There is nothing to be done. Only that horrid man –'

'What horrid man?' asked Charlotte.

There are some moments in life in which both men and women feel themselves imperatively called on to make a confidence; in which not to do so requires a disagreeable resolution and also a disagreeable suspicion. There are people of both sexes who never make confidences; who are never tempted by momentary circumstances to disclose their secrets; but such are generally dull, close, unimpassioned spirits, 'gloomy gnomes, who live in cold dark mines.' There was nothing of the gnome about Eleanor; and she therefore resolved to tell Charlotte Stanhope the whole story about Mr Slope.

'That horrid man; that Mr Slope,' said she: 'did you not see that he followed me out of the dining-room?'

'Of course I did, and was sorry enough; but I could not help it. I knew you would be annoyed. But you and Bertie managed it badly between you.'

'It was not his fault nor mine either. You know how I disliked the idea of coming in the carriage with that man.'

'I am sure I am very sorry if that has led to it.'

'I don't know what has led to it,' said Eleanor, almost crying again. 'But it has not been my fault.'

'But what has he done, my dear?'

'He's an abominable, horrid, hypocritical man, and it would serve him right to tell the bishop all about it.'

'Believe me, if you want to do him an injury, you had far better tell Mrs Proudie. But what did he do, Mrs Bold?'

'Ugh!' exclaimed Eleanor.

'Well, I must confess he's not very nice,' said Charlotte Stanhope.

'Nice!' said Eleanor. 'He is the most fulsome, fawning, abominable man I ever saw. What business had he to come to me? I that never gave him the slightest tittle of encouragement – I that always hated him, though I did take his part when others ran him down.'

'That's just where it is, my dear. He has heard that, and therefore fancied that of course you were in love with him.'

This was wormwood to Eleanor. It was in fact the very thing which all her friends had been saying for the last month past; and which experience now proved to be true. Eleanor resolved within herself that she would never again take any man's part. The world with all its villainy, and all its ill-nature, might wag as it liked; she would not again attempt to set crooked things straight.

'But what did he do, my dear?' said Charlotte, who was really rather interested in the subject.

'He – he – he –'

'Well – come, it can't have been anything so very horrid, for the man was not tipsy.'

'Oh, I am sure he was,' said Eleanor. 'I am sure he must have been tipsy.'

'Well, I declare I didn't observe it. But what was it, my love?'

'Why, I believe I can hardly tell you. He talked such horrid stuff that you never heard the like; about religion, and heaven, and love. Oh, dear – he is such a nasty man.'

'I can easily imagine the sort of stuff he would talk. Well – and then –?'

'And then – he took hold of me.'

'Took hold of you?'

'Yes – he somehow got close to me, and took hold of me –'

'By the waist?'

'Yes,' said Eleanor shuddering.

'And then –'

'Then I jumped away from him, and gave him a slap on the face; and ran away along the path, till I saw you.'

'Ha, ha, ha!' Charlotte Stanhope laughed heartily at the finale to the tragedy. It was delightful to her to think that Mr Slope had had his ears boxed. She did not quite appreciate the feeling which made her friend so unhappy at the result of the interview. To her thinking, the matter had ended happily enough as regarded the widow, who indeed was entitled to some sort of triumph among her friends. Whereas to Mr Slope would be due all those jibes and jeers which would naturally follow such an affair. His friends would ask him whether his ears tingled whenever he saw a widow; and he would be cautioned that beautiful things were made to be looked at, and not to be touched.

Such were Charlotte Stanhope's views on such matters; but she did not at the present moment clearly explain them to Mrs Bold. Her object was to endear herself to her friend; and therefore, having had her laugh, she was ready enough to offer sympathy. Could Bertie do anything? Should Bertie speak to the man, and warn him that in future he must behave with more decorum? Bertie, indeed, she declared, would be more angry than any one else when he heard to what insult Mrs Bold had been subjected.

'But you won't tell him?' said Mrs Bold with a look of horror.

'Not if you don't like it,' said Charlotte; 'but considering everything, I would strongly advise it. If you had a brother, you know, it would be unnecessary. But it is very right that Mr Slope should know that you have somebody by you that will, and can protect you.'

'But my father is here.'

'Yes, but it is so disagreeable for clergymen to have to quarrel with each other; and circumstanced as your father is just at this moment, it would be very inexpedient that there should be anything unpleasant between him and Mr Slope. Surely you and Bertie are intimate enough for you to permit him to take your part.'

Charlotte Stanhope was very anxious that her brother should at once on that very day settle matters with his future wife. Things had now come to that point between him and his father, and between him and his creditors, that he must either do so, or leave Barchester; either do that, or go back to his unwashed associates, dirty lodgings, and poor living at Carrara. Unless he could provide himself with an income, he must go to Carrara, or to ——. His father the prebendary had not said this in so many words, but had he done so, he could not have signified it more plainly.

Such being the state of the case, it was very necessary that no more time should be lost. Charlotte had seen her brother's apathy, when he neglected to follow Mrs Bold out of the room, with anger which she could hardly suppress. It was grievous to think that Mr Slope should have so distanced him. Charlotte felt that she had played her part with sufficient skill. She had brought them together and induced such a degree of intimacy, that her brother was really relieved from all trouble and labour in the matter. And moreover, it was quite plain that Mrs Bold was very fond of Bertie. And now it was plain enough also that he had nothing to fear from his rival Mr Slope.

There was certainly an awkwardness in subjecting Mrs Bold to a second offer on the same day. It would have been well perhaps to have put the matter off for a week, could a week have been spared. But circumstances are frequently too peremptory to be arranged as we would wish to arrange them; and such was the case now. This being so, could not this affair of Mr Slope's be turned to advantage? Could it not be made the excuse for bringing Bertie and Mrs Bold into still closer connection; into such close connection that they could not fail to throw themselves into each other's arms? Such was the game which Miss Stanhope now at a moment's notice resolved to play.

And very well she played it. In the first place, it was arranged that Mr Slope should not return in the Stanhopes' carriage to Barchester. It so happened that Mr Slope was already gone, but of that of course they knew nothing. The signora should be induced to go first, with only the servants and her sister, and Bertie should take Mr Slope's place in the second journey. Bertie was to be told in confidence of the whole affair, and when the carriage was gone off with its first load, Eleanor was to be left under Bertie's special protection, so as to insure her from any further aggression from Mr Slope. While the carriage was getting ready, Bertie was to seek out that gentleman and make him understand that he must provide himself with another conveyance back to Barchester. Their immediate object should be to walk about together in search of Bertie. Bertie, in short, was to be the Pegasus on whose wings they were to ride out of their present dilemma.

There was a warmth of friendship and cordial kindliness in all this, that was very soothing to the widow; but yet, though she gave way to it, she was hardly reconciled to doing so. It never occurred to her, that now that she had killed one dragon, another was about to spring up in her path; she had no remote idea that she would have to encounter another suitor in her proposed protector, but she hardly liked the thought of putting herself so much into the hands of young Stanhope. She felt that if she wanted protection, she should go to her father. She felt that she should ask him to provide a carriage for her back to Barchester. Mrs Clantantram she knew would give her a seat. She knew that she should not throw herself entirely upon friends whose friendship dated as it were but from yesterday. But yet she could not say 'no,' to one who was so sisterly in her kindness, so eager in her good nature, so comfortably sympathetic as Charlotte Stanhope. And thus she gave way to all the propositions made to her.

They first went into the dining-room, looking for their champion, and from thence to the drawing-room. Here they found Mr Arabin, still hanging over the signora's sofa; or, rather, they found him sitting near her head, as a physician might have sat, had the lady been his patient. There was no other person in the room. The guests were some in the tent, some few still in the dining-room, some at the bows and arrows, but most of them walking with Miss Thorne through the park, and looking at the games that were going on.

All that had passed, and was passing between Mr Arabin and the lady, it is unnecessary to give in detail. She was doing with him as she did with all others. It was her mission to make fools of men, and she was pursuing her mission with Mr Arabin. She had almost got him to own his love for Mrs Bold, and had subsequently almost induced him to acknowledge a passion for herself. He, poor man, was hardly aware what he was doing or saying, hardly conscious whether he was in heaven or hell. So little had he known of female attractions of that peculiar class which the signora owned, that he became affected with a kind of temporary delirium, when first subjected to its power. He lost his head rather than his heart, and toppled about mentally, reeling in his ideas as a drunken man does on his legs. She had whispered to him words that really meant nothing, but which coming from such beautiful lips, and accompanied by such lustrous glances, seemed to have a mysterious significance, which he felt though he could not understand.

In being thus be-sirened, Mr Arabin behaved himself very differently from Mr Slope. The signora had said truly, that the two men were the contrasts of each other; that the one was all for action, the other all for thought. Mr Slope, when this lady laid upon his senses the over-powering breath of her charms, immediately attempted to obtain some fruition, to achieve some mighty triumph. He began by catching at her hand, and progressed by kissing it. He made vows of love, and asked for vows in return. He promised everlasting devotion, knelt before her, and swore that had she been on Mount Ida, Juno would have had no cause to hate the offspring of Venus. But Mr Arabin uttered no oaths, kept his hand mostly in his trowsers pocket, and had no more thought of kissing Madam Neroni, than of kissing the Countess De Courcy.

As soon as Mr Arabin saw Mrs Bold enter the room, he blushed and rose from his chair; then he sat down again, and then again got up. The signora saw the blush at once, and smiled at the poor victim, but Eleanor was too much confused to see anything.

'Oh, Madeline,' said Charlotte, 'I want to speak to you particularly; we must arrange about the carriage, you know,' and she stooped down to whisper to her sister. Mr Arabin immediately withdrew to a little distance, and as Charlotte had in fact much to explain before she could make the new carriage arrangement intelligible, he had nothing to do but to talk to Mrs Bold.

'We have had a very pleasant party,' said he, using the tone he would have used had he delcared that the sun was shining very brightly, or the rain falling very fast.

'Very,' said Eleanor, who never in her life had passed a more unpleasant day.

'I hope Mr Harding has enjoyed himself.'

'Oh, yes, very much,' said Eleanor, who had not seen her father since she parted from him soon after her arrival.

'He returns to Barchester to-night, I suppose.'

'Yes, I believe so; that is, I think he is staying at Plumstead.'

'Oh, staying at Plumstead,' said Mr Arabin.

'He came from there this morning. I believe he is going back; he didn't exactly say, however.'

'I hope Mrs Grantly is quite well.'

'She seemed to be quite well. She is here; that is, unless she has gone away.'

'Oh, yes, to be sure. I was talking to her. Looking very well indeed.' Then there was a considerable pause; for Charlotte could not at once make Madeline understand why she was to be sent home in a hurry without her brother.

'Are you returning to Plumstead, Mrs Bold?' Mr Arabin merely asked this by way of making conversation, but he immediately perceived that he was approaching dangerous ground.

'No,' said Mrs Bold, very quietly; 'I am going home to Barchester.'

'Oh, ah, yes. I had forgotten that you had returned.' And then Mr Arabin, finding it impossible to say anything further, stood silent till Charlotte had completed her plans, and Mrs Bold stood equally silent, intently occupied as it appeared in the arrangement of her rings.

And yet these two people were thoroughly in love with each other; and though one was a middle-aged clergyman, and the other a lady at any rate past the wishy-washy bread-and-butter period of life, they were as unable to tell their own minds to each other as any Damon and Phillis, whose united ages would not make up that to which Mr Arabin had already attained.

Madeline Neroni consented to her sister's proposal, and then the two ladies again went off in quest of Bertie Stanhope.

⌘ FORTY-TWO ⌘

Ullathorne Sports – Act III

AND NOW MISS THORNE'S GUESTS WERE BEGINNING to take their departure, and the amusement of those who remained was becoming slack. It was getting dark, and ladies in morning costumes were thinking that if they were to appear by candle-light they ought to readjust themselves. Some young gentlemen had been heard to talk so loud that prudent mammas determined to retire judiciously, and the more discreet of the male sex, whose libations had been moderate, felt that there was not much more left for them to do.

Morning parties, as a rule, are failures. People never know how to get away from them gracefully. A picnic on an island or a mountain or in a wood may perhaps be permitted. There is no master of the mountain bound by courtesy to bid you stay while in his heart he is longing for your departure. But in a private house or in private grounds a morning party is a bore. One is called on to eat and drink at unnatural hours. One is obliged to give up the day which is useful, and is then left without resource for the evening which is useless. One gets home fagged and *désœuvré*, and yet at an hour too early for bed. There is no comfortable resource left. Cards in these genteel days are among the things tabooed, and a rubber of whist is impracticable.

All this began now to be felt. Some young people had come with some amount of hope that they might get up a dance in the evening, and were unwilling to leave till all such hope was at an end. Others, fearful of staying longer than was expected, had ordered their carriages early, and were doing their best to go, solicitous for their servants and horses. The countess and her noble brood were among the first to leave, and as regarded the Hon. George, it was certainly time that he did so. Her ladyship was in a great fret and fume. Those horrid roads would, she was sure, be the death of her if unhappily she were caught in them by the dark night. The lamps she was assured were good, but no lamp could withstand the jolting of the roads of East Barsetshire. The De Courcy property lay in the western division of the county.

Mrs Proudie could not stay when the countess was gone. So the bishop was searched for by the Revs Messrs Grey and Green, and found in one corner of the tent enjoying himself thoroughly in a disquisition on the hebdomadal board. He obeyed, however, the behests of his lady without finishing the sentence in which he was promising to Dr Gwynne that his authority at Oxford should remain unimpaired; and the episcopal horses turned their noses towards the palatial stables. Then the Grantlys went. Before they did so, Mr Harding managed to whisper a word into his daughter's ear. Of course, he said he would undeceive the Grantlys as to that foolish rumour about Mr Slope.

'No, no, no,' said Eleanor; 'pray do not – pray wait till I see you. You will be home in a day or two, and then I will explain to you everything.'

'I shall be home to-morrow,' said he.

'I am so glad,' said Eleanor. 'You will come and dine with me, and then we shall be so comfortable.'

Mr Harding promised. He did not exactly know what there was to be explained, or why Dr Grantly's mind should not be disabused of the mistake into which he had fallen; but nevertheless he promised. He owed some reparation to his daughter, and he thought that he might best make it by obedience.

And thus the people were thinning off by degrees, as Charlotte and Eleanor walked about in quest of Bertie. Their search might have been long, had they not happened to hear his voice. He was comfortably ensconced in the ha-ha, with his back to the sloping side, smoking a cigar, and eagerly engaged in conversation with some youngster from the further side of the county, whom he had never met before, who was also smoking under Bertie's pupilage, and listening with open ears to an account given by his companion of some of the pastimes of Eastern clime.

'Bertie, I am seeking you everywhere,' said Charlotte. 'Come up here at once.'

Bertie looked up out of the ha-ha, and saw the two ladies before him. As there was nothing for him but to obey, he got up and threw away his cigar. From the first moment of his acquaintance with her he had liked Eleanor Bold. Had he been left to his own devices, had she been penniless, and had it then been quite out of the question that he should marry her, he would most probably have fallen violently in love with her. But now he could not help regarding her somewhat as he did the marble workshops at Carrara, as he had done his easel and palette, as he had done the lawyer's chambers in London; in fact, as he had invariably regarded everything by which it had been proposed to him to obtain the means of living. Eleanor Bold appeared before him, no longer as a beautiful woman, but as a new profession called matrimony. It was a profession indeed requiring but little labour, and one in which an income was insured to him. But nevertheless he had been as it were goaded on to it; his sister had talked to him of Eleanor, just as she had talked of busts and portraits. Bertie did not dislike money, but he hated the very thought of earning it. He was now called away from his pleasant cigar to earn it, by offering himself as a husband to Mrs Bold. The work indeed was made easy enough; for in lieu of his having to seek the widow, the widow had apparently come to seek him.

He made some sudden absurd excuse to his auditor, and then throwing away his cigar, climbed up the wall of the ha-ha and joined the ladies on the lawn.

'Come and give Mrs Bold an arm,' said Charlotte, 'while I set you on a piece of duty which, as a preux chevalier, you must immediately perform. Your personal danger will, I fear, be insignificant, as your antagonist is a clergyman.'

Bertie immediately gave his arm to Eleanor, walking between her and his sister. He had lived too long abroad to fall into the Englishman's habit of offering each an arm to two ladies at the same time; a habit, by the bye, which foreigners regard as an approach to bigamy, or a sort of incipient Mormonism.

The little history of Mr Slope's misconduct was then told to Bertie by his sister, Eleanor's ears tingling the while. And well they might tingle. If it were necessary to speak of the outrage at all, why should it be spoken of to such a person as Mr Stanhope, and why in her own hearing? She knew she was wrong, and was unhappy and dispirited, and yet she could think of no way to extricate herself, no way to set herself right. Charlotte spared her as much as she possibly could, spoke of the whole thing as though Mr Slope had taken a glass of wine too much, said that of course there would be nothing more about it, but that steps must be taken to exclude Mr Slope from the carriage.

'Mrs Bold need be under no alarm about that,' said Bertie, 'for Mr Slope has gone this hour past. He told me that business made it necessary that he should start at once for Barchester.'

'He is not so tipsy, at any rate, but what he knows his fault,' said Charlotte. 'Well, my dear, that is one difficulty over. Now I'll leave you with your true knight, and get Madeline off as quickly as I can. The carriage is here, I suppose, Bertie?'

'It has been here for the last hour.'

'That's well. Good bye, my dear. Of course you'll come in to tea. I shall trust to you to bring her, Bertie; even by force if necessary.' And so saying, Charlotte ran off across the lawn, leaving her brother alone with the widow.

As Miss Stanhope went off, Eleanor bethought herself that, as Mr Slope had taken his departure, there no longer existed any necessity for separating Mr Stanhope from his sister Madeline, who so much needed his aid. It had been arranged that he should remain so as to preoccupy Mr Slope's place in the carriage, and act as a social policeman to effect the exclusion of that disagreeable gentleman. But Mr Slope had effected his own exclusion, and there was no possible reason now why Bertie should not go with his sister. At least Eleanor saw none, and she said as much.

'Oh, let Charlotte have her own way,' said he. 'She has arranged it, and there will be no end of confusion, if we make another change. Charlotte always arranges everything in our house; and rules us like a despot.'

'But the signora?' said Eleanor.

'Oh, the signora can do very well without me. Indeed, she will have to do without me,' he added, thinking rather of his studies in Carrara, than of his Barchester hymeneals.

'Why, you are not going to leave us?' asked Eleanor.

It has been said that Bertie Stanhope was a man without principle. He certainly was so. He had no power of using active mental exertion to keep himself from doing evil. Evil had no ugliness in his eyes; virtue no beauty. He was void of any of those feelings which actuate men to do good. But he was perhaps equally void of those which actuate men to do evil. He got into debt with utter recklessness, thinking nothing as to whether the tradesmen would ever be paid or not. But he did not invent active schemes of deceit for the sake of extracting the goods of others. If a man gave him credit, that was the man's look-out; Bertie Stanhope troubled himself nothing further. In borrowing money he did the same; he gave people references to 'his governor;' told them that the 'old chap' had a good income; and agreed to pay sixty per cent for the accommodation. All this he did without a scruple of conscience; but then he never contrived active villainy.

In this affair of his marriage, it had been represented to him as a matter of duty that he ought to put himself in possession of Mrs Bold's hand and fortune; and at first he had so regarded it. About her he had thought but little. It was the customary thing for men situated as he was to marry for money, and there was no reason why he should not do what others around him did. And so he consented. But now he began to see the matter in another light. He was setting himself down to catch this woman, as a cat sits to catch a mouse. He was to catch her, and swallow her up, her and her child, and her house and land, in order that he might live on her instead of on his father. There was a cold, calculating, cautious cunning about this quite at variance with Bertie's character. The prudence of the measure was quite as antagonistic to his feelings as the iniquity.

And then, should he be successful, what would be the reward? Having satisifed his creditors with half of the widow's fortune, he would be allowed to sit down quietly at Barchester, keeping economical house with the remainder. His duty would be to rock the cradle of the late Mr Bold's child, and his highest excitement a demure party at Plumstead rectory, should it ultimately turn out that the archdeacon would be sufficiently reconciled to receive him.

There was very little in the programme to allure such a man as Bertie Stanhope. Would not the Carrara workshop, or whatever worldly career fortune might have in store for him, would not almost anything be better than this? The lady herself was undoubtedly all that was desirable; but the most desirable lady becomes nauseous when she has to be taken as a pill. He was pledged to his sister, however, and let him quarrel with whom he would, it behoved him not to quarrel with her. If she were lost to him all would be lost that he could ever hope to derive henceforward from the paternal roof-tree. His mother was apparently indifferent to his weal or woe, to his wants or his warfare. His father's brow got blacker and blacker from day to day, as the old man looked at his hopeless son. And as for Madeline – poor Madeline, whom of all of them he liked the best – she had enough to do to shift for herself. No; come what might, he must cling to his sister and obey her behests, let them be ever so stern; or at the very least seem to obey them. Could not some happy deceit bring him through in this matter, so that he might save appearances with his sister, and yet not betray the widow to her ruin? What if he made a confederate of Eleanor? 'Twas in this spirit that Bertie Stanhope set about his wooing.

'But you are not going to leave Barchester?' asked Eleanor.

'I do not know,' he replied; 'I hardly know yet what I am going to do. But it is at any rate certain that I must do something.'

'You mean about your profession?' said she.

'Yes, about my profession, if you can call it one.'

'And is it not one?' said Eleanor. 'Were I a man, I know none I should prefer to it, expect painting. And I believe the one is as much in your power as the other.'

'Yes, just about equally so,' said Bertie, with a little touch of inward satire directed at himself. He knew in his heart that he would never make a penny by either.

'I have often wondered, Mr Stanhope, why you do not exert yourself more,' said Eleanor, who felt a friendly fondness for the man with whom she was walking. 'But I know it is very impertinent in me to say so.'

'Impertinent!' said he. 'Not so, but much too kind. It is much too kind in you to take any interest in so idle a scamp.'

'But you are not a scamp, though you are perhaps idle; and I do take an interest in you; a very great interest, she added, in a voice which almost made him resolve to change his mind. 'And when I call you idle, I know you are only so for the present moment. Why can't you settle steadily to work here in Barchester?'

'And make busts of the bishop, dean and chapter? or perhaps, if I achieve a great success, obtain a commission to put up an elaborate tombstone over a prebendary's widow, a dead lady with a Grecian nose, a bandeau, and an intricate lace veil; lying of course on a marble sofa, from among the legs of which Death will be creeping out and poking at his victim with a small toasting-fork.'

Eleanor laughed; but yet she thought that if the surviving prebendary paid the bill, the object of the artist as a professional man would, in a great measure, be obtained.

'I don't know about the dean and chapter and the prebendary's widow,' said Eleanor. 'Of course you must take them as they come. But the fact of your having a great cathedral in which such ornaments are required, could not but be in your favour.'

'No real artist could descend to the ornamentation of a cathedral,' said Bertie, who had his ideas of the high ecstatic ambition of art, as indeed all artists have, who are not in receipt of a good income. 'Buildings should be fitted to grace the sculpture, not the sculpture to grace the building.'

'Yes, when the work of art is good enough to merit it. Do you, Mr Stanhope, do something sufficiently excellent, and we ladies of Barchester will erect for it a fitting receptable. Come, what shall the subject be?'

'I'll put you in your pony chair, Mrs Bold, as Dannecker put Ariadne on her lion. Only you must promise to sit for me.'

'My ponies are too tame, I fear, and my broad-rimmed straw hat will not look so well in marble as the lace veil of the prebendary's wife.'

'If you will not consent to that, Mrs Bold, I will consent to try no other subject in Barchester.'

'You are determined, then, to push your fortune in other lands?'

'I am determined,' said Bertie, slowly and significantly, as he tried to bring up his mind to a great resolve; 'I am determined in this matter to be guided wholly by you.'

'Wholly by me!' said Eleanor, astonished at, and not quite liking, his altered manner.

'Wholly by you,' said Bertie, dropping his companion's arm, and standing before her on the path. In their walk they had come exactly to the spot in which Eleanor had been provoked into slapping Mr Slope's face. Could it be possible that this place was peculiarly unpropitious to her comfort? could it be possible that she should here have to encounter yet another amorous swain?

'If you will be guided by me, Mr Stanhope, you will set yourself down to steady and persevering work, and you will be ruled by your father as to the place in which it will be most advisable for you to do so.'

'Nothing could be more prudent, if only it were practicable. But now, if you will let me, I will tell you how it is that I will be guided by you, and why. Will you let me tell you?'

'I really do not know what you can have to tell.'

'No – you cannot know. It is impossible that you should. But we have been very good friends, Mrs Bold, have we not?'

'Yes, I think we have,' said she, observing in his demeanour an earnestness very unusual with him.

'You were kind enough to say just now that you took an interest in me, and I was perhaps vain enough to believe you.'

'There is no vanity in that; I do so as your sister's brother – and as my own friend also.'

'Well, I don't deserve that you should feel so kindly towards me,' said Bertie; 'but upon my word I am very grateful for it,' and he paused awhile, hardly knowing how to introduce the subject that he had in hand.

And it was no wonder that he found it difficult. He had to make known to his companion the scheme that had been prepared to rob her of her wealth; he had to tell her that he intended to marry her without loving her, or else that that he loved her without intending to marry her; and he had also to bespeak from her not only his own pardon, but also that of his sister, and induce Mrs Bold to protest in her future communion with Charlotte that an offer had been duly made to her and duly rejected.

Bertie Stanhope was not prone to be very diffident of his own conversational powers, but it did seem to him that he was about to tax them almost too far. He hardly knew where to begin, and he hardly knew where he should end.

By this time Eleanor was again walking on slowly by his side, not taking his arm as she had heretofore done, but listening very intently for whatever Bertie might have to say to her.

'I wish to be guided by you,' said he; 'and indeed, in this matter, there is no one else who can set me right.'

'Oh, that must be nonsense,' said she.

'Well, listen to me now, Mrs Bold; and if you can help it, pray don't be angry with me.'

'Angry!' said she.

'Oh, indeed you will have cause to be so. You know how very much attached to you my sister Charlotte is.'

Eleanor acknowledged that she did.

'Indeed she is; I never knew her to love any one so warmly on so short an acquaintance. You know also how well she loves me?'

Eleanor now made no answer, but she felt the blood tingle in her cheek as she gathered from what he said the probable result of this double-barrelled love on the part of Miss Stanhope.

'I am her only brother, Mrs Bold, and it is not to be wondered at that she should love me. But you do not yet know Charlotte – you do not know how entirely the well-being of our family hangs on her. Without her to manage for us, I do not know how we should get on from day to day. You cannot yet have observed all this.'

Eleanor had indeed observed a good deal of this; she did not however now say so, but allowed him to proceed with his story.

'You cannot therefore be surprised that Charlotte should be most anxious to do the best for us all.'

Eleanor said that she was not at all surprised.

'And she has had a very difficult game to play, Mrs Bold – a very difficult game. Poor Madeline's unfortunate marriage and terrible accident, my mother's ill health, my father's absence from England, and last, and worst perhaps, my own roving, idle spirit have almost been too much for her. You cannot wonder if among all her cares one of the foremost is to see me settled in the world.'

Eleanor on this occasion expressed no acquiescence. She certainly supposed that a formal offer was to be made, and could not but think that so singular an exordium was never before made by a gentleman in a similar position. Mr Slope had annoyed her by the excess of his ardour. It was quite clear that no such danger was to be feared from Mr Stanhope. Prudential motives alone actuated him. Not only was he about to make love because his sister told him, but he also took the precaution of explaining all this before he began. 'Twas thus, we may presume, that the matter presented itself to Mrs Bold.

When he had got so far, Bertie began poking the gravel with a little cane which he carried. He still kept moving on, but very slowly, and his companion moved slowly by his side, not inclined to assist him in the task the performance of which appeared to be difficult for him.

'Knowing how fond she is of yourself, Mrs Bold, cannot you imagine what scheme should have occurred to her?'

'I can imagine no better scheme, Mr Stanhope, than the one I proposed to you just now.'

'No,' said he, somewhat lack-a-daisically; 'I suppose that would be the best; but Charlotte thinks another plan might be joined with it. She wants me to marry you.'

A thousand remembrances flashed across Eleanor's mind all in a moment – how Charlotte had talked about and praised her brother, how she had continually contrived to throw the two of them together, how she had encouraged all manner of little intimacies, how she had with singular cordiality persisted in treating Eleanor as one of the family. All this had been done to secure her comfortable income for the benefit of one of the family!

Such a feeling as this is very bitter when it first impresses itself on a young mind. To the old such plots and plans, such matured schemes for obtaining the goods of this world without the trouble of earning them, such long-headed attempts to convert 'tuum' into 'meum,' are the ways of life to which they are accustomed. 'Tis thus that many live, and it therefore behoves all those who are well to do in the world to be on their guard against those who are not. With them it is the success that disgusts, not the attempt. But Eleanor had not yet learnt to look on her money as a source of danger; she had not begun to regard herself as fair game to be hunted down by hungry gentlemen. She had enjoyed the society of the Stanhopes, she had greatly liked the cordiality of Charlotte, and had been happy in her new friends. Now she saw the cause of all this kindness, and her mind was opened to a new phase of human life.

'Miss Stanhope,' said she, haughtily, 'has been contriving for me a great deal of honour, but she might have saved herself the trouble. I am not sufficiently ambitious.'

'Pray don't be angry with her, Mrs Bold,' said he, 'or with me either.'

'Certainly not with you, Mr Stanhope,' said she, with considerable sarcasm in her tone. 'Certainly not with you.'

'No – nor with her,' said he, imploringly.

'And why, may I ask you, Mr Stanhope, have you told me this singular story? For I may presume I may judge by your manner of telling it, that – that – that you and your sister are not exactly of one mind on the subject.'

'No, we are not.'

'And if so,' said Mrs Bold, who was now really angry with the unnecessary insult which she thought had been offered to her, 'and if so, why has it been worth your while to tell me all this?'

'I did once think, Mrs Bold – that you – that you –'

The widow now again became entirely impassive, and would not lend the slightest assistance to her companion.

'I did once think that you perhaps might – might have been taught to regard me as more than a friend.'

'Never!' said Mrs Bold, 'never. If I have ever allowed myself to do anything to encourage such an idea, I have been very much to blame –very much to blame indeed.'

'You never have,' said Bertie, who really had a good-natured anxiety to make what he said as little unpleasant as possible. 'You never have, and I have seen for some time that I had no chance; but my sister's hopes ran higher. I have not mistaken you, Mrs Bold, though perhaps she has.'

'Then why have you said all this to me?'

'Because I must not anger her.'

'And will not this anger her? Upon my word, Mr Stanhope, I do not understand the policy of your family. Oh, how I wish I was at home!' And as she expressed the wish, she could restrain herself no longer, but burst out into a flood of tears.

Poor Bertie was greatly moved. 'You shall have the carriage to yourself going home,' said he; 'at least you and my father. As for me I can walk, or for the matter of that it does not much signify what I do.' He perfectly understood that part of Eleanor's grief arose from the apparent necessity of going back to Barchester in the carriage with her second suitor.

This somewhat mollified her. 'Oh, Mr Stanhope,' said she, 'why should you have made me so miserable? What will you have gained by telling me all this?'

He had not even yet explained to her that she was to be a party to the little deception which he intended to play off upon his sister. This suggestion had still to be made, and as it was absolutely necessary, he proceeded to make it.

We need not follow him through the whole of his statement. At last, and not without considerable difficulty, he made Eleanor understand why he had let her into his confidence, seeing that he no longer intended her the honour of a formal offer. At last he made her comprehend the part which she was destined to play in this little family comedy.

But when she did understand it, she was only more angry with him than ever; more angry, not only with him, but with Charlotte also. Her fair name was to be bandied about between them in different senses, and each sense false. She was to be played off by the sister against the father; and then by the brother against the sister. Her dear friend Charlotte, with all her agreeable sympathy and affection, was striving to sacrifice her for the Stanhope family welfare; and Bertie, who, as he now proclaimed himself, was over head and ears in debt, completed the compliment of owning that he did not care to have his debts paid at so great a sacrifice to himself. Then she was asked to conspire together with this unwilling suitor, for the sake of making the family believe that he had in obedience to their commands done his best to throw himself thus away!

She lifted up her face when he had finished, and looking at him with much dignity, even through her tears, she said –

'I regret to say it, Mr Stanhope; but after what has passed, I believe that all intercourse between your family and myself had better cease.'

'Well, perhaps it had,' said Bertie naïvely; 'perhaps that will be better, at any rate for a time; and then Charlotte will think you are offended at what I have done.'

'And now I will go back to the house, if you please,' said Eleanor. 'I can find my way by myself, Mr Stanhope: after what has passed,' she added, 'I would rather go alone.'

'But I must find the carriage for you, Mrs Bold, and I must tell my father that you will return with him alone, and I must make some excuse to him for not going with you; and I must bid the servant put you down at your own house, for I suppose you will not now choose to see them again in the close.'

There was a truth about this, and a perspicuity in making arrangements for lessening her immediate embarrassment, which had some effect in softening Eleanor's anger. So she suffered herself to walk by his side over the now deserted lawn, till they came to the drawing-room window. There was something about Bertie Stanhope which gave him, in the estimation of every one, a different standing from that which any other man would occupy under similar circumstances. Angry as Eleanor was, and great as was her cause for anger, she was not half as angry with him as she would have been with any one else. He was apparently so simple, so good-natured, so unaffected and easy to talk to, that she had already half-forgiven him before he was at the drawing-room window. When they arrived there, Dr Stanhope was sitting nearly alone with Mr and Miss Thorne; one or two other unfortunates were there, who from one cause or another were still delayed in getting away; but they were every moment getting fewer in number.

As soon as he had handed Eleanor over to his father, Bertie started off to the front gate, in search of the carriage, and there waited leaning patiently against the front wall, and comfortably smoking a cigar, till it came up. When he returned to the room Dr Stanhope and Eleanor were alone with their hosts.

'At last, Miss Thorne,' said he cheerily, 'I have come to relieve you. Mrs Bold and my father are the last roses of the very delightful summer you have given us, and desirable as Mrs Bold's society always is, now at least you must be glad to see the last flowers plucked from the tree.'

Miss Thorne declared that she was delighted to have Mrs Bold and Dr Stanhope still with her; and Mr Thorne would have said the same, had he not been checked by a yawn, which he could not suppress.

'Father, will you give your arm to Mrs Bold?' said Bertie: and so the last adieux were made, and the prebendary led out Mrs Bold, followed by his son.

'I shall be home soon after you,' said he, as the two got into the carriage.

'Are you not coming in the carriage?' said the father.

'No; no; I have some one to see on the road, and shall walk. John, mind you drive to Mrs Bold's house first.'

Eleanor looking out of the window, saw him with his hat in his hand, bowing to her with his usual gay smile, as though nothing had happened to mar the tranquility of the day. It was many a long year before she saw him again. Dr Stanhope hardly spoke to her on her way home; and she was safely deposited by John at her own hall-door, before the carriage drove into the close.

And thus our heroine played the last act of that day's melodrame.

FORTY-THREE

Mr and Mrs Quiverful are made Happy.
Mr Slope is Encouraged by the Press

BEFORE SHE STARTED FOR ULLATHORNE, MRS PROUDIE, careful soul, caused two letters to be written, one by herself and one by her lord, to the inhabitants of Puddingdale vicarage, which made happy the hearth of those within it.

As soon as the departure of the horses left the bishop's stable-groom free for other services, that humble denizen of the diocese started on the bishop's own pony with the two despatches. We have had so many letters lately that we will spare ourselves these. That from the bishop was simply a request that Mr Quiverful would wait upon his lordship the next morning at 11 A.M.; and that from the lady was as simply a request that Mrs Quiverful would do the same by her, though it was couched in somewhat longer and more grandiloquent phraseology.

It had become a point of conscience with Mrs Proudie to urge the settlement of this great hospital question. She was resolved that Mr Quiverful should have it. She was resolved that there should be no more doubt or delay, no more refusals and resignations, no more secret negotiations carried on my Mr Slope on his own account in opposition to her behests.

'Bishop,' she said, immediately after breakfast, on the morning of that eventful day, 'have you signed the appointment yet?'

'No, my dear, not yet; it is not exactly signed as yet.'

'Then do it,' said the lady.

The bishop did it; and a very pleasant day indeed he spent at Ullathorne. And when he got home he had a glass of hot negus in his wife's sitting-room, and read the last number of the 'Little Dorrit' of the day with great inward satisfaction. Oh, husbands, oh, my marital friends, what great comfort is there to be derived from a wife well obeyed!

Much perturbation and flutter, high expectation and renewed hopes, were occasional at Puddingdale, by the receipt of these episcopal despatches. Mrs Quiverful, whose careful ear caught the sound of the pony's feet as he trotted up to the vicarage kitchen door, brought them in hurriedly to her husband. She was at the moment concocting the Irish stew destined to satisfy the noonday wants of fourteen young birds, let alone the parent couple. She had taken the letters from the man's hands between the folds of her capacious apron, so as to save them from the contamination of the stew, and in this guise she brought them to her husband's desk.

They at once divided the spoil, each taking that addressed to the other. 'Quiverful,' said she with impressive voice, 'you are to be at the palace at eleven to-morrow.'

'And so are you, my dear,' said he, almost gasping with the importance of the tidings: And then they exchanged letters.

'She'd never have sent for me again,' said the lady. 'if it wasn't all right.'

'Oh! my dear, don't be too certain,' said the gentleman. 'Only think if it should be wrong.'

'She'd never have sent for me, Q., if it wasn't all right,' again argued the lady. 'She's stiff and hard and proud as pie-crust, but I think she's right at bottom.' Such was Mrs Quiverful's verdict about Mrs Proudie, to which in after times she always adhered. People when they get their income doubled usually think that those through whose instrumentality this little ceremony is performed are right at bottom.

'Oh Letty!' said Mr Quiverful, rising from his well-worn seat.

'Oh Q.!' said Mrs Quiverful: and then the two, unmindful of the kitchen apron, the greasy fingers, and the adherent Irish stew, threw themselves warmly into each other's arms.

'For heaven's sake don't let any one cajole you out of it again,' said the wife.

'Let me alone for that,' said the husband, with a look of almost fierce determination, pressing his fist as he spoke rigidly on his desk, as though he had Mr Slope's head below his knuckles, and meant to keep it there.

'I wonder how soon it will be,' said she.

'I wonder whether it will be at all,' said he, still doubtful.

'Well, I won't say too much,' said the lady. 'The cup has slipped twice before, and it may fall altogether this time; but I'll not believe it. He'll give you the appointment to-morrow. You'll find he will.'

'Heaven send he may,' said Mr Quiverful, solemnly. And who that considers the weight of the burden on this man's back, will say that the prayer was an improper one? There were fourteen of them – fourteen of them living – as Mrs Quiverful had so powerfully urged in the presence of the bishop's wife. As long as promotion cometh from any human source, whether north or south, east or west, will not such a claim as this hold good, in spite of all our examination tests, *detur digniori's* and optimist tendencies? It is fervently to be hoped that it may. Till we can become divine we must be content to be human, lest in our hurry for a change we sink to something lower.

And then the pair sitting down lovingly together, talked over all their difficulties, as they so often did, and all their hopes, as they so seldom were enabled to do.

'You had better call on that man, Q., as you come away from the palace,' said Mrs Quiverful, pointing to an angry call for money from the Barchester draper, which the postman had left at the vicarage that morning. Cormorant that he was, unjust, hungry cormorant! When rumour first got abroad that the Quiverfuls were to go to the hospital this fellow with fawning eagerness had pressed his goods upon the wants of the poor clergyman. He had done so, feeling that he should be paid from the hospital funds, and flattering himself that a man with fourteen children, and money wherewithal to clothe them, could not but be an excellent customer. As soon as the second rumour reached him, he applied for his money angrily.

And 'the fourteen' – or such of them as were old enough to hope and discuss their hopes, talked over their golden future. The tall-grown girls whispered to each other of possible Barchester parties, of possible allowances for dress, of a possible piano – the one they had in the vicarage was so weather-beaten with the storms of years and children as to be no longer worthy of the name – of the pretty garden, and the pretty house. 'Twas of such things it most behoved them to whisper.

And the younger fry, they did not content themselves with whispers, but shouted to each other of their new playground beneath our dear ex-warden's well-loved elms, of their future own gardens, of marbles to be procured in the wished-for city, and of the rumour which had reached them of a Barchester school.

'Twas in vain that their cautious mother tried to instil into their breasts the very feeling she had striven to banish from that of their father; 'twas in vain that she repeated to the girls that 'there's many a slip 'twixt the cup and the lip;' 'twas in vain she attempted to make the children believe that they were to live at Puddingdale all their lives. Hopes mounted high and would not have themselves quelled. The neighbouring farmers heard the news, and came in to congratulate them. 'Twas Mrs Quiverful herself who had kindled the fire, and in the first outbreak of her renewed expectations she did it so thoroughly, that it was quite past her power to put it out again.

Poor matron! good honest matron! doing thy duty in the state to which thou hast been called, heartily if not contentedly; let the fire burn on – on this occasion the flames will not scorch; they shall warm thee and thine. 'Tis ordained that that husband of thine, that Q. of thy bosom, shall reign supreme for years to come over the bedesmen of Hiram's hospital.

And the last in all Barchester to mar their hopes, had he heard and seen all that passed at Puddingdale that day, would have been Mr Harding. What wants had he to set in opposition to those of such a regiment of young ravens? There are fourteen of them living! with him at any rate, let us say, that that argument would have been sufficient for the appointment of Mr Quiverful.

In the morning, Q. and his wife kept their appointments with that punctuality which bespeaks an expectant mind. The friendly farmer's gig was borrowed, and in that they went, discussing many things by the way. They had instructed the household to expect them back by one, and injunctions were given to the eldest pledge to have ready by that accustomed hour the remainder of the huge stew which the provident mother had prepared on the previous day. The hands of the kitchen clock came round to two, three, four, before the farmer's gig-wheels were again heard at the vicarage gate. With what palpitating hearts were the returning wanderers greeted!

'I suppose, children, you all thought we were never coming back any more?' said the mother, as she slowly let down her solid foot till it rested on the step of the gig. 'Well, such a day as we've had!' and then leaning heavily on a big boy's shoulder, she stepped once more on terra firma.

There was no need for more than the tone of her voice to tell them that all was right. The Irish stew might burn itself to cinders now.

Then there was such kissing and hugging, such crying and laughing. Mr Quiverful could not sit still at all, but kept walking from room to room, then out into the garden, then down the avenue into the road, and then back again to his wife. She, however, lost no time so idly.

'We must go to work at once, girls; and that in earnest. Mrs Proudie expects us to be in the hospital house on the 15th of October.'

Had Mrs Proudie expressed a wish that they should all be there on the next morning, the girls would have had nothing to say against it.

'And when will the pay begin?' asked the eldest boy.

'To-day, my dear,' said the gratified mother.

'Oh – that is jolly,' said the boy.

'Mrs Proudie insisted on our going down to the house,' continued the mother; 'and when there I thought I might save a journey by measuring some of the rooms and windows; so I got a knot of tape from Bobbins. Bobbins is as civil as you please, now.'

'I wouldn't thank him,' said Letty the younger.

'Oh, it's the way of the world, my dear. They all do just the same. You might just as well be angry with the turkey cock for gobbling at you. It's the bird's nature.' And as she enunciated to her bairns the upshot of her practical experience, she pulled from her pocket the portions of tape which showed the length and breadth of the various rooms at the hospital house.

And so we will leave her happy in her toils.

The Quiverfuls had hardly left the palace, and Mrs Proudie was still holding forth on the matter to her husband, when another visitor was announced in the person of Dr Gwynne. The master of Lazarus had asked for the bishop, and not for Mrs Proudie, and therefore, when he was shown into the study, he was surprised rather than rejoiced to find the lady there.

But we must go back a little, and it shall be but a little, for a difficulty begins to make itself manifest in the necessity of disposing of all our friends in the small remainder of this one volume. Oh, that Mr Longman would allow me a fourth! It should transcend the other three as the seventh heaven transcends all the lower stages of celestial bliss.

Going home in the carriage that evening from Ullathorne, Dr Gwynne had not without difficulty brought round his friend the archdeacon to a line of tactics much less bellicose than that which his own taste would have preferred. 'It will be unseemly in us to show ourselves in a bad humour: and moreover we have no power in this matter, and it will therefore be bad policy to act as though we had.' 'Twas thus the master of Lazarus argued. 'If,' he continued, 'the bishop be determined to appoint another to the hospital, threats will not prevent him, and threats should not be lightly used by an archdeacon to his bishop. If he will place a stranger in the hospital, we can only leave him to the indignation of others. It is probable that such a step may not eventually injure your father-in-law. I will see the bishop, if you will allow me – alone.' At this the archdeacon winced visibly; 'yes, alone; for so I shall be calmer: and then I shall at any rate learn what he does mean to do in the matter.'

The archdeacon puffed and blew, put up the carriage window and then put it down again, argued the matter up to his own gate, and at last gave way. Everybody was against him, his own wife, Mr Harding, and Dr Gwynne.

'Pray keep him out of hot water, Dr Gwynne,' Mrs Grantly had said to her guest. 'My dearest madam, I'll do my best,' the courteous master had replied. 'Twas thus he did it; and earned for himself the gratitude of Mrs Grantly.

And now we may return to the bishop's study.

Dr Gwynne had certainly not foreseen the difficulty which here presented itself. He – together with all the clerical world of England – had heard it rumoured about that Mrs Proudie did not confine herself to her wardrobes, still-rooms, and laundries; but yet it had never occurred to him that if he called on a bishop at one o'clock in the day, he could by any possibility find him closeted with his wife; or that if he did so, the wife would remain longer than necessary to make her curtsey. It appeared, however, as though in the present case Mrs Proudie had no idea of retreating.

The bishop had been very much pleased with Dr Gwynne on the preceding day, and of course thought that Dr Gwynne had been as much pleased with him. He attributed the visit solely to compliment, and thought it an extremely gracious and proper thing for the master of Lazarus to drive over from Plumstead specially to call at the palace so soon after his arrival in the country. The fact that they were not on the same side either in politics or doctrines made the compliment the greater. The bishop, therefore, was all smiles. And Mrs Proudie, who liked poeple with good handles to their names, was also very well disposed to welcome the master of Lazarus.

'We had a charming party at Ullathorne, Master, had we not?' said she. 'I hope Mrs Grantly got home without fatigue.'

Dr Gwynne said that they had all been a little tired, but were none the worse this morning.

'An excellent person, Miss Thorne,' suggested the bishop.

'And an exemplary Christian, I am told,' said Mrs Proudie.

Dr Gwynne declared that he was very glad to hear it.

'I have not seen her Sabbath-day schools yet,' continued the lady, 'but I shall make a point of doing so before long.'

Dr Gwynne merely bowed at this intimation. He had heard something of Mrs Proudie and her Sunday schools, both from Dr Grantly and Mr Harding.

'By the bye, Master,' continued the lady, 'I wonder whether Mrs Grantly would like me to drive over and inspect her Sabbath-day school. I hear that it is most excellently kept.'

Dr Gwynne really could not say. He had no doubt Mrs Grantly would be most happy to see Mrs Proudie any day Mrs Proudie would do her the honour of calling: that was, of course, if Mrs Grantly should happen to be at home.

A slight cloud darkened the lady's brow. She saw that her offer was not taken in good part. This generation of unregenerated vipers was still perverse, stiffnecked, and hardened in their iniquity. 'The archdeacon, I know,' said she, 'sets his face against these institutions.'

At this Dr Gwynne laughed slightly. It was but a smile. Had he given his cap for it he could not have helped it.

Mrs Proudie frowned again. ' "Suffer little children, and forbid them not," ' said she. 'Are we not to remember that, Dr Gwynne? "Take heed that ye despise not one of these little ones." Are we not to remember that, Dr Gwynne?' And at each of these questions she raised at him her menacing forefinger.

'Certainly, madam, certainly,' said the master, 'and so does the archdeacon, I am sure, on week days as well as on Sundays.'

'On week days you can't take heed not to despise them,' said Mrs Proudie, 'because then they are out in the fields. On week days they belong to their parents, but on Sundays they ought to belong to the clergyman.' And the finger was again raised.

The master began to understand and to share the intense disgust which the archdeacon always expressed when Mrs Proudie's name was mentioned. What was he to do with such a woman as this? To take his hat and go would have been his natural resource; but then he did not wish to be foiled in his object.

'My lord,' said he, 'I wanted to ask you a question on business, if you could spare me one moment's leisure. I know I must apologise for so disturbing you; but in truth I will not detain you five minutes.'

'Certainly, Master, certainly,' said the bishop; 'my time is quite yours – pray make no apology, pray make no apology.'

'You have a great deal to do just at the present moment, bishop. Do not forget how extremely busy you are at present,' said Mrs Proudie, whose spirit was now up; for she was angry with her visitor.

'I will not delay his lordship much above a minute,' said the master of Lazarus, rising from his chair, and expecting that Mrs Proudie would now go, or else that the bishop would lead the way into another room.

But neither event seemed likely to occur, and Dr Gwynne stood for a moment silent in the middle of the room.

'Perhaps it's about Hiram's hospital?' suggested Mrs Proudie.

Dr Gwynne, lost in astonishment, and not knowing what else on earth to do, confessed that his business with the bishop was connected with Hiram's hospital.

'His lordship has finally conferred the appointment on Mr Quiverful this morning,' said the lady.

Dr Gwynne made a simple reference to the bishop, and finding that the lady's statement was formally confirmed, he took his leave. 'That comes of the reform bill,' he said to himself as he walked down the bishop's avenue. 'Well, at any rate the Greek play bishops were not so bad as that.'

It has been said that Mr Slope, as he started for Ullathorne, received a despatch from his friend, Mr Towers, which had the effect of putting him in that high good-humour which subsequent events somewhat untowardly damped. It ran as follows. Its shortness will be its sufficient apology.

'MY DEAR SIR

I wish you every success. I don't know that I can help you, but if I can, I will.

'Yours ever,
'T.T.
'30/9/185 –'

There was more in this than in all Sir Nicholas Fitzwhiggin's flummery; more than in all the bishop's promises, even had they been ever so sincere; more than in any archbishop's good word, even had it been possible to obtain it. Tom Towers would do for him what he could.

Mr Slope had from his youth upwards been a firm believer in the public press. He had dabbled in it himself ever since he had taken his degree, and regarded it as the great arranger and distributor of all future British terrestrial affairs whatever. He had not yet arrived at the age, an age which sooner or later comes to most of us, which dissipates the golden dreams of youth. He delighted in the idea of wresting power from the hands of his country's magnates, and placing it in a custody which was at any rate nearer to his own reach. Sixty thousand broad sheets dispersing themselves daily among his reading fellow-citizens, formed in his eyes a better depôt for supremacy than a throne at Windsor, a cabinet in Downing Street, or even an assembly at Westminster. And on this subject we must not quarrel with Mr Slope, for the feeling is too general to be met with disrespect.

Tom Towers was as good, if not better than his promise. On the following morning the Jupiter, spouting forth public opinion with sixty thousand loud clarions, did proclaim to the world that Mr Slope was the fitting man for the vacant post. It was pleasant for Mr Slope to read the following lines in the Barchester news-room, which he did within thirty minutes after the morning train from London had reached the city.

'It is just now five years since we called the attention of our readers to the quiet city of Barchester. From that day to this, we have in no way meddled with the affairs of that happy ecclesiastical community. Since then, an old bishop has died there, and a young bishop has been installed; but we believe we did not do more than give some customary record of the interesting event. Nor are we now about to meddle very deeply in the affairs of the diocese. If any of the chapter feel a qualm of conscience on reading thus far, let it be quieted. Above all, let the mind of the new bishop be at rest. We are now not armed for war, but approach the reverend towers of the old cathedral with an olive-branch in our hands.

'It will be remembered that at the time alluded to, now five years past, we had occasion to remark on the state of a charity in Barchester called Hiram's hospital. We thought that it was maladministered, and that the very estimable and reverend gentleman who held the office of warden was somewhat too highly paid for duties which were somewhat too easily performed. This gentleman – and we say it in all sincerity and with no touch of sarcasm – had never looked on the matter in this light before. We do not wish to take praise to ourselves whether praise be due to us or not. But the consequence of our remark was, that the warden did look into the matter, and finding on so doing that he himself could come to no other opinion than that expressed by us, he very creditably threw up the appointment. The then bishop as creditably declined to fill the vacancy till the affair was put on a better footing. Parliament then took it up; and we have now the satisfaction of informing our readers that Hiram's hospital will be immediately re-opened under new auspices. Heretofore, provision was made for the maintenance of twelve old men. This will now be extended to the fair sex, and twelve elderly women, if any such can be found in Barchester, will be added to the establishment. There will be a matron; there will, it is hoped, be schools attached for the poorest of the children of the poor, and there will be a steward. The warden, for there will still be a warden, will receive an income more in keeping with the extent of the charity than that heretofore paid. The stipend we believe will be 450*l*. We may add that the excellent house which the former warden inhabited will still be attached to the situation.

'Barchester hospital cannot perhaps boast a world-wide reputation; but as we adverted to its state of decadence, we think it right also to advert to its renaissance. May it go on and prosper. Whether the salutary reform which has been introduced within its walls has been carried as far as could have been desired, may be doubtful. The important question of the school appears to be somewhat left to the discretion of the new warden. This might have been made the most important part of the establishment, and the new warden, whom we trust we shall not offend by the freedom of our remarks, might have been selected with some view to his fitness as schoolmaster. But we will not now look a gift horse in the mouth. May the hospital go on and prosper! The situation of warden has of course been offered to the gentleman who so honourably vacated it five years since; but we are given to understand that he has declined it. Whether the ladies who have been introduced, be in his estimation too much for his powers of control, whether it be that the diminished income does not offer to him sufficient temptation to resume his old place, or that he has in the meantime assumed other clerical duties, we do not know. We are, however, informed that he has refused the offer, and that the situation has been accepted by Mr Quiverful, the vicar of Puddingdale.

'So much we think is due to Hiram redivivus. But while we are on the subject of Barchester, we will venture with all respectful humility to express our opinion on another matter, connected with the ecclesiastical polity of that ancient city. Dr Trefoil, the dean, died yesterday. A short record of his death, giving his age, and the various pieces of preferment which he has at different times held, will be found in another column of this paper. The only fault we knew in him was his age, and as that is a crime of which we all hope to be guilty, we will not bear heavily on it. May he rest in peace! But though the great age of an expiring dean cannot be made matter of reproach, we are not inclined to look on such a fault as at all pardonable in a dean just brought to the birth. We do hope that the days of sexagenarian appointments are past. If we want deans, we must want them for some purpose. That purpose will necessarily be better fulfilled by a man of forty than by a man of sixty. If we are to pay deans at all, we are to pay them for some sort of work. That work, be it what it may, will be best performed by a workman in the prime of life. Dr Trefoil, we see, was eighty when he died. As we have as yet completed no plan for pensioning superannuated clergymen, we do not wish to get rid of any existing deans of that age. But we prefer having as few such as possible. If a man of seventy be now appointed, we beg to point out to Lord —— that he will be past all use in a year or two, if indeed he be not so at the present moment. His lordship will allow us to remind him that all men are not evergreens like himself.

'We hear that Mr Slope's name has been mentioned for this preferment.

Mr Slope is at present chaplain to the bishop. A better man could hardly be selected. He is a man of talent, young, active, and conversant with the affairs of the cathedral; he is moreover, we conscientiously believe, a truly pious clergyman. We know that his services in the city of Barchester have been highly appreciated. He is an eloquent preacher and a ripe scholar. Such a selection as this would go far to raise the confidence of the public in the present administration of church patronage, and would teach men to believe that from henceforth the establishment of our church will not afford easy couches to worn-out clerical voluptuaries.'

Standing at a reading-desk in the Barchseter news-room, Mr Slope digested this article with considerable satisfaction. What was therein said as to the hospital was now comparatively matter of indifference to him. He was certainly glad that he had not succeeded in restoring to the place the father of that virago who had so audaciously outraged all decency in his person; and was so far satisfied. But Mrs Proudie's nominee was appointed, and he was so far dissatisfied. His mind, however, was now soaring above Mrs Bold or Mrs Proudie. He was sufficiently conversant with the tactics of the Jupiter to know that the pith of the article would lie in the last paragraph. The place of honour was given to him, and it was indeed as honourable as even he could have wished. He was very grateful to his friend Mr Towers, and with full heart looked forward to the day when he might entertain him in princely style at his own full-spread board in the deanery dining-room.

It had been well for Mr Slope that Dr Trefoil had died in the autumn. Those caterers for our morning repast, the staff of the Jupiter, had been sorely put to it for the last month to find a sufficiency of proper pabulum. Just then there was no talk of a new American president. No wonderful tragedies had occurred on railway trains in Georgia, or elsewhere. There was a dearth of broken banks, and a dead dean with the necessity for a live one was a godsend. Had Dr Trefoil died in June, Mr Towers would probably not have known so much about the piety of Mr Slope.

And here we will leave Mr Slope for a while in his triumph; explaining, however, that his feelings were not altogether of a triumphant nature. His rejection by the widow, or rather the method of his rejection, galled him terribly. For days to come he positively felt the sting upon his cheek, whenever he thought of what had been done to him. He could not refrain from calling her by harsh names, speaking to himself as he walked through the streets of Barchester. When he said his prayers, he could not bring himself to forgive her. When he strove to do so, his mind recoiled from the attempt, and in lieu of forgiving ran off in a double spirit of vindictiveness dwelling on the extent of the injury he had received. And so his prayers dropped senseless from his lips.

And then the signora; what would he not have given to be able to hate her also? As it was, he worshipped the very sofa on which she was ever lying. And thus it was not all rose colour with Mr Slope, although his hopes ran high.

FORTY-FOUR

Mrs Bold at Home

POOR MRS BOLD, WHEN SHE GOT HOME from Ullathorne on the evening of Miss Thorne's party, was very unhappy, and moreover, very tired. Nothing fatigues the body so much as weariness of spirit, and Eleanor's spirit was indeed weary.

Dr Stanhope had civilly but not very cordially asked her in to tea, and her manner of refusal convinced the worthy doctor that he need not repeat the invitation. He had not exactly made himself a party to the intrigue which was to convert the late Mr Bold's patrimony into an income for his hopeful son, but he had been well aware what was going on. And he was well aware also, when he perceived that Bertie declined accompanying them home in the carriage, that the affair had gone off.

Eleanor was very much afraid that Charlotte would have darted out upon her, as the prebendary got out at his own door, but Bertie had thoughtfully saved her from this, by causing the carriage to go round by her own house. This also Dr Stanhope understood, and allowed to pass by without remark.

When she got home, she found Mary Bold in the drawing-room with the child in her lap. She rushed forward, and, throwing herself on her knees, kissed the little fellow till she almost frightened him.

'Oh, Mary, I am so glad you did not go. It was an odious party.'

Now the question of Mary's going had been one greatly mooted between them. Mrs Bold, when invited, had been the guest of the Grantlys, and Miss Thorne, who had chiefly known Eleanor at the hospital or at Plumstead rectory, had forgotten all about Mary Bold. Her sister-in-law had implored her to go under her wing, and had offered to write to Miss Thorne, or to call on her. But Miss Bold had declined. In fact, Mr Bold had not been very popular with such people as the Thornes, and his sister would not go among them unless she were specially asked to do so.

'Well then,' said Mary, cheerfully, 'I have the less to regret.'

'You have nothing to regret; but oh! Mary, I have – so much – so much' – and then she began kissing her boy, whom her caresses had aroused from his slumbers. When she raised her head, Mary saw that the tears were running down her cheeks.

'Good heavens, Eleanor, what is the matter? what has happened to you? Eleanor – dearest Eleanor – what is the matter?' and Mary got up with the boy still in her arms.

'Give him to me – give him to me,' said the young mother. 'Give him to me, Mary,' and she almost tore the child out of her sister's arms. The poor little fellow murmured somewhat at the disturbance, but nevertheless nestled himself close into his mother's bosom.

'Here, Mary, take the cloak from me. My own, own darling, darling, darling jewel. You are not false to me. Everybody else is false; everybody else is cruel. Mamma will care for nobody, nobody, nobody, but her own, own, own little man;' and she again kissed and pressed the baby and cried till the tears ran down over the child's face.

'Who has been cruel to you, Eleanor?' said Mary. 'I hope I have not.'

Now, in this matter, Eleanor had great cause for mental uneasiness. She could not certainly accuse her loving sister-in-law of cruelty; but she had to do that which was more galling; she had to accuse herself of imprudence against which her sister-in-law had warned her. Miss Bold had never encouraged Eleanor's acquaintance with Mr Slope, and she had positively discouraged the friendship of the Stanhopes as far as her usual gentle mode of speaking had permitted. Eleanor had only laughed at her, however, when she said that she disapproved of married women who lived apart from their husbands, and suggested that Charlotte Stanhope never went to church. Now, however Eleanor must either hold her tongue, which was quite impossible, or confess herself to have been utterly wrong, which was nearly equally so. So she staved off the evil day by more tears, and consoled herself by inducing little Johnny to rouse himself sufficiently to return her caresses.

'He is a darling – as true as gold. What would mamma do without him? Mamma would lie down and die if she had not her own Johnny Bold to give her comfort.' This and much more she said of the same kind, and for a time made no other answer to Mary's inquiries.

This kind of consolation from the world's deceit is very common.

Mothers obtain it from their children, and men from their dogs. Some men even do so from their walking-sticks, which is just as rational. How is it that we can take joy to ourselves in that we are not deceived by those who have not attained the art to deceive us? In a true man, if such can be found, or a true woman, much consolation may indeed be taken.

In the caresses of her child, however, Eleanor did receive consolation; and may ill befall the man who would begrudge it to her. The evil day, however, was only postponed. She had to tell her disagreeable tale to Mary, and she had also to tell it to her father. Must it not, indeed, be told to the whole circle of her acquaintance before she could be made to stand all right with them? At the present moment there was no one to whom she could turn for comfort. She hated Mr Slope; that was a matter of course, in that feeling she revelled. She hated and despised the Stanhopes; but that feeling distressed her greatly. She had, as it were, separated herself from her old friends to throw herself into the arms of this family; and then how had they intended to use her? She could hardly reconcile herself to her own father, who had believed ill of her. Mary Bold had turned Mentor. That she could have forgiven had the Mentor turned out to be in the wrong; but Mentors in the right are not to be pardoned. She could not but hate the archdeacon; and now she hated him worse than ever, for she must in some sort humble herself before him. She hated her sister, for she was part and parcel of the archdeacon. And she would have hated Mr Arabin if she could. He had pretended to regard her, and yet before her face he had hung over that Italian woman as though there had been no beauty in the world but hers – no other woman worth a moment's attention. And Mr Arabin would have to learn all this about Mr Slope! She told herself that she hated him, and she knew that she was lying to herself as she did so. She had no consolation but her baby, and of that she made the most. Mary, though she could not surmise what it was that had so violently affected her sister-in-law, saw at once that her grief was too great to be kept under control, and waited patiently till the child should be in his cradle.

'You'll have some tea, Eleanor,' she said.

'Oh, I don't care,' said she; though in fact she must have been very hungry, for she had eaten nothing at Ullathorne.

Mary quietly made the tea, and buttered the bread, laid aside the cloak, and made things look comfortable.

'He's fast asleep,' said she, 'you're very tired; let me take him up to bed.'

But Eleanor would not let her sister touch him. She looked wistfully at her baby's eyes, saw that they were lost in the deepest slumber, and then made a sort of couch for him on the sofa. She was determined that nothing should prevail upon her to let him out of her sight that night.

'Come, Nelly,' said Mary, 'don't be cross with me. I at least have done nothing to offend you.'

'I an't cross,' said Eleanor.

'Are you angry then? Surely you can't be angry with me.'

'No, I an't angry; at least not with you.'

'If you are not, drink the tea I have made for you. I am sure you must want it.'

Eleanor did drink it, and allowed herself to be persuaded. She ate and drank, and as the inner woman was recruited she felt a little more charitable towards the world at large. At last she found words to begin her story, and before she went to bed, she had made a clean breast of it and told everything – everything, that is, as to the lovers she had rejected: of Mr Arabin she said not a word.

'I know I was wrong,' said she, speaking of the blow she had given to Mr Slope; 'but I didn't know what he might do, and I had to protect myself.'

'He richly deserved it,' said Mary.

'Deserved it!' said Eleanor, whose mind as regarded Mr Slope was almost bloodthirsty. 'Had I stabbed him with a dagger, he would have deserved it. But what will they say about it at Plumstead?'

'I don't think I should tell them,' said Mary. Eleanor began to think that she would not.

There could have been no kinder comforter than Mary Bold. There was not the slightest dash of triumph about her when she heard of the Stanhope scheme, not did she allude to her former opinion when Eleanor called her late friend Charlotte a base, designing woman. She re-echoed all the abuse that was heaped on Mr Slope's head, and never hinted that she had said as much before. 'I told you so, I told you so!' is the croak of a true Job's comforter. But Mary, when she found her friend lying in her sorrow and scraping herself with potsherds, forbore to argue and to exult. Eleanor acknowledged the merit of the forbearance, and at length allowed herself to be tranquilised.

On the next day she did not go out of the house. Barchester she thought would be crowded with Stanhopes and Slopes; perhaps also with Arabins and Grantlys. Indeed there was hardly any one among her friends whom she could have met, without some cause of uneasiness.

In the course of the afternoon she heard that the dean was dead; and she also heard that Mr Quiverful had been finally appointed to the hospital.

In the evening her father came to her, and then the story, or as much of it as she could bring herself to tell him, had to be repeated. He was not in truth much surprised at Mr Slope's effrontery; but he was obliged to act as though he had been, to save his daughter's feelings. He was, however, anything but skilful in his deceit, and she saw through it.

'I see,' said she, 'that you think it only in the common course of things that Mr Slope should have treated me in this way.' She had said nothing to him about the embrace, nor yet of the way in which it had been met.

'I do not think it at all strange,' said he, 'that any one should admire my Eleanor.'

'It is strange to me,' said she, 'that any man should have so much audacity, without ever having received the slightest encouragement.'

To this Mr Harding answered nothing. With the archdeacon it would have been the text for a rejoinder, which would have disgraced Bildad the Shuhite.

'But you'll tell the archdeacon?' asked Mr Harding.

'Tell him what?' said she sharply.

'Or Susan?' continued Mr Harding. 'You'll tell Susan; you'll let them know that they wronged you in supposing that this man's addresses would be agreeable to you.'

'They may find that out their own way,' said she; 'I shall not ever willingly mention Mr Slope's name to either of them.'

'But I may.'

'I have no right to hinder you from doing anything that may be necessary to your own comfort, but pray do not do it for my sake. Dr Grantly never thought well of me, and never will. I don't know now that I am even anxious that he should do so.'

And then they went to the affair of the hospital. 'But is it true, papa?'

'What, my dear?' said he. 'About the dean? Yes, I fear quite true. Indeed I know there is no doubt about it.'

'Poor Miss Trefoil. I am so sorry for her. But I did not mean that,' said Eleanor. 'But about the hospital, papa?'

'Yes, my dear. I believe it is true that Mr Quiverful is to have it.'

'Oh, what a shame!'

'No, my dear, not at all, not at all a shame: I am sure I hope it will suit him.'

'But, papa, you know it is a shame. After all your hopes, all your expectations to get back to your old house, to see it given away in this way to a perfect stranger!'

'My dear, the bishop had a right to give it to whom he pleased.'

'I deny that, papa. He had no such right. It is not as though you were a candidate for a new piece of preferment. If the bishop has a grain of justice –'

'The bishop offered it to me on his terms, and as I did not like the terms, I refused it. After that, I cannot complain.'

'Terms! he had no right to make terms.'

'I don't know about that; but it seems he had the power. But to tell you the truth, Nelly, I am as well satisfied as it is. When the affair became the subject of angry discussion, I thoroughly wished to be rid of it altogether.'

'But you did want to go back to the old house, papa. You told me so yourself.'

'Yes, my dear, I did. For a short time I did wish it. And I was foolish in doing so. I am getting old now; and my chief worldly wish is for peace and rest. Had I gone back to the hospital, I should have had endless contentions with the bishop, contentions with his chaplain, and contentions with the archdeacon. I am not up to this now, I am not able to meet such troubles; and therefore I am not ill-pleased to find myself left to the little church of St Cuthbert's. I shall never starve,' added he, laughing, 'as long as you are here.'

'But will you come and live with me, papa?' she said earnestly, taking him by both his hands. 'If you will do that, if you will promise that, I will own that you are right.'

'I will dine with you to-day at any rate.'

'No, but live here altogether. Give up that close, odious little room in High Street.'

'My dear, it's a very nice little room; and you are really quite uncivil.'

'Oh, papa, don't joke. It's not a nice place for you. You say you are growing old, though I am sure you are not.'

'Am not I, my dear?'

'No, papa, not old – not to say old. But you are quite old enough to feel the want of a decent room to sit in. You know how lonely Mary and I are here. You know nobody ever sleeps in the big front bed-room. It is really unkind of you to remain up there alone, when you are so much wanted here.'

'Thank you, Nelly – thank you. But, my dear –'

'If you had been living here, papa, with us, as I really think you ought to have done, considering how lonely we are, there would have been none of all this dreadful affair about Mr Slope.'

Mr Harding, however, did not allow himself to be talked over into giving up his own and only little *pied à terre* in the High Street. He promised to come and dine with his daughter, and stay with her, and visit her, and do everything but absolutely live with her. It did not suit the peculiar feelings of the man to tell his daughter that though she had rejected Mr Slope, and been ready to reject Mr Stanhope, some other more favoured suitor would probably soon appear; and that on the appearance of such a suitor the big front bed-room might perhaps be more frequently in requisition than at present. But doubtless such an idea crossed his mind, and added its weight to the other reasons which made him decide on still keeping the close, odious little room in High Street.

The evening passed over quietly and in comfort. Eleanor was always happier with her father than with any one else. He had not, perhaps, any natural taste for baby-worship, but he was always ready to sacrifice himself, and therefore made an excellent third in a trio with his daughter and Mary Bold in singing the praises of the wonderful child.

They were standing together over their music in the evening, the baby having again been put to bed upon the sofa, when the servant brought in a very small note in a beautiful pink envelope. It quite filled the room with perfume as it lay upon the small salver. Mary Bold and Mrs Bold were both at the piano, and Mr Harding was sitting close to them, with the violoncello between his legs; so that the elegancy of the epistle was visible to them all.

'Please, ma'am, Dr Stanhope's coachman says he is to wait for an answer,' said the servant.

Eleanor got very red in the face as she took the note in her hand. She had never seen the writing before. Charlotte's epistles, to which she was well accustomed, were of a very different style and kind. She generally wrote on large note-paper; she twisted up her letters into the shape and sometimes into the size of cocked hats; she addressed them in a sprawling manly hand, and not unusually added a blot or a smudge, as though such were her own peculiar sign-manual. The address of this note was written in a beautiful female hand, and the gummed wafer bore on it an impress of a gilt coronet. Though Eleanor had never seen such a one before, she guessed that it came from the signora. Such epistles were very numerously sent out from any house in which the signora might happen to be dwelling, but they were rarely addressed to ladies. When the coachman was told by the lady's maid to take the letter to Mrs Bold, he openly expressed his opinion that there was some mistake about it. Whereupon the lady's maid boxed the coachman's ears. Had Mr Slope seen in how meek a spirit the coachman took the rebuke, he might have learnt a useful lesson, both in philosophy and religion.

The note was as follows. It may be taken as a faithful promise that no further letter whatever shall be transcribed at length in these pages.

'My dear mrs bold,

May I ask you, as a great favour, to call on me to-morrow? You can say what hour will best suit you; but quite early, if you can. I need hardly say that if I could call upon you I should not take this liberty with you.

'I partly know what occurred the other day, and I promise you that you shall meet with no annoyance if you will come to me. My brother leaves us for London to-day; from thence he goes to Italy.

'It will probably occur tro you that I should not thus intrude on you, unless I had that to say to you which may be of considerable moment. Pray therefore excuse me, even if you do not grant my request, and believe me,

'Very sincerely yours,

'M. Vesey Neroni.

'Thursday Evening.'

The three of then sat in consultation on this epistle for some ten or fifteen minutes, and then decided that Eleanor should write a line saying that she would see the signora the next morning, at twelve o'clock.

✄ FORTY-FIVE ✄

The Stanhopes at Home

We must now return to the stanhopes, and see how they behaved themselves on their return from Ullathorne. Charlotte, who came back in the first homeward journey with her sister, waited in palpitating expectation till the carriage drove up to the door a second time. She did not run down or stand at the window, or show in any outward manner that she looked for anything wonderful to occur; but, when she heard the carriage-wheels, she stood up with erect ears, listening for Eleanor's footfall on the pavement or the cheery sound of Bertie's voice welcoming her in. Had she heard either, she would have felt that all was right; but neither sound was there for her to hear. She heard only her father's slow step, as he ponderously let himself down from the carriage, and slowly walked along the hall, till he got into his own private room on the ground floor. 'Send Miss Stanhope to me,' he said to the servant.

'There's something wrong now,' said Madeline, who was lying on her sofa in the back drawing-room.

'It's all up with Bertie,' replied Charlotte. 'I know, I know,' she said to the servant, as he brought up the message. 'Tell my father I will be with him immediately.'

'Bertie's wooing has gone astray,' said Madeline; 'I knew it would.'

'It has been his own fault then. She was ready enough, I am quite sure,' said Charlotte, with that sort of ill-nature which is not uncommon when one woman speaks of another.

'What will you say to him now?' By 'him,' the signora meant their father.

'That will be as I find him. He was ready to pay two hundred pounds for Bertie, to stave off the worst of his creditors, if this marriage had gone on. Bertie must now have the money instead, and go and take his chance.'

'Where is he now?'

'Heaven knows! smoking in the bottom of Mr Thorne's ha-ha, or philandering with some of those Miss Chadwicks. Nothing will ever make an impression on him. But he'll be furious if I don't go down.'

'No; nothing ever will. But don't be long, Charlotte, for I want my tea.'

And so Charlotte went down to her father. There was a very black cloud on the old man's brow; blacker than his daughter could ever yet remember to have seen there. He was sitting in his own arm-chair, not comfortably over the fire, but in the middle of the room, waiting till she should come and listen to him.

'What has become of your brother?' he said, as soon as the door was shut.

'I should rather ask you,' said Charlotte. 'I left you both at Ullathorne, when I came away. What have you done with Mrs Bold?'

'Mrs Bold! nonsense. The woman has gone home as she ought to do. And heartily glad I am that she should not be sacrificed to so heartless a reprobate.'

'Oh, papa!'

'A heartless reprobate! Tell me now where he is, and what he is going to do. I have allowed myself to be fooled between you. Marriage, indeed! Who on earth that has money, or credit, or respect in the world to lose, would marry him?'

'It is no use your scolding me, papa. I have done the best I could for him and you.'

'And Madeline is nearly as bad,' said the prebendary, who was in truth very, very angry.

'Oh, I suppose we are all bad,' replied Charlotte.

The old man emitted a huge leonine sigh. If they were all bad, who had made them so? If they were unprincipled, selfish, and disreputable, who was to be blamed for the education which had had so injurious an effect?

'I know you'll ruin me among you,' said he.

'Why, papa, what nonsense that is. You are living within your income this minute, and if there are any new debts, I don't know of them. I am sure there ought to be none, for we are dull enough here.'

'Are those bills of Madeline's paid?'

'No, they are not. Who was to pay them?'

'Her husband may pay them.'

'Her husband! would you wish me to tell her you say so? Do you wish to turn her out of your house?'

'I wish she would know how to behave herself.'

'Why, what on earth has she done now? Poor Madeline! To-day is only the second time she has gone out since we came to this vile town.'

He then sat silent for a time, thinking in what shape he would declare his resolve. 'Well, papa,' said Charlotte, 'shall I stay here, or may I go upstairs and give mamma her tea?'

'You are in your brother's confidence. Tell me what he is going to do?'

'Nothing, that I am aware of.'

'Nothing – nothing! nothing but eat and drink, and spend every shilling of my money he can lay his hands upon. I have made up my mind, Charlotte. He shall eat and drink no more in this house.'

'Very well. Then I suppose he must go back to Italy.'

'He may go where he pleases.'

'That's easily said, papa; but what does it mean? You can't let him –'

'It means this,' said the doctor, speaking more loudly than was his wont, and with wrath flashing from his eyes; 'that as sure as God rules in heaven, I will not maintain him any longer in idleness.'

'Oh, ruling in heaven!' said Charlotte. 'It is no use talking about that. You must rule him here on earth; and the question is, how you can do it. You can't turn him out of the house penniless, to beg about the street.'

'He may beg where he likes.'

'He must go back to Carrara. That is the cheapest place he can live at, and nobody there will give him credit for above two or three hundred pauls. But you must let him have the means of going.'

'As sure as –'

'Oh, papa, don't swear. You know you must do it. You were ready to pay two hundred pounds for him if this marriage came off. Half that will start him to Carrara.'

'What? give him a hundred pounds!'

'You know we are all in the dark, papa,' said she, thinking it expedient to change the conversation. 'For anything we know, he may be at this moment engaged to Mrs Bold.'

'Fiddlestick,' said the father, who had seen the way in which Mrs Bold had got into the carriage, while his son stood apart without even offering her his hand.

'Well, then, he must go to Carrara,' said Charlotte.

Just at this moment the lock of the front door was heard, and Charlotte's quick ears detected her brother's cat-like step in the hall. She said nothing, feeling that for the present Bertie had better keep out of her father's way. But Dr Stanhope also heard the sound of the lock.

'Who's that?' he demanded. Charlotte made no reply, and he asked again, 'Who is that that has just come in? Open the door. Who is it?'

'I suppose it is Bertie.'

'Bid him come here,' said the father. But Bertie, who was close to the door and heard the call, required no further bidding, but walked in with a perfectly unconcerned and cheerful air. It was this peculiar *insouciance* which angered Dr Stanhope, even more than his son's extravagance.

'Well, sir?' said the doctor.

'And how did you get home, sir, with your fair companion?' said Bertie. 'I suppose she is not up-stairs, Charlotte?'

'Bertie,' said Charlotte, 'papa is in no humour for joking. He is very angry with you.'

'Angry!' said Bertie, raising his eyebrows, as though he had never yet given his parent cause for a single moment's uneasiness.

'Sit down, if you please, sir,' said Dr Stanhope very sternly, but not now very loudly. 'And I'll trouble you to sit down too, Charlotte. Your mother can wait for her tea a few minutes.'

Charlotte sat down on the chair nearest to the door, in somewhat of a perverse sort of manner; as much as though she would say – Well, here I am; you shan't say I don't do what I am bid; but I'll be whipped if I give way to you. And she was determined not to give way. She too was angry with Bertie; but she was not the less ready on that account to defend him from his father. Bertie also sat down. He drew his chair close to the library-table, upon which he put his elbow, and then resting his face comfortably on one hand, he began drawing little pictures on a sheet of paper with the other. Before the scene was over he had completed admirable figures of Miss Thorne, Mrs Proudie, and Lady De Courcy, and begun a family piece to comprise the whole set of the Lookalofts.

'Would it suit you, sir,' said the father, 'to give me some idea as to what your present intentions are? – what way of living you propose to yourself?'

'I'll do anything you can suggest, sir,' replied Bertie.

'No, I shall suggest nothing further. My time for suggesting has gone by. I have only one order to give, and that is, that you leave my house.'

'To-night?' said Bertie; and the simple tone of the question left the doctor without any adequately dignified method of reply.

'Papa does not quite mean to-night,' said Charlotte, 'at least I suppose not.'

'To-morrow, perhaps,' suggested Bertie.

'Yes, sir, to-morrow,' said the doctor. 'You shall leave this to-morrow.'

'Very well sir. Will the 4.30 P.M. train be soon enough?' and Bertie, as he asked, put the finishing touch to Miss Thorne's high-heeled boots.

'You may go how and when and where you please, so that you leave my house to-morrow. You have disgraced me, sir; you have disgraced yourself, and me, and your sisters.'

'I am glad at least, sir, that I have not disgraced my mother,' said Bertie.

Charlotte could hardly keep her countenance; but the doctor's brow grew still blacker than ever. Bertie was executing his *chef d'œuvre* in the delineation of Mrs Proudie's nose and mouth.

'You are a heartless reprobate sir; a heartless, thankless, good-for-nothing reprobate. I have done with you. You are my son – that I cannot help; but you shall have no more part or parcel in me as my child, nor I in you as your father.'

'Oh, papa, papa! you must not, shall not say so,' said Charlotte.

'I will say so, and do say so,' said the father, rising from his chair. 'And now leave the room, sir.'

'Stop, stop,' said Charlotte; 'why don't you speak, Bertie? why don't you look up and speak? It is your manner that makes papa so angry.'

'He is perfectly indifferent to all decency, to all propriety,' said the doctor; and then he shouted out, 'Leave the room, sir! Do you hear what I say?'

'Papa, papa, I will not let you part so. I know you will be sorry for it.' And then she added, getting up and whispering into his ear, 'Is he only to blame? Think of that. We have made our own bed, and, such as it is, we must lie on it. It is no use for us to quarrel among ourselves,' and as she finished her whisper Bertie finished off the countess's bustle, which was so well done that it absolutely seemed to be swaying to and fro on the paper with its usual lateral motion.

'My father is angry at the present time,' said Bertie, looking up for a moment from his sketches, 'because I am not going to marry Mrs Bold. What can I say on the matter? It is true that I am not going to marry her. In the first place –'

'That is not true, sir,' said Dr Stanhope; 'but I will not argue with you.'

'You were angry just this moment because I would not speak,' said Bertie, going on with a young Lookaloft.

'Give over drawing,' said Charlotte, going up to him and taking the paper from under his hand. The caricatures, however, she preserved, and showed them afterwards to the friends of the Thornes, the Proudies, and De Courcys. Bertie, deprived of his occupation, threw himself back in his chair and waited further orders.

'I think it will certainly be for the best that Bertie should leave this at once, perhaps to-morrow,' said Charlotte; 'but pray, papa, let us arrange some scheme together.'

'If he will leave this to-morrow, I will give him 10*l*., and he shall be paid 5*l*. a month by the banker at Carrara as long as he stays permanently in that place.'

'Well, sir! it won't be long,' said Bertie; 'for I shall be starved to death in about three months.'

'He must have marble to work with,' said Charlotte.

'I have plenty there in the studio to last me three months,' said Bertie. 'It will be no use attempting anything large in so limited a time; unless I do my own tombstone.'

Terms, however, were ultimately come to, somewhat more liberal than those proposed, and the doctor was induced to shake hands with his son, and bid him good night. Dr Stanhope would not go up to tea, but had it brought to him in his study by his daughter.

But Bertie went up-stairs and spent a pleasant evening. He finished the Lookalofts, greatly to the delight of his sisters, though the manner of portraying their *décolleté* dresses was not the most refined. Finding how matters were going, he by degrees allowed it to escape from him that he had not pressed his suit upon the widow in a very urgent way.

'I suppose, in point of fact, you never proposed at all?' said Charlotte.

'Oh, she understood that she might have me if she wished,' said he.

'And she didn't wish,' said the signora.

'You have thrown me over in the most shameful manner,' said Charlotte. 'I suppose you told her all about my little plan?'

'Well, it came out somehow; at least the most of it.'

'There's an end of that alliance,' said Charlotte; 'but it doesn't matter much. I suppose we shall all be back at Como soon.'

'I am sure I hope so,' said the signora; 'I'm sick of the sight of black coats. If that Mr Slope comes here any more, he'll be the death of me.'

'You've been the ruin of him, I think,' said Charlotte.

'And as for a second black-coated lover of mine, I am going to make a present of him to another lady with most singular disinterestedness.'

The next day, true to his promise, Bertie packed up and went off by the 4.30 P.M. train, with 20*l.* in his pocket, bound for the marble quarries of Carrara. And so he disappears from our scene.

At twelve o'clock on the day following that on which Bertie went, Mrs Bold, true also to her word, knocked at Dr Stanhope's door with a timid hand and palpitating heart. She was at once shown up to the back drawing-room, the folding doors of which were closed, so that in visiting the signora Eleanor was not necessarily thrown into any communion with those in the front room. As she went up the stairs, she saw none of the family, and was so far saved much of the annoyance which she had dreaded.

'This is very kind of you, Mrs Bold; very kind, after what has happened,' said the lady on the sofa with her sweetest smile.

'You wrote in such a strain that I could not but come to you.'

'I did, I did; I wanted to force you to see me.'

'Well, signora; I am here.'

'How cold you are to me. But I suppose I must put up with that. I know you think you have reason to be displeased with us all. Poor Bertie! if you knew all, you would not be angry with him.'

'I am not angry with your brother – not in the least. But I hope you did not send for me here to talk about him.'

'If you are angry with Charlotte, that is worse; for you have no warmer friend in all Barchester. But I did *not* send for you to talk about this – pray bring your chair nearer, Mrs Bold, so that I may look at you. It is so unnatural to see you keeping so far off from me.'

Eleanor did as she was bid, and brought her chair close to the sofa.

'And now, Mrs Bold, I am going to tell you something which you may perhaps think indelicate; but yet I know that I am right in doing so.'

Hereupon Mrs Bold said nothing, but felt inclined to shake in her chair. The signora, she knew, was not very particular, and that which to her appeared to be indelicate might to Mrs Bold appear to be extremely indecent.

'I believe you know Mr Arabin?'

Mrs Bold would have given the world not to blush, but her blood was not at her own command. She did blush up to her forehead, and the signora, who had made her sit in a special light in order that she might watch her, saw that she did so.

'Yes – I am acquainted with him. That is, slightly. He is an intimate friend of Dr Grantly, and Dr Grantly is my brother-in-law.'

'Well; if you know Mr Arabin, I am sure you must like him. I know and like him much. Everybody that knows him must like him.'

Mrs Bold felt it quite impossible to say anything in reply to this. Her blood was rushing about her body she knew not how or why. She felt as though she were swinging in her chair; and she knew that she was not only red in the face, but also almost suffocated with heat. However, she sat still and said nothing.

'How stiff you are with me, Mrs Bold,' said the signora; 'and I the while am doing for you all that one woman can do to serve another.'

A kind of thought came over the widow's mind that perhaps the signora's friendship was real, and that at any rate it could not hurt her; and another kind of thought, a glimmering of a thought, came to her also – that Mr Arabin was too precious to be lost. She despised the signora; but might she not stoop to conquer? It should be but the smallest fraction of a stoop!

'I don't want to be stiff,' she said, 'but your questions are so very singular.'

'Well, then, I will ask you one more singular still,' said Madeline Neroni, raising herself on her elbow and turning her own face full upon her companion's. 'Do you love him, love him with all your heart and soul, with all the love your bosom can feel? For I can tell you that he loves you, adores you, worships you, thinks of you and nothing else, is now thinking of you as he attempts to write his sermon for next Sunday's preaching. What would I not give to be loved in such a way by such a man, that is, if I were an object fit for any man to love!'

Mrs Bold got up from her seat and stood speechless before the woman who was now addressing her in this impassioned way. When the signora thus alluded to herself, the widow's heart was softened, and she put her own hand, as though caressingly, on that of her companion which was resting on the table. The signora grasped it and went on speaking.

'What I tell you is God's own truth; and it is for you to use it as may be best for your own happiness. But you must not betray me. He knows nothing of this. He knows nothing of my knowing his inmost heart. He is simple as a child in these matters. He told me his secret in a thousand ways because he could not dissemble; but he does not dream that he has told it. You know it now, and I advise you to use it.'

Eleanor returned the pressure of the other's hand with an infinitesimal *soupçon* of a squeeze.

'And remember,' continued the signora,' he is not like other men. You must not expect him to come to you with vows and oaths and pretty presents, to kneel at your feet, and kiss your shoe-strings. If you want that, there are plenty to do it; but he won't be one of them.' Eleanor's bosom nearly burst with a sigh; but Madeline, not heeding her, went on. 'With him, yea will stand for yea, and nay for nay. Though his heart should break for it, the woman who shall reject him once, will have rejected him once and for all. Remember that. And now, Mrs Bold. I will not keep you, for you are fluttered. I partly guess what use you will make of what I have said to you. If ever you are a happy wife in that man's house, we shall be far away; but I shall expect you to write me one line to say that you have forgiven the sins of the family.'

Eleanor half whispered that she would, and then, without uttering another word, crept out of the room, and down the stairs, opened the front door for heself without hearing or seeing any one, and found herself in the close.

It would be difficult to analyse Eleanor's feelings as she walked home. She was nearly stupefied by the things that had been said to her. She felt sore that her heart should have been so searched and riddled by a comparative stranger, by a woman whom she had never liked and never could like. She was mortified that the man whom she owned to herself that she loved should have concealed his love from her and shown it to another. There was much to vex her proud spirit. But there was, nevertheless, an under-stratum of joy in all this which buoyed her up wondrously. She tried if she could disbelieve what Madame Neroni had said to her; but she found that she could not. It was true; it must be true. She could not, would not, did not doubt it.

On one point she fully resolved to follow the advice given her. If it should ever please Mr Arabin to put such a question to her as that suggested, her 'yea' should be 'yea'. Would not all her miseries be at an end, if she could talk of them to him openly, with her head resting on his shoulder?

FORTY-SIX

Mr Slope's parting Interview with the Signora

ON THE FOLLOWING DAY THE SIGNORA WAS in her pride. She was dressed in her brightest of morning dresses, and had quite a *levée* round her couch. It was a beautifully bright October afternoon; all the gentlemen of the neighbourhood were in Barchester, and those who had the entry of Dr Stanhope's house were in the signora's back drawing-room. Charlotte and Mrs Stanhope were in the front room, and such of the lady's squires as could not for the moment get near the centre of attraction had to waste their fragrance on the mother and sister.

The first who came and the last to leave was Mr Arabin. This was the second visit he had paid to Madame Neroni since he had met her at Ullathorne. He came he knew not why, to talk about he knew not what. But, in truth, the feelings which now troubled him were new to him, and he could not analyse them. It may seem strange that he should thus come dangling about Madame Neroni because he was in love with Mrs Bold; but it was nevertheless the fact; and though he could not understand why he did so, Madame Neroni understood it well enough.

She had been gentle and kind to him, and had encouraged his staying. Therefore he stayed on. She pressed his hand when he first greeted her; she made him remain near her; and whispered to him little nothings. And then her eye, brilliant and bright, now mirthful, now melancholy, and invincible in either way! What man with warm feelings, blood unchilled, and a heart not guarded by a triple steel of experience could have withstood those eyes! The lady, it is true, intended to do him no mortal injury; she merely chose to inhale a slight breath of incense before she handed the casket over to another. Whether Mrs Bold would willingly have spared even so much is another question.

And then came Mr Slope. All the world now knew that Mr Slope was a candidate for the deanery, and that he was generally considered to be the favourite. Mr Slope, therefore, walked rather largely upon the earth. He gave to himself a portly air, such as might become a dean, spoke but little to other clergymen, and shunned the bishop as much as possible. How the meagre little prebendary, and the burly chancellor, and all the minor canons and vicars choral, ay, and all the choristers too, cowered and shook and walked about with long faces when they read or heard of that article in the Jupiter. Now were coming the days when nothing would avail to keep the impure spirit from the cathedral pulpit. That pulpit would indeed be his own. Precentors, vicars, and choristers might hang up their harps on the willows. Ichabod! Ichabod! the glory of their house was departing from them.

Mr Slope, great as he was with embryo grandeur, still came to see the signora. Indeed, he could not keep himself away. He dreamed of that soft hand which he had kissed so often, and of that imperial brow which his lips had once pressed, and he then dreamed also of further favours.

And Mr Thorne was there also. It was the first visit he had ever paid to the signora, and he made it not without due preparation. Mr Thorne was a gentleman usually precise in his dress, and prone to make the most of himself in an unpretending way. The gray hairs in his whiskers were eliminated perhaps once a month; those on his head were softened by a mixture which we will not call a dye; it was only a wash. His tailor lived in St James's Street, and his bootmaker at the corner of that street and Piccadilly. He was particular in the article of gloves, and the getting up of his shirts was a matter not lightly thought of in the Ullathorne laundry. On the occasion of the present visit he had rather overdone his usual efforts, and caused some little uneasiness to his sister, who had not hitherto received very cordially the proposition for a lengthened visit from the signora at Ullathorne.

There were others also there – young men about the city who had not much to do, and who were induced by the lady's charms to neglect that little; but all gave way to Mr Thorne, who was somewhat of a grand signior, as a country gentleman always is in a provincial city.

'Oh, Mr Thorne, this is so kind of you!' said the signora. 'You promised to come; but I really did not expect it. I thought you country gentlemen never kept your pledges.'

'Oh, yes, sometimes,' said Mr Thorne, looking rather sheepish, and making his salutations a little too much in the style of the last century.

'You deceive none but your consti – stit – stit; what do you call the people that carry you about in chairs and pelt you with eggs and apples when they make you a member of Parliament?'

'One another also, sometimes, signora,' said Mr Slope, with a deanish sort of smirk on his face. 'Country gentlemen do deceive one another sometimes, don't they, Mr Thorne?'

Mr Thorne gave him a look which undeaned him completely for the moment; but he soon remembered his high hopes, and recovering himself quickly, sustained his probable coming dignity by a laugh at Mr Thorne's expense.

'I never deceive a lady, at any rate,' said Mr Thorne; 'especially when the gratification of my own wishes is so strong an inducement to keep me true, as it now is.'

Mr Thorne went on thus awhile with antediluvian grimaces and compliments which he had picked up from Sir Charles Grandison, and the signora at every grimace and at every bow smiled a little smile and bowed a little bow. Mr Thorne, however, was kept standing at the foot of the couch, for the new dean sat in the seat of honour near the table. Mr Arabin the while was standing with his back to the fire, his coat tails under his arms, gazing at her with all his eyes – not quite in vain, for every now and again a glance came up at him, bright as a meteor out of heaven.

'Oh, Mr Thorne, you promised to let me introduce my little girl to you. Can you spare a moment? – will you see her now?'

Mr Thorne assured her that he could, and would see the young lady with the greatest pleasure in life. 'Mr Slope, might I trouble you to ring the bell?' said she; and when Mr Slope got up she looked at Mr Thorne and pointed to the chair. Mr Thorne, however, was much too slow to understand her, and Mr Slope would have recovered his seat had not the signora, who never chose to be unsuccessful, somewhat summarily ordered him out of it.

'Oh, Mr Slope, I must ask you to let Mr Thorne sit here just for a moment or two. I am sure you will pardon me. We can take a liberty with you this week. Next week, you know, when you move into the dean's house, we shall all be afraid of you.'

Mr Slope, with an air of much indifference, rose from his seat, and, walking into the next room, became greatly interested in Mrs Stanhope's worsted work.

And then the child was brought in. She was a little girl, about eight years of age, like her mother, only that her enormous eyes were black, and her hair quite jet. Her complexion, too, was very dark, and bespoke her foreign blood. She was dressed in the most outlandish and extravagant way in which clothes could be put on a child's back. She had great bracelets on her naked little arms, a crimson fillet braided with gold round her head, and scarlet shoes with high heels. Her dress was all flounces, and stuck out from her as though the object were to make it lie off horizontally from her little hips. It did not nearly cover her knees; but this was atoned for by a loose pair of drawers, which seemed made throughout of lace; then she had on pink silk stockings. It was thus that the last of the Neros was habitually dressed at the hour when visitors were wont to call.

'Julia, my love,' said the mother – Julia was ever a favourite name with the ladies of that family. 'Julia, my love, come here. I was telling you about the beautiful party poor mamma went to. This is Mr Thorne; will you give him a kiss, dearest?'

Julia put up her face to be kissed, as she did to all her mother's visitors; and then Mr Thorne found that he had got her, and, which was much more terrific to him, all her finery, into his arms. The lace and starch crumpled against his waistcoat and trowsers, the greasy black curls hung upon his cheek, and one of the bracelet clasps scratched his ear. He did not at all know how to hold so magnificent a lady, nor holding her what to do with her. However, he had on other occasions been compelled to fondle little nieces and nephews, and now set about the task in the mode he always had used.

'Diddle, diddle, diddle, diddle,' said he, putting the child on one knee, and working away with it as though he were turning a knife-grinder's wheel with his foot.

'Mamma, mamma,' said Julia, crossly, 'I don't want to be diddle diddled. Let me go, you naughty old man, you.'

Poor Mr Thorne put the child down quietly on the ground, and drew back his chair; Mr Slope, who had returned to the pole star that attracted him, laughed aloud; Mr Arabin winced and shut his eyes; and the signora pretended not to hear her daughter.

'Go to Aunt Charlotte, lovey,' said the mamma, 'and ask her if it is not time for you to go out.'

But little Miss Julia, though she had not exactly liked the nature of Mr Thorne's attention, was accustomed to be played with by gentlemen, and did not relish the idea of being sent so soon to her aunt.

'Julia, go when I tell you, my dear.' But Julia still went pouting about the signora. 'Charlotte, do come and take her,' said the signora. 'She must go out; and the days get so short now.' And thus ended the much-talked of interview between Mr Thorne and the last of the Neros.

Mr Thorne recovered from the child's crossness sooner than from Mr Slope's laughter. He could put up with being called an old man by an infant, but he did not like to be laughed at by the bishop's chaplain, even though that chaplain was about to become a dean. He said nothing, but he showed plainly enough that he was angry.

The signora was ready enough to avenge him. 'Mr Slope,' said she, 'I hear that you are triumphing on all sides.'

'How so?' said he, smiling. He did not dislike being talked to about the deanery, though, of course, he strongly denied the imputation.

'You carry the day both in love and war.' Mr Slope hereupon did not look quite so satisfied as he had done.

'Mr Arabin,' continued the signora, 'don't you think Mr Slope is a very lucky man?'

'Not more so than he deserves, I am sure,' said Mr Arabin.

'Only think, Mr Thorne, he is to be our new dean; of course we all know that.'

'Indeed, signora,' said Mr Slope, 'we all know nothing about it. I can assure you I myself –'

'He *is* to be the new dean – there is no manner of doubt of it, Mr Thorne.'

'Hum!' said Mr Thorne.

'Passing over the heads of old men like my father and Archdeacon Grantly –'

'Oh-oh!' said Mr Slope.

'The archdeacon would not accept it,' said Mr Arabin; whereupon Mr Slope smiled abominably, and said, as plainly as a look could speak, that the grapes were sour.

'Going over all our heads,' continued the signora; 'for, of course, I consider myself one of the chapter.'

'If I am ever dean,' said Mr Slope – 'that is, were I ever to become so, I should glory in such a canoness.'

'Oh, Mr Slope, stop; I haven't half done. There is another canoness for you to glory in. Mr Slope is not only to have the deanery, but a wife to put in it.'

Mr Slope again looked disconcerted.

'A wife with a large fortune too. It never rains but it pours, does it, Mr Thorne?'

'No, never,' said Mr Thorne, who did not quite relish talking about Mr Slope and his affairs.

'When will it be, Mr Slope?'

'When will what be?' said he.

'Oh! we know when the affair of the dean will be: a week will settle that. The new hat, I have no doubt, has been already ordered. But when will the marriage come off?'

'Do you mean mine or Mr Arabin's?' said he, striving to be facetious.

'Well, just then I meant yours, though, perhaps, after all, Mr Arabin's may be first. But we know nothing of him. He is too close for any of us. Now all is open and above board with you; which, by the bye, Mr Arabin, I beg to tell you I like much the best. He who runs can read that Mr Slope is a favoured lover. Come, Mr Slope, when is the widow to be made Mrs Dean?'

To Mr Arabin this badinage was peculiarly painful; and yet he could not tear himself away and leave it. He believed, still believed with that sort of belief which the fear of a thing engenders, that Mrs Bold would probably become the wife of Mr Slope. Of Mr Slope's little adventure in the garden he knew nothing. For aught he knew, Mr Slope might have had an adventure of quite a different character. He might have thrown himself at the widow's feet, been accepted, and then returned to town a jolly, thriving wooer. The signora's jokes were bitter enough to Mr Slope, but they were quite as bitter as Mr Arabin. He still stood leaning against the fire-place, fumbling with his hands in his trowsers pockets.

'Come, come, Mr Slope, don't be so bashful,' continued the signora. 'We all know that you proposed to the lady the other day at Ullathorne. Tell us with what words she accepted you. Was it with a simple "yes," or with two "no no's," which made an affirmative? or did silence give consent? or did she speak out with that spirit which so well becomes a widow, and say openly, "By my troth, sir, you shall make me Mrs Slope as soon as it is your pleasure to do so?" '

Mr Slope had seldom in his life felt himself less at his ease. There sat Mr Thorne, laughing silently. There stood his old antagonist, Mr Arabin, gazing at him with all his eyes. There round the door between the two rooms were clustered a little group of people, including Miss Stanhope and the Rev Messrs Gray and Green, all listening to his discomfiture. He knew that it depended solely on his own wit whether or no he could throw his joke back upon the lady. He knew that it stood him to do so if he possibly could; but he had not a word. ' 'Tis conscience that makes cowards of us all.' He felt on his cheek the sharp points of Eleanor's fingers, and did not know who might have seen the blow, who might have told the tale to this pestilent woman who took such delight in jeering him. He stood there, therefore, red as a carbuncle and mute as a fish; grinning just sufficiently to show his teeth; an object of pity.

But the signora had no pity; she knew nothing of mercy. Her present object was to put Mr Slope down, and she was determined to do it thoroughly, now that she had him in her power.

'What, Mr Slope, no answer? Why it can't possibly be that the woman has been fool enough to refuse you? She can't surely be looking out after a bishop. But I see how it is, Mr Slope. Widows are proverbially cautious, You should have let her alone till the new hat was on your head; till you could show her the key of the deanery.'

'Signora,' said he at last, trying to speak in a tone of dignified reproach, 'you really permit yourself to talk on solemn subjects in a very improper way.'

'Solemn subjects – what solemn subject? Surely a dean's hat is not such a solemn subject.'

'I have no aspirations such as those you impute to me. Perhaps you will drop the subject.'

'Oh certainly, Mr Slope; but one word first. Go to her again with the prime minister's letter in your pocket. I'll wager my shawl to your shovel she does not refuse you then.'

'I must say, signora, that I think you are speaking of the lady in a very unjustifiable manner.'

'And one other piece of advice, Mr Slope; I'll only offer you one other;' and then she commenced singing –

> 'It's gude to be merry and wise, Mr Slope;
>   Its gude to be honest and true;
> It's gude to be off with the old love – Mr Slope,
>   Before you are on with the new. –

'Ha, ha, ha!'

And the signora, throwing herself back on her sofa, laughed merrily. She little recked how those who heard her would, in their own imaginations, fill up the little history of Mr Slope's first love. She little cared that some among them might attribute to her the honour of his earlier admiration. She was tired of Mr Slope and wanted to get rid of him; she had ground for anger with him, and she chose to be revenged.

How Mr Slope got out of that room he never himself knew. He did succeed ultimately, and probably with some assistance, in getting his hat and escaping into the air. At last his love for the signora was cured.

Whenever he again thought of her in his dreams, it was not as of an angel with azure wings. He connected her rather with fire and brimstone, and though he could still believe her to be a spirit, he banished her entirely out of heaven, and found a place for her among the infernal gods. When he weighed in the balance, as he not seldom did, the two women to whom he had attached himself in Barchester, the pre-eminent place in his soul's hatred was usually allotted to the signora.

✂ FORTY-SEVEN ✂

The Dean Elect

DURING THE ENTIRE NEXT WEEK BARCHESTER WAS ignorant who was to be its new dean on Sunday morning. Mr Slope was decidedly the favourite; but he did not show himself in the cathedral, and then he sank a point or two in the betting. On Monday, he got a scolding from the bishop in the hearing of the servants, and down he went till nobody would have him at any price; but on Tuesday he received a letter, in an official cover, marked private, by which he fully recovered his place in the public favour. On Wednesday, he was said to be ill, and that did not look well; but on Thursday morning he went down to the railway station, with a very jaunty air; and when it was ascertained that he had taken a first-class ticket for London, there was no longer any room for doubt on the matter.

While matters were in this state of ferment at Barchester, there was not much mental comfort at Plumstead. Our friend the archdeacon had many grounds for inward grief. He was much displeased at the result of Dr Gwynne's diplomatic mission to the palace, and did not even scruple to say to his wife that had he gone himself, he would have managed the affair much better. His wife did not agree with him, but that did not mend the matter.

Mr Quiverful's appointment to the hospital was, however, a *fait accompli*, and Mr Harding's acquiescence in that appointment was not less so. Nothing would induce Mr Harding to make a public appeal against the bishop; and the Master of Lazarus quite approved of his not doing so.

'I don't know what has come to the Master,' said the archdeacon over and over again. 'He used to be ready enough to stand up for his order.'

'My dear archdeacon,' Mrs Grantly would say in reply, 'what is the use of always fighting? I really think the Master is right.' The Master, however, had taken steps of his own, of which neither the archdeacon nor his wife knew anything.

Then Mr Slope's successes were henbane to Dr Grantly; and Mrs Bold's improprieties were as bad. What would be all the world to Archdeacon Grantly if Mr Slope should become Dean of Barchester and marry his wife's sister! He talked of it, and talked of it till he was nearly ill. Mrs Grantly almost wished that the marriage were done and over, so that she might hear no more about it.

And there was yet another ground of misery which cut him to the quick, nearly as closely as either of the others. That paragon of a clergyman, whom he had bestowed upon St Ewold's, that college friend of whom he had boasted so loudly, that ecclesiastical knight before whose lance Mr Slope was to fall and bite the dust, that worthy bulwark of the church as it should be, that honoured representative of Oxford's best spirit, was – so at least his wife had told him half a dozen times –misconducting himself!

Nothing had been seen of Mr Arabin at Plumstead for the last week, but a good deal had, unfortunately, been heard of him. As soon as Mrs Grantly had found herself alone with the archdeacon, on the evening of the Ullathorne party, she had expressed herself very forcibly as to Mr Arabin's conduct on that occasion. He had, she declared, looked and acted and talked very unlike a decent parish clergyman. At first the archdeacon had laughed at this, and assured her that she need not trouble herself; that Mr Arabin would be found to be quite safe. But by degrees he began to find that his wife's eyes had been sharper than his own. Other people coupled the signora's name with that of Mr Arabin. The meagre little prebendary who lived in the close, told him to a nicety how often Mr Arabin had visited at Dr Stanhope's, and how long he had remained on the occasion of each visit. He had asked after Mr Arabin at the cathedral library, and an officious little vicar choral had offered to go and see whether he could be found at Dr Stanhope's. Rumour, when she has contrived to sound the first note on her trumpet, soon makes a loud peal audible enough. It was too clear that Mr Arabin had succumbed to the Italian woman, and that the archdeacon's credit would suffer fearfully if something were not done to rescue the brand from the burning. Besides, to give the archdeacon his due, he was really attached to Mr Arabin, and grieved greatly at his backsliding.

They were sitting, talking over their sorrows, in the drawing-room before dinner on the day after Mr Slope's departure for London; and on this occasion Mrs Grantly spoke out her mind freely. She had opinions of her own about parish clergymen, and now thought it right to give vent to them.

'If you would have been led by me, archdeacon, you would never have put a bachelor into St Ewold's.'

'But, my dear, you don't mean to say that all bachelor clergymen misbehave themselves.'

'I don't know that clergymen are so much better than other men,' said Mrs Grantly. 'It's all very well with a curate whom you have under your own eye, and whom you can get rid of if he persists in improprieties.'

'But Mr Arabin was a fellow, and couldn't have had a wife.'

'Then I would have found some one who could.'

'But, my dear, are fellows never to get livings?'

'Yes, to be sure they are, when they get engaged. I never would put a young man into a living unless he were married, or engaged to be married. Now here is Mr Arabin. The whole responsibility lies upon you.'

'There is not at this moment a clergyman in all Oxford more respected for morals and conduct than Arabin.'

'Oh, Oxford!' saaid the lady, with a sneer. 'What men choose to do at Oxford, nobody ever hears of. A man may do very well at Oxford who would bring disgrace on a parish; and, to tell you the truth, it seems to me that Mr Arabin is just such a man.'

The archdeacon groaned deeply, but he had no further answer to make.

'You really must speak to him, archdeacon. Only think what the Thornes will say if they hear that their parish clergyman spends his whole time philandering with this woman.'

The archdeacon groaned again. He was a courageous man, and knew well enough how to rebuke the younger clergymen of the diocese, when necessary. But there was that about Mr Arabin which made the doctor feel that it would be very difficult to rebuke him with good effect.

'You can advise him to find a wife for himself, and he will understand well enough what that means,' said Mrs Grantly.

The archdeacon had nothing for it but groaning. There was Mr Slope; he was going to be made dean; he was going to take a wife; he was about to achieve respectability and wealth; an excellent family mansion, and a family carriage; he would soon be among the comfortable *élite* of the ecclesiastical world of Barchester; whereas his own *protégé*, the true scion of the true church, by whom he had sworn, would be still but a poor vicar, and that with a very indifferent character for moral conduct! It might be all very well recommending Mr Arabin to marry, but how would Mr Arabin when married support a wife!

Things were ordering themselves thus in Plumstead drawing-room when Dr and Mrs Grantly were disturbed in their sweet discourse by the quick rattle of a carriage and pair of horses on the gravel sweep. The sound was not that of visitors, whose private carriages are generally brought up to country-house doors with demure propriety, but betokened rather the advent of some person or persons who were in a hurry to reach the house, and had no intention of immediately leaving it. Guests invited to stay a week, and who were conscious of arriving after the first dinner bell, would probably approach in such a manner. So might arrive an attorney with the news of a granduncle's death, or a son from college with all the fresh honours of a double first. No one would have had himself driven up to the door of a country house in such a manner who had the slightest doubt of his own right to force an entry.

'Who is it?' said Mrs Grantly, looking at her husband.

'Who on earth can it be?' said the archdeacon to his wife. He then quietly got up and stood with the drawing-room door open in his hand. 'Why, it's your father!'

It was indeed Mr Harding, and Mr Harding alone. He had come by himself in a post-chaise with a couple of horses from Barchester, arriving almost after dark, and evidently full of news. His visits had usually been made in the quietest manner; he had rarely presumed to come without notice, and had always been driven up in a modest old green fly, with one horse, that hardly made itself heard as it crawled up to the hall door.

'Good gracious, Warden, is it you?' said the archdeacon, forgetting in his surprise the events of the last few years. 'But come in; nothing the matter, I hope.'

'We are very glad you are come, papa,' said his daughter. 'I'll go and get your room ready at once.'

'I an't warden, archdeacon,' said Mr Harding. 'Mr Quiverful is warden.'

'Oh, I know, I know,' said the archdeacon, petulantly. 'I forgot all about it at the moment. Is anything the matter?'

'Don't go this moment, Susan,' said Mr Harding; 'I have something to tell you.'

'The dinner bell will ring in five minutes,' said she.

'Will it?' said Mr Harding. 'Then, perhaps, I had better wait.' He was big with news which he had come to tell, but which he knew could not be told without much discussion. He had hurried away to Plumstead as fast as two horses could bring him; and now, finding himself there, he was willing to accept the reprieve which dinner would give him.

'If you have anything of moment to tell us,' said the archdeacon, 'pray let us hear it at once. Has Eleanor gone off?'

'No, she has not,' said Mr Harding, with a look of great displeasure.

'Has Slope been made dean?'

'No, he has not; but –'

'But what?' said the archdeacon, who was becoming very impatient.

'They have –'

'They have what?' said the archdeacon.

'They have offered it to me,' said Mr Harding, with a modesty which almost prevented his speaking.

'Good heavens!' said the archdeacon, and sank back exhausted in an easy-chair.

'My dear, dear father,' said Mrs Grantly, and threw her arms round her father's neck.

'So I thought I had better come out and consult with you at once,' said Mr Harding.

'Consult!' shouted the archdeacon. 'But, my dear Harding, I congratulate you with my whole heart – with my whole heart; I do indeed. I never heard anything in my life that gave me so much pleasure;' and he got hold of both his father-in-law's hands, and shook them as though he were going to shake them off, and walked round and round the room, twirling a copy of the Jupiter over his head, to show his extreme exultation.

'But –' began Mr Harding.

'But me no buts,' said the archdeacon. 'I never was so happy in my life. It was just the proper thing to do. Upon my honour, I'll never say another word against Lord—the longest day I have to live.'

'That's Dr Gwynne's doing, you may be sure,' said Mrs Grantly, who greatly liked the Master of Lazarus, he being an orderly married man with a large family.

'I suppose it is,' said the archdeacon.

'Oh, papa, I am so truly delighted!' said Mrs Grantly, getting up and kissing her father.

'But, my dear,' said Mr Harding. – It was all in vain that he strove to speak; nobody would listen to him.

'Well, Mr Dean,' said the archdeacon, triumphing; 'the deanery gardens will be some consolation for the hospital elms. Well, poor Quiverful! I won't begrudge him his good fortune any longer.'

'No, indeed,' said Mrs Grantly. 'Poor woman, she has fourteen children. I am sure I am very glad they have got it.'

'So am I,' said Mr Harding.

'I would give twenty pounds,' said the archdeacon, 'to see how Mr Slope will look when he hears it.' The idea of Mr Slope's discomfiture formed no small part of the archdeacon's pleasure.

At last Mr Harding was allowed to go up-stairs and wash his hands, having, in fact, said very little of all that he had come out to Plumstead on purpose to say. Nor could anything more be said till the servants were gone after dinner. The joy of Dr Grantly was so uncontrollable that he could not refrain from calling his father-in-law Mr Dean before the men; and therefore it was soon matter of discussion in the lower regions how Mr Harding, instead of his daughter's future husband, was to be the new dean, and various were the opinions on the matter. The cook and butler, who were advanced in years, thought that it was just as it should be; but the footman and lady's maid, who were younger, thought it was a great shame that Mr Slope should lose his chance.

'He's a mean chap all the same,' said the footman; 'and it an't along of him that I says so. But I always did admire the missus's sister; and she'd well become the situation.'

While these were the ideas down-stairs, a very great difference of opinion existed above. As soon as the cloth was drawn and the wine on the table, Mr Harding made for himself an opportunity of speaking. It was, however, with much inward troubling that he said:–

'It's very kind of Lord—very kind, and I feel it deeply, most deeply. I am, I must confess, gratified by the offer –'

'I should think so,' said the archdeacon.

'But, all the same, I am afraid that I can't accept it.'

The decanter almost fell from the archdeacon's hand upon the table; and the start he made was so great as to make his wife jump up from her chair. Not accept the deanship! If it really ended in this, there would be no longer any doubt that his father-in-law was demented. The question now was whether a clergyman with low rank, and preferment amounting to less than 200*l.* a year, should accept high rank, 1200*l.* a year, and one of the most desirable positions which his profession had to afford!

'What!' said the archdeacon, gasping for breath, and staring at his guest as though the violence of his emotion had almost thrown him into a fit. 'What!'

'I do not find myself fit for new duties,' urged Mr Harding.

'New duties! what duties?' said the archdeacon, with unintended sarcasm.

'Oh, papa,' said Mrs Grantly, 'nothing can be easier than what a dean has to do. Surely you are more active than Dr Trefoil.'

'He won't have half as much to do as he has at present,' said Dr Grantly. 'Did you see what the Jupiter said the other day about young men?'

'Yes; and I saw that the Jupiter said all that it could to induce the appointment of Mr Slope. Perhaps you would wish to see Mr Slope made dean.'

Mr Harding made no reply to this rebuke, though he felt it strongly. He had not come over to Plumstead to have further contention with his son-in-law about Mr Slope, so he allowed it to pass by.

'I know I cannot make you understand my feeling,' he said, 'for we have been cast in different moulds. I may wish that I had your spirit and energy and power of combating; but I have not. Every day that is added to my life increases my wish for peace and rest.'

'And where on earth can a man have peace and rest if not in a deanery?' said the archdeacon.

'People will say that I am too old for it.'

'Good heavens! people! what people? What need you care for any people?'

'But I think myself I am too old for any new place.'

'Dear papa,' said Mrs Grantly, 'men ten years older than you are appointed to new situations day after day.'

'My dear,' said he, 'it is impossible that I should make you understand my feelings, nor do I pretend to any great virtue in the matter. The truth is, I want the force of character which might enable me to stand against the spirit of the times. The call on all sides now is for young men, and I have not the nerve to put myself in opposition to the demand. Were the Jupiter, when it hears of my appointment, to write article after article, setting forth my incompetency, I am sure it would cost me my reason. I ought to be able to bear with such things, you will say. Well, my dear, I own that I ought. But I feel my weakness, and I know that I can't. And, to tell you the truth, I know no more than a child what the dean has to do.'

'Pshaw!' exclaimed the archdeacon.

'Don't be angry with me, archdeacon: don't let us quarrel about it, Susan. If you knew how keenly I feel the necessity of having to disoblige you in this matter, you would not be angry with me.'

This was a dreadful blow to Dr Grantly. Nothing could possibly have suited him better than having Mr Harding in the deanery. Though he had never looked down on Mr Harding on account of his recent poverty, he did fully recognise the satisfaction of having those belonging to him in comfortable positions. It would be much more suitable that Mr Harding should be dean of Barchester than vicar of St Cuthbert's and precentor to boot. And then the great discomfiture of that arch enemy of all that was respectable in Barchester, of that new low-church clerical *parvenu* that had fallen amongst them, that alone would be worth more, almost, than the situation itself. It was frightful to think that such unhoped-for good fortune should be marred by the absurd crotchets and unwholesome hallucinations by which Mr Harding allowed himself to be led astray. To have the cup so near his lips and then to lose the drinking of it, was more than Dr Grantly could endure.

And yet it appeared as though he would have to endure it. In vain he threatened and in vain he coaxed. Mr Harding did not indeed speak with perfect decision of refusing the proffered glory, but he would not speak with anything like decision of accepting it. When pressed again and again, he would again and again allege that he was wholly unfitted to new duties. It was in vain that the archdeacon tried to insinuate, though he could not plainly declare, that there were no new duties to perform. It was in vain he hinted that in all cases of difficulty he, the archdeacon, was willing and able to guide a weak-minded dean. Mr Harding seemed to have a foolish idea, not only that there were new duties to do, but that no one should accept the place who was not himself prepared to do them.

The conference ended in an understanding that Mr Harding should at once acknowledge the letter he had received from the minister's private secretary, and should beg that he might be allowed two days to make up his mind; and that during those two days the matter should be considered.

On the following morning the archdeacon was to drive Mr Harding back to Barchester.

FORTY-EIGHT

Miss Thorne shows her Talent at Match-making

ON MR HARDING'S RETURN TO BARCHESTER FROM Plumstead, which was affected by him in due course in company with the archdeacon, more tidings of a surprising nature met him. He was, during the journey, subjected to such a weight of unanswerable argument, all of which went to prove that it was his bounden duty not to interfere with the paternal government that was so anxious to make him a dean, that when he arrived at the chemist's door in High Street, he hardly knew which way to turn himself in the matter. But, perplexed as he was, he was doomed to further perplexity. He found a note there from his daughter begging him most urgently to come to her immediately. But we must again go back a little in our story.

Miss Thorne had not been slow to hear the rumours respecting Mr Arabin, which had so much disturbed the happiness of Mrs Grantly. And she, also, was unhappy to think that her parish clergyman should be accused of worshipping a strange goddess. She, also, was of opinion, that rectors and vicars should all be married, and with that good-natured energy which was characteristic of her, she put her wits to work to find a fitting match for Mr Arabin. Mrs Grantly, in this difficulty, could think of no better remedy than a lecture from the archdeacon. Miss Thorne thought that a young lady, marriageable, and with a dowry, might be of more efficacy. In looking through the catalogue of her unmarried friends, who might possibly be in want of a husband, and might also be fit for such promotion as a country parsonage affords, she could think of no one more eligible than Mrs Bold; and, consequently, losing no time, she went into Barchester on the day of Mr Slope's discomfiture, the same day that her brother had had his interesting interview with the last of the Neros, and invited Mrs Bold to bring her nurse and baby to Ullathorne and make them a protracted visit.

Miss Thorne suggested a month or two, intending to use her influence afterwards in prolonging it so as to last out the winter, in order that Mr Arabin might have an opportunity of becoming fairly intimate with his intended bride. 'We'll have Mr Arabin too,' said Miss Thorne to herself; 'and before the spring they'll know each other; and in twelve or eighteen months' time, if all goes well, Mrs Bold will be domiciled at St Ewold's;' and then the kind-hearted lady gave herself some not undeserved praise for her match-making genius.

Eleanor was taken a little by surprise, but the matter ended in her promising to go to Ullathorne for at any rate a week or two; and on the day previous to that on which her father drove out to Plumstead, she had had herself driven out to Ullathorne.

Miss Thorne would not perplex her with her embryo lord on that same evening, thinking that she would allow her a few hours to make herself at home; but on the following morning Mr Arabin arrived. 'And now,' said Miss Thorne to herself, 'I must contrive to throw them in each other's way.' That same day, after dinner, Eleanor, with an assumed air of dignity which she could not maintain, with tears that she could not suppress, with a flutter which she could not conquer, and a joy which she could not hide, told Miss Thorne that she was engaged to marry Mr Arabin, and that it behoved her to get back home to Barchester as quick as she could.

To say simply that Miss Thorne was rejoiced at the success of the scheme, would give a very faint idea of her feelings on the occasion. My readers may probably have dreamt before now that they have had before them some terribly long walk to accomplish, some journey of twenty or thirty miles, an amount of labour frightful to anticipate, and that immediately on starting they have ingeniously found some accommodating short cut which has brought them without fatigue to their work's end in five minutes. Miss Thorne's waking feelings were somewhat of the same ntaure. My readers may perhaps have had to do with children, and may on some occasion have promised to their young charges some great gratification intended to come off, perhaps at the end of the winter, or at the beginning of summer. The impatient juveniles, however, will not wait, and clamorously demand their treat before they go to bed. Miss Thorne had a sort of feeling that her children were equally unreasonable. She was like an inexperienced gunner, who has ill calculated the length of the train that he has laid. The gunpowder exploded much too soon, and poor Miss Thorne felt that she was blown up by the strength of her own petard.

Miss Thorne had had lovers of her own, but they had been gentlemen of old-fashioned and deliberate habits. Miss Thorne's heart also had not always been hard, though she was still a virgin spinster; but it had never yielded in this way at the first assault. She had intended to bring together a middle-aged studious clergyman, and a discreet matron who might possibly be induced to marry again; and in doing so she had thrown fire among tinder. Well, it was all as it should be, but she did feel perhaps a little put out by the precipitancy of her own success; and perhaps a little vexed at the readiness of Mrs Bold to be wooed.

She said, however, nothing about it to any one, and ascribed it all to the altered manners of the new age. Their mothers and grandmothers were perhaps a little more deliberate; but it was admitted on all sides that things were conducted very differently now than in former times. For aught Miss Thorne knew of the matter, a couple of hours might be quite sufficient under the new régime to complete that for which she in her ignorance had allotted twelve months.

But we must not pass over the wooing so cavalierly. It has been told, with perhaps tedious accuracy, how Eleanor disposed of two of her lovers at

Ullathorne; and it must also be told with equal accuracy, and if possible with less tedium, how she encountered Mr Arabin.

It cannot be denied that when Eleanor accepted Miss Thorne's invitation, she remembered that Ullathorne was in the parish of St Ewold's. Since her interview with the signora she had done little else than think about Mr Arabin, and the appeal that had been made to her. She could not bring herself to believe or try to bring herself to believe, that what she had been told was untrue. Think of how she would, she could not but accept it as a fact that Mr Arabin was fond of her; and then when she went further, she asked herself the question, she could not but accept it as a fact also that she was fond of him. If it were destined for her to be the partner of his hopes and sorrows, to whom could she look for friendship so properly as to Miss Thorne? This invitation was like an ordained step towards the fulfilment of her destiny, and when she also heard that Mr Arabin was expected to be at Ullathorne on the following day, it seemed as though all the world were conspiring in her favour. Well, did she not deserve it? In that affair of Mr Slope, had not all the world conspired against her?

She could not, however, make herself easy and at home. When in the evening after dinner Miss Thorne expatiated on the excellence of Mr Arabin's qualities, and hinted that any little rumour which might be ill-naturedly spread abroad concerning him really meant nothing, Mrs Bold found herself unable to answer. When Miss Thorne went a little further and declared that she did not know a prettier vicarage-house in the county than St Ewold's, Mrs Bold remembering the projected bow-window and the projected priestess still held her tongue; though her ears tingled with the conviction that all the world knew that she was in love with Mr Arabin. Well; what would that matter if they could only meet and tell each other what each now longed to tell?

And they did meet. Mr Arabin came early in the day, and found the two ladies together at work in the drawing-room. Miss Thorne, who had she known all the truth would have vanished into air at once, had no conception that her immediate absence would be a blessing, and remained chatting with them till luncheon-time. Mr Arabin could talk about nothing but the Signora Neroni's beauty, would discuss no people but the Stanhopes. This was very distressing to Eleanor, and not very satisfactory to Miss Thorne. But yet there was evidence of innocence in his open avowal of admiration.

And then they had lunch, and then Mr Arabin went out on parish duty, and Eleanor and Miss Thorne were left to take a walk together.

'Do you think the Signora Neroni is so lovely as people say?' Eleanor asked as they were coming home.

'She is very beautiful certainly, very beautiful,' Miss Thorne answered; 'but I do not know that any one considers her lovely. She is a woman all men would like to look at; but few I imagine would be glad to take her to their hearths, even were she unmarried and not afflicted as she is.'

There was some little comfort in this. Eleanor made the most of it till she got back to the house. She was then left alone in the drawing-room, and just as it was getting dark Mr Arabin came in.

It was a beautiful afternoon in the beginning of October, and Eleanor was sitting in the window to get the advantage of the last daylight for her novel. There was a fire in the comfortable room, but the weather was not cold enough to make it attractive; and as she could see the sun set from where she sat, she was not very attentive to her book.

Mr Arabin when he entered stood awhile with his back to the fire in his usual way, merely uttering a few common-place remarks about the beauty of the weather, while he plucked up courage for more interesting converse. It cannot probably be said that he had resolved then and there to make an offer to Eleanor. Men we believe seldom make such resolves. Mr Slope and Mr Stanhope had done so, it is true; but gentlemen generally propose without any absolutely defined determination as to their doing so. Such was now the case with Mr Arabin.

'It is a lovely sunset,' said Eleanor, answering him on the dreadfully trite subject which he had chosen.

Mr Arabin could not see the sunset from the hearth-rug, so he had to go close to her.

'Very lovely,' said he, standing modestly so far away from her as to avoid touching the flounces of her dress. Then it appeared that he had nothing further to say; so after gazing for a moment in silence at the brightness of the setting sun, he returned to the fire.

Eleanor found that it was quite impossible for herself to commence a conversation. In the first place she could find nothing to say; words, which were generally plenty enough with her, would not come to her relief. And, moreover, do what she would, she could hardly prevent herself from crying.

'Do you like Ullathorne?' said Mr Arabin, speaking from the safely distant position which he had assumed on the heath-rug.

'Yes, indeed, very much!'

'I don't mean Mr and Mrs Thorne. I know you like them; but the style of the house. There is something about old-fashioned mansions, built as this is, and old-fashioned gardens, that to me is especially delightful.'

'I like everything old-fashioned,' said Eleanor; 'old-fashioned things are so much the honestest.'

'I don't know about that,' said Mr Arabin, gently laughing. 'That is an opinion on which very much may be said on either side. It is strange how widely the world is divided on a subject which so nearly concerns us all, and which is so close beneath our eyes. Some think that we are quickly progressing towards perfection, while others imagine that virtue is disappearing from the earth.'

'And you, Mr Arabin, what do you think?' said Eleanor. She felt somewhat surprised at the tone which his conversation was taking, and yet she was relieved at his saying something which enabled herself to speak without showing her own emotion.

'What do I think, Mrs Bold?' and then he rumbled his money with his hands in his trowsers pockets, and looked and spoke very little like a thriving lover. 'It is the bane of my life that on important subjects I acquire no fixed opinion. I think, and think, and go on thinking; and yet my thoughts were running ever in different directions. I hardly know whether or no we do lean more confidently than our fathers did on those high hopes to which we profess to aspire.'

'I think the world grows more worldly every day,' said Eleanor.

'That is because you see more of it than when you were younger. But we should hardly judge by what we see – we see so very little.' There was then a pause for a while, during which Mr Arabin continued to turn over his shillings and half-crowns. 'If we believe in Scripture, we can hardly think that mankind in general will now be allowed to retrograde.'

Eleanor, whose mind was certainly engaged otherwise than on the general state of mankind, made no answer to this. She felt thoroughly dissatisfied with herself. She could not force her thoughts away from the topic on which the signora had spoken to her in so strange a way, and yet she knew that she could not converse with Mr Arabin in an unrestrained natural tone till she did so. She was most anxious not to show to him any special emotion, and yet she felt that if he looked at her he would at once see that she was not at ease.

But he did not look at her. Instead of doing so, he left the fire-place and began walking up and down the room. Eleanor took up her book resolutely; but she could not read, for there was a tear in her eye, and do what she would it fell on her cheek. When Mr Arabin's back was turned to her she wiped it away; but another was soon coursing down her face in its place. They would come; not a deluge of tears that would have betrayed her at once, but one by one, single monitors. Mr Arabin did not observe her closely, and they passed unseen.

Mr Arabin, thus pacing up and down the room, took four or five turns before he spoke another word, and Eleanor sat equally silent with her face bent over her book. She was afraid that her tears would get the better of her, and was preparing for an escape from the room, when Mr Arabin in his walk stood opposite to her. He did not come close up, but stood exactly on the spot to which his course brought him, and then, with his hands under his coat tails, thus made his confession.

'Mrs Bold,' said he, 'I owe you retribution for a great offence of which I have been guilty towards you.' Eleanor's heart beat so that she could not trust herself to say that he had never been guilty of any offence. So Mr Arabin thus went on.

'I have thought much of it since, and I am now aware that I was wholly unwarranted in putting to you a question which I once asked you. It was indelicate on my part, and perhaps unmanly. No intimacy which may exist between myself and your connection, Dr Grantly, could justify it. Nor could the acquaintance which existed between ourselves.' This word acquaintance struck cold on Eleanor's heart. Was this to be her doom after all? 'I therefore think it right to beg your pardon in a humble spirit, and I now do so.'

What was Eleanor to say to him? She could not say much, because she was crying, and yet she must say something. She was most anxious to say that something graciously, kindly, and yet not in such a manner as to betray herself. She had never felt herself so much at a loss for words.

'Indeed I took no offence, Mr Arabin.'

'Oh, but you did! And had you not done so, you would not have been yourself. You were as right to be offended, as I was wrong so to offend you. I have not forgiven myself, but I hope to hear that you forgive me.'

She was now past speaking calmly, though she still continued to hide her tears, and Mr Arabin, after pausing a moment in vain for her reply, was walking off towards the door. She felt that she could not allow him to go unanswered without grievously sinning against all charity; so, rising from her seat, she gently touched his arm and said: 'Oh, Mr Arabin, do not go till I speak to you! I do forgive you. You know that I forgive you.'

He took the hand that had so gently touched his arm, and then gazed into her face as if he would peruse there, as though written in a book, the whole future destiny of his life; and as he did so, there was a sobre sad seriousness in his own countenance, which Eleanor found herself unable to sustain. She could only look down upon the carpet, let her tears trickle as they would, and leave her hand within his.

It was but for a minute that they stood so, but the duration of that minute was sufficient to make it ever memorable to them both. Eleanor was sure now that she was loved. No words, be their eloquence what it might, could be more impressive than that eager, melancholy gaze.

Why did he look so into her eyes? Why did he not speak to her? Could it be that he looked for her to make the first sign?

And he, though he knew but little of women, even he knew that he was loved. He had only to ask and it would be all his own, that inexpressible loveliness, those ever speaking but yet now mute eyes, that feminine brightness and eager loving spirit which had so attracted him since first he had encountered it at St Ewold's. It might, must all be his own now. On no other supposition was it possible that she should allow her hand to remain thus clasped within his own. He had only to ask. Ah! but that was the difficulty. Did a minute suffice for all this? Nay, perhaps it might be more than a minute.

'Mrs Bold –' at last he said, and then stopped himself.

If he could not speak, how was she to do so? He had called her by her name, the same name that any merest stranger would have used! She withdrew her hand from his, and moved as though to return to her seat. 'Eleanor!' he then said, in his softest tone, as though the courage of a lover were as yet but half assumed, as though he were still afraid of giving offence by the freedom which he took. She looked slowly, gently, almost piteously up into his face. There was at any rate no anger there to deter him.

'Eleanor!' he again exclaimed; and in a moment he had her clasped to his bosom. How this was done, whether the doing was with him or her, whether she had flown thither conquered by the tenderness of his voice, or he with a violence not likely to give offence had drawn her to his breast, neither of them knew; nor can I declare. There was now that sympathy between them which hardly admitted of individual motion. They were one and the same – one flesh – one spirit – one life.

'Eleanor, my own Eleanor, my own, my wife!' She ventured to look up at him through her tears, and he, bowing his face down over hers, pressed his lips upon her brow; his virgin lips, which since a beard first grew upon his chin, had never yet tasted the luxury of a woman's cheek.

She had been told that her yea must be yea, or her nay, nay; but she was called on for neither the one nor the other. She told Miss Thorne that she was engaged to Mr Arabin, but no such words had passed between them, no promises had been asked or given.

'Oh, let me go,' said she; 'let me go now. I am too happy to remain – let me go, that I may be alone.' He did not try to hinder her; he did not repeat the kiss; he did not press another on her lips. He might have done so had he been so minded. She was now all his own. He took his arm from round her waist, his arm that was trembling with a new delight, and let her go. She fled like a roe to her own chamber, and then, having turned the bolt, she enjoyed the full luxury of her love. She idolised, almost worshipped this man who had so meekly begged her pardon. And he was now her own. Oh, how she wept and cried and laughed, as the hopes and fears and miseries of the last few weeks passed in remembrance through her mind.

Mr Slope! That any one should have dared to think that she who had been chosen by him could possibly have mated herself with Mr Slope! That they should have dared to tell him, also, and subject her bright happiness to such needless risk! And then she smiled with joy as she thought of all the comforts that she could give him; not that he cared for comforts, but that it would be so delicious for her to give.

She got up and rang for her maid that she might tell her little boy of his new father; and in her own way she did tell him. She desired her maid to leave her, in order that she might be alone with her child; and then, while he lay sprawling on the bed, she poured forth the praises, all unmeaning to him, of the man she had selected to guard his infancy.

She could not be happy, however, till she had made Mr Arabin take the child to himself, and thus, as it were, adopt him as his own. The moment the idea struck her she took the baby up in her arms, and, opening her door, ran quickly down to the drawing-room. She at once found, by his step still pacing on the floor, that he was there; and a glance within the room told her that he was alone. She hesitated a moment, and then hurried in with her precious charge.

Mr Arabin met her in the middle of the room. 'There,' said she, breathless with her haste; 'there, take him – take him and love him.'

Mr Arabin took the little fellow from her, and kissing him again and again, prayed God to bless him. 'He shall be all as my own – all as my own,' said he. Eleanor, as she stooped to take back her child, kissed the hand that held him, and then rushed back with her treasure to her chamber.

It was thus that Mr Harding's younger daughter was won for the second time. At dinner neither she nor Mr Arabin were very bright, but their silence occasioned no remark. In the drawing-room, as we have before said, she told Miss Thorne what had occurred. The next morning she returned to Barchester, and Mr Arabin went over with his budget of news to the archdeacon. As Doctor Grantly was not there, he could only satisfy himself by telling Mrs Grantly how that he intended himself the honour of becoming her brother-in-law. In the ecstasy of her joy at hearing such tidings, Mrs Grantly vouchsafed him a warmer welcome than any he had yet received from Eleanor.

'Good heavens!' she exclaimed – it was the general exclamation of the rectory. 'Poor Eleanor! Dear Eleanor! What a monstrous injustice has been done her! – Well, it shall all be made up now.' And then she thought of the signora. 'What lies people tell,' she said to herself.

But people in this matter had told no lies at all.

※ FORTY-NINE ※

The Belzebub Colt

WHEN MISS THORNE LEFT THE DINING-ROOM, Eleanor had formed no intention of revealing to her what had occurred; but when she was seated beside her hostess on the sofa the secret dropped from her almost unawares. Eleanor was but a bad hypocrite, and she found herself quite unable to continue talking about Mr Arabin as though he were a stranger, while her heart was full of him. When Miss Thorne, pursuing her own scheme with discreet zeal, asked the young widow whether, in her opinion, it would not be a good thing for Mr Arabin to get married, she had nothing for it but to confess the truth. 'I suppose it would,' said Eleanor, rather sheepishly. Whereupon Miss Thorne amplified on the idea. 'Oh, Miss Thorne,' said Eleanor, 'he is going to be married: I am engaged to him.'

Now Miss Thorne knew very well that there had been no such

engagement when she had been walking with Mrs Bold in the morning. She had also heard enough to be tolerably sure that there had been no preliminaries to such an engagement. She was, therefore, as we have before described, taken a little by surprise. But, nevertheless, she embraced her guest, and cordially congratulated her.

Eleanor had no opportunity of speaking another word to Mr Arabin that evening, except such words as all the world might hear; and these, as may be supposed, were few enough. Miss Thorne did her best to leave them in privacy; but Mr Thorne, who knew nothing of what had occurred, and another guest, a friend of his, entirely interfered with her good intentions. So poor Eleanor had to go to bed without one sign of affection. Her state, nevertheless, was not to be pitied.

The next morning she was up early. It was probable, she thought, that by going down a little before the usual hour of breakfast, she might find Mr Arabin alone in the dining-room. Might it not be that he also would calculate that an interview would thus be possible? Thus thinking, Eleanor was dressed a full hour before the time fixed in the Ullathorne household for morning prayers. She did not at once go down. She was afraid to seem to be too anxious to meet her lover; though, heaven knows, her anxiety was intense enough. She therefore sat herself down at her window, and repeatedly looking at her watch, nursed her child till she thought she might venture forth.

When she found herself at the dining-room door, she stood a moment, hesitating to turn the handle; but when she heard Mr Thorne's voice inside she hesitated no longer. Her object was defeated, and she might now go in as soon as she liked without the slightest imputation on her delicacy. Mr Thorne and Mr Arabin were standing on the hearth-rug, discussing the merits of the Belzebub colt; or rather, Mr Thorne was discussing, and Mr Arabin was listening. That interesting animal had rubbed the stump of his tail against the wall of his stable, and occasioned much uneasiness to the Ullathorne master of the horse. Had Eleanor but waited another minute, Mr Thorne would have been in the stables.

Mr Thorne, when he saw his lady guest, repressed his anxiety. The Belzebub colt must do without him. And so the three stood, saying little or nothing to each other, till at last the master of the house, finding that he could no longer bear his present state of suspense respecting his favourite young steed, made an elaborate apology to Mrs Bold, and escaped. As he shut the door behind him, Eleanor almost wished that he had remained. It was not that she was afraid of Mr Arabin, but she hardly yet knew how to address him.

He, however, soon relieved her from her embarrassment. He came up to her, and taking both her hands in his, he said: 'So, Eleanor, you and I are to be man and wife. Is it so?'

She looked up into his face, and her lips formed themselves into a single syllable. She uttered no sound, but he could read the affirmative plainly in her face.

'It is a great trust,' said he; 'a very great trust.'

'It is – it is,' said Eleanor, not exactly taking what he had said in the sense that he had meant. 'It is a very, very great trust, and I will do my utmost to deserve it.'

'And I also will do my utmost to deserve it,' said Mr Arabin, very solemnly. And then, winding his arm around her waist, he stood there gazing at the fire, and she with her head leaning on his shoulder, stood by him, well satisfied with her position. They neither of them spoke, or found any want of speaking. All that was needful for them to say had been said. The yea, yea, had been spoken by Eleanor in her own way – and that way had been perfectly satisfactory to Mr Arabin.

And now it remained to them each to enjoy the assurance of the other's love. And how great that luxury is! How far it surpasses any other pleasure which God has allowed to his creatures! And to a woman's heart how doubly delightful!

When the ivy has found its tower, when the delicate creeper has found its strong wall, we know how the parasite plants grow and prosper. They were not created to stretch forth their branches alone, and endure without protection the summer's sun and the winter's storm. Alone they but spread themselves on the ground, and cower unseen in the dingy shade. But when they have found their firm supporters, how wonderful is their beauty; how all pervading and victorious! What is the turret without its ivy, or the high garden-wall without the jasmine which gives it its beauty and fragrance? The hedge without the honeysuckle is but a hedge.

There is a feeling still half existing, but now half conquered by the force of human nature, that a woman should be ashamed of her love till the husband's right to her compels her to acknowledge it. We would fain preach a different doctrine. A woman should glory in her love; but on that account let her take the more care that it be such as to justify her glory.

Eleanor did glory in hers, and she felt, and had cause to feel, that it deserved to be held as glorious. She could have stood there for hours with his arm round her, had fate and Mr Thorne permitted it. Each moment she crept nearer to his bosom, and felt more and more certain that there was her home. What now to her was the archdeacon's arrogance, her sister's coldness, or her dear father's weakness? What need she care for the duplicity of such friends as Charlotte Stanhope? She had found the strong shield that should guard her from all wrongs, the trusty pilot that should henceforward guide her through the shoals and rocks. She would give up the heavy burden of her independence, and once more assume the position of a woman, and the duties of a trusting and loving wife.

And he, too, stood there fully satisfied with his place. They were both looking intently on the fire, as though they could read there their future fate, till at last Eleanor turned her face towards his. 'How sad you are,' she said, smiling; and indeed his face was, if not sad, at least serious. 'How sad you are, love!'

'Sad,' said he, looking down at her; 'no, certainly not sad.' Her sweet loving eyes were turned towards him, and she smiled softly as he answered her. The temptation was too strong even for the demure propriety of Mr Arabin, and, bending over her, he pressed his lips to hers.

Immediately after this, Mr Thorne appeared, and they were both delighted to hear that the tail of the Belzebub colt was not materially injured.

It had been Mr Harding's intention to hurry over to Ullathorne as soon as possible after his return to Barchester, in order to secure the support of his daughter in his meditated revolt against the archdeacon as touching the deanery; but he was spared the additional journey by hearing that Mrs Bold had returned unexpectedly home. As soon as he had read her note he started off, and found her waiting for him in her own house.

How much each of them had to tell the other, and how certain each of them was that the story which he or she had to tell would astonish the other!

'My dear, I am so anxious to see you,' said Mr Harding, kissing his daughter.

'Oh, papa, I have so much to tell you!' said the daughter, returning the embrace.

'My dear, they have offered me the deanery!' said Mr Harding, anticipating by the suddenness of the revelation the tidings which Eleanor had to give him.

'Oh, papa,' said she, forgetting her own love and happiness in her joy at the surprising news; 'Oh, papa, can it be possible? Dear papa, how thoroughly, thoroughly happy that makes me!'

'But, my dear, I think it best to refuse it.'

'Oh, papa!'

'I am sure you will agree with me, Eleanor, when I explain it to you. You know, my dear, how old I am. If I live, I –'

'But, papa, I must tell you about myself.'

'Well, my dear.'

'I do so wonder how you'll take it.'

'Take what?'

'If you don't rejoice at it, if it doesn't make you happy, if you don't encourage me, I shall break my heart.'

'If that be the case, Nelly, I certainly will encourage you.'

'But I fear you won't. I do so fear you won't. And yet you can't but think I am the most fortunate woman living on God's earth.'

'Are you, dearest? Then I certainly will rejoice with you. Come, Nelly, come to me, and tell me what it is.'

'I am going –'

He led her to the sofa, and seating himself beside her, took both her hands in his. 'You are going to be married, Nelly. Is not that it?'

'Yes,' she said, faintly. 'That is if you will approve;' and then she blushed as she remembered the promise which she had so lately volunteered to him, and which she had so utterly forgotten in making her engagement with Mr Arabin.

Mr Harding thought for a moment who the man could be whom he was to be called upon to welcome as his son-in-law. A week since he would have had no doubt whom to name. In that case he would have been prepared to give his sanction, although he would have done so with a heavy heart. Now he knew that at any rate it would not be Mr Slope, though he was perfectly at a loss to guess who could possibly have filled the place. For a moment he thought that the man might be Bertie Stanhope, and his very soul sank within him.

'Well, Nelly?'

'Oh, papa, promise to me that, for my sake, you will love him.'

'Come, Nelly, come; tell me who it is.'

'But will you love him, papa?'

'Dearest, I must love any one that you love.' Then she turned her face to his, and whispered into his ear the name of Mr Arabin.

No man that she could have named could have more surprised or more delighted him. Had he looked round the world for a son-in-law to his taste, he could have selected no one whom he would have preferred to Mr Arabin. He was a clergyman; he held a living in the neighbourhood; he was of a set to which all Mr Harding's own partialities most closely adhered; he was the great friend of Dr Grantly; and he was, moreover, a man of whom Mr Harding knew nothing but what he approved. Nevertheless, his surprise was so great as to prevent the immediate expression of his joy. He had never thought of Mr Arabin in connection with his daughter; he had never imagined that they had any feeling in common. He had feared that his daughter had been made hostile to clergymen of Mr Arabin's stamp by her intolerance of the archdeacon's pretensions. Had he been put to wish, he might have wished for Mr Arabin for a son-in-law; but had he been put to guess, the name would never have occurred to him.

'Mr Arabin!' he exclaimed; 'impossible!'

'Oh, papa, for heaven's sake don't say anything against him! If you love me, don't say anything against him. Oh, papa, it's done, and mustn't be undone – oh, papa!'

Fickle Eleanor! where was the promise that she would make no choice for herself without her father's approval? She had chosen, and now demanded his acquiescence. 'Oh, papa, isn't he good? isn't he noble? isn't he religious, highminded, everything that a good man possibly can be?' and she clung to her father, beseeching him for his consent.

'My Nelly, my child, my own daughter! He is; he is noble and good and highminded; he is all that a woman can love and a man admire. He shall be my son, my own son. He shall be as close to my heart as you are. My Nelly, my child, my happy, happy child!'

We need not pursue the interview any further. By degrees they returned to the subject of the new promotion. Eleanor tried to prove to him, as the Grantlys had done, that his age could be no bar to his being a very excellent dean; but those arguments had now even less weight on him than before. He said little or nothing, but sat meditative. Every now and then he would kiss his daughter, and say 'yes,' or 'no,' or 'very true,' or 'well, my dear, I can't quite agree with you there,' but he could not be got to enter sharply into the question of 'to be, or not to be' dean of Barchester. Of her and her happiness, of Mr Arabin and his virtues, he would talk as much as Eleanor desired; and, to tell the truth, that was not a little; but about the deanery he would now say nothing further. He had got a new idea into his head – Why should not Mr Arabin be the new dean?

✂ FIFTY ✂

The Archdeacon is Satisfied with the State of Affairs

THE ARCHDEACON, IN HIS JOURNEY INTO BARCHESTER, had been assured by Mr Harding that all their prognostications about Mr Slope and Eleanor were groundless. Mr Harding, however, had found it very difficult to shake his son-in-law's faith in his own acuteness. The matter had, to Dr Grantly, been so plainly corroborated by such patent evidence, borne out by such endless circumstances, that he at first refused to take as true the positive statement which Mr Harding made to him of Eleanor's own disavowal of the impeachment. But at last he yielded in a qualified way. He brought himself to admit that he would at the present regard his past convictions as a mistake; but in doing this he so guarded himself, that if, at any future time, Eleanor should come forth to the world as Mrs Slope, he might still be able to say: 'There, I told you so. Remember what you said and what I said; and remember also for coming years, that I was right in this matter – as in all others.'

He carried, however, his concession so far as to bring himself to undertake to call at Eleanor's house, and he did call accordingly, while the father and daughter were yet in the middle of their conference. Mr Harding had had so much to hear and to say that he had forgotten to advertise Eleanor of the honour that awaited her, and she heard her brother-in-law's voice in the hall, while she was quite unprepared to see him.

'There's the archdeacon,' she said, springing up.

'Yes, my dear. He told me to tell you that he would come and see you; but, to tell the truth, I had forgotten all about it.'

Eleanor fled away, regardless of all her father's entreaties. She could not now, in the first hours of her joy, bring herself to bear all the archdeacon's retractions, apologies, and congratulations. He would have so much to say, and would be so tedious in saying it; consequently, the archdeacon, when he was shown into the drawing-room, found no one there but Mr Harding.

'You must excuse Eleanor,' said Mr Harding.

'Is anything the matter?' asked the doctor, who at once anticipated that the whole truth about Mr Slope had at last come out.

'Well, something is the matter. I wonder now whether you will be much surprised?'

The archdeacon saw by his father-in-law's manner that after all he had nothing to tell him about Mr Slope. 'No,' said he, 'certainly not – nothing will ever surprise me again.' Very many men now-a-days, besides the archdeacon, adopt or affect to adopt the *nil admirari* doctrine; but nevertheless, to judge from their appearance, they are just as subject to sudden emotions as their grandfathers and grandmothers were before them.

'What do you think Mr Arabin has done?'

'Mr Arabin! It's nothing about that daughter of Stanhope's, I hope?'

'No, not that woman,' said Mr Harding, enjoying his joke in his sleeve.

'Not that woman! Is he going to do anything about any woman? Why can't you speak out if you have anything to say? There is nothing I hate so much as these sort of mysteries.'

'There shall be no mystery with you, archdeacon; though of course, it must go no further at present.'

'Well.'

'Except Susan. You must promise me you'll tell no one else.'

'Nonsense!' exclaimed the archdeacon, who was becoming angry in his suspense. 'You can't have any secret about Mr Arabin.'

'Only this – that he and Eleanor are engaged.'

It was quite clear to see, by the archdeacon's face, that he did not believe a word of it. 'Mr Arabin! It's impossible!'

'Eleanor, at any rate, has just now told me so.'

'It's impossible,' repeated the archdeacon.

'Well, I can't say I think it impossible. It certainly took me by surprise; but that does not make it impossible.'

'She must be mistaken.'

Mr Harding assured him that there was no mistake; that he would find, on returning home, that Mr Arabin had been at Plumstead with the express object of making the same declaration, that even Miss Thorne knew all about it; and that, in fact, the thing was as clearly settled as any such arrangement between a lady and a gentleman could well be.

'Good heavens!' said the archdeacon, walking up and down Eleanor's drawing-room. 'Good heavens! Good heavens!'

Now, these exclamations certainly betokened faith. Mr Harding properly gathered from it that, at last, Dr Grantly did believe the fact. The first utterance clearly evinced a certain amount of distaste at the information he had received; the second, simply indicated surprise; in the tone of the third, Mr Harding fancied that he could catch a certain gleam of satisfaction.

The archdeacon had truly expressed the workings of his mind. He could not but be disgusted to find how utterly astray he had been in all his anticipations. Had he only been lucky enough to have suggested this marriage himself when he first brought Mr Arabin into the country, his character for judgment and wisdom would have received an addition which would have classed him at any rate next to Solomon. And why had he not done so? Might he not have foreseen that Mr Arabin would want a wife in his parsonage? He had foreseen that Eleanor would want a husband; but should he not also have perceived that Mr Arabin was a man much more likely to attract her than Mr Slope? The archdeacon found that he had been at fault, and of course could not immediately get over his discomfiture.

Then his surprise was intense. How sly this pair of young turtle doves had been with him. How egregiously they had hoaxed him. He had preached to Eleanor against her fancied attachment to Mr Slope, at the very time that she was in love with his own protégé, Mr Arabin; and had absolutely taken that same Mr Arabin into his confidence with reference to his dread of Mr Slope's alliance. It was very natural that the archdeacon should feel surprise.

But there was also great ground for satisfaction. Looking at the match by itself, it was the very thing to help the doctor out of his difficulties. In the first place, the assurance that he should never have Mr Slope for his brother-in-law, was in itself a great comfort. Then Mr Arabin was, of all men, the one with whom it would best suit him to be so intimately connected. But the crowning comfort was the blow which this marriage would give to Mr Slope. He had now certainly lost his wife; rumour was beginning to whisper that he might possibly lose his position in the palace; and if Mr Harding would only be true, the great danger of all would be surmounted. In such case it might be expected that Mr Slope would own himself vanquished, and take himself altogether away from Barchester. And so the archdeacon would again be able to breathe pure air.

'Well, well,' said he. 'Good heavens! good heavens!' and the tone of the fifth exclamation made Mr Harding fully aware that content was reigning in the archdeacon's bosom.

And then slowly, gradually, and craftily Mr Harding propounded his own new scheme. Why should not Mr Arabin be the new dean?

Slowly, gradually, and thoughtfully Dr Grantly fell into his father-in-law's views. Much as he liked Mr Arabin, sincere as was his admiration for that gentleman's ecclesiatical abilities, he would not have sanctioned a measure which would rob his father-in-law of his fairly-earned promotion, were it at all practicable to induce his father-in-law to accept the promotion which he had earned. But the archdeacon had, on a former occasion, received proof of the obstinacy with which Mr Harding could adhere to his own views in opposition to the advice of all his friends. He knew tolerably well that nothing would induce the meek, mild man before him to take the high place offered to him, if he thought it wrong to do so. Knowing this, he also said to himself more than once: 'Why should not Mr Arabin be Dean of Barchester?' It was at last arranged between them that they would together start to London by the earliest train on the following morning, making a little *détour* to Oxford on their journey. Dr Gwynne's counsels, they imagined, might perhaps be of assistance to them.

These matters settled, the archdeacon hurried off, that he might return to Plumstead and prepare for his journey. The day was extremely fine, and he came into the city in an open gig. As he was driving up the High Street he encountered Mr Slope at a crossing. Had he not pulled up rather sharply, he would have run over him. The two had never spoken to each other since they had met on a memorable occasion in the bishop's study. They did not speak now; but they looked each other full in the face, and Mr Slope's countenance was as impudent, as triumphant, as defiant as ever. Had Dr Grantly not known to the contrary, he would have imagined that his enemy had won the deanship, the wife, and all the rich honours, for which he had been striving. As it was, he had lost everything that he had in the world, and had just received his *congé* from the bishop.

In leaving the town the archdeacon drove by the well-remembered entrance of Hiram's hospital. There, at the gate, was a large, untidy, farmer's wagon, laden with untidy-looking furniture; and there, inspecting the arrival, was good Mrs Quiverful – not dressed in her Sunday best – not very clean in her apparel – not graceful as to her bonnet and shawl; or, indeed, with many feminine charms as to her whole appearance. She was busy at domestic work in her new house, and had just ventured out, expecting to see no one on the arrival of the family chattels. The archdeacon was down upon her before she knew where she was.

Her acquaintance with Dr Grantly or his family was very slight indeed. The archdeacon, as a matter of course, knew every clergyman in the archdeaconry, it may almost be said in the diocese, and had some acquaintance, more or less intimate, with their wives and families. With Mr Quiverful he had been concerned on various matters of business; but of Mrs Q he had seen very little. Now, however, he was in too gracious a mood to pass her by unnoticed. The Quiverfuls, one and all, had looked for the bitterest hostility from Dr Grantly; they knew his anxiety that Mr Harding should return to his old home at the hospital, and they did not know that a new home had been offered to him at the deanery. Mrs

Quiverful was therefore not a little surprised and not a little rejoiced also, at the tone in which she was addressed.

'How do you do, Mrs Quiverful? – how do you do?' said he, stretching his left hand out of the gig, as he spoke to her. 'I am very glad to see you employed in so pleasant and useful a manner; very glad indeed.'

Mrs Quiverful thanked him, and shook hands with him, and looked into his face suspiciously. She was not sure whether the congratulations and kindness were or were not ironical.

'Pray tell Mr Quiverful from me,' he continued, 'that I am rejoiced at his appointment. It's a comfortable place, Mrs Quiverful, and a comfortable house, and I am very glad to see you in it. Good-bye – good-bye.' And he drove on, leaving the lady well pleased and astonished at his good-nature. On the whole things were going well with the archdeacon, and he could afford to be charitable to Mrs Quiverful. He looked forth from his gig smilingly on all the world, and forgave every one in Barchester their sins, excepting only Mrs Proudie and Mr Slope. Had he seen the bishop, he would have felt inclined to pat even him kindly on the head.

He determined to go home by St Ewold's. This would take him some three miles out of his way; but he felt that he could not leave Plumstead comfortably without saying one word of good fellowship to Mr Arabin. When he reached the parsonage the vicar was still out; but, from what he had heard, he did not doubt but that he would meet him on the road between their two houses. He was right in this, for about halfway home, at a narrow turn, he came upon Mr Arabin, who was on horseback.

'Well, well, well, well;' said the archdeacon, loudly, joyously, and with supreme good humour; 'well, well, well, well; so, after all, we have no further cause to fear Mr Slope.'

'I hear from Mrs Grantly that they have offered the deanery to Mr Harding,' said the other.

'Mr Slope has lost more than the deanery, I find,' and then the archdeacon laughed jocosely. 'Come, come, Arabin, you have kept your secret well enough. I know all about it now.'

'I have had no secret, archdeacon,' said the other with a quiet smile. 'None at all – not for a day. It was only yesterday that I knew my own good fortune, and to-day I went over to Plumstead to ask your approval. From what Mrs Grantly has said to me, I am led to hope that I shall have it.'

'With all my heart, with all my heart,' said the archdeacon cordially, holding his friend fast by the hand. 'It's just as I would have it. She is an excellent young woman; she will not come to you empty-handed; and I think she will make you a good wife. If she does her duty by you as her sister does by me, you'll be a happy man; that's all I can say.' And as he finished speaking, a tear might have been observed in each of the doctor's eyes.

Mr Arabin warmly returned the archdeacon's grasp, but he said little. His heart was too full for speaking, and he could not express the gratitude which he felt. Dr Grantly understood him as well as though he had spoken for an hour.

'And mind, Arabin,' said he, 'no one but myself shall tie the knot. We'll get Eleanor out to Plumstead, and it shall come off there. I'll make Susan stir herself, and we'll do it in style. I must be off to London to-morrow on special business. Harding goes with me. But I'll be back before your bride has got her wedding dress ready.' And so they parted.

On his journey home the archdeacon occupied his mind with preparations for the marriage festivities. He made a great resolve that he would atone to Eleanor for all the injury he had done her by the munificence of his future treatment. He would show her what was the difference in his eyes between a Slope and an Arabin. On one other thing also he decided with a firm mind: if the affair of the dean should not be settled in Mr Arabin's favour, nothing should prevent him putting a new front and bow-window to the dining-room at St Ewold's parsonage.

'So we're sold after all, Sue,' said he to his wife, accosting her with a kiss as soon as he entered his house. He did not call his wife Sue above twice or thrice in a year, and these occasions were great high days.

'Eleanor has had more sense than we gave her credit for,' said Mrs Grantly.

And there was great content in Plumstead rectory that evening; and Mrs Grantly promised her husband that she would now open her heart, and take Mr Arabin into it. Hitherto she had declined to do so.

✖ FIFTY-ONE ✖

Mr Slope Bids Farewell to the Palace
and its Inhabitants

WE MUST NOW TAKE LEAVE OF MR Slope, and of the bishop also, and of Mrs Proudie. These leave-takings in novels are as disagreeable as they are in real life; not so sad, indeed, for they want the reality of sadness; but quite as perplexing, and generally less satisfactory. What novelist, what Fielding, what Scott, what George Sand, or Sue, or Dumas, can impart an interest to the last chapter of his fictitious history? Promises of two children and superhuman happiness are of no avail, nor assurance of extreme respectability carried to an age far exceeding that usually allotted to mortals. The sorrows of our heroes and heroines, they are your delight, oh public! their sorrows, or their sins, or their absurdies; not their virtues, good sense, and consequent rewards. When we begin to tint our final pages with *couleur de rose*, as in according with fixed rule we must do, we altogether extinguish our own powers of pleasing. When we become dull we offend your intellect; and we must become dull or we should offend your taste. A late writer, wishing to sustain his interest to the last page, hung his hero at the end of the third volume. The consequence was, that no one would read his novel. And who can apportion out and dovetail his incidents, dialogues, characters, and descriptive morsels, so as to fit them all exactly into 439 pages, without either compressing them unnaturally, or extending them artificially at the end of his labour? Do I not myself know that I am at this moment in want of a dozen pages, and that I am sick with cudgelling my brains to find them? And then when everything is done, the kindest-hearted critic of them all invariably twits us with the incompetency and lameness of our conclusion. We have either become idle and neglected it, or tedious and over-laboured it. It is insipid or unnatural, over-strained or imbecile. It means nothing, or attempts too much. The last scene of all, as all last scenes we fear must be,

> Is second childishness, and mere oblivion,
> Sans teeth, sans eyes, sans taste, sans everything.

I can only say that if some critic, who thoroughly knows his work, and has laboured on it till experience has made him perfect, will write the last fifty pages of a novel in the way they should be written. I, for one, will in future do my best to copy the example. Guided by my own lights only, I confess that I despair of success.

For the last week or ten days, Mr Slope had seen nothing of Mrs Proudie, and very little of the bishop. He still lived in the palace, and still went through his usual routine work; but the confidential doings of the diocese had passed into other hands. He had seen this clearly, and marked it well; but it had not much disturbed him. He had indulged in other hopes till the bishop's affairs had become dull to him, and he was moreover aware that, as regarded the diocese, Mrs Proudie had checkmated him. It has been explained, in the beginning of these pages, how three or four were contending together as to who, in fact, should be bishop of Barchester. Each of these had now admitted to himself (or boasted to herself) that Mrs Proudie was victorious in the struggle. They had gone through a competitive examination of considerable severity, and she had come forth the winner, *facile princeps*. Mr Slope had, for a moment, run her hard, but it was only for a moment. It had become, as it were, acknowledged that Hiram's hospital should be the testing point between them, and now Mr Quiverful was already in the hospital, the proof of Mrs Proudie's skill and courage.

All this did not break down Mr Slope's spirit, because he had other hopes. But, alas, at last there came to him a note from his friend Sir Nicholas, informing him that the deanship was disposed of. Let us give Mr Slope his due. He did not lie prostrate under this blow, or give himself up to vain lamentations; he did not henceforward despair of life, and call upon gods above and gods below to carry him off. He sat himself down in his chair, counted out what monies he had in hand for present purposes, and what others were coming in to him, bethought himself as to the best sphere for his future exertions, and at once wrote off a letter to a rich sugar-refiner's wife in Baker Street, who, as he well knew, was much given to the entertainment and encouragement of serious young evangelical clergymen. He was again, he said, 'upon the world, having found the air of a cathedral town, and the very nature of cathedral services, uncongenial to his spirit;' and then he sat awhile, making firm resolves as to his manner of parting from the bishop, also as to his future conduct.

> At last he rose, and twitched his mantle blue (black),
> To-morrow to fresh woods and pastures new.

Having received a formal command to wait upon the bishop, he rose and proceeded to obey it. He rang the bell and desired the servant to inform his master that if it suited his lordship, he, Mr Slope, was ready to wait upon him. The servant, who well understood that Mr Slope was no longer in the ascendant, brought back a message, saying that 'his lordship desired that Mr Slope would attend him immediately in his study.' Mr Slope waited about ten minutes more to prove his independence, and then he went into the bishop's room. There, as he had expected, he found Mrs Proudie, together with her husband.

'Hum, ha – Mr Slope, pray take a chair,' said the gentleman bishop.

'Pray be seated, Mr Slope,' said the lady bishop.

'Thank ye, thank ye,' said Mr Slope, and walking round to the fire, he threw himself into one of the arm-chairs that graced the hearth-rug.

'Mr Slope,' said the bishop, 'it has become necessary that I should speak to you definitively on a matter that has for some time been pressing itself on my attention.'

'May I ask whether the subject is any way connected with myself?' said Mr Slope.

'It is so – certainly – yes, it certainly is connected with yourself, Mr Slope.'

'Then, my lord, if I may be allowed to express a wish, I would prefer that no discussion on the subject should take place between us in the presence of a third person.'

'Don't alarm yourself, Mr Slope,' said Mrs Proudie, 'no discussion is at all necessary. The bishop merely intends to express his own wishes.'

'I merely intend, Mr Slope, to express my own wishes – no discussion will be at all necessary,' said the bishop, reiterating his wife's words.

'That is more, my lord, than we any of us can be sure of,' said Mr Slope; 'I cannot, however, force Mrs Proudie to leave the room; nor can I refuse to remain here if it be your lordship's wish that I should do so.'

'It is his lordship's wish, certainly,' said Mrs Proudie.

'Mr Slope,' began the bishop, in a solemn, serious voice, 'it grieves me to have to find fault. It grieves me much to have to find fault with a clergyman; but especially so with a clergyman in your position.'

'Why, what have I done amiss, my lord?' demanded Mr Slope, boldly.

'What have you done amiss, Mr Slope?' said Mrs Proudie, standing erect before the culprit, and raising that terrible forefinger. 'Do you dare to ask the bishop what you have done amiss? does not your conscience –'

'Mrs Proudie, pray let it be understood, once for all, that I will have no words with you.'

'Ah, sir, but you will have words,' said she; 'you must have words. Why have you had so many words with that Signora Neroni? Why have you disgraced yourself, you a clergyman too, by constantly consorting with such a woman as that – with a married woman – with one altogether unfit for a clergyman's society?'

'At any rate, I was introduced to her in your drawing-room,' retorted Mr Slope.

'And shamefully you behaved there,' said Mrs Proudie, 'most shamefully. I was wrong to allow you to remain in the house a day after what I then saw. I should have insisted on your instant dismissal.'

'I have yet to learn, Mrs Proudie, that you have the power to insist either on my going from hence or on my staying here.'

'What!' said the lady; 'I am not to have the privilege of saying who shall and who shall not frequent my own drawing-room! I am not to save my servants and dependants from having their morals corrupted by improper conduct! I am not to save my own daughters from impurity! I will let you see, Mr Slope, whether I have the power or whether I have not. You will have the goodness to understand that you no longer fill any situation about the bishop; and as your room will be immediately wanted in the palace for another chaplain, I must ask you to provide yourself with apartments as soon as may be convenient to you.'

'My lord,' said Mr Slope, appealing to the bishop, and so turning his back completely on the lady, 'will you permit me to to ask that I may have from your own lips any decision that you may have come to on this matter?'

'Certainly, Mr Slope, certainly,' said the bishop; 'that is but reasonable. Well, my decision is that you had better look for some other preferment. For the situation which you have lately held I do not think that you are well suited.'

'And what, my lord, has been my fault?'

'That Signora Neroni is one fault,' said Mrs Proudie; 'and a very abominable fault she is; very abominable and very disgraceful. Fie, Mr Slope, fie! You an evangelical clergyman indeed!'

'My lord, I desire to know for what fault I am turned out of your lordship's house.'

'You hear what Mrs Proudie says,' said the bishop.

'When I publish the history of this transaction, my lord, as I decidedly shall do in my own vindication, I presume you will not wish me to state that you have discarded me at your wife's bidding – because she has objected to my being acquainted with another lady, the daughter of one of the prebendaries of the chapter?'

'You may publish what you please, sir,' said Mrs Proudie. 'But you will not be insane enough to publish any of your doings in Barchester. Do you think I have not heard of your kneelings at that creature's feet – that is if she has any feet – and of your constant slobbering over her hand? I advise you to beware, Mr Slope, of what you do and say. Clergymen have been unfrocked for less than what you have been guilty of.'

'My lord, if this goes on I shall be obliged to indict this woman – Mrs Proudie I mean – for defamation of character.'

'I think, Mr Slope, you had better now retire,' said the bishop. 'I will enclose to you a cheque for any balance that may be due to you; and, under the present circumstances, it will of course be better for all parties that you should leave the palace at the earliest possible moment. I will allow you for your journey back to London, and for your maintenance in Barchester for a week from this date.'

'If, however, you wish to remain in this neighbourhood,' said Mrs Proudie, 'and will solemnly pledge yourself never again to see that woman, and will promise also to be more circumspect in your conduct, the bishop will mention your name to Mr Quiverful, who now wants a curate at Puddingdale. The house is, I imagine, quite sufficient for your requirements: and there will moreover be a stipend of fifty pounds a year.'

'May God forgive you, madam, for the manner in which you have treated me,' said Mr Slope, looking at her with a very heavenly look; 'and remember this, madam, that you yourself may still have a fall;' and he looked at her with a very worldly look. 'As to the bishop, I pity him!' And so saying, Mr Slope left the room. Thus ended the intimacy of the Bishop of Barchester with his first confidential chaplain.

Mrs Proudie was right in this; namely, that Mr Slope was not insane enough to publish to the world any of his doings in Barchester. He did not trouble his friend Mr Towers with any written statement of the iniquity of Mrs Proudie, or the imbecility of her husband. He was aware that it would be wise in him to drop for the future all allusions to his doings in the cathedral city. Soon after the interview just recorded, he left Barchester, shaking the dust off his feet as he entered the railway carriage; and he gave no longing lingering look after the cathedral towers, as the train hurried him quickly out of their sight.

It is well known that the family of the Slopes never starve: they always fall on their feet like cats, and let them fall where they will, they live on the fat of the land. Our Mr Slope did so. On his return to town he found that the sugar-refiner had died, and that his widow was inconsolable: or, in other words, in want of consolation. Mr Slope consoled her, and soon found himself settled with much comfort in the house in Baker Street. He possessed himself, also, before long, of a church in the vicinity of the New Road, and became known to fame as one of the most eloquent preachers and pious clergymen in that part of the metropolis. There let us leave him.

Of the bishop and his wife very little further need be said. From that time forth nothing material occurred to interrupt the even course of their domestic harmony. Very speedily, a further vacancy on the bench of bishops gave to Dr Proudie the seat in the House of Lords, which he at first so anxiously longed for. But by this time he had become a wiser man. He did certainly take his seat, and occasionally registered a vote in favour of Government views on ecclesiastical matters. But he had thoroughly learnt that his proper sphere of action lay in close contiguity with Mrs Proudie's wardrobe. He never again aspired to disobey, or seemed even to wish for autocratic diocesan authority. If ever he thought of freedom, he did so, as men think of the millennium, as of a good time which may be coming, but which nobody expects to come in their day. Mrs Proudie might be said still to bloom, and was, at any rate, strong; and the bishop had no reason to apprehend that he would be speedily visited with the sorrows of a widower's life.

He is still Bishop of Barchester. He has so graced that throne, that the Government has been averse to translate him, even to higher dignities. There may he remain, under safe pupilage, till the new-fangled manners of the age have discovered him to be superannuated, and bestowed on him a pension. As for Mrs Proudie, our prayers for her are that she may live for ever.

✂ FIFTY-TWO ✂

The New Dean takes Possession of the Deanery, and the New Warden of the Hospital

MR HARDING AND THE ARCHDEACON TOGETHER MADE their way to Oxford, and there, by dint of cunning argument, they induced the Master of Lazarus also to ask himself this momentous question: 'Why should not Mr Arabin be Dean of Barchester?' He of course, for a while tried his hand at persuading Mr Harding that he was foolish, over-scrupulous, self-willed, and weak-minded; but he tried in vain. If Mr Harding would not give way to Dr Grantly, it was not likely he would give way to Dr Gwynne; more especially now that so admirable a scheme as that of inducting Mr Arabin into the deanery had been set on foot. When the master found that his eloquence was vain and heard also that Mr Arabin was about to become Mr Harding's son-in-law, he confessed that he also would, under such circumstances, be glad to see his old friend and protégé, the fellow of his college, placed in the comfortable position that was going a-begging.

'It might be the means, you know, Master, of keeping Mr Slope out,' said the archdeacon with grave caution.

'He has no more chance of it,' said the master, 'than our college chaplain. I know more about it than that.'

Mrs Grantly had been right in her surmise. It was the Master of Lazarus who had been instrumental in representing in high places the claims which Mr Harding had upon the Government, and he now consented to use his best endeavours towards getting the offer transferred to Mr Arabin. The three of them went on to London together, and there they remained a week, to the great disgust of Mrs Grantly, and most probably also of Mrs Gwynne. The minister was out of town in one direction, and his private secretary in another. The clerks who remained could do nothing in such a matter as this, and all was difficulty and confusion. The two doctors seemed to have plenty to do; they bustled here and they bustled there, and complained at their club in the evenings that they had been driven off their legs; but Mr Harding had no occupation. Once or twice he suggested that he might perhaps return to Barchester. His request, however, was peremptorily refused, and he had nothing for it but to while away his time in Westminster Abbey.

At length an answer from the great man came. The Master of Lazarus had made his proposition through the Bishop of Belgravia. Now this bishop, though but newly gifted with his diocesan honours, was a man of much weight in the clerico-political world. He was, if not as pious, at any rate as wise as St Paul, and had been with so much effect all things to all men, that though he was great among the dons of Oxford, he had been selected for the most favourite seat on the bench by a Whig Prime Minister. To him Dr Gwynne had made known his wishes and his arguments, and the bishop had made them known to the Marquis of Kensington Gore. The marquis, who was Lord High Steward of the Pantry Board, and who by most men was supposed to hold the highest office out of the cabinet, trafficked much in affairs of this kind. He not only suggested the arrangement to the minister over a cup of coffee, standing on a drawing-room rug in Windsor Castle, but he also favourably mentioned Mr Arabin's name in the ear of a distinguished person.

And so the matter was arranged. The answer of the great man came, and Mr Arabin was made Dean of Barchester. The three clergymen who had come up to town on this important mission dined together with great glee on the day on which the news reached them. In a silent, decent, clerical manner, they toasted Mr Arabin with full bumpers of claret. The satisfaction of all of them was supreme. The Master of Lazarus had been successful in his attempt, and success is dear to us all. The archdeacon had trampled upon Mr Slope, and had lifted to high honours the young clergyman whom he had induced to quit the retirement and comfort of the university. So at least the archdeacon thought; though, to speak sooth, not be, but circumstances, had trampled on Mr Slope. But the satisfaction of Mr Harding was, of all, perhaps, the most complete. He laid aside his usual melancholy manner, and brought forth little quiet jokes from the inmost mirth of his heart; he poked his fun at the archdeacon about Mr Slope's marriage, and quizzed him for his improper love for Mrs Proudie. On the following day they all returned to Barchester.

It was arranged that Mr Arabin should know nothing of what had been done till he received the minister's letter from the hands of his embryo father-in-law. In order that no time might be lost, a message had been sent to him by the preceding night's post, begging him to be at the deanery at the hour that the train from London arrived. There was nothing in this which surprised Mr Arabin. It had somehow got about through all Barchester that Mr Harding was the new dean, and all Barchester was prepared to welcome him with pealing bells and full hearts. Mr Slope had certainly had a party; there had certainly been those in Barchester who were prepared to congratulate him on his promotion with assumed sincerity, but even his own party was not broken-hearted by his failure. The inhabitants of the city, even the high-souled ecstatic young ladies of thirty-five, had begun to comprehend that their welfare, and the welfare of the place, was connected in some mysterious manner with daily chants and bi-weekly anthems. The expenditure of the palace had not added much to the popularity of the bishop's side of the question; and, on the whole, there was a strong reaction. When it became known to all the world that Mr Harding was to be the new dean, all the world rejoiced heartily.

Mr Arabin, we have said, was not surprised at the summons which called him to the deanery. He had not as yet seen Mr Harding since Eleanor had accepted him, nor had he seen him since he had learnt his future father-in-law's preferment. There was nothing more natural, more necessary, than that they should meet each other at the earliest possible moment. Mr Arabin was waiting in the deanery parlour when Mr Harding and Dr Grantly were driven up from the station.

There was some excitement in the bosoms of them all, as they met and shook hands; by far too much to enable either of them to begin his story and tell it in a proper equable style of narrative. Mr Harding was some minutes quite dumbfounded, and Mr Arabin could only talk in short, spasmodic sentences about his love and good fortune. He slipped in, as best he could, some sort of congratulation about the deanship, and then went on with his hopes and fears – hopes that he might be received as a son, and fears that he hardly deserved such good fortune. Then he went back to the dean; it was the most thoroughly satisfactory appointment, he said, of which he had ever heard.

'But! but! but –' said Mr Harding; and then failing to get any further, he looked imploringly at the archdeacon.

'The truth is, Arabin,' said the doctor, 'that, after all, you are not destined to be son-in-law to a dean. Nor am I either: more's the pity.'

Mr Arabin looked at him for explanation. 'Is not Mr Harding to be the new dean?'

'It appears not,' said the archdeacon. Mr Arabin's face fell a little, and he looked from one to the other. It was plainly to be seen from them both that there was no cause of unhappiness in the matter, at least not of unhappiness to them; but there was as yet no elucidation of the mystery.

'Think how old I am,' said Mr Harding, imploringly.

'Fiddlestick!' said the archdeacon.

'That's all very well, but it won't make a young man of me,' said Mr Harding.

'And who is to be dean?' asked Mr Arabin.

'Yes, that's the question,' said the archdeacon. 'Come, Mr Precentor, since you obstinately refuse to be anything else, let us know who is to be the man. He has got the nomination in his pocket.'

With eyes brim full of tears, Mr Harding pulled out the letter and handed it to his future son-in-law. He tried to make a little speech, but failed altogether. Having given up the document, he turned round to the wall, feigning to blow his nose, and then sat himself down on the old dean's dingy horse-hair sofa. And here we find it necessary to bring our account of the interview to an end.

Nor can we pretend to describe the rapture with which Mr Harding was received by his daughter. She wept with grief and wept with joy; with grief that her father should, in his old age, still be without that rank and worldly position which, according to her ideas, he had so well earned; and with joy in that he, her darling father, should have bestowed on that other dear one the good things of which he himself would not open his hand to take possession. And here Mr Harding again showed his weakness. In the *mêlée* of this exposal of their loves and reciprocal affection, he found himself unable to resist the entreaties of all parties that the lodgings in the High Street should be given up. Eleanor would not live in the deanery, she said, unless her father lived there also. Mr Arabin would not be dean, unless Mr Harding would be co-dean with him. The archdeacon declared that his father-in-law should not have his own way in everything, and Mrs Grantly carried him off to Plumstead, that he might remain there till Mr and Mrs Arabin were in a state to receive him in their own mansion.

Pressed by such arguments as these, what could a weak old man do but yield?

But there was yet another task which it behoved Mr Harding to do before he could allow himself to be at rest. Little has been said in these pages of the state of those remaining old men who had lived under his sway at the hospital. But not on this account must it be presumed that he had forgotten them, or that in their state of anarchy and in their want of due government he had omitted to visit them. He visited them constantly, and had latterly given them to understand that they would soon be required to subscribe their adherence to a new master. There were now but five of them, one of them having been but quite lately carried to his rest – but five of the full number, which had hitherto been twelve, and which was now to be raised to twenty-four, including women. Of these old Bunce, who for many years had been the favourite of the late warden, was one; and Abel Handy, who had been the humble means of driving that warden from his home, was another.

Mr Harding now resolved that he himself would introduce the new warden to the hospital. He felt that many circumstances might conspire to make the men receive Mr Quiverful with aversion and disrespect; he felt also that Mr Quiverful might himself feel some qualms of conscience if he entered the hospital with an idea that he did so in hostility to his predecessor. Mr Harding therefore determined to walk in, arm in arm with Mr Quiverful, and to ask from these men their respectful obedience to their new master.

On returning to Barchester, he found that Mr Quiverful had not yet slept in the hospital house, or entered on his new duties. He accordingly made known to that gentleman his wishes, and his proposition was not rejected.

It was a bright clear morning, though in November, that Mr Harding and Mr Quiverful, arm in arm, walked through the hospital gate. It was one trait in our old friend's character that he did nothing with parade. He omitted, even in the more important doings of his life, that sort of parade by which most of us deem it necessary to grace our important doings. We have housewarmings, christenings, and gala days; we keep, if not our own birthdays, those of our children; we are apt to fuss ourselves if called upon to change our residences, and have, almost all of us, our little state occasions. Mr Harding had no state occasions. When he left his old house, he went forth from it with the same quiet composure as though he were merely taking his daily walk; and now that he re-entered it with another warden under his wing, he did so with the same quiet step and calm demeanour. He was a little less upright than he had been five years, nay, it was now nearly six years ago; he walked perhaps a little slower; his footfall was perhaps a thought less firm; otherwise one might have said that he was merely returning with a friend under his arm.

This friendliness was everything to Mr Quiverful. To him, even in his poverty, the thought that he was supplanting a brother clergyman so kind and courteous as Mr Harding, had been very bitter. Under his circumstances it had been impossible for him to refuse the proffered boon; he could not reject the bread that was offered to his children, or refuse to ease the heavy burden that had so long oppressed that poor wife of his; nevertheless, it had been very grievous to him to think that in going to the hospital he might encounter the ill will of his brethren in the diocese. All this Mr Harding had fully comprehended. It was for such feelings as these, for the nice comprehension of such motives, that his heart and intellect were peculiarly fitted. In most matters of worldly import the archdeacon set down his father-in-law as little better than a fool. And perhaps he was right. But in some other matters, equally important if they be rightly judged, Mr Harding, had he been so minded, might with as much propriety have set down his son-in-law for a fool. Few men, however, are constituted as was Mr Harding. He had that nice appreciation of the feelings of others which belongs of right exclusively to women.

Arm in arm they walked into the inner quadrangle of the building, and there the five old men met them. Mr Harding shook hands with them all, and then Mr Quiverful did the same. With Bunce Mr Harding shook hands twice, and Mr Quiverful was about to repeat the same ceremony, but the old man gave him no encouragement.

'I am very glad to know that at last you have a new warden,' said Mr Harding in a very cheery voice.

'We be very old for any change,' said one of them; 'but we do suppose it be all for the best.'

'Certainly – certainly it is for the best,' said Mr Harding. 'You will again have a clergyman of your own church under the same roof with you, and a very excellent clergyman you will have. It is a great satisfaction to me to know that so good a man is coming to take care of you, and that it is no stranger, but a friend of my own, who will allow me from time to time to come in and see you.'

'We be very thankful to your reverence,' said another of them.

'I need not tell you, my good friends,' said Mr Quiverful, 'how extremely grateful I am to Mr Harding for his kindness to me – I must say his uncalled for, unexpected kindness.'

'He be always very kind,' said a third.

'What I can do to fill the void which he left here, I will do. For your sake and my own I will do so, and especially for his sake. But to you who have known him, I can never be the same well-loved friend and father that he has been.'

'No, sir, no,' said old Bunce, who hitherto had held his peace; 'no one can be that. Not if the new bishop sent a hangel to us out of heaven. We doesn't doubt you'll do your best, sir, but you'll not be like the old master; not to us old ones.'

'Fie, Bunce, fie! how dare you talk in that way?' said Mr Harding; but as he scolded the old man he still held him by his arm, and pressed it with warm affection.

There was no getting up any enthusiasm in the matter. How could five old men tottering away to their final resting-place be enthusiastic on the reception of a stranger? What could Mr Quiverful be to them, or they to Mr Quiverful? Had Mr Harding indeed come back to them, some last flicker of joyous light might have shone forth on their aged cheeks; but it was in vain to bid them rejoice because Mr Quiverful was about to move his fourteen children from Puddingdale into the hospital house. In reality they did no doubt receive advantage, spiritual as well as corporal; but this they could neither anticipate nor acknowledge.

It was a dull affair enough, this introduction of Mr Quiverful; but still it had its effect. The good which Mr Harding intended did not fall to the ground. All the Barchester world, including the five old bedesmen, treated Mr Quiverful with the more respect, because Mr Harding had thus walked in arm in arm with him, on his first entrance to his duties.

And here in their new abode we will leave Mr and Mrs Quiverful and their fourteen children. May they enjoy the good things which Providence has at length given to them!

❊ FIFTY-THREE ❊

Conclusion

THE END OF A NOVEL, LIKE THE end of a children's dinner-party, must be made up of sweetmeats and sugar-plums. There is now nothing else to be told but the gala doings of Mr Arabin's marriage, nothing more to be described than the wedding dresses, no further dialogue to be recorded than that which took place between the archdeacon who married them, and Mr Arabin and Eleanor who were married. 'Wilt thou have this woman to thy wedded wife,' and 'Wilt thou have this man to thy wedded husband, to live together according to God's ordinance?' Mr Arabin and Eleanor each answered, 'I will.' We have no doubt that they will keep their promises; the more especially as the Signora Neroni had left Barchester before the ceremony was performed.

Mrs Bold had been somewhat more than two years a widow before she was married to her second husband, and little Johnny was then able with due assistance to walk on his own legs into the drawing-room to receive the salutations of the assembled guests. Mr Harding gave away the bride, the archdeacon performed the service, and the two Miss Grantlys, who were joined in their labours by other young ladies of the neighbourhood, performed the duties of bridesmaids with equal diligence and grace. Mrs Grantly superintended the breakfast and bouquets, and Mary Bold distributed the cards and cake. The archdeacon's three sons had also come home for the occasion. The eldest was great with learning, being regarded by all who knew him as a certain future double first. The second, however, bore the palm on this occasion, being resplendent in a new

374

uniform. The third was just entering the university, and was probably the proudest of the three.

But the most remarkable feature in the whole occasion was the excessive liberality of the archdeacon. He literally made presents to everybody. As Mr Arabin had already moved out of the parsonage of St Ewold's, that scheme of elongating the dining-room was of course abandoned; but he would have refurnished the whole deanery had he been allowed. He sent down a magnificent piano by Erard, gave Mr Arabin a cob which any dean in the land might have been proud to bestride, and made a special present to Eleanor of a new pony chair that had gained a prize in the Exhibition. Nor did he even stay his hand here; he bought a set of cameos for his wife, and a sapphire bracelet for Miss Bold; showered pearls and workboxes on his daughters, and to each of his sons he presented a cheque for 20*l*. On Mr Harding he bestowed a magnificent violoncello with all the new-fashioned arrangements and expensive additions, which, on account of these novelties, that gentleman could never use with satisfaction to his audience or pleasure to himself.

Those who knew the archdeacon well, perfectly understood the cause of his extravagance. 'Twas thus that he sang his song of triumph over Mr Slope. This was his pæan, his hymn of thanksgiving, his loud oration. He had girded himself with his sword, and gone forth to the war; now he was returning from the field laden with the spoils of the foe. The cob and the cameos, the violoncello and the pianoforte, were all as it were trophies reft from the tent of his now conquered enemy.

The Arabins after their marriage went abroad for a couple of months, according to the custom in such matters now duly established, and then commenced their deanery life under good auspices. And nothing can be more pleasant than the present arrangement of ecclesiastical affairs in Barchester. The titular bishop never interfered, and Mrs Proudie not often. Her sphere is more extended, more noble, and more suited to her ambition than that of a cathedral city. As long as she can do what she pleases with the diocese, she is willing to leave the dean and chapter to themselves. Mr Slope tried his hand at subverting the old-established customs of the close, and from his failure she has learnt experience. The burly chancellor and the meagre little prebendary are not teased by any application respecting Sabbath-day schools, the dean is left to his own dominions, and the intercourse between Mrs Proudie and Mrs Arabin is confined to a yearly dinner given by each to the other. At these dinners Dr Grantly will not take a part; but he never fails to ask for and receive a full acount of all that Mrs Proudie either does or says.

His ecclesiastical authority has been greatly shorn since the palmy days in which he reigned supreme as mayor of the palace to his father, but nevertheless such authority as is now left to him he can enjoy without interference. He can walk down the High Street of Barchester without feeling that those who see him are comparing his claims with those of Mr Slope. The intercourse between Plumstead and the deanery is of the most constant and familiar description. Since Eleanor has been married to a clergyman, and especially to a dignitary of the church, Mrs Grantly has found many more points of sympathy with her sister; and on a coming occasion, which is much looked forward to by all parties, she intends to spend a month or two at the deanery. She never thought of spending a month in Barchester when little Johnny Bold was born!

The two sisters do not quite agree on matters of church doctrine, though their differences are of the most amicable description. Mr Arabin's church is two degrees higher than that of Mrs Grantly. This may seem strange to those who will remember that Eleanor was once accused of partiality to Mr Slope; but it is no less the fact. She likes her husband's silken vest, she likes his adherence to the rubric, she specially likes the eloquent philosophy of his sermons, and she likes the red letters in her own prayer-book. It must not be presumed that she has a taste for candles, or that she is at all astray about the real presence; but she has an inkling that way. She sent a handsome subscription towards certain very heavy ecclesiastical legal expenses which have lately been incurred in Bath, her name of course not appearing; she assumes a smile of gentle ridicule when the Archbishop of Canterbury is named, and she has put up a memorial window in the cathedral.

Mrs Grantly, who belongs to the high and dry church, the high church as it was some fifty years since, before tracts were written and young clergymen took upon themselves the highly meritorious duty of cleaning churches, rather laughs at her sister. She shrugs her shoulders, and tells Miss Thorne that she supposes Eleanor will have an oratory in the deanery before she has done. But she is not on that account a whit displeased. A few high church vagaries do not, she thinks, sit amiss on the shoulders of a young dean's wife. It shows at any rate that her heart is in the subject; and it shows moreover that she is removed, wide as the poles asunder, from that cesspool of abomination in which it was once suspected that she would wallow and grovel. Anathema maranatha! Let anything else be held as blessed, so that that be well cursed. Welcome kneelings and bowings, welcome matins and complines, welcome bell, book, and candle, so that Mr Slope's dirty surplices and ceremonial Sabbaths be held in due execration!

If it be essentially and absolutely necessary to choose between the two, we are inclined to agree with Mrs Grantly that the bell, book, and candle are the lesser evil of the two. Let it however be understood that no such necessity is admitted in these pages.

Dr Arabin (we suppose he must have become a doctor when he became a dean) is more moderate and less outspoken on doctrinal points than his wife, as indeed in his station it behoves him to be. He is a studious, thoughtful, hard-working man. He lives constantly at the deanery, and preaches nearly every Sunday. His time is spent in sifting and editing old ecclesiastical literature, and in producing the same articles new. At Oxford he is generally regarded as the most promising clerical ornament of the age. He and his wife live together in perfect mutual confidence. There is but one secret in her bosom which he has not shared. He has never yet learned how Mr Slope had his ears boxed.

The Stanhopes soon found that Mr Slope's power need no longer operate to keep them from the delight of their Italian villa. Before Eleanor's marriage they had all migrated back to the shores of Como. They had not been resettled long before the signora received from Mrs Arabin a very pretty though very short epistle, in which she was informed of the fate of the writer. This letter was answered by another, bright, charming, and witty, as the signora's letters always were; and so ended the friendship between Eleanor and the Stanhopes.

One word of Mr Harding, and we have done.

He is still Precentor of Barchester, and still pastor of the little church of St Cuthbert's. In spite of what he has so often said himself, he is not even yet an old man. He does such duties as fall to his lot well and conscientiously, and is thankful that he has never been tempted to assume others for which he might be less fitted.

The Author now leaves him in the hands of his readers; not as a hero, not as a man to be admired and talked of, not as a man who should be toasted at public dinners and spoken of with conventional absurdity as a perfect divine, but as a good man without guile, believing humbly in the religion which he has striven to teach, and guided by the precepts which he has striven to learn.

THE END

MISS
MACKENZIE

✤ ONE ✤

The Mackenzie Family

I FEAR I MUST TROUBLE MY READER with some few details as to the early life of Miss Mackenzie – details which will be dull in the telling, but which shall be as short as I can make them. Her father, who had in early life come from Scotland to London, had spent all his days in the service of his country. He became a clerk in Somerset House at the age of sixteen, and was a clerk in Somerset House when he died at the age of sixty. Of him no more shall be said than that his wife had died before him, and that he, at dying, left behind him two sons and a daughter.

Thomas Mackenzie, the eldest of those two sons, had engaged himself in commercial pursuits – as his wife was accustomed to say when she spoke of her husband's labours; or went into trade, and kept a shop, as was more generally asserted by those of the Mackenzie circle who were wont to speak their minds freely. The actual and unvarnished truth in the matter shall now be made known. He, with his partner, made and sold oilcloth, and was possessed of premises in the New Road, over which the names of 'Rubb and Mackenzie' were posted in large letters. As you, my reader, might enter therein, and purchase a yard and a half of oilcloth, if you were so minded, I think that the free-spoken friends of the family were not far wrong. Mrs Thomas Mackenzie, however, declared that she was calumniated, and her husband cruelly injured; and she based her assertions on the fact that 'Rubb and Mackenzie' had wholesale dealings, and that they sold their article to the trade, who re-sold it. Whether or no she was ill-treated in the matter, I will leave my readers to decide, having told them all that it is necessary for them to know, in order that a judgement may be formed.

Walter Mackenzie, the second son, had been placed in his father's office, and he also had died before the time at which our story is supposed to commence. He had been a poor sickly creature, always ailing, gifted with an affectionate nature, and a great respect for the blood of the Mackenzies, but not gifted with much else that was intrinsically his own. The blood of the Mackenzies was, according to his way of thinking, very pure blood indeed; and he had felt strongly that his brother had disgraced the family by connecting himself with that man Rubb, in the New Road. He had felt this the more strongly, seeing that 'Rubb and Mackenzie' had not done great things in their trade. They had kept their joint commercial head above water, but had sometimes barely succeeded in doing that. They had never been bankrupt, and that, perhaps, for some years was all that could be said. If a Mackenzie did go into trade, he should, at any rate, have done better than this. He certainly should have done better than this, seeing that he started in life with a considerable sum of money.

Old Mackenzie – he who had come from Scotland – had been the first-cousin of Sir Walter Mackenzie, baronet, of Incharrow, and he had married the sister of Sir John Ball, baronet, of the Cedars, Twickenham. The young Mackenzies, therefore, had reason to be proud of their blood. It is true that Sir John Ball was the first baronet, and that he had simply been a political Lord Mayor in strong political days – a political Lord Mayor in the leather business; but, then, his business had been undoubtedly wholesale; and a man who gets himself to be made a baronet cleanses himself from the stains of trade, even though he have traded in leather. And then, the present Mackenzie baronet was the ninth of the name; so that on the higher and nobler side of the family, our Mackenzies may be said to have been very strong indeed. This strength the two clerks in Somerset House felt and enjoyed very keenly; and it may therefore be understood that the oilcloth manufactory was much out of favour with them.

When Tom Mackenzie was twenty-five – 'Rubb and Mackenzie' as he afterwards became – and Walter, at the age of twenty-one, had been for a year or two placed at a desk in Somerset House, there died one Jonathan Ball, a brother of the baronet Ball, leaving all he had in the world to the two brother Mackenzies. This all was by no means a trifle, for each brother received about twelve thousand pounds when the opposing lawsuits instituted by the Ball family were finished. These opposing lawsuits were carried on with great vigour, but with no success on the Ball side, for three years. By that time, Sir John Ball, of the Cedars, was half ruined, and the Mackenzies got their money. It is needless to say much to the reader of the manner in which Tom Mackenzie found his way into trade – how, in the first place, he endeavoured to resume his Uncle Jonathan's share in the leather business, instigated thereto by a desire to oppose his Uncle John – Sir John, who was opposing him in the matter of the will – how he lost money in this attempt, and ultimately embarked, after some other fruitless speculations, the residue of his fortune in partnership with Mr Rubb. All that happened long ago. He was now a man of nearly fifty, living with his wife and family – a family of six or seven children – in a house in Gower Street, and things had not gone with him very well.

Nor is it necessary to say very much of Walter Mackenzie, who had been four years younger than his brother. He had stuck to the office in spite of his wealth; and as he had never married, he had been a rich man. During his father's lifetime, and when he was quite young, he had for a while shone in the world of fashion, having been patronised by the Mackenzie baronet, and by others who thought that a clerk from Somerset House with twelve thousand pounds must be a very estimable fellow. He had not, however, shone in a very brilliant way. He had gone to parties for a year or two, and during those years had essayed the life of a young man about town, frequenting theatres and billiard-rooms, and doing a few things which he should have left undone, and leaving undone a few things which should not have been so left. But, as I have said, he was weak in body as well as weak in mind. Early in life he became an invalid; and though he kept his place in Somerset House till he died, the period of his shining in the fashionable world came to a speedy end.

Now, at length, we will come to Margaret Mackenzie, the sister, our heroine, who was eight years younger than her brother Walter, and twelve years younger than Mr Rubb's partner. She had been little more than a child when her father died; or I might more correctly say, that though she had then reached an age which makes some girls young women, it had not as yet had that effect upon her. She was then nineteen; but her life in her father's house had been dull and monotonous; she had gone very little into company, and knew very little of the ways of the world. The Mackenzie baronet people had not noticed her. They had failed to make much of Walter with his twelve thousand pounds, and did not trouble themselves with Margaret, who had no fortune of her own. The Ball baronet people were at extreme variance with all her family, and, as a matter of course, she received no countenance from them. In those early days she did not receive much countenance from any one; and perhaps I may say that she had not shown much claim for such countenance as is often given to young ladies by their richer relatives. She was neither beautiful nor clever, nor was she in any special manner made charming by any of those softnesses and graces of youth which to some girls seem to atone for a want of beauty and cleverness. At the age of nineteen, I may almost say that Margaret Mackenzie was ungainly. Her brown hair was rough, and did not form itself into equal lengths. Her cheek-bones were somewhat high, after the manner of the Mackenzies. She was thin and straggling in her figure, with bones larger than they should have been for purposes of youthful grace. There was not wanting a certain brightness to her grey eyes, but it was a brightness as to the use of which she had no early knowledge. At this time her father lived at Camberwell, and I doubt whether the education which Margaret received at Miss Green's establishment for young ladies in that suburb was of a kind to make up by art for that which nature had not given her. This school, too, she left at an early age – at a very early age, as her age went. When she was nearly sixteen, her father, who was then almost an old man, became ill, and the next three years she spent in nursing him. When he died, she was transferred to her younger brother's house – to a house which he had taken in one of the quiet streets leading down from the Strand to the river, in order that he might be near his office. And here for fifteen years she had lived, eating his bread and nursing him, till he also died, and so she was alone in the world.

During those fifteen years her life had been very weary. A moated grange in the country is bad enough for the life of any Mariana, but a moated grange in town is much worse. Her life in London had been altogether of the moated grange kind, and long before her brother's death it had been very wearisome to her. I will not say that she was always waiting for some one that came not, or that she declared herself to be aweary, or that she wished that she were dead. But the mode of her life was as near that as prose may be near to poetry, or truth to romance. For the coming of one, who, as things fell out in that matter, soon ceased to come at all to her, she had for a while been anxious. There was a young clerk then in Somerset House, one Harry Handcock by name, who had visited her brother in the early days of that long sickness. And Harry Handcock had seen beauty in those grey eyes, and the straggling, uneven locks had by that time settled themselves into some form of tidiness, and the big joints, having been covered, had taken upon themselves softer womanly motions, and the sister's tenderness to the brother had been appreciated. Harry Handcock had spoken a word or two, Margaret being then five-and-twenty, and Harry ten years her senior. Harry had spoken, and Margaret had listened only too willingly. But the sick brother upstairs had become cross and peevish. Such a thing should never take place with his consent, and Harry Handcock had ceased to speak tenderly.

He had ceased to speak tenderly, though he didn't cease to visit the quiet house in Arundel Street. As far as Margaret was concerned he might as well have ceased to come; and in her heart she sang that song of Mariana's, complaining bitterly of her weariness; though the man was seen then in her brother's sickroom regularly once a week. For years this went on. The brother would crawl out to his office in summer, but would never leave his bedroom in the winter months. In those days these things were allowed in public offices; and it was not till very near the end of his life that certain stern official reformers hinted at the necessity of his retiring on a pension. Perhaps it was that hint that killed him. At any rate, he died in harness – if it can in truth be said of him that he ever wore harness. Then, when he was dead, the days were gone in which Margaret Mackenzie cared for Harry Handcock. Harry Handcock was still a bachelor, and when the nature of his late friend's will was ascertained, he said a word or two to show that he thought he was not yet too old for matrimony. But Margaret's weariness could not now be cured in that way. She would have taken him while she had nothing, or would have taken him in those early days had fortune filled her lap with gold. But she had seen Harry Handcock at least weekly for the last ten years, and having seen him without any speech of love, she was not now prepared for the renewal of such speaking.

When Walter Mackenzie died there was a doubt through all the Mackenzie circle as to what was the destiny of his money. It was well known that he had been a prudent man, and that he was possessed of a freehold estate which gave him at least six hundred a year. It was known also that he had money saved beyond this. It was known, too, that Margaret had nothing, or next to nothing, of her own. The old Mackenzie had had no fortune left to him, and had felt it to be a grievance that his sons had not joined their richer lots to his poorer lot. This, of course, had been no fault of Margaret's, but it had made him feel justified in leaving his daughter as a burden upon his younger son. For the last fifteen years she had eaten bread to which she had no positive claim; but if ever woman earned the morsel which she required, Margaret Mackenzie had earned her morsel during her untiring attendance upon her brother. Now she was left to her own resources, and as she went silently about the house during those sad hours which intervened between the death of her brother and his burial, she was altogether in ignorance whether any means of subsistence had been left to her. It was known that Walter Mackenzie had more than once altered his will – that he had, indeed, made many wills – according as he was at such moments on terms of more or less friendship with his brother; but he had never told to any one what was the nature of any bequest that he had made. Thomas Mackenzie had thought of both his brother and sister as poor creatures, and had been thought of by them as being but a poor creature himself. He had become a shopkeeper, so they declared, and it must be admitted that Margaret had shared the feeling which regarded her brother Tom's trade as being disgraceful. They, of Arundel Street, had been idle, reckless, useless beings – so Tom had often declared to his wife – and only by fits and starts had there existed any friendship between him and either of them. But the firm of Rubb and Mackenzie was not growing richer in those days, and both Thomas and his wife had felt themselves forced into a certain amount of conciliatory demeanour by the claims of their seven surviving children. Walter, however, said no word to any one of his money; and when he was followed to his grave by his brother and nephews, and by Harry Handcock, no one knew of what nature would be the provision made for his sister.

'He was a great sufferer,' Harry Handcock had said, at the only interview which took place between him and Margaret after the death of her brother and before the reading of the will.

'Yes indeed, poor fellow,' said Margaret, sitting in the darkened dining-room, in all the gloom of her new mourning.

'And you yourself, Margaret, have had but a sorry time of it.' He still called her Margaret from old acquaintance, and had always done so.

'I have had the blessing of good health,' she said, 'and have been very thankful. It has been a dull life, though, for the last ten years.'

'Women generally lead dull lives, I think.' Then he had paused for a while, as though something were on his mind which he wished to consider before he spoke again. Mr Handcock, at this time, was bald and very stout. He was a strong healthy man, but had about him, to the outward eye, none of the aptitudes of a lover. He was fond of eating and drinking, as no one knew better than Margaret Mackenzie; and had altogether dropped the poetries of life, if at any time any of such poetries had belonged to him. He was, in fact, ten years older than Margaret Mackenzie; but he now looked to be almost twenty years her senior. She was a woman who at thirty-five had more of the graces of womanhood than had belonged to her at twenty. He was a man who at forty-five had lost all that youth does for a man. But still I think that she would have fallen back upon her former love, and found that to be sufficient, had he asked her to do so even now. She would have felt herself bound by her faith to do so, had he said that such was his wish, before the reading of her brother's will. But he did no such thing. 'I hope he will have made you comfortable,' he said.

'I hope he will have left me above want,' Margaret had replied – and that had then been all. She had, perhaps, half-expected something more from him, remembering that the obstacle which had separated them was now removed. But nothing more came, and it would hardly be true to say that she was disappointed. She had no strong desire to marry Harry Handcock whom no one now called Harry any longer; but yet, for the sake of human nature, she bestowed a sigh upon his coldness, when he carried his tenderness no further than a wish that she might be comfortable.

There had of necessity been much of secrecy in the life of Margaret Mackenzie. She had possessed no friend to whom she could express her thoughts and feelings with confidence. I doubt whether any living being knew that there now existed, up in that small back bedroom in Arundel Street, quires of manuscript in which Margaret had written her thoughts and feelings – hundreds of rhymes which had never met any eye but her own; and outspoken words of love contained in letters which had never been sent, or been intended to be sent, to any destination. Indeed these letters had been commenced with no name, and finished with no signature. It would be hardly true to say that they had been intended for Harry Handcock, even at the warmest period of her love. They had rather been trials of her strength – proofs of what she might do if fortune should ever be so kind to her as to allow of her loving. No one had ever guessed all this, or had dreamed of accusing Margaret of romance. No one capable of testing her character had known her. In latter days she had now and again dined in Gower Street, but her sister-in-law, Mrs Tom, had declared her to be a silent, stupid old maid. As a silent, stupid old maid, the Mackenzies of Rubb and Mackenzie were disposed to regard her. But how should they treat this stupid old maid of an aunt, if it should now turn out that all the wealth of the family belonged to her?

When Walter's will was read such was found to be the case. There was no doubt, or room for doubt, in the matter. The will was dated but two months before his death, and left everything to Margaret, expressing a conviction on the part of the testator that it was his duty to do so, because of his sister's unremitting attention to himself. Harry Handcock was requested to act as executor, and was requested also to accept a gold watch and a present of two hundred pounds. Not a word was there in the whole will of his brother's family; and Tom, when he went home with a sad heart, told his wife that all this had come of certain words which she had spoken when last she had visited the sick man. 'I knew it would be so,' said Tom to his wife. 'It can't be helped now, of course. I knew you could not keep your temper quiet, and always told you not to go near him.' How the wife answered, the course of our story at the present moment does not require me to tell. That she did answer with sufficient spirit, no one, I should say, need doubt; and it may be surmised that things in Gower Street were not comfortable that evening.

Tom Mackenzie had communicated the contents of the will to his sister, who had declined to be in the room when it was opened. 'He has left you everything – just everything,' Tom had said. If Margaret made any word of reply, Tom did not hear it. 'There will be over eight hundred a year, and he has left you all the furniture,' Tom continued. 'He has been very good,' said Margaret, hardly knowing how to express herself on such an occasion. 'Very good to you,' said Tom, with some little sarcasm in his voice. 'I mean good to me,' said Margaret. Then he told her that Harry Handcock had been named as executor. 'There is no more about him in the will, is there?' said Margaret. At the moment, not knowing much about executors, she had fancied that her brother had, in making such appointment, expressed some further wish about Mr Handcock. Her brother explained to her that the executor was to have two hundred pounds and a gold watch, and then she was satisfied.

'Of course, it's a very sad look-out for us,' Tom said; 'but I do not on that account blame you.'

'If you did you would wrong me,' Margaret answered, 'for I never once during all the years that we lived together spoke to Walter one word about his money.'

'I do not blame you,' the brother rejoined; and then no more had been said between them.

He had asked her even before the funeral to go up to Gower Street and stay with them, but she had declined. Mrs Tom Mackenzie had not asked her. Mrs Tom Mackenzie had hoped, then – had hoped and had inwardly resolved – that half, at least, of the dying brother's money would have come to her husband; and she had thought that if she once encumbered herself with the old maid, the old maid might remain longer than was desirable. 'We should never get rid of her,' she had said to her eldest daughter, Mary Jane. 'Never, mamma,' Mary Jane had replied. The mother and daughter had thought that they would be on the whole safer in not pressing any such invitation. They had not pressed it, and the old maid had remained in Arundel Street.

Before Tom left the house, after the reading of the will, he again invited his sister to his own home. An hour or two had intervened since he had told her of her position in the world, and he was astonished at finding how composed and self-assured she was in the tone and manner of her answer. 'No, Tom, I think I had better not,' she said. 'Sarah will be somewhat disappointed.'

'You need not mind that,' said Tom.

'I think I had better not. I shall be very glad to see her if she will come to me; and I hope you will come, Tom; but I think I will remain here till I have made up my mind what to do.' She remained in Arundel Street for the next three months, and her brother saw her frequently; but Mrs Tom Mackenzie never went to her, and she never went to Mrs Tom Mackenzie. 'Let it be even so,' said Mrs Tom; 'they shall not say that I ran after her and her money. I hate such airs.' 'So do I, mamma,' said Mary Jane, tossing her head. 'I always said that she was a nasty old maid.'

On that same day – the day on which the will was read – Mr Handcock had also come to her. 'I need not tell you,' he had said, as he pressed her hand, 'how rejoiced I am – for your sake, Margaret.' Then she had returned the pressure, and had thanked him for his friendship. 'You know that I have been made executor to the will,' he continued. 'He did this simply to save you from trouble. I need only promise that I will do anything and everything that you can wish.' Then he left her, saying nothing of his suit on that occasion.

Two months after this – and during those two months he had necessarily seen her frequently – Mr Handcock wrote to her from his office in Somerset House, renewing his old proposals of marriage. His letter was short and sensible, pleading his cause as well, perhaps, as any words were capable of pleading it at this time; but it was not successful. As to her money he told her that no doubt he regarded it now as a great addition to their chance of happiness, should they put their lots together; and as to his love for her, he referred her to the days in which he had desired to make her his wife without a shilling of fortune. He had never changed, he said; and if her heart was as constant as his, he would make good now the proposal which she had once been willing to accept. His income was not equal to hers, but it was not inconsiderable, and therefore as regards means they would be very comfortable. Such were his arguments, and Margaret, little as she knew of the world, was able to perceive that he expected that they would succeed with her.

Little, however, as she might know of the world, she was not prepared to sacrifice herself and her new freedom, and her new power and her new wealth, to Mr Harry Handcock. One word said to her when first she was free and before she was rich, would have carried her. But an argumentative, well-worded letter, written to her two months after the fact of her freedom and the fact of her wealth had sunk into his mind, was powerless on her. She had looked at her glass and had perceived that years had improved her, whereas years had not improved Harry Handcock. She had gone back over her old aspirations, aspirations of which no whisper had ever been uttered, but which had not the less been strong within her, and had told herself that she could not gratify them by a union with Mr Handcock. She thought, or rather hoped, that society might still open to her its portals – not simply the society of the Handcocks from Somerset House, but that society of which she had read in novels during the day, and of which she had dreamed at night. Might it not yet be given to her to know clever people, nice people, bright people, people who were not heavy and fat like Mr Handcock, or sick and wearisome like her poor brother Walter, or vulgar and quarrelsome like her relatives in Gower Street? She reminded herself that she was the niece of one baronet, and the first-cousin once removed of another, that she had eight hundred a year, and liberty to do with it whatsoever she pleased; and she reminded herself, also, that she had higher tastes in the world than Mr Handcock. Therefore she wrote to him an answer, much longer than his letter, in which she explained to him that the more than ten years' interval which had elapsed since words of love had passed between them had – had – had – changed the nature of her regard. After much hesitation, that was the phrase which she used.

And she was right in her decision. Whether or no she was doomed to be disappointed in her aspirations, or to be partially disappointed and partially gratified, these pages are written to tell. But I think we may conclude that she would hardly have made herself happy by marrying Mr Handcock while such aspirations were strong upon her. There was nothing on her side in favour of such a marriage but a faint remembrance of auld lang syne.

She remained three months in Arundel Street, and before that period was over she made a proposition to her brother Tom, showing to what extent she was willing to burden herself on behalf of his family. Would he allow her, she asked, to undertake the education and charge of his second daughter, Susanna? She would not offer to adopt her niece, she said, because it was on the cards that she herself might marry; but she would promise to take upon herself the full expense of the girl's education, and all charge of her till such education should be completed. If then any future guardianship on her part should have become incompatible with her own circumstances, she should give Susanna five hundred pounds. There was an air of business about this which quite startled Tom Mackenzie, who, as has before been said, had taught himself in old days to regard his sister as a poor creature. There was specially an air of business about her allusion to her own future state. Tom was not at all surprised that his sister should think of marrying, but he was much surprised that she should dare to declare her thoughts. 'Of course she will marry the first fool that asks her,' said Mrs Tom. The father of the large family, however, pronounced the offer to be too good to be refused. 'If she does, she will keep her word about the five hundred pounds,' he said. Mrs Tom, though she demurred, of course gave way; and when Margaret Mackenzie left London for Littlebath, where lodgings had been taken for her, she took her niece Susanna with her.

✂ TWO ✂

Miss Mackenzie goes to Littlebath

I FEAR THAT MISS MACKENZIE, WHEN SHE betook herself to Littlebath, had before her mind's eye no sufficiently settled plan of life. She wished to live pleasantly, and perhaps fashionably; but she also desired to live respectably, and with a due regard to religion. How she was to set about doing this at Littlebath, I am afraid she did not quite know. She told herself over and over again that wealth entailed duties as well as privileges; but she had no clear idea what were the duties so entailed, or what were the privileges. How could she have obtained any clear idea on the subject in that prison which she had inhabited for so many years by her brother's bedside?

She had indeed been induced to migrate from London to Littlebath by an accident which should not have been allowed to actuate her. She had been ill, and the doctor, with that solicitude which doctors sometimes feel for ladies who are well to do in the world, had recommended change of air. Littlebath, among the Tantivy hills, would be the very place for her. There were waters at Littlebath which she might drink for a month or two with great advantage to her system. It was then the end of July, and everybody that was anybody was going out of town. Suppose she were to go to Littlebath in August, and stay there for a month, or perhaps two months, as she might feel inclined. The London doctor knew a Littlebath doctor, and would be so happy to give her a letter. Then she spoke to the clergyman of the church she had lately attended in London who also had become more energetic in his assistance since her brother's death than he had been before, and he also could give her a letter to a gentleman of his cloth at Littlebath. She knew very little in private life of the doctor or of the clergyman in London, but not the less, on that account, might their introductions be of service to her in forming a circle of acquaintance at Littlebath. In this way she first came to think of Littlebath, and from this beginning she had gradually reached her decision.

Another little accident, or two other little accidents, had nearly induced her to remain in London – not in Arundel Street, which was to her an odious locality, but in some small genteel house in or about Brompton. She had written to the two baronets to announce to them her brother's death, Tom Mackenzie, the surviving brother, having positively refused to hold any communication with either of them. To both these letters, after some interval, she received courteous replies. Sir Walter Mackenzie was a very old man, over eighty, who now never stirred away from Incharrow, in Ross-shire. Lady Mackenzie was not living. Sir Walter did not write himself, but a letter came from Mrs Mackenzie, his eldest son's wife, in which she said that she and her husband would be up in London in the course of the next spring, and hoped that they might then have the pleasure of making their cousin's acquaintance. This letter, it was true, did not come till the beginning of August, when the Littlebath plan was nearly formed; and Margaret knew that her cousin, who was in Parliament, had himself been in London almost up to the time at which it was written, so that he might have called had he chosen. But she was prepared to forgive much. There had been cause for offence; and if her great relatives were now prepared to take her by the hand, there could be no reason why she should not consent to be so taken. Sir John Ball, the other baronet, had absolutely come to her, and had seen her. There had been a regular scene of reconciliation, and she had gone down for a day and night to the Cedars. Sir John also was an old man, being over seventy, and Lady Ball was nearly as old. Mr Ball, the future baronet, had also been there. He was a widower, with a large family and small means. He had been, and of course still was, a barrister; but as a barrister he had never succeeded, and was now waiting sadly till he should inherit the very moderate fortune which would come to him at his father's death. The Balls, indeed, had not done well with their baronetcy, and their cousin found them living with a degree of strictness, as to small expenses, which she herself had never been called upon to exercise. Lady Ball indeed had a carriage – for what would a baronet's wife do without one? – but it did not very often go out. And the Cedars was an old place, with grounds and paddocks appertaining; but the ancient solitary gardener could not make much of the grounds, and the grass of the paddocks was always sold. Margaret, when she was first asked to go to the Cedars, felt that it would be better for her to give up her migration to Littlebath. It would be much, she thought, to have her relations near to her. But she had found Sir John and Lady Ball to be very dull, and her cousin, the father of the large family, had spoken to her about little except money. She was not much in love with the Balls when she returned to London, and the Littlebath plan was allowed to go on.

She made a preliminary journey to that place, and took furnished lodgings in the Paragon. Now it is known to all the world that the Paragon is the nucleus of all that is pleasant and fashionable at Littlebath. It is a long row of houses with two short rows abutting from the ends of the long row, and every house in it looks out upon the Montpelier Gardens. If not built of stone, these houses are built of such stucco that the Margaret Mackenzies of the world do not know the difference. Six steps, which are of undoubted stone, lead up to each door. The areas are grand with high railings. The flagged way before the houses is very broad, and at each corner there is an extensive sweep, so that the carriages of the Paragonites may be made to turn easily. Miss Mackenzie's heart sank a little within her at the sight of all this grandeur, when she was first taken to the Paragon by her new friend the doctor. But she bade her heart be of good courage, and looked at the first floor – divided into dining-room and drawing-room – at the large bedroom upstairs for herself, and two small rooms for her niece and her maid-servant – at the kitchen in which she was to have a partial property, and did not faint at the splendour. And yet how different it was from those dingy rooms in Arundel Street! So different that she could hardly bring herself to think that this bright abode could become her own.

'And what is the price, Mrs Richards?' Her voice almost did fail her as she asked this question. She was determined to be liberal; but money of her own had hitherto been so scarce with her that she still dreaded the idea of expense.

'The price, mem, is well beknown to all as knows Littlebath. We never alters. Ask Dr Pottinger else.'

Miss Mackenzie did not at all wish to ask Dr Pottinger, who was at this moment standing in the front room, while she and her embryo landlady were settling affairs in the back room.

'But what is the price, Mrs Richards?'

'The price, mem, is two pound ten a week, or nine guineas if taken by the month – to include the kitchen fire.'

Margaret breathed again. She had made her little calculations over and over again, and was prepared to bid as high as the sum now named for such a combination of comfort and splendour as Mrs Richards was able to offer to her. One little question she asked, putting her lips close to Mrs Richards' ear so that her friend the doctor should not hear her through the doorway, and then jumped back a yard and a half, awe-struck by the energy of her landlady's reply.

'B—— in the Paragon!' Mrs Richards declared that Miss Mackenzie did not as yet know Littlebath. She bethought herself that she did know Arundel Street, and again thanked Fortune for all the good things that had been given to her.

Miss Mackenzie feared to ask any further questions after this, and took the rooms out of hand by the month.

'And very comfortable you'll find yourself,' said Dr Pottinger, as he walked back with his new friend to the inn. He had perhaps been a little disappointed when he saw that Miss Mackenzie showed every sign of good health; but he bore it like a man and a Christian, remembering, no doubt, that let a lady's health be ever so good, she likes to see a doctor sometimes, especially if she be alone in the world. He offered her, therefore, every assistance in his power.

'The assembly rooms were quite close to the Paragon,' he said.

'Oh, indeed!' said Miss Mackenzie, not quite knowing the purport of assembly rooms.

'And there are two or three churches within five minutes' walk.' Here Miss Mackenzie was more at home, and mentioned the name of the Rev. Mr Stumfold, for whom she had a letter of introduction, and whose church she would like to attend.

Now Mr Stumfold was a shining light at Littlebath, the man of men, if he was not something more than mere man, in the eyes of the devout inhabitants of that town. Miss Mackenzie had never heard of Mr Stumfold till her clergyman in London had mentioned his name, and even now had no idea that he was remarkable for any special views in Church matters. Such special views of her own she had none. But Mr Stumfold at Littlebath had very special views, and was very specially known for them. His friends said that he was evangelical, and his enemies said that he was Low Church. He himself was wont to laugh at these names – for he was a man who could laugh – and to declare that his only ambition was to fight the devil under whatever name he might be allowed to carry on that battle. And he was always fighting the devil by opposing those pursuits which are the life and mainstay of such places as Littlebath. His chief enemies were card-playing and dancing as regarded the weaker sex, and hunting and horse-racing – to which, indeed, might be added everything under the name of sport – as regarded the stronger. Sunday comforts were also enemies which he hated with a vigorous hatred, unless three full services a day, with sundry intermediate religious readings and exercitations of the spirit, may be called Sunday comforts. But not on this account should it be supposed that Mr Stumfold was a dreary, dark, sardonic man. Such was by no means the case. He could laugh loud. He could be very jovial at dinner parties. He could make his little jokes about little pet wickednesses. A glass of wine, in season, he never refused. Picnics he allowed, and the flirtation accompanying them. He himself was driven about behind a pair of horses, and his daughters were horsewomen. His sons, if the world spoke truth, were Nimrods; but that was in another county, away from the Tantivy hills, and Mr Stumfold knew nothing of it. In Littlebath Mr Stumfold reigned over his own set as a tyrant, but to those who obeyed him he was never austere in his tyranny.

When Miss Mackenzie mentioned Mr Stumfold's name to the doctor, the doctor felt that he had been wrong in his allusion to the assembly rooms. Mr Stumfold's people never went to assembly rooms. He, a doctor of medicine, of course went among saints and sinners alike, but in such a place as Littlebath he had found it expedient to have one tone for the saints and another for the sinners. Now the Paragon was generally inhabited by sinners, and therefore he had made his hint about the assembly rooms. He at once pointed out Mr Stumfold's church, the spire of which was to be seen as they walked towards the inn, and said a word in praise of that good man. Not a syllable would he again have uttered as to the wickednesses of the place, had not Miss Mackenzie asked some questions as to those assembly rooms.

'How did people get to belong to them? Were they pleasant? What did they do there? Oh – she could put her name down, could she? If it was anything in the way of amusement she would certainly like to put her name down.' Dr Pottinger, when on that afternoon he instructed his wife to call on Miss Mackenzie as soon as that young lady should be settled, explained that the stranger was very much in the dark as to the ways and manners of Littlebath.

'What! go to the assembly rooms, and sit under Mr Stumfold!' said Mrs Pottinger. 'She never can do both, you know.'

Miss Mackenzie went back to London, and returned at the end of a week with her niece, her new maid, and her boxes. All the old furniture had been sold, and her personal belongings were very scanty. The time had now come in which personal belongings would accrue to her, but when she reached the Paragon one big trunk and one small trunk contained all that she possessed. The luggage of her niece Susanna was almost as copious as her own. Her maid had been newly hired, and she was almost ashamed of the scantiness of her own possessions in the eyes of her servant.

The way in which Susanna had been given up to her had been oppressive, and at one moment almost distressing. That objection which each lady had to visit the other – Miss Mackenzie, that is, and Susanna's mamma – had never been overcome, and neither side had given way. No visit of affection or of friendship had been made. But as it was needful that the transfer of the young lady should be effected with some solemnity, Mrs Mackenzie had condescended to bring her to her future guardian's lodgings on the day before that fixed for the journey to Littlebath. To so much degradation – for in her eyes it was degradation – Mrs Mackenzie had consented to subject herself; and Mr Mackenzie was to come on the following morning, and take his sister and daughter to the train.

The mother, as soon as she found herself seated and almost before she had recovered the breath lost in mounting the lodging-house stairs, began the speech which she had prepared for delivery on the occasion. Miss Mackenzie, who had taken Susanna's hand, remained with it in her own during the greater part of the speech. Before the speech was done the poor girl's hand had been dropped, but in dropping it the aunt was not guilty of any unkindness. ' Margaret,' said Mrs Mackenzie, 'this is a trial, a very great trial to a mother, and I hope that you feel it as I do.'

'Sarah,' said Miss Mackenzie, 'I will do my duty by your child.'

'Well; yes; I hope so. If I thought you would not do your duty by her, no consideration of mere money would induce me to let her go to you. But I do hope, Margaret, you will think of the greatness of the sacrifice we are making. There never was a better child than Susanna.'

'I am very glad of that, Sarah.'

'Indeed, there never was a better child than any of 'em; I will say that for them before the child herself; and if you do your duty by her, I'm quite sure she'll do hers by you. Tom thinks it best that she should go; and, of course, as all the money which should have gone to him has come to you' – it was here, at this point that Susanna's hand was dropped – 'and as you haven't got a chick nor a child, nor yet anybody else of your own, no doubt it is natural that you should wish to have one of them.'

'I wish to do a kindness to my brother,' said Miss Mackenzie – ' and to my niece.'

'Yes; of course; I understand. When you would not come up to see us, Margaret, and you all alone, and we with a comfortable home to offer you, of course I knew what your feelings were towards me. I don't want anybody to tell me that! Oh dear, no! "Tom," said I when he asked me to go down to Arundel Street, "not if I know it." Those were the very words I uttered: "Not if I know it, Tom!" And your papa never asked me to go again – did he, Susanna? Nor I couldn't have brought myself to. As you are so frank, Margaret, perhaps candour is the best on both sides. Now I am going to leave my darling child in your hands, and if you have got a mother's heart within your bosom, I hope you will do a mother's duty by her.'

More than once during this oration Miss Mackenzie had felt inclined to speak her mind out, and to fight her own battle; but she was repressed by the presence of the girl. What chance could there be of good feeling, of aught of affection between her and her ward, if on such an occasion as this the girl were made the witness of a quarrel between her mother and her aunt? Miss Mackenzie's face had become red, and she had felt herself to be angry; but she bore it all with good courage.

'I will do my best,' said she. 'Susanna, come here and kiss me. Shall we be great friends?' Susanna went and kissed her; but if the poor girl attempted any answer it was not audible. Then the mother threw herself on the daughter's neck, and the two embraced each other with many tears.

'You'll find all her things very tidy, and plenty of 'em,' said Mrs Mackenzie through her tears. 'I'm sure we've worked hard enough at 'em for the last three weeks.'

'I've no doubt we shall find it all very nice,' said the aunt.

'We wouldn't send her away to disgrace us, were it ever so; though of course in the way of money it would make no difference to you if she had come without a thing to her back. But I've that spirit I couldn't do it, and so I told Tom.' After this Mrs Mackenzie once more embraced her daughter, and then took her departure.

Miss Mackenzie, as soon as her sister-in-law was gone, again took the girl's hand in her own. Poor Susanna was in tears, and indeed there was enough in her circumstances at the present moment to justify her in weeping. She had been given over to her new destiny in no joyous manner.

'Susanna,' said Aunt Margaret, with her softest voice, 'I'm so glad you have come to me. I will love you very dearly if you will let me.'

The girl came and clustered close against her as she sat on the sofa, and so contrived as to creep in under her arm. No one had ever crept in under her arm, or clung close to her before. Such outward signs of affection as that had never been hers, either to give or to receive.

'My darling,' she said, 'I will love you so dearly.'

Susanna said nothing, not knowing what words would be fitting for such an occasion, but on hearing her aunt's assurance of affection, she clung still closer to her, and in this way they became happy before the evening was over.

This adopted niece was no child when she was thus placed under her aunt's charge. She was already fifteen, and though she was young-looking for her age – having none of that precocious air of womanhood which some girls have assumed by that time – she was a strong healthy well-grown lass, standing stoutly on her legs, with her head well balanced, with a straight back, and well-formed though not slender waist. She was sharp about the shoulders and elbows, as girls are – or should be – at that age; and her face was not formed into any definite shape of beauty, or its reverse. But her eyes were bright – as were those of all the Mackenzies – and her mouth was not the mouth of a fool. If her cheek-bones were a little high, and the lower part of her face somewhat angular, those peculiarities were probably not distasteful to the eyes of her aunt.

'You're a Mackenzie all over,' said the aunt, speaking with some little touch of the northern burr in her voice, though she herself had never known anything of the north.

'That's what mamma's brothers and sisters always tell me. They say I am Scotchy.'

Then Miss Mackenzie kissed the girl again. If Susanna had been sent to her because she had in her gait and appearance more of the land of cakes than any of her brothers and sisters, that at any rate should do her no harm in the estimation of her aunt. Thus in this way they became friends.

On the following morning Mr Mackenzie came and took them down to the train.

'I suppose we shall see you sometimes up in London?' he said, as he stood by the door of the carriage.

'I don't know that there will be much to bring me up,' she answered.

'And there won't be much to keep you down in the country,' said he. 'You don't know anybody at Littlebath, I believe?'

'The truth is, Tom, that I don't know anybody anywhere. I'm likely to know as many people at Littlebath as I should in London. But situated as I am, I must live pretty much to myself wherever I am.'

Then the guard came bustling along the platform, the father kissed his daughter for the last time, and kissed his sister also, and our heroine with her young charge had taken her departure, and commenced her career in the world.

For many a mile not a word was spoken between Miss Mackenzie and her niece. The mind of the elder of the two travellers was very full of thought – of thought and of feeling too, so that she could not bring herself to speak joyously to the young girl. She had her doubts as to the wisdom of what she was doing. Her whole life, hitherto, had been sad, sombre, and, we may almost say, silent. Things had so gone with her that she had had no power of action on her own behalf. Neither with her father, nor with her brother, though both had been invalids, had anything of the management of affairs fallen into her hands. Not even in the hiring or discharging of a cookmaid had she possessed any influence. No power of the purse had been with her – none of that power which belongs legitimately to a wife because a wife is a partner in the business. The two sick men whom she had nursed had liked to retain in their own hands the little privileges which their position had given them. Margaret, therefore, had been a nurse in their houses, and nothing more than a nurse. Had this gone on for another ten years she would have lived down the ambition of any more exciting career, and would have been satisfied, had she then come into the possession of the money which was now hers, to have ended her days nursing herself – or more probably, as she was by nature unselfish, she would have lived down her pride as well as her ambition, and would have gone to the house of her brother and have expended herself in nursing her nephews and nieces. But luckily for her – or unluckily, as it may be – this money had come to her before her time for withering had arrived. In heart, and energy, and desire, there was still much of strength left to her. Indeed it may be said of her, that she had come so late in life to whatever of ripeness was to be vouchsafed to her, that perhaps the period of her thraldom had not terminated itself a day too soon for her advantage. Many of her youthful verses she had destroyed in the packing up of those two modest trunks; but there were effusions of the spirit which had flown into rhyme within the last twelve months, and which she still preserved. Since her brother's death she had confined herself to simple prose, and for this purpose she kept an ample journal. All this is mentioned to show that at the age of thirty-six Margaret Mackenzie was still a young woman.

She had resolved that she would not content herself with a lifeless life, such as those few who knew anything of her evidently expected from her. Harry Handcock had thought to make her his head nurse; and the Tom Mackenzies had also indulged some such idea when they gave her that first invitation to come and live in Gower Street. A word or two had been said at the Cedars which led her to suppose that the baronet's family there would have admitted her, with her eight hundred a year, had she chosen to be so admitted. But she had declared to herself that she would make a struggle to do better with herself and with her money than that. She would go into the world, and see if she could find any of those pleasantnesses of which she had read in books. As for dancing, she was too old, and never yet in her life had she stood up as a worshipper of Terpsichore. Of cards she knew nothing; she had never even seen them used. To the performance of plays she had been once or twice in her early days, and now regarded a theatre not as a sink of wickedness after the manner of the Stumfoldians, but as a place of danger because of difficulty of ingress and egress, because the ways of a theatre were far beyond her ken. The very mode in which it would behove her to dress herself to go out to an ordinary dinner party, was almost unknown to her. And yet, in spite of all this, she was resolved to try.

Would it not have been easier for her – easier and more comfortable – to have abandoned all ideas of the world, and have put herself at once under the tutelage and protection of some clergyman who would have told her how to give away her money, and prepare herself in the right way for a comfortable death-bed? There was much in this view of life to recommend it. It would be very easy, and she had the necessary faith. Such a clergyman, too, would be a comfortable friend, and, if a married man, might be a very dear friend. And there might, probably, be a clergyman's wife, who would go about with her, and assist in that giving away of her money. Would not this be the best life after all? But in order to reconcile herself altogether to such a life as that, it was necessary that she should be convinced that the other life was abominable, wicked, and damnable. She had seen enough of things – had looked far enough into the ways of the world – to perceive this. She knew that she must go about such work with strong convictions, and as yet she could not bring herself to think that 'dancing and delights' were damnable. No doubt she would come to have such belief if told so often enough by some persuasive divine; but she was not sure that she wished to believe it.

After doubting much, she had determined to give the world a trial, and, feeling that London was too big for her, had resolved upon Littlebath. But now, having started herself upon her journey, she felt as some mariner might who had put himself out alone to sea in a small boat, with courage enough for the attempt, but without that sort of courage which would make the attempt itself delightful.

And then this girl that was with her! She had told herself that it would not be well to live for herself alone, that it was her duty to share her good things with some one, and therefore she had resolved to share them with her niece. But in this guardianship there was danger, which frightened her as she thought of it.

'Are you tired yet, my dear?' said Miss Mackenzie, as they got to Swindon.

'Oh dear, no; I'm not at all tired.'

'There are cakes in there, I see. I wonder whether we should have time to buy one.'

After considering the matter for five minutes in doubt, Aunt Margaret did rush out, and did buy the cakes.

❧ THREE ❧

Miss Mackenzie's First Acquaintances

IN THE FIRST FORTNIGHT OF MISS MACKENZIE'S sojourn at Littlebath, four persons called upon her; but though this was a success as far as it went, those fourteen days were very dull. During her former short visit to the place she had arranged to send her niece to a day school which had been recommended to her as being very genteel, and conducted under moral and religious auspices of most exalted character. Hither Susanna went every morning after breakfast, and returned home in these summer days at eight o'clock in the evening. On Sundays also, she went to morning church with the other girls; so that Miss Mackenzie was left very much to herself.

Mrs Pottinger was the first to call, and the doctor's wife contented herself with simple offers of general assistance. She named a baker to Miss Mackenzie, and a dressmaker; and she told her what was the proper price to be paid by the hour for a private brougham or for a public fly. All this was useful, as Miss Mackenzie was in a state of densest ignorance; but it did not seem that much in the way of amusement would come from the acquaintance of Mrs Pottinger. That lady said nothing about the assembly rooms, nor did she speak of the Stumfoldian manner of life. Her husband had no doubt explained to her that the stranger was not as yet a declared disciple in either school. Miss Mackenzie had wished to ask a question about the assemblies, but had been deterred by fear. Then came Mr Stumfold in person, and, of course, nothing about the assembly rooms was said by him. He made himself very pleasant, and Miss Mackenzie almost resolved to put herself into his hands. He did not look sour at her, nor did he browbeat her with severe words, nor did he exact from her the performance of any hard duties. He promised to find her a seat in his church, and told her what were the hours of service. He had three 'Sabbath services', but he thought that regular attendance twice every Sunday was enough for people in general. He would be delighted to be of use, and Mrs Stumfold should come and call. Having promised this, he went his way. Then came Mrs Stumfold, according to promise, bringing with her one Miss Baker, a maiden lady. From Mrs Stumfold our friend got very little assistance. Mrs Stumfold was hard, severe, and perhaps a little grand. She let fall a word or two which intimated her conviction that Miss Mackenzie was to become at all points a Stumfoldian, since she had herself invoked the countenance and assistance of the great man on her first arrival; but beyond this, Mrs Stumfold afforded no comfort. Our friend could not have explained to herself why it was so, but after having encountered Mrs Stumfold, she was less inclined to become a disciple than she had been when she had seen only the great master himself. It was not only that Mrs Stumfold, as judged by externals, was felt to be more severe than her husband evangelically, but she was more severe also ecclesiastically. Miss Mackenzie thought that she could probably obey the ecclesiastical man, but that she would certainly rebel against the ecclesiastical woman.

There had been, as I have said, a Miss Baker with the female minister, and Miss Mackenzie had at once perceived that had Miss Baker called alone, the whole thing would have been much more pleasant. Miss Baker had a soft voice, was given to a good deal of gentle talking, was kind in her manner, and prone to quick intimacies with other ladies of her own nature. All this Miss Mackenzie felt rather than saw, and would have been delighted to have had Miss Baker without Mrs Stumfold. She could, she knew, have found out all about everything in five minutes, had she and Miss Baker been able to sit close together and to let their tongues loose. But Miss Baker, poor soul, was in these days thoroughly subject to the female Stumfold influence, and went about the world of Littlebath in a repressed manner that was truly pitiable to those who had known her before the days of her slavery.

But, as she rose to leave the room at her tyrant's bidding, she spoke a word of comfort. 'A friend of mine, Miss Mackenzie, lives next door to you, and she has begged me to say that she will do herself the pleasure of calling on you, if you will allow her.'

The poor woman hesitated as she made her little speech, and once cast her eye round in fear upon her companion.

'I'm sure I shall be delighted,' said Miss Mackenzie.

'That's Miss Todd, is it?' said Mrs Stumfold; and it was made manifest by Mrs Stumfold's voice that Mrs Stumfold did not think much of Miss Todd.

'Yes; Miss Todd. You see she is so close a neighbour,' said Miss Baker, apologetically.

Mrs Stumfold shook her head, and then went away without further speech.

Miss Mackenzie became at once impatient for Miss Todd's arrival, and was induced to keep an eye restlessly at watch on the two neighbouring doors in the Paragon, in order that she might see Miss Todd at the moment of some entrance or exit. Twice she did see a lady come out from the house next her own on the right, a stout jolly-looking dame, with a red face and a capacious bonnet, who closed the door behind her with a slam, and looked as though she would care little for either male Stumfold or female. Miss Mackenzie, however, made up her mind that this was not Miss Todd. This lady, she thought, was a married lady; on one occasion there had been children with her, and she was, in Miss Mackenzie's judgment, too stout, too decided, and perhaps too loud to be a spinster. A full week passed by before this question was decided by the promised visit – a week during which the new comer never left her house at any hour at which callers could be expected to call, so anxious was she to become acquainted with her neighbour; and she had almost given the matter up in despair, thinking that Mrs Stumfold had interfered with her tyranny, when, one day immediately after lunch – in these days Miss Mackenzie always lunched, but seldom dined – when one day immediately after lunch, Miss Todd was announced.

Miss Mackenzie immediately saw that she had been wrong. Miss Todd was the stout, red-faced lady with the children. Two of the children, girls of eleven and thirteen, were with her now. As Miss Todd walked across the room to shake hands with her new acquaintance, Miss Mackenzie at once recognised the manner in which the street door had been slammed, and knew that it was the same firm step which she had heard on the pavement half down the Paragon.

'My friend, Miss Baker, told me you had come to live next door to me,' began Miss Todd, 'and therefore I told her to tell you that I should come and see you. Single ladies, when they come here, generally like some one to come to them. I'm single myself, and these are my nieces. You've got a niece, I believe, too. When the Popes have nephews, people say all manner of ill-natured things. I hope they ain't so uncivil to us.'

Miss Mackenzie smirked and smiled, and assured Miss Todd that she was very glad to see her. The allusion to the Popes she did not understand.

'Miss Baker came with Mrs Stumfold, didn't she?' continued Miss Todd. 'She doesn't go much anywhere now without Mrs Stumfold, unless when she creeps down to me. She and I are very old friends. Have you known Mr Stumfold long? Perhaps you have come here to be near him; a great many ladies do,'

In answer to this, Miss Mackenzie explained that she was not a follower of Mr Stumfold in that sense. It was true that she had brought a letter to him, and intended to go to his church. In consequence of that letter, Mrs Stumfold had been good enough to call upon her.

'Oh yes: she'll come to you quick enough. Did she come with her carriage and horses?'

'I think she was on foot,' said Miss Mackenzie.

'Then I should tell her of it. Coming to you, in the best house in the Paragon, on your first arrival, she ought to have come with her carriage and horses.'

'Tell her of it!' said Miss Mackenzie.

'A great many ladies would, and would go over to the enemy before the month was over, unless she brought the carriage in the meantime. I don't advise you to do so. You haven't got standing enough in the place yet, and perhaps she could put you down.'

'But it makes no difference to me how she comes.'

'None in the least, my dear, or to me either. I should be glad to see her even in a wheelbarrow for my part. But you mustn't suppose that she ever comes to me. Lord bless you! no. She found me out to be past all grace ever so many years ago.'

'Mrs Stumfold thinks that Aunt Sally is the old gentleman himself,' said the elder of the girls.

'Ha, ha, ha,' laughed the aunt. 'You see, Miss Mackenzie, we run very much into parties here, as they do in most places of this kind, and if you mean to go thoroughly in with the Stumfold party you must tell me so, candidly, and there won't be any bones broken between us. I shan't like you the less for saying so: only in that case it won't be any use our trying to see much of each other.'

Miss Mackenzie was somewhat frightened, and hardly knew what answer to make. She was very anxious to have it understood that she was not, as yet, in bond under Mrs Stumfold – that it was still a matter of choice to herself whether she would be a saint or a sinner; and she would have been so glad to hint to her neighbour that she would like to try the sinner's line, if it were only for a month or two; only Miss Todd frightened her! And when the girl told her that Miss Todd was regarded, ex parte Stumfold, as being the old gentleman himself, Miss Mackenzie again thought for an instant that there would be safety in giving way to the evangelico-ecclesiastical influence, and that perhaps life might be pleasant enough to her if she could be allowed to go about in couples with that soft Miss Baker.

'As you have been so good as to call,' said Miss Mackenzie, 'I hope you will allow me to return your visit.'

'Oh, dear, yes – shall be quite delighted to see you. You can't hurt me, you know. The question is, whether I shan't ruin you. Not that I and Mr Stumfold ain't great cronies. He and I meet about on neutral ground, and are the best friends in the world. He knows I'm a lost sheep – a gone 'coon, as the Americans say – so he pokes his fun at me, and we're as jolly as sandboys. But St Stumfolda is made of sterner metal, and will not put up with any such female levity. If she pokes her fun at any sinners, it is at gentlemen sinners; and grim work it must be for them, I should think. Poor Mary Baker! the best creature in the world. I'm afraid she has a bad time of it. But then, you know, perhaps that is the sort of thing you like.'

'You see I know so very little of Mrs Stumfold,' said Miss Mackenzie.

'That's a misfortune will soon be cured if you let her have her own way. You ask Mary Baker else. But I don't mean to be saying anything bad behind anybody's back; I don't indeed. I have no doubt these people are very good in their way; only their ways are not my ways; and one doesn't like to be told so often that one's own way is broad, and that it leads – you know where. Come, Patty, let us be going. When you've made up your mind, Miss Mackenzie, just you tell me. If you say, "Miss Todd, I think you're too wicked for me," I shall understand it. I shan't be in the least offended. But if my way isn't – isn't too broad, you know, I shall be very happy to see you.'

Hereupon Miss Mackenzie plucked up courage and asked a question.

'Do you ever go to the assembly rooms, Miss Todd?'

Miss Todd almost whistled before she gave her answer. 'Why, Miss Mackenzie, that's where they dance and play cards, and where the girls flirt and the young men make fools of themselves. I don't go there very often myself, because I don't care about flirting, and I'm too old for dancing. As for cards, I get plenty of them at home. I think I did put down my name and paid something when I first came here, but that's ever so many years ago. I don't go to the assembly rooms now.'

As soon as Miss Todd was gone, Miss Mackenzie went to work to reflect seriously upon all she had just heard. Of course, there could be no longer any question of her going to the assembly rooms. Even Miss Todd, wicked as she was, did not go there. But should she, or should she not, return Miss Todd's visit? If she did she would be thereby committing herself to what Miss Todd had profanely called the broad way. In such case any advance in the Stumfold direction would be forbidden to her. But if she did not call on Miss Todd, then she would have plainly declared that she intended to be such another disciple as Miss Baker, and from that decision there would be no recall. On this subject she must make up her mind, and in doing so she laboured with all her power. As to any charge of incivility which might attach to her for not returning the visit of a lady who had been so civil to her, of that she thought nothing. Miss Todd had herself declared that she would not be in the least offended. But she liked this new acquaintance. In owning all the truth about Miss Mackenzie, I must confess that her mind hankered after the things of this world. She thought that if she could only establish herself as Miss Todd was established, she would care nothing for the Stumfolds, male or female.

But how was she to do this? An establishment in the Stumfold direction might be easier.

In the course of the next week two affairs of moment occurred to Miss Mackenzie. On the Wednesday morning she received from London a letter of business which caused her considerable anxiety, and on the Thursday afternoon a note was brought to her from Mrs Stumfold – or rather an envelope containing a card on which was printed an invitation to drink tea with that lady on that day week. This invitation she accepted without much doubt. She would go and see Mrs Stumfold in her house, and would then be better able to decide whether the mode of life practised by the Stumfold party would be to her taste. So she wrote a reply, and sent it by her maid-servant, greatly doubting whether she was not wrong in writing her answer on common note-paper, and whether she also should not have supplied herself with some form or card for the occasion.

The letter of business was from her brother Tom, and contained an application for the loan of some money – for the loan, indeed, of a good deal of money. But the loan was to be made not to him but to the firm of Rubb and Mackenzie, and was not to be a simple lending of money on the faith of that firm, for purposes of speculation or ordinary business. It was to be expended in the purchase of the premises in the New Road, and Miss Mackenzie was to have a mortgage on them, and was to receive five per cent for the money which she should advance. The letter was long, and though it was manifest even to Miss Mackenzie that he had written the first page with much hesitation, he had waxed strong as he had gone on, and had really made out a good case. 'You are to understand,' he said, 'that this is, of course, to be done through your own lawyer, who will not allow you to make the loan unless he is satisfied with the security. Our landlords are compelled to sell the premises, and unless we purchase them ourselves, we shall in all probability be turned out, as we have only a year or two more under our present lease. You could purchase the whole thing yourself, but in that case you would not be sure of the same interest for your money.' He then went on to say that Samuel Rubb, junior, the son of old Rubb, should run down to Littlebath in the course of next week, in order that the whole thing might be made clear to her. Samuel Rubb was not the partner whose name was included in the designation of the firm, but was a young man – 'a comparatively young man' – as her brother explained, who had lately been admitted to a share in the business.

This letter put Miss Mackenzie into a twitter. Like all other single ladies, she was very nervous about her money. She was quite alive to the beauty of a high rate of interest, but did not quite understand that high interest and impaired security should go hand in hand together. She wished to oblige her brother, and was aware that she had money as to which her lawyers were looking out for an investment. Even this had made her unhappy, as she was not quite sure whether her lawyers would not spend the money. She knew that lone women were terribly robbed sometimes, and had almost resolved upon insisting that the money should be put into the Three per Cents. But she had gone to work with figures, and having ascertained that by doing so twenty-five pounds a year would be docked off from her computed income, she had given no such order. She now again went to work with her figures, and found that if the loan were accomplished it would add twenty-five pounds a year to her computed income. Mortgages, she knew, were good things, strong and firm, based upon landed security, and very respectable. So she wrote to her lawyers, saying that she would be glad to oblige her brother if there were nothing amiss. Her lawyers wrote back, advising her to refer Mr Rubb, junior, to them. On the day named in her brother's letter, Mr Samuel Rubb, junior, arrived at Littlebath, and called upon Miss Mackenzie in the Paragon.

Miss Mackenzie had been brought up with contempt and almost with hatred for the Rubb family. It had, in the first instance, been the work of old Samuel Rubb to tempt her brother Tom into trade; and he had tempted Tom into a trade that had not been fat and prosperous, and therefore pardonable, but into a trade that had been troublesome and poor. Walter Mackenzie had always spoken of these Rubbs with thorough disgust, and had persistently refused to hold any intercourse with them. When, therefore, Mr Samuel Rubb was announced, our heroine was somewhat inclined to seat herself upon a high horse.

Mr Samuel Rubb, junior, came upstairs, and was by no means the sort of person in appearance that Miss Mackenzie had expected to see. In the first place, he was, as well as she could guess, about forty years of age; whereas she had expected to see a young man. A man who went about the world especially designated as junior, ought, she thought, to be very young. And then Mr Rubb carried with him an air of dignity, and had about his external presence a something of authority which made her at once seat herself a peg lower than she had intended. He was a good-looking man, nearly six feet high, with great hands and feet, but with a great forehead also, which atoned for his hands and feet. He was dressed throughout in black, as tradesmen always are in these days; but, as Miss Mackenzie said to herself, there was certainly no knowing that he belonged to the oilcloth business from the cut of his coat or the set of his trousers. He began his task with great care, and seemed to have none of the hesitation which had afflicted her brother in writing his letter. The investment, he said, would, no doubt, be a good one. Two thousand four hundred pounds was the sum wanted, and he understood that she had that amount lying idle. Their lawyer had already seen her lawyer, and there could be no doubt as to the soundness of the mortgage. An assurance company with whom the firm had dealings was quite ready to advance the money on the proposed security, and at the proposed rate of interest, but in such a matter as that, Rubb and Mackenzie did not wish to deal with an assurance company. They desired that all control over the premises should either be in their own hands, or in the hands of someone connected with them.

By the time that Mr Samuel Rubb had done, Miss Mackenzie found herself to have dismounted altogether from her horse, and to be pervaded by some slight fear that her lawyers might allow so favourable an opportunity for investing her money to slip through their hands.

Then, on a sudden, Mr Rubb dropped the subject of the loan, and Miss Mackenzie, as he did so, felt herself to be almost disappointed. And when she found him talking easily to her about matters of external life, although she answered him readily, and talked to him also easily, she entertained some feeling that she ought to be offended. Mr Rubb, junior, was a tradesman who had come to her on business, and having done his business, why did he not go away? Nevertheless, Miss Mackenzie answered him when he asked questions, and allowed herself to be seduced into a conversation.

'Yes, upon my honour,' he said, looking out of the window into the Montpelier Gardens, 'a very nice situation indeed. How much better they do these things in such a place as this than we do up in London! What dingy houses we live in, and how bright they make the places here!'

'They are not crowded so much, I suppose,' said Miss Mackenzie.

'It isn't only that. The truth is, that in London nobody cares what his house looks like. The whole thing is so ugly that anything not ugly would be out of place. Now, in Paris – you have been in Paris, Miss Mackenzie?'

In answer to this, Miss Mackenzie was compelled to own that she had never been in Paris.

'Ah, you should go to Paris, Miss Mackenzie; you should, indeed. Now, you're a lady that have nothing to prevent your going anywhere. If I were you, I'd go almost everywhere; but above all, I'd go to Paris. There's no place like Paris.'

'I suppose not,' said Miss Mackenzie.

By this time Mr Rubb had returned from the window, and had seated himself in the easy chair in the middle of the room. In doing so he thrust out both his legs, folded his hands one over the other, and looked very comfortable.

'Now I'm a slave to business,' he said. 'That horrid place in the New Road, which we want to buy with your money, has made a prisoner of me for the last twenty years. I went into it as the boy who was to do the copying, when your brother first became a partner. Oh dear, how I did hate it!'

'Did you now?'

'I should rather think I did. I had been brought up at the Merchant Taylors' and they intended to send me to Oxford. That was five years before they began the business in the New Road. Then came the crash which our house had at Manchester; and when we had picked up the pieces, we found that we had to give up university ideas. However, I'll make a business of it before I'm done; you see if I don't, Miss Mackenzie. Your brother has been with us so many years that I have quite a pleasure in talking to you about it.'

Miss Mackenzie was not quite sure that she reciprocated the pleasure; for, after all, though he did look so much better than she had expected, he was only Rubb, junior, from Rubb and Mackenzie's; and any permanent acquaintance with Mr Rubb would not suit the line of life in which she was desirous of moving. But she did not in the least know how to stop him, or how to show him that she had intended to receive him simply as a man of business. And then it was so seldom that anyone came to talk to her, that she was tempted to fall away from her high resolves. 'I have not known much of my brother's concerns,' she said, attempting to be cautious.

Then he sat for another hour, making himself very agreeable, and at the end of that time she offered him a glass of wine and a biscuit, which he accepted. He was going to remain two or three days in the neighbourhood, he said, and might he call again before he left? Miss Mackenzie told him that he might. How was it possible that she should answer such a question in any other way? Then he got up, and shook hands with her, told her that he was so glad he had come to Littlebath, and was quite cordial and friendly. Miss Mackenzie actually found herself laughing with him as they stood on the floor together, and though she knew that it was improper, she liked it. When he was gone she could not remember what it was that had made her laugh, but she remembered that she had laughed. For a long time past very little laughter had come to her share.

When he was gone she prepared herself to think about him at length. Why had he talked to her in that way? Why was he going to call again? Why was Rubb, junior, from Rubb and Mackenzie's, such a pleasant fellow? After all, he retailed oilcloth at so much a yard; and little as she knew of the world, she knew that she, with ever so much good blood in her veins, and with ever so many hundreds a year of her own, was entitled to look for acquaintances of a higher order than that. She, if she were entitled to make any boast about herself – and she was by no means inclined to such boastings – might at any rate boast that she was a lady. Now, Mr Rubb was not a gentleman. He was not a gentleman by position. She knew that well enough, and she thought that she had also discovered that he was not quite a gentleman in his manners and mode of speech. Nevertheless she had liked him, and had laughed with him, and the remembrance of this made her sad.

That same evening she wrote a letter to her lawyer, telling him that she was very anxious to oblige her brother, if the security was good. And then she went into the matter at length, repeating much of what Mr Rubb had said to her, as to the excellence of mortgages in general, and of this mortgage in particular. After that she dressed herself with great care, and went out to tea at Mrs Stumfold's. This was the first occasion in her life in which she had gone to a party, the invitation to which had come to her on a card, and of course she felt herself to be a little nervous.

✂ FOUR ✂

Miss Mackenzie Commences her Career

MISS MACKENZIE HAD BEEN THREE WEEKS AT Littlebath when the day arrived on which she was to go to Mrs Stumfold's party, and up to that time she had not enjoyed much of the society of that very social place. Indeed, in these pages have been described with accuracy all the advancement which she had made in that direction. She had indeed returned Miss Todd's call, but had not found that lady at home. In doing this she had almost felt herself to be guilty of treason against the new allegiance which she seemed to have taken upon herself in accepting Mrs Stumfold's invitation; and she had done it at last not from any firm resolve of which she might have been proud, but had been driven to it by ennui, and by the easy temptation of Miss Todd's neighbouring door. She had, therefore, slipped out, and finding her wicked friend to be not at home, had hurried back again. She had, however, committed herself to a card, and she knew that Mrs Stumfold would hear of it through Miss Baker. Miss Baker's visit she had not returned, being in doubt where Miss Baker lived, being terribly in doubt also whether the Median rules of fashion demanded of her that she should return the call of a lady who had simply come to her with another caller. Her hesitation on this subject had been much, and her vacillations many, but she had thought it safer to abstain. For the last day or two she had been expecting the return of Mr Rubb, junior – keeping herself a prisoner, I fear, during the best hours of the day, so that she might be there to receive him when he did come; but though she had so acted, she had quite resolved to be very cold with him, and very cautious, and had been desirous of seeing him solely with a view to the mercantile necessities of her position. It behoved her certainly to attend to business when business came in her way, and therefore she would take care to be at home when Mr Rubb should call.

She had been to church twice a day on each of the Sundays that she had passed in Littlebath, having in this matter strictly obeyed the hints which Mr Stumfold had given for her guidance. No doubt she had received benefit from the discourses which she had heard from that gentleman each morning; and, let us hope, benefit also from the much longer discourses which she had heard from Mr Stumfold's curate on each evening. The Rev. Mr Maguire was very powerful, but he was also very long; and Miss Mackenzie, who was hardly as yet entitled to rank herself among the thoroughly converted, was inclined to think that he was too long. She was, however, patient by nature, and willing to bear much, if only some little might come to her in return. What of social comfort she had expected to obtain from her churchgoings I cannot quite define; but I think that she had unconsciously expected something from them in that direction, and that she had been disappointed.

But now, at nine o'clock on this appointed evening, she was of a certainty and in very truth going into society. The card said half-past eight; but the Sun had not yoked his horses so far away from her Tyre, remote as that Tyre had been, as to have left her in ignorance that half-past eight meant nine. When her watch showed her that half-past eight had really come, she was fidgety, and rang the bell to inquire whether the man might have probably forgotten to send the fly; and yet she had been very careful to tell the man that she did not wish to be at Mrs Stumfold's before nine.

'He understands, Miss,' said the servant; 'don't you be afeard; he's a-doing of it every night.'

Then she became painfully conscious that even the maid-servant knew more of the social ways of the place than did she.

When she reached the top of Mrs Stumfold's stairs, her heart was in her mouth, for she perceived immediately that she had kept people waiting. After all, she had trusted to false intelligence in that matter of the hour. Half-past eight had meant half-past eight, and she ought to have known that this would be so in a house so upright as that of Mrs Stumfold. That lady met her at the door, and smiling – blandly, but, perhaps I might be permitted to say, not so blandly as she might have smiled – conducted the stranger to a seat.

'We generally open with a little prayer, and for that purpose our dear friends are kind enough to come to us punctually.'

Then Mr Stumfold got up, and pressed her hand very kindly.

'I'm so sorry,' Miss Mackenzie had uttered.

'Not in the least,' he replied. 'I knew you couldn't know, and therefore we ventured to wait a few minutes. The time hasn't been lost, as Mr Maguire has treated us to a theological argument of great weight.'

Then all the company laughed, and Miss Mackenzie perceived that Mr Stumfold could joke in his way. She was introduced to Mr Maguire, who also pressed her hand; and then Miss Baker came and sat by her side. There was, however, at that moment no time for conversation. The prayer was begun immediately, Mr Stumfold taking this duty himself. Then Mr Maguire read half a chapter in the Bible, and after that Mr Stumfold explained it. Two ladies asked Mr Stumfold questions with great pertinacity, and these questions Mr Stumfold answered very freely, walking about the room the while, and laughing often as he submitted himself to their interrogations. And Miss Mackenzie was much astonished at the special freedom of his manner – how he spoke of St Paul as Paul, declaring the saint to have been a good fellow; how he said he liked Luke better than Matthew, and how he named even a holier name than these with infinite ease and an accustomed familiarity which seemed to delight the other ladies; but which at first shocked her in her ignorance.

'But I'm not going to have anything more to say to Peter and Paul at present,' he declared at last. 'You'd keep me here all night, and the tea will be spoilt.'

Then they all laughed again at the absurd idea of this great and good man preferring his food – his food of this world – to that other food which it was his special business to dispense. There is nothing which the Stumfoldian ladies of Littlebath liked so much as these little jokes which bordered on the profanity of the outer world, which made them feel themselves to be almost as funny as the sinners, and gave them a slight taste, as it were, of the pleasures of iniquity.

'Wine maketh glad the heart of woman, Mrs Jones,' Mr Stumfold would say as he filled for the second time the glass of some old lady of his set; and the old lady would chirrup and wink, and feel that things were going almost as jollily with her as they did with that wicked Mrs Smith, who spent every night of her life playing cards, or as they had done with that horrid Mrs Brown, of whom such terrible things were occasionally whispered when two or three ladies found themselves sufficiently private to whisper them; that things were going almost as pleasant here in this world, although accompanied by so much safety as to the future in her own case, and so much danger in those other cases! I think it was this aptitude for feminine rakishness which, more than any of his great virtues, more even than his indomitable industry, made Mr Stumfold the most popular man in Littlebath. A dozen ladies on the present occasion skipped away to the tea-table in the back drawing-room with a delighted alacrity, which was all owing to the unceremonious treatment which St Peter and St Paul had received from their pastor.

Miss Mackenzie had just found time to cast an eye round the room and examine the scene of Mr Stumfold's pleasantries while Mr Maguire was reading. She saw that there were only three gentlemen there besides the two clergymen. There was a very old man who sat close wedged in between Mrs Stumfold and another lady, by whose joint dresses he was almost obliterated. This was Mr Peters, a retired attorney. He was Mrs Stumfold's father, and from his coffers had come the superfluities of comfort which Miss Mackenzie saw around her. Rumour, even among the saintly people of Littlebath, said that Mr Peters had been a sharp practitioner in his early days – that he had been successful in his labours was admitted by all.

'No doubt he has repented,' Miss Baker said one day to Miss Todd.

'And if he has not, he has forgotten all about it, which generally means the same thing,' Miss Todd had answered.

Mr Peters was now very old, and I am disposed to think he had forgotten all about it.

The other two gentlemen were both young, and they stood very high in the graces of all the company there assembled. They were high in the graces of Mr Stumfold, but higher still in the graces of Mrs Stumfold, and were almost worshipped by one or two other ladies whose powers of external adoration were not diminished by the possession of husbands. They were, both of them, young men who had settled themselves for a time at Littlebath that they might be near Mr Stumfold, and had sufficient of worldly wealth to enable them to pass their time in semi-clerical pursuits.

Mr Frigidy, the elder, intended at some time to go into the Church, but had not as yet made sufficient progress in his studies to justify him in hoping that he could pass a bishop's examination. His friends told him of Islington and St Bees, of Durham, Birkenhead, and other places where the thing could be done for him; but he hesitated, fearing whether he might be able to pass even the initiatory gates of Islington. He was a good young man, at peace with all the world – except Mr Startup. With Mr Startup the veracious chronicler does not dare to assert that Mr Frigidy was at peace. Now Mr Startup was the other young man whom Miss Mackenzie saw in that room.

Mr Startup was also a very good young man, but he was of a fiery calibre, whereas Frigidy was naturally mild. Startup was already an open-air preacher, whereas Frigidy lacked nerve to speak a word above his breath. Startup was not a clergyman because certain scruples impeded and prevented him, while in the bosom of Frigidy there existed no desire so strong as that of having the word reverend attached to his name. Startup, though he was younger than Frigidy, could talk to seven ladies at once with ease, but Frigidy could not talk to one without much assistance from that lady herself. The consequence of this was that Mr Frigidy could not bring himself to love Mr Startup – could not enable himself to justify a veracious chronicler in saying that he was at peace with all the world, Startup included.

The ladies were too many for Miss Mackenzie to notice them specially as she sat listening to Mr Maguire's impressive voice. Mr Maguire she did notice, and found him to be the possessor of a good figure, of a fine head of jet black hair, of a perfect set of white teeth, of whiskers which were also black and very fine, but streaked here and there with a grey hair – and of the most terrible squint in his right eye which ever disfigured a face that in all other respects was fitted for an Apollo. So egregious was the squint that Miss Mackenzie could not keep herself from regarding it, even while

411

Mr Stumfold was expounding. Had she looked Mr Maguire full in the face at the beginning, I do not think it would so much have mattered to her; but she had seen first the back of his head, and then his profile, and had unfortunately formed a strong opinion as to his almost perfect beauty. When, therefore, the defective eye was disclosed to her, her feelings were moved in a more than ordinary manner. How was it that a man graced with such a head, with such a mouth and chin and forehead, nay, with such a left eye, could be cursed with such a right eye! She was still thinking of this when the frisky movement into the tea-room took place around her.

When at this moment Mr Stumfold offered her his arm to conduct her through the folding doors, this condescension on his part almost confounded her. The other ladies knew that he always did so to a newcomer, and therefore thought less of it. No other gentleman took any other lady, but she was led up to a special seat – a seat of honour as it were, at the left hand side of a huge silver kettle. Immediately before the kettle sat Mrs Stumfold. Immediately before another kettle, at another table, sat Miss Peters, a sister of Mrs Stumfold's. The back drawing-room in which they were congregated was larger than the other, and opened behind into a pretty garden. Mr Stumfold's lines in falling thus among the Peters, had fallen to him in pleasant places. On the other side of Miss Mackenzie sat Miss Baker, and on the other side of Mrs Stumfold stood Mr Startup, talking aloud and administering the full tea-cups with a conscious grace. Mr Stumfold and Mr Frigidy were at the other table, and Mr Maguire was occupied in passing promiscuously from one to the other. Miss Mackenzie wished with all her heart that he would seat himself somewhere with his face turned away from her, for she found it impossible to avert her eyes from his eye. But he was always there, before her sight, and she began to feel that he was an evil spirit – her evil spirit, and that he would be too many for her.

Before anybody else was allowed to begin, Mrs Stumfold rose from her chair with a large and completely filled bowl of tea, with a plate also laden with buttered toast, and with her own hands and on her own legs carried these delicacies round to her papa. On such an occasion as this no servant, no friend, no Mr Startup, was allowed to interfere with her filial piety.

'She does it always,' said an admiring lady in an audible whisper from the other side of Miss Baker. 'She does it always.'

The admiring lady was the wife of a retired coachbuilder, who was painfully anxious to make her way into good evangelical society at Littlebath.

'Perhaps you will put in the sugar for yourself,' said Mrs Stumfold to Miss Mackenzie as soon as she returned. On this occasion Miss Mackenzie received her cup the first after the father of the house, but the words spoken to her were stern to the ear.

'Perhaps you will put in the sugar yourself. It lightens the labour.'

Miss Mackenzie expressed her willingness to do so and regretted that Mrs Stumfold should have to work so hard. Could she be of assistance?

'I'm quite used to it, thank you,' said Mrs Stumfold.

The words were not uncivil, but the tone was dreadfully severe, and Miss Mackenzie felt painfully sure that her hostess was already aware of the card that had been left at Miss Todd's door.

Mr Startup was now actively at work.

'Lady Griggs's and Miss Fleebody's – I know. A great deal of sugar for her ladyship, and Miss Fleebody eats muffin. Mrs Blow always takes pound-cake, and I'll see that there's one near her. Mortimer' – Mortimer was the footman – 'is getting more bread and butter. Maguire, you have two dishes of sweet biscuits over there; give us one here. Never mind me, Mrs Stumfold; I'll have my innings presently.'

All this Mr Frigidy heard with envious ears as he sat with his own tea-cup before him at the other table. He would have given the world to have been walking about the room like Startup, making himself useful and conspicuous; but he couldn't do it – he knew that he couldn't do it. Later in the evening, when he had been sitting by Miss Trotter for two hours – and he had very often sat by Miss Trotter before – he ventured upon a remark.

'Don't you think that Mr Startup makes himself a little forward?'

'Oh dear yes, very,' said Miss Trotter. 'I believe he's an excellent young man, but I always did think him forward, now you mention it. And sometimes I've wondered how dear Mrs Stumfold could like so much of it. But do you know, Mr Frigidy, I am not quite sure that somebody else does like it. You know who I mean.'

Miss Trotter said much more than this, and Mr Frigidy was comforted, and believed that he had been talking.

When Mrs Stumfold commenced her conversation with Mr Startup, Miss Baker addressed herself to Miss Mackenzie; but there was at first something of stiffness in her manner – as became a lady whose call had not been returned.

'I hope you like Littlebath,' said Miss Baker.

Miss Mackenzie, who began to be conscious that she had done wrong, hesitated as she replied that she liked it pretty well.

'I think you'll find it pleasant,' said Miss Baker; and then there was a pause. There could not be two women more fitted for friendship than were these, and it was much to be hoped, for the sake of our poor, solitary heroine especially, that this outside crust of manner might be broken up and dispersed.

'I dare say I shall find it pleasant, after a time,' said Miss Mackenzie. Then they applied themselves each to her own bread and butter.

'You have not seen Miss Todd, I suppose, since I saw you?' Miss Baker asked this question when she perceived that Mrs Stumfold was deep in some secret conference with Mr Startup. It must, however, be told to Miss Baker's credit, that she had persistently maintained her friendship with Miss Todd, in spite of all the Stumfoldian influences. Miss Mackenzie, at the moment less brave, looked round aghast, but seeing that her hostess was in deep conference with her prime minister, she took heart of grace. 'I called, and I did not see her.'

'She promised me she would call,' said Miss Baker.

'And I returned her visit, but she wasn't at home,' said Miss Mackenzie.

'Indeed,' said Miss Baker; and then there was silence between them again.

But, after a pause, Miss Mackenzie again took heart of grace. I do not think that there was, of nature, much of the coward about her. Indeed, the very fact that she was there alone at Littlebath, fighting her own battle with the world, instead of having allowed herself to be swallowed up by the Harry Handcocks, and Tom Mackenzies, proved her to be anything but a coward. 'Perhaps, Miss Baker, I ought to have returned your visit,' said she.

'That was just as you like,' said Miss Baker with her sweetest smile.

'Of course, I should have liked it, as I thought it so good of you to come. But as you came with Mrs Stumfold, I was not quite sure whether it might be intended; and then I didn't know – did not exactly know – where you lived.'

After this the two ladies got on very comfortably, so long as they were left sitting side by side. Miss Baker imparted to Miss Mackenzie her full address, and Miss Mackenzie, with that brightness in her eyes which they always assumed when she was eager, begged her new friend to come to her again.

'Indeed, I will,' said Miss Baker. After that they were parted by a general return to the front room.

And now Miss Mackenzie found herself seated next to Mr Maguire. She had been carried away in the crowd to a further corner, in which there were two chairs, and before she had been able to consider the merits or demerits of the position, Mr Maguire was seated close beside her. He was seated close beside her in such a way as to make the two specially separated from all the world beyond, for in front of them stood a wall of crinoline – a wall of crinoline divided between four or five owners, among whom was shared the eloquence of Mr Startup, who was carrying on an evangelical flirtation with the whole of them in a manner that was greatly pleasing to them, and enthusiastically delightful to him. Miss Mackenzie, when she found herself thus entrapped, looked into Mr Maguire's eye with dismay. Had that look been sure to bring down upon her the hatred of that reverend gentleman, she could not have helped it. The eye fascinated her, as much as it frightened her. But Mr Maguire was used to have his eye inspected, and did not hate her. He fixed it apparently on the corners of the wall, but in truth upon her, and then he began:

'I am so glad that you have come among us, Miss Mackenzie.'

'I'm sure that I'm very much obliged.'

'Well; you ought to be. You must not be surprised at my saying so, though it sounds uncivil. You ought to feel obliged, and the obligation should be mutual. I am not sure, that when all things are considered, you could find yourself in any better place in England, than in the drawing-room of my friend Stumfold; and, if you will allow me to say so, my friend Stumfold could hardly use his drawing-room better, than by entertaining you.'

'Mr Stumfold is very good, and so is she.'

'Mr Stumfold is very good; and as for Mrs Stumfold, I look upon her as a very wonderful woman – quite a wonderful woman. For grasp of intellect, for depth of thought, for tenderness of sentiment – perhaps you mightn't have expected that, but there it is – for tenderness of sentiment, for strength of faith, for purity of life, for genial hospitality, and all the domestic duties, Mrs Stumfold has no equal in Littlebath, and perhaps few superiors elsewhere.'

Here Mr Maguire paused, and Miss Mackenzie, finding herself obliged to speak, said that she did not at all doubt it.

'You need not doubt it, Miss Mackenzie. She is all that, I tell you; and more, too. Her manners may seem a little harsh to you at first. I know it is so sometimes with ladies before they know her well; but it is only skin-deep, Miss Mackenzie – only skin-deep. She is so much in earnest about her work, that she cannot bring herself to be light and playful as he is. Now, he is as full of play as a young lamb.'

'He seems to be very pleasant.'

'And he is always just the same. There are people, you know, who say that religion is austere and melancholy. They never could say that if they knew my friend Stumfold. His life is devoted to his clerical duties. I know no man who works harder in the vineyard than Stumfold. But he always works with a smile on his face. And why not, Miss Mackenzie? when you think of it, why not?'

'I dare say it's best not to be unhappy,' said Miss Mackenzie. She did not speak till she perceived that he had paused for her answer.

'Of course we know that this world can make no one happy. What are we that we should dare to be happy here?'

Again he paused, but Miss Mackenzie feeling that she had been ill-treated and trapped into a difficulty at her last reply, resolutely remained silent.

'I defy any man or woman to be happy here,' said Mr Maguire, looking at her with one eye and at the corner of the wall with the other in a manner that was very terrible to her. 'But we may be cheerful – we may go about our work singing psalms of praise instead of songs of sorrow. Don't you agree with me, Miss Mackenzie, that psalms of praise are better than songs of sorrow?'

'I don't sing at all, myself,' said Miss Mackenzie.

'You sing in your heart, my friend; I am sure you sing in your heart. Don't you sing in your heart?' Here again he paused.

'Well; perhaps in my heart, yes.'

'I know you do, loud psalms of praise upon a ten-stringed lute. But Stumfold is always singing aloud, and his lute has twenty strings.' Here the voice of the twenty-stringed singer was heard across the large room asking the company a riddle.

'Why was Peter in prison like a little boy with his shoes off?'

'That's so like him,' said Mr Maguire.

All the ladies in the room were in a fever of expectation, and Mr Stumfold asked the riddle again.

'He won't tell them till we meet again; but there isn't one here who won't study the life of St Peter during the next week. And what they'll learn in that way they'll never forget.'

'But why was he like a little boy with his shoes off?' asked Miss Mackenzie.

'Ah! that's Stumfold's riddle. You must ask Mr Stumfold, and he won't tell you till next week. But some of the ladies will be sure to find it out before then. Have you come to settle yourself altogether at Littlebath, Miss Mackenzie?'

This question he asked very abruptly, but he had a way of looking at her when he asked a question, which made it impossible for her to avoid an answer.

'I suppose I shall stay here for some considerable time.'

'Do, do,' said he with energy. 'Do; come and live among us, and be one of us; come and partake with us at the feast which we are making ready; come and eat of our crusts, and dip with us in the same dish; come and be of our flock, and go with us into the pleasant pastures, among the lanes and green hedges which appertain to the farm of the Lord. Come and walk with us through the Sabbath cornfields, and pluck the ears when you are a-hungered, disregarding the broad phylacteries. Come and sing with us songs of a joyful heart, and let us be glad together. What better can you do, Miss Mackenzie? I don't believe there is a more healthy place in the world than Littlebath, and, considering that the place is fashionable, things are really very reasonable.'

He was rapid in his utterance, and so full of energy, that Miss Mackenzie did not quite follow him in his quick transitions. She hardly understood whether he was advising her to take up an abode in a terrestrial Eden or a celestial Paradise; but she presumed that he meant to be civil, so she thanked him and said she thought she would. It was a thousand pities that he should squint so frightfully, as in all other respects he was a good-looking man. Just at this moment there seemed to be a sudden breaking up of the party.

'We are all going away,' said Mr Maguire. 'We always do when Mrs Stumfold gets up from her seat. She does it when she sees that her father is nodding his head. You must let me out, because I've got to say a prayer. By-the-bye, you'll allow me to walk home with you, I hope. I shall be so happy to be useful.'

Miss Mackenzie told him that the fly was coming for her, and then he scrambled away into the middle of the room.

'We always walk home from these parties,' said Miss Baker, who had, however, on this occasion, consented to be taken away by Miss Mackenzie in the fly. 'It makes it come so much cheaper, you know.'

'Of course it does; and it's quite as nice if everybody does it. But you don't walk going there?'

'Not generally,' said Miss Baker; 'but there are some of them who do that. Miss Trotter always walks both ways, if it's ever so wet.' Then there were a few words said about Miss Trotter which were not altogether good-natured.

Miss Mackenzie, as soon as she was at home, got down her Bible and puzzled herself for an hour over that riddle of Mr Stumfold's; but with all her trouble she could not find why St Peter in prison was like a little boy with his shoes off.

⚜ FIVE ⚜

Showing how Mr Rubb, Junior, Progressed at Littlebath

A FULL WEEK HAD PASSED BY AFTER Mrs Stumfold's tea-party before Mr Rubb called again at the Paragon; and in the meantime Miss Mackenzie had been informed by her lawyer that there did not appear to be any objection to the mortgage, if she liked the investment for her money.

'You couldn't do better with your money – you couldn't indeed,' said Mr Rubb, when Miss Mackenzie, meaning to be cautious, started the conversation at once upon matters of business.

Mr Rubb had not been in any great hurry to repeat his call, and Miss Mackenzie had resolved that if he did come again she would treat him simply as a member of the firm with whom she had to transact certain monetary arrangements. Beyond that she would not go; and as she so resolved, she repented herself of the sherry and biscuit.

The people whom she had met at Mr Stumfold's had been all ladies and gentlemen; she, at least, had supposed them to be so, not having as yet received any special information respecting the wife of the retired coachbuilder. Mr Rubb was not a gentleman; and though she was by no means inclined to give herself airs – though, as she assured herself, she believed Mr Rubb to be quite as good as herself – yet there was, and must always be, a difference among people. She had no inclination to be proud; but if Providence had been pleased to place her in one position, it did not behove her to degrade herself by assuming a position that was lower. Therefore, on this account, and by no means moved by any personal contempt towards Mr Rubb, or the Rubbs of the world in general, she was resolved that she would not ask him to take any more sherry and biscuits.

Poor Miss Mackenzie! I fear that they who read this chronicle of her life will already have allowed themselves to think worse of her than she deserved. Many of them, I know, will think far worse of her than they should think. Of what faults, even if we analyse her faults, has she been guilty? Where she has been weak, who among us is not, in that, weak also? Of what vanity has she been guilty with which the least vain among us might not justly tax himself? Having been left alone in the world, she has looked to make friends for herself; and in seeking for new friends she has wished to find the best that might come in her way.

Mr Rubb was very good-looking; Mr Maguire was afflicted by a terrible squint. Mr Rubb's mode of speaking was pleasant to her; whereas she was by no means sure that she liked Mr Maguire's speech. But Mr Maguire was by profession a gentleman. As the discreet young man, who is desirous of rising in the world, will eschew skittles, and in preference go out to tea at his aunt's house – much more delectable as skittles are to his own heart – so did Miss Mackenzie resolve that it would become her to select Messrs Stumfold and Maguire as her male friends, and to treat Mr Rubb simply as a man of business. She was denying herself skittles and beer, and putting up with tea and an old aunt, because she preferred the proprieties of life to its pleasures. Is it right that she should be blamed for such self-denial? But now the skittles and beer had come after her, as those delights will sometimes pursue the prudent youth who would fain avoid them. Mr Rubb was there, in her drawing-room, looking extremely well, shaking hands with her very comfortably, and soon abandoning his conversation on that matter of business to which she had determined to confine herself. She was angry with him, thinking him to be very free and easy; but, nevertheless, she could not keep herself from talking to him.

'You can't do better than five per cent,' he had said to her, 'not with first-class security, such as this is.'

All that had been well enough. Five per cent and first-class security were, she knew, matters of business; and though Mr Rubb had winked his eye at her as he spoke of them, leaning forward in his chair and looking at her not at all as a man of business, but quite in a friendly way, yet she had felt that she was so far safe. She nodded her head also, merely intending him to understand thereby that she herself understood something about business. But when he suddenly changed the subject, and asked her how she liked Mr Stumfold's set, she drew herself up suddenly and placed herself at once upon her guard.

'I have heard a great deal about Mr Stumfold,' continued Mr Rubb, not appearing to observe the lady's altered manner, 'not only here and where I have been for the last few days, but up in London also. He is quite a public character, you know.'

'Clergymen in towns, who have large congregations, always must so be, I suppose.'

'Well, yes; more or less. But Mr Stumfold is decidedly more, and not less. People say he is going in for a bishopric.'

'I had not heard it,' said Miss Mackenzie, who did not quite understand what was meant by going in for a bishopric.

'Oh, yes, and a very likely man he would have been a year or two ago. But they say the prime minister has changed his tap lately.'

'Changed his tap!' said Miss Mackenzie.

'He used to draw his bishops very bitter, but now he draws them mild and creamy. I dare say Stumfold did his best, but he didn't quite get his hay in while the sun shone.'

'He seems to me to be very comfortable where he is,' said Miss Mackenzie.

'I dare say. It must be rather a bore for him having to live in the house with old Peters. How Peters scraped his money together, nobody ever knew yet; and you are aware, Miss Mackenzie, that old as he is, he keeps it all in his own hands. That house, and everything that is in it, belongs to him; you know that, I dare say.'

Miss Mackenzie, who could not keep herself from being a little interested in these matters, said that she had not known it.

'Oh dear, yes! and the carriage too. I've no doubt Stumfold will be all right when the old fellow dies. Such men as Stumfold don't often make mistakes about their money. But as long as old Peters lasts I shouldn't think it can be quite serene. They say that she is always cutting up rough with the old man.'

'She seemed to me to behave very well to him,' said Miss Mackenzie, remembering the carriage of the teacup.

'I dare say it is so before company, and of course that's all right; it's much better that the dirty linen should be washed in private. Stumfold is a clever man, there's no doubt about that. If you've been much to his house, you've probably met his curate, Mr Maguire.'

'I've only been there once, but I did meet Mr Maguire.'

'A man that squints fearfully. They say he's looking out for a wife too, only she must not have a father living, as Mrs Stumfold has. It's astonishing how these parsons pick up all the good things that are going in the way of money.' Miss Mackenzie, as she heard this, could not but remember that she might be regarded as a good thing going in the way of money, and became painfully aware that her face betrayed her consciousness.

'You'll have to keep a sharp look out,' continued Mr Rubb, giving her a kind caution, as though he were an old familiar friend.

'I don't think there's any fear of that kind,' said Miss Mackenzie, blushing.

'I don't know about fear, but I should say that there is great probability; of course I am only joking about Mr Maguire. Like the rest of them, of course, he wishes to feather his own nest; and why shouldn't he? But you may be sure of this, Miss Mackenzie, a lady with your fortune, and, if I may be allowed to say so, with your personal attractions, will not want for admirers.'

Miss Mackenzie was very strongly of opinion that Mr Rubb might not be allowed to say so. She thought that he was behaving with an unwarrantable degree of freedom in saying anything of the kind; but she did not know how to tell him either by words or looks that such was the case. And, perhaps, though the impertinence was almost unendurable, the idea conveyed was not altogether so grievous; it had certainly never hitherto occurred to her that she might become a second Mrs Stumfold; but, after all, why not? What she wanted was simply this, that something of interest should be added to her life. Why should not she also work in the vineyard, in the open quasiclerical vineyard of the Lord's people, and also in the private vineyard of some one of the people's pastors? Mr Rubb was very impertinent, but it might, perhaps, be worth her while to think of what he said. As regarded Mr Maguire, the gentleman whose name had been specially mentioned, it was quite true that he did squint awfully.

'Mr Rubb,' said she, 'if you please, I'd rather not talk about such things as that.'

'Nevertheless, what I say is true, Miss Mackenzie; I hope you don't take it amiss that I venture to feel an interest about you.'

'Oh! no,' said she; 'not that I suppose you do feel any special interest about me.'

'But indeed I do, and isn't it natural? If you will remember that your only brother is the oldest friend that I have in the world, how can it be otherwise? Of course he is much older than me, and very much older than you, Miss Mackenzie.'

'Just twelve years,' said she, very stiffly.

'I thought it had been more, but in that case you and I are nearly of an age. As that is so, how can I fail to feel an interest about you? I have neither mother, nor sister, nor wife of my own; a sister, indeed, I have, but she's married at Singapore, and I have not seen her for seventeen years.'

'Indeed.'

'No, not for seventeen years; and the heart does crave for some female friend, Miss Mackenzie.'

'You ought to get a wife, Mr Rubb.'

'That's what your brother always says. "Samuel," he said to me just before I left town, "you're settled with us now; your father has as good as given up to you his share of the business, and you ought to get married." Now, Miss Mackenzie, I wouldn't take that sort of thing from any man but your brother; it's very odd that you should say exactly the same thing too.'

'I hope I have not offended you.'

'Offended me! no, indeed, I'm not such a fool as that. I'd sooner know that you took an interest in me than any woman living. I would, indeed. I dare say you don't think much of it, but when I remember that the names of Rubb and Mackenzie have been joined together for more than twenty years, it seems natural to me that you and I should be friends.'

Miss Mackenzie, in the few moments which were allowed to her for reflection before she was obliged to answer, again admitted to herself that he spoke the truth. If there was any fault in the matter the fault was with her brother Tom, who had joined the name of Mackenzie with the name of Rubb in the first instance. Where was this young man to look for a female friend if not to his partner's family, seeing that he had neither wife nor mother of his own, nor indeed a sister, except one out at Singapore, who was hardly available for any of the purposes of family affection? And yet it was hard upon her. It was through no negligence on her part that poor Mr Rubb was so ill provided. 'Perhaps it might have been so if I had continued to live in London,' said Miss Mackenzie; 'but as I live at Littlebath' – Then she paused, not knowing how to finish her sentence.

'What difference does that make? The distance is nothing if you come to think of it. Your hall door is just two hours and a quarter from our place of business in the New Road; and it's one pound five and nine if you go by first-class and cabs, or sixteen and ten if you put up with second-class and omnibuses. There's no other way of counting. Miles mean nothing now-a-days.'

'They don't mean much, certainly.'

'They mean nothing. Why, Miss Mackenzie, I should think it no trouble at all to run down and consult you about anything that occurred, about any matter of business that weighed at all heavily, if nothing prevented me except distance. Thirty shillings more than does it all, with a return ticket, including a bit of lunch at the station.'

'Oh! and as for that –'

'I know what you mean, Miss Mackenzie, and I shall never forget how kind you were to offer me refreshment when I was here before.'

'But, Mr Rubb, I hope you won't think of doing such a thing. What good could I do you? I know nothing about business; and really, to tell the truth, I should be most unwilling to interfere – that is, you know, to say anything about anything of the kind.'

'I only meant to point out that the distance is nothing. And as to what you were advising me about getting married –'

'I didn't mean to advise you, Mr Rubb!'

'I thought you said so.'

'But, of course, I did not intend to discuss such a matter seriously.'

'It's a most serious subject to me, Miss Mackenzie.'

'No doubt; but it's one I can't know anything about. Men in business generally do find, I think, that they get on better when they are married.'

'Yes, they do.'

'That's all I meant to say, Mr Rubb.'

After this he sat silent for a few minutes, and I am inclined to think that he was weighing in his mind the expediency of asking her to become Mrs Rubb, on the spur of the moment. But if so, his mind finally gave judgment against the attempt, and in giving such judgment his mind was right. He would certainly have so startled her by the precipitancy of such a proposition, as to have greatly endangered the probability of any further intimacy with her. As it was, he changed the conversation, and began to ask questions as to the welfare of his partner's daughter. At this period of the day Susanna was at school, and he was informed that she would not be home till the evening. Then he plucked up courage and begged to be allowed to come again – just to look in at eight o'clock, so that he might see Susanna. He could not go back to London comfortably, unless he could give some tidings of Susanna to the family in Gower Street. What was she to do? Of course she was obliged to ask him to drink tea with them. 'That would be so pleasant,' he said; and Miss Mackenzie owned to herself that the gratification expressed in his face as he spoke was very becoming.

When Susanna came home she did not seem to know much of Mr Rubb, junior, or to care much about him. Old Mr Rubb lived, she knew, near the place of business in the New Road, and sometimes he came to Gower Street, but nobody liked him. She didn't remember that she had ever seen Mr Rubb, junior, at her mother's house but once, when he came to dinner. When she was told that Mr Rubb was very anxious to see her, she chucked up her head and said that the man was a goose.

He came, and in a very few minutes he had talked over Susanna. He brought her a little present – a work-box – which he had bought for her at Littlebath; and though the work-box itself did not altogether avail, it paved the way for civil words, which were more efficacious. On this occasion he talked more to his partner's daughter than to his partner's sister, and promised to tell her mamma how well she was looking, and that the air of Littlebath had brought roses to her cheeks.

'I think it is a healthy place,' said Miss Mackenzie.

'I'm quite sure it is,' said Mr Rubb. 'And you like Mrs Crammer's school, Susanna?'

She would have preferred to have been called Miss Mackenzie, but was not disposed to quarrel with him on the point.

'Yes, I like it very well,' she said. 'The other girls are very nice; and if one must go to school, I suppose it's as good as any other school.'

'Susanna thinks that going to school at all is rather a nuisance,' said Miss Mackenzie.

'You'd think so too, aunt, if you had to practise every day for an hour in the same room with four other pianos. It's my belief that I shall hate the sound of a piano the longest day that I shall live.'

'I suppose it's the same with all young ladies,' said Mr Rubb.

'It's the same with them all at Mrs Crammer's. There isn't one there that does not hate it.'

'But you wouldn't like not to be able to play,' said her aunt.

'Mamma doesn't play, and you don't play; and I don't see what's the use of it. It won't make anybody like music to hear four pianos all going at the same time, and all of them out of tune.'

'You must not tell them in Gower Street, Mr Rubb, that Susanna talks like that,' said Miss Mackenzie.

'Yes, you may, Mr Rubb. But you must tell them at the same time that I am quite happy, and that Aunt Margaret is the dearest woman in the world.'

'I'll be sure to tell them that,' said Mr Rubb. Then he went away, pressing Miss Mackenzie's hand warmly as he took his leave; and as soon as he was gone, his character was of course discussed.

'He's quite a different man, aunt, from what I thought; and he's not at all like old Mr Rubb. Old Mr Rubb, when he comes to drink tea in Gower Street, puts his handkerchief over his knees to catch the crumbs.'

'There's no great harm in that, Susanna.'

'I don't suppose there's any harm in it. It's not wicked. It's not wicked to eat gravy with your knife.'

'And does old Mr Rubb do that?'

'Always. We used to laugh at him, because he is so clever at it. He never spills any; and his knife seems to be quite as good as a spoon. But this Mr Rubb doesn't do things of that sort.'

'He's younger, my dear.'

'But being younger doesn't make people more ladylike of itself.'

'I did not know that Mr Rubb was exactly ladylike.'

'That's taking me up unfairly; isn't it, aunt? You know what I meant;

423

and only fancy that the man should go out and buy me a work-box. That's more than old Mr Rubb ever did for any of us, since the first day he knew us. And, then, didn't you think that young Mr Rubb is a handsome man, aunt?'

'He's all very well, my dear.'

'Oh; I think he is downright handsome; I do, indeed. Miss Dumpus – that's Mrs Crammer's sister – told us the other day, that I was wrong to talk about a man being handsome; but that must be nonsense, aunt?'

'I don't see that at all, my dear. If she told you so, you ought to believe that it is not nonsense.'

'Come, aunt; you don't mean to tell me that you would believe all that Miss Dumpus says. Miss Dumpus says that girls should never laugh above their breath when they are more than fourteen years old. How can you make a change in your laughing just when you come to be fourteen? And why shouldn't you say a man's handsome, if he is handsome?'

'You'd better go to bed, Susanna.'

'That won't make Mr Rubb ugly. I wish you had asked him to come and dine here on Sunday; so that we might have seen whether he eats his gravy with his knife. I looked very hard to see whether he'd catch his crumbs in his handkerchief.'

Then Susanna went to her bed, and Miss Mackenzie was left alone to think over the perfections and imperfections of Mr Samuel Rubb, junior.

From that time up to Christmas she saw no more of Mr Rubb; but she heard from him twice. His letters, however, had reference solely to business, and were not of a nature to produce either anger or admiration. She had also heard more than once from her lawyer; and a question had arisen as to which she was called upon to trust to her own judgment for a decision. Messrs Rubb and Mackenzie had wanted the money at once, whereas the papers for the mortgage were not ready. Would Miss Mackenzie allow Messrs Rubb and Mackenzie to have the money under these circumstances? To this inquiry from her lawyer she made a rejoinder asking for advice. Her lawyer told her that he could not recommend her, in the ordinary way of business, to make any advance of money without positive security; but, as this was a matter between friends and near relatives, she might perhaps be willing to do it; and he added that, as far as his own opinion went, he did not think that there would be any great risk. But then it all depended on this – did she want to oblige her friends and near relatives? In answer to this question she told herself that she certainly did wish to do so; and she declared – also to herself – that she was willing to advance the money to her brother, even though there might be some risk. The upshot of all this was that Messrs Rubb and Mackenzie got the money some time in October, but that the mortgage was not completed when Christmas came. It was on this matter that Mr Rubb, junior, had written to Miss Mackenzie, and his letter had been of a nature to give her a feeling of perfect security in the transaction. With her brother she had had no further correspondence; but this did not surprise her, as her brother was a man much less facile in his modes of expression than his younger partner.

As the autumn had progressed at Littlebath, she had become more and more intimate with Miss Baker, till she had almost taught herself to regard that lady as a dear friend. She had fallen into the habit of going to Mrs Stumfold's tea-parties every fortnight, and was now regarded as a regular Stumfoldian by all those who interested themselves in such matters. She had begun a system of district visiting and Bible reading with Miss Baker, which had at first been very agreeable to her. But Mrs Stumfold had on one occasion called upon her and taken her to task – as Miss Mackenzie had thought, rather abruptly – with reference to some lack of energy or indiscreet omission of which she had been judged to be guilty by that highly-gifted lady. Against this Miss Mackenzie had rebelled mildly, and since that things had not gone quite so pleasantly with her. She had still been honoured with Mrs Stumfold's card of invitation, and had still gone to the tea-parties on Miss Baker's strenuously-urged advice; but Mrs Stumfold had frowned, and Miss Mackenzie had felt the frown; Mrs Stumfold had frowned, and the retired coach-builder's wife had at once snubbed the culprit, and Mr Maguire had openly expressed himself to be uneasy.

'Dearest Miss Mackenzie,' he had said, with charitable zeal, 'if there has been anything wrong, just beg her pardon, and you will find that everything has been forgotten at once; a more forgiving woman than Mrs Stumfold never lived.'

'But suppose I have done nothing to be forgiven,' urged Miss Mackenzie.

Mr Maguire looked at her, and shook his head, the exact meaning of the look she could not understand, as the peculiarity of his eyes created confusion; but when he repeated twice to her the same words, 'The heart of man is exceeding treacherous,' she understood that he meant to condemn her.

'So it is, Mr Maguire, but that is no reason why Mrs Stumfold should scold me.'

Then he got up and left her, and did not speak to her again that evening, but he called on her the next day, and was very affectionate in his manner. In Mr Stumfold's mode of treating her she had found no difference.

With Miss Todd, whom she met constantly in the street, and who always nodded to her very kindly, she had had one very remarkable interview.

'I think we had better give it up, my dear,' Miss Todd had said to her. This had been in Miss Baker's drawing-room.

'Give what up?' Miss Mackenzie had asked.

'Any idea of our knowing each other. I'm sure it never can come to anything, though for my part I should have been so glad. You see you can't serve God and Mammon, and it is settled beyond all doubt that I'm Mammon. Isn't it, Mary?'

Miss Baker, to whom this appeal was made, answered it only by a sigh.

'You see,' continued Miss Todd, 'that Miss Baker is allowed to know me, though I am Mammon, for the sake of auld lang syne. There have been so many things between us that it wouldn't do for us to drop each other. We have had the same lovers; and you know, Mary, that you've been very near coming over to Mammon yourself. There's a sort of understanding that Miss Baker is not to be required to cut me. But they would not allow that sort of liberty to a new comer; they wouldn't, indeed.'

'I don't know that anybody would be likely to interfere with me,' said Miss Mackenzie.

'Yes, they would, my dear. You didn't quite know yourself which way it was to be when you first came here, and if it had been my way, I should have been most happy to have made myself civil. You have chosen now, and I don't doubt but what you have chosen right. I always tell Mary Baker that it does very well for her, and I dare say it will do very well for you too. There's a great deal in it, and only that some of them do tell such lies I think I should have tried it myself. But, my dear Miss Mackenzie, you can't do both.'

After this Miss Mackenzie used to nod to Miss Todd in the street, but beyond that there was no friendly intercourse between those ladies.

At the beginning of December there came an invitation to Miss Mackenzie to spend the Christmas holidays away from Littlebath, and as she accepted this invitation, and as we must follow her to the house of her friends, we will postpone further mention of the matter till the next chapter.

✂ SIX ✂

Miss Mackenzie goes to the Cedars

ABOUT THE MIDDLE OF DECEMBER MRS MACKENZIE, of Gower Street, received a letter from her sister-in-law at Littlebath, in which it was proposed that Susanna should pass the Christmas holidays with her father and mother. 'I myself,' said the letter, 'am going for three weeks to the Cedars. Lady Ball has written to me, and as she seems to wish it, I shall go. It is always well, I think, to drop family dissensions.' The letter said a great deal more, for Margaret Mackenzie, not having much business on hand, was fond of writing long letters; but the upshot of it was, that she would leave Susanna in Gower Street, on her way to the Cedars, and call for her on her return home.

'What on earth is she going there for?' said Mrs Tom Mackenzie.

'Because they have asked her,' replied the husband.

'Of course they have asked her; but that's no reason she should go. The Balls have behaved very badly to us, and I should think much better of her if she stayed away.'

To this Mr Mackenzie made no answer, but simply remarked that he would be rejoiced in having Susanna at home on Christmas Day.

'That's all very well, my dear,' said Mrs Tom, 'and of course so shall I. But as she has taken the charge of the child I don't think she ought to drop her down and pick her up just whenever she pleases. Suppose she was to take it into her head to stop at the Cedars altogether, what are we to do then? – just have the girl returned upon our hands, with all her ideas of life confused and deranged. I hate such ways.'

'She has promised to provide for Susanna, whenever she may not continue to give her a home.'

'What would such a promise be worth if John Ball got hold of her money? That's what they're after, as sure as my name is Martha; and what she's after too, very likely. She was there once before she went to Littlebath at all. They want to get their uncle's money back, and she wants to be a baronet's wife.'

The same view of the matter was perhaps taken by Mr Rubb, junior, when he was told that Miss Mackenzie was to pass through London on her way to the Cedars, though he did not express his fears openly, as Mrs Mackenzie had done.

'Why don't you ask your sister to stay in Gower Street?' he said to his partner.

'She wouldn't come.'

'You might at any rate ask her.'

'What good would it do?'

'Well; I don't know that it would do any good; but it wouldn't do any harm. Of course it's natural that she should wish to have friends about her; and it will only be natural too that she should marry some one.'

'She may marry whom she pleases for me.'

'She will marry whom she pleases; but I suppose you don't want to see her money go to the Balls.'

'I shouldn't care a straw where her money went,' said Thomas Mackenzie, 'if I could only know that this sum which we have had from her was properly arranged. To tell you the truth, Rubb, I'm ashamed to look my sister in the face.'

'That's nonsense. Her money is as right as the bank; and if in such matters as that brothers and sisters can't take liberties with each other, who the deuce can?'

'In matters of money nobody should ever take a liberty with anybody,' said Mr Mackenzie.

He knew, however, that a great liberty had been taken with his sister's money, and that his firm had no longer the power of providing her with the security which had been promised to her.

Mr Mackenzie would take no steps, at his partner's instance, towards arresting his sister in London; but Mr Rubb was more successful with Mrs Mackenzie, with whom, during the last month or two, he had contrived to establish a greater intimacy than had ever previously existed between the two families. He had been of late a good deal in Gower Street, and Mrs Mackenzie had found him to be a much pleasanter and better educated man than she had expected. Such was the language in which she expressed her praise of him, though I am disposed to doubt whether she herself was at all qualified to judge of the education of any man. He had now talked over the affairs of Margaret Mackenzie with her sister-in-law, and the result of that talking was that Mrs Mackenzie wrote a letter to Littlebath, pressing Miss Mackenzie to stay a few days in Gower Street, on her way through London. She did this as well as she knew how to do it; but still there was that in the letter which plainly told an apt reader that there was no reality in the professions of affection made in it. Miss Mackenzie became well aware of the fact as she read her sister's words. Available hypocrisy is a quality very difficult of attainment and of all hypocrisies, epistolary hypocrisy is perhaps the most difficult. A man or woman must have studied the matter very thoroughly, or be possessed of great natural advantages in that direction, who can so fill a letter with false expressions of affection, as to make any reader believe them to be true. Mrs Mackenzie was possessed of no such skill.

'Believe her to be my affectionate sister-in-law! I won't believe her to be anything of the kind,' Margaret so spoke of the writer to herself, when she had finished the letter; but, nevertheless, she answered it with kind language, saying that she could not stay in town as she passed through to the Cedars, but that she would pass one night in Gower Street when she called to pick up Susanna on her return home.

It is hard to say what pleasure she promised herself in going to the Cedars, or why she accepted that invitation. She had, in truth, liked neither the people nor the house, and had felt herself to be uncomfortable while she was there. I think she felt it to be a duty to force herself to go out among people who, though they were personally disagreeable to her, might be socially advantageous. If Sir John Ball had not been a baronet, the call to the Cedars would not have been so imperative on her. And yet she was not a tufthunter, nor a toady. She was doing what we all do – endeavouring to choose her friends from the best of those who made overtures to her of friendship. If other things be equal, it is probable that a baronet will be more of a gentleman and a pleasanter fellow than a manufacturer of oilcloth. Who is there that doesn't feel that? It is true that she had tried the baronet, and had not found him very pleasant, but that might probably have been her own fault. She had been shy and stiff, and perhaps ill-mannered, or had at least accused herself of these faults; and therefore she resolved to go again.

She called with Susanna as she passed through London, and just saw her sister-in-law.

'I wish you could have stayed,' said Mrs Mackenzie.

'I will for one night, as I return, on the 10th of January,' said Miss Mackenzie.

Mrs Mackenzie could not understand what Mr Rubb had meant by saying that that old maid was soft and pleasant, nor could she understand Susanna's love for her aunt. 'I suppose men will put up with anything for the sake of money,' she said to herself; 'and as for children, the truth is, they'll love anybody who indulges them.'

'Aunt is so kind,' Susanna said. 'She's always kind. If you wake her up in the middle of the night, she's kind in a moment. And if there's anything good to eat, it will make her eyes quite shine if she sees that anybody else likes it. I have known her sit for half an hour ever so uncomfortable, because she would not disturb the cat.'

'Then she must be a fool, my dear,' said Mrs Mackenzie.

'She isn't a fool, mamma; I'm quite sure of that,' said Susanna.

Miss Mackenzie went on to the Cedars, and her mind almost misgave her in going there, as she was driven up through the dull brick lodges, which looked as though no paint had touched them for the last thirty years, up to the front door of the dull brick house, which bore almost as dreary a look of neglect as the lodges. It was a large brick house of three stories, with the door in the middle, and three windows on each side of the door, and a railed area with a kitchen below the ground. Such houses were built very commonly in the neighbourhood of London some hundred and fifty years ago, and they may still be pleasant enough to the eye if there be ivy over them, and if they be clean with new paint, and spruce with the outer care of gardeners and the inner care of housemaids; but old houses are often like old ladies, who require more care in their dressing than they who are younger. Very little care was given to the Cedars, and the place therefore always looked ill-dressed. On the right hand as you entered was the dining-room, and the three windows to the left were all devoted to the hall. Behind the dining-room was Sir John's study, as he called it, and behind or beyond the hall was the drawing-room, from which four windows looked out into the garden. This might have been a pretty room had any care been taken to make anything pretty at the Cedars. But the furniture was old, and the sofas were hard, and the tables were rickety, and the curtains which had once been red had become brown with the sun. The dinginess of the house had not struck Miss

Mackenzie so forcibly when she first visited it, as it did now. Then she had come almost direct from Arundel Street, and the house in Arundel Street had itself been very dingy. Mrs Stumfold's drawing-rooms were not dingy, nor were her own rooms in the Paragon. Her eye had become accustomed to better things, and she now saw at once how old were the curtains, and how lamentably the papers wanted to be renewed on the walls. She had, however, been drawn from the neighbouring station to the house in the private carriage belonging to the establishment, and if there was any sense of justice in her, it must be presumed that she balanced the good things with the bad.

But her mind misgave her, not because the house was outwardly dreary, but in fear of the inward dreariness of the people – or in fear rather of their dreariness and pride combined. Old Lady Ball, though naturally ill-natured, was not ill-mannered, nor did she give herself any special airs; but she knew that she was a baronet's wife, that she kept her carriage, and that it was an obligation upon her to make up for the poverty of her house by some little haughtiness of demeanour. There are women, high in rank, but poor in pocket, so gifted with the peculiar grace of aristocracy, that they show by every word spoken, by every turn of the head, by every step taken, that they are among the high ones of the earth, and that money has nothing to do with it. Old Lady Ball was not so gifted, nor had she just claim to such gifts. But some idea on the subject pervaded her mind, and she made efforts to be aristocratic in her poverty. Sir John was a discontented, cross old man, who had succeeded greatly in early life, having been for nearly twenty years in Parliament, but had fallen into adversity in his older days. The loss of that very money of which his niece, Miss Mackenzie was possessed, was, in truth, the one great misfortune which he deplored; but that misfortune had had ramifications and extensions with which the reader need not trouble himself; but which, altogether, connected as they were with certain liberal aspirations which he had entertained in early life, and certain political struggles made during his parliamentary career, induced him to regard himself as a sort of Prometheus. He had done much for the world, and the world in return had made him a baronet without any money! He was a very tall, thin, gray-haired, old man, stooping much, and worn with age, but still endowed with some strength of will, and great capability of making himself unpleasant. His son was a bald-headed, stout man, somewhat past forty, who was by no means without cleverness, having done great things as a young man at Oxford; but in life he had failed. He was a director of certain companies in London, at which he used to attend, receiving his guinea for doing so, and he had some small capital – some remnant of his father's trade wealth, which he nursed with extreme care, buying shares here and there and changing his money about as his keen outlook into City affairs directed him. I do not suppose that he had much talent for the business, or he would have grown rich; but a certain careful zeal carried him on without direct loss, and gave him perhaps five per cent for his capital, whereas he would have received no more than four and a half had he left it alone and taken his dividends without troubling himself. As the difference did not certainly amount to a hundred a-year, it can hardly be said that he made good use of his time. His zeal deserved a better success. He was always thinking of his money; excusing himself to himself and to others by the fact of his nine children. For myself I think that his children were no justification to him; as they would have been held to be none, had he murdered and robbed his neighbours for their sake.

There had been a crowd of girls in the house when Miss Mackenzie had paid her former visit to the Cedars – so many that she had carried away no remembrance of them as individuals. But at that time the eldest son, a youth now just of age, was not at home. This hope of the Balls, who was endeavouring to do at Oxford as his father had done, was now with his family, and came forward to meet his cousin as the old carriage was driven up to the door. Old Sir John stood within, in the hall, mindful of the window air, and Lady Ball, a little mindful of her dignity, remained at the drawing- room door. Even though Miss Mackenzie had eight hundred a-year, and was nearly related to the Incharrow family, a further advance than the drawing-room door would be inexpedient; for the lady, with all her virtues, was still sister to the man who dealt in retail oilcloth in the New Road!

Miss Mackenzie thought nothing of this, but was well contented to be received by her hostess in the drawing-room.

'It's a dull house to come to, my dear,' said Lady Ball; 'but blood is thicker than water, they say, and we thought that perhaps you might like to be with your cousins at Christmas.'

'I shall like it very much,' said Miss Mackenzie.

'I suppose you must find it rather sad, living alone at Littlebath, away from all your people?'

'I have my niece with me, you know.'

'A niece, have you? That's one of the girls from Gower Street, I suppose? It's very kind of you, and I dare say, very proper.'

'But Littlebath is a very gay place, I thought,' said John Ball, the third and youngest of the name. 'We always hear of it at Oxford as being the most stunning place for parties anywhere near.'

'I suppose you play cards every night of your life,' said the baronet.

'No; I don't play cards,' said Miss Mackenzie. 'Many ladies do, but I'm not in that set.'

'What set are you in?' said Sir John.

'I don't think I am in any set. I know Mr Stumfold, the clergyman there, and I go to his house sometimes.'

'Oh, ah; I see,' said Sir John. 'I beg your pardon for mentioning cards. I shouldn't have done it, if I had known that you were one of Mr Stumfold's people.'

'I am not one of Mr Stumfold's people especially,' she said, and then she went upstairs.

The other John Ball came back from London just in time for dinner – the middle one of the three, whom we will call Mr Ball. He greeted his cousin very kindly, and then said a word or two to his mother about shares. She answered him, assuming a look of interest in his tidings.

'I don't understand it; upon my word, I don't,' said he. 'Some of them will burn their fingers before they've done. I don't dare do it; I know that.'

In the evening, when John Ball – or Jack, as he was called in the family – had left the drawing-room, and the old man was alone with his son, they discussed the position of Margaret Mackenzie.

'You'll find she has taken up with the religious people there,' said the father.

'It's just what she would do,' said the son.

'They're the greatest thieves going. When once they have got their eyes upon money, they never take them off again.'

'She's not been there long enough yet to give any one a hold upon her.'

'I don't know that, John; but, if you'll take my advice, you'll find out the truth at once. She has no children, and if you've made up your mind about it, you'll do no good by delay.'

'She's a very nice woman, in her way.'

'Yes, she's nice enough. She's not a beauty; eh, John? and she won't set the Thames on fire.'

'I don't wish her to do so; but I think she'd look after the girls, and do her duty.'

'I dare say; unless she has taken to run after prayer-meetings every hour of her life.'

'They don't often do that after they're married, sir.'

'Well; I know nothing against her. I never thought much of her brothers, and I never cared to know them. One's dead now, and as for the other, I don't suppose he need trouble you much. If you've made up your mind about it, I think you might as well ask her at once.' From all which it may be seen that Miss Mackenzie had been invited to the Cedars with a direct object on the part of Mr Ball.

But though the old gentleman thus strongly advised instant action, nothing was done during Christmas week, nor had any hint been given up to the end of the year. John Ball, however, had not altogether lost his time, and had played the part of middle-aged lover better than might have been expected from one the whole tenor of whose life was so thoroughly unromantic. He did manage to make himself pleasant to Miss

Mackenzie, and so far ingratiated himself with her that he won much of her confidence in regard to money matters.

'But that's a very large sum of money?' he said to her one day as they were sitting together in his father's study. He was alluding to the amount which she had lent to Messrs Rubb and Mackenzie, and had become aware of the fact that as yet Miss Mackenzie held no security for the loan. 'Two thousand five hundred pounds is a very large sum of money.'

'But I'm to get five per cent, John.' They were first cousins, but it was not without some ceremonial difficulty that they had arrived at each other's Christian names.

'My dear Margaret, their word for five per cent is no security. Five per cent is nothing magnificent. A lady situated as you are should never part with her money without security – never: but if she does, she should have more than five per cent.'

'You'll find it's all right, I don't doubt,' said Miss Mackenzie, who, however, was beginning to have little inward tremblings of her own.

'I hope so; but I must say, I think Mr Slow has been much to blame. I do, indeed.' Mr Slow was the attorney who had for years acted for Walter Mackenzie and his father, and was now acting for Miss Mackenzie. 'Will you allow me to go to him and see about it?'

'It has not been his fault. He wrote and asked me whether I would let them have it, before the papers were ready, and I said I would.'

'But may I ask about it?'

Miss Mackenzie paused before she answered:

'I think you had better not, John. Remember that Tom is my own brother, and I should not like to seem to doubt him. Indeed, I do not doubt him in the least – nor yet Mr Rubb.'

'I can assure you that it is a very bad way of doing business,' said the anxious lover.

By degrees she began to like her cousin John Ball. I do not at all wish the reader to suppose that she had fallen in love with that bald-headed, middle-aged gentleman, or that she even thought of him in the light of a possible husband; but she found herself to be comfortable in his company, and was able to make a friend of him. It is true that he talked to her more of money than anything else; but then it was her money of which he talked, and he did it with an interest that could not but flatter her. He was solicitous about her welfare, gave her bits of advice, did one or two commissions for her in town, called her Margaret, and was kind and cousinly. The Cedars, she thought, was altogether more pleasant than she had found the place before. Then she told herself that on the occasion of her former visit she had not been there long enough to learn to like the place or the people. Now she knew them, and though she still dreaded her uncle and his cross sayings, and though that driving out with her aunt in the old carriage was tedious, she would have been glad to prolong her stay there, had she not bound herself to take Susanna back to school at Littlebath on a certain day. When that day came near – and it did come very near before Mr Ball spoke out – they pressed her to prolong her stay. This was done by both Lady Ball and by her son.

'You might as well remain with us another fortnight,' said Lady Ball during one of these drives. It was the last drive which Miss Mackenzie had through Twickenham lanes during that visit to the Cedars.

'I can't do it, aunt, because of Susanna.'

'I don't see that at all. You're not to make yourself a slave to Susanna.'

'But I'm to make myself a mother to her as well as I can.'

'I must say you have been rather hasty, my dear. Suppose you were to change your mode of life, what would you do?'

Then Miss Mackenzie, blushing slightly in the obscure corner of the carriage as she spoke, explained to Lady Ball that clause in her agreement with her brother respecting the five hundred pounds.

'Oh, indeed,' said Lady Ball.

The information thus given had been manifestly distasteful, and the conversation was for a while interrupted; but Lady Ball returned to her request before they were again at home.

'I really do think you might stop, Margaret. Now that we have all got to know each other, it will be a great pity that it all should be broken up.'

'But I hope it won't be broken up, aunt.'

'You know what I mean, my dear. When people live so far off they can't see each other constantly; and now you are here, I think you might stay a little longer. I know there is not much attraction –'

'Oh, aunt, don't say that! I like being here very much.'

'Then, why can't you stay? Write and tell Mrs Tom that she must keep Susanna at home for another week or so. It can't matter.'

To this Miss Mackenzie made no immediate answer.

'It is not only for myself I speak, but John likes having you here with his girls; and Jack is so fond of you; and John himself is quite different while you are here. Do stay!'

Saying which Lady Ball put out her hand caressingly on Miss Mackenzie's arm.

'I'm afraid I mustn't,' said Miss Mackenzie, very slowly. 'Much as I should like it, I'm afraid I mustn't do it. I've pledged myself to go back with Susanna, and I like to be as good as my word.'

Lady Ball drew herself up.

'I never went so much out of my way to ask any one to stay in my house before,' she said.

'Dear aunt! don't be angry with me.'

'Oh no! I'm not angry. Here we are. Will you get out first?'

Whereupon Lady Ball descended from the carriage. and walked into the house with a good deal of dignity.

'What a wicked old woman she was!' virtuous readers will say; 'what a wicked old woman to endeavour to catch that poor old maid's fortune for her son!'

But I deny that she was in any degree a wicked old woman on that score. Why should not the two cousins marry, and do very well together with their joint means? Lady Ball intended to make a baronet's wife of her. If much was to be taken, was not much also to be given?

'You are going to stay, are you not?' Jack said to her that evening, as he wished her good-night. She was very fond of Jack, who was a nice-looking, smooth-faced young fellow, idolised by his sisters over whom he tyrannised, and bullied by his grandfather, before whom he quaked.

'I'm afraid not, Jack; but you shall come and see me at Littlebath, if you will.'

'I should like it, of all things; but I do wish you'd stay: the house is so much nicer when you are in it!'

But of course she could not stay at the request of the young lad, when she had refused the request of the lad's grandmother.

After this she had one day to remain at the Cedars. It was a Thursday, and on the Friday she was to go to her brother's house on her way to Littlebath. On the Thursday morning Mr Ball waylaid her on the staircase, as she came down to breakfast, and took her with him into the drawing-room. There he made his request, standing with her in the middle of the room.

'Margaret,' he said, 'must you go away and leave us?'

'I'm afraid I must, John,' she said.

'I wish we could make you think better of it.'

'Of course I should like to stay, but –'

'Yes, there's always a but. I should have thought that, of all people in the world, you were the one most able to do just what you please with your time.'

'We have all got duties to do, John.'

'Of course we have; but why shouldn't it be your duty to make your relations happy? If you could only know how much I like your being here?'

Had it not been that she did not dare to do that for the son which she had refused to the mother, I think that she would have given way. As it was, she did not know how to yield, after having persevered so long.

'You are all so kind,' she said, giving him her hand, 'that it goes to my heart to refuse you; but I'm afraid I can't. I do not wish to give my brother's wife cause to complain of me.'

'Then,' said Mr Ball, speaking very slowly, 'I must ask this favour of you, that you will let me see you alone for half an hour after dinner this evening.'

'Certainly,' said Miss Mackenzie.

'Thank you, Margaret. After tea I will go into the study, and perhaps you will follow me.'

SEVEN

Miss Mackenzie leaves the Cedars

THERE WAS SOMETHING SO SERIOUS IN HER cousin's request to her, and so much of gravity in his mode of making it, that Miss Mackenzie could not but think of it throughout the day. On what subject did he wish to speak to her in so solemn and special a manner? An idea of the possibility of an offer no doubt crossed her mind and fluttered her, but it did not do more than this; it did not remain fixed with her, or induce her to resolve what answer she would give if such offer were made. She was afraid to allow herself to think that such a thing could happen, and put the matter away from her – uneasily, indeed, but still with so much resolution as to leave her with a conviction that she need not give any consideration to such an hypothesis.

And she was not at a loss to suggest to herself another subject. Her cousin had learned something about her money which he felt himself bound to tell her, but which he would not have told her now had she consented to remain at the Cedars. There was something wrong about the loan. This made her seriously unhappy, for she dreaded the necessity of discussing her brother's conduct with her cousin.

During the whole of the day Lady Ball was very courteous, but rather distant. Lady Ball had said to herself that Margaret would have stayed had she been in a disposition favourable to John Ball's hopes. If she should decline the alliance with which the Balls proposed to honour her, then Lady Ball was prepared to be very cool. There would be an ingratitude in such a proceeding after the open-armed affection which had been shown to her which Lady Ball could not readily bring herself to forgive. Sir John, once or twice during the day, took up his little sarcasms against her supposed religious tendencies at Littlebath.

'You'll be glad to get back to Mr Stumfold,' he said.

'I shall be glad to see him, of course,' she answered, 'as he is a friend.'

'Mr Stumfold has a great many lady friends at Littlebath,' he continued.

'Yes, a great many,' said Miss Mackenzie, understanding well that she was being bullied.

'What a pity that there can be only one Mrs Stumfold,' snarled the baronet; 'it's often a wonder to me how women can be so foolish.'

'And it's often a wonder to me,' said Miss Mackenzie, 'how gentlemen can be so ill-natured.'

She had plucked up her spirits of late, and had resented Sir John's ill-humour.

At the usual hour Mr Ball came home to dinner, and Miss Mackenzie, as soon as she saw him, again became fluttered. She perceived that he was not at his ease, and that made her worse. When he spoke to the girls he seemed hardly to mind what he was saying, and he greeted his mother without any whispered tidings as to the share-market of the day.

Margaret asked herself if it could be possible that anything was very wrong about her own money. If the worst came to the worst she could but have lost that two thousand five hundred pounds and she would be able to live well enough without it. If her brother had asked her for it, she would have given it to him. She would teach herself to regard it as a gift, and then the subject would not make her unhappy.

They all came down to dinner, and they all went in to tea, and the tea-things were taken away, and then John Ball arose. During tea-time neither he nor Miss Mackenzie had spoken a word, and when she got up to follow him, there was a solemnity about the matter which ought to have been ludicrous to any of those remaining, who might chance to know what was about to happen. It must be supposed that Lady Ball at any rate did know, and when she saw her middle-aged niece walk slowly out of the room after her middle-aged son, in order that a love proposal might be made from one to the other with advantage, she must, I should think, have perceived the comic nature of the arrangement. She went on, however, very gravely with her knitting, and did not even make an attempt to catch her husband's eye.

'Margaret,' said John Ball, as soon as he had shut the study door; 'but, perhaps, you had better sit down.'

Then she sat down, and he came and seated himself opposite to her; opposite her, but not so close as to give him any of the advantages of a lover.

'Margaret, I don't know whether you have guessed the subject on which I wish to speak to you; but I wish you had.'

'Is it about the money?' she asked.

'The money! What money? The money you have lent to your brother? Oh, no.'

Then, at that moment, Margaret did, I think, guess.

'It's not at all about the money,' he said, and then he sighed

He had at one time thought of asking his mother to make the proposition for him, and now he wished that he had done so.

'No, Margaret, it's something else that I want to say. I believe you know my condition in life pretty accurately.'

'In what way, John?'

'I am a poor man; considering my large family, a very poor man. I have between eight and nine hundred a year, and when my father and mother are both gone I shall have nearly as much more; but I have nine children, and as I must keep up something of a position, I have a hard time of it sometimes, I can tell you.'

Here he paused, as though he expected her to say something; but she had nothing to say and he went on.

'Jack is at Oxford, as you know, and I wish to give him any chance that a good education may afford. It did not do much for me, but he may be more lucky. When my father is dead, I think I shall sell this place; but I have not quite made up my mind about that – it must depend on circumstances. As for the girls, you see that I do what I can to educate them.'

'They seem to me to be brought up very nicely; nothing could be better.'

'They are good girls, very good girls, and so is Jack a very good fellow.'

'I love Jack dearly,' said Miss Mackenzie, who had already come to a half-formed resolution that Jack Ball should be heir to half her fortune, her niece Susanna being heiress to the other half.

'Do you? I'm so glad of that.' And there was actually a tear in the father's eye.

'And so I do the girls,' said Margaret. 'It's something so nice to feel that one has people really belonging to one that one may love. I hope they'll know Susanna some day, for she's a very nice girl – a very dear girl.'

'I hope they will,' said Mr Ball; but there was not much enthusiasm in the expression of this hope.

Then he got up from his chair, and took a turn across the room. 'The truth is, Margaret, that there's no use in my beating about the bush. I shan't say what I've got to say a bit the better for delaying it. I want you to be my wife, and to be mother to those children. I like you better than any woman I've seen since I lost Rachel, but I shouldn't dare to make you such an offer if you had not money of your own. I could not marry unless my wife had money, and I would not marry any woman unless I felt I could love her – not if she had ever so much. There! now you know it all. I suppose I have not said it as I ought to do, but if you're the woman I take you for that won't make much difference.'

For my part I think that he said what he had to say very well. I do not know that he could have done it much better. I do not know that any other form of words would have been more persuasive to the woman he was addressing. Had he said much of his love, or nothing of his poverty; or had he omitted altogether any mention of her wealth, her heart would have gone against him at once. As it was he had produced in her mind such a state of doubt, that she was unable to answer him on the moment.

'I know,' he went on to say, 'that I haven't much to offer you.' He had now seated himself again, and as he spoke he looked upon the ground.

'It isn't that, John,' she answered; 'you have much more to give than I have a right to expect.'

'No,' he said. 'What I offer you is a life of endless trouble and care. I know all about it myself. It's all very well to talk of a competence and a big house, and if you were to take me, perhaps we might keep the old place on and furnish it again, and my mother thinks a great deal about the title. For my part I think it's only a nuisance when a man has not got a fortune with it, and I don't suppose it will be any pleasure to you to be called Lady Ball. You'd have a life of fret and worry, and would not have half so much money to spend as you have now. I know all that, and have thought a deal about it before I could bring myself to speak to you. But, Margaret, you would have duties which would, I think, in themselves, have a pleasure for you. You would know what to do with your life, and would be of inestimable value to many people who would love you dearly. As for me, I never saw any other woman whom I could bring myself to offer as a mother to my children.' All this he said looking down at the floor, in a low, dull, droning voice, as though every sentence spoken were to have been the last. Then he paused, looked into her face for a moment, and after that, allowed his eyes again to fall on the ground.

Margaret was, of course, aware that she must make him some answer, and she was by no means prepared to give him one that would be favourable. Indeed, she thought she knew that she could not marry him, because she felt that she did not love him with affection of the sort which would be due to a husband. She told herself that she must refuse his offer. But yet she wanted time, and above all things, she wished to find words which would not be painful to him. His dull droning voice, and the honest recital of his troubles, and of her troubles if she were to share his lot, had touched her more nearly than any vows of love would have done. When he told her of the heavy duties which might fall to her lot as his wife, he almost made her think that it might be well for her to marry him, even though she did not love him. 'I hardly know how to answer you, you have taken me so much by surprise,' she said.

'You need not give me an answer at once,' he replied; 'you can think of it.' As she did not immediately say anything, he presumed that she assented to this proposition. 'You won't wonder now,' he said, 'that I wished you to stay here, or that my mother wished it.'

'Does Lady Ball know?' she asked.

'Yes, my mother does know.'

'What am I to say to her?'

'Shall I tell you, Margaret, what to say? Put your arms round her neck, and tell her that you will be her daughter.'

'No, John; I cannot do that; and perhaps I ought to say now that I don't think it will ever be possible. It has all so surprised me, that I haven't known how to speak; and I am afraid I shall be letting you go from me with a false idea. Perhaps I ought to say at once that it cannot be.'

'No, Margaret, no. It is much better that you should think of it. No harm can come of that.'

'There will be harm if you are disappointed.'

'I certainly shall be disappointed if you decide against me; but not more violently so, if you do it next week than if you do it now. But I do hope that you will not decide against me.'

'And what am I to do?'

'You can write to me from Littlebath.'

'And how soon must I write?'

'As soon as you can make up your mind. But, Margaret, do not decide against me too quickly. I do not know that I shall do myself any good by promising you that I will love you tenderly.' So saying he put out his hand, and she took it; and they stood there looking into each other's eyes, as young lovers might have done – as his son might have looked into those of her daughter, had she been married young and had children of her own. In the teeth of all those tedious money dealings in the City there was some spice of romance left within his bosom yet!

But how was she to get herself out of the room? It would not do for such a Juliet to stay all the night looking into the eyes of her ancient Romeo. And how was she to behave herself to Lady Ball, when she should again find herself in the drawing-room, conscious as she was that Lady Ball knew all about it? And how was she to conduct herself before all those young people whom she had left there? And her proposed father-in-law, whom she feared so much, and in truth disliked so greatly – would he know all about it, and thrust his ill-natured jokes at her? Her lover should have opened the door for her to pass through; but instead of doing so, as soon as she had withdrawn her hand from his, he placed himself on the rug, and leaned back in silence against the chimney-piece.

'I suppose it wouldn't do,' she said, 'for me to go off to bed without seeing them.'

'I think you had better see my mother,' he replied, 'else you will feel awkward in the morning.'

Then she opened the door for herself, and with frightened feet crept back to the drawing-room. She could hardly bring herself to open the second door; but when she had done so, her heart was greatly released, as, looking in, she saw that her aunt was the only person there.

'Well, Margaret,' said the old lady, walking up to her; 'well?'

'Dear aunt, I don't know what I am to say to you. I don't know what you want.'

'I want you to tell me you have consented to become John's wife.'

'But I have not consented. Think how sudden it has been, aunt!'

'Yes, yes; I can understand that. You could not tell him at once that you would take him; but you won't mind telling me.'

'I would have told him so in an instant, if I had made up my mind. Do you think I would wish to keep him in suspense on such a matters? If I could have felt that I could love him as his wife, I would have told him so instantly – instantly.'

'And why not love him as his wife – why not?' Lady Ball, as she asked the question, was almost imperious in her eagerness.

'Why not, aunt? It is not easy to answer such a question as that. A woman, I suppose, can't say why she doesn't love a man, nor yet why she does. You see, it's so sudden. I hadn't thought of him in that way.'

'You've known him now for nearly a year, and you've been in the house with him for the last three weeks. If you haven't seen that he has been attached to you, you are the only person in the house that has been so blind.'

'I haven't seen it at all, aunt.'

'Perhaps you are afraid of the responsibility,' said Lady Ball.

'I should fear it certainly; but that alone would not deter me. I would endeavour to do my best.'

'And you don't like living in the same house with me and Sir John.'

'Indeed, yes; you are always good to me; and as to my uncle, I know he does not mean to be unkind. I should not fear that.'

'The truth is, I suppose, Margaret, that you do not like to part with your money.'

'That's unjust, aunt. I don't think I care more for my money than another woman.'

'Then what is it? He can give you a position in the world higher than any you could have had a hope to possess. As Lady Ball you will be equal in all respects to your own far-away cousin, Lady Mackenzie.'

'That has nothing to do with it, aunt.'

'Then what is it?' asked Lady Ball again. 'I suppose you have no absolute objection to be a baronet's wife.'

'Suppose, aunt, that I do not love him?'

'Pshaw!' said the old woman.

'But it isn't pshaw,' said Miss Mackenzie. 'No woman ought to marry a man unless she feels that she loves him.'

'Pshaw!' said Lady Ball again.

They had both been standing; and as everybody else was gone Miss Mackenzie had determined that she would go off to bed without settling herself in the room. So she prepared herself for her departure.

'I'll say good-night now, aunt. I have still some of my packing to do, and I must be up early.'

'Don't be in a hurry, Margaret. I want to speak to you before you leave us, and I shall have no other opportunity. Sit down, won't you?'

Then Miss Mackenzie seated herself, most unwillingly.

'I don't know that there is anyone nearer to you than I am, my dear; at any rate, no woman; and therefore I can say more than any other person. When you talk of not loving John, does that mean – does it mean that you are engaged to anyone else?'

'No, it does not.'

'And it does not mean that there is anyone else whom you are thinking of marrying?'

'I am not thinking of marrying anyone.'

'Or that you love any other man?'

'You are cross-questioning me, aunt, more than is fair.'

'Then there is some one?'

'No, there is nobody. What I say about John I don't say through any feeling for anybody else'

'Then, my dear, I think that a little talk between you and me may make this matter all right. I'm sure you don't doubt John when he says that he loves you very dearly. As for your loving him, of course that would come. It is not as if you two were two young people, and that you wanted to be billing and cooing. Of course you ought to be fond of each other, and like each other's company; and I have no doubt that you will. You and I would, of course, be thrown very much together, and I'm sure I'm very fond of you. Indeed, Margaret, I have endeavoured to show that I am.'

'You've been very kind, aunt.'

'Therefore as to your loving him, I really don't think there need be any doubt about that. Then, my dear, as to the other part of the arrangement – the money and all that. If you were to have any children, your own fortune would be settled on them; at least, that could be arranged, if you required it; though, as your fortune all came from the Balls, and is the very money with which the title was intended to be maintained, you probably would not be very exacting about that. Stop a moment, my dear, and let me finish before you speak. I want you particularly to think of what I say, and to remember that all your money did come from the Balls. It has been very hard upon John, you must feel that. Look at him with his heavy family, and how he works for them!'

'But my uncle Jonathan died and left his money to my brothers before John was married. It is twenty-five years ago.'

'Well I remember it, my dear! John was just engaged to Rachel, and the marriage was put off because of the great cruelty of Jonathan's will. Of course I am not blaming you.'

'I was only ten years old, and uncle Jonathan did not leave me a penny. My money came to me from my brother; and, as far as I can understand, it is nearly double as much as he got from Sir John's brother.'

'That may be; but John would have doubled it quite as readily as Walter Mackenzie. What I mean to say is this, that as you have the money which in the course of nature would have come to John, and which would have been his now if a great injustice had not been done –'

'It was done by a Ball, and not by a Mackenzie.'

'That does not alter the case in the least. Your feelings should be just the same in spite of that. Of course the money is yours and you can do what you like with it. You can give it to young Mr Samuel Rubb, if you please.'

Stupid old woman! 'But I think you must feel that you should repair the injury which was done, as it is in your power to do so. A fine position is offered you. When poor Sir John goes, you will become Lady Ball, and be the mistress of this house, and have your own carriage.' Terribly stupid old woman! 'And you would have friends and relatives always round you, instead of being all alone at such a place as Littlebath, which must, I should say, be very sad. Of course there would be duties to perform to the dear children; but I don't think so ill of you, Margaret, as to suppose for an instant that you would shrink from that. Stop one moment, my dear, and I shall have done. I think I have said all now; but I can well understand that when John spoke to you, you could not immediately give him a favourable answer. It was much better to leave it till to-morrow. But you can't have any objection to speaking out to me, and I really think you might make me happy by saying that it shall be as I wish.'

It is astonishing the harm that an old woman may do when she goes well to work, and when she believes she can prevail by means of her own peculiar eloquence. Lady Ball had so trusted to her own prestige, to her own ladyship, to her own carriage and horses, and to the rest of it, and had also so misjudged Margaret's ordinary mild manner, that she had thought to force her niece into an immediate acquiescence by her mere words. The result, however, was exactly the contrary to this. Had Miss Mackenzie been left to herself after the interview with Mr Ball: had she gone upstairs to sleep upon his proposal, without any disturbance to those visions of sacrificial duty which his plain statement had produced: had she been allowed to leave the house and think over it all without any other argument to her than those which he had used, I think that she would have accepted him. But now she was up in arms against the whole thing. Her mind, clear as it was, was hardly lucid enough to allow of her separating the mother and son at this moment. She was claimed as a wife into the family because they thought that they had a right to her fortune; and the temptations offered, by which they hoped to draw her into her duty, were a beggarly title and an old coach! No! The visions of sacrificial duty were all dispelled. There was doubt before, but now there was no doubt.

'I think I will go to bed, aunt,' she said very calmly, 'and I will write to John from Littlebath.'

'And cannot you put me out of my suspense?'

'If you wish it, yes. I know that I must refuse him. I wish that I had told him so at once, as then there would have been an end of it.'

'You don't mean that you have made up your mind?'

'Yes, aunt, I do. I should be wrong to marry a man that I do not love; and as for the money, aunt, I must say that I think you are mistaken.'

'How mistaken?'

'You think that I am called upon to put right some wrong that you think was done you by Sir John's brother. I don't think that I am under any such obligation. Uncle Jonathan left his money to his sister's children instead of to his brother's children. If his money had come to John, you would not have admitted that we had any claim, because we were nephews and nieces.'

'The whole thing would have been different.'

'Well, aunt, I am very tired, and if you'll let me, I'll go to bed.'

'Oh, certainly.'

Then, with anything but warm affection, the aunt and niece parted, and Miss Mackenzie went to her bed with a firm resolution that she would not become Lady Ball.

It had been arranged for some time back that Mr Ball was to accompany his cousin up to London by the train; and though under the present circumstances that arrangement was not without a certain amount of inconvenience, there was no excuse at hand for changing it. Not a word was said at breakfast as to the scenes of last night. Indeed, no word could very well have been said, as all the family was present, including Jack and the girls. Lady Ball was very quiet, and very dignified; but Miss Mackenzie perceived that she was always called 'Margaret,' and not 'my dear,' as had been her aunt's custom. Very little was said by any one, and not a great deal was eaten.

'Well; when are we to see you back again?' said Sir John, as Margaret arose from her chair on being told that the carriage was there.

'Perhaps you and my aunt will come down some day and see me at Littlebath?' said Miss Mackenzie.

'No; I don't think that's very likely,' said Sir John.

Then she kissed all the children, till she came to Jack.

'I am going to kiss you, too,' she said to him.

'No objection in life,' said Jack. 'I sha'n't complain about that.'

'You'll come and see me at Littlebath?' said she.

'That I will if you'll ask me.'

Then she put her face to her aunt, and Lady Ball permitted her cheek to be touched. Lady Ball was still not without hope, but she thought that the surest way was to assume a high dignity of demeanour, and to exhibit a certain amount of displeasure. She still believed that Margaret might be frightened into the match. It was but a mile and a half to the station, and for that distance Mr Ball and Margaret sat together in the carriage. He said nothing to her as to his proposal till the station was in view, and then only a word.

'Think well of it, Margaret, if you can.'

'I fear I cannot think well of it,' she answered. But she spoke so low, that I doubt whether he completely heard her words. The train up to London was nearly full, and there he had no opportunity of speaking to her. But he desired no such opportunity. He had said all that he had to say, and was almost well pleased to know that a final answer was to be given to him, not personally, but by letter. His mother had spoken to him that morning, and had made him understand that she was not well pleased with Margaret; but she had said nothing to quench her son's hopes.

'Of course she will accept you,' Lady Ball had said, 'but women like her never like to do anything without making a fuss about it.'

'To me, yesterday, I thought she behaved admirably,' said her son.

At the station at London he put her into the cab that was to take her to Gower Street, and as he shook hands with her through the window, he once more said the same words:

'Think well of it, Margaret, if you can.'

✖ EIGHT ✖

Mrs Tom Mackenzie's Dinner Party

MRS TOM WAS EVER SO GRACIOUS ON the arrival of her sister-in-law, but even in her graciousness there was something which seemed to Margaret to tell of her dislike. Near relatives, when they are on good terms with each other, are not gracious. Now, Mrs Tom, though she was ever so gracious, was by no means cordial. Susanna, however, was delighted to see her aunt, and Margaret, when she felt the girl's arms round her neck, declared to herself that that should suffice for her – that should be her love, and it should be enough. If indeed, in after years, she could make Jack love her too, that would be better still. Then her mind went to work upon a little marriage scheme that would in due time make a baronet's wife of Susanna. It would not suit her to become Lady Ball, but it might suit Susanna.

'We are going to have a little dinner party to-day,' said Mrs Tom.

'A dinner party!' said Margaret. 'I didn't look for that, Sarah.'

'Perhaps I ought not to call it a party, for there are only one or two coming. There's Dr Slumpy and his wife; I don't know whether you ever met Dr Slumpy. He has attended us for ever so long; and there is Miss Colza, a great friend of mine. Mademoiselle Colza I ought to call her, because her father was a Portuguese. Only as she never saw him, we call her Miss. And there's Mr Rubb – Samuel Rubb, junior. I think you met him at Littlebath.'

'Yes; I know Mr Rubb.'

'That's all; and I might as well say how it will be now. Mr Rubb will take you down to dinner. Tom will take Mrs Slumpy, and the doctor will take me. Young Tom' – Young Tom was her son, who was now beginning his career at Rubb and Mackenzie's – 'Young Tom will take Miss Colza, and

Mary Jane and Susanna will come down by themselves. We might have managed twelve, and Tom did think of asking Mr Handcock and one of the other clerks, but he did not know whether you would have liked it.'

'I should not have minded it. That is, I should have been very glad to meet Mr Handcock, but I don't care about it.'

'That's just what we thought, and therefore we did not ask him. You'll remember, won't you, that Mr Rubb takes you down?' After that Miss Mackenzie took her nieces to the Zoological Gardens, leaving Mary Jane at home to assist her mother in the cares for the coming festival, and thus the day wore itself away till it was time for them to prepare themselves for the party.

Miss Colza was the first to come. She was a young lady somewhat older than Miss Mackenzie; but the circumstances of her life had induced her to retain many of the propensities of her girlhood. She was as young looking as curls and pink bows could make her, and was by no means a useless guest at a small dinner party, as she could chatter like a magpie. Her claims to be called 'Mademoiselle' were not very strong, as she had lived in Finsbury Square all her life. Her father was connected in trade with the Rubb and Mackenzie firm, and dealt, I think, in oil. She was introduced with great ceremony, and having heard that Miss Mackenzie lived at Littlebath, went off at score about the pleasures of that delicious place.

'I do so hate London, Miss Mackenzie.'

'I lived here all my life, and I can't say I liked it.'

'It is such a crowd, isn't it? and yet so dull. Give me Brighton! We were down for a week in November, and it was nice.'

'I never saw Brighton.'

'Oh, do go to Brighton. Everybody goes there now; you really do see the world at Brighton. Now, in London one sees nothing.'

Then came in Mr Rubb, and Miss Colza at once turned her attention to him. But Mr Rubb shook Miss Colza off almost unceremoniously, and seated himself by Miss Mackenzie. Immediately afterwards arrived the doctor and his wife. The doctor was a very silent man, and as Tom Mackenzie himself was not given to much talking, it was well that Miss Colza should be there. Mrs Slumpy could take her share in conversation with an effort, when duly assisted; but she could not lead the van, and required more sprightly aid than her host was qualified to give her. Then there was a whisper between Tom and Mrs Tom and the bell was rung, and the dinner was ordered. Seven had been the time named, and a quarter past seven saw the guests assembled in the drawing-room. A very dignified person in white cotton gloves had announced the names, and the same dignified person had taken the order for dinner. The dignified person had then retreated downstairs slowly, and what was taking place for the next half-hour poor Mrs Mackenzie, in the agony of her mind, could not surmise. She longed to go and see, but did not dare. Even for Dr

Slumpy, or even for his wife, had they been alone with her she would not have cared much. Miss Colza she could have treated with perfect indifference – could even have taken her down into the kitchen with her. Rubb, her own junior partner, was nothing, and Miss Mackenzie was simply her sister-in-law. But together they made a party. Moreover she had on her best and stiffest silk gown, and so armed she could not have been effective in the kitchen. And so came a silence for some minutes, in spite of the efforts of Miss Colza. At last the hostess plucked up her courage to make a little effort.

'Tom,' she said, 'I really think you had better ring again.'

'It will be all right, soon,' said Tom, considering that upon the whole it would be better not to disturb the gentleman downstairs just yet.

'Upon my word, I never felt it so cold in my life as I did to-day,' he said, turning on Dr Slumpy for the third time with that remark.

'Very cold,' said Dr Slumpy, pulling out his watch and looking at it.

'I really think you'd better ring the bell,' said Mrs Tom.

Tom, however, did not stir, and after another period of five minutes dinner was announced. It may be as well, perhaps, to explain, that the soup had been on the table for the last quarter of an hour or more, but that after placing the tureen on the table, the dignified gentleman downstairs had come to words with the cook, and had refused to go on further with the business of the night until that ill-used woman acceded to certain terms of his own in reference to the manner in which the foods should be served. He had seen the world, and had lofty ideas, and had been taught to be a tyrant by the weakness of those among whom his life had been spent. The cook had alleged that the dinner, as regarded the eating of it, would certainly be spoilt. As to that, he had expressed a mighty indifference. If he was to have any hand in them, things were to be done according to certain rules, which, as he said, prevailed in the world of fashion. The cook, who had a temper and who regarded her mistress, stood out long and boldly, but when the housemaid, who was to assist Mr Grandairs upstairs, absolutely deserted her, and sitting down began to cry, saying: 'Sairey, why don't you do as he tells you? What signifies its being greasy if it hain't never to go hup?' then Sarah's courage gave way, and Mr Grandairs, with all the conqueror in his bosom, announced that dinner was served.

It was a great relief. Even Miss Colza's tongue had been silent, and Mr Rubb had found himself unable to carry on any further small talk with Miss Mackenzie. The minds of men and women become so tuned to certain positions, that they go astray and won't act when those positions are confused. Almost every man can talk for fifteen minutes, standing in a drawing-room, before dinner; but where is the man who can do it for an hour? It is not his appetite that impedes him, for he could well have borne to dine at eight instead of seven; nor is it that matter lacks him, for at other times his eloquence does not cease to flow so soon. But at that special point of the day he is supposed to talk for fifteen minutes, and if any prolonged call is then made upon him, his talking apparatus falls out of order and will not work. You can sit still on a Sunday morning, in the cold, on a very narrow bench, with no comfort appertaining, and listen for half an hour to a rapid outflow of words, which, for any purpose of instruction or edification, are absolutely useless to you. The reading to you of the 'Quæ genus,' or 'As in præsenti,' could not be more uninteresting. Try to undergo the same thing in your own house on a Wednesday afternoon, and see where you will be. To those ladies and gentlemen who had been assembled in Mrs Mackenzie's drawing-room this prolonged waiting had been as though the length of the sermon had been doubled, or as if it had fallen on them at some unexpected and unauthorised time.

But now they descended, each gentleman taking his allotted lady, and Colza's voice was again heard. At the bottom of the stairs, just behind the dining-room door, stood the tyrant, looking very great, repressing with his left hand the housemaid who was behind him. She having observed Sarah at the top of the kitchen stairs telegraphing for assistance, had endeavoured to make her way to her friend while Tom Mackenzie and Mrs Slumpy were still upon the stairs; but the tyrant, though he had seen the cook's distress, had refused and sternly kept the girl a prisoner behind him. Ruat dinner, fiat genteel deportment.

The order of the construction of the dinner was no doubt à la Russe; and why should it not have been so, as Tom Mackenzie either had or was supposed to have as much as eight hundred a year? But I think it must be confessed that the architecture was in some degree composite. It was à la Russe, because in the centre there was a green arrangement of little boughs with artificial flowers fixed on them, and because there were figs and raisins, and little dishes with dabs of preserve on them, all around the green arrangement; but the soups and fish were on the table, as was also the wine, though it was understood that no one was to be allowed to help himself or his neighbour to the contents of the bottle. When Dr Slumpy once made an attempt at the sherry, Grandairs was down upon him instantly, although laden at the time with both potatoes and sea-kale; after that he went round and frowned at Dr Slumpy, and Dr Slumpy understood the frown.

That the soup should be cold, everybody no doubt expected. It was clear soup. Made chiefly of Marsala, and purchased from the pastry cook's in Store Street. Grandairs, no doubt, knew all about it, as he was connected with the same establishment. The fish – Mrs Mackenzie had feared greatly about her fish, having necessarily trusted its fate solely to her own cook – was very ragged in its appearance, and could not be very warm; the melted butter too was thick and clotted, and was brought round with the other condiments too late to be of much service; but still the fish was eatable, and Mrs Mackenzie's heart, which had sunk very low as the unconsumed soup was carried away, rose again in her bosom. Poor woman! she had done her best, and it was hard that she should suffer. One little effort she made at the moment to induce Elizabeth to carry round the sauce, but Grandairs had at once crushed it; he had rushed at the girl and taken the butter-boat from her hand. Mrs Mackenzie had seen it all; but what could she do, poor soul?

The thing was badly managed in every way. The whole hope of conversation round the table depended on Miss Colza, and she was deeply offended by having been torn away from Mr Rubb. How could she talk seated between the two Tom Mackenzies? From Dr Slumpy Mrs Mackenzie could not get a word. Indeed, with so great a weight on her mind, how could she be expected to make any great effort in that direction? But Mr Mackenzie might have done something, and she resolved that she would tell him so before he slept that night. She had slaved all day in order that he might appear respectable before his own relatives, at the bottom of his own table – and now he would do nothing! 'I believe he is thinking of his own dinner!' she said to herself. If her accusation was just his thoughts must have been very sad.

In a quiet way Mr Rubb did talk to his neighbour. Upstairs he had spoken a word or two about Littlebath, saying how glad he was that he had been there. He should always remember Littlebath as one of the pleasantest places he had ever seen. He wished that he lived at Littlebath; but then what was the good of his wishing anything, knowing as he did that he was bound for life to Rubb and Mackenzie's counting house!

'And you will earn your livelihood there,' Miss Mackenzie had replied.

'Yes; and something more than that I hope. I don't mind telling you – a friend like you – that I will either spoil a horn or make a spoon. I won't go on in the old groove, which hardly gives any of us salt to our porridge. If I understand anything of English commerce, I think I can see my way to better things than that.' Then the period of painful waiting had commenced, and he was unable to say anything more.

That had been upstairs. Now below, amidst all the troubles of Mrs Mackenzie and the tyranny of Grandairs, he began again:

'Do you like London dinner parties?'

'I never was at one before.'

'Never at one before! I thought you had lived in London all your life.'

'So I have; but we never used to dine out. My brother was an invalid.'

'And do they do the thing well at Littlebath?'

'I never dined out there. You think it very odd, I dare say, but I never was at a dinner party in my life – not before this.'

'Don't the Balls see much company?'

'No, very little; none of that kind.'

'Dear me. It comes so often to us here that we get tired of it. I do, at least. I'm not always up to this kind of thing. Champagne – if you please. Miss Mackenzie, you will take some champagne?'

Now had come the crisis of the evening, the moment that was all important, and Grandairs was making his round in all the pride of his vocation. But Mrs Mackenzie was by no means so proud at the present conjuncture of affairs. There was but one bottle of champagne. 'So little wine is drank now, that, what is the good of getting more? Of course the children won't have it.' So she had spoken to her husband. And who shall blame her or say where economy ends, or where meanness begins? She had wanted no champagne herself, but had wished to treat her friends well. She had seized a moment after Grandairs had come, and Mrs Slumpy was not yet there, to give instructions to the great functionary.

'Don't mind me with the champagne, nor yet Mr Tom, nor the young ladies.'

Thus she had reduced the number to six, and had calculated that the bottle would certainly be good for that number, with probably a second glass for the doctor and Mr Rubb. But Grandairs had not condescended to be put out of his way by such orders as these. The bottle had first come to Miss Colza, and then Tom's glass had been filled, and Susanna's – through no fault of theirs, innocent bairns, 'but on purpose!' as Mrs Mackenzie afterwards declared to her husband when speaking of the man's iniquity. And I think it had been done on purpose. The same thing occurred with Mary Jane – till Mrs Mackenzie, looking on, could have cried. The girl's glass was filled full, and she did give a little shriek at last. But what availed shrieking? When the bottle came round behind Mrs Mackenzie back to Dr Slumpy, it was dry, and the wicked wretch held the useless nozzle triumphantly over the doctor's glass.

'Give me some sherry, then,' said the doctor.

The little dishes which had been brought round after the fish, three in number – and they in the proper order of things should have been spoken of before the champagne – had been in their way successful. They had been so fabricated, that all they who attempted to eat of their contents became at once aware that they had got hold of something very nasty, something that could hardly have been intended by Christian cooks as food for men; but, nevertheless, there had been something of glory attending them. Little dishes require no concomitant vegetables, and therefore there had been no scrambling. Grandairs brought one round after the other with much majesty, while Elizabeth stood behind looking on in wonder. After the second little dish Grandairs changed the plates, so that it was possible to partake of two, a feat which was performed by Tom Mackenzie the younger. At this period Mrs Mackenzie, striving hard for equanimity, attempted a word or two with the doctor. But immediately upon that came the affair of the champagne, and she was crushed, never to rise again.

Mr Rubb at this time had settled down into so pleasant a little series of whispers with his neighbour, that Miss Colza resolved once more to exert herself, not with the praiseworthy desire of assisting her friend Mrs Mackenzie, but with malice prepense in reference to Miss Mackenzie.

Miss Mackenzie seemed to be having 'a good time' with her neighbour Samuel Rubb, junior, and Miss Colza, who was a woman of courage, could not see that and not make an effort. It cannot be told here what passages there had been between Mr Rubb and Miss Colza. That there had absolutely been passages I beg the reader to understand. 'Mr Rubb,' she said, stretching across the table, 'do you remember when, in this very room, we met Mr and Mrs Talbot Green?'

'Oh yes, very well,' said Mr Rubb, and then turning to Miss Mackenzie, he went on with his little whispers.

'Mr Rubb,' continued Miss Colza, 'does anybody put you in mind of Mrs Talbot Green?'

'Nobody in particular. She was a thin, tall, plain woman, with red hair, wasn't she? Who ought she to put me in mind of?'

'Oh dear! how can you forget so? That wasn't her looks at all. We all agreed that she was quite interesting-looking. Her hair was just fair, and that was all. But I shan't say anything more about it.'

'But who do you say is like her?'

'Miss Colza means Aunt Margaret,' said Mary Jane.

'Of course I do,' said Miss Colza. 'But Mrs Talbot Green was not at all the person that Mr Rubb has described; we all thought her very nice-looking. Mr Rubb, do you remember how you would go on talking to her, till Mr Talbot Green did not like it at all?'

'No, I don't.'

'Oh, but you did; and you always do.'

Then Miss Colza ceased, having finished that effort. But she made others from time to time as long as they remained in the dining-room, and by no means gave up the battle. There are women who can fight such battles when they have not an inch of ground on which to stand.

After the little dishes there came, of course, a saddle of mutton, and, equally of course, a pair of boiled fowls. There was also a tongue; but the à la Russe construction of the dinner was maintained by keeping the tongue on the sideboard, while the mutton and chickens were put down to be carved in the ordinary way. The ladies all partook of the chickens, and the gentlemen all of the mutton. The arrangement was very tedious, as Dr Slumpy was not as clever with the wings of the fowls as he perhaps would have been had he not been defrauded in the matter of the champagne; and then every separate plate was carried away to the sideboard with reference to the tongue. Currant jelly had been duly provided, and, if Elizabeth had been allowed to dispense it, might have been useful. But Grandairs was too much for the jelly, as he had been for the fish-sauce, and Dr Slumpy in vain looked up, and sighed, and waited. A man in such a condition measures the amount of cold which his meat may possibly endure against the future coming of the potatoes, till he falls utterly to the ground between two stools. So was it now with Dr Slumpy. He gave one last sigh as he saw the gravy congeal upon his plate, but, nevertheless, he had finished the unpalatable food before Grandairs had arrived to his assistance.

Why tell of the ruin of the maccaroni, of the fine-coloured pyramids of shaking sweet things which nobody would eat, and by the non-consumption of which nothing was gained, as they all went back to the pastrycook's – or of the ice-puddings flavoured with onions? It was all misery, wretchedness, and degradation. Grandairs was king, and Mrs Mackenzie was the lowest of his slaves. And why? Why had she done this thing? Why had she, who, to give her her due, generally held her own in her own house pretty firmly – why had she lowered her neck and made a wretched thing of herself? She knew that it would be so when she first suggested to herself the attempt. She did it for fashion's sake, you will say. But there was no one there who did not as accurately know as she did herself, how absolutely beyond fashion's way lay her way. She was making no fight to enter some special portal of the world, as a lady may do who takes a house suddenly in Mayfair, having come from God knows where. Her place in the world was fixed, and she made no contest as to the fixing. She hoped for no great change in the direction of society. Why on earth did she perplex her mind and bruise her spirit, by giving a dinner à la anything? Why did she not have the roast mutton alone, so that all her guests might have eaten and have been merry?

She could not have answered this question herself, and I doubt whether I can do so for her. But this I feel, that unless the question can get itself answered, ordinary Englishmen must cease to go and eat dinners at each other's houses. The ordinary Englishman, of whom we are now speaking, has eight hundred a year; he lives in London; and he has a wife and three or four children. Had he not better give it up and go back to his little bit of fish and his leg of mutton? Let him do that boldly, and he will find that we, his friends, will come to him fast enough; yes, and will make a gala day of it. By Heavens, we have no gala time of it when we go to dine with Mrs Mackenzie à la Russe! Lady Mackenzie, whose husband has ever so many thousands a year, no doubt does it very well. Money, which cannot do everything – which, if well weighed, cannot in its excess perhaps do much – can do some things. It will buy diamonds and give grand banquets. But paste diamonds, and banquets which are only would-be grand, are among the poorest imitations to which the world has descended.

'So you really go to Littlebath to-morrow,' Mr Rubb said to Miss Mackenzie, when they were again together in the drawing-room.

'Yes, to-morrow morning. Susanna must be at school the next day.'

'Happy Susanna! I wish I were going to school at Littlebath. Then I shan't see you again before you go.'

'No; I suppose not.'

'I am so sorry, because I particularly wished to speak to you – most particularly. I suppose I could not see you in the morning? But, no; it would not do. I could not get you alone without making such a fuss of the thing.'

'Couldn't you say it now?' asked Miss Mackenzie.

'I will, if you'll let me; only I suppose it isn't quite the thing to talk about business at an evening party; and your sister-in-law, if she knew it, would never forgive me.'

'Then she shan't know it, Mr Rubb.'

'Since you are so good, I think I will make bold. Carpe diem, as we used to say at school, which means that one day is as good as another, and, if so why not any time in the day? Look here, Miss Mackenzie – about that money, you know.'

And Mr Rubb got nearer to her on the sofa as he whispered the word money into her ear. It immediately struck her that her own brother Tom had said not a word to her about the money, although they had been together for the best part of an hour before they had gone up to dress.

'I suppose Mr Slow will settle all that,' said Miss Mackenzie.

'Of course – that is to say, he has nothing further to settle just as yet. He has our bond for the money, and you may be sure it's all right. The property is purchased, and is ours – our own at this moment, thanks to you. But landed property is so hard to convey. Perhaps you don't understand much about that! and I'm sure I don't. The fact is, the title deeds at present are in other hands, a mere matter of form; and I want you to understand that the mortgage is not completed for that reason.'

'I suppose it will be done soon?'

'It may, or it may not; but that won't affect your interest, you know.'

'I was thinking of the security.'

'Well, the security is not as perfect as it should be. I tell you that honestly; and if we were dealing with strangers we should expect to be called on to refund. And we should refund instantly, but at a great sacrifice, a ruinous sacrifice. Now, I want you to put so much trust in us – in me, if I may be allowed to ask you to do so – as to believe that your money is substantially safe. I cannot explain it all now; but the benefit which you have done us is immense.'

'I suppose it will all come right, Mr Rubb.'

'It will all come right, Miss Mackenzie.'

Then there was extracted from her something which he was able to take as a promise that she would not stir in the matter for a while, but would take her interest without asking for any security as to her principal.

The conversation was interrupted by Miss Colza, who came and stood opposite to them.

'Well, I'm sure,' she said; 'you two are very confidential.'

'And why shouldn't we be confidential, Miss Colza?' asked Mr Rubb.

'Oh, dear! no reason in life, if you both like it.'

Miss Mackenzie was not sure that she did like it. But again she was not sure that she did not, when Mr Rubb pressed her hand at parting, and told her that her great kindness had been of the most material service to the firm. 'He felt it,' he said, 'if nobody else did.' That also might be a sacrificial duty and therefore gratifying.

The next morning she and Susanna left Gower Street at eight, spent an interesting period of nearly an hour at the railway station, and reached Littlebath in safety at one.

❧ NINE ❧

Miss Mackenzie's Philosophy

MISS MACKENZIE REMAINED QUIET IN HER ROOM for two days after her return before she went out to see anybody. These last Christmas weeks had certainly been the most eventful period of her life, and there was very much of which it was necessary that she should think. She had, she thought, made up her mind to refuse her cousin's offer; but the deed was not yet done. She had to think of the mode in which she must do it; and she could not but remember, also, that she might still change her mind in that matter if she pleased. The anger produced in her by Lady Ball's claim, as it were, to her fortune, had almost evaporated; but the memory of her cousin's story of his troubles was still fresh. 'I have a hard time of it sometimes, I can tell you.' Those words and others of the same kind were the arguments which had moved her, and made her try to think that she could love him. Then she remembered his bald head and the weary, careworn look about his eyes, and his little intermittent talk, addressed chiefly to his mother, about the money-market – little speeches made as he would sit with the newspaper in his hand:

'The Confederate loan isn't so bad, after all. I wish I'd taken a few.'

'You know you'd never have slept if you had,' Lady Ball would answer.

All this Miss Mackenzie now turned in her mind, and asked herself whether she could be happy in hearing such speeches for the remainder of her life.

'It is not as if you two were young people, and wanted to be billing and cooing,' Lady Ball had said to her the same evening.

Miss Mackenzie, as she thought of this, was not so sure that Lady Ball was right. Why should she not want billing and cooing as well as another? It was natural that a woman should want some of it in her life, and she had had none of it yet. She had had a lover, certainly, but there had been no billing and cooing with him. Nothing of that kind had been possible in her brother Walter's house.

And then the question naturally arose to her whether her aunt had treated her justly in bracketing her with John Ball in that matter of age. John Ball was ten years her senior; and ten years, she knew, was a very proper difference between a man and his wife. She was by no means inclined to plead, even to herself, that she was too young to marry her cousin; there was nothing in their ages to interfere, if the match was in other respects suitable. But still, was not he old for his age, and was not she young for hers? And if she should ultimately resolve to devote herself and what she had left of youth to his children and his welfare, should not the sacrifice be recognised? Had Lady Ball done well to speak of her as she certainly might well speak of him? Was she beyond all aptitude for billing and cooing, if billing and cooing might chance to come in her way?

Thinking of this during the long afternoon, when Susanna was at school, she got up and looked at herself in the mirror. She moved up her hair from off her ears, knowing where she would find a few that were grey, and shaking her head, as though owning to herself that she was old; but as her fingers ran almost involuntarily across her locks, her touch told her that they were soft and silken; and she looked into her own eyes, and saw that they were bright; and her hand touched the outline of her cheek, and she knew that something of the fresh bloom of youth was still there; and her lips parted, and there were her white teeth; and there came a smile and a dimple, and a slight purpose of laughter in her eye, and then a tear. She pulled her scarf tighter across her bosom, feeling her own form, and then she leaned forward and kissed herself in the glass.

He was very careworn, soiled as it were with the world, tired out with the dusty, weary life's walk which he had been compelled to take. Of romance in him there was nothing left, while in her the aptitude for romance had only just been born. It was not only that his head was bald, but that his eye was dull, and his step slow. The juices of life had been pressed out of him; his thoughts were all of his cares, and never of his hopes. It would be very sad to be the wife of such a man; it would be very sad, if there were no compensation; but might not the sacrificial duties give her that atonement which she would require? She would fain do something with her life and her money – some good, some great good to some other person. If that good to another person and billing and cooing might go together, it would be very pleasant. But she knew there was danger in such an idea. The billing and cooing might lead altogether to evil. But there could be no doubt that she would do good service if she married her cousin; her money would go to good purposes, and her care to those children would be invaluable. They were her cousins, and would it not be sweet to make of herself a sacrifice?

And then – Reader! remember that she was no saint, and that hitherto very little opportunity had been given to her of learning to discriminate true metal from dross. Then – she thought of Mr Samuel Rubb, junior. Mr Samuel Rubb, junior, was a handsome man, about her own age; and she felt almost sure that Mr Samuel Rubb, junior, admired her. He was not worn out with life; he was not broken with care; he would look forward into the world, and hope for things to come. One thing she knew to be true – he was not a gentleman. But then, why should she care for that? The being a gentleman was not everything. As for herself, might there not be strong reason to doubt whether those who were best qualified to judge would call her a lady? Her surviving brother kept an oilcloth shop, and the brother with whom she had always lived had been so retired from the world that neither he nor she knew anything of its ways. If love could be gained, and anything of romance; if some active living mode of life could thereby be opened to her, would it not be well for her to give up that idea of being a lady? Hitherto her rank had simply enabled her to become a Stumfoldian; and then she remembered that Mr Maguire's squint was very terrible! How she should live, what she should do with herself, were matters to her of painful thought; but she looked in the glass again, and resolved that she would decline the honour of becoming Mrs Ball.

On the following morning she wrote her letter, and it was written thus:

'7 Paragon, Littlebath, January, 186–.

'MY DEAR JOHN,

I have been thinking a great deal about what you said to me, and I have made up my mind that I ought not to become your wife. I know that the honour you have proposed to me is very great, and that I may seem to be ungrateful in declining it; but I cannot bring myself to feel that sort of love for you which a wife should have for her husband. I hope this will not make you displeased with me. It ought not to do so, as my feelings towards you and to your children are most affectionate.

'I know my aunt will be angry with me. Pray tell her from me, with my best love, that I have thought very much of all she said to me, and that I feel sure that I am doing right. It is not that I should be afraid of the duties which would fall upon me as your wife; but that the woman who undertakes those duties should feel for you a wife's love. I think it is best to speak openly, and I hope that you will not be offended.

'Give my best love to my uncle and aunt, and to the girls, and to Jack, who will, I hope, keep his promise of coming and seeing me.

'Your very affectionate cousin,

'MARGARET MACKENZIE'

'There,' said John Ball to his mother, when he had read the letter, 'I knew it would be so; and she is right. Why should she give up her money and her comfort and her ease, to look after my children?'

Lady Ball took the letter and read it, and pronounced it to be all nonsense.

'It may be all nonsense,' said her son; 'but such as it is, it is her answer.'

'I suppose you'll have to go down to Littlebath after her,' said Lady Ball.

'I certainly shall not do that. It would do no good; and I'm not going to persecute her.'

'Persecute her! What nonsense you men do talk! As if any woman in her condition could be persecuted by being asked to become a baronet's wife. I suppose I must go down.'

'I beg that you will not, mother.'

'She is just one of those women who are sure to stand off, not knowing their own minds. The best creature in the world, and really very clever, but weak in that respect! She has not had lovers when she was young, and she thinks that a man should come dallying about her as though she were eighteen. It only wants a little perseverance, John, and if you'll take my advice, you'll go down to Littlebath after her.'

But John, in this matter, would not follow his mother's advice, and declared that he would take no further steps. 'He was inclined,' he said, 'to think that Margaret was right. Why should any woman burden herself with nine children?'

Then Lady Ball said a great deal more about the Ball money, giving it as her decided opinion that Margaret owed herself and her money to the Balls. As she could not induce her son to do anything, she wrote a rejoinder to her niece.

'My dearest Margaret,' she said, 'Your letter has made both me and John very unhappy. He has set his heart upon making you his wife, and I don't think will ever hold up his head again if you will not consent. I write now instead of John, because he is so much oppressed. I wish you had remained here, because then we could have talked it over quietly. Would it not be better for you to be here than living alone at Littlebath? for I cannot call that little girl who is at school anything of a companion. Could you not leave her as a boarder, and come to us for a month? You would not be forced to pledge yourself to anything further; but we could talk it over.'

It need hardly be said that Miss Mackenzie, as she read this, declared to herself that she had no desire to talk over her own position with Lady Ball any further.

'John is afraid,' the letter went on to say, 'that he offended you by the manner of his proposition; and that he said too much about the children, and not enough about his own affection. Of course he loves you dearly. If you knew him as I do, which of course you can't as yet, though I hope you will, you would be aware that no consideration, either of money or about the children, would induce him to propose to any woman unless he loved her. You may take my word for that.'

There was a great deal more in the letter of the same kind, in which Lady Ball pressed her own peculiar arguments; but I need hardly say that they did not prevail with Miss Mackenzie. If the son could not induce his cousin to marry him, the mother certainly never would do so. It did not take her long to answer her aunt's letter. She said that she must, with many thanks, decline for the present to return to the Cedars, as the charge which she had taken of her niece made her presence at Littlebath necessary. As to the answer which she had given to John, she was afraid she could only say that it must stand. She had felt a little angry with Lady Ball; and though she tried not to show this in the tone of her letter, she did show it.

'If I were you I would never see her or speak to her again,' said Lady Ball to her son.

'Very likely I never shall,' he replied.

'Has your love-making with that old maid gone wrong, John?' the father asked.

But John Ball was used to his father's ill nature, and never answered it.

Nothing special to our story occurred at Littlebath during the next two or three months, except that Miss Mackenzie became more and more intimate with Miss Baker, and more and more anxious to form an acquaintance with Miss Todd. With all the Stumfoldians she was on terms of mitigated friendship, and always went to Mrs Stumfold's fortnightly tea-drinkings. But with no lady there – always excepting Miss Baker – did she find that she grew into familiarity. With Mrs Stumfold no one was familiar. She was afflicted by the weight of her own position, as we suppose the Queen to be, when we say that her Majesty's altitude is too high to admit of friendships. Mrs Stumfold never condescended – except to the bishop's wife who, in return, had snubbed Mrs Stumfold. But living, as she did, in an atmosphere of flattery and toadying, it was wonderful how well she preserved her equanimity, and how she would talk and perhaps think of herself, as a poor, erring human being. When, however, she insisted much upon this fact of her humanity, the coachmaker's wife would shake her head, and at last stamp her foot in anger, swearing that though everybody was of course dust, and grass, and worms; and though, of course, Mrs Stumfold must, by nature, be included in that everybody; yet dust, and grass, and worms nowhere exhibited themselves with so few of the stains of humanity on them as they did within the bosom of Mrs Stumfold. So that, though the absolute fact of Mrs Stumfold being dust, and grass, and worms, could not, in regard to the consistency of things, be denied, yet in her dustiness, grassiness, and worminess she was so little dusty, grassy, and wormy, that it was hardly fair, even in herself, to mention the fact at all.

'I know the deceit of my own heart,' Mrs Stumfold would say.

'Of course you do, Mrs Stumfold,' the coachmaker's wife replied. 'It is dreadful deceitful, no doubt. Where's the heart that ain't? But there's a difference in hearts. Your deceit isn't hard like most of 'em. You know it, Mrs Stumfold, and wrestle with it, and get your foot on the neck of it, so that, as one may say, it's always being killed and got the better of.'

During these months Miss Mackenzie learned to value at a very low rate the rank of the Stumfoldian circle into which she had been admitted. She argued the matter with herself, saying that the coachbuilder's wife and others were not ladies. In a general way she was, no doubt, bound to assume them to be ladies; but she taught herself to think that such ladyhood was not of itself worth a great deal. It would not be worth the while of any woman to abstain from having some Mr Rubb or the like, and from being the lawful mother of children in the Rubb and Mackenzie line of life, for the sake of such exceptional rank as was to be maintained by associating with the Stumfoldians. And, as she became used to the things and persons around her, she indulged herself in a considerable amount of social philosophy, turning over ideas in her mind for which they, who saw merely the lines of her outer life, would hardly have given her credit. After all, what was the good of being a lady? Or was there any good in it at all? Could there possibly be any good in making a struggle to be a lady? Was it not rather one of those things which are settled for one externally, as are the colour of one's hair and the size of one's bones, and which should be taken or left alone, as Providence may have directed? 'One cannot add a cubit to one's height, nor yet make oneself a lady;' that was the nature of Miss Mackenzie's argument with herself.

And, indeed, she carried the argument further than that. It was well to be a lady. She recognised perfectly the delicacy and worth of the article. Miss Baker was a lady; as to that there was no doubt. But, then, might it not also be very well not to be a lady; and might not the advantages of the one position be compensated with equal advantages in the other? It is a grand thing to be a queen; but a queen has no friends. It is fine to be a princess; but a princess has a very limited choice of husbands. There was something about Miss Baker that was very nice; but even Miss Baker was very melancholy, and Miss Mackenzie could see that that melancholy had come from wasted niceness. Had she not been so much the lady, she might have been more the woman. And there could be no disgrace in not being a lady, if such ladyhood depended on external circumstances arranged for one by Providence. No one blames one's washerwoman for not being a lady. No one wishes one's housekeeper to be a lady; and people are dismayed, rather than pleased, when they find that their tailors' wives want to be ladies. What does a woman get by being a lady? If fortune have made her so, fortune has done much for her. But the good things come as the natural concomitants of her fortunate position. It is not because she is a lady that she is liked by her peers and peeresses. But those choice gifts which have made her a lady have made her also to be liked. It comes from the outside, and for it no struggle can usefully be made. Such was the result of Miss Mackenzie's philosophy.

One may see that all these self-inquiries tended Rubb-wards. I do not mean that they were made with any direct intention on her part to reconcile herself to a marriage with Mr Samuel Rubb, or that she even thought of such an event as probable. He had said nothing to her to justify such thought, and as yet she knew but very little of him. But they all went to reconcile her to that sphere of life which her brother Tom had chosen, and which her brother Walter had despised. They taught her to believe that a firm footing below was better than what might, after a life's struggle, be found to be but a false footing above. And they were brightened undoubtedly by an idea that some marriage in which she could love and be loved was possible to her below, though it would hardly be possible to her above.

Her only disputant on the subject was Miss Baker, and she startled that lady much by the things which she said. Now, with Miss Baker, not to be a lady was to be nothing. It was her weakness, and I may also say her strength. Her ladyhood was of that nature that it took no soil from outer contact. It depended, even within her own bosom, on her own conduct solely, and in no degree on the conduct of those among whom she might chance to find herself. She thought it well to pass her evenings with Mr Stumfold's people, and he at any rate had the manners of a gentleman. So thinking, she felt in no wise disgraced because the coachbuilder's wife was a vulgar, illiterate woman. But there were things, not bad in themselves, which she herself would never have done, because she was a lady. She would have broken her heart rather than marry a man who was not a gentleman. It was not unlady-like to eat cold mutton, and she ate it. But she would have shuddered had she been called on to eat any mutton with a steel fork. She had little generous ways with her, because they were the ways of ladies, and she paid for them from off her own back and out of her own dish. She would not go out to tea in a street cab, because she was a lady and alone; but she had no objection to walk, with her servant with her if it was dark. No wonder that such a woman was dismayed by the philosophy of Miss Mackenzie.

And yet they had been brought together by much that was alike in their dispositions. Miss Mackenzie had now been more than six months an inhabitant of Littlebath, and six months at such places is enough for close intimacies. They were both quiet, conscientious, kindly women, each not without some ambition of activity, but each a little astray as to the way in which that activity should be shown. They were both alone in the world, and Miss Baker during the last year or two had become painfully so from the fact of her estrangement from her old friend Miss Todd. They both wished to be religious, having strong faith in the need of the comfort of religion; but neither of them were quite satisfied with the Stumfoldian creed. They had both, from conscience, eschewed the vanities of the world; but with neither was her conscience quite satisfied that such eschewal was necessary, and each regretted to be losing pleasures which might after all be innocent.

'If I'm to go to the bad place,' Miss Todd had said to Miss Baker, 'because I like to do something that won't hurt my old eyes of an evening, I don't see the justice of it. As for calling it gambling, it's a falsehood, and your Mr Stumfold knows that as well as I do. I haven't won or lost ten pounds in ten years, and I've no more idea of making money by cards than I have by sweeping the chimney. Tell me why are cards wicked? Drinking, and stealing, and lying, and backbiting, and naughty love-making – but especially backbiting – backbiting – backbiting – those are the things that the Bible says are wicked. I shall go on playing cards, my dear, till Mr Stumfold can send me chapter and verse forbidding it.'

Then Miss Baker, who was no doubt weak, had been unable to answer her, and had herself hankered after the flesh-pots of Egypt and the delights of the unregenerated.

All these things Miss Baker and Miss Mackenzie discussed, and Miss Baker learned to love her younger friend in spite of her heterodox philosophy. Miss Mackenzie was going to give a tea-party – nothing as yet having been quite settled, as there were difficulties in the way; but she propounded to Miss Baker the possibility of asking Miss Todd and some few of the less conspicuous Toddites. She had her ambition, and she wished to see whether even she might not do something to lessen the gulf which separated those who loved the pleasures of the world in Littlebath from the bosom of Mr Stumfold.

'You don't know what you are going to do,' Miss Baker said.

'I'm not going to do any harm.'

'That's more than you can say, my dear.' Miss Baker had learnt from Miss Todd to call her friends 'my dear.'

'You are always so afraid of everything,' said Miss Mackenzie.

'Of course I am – one has to be afraid. A single lady can't go about and do just as she likes, as a man can do, or a married woman.'

'I don't know about a man; but I think a single woman ought to be able to do more what she likes than a married woman. Suppose Mrs Stumfold found that I had got old Lady Ruff to meet her, what could she do to me?'

Old Lady Ruff was supposed to be the wickedest old card-player in all Littlebath, and there were strange stories afloat of the things she had done. There were Stumfoldians who declared that she had been seen through the blinds teaching her own maid piquet on a Sunday afternoon;

but any horror will get itself believed nowadays. How could they have known that it was not beggar-my-neighbour? But piquet was named because it is supposed in the Stumfoldian world to be the wickedest of all games.

'I don't suppose she'd do much,' said Miss Baker; 'no doubt she would be very much offended.'

'Why shouldn't I try to convert Lady Ruff?'

'She's over eighty, my dear.'

'But I suppose she's not past all hope. The older one is the more one ought to try. But, of course, I'm only joking about her. Would Miss Todd come if you were to ask her?'

'Perhaps she would, but I don't think she'd be comfortable; or if she were, she'd make the others uncomfortable. She always does exactly what she pleases.'

'That's just why I think I should like her. I wish I dared to do what I pleased! We all of us are such cowards. Only that I don't dare, I'd go off to Australia and marry a sheep farmer.'

'You would not like him when you'd got him – you'd find him very rough.'

'I shouldn't mind a bit about his being rough. I'd marry a shoe-black tomorrow if I thought I could make him happy, and he could make me happy.'

'But it wouldn't make you happy.'

'Ah! that's just what we don't know. I shan't marry a shoe-black, because I don't dare. So you think I'd better not ask Miss Todd. Perhaps she wouldn't get on well with Mr Maguire.'

'I had them both together once, my dear, and she made herself quite unbearable. You've no idea what kind of things she can say.'

'I should have thought Mr Maguire would have given her as good as she brought,' said Miss Mackenzie.

'So he did; and then Miss Todd got up and left him, saying out loud, before all the company, that it was not fair for him to come and preach sermons in such a place as that. I don't think they have ever met since.'

All this made Miss Mackenzie very thoughtful. She had thrown herself into the society of the saints, and now there seemed to be no escape for her; she could not be wicked even if she wished it. Having got into her convent, and, as it were, taken the vows of her order, she could not escape from it.

'That Mr Rubb that I told you of is coming down here,' she said, still speaking to Miss Baker of her party.

'Oh, dear! will he be here when you have your friends here?'

'That's what I intended; but I don't think I shall ask anybody at all. It is so stupid always seeing the same people.'

'Mr Rubb is – is – is –?'

'Yes; Mr Rubb is a partner in my brother's house, and sells oilcloth, and things of that sort, and is not by any means aristocratic. I know what you mean.'

'Don't be angry with me, my dear.'

'Angry! I am not a bit angry. Why should I be angry? A man who keeps a shop is not, I suppose, a gentleman. But then, you know, I don't care about gentlemen – about any gentleman, or any gentlemen.'

Miss Baker sighed, and then the conversation dropped. She had always cared about gentlemen – and once in her life, or perhaps twice, had cared about a gentleman.

Yes; Mr Rubb was coming down again. He had written to say that it was necessary that he should again see Miss Mackenzie about the money. The next morning after the conversation which has just been recorded, Miss Mackenzie got another letter about the same money, of which it will be necessary to say more in the next chapter.

⚹ TEN ⚹

Plenary Absolutions

THE LETTER WHICH MISS MACKENZIE RECEIVED WAS from old Mr Slow, her lawyer; and it was a very unpleasant letter. It was so unpleasant that it made her ears tingle when she read it and remembered that the person to whom special allusion was made was one whom she had taught herself to regard as her friend. Mr Slow's letter was as follows:

'7 Little St Dunstan Court,
'April, 186 –.

'DEAR MADAM,

I think it proper to write to you specially, about the loan made by you to Messrs Rubb and Mackenzie, as the sum lent is serious, and as there has been conduct on the part of some one which I regard as dishonest. I find that what we have done in the matter has been regulated rather by the fact that you and Mr Mackenzie are brother and sister, than by the ordinary course of such business; and I perceive that we had special warrant given to us for this by you in your letter of the 23rd November last; but, nevertheless, it is my duty to explain to you that Messrs Rubb and Mackenzie, or – as I believe to be the case, Mr Samuel Rubb, junior, of that firm – have not dealt with you fairly. The money was borrowed for the purpose of buying certain premises, and, I believe, was laid out in that way. But it was borrowed on the special understanding that you, as the lender, were to have the title-deeds of that property, and the first mortgage upon them. It was alleged, when the purchase was being made, that the money was wanted before the mortgage could be effected, and you desired us to advance it. This we did, aware of the close family connection between yourself and one of the firm. Of course, on your instruction, we should have done this had there been no such relationship, but in that case we should have made further inquiry, and, probably, have ventured to advise you. But though the money was so advanced without the completion of the mortgage, it was advanced on the distinct understanding that the security proffered in the first instance was to be forthcoming without delay. We now learn that the property is mortgaged to other parties to its full value, and that no security for your money is to be had.

'I have seen both Mr Mackenzie and Mr Rubb, junior. As regards your brother, I believe him to have been innocent of any intention of the deceit, for deceit there certainly has been. Indeed, he does not deny it. He offers to give you any security on the business, such as the stock-in-trade or the like, which I may advise you to take. But such would in truth be of no avail to you as security. He, your brother, seemed to be much distressed by what has been done, and I was grieved on his behalf. Mr Rubb – the younger Mr Rubb – expressed himself in a very different way. He at first declined to discuss the matter with me; and when I told him that if that was his way I would certainly expose him, he altered his tone a little, expressing regret that there should be delay as to the security, and wishing me to understand that you were yourself aware of all the facts.

'There can be no doubt that deceit has been used towards you in getting your money, and that Mr Rubb has laid himself open to proceedings which, if taken against him, would be absolutely ruinous to him. But I fear they would be also ruinous to your brother. It is my painful duty to tell you that your money so advanced is on a most precarious footing. The firm, in addition to their present liabilities, are not worth half the money; or, I fear I may say, any part of it. I presume there is a working profit, as two families live upon the business. Whether, if you were to come upon them as a creditor, you could get your money out of their assets, I cannot say; but you, perhaps, will not feel yourself disposed to resort to such a measure. I have considered it my duty to tell you all the facts, and though your distinct authority to us to advance the money absolves us from responsibility, I must regret that we did not make further inquiries before we allowed so large a sum of money to pass out of our hands.

'I am, dear Madam,
'Your faithful servant,
'JONATHAN SLOW.'

Mr Rubb's promised visit was to take place in eight or ten days from the date on which this letter was received. Miss Mackenzie's ears, as I have said, tingled as she read it. In the first place, it gave her a terrible picture of the precarious state of her brother's business. What would he do – he with his wife, and all his children, if things were in such a state as Mr Slow described them? And yet a month or two ago he was giving champagne and iced puddings for dinner! And then what words that discreet old gentleman, Mr Slow, had spoken about Mr Rubb, and what things he had hinted over and above what he had spoken! Was it not manifest that he conceived Mr Rubb to have been guilty of direct fraud?

Miss Mackenzie at once made up her mind that her money was gone! But, in truth, this did not much annoy her. She had declared to herself once before that if anything was wrong about the money she would regard it as a present made to her brother; and when so thinking of it, she had, undoubtedly, felt that it was, not improbably, lost to her. It was something over a hundred a year to be deducted from her computed income, but she would still be able to live at the Paragon quite as well as she had intended, and be able also to educate Susanna. Indeed, she could do this easily and still save money, and, therefore, as regarded the probable loss, why need she be unhappy?

Before the morning was over she had succeeded in white-washing Mr Rubb in her own mind. It is, I think, certainly the fact that women are less pervious to ideas of honesty than men are. They are less shocked by dishonesty when they find it, and are less clear in their intellect as to that which constitutes honesty. Where is the woman who thinks it wrong to smuggle? What lady's conscience ever pricked her in that she omitted the armorial bearings on her silver forks from her tax papers? What wife ever ceased to respect her husband because he dealt dishonestly in business? Whereas, let him not go to church, let him drink too much wine, let him go astray in his conversation, and her wrath arises against these faults. But this lack of feminine accuracy in the matter of honesty tends rather to charity in their judgment of others, than to deeds of fraud on the part of women themselves.

Miss Mackenzie, who desired nothing that was not her own, who scrupulously kept her own hands from all picking and stealing, gave herself no peace, after reading the lawyer's letter, till she was able to tell herself that Mr Rubb was to be forgiven for what he had done. After all, he had, no doubt, intended that she should have the promised security. And had not he himself come to her in London and told her the whole truth – or, if not the whole truth, as much of it as was reasonable to expect that he should be able to tell her at an evening party after dinner? Of course Mr Slow was hard upon him. Lawyers always were hard. If she chose to give Messrs Rubb and Mackenzie two thousand five hundred pounds out of her pocket, what was that to him? So she went on, till at last she was angry with Mr Slow for the language he had used.

It was, however, before all things necessary that she should put Mr Slow right as to the facts of the case. She had, no doubt, condoned whatever Mr Rubb had done. Mr Rubb undoubtedly had her sanction for keeping her money without security. Therefore, by return of post, she wrote the following short letter, which rather astonished Mr Slow when he received it –

'Littlebath, April, 186–.

'DEAR SIR,

I am much obliged by your letter about the money; but the truth is that I have known for some time that there was to be no mortgage. When I was in town I saw Mr Rubb at my brother's house, and it was understood between us then that the matter was to remain as it is. My brother and his partner are very welcome to the money.

'Believe me to be,

'Yours sincerely,

'MARGARET MACKENZIE.

The letter was a false letter; but I suppose Miss Mackenzie did not know that she was writing falsely. The letter was certainly false, because when she spoke of the understanding ' between us,' having just mentioned her brother and Mr Rubb, she intended the lawyer to believe that the understanding was between them three; whereas, not a word had been said about the money in her brother's hearing, nor was he aware that his partner had spoken of the money.

Mr Slow was surprised and annoyed. As regarded his comfort as a lawyer, his client's letter was of course satisfactory. It absolved him not only from all absolute responsibility, but also from the feeling which no doubt had existed within his own breast, that he had in some sort neglected the lady's interest. But, nevertheless, he was annoyed. He did not believe the statement that Rubb and Mackenzie had had permission to hold the money without mortgage, and thought that neither of the partners had themselves so conceived when he had seen them. They had, however, been too many for him – and too many also for the poor female who had allowed herself to be duped out of her money. Such were Mr Slow's feelings on the matter, and then he dismissed the subject from his mind.

The next day, about noon, Miss Mackenzie was startled almost out of her propriety by the sudden announcement at the drawing-room door of Mr Rubb. Before she could bethink herself how she would behave herself, or whether it would become her to say anything of Mr Slow's letter to her, he was in the room.

'Miss Mackenzie,' he said, hurriedly – and yet he had paused for a moment in his hurry till the servant had shut the door – 'may I shake hands with you?'

There could, Miss Mackenzie thought, be no objection to so ordinary a ceremony; and, therefore, she said, 'Certainly,' and gave him her hand.

'Then I am myself again,' said Mr Rubb; and having so said, he sat down.

Miss Mackenzie hoped that there was nothing the matter with him, and then she also sat down at a considerable distance.

'There is nothing the matter with me,' said he, 'as you are still so kind to me. But tell me, have you not received a letter from your lawyer?'

'Yes, I have.'

'And he has done all in his power to blacken me? I know it. Tell me, Miss Mackenzie, has he not blackened me? Has he not laid things to my charge of which I am incapable? Has he not accused me of getting money from you under false pretences – than do which, I'd sooner have seen my own brains blown out? I would, indeed.'

'He has written to me about the money, Mr Rubb.'

'Yes; he came to me, and behaved shamefully to me; and he saw your brother, too, and has been making all manner of ignominious inquiries. Those lawyers can never understand that there can be anything of friendly feeling about money. They can't put friendly feelings into their unconscionable bills. I believe the world would go on better if there was no such thing as an attorney in it. I wonder who invented them, and why?'

Miss Mackenzie could give him no information on this point, and therefore he went on:

'But you must tell me what he has said, and what it is he wants us to do. For your sake, if you ask us, Miss Mackenzie, we'll do anything. We'll sell the coats off our backs, if you wish it. You shall never lose one shilling by Rubb and Mackenzie as long as I have anything to do with the firm. But I'm sure you will excuse me if I say that we can do nothing at the bidding of that old cormorant.'

'I don't know that there's anything to be done, Mr Rubb.'

'Is not there? Well, it's very generous in you to say so; and you always are generous. I've always told your brother, since I had the honour of knowing you, that he had a sister to be proud of. And, Miss Mackenzie, I'll say more than that; I've flattered myself that I've had a friend to be proud of. But now I must tell you why I've come down to-day; you know I was to have been here next week. Well, when Mr Slow came to me and I found what was up, I said to myself at once that it was right you should know exactly – exactly – how the matter stands. I was going to explain it next week, but I wouldn't leave you in suspense when I knew that that lawyer was going to trouble you.'

'It hasn't troubled me, Mr Rubb.'

'Hasn't it though, really? That's so good of you again! Now the truth is – but it's pretty nearly just what I told you that day after dinner, when you agreed, you know, to what we had done.'

Here he paused, as though expecting an answer.

'Yes, I did agree.'

'Just at present, while certain other parties have a right to hold the title-deeds, and I can't quite say how long that may be, we cannot execute a mortgage in your favour. The title-deeds represent the property. Perhaps you don't know that.'

'Oh yes, I know as much as that.'

'Well then, as we haven't the title-deeds, we can't execute the mortgage. Perhaps you'll say you ought to have the title-deeds.'

'No, Mr Rubb, I don't want to say anything of the kind. If my money can be of any assistance to my brother – to my brother and you – you are welcome to the use of it, without any mortgage. I will show you a copy of the letter I sent to Mr Slow.'

'Thanks; a thousand thanks! and may I see the letter which Mr Slow wrote?'

'No, I think not. I don't know whether it would be right to show it to you.'

'I shouldn't think of doing anything about it; that is, resenting it, you know. Only then we should all be on the square together.'

'I think I'd better not. Mr Slow, when he wrote it, probably did not mean that I should show it to you.'

'You're right; you're always right. But you'll let me see your answer.'

Then Miss Mackenzie went to her desk, and brought him a copy of the note she had written to the lawyer. He read it very carefully, twice over; and then she could see, when he refolded the paper, that his eyes were glittering with satisfaction.

'Miss Mackenzie, Miss Mackenzie,' he said, 'I think that you are an angel! '

And he did think so. In so much at that moment he was at any rate sincere. She saw that he was pleased, and she was pleased herself.

'There need be no further trouble about it,' she said; and as she spoke she rose from her seat.

And he rose, too, and came close to her. He came close to her, hesitated for a moment, and then, putting one hand behind her waist, though barely touching her, he took her hand with his other hand. She thought that he was going to kiss her lips, and for a moment or two he thought so too; but either his courage failed him or else his discretion prevailed. Whether it was the one or the other, must depend on the way in which she would have taken it. As it was, he merely raised her hand and kissed that. When she could look into his face his eyes were full of tears.

'The truth is,' said he, 'that you have saved us from ruin – that's the real truth. Damn all lying! '

She started at the oath, but in an instant she had forgiven him that too. There was a sound of reality about it, which reconciled her to the indignity; though, had she been true to her faith as a Stumfoldian, she ought at least to have fainted at the sound.

'I hardly know what I am saying, Miss Mackenzie, and I beg your pardon; but the fact is you could sell us up if you pleased. I didn't mean it when I first got your brother to agree as to asking you for the loan; I didn't indeed; but things were going wrong with us, and just at that moment they went more wrong than ever; and then came the temptation, and we were able to make everything right by giving up the title-deeds of the premises. That's how it was, and it was I that did it. It wasn't your brother; and though you may forgive me, he won't.'

This was all true, but how far the truth should be taken towards palliating the deed done, I must leave the reader to decide; and the reader will doubtless perceive that the truth did not appear until Mr Rubb had ascertained that its appearance would not injure him. I think, however, that it came from his heart, and that it should count for something in his favour. The tear which he rubbed from his eye with his hand counted very much in his favour with Miss Mackenzie; she had not only forgiven him now, but she almost loved him for having given her something to forgive. With many women I doubt whether there be any more effectual way of touching their hearts than ill-using them and then confessing it. If you wish to get the sweetest fragrance from the herb at your feet, tread on it and bruise it.

She had forgiven him, and taken him absolutely into favour, and he had kissed her hand, having all but embraced her as he did so; but on the present occasion he did not get beyond that. He lacked the audacity to proceed at once from the acknowledgment of his fault to a declaration of his love; but I hardly think that he would have injured himself had he done so. He should have struck while the iron was hot, and it was heated now nearly to melting; but he was abashed by his own position, and having something real in his heart, having some remnant of generous feeling left about him, he could not make such progress as he might have done had he been cool enough to calculate all his advantages.

'Don't let it trouble you any more,' Miss Mackenzie said, when he had dropped her hand.

'But it does trouble me, and it will trouble me.'

'No,' she said, with energy, 'it shall not; let there be an end of it. I will write to Tom, and tell him that he is welcome to the money. Isn't he my brother? You are both welcome to it. If it has been of service to you, I am very happy that it should be so. And now, Mr Rubb, if you please, we won't have another word about it.'

'What am I to say? '

'Not another word.'

It seemed as though he couldn't speak another word, for he went to the window and stood there silently, looking into the street. As he did so, there came another visitor to Miss Mackenzie, whose ringing at the doorbell had not been noticed by them, and Miss Baker was announced while Mr Rubb was still getting the better of his feelings. Of course he turned round when he heard the lady's name, and of course he was introduced by his hostess. Miss Mackenzie was obliged to make some apology for the gentleman's presence.

'Mr Rubb was expected next week, but business brought him down today unexpectedly.'

'Quite unexpectedly,' said Mr Rubb, making a violent endeavour to recover his equanimity.

Miss Baker looked at Mr Rubb, and disliked him at once. It should be remembered that she was twenty years older than Miss Mackenzie, and that she regarded the stranger, therefore, with a saner and more philosophical judgment than her friend could use – with a judgment on which the outward comeliness of the man had no undue influence; and it should be remembered also that Miss Baker, from early age, and by all the association of her youth, had been taught to know a gentleman when she saw him. Miss Mackenzie, who was by nature the cleverer woman of the two, watched her friend's face, and saw by a glance that she did not like Mr Rubb, and then, within her own bosom, she called her friend an old maid.

'We're having uncommonly fine weather for the time of year,' said Mr Rubb.

'Very fine weather,' said Miss Baker. 'I've called, my dear, to know whether you'll go in with me next door and drink tea this evening?'

'What, with Miss Todd?' asked Miss Mackenzie, who was surprised at the invitation.

'Yes, with Miss Todd. It is not one of her regular nights, you know, and her set won't be there. She has some old friends with her – a Mr Wilkinson, a clergyman, and his wife. It seems that her old enemy and your devoted slave, Mr Maguire, knows Mr Wilkinson, and he's going to be there.'

'Mr Maguire is no slave of mine, Miss Baker.'

'I thought he was; at any rate his presence will be a guarantee that Miss Todd will be on her best behaviour, and that you needn't be afraid.'

'I'm not afraid of anything of that sort.'

'But will you go? '

'Oh, yes, if you are going.'

'That's right; and I'll call for you as I pass by. I must see her now, and tell her. Good-morning, Sir;' whereupon Miss Baker bowed very stiffly to Mr Rubb.

'Good-morning, Ma'am,' said Mr Rubb, bowing very stiffly to Miss Baker.

When the lady was gone, Mr Rubb sat himself again down on the sofa, and there he remained for the next half-hour. He talked about the business of the firm, saying how it would now certainly be improved; and he talked about Tom Mackenzie's family, saying what a grand thing it was for Susanna to be thus taken in hand by her aunt; and he asked a question or two about Miss Baker, and then a question or two about Mr Maguire, during which questions he learned that Mr Maguire was not as yet a married man; and from Mr Maguire he got on to the Stumfolds, and learned somewhat of the rites and ceremonies of the Stumfoldian faith. In this way he prolonged his visit till Miss Mackenzie began to feel that he ought to take his leave.

Miss Baker had gone at once to Miss Todd, and had told that lady that Miss Mackenzie would join her tea-party. She had also told how Mr Rubb, of the firm of Rubb and Mackenzie, was at this moment in Miss Mackenzie's drawing-room.

'I'll ask him to come, too,' said Miss Todd. Then Miss Baker had hesitated, and had looked grave.

'What's the matter? ' said Miss Todd.

'I'm not quite sure you'll like him,' said Miss Baker.

'Probably not,' said Miss Todd; 'I don't like half the people I meet, but that's no reason I shouldn't ask him.'

'But he is – that is, he is not exactly –'

'What is he, and what is he not, exactly?' asked Miss Todd.

'Why, he is a tradesman, you know,' said Miss Baker.

'There's no harm that I know of in that,' said Miss Todd. 'My uncle that left me my money was a tradesman.'

'No,' said Miss Baker, energetically; 'he was a merchant in Liverpool.'

'You'll find it very hard to define the difference, my dear,' said Miss Todd. 'At any rate I'll ask the man to come; – that is, if it won't offend you.'

'It won't in the least offend me,' said Miss Baker.

So a note was at once written and sent in to Miss Mackenzie, in which she was asked to bring Mr Rubb with her on that evening. When the note reached Miss Mackenzie, Mr Rubb was still with her.

Of course she communicated to him the invitation. She wished that it had not been sent; she wished that he would not accept it – though on that head she had no doubt; but she had not sufficient presence of mind to keep the matter to herself and say nothing about it. Of course he was only too glad to drink tea with Miss Todd. Miss Mackenzie attempted some slight manoeuvre to induce Mr Rubb to go direct to Miss Todd's house; but he was not such an ass as that; he knew his advantage, and kept it, insisting on his privilege of coming there, to Miss Mackenzie's room, and escorting her. He would have to escort Miss Baker also; and things, as he thought, were looking well with him. At last he rose to go, but he made good use of the privilege of parting. He held Miss Mackenzie's hand, and pressed it.

'You mustn't be angry,' he said, 'if I tell you that you are the best friend I have in the world.'

'You have better friends than me,' she said, 'and older friends.'

'Yes; older friends; but none – not one, who has done for me so much as you have; and certainly none for whom I have so great a regard. May God bless you, Miss Mackenzie!'

'May God bless you, too, Mr Rubb!'

What else could she say? When his civility took so decorous a shape, she could not bear to be less civil than he had been, or less decorous. And yet it seemed to her that in bidding God bless him with that warm pressure of the hand, she had allowed to escape from her an appearance of affection which she had not intended to exhibit.

'Thank you; thank you,' said he; and then at last he went.

She seated herself slowly in her own chair near the window – the chair in which she was accustomed to sit for many solitary hours, and asked herself what it all meant. Was she allowing herself to fall in love with Mr Rubb, and if so, was it well that it should be so? This would be bringing to the sternest proof of reality her philosophical theory on social life. It was all very well for her to hold a bold opinion in discussions with Miss Baker as to a 'man being a man for a' that,' even though he might not be a gentleman; but was she prepared to go the length of preferring such a man to all the world? Was she ready to go down among the Rubbs, for now and ever, and give up the society of such women as Miss Baker? She knew that it was necessary that she should come to some resolve on the matter, as Mr Rubb's purpose was becoming too clear to her. When an unmarried gentleman of forty tells an unmarried lady of thirty-six that she is the dearest friend he has in the world, he must surely intend that they shall, neither of them, remain unmarried any longer. Then she thought also of her cousin, John Ball; and some vague shadow of thought passed across her mind also in respect of the Rev. Mr Maguire.

✖ ELEVEN ✖

Miss Todd Entertains some Friends at Tea

I BELIEVE THAT A DESIRE TO GET married is the natural state of a woman at the age of – say from twenty-five to thirty-five, and I think also that it is good for the world in general that it should be so. I am now speaking, not of the female population at large, but of women whose position in the world does not subject them to the necessity of earning their bread by the labour of their hands. There is, I know, a feeling abroad among women that this desire is one of which it is expedient that they should become ashamed; that it will be well for them to alter their natures in this respect, and learn to take delight in the single state. Many of the most worthy women of the day are now teaching this doctrine, and are intent on showing by precept and practice that an unmarried woman may have as sure a hold on the world, and a position within it as ascertained, as may an unmarried man. But I confess to an opinion that human nature will be found to be too strong for them. Their school of philosophy may be graced by a few zealous students – by students who will be subject to the personal influence of their great masters – but it will not be successful in the outer world. The truth in the matter is too clear. A woman's life is not perfect or whole till she has added herself to a husband.

Nor is a man's life perfect or whole till he has added to himself a wife; but the deficiency with the man, though perhaps more injurious to him than its counterpart is to the woman, does not, to the outer eye, so manifestly unfit him for his business in the world. Nor does the deficiency make itself known to him so early in life, and therefore it occasions less of regret – less of regret, though probably more of misery. It is infinitely for his advantage that he should be tempted to take to himself a wife; and, therefore, for his sake if not for her own, the philosophic preacher of single blessedness should break up her class-rooms, and bid her pupils go and do as their mothers did before them.

They may as well give up their ineffectual efforts, and know that nature is too strong for them. The desire is there; and any desire which has to be repressed with an effort, will not have itself repressed unless it be in itself wrong. But this desire, though by no means wrong, is generally accompanied by something of a feeling of shame. It is not often acknowledged by the woman to herself, and very rarely acknowledged in simple plainness to another. Miss Mackenzie could not by any means bring herself to own it, and yet it was there strong within her bosom. A man situated in outer matters as she was situated, possessed of good means, hampered by no outer demands, would have declared to himself clearly that it would be well for him to marry. But he would probably be content to wait a while and would, unless in love, feel the delay to be a luxury. But Miss Mackenzie could not confess as much, even to herself – could not let herself know that she thought as much; but yet she desired to be married, and dreaded delay. She desired to be married, although she was troubled by some half-formed idea that it would be wicked. Who was she, that she should be allowed to be in love? Was she not an old maid by prescription, and, as it were, by the force of ordained circumstances? Had it not been made very clear to her when she was young that she had no right to fall in love, even with Harry Handcock? And although in certain moments of ecstasy, as when she kissed herself in the glass, she almost taught herself to think that feminine charms and feminine privileges had not been all denied to her, such was not her permanent opinion of herself. She despised herself. Why, she knew not; and probably did not know that she did so. But, in truth, she despised herself, thinking herself to be too mean for a man's love.

She had been asked to marry him by her cousin Mr Ball, and she had almost yielded. But had she married him it would not have been because she thought herself good enough to be loved by him, but because she held herself to be so insignificant that she had no right to ask for love. She would have taken him because she could have been of use, and because she would have felt that she had no right to demand any other purpose in the world. She would have done this, had she not been deterred by the rude offer of other advantages which had with so much ill judgment been made to her by her aunt.

Now, here was a lover who was not old and careworn, who was personally agreeable to her, with whom something of the customary romance of the world might be possible. Should she take him? She knew well that there were drawbacks. Her perceptions had not missed to notice the man's imperfections, his vulgarities, his false promises, his little pushing ways. But why was she to expect him to be perfect, seeing, as she so plainly did, her own imperfections? As for her money, of course he wanted her money. So had Mr Ball wanted her money. What man on earth could have wished to marry her unless she had had money? It was thus that she thought of herself. And he had robbed her! But that she had forgiven; and, having forgiven it, was too generous to count it for anything. But, nevertheless, she was ambitious. Might there not be a better, even than Mr Rubb?

Mr Maguire squinted horribly; so horribly that the form and face of the man hardly left any memory of themselves except the memory of the squint. His dark hair, his one perfect eye, his good figure, his expressive mouth, were all lost in that dreadful perversion of vision. It was a misfortune so great as to justify him in demanding that he should be judged by different laws than those which are used as to the conduct of the world at large. In getting a wife he might surely use his tongue with more freedom than another man, seeing that his eye was so much against him. If he were somewhat romantic in his talk, or even more than romantic, who could find fault with him? And if he used his clerical vocation to cover the terrors of that distorted pupil, can any woman say that he should be therefore condemned? Miss Mackenzie could not forget his eye, but she thought that she had almost brought herself to forgive it. And, moreover, he was a gentleman, not only by Act of Parliament, but in outward manners. Were she to become Mrs Maguire, Miss Baker would certainly come to her house, and it might be given to her to rival Mrs Stumfold – in running which race she would be weighted by no Mr Peters.

It is true that Mr Maguire had never asked her to marry him, but she believed that he would ask her if she gave him any encouragement. Now it was to come to pass, by a wonderful arrangement of circumstances, that she was to meet these two gentlemen together. It might well be, that on this very occasion, she must choose whether it should be either or neither.

Mr Rubb came, and she looked anxiously at his dress. He had on bright yellow kid gloves, primrose he would have called them, but, if there be such things as yellow gloves, they were yellow; and she wished that she had the courage to ask him to take them off. This was beyond her, and there he sat, with his gloves almost as conspicuous as Mr Maguire's eye. Should she, however, ever become Mrs Rubb, she would not find the gloves to be there permanently; whereas the eye would remain. But then the gloves were the fault of the one man, whereas the eye was simply the misfortune of the other. And Mr Rubb's hair was very full of perfumed grease, and sat on each side of his head in a conscious arrangement of waviness that was detestable. As she looked at Mr Rubb in all the brightness of his evening costume, she began to think that she had better not. At last Miss Baker came, and they started off together. Miss Mackenzie saw that Miss Baker eyed the man, and she blushed. When they got down upon the doorstep, Samuel Rubb, junior, absolutely offered an arm simultaneously to each lady! At that moment Miss Mackenzie hated him in spite of her special theory.

'Thank you,' said Miss Baker, declining the arm; 'it is only a step.'

Miss Mackenzie declined it also.

'Oh, of course,' said Mr Rubb. 'If it's only next door it does not signify.'

Miss Todd welcomed them cordially, gloves and all. 'My dear,' she said to Miss Baker, 'I haven't seen you for twenty years. Miss Mackenzie, this is very kind of you. I hope we sha'n't do you any harm, as we are not going to be wicked to-night.'

Miss Mackenzie did not dare to say that she would have preferred to be wicked, but that is what she would have said if she had dared.

'Mr Rubb, I'm very happy to see you,' continued Miss Todd, accepting her guest's hand, glove and all. 'I hope they haven't made you believe that you are going to have any dancing, for, if so, they have hoaxed you shamefully.' Then she introduced them to Mr and Mrs Wilkinson.

Mr Wilkinson was a plain-looking clergyman, with a very pretty wife. 'Adela,' Miss Todd said to Mrs Wilkinson, 'you used to dance, but that's all done with now, I suppose.'

'I never danced much,' said the clergyman's wife, 'but have certainly given it up now, partly because I have no one to dance with.'

'Here's Mr Rubb quite ready. He'll dance with you, I'll be bound, if that's all.'

Mr Rubb became very red, and Miss Mackenzie, when she next took courage to look at him, saw that the gloves had disappeared.

There came also a Mr and Mrs Fuzzybell, and immediately afterwards Mr Maguire, whereupon Miss Todd declared her party to be complete.

'Mrs Fuzzybell, my dear, no cards!' said Miss Todd, quite out loud, with a tragic-comic expression in her face that was irresistible. 'Mr Fuzzybell, no cards!' Mrs Fuzzybell said that she was delighted to hear it. Mr Fuzzybell said that it did not signify. Miss Baker stole a glance at Mr Maguire, and shook in her shoes. Mr Maguire tried to look as though he had not heard it.

'Do you play cards much here?' asked Mr Rubb.

'A great deal too much, Sir,' said Miss Todd, shaking her head.

'Have you many Dissenters in your parish, Mr Wilkinson?' asked Mr Maguire.

'A good many,' said Mr Wilkinson.

'But no Papists?' suggested Mr Maguire.

'No, we have no Roman Catholics.'

'That is such a blessing!' said Mr Maguire, turning his eyes up to Heaven in a very frightful manner. But he had succeeded for the present in putting down Miss Todd and her cards.

They were now summoned round the tea-table – a genuine tea-table at which it was expected that they should eat and drink. Miss Mackenzie was seated next to Mr Maguire on one side of the table, while Mr Rubb sat on the other between Miss Todd and Miss Baker. While they were yet taking their seats, and before the operations of the banquet had commenced, Susanna entered the room. She also had been specially invited, but she had not returned from school in time to accompany her aunt. The young lady had to walk round the room to shake hands with everybody, and when she came to Mr Rubb, was received with much affectionate urgency. He turned round in his chair and was loud in his praises. 'Miss Mackenzie,' said he, speaking across the table, 'I shall have to report in Gower Street that Miss Susanna has become quite the lady.' From that moment Mr Rubb had an enemy close to the object of his affections, who was always fighting a battle against him.

Susanna had hardly gained her seat, before Mr Maguire seized an opportunity which he saw might soon be gone, and sprang to his legs. 'Miss Todd,' said he, 'may I be permitted to ask a blessing?'

'Oh, certainly,' said Miss Todd; 'but I thought one only did that at dinner.'

Mr Maguire, however, was not the man to sit down without improving the occasion.

'And why not for tea also?' said he. 'Are they not gifts alike?'

'Very much alike,' said Miss Todd, 'and so is a cake at a pastry-cook's. But we don't say grace over our buns.'

'We do, in silence,' said Mr Maguire, still standing; 'and therefore we ought to have it out loud here.'

'I don't see the argument; but you're very welcome.'

'Thank you,' said Mr Maguire; and then he said his grace. He said it with much poetic emphasis, and Miss Mackenzie, who liked any little additional excitement, thought that Miss Todd had been wrong.

'You've a deal of society here, no doubt,' said Mr Rubb to Miss Baker, while Miss Todd was dispensing her tea.

'I suppose it's much the same as other places,' said Miss Baker. 'Those who know many people can go out constantly if they like it.'

'And it's so easy to get to know people,' said Mr Rubb. 'That's what makes me like these sort of places so much. There's no stiffness and formality, and all that kind of thing. Now in London, you don't know your next neighbour, though you and he have lived there for ten years.'

'Nor here either, unless chance brings you together.'

'Ah; but there is none of that horrid decorum here,' said Mr Rubb. 'There's nothing I hate like decorum. It prevents people knowing each other, and being jolly and happy together. Now, the French know more about society than any people, and I'm told they have none of it.'

'I'm sure I can't say,' said Miss Baker.

'It's given up to them that they've got rid of it altogether,' said Mr Rubb.

'Who have got rid of what?' asked Miss Todd, who saw that her friend was rather dismayed by the tenor of Mr Rubb's conversation.

'The French have got rid of decorum,' said Mr Rubb.

'Altogether, I believe,' said Miss Todd.

'Of course they have. It's given up to them that they have. They're the people that know how to live!'

'You'd better go and live among them, if that's your way of thinking,' said Miss Todd.

'I would at once, only for the business,' said Mr Rubb. 'If there's anything I hate, it's decorum. How pleasant it was for me to be asked in to take tea here in this social way!'

'But I hope decorum would not have forbidden that,' said Miss Todd.

'I rather think it would though, in London.'

'Where you're known, you mean?' asked Miss Todd.

'I don't know that that makes any difference; but people don't do that sort of thing. Do they, Miss Mackenzie? You've lived in London most of your life, and you ought to know.'

Miss Mackenzie did not answer the appeal that was made to her. She was watching Mr Rubb narrowly, and knew that he was making a fool of himself. She could perceive also that Miss Todd would not spare him. She could forgive Mr Rubb for being a fool. She could forgive him for not knowing the meaning of words, for being vulgar and assuming; but she could hardly bring herself to forgive him in that he did so as her friend, and as the guest whom she had brought thither. She did not declare to herself that she would have nothing more to do with him, because he was an ass; but she almost did come to this conclusion, lest he should make her appear to be an ass also.

'What is the gentleman's name?' asked Mr Maguire, who, under the protection of the urn, was able to whisper into Miss Mackenzie's ear.

'Rubb,' said she.

'Oh, Rubb; and he comes from London?'

'He is my brother's partner in business,' said Miss Mackenzie.

'Oh, indeed. A very worthy man, no doubt. Is he staying with – with you, Miss Mackenzie?'

Then Miss Mackenzie had to explain that Mr Rubb was not staying with her – that he had come down about business, and that he was staying at some inn.

'An excellent man of business; I'm sure,' said Mr Maguire. 'By-the-bye, Miss Mackenzie, if it be not improper to ask, have you any share in the business?'

Miss Mackenzie explained that she had no share in the business; and then blundered on, saying how Mr Rubb had come down to Littlebath about money transactions between her and her brother.

'Oh, indeed,' said Mr Maguire; and before he had done, he knew very well that Mr Rubb had borrowed money of Miss Mackenzie.

'Now, Mrs Fuzzybell, what are we to do?' said Miss Todd, as soon as the tea-things were gone.

'We shall do very well,' said Mrs Fuzzybell; 'we'll have a little conversation.'

'If we could all banish decorum, like Mr Rubb, and amuse ourselves, wouldn't it be nice? I quite agree with you, Mr Rubb; decorum is a great bore; it prevents our playing cards to-night.'

'As for cards, I never play cards myself,' said Mr Rubb.

'Then, when I throw decorum overboard, it sha'n't be in company with you, Mr Rubb.'

'We were always taught to think that cards were objectionable.'

'You were told they were the devil's books, I suppose,' said Miss Todd.

'Mother always objected to have them in the house,' said Mr Rubb.

'Your mother was quite right,' said Mr Maguire; 'and I hope that you will never forget or neglect your parent's precepts. I'm not meaning to judge you, Miss Todd –'

'But that's just what you are meaning to do, Mr Maguire.'

'Not at all; very far from it. We've all got our wickednesses and imperfections.'

'No, no, not you, Mr Maguire. Mrs Fuzzybell, you don't think that Mr Maguire has any wickednesses and imperfections?'

'I'm sure I don't know,' said Mrs Fuzzybell, tossing her head.

'Miss Todd,' said Mr Maguire, 'when I look into my own heart, I see well how black it is. It is full of iniquity; it is a grievous sore that is ever running, and will not be purified.'

'Gracious me, how unpleasant!' said Miss Todd.

'I trust that there is no one here who has not a sense of her own wickedness.'

'Or of his,' said Miss Todd.

'Or of his,' and Mr Maguire looked very hard at Mr Fuzzybell. Mr Fuzzybell was a quiet, tame old gentleman, who followed his wife's heels about wherever she went; but even he, when attacked in this way, became very fierce, and looked back at Mr Maguire quite as severely as Mr Maguire looked at him.

'Or of his,' continued Mr Maguire; 'and therefore far be it from me to think hardly of the amusements of other people. But when this gentleman tells me that his excellent parent warned him against the fascination of cards, I cannot but ask him to remember those precepts to his dying bed.'

'I won't say what I may do later in life, ' said Mr Rubb.

'When he becomes like you and me, Mrs Fuzzybell,' said Miss Todd.

'When one does get older,' said Mr Rubb.

'And has succeeded in throwing off all decorum,' said Miss Todd.

'How can you say such things?' asked Miss Baker, who was shocked by the tenor of the conversation.

'It isn't I, my dear; it's Mr Rubb and Mr Maguire, between them. One says he has thrown off all decorum and the other declares himself to be a mass of iniquity. What are two poor old ladies like you and I to do in such company?'

Miss Mackenzie, when she heard Mr Maguire declare himself to be a running sore, was even more angry with him than with Mr Rubb. He, at any rate, should have known better. After all, was not Mr Ball better than either of them, though his head was bald and his face worn with that solemn, sad look of care which always pervaded him?

In the course of the evening she found herself seated apart from the general company, with Mr Maguire beside her. The eye that did not squint was towards her, and he made an effort to be agreeable to her that was not altogether ineffectual.

'Does not society sometimes make you very sad?' he said.

Society had made her sad to-night, and she answered him in the affirmative.

'It seems that people are so little desirous to make other people happy,' she replied.

'It was just that idea that was passing through my own mind. Men and women are anxious to give you the best they have, but it is in order that you may admire their wealth or their taste; and they strive to be witty, amusing, and sarcastic! but that, again, is for the éclat they are to gain. How few really struggle to make those around them comfortable!'

'It comes, I suppose, from people having such different tastes,' said Miss Mackenzie, who, on looking round the room, thought that the people assembled there were peculiarly ill-assorted.

'As for happiness,' continued Mr Maguire, 'that is not to be looked for from society. They who expect their social hours to be happy hours will be grievously disappointed.'

'Are you not happy at Mrs Stumfold's?'

'At Mrs Stumfold's? Yes – sometimes, that is; but even there I always seem to want something. Miss Mackenzie, has it never occurred to you that the one thing necessary in this life, the one thing – beyond a hope for the next, you know, the one thing is – ah, Miss Mackenzie, what is it?'

'Perhaps you mean a competence,' said Miss Mackenzie.

'I mean some one to love,' said Mr Maguire.

As he spoke he looked with all the poetic vigour of his better eye full into Miss Mackenzie's face, and Miss Mackenzie, who then could see nothing of the other eye, felt the effect of the glance somewhat as he intended that she should feel it. When a lady who is thinking about getting married is asked by a gentleman who is frequently in her thoughts whether she does not want some one to love, it is natural that she should presume that he means to be particular; and it is natural also that she should be in some sort gratified by that particularity. Miss Mackenzie was, I think, gratified, but she did not express any such feeling.

'Is not that your idea also?' said he – 'some one to love; is not that the great desideratum here below!' And the tone in which he repeated the last words was by no means ineffective.

'I hope everybody has that,' said she.

'I fear not; not anyone to love with a perfect love. Who does Miss Todd love?'

'Miss Baker.'

'Does she? And yet they live apart, and rarely see each other. They think differently on all subjects. That is not the love of which I am speaking. And you, Miss Mackenzie, are you sure that you love anyone with that perfect all-trusting, love?'

'I love my niece Susanna best,' said she.

'Your niece, Susanna! She is a sweet child, a sweet girl; she has everything to make those love her who know her; but –'

'You don't think anything amiss of Susanna, Mr Maguire?'

'Nothing, nothing; Heaven forbid, dear child! And I think so highly of you for your generosity in adopting her.'

'I could not do less than take one of them, Mr Maguire.'

'But I meant a different kind of love from that. Do you feel that your regard for your niece is sufficient to fill your heart?'

'It makes me very comfortable.'

'Does it? Ah! me; I wish I could make myself comfortable.'

'I should have thought, seeing you so much in Mrs Stumfold's house –'

'I have the greatest veneration for that woman, Miss Mackenzie! I have sometimes thought that of all the human beings I have ever met, she is the most perfect; she is human, and therefore a sinner, but her sins never meet my eyes.'

Miss Mackenzie, who did not herself regard Mrs Stumfold as being so much better than her neighbours, could not receive this with much rapture.

'But,' continued Mr Maguire, 'she is as cold – as cold – as cold as ice.'

As the lady in question was another man's wife, this did not seem to Miss Mackenzie to be of much consequence to Mr Maguire, but she allowed him to go on.

'Stumfold I don't think minds it; he is of that joyous disposition that all things work to good for him. Even when she's most obdurate in her sternness to him –'

'Law! Mr Maguire, I did not think she was ever stern to him.'

'But she is, very hard. Even then I don't think he minds it much. But, Miss Mackenzie, that kind of companion would not do for me at all. I think a woman should be soft and soothing, like a dove.'

She did not stop to think whether doves are soothing, but she felt that the language was pretty.

Just at this moment she was summoned by Miss Baker, and looking up she perceived that Mr and Mrs Fuzzybell were already leaving the room.

'I don't know why you need disturb Miss Mackenzie,' said Miss Todd, 'she has only got to go next door, and she seems very happy just now.'

'I would sooner go with Miss Baker,' said Miss Mackenzie.

'Mr Maguire would see you home,' suggested Miss Todd.

But Miss Mackenzie of course went with Miss Baker, and Mr Rubb accompanied them.

'Good-night, Mr Rubb,' said Miss Todd; 'and don't make very bad reports of us in London.'

'Oh! no; indeed I won't.'

'For though we do play cards, we still stick to decorum, as you must have observed to-night.'

At Miss Mackenzie's door there was an almost overpowering amount of affectionate farewells. Mr Maguire was there as well as Mr Rubb, and both gentlemen warmly pressed the hand of the lady they were leaving. Mr Rubb was not quite satisfied with his evening's work, because he had not been able to get near to Miss Mackenzie; but, nevertheless, he was greatly gratified by the general manner in which he had been received, and was much pleased with Littlebath and its inhabitants. Mr Maguire, as he walked home by himself, assured himself that he might as well now put the question; he had been thinking about it for the last two months, and had made up his mind that matrimony would be good for him.

Miss Mackenzie, as she went to bed, told herself that she might have a husband if she pleased; but then, which should it be? Mr Rubb's manners were very much against him; but of Mr Maguire's eye she had caught a gleam as he turned from her on the doorsteps, which made her think of that alliance with dismay.

TWELVE

Mrs Stumfold Interferes

ON THE MORNING FOLLOWING MISS TODD'S TEA-PARTY, Mr Rubb called on Miss Mackenzie and bade her adieu. He was, he said, going up to London at once, having received a letter which made his presence there imperative. Miss Mackenzie could, of course, do no more than simply say good-bye to him. But when she had said so he did not even then go at once. He was standing with his hat in hand, and had bade her farewell; but still he did not go. He had something to say, and she stood there trembling, half fearing what the nature of that something might be.

'I hope I may see you again before long,' he said at last.

'I hope you may,' she replied.

'Of course I shall. After all that's come and gone, I shall think nothing of running down, if it were only to make a morning call.'

'Pray don't do that, Mr Rubb.'

'I shall, as a matter of course. But in spite of that, Miss Mackenzie, I can't go away without saying another word about the money. I can't indeed.'

'There needn't be any more about that, Mr Rubb.'

'But there must be, Miss Mackenzie; there must, indeed; at least, so much as this. I know I've done wrong about that money.'

'Don't talk about it. If I choose to lend it to my brother and you without security, there's nothing very uncommon in that.'

'No; there ain't; at least perhaps there ain't. Though as far as I can see, brothers and sisters out in the world are mostly as hard to each other where money is concerned as other people. But the thing is, you didn't mean to lend it without security.'

'I'm quite contented as it is.'

'And I did wrong about it all through; I feel it so that I can't tell you. I do, indeed. But I'll never rest till that money is paid back again. I never will.'

Then, having said that, he went away. When early on the preceding evening he had put on bright yellow gloves, making himself smart before the eyes of the lady of his love, it must be presumed that he did so with some hope of success. In that hope he was altogether betrayed. When he came and confessed his fraud about the money, it must be supposed that in doing so he felt that he was lowering himself in the estimation of her whom he desired to win for his wife. But, had he only known it, he thereby took the most efficacious step towards winning her esteem. The gloves had been nearly fatal to him; but those words – 'I feel it so that I can't tell you,' redeemed the evil that the gloves had done. He went away, however, saying nothing more then, and failing to strike while the iron was hot.

Some six weeks after this Mrs Stumfold called on Miss Mackenzie, making a most important visit. But it should be first explained, before the nature of that visit is described, that Miss Mackenzie had twice been to Mrs Stumfold's house since the evening of Miss Todd's party, drinking tea there on both occasions, and had twice met Mr Maguire. On the former occasion they two had had some conversation, but it had been of no great moment. He had spoken nothing then of the pleasures of love, nor had he made any allusion to the dove-like softness of women. On the second meeting he had seemed to keep aloof from her altogether, and she had begun to tell herself that that dream was over, and to scold herself for having dreamed at all – when he came close up behind and whispered a word in her ear.

'You know,' he said, 'how much I would wish to be with you, but I can't now.'

She had been startled, and had turned round, and had found herself close to his dreadful eye. She had never been so close to it before, and it frightened her. Then again he came to her just before she left, and spoke to her in the same mysterious way:

'I will see you in a day or two,' he said, 'but never mind now;' and then he walked away. She had not spoken a word to him, nor did she speak a word to him that evening.

Miss Mackenzie had never before seen Mrs Stumfold since her first visit of ceremony, except in that lady's drawing-room, and was surprised when she heard the name announced. It was an understood thing that Mrs Stumfold did not call on the Stumfoldians unless she had some great and special reason for doing so – unless some erring sister required admonishing, or the course of events in the life of some Stumfoldian might demand special advice. I do not know that any edict of this kind had actually been pronounced, but Miss Mackenzie, though she had not yet been twelve months in Littlebath, knew that this arrangement was generally understood to exist. It was plain to be seen by the lady's face, as she entered the room, that some special cause had brought her now. It wore none of those pretty smiles with which morning callers greet their friends before they begin their first gentle attempts at miscellaneous conversation. It was true that she gave her hand to Miss Mackenzie, but she did even this with austerity; and when she seated herself – not on the sofa as she was invited to do, but on one of the square, hard, straight-backed chairs – Miss Mackenzie knew well that pleasantness was not to be the order of the morning.

'My dear Miss Mackenzie,' said Mrs Stumfold, 'I hope you will pardon me if I express much tender solicitude for your welfare.'

Miss Mackenzie was so astonished at this mode of address, and at the tone in which it was uttered, that she made no reply to it. The words themselves had in them an intention of kindness, but the voice and look of the lady were, if kind, at any rate not tender.

'You came among us,' continued Mrs Stumfold, ' and became one of us, and we have been glad to welcome you.'

'I'm sure I've been much obliged.'

'We are always glad to welcome those who come among us in a proper spirit. Society with me, Miss Mackenzie, is never looked upon as an end in itself. It is only a means to an end. No woman regards society more favourably than I do. I think it offers to us one of the most efficacious means of spreading true gospel teaching. With these views I have always thought it right to open my house in a spirit, as I hope, of humble hospitality – and Mr Stumfold is of the same opinion. Holding these views, we have been delighted to see you among us, and, as I have said already, to welcome you as one of us.'

There was something in this so awful that Miss Mackenzie hardly knew how to speak, or let it pass without speaking. Having a spirit of her own she did not like being told that she had been, as it were, sat upon and judged, and then admitted into Mrs Stumfold's society as a child may be admitted into a school after an examination. And yet on the spur of the moment she could not think what words might be appropriate for her answer. She sat silent, therefore, and Mrs Stumfold again went on.

'I trust that you will acknowledge that we have shown our good will towards you, our desire to cultivate a Christian friendship with you, and that you will therefore excuse me if I ask you a question which might otherwise have the appearance of interference. Miss Mackenzie, is there anything between you and my husband's curate, Mr Maguire?'

Miss Mackenzie's face became suddenly as red as fire, but for a moment or two she made no answer. I do not know whether I may as yet have succeeded in making the reader understand the strength as well as the weakness of my heroine's character; but Mrs Stumfold had certainly not succeeded in perceiving it. She was accustomed, probably, to weak, obedient women – to women who had taught themselves to believe that submission to Stumfoldian authority was a sign of advanced Christianity; and in the mild-looking, quiet-mannered lady who had lately come among them, she certainly did not expect to encounter a rebel. But on such matters as that to which the female hierarch of Littlebath was now alluding, Miss Mackenzie was not by nature adapted to be submissive.

'Is there anything between you and Mr Maguire?' said Mrs Stumfold again. 'I particularly wish to have a plain answer to that question.'

Miss Mackenzie, as I have said, became very red in the face. When it was repeated, she found herself obliged to speak. 'Mrs Stumfold, I do not know that you have any right to ask me such a question as that.'

'No right! No right to ask a lady who sits under Mr Stumfold whether or not she is engaged to Mr Stumfold's own curate! Think again of what you are saying, Miss Mackenzie!' And there was in Mrs Stumfold's voice as she spoke an expression of offended majesty, and in her countenance a look of awful authority, sufficient no doubt to bring most Stumfoldian ladies to their bearings.

'You said nothing about being engaged to him.'

'Oh, Miss Mackenzie!'

'You said nothing about being engaged to him but if you had I should have made the same answer. You asked me if there was anything between me and him; and I think it was a very offensive question.'

'Offensive! I am afraid, Miss Mackenzie, you have not your spirit subject to a proper control. I have come here in all kindness to warn you against danger, and you tell me that I am offensive! What am I to think of you?'

'You have no right to connect my name with any gentleman's. You can't have any right merely because I go to Mr Stumfold's church. It's quite preposterous. If I went to Mr Paul's church' – Mr Paul was a very High Church young clergyman who had wished to have candles in his church, and of whom it was asserted that he did keep a pair of candles on an inverted box in a closet inside his bedroom – 'if I went to Mr Paul's church, might his wife, if he had one, come and ask me all manner of questions like that?'

Now Mr Paul's name stank in the nostrils of Mrs Stumfold. He was to her the thing accursed. Had Miss Mackenzie quoted the Pope, or Cardinal Wiseman or even Dr Newman, it would not have been so bad. Mrs Stumfold had once met Mr Paul, and called him to his face the most abject of all the slaves of the scarlet woman. To this courtesy Mr Paul, being a good-humoured and somewhat sportive young man, had replied that she was another. Mrs Stumfold had interpreted the gentleman's meaning wrongly, and had ever since gnashed with her teeth and fired great guns with her eyes whenever Mr Paul was named within her hearing. 'Ribald ruffian,' she had once said of him; 'but that he thinks his priestly rags protect him, he would not have dared to insult me.' It was said that she had complained to Stumfold; but Mr Stumfold's sacerdotal clothing, whether ragged or whole, prevented him also from interfering, and nothing further of a personal nature had occurred between the opponents.

But Miss Mackenzie, who certainly was a Stumfoldian by her own choice, should not have used the name. She probably did not know the whole truth as to that passage of arms between Mr Paul and Mrs Stumfold, but she did know that no name in Littlebath was so odious to the lady as that of the rival clergyman.

'Very well, Miss Mackenzie,' said she, speaking loudly in her wrath;

'then let me tell you that you will come by your ruin – yes, by your ruin. You poor unfortunate woman, you are unfit to guide your own steps, and will not take counsel from those who are able to put you in the right way!'

'How shall I be ruined?' said Miss Mackenzie, jumping up from her seat.

'How? Yes. Now you want to know. After having insulted me in return for my kindness in coming to you, you ask me questions. If I tell you how, no doubt you will insult me again.'

' I haven't insulted you, Mrs Stumfold. And if you don't like to tell me, you needn't. I'm sure I did not want you to come to me and talk in this way.'

'Want me! Who ever does want to be reproved for their own folly? I suppose what you want is to go on and marry that man, who may have two or three other wives for what you know, and put yourself and your money into the hands of a person whom you never saw in your life above a few months ago, and of whose former life you literally know nothing. Tell the truth, Miss Mackenzie, isn't that what you desire to do?'

'I find him acting as Mr Stumfold's curate.'

'Yes; and when I come to warn you, you insult me. He is Mr Stumfold's curate, and in many respects he is well fitted for his office.'

'But has he two or three wives already, Mrs Stumfold?'

'I never said that he had.'

'I thought you hinted it.'

'I never hinted it, Miss Mackenzie. If you would only be a little more careful in the things which you allow yourself to say, it would be better for yourself; and better for me too, while I am with you.'

'I declare you said something about two or three wives; and if there is anything of that kind true of a gentleman and a clergyman, I don't think he ought to be allowed to go about as a single gentleman. I mean as a curate. Mr Maguire is nothing to me – nothing whatever; and I don't see why I should have been mixed up with him; but if there is anything of that sort –'

'But there isn't.'

'Then, Mrs Stumfold, I don't think you ought to have mentioned two or three wives. I don't, indeed. It is such a horrid idea – quite horrid! And I suppose, after all, the poor man has not got one?'

'If you had allowed me, I should have told you all, Miss Mackenzie, Mr Maguire is not married, and never has been married, as far as I know.'

'Then I do think what you said of him was very cruel.'

'I said nothing; as you would have known, only you are so hot. Miss Mackenzie, you quite astonish me; you do, indeed. I had expected to find you temperate and calm; instead of that, you are so impetuous, that you will not listen to a word. When it first came to my ears that there might be something between you and Mr Maguire –'

'I will not be told about something. What does something mean, Mrs Stumfold?'

'When I was told of this,' continued Mrs Stumfold, determined that she would not be stopped any longer by Miss Mackenzie's energy; 'when I was told of this, and, indeed, I may say saw it –'

'You never saw anything, Mrs Stumfold.'

'I immediately perceived that it was my duty to come to you; to come to you and tell you that another lady has a prior claim upon Mr Maguire's hand and heart.'

'Oh, indeed.'

'Another young lady,' – with an emphasis on the word young – 'whom he first met at my house, who was introduced to him by me – a young lady not above thirty years of age, and quite suitable in every way to be Mr Maguire's wife. She may not have quite so much money as you; but she has a fair provision, and money is not everything; a lady in every way suitable –'

'But is this suitable young lady, who is only thirty years of age, engaged to him?'

'I presume, Miss Mackenzie, that in speaking to you, I am speaking to a lady who would not wish to interfere with another lady who has been before her. I do hope that you cannot be indifferent to the ordinary feelings of a female Christian on that subject. What would you think if you were interfered with, though, perhaps, as you had not your fortune in early life, you may never have known what that was.'

This was too much even for Miss Mackenzie.

'Mrs Stumfold,' she said, again rising from her seat, 'I won't talk about this any more with you. Mr Maguire is nothing to me; and, as far as I can see, if he was, that would be nothing to you.'

'But it would – a great deal.'

'No, it wouldn't. You may say what you like to him, though, for the matter of that, I think it a very indelicate thing for a lady to go about raising such questions at all. But perhaps you have known him a long time, and I have nothing to do with what you and he choose to talk about. If he is behaving bad to any friend of yours, go and tell him so. As for me, I won't hear anything more about it.'

As Miss Mackenzie continued to stand, Mrs Stumfold was forced to stand also, and soon afterwards found herself compelled to go away. She had, indeed, said all that she had come to say, and though she would willingly have repeated it again had Miss Mackenzie been submissive, she did not find herself encouraged to do so by the rebellious nature of the lady she was visiting.

'I have meant well, Miss Mackenzie,' she said as she took her leave, 'and I hope that I shall see you just the same as ever on my Thursdays.'

To this Miss Mackenzie made answer only by a curtsey, and then Mrs Stumfold went her way.

Miss Mackenzie, as soon as she was left to herself, began to cry. If Mrs Stumfold could have seen her, how it would have soothed and rejoiced that lady's ruffled spirit! Miss Mackenzie would sooner have died than have wept in Mrs Stumfold's presence, but no sooner was the front door closed than she began. To have been attacked at all in that way would have been too much for her, but to have been called old and unsuitable – for that was, in truth, the case; to hear herself accused of being courted solely for her money, and that when in truth she had not been courted at all; to have been informed that a lover for her must have been impossible in those days when she had no money! was not all this enough to make her cry? And then, was it the truth that Mr Maguire ought to marry some one else? If so, she was the last woman in Littlebath to interfere between him and that other one. But how was she to know that this was not some villainy on the part of Mrs Stumfold? She felt sure, after what she had now seen and heard, that nothing in that way would be too bad for Mrs Stumfold to say or do. She never would go to Mrs Stumfold's house again; that was a matter of course; but what should she do about Mr Maguire? Mr Maguire might never speak to her in the way of affection – probably never would do so; that she could bear; but how was she to bear the fact that every Stumfoldian in Littlebath would know all about it? On one thing she finally resolved, that if ever Mr Maguire spoke to her on the subject, she would tell him everything that had occurred. After that she cried herself to sleep.

On that afternoon she felt herself to be very desolate and much in want of a friend. When Susanna came back from school in the evening she was almost more desolate than before. She could say nothing of her troubles to one so young, nor yet could she shake off the thought of them. She had been bold enough while Mrs Stumfold had been with her, but now that she was alone, or almost worse than alone, having Susanna with her – now that the reaction had come, she began to tell herself that a continuation of this solitary life would be impossible to her. How was she to live if she was to be trampled upon in this way? Was it not almost necessary that she should leave Littlebath? And yet if she were to leave Littlebath, whither should she go, and how should she muster courage to begin everything over again? If only it had been given her to have one friend – one female friend to whom she could have told everything! She thought of Miss Baker, but Miss Baker was a staunch Stumfoldian; and what did she know of Miss Baker that gave her any right to trouble Miss Baker on such a subject? She would almost rather have gone to Miss Todd, if she had dared.

She laid awake crying half the night. Nothing of the kind had ever occurred to her before. No one had ever accused her of any impropriety; no one had ever thrown it in her teeth that she was longing after fruit that ought to be forbidden to her. In her former obscurity and dependence she had been safe. Now that she had begun to look about her and hope for joy in the world, she had fallen into this terrible misfortune! Would it not have been better for her to have married her cousin John Ball, and thus have had a clear course of duty marked out for her? Would it not have been better for her even to have married Harry Handcock than to have come to this misery? What good would her money do her, if the world was to treat her in this way?

And then, was it true? Was it the fact that Mr Maguire was ill-treating some other woman in order that he might get her money? In all her misery she remembered that Mrs Stumfold would not commit herself to any such direct assertion, and she remembered also that Mrs Stumfold had especially insisted on her own part of the grievance – on the fact that the suitable young lady had been met by Mr Maguire in her drawing-room. As to Mr Maguire himself, she could reconcile herself to the loss of him. Indeed she had never yet reconciled herself to the idea of taking him. But she could not endure to think that Mrs Stumfold's interference should prevail, or, worse still, that other people should have supposed it to prevail.

The next day was Thursday – one of Mrs Stumfold's Thursdays – and in the course of the morning Miss Baker came to her, supposing that, as a matter of course, she would go to the meeting.

'Not to-night, Miss Baker,' said she.

'Not going! and why not?'

'I'd rather not go out to-night.'

'Dear me, how odd. I thought you always went to Mrs Stumfold's. There's nothing wrong, I hope?'

Then Miss Mackenzie could not restrain herself, and told Miss Baker everything. And she told her story, not with whines and lamentations, as she had thought of it herself while lying awake during the past night, but with spirited indignation. 'What right had she to come to me and accuse me?'

'I suppose she meant it for the best,' said Miss Baker.

'No, Miss Baker, she meant it for the worst. I am sorry to speak so of your friend, but I must speak as I find her. She intended to insult me. Why did she tell me of my age and my money? Have I made myself out to be young? or misbehaved myself with the means which Providence has given me? And as to the gentleman, have I ever conducted myself so as to merit reproach? I don't know that I was ever ten minutes in his company that you were not there also.'

'It was the last accusation I should have brought against you,' whimpered Miss Baker.

'Then why has she treated me in this way? What right have I given her to be my advisor, because I go to her husband's church? Mr Maguire is my friend, and it might have come to that, that he should be my husband. Is there any sin in that, that I should be rebuked?'

'It was for the other lady's sake, perhaps.'

'Then let her go to the other lady, or to him. She has forgotten herself in coming to me, and she shall know that I think so.'

Miss Baker, when she left the Paragon, felt for Miss Mackenzie more of respect and more of esteem also than she had ever felt before. But Miss Mackenzie, when she was left alone, went upstairs, threw herself on her bed, and was again dissolved in tears.

✼ THIRTEEN ✼

Mr Maguire's Courtship

AFTER THE SCENE BETWEEN MISS MACKENZIE AND Miss Baker more than a week passed by before Miss Mackenzie saw any of her Littlebath friends; or, as she called them with much sadness when speaking of them to herself, her Littlebath acquaintances. Friends, or friend, she had none. It was a slow, heavy week with her, and it is hardly too much to say that every hour in it was spent in thinking of the attack which Mrs Stumfold had made upon her. When the first Sunday came, she went to church, and saw there Miss Baker, and Mrs Stumfold, and Mr Stumfold and Mr Maguire. She saw, indeed, many Stumfoldians, but it seemed that their eyes looked at her harshly, and she was quite sure that the coachmaker's wife treated her with marked incivility as they left the porch together. Miss Baker had frequently waited for her on Sunday mornings, and walked the length of two streets with her; but she encountered no Miss Baker near the church gate on this morning, and she was sure that Mrs Stumfold had prevailed against her. If it was to be thus with her, had she not better leave Littlebath as soon as possible? In the same solitude she lived the whole of the next week; with the same feelings did she go to church on the next Sunday; and then again was she maltreated by the up-turned nose and half-averted eyes of the coachmaker's wife.

Life such as this would be impossible to her. Let any of my readers think of it, and then tell themselves whether it could be possible. Mariana's solitude in the moated grange was as nothing to hers. In granges, and such like rural retreats, people expect solitude; but Miss Mackenzie had gone to Littlebath to find companionship. Had she been utterly disappointed, and found none, that would have been bad; but she had found it and then lost it. Mariana, in her desolateness, was still waiting for the coming of some one; and so was Miss Mackenzie waiting, though she hardly knew for whom. For me, if I am to live in a moated grange, let it be in the country. Moated granges in the midst of populous towns are very terrible.

But on the Monday morning – the morning of the second Monday after the Stumfoldian attach – Mr Maguire came, and Mariana's weariness was, for the time, at an end. Susanna had hardly gone, and the breakfast things were still on the table, when the maid brought her up word that Mr Maguire was below, and would see her if she would allow him to come up. She had heard no ring at the bell, and having settled herself with a novel in the arm-chair, had almost ceased for the moment to think of Mr Maguire or of Mrs Stumfold. There was something so sudden in the request now made to her, that it took away her breath.

'Mr Maguire, Miss, the clergyman from Mr Stumfold's church,' said the girl again.

It was necessary that she should give an answer, though she was ever so breathless.

'Ask Mr Maguire to walk up,' she said; and then she began to bethink herself how she would behave to him.

He was there, however, before her thoughts were of much service to her, and she began by apologising for the breakfast things.

'It is I that ought to beg your pardon for coming so early,' said he; 'but my time at present is so occupied that I hardly know how to find half an hour for myself; and I thought you would excuse me.'

'Oh, certainly,' said she; and then sitting down she waited for him to begin.

It would have been clear to any observer, had there been one present, that Mr Maguire had practised his lesson. He could not rid himself of those unmistakable signs of preparation which every speaker shows when he has been guilty of them. But this probably did not matter with Miss Mackenzie, who was too intent on the part she herself had to play to notice his imperfections.

'I saw that you observed, Miss Mackenzie,' he said, 'that I kept aloof from you on the two last evenings on which I met you at Mrs Stumfold's.'

'That's a long time ago, Mr Maguire,' she answered. 'It's nearly a month since I went to Mrs Stumfold's house.'

'I know that you were not there on the last Thursday. I noticed it. I could not fail to notice it. Thinking so much of you as I do, of course I did notice it. Might I ask you why you did not go?'

'I'd rather not say anything about it,' she replied, after a pause.

'Then there has been some reason? Dear Miss Mackenzie, I can assure you I do not ask you without a cause.'

'If you please, I will not speak upon that subject. I had much rather not, indeed, Mr Maguire.'

'And shall I not have the pleasure of seeing you there on next Thursday?'

'Certainly not.'

'Then you have quarrelled with her, Miss Mackenzie?'

He said nothing now of the perfections of that excellent woman, of whom not long since he had spoken in terms almost too strong for any simple human virtues.

'I'd rather not speak of it. It can't do any good. I don't know why you should ask me whether I intend to go there any more, but as you have, I have answered you.'

Then Mr Maguire got up from his chair, and walked about the room, and Miss Mackenzie, watching him closely, could see that he was much moved. But, nevertheless, I think he had made up his mind to walk about the room beforehand. After a while he paused, and, still standing, spoke to her again across the table.

'May I ask you this question? Has Mrs Stumfold said anything to you about me?'

'I'd rather not talk about Mrs Stumfold.'

'But, surely, I may ask that. I don't think you are the woman to allow anything said behind a person's back to be received to his detriment.'

'Whatever one does hear about people one always hears behind their backs.'

'Then she has told you something, and you have believed it?'

She felt herself to be so driven by him that she did not know how to protect herself. It seemed to her that these clerical people of Littlebath had very little regard for the feelings of others in their modes of following their own pursuits.

'She has told you something of me, and you have believed her?' repeated Mr Maguire. 'Have I not a right to ask you what she has said?'

'You have no right to ask me anything.'

'Have I not, Miss Mackenzie? Surely that is hard. Is it not hard that I should be stabbed in the dark, and have no means of redressing myself? I did not expect such an answer from you – indeed I did not.'

'And is not it hard that I should be troubled in this way? You talk of stabbing. Who has stabbed you? Is it not your own particular friend, whom you described to me as the best person in all the world? If you and she fall out why should I be brought into it? Once for all, Mr Maguire, I won't be brought into it.'

Now he sat down and again paused before he went on with his talk.

'Miss Mackenzie,' he said, when he did speak. 'I had not intended to be so abrupt as I fear you will think me in that which I am about to say; but I believe you will like plain measures best.'

'Certainly I shall, Mr Maguire.'

'They are the best, always. If, then, I am plain with you, will you be plain with me also? I think you must guess what it is I have to say to you.'

'I hate guessing anything, Mr Maguire.'

'Very well; then I will be plain. We have now known each other for nearly a year, Miss Mackenzie.'

'A year, is it? No, not a year. This is the beginning of June, and I did not come here till the end of last August. It's about nine months, Mr Maguire.'

'Very well; nine months. Nine months may be as nothing in an acquaintance, or it may lead to the closest friendship.'

'I don't know that we have met so very often. You have the parish to attend to, Mr Maguire.'

'Of course I have – or rather I had, for I have left Mr Stumfold.'

'Left Mr Stumfold! Why, I heard you preach yesterday.'

'I did preach yesterday, and shall till he has got another assistant. But he and I are parted as regards all friendly connection.'

'But isn't that a pity? '

'Miss Mackenzie, I don't mind telling you that I have found it impossible to put up with the impertinence of that woman' – and now, as he spoke, there came a distorted fire out of his imperfect eye – 'impossible! If you knew what I have gone through in attempting it! But that's over. I have the greatest respect for him in the world; a very thorough esteem. He is a hard-working man, and though I do not always approve the style of his wit – of which, by-the-bye, he thinks too much himself – still I acknowledge him to be a good spiritual pastor. But he has been unfortunate in his marriage. No doubt he has got money, but money is not everything.'

'Indeed, it is not, Mr Maguire.'

'How he can live in the same house with that Mr Peters, I can never understand. The quarrels between him and his daughter are so incessant that poor Mr Stumfold is unable to conceal them from the public.'

'But you have spoken so highly of her.'

'I have endeavoured, Miss Mackenzie – I have endeavoured to think well of her. I have striven to believe that it was all gold that I saw. But let that pass. I was forced to tell you that I am going to leave Mr Stumfold's church, or I should not now have spoken about her or him. And now comes the question, Miss Mackenzie.'

'What is the question, Mr Maguire?'

'Miss Mackenzie – Margaret, will you share your lot with mine? It is true that you have money. It is true that I have none – not even a curacy now. But I don't think that any such consideration as that would weigh with you for a moment, if you can find it in your heart to love me.'

Miss Mackenzie sat thinking for some minutes before she gave her answer – or striving to think; but she was so completely under the terrible fire of his eye, that any thought was very difficult.

'I am not quite sure about that,' she said after a while. 'I think, Mr Maguire, that there should be a little money on both sides. You would hardly wish to live altogether on your wife's fortune.'

'I have my profession,' he replied, quickly.

'Yes, certainly; and a noble profession it is – the most noble,' said she.

'Yes, indeed; the most noble.'

'But somehow –'

'You mean the clergymen are not paid as they should be. No, they are not, Miss Mackenzie. And is it not a shame for a Christian country like this that it should be so? But still, as a profession, it has its value. Look at Mrs Stumfold; where would she be if she were not a clergyman's wife? The position has its value. A clergyman's wife is received everywhere, you know.'

'A man before he talks of marriage ought to have something of his own, Mr Maguire, besides –'

'Besides what?'

'Well, I'll tell you. As you have done me this honour, I think that I am now bound to tell you what Mrs Stumfold said to me. She had no right to connect my name with yours or with that of any other gentleman, and my quarrel with her is about that. As to what she said about you, that is your affair and not mine.'

Then she told him the whole of that conversation which was given in the last chapter, not indeed repeating the hint about the three or four wives, but recapitulating as clearly as she could all that had been said about the suitable young lady.

'I knew it,' said he; 'I knew it. I knew it as well as though I had heard it. Now what am I to think of that woman, Miss Mackenzie?'

'Of which woman?'

'Of Mrs Stumfold, of course. It's all jealousy: every bit of it jealousy.'

'Jealousy! Do you mean that she – that she –'

'Not jealousy of that kind, Miss Mackenzie. Oh dear, no. She's as pure as the undriven snow, I should say, as far as that goes. But she can't bear to think that I should rise in the world.'

'I thought she wanted to marry you to a suitable lady, and young, with a fair provision.'

'Pshaw! The lady has about seventy pounds a-year! But that would signify nothing if I loved her, Miss Mackenzie.'

'There has been something, then?'

'Yes; there has been something. That is, nothing of my doing – nothing on earth. Miss Mackenzie, I am as innocent as the babe unborn.'

As he said this she could not help looking into the horrors of his eyes, and thinking that innocent was not the word for him.

'I'm as innocent as the babe unborn. Why should I be expected to marry a lady merely because Mrs Stumfold tells me that there she is? And it's my belief that old Peters has got their money somewhere, and won't give it up, and that that's the reason of it.'

'But did you ever say you would marry her?'

'What! Miss Floss, never! I'll tell you the whole story, Miss Mackenzie; and if you want to ask any one else, you can ask Mrs Perch.' Mrs Perch was the coach-builder's wife. 'You've seen Miss Floss at Mrs Stumfold's, and must know yourself whether I ever noticed her any more than to be decently civil.'

'Is she the lady that's so thin and tall?'

'Yes.'

'With the red hair?'

'Well, it's sandy, certainly. I shouldn't call it just red myself.'

'Some people like red hair, you know,' said Miss Mackenzie, thinking of the suitable lady. Miss Mackenzie was willing at that moment to forfeit all her fortune if Miss Floss was not older than she was!

'And that is Miss Floss, is it?'

'Yes, and I don't blame Mrs Stumfold for wishing to get a husband for her friend, but it is hard upon me.'

'Really, Mr Maguire, I think that perhaps you couldn't do better.'

'Better than what?'

'Better than take Miss Floss. As you say, some people like red hair. And she is very suitable, certainly. And, Mr Maguire, I really shouldn't like to interfere – I shouldn't indeed.'

'Miss Mackenzie, you're joking, I know.'

'Not in the least, Mr Maguire. You see there has been something about it.'

'There has been nothing.'

'There's never smoke without fire; and I don't think a lady like Mrs Stumfold would come here and tell me all that she did, if it hadn't gone some way. And you owned just now that you admired her.'

'I never owned anything of the kind. I don't admire her a bit. Admire her! Oh, Miss Mackenzie, what do you think of me?'

Miss Mackenzie said that she really didn't know what to think.

Then, having as he thought altogether disposed of Miss Floss, he began again to press his suit. And she was weak; for though she gave him no positive encouragement, neither did she give him any positive denial. Her mind was by no means made up, and she did not know whether she wished to take him or to leave him. Now that the thing had come so near, what guarantee had she that he would be good to her if she gave him everything that she possessed? As to her cousin John Ball, she would have had many guarantees. Of him she could say that she knew what sort of a man he was; but what did she know of Mr Maguire? At that moment, as he sat there pleading his own cause with all the eloquence at his command, she remembered that she did not even know his Christian name. He had always in her presence been called Mr Maguire. How could she say that she loved a man whose very name she had not as yet heard?

But still, if she left all her chances to run from her, what other fate would she have but that of being friendless all her life? Of course she must risk much if she was ever minded to change her mode of life. She had said something to him as to the expediency of there being money on both sides, but as she said it she knew that she would willingly have given up her money could she only have been sure of her man. Was not her income enough for both? What she wanted was companionship, and love if it might be possible; but if not love, then friendship. This, had she known where she could purchase it with certainty, she would willingly have purchased with all her wealth.

'If I have surprised you, will you say that you will take time to think of it?' pleaded Mr Maguire.

Miss Mackenzie, speaking in the lowest possible voice, said that she would take time to think of it.

When a lady says that she will take time to think of such a proposition, the gentleman is generally justified in supposing that he has carried his cause. When a lady rejects a suitor, she should reject him peremptorily. Anything short of such peremptory reaction is taken for acquiescence. Mr Maguire consequently was elated, called her Margaret, and swore that he loved her as he had never loved woman yet.

'And when may I come again?' he asked.

Miss Mackenzie begged that she might be allowed a fortnight to think of it.

'Certainly,' said the happy man.

'And you must not be surprised,' said Miss Mackenzie, 'if I make some inquiry about Miss Floss.'

'Any inquiry you please,' said Mr Maguire. 'It is all in that woman's brain; it is indeed. Miss Floss, perhaps, has thought of it; but I can't help that, can I? I can't help what has been said to her. But if you mean anything as to a promise from me, Margaret, on my word as a Christian minister of the Gospel, there has been nothing of the kind.'

She did not much mind his calling her Margaret; it was in itself such a trifle; but when he made a fuss about kissing her hand it annoyed her.

'Only your hand,' he said, beseeching the privilege.

'Pshaw,' she said, 'what's the good?'

She had sense enough to feel that with such lovemaking as that between her and her lover there should be no kissing till after marriage; or at any rate, no kissing of hands, as is done between handsome young men of twenty-three and beautiful young ladies of eighteen, when they sit in balconies on moonlight nights. A good honest kiss, mouth to mouth, might not be amiss when matters were altogether settled; but when she thought of this, she thought also of his eye and shuddered. His eye was not his fault, and a man should not be left all his days without a wife because he squints; but still, was it possible? could she bring herself to endure it?

He did kiss her hand, however, and then went. As he stood at the door he looked back fondly and exclaimed –

'On Monday fortnight, Margaret; on Monday fortnight.'

'Goodness gracious, Mr Maguire,' she answered, 'do shut the door;' and then he vanished.

As soon as he was gone she remembered that his name was Jeremiah. She did not know how she had learned it, but she knew that such was the fact. If it did come to pass how was she to call him? She tried the entire word Jeremiah, but it did not seem to answer. She tried Jerry also, but that was worse. Jerry might have been very well had they come together fifteen years earlier in life, but she did not think that she could call him Jerry now. She supposed it must be Mr Maguire; but if so, half the romance of the thing would be gone at once!

She felt herself to be very much at sea, and almost wished that she might be like Mariana again, waiting and aweary, so grievous was the necessity of having to make up her mind on such a subject. To whom should she go for advice? She had told him that she would make further inquiries about Miss Floss, but of whom was she to make them? The only person to whom she could apply was Miss Baker, and she was almost sure that Miss Baker would despise her for thinking of marrying Mr Maguire.

But after a day or two she did tell Miss Baker, and she saw at once that Miss Baker did despise her. But Miss Baker, though she manifestly did despise her, promised her some little aid. Miss Todd knew everything and everybody. Might Miss Baker tell Miss Todd? If there was anything wrong, Miss Todd would ferret it out to a certainty. Miss Mackenzie, hanging down her head, said that Miss Baker might tell Miss Todd. Miss Baker, when she left Miss Mackenzie, turned at once into Miss Todd's house, and found her friend at home.

'It surprises me that any woman should be so foolish,' said Miss Baker.

'Come, come, my dear, don't you be hard upon her. We have all been foolish in our days. Do you remember, when Sir Lionel used to be here, how foolish you and I were?'

'It's not the same thing at all,' said Miss Baker. 'Did you ever see a man with such an eye as he has got?'

'I shouldn't mind his eye, my dear; only I'm afraid he's got no money.'

Miss Todd, however, promised to make inquiries, and declared her intention of communicating what intelligence she might obtain direct to Miss Mackenzie. Miss Baker resisted this for a little while, but ultimately submitted, as she was wont to do, to the stronger character of her friend.

Miss Mackenzie had declared that she must have a fortnight to think about it, and Miss Todd therefore knew that she had nearly a fortnight for her inquiries. The reader may be sure that she did not allow the grass to grow under her feet. With Miss Mackenzie the time passed slowly enough, for she could only sit on her sofa and doubt, resolving first one way and then another; but Miss Todd went about Littlebath, here and there, among friends and enemies, filling up all her time; and before the end of the fortnight she certainly knew more about Mr Maguire than did anybody else in Littlebath.

She did not see Miss Mackenzie till the Saturday, the last Saturday before the all-important Monday; but on that day she went to her.

'I suppose you know what I'm come about, my dear,' she said.

Miss Mackenzie blushed, and muttered something about Miss Baker.

'Yes, my dear; Miss Baker was speaking to me about Mr Maguire. You needn't mind speaking out to me, Miss Mackenzie. I can understand all about it; and if I can be of any assistance, I shall be very happy. No doubt you feel a little shy, but you needn't mind with me.'

'I'm sure you're very good.'

'I don't know about that, but I hope I'm not very bad. The long and the short of it is, I suppose, that you think you might as well – might as well take Mr Maguire.'

Miss Mackenzie felt thoroughly ashamed of herself. She could not explain to Miss Todd all her best motives; and then, those motives which were not the best were made to seem so very weak and mean by the way in which Miss Todd approached them. When she thought of the matter alone, it seemed to her that she was perfectly reasonable in wishing to be married, in order that she might escape the monotony of a lonely life; and she thought that if she could talk to Miss Todd about the subject gently, for a quarter of an hour at a time every day for two or three months, it was possible that she might explain her views with credit to herself; but how could she do this to anyone so very abruptly? She could only confess that she did want to marry the man, as the child confesses her longing for a tart.

'I have thought about it, certainly,' she said.

'Quite right,' said Miss Todd; 'quite right if you like him. Now for me, I'm so fond of my own money and my own independence, that I've never had a fancy that way – not since I was a girl.'

'But you're so different, Miss Todd; you've got such a position of your own.'

And Miss Mackenzie, who was at present desirous of marrying a very strict evangelical clergyman, thought with envy of the social advantages and pleasant iniquities of her wicked neighbour.

'Oh, I don't know. I've a few friends, but that comes of being here so long. And then, you see, I ain't particular as you are. I always see that when a lady goes in to be evangelical, she soon finds a husband to take care of her; that is, if she has got any money. It all goes on very well, and I've no doubt they're right. There's my friend Mary Baker, she's single still; but then she began very late in life. Now about Mr Maguire.'

'Well, Miss Todd.'

'In the first place, I really don't think he has got much that he can call his own.'

'He hasn't got anything, Miss Todd; he told me so himself.'

'Did he, indeed?' said Miss Todd; 'then let me tell you he is a deal honester than they are in general.'

' Oh, he told me that. I know he's got no income in the world besides his curacy, and that he has thrown up.'

'And therefore you are going to give him yours.'

'I don't know about that, Miss Todd; but it wasn't about money that I was doubting. What I've got is enough for both of us, if his wants are not greater than mine. What is the use of money if people cannot be happy together with it? I don't care a bit for money, Miss Todd; that is, not for itself. I shouldn't like to be dependent on a stranger; I don't know that I would like to be dependent again even on a brother; but I should take no shame to be dependent on a husband if he was good to me.'

'That's just it; isn't it?'

'There's quite enough for him and me.'

'I must say you look at the matter in the most disinterested way. I couldn't bring myself to take it up like that.'

'You haven't lived the life that I have, Miss Todd, and I don't suppose you ever feel solitary as I do.'

'Well, I don't know. We single women have to be solitary sometimes – and sometimes sad.'

'But you're never sad, Miss Todd.'

'Have you never heard there are some animals, that, when they're sick, crawl into holes, and don't ever show themselves among the other animals? Though it is only the animals that do it, there's a pride in that which I like. What's the good of complaining if one's down in the mouth? When one gets old and heavy and stupid, one can't go about as one did when one was young; and other people won't care to come to you as they did then.'

'But I had none of that when I was young, Miss Todd.'

'Hadn't you? Then I won't say but what you may be right to try and begin now. But, law! what am I talking of? I am old enough to be your mother.'

'I think it so kind of you to talk to me at all.'

'Well, now about Mr Maguire. I don't think he's possessed of much of the fat of the land; but that you say you know already?'

'Oh yes, I know all that.'

'And it seems he has lost his curacy?'

'He threw that up himself.'

'I shouldn't be surprised – but mind I don't say this for certain – but I shouldn't be surprised if he owed a little money.'

Miss Mackenzie's face became rather long.

'What do you call a little, Miss Todd?'

'Two or three hundred pounds. I don't call that a great deal.'

'Oh dear, no!' and Miss Mackenzie's face again became cheerful. 'That could be settled without any trouble.'

'Upon my word you are the most generous woman I ever saw.'

'No, I'm not that.'

'Or else you must be very much in love?'

'I don't think I am that either, Miss Todd; only I don't care much about money if other things are suitable. What I chiefly wanted to know was –'

'About that Miss Floss?'

'Yes, Miss Todd.'

'My belief is there never was a greater calumny, or what I should call a stronger attempt at a do. Mind I don't think much of your St Stumfolda, and never did. I believe the poor man has never said a word to the woman. Mrs Stumfold has put it into her head that she could have Mr Maguire if she chose to set her cap at him, and, I dare say, Miss Floss has been dutiful to her saint. But, Miss Mackenzie, if nothing else hinders you, don't let that hinder you.' Then Miss Todd, having done her business and made her report, took her leave.

This was on Saturday. The next day would be Sunday, and then on the following morning she must make her answer. All that she had heard about Mr Maguire was, to her thinking, in his favour. As to his poverty, that he had declared himself, and that she did not mind. As to a few hundred pounds of debt, how was a poor man to have helped such a misfortune? In that matter of Miss Floss he had been basely maligned – so much maligned, that Miss Mackenzie owed him all her sympathy. What excuse could she now have for refusing him?

When she went to bed on the Sunday night such were her thoughts and her feelings.

✂ FOURTEEN ✂

Tom Mackenzie's Bed-Side

THERE WAS A STUMFOLDIAN EDICT, ULTRA-MEDIAN-AND-PERSIAN in its strictness, ordaining that no Stumfoldian in Littlebath should be allowed to receive a letter on Sundays. And there also existed a co-ordinate rule on the part of the Postmaster-General – or, rather, a privilege granted by that functionary – in accordance with which Stumfoldians, and other such sects of Sabbatarians, were empowered to prohibit the letter-carriers from contaminating their special knockers on Sunday mornings. Miss Mackenzie had given way to this easily, seeing nothing amiss in the edict, and not caring much for her Sunday letters. In consequence, she received on the Monday mornings those letters which were due to her on Sundays, and on this special Monday morning she received a letter, as to which the delay was of much consequence. It was to tell her that her brother Tom was dying, and to pray that she would be up in London as early on the Monday as was practicable. Mr Samuel Rubb, junior, who had written the letter in Gower Street, had known nothing of the Sabbatical edicts of the Stumfoldians.

'It is an inward tumour,' said Mr Rubb, 'and has troubled him long, though he has said nothing about it. It is now breaking, and the doctor says he can't live. He begs that you will come to him, as he has very much to say to you. Mrs Tom would have written, but she is so much taken up, and is so much beside herself, that she begs me to say that she is not able; but I hope it won't be less welcome coming from me. The second pair back will be ready for you, just as if it were your own. I would be waiting at the station on Monday, if I knew what train you would come by.'

This she received while at breakfast on the Monday morning, having sat down a little earlier than usual, in order that the tea-things might be taken away so as to make room for Mr Maguire.

Of course she must go up to town instantly, by the first practicable train. She perceived at once that she would have to send a message by telegraph, as they would have expected to hear from her that morning. She got the railway guide, and saw that the early express train had already gone. There was, however, a mid-day train which would reach Paddington in the afternoon. She immediately got her bonnet and went off to the telegraph office, leaving word with the servant, that if any one called 'he' was to be told that she had received sudden tidings which took her up to London. On her return she found that 'he' had not been there yet, and now she could only hope that he would not come till after she had started. It would, of course, be impossible, at such a moment as this, to make any answer to such a proposition as Mr Maguire's.

He came, and when the servant gave him the message at the door, he sent up craving permission to see her but for a moment. She could not refuse him, and went down to him in the drawing-room, with her shawl and bonnet.

'Dearest Margaret,' said he, 'what is this?' and he took both her hands.

'I have received word that my brother, in London, is very ill – that he is dying, and I must go to him.'

He still held her hands, standing close to her, as though he had some special right to comfort her.

'Cannot I go with you?' he said. 'Let me; do let me.'

'Oh, no, Mr Maguire; it is impossible. What could you do? I am going to my brother's house.'

'But have I not a right to be of help to you at such a time?' he asked.

'No, Mr Maguire; no right; certainly none as yet.'

'Oh! Margaret.'

'I'm sure you will see that I cannot talk of anything of that sort now.'

'But you will not be back for ever so long.'

'I cannot tell.'

'Oh! Margaret; you will not leave me in suspense? After bidding me wait a fortnight, you will not go away without telling me that you will be mine when you come back? One word will do it.'

'Mr Maguire, you really must excuse me now.'

'One word, Margaret; only one word,' and he still held her.

'Mr Maguire,' she said, tearing her hand from him, 'I am astonished at you. I tell you that my brother is dying and you hold me here, and expect me to give you an answer about nonsense. I thought you were more manly.'

He saw that there was a flash in her eye as he stepped back; so he begged her pardon, and muttering something about hoping to hear from her soon, took his leave. Poor man! I do not see why she should not have accepted him, as she had made up her mind to do so. And to him, with his creditors, and in his present position, any certainty in this matter would have made so much difference!

At the Paddington station Miss Mackenzie was met by her other lover, Mr Rubb. Mr Rubb, however, had never yet declared himself as holding this position, and did not do so on the present occasion. Their conversation in the cab was wholly concerning her brother's state, or nearly so. It seemed that there was no hope. Mr Rubb said that very clearly. As to time the doctor would say nothing certain; but he had declared that it might occur any day. The patient could never leave his bed again; but as his constitution was strong, he might remain in his present condition some weeks. He did not suffer much pain, or, at any rate, did not complain of much; but was very sad. Then Mr Rubb said one other word.

'I am afraid he is thinking of his wife and children.'

'Would there be nothing for them out of the business?' asked Miss Mackenzie.

The junior partner at first shook his head, saying nothing. After a few minutes he did speak in a low voice. 'If there be anything, it will be very little – very little.'

Miss Mackenzie was rejoiced that she had given no definite promise to Mr Maguire. There seemed to be now a job for her to do in the world which would render it quite unnecessary that she should look about for a husband. If her brother's widow were left penniless, with seven children, there would be no longer much question as to what she would do with her money. Perhaps the only person in the world that she cordially disliked was her sister-in-law. She certainly knew no other woman whose society would be so unpalatable to her. But if things were so as Mr Rubb now described them, there could be no doubt about her duty. It was very well indeed that her answer to Mr Maguire had been postponed to that Monday.

She found her sister-in-law in the dining-room, and Mrs Mackenzie, of course, received her with a shower of tears. 'I did think you would have come, Margaret, by the first train.'

Then Margaret was forced to explain all about the letter and the Sunday arrangements at Littlebath; and Mrs Tom was stupid and wouldn't understand, but persisted in her grievance, declaring that Tom was killing himself with disappointment.

'And there's Dr Slumpy just this moment gone without a word to comfort one – not even to say about when it will be. I suppose you'll want your dinner before you go up to see him. As for us we've had no dinners, or anything regular; but, of course, you must be waited on.' Miss Mackenzie simply took off her bonnet and shawl, and declared herself ready to go upstairs as soon as her brother would be ready to see her.

'It's fret about money has done it all, Margaret,' said the wife. 'Since the day that Walter's shocking will was read, he's never been himself for an hour. Of course he wouldn't show it to you; but he never has.'

Margaret turned short round upon her sister-in-law on the stairs.

'Sarah,' said she, and then she stopped herself. 'Never mind; it is natural, no doubt, you should feel it; but there are times and places when one's feelings should be kept under control.'

'That's mighty fine,' said Mrs Mackenzie; 'but, however, if you'll wait here, I'll go up to him.'

In a few minutes more Miss Mackenzie was standing by her brother's bedside, holding his hand in hers.

'I knew you would come, Margaret,' he said.

'Of course I should come; who doubted it? But never mind that, for here I am.'

'I only told her that we expected her by the earlier train,' said Mrs Tom.

'Never mind the train as long as she's here,' said Tom. 'You've heard how it is with me, Margaret?'

Then Margaret buried her face in the bed-clothes and wept, and Mrs Tom, weeping also, hid herself behind the curtains.

There was nothing said then about money or the troubles of the business, and after a while the two women went down to tea. In the dining-room they found Mr Rubb, who seemed to be quite at home in the house. Cold meat was brought up for Margaret's dinner, and they all sat down to one of those sad sick-house meals which he or she who has not known must have been lucky indeed. To Margaret it was nothing new. All the life that she remembered, except the last year, had been spent in nursing her other brother; and now to be employed about the bed-side of a sufferer was as natural to her as the air she breathed.

'I will sit with him to-night, Sarah, if you will let me,' she said; and Sarah assented.

It was still daylight when she found herself at her post. Mrs Mackenzie had just left the room to go down among the children, saying that she would return again before she left him for the night. To this the invalid remonstrated, begging his wife to go to bed.

'She has not had her clothes off for the last week,' said the husband.

'It don't matter about my clothes,' said Mrs Tom, still weeping. She was always crying when in the sick room, and always scolding when out of it; thus complying with the two different requisitions of her nature. The matter, however, was settled by an assurance on her part that she would go to bed, so that she might be stirring early.

There are women who seem to have an absolute pleasure in fixing themselves for business by the bedside of a sick man. They generally commence their operations by laying aside all fictitious feminine charms, and by arraying themselves with a rigid, unconventional, unenticing propriety. Though they are still gentle – perhaps more gentle than ever in their movements – there is a decision in all they do very unlike their usual mode of action. The sick man, who is not so sick but what he can ponder on the matter, feels himself to be like a baby, whom he has seen the nurse to take from its cradle, pat on the back, feed, and then return to its little couch, all without undue violence or tyranny, but still with a certain consciousness of omnipotence as far as that child was concerned. The vitality of the man is gone from him, and he, in his prostrate condition, debarred by all the features of his condition from spontaneous exertion, feels himself to be more a woman than the woman herself. She, if she be such a one as our Miss Mackenzie, arranges her bottles with precision; knows exactly how to place her chair, her lamp, and her teapot; settles her cap usefully on her head, and prepares for the night's work certainly with satisfaction. And such are the best women of the world – among which number I think that Miss Mackenzie has a right to be counted.

A few words of affection were spoken between the brother and sister, for at such moments brotherly affection returns, and the estrangements of life are all forgotten in the old memories. He seemed comforted to feel her hand upon the bed, and was glad to pronounce her name, and spoke to her as though she had been the favourite of the family for years, instead of the one member of it who had been snubbed and disregarded. Poor man, who shall say that there was anything hypocritical or false in this? And yet, undoubtedly, it was the fact that Margaret was now the only wealthy one among them, which had made him send to her, and think of her, as he lay there in his sickness.

When these words of love had been spoken, he turned himself on his pillow, and lay silent for a long while – for hours, till the morning sun had risen, and the daylight was again seen through the window curtain. It was not much after midsummer, and the daylight came to them early. From time to time she had looked at him, and each hour in the night she had crept round to him, and given him that which he needed. She did it all with a certain system, noiselessly, but with an absolute assurance on her own part that she carried with her an authority sufficient to ensure obedience. On that ground, in that place, I think that even Miss Todd would have succumbed to her.

But when the morning sun had driven the appearance of night from the room, making the paraphernalia of sickness more ghastly than they had been under the light of the lamp, the brother turned himself back again, and began to talk of those things which were weighing on his mind.

'Margaret,' he said, 'it's very good of you to come, but as to myself, no one's coming can be of any use to me.'

'It is all in the hands of God, Tom.'

'No doubt, no doubt,' said he, sadly, not daring to argue such a point with her, and yet feeling but little consolation from her assurance. 'So is the bullock in God's hands when the butcher is going to knock him on the head, but yet we know that the beast will die. Men live and die from natural causes, and not by God's interposition.'

'But there is hope; that is what I mean. If God pleases –'

'Ah, well. But, Margaret, I fear that he will not please; and what am I to do about Sarah and the children?'

This was a question that could be answered by no general platitude – by no weak words of hopeless consolation. Coming from him to her, it demanded either a very substantial answer, or else no answer at all. What was he to do about Sarah and the children? Perhaps there came a thought across her mind that Sarah and the children had done very little for her – had considered her very little, in those old, weary days, in Arundel Street. And those days were not, as yet, so very old. It was now not much more than twelve months since she had sat by the deathbed of her other brother – since she had expressed to herself, and to Harry Handcock, a humble wish that she might find herself to be above absolute want.

'I do not think you need fret about that, Tom,' she said, after turning these things over in her mind for a minute or two.

'How, not fret about them? But I suppose you know nothing of the state of the business. Has Rubb spoken to you?'

'He did say some word as we came along in the cab.'

'What did he say?'

'He said –'

'Well, tell me what he said. He said, that if I died – what then? You must not be afraid of speaking of it openly. Why, Margaret, they have all told me that it must be in a month or two. What did Rubb say?'

'He said that there would be very little coming out of the business – that is, for Sarah and the children – if anything were to happen to you.'

'I don't suppose they'd get anything. How it has been managed I don't know. I have worked like a galley slave at it, but I haven't kept the books, and I don't know how things have gone so badly. They have gone badly – very badly.'

'Has it been Mr Rubb's fault?'

'I won't say that; and, indeed, if it has been any man's fault it has been the old man's. I don't want to say a word against the one that you know. Oh, Margaret!'

'Don't fret yourself now, Tom.'

'If you had seven children, would not you fret yourself? And I hardly know how to speak to you about it. I know that we have already had ever so much of your money, over two thousand pounds; and I fear you will never see it again.'

'Never mind, Tom; it is yours, with all my heart. Only, Tom, as it is so badly wanted, I would rather it was yours than Mr Rubb's. Could I not do something that would make that share of the building yours?'

He shifted himself uneasily in his bed, and made her understand that she had distressed him.

'But perhaps it will be better to say nothing more about that,' said she.

'It will be better that you should understand it all. The property belongs nominally to us, but it is mortgaged to the full of its value. Rubb can explain it all, if he will. Your money went to buy it, but other creditors would not be satisfied without security. Ah, dear! it is so dreadful to have to speak of all this in this way.'

'Then don't speak of it, Tom.'

'But what am I to do?'

'Are there no proceeds from the business?'

'Yes, for those who work in it; and I think there will be something coming out of it for Sarah – something, but it will be very small. And if so, she must depend for it solely on Mr Rubb.'

'On the young one?'

'Yes; on the one that you know.'

There was a great deal more said, and of course everyone will know how such a conversation was ended, and will understand with what ample assurance as to her own intentions Margaret promised that the seven children should not want. As she did so, she made certain rapid calculations in her head. She must give up Mr Maguire. There was no doubt about that. She must give up all idea of marrying any one, and, as she thought of this, she told herself that she was perhaps well rid of a trouble. She had already given away to the firm of Rubb and Mackenzie above a hundred a-year out of her income. If she divided the remainder with Mrs Tom, keeping about three hundred and fifty pounds a-year for herself and Susanna, she would, she thought, keep her promise well, and yet retain enough for her own comfort and Susanna's education. It would be bad for the prospects of young John Ball, the third of the name, whom she had taught herself to regard as her heir; but young John Ball would know nothing of the good things he had lost. As to living with her sister-in-law Sarah, and sharing her house and income with the whole family, that she declared to herself nothing should induce her to do. She would give up half of all that she had, and that half would be quite enough to save her brother's children from want. In making the promise to her brother she said nothing about proportions, and nothing as to her own future life. 'What I have,' she said, 'I will share with them and you may rest assured that they shall not want.' Of course he thanked her as dying men do thank those who take upon themselves such charges; but she perceived as he did so, or thought that she perceived, that he still had something more upon his mind.

Mrs Tom came and relieved her in the morning, and Miss Mackenzie was obliged to put off for a time that panoply of sick-room armour which made her so indomitable in her brother's bedroom. Downstairs she met Mr Rubb, who talked to her much about her brother's affairs, and much about the oilcloth business. speaking as though he were desirous that the most absolute confidence should exist between him and her. But she said no word of her promise to her brother, except that she declared that the money lent was now to be regarded as a present made by her to him personally.

'I am afraid that that will avail nothing,' said Mr Rubb, junior, 'for the amount now stands as a debt due by the firm to you, and the firm, which would pay you the money if it could, cannot pay it to your brother's estate any more than it can to yours.'

'But the interest,' said Miss Mackenzie.

'Oh, yes! the interest can be paid,' said Mr Rubb, junior, but the tone of his voice did not give much promise that this interest would be forthcoming with punctuality.

She watched again that night; and on the next day, in the afternoon, she was told that a gentleman wished to see her in the drawing-room. Her thoughts at once pointed to Mr Maguire, and she went downstairs prepared to be very angry with that gentleman. But on entering the room she found her cousin, John Ball. She was, in truth, glad to see him; for, after all, she thought that she liked him the best of all the men or women that she knew. He was always in trouble, but then she fancied that with him she at any rate knew the worst. There was nothing concealed with him – nothing to be afraid of. She hoped that they might continue to know each other intimately as cousins. Under existing circumstances they could not, of course, be anything more to each other than that.

'This is very kind of you, John,' she said, taking his hand. 'How did you know I was here?'

'Mr Slow told me. I was with Mr Slow about business of yours. I'm afraid from what I hear that you find your brother very ill.'

'Very ill, indeed, John – ill to death.'

She then asked after her uncle and aunt, and the children, at the Cedars.

They were much as usual, he said; and he added that his mother would be very glad to see her at the Cedars; only he supposed there was no hope of that.

'Not just at present, John. You see I am wholly occupied here.'

'And will he really die, do you think?'

'The doctors say so.'

'And his wife and children – will they be provided for?'

Margaret simply shook her head, and John Ball, as he watched her, felt assured that his uncle Jonathan's money would never come in his way, or in the way of his children. But he was a man used to disappointment, and he bore this with mild sufferance.

Then he explained to her the business about which he had specially come to her. She had entrusted him with certain arrangements as to a portion of her property, and he came to tell her that a certain railway company wanted some houses which belonged to her, and that by Act of Parliament she was obliged to sell them.

'But the Act of Parliament will make the railway company pay for them, won't it, John?'

Then he went on to explain to her that she was in luck's way, 'as usual,' said the poor fellow, thinking of his own misfortunes, and that she would greatly increase her income by the sale. Indeed, it seemed to her that she would regain pretty nearly all she had lost by the loan to Rubb and Mackenzie. 'How very singular,' thought she to herself. Under these circumstances, it might, after all, be possible that she should marry Mr Maguire, if she wished it.

When Mr Ball had told his business he did not stay much longer. He said no word of his own hopes, if hopes they could be called any longer. As he left her, he just referred to what had passed between them. ' This is no time, Margaret,' said he, 'to ask you whether you have changed your mind?'

'No, John; there are other things to think of now; are there not? And, besides, they will want here all that I can do for them.'

She spoke to him with an express conviction that what was wanted of her by him, as well as by others, was her money, and it did not occur to him to contradict her.

'He might have asked to see me, I do think,' said Mrs Tom, when John Ball was gone. 'But there always was an upsetting pride about those people at the Cedars which I never could endure. And they are as poor as church mice. When poverty and pride go together I do detest them. I suppose he came to find out all about us, but I hope you told him nothing.'

To all this Miss Mackenzie made no answer at all.

FIFTEEN

The Tearing of the Verses

THINGS WENT ON IN GOWER STREET FOR three or four weeks in the same way, and then Susanna was fetched home from Littlebath. Miss Mackenzie would have gone down herself but that she was averse to see Mr Maguire. She therefore kept on her Littlebath lodgings, though Mrs Tom said much to her of the wasteful extravagance in doing so. It was at last settled that Mr Rubb should go down to Littlebath and bring Susanna back with him; and this he did, not at all to that young lady's satisfaction. It was understood that Susanna did not leave the school, at which she had lately been received as a boarder; but the holidays had come, and it was thought well that she should see her father. During this time Miss Mackenzie received two letters from Mr Maguire. In the first he pleaded hard for an answer to his offer. He had, he said, now relinquished his curacy, having found the interference of that terrible woman to be unendurable. He had left his curacy, and was at present without employment. Under such circumstances, 'his Margaret' would understand how imperative it was that he should receive an answer. A curacy, or, rather, a small incumbency, had offered itself among the mines in Cornwall; but he could not think of accepting this till he should know what 'his Margaret' might say to it.

To this Margaret answered most demurely, and perhaps a little slily. She said that her brother's health and affairs were at present in such a condition as to allow her to think of nothing else; that she completely understood Mr Maguire's position, and that it was essential that he should not be kept in suspense. Under these combined circumstances she had no alternative but to release him from the offer he had made. This she did with the less unwillingness as it was probable that her pecuniary position would be considerably altered by the change in her brother's family which they were now expecting almost daily. Then she bade him farewell, with many expressions of her esteem, and said that she hoped he might be happy among the mines in Cornwall.

Such was her letter; but it did not satisfy Mr Maguire, and he wrote a second letter. He had declined, he said, the incumbency among the mines, having heard of something which he thought would suit him better in Manchester. As to that, there was no immediate hurry, and he proposed remaining at Littlebath for the next two months, having been asked to undertake temporary duty in a neighbouring church for that time. By the end of the two months he hoped that 'his Margaret' would be able to give him an answer in a different tone. As to her pecuniary position, he would leave that, he said, 'all to herself.'

To this second letter Miss Mackenzie did not find it necessary to send any reply. The domestics in the Mackenzie family were not at this time numerous, and the poor mother had enough to do with her family downstairs. No nurse had been hired for the sick man, for nurses cannot be hired without money, and money with the Tom Mackenzies was scarce. Our Miss Mackenzie would have hired a nurse, but she thought it better to take the work entirely into her own hands. She did so, and I think we may say that her brother did not suffer by it. As she sat by his bedside, night after night, she seemed to feel that she had fallen again into her proper place, and she looked back upon the year she had spent at Littlebath almost with dismay. Since her brother's death, three men had offered to marry her, and there was a fourth from whom she had expected such an offer. She looked upon all this with dismay, and told herself that she was not fit to sail, under her own guidance, out in the broad sea, amidst such rocks as those. Was not some humbly feminine employment, such as that in which she was now engaged, better for her in all ways? Sad as was the present occasion, did she not feel a satisfaction in what she was doing, and an assurance that she was fit for her position? Had she not always been ill at ease, and out of her element, while striving at Littlebath to live the life of a lady of fortune? She told herself that it was so, and that it would be better for her to be a hard-working, dependent woman, doing some tedious duty day by day, than to live a life of ease which prompted her to longings for things unfitted to her.

She had brought a little writing-desk with her that she had carried from Arundel Street to Littlebath, and this she had with her in the sick man's bedroom. Sitting there through the long hours of night, she would open this and read over and over again those remnants of the rhymes written in her early days which she had kept when she made her great bonfire. There had been quires of such verses, but she had destroyed all but a few leaves before she started for Littlebath. What were left, and were now read, were very sweet to her, and yet she knew that they were wrong and meaningless. What business had such a one as she to talk of the sphere's tune and the silvery moon, of bright stars shining and hearts repining? She would not for worlds have allowed any one to know what a fool she had been – either Mrs Tom, or John Ball, or Mr Maguire, or Miss Todd. She would have been covered with confusion if her rhymes had fallen into the hands of any one of them.

And yet she loved them well, as a mother loves her only idiot child. They were her expressions of the romance and poetry that had been in her; and though the expressions doubtless were poor, the romance and poetry of her heart had been high and noble. How wrong the world is in connecting so closely as it does the capacity for feeling and the capacity for expression – in thinking that capacity for the one implies capacity for the other, or incapacity for the one incapacity also for the other; in confusing the technical art of the man who sings with the unselfish tenderness of the man who feels! But the world does so connect them; and, consequently, those who express themselves badly are ashamed of their feelings.

She read her poor lines again and again, throwing herself back into the days and thoughts of former periods, and telling herself that it was all over. She had thought of encouraging love, and love had come to her in the shape of Mr Maguire, a very strict evangelical clergyman, without a cure or an income, somewhat in debt, and with, oh! such an eye! She tore the papers, very gently, into the smallest fragments. She tore them again and again, swearing to herself as she did so that there should be an end of all that; and, as there was no fire at hand, she replaced the pieces in her desk. During this ceremony of the tearing she devoted herself to the duties of a single life, to the drudgeries of ordinary utility, to such works as those she was now doing. As to any society, wicked or religious – wicked after the manner of Miss Todd, or religious after the manner of St Stumfolda – it should come or not, as circumstances might direct. She would go no more in search of it. Such were the resolves of a certain night, during which the ceremony of the tearing took place.

It came to pass at this time that Mr Rubb, junior, visited his dying partner almost daily, and was always left alone with him for some time. When these visits were made Miss Mackenzie would descend to the room in which her sister-in-law was sitting, and there would be some conversation between them about Mr Rubb and his affairs. Much as these two women disliked each other, there had necessarily arisen between them a certain amount of confidence. Two persons who are much thrown together, to the exclusion of other society, will tell each other their thoughts, even though there be no love between them.

'What is he saying to him all these times when he is with him?' said Mrs Tom one morning, when Miss Mackenzie had come down on the appearance of Mr Rubb in the sick room.

'He is talking about the business, I suppose.'

'What good can that do? Tom can't say anything about that, as to how it should be done. He thinks a great deal about Sam Rubb; but it's more than I do.'

'They must necessarily be in each other's confidence, I should say.'

'He's not in my confidence. My belief is he's been a deal too clever for Tom; and that he'll turn out to be too clever – for me, and – my poor orphans.' Upon which Mrs Tom put her handkerchief up to her eyes. 'There; he's coming down,' continued the wife. 'Do you go up now, and make Tom tell you what it is that Sam Rubb has been saying to him.'

Margaret Mackenzie did go up as she heard Mr Rubb close the front door; but she had no such purpose as that with which her sister-in-law had striven to inspire her. She had no wish to make the sick man tell her anything that he did not wish to tell. In considering the matter within her own breast, she owned to herself that she did not expect much from the Rubbs in aid of the wants of her nephews and nieces; but what would be the use of troubling a dying man about that? She had agreed with herself to believe that the oilcloth business was a bad affair, and that it would be well to hope for nothing from it. That her brother to the last should harass himself about the business was only natural; but there could be no reason why she should harass him on the same subject. She had recognised the fact that his widow and children must be supported by her; and had she now been told that the oilcloth factory had been absolutely abandoned as being worth nothing, it would not have caused her much disappointment. She thought a great deal more of the railway company that was going to buy her property under such favourable circumstances.

She was, therefore, much surprised when her brother began about the business as soon as she had seated herself. I do not know that the reader need be delayed with any of the details that he gave her, or with the contents of the papers which he showed her. She, however, found herself compelled to go into the matter, and compelled also to make an endeavour to understand it. It seemed that everything hung upon Samuel Rubb, junior, except the fact that Samuel Rubb's father, who now never went near the place, got more than half the net profits; and the further fact, that the whole thing would come to an end if this payment to old Rubb were stopped.

'Tom,' said she, in the middle of it all, when her head was aching with figures, 'if it will comfort you, and enable you to put all these things away, you may know that I will divide everything I have with Sarah.'

He assured her that her kindness did comfort him; but he hoped better than that; he still thought that something better might be arranged if she would only go on with her task. So she went on painfully toiling through figures.

'Sam drew them up on purpose for you, yesterday afternoon,' said he.

'Who did it?' she asked.

'Samuel Rubb.'

He then went on to declare that she might accept all Samuel Rubb's figures as correct.

She was quite willing to accept them, and she strove hard to understand them. It certainly did seem to her that when her money was borrowed somebody must have known that the promised security would not be forthcoming; but perhaps that somebody was old Rubb, whom, as she did not know him, she was quite ready to regard as the villain in the play that was being acted. Her own money, too, was a thing of the past. That fault, if fault there had been, was condoned; and she was angry with herself in that she now thought of it again.

'And now,' said her brother, as soon as she had put the papers back, and declared that she understood them. 'Now I have something to say to you which I hope you will hear without being angry.' He raised himself on his bed as he said this, doing so with difficulty and pain, and turning his face upon her so that he could look into her eyes. 'If I didn't know that I was dying I don't think that I could say it to you.'

'Say what, Tom?'

She thought of what most terrible thing it might be possible that he should have to communicate. Could it be that he had got hold, or that Rubb and Mackenzie had got hold, of all her fortune, and turned it into unprofitable oilcloth? Could they in any way have made her responsible for their engagements? She wished to trust them; she tried to avoid suspicion; but she feared that things were amiss.

'Samuel Rubb and I have been talking of it, and he thinks it had better come from me,' said her brother.

'What had better come?' she asked.

'It is his proposition, Margaret.' Then she knew all about it, and felt great relief. Then she knew all about it, and let him go on till he had spoken his speech.

'God knows how far he may be indulging a false hope, or deceiving himself altogether; but he thinks it possible that you might – might become fond of him. There, Margaret, that's the long and the short of it. And when I told him that he had better say that himself, he declared that you would not bring yourself to listen to him while I am lying here dying.'

'Of course I would not.'

'But, look here, Margaret; I know you would do much to comfort me in my last moments.'

'Indeed, I would, Tom.'

'I wouldn't ask you to marry a man you didn't like – not even if it were to do the children a service; but if that can be got over, the other feeling should not restrain you when it would be the greatest possible comfort to me.'

'But how could it serve you, Tom?'

'If that could be arranged, Rubb would give up to Sarah during his father's life all the proceeds of the business, after paying the old man. And when he dies, and he is very old now, the five hundred a-year would be continued to her. Think what that would be, Margaret.'

'But, Tom, she shall have what will make her comfortable without waiting for any old man's death. It shall be quite half of my income. If that is not enough it shall be more. Will not that do for her?'

Then her brother strove to explain as best he could that the mere money was not all he wanted. If his sister did not like this man, if she had no wish to become a married woman, of course, he said, the plan must fall to the ground. But if there was anything in Mr Rubb's belief that she was not altogether indifferent to him, if such an arrangement could be made palatable to her, then he would be able to think that he, by the work of his life, had left something behind him to his wife and family.

'And Sarah would be more comfortable,' he pleaded. 'Of course, she is grateful to you, as I am, and as we all are. But given bread is bitter bread, and if she could think it came to her, of her own right –'

He said ever so much more, but that ever so much more was quite unnecessary. His sister understood the whole matter. It was desirable that she, by her fortune, should enable the widow and orphans of her brother to live in comfort; but it was not desirable that this dependence on her should be plainly recognised. She did not, however, feel herself to be angry or hurt. It would, no doubt, be better for the family that they should draw their income in an apparently independent way from their late father's business than that they should owe their support to the charity of an aunt. But then, how about herself? A month or two ago, before the Maguire feature in her career had displayed itself so strongly, an overture from Mr Rubb might probably not have been received with disfavour. But now, while she was as it were half engaged to another man, she could not entertain such a proposition. Her womanly feeling revolted from it. No doubt she intended to refuse Mr Maguire. No doubt she had made up her mind to that absolutely, during the ceremony of tearing up her verses. And she had never had much love for Mr Maguire, and had felt some – almost some, for Mr Rubb. In either case she was sure that, had she married the man – the one man or the other – she would instantly have become devoted to him. And I, who chronicle her deeds and endeavour to chronicle her thoughts, feel equally sure that it would have been so. There was something harsh in it, that Mr Maguire's offer to her should, though never accepted, debar her from the possibility of marrying Mr Rubb, and thus settling all the affairs of her family in a way that would have been satisfactory to them and not altogether unsatisfactory to her; but she was aware that it did so. She felt that it was so, and then threw herself back for consolation upon the security which would still be hers, and the want of security which must attach itself to a marriage with Mr Rubb. He might make ducks, and drakes, and oilcloth of it all; and then there would be nothing left for her, for her sister-in-law, or for the children.

'May I tell him to speak to yourself?' her brother asked, while she was thinking of all this.

'No, Tom; it would do no good.'

'You do not fancy him, then.'

'I do not know about fancying; but I think it will be better for me to remain as I am. I would do anything for you and Sarah, almost anything; but I cannot do that.'

'Then I will say nothing further.'

'Don't ask me to do that.'

And he did not ask her again, but turned his face from her and thought of the bitterness of his death-bed.

That evening, when she went down to tea, she met Samuel Rubb standing at the drawing-room door.

'There is no one here,' he said; 'will you mind coming in? Has your brother spoken to you?'

She had followed him into the room, and he had closed the door as he asked the question.

'Yes, he has spoken to me.'

She could see that the man was trembling with anxiety and eagerness, and she almost loved him that he was anxious and eager. Mr Maguire, when he had come a wooing, had not done it badly altogether, but there had not been so much reality as there was about Sam Rubb while he stood there shaking, and fearing, and hoping.

'Well,' said he, 'may I hope – may I think it will be so? may I ask you to be mine?'

He was handsome in her eyes, though perhaps, delicate reader, he would not have been handsome in yours. She knew that he was not a gentleman; but what did that matter? Neither was her sister-in-law Sarah a lady. There was not much in that house in Gower Street that was after the manner of gentlemen and ladies. She was ready to throw all that to the dogs, and would have done so but for Mr Maguire. She felt that she would like to have allowed herself to love him in spite of the tearing of the verses. She felt this, and was very angry with Mr Maguire. But the facts were stern, and there was no hope for her.

'Mr Rubb,' she said, 'there can be nothing of that kind.'

'Can't there really, now?' said he.

She assured him in her strongest language, that there could be nothing of that kind, and then went down to the dining-room.

He did not venture to follow her, but made his way out of the house without seeing anyone else.

Another fortnight went by, and then, towards the close of September, came the end of all things in this world for poor Tom Mackenzie. He died in the middle of the night in his wife's arms, while his sister stood by holding both their hands. Since the day on which he had endeavoured to arrange a match between his partner and his sister he had spoken no word of business, at any rate to the latter, and things now stood on that footing which she had then attempted to give them. We all know how silent on such matters are the voices of all in the bereft household, from the hour of death till that other hour in which the body is consigned to its kindred dust. Women make mourning, and men creep about listlessly, but during those few sad days there may be no talk about money. So it was in Gower Street. The widow, no doubt, thought much of her bitter state of dependence, thought something, perhaps, of the chance there might be that her husband's sister would be less good than her word, now that he was gone – meditated with what amount of submission she must accept the generosity of the woman she had always hated; but she was still mistress of that house till the undertakers had done their work; and till that work had been done, she said little of her future plans.

'I'd earn my bread, if I knew how,' she began, putting her handkerchief up to her eyes, on the afternoon of the very day on which he was buried.

'There will be no occasion for that, Sarah,' said Miss Mackenzie, 'there will be enough for us all.'

'But I would if I knew how. I wouldn't mind what I did; I'd scour floors rather than be dependent, I've that spirit in me; and I've worked, and moiled, and toiled with those children; so I have.'

Miss Mackenzie then told her that she had solemnly promised her brother to divide her income with his widow, and informed her that she intended to see Mr Slow, the lawyer, on the following day, with reference to the doing of this.

'If there is anything from the factory, that can be divided too,' said Miss Mackenzie.

'But there won't. The Rubbs will take all that; of course they will. And Tom put into it near upon ten thousand pounds!'

Then she began to cry again, but soon interrupted her tears to ask what was to become of Susanna. Susanna, who was by, looked anxiously up into her aunt's eyes.

'Susanna and I,' said the aunt, 'have thrown in our lot together, and we mean to remain so; don't we, dear?

'If mamma will let me.'

'I'm sure it's very good of you to take one off my hands,' said the mother, 'for even one will be felt.'

Then came a note to Miss Mackenzie from Lady Ball, asking her to spend a few days at the Cedars before she returned to Littlebath – that is, if she did return – and she consented to do this. While she was there Mr Slow could prepare the necessary arrangements for the division of the property, and she could then make up her mind as to the manner and whereabouts of her future life. She was all at sea again, and knew not how to choose. If she were a Romanist, she would go into a convent; but Protestant convents she thought were bad, and peculiarly unfitted for the followers of Mr Stumfold. She had nothing to bind her to any spot, and something to drive her from every spot of which she knew anything.

Before she went to the Cedars Mr Rubb came to Gower Street and bade her farewell.

'I had allowed myself to hope, Miss Mackenzie,' said he, 'I had, indeed; I suppose I was very foolish.'

'I don't know as to being foolish, Mr Rubb, unless it was in caring about such a person as me.'

'I do care for you, very much; but I suppose I was wrong to think you would put up with such as I am. Only I did think that perhaps, seeing that we had been partners with your brother so long – All the same, I know that the Mackenzies are different from the Rubbs.'

'That has nothing to do with it; nothing in the least.'

'Hasn't it now? Then, perhaps, Miss Mackenzie, at some future time –'

Miss Mackenzie was obliged to tell him that there could not possibly be any other answer given to him at any future time than that which she gave him now. He suggested that perhaps he might be allowed to try again when the first month or two of her grief for her brother should be over; but she assured him that it would be useless. At the moment of her conference with him, she did this with all her energy; and then, as soon as she was alone, she asked herself why she had been so energetical. After all, marriage was an excellent state in which to live. The romance was doubtless foolish and wrong, and the tearing of the papers had been discreet, yet there could be no good reason why she should turn her back upon sober wedlock. Nevertheless, in all her speech to Mr Rubb she did do so. There was something in her position as connected with Mr Maguire which made her feel that it would be indelicate to entertain another suitor before that gentleman had received a final answer.

As she went away from Gower Street to the Cedars she thought of this very sadly, and told herself that she had been like the ass who starved between two bundles of hay, or as the boy who had fallen between two stools.

✖ SIXTEEN ✖

Lady Ball's Grievance

MISS MACKENZIE, BEFORE SHE LEFT GOWER STREET, was forced to make some arrangements as to her affairs at Littlebath, and these were ultimately settled in a manner that was not altogether palatable to her. Mr Rubb was again sent down, having Susanna in his charge, and he was empowered to settle with Miss Mackenzie's landlady and give up the lodgings. There was much that was disagreeable in this. Miss Mackenzie having just rejected Mr Rubb's suit, did not feel quite comfortable in giving him a commission to see all her stockings and petticoats packed up and brought away from the lodgings. Indeed, she could give him no commission of the kind, but intimated her intention of writing to the lodging-house keeper. He, however, was profuse in his assurances that nothing should be left behind, and if Miss Mackenzie would tell him anything of the way in which the things ought to be packed, he would be so happy to attend to her! To him Miss Mackenzie would give no such instructions, but, doubtless, she gave many to Susanna.

As to Susanna, it was settled that she should remain as a boarder at the

Littlebath school, at any rate for the next half-year. After that there might be great doubt whether her aunt could bear the expense of maintaining her in such a position.

Miss Mackenzie had reconciled herself to going to the Cedars because she would thus have an opportunity of seeing her lawyer and arranging about her property, whereas had she been down at Littlebath there would have been a difficulty. And she wanted some one whom she could trust to act for her, some one besides the lawyer, and she thought that she could trust her cousin, John Ball. As to getting away from all her suitors that was impossible. Had she gone to Littlebath there was one there; had she remained with her sister-in-law, she would have been always near another; and, on going to the Cedars, she would meet the third. But she could not on that account absolutely isolate herself from everybody that she knew in the world. And, perhaps, she was getting somewhat used to her suitors, and less liable than she had been to any fear that they could force her into action against her own consent. So she went to the Cedars, and, on arriving there, received from her uncle and aunt but a moderate amount of condolence as to the death of her brother.

Her first and second days in her aunt's house were very quiet. Nothing was said of John's former desires, and nothing about her own money or her brother's family. On the morning of the third day she told her cousin that she would, on the next morning, accompany him to town if he would allow her. 'I am going to Mr Slow's,' said she, 'and perhaps you could go with me.' To this he assented willingly, and then, after a pause, surmised that her visit must probably have reference to the sale of her houses to the railway company. 'Partly to that,' she said, 'but it chiefly concerns arrangements for my brother's family.'

To this John Ball said nothing, nor did Lady Ball, who was present, then speak. But Miss Mackenzie could see that her aunt looked at her cousin, opening her eyes, and expressing concern. John Ball himself allowed no change to come upon his face, but went on deliberately with his bread and butter. 'I shall be very happy to go with you,' he said, 'and will either come and call for you when you have done, or stay with you while you are there, just as you like.'

'I particularly want you to stay with me,' said she, 'and as we go up to town I will tell you all about it.'

She observed that before her cousin left the house on that day, his mother got hold of him and was alone with him for nearly half an hour. After that, Lady Ball was alone with Sir John, in his own room, for another half hour. The old baronet had become older, of course, and much weaker, since his niece had last been at the Cedars, and was now seldom seen about the house till the afternoon.

Of all the institutions at the Cedars that of the carriage was the most important. Miss Mackenzie found that the carriage arrangement had been fixed upon a new and more settled basis since her last visit. Then it used to go out perhaps as often as three times a week. But there did not appear to be any fixed rule. Like other carriages, it did, to a certain degree, come when it was wanted. But now there was, as I have said, a settled basis. The carriage came to the door on Tuesdays, Thursdays, and Saturdays, exactly at two o'clock, and Sir John with Lady Ball were driven about till four.

On the first Tuesday of her visit Miss Mackenzie had gone with her uncle and aunt, and even she had found the pace to be very slow, and the whole affair to be very dull. Her uncle had once enlivened the thing by asking her whether she had found any lovers since she went to Littlebath, and this question had perplexed her very much. She could not say that she had found none, and as she was not prepared to acknowledge that she had found any, she could only sit still and blush.

'Women have plenty of lovers when they have plenty of money,' said the baronet.

'I don't believe that Margaret thinks of anything of the kind,' said Lady Ball.

After that Margaret determined to have as little to do with the carriage as possible, and on that evening she learned from her cousin that the horses had been sold to the man who farmed the land, and were hired every other day for two hours' work.

It was on the Thursday morning that Miss Mackenzie had spoken of going into town on the morrow, and on that day when her aunt asked her about the driving, she declined.

'I hope that nothing your uncle said on Tuesday annoyed you?'

'Oh dear, no; but if you don't mind it, I'd rather stay at home.'

'Of course you shall if you like it,' said her aunt; 'and by-the-by, as I want to speak to you, and as we might not find time after coming home, if you don't mind it I'll do it now.'

Of course Margaret said that she did not mind it, though in truth she did mind it, and was afraid of her aunt.

'Well then, Margaret, look here. I want to know something about your brother's affairs. From what I have heard, I fear they were not very good.'

'They were very bad, aunt – very bad indeed.'

'Dear, dear; you don't say so. Sir John always feared that it would be so when Thomas Mackenzie mixed himself up with those Rubbs. And there has gone half of Jonathan Ball's money – money which Sir John made! Well, well!'

Miss Mackenzie had nothing to say to this; and as she had nothing to say to it she sat silent, making no attempt at any words.

'It does seem hard; don't it, my dear?'

'It wouldn't make any difference to anybody now – to my uncle, I mean, or to John, if the money was not gone.'

'That's quite true; quite true; only it does seem to be a pity. However, that half of Jonathan's money which you have got, is not lost, and there's some comfort in that.'

Miss Mackenzie was not called upon to make any answer to this; for although she had lost a large sum of money by lending it to her brother, nevertheless she was still possessed of a larger sum of money than that which her brother Walter had received from Jonathan Ball.

'And what are they going to do, my dear – the children, I mean, and the widow? I suppose there'll be something for them out of the business?'

'I don't think there'll be anything, aunt. As far as I can understand there will be nothing certain. They may probably get a hundred and twenty-five pounds a-year.' This she named, as being the interest of the money she had lent – or given.

'A hundred and twenty-five pounds a-year. That isn't much, but it will keep them from absolute want.'

'Would it, aunt?'

'Oh, yes; at least, I suppose so. I hope she's a good manager. She ought to be, for she's a very disagreeable woman. You told me that yourself, you know.'

Then Miss Mackenzie, having considered for one moment, resolved to make a clean breast of it all, and this she did with the fewest possible words.

'I'm going to divide what I've got with them, and I hope it will make them comfortable.'

'What!' exclaimed her aunt.

'I'm going to give Sarah half what I've got, for her and her children. I shall have enough to live on left.'

'Margaret, you don't mean it?'

'Not mean it? why not, aunt? You would not have me let them starve. Besides, I promised my brother when he was dying.'

'Then I must say he was very wrong, very wicked, I may say, to exact any such promise from you; and no such promise is binding. If you ask Sir John, or your lawyer, they will tell you so. What! exact a promise from you to the amount of half your income. It was very wrong.'

'But, aunt, I should do the same if I had made no promise.'

'No, you wouldn't, my dear. Your friends wouldn't let you. And indeed your friends must prevent it now. They will not hear of such a sacrifice being made.'

'But, aunt –'

'Well, my dear.'

'It's my own, you know.' And Margaret, as she said this, plucked up her courage, and looked her aunt full in the face.

'Yes, it is your own, by law; but I don't suppose, my dear, that you are of that disposition or that character that you'd wish to set all the world at defiance, and make everybody belonging to you feel that you had disgraced yourself.'

'Disgraced myself by relieving my brother's family!'

'Disgraced yourself by giving to that woman money that has come to you as your fortune has come. Think of it, where it came from!'

'It came to me from my brother Walter.'

'And where did he get it? And who made it? And don't you know that your brother Tom had his share of it, and wasted it all? Did it not all come from the Balls? And yet you think so little of that, that you are going to let that woman rob you of it – rob you and my grandchildren; for that, I tell you, is the way in which the world will look at it. Perhaps you don't know it, but all that property was as good as given to John at one time. Who was it first took you by the hand when you were left all alone in Arundel Street? Oh, Margaret, don't go and be such an ungrateful, foolish creature!'

Margaret waited for a moment, and then she answered –

'There's nobody so near to me as my own brother's children.'

'As to that, Margaret, there isn't much difference in nearness between your uncle and your nephews and nieces. But there's a right and a wrong in these things, and when money is concerned, people are not justified in indulging their fancies. Everything here has been told to you. You know how John is situated with his children. And after what there has been between you and him, and after what there still might be if you would have it so, I own that I am astonished – fairly astonished. Indeed, my dear, I can only look on it as simple weakness on your part. It was but the other day that you told me you had done all that you thought necessary by your brother in taking Susanna.'

'But that was when he was alive, and I thought he was doing well.'

'The fact is, you have been there and they've talked you over. It can't be that you love children that you never saw till the other day; and as for the woman, you always hated her.'

'Whether I love her or hate her has nothing to do with it.'

'Margaret, will you promise me this, that you will see Mr Slow and talk to him about it before you do anything?'

'I must see Mr Slow before I can do anything; but whatever he says, I shall do it all the same.'

'Will you speak to your uncle?'

'I had rather not.'

'You are afraid to tell him of this; but of course he must be told. Will you speak to John?'

'Certainly; I meant to do so going to town tomorrow.'

'And if he tells you you are wrong –'

'Aunt, I know I am not wrong. It is nonsense to say that I am wrong in –'

'That's disrespectful, Margaret!'

'I don't want to be disrespectful, aunt; but in such a case as this I know that I have a right to do what I like with my own money. If I was going to give it away to any other friend, if I was going to marry, or anything like that,' – she blushed at the remembrance of the iniquities she had half intended as she said this – 'then there might be some reason for you to scold me; but with a brother and a brother's family it can't be wrong. If you had a brother, and had been with him when he was dying, and he had left his wife and children looking to you, you would have done the same.'

Upon this Lady Ball got up from her chair and walked to the door. Margaret had been more impetuous and had answered her with much more confidence than she had expected. She was determined now to say one more word, but so to say it that it should not be answered – to strike one more blow, but so to strike it that it should not be returned.

'Margaret,' she said, as she stood with the door open in her hands, 'if you will reflect where the money came from, your conscience will tell you without much difficulty where it should go to. And when you think of your brother's children, whom this time last year you had hardly seen, think also of John Ball's children, who have welcomed you into this house as their dearest relative. In one sense, certainly, the money is yours, Margaret; but in another sense, and that the highest sense, it is not yours to do what you please with it.'

Then Lady Ball shut the door rather loudly, and sailed away along the hall. When the passages were clear, Miss Mackenzie made her way up into her own room, and saw none of the family till she came down just before dinner.

She sat for a long time in the chair by her bed-side thinking of her position. Was it true after all that she was bound by a sense of justice to give any of her money to the Balls? It was true that in one sense it had been taken from them, but she had had nothing to do with the taking. If her brother Walter had married and had children, then the Balls would have not expected the money back again. It was ever so many years – five-and-twenty years, and more since the legacy had been made by Jonathan Ball to her brother, and it seemed to her that her aunt had no common sense on her side in the argument. Was it possible that she should allow her own nephews and nieces to starve while she was rich? She had, moreover, made a promise – a promise to one who was now dead, and there was a solemnity in that which carried everything else before it. Even though the thing might be unjust, still she must do it.

But she was to give only half her fortune to her brother's family; there would still be the half left for herself, for herself or for these Balls if they wanted it so sorely. She was beginning to hate her money. It had brought to her nothing but tribulation and disappointment. Had Walter left her a hundred a year, she would, not having then dreamed of higher things, have been amply content. Would it not be better that she should take for herself some modest competence, something on which she might live without trouble to her relatives, without trouble to her friends she had first said – but as she did so she told herself with scorn that friends she had none – and then let the Balls have what was left her after she had kept her promise to her brother? Anything would be better than such persecution as that to which her aunt had subjected her.

At last she made up her mind to speak of it all openly to her cousin. She had an idea that in such matters men were more trustworthy than women, and perhaps less greedy. Her cousin would, she thought, be more just to her than her aunt had been. That her aunt had been very unjust – cruel and unjust – she felt assured.

She came down to dinner, and she could see by the manner of them all that the matter had been discussed since John Ball's return from London. Jack, the eldest son, was not at home, and the three girls who came next to Jack dined with their father and grandfather. To them Margaret endeavoured to talk easily, but she failed. They had never been favourites with her as Jack was, and, on this occasion, she could get very little from them that was satisfactory to her. John Ball was courteous to her, but he was very silent throughout the whole evening. Her aunt showed her displeasure by not speaking to her, or speaking barely with a word. Her uncle, of whose voice she was always in fear, seemed to be more cross, and when he did speak, more sarcastic than ever. He asked her whether she intended to go back to Littlebath.

'I think not,' said she.

'Then that has been a failure, I suppose,' said the old man.

'Everything is a failure, I think,' said she, with tears in her eyes.

This was in the drawing-room, and immediately her cousin John came and sat by her. He came and sat there, as though he had intended to speak to her; but he went away again in a minute or two without having uttered a word. Things went on in the same way till they moved off to bed, and then the formal adieus for the night were made with a coldness that amounted, on the part of Lady Ball, almost to inhospitality.

'Good-night, Margaret,' she said, as she just put out the tip of her finger.

'Good-night, my dear,' said Sir John. 'I don't know what's the matter with you, but you look as though you'd been doing something that you were ashamed of.'

Lady Ball was altogether injudicious in her treatment of her niece. As to Sir John, it made probably very little difference. Miss Mackenzie had perceived, when she first came to the Cedars, that he was a cross old man, and that he had to be endured as such by any one who chose to go into that house. But she had depended on Lady Ball for kindness of manner, and had been tempted to repeat her visits to the house because her aunt had, after her fashion, been gracious to her. But now there was rising in her breast a feeling that she had better leave the Cedars as soon as she could shake the dust off her feet, and see nothing more of the Balls. Even the Rubb connection seemed to her to be better than the Ball connection, and less exaggerated in its greediness. Were it not for her cousin John, she would have resolved to go on the morrow. She would have faced the indignation of her aunt, and the cutting taunts of her uncle, and have taken herself off at once to some lodging in London. But John Ball had meant to be kind to her when he came and sat close to her on the sofa, and her soft heart relented towards him.

Lady Ball had in truth mistaken her niece's character. She had found her to be unobtrusive, gentle, and unselfish; and had conceived that she must therefore be weak and compliant. As to many things she was compliant, and as to some things she was weak; but there was in her composition a power of resistance and self-sustenance on which Lady Ball had not counted. When conscious of absolute ill-usage, she could fight well, and would not bow her neck to any Mrs Stumfold or to any Lady Ball.

❋ SEVENTEEN ❋

Mr Slow's Chambers

SHE CAME DOWN LATE TO BREAKFAST ON the following morning, not being present at prayers, and when she came down she wore a bonnet.

'I got myself ready, John, for fear I should keep you waiting.'

Her aunt spoke to her somewhat more graciously than on the preceding evening, and accepted her apology for being late.

Just as she was about to start Lady Ball took her apart and spoke one word to her.

'No one can tell you better what you ought to do than your cousin John; but pray remember that he is far too generous to say a word for himself.'

Margaret made no answer, and then she and her cousin started on foot across the grounds to the station. The distance was nearly a mile, and during the walk no word was said between them about the money. They got into the train that was to take them up to London, and sat opposite to each other. It happened that there was no passenger in either of the seats next to him or her, so that there was ample opportunity for them to hold a private conversation; but Mr Ball said nothing to her, and she, not knowing how to begin, said nothing to him. In this way they reached the London station at Waterloo Bridge, and then he asked her what she proposed to do next.

'Shall we go to Mr Slow's at once?' she asked.

To this he assented, and at her proposition they agreed to walk to the lawyer's chambers. These were on the north side of Lincoln's Inn Fields, near the Turnstile, and Mr Ball remarked that the distance was again not much above a mile. So they crossed the Strand together, and made their way by narrow streets into Drury Lane, and then under a certain archway into Lincoln's Inn Fields. To Miss Mackenzie, who felt that something ought to be said, the distance and time occupied seemed to be very short.

'Why, this is Lincoln's Inn Fields!' she exclaimed, as she came out upon the west side.

'Yes; this is Lincoln's Inn Fields, and Mr Slow's chambers are over there.'

She knew very well where Mr Slow's chambers were situated, but she paused on the pavement, not wishing to go thither quite at once.

'John,' she said, 'I thought that perhaps we might have talked over all this before we saw Mr Slow.'

'Talked over all what?'

'About the money that I want to give to my brother's family. Did not my aunt tell you of it?.'

'Yes; she told me that you and she had differed.'

'And she told you what about?'

'Yes,' said he, slowly; 'she told me what about.'

'And what ought I to do, John?'

As she asked the question she caught hold of the lappet of his coat, and looked up into his face as though supplicating him to give her the advantage of all his discretion and all his honesty.

They were still standing on the pavement, where the street comes out from under the archway. She was gazing into his face, and he was looking away from her, over towards the inner railings of the square, with heavy brow and dull eye and motionless face. She was very eager, and he seemed to be simply patient, but nevertheless he was working hard with his thoughts, striving to determine how best he might answer her. His mother had told him that he might model this woman to his will, and had repeated to him that story which he had heard so often of the wrong that had been done to him by his uncle Jonathan. It may be said that there was no need for such repetition, as John Ball had himself always thought quite enough of that injury. He had thought of it for the last twenty years, almost hourly, till it was graven upon his very soul. He had been a ruined, wretched, moody man, because of his uncle Jonathan's will. There was no need, one would have said, to have stirred him on that subject. But his mother, on this morning, in the ten minutes before prayer-time, had told him of it all again, and had told him also that the last vestige of his uncle's money would now disappear from him unless he interfered to save it.

'On this very day it must be saved; and she will do anything you tell her,' said his mother. 'She regards you more than anyone else. If you were to ask her again now, I believe she would accept you this very day. At any rate, do not let those people have the money.'

And yet he had not spoken to Margaret on the subject during the journey, and would now have taken her to the lawyer's chambers without a word, had she not interrupted him and stopped him.

Nevertheless he had been thinking of his uncle, and his uncle's will, and his uncle's money, throughout the morning. He was thinking of it at that moment when she stopped him – thinking how hard it all was, how cruel that those people in the New Road should have had and spent half his uncle's fortune, and that now the remainder, which at one time had seemed to be near the reach of his own children, should also go to atone for the negligence and fraud of those wretched Rubbs.

We all know with how strong a bias we regard our own side of any question, and he regarded his side in this question with a very strong bias. Nevertheless he had refrained from a word, and would have refrained, had she not stopped him.

When she took hold of him by the coat, he looked for a moment into her face, and thought that in its trouble it was very sweet. She leaned somewhat against him as she spoke, and he wished that she would lean against him altogether. There was about her a quiet power of endurance, and at the same time a comeliness and a womanly softness which seemed to fit her altogether for his wants and wishes. As he looked with his dull face across into the square, no physiognomist would have declared of him that at that moment he was suffering from love, or thinking of a woman that was dear to him. But it was so with him, and the physiognomist, had one been there, would have been wrong. She had now asked him a question, which he was bound to answer in some way – 'What ought I to do, John?'

He turned slowly round and walked with her, away from their destination, round by the south side of the square, and then up along the blank wall on the east side, nearly to the passage into Holborn, and back again all round the enclosed space. She, while she was speaking to him and listening to him, hardly remembered where she was or whither she was going.

'I thought,' said he, in answer to her question, 'that you intended to ask Mr Slow's advice?'

'I didn't mean to do more than tell him what should be done. He is not a friend, you know, John.'

'It's customary to ask lawyers their advice on such subjects.'

'I'd rather have yours, John. But, in truth, what I want you to say is, that I am right in doing this – right in keeping my promise to my brother, and providing for his children.'

'Like most people, Margaret, you want to be advised to follow your own counsel.'

'God knows that I want to do right, John. I want to do nothing else, John, but what's right. As to this money, I care but little for it for myself.'

'It is your own, and you have a right to enjoy it.'

'I don't know much about enjoyment. As to enjoyment, it seems to me to be pretty much the same whether a person is rich or poor. I always used to hear that money brought care, and I'm sure I've found it so since I had any.'

'You've got no children, Margaret.'

'No; but there are all those orphans. Am I not bound to look upon them as mine, now that he has gone? If they don't depend on me, whom are they to depend on?'

'If your mind is made up, Margaret, I have nothing to say against it. You know what my wishes are. They are just the same now as when you were last with us. It isn't only for the money I say this, though, of course, that must go a long way with a man circumstanced as I am; but, Margaret, I love you dearly. and if you can make up your mind to be my wife, I would do my best to make you happy.'

'I hadn't meant you to talk in that way, John,' said Margaret.

But she was not much flurried. She was now so used to these overtures that they did not come to her as much out of the common way. And she gave herself none of that personal credit which women are apt to take to themselves when they find they are often sought in marriage. She looked upon her lovers as so many men to whom her income would be convenient, and felt herself to be almost under an obligation to them for their willingness to put up with the incumbrance which was attached to it.

'But it's the only way I can talk when you ask me about this,' said he. Then he paused for a moment before he added, 'How much is it you wish to give to your brother's widow?'

'Half what I've got left.'

'Got left! You haven't lost any of your money have you, Margaret?'

Then she explained to him the facts as to the loan, and took care to explain to him also, very fully, the compensatory fact of the purchase by the railway company. 'And my promise to him was made after I had lent it, you know,' she urged.

'I do think it ought to be deducted; I do indeed,' he said. 'I am not speaking on my own behalf now, as for the sake of my children, but simply as a man of business. As for myself, though I do think I have been hardly used in the matter of my uncle's money, I'll try to forget it. I'll try at any rate to do without it. When I first knew you, and found – found that I liked you so much, I own that I did have hopes. But if it must be, there shall be an end of that. The children don't starve, I suppose.'

'Oh, John!'

'As for me, I won't hanker after your money. But. for your own sake, Margaret –'

'There will be more than enough for me, you know; and, John –'

She was going to make him some promise; to tell him something of her intention towards his son, and to make some tender of assistance to himself; being now in that mind to live on the smallest possible pittance, of which I have before spoken, when he ceased speaking or listening, and hurried her on to the attorney's chambers.

'Do what you like with it. It is your own,' said he. 'And we shall do no good by talking about it any longer out here.'

So at last they made their way up to Mr Slow's rooms, on the first floor in the old house in Lincoln's Inn Fields, and were informed that that gentleman was at home. Would they be pleased to sit down in the waiting-room?

There is, I think, no sadder place in the world than the waiting-room attached to an attorney's chambers in London. In this instance it was a three-cornered room, which had got itself wedged in between the house which fronted to Lincoln's Inn Fields, and some buildings in a narrow lane that ran at the back of the row. There was no carpet in it, and hardly any need of one, as the greater part of the floor was strewed with bundles of dusty papers. There was a window in it, which looked out from the point of the further angle against the wall of the opposite building. The dreariness of this aspect had been thought to be too much for the minds of those who waited, and therefore the bottom panes had been clouded, so that there was in fact no power of looking out at all. Over the fireplace there was a table of descents and relationship, showing how heirship went; and the table was very complicated, describing not only the heirship of ordinary real and personal property, but also explaining the wonderful difficulties of gavelkind, and other mysteriously traditional laws. But the table was as dirty as it was complicated, and the ordinary waiting reader could make nothing of it. There was a small table in the room, near the window, which was always covered with loose papers; but these loose papers were on this occasion again covered with sheets of parchment, and a pale-faced man, of about thirty, whose beard had never yet attained power to do more than sprout, was sitting at the table, and poring over the parchments. Round the room, on shelves, there was a variety of iron boxes, on which were written the names of Mr Slow's clients – of those clients whose property justified them in having special boxes of their own. But these boxes were there, it must be supposed, for temporary purposes – purposes which might be described as almost permanently temporary – for those boxes which were allowed to exist in absolute permanence of retirement, were kept in an iron room downstairs, the trap-door into which had yawned upon Miss Mackenzie as she was shown into the waiting-room. There was, however, one such box open, on the middle of the floor, and sundry of the parchments which had been taken from it were lying around it.

There were but two chairs in the room besides the one occupied by the man at the table, and these were taken by John Ball and his cousin. She sat herself down, armed with patience, indifferent to the delay and indifferent to the dusty ugliness of everything around her, as women are on such occasions. He, thinking much of his time, and somewhat annoyed at being called upon to wait, sat with his chin resting on his umbrella between his legs, and as he did so he allowed his eyes to roam around among the names upon the boxes. There was nothing on any one of those up on the shelves that attracted him. There was the Marquis of B——, and Sir C. D.——, and the Dowager Countess of E.—— Seeing this, he speculated mildly whether Mr Slow put forward the boxes of his aristocratic customers to show how well he was doing in the world. But presently his eye fell from the shelf and settled upon the box on the floor. There, on that box, he saw the name of Walter Mackenzie.

This did not astonish him, as he immediately said to himself that these papers were being searched with reference to the business on which his cousin was there that day; bur suddenly it occurred to him that Margaret had given him to understand that Mr Slow did not expect her. He stepped over to her, therefore, one step over the papers, and asked her the question, whispering it into her ear.

'No,' said she, 'I had no appointment. I don't think he expects me.'

He returned to his seat, and again sitting down with his chin on the top of his umbrella, surveyed the parchments that lay upon the ground. Upon one of them, that was not far from his feet, he read the outer endorsements written as such endorsements always are, in almost illegible old English letters–

'Jonathan Ball, to John Ball, junior – Deed of Gift.'

But, after all, there was nothing more than a coincidence in this. Of course Mr Slow would have in his possession all the papers appertaining to the transfer of Jonathan Ball's property to the Mackenzies; or, at any rate, such as referred to Walter's share of it. Indeed, Mr Slow, at the time of Jonathan Ball's death, acted for the two brothers, and it was probable that all the papers would be with him. John Ball had known that there had been some intention on his uncle's part, before the quarrel between his father and his uncle, to make over to him, on his coming of age, a certain property in London, and he had been told that the money which the Mackenzies had inherited had ultimately come from this very property. His uncle had been an eccentric, quarrelsome man, prone to change his mind often, and not regardful of money as far as he himself was concerned. John Ball remembered to have heard that his uncle had intended him to become possessed of certain property in his own right the day that he became of age, and that this had all been changed because of the quarrel which had taken place between his uncle and his father. His father now never spoke of this, and for many years past had seldom mentioned it. But from his mother he had often heard of the special injury which he had undergone.

'His uncle,' she had said, 'had given it, and had taken it back again – had taken it back that he might waste it on those Mackenzies.'

All this he had heard very often, but he had never known anything of a deed of gift. Was it not singular, he thought, that the draft of such a deed should be lying at his foot at this moment.

He showed nothing of this in his face, and still sat there with his chin resting on his umbrella. But certainly stronger ideas than usual of the great wrongs which he had suffered did come into his head as he looked upon the paper at his feet. He began to wonder whether he would be justified in taking it up and inspecting it. But as he was thinking of this the pale-faced man rose from his chair, and after moving among the papers on the ground for an instant, selected this very document, and carried it with him to his table. Mr Ball, as his eyes followed the parchment, watched the young man dust it and open it, and then having flattened it with his hand, glance over it till he came to a certain spot. The pale-faced clerk, accustomed to such documents, glanced over the ambages, the 'whereases,' the 'aforesaids,' the rich exuberance of 'admors.,' 'exors.,' and 'assigns,' till he deftly came to the pith of the matter, and then he began to make extracts, a date here and a date there. John Ball watched him all the time, till the door was opened, and old Mr Slow himself appeared in the room.

He stepped across the papers to shake hands with his client, and then shook hands also with Mr Ball, whom he knew. His eye glanced at once down to the box, and after that over towards the pale-faced clerk. Mr Ball perceived that the attorney had joined in his own mind the operation that was going on with these special documents, and the presence of these two special visitors; and that he, in some measure, regretted the coincidence. There was something wrong, and John Ball began to consider whether the old lawyer could be an old scoundrel. Some lawyers, he knew, were desperate scoundrels. He said nothing, however; but, obeying Mr Slow's invitation, followed him and his cousin into the sanctum sanctorum of the chambers.

'They didn't tell me you were here at first,' said the lawyer, in a tone of vexation, 'or I wouldn't have had you shown in there.'

John Ball thought that this was, doubtless, true, and that very probably they might not have been put in among those papers had Mr Slow known what was being done.

'The truth is,' continued the lawyer, 'the Duke of F——'s man of business was with me, and they did not like to interrupt me.'

Mr Slow was a grey-haired old man, nearer eighty than seventy, who, with the exception of a fortnight's holiday every year which he always spent at Margate, had attended those same chambers in Lincoln's Inn Fields daily for the last sixty years. He was a stout, thickset man, very leisurely in all his motions, who walked slowly, talked slowly, read slowly, wrote slowly, and thought slowly; but who, nevertheless, had the reputation of doing a great deal of business, and doing it very well. He had a partner in the business, almost as old as himself, named Bideawhile; and they who knew them both used to speculate which of the two was the most leisurely. It was, however, generally felt that, though Mr Slow was the slowest in his speech, Mr Bideawhile was the longest in getting anything said. Mr Slow would often beguile his time with unnecessary remarks; but Mr Bideawhile was so constant in beguiling his time, that men wondered how, in truth, he ever did anything at all. Of both of them it may be said that no men stood higher in their profession, and that Mr Ball's suspicions, had they been known in the neighbourhood of Lincoln's Inn, would have been scouted as utterly baseless. And, for the comfort of my readers, let me assure them that they were utterly baseless. There might, perhaps, have been a little vanity about Mr Slow as to the names of his aristocratic clients; but he was an honest, painstaking man, who had ever done his duty well by those who had employed him.

Is it not remarkable that the common repute which we all give to attorneys in the general is exactly opposite to that which every man gives to his own attorney in particular? Whom does anybody trust so implicitly as he trusts his own attorney? And yet is it not the case that the body of attorneys is supposed to be the most roguish body in existence?

The old man seemed now to be a little fretful, and said something more about his sorrow at their having been sent into that room.

'We are so crowded,' he said, 'that we hardly know how to stir ourselves.'

Miss Mackenzie said it did not signify in the least. Mr Ball said nothing, but seated himself with his chin again resting on his umbrella.

'I was so sorry to see in the papers an account of your brother's death,' said Mr Slow.

'Yes, Mr Slow; he has gone, and left a wife and very large family.'

'I hope they are provided for, Miss Mackenzie.'

'No, indeed; they are not provided for at all. My brother had not been fortunate in business.'

'And yet he went into it with a large capital – with a large capital in such a business as that.'

John Ball, with his chin on the umbrella, said nothing. He said nothing, but he winced as he thought whence the capital had come. And he thought, too, of those much-meaning words: 'Jonathan Ball to John Ball, junior – Deed of gift.'

'He had been unfortunate,' said Miss Mackenzie, in an apologetic tone.

'And what will you do about your loan?' said Mr Slow, looking over to John Ball when he asked the question, as though inquiring whether all Miss Mackenzie's affairs were to be talked over openly in the presence of that gentleman.

'That was a gift,' said Miss Mackenzie.

'A deed of gift,' thought John Ball to himself. 'A deed of gift!'

'Oh, indeed! Then there's an end of that, I suppose,' said Mr Slow.

'Exactly so. I have been explaining to my cousin all about it. I hope the firm will be able to pay my sister-in-law the interest on it, but that does not seem sure.'

'I am afraid I cannot help you there, Miss Mackenzie.'

'Of course not. I was not thinking of it. But what I've come about is this.' Then she told Mr Slow the whole of her project with reference to her fortune; how, on his death-bed, she had promised to give half of all that she had to her brother's wife and family, and how she had come there to him, with her cousin, in order that he might put her in the way of keeping her promise.

Mr Slow sat in silence and patiently heard her to the end. She, finding herself thus encouraged to speak, expatiated on the solemnity of her promise, and declared that she could not be comfortable till she had done all that she had undertaken to perform. 'And I shall have quite enough for myself afterwards, Mr Slow, quite enough.'

Mr Slow did not say a word till she had done, and even then he seemed to delay his speech. John Ball never raised his face from his umbrella, but sat looking at the lawyer, whom he still suspected of roguery. And if the lawyer were a rogue, what then about his cousin? It must not be supposed that he suspected her; but what would come of her, if the fortune she held were, in truth, not her own?

'I have told my cousin all about it,' continued Margaret, 'and I believe that he thinks I am doing right. At any rate, I would do nothing without his knowing it.'

'I think she is giving her sister-in-law too much,' said John Ball.

'I am only doing what I promised,' urged Margaret.

'I think that the money which she lent to the firm should, at any rate, be deducted,' said John Ball, speaking this with a kind of proviso to himself, that the words so spoken were intended to be taken as having any meaning only on the presumption that that document which he had seen in the other room should turn out to be wholly inoperative and inefficient at the present moment. In answer to these side-questions or corollary points as to the deduction or non-deduction of the loan, Mr Slow answered not a word; but when there was silence between them, he did make answer as to the original proposition.

'Miss Mackenzie,' he said, 'I think you had better postpone doing anything in this matter for the present.'

'Why postpone it?' said she.

'Your brother's death is very recent. It happened not above a fortnight since, I think.'

'And I want to have this settled at once, so that there shall be no distress. What's the good of waiting?'

'Such things want thinking of, Miss Mackenzie.'

'But I have thought of it. All I want now is to have it done.'

A slight smile came across the puckered grey face of the lawyer as he felt the imperative nature of the instruction given to him. The lady had come there not to be advised, but to have her work done for her out of hand. But the smile was very melancholy, and soon passed away.

'Is the widow in immediate distress?' asked Mr Slow.

Now the fact was that Miss Mackenzie herself had been in good funds, having had ready money in her hands from the time of her brother Walter's death; and for the last year she had by no means spent her full income. She had, therefore, given her sister-in-law money, and had paid the small debts which had come in, as such small debts will come in, directly the dead man's body was under ground. Nay, some had come in and had been paid while the man was yet dying. She exclaimed, therefore, that her sister-in-law was not absolutely in immediate want.

'And does she keep the house?' asked the lawyer.

Then Miss Mackenzie explained that Mrs Tom intended, if possible, to keep the house, and to take some lady in to lodge with her.

'Then there cannot be any immediate hurry,' urged the lawyer; 'and as the sum of money in question is large, I really think the matter should be considered.'

But Miss Mackenzie still pressed it. She was very anxious to make him understand – and of course he did understand at once – that she had no wish to hurry him in his work. All that she required of him was an assurance that he accepted her instructions, and that the thing should be done with not more than the ordinary amount of legal delay.

'You can pay her what you like out of your own income,' said the lawyer.

'But that is not what I promised,' said Margaret Mackenzie.

Then there was silence among them all. Mr Ball had said very little since he had been sitting in that room, and now it was not he who broke the silence. He was still thinking of that deed of gift, and wondering whether it had anything to do with Mr Slow's unwillingness to undertake the commission which Margaret wished to give him. At last Mr Slow got up from his chair, and spoke as follows:

'Mr Ball, I hope you will excuse me; but I have a word or two to say to Miss Mackenzie, which I had rather say to her alone.'

'Certainly,' said Mr Ball, rising and preparing to go.

'You will wait for me, John,' said Miss Mackenzie, asking this favour of him as though she were very anxious that he should grant it.

Mr Slow said that he might be closeted with Miss Mackenzie for some little time, perhaps for a quarter of an hour or twenty minutes. John Ball looked at his watch, and then at his cousin's face, and then promised that he would wait. Mr Slow himself took him into the outer office, and then handed him a chair; but he observed that he was not allowed to go back into the waiting-room.

There he waited for three-quarters of an hour, constantly looking at his watch, and thinking more and more about that deed of gift. Surely it must be the case that the document which he had seen had some reference to this great delay. At last he heard a door open, and a step along a passage, and then another door was opened, and Mr Slow reappeared with Margaret Mackenzie behind him. John Ball's eyes immediately fell on his cousin's face, and he could see that it was very pale. The lawyer's wore that smile which men put on when they wish to cover the disagreeable seriousness of the moment.

'Good morning, Miss Mackenzie,' said he, pressing his client's hand.

'Good morning, sir,' said she.

The lawyer and Mr Ball then touched each other's hands, and the former followed his cousin down the steps out into the square.

✂ EIGHTEEN ✂

Tribulation

WHEN THEY WERE ONCE MORE OUT IN the square, side by side, Miss Mackenzie took hold of her cousin's arm and walked on for a few steps in silence, in the direction of Great Queen Street – that is to say, away from the city, towards which she knew her cousin would go in pursuit of his own business. And indeed the hour was now close at hand in which he should be sitting as a director at the Shadrach Fire Assurance Office. If not at the Shadrach by two, or, with all possible allowance for the short-coming of a generally punctual director, by a quarter past two, he would be too late for his guinea; and now, as he looked at his watch, it wanted only ten minutes to two. He was very particular about these guineas, and the chambers of the Shadrach were away in Old Broad Street. Neverthe-less he walked on with her.

'John,' she said, when they had walked half the length of that side of the square, 'I have heard dreadful news.'

Then that deed of gift was, after all, a fact; and Mr Slow, instead of being a rogue, must be the honestest old lawyer in London! He must have been at work in discovering the wrong that had been done, and was now about to reveal it to the world. Some such idea as this had glimmered across Mr Ball's mind as he had sat in Mr Slow's outer office, with his chin still resting on his umbrella.

But though some such idea as this did cross his mind, his thought on the instant was of his cousin.

'What dreadful news, Margaret?'

'It is about my money.'

'Stop a moment, Margaret. Are you sure that you ought to tell it to me?'

'If I don't, to whom shall I tell it? And how can I bear it without telling it to some one?'

'Did Mr Slow bid you speak of it to me?'

'No; he bade me think much of it before I did so, as you are concerned. And he said that you might perhaps be disappointed.'

Then they walked on again in silence. John Ball found his position to be very difficult, and hardly knew how to speak to her, or how to carry himself. If it was to be that this money was to come back to him; if it was his now in spite of all that had come and gone; if the wrong done was to be righted, and the property wrested from him was to be restored – restored to him who wanted it so sorely – how could he not triumph in such an act of tardy restitution? He remembered all the particulars at this moment. Twelve thousand pounds of his uncle Jonathan's money had gone to Walter Mackenzie. The sum once intended for him had been much more than that – more he believed than double that; but if twelve thousand pounds was now restored to him, how different would it make the whole tenor of his life; Mr Slow said that he might be disappointed; but then Mr Slow was not his lawyer. Did he not owe it to his family immediately to go to his own attorney? Now he thought no more of his guinea at the Shadrach, but walked on by his cousin's side with his mind intently fixed on his uncle's money. She was still leaning on his arm.

'Tell me, John, what shall I do?' said she, looking up into his face.

Would it not be better for them, better for the interests of them both, that they should be separated? Was it probable, or possible, that with interests so adverse, they should give each other good advice? Did it not behove him to explain to her that till this should be settled between them, they must necessarily regard each other as enemies? For a moment or two he wished himself away from her, and was calculating how he might escape. But then, when he looked down at her, and saw the softness of her eye, and felt the confidence implied in the weight of her hand upon his arm, his hard heart was softened, and he relented.

'It is difficult to tell you what you should do,' he said. 'At present nothing seems to be known. He has said nothing for certain.'

'But I could understand him,' she said, in reply; 'I could see by his face, and I knew by the tone of his voice, that he was almost certain. I know that he is sure of it. John, I shall be a beggar, an absolute beggar! I shall have nothing; and those poor children will be beggars, and their mother. I feel as though I did not know where I am, or what I am doing.'

Then an idea came into his head. If this money was not hers, it was his. If it was not his, then it was hers. Would it not be well that they should solve all the difficulty by agreeing then and there to be man and wife? It was true that since his Rachel's death he had seen no woman whom he so much coveted to have in his home as this one who now leaned on his arm. But, as he thought of it, there seemed to be a romance about such a step which would not befit him. What would his mother and father say to him if, after all his troubles, he was at last to marry a woman without a farthing? And then, too, would she consent to give up all further consideration for her brother's family? Would she agree to abandon her idea of assisting them, if ultimately it should turn out that the property was hers? No; there was certainly a looseness about such a plan which did not befit him; and, moreover, were he to attempt it, he would probably not succeed.

But something must be done, now at this moment. The guinea at the Shadrach was gone for ever, and therefore he could devote himself for the day to his cousin.

'Are you to hear again from Mr Slow?' he said.

'I am to go to him this day week.'

'And then it will be decided?'

'John, it is decided now; I am sure of it. I feel that it is all gone. A careful man like that would never have spoken as he did, unless he was sure. It will be all yours, John.'

'So would have been that which your brother had,' said he.

'I suppose so. It is dreadful to think of; very dreadful. I can only promise that I will spend nothing till it is decided. John, I wish you would take from me what I have, lest it should go.' And she absolutely had her hand upon her purse in her pocket.

'No,' said he slowly, 'no; you need think of nothing of that sort.'

'But what am I to do? Where am I to go while this week passes by?'

'You will stay where you are, of course.'

'Oh John! if you could understand! How am I to look my aunt in the face. Don't you know that she would not wish to have me there at all if I was a poor creature without anything?' The poor creature did not know herself how terribly heavy was the accusation she was bringing against her aunt. 'And what will she say when she knows that the money I have spent has never really been my own?'

Then he counselled her to say nothing about it to her aunt till after her next visit to Mr Slow's and made her understand that he, himself, would not mention the subject at the Cedars till the week was passed. He should go, he said, to his own lawyer, and tell him the whole story as far as he knew it. It was not that he in the least doubted Mr Slow's honesty or judgment, but it would be better that the two should act together. Then when the week was over, he and Margaret would once more go to Lincoln's Inn Fields.

'What a week I shall have!' said she.

'It will be a nervous time for us both,' he answered.

'And what must I do after that?' This question she asked, not in the least as desirous of obtaining from him any assurance of assistance, but in the agony of her spirit, and in sheer dismay as to her prospects.

'We must hope for the best,' he said. 'God tempers the wind to the shorn lamb.' He had often thought of the way in which he had been shorn, but he did not, at this moment, remember that the shearing had never been so tempered as to be acceptable to his own feelings.

'And in God only can I trust,' she answered. As she said this, her mind went away to Littlebath, and the Stumfoldians, and Mr Maguire. Was there not great mercy in the fact, that this ruin had not found her married to that unfortunate clergyman? And what would they all say at Littlebath when they heard the story? How would Mrs Stumfold exult over the downfall of the woman who had rebelled against her! how would the nose of the coachmaker's wife rise in the air! and how would Mr Maguire rejoice that this great calamity had not fallen upon him! Margaret Mackenzie's heart and spirit had been sullied by no mean feeling with reference to her own wealth. It had never puffed her up with exultation. But she calculated on the meanness of others, as though it was a matter of course, not, indeed, knowing that it was meanness, or blaming them in any way for that which she attributed to them. Four gentlemen had wished to marry her during the past year. It never occurred to her now, that any one of these four would on that account hold out a hand to help her. In losing her money she would have lost all that was desirable in their eyes, and this seemed to her to be natural.

They were still walking round Lincoln's Inn Fields. 'John,' she exclaimed suddenly, 'I must go to them in Gower Street.'

'What, now, to-day?'

'Yes, now, immediately. You need not mind me; I can get back to Twickenham by myself. I know the trains.'

'If I were you, Margaret, I would not go till all this is decided.'

'It is decided, John; I know it is. And how can I leave them in such a condition, spending money which they will never get? They must know it some time, and the sooner the better. Mr Rubb must know it too. He must understand that he is more than ever bound to provide them with an income out of the business.'

'I would not do it to-day if I were you.'

'But I must, John; this very day. If I am not home by dinner, tell them that I had to go to Gower Street. I shall at any rate be there in the evening. Do not you mind coming back with me.'

They were then at the gate leading into the New Square, and she turned abruptly round, and hurried away from him up into Holborn, passing very near to Mr Slow's chambers. John Ball did not attempt to follow her, but stood there awhile looking after her. He felt, in his heart, and knew by his judgment, that she was a good woman, true, unselfish, full of love, clever too in her way, quick in apprehension, and endowed with an admirable courage. He had heard her spoken of at the Cedars as a poor creature who had money. Nay, he himself had taken a part in so speaking of her. Now she had no money, but he knew well that she was a creature the very reverse of poor. What should he do for her? In what way should he himself behave towards her? In the early days of his youth, before the cares of the world had made him hard, he had married his Rachel without a penny, and his father had laughed at him, and his mother had grieved over him. Tough and hard, and careworn as he was now, defiled by the price of stocks, and saturated with the poison of the money market, then there had been in him a touch of romance and a dash of poetry, and he had been happy with his Rachel. Should he try it again now? The woman would surely love him when she found that he came to her in her poverty as he had before come to her in her wealth. He watched her till she passed out of his sight along the wall leading to Holborn, and then he made his way to the City through Lincoln's Inn and Chancery Lane.

Margaret walked straight into Holborn, and over it towards Red Lion Square. She crossed the line of the omnibuses, feeling that now she must spend no penny which she could save. She was tired, for she had already walked much that morning, and the day was close and hot; but nevertheless she went on quickly, through Bloomsbury Square and Russell Square, to Gower Street. As she got near to the door her heart almost failed her; but she went up to it and knocked boldly. The thing should be done, let the pain of doing it be what it might.

'Laws, Miss Margaret! is that you?' said the maid.

'Yes, missus is at home. She'll see you, of course, but she's hard at work on the furniture.'

Then she went directly up into the drawing-room and there she found her sister-in-law, with her dress tucked up to her elbows, with a cloth in her hand, rubbing the chairs.

'What, Margaret! Whoever expected to see you? If we are to let the rooms, it's as well to have the things tidy, isn't it? Besides, a person bears it all the better when there's anything to do.'

Then Mary Jane, the eldest daughter, came in from the bed-room behind the drawing-room, similarly armed for work.

Margaret sat down wearily upon the sofa, having muttered some word in answer to Mrs Tom's apology for having been found at work so soon after her husband's death.

'Sarah,' she said, 'I have come to you to-day because I had something to say to you about business.'

'Oh, to be sure! I never thought for a moment you had come for pleasure, or out of civility, as it might be. Of course I didn't expect that when I saw you.'

'Sarah, will you come upstairs with me into your own room?'

'Upstairs, Margaret? Oh yes, if you please. We shall be down directly, my dear, and I dare say Margaret will stay to tea. We tea early, because, since you went, we have dined at one.'

Then Mrs Tom led the way up to the room in which Margaret had watched by her dying brother's bed-side.

'I'm come in here,' said Mrs Tom, again apologising, 'because the children had to come out of the room behind the drawing-room. Miss Colza is staying with us, and she and Mary Jane have your room.'

Margaret did not care much for all this; but the solemnity of the chamber in which, when she last saw it, her brother's body was lying, added something to her sadness at the moment.

'Sarah,' she said, endeavouring to warn her sister-in-law by the tone of her voice that her news was bad news, 'I have just come from Mr Slow.'

'He's the lawyer, isn't he?'

'Yes, he's the lawyer. You know what I promised my brother. I went to him to make arrangements for doing it, and when there I heard – oh, Sarah, such dreadful news!'

'He says you're not to do it, I suppose!' And in the woman's voice and eyes there were signs of anger, not against Mr Slow alone, but also against Miss Mackenzie. 'I knew how it would be. But, Margaret, Mr Slow has got nothing to do with it. A promise is a promise; and a promise made to a dying man! Oh, Margaret!'

'If I had it to give I would give it as surely as I am standing here. When I told my brother it should be so, he believed me at once.'

'Of course he believed you.'

'But Sarah, they tell me now that I have nothing to give.'

'Who tells you so?'

'The lawyer. I cannot explain it all to you; indeed, I do not as yet understand it myself; but I have learned this morning that the property which Walter left me was not his to leave. It had been given away before Mr Jonathan Ball died.'

'It's a lie!' said the injured woman – the woman who was the least injured, but who, with her children, had perhaps the best excuse for being ill able to bear the injury. 'It must be a lie. It's more than twenty years ago. I don't believe and won't believe that it can be so. John Ball must have something to do with this.'

'The property will go to him, but he has had nothing to do with it. Mr Slow found it out.'

'It can't be so, not after twenty years. Whatever they may have done from Walter, they can't take it away from you; not if you've spirit enough to stand up for your rights. If you let them take it in that way, I can't tell you what I shall think of you.'

'It is my own lawyer that says so.'

'Yes, Mr Slow; the biggest rogue of them all. I always knew that of him, always. Oh, Margaret, think of the children! What are we to do? What are we to do?' And sitting down on the bedside, she put her dirty apron up to her eyes.

'I have been thinking of them ever since I heard it,' said Margaret.

'But what good will thinking do? You must do something. Oh! Margaret, after all that you said to him when he lay there dying!' and the woman, with some approach to true pathos, put her hand on the spot where her husband's head had rested. 'Don't let his children come to beggary because men like that choose to rob the widow and the orphan.'

'Every one has a right to what is his own,' said Margaret. 'Even though widows should be beggars, and orphans should want.'

'That's very well of you, Margaret. It's very well for you to say that, who have friends like the Balls to stand by you. And, perhaps, if you will let him have it all without saying anything, he will stand by you firmer than ever. But who is there to stand by me and my children? It can't be that after twenty years your fortune should belong to anyone else. Why should it have gone on for more than twenty years, and nobody have found it out? I don't believe it can come so, Margaret, unless you choose to let them do it. I don't believe a word of it.'

There was nothing more to be said upon that subject at present. Mrs Tom did indeed say a great deal more about it, sometimes threatening Margaret, and sometimes imploring her; but Miss Mackenzie herself would not allow herself to speak of the thing otherwise than as an ascertained fact. Had the other woman been more reasonable or less passionate in her lamentations Miss Mackenzie might have trusted herself to tell her that there was yet a doubt. But she herself felt that the doubt was so small, and that, in Mrs Tom's mind, it would be so magnified into nearly a certainty on the other side, that she thought it most discreet not to refer to the exact amount of information which Mr Slow had given to her.

'It will be best for us to think, Sarah,' she said, trying to turn the other's mind away from the coveted income which she would never possess – 'to think what you and the children had better do.'

'Oh, dear! oh, dear! oh, dear!'

'It is very bad; but there is always something to be done. We must lose no time in letting Mr Rubb know the truth. When he hears how it is, he will understand that something must be done for you out of the firm.'

'He won't do anything. He's downstairs now, flirting with that girl in the drawing-room, instead of being at his business.'

'If he's downstairs, I will see him.'

As Mrs Mackenzie made no objection to this, Margaret went downstairs, and when she came near the passage at the bottom, she heard the voices of people talking merrily in the parlour. As her hand was on the lock of the door, words from Miss Colza became very audible. 'Now, Mr Rubb, be quiet.' So she knocked at the door, and having been invited by Mr Rubb to come in, she opened it.

It may be presumed that the flirting had not gone to any perilous extent, as there were three or four children present. Nevertheless Miss Colza and Mr Rubb were somewhat disconcerted, and expressed their surprise at seeing Miss Mackenzie.

'We all thought you were staying with the baronet's lady,' said Miss Colza.

Miss Mackenzie explained that she was staying at Twickenham, but that she had come up to pay a visit to her sister-in-law. 'And I've a word or two I want to say to you, Mr Rubb, if you'll allow me.'

'I suppose, then, I'd better make myself scarce,' said Miss Colza.

As she was not asked to stay, she did make herself scarce, taking the children with her up among the tables and chairs in the drawing-room. There she found Mary Jane, but she did not find Mrs Mackenzie, who had thrown herself on the bed in her agony upstairs.

Then Miss Mackenzie told her wretched story to Mr Rubb – telling it for the third time. He was awe-struck as he listened, but did not once attempt to deny the facts, as had been done by Mrs Mackenzie.

'And is it sure?' he asked, when her story was over.

'I don't suppose it is quite sure yet. Indeed, Mr Slow said it was not quite sure. But I have not allowed myself to doubt it, and I do not doubt it.'

'If he himself had not felt himself sure, he would not have told you.'

'Just so, Mr Rubb. That is what I think; and therefore I have given my sister-in-law no hint that there is a chance left. I think you had better not do so either.'

'Perhaps not,' said he. He spoke in a low voice, almost whispering, as though he were half scared by the tidings he had heard.

'It is very dreadful,' she said; 'very dreadful for Sarah and the children.'

'And for you too, Miss Mackenzie.'

'But about them, Mr Rubb. What can you do for them out of the business'

He looked very blank, and made no immediate answer.

'I know you will feel for their position,' she said. 'You do; do you not?'

'Indeed I do, Miss Mackenzie.'

'And you will do what you can. You can at any rate ensure them the interest of the money – of the money you know that came from me.'

Still Mr Rubb sat in silence, and she thought that he must be stony-hearted. Surely he might undertake to do that, knowing, as he so well knew, the way in which the money had been obtained, and knowing also that he had already said that so much should be forthcoming out of the firm to make up a general income for the family of his late partner.

'Surely there will be no doubt about that, Mr Rubb.'

'The Balls will claim the debt,' said he hoarsely; and then, in answer to her inquiries, he explained that the sum she had lent had not, in truth, been hers to lend. It had formed part of the money that John Ball could claim, and Mr Slow held in his hands an acknowledgement of the debt from Rubb and Mackenzie. Of course, Mr Ball would claim that the interest should be paid to him; and he would claim the principal too, if, on inquiry, he should find that the firm would be able to raise it. 'I don't know that he wouldn't be able to come upon the firm for the money your brother put into the business,' said he gloomily. 'But I don't think he'll be such a fool as that. He'd get nothing by it.'

'Then may God help them! ' said Miss Mackenzie.

'And what will you do?' he asked.

She shook her head, but made him no answer. As for herself she had not begun to form a plan. Her own condition did not seem to her to be nearly so dreadful as that of all these young children.

'I wish I knew how to help you,' said Samuel Rubb.

'There are some positions, Mr Rubb, in which no one but God can help one. But, perhaps – perhaps you may still do something for the children.'

'I will try, Miss Mackenzie.'

'Thank you, and may God bless you; and He will bless you if you try. "Who giveth a drop of water to one of them in my name, giveth it also to me." You will think of that, will you not?'

'I will think of you, and do the best that I can.'

'I had hoped to have made them so comfortable! But God's will be done; God's will be done. I think I had better go now, Mr Rubb. There will be no use in my going to her upstairs again. Tell her from me, with my love, that she shall hear from me when I have seen the lawyer. I will try to come to her, but perhaps I may not be able. Good-bye, Mr Rubb.'

'Good-bye, Miss Mackenzie. I hope we shall see each other sometimes.'

'Perhaps so. Do what you can to support her. She will want all that her friends can do for her.' So saying she went out of the room, and let herself out of the front door into the street, and began her walk back to the Waterloo Station.

She had not broken bread in her sister-in-law's house, and it was now nearly six o'clock. She had taken nothing since she had breakfasted at Twickenham, and the affairs of the day had been such as to give her but little time to think of such wants. But now as she made her weary way through the streets she became sick with hunger, and went into a baker's shop for a bun. As she ate it she felt that it was almost wrong in her to buy even that. At the present moment nothing that she possessed seemed to her to be, by right, her own. Every shilling in her purse was the property of John Ball, if Mr Slow's statement were true. Then, when the bun was finished, as she went down by Bloomsbury church and the region of St Giles's back to the Strand, she did begin to think of her own position. What should she do, and how should she commence to do it? She had declared to herself but lately that the work for which she was fittest was that of nursing the sick. Was it not possible that she might earn her bread in this way? Could she not find such employment in some quarter where her labour would be worth the food she must eat and the raiment she would require? There was a hospital somewhere in London with which she thought she had heard that John Ball was connected. Might not he obtain for her a situation such as that?

It was past eight when she reached the Cedars, and then she was very tired – very tired and nearly sick also with want. She went first of all up to her room, and then crept down into the drawing-room, knowing that she should find them at tea. When she entered there was a large party round the table, consisting of the girls and children and Lady Ball. John Ball, who never took tea, was sitting in his accustomed place near the lamp, and the old baronet was half asleep in his arm-chair.

'If you were going to dine in Gower Street, Margaret, why didn't you say so?' said Lady Ball.

In answer to this, Margaret burst out into tears. It was not the unkindness of her aunt's voice that upset her so much as her own weakness, and the terrible struggle of the long day.

'What on earth is the matter?' said Sir John.

One of the girls brought her a cup of tea, but she felt herself to be too weak to take it in her hand, and made a sign that it should be put on the table. She was not aware that she had ever fainted, but a fear came upon her that she might do so now. She rallied herself and struggled, striving to collect her strength.

'Do you know what is the matter with her, John?' said Lady Ball.

Then John Ball asked her if she had had dinner, and when she did not answer him he saw how it was.

'Mother,' he said, 'she has had no food all day; I will get it for her.'

'If she wants anything, the servants can bring it to her, John,' said the mother.

But he would not trust the servants in this matter, but went out himself and fetched her meat and wine, and pressed her to take it, and sat himself beside her, and spoke kind words into her ear, and at last, in some sort, she was comforted.

NINETEEN

Showing how Two of Miss Mackenzie's
Lovers Behaved

MR BALL, ON HIS RETURN HOME to the Cedars, had given no definite answer to his mother's inquiries as to the day's work in London, and had found it difficult to make any reply to her that would for the moment suffice. She was not a woman easily satisfied with evasive answers; but, nevertheless, he told her nothing of what had occurred, and left her simply in a bad humour. This conversation had taken place before dinner, but after dinner she asked him another question.

'John, you might as well tell me this; are you engaged to Margaret Mackenzie?'

'No, I am not,' said her son, angrily.

After that his mother's humour had become worse than before, and in that state her niece had found her when she returned home in the evening, and had suffered in consequence.

On the next morning Miss Mackenzie sent down word to say she was not well, and would not come down to breakfast. It so happened that John Ball was going into town on this day also, the Abednego Life Office holding its board day immediately after that of the Shadrach Fire Office, and therefore he was not able to see her before she encountered his mother. Lady Ball went up to her in her bedroom immediately after breakfast, and there remained with her for some time. Her aunt at first was tender with her, giving her tea and only asking her gentle little questions at intervals; but as the old lady became impatient at learning nothing, she began a system of cross-questions, and at last grew to be angry and disagreeable. Her son had distinctly told her that he was not engaged to his cousin, and had in fact told her nothing else distinctly; but she, when she had seen how careful he had been in supplying Margaret's wants himself, with what anxious solicitude he had pressed wine on her; how he had sat by her saying soft words to her – Lady Ball, when she remembered this, could not but think that her son had deceived her. And if so, why had he wished to deceive her? Could it be that he had allowed her to give away half her money, and had promised to marry her with the other half? There were moments in which her dear son John could be very foolish, in spite of that life-long devotion to the price of stocks, for which he was conspicuous. She still remembered, as though it were but the other day, how he had persisted in marrying Rachel, though Rachel brought nothing with her but a sweet face, a light figure, a happy temper, and the clothes on her back. To all mothers their sons are ever young, and to old Lady Ball John Ball was still young, and still, possibly, capable of some such folly as that of which she was thinking. If it were not so, if there were not something of that kind in the wind why should he – why should she – be so hard and uncommunicative in all their answers? There lay her niece, however, sick with the headache, and therefore weak, and very much in Lady Ball's power. The evil to be done was great, and the necessity for preventing it might be immediate. And Lady Ball was a lady who did not like to be kept in the dark in reference to anything concerning her family. Having gone downstairs, therefore, for an hour or so to look after her servants, or, as she had said, to allow Margaret to have a little sleep, she returned again to the charge, and sitting close to Margaret's pillow, did her best to find out the truth.

If she could only have known the whole truth; how her son's thoughts were running throughout the day, even as he sat at the Abednego board, not on Margaret with half her fortune, but on Margaret with none! how he was recalling the sweetness of her face as she looked up to him in the square, and took him by his coat, and her tears as she spoke of the orphan children, and the grace of her figure as she had walked away from him, and the persistency of her courage in doing what she thought to be right! how he was struggling within himself with an endeavour, a vain endeavour, at a resolution that such a marriage as that must be out of the question! Had Lady Ball known all that, I think she would have flown to the offices of the Abednego after her son, and never have left him till she had conquered his heart and trampled his folly under her feet.

But she did not conquer Margaret Mackenzie. The poor creature lying there, racked, in truth, with pain and sorrow, altogether incapable of any escape from her aunt's gripe, would not say a word that might tend to ease Lady Ball's mind. If she had told all that she knew, all that she surmised, how would her aunt have rejoiced? That the money should come without the wife would indeed have been a triumph! And Margaret in telling all would have had nothing to tell of those terribly foolish thoughts which were then at work in the City. To her such a state of things as that which I have hinted would have seemed quite as improbable, quite as unaccountable, as it would have done to her aunt. But she did not tell all, nor in truth did she tell anything.

'And John was with you at the lawyer's,' said Lady Ball, attempting her cross-examination for the third time.

'Yes; he was with me there.'

'And what did he say when you asked Mr Slow to make such a settlement as that?'

'He didn't say anything, aunt. The whole thing was put off.'

'I know it was put off; of course it was put off. I didn't suppose any respectable lawyer in London would have dreamed of doing such a thing. But what I want to know is, how it was put off. What did Mr Slow say?'

'I am to see him again next week.'

'But not to get him to do anything of that kind?'

'I can't tell, aunt, what he is to do then.'

'But what did he say when you made such a proposition as that? Did he not tell you that it was quite out of the question?'

'I don't think he said that, aunt.'

'Then what did he say? Margaret, I never saw such a person as you are. Why should you be so mysterious? There can't be anything you don't want me to know, seeing how very much I am concerned; and I do think you ought to tell me all that occurred, knowing, as you do, that I have done my very best to be kind to you.

'Indeed there isn't anything I can tell – not yet.'

Then Lady Ball remained silent at the bed-head for the space, perhaps, of ten minutes, meditating over it all. If her son was, in truth, engaged to this woman, at any rate she would find that out. If she asked a point-blank question on that subject, Margaret would not be able to leave it unanswered, and would hardly be able to give a directly false answer.

'My dear,' she said, 'I think you will not refuse to tell me plainly whether there is anything between you and John. As his mother, I have a right to know?'

'How anything between us?' said Margaret, raising herself on her elbow.

'Are you engaged to marry him?'

'Oh, dear! no.'

'And there is nothing of that sort going on?'

'Nothing at all.'

'You are determined still to refuse him?'

'It is quite out of the question, aunt. He does not wish it at all. You may be sure that he has quite changed his mind about it.'

'But he won't have changed his mind if you have given up your plan about your sister-in-law.'

'He has changed it altogether, aunt. You needn't think anything more about that. He thinks no more about it.'

Nevertheless he was thinking about it this very moment, as he voted for accepting a doubtful life at the Abednego, which was urged on the board by a director, who, I hope, had no intimate personal relations with the owner of the doubtful life in question.

Lady Ball did not know what to make of it. For many years past she had not seen her son carry himself so much like a lover as he had done when he sat himself beside his cousin pressing her to drink her glass of sherry. Why was he so anxious for her comfort? And why, before that, had he been so studiously reticent as to her affairs?

'I can't make anything out of you,' said Lady Ball, getting up from her chair with angry alacrity; 'and I must say that I think it very ungrateful of you, seeing all that I have done for you.'

So saying, she left the room.

What, oh, what would she think when she should come to know the truth? Margaret told herself as she lay there, holding her head between her hands, that she was even now occupying that room and enjoying the questionable comfort of that bed under false pretences. When it was known that she was absolutely a pauper, would she then be made welcome to her uncle's house? She was now remaining there without divulging her circumstances, under the advice and by the authority of her cousin; and she had resolved to be guided by him in all things as long as he would be at the trouble to guide her. On whom else could she depend? But, nevertheless, her position was very grievous to her, and the more so now that her aunt had twitted her with ingratitude. When the servant came to her, she felt that she had no right to the girl's services; and when a message was brought to her from Lady Ball, asking whether she would be taken out in the carriage, she acknowledged to herself that such courtesy to her was altogether out of place.

On that evening her cousin said nothing to her, and on the next day he went again up to town.

'What, four days running, John!' said Lady Ball, at breakfast.

'I have particular business to-day, mother,' said he.

On that evening, when he came back, he found a moment to take Margaret by the hand and tell her that his own lawyer also was to meet them at Mr Slow's chambers on the day named. He took her thus, and held her hand closely in his while he was speaking, but he said nothing to her more tender than the nature of such a communication required.

'You and John are terribly mysterious,' said Lady Ball to her, a minute or two afterwards. 'If there is anything I do hate it's mystery in families. We never had any with us till you came.'

On the next day a letter reached her which had been redirected from Gower Street. It was from Mr Maguire; and she took it up into her own room to read it and answer it. The letter and reply were as follows:

'Littlebath, Oct., 186–.

DEAREST MARGARET,

I hope the circumstances of the case will, in your opinion, justify me in writing to you again, though I am sorry to intrude upon you at a time when your heart must yet be sore with grief for the loss of your lamented brother. Were we now all in all to each other, as I hope we may still be before long, it would be my sweet privilege to wipe your eyes, and comfort you in your sorrow, and bid you remember that it is the Lord who giveth and the Lord who taketh away. Blessed be the name of the Lord. I do not doubt that you have spoken to yourself daily in those words, nay, almost hourly, since your brother was taken from you. I had not the privilege of knowing him, but if he was in any way like his sister, he would have been a friend whom I should have delighted to press to my breast and carry in my heart of hearts.

'But now, dearest Margaret, will you allow me to intrude upon you with another theme? Of course you well know the subject upon which, at present, I am thinking more than on any other. May I be permitted to hope that that subject sometimes presents itself to you in a light that is not altogether disagreeable. When you left Littlebath so suddenly, carried away on a mission of love and kindness, you left me, as you will doubtlessly remember, in a state of some suspense. You had kindly consented to acknowledge that I was not altogether indifferent to you.'

'That's not true,' said Margaret to herself, almost out loud; 'I never told him anything of the kind.'

'And it was arranged that on that very day we were to have had a meeting, to which – shall I confess it? – I looked forward as the happiest moment of my life. I can hardly tell you what my feelings were when I found that you were going, and that I could only just say to you, farewell. If I could only have been with you when that letter came I think I could have softened your sorrow, and perhaps then, in your gentleness, you might have said a word which would have left me nothing to wish for in this world. But it has been otherwise ordered, and, Margaret, I do not complain.

'But what makes me write now is the great necessity that I should know exactly how I stand. You said something in your last dear letter which gave me to understand that you wished to do something for your brother's family. Promises made by the bed-sides of the dying are always dangerous, and in the cases of Roman Catholics have been found to be replete with ruin.'

Mr Maguire, no doubt, forgot that in such cases the promises are made by, and not to, the dying person.

'Nevertheless, I am far from saying that they should not be kept in a modified form, and you need not for a moment think that I, if I may be allowed to have an interest in the matter, would wish to hinder you from doing whatever may be becoming. I think I may promise you that you will find no mercenary spirit in me, although, of course, I am bound, looking forward to the tender tie which will, I hope, connect us, to regard your interests above all other worldly affairs. If I may then say a word of advice, it is to recommend that nothing permanent be done till we can act together in this matter. Do not, however, suppose that anything you can do or have done, can alter the nature of my regard.

'But now, dearest Margaret, will you not allow me to press for an immediate answer to my appeal? I will tell you exactly how I am circumstanced, and then you will see how strong is my reason that there should be no delay. Very many people here, I may say all the élite of the evangelical circles, including Mrs Perch' – Mrs Perch was the coachmaker's wife, who had always been so true to Mrs Stumfold –'desired that I should establish a church here, on my own bottom, quite independent of Mr Stumfold. The Stumfolds would then soon have to leave Littlebath, there is no doubt of that, and she has already made herself so unendurable, and her father and she together are so distressing, that the best of their society has fallen away from them. Her treatment to you was such that I could never endure her afterwards. Now the opening for a clergyman with pure Gospel doctrines would be the best thing that has turned up for a long time. The church would be worth over six hundred a year, besides the interest of the money which would have to be laid out. I could have all this commenced at once, and secure the incumbency, if I could myself head the subscription list with two thousand pounds. It should not be less than that. You will understand that the money would not be given, though, no doubt, a great many persons would, in this way, be induced to give theirs. But the pew rents would go in the first instance to provide interest for the money not given, but lent; as would of course be the case with your money, if you would advance it.

'I should not think of such a plan as this if I did not feel that it was the best thing for your interests; that is, if, as I fondly hope, I am ever to call you mine. Of course, in that case, it is only common prudence on my part to do all I can to insure for myself such a professional income, for your sake. For, dearest Margaret, my brightest earthly hope is to see you with everything comfortable around you. If that could be arranged, it would be quite within our means to keep some sort of carriage.'

Here would be a fine opportunity for rivalling Mrs Stumfold! That was the temptation with which he hoped to allure her.

'But the thing must be done quite immediately, therefore let me pray you not to postpone my hopes with unnecessary delay. I know it seems unromantic to urge a lady with any pecuniary considerations, but I think that under the circumstances, as I have explained them, you will forgive me.

'Believe me to be, dearest Margaret,
'Yours, with truest,
'Most devoted affection,
'JEREH. MAGUIRE.

One man had wanted her money to buy a house on a mortgage, and another now asked for it to build a church, giving her, or promising to give her, the security of the pew rents. Which of the two was the worst? They were both her lovers, and she thought that he was the worst who first made his love and then tried to get her money. These were the ideas which at once occurred to her upon her reading Mr Maguire's letter. She had quite wit enough to see through the whole project; how outsiders were to be induced to give their money, thinking that all was to be given; whereas those inside the temple – those who knew all about it – were simply to make for themselves a good speculation. Her cousin John's constant solicitude for money was bad; but, after all, it was not so bad as this. She told herself at once that the letter was one which would of itself have ended everything between her and Mr Maguire, even had nothing occurred to put an absolute and imperative stop to the affair. Mr Maguire pressed for an early answer, and before she left the room she sat down and wrote it.

'The Cedars, Twickenham, October, 186–.

'DEAR SIR'

Before she wrote the words, 'Dear Sir,' she had to think much of them, not having had as yet much experience in writing letters to gentlemen; but she concluded at last that if she simply wrote 'Sir,' he would take it as an insult, and that if she wrote 'My dear Mr Maguire,' it would, under the circumstances, be too affectionate.

'DEAR SIR

I have got your letter to-day, and I hasten to answer it at once. All that to which you allude between us must be considered as being altogether over, and I am very sorry that you should have had so much trouble. My circumstances are altogether changed. I cannot explain how, as it would make my letter very long; but you may be assured that such is the case, and to so great an extent that the engagement you speak of would not at all suit you at present. Pray take this as being quite true, and believe me to be

'Your very humble servant,
'MARGARET MACKENZIE.'

I feel that the letter was somewhat curt and dry as an answer to an effusion so full of affection as that which the gentleman had written; and the fair reader, when she remembers that Miss Mackenzie had given the gentleman considerable encouragement, will probably think that she should have expressed something like regret at so sudden a termination to so tender a friendship. But she, in truth, regarded the offer as having been made to her money solely, and as in fact no longer existing as an offer, now that her money itself was no longer in existence. She was angry with Mr Maguire for the words he had written about her brother's affairs; for his wish to limit her kindness to her nephews and nieces, and also for his greediness in being desirous of getting her money at once; but as to the main question, she thought herself bound to answer him plainly, as she would have answered a man who came to buy from her a house, which house was no longer in her possession.

Mr Maguire when he received her letter, did not believe a word of it. He did not in the least believe that she had actually lost everything that had once belonged to her, or that he, if he married her now, would obtain less than he would have done had he married her before her brother's death. But he thought that her brother's family and friends had got hold of her in London; that Mr Rubb might very probably have done it; and that they were striving to obtain command of her money, and were influencing her to desert him. He thinking so, and being a man of good courage, took a resolution to follow his game, and to see whether even yet he might not obtain the good things which had made his eyes glisten and his mouth water. He knew that there was very much against him in the race that he was desirous of running, and that an heiress with – he did not know how much a year, but it had been rumoured among the Stumfoldians that it was over a thousand – might not again fall in his way. There were very many things against him, of which he was quite conscious. He had not a shilling of his own, and was in receipt of no professional income. He was not altogether a young man. There was in his personal appearance a defect which many ladies might find it difficult to overcome; and then that little story about his debts, which Miss Todd had picked up, was not only true, but was some degrees under the truth. No doubt, he had a great wish that his wife should be comfortable; but he also, for himself, had long been pining after those eligible comforts, which when they appertain to clergymen, the world, with so much malice, persists in calling the flesh-pots of Egypt. Thinking of all this, of the position he had already gained in spite of his personal disadvantages, and of the great chance there was that his Margaret might yet be rescued from the Philistines, he resolved upon a journey to London.

In the meantime Miss Mackenzie's other lover had not been idle, and he also was resolved by no means to give up the battle.

It cannot be said that Mr Rubb was not mercenary in his views, but with his desire for the lady's money was mingled much that was courageous, and something also that was generous. The whole truth had been told to him as plainly as it had been told to Mr Ball, and nevertheless he determined to persevere. He went to work diligently on that very afternoon, deserting the smiles of Miss Colza, and made such inquiries into the law of the matter as were possible to him; and they resulted, as far as Miss Mackenzie was concerned, in his appearing late one afternoon at the front door of Sir John Ball's house. On the day following this Miss

Mackenzie was to keep her appointment with Mr Slow, and her cousin was now up in London among the lawyers.

Miss Mackenzie was sitting with her aunt when Mr Rubb called. They were both in the drawing-room; and Lady Ball, who had as yet succeeded in learning nothing, and who was more than ever convinced that there was much to learn, was not making herself pleasant to her companion. Throughout the whole week she had been very unpleasant. She did not quite understand why Margaret's sojourn at the Cedars had been and was to be so much prolonged. Margaret, feeling herself compelled to say something on the subject, had with some hesitation told her aunt that she was staying till she had seen her lawyer again, because her cousin wished her to stay.

In answer to this, Lady Ball had of course told her that she was welcome. Her ladyship had then cross-questioned her son on that subject also, but he had simply said that as there was law business to be done, Margaret might as well stay at Twickenham till it was completed.

'But, my dear,' Lady Ball had said, 'her law business might go on for ever, for what you know.'

'Mother,' said the son, sternly, 'I wish her to stay here at present, and I suppose you will not refuse to permit her to do so.'

After this, Lady Ball could go no further.

On the day on which Mr Rubb was announced in the drawing-room, the aunt and niece were sitting together. 'Mr Rubb – to see Miss Mackenzie,' said the old servant, as he opened the door.

Miss Mackenzie got up, blushing to her forehead, and Lady Ball rose from her chair with an angry look, as though asking the oilcloth manufacturer how he dared to make his way in there. The name of the Rubbs had been specially odious to all the family at the Cedars since Tom Mackenzie had carried his share of Jonathan Ball's money into the firm in the New Road. And Mr Rubb's appearance was not calculated to mitigate this anger. Again he had got on those horrid yellow gloves, and again had dressed himself up to his idea of the garb of a man of fashion. To Margaret's eyes, in the midst of her own misfortunes, he was a thing horrible to behold, as he came into that drawing-room. When she had seen him in his natural condition, at her brother's house, he had been at any rate unobjectionable to her; and when, on various occasions, he had talked to her about his own business, pleading his own cause and excusing his own fault, she had really liked him. There had been a moment or two, the moments of his bitterest confessions, in which she had in truth liked him much. But now! What would she not have given that the old servant should have taken upon himself to declare that she was not at home.

But there he was in her aunt's drawing-room, and she had nothing to do but to ask him to sit down.

'This is my aunt, Lady Ball,' said Margaret.

'I hope I have the honour of seeing her ladyship quite well,' said Mr Rubb, bowing low before he ventured to seat himself.

Lady Ball would not condescend to say a word, but stared at him in a manner that would have driven him out of the room had he understood the nature of such looks on ladies' faces.

'I hope my sister-in-law and the children are well,' said Margaret, with a violent attempt to make conversation.

'Pretty much as you left them, Miss Mackenzie; she takes on a good deal; but that's only human nature; eh, my lady?'

But her ladyship still would not condescend to speak a word.

Margaret did not know what further to say. All subjects on which it might have been possible for her to speak to Mr Rubb were stopped from her in the presence of her aunt. Mr Rubb knew of that great calamity of which, as yet, Lady Ball knew nothing – of that great calamity to the niece, but great blessing, as it would be thought by the aunt. And she was in much fear lest Mr Rubb should say something which might tend to divulge the secret.

'Did you come by the train?' she said, at last, reduced in her agony to utter the first unmeaning question of which she could think.

'Yes, Miss Mackenzie, I came by the train, and I am going back by the 5.45, if I can just be allowed to say a few words to you first.'

'Does the gentleman mean in private?' asked Lady Ball.

'If you please, my lady,' said Mr Rubb, who was beginning to think that he did not like Lady Ball.

'If Miss Mackenzie wishes it, of course she can do so.'

'It may be about my brother's affairs,' said Margaret, getting up.

'It is nothing to me, my dear, whether they are your brother's or your own,' said Lady Ball; 'you had better not interrupt your uncle in the study; but I daresay you'll find the dining-room disengaged.'

So Miss Mackenzie led the way into the dining-room, and Mr Rubb followed. There they found some of the girls, who stared very hard at Mr Rubb, as they left the room at their cousin's request. As soon as they were left alone Mr Rubb began his work manfully.

'Margaret,' said he, 'I hope you will let me call you so now that you are in trouble?'

To this she made no answer.

'But perhaps your trouble is over? Perhaps you have found out that it isn't as you told us the other day?'

'No, Mr Rubb; I have found nothing of that kind; I believe it is as I told you.'

'Then I'll tell you what I propose. You haven't given up the fight, have you? You have not done anything?'

'I have done nothing as yet.'

'Then I'll tell you my plan. Fight it out.'

'I do not want to fight for anything that is not my own.'

'But it is your own. It is your own of rights, even though it should not be so by some quibble of the lawyers'. I don't believe twelve Englishmen would be found in London to give it to anybody else; I don't indeed.'

'But my own lawyer tells me it isn't mine, Mr Rubb.'

'Never mind him; don't you give up anything. Don't you let them make you soft. When it comes to money nobody should give up anything. Now I'll tell you what I propose.'

She now sat down and listened to him, while he stood over her. It was manifest that he was very eager, and in his eagerness he became loud, so that she feared his words might be heard out of the room.

'You know what my sentiments are,' he said. At that moment she did not remember what his sentiments were, nor did she know what he meant. 'They're the same now as ever. Whether you have got your fortune, or whether you've got nothing, they're the same. I've seen you tried alongside of your brother, when he was a-dying, and, Margaret, I like you now better than ever I did.'

'Mr Rubb, at present, all that cannot mean anything.'

'But doesn't it mean anything? By Jove! it does though. It means just this, that I'll make you Mrs Rubb to-morrow, or as soon as Doctors' Commons, and all that, will let us do it; and I'll chance the money afterwards. Do you let it just go easy, and say nothing, and I'll fight them. If the worst comes to the worst, they'll be willing enough to cry halves with us. But, Margaret, if the worst does come to be worse than that you won't find me hard to you on that account. I shall always remember who helped me when I wanted help.'

'I am sure, Mr Rubb, I am much obliged to you.'

'Don't talk about being obliged, but get up and give me your hand, and say it shall be a bargain.' Then he tried to take her by the hand and raise her from the chair up towards him.

'No, no, no!' said she.

'But I say yes. Why should it be no? If there never should come a penny out of this property I will put a roof over your head, and will find you victuals and clothes respectably. Who will do better for you than that? And as for the fight, by Jove! I shall like it. You'll find they'll get nothing out of my hands till they have torn away my nails.'

Here was a new phase in her life. Here was a man willing to marry her even though she had no assured fortune.

'Margaret,' said he, pleading his cause again, 'I have that love for you that I would take you though it was all gone, to the last farthing.'

'It is all gone.'

'Let that be as it may, we'll try it. But though it should be all gone, every shilling of it, still, will you be my wife?'

It was altogether a new phase, and one that was inexplicable to her. And this came from a man to whom she had once thought that she might bring herself to give her hand and her heart, and her money also. She did not doubt that if she took him at his word he would be good to her, and provide her with shelter, and food and raiment, as he had promised her. Her heart was softened towards him, and she forgot his gloves and his shining boots. But she could not bring herself to say that she would love him, and be his wife. It seemed to her now that she was under the guidance of her cousin, and that she was pledged to do nothing of which he would disapprove. He would not approve of her accepting the hand of a man who would be resolved to litigate this matter with him.

'It cannot be,' she said. 'I feel how generous you are, but it cannot be.'

'And why shouldn't it be?'

'Oh, Mr, Rubb, there are things one cannot explain.'

'Margaret, think of it. How are you to do better?'

'Perhaps not; probably not. In many ways I am sure I could not do better. But it cannot be.'

Not then, nor for the next twenty minutes, but at last he took his answer and went. He did this when he found that he had no more minutes to spare if he intended to return by the 5.45 train. Then, with an angry gesture of his head, he left her, and hurried across to the front door. Then, as he went out, Mr John Ball came in.

'Good evening, sir,' said Mr Rubb. 'I am Mr Samuel Rubb. I have just been seeing Miss Mackenzie, on business. Good evening, sir.'

John Ball said never a word, and Samuel Rubb hurried across the grounds to the railway station.

✠ TWENTY ✠

Showing How the Third Lover Behaved

'WHAT HAS THAT MAN BEEN HERE FOR?' Those were the first words which Mr Ball spoke to his cousin after shutting the hall-door behind Mr Rubb's back. When the door was closed he turned round and saw Margaret as she was coming out of the dining-room, and in a voice that sounded to her as though he were angry, asked her the above question.

'He came to see me, John,' said Miss Mackenzie, going back into the dining-room. 'He was my brother's partner.'

'He said he came upon business; what business could he have?'

It was not very easy for her to tell him what had been Mr Rubb's business. She had no wish to keep anything secret from her cousin, but she did not know how to describe the scene which had just taken place, or how to acknowledge that the man had come there to ask her to marry him.

'Does he know anything of this matter of your money?' continued Mr Ball.

'Oh yes; he knows it all. He was in Gower Street when I told my sister-in-law.'

'And he came to advise you about it?'

'Yes; he did advise me about it. But his advice I shall not take.'

'And what did he advise?'

Then Margaret told him that Mr Rubb had counselled her to fight it out to the last, in order that a compromise might at any rate be obtained.

'If it has no selfish object in view I am far from saying that he is wrong,' said John Ball. 'It is what I should advise a friend to do under similar circumstances.'

'It is not what I shall do, John.'

'No; you are like a lamb that gives itself up to the slaughterer. I have been with one lawyer or the other all day, and the end of it is that there is no use on earth in your going to London tomorrow, nor, as far as I can see, for another week to come. The two lawyers together have referred the case to counsel for opinion – for an amicable opinion as they call it. From what they all say, Margaret, it seems to me clear that the matter will go against you.'

'I have expected nothing else since Mr Slow spoke to me.'

'But no doubt you can make a fight, as your friend says.'

'I don't want to fight, John; you know that.'

'Mr Slow won't let you give it up without a contest. He suggested a compromise – that you and I should divide it. But I hate compromises.' She looked up into his face but said nothing. 'The truth is, I have been so wronged in the matter, the whole thing has been so cruel, it has, all of it together, so completely ruined me and my prospects in life, that were it any one but you, I would sooner have a lawsuit than give up one penny of what is left.' Again she looked at him, but he went on speaking of it without observing her. 'Think what it has been, Margaret! The whole of this property was once mine! Not the half of it only that has been called yours, but the whole of it! The income was actually paid for one half-year to a separate banking account on my behalf, before I was of age. Yes, paid to me, and I had it! My uncle Jonathan had no more legal right to take it away from me than you have to take the coat off my back. Think of that, and of what four-and-twenty thousand pounds would have done for me and my family from that time to this. There have been nearly thirty years of this robbery!'

'It was not my fault, John.'

'No; it was not your fault. But if your brothers could pay me back all that they really owe me, all that the money would now be worth, it would come to nearly a hundred thousand pounds. After that, what is a man to say when he is asked to compromise? As far as I can see, there is not a shadow of doubt about it. Mr Slow does not pretend that there is a doubt. How they can fail to see the justice of it is what passes my understanding!'

'Mr Slow will give up at once, I suppose, if I ask him?'

'I don't want you to ask him. I would rather that you didn't say a word to him about it. There is a debt too from that man Rubb which they advise me to abandon.'

In answer to this, Margaret could say nothing, for she knew well that her trust in the interest of that money was the only hope she had of any maintenance for her sister-in-law.

After a few minutes' silence he again spoke to her. 'He desires to know whether you want money for immediate use.'

'Who wants to know?'

'Mr Slow.'

'Oh no, John. I have money at the bankers', but I will not touch it.'

'How much is there at the bankers?'

'There is more than three hundred pounds; but very little more; perhaps three hundred and ten.'

'You may have that.'

'John, I don't want anything that is not my own; not though I had to walk out to earn my bread in the streets to-morrow.'

'That is your own, I tell you. The tenants have been ordered not to pay any further rents, till they receive notice. You can make them pay, nevertheless, if you wish it; at least, you might do so, till some legal steps were taken.'

'Of course, I shall do nothing of the kind. It was Mr Slow's people who used to get the money. And am I not to go up to London to-morrow?'

'You can go if you choose, but you will learn nothing. I told Mr Slow that I would bid you wait till I heard from him again. It is time now for us to get ready for dinner.'

Then, as he was going to leave the room, she took him by the coat and held him again – held him as fast as she had done on the pavement in Lincoln's Inn Fields. There was a soft, womanly, trusting weakness in the manner of her motion as she did this, which touched him now as it had touched him then.

'John,' she said, 'if there is to be so much delay, I must not stay here.'

'Why not, Margaret?'

'My aunt does not like my staying; I can see that; and I don't think it is fair to do so while she does not know all about it. It is something like cheating her out of the use of the house.'

'Then I will tell her.'

'What, all? Had I not better go first?'

'No; you cannot go. Where are you to go to? I will tell her everything tonight. I had almost made up my mind to do so already. It will be better that they should both know it – my father and my mother. My father probably will be required to say all that he knows about the matter.'

'I shall be ready to go at once if she wishes it,' said Margaret.

To this he made no answer, but went upstairs to his bedroom, and there, as he dressed, thought again, and again, and again of his cousin Margaret. What should he do for her, and in what way should he treat her? The very name of the Mackenzies he had hated of old, and their names were now more hateful to him than ever. He had correctly described his own feelings towards them when he said, either truly or untruly, that they had deprived him of that which would have made his whole life prosperous instead of the reverse. And it seemed as though he had really thought that they had been in fault in this – that they had defrauded him. It did not, apparently, occur to him that the only persons he could blame were his uncle Jonathan and his own lawyers, who, at his uncle's death, had failed to discover on his behalf what really were his rights. Walter Mackenzie had been a poor creature who could do nothing. Tom Mackenzie had been a mean creature who had allowed himself to be cozened in a petty trade out of the money which he had wrongfully acquired. They were odious to him, and he hated their memories. He would fain have hated all that belonged to them, had he been able. But he was not able to hate this woman who clung to him, and trusted him, and felt no harsh feelings towards him, though he was going to take from her everything that had been hers. She trusted him for advice even though he was her adversary! Would he have trusted her or any other human being under such circumstances? No, by heavens! But not the less on that account did he acknowledge to himself that this confidence in her was very gracious.

That evening passed by very quietly as far as Miss Mackenzie was concerned. She had some time since, immediately on her last arrival at the Cedars, offered to relieve her aunt from the trouble of making tea, and the duty had then been given up to her. But since Lady Ball's affair in obtaining possession of her niece's secret, the post of honour had been taken away.

'You don't make it as your uncle likes it,' Lady Ball had said.

She made her little offer again on this evening, but it was rejected.

'Thank you, no; I believe I had better do it myself,' had been the answer.

'Why can't you let Margaret make tea? I'm sure she does it very well,' said John.

'I don't see that you can be a judge, seeing that you take none,' his mother replied; 'and if you please, I'd rather make the tea in my own house as long as I can.'

This little allusion to her own house was, no doubt, a blow at her son, to punish him in that he had dictated to her in that matter of the continued entertainment of her guest; but Margaret also felt it to be a blow at her, and resolved that she would escape from the house with as little further delay as might be possible. Beyond this, the evening was very quiet, till Margaret, a little after tea, took her candle and went off wearily to her room.

But then the business of the day as regarded the Cedars began; for John Ball, before he went to bed, told both his father and his mother the whole story – the story, that is, as far as the money was concerned, and also as far as Margaret's conduct to him was concerned; but of his own feelings towards her he said nothing.

'She has behaved admirably, mother,' he said; 'you must acknowledge that, and I think that she is entitled to all the kindness we can show her.'

'I have been kind to her,' Lady Ball answered.

This had taken place in Lady Ball's own room, after they had left Sir John. The tidings had taken the old man so much by surprise, that he had said little or nothing. Even his caustic ill-nature had deserted him, except on one occasion, when he remarked that it was like his brother Jonathan to do as much harm with his money as was within his reach.

'My memory in such a matter is worth nothing – absolutely nothing,' the old man had said. 'I always supposed something was wrong. I remember that. But I left it all to the lawyers.'

In Lady Ball's room the conversation was prolonged to a late hour of the night, and took various twists and turns, as such conversations will do.

'What are we to do about the young woman?' That was Lady Ball's main question, arising, no doubt, from the reflection that the world would lean very heavily on them if they absolutely turned her out to starve in the streets.

John Ball made no proposition in answer to this, having not as yet made up his mind as to what his own wishes were with reference to the young woman. Then his mother made her proposition.

'Of course that money due by the Rubbs must be paid. Let her take that.' But her son made no reply to this other than that he feared the Rubbs were not in a condition to pay the money.

'They would pay her the interest at any rate,' said Lady Ball, 'till she had got into some other way of life. She would do admirably for a companion to an old lady, because her manners are good, and she does not want much waiting upon herself.'

On the next morning Miss Mackenzie trembled in her shoes as she came down to breakfast. Her uncle, whom she feared the most, would not be there; but the meeting with her aunt, when her aunt would know that she was a pauper and that she had for the last week been an impostor, was terrible to her by anticipation. But she had not calculated that her aunt's triumph in this newly-acquired wealth for the Ball family would, for the present, cover any other feeling that might exist. Her aunt met her with a gracious smile, was very urbane in selecting a chair for her at prayers close to her own, and pressed upon her a piece of buttered toast out of a little dish that was always prepared for her ladyship's own consumption. After breakfast John Ball again went to town. He went daily to town during the present crisis; and, on this occasion, his mother made no remark as to the urgency of his business. When he was gone Lady Ball began to potter about the house, after her daily custom, and was longer in her pottering than was usual with her. Miss Mackenzie helped the younger children in their lessons, as she often did; and when time for luncheon came, she had almost begun to think that she was to be allowed to escape any conversation with her aunt touching the great money question. But it was not so. At one she was told that luncheon and the children's dinner was postponed till two, and she was asked by the servant to go up to Lady Ball in her own room.

'Come and sit down, my dear,' said Lady Ball, in her sweetest voice. 'It has got to be very cold, and you had better come near the fire.' Margaret did as she was bidden, and sat herself down in the chair immediately opposite to her aunt.

'This is a wonderful story that John has told me,' continued her aunt – 'very wonderful.'

'It is sad enough for me,' said Margaret, who did not feel inclined to be so self-forgetful in talking to her aunt as she had been with her cousin.

'It is sad for you, Margaret, no doubt. But I am sure you have within you that conscientious rectitude of purpose that you would not wish to keep anything for yourself that in truth belongs to another.'

To this Margaret answered nothing, and her aunt went on.

'It is a great change to you, no doubt; and, of course, that is the point on which I wish to speak to you most especially. I have told John that something must be done for you.'

This jarred terribly on poor Margaret's feelings. Her cousin had said nothing, not a word as to doing anything for her. The man who had told her of his love, and asked her to be his wife, not twelve months since – who had pressed her to be of all women the dearest to him and the nearest – had talked to her of her ruin without offering her aid, although this ruin to her would enrich him very greatly. She had expected nothing from him, had wanted nothing from him; but by degrees, when absent from him, the feeling had grown upon her that he had been hard to her in abstaining from expressions of commiseration. She had yielded to him in the whole affair, assuring him that nothing should be done by her to cause him trouble; and she would have been grateful to him if in return he had said something to her of her future mode of life. She had intended to speak to him about the hospital; but she had thought that she might abstain from doing so till he himself should ask some question as to her plans. He had asked no such question, and she was now almost

560

determined to go away without troubling him on the subject. But if he, who had once professed to love her, would make no suggestion as to her future life, she could ill bear that any offer of the kind should come from her aunt, who, as she knew, had only regarded her for her money.

'I would rather,' she replied, 'that nothing should be said to him on the subject.'

'And why not, Margaret?'

'I desire that I may be no burden to him or anybody. I will go away and earn my bread; and even if I cannot do that, my relations shall not be troubled by hearing from me.'

She said this without sobbing, but not without that almost hysterical emotion which indicates that tears are being suppressed with pain.

'That is false pride, my dear.'

'Very well, aunt. I daresay it is false; but it is my pride. I may be allowed to keep my pride, though I can keep nothing else.'

'What you say about earning your bread is very proper; and I and John and your uncle also have been thinking of that. But I should be glad if some additional assistance should be provided for you, in the event of old age, you know, or illness. Now, as to earning your bread, I remarked to John that you were peculiarly qualified for being a lady's companion.'

'For being what, aunt?'

'For being companion to some lady in the decline of life, who would want to have some nice mannered person always with her. You have the advantage of being ladylike and gentle, and I think that you are patient by disposition.'

'Aunt,' said Miss Mackenzie, and her voice as she spoke was hardly gentle, nor was it indicative of much patience. Her hysterics also, seemed for the time to have given way to her strong passionate feeling. 'Aunt,' she said, 'I would sooner take a broom in my hand, and sweep a crossing in London, than lead such a life as that. What! make myself the slave of some old woman, who would think that she had bought the power of tyrannising over me by allowing me to sit in the same room with her? No, indeed! It may very likely be the case that I may have to serve such a one in the kitchen, but it shall be in the kitchen, and not in the drawing-room. I have not had much experience in life, but I have had enough to learn that lesson!'

Lady Ball, who during the first part of the conversation had been unrolling and winding a great ball of worsted, now sat perfectly still, holding the ball in her lap, and staring at her niece. She was a quick-witted woman, and it no doubt occurred to her that the great objection to living with an old lady, which her niece had expressed so passionately, must have come from the trial of that sort of life which she had had at the Cedars. And there was enough in Miss Mackenzie's manner to justify Lady Ball in thinking that some such expression of feeling as this had been intended by her. She had never before heard Margaret speak out so freely, even in the days of her undoubted heiress-ship; and now, though she greatly disliked her niece, she could not avoid mingling something of respect and something almost amounting to fear with her dislike. She did not dare to go on unwinding her worsted, and giving the advantage of her condescension to a young woman who spoke out at her in that way.

'I thought I was advising you for the best,' she said,' and I hoped that you would have been thankful.'

'I don't know what may be for the best,' said Margaret, again bordering upon the hysterical in the tremulousness of her voice, 'but that I'm sure would be for the worst. However, I've made up my mind to nothing as yet.'

'No, my dear; of course not; but we all must think of it, you know.'

Her cousin John had not thought of it, and she did not want any one else to do so. She especially did not want her aunt to think of it. But it was no doubt necessary that her aunt should consider how long she would be required to provide a home for her impoverished niece, and Margaret's mind at once applied itself to that view of the subject. 'I have made up my mind that I will go to London next week, and then I must settle upon something.'

'You mean when you go to Mr Slow's?'

'I mean that I shall go for good. I have a little money by me, which John says I may use, and I shall take a lodging till – till – till –' Then she could not go on any further.

'You can stay here, Margaret, if you please – that is till something more is settled about all this affair.'

'I will go on Monday, aunt. I have made up my mind to that.' It was now Saturday. 'I will go on Monday. It will be better for all parties that I should be away.' Then she got up, and waiting no further speech from her aunt, took herself off to her own room.

She did not see her aunt again till dinner-time, and then neither of them spoke to each other. Lady Ball thought that she had reason to be offended, and Margaret would not be the first to speak. In the evening, before the whole family, she told her cousin that she had made up her mind to go up to London on Monday. He begged her to reconsider her resolution, but when she persisted that she would do so, he did not then argue the question any further. But on the Sunday he implored her not to go as yet, and did obtain her consent to postpone her departure till Tuesday. He wished, he said, to be at any rate one day more in London before she went. On the Sunday she was closeted with her uncle who also sent for her, and to him she suggested her plan of becoming nurse at a hospital. He remarked that he hoped that would not be necessary.

'Something will be necessary,' she said, 'as I don't mean to eat anybody's bread but my own.'

In answer to this he said that he would speak to John, and then that interview was over. On the Monday morning John Ball said something respecting Margaret to his mother which acerbated that lady more than ever against her niece. He had not proposed that anything special should be done; but he had hinted, when his mother complained of Margaret, that Margaret's conduct was everything that it ought to be.

'I believe you would take anybody's part against me,' Lady Ball had said, and then as a matter of course she had been very cross. The whole of that day was terrible to Miss Mackenzie, and she resolved that nothing said by her cousin should induce her to postpone her departure for another day.

In order to insure this by a few minutes' private conversation with him, and also with the view of escaping for some short time from the house, she walked down to the station in the evening to meet her cousin. The train by which he arrived reached Twickenham at five o'clock, and the walk occupied about twenty minutes. She met him just as he was coming out of the station gate, and at once told him that she had come there for the sake of walking back with him and talking to him. He thanked her, and said that he was very glad to meet her. He also wanted to speak to her very particularly. Would she take his arm?

She took his arm, and then began with a quick tremulous voice to tell him of her sufferings at the house. She threw no blame on her aunt that she could avoid, but declared it to be natural that under such circumstances as those now existing her prolonged sojourn at her aunt's house should be unpleasant to both of them. In answer to all this, John Ball said nothing, but once or twice lifted up his left hand so as to establish Margaret's arm more firmly on his own. She hardly noticed the motion, but yet she was aware that it was intended for kindness, and then she broke forth with a rapid voice as to her plan about the hospital. 'I think we can manage better than that, at any rate,' said he, stopping her in the path when this proposal met his ear. But she went on to declare that she would like it, that she was strong and qualified for such work, that it would satisfy her aspirations, and be fit for her. And then, after that, she declared that nothing should induce her to undertake the kind of life that had been suggested by her aunt. 'I quite agree with you there,' said he; 'quite. I hate tabbies as much as you do.'

They had now come to a little gate, of which John Ball kept a key, and which led into the grounds belonging to the Cedars. The grounds were rather large, and the path through them extended for half a mile, but the land was let off to a grazier. When inside the wall, however, they were private; and Mr Ball, as soon as he had locked the gate behind him, stopped her in the dark path, and took both her hands in his. The gloom of the evening had now come round them, and the thick trees which formed the belt of the place, joined to the high wall, excluded from them nearly all what light remained.

'And now,' said he, 'I will tell you my plan.'

'What plan?' said she; but her voice was very low.

'I proposed it once before, but you would not have it then.'

When she heard this, she at once drew both her hands from him, and stood before him in an agony of doubt. Even in the gloom, the trees were going round her, and everything, even her thoughts, were obscure and misty.

'Margaret,' said he, 'you shall be my wife, and the mother of my children, and I will love you as I loved Rachel before. I loved you when I asked you at Christmas, but I did not love you then as I love you now.'

She still stood before him, but answered him not a word. How often since the tidings of her loss had reached her had the idea of such a meeting as this come before her! how often had she seemed to listen to such words as those he now spoke to her! Not that she had expected it, or hoped for it, or even thought of it as being in truth possible; but her imagination had been at work, during the long hours of the night, and the romance of the thing had filled her mind, and the poetry of it had been beautiful to her. She had known – she had told herself that she knew – that no man would so sacrifice himself; certainly no such man as John Ball, with all his children and his weary love of money! But now the poetry had come to be fact, and the romance had turned itself into reality, and the picture formed by her imagination had become a living truth. The very words of which she had dreamed had been spoken to her.

'Shall it be so, my dear?' he said, again taking one of her hands. 'You want to be a nurse; will you be my nurse? Nay; I will not ask, but it shall be so. They say that the lovers who demand are ever the most successful. I make my demand. Tell me, Margaret, will you obey me?'

He had walked on now, but in order that his time might be sufficient, he led her away from the house. She was following him, hardly knowing whither she was going.

'Susanna,' said he, 'shall come and live with the others; one more will make no difference.'

'And my aunt?' said Margaret.

It was the first word she had spoken since the gate had been locked behind her, and this word was spoken in a whisper.

'I hope my mother may feel that such a marriage will best conduce to my happiness; but, Margaret, nothing that my mother can say will change me. You and I have known something of each other now. Of you, from the way in which things have gone, I have learned much. Few men, I take it, see so much of their future wives as I have seen of you. If you can love me as your husband, say so at once honestly, and then leave the rest to me.'

'I will,' she said, again whispering; and then she clung to his hand, and for a minute or two he had his arm round her waist. Then he took her, and kissed her lips, and told her that he would take care of her, and watch for her, and keep her, if possible, from trouble.

Ah, me, how many years had rolled by since last she had been kissed in that way! Once, and once only, had Harry Handcock so far presumed, and so far succeeded. And now, after a dozen years or more, that game had begun again with her! She had boxed Harry Handcock's ears when he had kissed her; but now, from her lover of to-day, she submitted to the ceremony very tamely.

'Oh, John,' she said, 'how am I to thank you?' But the thanks were tendered for the promise of his care, and not for the kiss.

I think there was but little more said between them before they reached the door-step. When there, Mr Ball, speaking already with something of marital authority, gave her his instructions.

'I shall tell my mother this evening,' he said, 'as I hate mysteries; and I shall tell my father also. Of course there may be something disagreeable said before we all shake down happily in our places, but I shall look to you, Margaret, to be firm.'

'I shall be firm,' she said, 'if you are.'

'I shall be firm,' was the reply; and then they went into the house.

❈ TWENTY-ONE ❈

Mr Maguire goes to London on Business

MR MAGUIRE MADE UP HIS MIND TO go to London, to look after his lady-love, but when he found himself there he did not quite know what to do. It is often the case with us that we make up our minds for great action – that in some special crisis of our lives we resolve that something must be done, and that we make an energetic start; but we find very soon that we do not know how to go on doing anything. It was so with Mr Maguire. When he had secured a bed at a small public house near the Great Western railway station – thinking, no doubt that he would go to the great hotel on his next coming to town, should he then have obtained the lady's fortune – he scarcely knew what step he would next take. Margaret's last letter had been written to him from the Cedars, but he thought it probable that she might only have gone there for a day or two. He knew the address of the house in Gower Street, and at last resolved that he would go boldly in among the enemy there; for he was assured that the family of the lady's late brother were his special enemies in this case. It was considerably past noon when he reached London, and it was about three when, with a hesitating hand, but a loud knock, he presented himself at Mrs Mackenzie's door.

He first asked for Miss Mackenzie, and was told that she was not staying there. Was he thereupon to leave his card and go away? He had told himself that in this pursuit of the heiress he would probably be called upon to dare much, and if he did not begin to show some daring at once, how could he respect himself, or trust to himself for future daring? So he boldly asked for Mrs Mackenzie, and was at once shown into the parlour. There sat the widow, in her full lugubrious weeds, there sat Miss Colza, and there sat Mary Jane, and they were all busy hemming, darning, and clipping; turning old sheets into new ones; for now it was more than ever necessary that Mrs Mackenzie should make money at once by taking in lodgers. When Mr Maguire was shown into the room each lady rose from her chair, with her sheet in her hands and in her lap, and then, as he stood before them, at the other side of the table, each lady again sat down.

'A gentleman as is asking for Miss Margaret,' the servant had said; that same cook to whom Mr Grandairs had been so severe on the occasion of Mrs Mackenzie's dinner party. The other girl had been unnecessary to them in their poverty, and had left them.

'My name is Maguire, the Rev. Mr Maguire, from Littlebath, where I had the pleasure of knowing Miss Mackenzie.'

Then the widow asked him to take a chair, and he took a chair.

'My sister-in-law is not with us at present,' said Mrs Mackenzie.

'She is staying for a visit with her aunt, Lady Ball, at the Cedars, Twickenham,' said Mary Jane, who had contrived to drop her sheet, and hustle it under the table with her feet, as soon as she learned that the visitor was a clergyman.

'Lady Ball is the lady of Sir John Ball, Baronet,' said Miss Colza, whose good nature made her desirous of standing up for the honour of the family with which she was, for the time, domesticated.

'I knew she had been at Lady Ball's,' said the clergyman, 'as I heard from her from thence; but I thought she had probably returned.'

'Oh dear, no,' said the widow, 'she ain't returned here, nor don't mean. We haven't the room for her, and that's the truth. Have we, Mary Jane?'

'That we have not, mamma; and I don't think aunt Margaret would think of such a thing.'

Then, thought Mr Maguire, the Balls must have got hold of the heiress, and not the Mackenzies, and my battle must be fought at the Cedars, and not here. Still, as he was there, he thought possibly he might obtain some further information; and this would be the easier, if, as appeared to be the case, there was enmity between the Gower Street family and their relative.

'Has Miss Mackenzie gone to live permanently at the Cedars?' he asked.

'Not that I know of,' said the widow.

'It isn't at all unlikely, mamma, that it may be so, when you consider everything. It's just the sort of way in which they'll most likely get over her.'

'Mary Jane, hold your tongue,' said her mother; 'you shouldn't say things of that sort before strangers.'

'Though I may not have the pleasure of knowing you and your amiable family,' said Mr Maguire, smiling his sweetest, 'I am by no means a stranger to Miss Mackenzie.'

Then the ladies all looked at him, and thought they had never seen anything so terrible as that squint.

'Miss Mackenzie is making a long visit at the Cedars,' said Miss Colza, 'that is all we know at present. I am told the Balls are very nice people, but perhaps a little worldly-minded; that's to be expected, however, from people who live out of the west-end from London. I live in Finsbury Square, or at least, I did before I came here, and I ain't a bit ashamed to own it. But of course the west-end is the nicest.'

Then Mr Maguire got up, saying that he should probably do himself the pleasure of calling on Miss Mackenzie at the Cedars, and went his way.

'I wonder what he's after,' said Mrs Mackenzie, as soon as the door was shut.

'Perhaps he came to tell her to bear it all with Christian resignation,' said Miss Colza; 'they always do come when anything's in the wind like that; they like to know everything before anybody else.'

'It's my belief he's after her money,' said Mrs Mackenzie.

'With such a squint as that!' said Mary Jane; 'I wouldn't have him though he was made of money, and I hadn't a farthing.'

'Beauty is but skin deep,' said Miss Colza.

'And it's manners to wait till you are asked,' said Mrs Mackenzie.

Mary Jane chucked up her head with disdain, thereby indicating that though she had not been asked, and though beauty is but skin deep, still she held the same opinion.

Mr Maguire, as he went away to a clerical advertising office in the neighbourhood of Exeter Hall, thought over the matter profoundly. It was clear enough to him that the Mackenzies of Gower Street were not interfering with him; very probably they might have hoped and attempted to keep the heiress among them; that assertion that there was no room for her in the house – as though they were and ever had been averse to having her with them – seemed to imply that such was the case. It was the natural language of a disappointed woman. But if so, that hope was now over with them. And then the young lady had plainly exposed the suspicions which they all entertained as to the Balls. These grand people at the Cedars, this baronet's family at Twickenham, must have got her to come among them with the intention of keeping her there. It did not occur to him that the baronet or the baronet's son would actually want Miss Mackenzie's money. He presumed baronets to be rich people; but still they might very probably be as dogs in the manger, and desirous of preventing their relative from doing with her money that active service to humanity in general which would be done were she to marry a deserving clergyman who had nothing of his own.

He made his visit to the advertising office, and learned that clergymen without cures were at present drugs in the market. He couldn't understand how this should be the case, seeing that the newspapers were constantly declaring that the supply of university clergymen were becoming less and less every day. He had come from Trinity, Dublin and after the success of his career at Littlebath, was astonished that he should not be snapped at by the retailers of curacies.

On the next day he visited Twickenham. Now, on the morning of that very day Margaret Mackenzie first woke to the consciousness that she was the promised wife of her cousin John Ball. There was great comfort in the thought.

It was not only, nor even chiefly, that she who, on the preceding morning, had awakened to the remembrance of her utter destitution, now felt that all those terrible troubles were over. It was not simply that her great care had been vanquished for her. It was this, that the man who had a second time come to her asking for her love, had now given her all-sufficient evidence that he did so for the sake of her love. He, who was so anxious for money, had shown her that he could care for her more even than he cared for gold. As she thought of this, and made herself happy in the thought, she would not rise at once from her bed, but curled herself in the clothes and hugged herself in her joy.

'I should have taken him before, at once, instantly, if I could have thought that it was so,' she said to herself; 'but this is a thousand times better.'

Then she found that the pillow beneath her cheek was wet with her tears.

On the preceding evening she had been very silent and demure, and her betrothed had also been silent. There had been no words about the tea-making, and Lady Ball had been silent also. As far as she knew, Margaret was to go on the following day, but she would say nothing on the subject. Margaret, indeed, had commenced her packing, and did not know when she went to bed whether she was to go or not. She rather hoped that she might be allowed to go, as her aunt would doubtless be disagreeable; but in that, and in all matters now, she would of course be guided implicitly by Mr Ball. He had told her to be firm, and of her own firmness she had no doubt whatever. Lady Ball, with all her anger, or with all her eloquence. should not talk her out of her husband. She could be firm, and she had no doubt that John Ball could be firm also.

Nevertheless, when she was dressing, she did not fail to tell herself that she might have a bad time of it that morning – and a bad time of it for some days to come, if it was John's intention that she should remain at the Cedars. She was convinced that Lady Ball would not welcome her as a daughter-in-law now as she would have done when the property was thought to belong to her. What right had she to expect such welcome? No doubt some hard things would be said to her; but she knew her own courage, and was sure that she could bear any hard things with such a hope within her breast as that which she now possessed. She left her room a little earlier than usual, thinking that she might thus meet her cousin and receive his orders. And in this she was not disappointed; he was in the hall as she came down, and she was able to smile on him, and press his hand, and make her morning greetings to him with some tenderness in her voice. He looked heavy about the face, and almost more careworn than usual, but he took her hand and led her into the breakfast-room.

'Did you tell your mother, John? ' she said, standing very close to him, almost leaning upon his shoulder.

He, however, did not probably want such signs of love as this, and moved a step away from her.

'Yes,' said he, 'I told both my father and my mother. What she says to you, you must hear, and bear it quietly for my sake.'

'I will,' said Margaret.

'I think that she is unreasonable, but still she is my mother.'

'I shall always remember that, John.'

'And she is old, and things have not always gone well with her. She says, too, that you have been impertinent to her.'

Margaret's face became very red at this charge, but she made no immediate reply.

'I don't think you could mean to be impertinent.'

'Certainly not, John; but, of course, I shall feel myself much more bound to her now than I was before.'

'Yes, of course; but I wish that nothing had occurred to make her so angry with you.'

'I don't think that I was impertinent, John, though perhaps it might seem so. When she was talking about my being a companion to a lady, I perhaps answered her sharply. I was so determined that I wouldn't lead that sort of life, that, perhaps I said more than I should have done. You know, John, that it hasn't been quite pleasant between us for the last few days.'

John did know this, and he knew also that there was not much probability of pleasantness for some days to come. His mother's last words to him on the preceding evening, as he was leaving her after having told his story, did not give much promise of pleasantness for Margaret. 'John,' she had said, 'nothing on earth shall induce me to live in the same house with Margaret Mackenzie as your wife. If you choose to break up everything for her sake, you can do it. I cannot control you. But remember, it will be your doing.'

Margaret then asked him what she was to do, and where she was to live. She would fain have asked him when they were to be married, but she did not dare to make inquiry on that point. He told her that, for the present, she must remain at the Cedars. If she went away it would be regarded as an open quarrel, and moreover, he did not wish that she should live by herself in London lodgings. 'We shall be able to see how things go for a day or two,' he said. To this she submitted without a murmur, and then Lady Ball came into the room.

They were both very nervous in watching her first behaviour, but were not at all prepared for the line of conduct which she adopted. John Ball and Margaret had separated when they heard the rustle of her dress. He had made a step towards the window, and she had retreated to the other side of the fire-place. Lady Ball, on entering the room, had been nearest to Margaret, but she walked round the table away from her usual place for prayers, and accosted her son.

'Good-morning, John,' she said, giving him her hand.

Margaret waited a second or two, and then addressed her aunt.

'Good-morning, aunt,' she said, stepping half across the rug.

But her aunt, turning her back to her, moved into the embrasure of the window. It had been decided that there was to be an absolute cut between them! As long as she remained in that house Lady Ball would not speak to her. John said nothing, but a black frown came upon his brow. Poor Margaret retired, rebuked, to her corner by the chimney. Just at that moment the girls and children rushed in from the study, with the daily governess who came every morning, and Sir John rang for the servants to come to prayers.

I wonder whether that old lady's heart was at all softened as she prayed? whether it ever occurred to her to think that there was any meaning in that form of words she used, when she asked her God to forgive her as she might forgive others? Not that Margaret had in truth trespassed against her at all; but, doubtless, she regarded her niece as a black trespasser, and as being quite qualified for forgiveness, could she have brought herself to forgive. But I fear that the form of words on that occasion meant nothing, and that she had been delivered from no evil during those moments she had been on her knees. Margaret sat down in her accustomed place, but no notice was taken of her by her aunt. When the tea had been poured out, John got up from his seat and asked his mother which was Margaret's cup.

'My dear,' said she, 'if you will sit down, Miss Mackenzie shall have her tea.'

'I will take it to her,' said he.

'John,' said his mother, drawing her chair somewhat away from the table, 'if you flurry me in this way, you will drive me out of the room.'

Then he had sat down, and Margaret received her cup in the usual way. The girls and children stared at each other, and the governess, who always breakfasted at the house, did not dare to lift her eyes from off her plate.

Margaret longed for an opportunity of starting with John Ball, and walking with him to the station, but no such opportunity came in her way. It was his custom always to go up to his father before he left home, and on this occasion Margaret did not see him after he quitted the breakfast table. When the clatter of the knives and cups was over, and the eating and drinking was at an end, Lady Ball left the room and Margaret began to think what she would do. She could not remain about the house in her aunt's way, without being spoken to, or speaking. So she went to her room, resolving that she would not leave it till the carriage had taken off Sir John and her aunt. Then she would go out for a walk, and would again meet her cousin at the station.

From her bedroom window she could see the sweep before the front of the house, and at two o'clock she saw and heard the lumbering of the carriage as it came to the door, and then she put on her hat to be ready for her walk; but her uncle and aunt did not, as it seemed, come out, and the carriage remained there as a fixture. This had been the case for some twenty minutes, when there came a knock at her own door, and the maid-servant told her that her aunt wished to see her in the drawing-room.

'To see me?' said Margaret, thoroughly surprised, and not a little dismayed.

'Yes, Miss; and there's a gentleman there who asked for you when he first come.'

Now, indeed, she was dismayed. Who could be the gentleman? Was it Mr Slow, or a myrmidon from Mr Slow's legal abode? Or was it Mr Rubb with his yellow gloves again? Whoever it was there must be something very special in his mission, as her aunt had, in consequence, deferred her drive, and was also apparently about to drop her purpose of cutting her niece's acquaintance in her own house.

But we will go back to Mr Maguire. He had passed the evening and the morning in thinking over the method of his attack, and had at last resolved that he would be very bold. He would go down to the Cedars, and claim Margaret as his affianced bride. He went, therefore, down to the Cedars, and in accordance with his plan as arranged, he gave his card to the servant, and asked if he could see Sir John Ball alone. Now, Sir John

Ball never saw any one on business, or, indeed, not on business; and, after a while, word was brought out to Mr Maguire that he could see Lady Ball, but that Sir John was not well enough to receive any visitors. Lady Ball, Mr Maguire thought, would suit him better than Sir John. He signified his will accordingly, and on being shown into the drawing-room, found her ladyship there alone.

It must be acknowledged that he was a brave man, and that he was doing a bold thing. He knew that he should find himself among enemies, and that his claim would be ignored and ridiculed by the persons whom he was about to attack; he knew that everybody, on first seeing him, was affrighted and somewhat horrified; he knew too – at least, we must presume that he knew – that the lady herself had given him no promise. But he thought it possible, nay, almost probable, that she would turn to him if she saw him again; that she might own him as her own; that her feelings might be strong enough in his favour to induce her to throw off the thraldom of her relatives, and that he might make good his ground in her breast, even if he could not bear her away in triumph out of the hands of his enemies.

When he entered the room Lady Ball looked at him and shuddered. People always did shudder when they saw him for the first time.

'Lady Ball,' said he, 'I am the Rev. Mr Maguire, of Littlebath.'

She was holding his card in her hand, and having notified to him that she was aware of the fact he had mentioned, asked him to sit down.

'I have called,' said he, taking his seat, 'hoping to be allowed to speak to you on a subject of extreme delicacy.'

'Indeed,' said Lady Ball, thinking to catch his eye, and failing in the effort.

'I may say of very extreme delicacy. I believe your niece, Miss Margaret Mackenzie, is staying here?' In answer to this, Lady Ball acknowledged that Miss Mackenzie was now at the Cedars.

'Have you any objection, Lady Ball, to allowing me to see her in your presence?'

Lady Ball was a quick-thinking, intelligent, and, at the same time, prudent old lady, and she gave no answer to this before she had considered the import of the question. Why should this clergyman want to see Margaret?. And would his seeing her conduce most to her own success, or to Margaret's? Then there was the fact that Margaret was of an age which entitled her to the right of seeing any visitor who might call on her. Thinking over all this as best she could in the few moments at her command, and thinking also of this clergyman's stipulation that she was to be present at the interview, she said that she had no objection whatever. She would send for Miss Mackenzie.

She rose to ring the bell, but Mr Maguire, also rising from his chair, stopped her hand.

'Pardon me for a moment,' said he. 'Before you call Margaret to come down I would wish to explain to you for what purpose I have come here.'

Lady Ball, when she heard the man call her niece by her Christian name, listened with all her ears. Under no circumstances but one could such a man call such a woman by her Christian name in such company.

'Lady Ball,' he said, 'I do not know whether you may be aware of it or no, but I am engaged to marry your niece.'

Lady Ball, who had not yet resumed her seat, now did so.

'I had not heard of it,' she said.

'It may be so,' said Mr Maguire.

'It is so,' said Lady Ball.

'Very probably. There are many reasons which operate upon young ladies in such a condition to keep their secret even from their nearest relatives. For myself, being a clergyman of the Church of England, professing evangelical doctrines, and therefore, as I had need not say, averse to everything that may have about it even a seeming of impropriety, I think it best to declare the fact to you, even though in doing so I may perhaps give some offence to dear Margaret.'

It must, I think, be acknowledged that Mr Maguire was true to himself, and that he was conducting his case at any rate with courage.

Lady Ball was doubtful what she would do. It was on her tongue to tell the man that her niece's fortune was gone. But she remembered that she might probably advance her own interests by securing an interview between the two lovers of Littlebath in her own presence. She never for a moment doubted that Mr Maguire's statement was true. It never occurred to her that there had been no such engagement. She felt confident from the moment in which Mr Maguire's important tidings had reached her ears that she had now in her hands the means of rescuing her son. That Mr Maguire would cease to make his demand for his bride when he should hear the truth, was of course to be expected; but her son would not be such an idiot, such a soft fool, as to go on with his purpose when he should learn that such a secret as this had been kept back from him. She had refused him, and taken up with this horrid, greasy, evil-eyed parson when she was rich; and then, when she was poor – even before she had got rid of her other engagement, she had come back upon him, and, playing upon his pity, had secured him in her toils. Lady Ball felt well inclined to thank the clergyman for coming to her relief at such a moment.

'It will be best that I should ask my niece to come down to you,' said she, getting up and walking out of the room.

But she did not go up to her niece. She first went to Sir John and quieted his impatience with reference to the driving, and then, after a few minutes' further delay for consideration, she sent the servant up to her niece. Having done this she returned to the drawing-room, and found Mr Maguire looking at the photographs on the table.

'It is very like dear Margaret, very like her, indeed,' said he, looking at one of Miss Mackenzie. 'The sweetest face that ever my eyes rested on! May I ask you if you have just seen your niece, Lady Ball?'

'No, sir, I have not seen her; but I have sent for her.'

There was still some little delay before Margaret came down. She was much fluttered, and wanted time to think, if only time could be allowed to her. Perhaps there had come a man to say that her money was not gone. If so, with what delight would she give it all to her cousin John! That was her first thought. But if so, how then about the promise made to her dying brother? She almost wished that the money might not be hers. Looking to herself only, and to her own happiness, it would certainly be better for her that it should not be hers. And if it should be Mr Rubb with the yellow gloves! But before she could consider that alternative she had opened the door, and there was Mr Maguire standing ready to receive her.

'Dearest Margaret!' he exclaimed. 'My own love!' And there he stood, with his arms open, as though he expected Miss Mackenzie to rush into them. He was certainly a man of very great courage.

'Mr Maguire!' said she, and she stood still near the door. Then she looked at her aunt, and saw that Lady Ball's eyes were keenly fixed upon her. Something like the truth, some approximation to the facts as they were, flashed upon her in a moment, and she knew that she had to bear herself in this difficulty with all her discretion and all her fortitude.

'Margaret,' exclaimed Mr Maguire, 'will you not come to me?'

'What do you mean, Mr Maguire?' said she, still standing aloof from him, and retreating somewhat nearer to the door.

'The gentleman says that you are engaged to marry him,' said Lady Ball.

Margaret, looking again into her aunt's face, saw the smile of triumph that sat there, and resolved at once to make good her ground.

'If he has said that, he has told an untruth – an untruth both unmanly and unmannerly. You hear, sir, what Lady Ball has stated. Is it true that you have made such an assertion?'

'And will you contradict it, Margaret? Oh, Margaret! Margaret! you cannot contradict it.'

The reader must remember that this clergyman no doubt thought and felt that he had a good deal of truth on his side. Gentlemen when they make offers to ladies, and are told by ladies that they may come again, and that time is required for consideration, are always disposed to think that the difficulties of the siege are over. And in nine cases out of ten it is so. Mr Maguire, no doubt, since the interview in question, had received letters from the lady which should at any rate have prevented him from uttering any such assertion as that which he had now made; but he looked upon those letters as the work of the enemy, and chose to go back for his authority to the last words which Margaret had spoken to him. He knew that he was playing an intricate game – that all was not quite on the square; but he thought that the enemy was playing him false, and that falsehood in return was therefore fair. This that was going on was a robbery of the Church, a spoiling of Israel, a touching with profane hands of things that had already been made sacred.

'But I do contradict it,' said Margaret, stepping forward into the room, and almost exciting admiration in Lady Ball's breast by her demeanour. 'Aunt,' said she, 'as this gentleman has chosen to come here with such a story as this, I must tell you all the facts.'

'Has he ever been engaged to you?' asked Lady Ball.

'Never.'

'Oh, Margaret!' again exclaimed Mr Maguire.

'Sir, I will ask you to let me tell my aunt the truth. When I was at Littlebath, before I knew that my fortune was not my own' – as she said this she looked hard into Mr Maguire's face – 'before I had become penniless, as I am now' – then she paused again, and still looking at him, saw with inward pleasure the elongation of her suitor's face, 'this gentleman asked me to marry him.'

'He did ask you?' said Lady Ball.

'Of course I asked her,' urged Mr Maguire. 'There can be no denying that on either side.'

He did not now quite know what to do. He certainly did not wish to impoverish the Church by marrying Miss Mackenzie without any fortune. But might it not all be a trick? That she had been rich he knew, and how could she have become poor so quickly?

'He did ask me, and I told him that I must take a fortnight to consider of it.'

'You did not refuse him, then?' said Lady Ball.

'Not then, but I have done so since by letter. Twice I have written to him, telling him that I had nothing of my own, and that there could be nothing between us.'

'I got her letters,' said Mr Maguire, turning round to Lady Ball. 'I certainly got her letters. But such letters as those, if they are written under dictation –'

He was rather anxious that Lady Bell should quarrel with him. In the programme which he had made for himself when he came to the house, a quarrel to the knife with the Ball family was a part of his tactics. His programme, no doubt, was disturbed by the course which events had taken, but still a quarrel with Lady Ball might be the best for him. If she were to quarrel with him, it would give him some evidence that this story about the loss of the money was untrue. But Lady Ball would not quarrel with him. She sat still and said nothing. 'Nobody dictated them,' said Margaret. 'But now you are here, I will tell you the facts. The money which I thought was mine, in truth belongs to my cousin, Mr John Ball, and I –'

So far she spoke loudly, With her face raised, and her eyes fixed upon him. Then as she concluded, she dropped her voice and eyes together. 'And I am now engaged to him as his wife.'

'Oh, indeed!' said Mr Maguire.

'That statement must be taken for what it is worth,' said Lady Ball, rising from her seat. 'Of what Miss Mackenzie says now, I know nothing. I sincerely hope that she may find that she is mistaken.'

'And now, Margaret,' said Mr Maguire, 'may I ask to see you for one minute alone?'

'Certainly not,' said she. 'If you have anything more to say I will hear it in my aunt's presence.' She waited a few moments, but as he did not speak, she took herself back to the door and made her escape to her own room.

How Mr Maguire took himself out of the house we need not stop to inquire. There must, I should think, have been some difficulty in the manoeuvre. It was considerably past three when Sir John was taken out for his drive, and while he was in the carriage his wife told him what had occurred.

✶ TWENTY-TWO ✶

Still at the Cedars

MARGARET, WHEN SHE HAD REACHED HER OWN room, and seated herself so that she could consider all that had occurred in quietness, immediately knew her own difficulty. Of course Lady Ball would give her account of what had occurred to her son, and of course John would be angry when he learned that there had been any purpose of marriage between her and Mr Maguire. She herself took a different view of the matter now than that which had hitherto presented itself. She had not thought much of Mr Maguire or his proposal. It had been made under a state of things differing much from that now existing, and the change that had come upon her affairs had seemed to her to annul the offer. She had learned to regard it almost as though it had never been. There had been no engagement; there had hardly been a purpose in her own mind; and the moment had never come in which she could have spoken of it to her cousin with propriety.

That last, in truth, was her valid excuse for not having told him the whole story. She had hardly been with him long enough to do more than accept the offer he had himself made. Of course she would have told him of Mr Maguire – of Mr Maguire and of Mr Rubb also, when first an opportunity might come for her to do so. She had no desire to keep from his knowledge any tittle of what had occurred. There had been nothing of which she was ashamed. But not the less did she feel that it would have been well for her that she should have told her own story before that horrid man had come to the Cedars. The story would now first be told to him by her aunt, and she knew well the tone in which it would be told.

It occurred to her that she might even yet go and meet him at the station. But if so, she must tell him at once, and he would know that she had done so because she was afraid of her aunt, and she disliked the idea of excusing herself before she was accused. If he really loved her, he would listen to her, and believe her. If he did not – why then let Lady Ball have her own way. She had promised to be firm, and she would keep her promise; but she would not intrigue with the hope of making him firm. If he was infirm of purpose, let him go. So she sat in her room, even when she heard the door close after his entrance, and did not go down till it was time for her to show herself in the drawing-room before dinner. When she entered the room was full. He nodded at her with a pleasant smile, and she made up her mind that he had heard nothing as yet. Her uncle had excused himself from coming to table, and her aunt and John were talking together in apparent eagerness about him. For one moment her cousin spoke to her before dinner.

'I am afraid,' he said, 'that my father is sinking fast.'

Then she felt quite sure that he had as yet heard nothing about Mr Maguire.

But it was late in the evening, when other people had gone to bed, that Lady Ball was in the habit of discussing family affairs with her son, and doubtless she would do so to-night. Margaret, before she went up to her room, strove hard to get from him a few words of kindness, but it seemed as though he was not thinking of her.

'He is full of his father,' she said to herself.

When her bed-candle was in her hand she did make an opportunity to speak to him.

'Has Mr Slow settled anything more as yet? ' she asked.

'Well, yes. Not that he has settled anything, but he has made a proposition to which I am willing to agree. I don't go up to town tomorrow, and we will talk it over. If you will agree to it, all the money difficulties will be settled.'

'I will agree to anything that you tell me is right.'

'I will explain it all to you to-morrow; and, Margaret, I have told Mr Slow what are my intentions – our intentions, I ought to say.' She smiled at him with that sweet smile of hers, as though she thanked him for speaking of himself and her together, and then she took herself away. Surely, after speaking to her in that way, he would not allow any words from his mother to dissuade him from his purpose?

She could not go to bed. She knew that her fate was being discussed, and she knew that her aunt at that very time was using every argument in her power to ruin her. She felt, moreover, that the story might be told in such a way as to be terribly prejudicial to her. And now, when his father was so ill, might it not be very natural that he should do almost anything to lessen his mother's troubles? But to her it would be absolute ruin; such ruin that nothing which she had yet endured would be in any way like it. The story of the loss of her money had stunned her, but it had not broken her spirit. Her misery from that had arisen chiefly from the wants of her brother's family. But if he were now to tell her that all must be over between them, her very heart would be broken.

She could not go to bed while this was going on, so she sat listening, till she should hear the noise of feet about the house. Silently she loosened the lock of her own door, so that the sound might more certainly come to her, and she sat thinking what she might best do. It had not been quite eleven when she came upstairs, and at twelve she did not hear anything. And yet she was almost sure that they must be still together in that small room downstairs, talking of her and of her conduct. It was past one before she heard the door of the room open. She heard it so plainly, that she wondered at herself for having supposed for a moment that they could have gone without her noticing them. Then she heard her cousin's heavy step coming upstairs. In passing to his room he would not go actually by her door, but would be very near it. She looked through the chink, having carefully put away her own candle, and could see his face as he came upon the top stair. It wore a look of trouble and of pain, but not, as she thought, of anger. Her aunt, she knew, would go to her room by the back stairs, and would go through the kitchen and over the whole of the lower house, before she would come out on the landing to which Margaret's room opened. Then, seeing her cousin, the idea occurred to her that she would have it all over on that very night. If he had heard that which changed his purpose, why should she be left in suspense? He should tell her at once, and at once she would prepare herself for her future life.

So she opened the door a little way, and called to him.

'John,' she said, 'is that you?'

She spoke almost in a whisper; but, nevertheless, he heard her very clearly, and at once turned towards her room.

'Come in, John,' she said, opening the door wider. 'I wish to speak to you. I have been waiting till you should come up.'

She had taken off her dress, and had put on in place of it a white dressing-gown; but of this she had not thought till he was already within the room. 'I hope you won't mind finding me like this, but I did so want to speak to you to-night.'

He, as he looked at her, felt that he had no objection to make to her appearance. If that had been his only trouble concerning her he would have been well satisfied. When he was within the room, she closed the lock of the door very softly, and then began to question him.

'Tell me,' she said, 'what my aunt has been saying to you about that man that came here to-day.'

He did not answer her at once, but stood leaning against the bed.

'I know she has been telling you,' continued Margaret. 'I know she would not let you go to bed without accusing me. Tell me, John, what she has told you.'

He was very slow to speak. As he had sat listening to his mother's energetic accusation against the woman he had promised to marry, hearing her bring up argument after argument to prove that Margaret had, in fact, been engaged to that clergyman – that she had intended to marry that man while she had money, and had not, up to that day, made him fully understand that she would not do so – he had himself said little or nothing, claiming to himself the use of that night for consideration. The circumstances against Margaret he owned to be very strong. He felt angry with her for having had any lover at Littlebath. It was but the other day, during her winter visit to the Cedars, that he had himself proposed to her, and that she had rejected him. He had now renewed his proposal, and he did not like to think that there had been any one else between his overtures. And he could not deny the strength of his mother's argument when she averred that Mr Maguire would not have come down there unless he had had, as she said, every encouragement. Indeed, throughout the whole affair, Lady Ball believed Mr Maguire, and disbelieved her niece; and something of her belief, and something also of her disbelief, communicated itself to her son. But, still, he reserved to himself the right of postponing his own opinion till the morrow; and as he was coming upstairs, when Margaret saw him through the chink of the door, he was thinking of her smiles, of her graciousness, and her goodness. He was remembering the touch of her hand when they were together in the square, and the feminine sweetness with which she had yielded to him every point regarding her fortune. When he did not speak to her at once, she questioned him again.

'I know she has told you that Mr Maguire has been here, and that she has accused me of deceiving you.'

'Yes, Margaret, she has.'

'And what have you said in return; or rather, what have you thought?'

He had been leaning, or half sitting, on the bed, and she had placed herself beside him. How was it that she had again taken him by the coat, and again looked up into his face with those soft, trusting eyes? Was it a trick with her? Had she ever taken that other man by the coat in the same way, and smitten him also with the battery of her eyes? The loose sleeve of her dressing-gown had fallen back, and he could see that her arm was round and white, and very fair. Was she conversant with such tricks as these? His mother had called her clever and cunning as a serpent. Was it so? Had his mother seen with eyes clearer than his own, and was he now being surrounded by the meshes of a false woman's web? He moved away from her quickly, and stood upon the hearth-rug with his back to the empty fire grate.

Then she stood up also.

'John,' she said, 'if you have condemned me, say so. I shall defend myself for the sake of my character, but I shall not ask you to come back to me.'

But he had not condemned her. He had not condemned her altogether, neither had he acquitted her. He was willing enough to hear her defence, as he had heard his mother's accusation; but he was desirous of hearing it without committing himself to any opinion.

'I have been much surprised,' he said, 'by what my mother has now told me – very much surprised indeed. If Mr Maguire had any claim upon your hand, should you not have told me?'

'He had no claim; but no doubt it was right that I should tell you. I was bound by my duty to tell you everything that had occurred.'

'Of course you were – and yet you did not do it.'

'But I was not so bound before what you said to me in the shrubbery last night? Remember, John, it was but last night. Have I had a moment to speak to you?'

'If there was any question of engagement between you and him, you should have told it me then, on the instant.'

'But there was no question. He came to me one day and made me an offer. I will tell you everything, and I think you will believe me. I found him holding a position of respect, at Littlebath, and I was all alone in the world. Why should I not listen to him? I gave him no answer, but told him to speak to me again after a while. Then came my poor brother's illness and death; and after that came, as you know, the loss of all my money. In the meantime Mr Maguire had written, but as I knew that my brother's family must trust to me for their support – that, at least, John was my hope then – I answered him that my means were not the same as before, and that everything must be over. Then he wrote to me again after I had lost my money, and once I answered him. I wrote to him so that he should know that nothing could come of it. Here are all his letters, and I have a copy of the last I wrote to him.' So saying, she pulled the papers out of her desk – the desk in which still lay the torn shreds of her poetry – and handed them to him. 'After that, what right had he to come here and make such a statement as he did to my aunt? How can he be a gentleman, and say what was so false?'

'No one says that he is a gentleman,' replied John Ball, as he took the proffered papers.

'I have told you all now,' said she; and as she spoke, a gleam of anger flashed from her eyes, for she was not in all respects a Griselda such as she of old. 'I have told you all now, and if further excuse be wanting, I have none further to make.'

Slowly he read the letters, still standing up on the hearth-rug, and then he folded them again into their shapes, and slowly gave them back to her.

'There is no doubt,' said he, 'as to his being a blackguard. He was hunting for your money, and now that he knows you have got none, he will trouble you no further.' Then he made a move from the place on which he stood, as if he were going.

'And is that to be all, John?' she said.

'I shall see you to-morrow,' he replied. 'I am not going to town.'

'But is that to be all to-night?'

'It is very late,' and he looked at his watch. 'I do not see that any good can come of talking more about it now. Good-night to you.'

'Good-night,' she said. Then she waited till the door was closed, and when he was gone she threw herself upon the bed. Alas! alas! Now once more was she ruined, and her present ruin was ruin indeed.

She threw herself on the bed, and sobbed as though she would have broken her heart in the bitterness of her spirit. She had told him the plainest, simplest truest story, and he had received it without one word of comment in her favour – without one sign to show that her truthfulness had been acknowledged by him! He had told her that this man, who had done her so great an injury, was a blackguard; but of her own conduct he had not allowed himself to speak. She knew that his judgment had gone against her, and though she felt it to be hard – very hard – she resolved that she would make no protest against it. Of course she would leave the Cedars. Only a few hours since she had assured herself that it was her duty henceforward to obey him in everything. But that was now all changed. Whatever he might say to the contrary, she would go. If he chose to follow her whither she went, and again ask her to be his wife she would receive him with open arms. Oh, yes; let him only once again own that she was worthy of him, and then she would sit at his feet and confess her folly, and ask his pardon a thousand times for the trouble she had given him. But unless he were to do this she would never again beg for favour. She had made her defence, and had, as she felt, made it in vain. She would not condescend to say one other word in excuse of her conduct.

As for her aunt, all terms between Lady Ball and herself must be at an end. Lady Ball had passed a day with her in the house without speaking to her, except when that man had come, and then she had taken part with him! Her aunt, she thought, had been untrue to hospitality in not defending the guest within her own walls; she had been untrue to her own blood, in not defending her husband's niece; but, worse than all that, ten times worse, she had been untrue as from one woman to another! Margaret, as she thought of this, rose from the bed and walked wildly through the room unlike any Griselda. No; she would have no terms with Lady Ball. Lady Ball had understood it all, though John had not done so! She had known how it all was, and had pretended not to know. Because she had an object of her own to gain, she had allowed these calumnies to be believed! Let come what might, they should all know that Margaret Mackenzie, poor, wretched, destitute as she was, had still spirit enough to resent such injuries as these.

In the morning she sent down word by one of her young cousins that she would not come to breakfast, and she asked that some tea might be sent up to her.

'Is she in bed, my dear?' asked Lady Ball.

'No, she is not in bed,' said Jane Ball. 'She is sitting up, and has got all her things about the room as though she were packing.'

'What nonsense!' said Lady Ball; 'why does she not come down?'

Then Isabella, the eldest girl, was sent up to her, but Margaret refused to show herself.

'She says she would rather not; but she wants to know if papa will walk out with her at ten.'

Lady Ball again said that this was nonsense, but tea and toast were at last supplied to her, and her cousin promised to be ready at the hour named. Exactly at ten o'clock, Margaret opened the schoolroom door, and asked one of the girls to tell her father that she would be found on the walk leading to the long shrubbery.

There on the walk she remained, walking slowly backwards and forwards over a space of twenty yards, till he joined her. She gave him her hand, and then turned towards the long shrubbery, and he, following her direction, walked at her side.

'John,' she said, 'you will not be surprised at my telling you that, after what has occurred, I shall leave this place to-day.'

'You must not do that,' he said.

'Ah, but I must do it. There are some things John, which no woman should bear or need bear. After what has occurred it is not right that I should incur your mother's displeasure any longer. All my things are ready. I want you to have them taken down to the one o'clock train.'

'No, Margaret; I will not consent to that.'

'But, John, I cannot consent to anything else. Yesterday was a terrible day for me. I don't think you can know how terrible. What I endured then no one has a right to expect that I should endure any longer. It was necessary that I should say something to you of what had occurred, and that I said last night. I have no further call to remain here, and, most positively, I shall go to-day.'

He looked into her face and saw that she was resolved, but yet he was not minded to give way. He did not like to think that all authority over her was passing out of his hands. During the night he had not made up his mind to pardon her at once. Nay, he had not yet told himself that he would pardon her at all. But he was prepared to receive her tears and excuses, and we may say that, in all probability, he would have pardoned her had she wept before him and excused herself. But though she could shed tears on this matter – though, doubtless, there were many tears to be shed by her – she would shed no more before him in token of submission. If he would first submit, then, indeed, she might weep on his shoulder or laugh on his breast, as his mood might dictate.

'Margaret,' he said, 'we have very much to talk over before you can go.'

'There will be time for that between this and one. Look here, John; I have made up my mind to go. After what took place yesterday, it will be better for us all that we should be apart.'

'I don't see that, unless, indeed, you are determined to quarrel with us altogether. I suppose my wishes in the matter will count for something.'

'Yesterday morning they would have counted for everything; but not this morning.'

'And why not, Margaret?'

This was a question to which it was so difficult to find a reply, that she left it unanswered. They both walked on in silence for some paces, and then she spoke again.

'You said yesterday that you had been with Mr Slow, and that you had something to tell me. If you still wish to tell me anything, perhaps you can do so now.'

'Everything seems to be so much changed,' said he, speaking very gloomily.

'Yes,' said she; 'things are changed. But my confidence in Mr Slow, and in you, is not altered. If you like it, you can settle everything about the money without consulting me. I shall agree to anything about that.'

'I was going to propose that your brother's family should have the debt due by the Rubbs. Mr Slow thinks he might so manage as to secure the payment of the interest.'

'Very well; I shall be delighted that it should be so. I had hoped that they would have had more, but that of course is all over. I cannot give them what is not mine.'

But this arrangement, which would have been pleasant enough before – which seemed to be very pleasant when John Ball was last in Mr Slow's chambers, telling that gentleman that he was going to make everything smooth by marrying his cousin – was not by any means so pleasant now. He had felt, when he was mentioning the proposed arrangement to Margaret, that the very naming of it seemed to imply that Mr Maguire and his visit were to go for nothing. If Mr Maguire and his visit were to go for much – to go for all that which Lady Ball wished to make of them – then, in such a case as that, the friendly arrangement in question would not hold water. If that were to be so, they must all go to work again, and Mr Slow must be told to do the best in his power for his own client. John Ball was by no means resolved to obey his mother implicitly and make so much of Mr Maguire and his visit as all this; but how could he help doing so if Margaret would go away? He could not as yet bring himself to tell her that Mr Maguire and the visit should go altogether for nothing. He shook his head in his trouble, and pished and pshawed.

'The truth is, Margaret, you can't go to-day.'

'Indeed I shall, John,' said she, smiling. 'You would hardly wish to keep me a prisoner, and the worst you could do would be to keep my luggage from me.'

'Then I must say that you are very obstinate.'

'It is not very often that I resolve to have my own way; but I have resolved now, and you should not try to balk me.'

They had now come round nearly to the house, and she showed, by the direction that she took, that she was going in.

'You will go?' said he.

'Yes,' said she; 'I will go. My address will be at the old house in Arundel Street. Shall I see you again before I go?' she asked him, when she stood on the doorstep. 'Perhaps you will be busy, and I had better say goodbye.'

'Good-bye,' said he, very gloomily; but he took her hand.

'I suppose I had better not disturb my uncle. You will give him my love. And, John, you will tell some one about my luggage; will you not?'

He muttered some affirmative, and then went round from the front of the house, while she entered the hall.

It was now half-past eleven, and she intended to start at half-past twelve. She went into the drawing-room and not finding her aunt, rang the bell. Lady Ball was with Sir John, she was told. She then wrote a note on a scrap of paper, and sent it in:

'DEAR AUNT,

I leave here at half-past twelve. Perhaps you would like to see me before I go.

'M. M.'

Then, while she was waiting for an answer, she went into the school room, and said good-bye to all the children.

'But you are coming back, aunt Meg,' said the youngest girl.

Margaret stooped down to kiss her, and, when the child saw and felt the tears, she asked no further questions.

'Lady Ball is in the drawing-room, Miss,' a servant said at that moment, and there she went to fight her last battle!

'What's the meaning of this, Margaret?' said her aunt.

'Simply that I am going. I was to have gone on Monday, as you will remember.'

'But it was understood that you were to stop.'

For a moment or two Margaret said nothing.

'I hate these sudden changes,' said Lady Ball; 'they are hardly respectable. I don't think you should leave the house in this way, without having given notice to any one. What will the servants think of it?'

'They will probably think the truth, aunt. They probably thought that, when they saw that you did not speak to me yesterday morning. You can hardly imagine that I should stay in the house under such circumstances as that.'

'You must do as you like, of course.'

'In this instance I must, aunt. I suppose I cannot see my uncle?'

'It is quite out of the question.'

'Then I will say good-bye to you. I have said good-bye to John. Good-bye, aunt,' and Margaret put out her hand.

But Lady Ball did not put out hers.

'Good-bye, Margaret,' she said. 'There are circumstances under which it is impossible for a person to make any expression of feeling that may be taken for approbation. I hope a time may come when these things shall have passed away, and that I may be able to see you again.' Margaret's eyes, as she made her way out of the room were full of tears, and when she found herself outside the hall door, and at the bottom of the steps, she was obliged to put her handkerchief up to them. Before her on the road was a boy with a donkey cart and her luggage. She looked round furtively, half-fearing, half hoping - hardly expecting, but yet thinking, that she might again see her cousin. But he did not show himself to her as she walked down to the railway station by herself. As she went she told herself that she was right; she applauded her own courage, but what, oh! what was she to do? Everything now was over for her. Her fortune was gone. The man whom she had learned to love had left her. There was no place in the world on which her feet might rest till she had made one for herself by the work of her hands. And as for friends – was there a single being in the world whom she could now call her friend?

❋ TWENTY-THREE ❋

The Lodgings of Mrs Buggins, *née* Protheroe

IT WAS NEARLY THE END OF OCTOBER when Miss Mackenzie left the Cedars and at that time of the year there is not much difficulty in getting lodgings in London. The house which her brother Walter occupied in Arundel Street had, at his death, remained in the hands of an old servant of his, who had bought her late master's furniture with her savings, and had continued to live there, letting out the house in lodgings. Her former mistress had gone to see her once or twice during the past year, and it had been understood between them, that if Miss Mackenzie ever wanted a room for a night or two in London, she could be accommodated at the old house. She would have preferred to write to Hannah Protheroe – or Mrs Protheroe, as she was now called by brevet rank since she had held a house of her own – had time permitted her to do so. But time and the circumstances did not permit this, and therefore she had herself driven to Arundel Street without any notice.

Mrs Protheroe received her with open arms, and with many promises of comfort and attendance – as was to be expected, seeing that Mrs Protheroe was, as she thought, receiving into her house the rich heiress. She proffered at once the use of her drawing-room and of the best bedroom, and declared that as the house was now empty, with the exception of one young gentleman from Somerset House upstairs, she would be able to devote herself almost exclusively to Miss Mackenzie. Things were much changed from those former days in which Hannah Protheroe used frequently to snub Margaret Mackenzie, being almost of equal standing in the house with her young mistress. And now Margaret was called upon to explain, that low as her standing might have been then, at this present moment it was even lower. She had indeed the means of paying for her lodgings, but these she was called upon to husband with the minutest economy. The task of telling all this was difficult. She began it by declining the drawing-room, and by saying that a bedroom upstairs would suffice for her.

'You haven't heard, Hannah, what has happened to me,' she said, when Mrs Protheroe expressed her surprise at this decision. 'My brother's will was no will at all. I do not get any of his property. It all goes under some other will to my cousin, Mr John Ball.'

By these tidings Hannah was of course prostrated, and driven into a state of excitement that was not without its pleasantness as far as she was concerned. Of course she objected that the last will must be the real will, and in this way the matter came to full discussion between them.

'And, after all, that John Ball is to have everything!' said Mrs Protheroe, holding up both her hands. By this time Hannah Protheroe had got herself comfortably into a chair, and no doubt her personal pleasure in the evening's occupation was considerably enhanced by the unconscious feeling that she was the richer woman of the two. But she behaved very well, and I am inclined to think, in preparing buttered muffins for her guest, she was more particular in the toasting, and more generous with the butter, than she would have been had she been preparing the dainty for drawing-room use. And when she learned that Margaret had eaten nothing since breakfast, she herself went out and brought in a sweetbread with her own hand, though she kept a servant whom she might have sent to the shop. And, for the honour of lodging-house keepers, I protest that that sweetbread never made its appearance in any bill.

'You will be more comfortable down here with me, won't you, my dear, than up there, with not a creature to speak to?'

In this way Mrs Protheroe made her apology for giving Miss Mackenzie her tea downstairs, in a little back parlour behind the kitchen. It was a tidy room, with two wooden armchairs, and a bit of carpet over the flags in the centre, and a rug before the fire. Margaret did not inquire why it smelt of tobacco, nor did Mrs Protheroe think it necessary to give any explanation why she went up herself at half-past seven to answer the bell at the area; nor did she say anything then of the office messenger from Somerset House, who often found this little room convenient for his evening pipe. So was passed the first evening after our Griselda had left the Cedars.

The next day she sat at home doing nothing – still talking to Hannah Protheroe, and thinking that perhaps John Ball might come. But he did not come. She dined downstairs, at one o'clock, in the same room behind the kitchen, and then she had tea at six. But as Hannah intimated that perhaps a gentleman friend would look in during the evening, she was obliged to betake herself, after tea, to the solitude of her own room. As Hannah was between fifty and sixty, and nearer the latter age than the former, there could be no objection to her receiving what visitors she pleased. The third day passed with Miss Mackenzie the same as the second, and still no cousin came to see her. The next day, being Sunday, she diversified by going to church three times; but on the Sunday she was forced to dine alone, as the gentleman friend usually came in on that day to eat his bit of mutton with his friend, Mrs Protheroe.

'A most respectable man, in the Admiralty branch, Miss Margaret, and will have a pension of twenty-seven shillings and sixpence a week in a year or two. And it is so lonely by oneself, you know.'

Then Miss Mackenzie knew that Hannah Protheroe intended to become Hannah Buggins, and she understood the whole mystery of the tobacco smoke.

On the Monday she went to the house in Gower Street, and communicated to them the fact that she had left the Cedars. Miss Colza was in the room with her sister-in-law and nieces, and as it was soon evident that Miss Colza knew the whole history of her misfortune with reference to the property, she talked about her affairs before Miss Colza as though that young lady had been one of her late brother's family. But yet she felt that she did not like Miss Colza, and once or twice felt almost inclined to resent certain pushing questions which Miss Colza addressed to her.

'And have you quarrelled with all the Ball family?' the young lady asked, putting great emphasis on the word all.

'I did not say that I had quarrelled with any of them,' said Miss Mackenzie.

'Oh! I beg pardon. I thought as you came away so sudden like, and as you didn't see any of them since, you know –'

'It is a matter of no importance whatever,' said Miss Mackenzie.

'No: none in the least,' said Miss Colza. And in this way they made up their minds to hate each other.

But what did the woman mean by talking in this way of all the Balls, as though a quarrel with one of the family was a thing of more importance than a quarrel with any of the others? Could she know, or could she even guess, anything of John Ball and of the offer he had made? But this mystery was soon cleared up in Margaret's mind, when, at Mrs Mackenzie's request, they two went upstairs into that lady's bedroom for a little private conversation.

The conversation was desired for purposes appertaining solely to the convenience of the widow. She wanted some money, and then, with tears in her eyes, she demanded to know what was to be done. Miss Colza paid her eighteen shillings a week for board and lodging, and that was now two weeks in arrear; and one bedroom was let to a young man employed in the oilcloth factory, at seven shillings a week.

'And the rent is ninety pounds, and the taxes twenty-two,' said Mrs Mackenzie, with her handkerchief up to her eyes; 'and there's the taxman come now for seven pound ten, and where I'm to get it, unless I coined my blood, I don't know.'

Margaret gave her two sovereigns which she had in her purse, and promised to send her a cheque for the amount of the taxes due. Then she told as much as she could tell of that proposal as to the interest of the money due from the firm in the New Road.

'If it could only be made certain,' said the widow, who had fallen much from her high ideas since Margaret had last seen her. Things were greatly changed in that house since the day on which the dinner, à la Russe, had been given under the auspices of Mr Grandairs. 'If it can only be made certain. They still keep his name up in the firm. There it is as plain as life over the place of business' – she would not even yet call it a shop – 'Rubb and Mackenzie; and yet they won't let me know anything as to how matters are going on. I went there the other day, and they would tell me nothing. And as for Samuel Rubb, he hasn't been here this last fortnight, and I've got no one to see me righted. If you were to ask Mr Slow, wouldn't he be able to see me righted?'

Margaret declared that she hardly knew whether that would come within Mr Slow's line of business, and that she did not feel herself competent to give advice on such a point as that. She then explained, as best she could, that her own affairs were not as yet settled, but that she was led to hope, from what had been said to her, that the interest due by the firm on the money borrowed might become a fixed annual income for Mrs Mackenzie's benefit.

After that it came out that Mr Maguire had again been in Gower Street.

'And he was alone, for the best part of half an hour, with that young woman downstairs,' said Mrs Mackenzie.

'And you saw him?' Margaret asked.

'Oh, yes; I saw him afterwards.'

'And what did he say?'

'He didn't say much to me. Only he gave me to understand – at least, that is what I suppose he meant – that you and he – He meant to say, that you and he had been courting, I suppose.'

Then Margaret understood why Miss Colza had desired to know whether she had quarrelled with all the Balls. In her open and somewhat indignant speech in the drawing-room at the Cedars, she had declared before Mr Maguire, in her aunt's presence, that she was engaged to marry her cousin, John Ball. Mr Maguire had now enlisted Miss Colza in his service, and had told Miss Colza what had occurred. But still Miss Mackenzie did not thoroughly understand the matter. Why, she asked herself, should Mr Maguire trouble himself further, now that he knew that she had no fortune? But, in truth, it was not so easy to satisfy Mr Maguire on that point, as it was to satisfy Miss Mackenzie herself. He believed that the relatives of his lady-love were robbing her, or that they were, at any rate, taking advantage of her weakness. If it might be given to him to rescue her and her fortune from them, then, in such case as that, surely he would get his reward. The reader will therefore understand why Miss Colza was anxious to know whether Miss Mackenzie had quarrelled with all the Balls.

Margaret's face became unusually black when she was told that she and Mr Maguire had been courting, but she did not contradict the assertion. She did, however, express her opinion of that gentleman.

'He is a mean, false, greedy man,' she said, and then paused a moment; 'and he has been the cause of my ruin.' She would not, however, explain what she meant by this, and left the house, without going back to the room in which Miss Colza was sitting.

About a week afterwards she got a letter from Mr Slow, in which that gentleman – or rather the firm, for the letter was signed Slow and Bideawhile – asked her whether she was in want of immediate funds. The affair between her and her cousin was not yet, they said, in a state for final settlement, but they would be justified in supplying her own immediate wants out of the estate. To this she sent a reply, saying that she had money for her immediate wants, but that she would feel very grateful if anything could be done for Mrs Mackenzie and her family. Then she got a further letter, very short, saying that a half-year's interest on the loan had, by Mr Ball's consent, been paid to Mrs Mackenzie by Rubb and Mackenzie.

On the day following this, when she was sitting up in her bedroom,

Mrs Protheroe came to her, dressed in wonderful habiliments. She wore a dark-blue bonnet, filled all round with yellow flowers, and a spotted silk dress, of which the prevailing colour was scarlet. She was going, she said, to St Mary-le-Strand, 'to be made Mrs Buggins of.' She tried to carry it off with bravado when she entered the room, but she left it with a tear in her eye, and a whimper in her throat. 'To be sure, I'm an old woman,' she said before she went. 'Who has said that I ain't? Not I; nor yet Buggins. We is both of us old. But I don't know why we is to be desolate and lonely all our days, because we ain't young. It seems to me that the young folks is to have it all to themselves, and I'm sure I don't know why.' Then she went, clearly resolved, that as far as she was concerned, the young people shouldn't have it all to themselves; and as Buggins was of the same way of thinking, they were married at St Mary-le-Strand that very morning.

And this marriage would have been of no moment to us or to our little history, had not Mr Maguire chosen that morning, of all mornings in the year, to call on Miss Mackenzie in Arundel Street. He had obtained her address – of course, from Miss Colza; and, not having been idle the while in pushing his inquiries respecting Miss Mackenzie's affairs, had now come to Arundel Street to carry on the battle as best he might. Margaret was still in her room as he came, and as the girl could not show the gentleman up there, she took him into an empty parlour, and brought the tidings up to the lodger. Mr Maguire had not sent up his name; but a personal description by the girl at once made Margaret know who was there.

'I won't see him,' said she, with heightened colour, grieving greatly that the strong-minded Hannah Protheroe – or Buggins, as it might probably be by that time – was not at home. 'Martha, don't let him come up. Tell him to go away at once.'

After some persuasion, the girl went down with the message, which she softened to suit her own idea of propriety. But she returned, saying that the gentleman was very urgent. He insisted that he must see Miss Mackenzie, if only for an instant, before he left the house.

'Tell him,' said Margaret, 'that nothing shall induce me to see him. I'll send for a policeman. If he won't go when he's told, Martha, you must go for a policeman.'

Martha, when she heard that, became frightened about the spoons and coats, and ran down again in a hurry. Then she came up again with a scrap of paper, on which a few words had been written with a pencil. This was passed through a very narrow opening in the door, as Margaret stood with it guarded, fearing lest the enemy might carry the point by an assault.

'You are being robbed,' said the note, 'you are, indeed – and my only wish is to protect you.'

'Tell him that there is no answer, and that I will receive no more notes from him,' said Margaret. Then, at last, when he received that message, Mr Maguire went away.

About a week after that, another visitor came to Miss Mackenzie, and him she received. But he was not the man for whose coming she in truth longed. It was Mr Samuel Rubb who now called, and when Mrs Buggins told her lodger that he was in the parlour, she went down to see him willingly. Her life was now more desolate than it had been before the occurrence of that ceremony in the church of St Mary-le-Strand; for, though she had much respect for Mr Buggins, of whose character she had heard nothing that was not good, and though she had given her consent as to the expediency of the Buggins' alliance, she did not find herself qualified to associate with Mr Buggins.

'He won't say a word, Miss,' Hannah had pleaded, 'and he'll run and fetch for you like a dog.'

But even when recommended so highly for his social qualities, Buggins, she felt, would be antipathetic to her; and, with many false assurances that she did not think it right to interrupt a newly-married couple, she confined herself on those days to her own room.

But when Mr Rubb came, she went down to see him. How much Mr Rubb knew of her affairs – how far he might be in Miss Colza's confidence – she did not know; but his conduct to her had not been offensive, and she had been pleased when she learned that the first half year's interest had been paid to her sister-in-law.

'I'm sorry to hear of all this, Miss Mackenzie,' said he, when he came forward to greet her. He had not thought it necessary, on this occasion, to put on his yellow gloves or his shiny boots, and she liked him the better on that account.

'Of all what, Mr Rubb?' said she.

'Why, about you and the family at the Cedars. If what I hear is true, they've just got you to give up everything, and then dropped you.'

'I left Sir John Ball's house on my own account, Mr Rubb; I was not turned out.'

'I don't suppose they'd do that. They wouldn't dare to do that; not so soon after getting hold of your money. Miss Mackenzie, I hope I shall not anger you; but it seems to me to be the most horridly wicked piece of business I ever heard of.'

'You are mistaken, Mr Rubb. You forget that the thing was first found out by my own lawyer.'

'I don't know how that may be, but I can't bring myself to believe that it all is as they say it is; I can't, indeed.'

She merely smiled, and shook her head. Then he went on speaking.

'I hope I'm not giving offence. It's not what I mean, if I am.'

'You are not giving any offence, Mr Rubb; only I think you are mistaken about my relatives at Twickenham.'

'Of course, I may be; there's no doubt of that. I may be mistaken, like another. But, Miss Mackenzie, by heavens, I can't bring myself to think it.' As he spoke in this energetic way, he rose from his chair, and stood opposite to her. 'I cannot bring myself to think that the fight should be given up.'

'But there has been no fight.'

'There ought to be a fight, Miss Mackenzie; I know that there ought. I believe I'm right in supposing, if all this is allowed to go by the board as it is going, that you won't have, so to say, anything of your own.'

'I shall have to earn my bread like other people; and, indeed, I am endeavouring now to put myself in the way of doing so.'

'I'll tell you how you shall earn it. Come and be my wife. I think we've got a turn for good up at the business. Come and be my wife. That's honest, any way.'

'You are honest,' said she, with a tear in her eye.

'I am honest now,' said he, 'though I was not honest to you once': and I think there was a tear in his eye also.

'If you mean about that money that you have borrowed, I am very glad of it – very glad of it. It will be something for them in Gower Street.'

'Miss Mackenzie, as long as I have a hand to help myself with, they shall have that at least. But now, about this other thing. Whether there's nothing to come or anything, I'll be true to my offer. I'll fight for it, if there's to be a fight, and I'll let it go if there's to be no fight. But whether one way or whether the other, there shall be a home for you when you say the word. Say it now. Will you be my wife?'

'I cannot say that word, Mr Rubb.'

'And why not?'

'I cannot say it; indeed, I cannot.'

'Is it Mr Ball that prevents you?'

'Do not ask me questions like that. Indeed, indeed, indeed, I cannot do as you ask me.'

'You despise me, like enough, because I am only a tradesman?'

'What am I myself, that I should despise any man? No, Mr Rubb, I am thankful and grateful to you; but it cannot be.'

Then he took up his hat, and, turning away from her without any word of adieu, made his way out of the house.

'He really do seem a nice man, Miss,' said Mrs Buggins. 'I wonder you wouldn't have him liefer than go into one of them hospitals.'

Whether Miss Mackenzie had any remnant left of another hope, or whether all such hope had gone, we need not perhaps inquire accurately. Whatever might be the state of her mind on that score, she was doing her best to carry out her purpose with reference to the plan of nursing; and as she could not now apply to her cousin, she had written to Mr Slow upon the subject.

Late in November yet another gentleman came to see her, but when he came she was unfortunately out. She had gone up to the house in Gower Street, and had there been so cross-questioned by the indefatigable Miss Colza that she had felt herself compelled to tell her sister-in-law that she could not again come there as long as Miss Colza was one of the family. It was manifest to her that these questions had been put on behalf of Mr Maguire, and she had therefore felt more indignant than she would have been had they originated in the impertinent curiosity of the woman herself. She also informed Mrs Mackenzie that, in obedience to instructions from Mr Slow, she intended to postpone her purpose with reference to the hospital till some time early in the next year. Mr Slow had sent a clerk to her to explain that till that time such amicable arrangement as that to which he looked forward to make could not be completed. On her return from this visit to Gower Street she found the card – simply the card – of her cousin, John Ball.

Why had she gone out? Why had she not remained a fixture in the house, seeing that it had always been possible that he should come? But why! oh, why! had he treated her in this way, leaving his card at her home, as though that would comfort her in her grievous desolation? It would have been far better that he should have left there no intimation of his coming. She took the card, and in her anger threw it from her into the fire.

But yet she waited for him to come again. Not once during the next ten days, excepting on the Sunday, did she go out of the house during the hours that her cousin would be in London. Very sad and monotonous was her life, passed alone in her own bedroom. And it was the more sad, because Mrs Buggins somewhat resented the manner in which her husband was treated. Mrs Buggins was still attentive, but she made little speeches about Buggins' respectability, and Margaret felt that her presence in the house was an annoyance.

At last, at the end of the ten days, John Ball came again, and Margaret, with a fluttering heart, descended to meet him in the empty parlour.

She was the first to speak. As she had come downstairs, she had made up her mind to tell him openly what were her thoughts.

'I had hoped to have seen you before this, John,' she said, as she gave him her hand.

'I did call before. Did you not get my card?'

'Oh, yes; I got your card. But I had expected to see you before that. The kind of life that I am leading here is very sad, and cannot be long continued.'

'I would have had you remain at the Cedars, Margaret; but you would not be counselled by me.'

'No; not in that, John.'

'I only mention it now to excuse myself. But you are not to suppose that

I am not anxious about you, because I have not seen you. I have been with Mr Slow constantly. These law questions are always very tedious in being settled.'

'But I want nothing for myself.'

'It behoves Mr Slow, for that very reason, to be the more anxious on your behalf; and, if you will believe me, Margaret, I am quite as anxious as he is. If you had remained with us, I could have discussed the matter with you from day to day; but, of course, I cannot do so while you are here.'

As he was talking in this way, everything with reference to their past intercourse came across her mind. She could not tell him that she had been anxious to see him, not with reference to the money, but that he might tell her that he did not find her guilty on that charge which her aunt had brought against her concerning Mr Maguire. She did not want assurances of solicitude as to her future means of maintenance. She cared little or nothing about her future maintenance, if she could not get from him one kind word with reference to the past. But he went on talking to her about Mr Slow, and the interest, and the property, and the law, till, at last, in her anger, she told him that she did not care to hear further about it, till she should be told at last what she was to do.

'As I have got nothing of my own,' she said, 'I want to be earning my bread, and I think that the delay is cruel.'

'And do you think,' said he, 'that the delay is not cruel to me also?'

She thought that he alluded to the fact that he could not yet obtain possession of the income for his own purposes.

'You may have it all at once, for me,' she said.

'Have all what?' he replied. 'Margaret, I think you fail to see the difficulties of my position. In the first place, my father is on his deathbed!'

'Oh, John, I am sorry for that.'

'And, then, my mother is very bitter about all this. And how can I, at such a time, tell her that her opinion is to go for nothing? I am bound to think of my own children, and cannot abandon my claim to the property.'

'No one wants you to abandon it. At least, I do not.'

'What am I to do, then? This Mr Maguire is making charges against me.'

'Oh, John!'

'He is saying that I am robbing you, and trying to cover the robbery by marrying you. Both my own lawyer, and Mr Slow, have told me that a plain statement of the whole case must be prepared, so that any one who cares to inquire may learn the whole truth, before I can venture to do anything which might otherwise compromise my character. You do not think of all this, Margaret, when you are angry with me.' Margaret, hanging down her head, confessed that she had not thought of it.

'The difficulty would have been less, had you remained at the Cedars.'

Then she again lifted her head, and told him that that would have been impossible. Let things go as they might, she knew that she had been right in leaving her aunt's house.

There was not much more said between them, nor did he give her any definite promise as to when he would see her again. He told her that she might draw on Mr Slow for money if she wanted it, but that she again declined. And he told her also not to withdraw Susanna Mackenzie from her school at Littlebath – at any rate, not for the present; and intimated also that Mr Slow would pay the schoolmistress's bill. Then he took his leave of her. He had spoken no word of love to her; but yet she felt, when he was gone, that her case was not as hopeless now as it had seemed to be that morning.

✖ TWENTY-FOUR ✖

The Little Story of the Lion and the Lamb

DURING THOSE THREE MONTHS OF OCTOBER, NOVEMBER, and December, Mr Maguire was certainly not idle. He had, by means of pertinacious inquiry, learned a good deal about Miss Mackenzie; indeed, he had learned most of the facts which the reader knows, though not quite all of them. He had seen Jonathan Ball's will, and he had seen Walter Mackenzie's will. He had ascertained, through Miss Colza, that John Ball now claimed the property by some deed said to have been executed by Jonathan Ball previous to the execution of his will; and he had also learned, from Miss Mackenzie's own lips, in Lady Ball's presence, that she had engaged herself to marry the man who was thus claiming her property. Why should Mr Ball want to marry her – who would in such a case be penniless – but that he felt himself compelled in that way to quell all further inquiry into the thing that he was doing? And why should she desire to marry him, but that in this way she might, as it were, go with her own property, and not lose the value of it herself when compelled to surrender it to her cousin? That she would have given herself, with all her property, to him – Maguire – a few months ago, Mr Maguire felt fully convinced, and, as I have said before, had some ground for such conviction. He had learned also from Miss Colza, that Miss Mackenzie had certainly quarrelled with Lady Ball, and that she had, so Miss Colza believed, been turned out of the house at the Cedars. Whether Mr Ball had or had not abandoned his matrimonial prospects, Miss Colza could not quite determine. Having made up her mind to hate Miss Mackenzie, and therefore, as was natural, thinking that no gentleman could really like such 'a poor dowdy creature,' she rather thought that he had abandoned his matrimonial prospects. Mr Maguire had thus learned much on the subject; but he had not learned this – that John Ball was honest throughout in the matter, and that the lawyers employed in it were honest also.

And now, having got together all this information, and he himself being in a somewhat precarious condition as to his own affairs, Mr Maguire resolved upon using his information boldly. He had a not incorrect idea of the fitness of things, and did not fail to tell himself that were he at that moment in possession of those clerical advantages which his labours in the vineyard should have earned for him, he would not have run the risk which he must undoubtedly incur by engaging himself in this matter. Had he a full church at Littlebath depending on him, had Mr Stumfold's chance and Mr Stumfold's success been his, had he still even been an adherent of the Stumfoldian fold, he would have paused before he rushed to the public with an account of Miss Mackenzie's grievance. But as matters stood with him, looking round upon his own horizon, he did not see that he had any course before him more likely to lead to good pecuniary results, than this.

The reader has been told how Mr Maguire went to Arundel Street, and how he was there received. But that reception did not at all daunt his courage. It showed him that the lady was still under the Ball influence, and that his ally, Miss Colza, was probably wrong in supposing that the Ball marriage was altogether off. But this only made him the more determined to undermine that influence, and to prevent that marriage. If he could once succeed in convincing the lady that her best chance of regaining her fortune lay in his assistance, or if he could even convince her that his interference must result, either with or without her good wishes, in dividing her altogether from the Ball alliance, then she would be almost compelled to throw herself into his arms. That she was violently in love with him he did not suppose, nor did he think it at all more probable that she should be violently in love with her cousin. He put her down in his own mind as one of those weak, good women, who can bring themselves easily to love any man, and who are sure to make useful wives, because they understand so thoroughly the nature of obedience. If he could secure for her her fortune, and could divide her from John Ball, he had but little doubt that she would come to him, in spite of the manner in which she had refused to receive him in Arundel Street. Having considered all this, after the mode of thinking which I have attempted to describe, he went to work with such weapons as were readiest to his hands.

As a first step, he wrote boldly to John Ball. In this letter he reasserted the statement he had made to Lady Ball as to Miss Mackenzie's engagement to himself, and added some circumstances which he had not mentioned to Lady Ball. He said, that having become engaged to that lady, he had, in consequence, given up his curacy at Littlebath, and otherwise so disarranged his circumstances, as to make it imperative upon him to take the steps which he was now taking. He had come up to London, expecting to find her anxious to receive him in Gower Street, and had then discovered that she had been taken away to the Cedars. He could not, he said, give any adequate description of his surprise, when, on arriving there, he heard from the mouth of his own Margaret that she was now engaged to her cousin. But if his surprise then had been great and terrible, how much greater and more terrible must it have been when, step by step, the story of that claim upon her fortune revealed itself to him! He pledged himself, in his letter, as a gentleman and as a Christian minister, to see the matter out. He would not allow Miss Mackenzie to be despoiled of her fortune and her hand – both of which he had a right to regard as his own – without making known to the public a transaction which he regarded as nefarious. Then there was a good deal of eloquent indignation the nature and purport of which the reader will probably understand.

Mr Ball did not at all like this letter. He had that strong feeling of disinclination to be brought before the public with reference to his private affairs, which is common to all Englishmen; and he specially had a dislike to this, seeing that there would be a question not only as to money, but also as to love. A gentleman does not like to be accused of a dishonest attempt to possess himself of a lady's property; but, at the age of fifty, even that is almost better than one which charges him with such attempt against a lady's heart. He knew that he was not dishonest, and therefore could endure the first. He was not quite sure that he was not, or might not become, ridiculous, and therefore feared the latter very greatly. He could not ignore the letter, and there was nothing for it but to show it to his lawyer. Unfortunately, he had told this lawyer, on the very day of Mr Maguire's visit to the Cedars, that all was to be made smooth by his marriage with Miss Mackenzie; and now, with much misery and many inward groanings, he had to explain all this story of Mr Maguire. It was the more painful in that he had to admit that an offer had been made to the lady by the clergyman, and had not been rejected.

'You don't think there was more than that?' asked the lawyer, having paved the way for his question with sundry apologetic flourishes.

'I am sure there was not,' said John Ball. 'She is as true as the Gospel, and he is as false as the devil.'

'Oh, yes,' said the lawyer; 'there's no doubt about his falsehood. He's one of those fellows for whom nothing is too dirty. Clergymen are like women. As long as they're pure, they're a long sight purer than other men; but when they fall, they sink deeper.'

'You needn't be afraid of taking her word,' said John Ball. 'If all women were as pure as she is, there wouldn't be much amiss with them.' His eyes glittered as he spoke of her, and it was a pity that Margaret could not have heard him then, and seen him there.

'You don't think she has been – just a little foolish, you know?'

'I think she was very foolish in not bidding such a man to go about his business, at once. But she has not been more so than what she owns. She is as brave as she is good, and I don't think she would keep anything back.'

The result was that a letter was written by the lawyer to Mr Maguire, telling Mr Maguire that any further communication should be made to him; and also making a slight suggestion as to the pains and penalties which are incurred in the matter of a libel. Mr Maguire had dated his letter from Littlebath, and there the answer reached him. He had returned thither, having found that he could take no further immediate steps towards furthering his cause in London.

And now, what steps should he take next? More than once he thought of putting his own case into the hands of a lawyer; but what was a lawyer to do for him? An action for breach of promise was open to him, but he had wit enough to feel that there was very little chance of success for him in that line. He might instruct a lawyer to look into Miss Mackenzie's affairs, and he thought it probable that he might find a lawyer to take such instructions. But there would be much expense in this, and, probably, no result. Advancing logically from one conclusion to another, he at last resolved that he must rush boldly into print, and lay the whole iniquity of the transaction open to the public.

He believed – I think he did believe – that the woman was being wronged. Some particle of such belief he had, and fostering himself with this, he sat himself down, and wrote a leading article.

Now there existed in Littlebath at this time a weekly periodical called the *Christian Examiner*, with which Mr Maguire had for some time had dealings. He had written for the paper, taking an earnest part in local religious subjects; and the paper, in return, had very frequently spoken highly of Mr Maguire's eloquence, and of Mr Maguire's energy. There had been a give and take in this, which all people understand who are conversant with the provincial, or perhaps I might add, with the metropolitan press of the country. The paper in question was not a wicked paper, nor were the gentlemen concerned in its publication intentionally scurrilous or malignant; but it was subject to those great temptations which beset all class newspapers of the kind, and to avoid which seems to be almost more difficult, in handling religious subjects, than in handling any other. The editor of a *Christian Examiner*, if, as is probable, he have, of his own, very strong and one-sided religious convictions, will think that those who differ from him are in a perilous way, and so thinking, will feel himself bound to tell them so. The man who advocates one line of railway instead of another, or one prime minister as being superior to all others, does not regard his opponents as being fatally wrong – wrong for this world and for the next – and he can restrain himself. But how is a newspaper writer to restrain himself when his opponent is incurring everlasting punishment, or, worse still, carrying away others to a similar doom, in that they read, and perhaps even purchase, that which the lost one has written? In this way the contents of religious newspapers are apt to be personal; and heavy, biting, scorching attacks, become the natural vehicle of *Christian Examiners*.

Mr Maguire sat down and wrote his leading article, which on the following Saturday appeared in all the glory of large type. The article shall not be repeated here at length, because it contained sundry quotations from Holy Writ which may as well be omitted, but the purport of it shall be explained. It commenced with a dissertation against an undue love of wealth – the *auri sacra fames*, as the writer called it; and described with powerful unction the terrible straits into which, when indulged, it led the vile, wicked, ugly, hideous, loathsome, devilish human heart. Then there was an eloquent passage referring to worms and dust and grass, and a quotation respecting treasures both corruptible and incorruptible. Not at once, but with crafty gradations, the author sloped away to the point of his subject. How fearful was it to watch the way in which the strong, wicked ones – the roaring lions of the earth, beguiled the ignorance of the innocent, and led lonely lambs into their slaughter-houses. All this, much amplified, made up half the article; and then, after the manner of a pleasant relater of anecdotes, the clerical story-teller began his little tale. When, however, he came to the absolute writing of the tale, he found it to be prudent for the present to omit the names of his hero and heroine – to omit, indeed, the names of all the persons concerned. He had first intended boldly to dare it all, and perhaps would yet have done so had he been quite sure of his editor. But his editor he found might object to these direct personalities at the first sound of the trumpet, unless the communication were made in the guise of a letter, with Mr Maguire's name at the end of it. After a while the editor might become hot in the fight himself, and then the names could be blazoned forth. And there existed some chance – some small chance – that the robber-lion, John Ball, might be induced to drop his lamb from his mouth when he heard this premonitory blast, and then the lion's prey might be picked up by – 'the bold hunter,' Mr Maguire would probably have said, had he been called upon to finish the sentence himself; anyone else might, perhaps, say, by the jackal. The little story was told, therefore, without the mention of any names. Mr Maguire had read other little stories told in another way in other newspapers, of greater weight, no doubt, than the Littlebath *Christian Examiner*, and had thought that he could wield a thunderbolt as well as any other Jupiter; but in wielding thunderbolts, as in all other operations of skill, a man must first try his 'prentice hand with some reticence; and thus he reconciled himself to prudence, not without some pangs of conscience which accused him inwardly of cowardice.

'Not long ago there was a lady in this town, loved and respected by all who knew her.' Thus he began, and then gave a not altogether inaccurate statement of the whole affair, dropping, of course, his own share in the concern, and accusing the vile, wicked, hideous, loathsome human heart of the devouring lion, who lived some miles to the west end of London, of a brutal desire and a hellish scheme to swallow up the inheritance of the innocent, loved, and respected lamb, in spite of the closest ties of consanguinity between them. And then he went on to tell how, with a base desire of covering up from the eyes of an indignant public his bestial greediness in having made this dishonest meal, the lion had proposed to himself the plan of marrying the lamb! It was a pity that Maguire had not learned – that Miss Colza had not been able to tell him – that the lion had once before expressed his wish to take the lamb for his wife. Had he known that, what a picture he would have drawn of the disappointed vindictive king of the forest, as lying in his lair at Twickenham he meditated his foul revenge! This unfortunately was unknown to Mr Maguire and unsuspected by him.

But the article did not end here. The indignant writer of it went on to say that he had buckled on his armour in support of the lamb, and that he was ready to meet the lion either in the forest or in any social circle; either in the courts of law or before any Christian arbitrator. With loud trumpetings, he summoned the lion to appear and plead guilty, or to stand forward, if he dared, and declare himself innocent with his hand on his heart. If the lion could prove himself to be innocent the writer of that article offered him the right hand of fellowship, an offer which the lion would not, perhaps, regard as any strong inducement; but if the lion were not innocent – if, as the writer of that article was well aware was the case, the lion was basely, greedily, bestially guilty, then the writer of that article pledged himself to give the lion no peace till he had disgorged his prey, and till the lamb was free to come back, with all her property, to that Christian circle in Littlebath which had loved her so warmly and respected her so thoroughly.

Such was the nature of the article, and the editor put it in. After all, what, in such matters, is an editor to do? Is it not his business to sell his paper? And if the editor of a *Christian Examiner* cannot trust the clergyman he has sat under, whom can he trust? Some risk an editor is obliged to run, or he will never sell his paper. There could be little doubt that such an article as this would be popular among the religious world of Littlebath, and that it would create a demand. He had his misgivings – had that poor editor. He did not feel quite sure of his lion and his lamb. He talked the matter over vehemently with Mr Maguire in the little room in which he occupied himself with his scissors and his paste; but ultimately the article was inserted. Who does not know that interval of triumph which warms a man's heart when he has delivered his blow, and the return blow has not been yet received? The blow has been so well struck that it must be successful, nay, may probably be death-dealing. So felt Mr Maguire when two dozen copies of the *Christian Examiner* were delivered at his lodgings on the Saturday morning. The article, though printed as a leading article, had been headed as a little story – 'The Lion and the Lamb' – so that it might more readily attract attention. It read very nicely in print. It had all that religious unction which is so necessary for *Christian Examiners*, and with it that spice of devilry, so delicious to humanity that without it even *Christian Examiners* cannot be made to sell themselves. He was very busy with his two dozen damp copies before him – two dozen which had been sent to him, by agreement, as the price of his workmanship. He made them up and directed them with his own hand. To the lion and the lamb he sent two copies, two to each. To Mr Slow he sent a copy, and another to Messrs Slow and Bideawhile, and a third to the other lawyer. He sent a copy to Lady Ball and one to Sir John. Another he sent to the old Mackenzie, baronet at Incharrow, and two more to the baronet's eldest son, and the baronet's eldest son's wife. A copy he sent to Mrs Tom Mackenzie, and a copy to Miss Colza; and a copy also he sent to Mrs Buggins. And he sent a copy to the Chairman of the Board at the Shadrach Fire Office, and another to the Chairman at the Abednego Life Office. A copy he sent to Mr Samuel Rubb, junior, and a copy to Messrs Rubb and Mackenzie. Out of his own pocket he supplied the postage stamps, and with his own hand he dropped the papers into the Littlebath post-office.

Poor Miss Mackenzie, when she read the article, was stricken almost to the ground. How she did hate the man whose handwriting on the address she recognised at once! What should she do? In her agony she almost resolved that she would start at once for the Cedars and profess her willingness to go before all the magistrates in London and Littlebath, and swear that her cousin was no lion and that she was no lamb. At that moment her feelings towards the Christians and *Christian Examiners* of Littlebath were not the feelings of a Griselda. I think she could have spoken her mind freely had Mr Maguire come in her way. Then, when she saw Mrs Buggins's copy, her anger blazed up afresh, and her agony became more intense. The horrid man must have sent copies all over the world, or he would never have thought of sending a copy to Mrs Buggins!

But she did not go to the Cedars. She reflected that when there she might probably find her cousin absent, and in such case she would hardly know how to address herself to her aunt. Mr Ball, too, might perhaps come to her, and for three days she patiently awaited his coming. On the evening of the third day there came to her, not Mr Ball, but a clerk from Mr Slow, the same clerk who had been with her before, and he made an appointment with her at Mr Slow's office on the following morning. She was to meet Mr Ball there, and also to meet Mr Ball's lawyer. Of course she consented to go, and of course she was on Mr Slow's staircase exactly at the time appointed. Of what she was thinking as she walked round Lincoln's Inn Fields to kill a quarter of an hour which she found herself to have on hand, we will not now inquire.

She was shown at once into Mr Slow's room, and the first thing that met her eyes was a copy of that horrible *Christian Examiner*, lying on the table before him. She knew it instantly, and would have known it had she simply seen a corner of the printing. To her eyes and to her mind, no other printed paper had ever been so ugly and so vicious. But she saw that there was also another newspaper under the *Christian Examiner*. Mr Slow brought her to the fire, and gave her a chair, and was very courteous. In a few moments came the other lawyer, and with him came John Ball.

Mr Slow opened the conference, all the details of which need not be given here. He first asked Miss Mackenzie whether she had seen that wicked libel. She, with much energy and, I may almost say, with virulence, declared that the horrid paper had been sent to her. She hoped that nobody suspected that she had known anything about it. In answer to this, they all assured her that she need not trouble herself on that head. Mr Slow then told her that a London paper had copied the whole story of the 'Lion and the Lamb,' expressing a hope that the lion would be exposed if there was any truth in it, and the writer would be exposed if there was none.

'The writer was Mr Maguire, a clergyman,' said Miss Mackenzie, with indignation.

'We all know that,' said Mr Slow, with a slight smile on his face. Then he went on reading the remarks of the London paper, which declared that the Littlebath *Christian Examiner*, having gone so far, must, of necessity, go further. The article was calculated to give the greatest pain to, no doubt, many persons; and the innocence or guilt of 'the Lion,' as poor John Ball was called, must be made manifest to the public.

'And now, my dear Miss Mackenzie, I will tell you what we propose to do,' said Mr Slow. He then explained that it was absolutely necessary that a question of law should be tried and settled in a court of law, between her and her cousin. When she protested against this, he endeavoured to explain to her that the cause would be an amicable cause, a simple reference, in short, to a legal tribunal. Of course, she did not understand this, and, of course, she still protested; but after a while, when she began to perceive that her protest was of no avail, she let that matter drop. The cause should be brought on as soon as possible, but could not be decided till late in the spring. She was told that she had better make no great change in her own manner of life till that time, and was again informed that she could have what money she wanted for her own maintenance. She refused to take any money: but when the reference was made to some proposed change in her life, she looked wistfully into her cousin's face. He, however, had nothing to say then, and kept his eyes intently fixed upon the carpet.

Mr Slow then took up the *Christian Examiner*, and declared to her what was their intention with reference to that. A letter should be written from his house to the editor of the London newspaper, giving a plain statement of the case, with all the names, explaining that all the parties were acting in perfect concert, and that the matter was to be decided in the only way which could be regarded as satisfactory. In answer to this, Miss Mackenzie, almost in tears, pointed out how distressing would be the publicity thus given to her name 'particularly' – she said, 'particularly –' But she could not go on with the expression of her thoughts, or explain that so public a reference to a proposal of marriage from her cousin must be doubly painful to her, seeing that the idea of such a marriage had been abandoned. But Mr Slow understood all this, and, coming over to her, took her gently by the hand.

'My dear,' he said, 'you may trust me in this as though I were your father. I know that such publicity is painful; but, believe me, it is the best that we can do.'

Of course she had no alternative but to yield.

When the interview was over, her cousin walked home with her to Arundel Street, and said much to her as to the necessity for this trial. He said so much, that she, at last, dimly understood that the matter could not be set at rest by her simple renouncing of the property. Her own lawyer could not allow her to do so; nor could he, John Ball, consent to receive the property in such a manner. 'You see, by that newspaper, what people would say of me.'

But had he not the power of making everything easy by doing that which he himself had before proposed to do? Why did he not again say, 'Margaret, come and be my wife?' She acknowledged to herself that he had a right to act as though he had never said those words – that the facts elicited by Mr Maguire's visit to the Cedars were sufficient to absolve him from his offer. But yet she thought that they should have been sufficient also to induce him to renew it.

On that occasion, when he left her at the door in Arundel Street, he had not renewed his offer.

❊ TWENTY-FIVE ❊

Lady Ball in Arundel Street

ON CHRISTMAS DAY MISS MACKENZIE WAS PRESSED very hard to eat her Christmas dinner with Mr and Mrs Buggins, and she almost gave way.

She had some half-formed idea in her head that should she once sit down to table with Buggins, she would have given up the fight altogether. She had no objection to Buggins, and had, indeed, no strong objection to put herself on a par with Buggins; but she felt that she could not be on a par with Buggins and with John Ball at the same time. Why it should be that in associating with the man she would take a step downwards, and might yet associate with the man's wife without taking any step downwards, she did not attempt to explain to herself. But I think that she could have explained it had she put herself to the task of analysing the question, and that she felt exactly the result of such analysis without making it. At any rate, she refused the invitation persistently, and ate her wretched dinner alone in her bedroom.

She had often told herself, in those days of her philosophy at Littlebath, that she did not care to be a lady; and she told herself now the same thing very often when she was thinking of the hospital. She cosseted herself with no false ideas as to the nature of the work which she proposed to undertake. She knew very well that she might have to keep rougher company than that of Buggins if she put her shoulder to that wheel. She was willing enough to do this, and had been willing to encounter such company ever since she left the Cedars. She was prepared for the roughness. But she would not put herself beyond the pale, as it were, of her cousin's hearth, moved simply by a temptation to relieve the monotony of her life. When the work came within her reach she would go to it, but till then she would bear the wretchedness of her dull room upstairs. She wondered whether he ever thought how wretched she must be in her solitude.

On New Year's Day she heard that her uncle was dead. She was already in mourning for her brother, and was therefore called upon to make no change in that respect. She wrote a note of condolence to her aunt, in which she strove much, and vainly, to be cautious and sympathetic at the same time, and in return received a note, in which Lady Ball declared her purpose of coming to Arundel Street to see her niece as soon as she found herself able to leave the house. She would, she said, give Margaret warning the day beforehand, as it would be very sad if she had her journey all for nothing.

Her aunt, Lady Ball, was coming to see her in Arundel Street! What could be the purpose of such a visit after all that had passed between them? And why should her aunt trouble herself to make it at a period of such great distress? Lady Ball must have some very important plan to propose, and poor Margaret's heart was in a flutter. It was ten days after this before the second promised note arrived, and then Margaret was asked to say whether she would be at home and able to receive her aunt's visit at ten minutes past two on the day but one following. Margaret wrote back to say that she would be at home at ten minutes past two on the day named.

Her aunt was old, and she again borrowed the parlour, though she was not now well inclined to ask favours from Mrs Buggins. Mrs Buggins had taken to heart the slight put upon her husband, and sometimes made nasty little speeches.

'Oh dear, yes, in course, Miss Margaret; not that I ever did think much of them Ballses, and less than ever now, since the gentleman was kind enough to send me the newspaper. But she's welcome to the room, seeing as how Mr Tiddy will be in the City, of course; and you're welcome to it, too, though you do keep yourself so close to yourself, which won't ever bring you round to have your money again; that it won't.'

Lady Ball came and was shown into the parlour, and her niece went down to receive her.

'I would have been here before you came, aunt, only the room is not mine.'

In answer to this, Lady Ball said that it did very well. Any room would answer the present purpose. Then she sat down on the sofa from which she had risen. She was dressed, of course, in the full weeds of her widowhood, and the wide extent of her black crape was almost awful in Margaret's eyes. She did not look to be so savage as her niece had sometimes seen her, but there was about her a ponderous accumulation of crape, which made her even more formidable than she used to be. It would be almost impossible to refuse anything to a person so black, so grave, so heavy, and so big.

'I have come to you, my dear,' she said, 'as soon as I possibly could after the sad event which we have had at home.'

In answer to this, Margaret said that she was much obliged, but she hoped that her aunt had put herself to no trouble. Then she said a word or two about her uncle – a word or two that was very difficult, as of course it could mean nothing.

'Yes,' said the widow, 'he has been taken from us after a long and useful life. I hope his son will always show himself to be worthy of such a father.'

After that there was silence in the room for a minute or two, during which Margaret waited for her aunt to begin; but Lady Ball sat there solid, grave, and black, as though she thought that her very presence, without any words, might be effective upon Margaret as a preliminary mode of attack. Margaret herself could find nothing to say to her aunt, and she, therefore, also remained silent. Lady Ball was so far successful in this, that when three minutes were over her niece had certainly been weakened by the oppressive nature of the meeting. She had about her less of vivacity, and perhaps also less of vitality, than when she first entered the room.

'Well, my dear,' said her aunt at last, 'there are things, you know, which must be talked about, though they are ever so disagreeable; 'and then she pulled out of her pocket that abominable number of the Littlebath *Christian Examiner*.

'Oh, aunt, I hope you are not going to talk about that.'

'My dear, that is cowardly; it is, indeed. How am I to help talking about it? I have come here, from Twickenham, on purpose to talk about it.'

'Then, aunt, I must decline; I must, indeed.'

'My dear!'

'I must, indeed, aunt.'

Let a man or a woman's vitality be ever so thoroughly crushed and quenched by fatigue or oppression – or even by black crape – there will always be some mode of galvanising which will restore it for a time, some specific either of joy or torture which will produce a return of temporary energy. This Littlebath newspaper was a battery of sufficient power to put Margaret on her legs again, though she perhaps might not be long able to keep them.

'It is a vile, lying paper, and it was written by a vile, lying man, and I hope you will put it up and say nothing about it.'

'It is a vile, lying paper, Margaret; but the lies are against my son, and not against you.'

'He is a man, and knows what he is about, and it does not signify to him. But, aunt, I won't talk about it, and there's an end of it.'

'I hope he does know what he is about' said Lady Ball. 'I hope he does. But you, as you say, are a woman, and therefore it specially behoves you to know what you are about.'

'I am not doing anything to anybody,' said Margaret.

Lady Ball had now refolded the offensive newspaper, and restored it to her pocket. Perhaps she had done as much with it as she had from the first intended. At any rate, she brought it forth no more, and made no further intentionally direct allusion to it. 'I don't suppose you really wish to do any injury to anybody,' she said.

'Does anybody accuse me of doing them an injury?' Margaret asked.

'Well, my dear, if I were to say that I accused you, perhaps you would misunderstand me. I hope – I thoroughly expect, that before I leave you, I may be able to say that I do not accuse you. If you will only listen to me patiently for a few minutes, Margaret – which I couldn't get you to do, you know, before you went away from the Cedars in that very extraordinary manner – I think I can explain to you something which –'
Here Lady Ball became embarrassed, and paused; but Margaret gave her no assistance, and therefore she began a new sentence. 'In point of fact, I want you to listen to what I say, and then, I think – I do think – you will do as we would have you.'

Whom did she include in that word 'we'? Margaret had still sufficient vitality not to let the word pass by unquestioned.

'You mean yourself and John?' said she.

'I mean the family,' said Lady Ball rather sharply. 'I mean the whole family, including those dear girls to whom I have been in the position of a mother since my son's wife died. It is in the name of the Ball family that I now speak, and surely I have a right.'

Margaret thought that Lady Ball had no such right, but she would not say so at that moment.

'Well, Margaret, to come to the point at once, the fact is this. You must renounce any idea that you may still have of becoming my son's wife.' Then she paused.

'Has John sent you here to say this?' demanded Margaret.

'I don't wish you to ask any such question as that. If you had any real regard for him I don't think you would ask it. Consider his difficulties, and consider the position of those poor children! If he were your brother, would you advise him, at his age, to marry a woman without a farthing, and also to incur the certain disgrace which would attach to his name after – after all that has been said about it in this newspaper?' – then, Lady Ball put her hand upon her pocket – 'in this newspaper, and in others?'

This was more than Margaret could bear. 'There would be no disgrace,' said she, jumping to her feet.

'Margaret, if you put yourself into a passion, how can you understand reason? You ought to know, yourself, by the very fact of your being in a passion, that you are wrong. Would there be no disgrace, after all that has come out about Mr Maguire?'

'No, none – none!' almost shouted this modern Griselda. 'There could be no disgrace. I won't admit it. As for his marrying me, I don't expect it. There is nothing to bind him to me. If he doesn't come to me I certainly shall not go to him. I have looked upon it as all over between him and me; and as I have not troubled him with any importunities, nor yet you, it is cruel in you to come to me in this way. He is free to do what he likes – why don't you go to him? But there would be no disgrace.'

'Of course he is free. Of course such a marriage never can take place now. It is quite out of the question. You say that it is all over, and you are quite right. Why not let this be settled in a friendly way between you and me, so that we might be friends again? I should be so glad to help you in your difficulties if you would agree with me about this.'

'I want no help.'

'Margaret, that is nonsense. In your position you are very wrong to set your natural friends at defiance. If you will only authorise me to say that you renounce this marriage –'

'I will not renounce it,' said Margaret, who was still standing up. 'I will not renounce it. I would sooner lose my tongue than let it say such a word. You may tell him, if you choose to tell him anything, that I demand nothing from him; nothing. All that I once thought mine is now his, and I demand nothing from him. But when he asked me to be his wife he told me to be firm, and in that I will obey him. He may renounce me, and I shall have nothing with which to reproach him; but I will never renounce him – never.' And then the modern Griselda, who had been thus galvanised into vitality, stood over her aunt in a mood that was almost triumphant.

'Margaret, I am astonished at you,' said Lady Ball, when she had recovered herself.

'I can't help that, aunt.'

'And now let me tell you this. My son is, of course, old enough to do as he pleases. If he chooses to ruin himself and his children by marrying, anybody – even if it were out of the streets – I can't help it. Stop a moment and hear me to the end.' This she said, as her niece had made a movement as though towards the door. 'I say, even if it were out of the streets, I couldn't help it. But nothing shall induce me to live in the same house with him if he marries you. It will be on your conscience for ever that you have brought ruin on the whole family, and that will be your punishment. As for me, I shall take myself off to some solitude, and – there – I – shall – die.' Then Lady Ball put her handkerchief up to her face and wept copiously.

Margaret stood still, leaning upon the table, but she spoke no word, either in answer to the threat or to the tears. Her immediate object was to take herself out of the room, but this she did not know how to achieve. At last her aunt spoke again: 'If you please, I will get you to ask your landlady to send for a cab.' Then the cab was procured, and Buggins, who had come home for his dinner, handed her ladyship in. Not a word had been spoken during the time that the cab was being fetched, and when Lady Ball went down the passage, she merely said, 'I wish you good-bye, Margaret.'

'Good-bye,' said Margaret, and then she escaped to her own bedroom.

Lady Ball had not done her work well. It was not within her power to induce Margaret to renounce her engagement, and had she known her niece better, I do not think that she would have made the attempt. She did succeed in learning that Margaret had received no renewal of an offer from her son – that there was, in fact, no positive engagement now existing between them; and with this, I think, she should have been satisfied. Margaret had declared that she demanded nothing from her cousin, and with this assurance Lady Ball should have been contented. But she had thought to carry her point, to obtain the full swing of her will, by means of a threat, and had forgotten that in the very words of her own menace she conveyed to Margaret some intimation that her son was still desirous of doing that very thing which she was so anxious to prevent. There was no chance that her threat should have any effect on Margaret. She ought to have known that the tone of the woman's mind was much too firm for that. Margaret knew – was as sure of it as any woman could be sure – that her cousin was bound to her by all ties of honour. She believed, too, that he was bound to her by love, and that if he should finally desert it, he would be moved to do so by mean motives. It was no anger on the score of Mr Maguire that would bring him to such a course, no suspicion that she was personally unworthy of being his wife. Our Griselda, with all her power of suffering and willingness to suffer, understood all that, and was by no means disposed to give way to any threat from Lady Ball.

When she was upstairs, and once more in solitude, she disgraced herself again by crying. She could be strong enough when attacked by others, but could not be strong when alone. She cried and sobbed upon her bed, and then, rising, looked at herself in the glass, and told herself that she was old and ugly, and fitted only for that hospital nursing of which she had been thinking. But still there was something about her heart that bore her up. Lady Ball would not have come to her, would not have exercised her eloquence upon her, would not have called upon her to renounce this engagement, had she not found all similar attempts upon her own son to be ineffectual. Could it then be so, that, after all, her cousin would be true to her? If it were so, if it could be so, what would she not do for him and for his children? If it were so, how blessed would have been all these troubles that had brought her to such a haven at last! Then she tried to reconcile his coldness to her with that which she so longed to believe might be the fact. She was not to expect him to be a lover such as are young men. Was she young herself, or would she like him better if he were to assume anything of youth in his manners? She understood that life with him was a serious thing, and that it was his duty to be serious and grave in what he did. It might be that it was essential to his character, after all that had passed, that the question of the property should be settled finally, before he could come to her, and declare his wishes. Thus flattering herself, she put away from her her tears, and dressed herself, smoothing her hair, and washing away the traces of her weeping; and then again she looked at herself in the glass to see if it were possible that she might be comely in his eyes.

The months of January and February slowly wore themselves away, and during the whole of that time Margaret saw her cousin but once, and then she met him at Mr Slow's chambers. She had gone there to sign some document, and there she had found him. She had then been told that she would certainly lose her cause. No one who had looked into the matter had any doubt of that. It certainly was the case that Jonathan Ball had bequeathed property which was not his at the time he made the will, but which at the time of his death, in fact, absolutely belonged to his nephew, John Ball. Old Mr Slow, as he explained this now for the seventh or eighth time, did it without a tone of regret in his voice, or a sign of sorrow in his eye. Margaret had become so used to the story now, that it excited no strong feelings within her. Her wish, she said, was, that the matter should be settled. The lawyer, with almost a smile on his face, but still shaking his head, said that he feared it could not be settled before the end of April. John Ball sat by, leaning his face, as usual, upon his umbrella, and saying nothing. It did, for a moment, strike Miss Mackenzie as singular, that she should be reduced from affluence to absolute nothingness in the way of property, in so very placid a manner. Mr Slow seemed to be thinking that he was, upon the whole, doing rather well for his client.

'Of course you understand, Miss Mackenzie, that you can have any money you require for your present personal wants.'

This had been said to her so often, that she took it as one of Mr Slow's legal formulas, which meant nothing to the laity.

On that occasion also Mr Ball walked home with her, and was very eloquent about the law's delays. He also seemed to speak as though there was nothing to be regretted by anybody, except the fact that he could not get possession of the property as quick as he wished. He said not a word of anything else, and Margaret, of course, submitted to be talked to by him rather than to talk herself. Of Lady Ball's visit he said not a word, nor did she. She asked after the children, and especially after Jack. One word she did say:

'I had hoped Jack would have come to see me at my lodging's.'

'Perhaps he had better not,' said Jack's father, 'till all is settled. We have had much to trouble us at home since my father's death.'

Then of course she dropped that subject. She had been greatly startled on that day on hearing her cousin called Sir John by Mr Slow. Up to that moment it had never occurred to her that the man of whom she was so constantly thinking as her possible husband was a baronet. To have been Mrs Ball seemed to her to have been possible; but that she should become Lady Ball was hardly possible. She wished that he had not been called Sir John. It seemed to her to be almost natural that people should be convinced of the impropriety of such a one as her becoming the wife of a baronet.

During this period she saw her sister-in-law once or twice, who on those occasions came down to Arundel Street. She herself would not go to Gower Street, because of the presence of Miss Colza. Miss Colza still continued to live there, and still continued very much in arrear in her contributions to the household fund. Mrs Mackenzie did not turn her out, because she would – so she said – in such case get nothing. Mrs Tom was by this time quite convinced that the property would, either justly or unjustly, go into the hands of John Ball, and she was therefore less anxious to make any sacrifice to please her sister-in-law.

'I'm sure I don't see why you should be so bitter against her,' said Mrs Tom. ' I don't suppose she told the clergyman a word that wasn't true.'

Miss Mackenzie declined to discuss the subject, and assured Mrs Tom that she only recommended the banishment of Miss Colza because of her apparent unwillingness to pay.

'As for the money,' said Mrs Tom, 'I expect Mr Rubb to see to that. I suppose he intends to make her Mrs Rubb sooner or later.'

Miss Mackenzie, having some kindly feeling towards Mr Rubb, would have preferred to hear that Miss Colza was likely to become Mrs Maguire. During these visits, Mrs Tom got more than one five-pound note from her sister-in-law, pleading the difficulty she had in procuring breakfast for lodgers without any money for the baker. Margaret protested against these encroachments, but, still, the money would be forthcoming.

Once, towards the end of February, Mrs Buggins seduced her lodger down into her parlour in the area, and Miss Mackenzie thought she perceived that something of the old servant's manners had returned to her. She was more respectful than she had been of late, and made no attempts at smart, ill-natured speeches.

'It's a weary life, Miss, this you're living here, isn't it?' said she.

Margaret said that it was weary, but that there could be no change till the lawsuit should be settled. It would be settled, she hoped, in April.

'Bother it for a lawsuit,' said Mrs Buggins. 'They all tells me that it ain't any lawsuit at all, really.'

'It's an amicable lawsuit,' said Miss Mackenzie.

'I never see such amicableness! 'Tis a wonder to hear, Miss, how everybody is talking about it everywheres. Where we was last night – that is, Buggins and I – most respectable people in the copying line – it isn't only he as does the copying, but she too; nurses the baby, and minds the kitchen fire, and goes on, sheet after sheet, all at the same time; and a very tidy thing they make of it, only they do straggle their words so – well, they were saying as it's one of the most remarkablest cases as ever was know'd.'

'I don't see that I shall be any the better because it's talked about.'

'Well, Miss Margaret, I'm not so sure of that. It's my belief that if one only gets talked about enough, one may have a'most anything one chooses to ask for.'

'But I don't want to ask for anything.'

'But if what we heard last night is all true, there's somebody else that does want to ask for something, or, as has asked, as folks say.'

Margaret blushed up to the eyes, and then protested that she did not know what Mrs Buggins meant.

'I never dreamed of it, my dear; indeed, I didn't, when the old lady come here with her tantrums; but now, it's as plain as a pikestaff. If I'd a' known anything about that, my dear, I shouldn't have made so free about Buggins; indeed, I shouldn't.'

'You're talking nonsense, Mrs Buggins; indeed, you are.'

'They have the whole story all over the town at any rate, and in the lane, and all about the courts; and they declare it don't matter a toss of a halfpenny which way the matter goes, as you're to become Lady Ball the very moment the case is settled.'

Miss Mackenzie protested that Mrs Buggins was a stupid woman – the stupidest woman she had ever heard or seen; and then hurried up into her own room to hug herself in her joy, and teach herself to believe that what so many people said must at last come true.

Three days after this, a very fine, private carriage, with two servants on a hammer cloth, drove up to the door in Arundel Street, and the maid-servant, hurrying upstairs, told Miss Mackenzie that a beautifully-dressed lady downstairs was desirous of seeing her immediately.

✕ TWENTY-SIX ✕

Mrs Mackenzie of Cavendish Square

'MY DEAR,' SAID THE BEAUTIFULLY-DRESSED LADY, 'you don't know me, I think;' and the beautifully-dressed lady came up to Miss Mackenzie very cordially, took her by the hand, smiled upon her, and seemed to be a very good-natured person indeed. Margaret told the lady that she did not know her, and at that moment was altogether at a loss to guess who the lady might be. The lady might be forty years of age, but was still handsome, and carried with her that easy, self-assured, well balanced manner, which, if it be not overdone, goes so far to make up for beauty, if beauty itself be wanting.

'I am your cousin, Mrs Mackenzie – Clara Mackenzie. My husband is Walter Mackenzie, and his father is Sir Walter Mackenzie, of Incharrow. Now you will know all about me.'

'Oh, yes, I know you,' said Margaret.

'I ought, I suppose, to make ever so many apologies for not coming to you before; but I did call upon you, ever so long ago; I forget when, and after that you went to live at Littlebath. And then we heard of you as being with Lady Ball, and for some reason, which I don't quite understand, it has always been supposed that Lady Ball and I were not to know each other. And now I have heard this wonderful story about your fortune, and about everything else, too, my dear; and it seems all very beautiful, and very romantic; and everybody says that you have behaved so well; and so, to make a long story short, I have come to find you out in your hermitage, and to claim cousinship, and all that sort of thing.'

'I'm sure I'm very much obliged to you, Mrs Mackenzie –'

'Don't say it in that way, my dear, or else you'll make me think you mean to turn a cold shoulder on me for not coming to you before.'

'Oh, no.'

'But we've only just come to town; and though of course I heard the story down in Scotland –'

'Did you?'

'Did I? Why, everybody is talking about it, and the newspapers have been full of it.'

'Oh, Mrs Mackenzie, that is so terrible.'

'But nobody has said a word against you. Even that stupid clergyman, who calls you the lamb, has not pretended to say that you were his lamb. We had the whole story of the Lion and the Lamb in the *Inverary Interpreter*, but I had no idea that it was you, then. But the long and the short of it is, that my husband says he must know his cousin; and to tell the truth, it was he that sent me; and we want you to come and stay with us in Cavendish Square till the lawsuit is over, and everything is settled.'

Margaret was so startled by the proposition, that she did not know how to answer it. Of course she was at first impressed with a strong idea of the impossibility of her complying with such a request, and was simply anxious to find some proper way of refusing it. The Incharrow Mackenzies were great people who saw much company, and it was, she thought, quite out of the question that she should go to their house. At no time of her career would she have been, as she conceived, fit to live with such grand persons; but at the present moment, when she grudged herself even a new pair of gloves out of the money remaining to her, while she was still looking forward to a future life passed as a nurse in a hospital, she felt that there would be an absolute unfitness in such a visit.

'You are very kind,' she said at last with faltering voice, as she meditated in what words she might best convey her refusal.

'No, I'm not a bit kind; and I know from the tone of your voice that you are meditating a refusal. But I don't mean to accept it. It is much better that you should be with us while all this is going on, than that you should be living here alone. And there is no one with whom you could live during this time so properly, as with those who are your nearest relatives.'

'But, Mrs Mackenzie –'

'I suppose you are thinking now of another cousin, but it's not at all proper that you should go to his house – not as yet, you know. And you need not suppose that he'll object because of what I said about Lady Ball and myself. The Capulets and the Montagues don't intend to keep it up for ever; and, though we have never visited Lady Ball, my husband and the present Sir John know each other very well.'

Mrs Mackenzie was not on that occasion able to persuade Margaret to come at once to Cavendish Square, and neither was Margaret able to give a final refusal. She did not intend to go, but she could not bring herself to speak a positive answer in such a way as to have much weight with Mrs Mackenzie. That lady left her at last, saying that she would send her husband, and promising Margaret that she would herself come in ten days to fetch her.

'Oh no,' said Margaret; 'it will be very good-natured of you to come, but not for that.'

'But I shall come, and shall come for that,' said Mrs Mackenzie; and at the end of the ten days she did come, and she did carry her husband's cousin back with her to Cavendish Square.

In the meantime Walter Mackenzie had called in Arundel Street, and had seen Margaret. But there had been given to her advice by a counsellor whom she was more inclined to obey than any of the Mackenzies. John Ball had written to her, saying that he had heard of the proposition, and recommending her to accept the invitation given to her.

'Till all this trouble about the property is settled,' said he, 'it will be much better that you should be with your cousins than living alone in Mrs Buggins' lodgings.'

After receiving this Margaret held out no longer but was carried off by the handsome lady in the grand carriage, very much to the delight of Mrs Buggins.

Mrs Buggins' respect for Miss Mackenzie had returned altogether since she had heard of the invitation to Cavendish Square, and she apologised, almost without ceasing, for the liberty she had taken in suggesting that Margaret should drink tea with her husband.

'And indeed, Miss, I shouldn't have proposed such a thing, were it ever so, if I had suspected for a hinstant how things were a going to be. For Buggins is a man as knows his place, and never puts himself beyond it! But you was that close, Miss –'

In answer to this Margaret would say that it didn't signify, and that it wasn't on that account; and I have no doubt but that the two women thoroughly understood each other.

There was a subject on which, in spite of all her respect, Mrs Buggins ventured to give Miss Mackenzie much advice, and to insist on that advice strongly. Mrs Buggins was very anxious that the future 'baronet's lady' should go out upon her grand visit with a proper assortment of clothing. That argument of the baronet's lady was the climax of Mrs Buggins' eloquence: 'You, my dear, as is going to be one baronet's lady is going to a lady who is going to be another baronet's lady, and it's only becoming you should go as is becoming.'

Margaret declared that she was not going to be anybody's lady, but Mrs Buggins altogether pooh-poohed this assertion.

'That, Miss, is your predestination,' said Mrs Buggins, 'and well you'll become it. And as for money, doesn't that old party who found it all out say reg'lar once a month that there's whatever you want to take for your own necessaries? and you that haven't had a shilling from him yet! If it was me, I'd send him in such a bill for necessaries as 'ud open that old party's eyes a bit, and hurry him up with his lawsuits.'

The matter was at last compromised between her and Margaret, and a very moderate expenditure for smarter clothing was incurred.

On the day appointed Mrs Mackenzie again came, and Margaret was carried off to Cavendish Square. Here she found herself suddenly brought into a mode of life altogether different from anything she had as yet experienced. The Mackenzies were people who went much into society, and received company frequently at their own house. The first of these evils for a time Margaret succeeded in escaping, but from the latter she had no means of withdrawing herself. There was very much to astonish her at this period of her life, but that which astonished her perhaps more than anything else was her own celebrity. Everybody had heard of the Lion and the Lamb, and everybody was aware that she was supposed to represent the milder of those two favourite animals. Everybody knew the story of her property, or rather of the property which had never in truth been hers, and which was now being made to pass out of her hands by means of a lawsuit, of which everybody spoke as though it were the best thing in the world for all the parties concerned. People, when they mentioned Sir John Ball to her – and he was often so mentioned – never spoke of him in harsh terms, as though he were her enemy. She observed that he was always named before her in that euphuistic language which we naturally use when we speak to persons of those who are nearest to them and dearest to them. The romance of the thing, and not the pity of it, was the general subject of discourse, so that she could not fail to perceive that she was generally regarded as the future wife of Sir John Ball.

It was the sudden way in which all this had come upon her that affected her so greatly. While staying in Arundel Street she had been altogether ignorant that the story of the Lion and the Lamb had become public, or that her name had been frequent in men's mouths. When Mrs Buggins had once told her that she was thus becoming famous, she had ridiculed Mrs Buggins' statement. Mrs Buggins had brought home word from some tea-party that the story had been discussed among her own friends; but Miss Mackenzie had regarded that as an accident. A lawyer's clerk or two about Chancery Lane or Carey Street might by chance hear of the matter in the course of their daily work – that it should be so, and that such people talked of her affairs distressed her; but that had, she was sure, been all. Now, however, in her new home she had learned that Mr Maguire's efforts had become notorious, and that she and her history were public property. When all this first became plain to her, it overwhelmed her so greatly that she was afraid to show her face; but this feeling gradually wore itself away, and she found herself able to look around upon the world again, and ask herself new questions of the future, as she had done when she had first found herself to be the possessor of her fortune.

When she had been about three weeks with the Mackenzies, Sir John Ball came to see her. He had written to her once before that, but his letter had referred simply to some matter of business. When he was shown into the drawing-room in Cavendish Square, Mrs Mackenzie and Margaret were both there, but the former in a few minutes got up and left the room. Margaret had wished with all her heart that her hostess would remain with them. She was sure that Sir John Ball had nothing to say that she would care to hear, and his saying nothing would seem to be of no special moment while three persons were in the room. But his saying nothing when special opportunity for speaking had been given to him would be of moment to her. Her destiny was in his hands to such a degree that she felt his power over her to amount almost to a cruelty. She longed to ask him what her fate was to be, but it was a question that she could not put to him. She knew that he would not tell her now; and she knew also that the very fact of his not telling her would inflict upon her a new misery, and deprive her of the comfort which she was beginning to enjoy. If he could not tell her at once how all this was to be ended, it would be infinitely better for her that he should remain away from her altogether.

As soon as Mrs Mackenzie had left the room he began to describe to her his last interview with the lawyers. She listened to him, and pretended to interest herself, but she did not care two straws about the lawyers. Point after point he explained to her, showing the unfortunate ingenuity with which his uncle Jonathan had contrived to confuse his affairs, and Margaret attempted to appear concerned. But her mind had now for some months past refused to exert itself with reference to the mode in which Mr Jonathan Ball had disposed of his money. Two years ago she had been told that it was hers; since that, she had been told that it was not hers. She had felt the hardship of this at first; but now that feeling was over with her, and she did not care to hear more about it. But she did care very much to know what was to be her future fate.

'And when will be the end of it, John?' she asked him.

'Ha! that seems so hard to say. They did name the first of April, but it won't be so soon as that. Mr Slow said to-day about the end of April, but his clerk seems to think it will be the middle of May.'

'It is very provoking,' said Margaret.

'Yes, it is,' said John Ball, 'very provoking; I feel it so. It worries me so terribly that I have no comfort in life. But I suppose you find everything very nice here.'

'They are very kind to me.'

'Very kind, indeed. It was quite the proper thing for them to do; and when I heard that Mrs Mackenzie had been to you in Arundel Street, I was delighted.'

Margaret did not dare to tell him that she would have preferred to have been left in Arundel Street; but that, at the moment, was her feeling. If, when all this was over, she would still have to earn her bread, it would have been much better for her not to have come among her rich relations. What good would it then do her to have lived two or three months in Cavendish Square?

'I wish it were all settled, John,' she said; and as she spoke there was a tear standing in the corner of each eye.

'I wish it were, indeed,' said John Ball; but I think that he did not see the tears.

It was on her tongue to speak some word about the hospital; but she felt that if she did so now, it would be tantamount to asking him that question which it did not become her to ask; so she repressed the word, and sat in silence.

'When the day is positively fixed for the hearing,' said he, 'I will be sure to let you know.'

'I wish you would let me know nothing further about it, John, till it is all settled.'

'I sometimes almost fancy that I wish the same thing,' said he, with a faint attempt at a smile; and after that he got up and went his way.

This was not to be endured. Margaret declared to herself that she could not live and bear it. Let the people around her say what they would, it could not be that he would treat her in this way if he intended to make her his wife. It would be better for her to make up her mind that it was not to be so, and to insist on leaving the Mackenzies' house. She would go, not again to Arundel Street, but to some lodging further away, in some furthest recess of London, where no one would come to her and flurry her with false hopes, and there remain till she might be allowed to earn her bread. That was the mood in which Mrs Mackenzie found her late in the afternoon on the day of Sir John Ball's visit. There was to be a dinner party in the house that evening, and Margaret began by asking leave to absent herself.

'Nonsense, Margaret,' said Mrs Mackenzie; 'I won't have anything of the kind.'

'I cannot come down, Mrs Mackenzie; I cannot, indeed.'

'That is absolute nonsense. That man has been saying something unkind to you. Why do you mind what he says?'

'He has not said anything unkind; he has not said anything at all.'

'Oh, that's the grief, is it?'

'I don't know what you mean by grief; but if you were situated as I am you would perceive that you were in a false position.'

'I am sure he has been saying something unkind to you.'

Margaret hardly knew how to tell her thoughts and feelings, and yet she wished to tell them. She had resolved that she would tell the whole to

Mrs Mackenzie, having convinced herself that she could not carry out her plan of leaving Cavendish Square without some explanation of the kind. She did not know how to make her speech with propriety, so she jumped at the difficulty boldly. 'The truth is, Mrs Mackenzie, that he has no more idea of marrying me than he has of marrying you.'

'Margaret, how can you talk such nonsense?'

'It is not nonsense; it is true; and it will be much better that it should all be understood at once. I have nothing to blame him for, nothing; and I don't blame him; but I cannot bear this kind of life any longer. It is killing me. What business have I to be living here in this way, when I have got nothing of my own, and have no one to depend on but myself?'

'Then he must have said something to you; but, whatever it was, you cannot but have misunderstood him.'

'No; he has said nothing, and I have not misunderstood him.' Then there was a pause.

'He has said nothing to me, and I am bound to understand what that means.'

'Margaret, I want to put one question to you,' said Mrs Mackenzie, speaking with a serious air that was very unusual with her – 'and you will understand, dear, that I only do so because of what you are saying now.'

'You may put any question you please to me,' said Margaret.

'Has your cousin ever asked you to be his wife, or has he not?'

'Yes, he has. He has asked me twice.'

'And what answer did you make him?'

'When I thought all the property was mine, I refused him. Then, when the property became his, he asked me again, and I accepted him. Sometimes, when I think of that, I feel so ashamed of myself, that I hardly dare to hold up my head.'

'But you did not accept him simply because you had lost your money.'

'No; but it looks so like it; does it not? And of course he must think that I did so.'

'I am quite sure he thinks nothing of the kind. But he did ask you, and you did accept him?'

'Oh, yes.'

'And since that, has he ever said anything to you to signify that the match should be broken off?'

'The very day after he had asked me, Mr Maguire came to the Cedars and saw me, and Lady Ball was there too. And he was very false, and told my aunt things that were altogether untrue. He said that – that I had promised to marry him, and Lady Ball believed him.'

'But did Mr Ball believe him?'

'My aunt said all that she could against me, and when John spoke to me the next day, it was clear that he was very angry with me.'

'But did he believe you or Mr Maguire when you told him that Mr Maguire's story was a falsehood from beginning to end?'

'But it was not a falsehood from beginning to end. That's where I have been so very, very unfortunate; and perhaps I ought to say, as I don't want to hide anything from you, so very, very wrong. The man did ask me to marry him, and I had given him no answer.'

'Had you thought of accepting him?'

'I had not thought about that at all, when he came to me. So I told him that I would consider it all, and that he must come again.'

'And he came again.'

'Then my brother's illness occurred, and I went to London. After that Mr Maguire wrote to me two or three times, and I refused him in the plainest language that I could use. I told him that I had lost all my fortune, and then I was sure that there would be an end of any trouble from him; but he came to the Cedars on purpose to do me all this injury; and now he has put all these stories about me into the newspapers, how can I think that any man would like to make me his wife? I have no right to be surprised that Lady Ball should be so eager against it.'

'But did Mr Ball believe you when you told him the story?'

'I think he did believe me.'

'And what did he say?'

Margaret did not answer at once, but sat with her fingers up among her hair upon her brow:

'I am trying to think what were his words,' she said, 'but I cannot remember. I spoke more than he did. He said that I should have told him about Mr Maguire, and I tried to explain to him that there had been no time to do so. Then I said that he could leave me if he liked.'

'And what did he answer?'

'If I remember rightly, he made no answer. He left me saying that he would see me again the next day. But the next day I went away. I would not remain in the house with Lady Ball after what she had believed about me. She took that other man's part against me, and therefore I went away.'

'Did he say anything as to your going?'

'He begged me to stay, but I would not stay. I thought it was all over then. I regarded him as being quite free from any engagement, and myself as being free from any necessity of obeying him. And it was all over. I had no right to think anything else.'

'And what came next?'

'Nothing. Nothing else has happened, except that Lady Ball came to me in Arundel Street, asking me to renounce him.'

'And you refused?'

'Yes; I would do nothing at her bidding. Why should I? She had been my enemy throughout, since she found that the money belonged to her son and not to me.'

'And all this time you have seen him frequently?'

'I have seen him sometimes about the business.'

'And he has never said a word to you about your engagement to him?'

'Never a word.'

'Nor you to him?'

'Oh, no! how could I speak to him about it?'

'I would have done so. I would not have had my heart crushed within me. But perhaps you were right. Perhaps it was best to be patient.'

'I know that I have been wrong to expect anything or to hope for anything,' said Margaret. 'What right have I to hope for anything when I refused him while I was rich?'

'That has nothing to do with it.'

'When he asked me again, he only did it because he pitied me. I don't want to be any man's wife because he pities me.'

'But you accepted him.'

'Yes; because I loved him.'

'And now?' Again Miss Mackenzie sat silent, still moving her fingers among the locks upon her brow. 'And now, Margaret?' repeated Mrs Mackenzie.

'What's the use of it now?'

'But you do love him?'

'Of course I love him. How shall it be otherwise? What has he done to change my love? His feelings have changed, and I have no right to blame him. He has changed; and I hate myself, because I feel that in coming here I have, as it were, run after him. I should have put myself in some place where no thought of marrying him should ever have come again to me.'

'Margaret, you are wrong throughout.'

'Am I? Everybody always says that I am always wrong.'

'If I can understand anything of the matter, Sir John Ball has not changed.'

'Then, why – why – why?'

'Ah, yes, exactly; why? Why is it that men and women cannot always understand each other; that they will remain for hours in each other's presence without the power of expressing, by a single word, the thoughts that are busy within them? Who can say why it is so? Can you get up and make a clean breast of it all to him?'

'But I am a woman, and am very poor.'

'Yes, and he is a man, and, like most men, very dumb when they have anything at heart which requires care in the speaking. He knows no better than to let things be as they are; to leave the words all unspoken till he can say to you, "Now is the time for us to go and get ourselves married;" just as he might tell you that now was the time to go and dine.'

'But will he ever say that?'

'Of course he will. If he does not say so when all this business is off his mind, when Mr Maguire and his charges are put at rest, when the lawyers have finished their work, then come to me and tell me that I have deceived you. Say to me then, "Clara Mackenzie, you have put me wrong, and I look to you to put me right." You will find I will put you right.'

In answer to this, Margaret was able to say nothing further. She sat for a while with her face buried in her hands thinking of it all, asking herself whether she might dare to believe it all. At last, however, she went up to dress for dinner; and when she came down to the drawing-room there was a smile upon her face.

After that a month or six weeks passed in Cavendish Square, and there was, during all that time, no further special reference to Sir John Ball or his affairs. Twice he was asked to dine with the Mackenzies, and on both occasions he did so. On neither of those evenings did he say very much to Margaret; but, on both of them he said some few words, and it was manifestly his desire that they should be regarded as friends.

And as the spring came on, Margaret's patience returned to her, and her spirits were higher than they had been at any time since she first discovered that success among the Stumfoldians at Littlebath did not make her happy.

✎ TWENTY-SEVEN ✎

The Negro Soldiers' Orphan Bazaar

IN THE SPRING DAYS OF THE EARLY May there came up in London that year a great bazaar – a great charity bazaar on behalf of the orphan children of negro soldiers who had fallen in the American war. Tidings had come to this country that all slaves taken in the revolted States had been made free by the Northern invaders, and that these free men had been called upon to show their immediate gratitude by becoming soldiers in the Northern ranks. As soldiers they were killed in battle, or died, and as dead men they left orphans behind them. Information had come that many of these orphans were starving, and hence had arisen the cause for the Negro Soldiers' Orphan Bazaar. There was still in existence at that time, down at South Kensington, some remaining court or outstanding building which had belonged to the Great International Exhibition, and here the bazaar was to be held. I do not know that I can trace the way in which the idea grew and became great, or that anyone at the time was able to attribute the honour to the proper founder. Some gave it all to the Prince of Wales, declaring that his royal highness had done it out of his own head; and others were sure that the whole business had originated with a certain philanthropical Mr Manfred Smith who had lately come up in the world, and was supposed to have a great deal to do with most things. Be that as it may, this thing did grow and become great, and there was a list of lady patronesses which included some duchesses, one marchioness, and half the countesses in London. It was soon manifest to the eyes of those who understood such things, that the Negro Soldiers' Orphan Bazaar was to be a success, and therefore there was no difficulty whatsoever in putting the custody of the stalls into the hands of proper persons. The difficulty consisted in rejecting offers from persons who undoubtedly were quite proper for such an occasion. There came to be interest made for permission to serve, and boastings were heard of unparalleled success in the bazaar line. The Duchess of St Bungay had a happy bevy of young ladies who were to act as counter attendants under her grace; and who so happy as any young lady who could get herself put upon the duchess's staff? It was even rumoured that a certain very distinguished person would have shown herself behind a stall, had not a certain other more distinguished person expressed an objection: and while the rumour was afloat as to the junior of those two distinguished persons, the young-ladydom of London was frantic in its eagerness to officiate. Now at that time there had become attached to the name of our poor Griselda a romance with which the west-end of London had become wonderfully well acquainted. The story of the Lion and the Lamb was very popular. Mr Maguire may be said to have made himself odious to the fashionable world at large, and the fate of poor Margaret Mackenzie with her lost fortune, and the additional misfortune of her clerical pledged protector, had recommended itself as being truly interesting to all the feeling hearts of the season. Before May was over, gentlemen were enticed to dinner parties by being told – and untruly told – that the Lamb had been 'secured;' as on the previous year they had been enticed by a singular assurance as to Bishop Colenso; and when Margaret on one occasion allowed herself to be taken to Covent Garden Theatre, every face from the stalls was turned towards her between the acts.

Who then was more fit to take a stall, or part of a stall at the Negro Soldiers' Orphan Bazaar, than our Griselda? When the thing loomed so large, lady patronesses began to be aware that mere nobodies would hardly be fit for the work. There would have been little or no difficulty in carrying out a law that nobody should take a part in the business who had not some handle to her name, but it was felt that such an arrangement as that might lead to failure rather than glory. The commoner world must be represented but it should be represented only by ladies who had made great names for themselves. Mrs Conway Sparkes, the spiteful poetess, though she was old and ugly as well as spiteful, was to have a stall and a bevy, because there was thought to be no doubt about her poetry. Mrs Chaucer Munro had a stall and a bevy; but I cannot clearly tell her claim to distinction, unless it was that she had all but lost her character four times, but had so saved it on each of those occasions that she was just not put into the Index Expurgatorius of fashionable society in London. It was generally said by those young men who discussed the subject, that among Mrs Chaucer Munro's bevy would be found the most lucrative fascination of the day. And then Mrs Mackenzie was asked to take a stall, or part of a stall, and to bring Griselda with her as her assistant. By this time the Lamb was most generally known as 'Griselda' among fashionable people.

Now Mrs Mackenzie was herself a woman of fashion, and quite open to the distinction of having a part assigned to her at the great bazaar of the season. She did not at all object to a booth on the left hand of the Duchess of St Bungay, although it was just opposite to Mrs Chaucer Munro. She assented at once.

'But you must positively bring Griselda,' said Lady Glencora Palliser, by whom the business of this mission was conducted.

'Of course, I understand that,' said Mrs Mackenzie. 'But what if she won't come?'

'Griseldas are made to do anything,' said Lady Glencora, 'and of course she must come.'

Having settled the difficulty in this way, Lady Glencora went her way, and Mrs Mackenzie did not allow Griselda to go to her rest that night till she had extracted from her a promise of acquiescence, which, I think, never would have been given had Miss Mackenzie understood anything of the circumstances under which her presence was desired.

But the promise was given, and Margaret knew little or nothing of what was expected from her till there came up, about a fortnight before the day of the bazaar, the great question of her dress for the occasion. Previous to that she would fain have been energetic in collecting and making things for sale at her stall, for she really taught herself to be anxious that the negro soldiers' orphans should have provision made for them; but, alas! her energy was all repressed, and she found that she was not to be allowed to do anything in that direction.

'Things of that sort would not go down at all now-a-days, Margaret,' said Mrs Mackenzie. 'Nobody would trouble themselves to carry them away. There are tradesmen who furnish the stalls, and mark their own prices, and take back what is not sold. You charge double the tradesman's price, that's all.'

Margaret, when her eyes were thus opened, of course ceased to make little pincushions, but she felt that her interest in the thing was very much lowered. But a word must be said as to that question of the dress. Miss Mackenzie, when she was first interrogated as to her intentions, declared her purpose of wearing a certain black silk dress which had seen every party at Mrs Stumfold's during Margaret's Littlebath season. To this her cousin demurred, and from demurring proceeded to the enunciation of a positive order. The black silk dress in question should not be worn. Now Miss Mackenzie chose to be still in mourning on the second of June, the day of the bazaar, her brother having died in September, and had no fitting garment, so she said, other than the black silk in question. Whereupon Mrs Mackenzie, without further speech to her cousin on the subject, went out and purchased a muslin covered all over with the prettiest little frecks of black, and sent a milliner to Margaret, and provided a bonnet of much the same pattern, the gayest, lightest, jauntiest, falsest, most make-belief-mourning bonnet that ever sprang from the art of a designer in bonnets – and thus nearly broke poor Margaret's heart.

'People should never have things given them, who can't buy for themselves,' she said, with tears in her eyes, 'because of course they know what it means.'

'But, my dearest,' said Mrs Mackenzie, 'young ladies who never have any money of their own at all always accept presents from all their relations. It is their special privilege.'

'Oh, yes, young ladies; but not women like me who are waiting to find out whether they are ruined or not.'

The difficulty, however, was at last overcome, and Margaret, with many inward upbraidings of her conscience, consented to wear the black-freckled dress.

'I never saw anybody look so altered in my life,' said Mrs Mackenzie, when Margaret, apparelled, appeared in the Cavendish Square drawing-room on the morning in question. 'Oh, dear, I hope Sir John Ball will come to look at you.'

'Nonsense! he won't be such a fool as to do anything of the kind.'

'I took care to let him know that you would be there;' said Mrs Mackenzie.

'You didn't?'

'But I did, my dear.'

'Oh, dear, what will he think of me?' ejaculated Margaret; but nevertheless I fancy that there must have been some elation in her bosom when she regarded herself and the freckled muslin in the glass.

Both Mrs Mackenzie and Miss Mackenzie had more than once gone down to the place to inspect the ground and make themselves familiar with the position they were to take. There were great stalls and little stalls, which came alternately; and the Mackenzie stall stood next to a huge centre booth at which the duchess was to preside. On their other hand was the stall of old Lady Ware, and opposite to them, as has been before said, the doubtful Mrs Chaucer Munro was to hold difficult sway over her bevy of loud nymphs. Together with Mrs Mackenzie were two other Miss Mackenzies, sisters of her husband, handsome, middle-aged women, with high cheek-bones and fine brave-looking eyes. All the Mackenzies, except our Griselda, were dressed in the tartan of their clan; and over the stall there was some motto in Gaelic, 'Dhu dhaith donald dhuth,' which nobody could understand, but which was not the less expressive. Indeed, the Mackenzie stall was got up very well; but then was it not known and understood that Mrs Mackenzie did get up things very well? It was acknowledged on all sides that the Lamb, Griselda, was uncommonly well got up on this occasion.

It was understood that the ladies were to be assembled in the bazaar at half-past two, and that the doors were to be thrown open to the public at three o'clock. Soon after half-past two Mrs Mackenzie's carriage was at the door, and the other Mackenzies having come up at the same time, the Mackenzie phalanx entered the building together. There were many others with them, but as they walked up they found the Countess of Ware standing alone in the centre building, with her four daughters behind her. She had on her head a wonderful tiara, which gave to her appearance a ferocity almost greater than was natural to her. She was a woman with square jaws, and a big face, and stout shoulders: but she was not, of her own unassisted height, very tall. But of that tiara and its altitude she was proud, and as she stood in the midst of the stalls, brandishing her umbrella-sized parasol in her anger, the ladies, as they entered, might well be cowed by her presence.

'When ladies say half-past two,' said she, 'they ought to come at half-past two. Where is the Duchess of St Bungay? I shall not wait for her.'

But there was a lady there who had come in behind the Mackenzies, whom nothing ever cowed. This was the Lady Glencora Palliser, the great heiress who had married the heir of a great duke, pretty, saucy, and occasionally intemperate, in whose eyes Lady Ware with her ferocious tiara was simply an old woman in a ridiculous head-gear. The countess had apparently addressed herself to Mrs Mackenzie, who had been the foremost to enter the building, and our Margaret had already begun to tremble. But Lady Glencora stepped forward, and took the brunt of the battle upon herself.

'Nobody ever yet was so punctual as my Lady Ware,' said Lady Glencora.

'It is very annoying to be kept waiting on such occasions,' said the countess.

'But my dear Lady Ware, who keeps you waiting? There is your stall, and why on earth should you stand here and call us all over as we come in, like naughty schoolboys?'

'The duchess said expressly that she would be here at half-past two.'

'Who ever expects the dear duchess to keep her word?' said Lady Glencora.

'Or whoever cared whether she does or does not?' said Mrs Chaucer Munro, who, with her peculiar bevy, had now made her way up among the front rank.

Then to have seen the tiara of Lady Ware, as it wagged and nodded while she looked at Mrs Munro, and to have witnessed the high moral tone of the ferocity with which she stalked away to her own stall with her daughters behind her – a tragi-comedy which it was given to no male eyes to behold – would have been worth the whole after-performance of the bazaar. No male eyes beheld that scene, as Mr Manfred Smith, the manager, had gone out to look for his duchess, and missing her carriage in the crowd, did not return till the bazaar had been opened. That Mrs Chaucer Munro did not sink, collapsed, among her bevy, must have been owing altogether to that callousness which a long habit of endurance produces. Probably she did feel something as at the moment there came no titter from any other bevy corresponding to the titter which was raised by her own. She and her bevy retired to their allotted place, conscious that their time for glory could not come till the male world should appear upon the scene. But Lady Ware's tiara still wagged and nodded behind her counter, and Margaret, looking at her, thought that she must have come there as the grand duenna of the occasion.

Just at three o'clock the poor duchess hurried into the building in a terrible flurry, and went hither and thither among the stalls, not knowing at first where was her throne. Unkind chance threw her at first almost into the booth of Mrs Conway Sparkes, the woman whom of all women she hated the most; and from thence she recoiled into the arms of Lady Hartletop who was sitting serene, placid, and contented in her appointed place.

'Opposite, I think, duchess,' Mrs Conway Sparkes had said. 'We are only the small fry here.'

'Oh, ah; I beg pardon. They told me the middle, to the left.'

'And this is the middle to the right,' said Mrs Conway Sparkes. But the duchess had turned round since she came in, and could not at all understand where she was.

'Under the canopy, duchess,' just whispered Lady Hartletop. Lady Hartletop was a young woman who knew her right hand from her left under all circumstances of life, and who never made any mistakes. The duchess looked up in her confusion to the centre of the ceiling, but could see no canopy. Lady Hartletop had done all that could be required of her, and if the duchess were to die amidst her difficulties it would not be her fault. Then came forth the Lady Glencora, and with true charity conducted the lady-president to her chair, just in time to avoid the crush, which ensued upon the opening of the doors.

The doors were opened, and very speedily the space of the bazaar between the stalls became too crowded to have admitted the safe passage of such a woman as the Duchess of St Bungay; but Lady Glencora, who was less majestic in her size and gait, did not find herself embarrassed. And now there arose, before the general work of fleecing the wether lambs had well commenced, a terrible discord, as of a brass band with broken bassoons, and trumpets all out of order, from the further end of the building – a terrible noise of most unmusical music, such as Bartholomew Fair in its loudest days could hardly have known. At such a diapason one would have thought that the tender ears of May Fair and Belgravia would have been crushed and cracked and riven asunder; that female voices would have shrieked, and the intensity of fashionable female agony would have displayed itself in all its best recognised forms. But the crash of brass was borne by them as though they had been rough schoolboys delighting in a din. The duchess gave one jump, and then remained quiet and undismayed. If Lady Hartletop heard it, she did not betray the hearing. Lady Glencora for a moment put her hands to her ears as she laughed, but she did it as though the prettiness of the motion were its only one cause. The fine nerves of Mrs Conway Sparkes, the poetess, bore it all without flinching; and Mrs Chaucer Munro with her bevy rushed forward so that they might lose nothing of what was coming.

'What are they going to do?' said Margaret to her cousin, in alarm.

'It's the play part of the thing. Have you not seen the bills?' Then Margaret looked at a great placard which was exhibited near to her, which, though by no means intelligible to her, gave her to understand that there was a show in progress. The wit of the thing seemed to consist chiefly in the wonderful names chosen. The King of the Cannibal Islands was to appear on a white charger. King Chrononhotonthologos was to be led in chains by Tom Thumb. Achilles would drag Hector thrice round the walls of Troy; and Queen Godiva would ride through Coventry, accompanied by Lord Burghley and the ambassador from Japan. It was also signified that in some back part of the premises a theatrical entertainment would be carried on throughout the afternoon, the King of the Cannibal Islands, with his royal brother and sister Chrononhoton-thologos and Godiva, taking principal parts; but as nobody seemed to go to the theatre the performers spent their time chiefly in making processions through and amidst the stalls, when, as the day waxed hot, and the work became heavy, they seemed to be taken much in dudgeon by the various bevies with whose business they interfered materially.

On this, their opening march, they rushed into the bazaar with great energy, and though they bore no resemblance to the characters named in the playbill, and though there was among them neither a Godiva, a Hector, a Tom Thumb, or a Japanese, nevertheless, as they were dressed in paint and armour after the manner of the late Mr Richardson's heroes, and as most of the ladies had probably been without previous oppor-tunity of seeing such delights, they had their effect. When they had made their twenty-first procession the thing certainly grew stale, and as they brought with them an infinity of dirt, they were no doubt a nuisance. But no one would have been inclined to judge these amateur actors with harshness who knew how much they themselves were called on to endure, who could appreciate the disgusting misery of a hot summer afternoon spent beneath dust and paint and tin-plate armour, and who would remember that the performers received payment neither in *éclat* nor in thanks, nor even in the smiles of beauty.

'Can't somebody tell them not to come any more?' said the duchess, almost crying with vexation towards the end of the afternoon.

Then Mr Manfred Smith, who managed everything, went to the rear, and the king and warriors were sent away to get beer or cooling drinks at their respective clubs.

Poor Mr Manfred Smith! He had not been present at the moment in which he was wanted to lead the duchess to her stall, and the duchess never forgave him. Instead of calling him by his name from time to time, and enabling him to shine in public as he deserved to shine – for he had worked at the bazaar for the last six weeks as no professional man ever worked at his profession – the duchess always asked for 'somebody' when she wanted Mr Smith, and treated him when he came as though he had been a servant hired for the occasion. One very difficult job of work was given to him before the day was done; 'I wish you'd go over to those young women,' said the duchess, 'and say that if they make so much noise, I must go away.'

The young women in question were Mrs Chaucer Munro and her bevy, and the commission was one which poor Manfred Smith found it difficult to execute.

'Mrs Munro,' said he, 'you'll be sorry to hear – that the duchess – has got – a headache, and she thinks we all might be a little quieter.'

The shouts of the loud nymphs were by this time high. 'Pooh!' said one of them. 'Headache indeed!' said another. 'Bother her head!' said a third. 'If the duchess is ill, perhaps she had better retire,' said Mrs Chaucer Munro. Then Mr Manfred Smith walked off sorrowfully towards the door, and seating himself on the stool of the money-taker by the entrance, wiped off the perspiration from his brow. He had already put on his third pair of yellow kid gloves for the occasion, and they were soiled and torn and disreputable; his polished boots were brown with dust; the magenta ribbon round his neck had become a moist rope; his hat had been thrown down and rumpled; a drop of oil had made a spot upon his trousers; his whiskers were draggled and out of order, and his mouth was full of dirt. I doubt if Mr Manfred Smith will ever undertake to manage another bazaar.

The duchess I think was right in her endeavour to mitigate the riot among Mrs Munro's nymphs. Indeed there was rioting among other nymphs than hers, though her noise and their noise was the loudest; and it was difficult to say how there should not be riot, seeing what was to be the recognised manner of transacting business. At first there was something of prettiness in the rioting. The girls, who went about among the crowd, begging men to put their hands into lucky bags, trading in rose-buds, and asking for half-crowns for cigar lighters, were fresh in their muslins, pretty with their braided locks, and perhaps not impudently over-pressing in their solicitations to male strangers. While they were not as yet either aweary or habituated to the necessity of importunity, they remembered their girlhood and their ladyhood, their youth and their modesty, and still carried with them something of the bashfulness of maidenhood; and the young men, the wether lambs, were as yet flush with their half-crowns, and the elder sheep had not quite dispensed the last of their sovereigns or buttoned up their trousers pockets. But as the work went on, and the dust arose, and the prettinesses were destroyed, and money became scarce, and weariness was felt, and the heat showed itself, and the muslins sank into limpness, and the ribbons lost their freshness, and braids of hair grew rough and loose, and sidelocks displaced themselves – as girls became used to soliciting and forgetful of their usual reticences in their anxiety for money, the charm of the thing went, and all was ugliness and rapacity. Young ladies no longer moved about, doing works of charity; but harpies and unclean birds were greedy in quest of their prey.

'Put a letter in my post-office,' said one of Mrs Munro's bevy, who officiated in a postal capacity behind a little square hole, to a young man on whom she pounced out and had caught him and brought up, almost with violence.

The young man tendered some scrap of paper and a sixpence.

'Only sixpence!' said the girl.

A cabman could not have made the complaint with a more finished accent of rapacious disgust.

'Never mind,' said the girl, 'I'll give you an answer.'

Then, with inky fingers and dirty hands, she tendered him some scrawl, and demanded five shillings postage. 'Five shillings!' said the young man. 'Oh, I'm d——'

Then he gave her a shilling and walked away. She ventured to give one little halloa after him, but she caught the duchess's eye looking at her, and was quiet.

I don't think there was much real flirting done. Men won't flirt with draggled girls, smirched with dust, weary with work, and soiled with heat; and especially they will not do so at the rate of a shilling a word. When the whole thing was over, Mrs Chaucer Munro's bevy, lying about on the benches in fatigue before they went away, declared that, as far as they were concerned, the thing was a mistake. The expenditure in gloves and muslin had been considerable, and the returns to them had been very small. It is not only that men will not flirt with draggled girls, but they will carry away with them unfortunate remembrances of what they have seen and heard. Upon the whole it may be doubted whether any of the bevies were altogether contented with the operations on the occasion of the Negro Soldiers' Orphan Bazaar.

Miss Mackenzie had been, perhaps, more fortunate than some of the others. It must, however, be remembered that there are two modes of conducting business at these bazaars. There is the travelling merchant, who roams about, and there is the stationary merchant, who remains always behind her counter. It is not to be supposed that the Duchess of St Bungay spent the afternoon rushing about with a lucky bag. The duchess was a stationary trader, and so were all the ladies who belonged to the Mackenzie booth. Miss Mackenzie, the lamb, had been much regarded, and consequently the things at her disposal had been quickly sold. It had all seemed to her to be very wonderful, and as the fun grew fast and furious, as the young girls became eager in their attacks, she made up her mind that she would never occupy another stall at a bazaar. One incident, and but one, occurred to her during the day; and one person came to her that she knew, and but one. It was nearly six, and she was beginning to think that the weary work must soon be over, when, on a sudden, she found Sir John Ball standing beside her.

'Oh, John!' she said, startled by his presence, 'who would have thought of seeing you here?'

'And why not me as well as any other fool of my age?'

'Because you think it is foolish,' she answered, 'and I suppose the others don't.'

'Why should you say that I think it foolish? At any rate, I'm glad to see you looking so nice and happy.'

'I don't know about being happy,' said Margaret – 'or nice either for the matter of that.'

But there was a smile on her face as she spoke, and Sir John smiled also when he saw it.

'Doesn't she look well in that bonnet?' said Mrs Mackenzie, turning round to the side of the counter at which he was standing. 'It was my choice, and I absolutely made her wear it. If you knew the trouble I had!'

'It is very pretty,' said Sir John.

'Is it not? And are you not very much obliged to me? I'm sure you ought to be, for nobody before has ever taken the trouble of finding out what becomes her most. As for herself, she's much too well-behaved a young woman to think of such vanities.'

'Not at present, certainly,' said Margaret.

'And why not at present? She looks on those lawyers and their work as though there was something funereal about them. You ought to teach her better, Sir John.'

'All that will be over in a day or two now,' said he.

'And then she will shake off her dowdiness and her gloom together,' said Mrs Mackenzie. 'Do you know I fancy she has a liking for pretty things at heart as well as another woman.'

'I hope she has,' said he.

'Of course you do. What is a woman worth without it? Don't be angry, Margaret, but I say a woman is worth nothing without it, and Sir John will agree with me if he knows anything about the matter. But, Margaret, why don't you make him buy something? He can't refuse you if you ask him.'

If Miss Mackenzie could thereby have provided for all the negro soldiers' orphans in existence, I do not think that she could at that moment have solicited him to make a purchase.

'Come, Sir John,' continued Mrs Mackenzie, 'you must buy something of her. What do you say to this paper-knife?'

'How much does the paper-knife cost?' said he, still smiling. It was a large, elaborate, and perhaps, I may say, unwieldy affair, with a great elephant at the end of it.

'Oh! that is terribly dear,' said Margaret, 'it costs two pounds ten.'

Thereupon he put his hand into his pocket, and taking out his purse, gave her a five-pound note.

'We never give change,' said Mrs Mackenzie: 'do we, Margaret?'

'I'll give him change,' said Margaret.

'I'll be extravagant for once,' said Sir John, 'and let you keep the whole.'

'Oh, John!' said Margaret.

'You have no right to scold him yet,' said Mrs Mackenzie.

Margaret, when she heard this, blushed up to her forehead, and in her confusion forgot all about the paper-knife and the money. Sir John, I fancy, was almost as much confused himself, and was quite unable to make any fitting reply. But, just at that moment, there came across two harpies from the realms of Mrs Chaucer Munro, eagerly intent upon their prey.

'Here are the lion and the lamb together,' said one harpy. 'The lion must buy a rose to give to the lamb. Sir Lion, the rose is but a poor half-crown.' And she tendered him a battered flower, leering at him from beneath her draggled, dusty bonnet as she put forth her untempting hand for the money.

'Sir Lion, Sir Lion,' said the other harpy, 'I want your name for a raffle.'

But the lion was off, having pushed the first harpy aside somewhat rudely. That tale of the Lion and the Lamb had been very terrible to him; but never till this occasion had any one dared to speak of it directly to his face. But what will not a harpy do who has become wild and dirty and disgusting in the pursuit of half-crowns?

'Now he is angry,' said Margaret. 'Oh, Mrs Mackenzie, why did you say that?'

'Yes; he is angry,' said Mrs Mackenzie, 'but not with you or me. Upon my word, I thought he would have pushed that girl over; and if he had, he would only have served her right.'

'But why did you say that? You shouldn't have said it.'

'About your not scolding him yet? I said it, my dear, because I wanted to make myself certain. I was almost certain before, but now I am quite certain.'

'Certain of what, Mrs Mackenzie?'

'That you'll be a baronet's wife before me, and entitled to be taken out of a room first as long as dear old Sir Walter is alive.'

Soon after that the bazaar was brought to an end, and it was supposed to have been the most successful thing of the kind ever done in London. Loud boasts were made that more than eight hundred pounds had been cleared; but whether any orphans of any negro soldiers were ever the better for the money I am not able to say.

TWENTY-EIGHT

Showing How the Lion was Stung by the Wasp

IT MAY BE REMEMBERED THAT MR MAGUIRE, when he first made public that pretty story of the Lion and the Lamb, declared that he would give the lion no peace till that beast had disgorged his prey, and that he had pledged himself to continue the fight till he should have succeeded in bringing the lamb back to the pleasant pastures of Littlebath. But Mr Maguire found some difficulty in carrying out his pledge. He was willing enough to fight, but the weapons with which to do battle were wanting to him. The *Christian Examiner*, having got so far into the mess, and finding that a ready sale did in truth result from any special article as to the lion and the lamb, was indeed ready to go on with the libel. The *Christian Examiner* probably had not much to lose. But there arose a question whether fighting simply through the columns of the *Christian Examiner* was not almost tantamount to no fight at all. He wanted to bring an action against Sir John Ball, to have Sir John Ball summoned into court and examined about the money, to hear some truculent barrister tell Sir John Ball that he could not conceal himself from the scorn of an indignant public behind the spangles of his parvenu baronetcy. He had a feeling that the lion would be torn to pieces, if only a properly truculent barrister could be got to fix his claws into him. But, unfortunately, no lawyer – not even Solomon Walker, the Low Church attorney at Littlebath – would advise him that he had any ground for an action. If indeed he chose to proceed against the lady for a breach of promise of marriage, then the result would depend on the evidence. In such case as that the Low Church attorney at Littlebath was willing to take the matter up. 'But Mr Maguire was, of course, aware,' said Solomon Walker, 'that there was a prejudice in the public mind against gentlemen appearing as parties to such suits.' Mr Maguire was also aware that he could adduce no evidence of the fact beyond his own unsupported, and, in such case, untrue word, and declared therefore to the attorney, in a very high tone indeed, that on no account would he take any step to harass the lady. It was simply against Sir John Ball that he wished to proceed. 'Things would come out in that trial, Mr Walker,' he said, 'which would astonish you and all the legal world. A rapacious scheme of villainy has been conceived and brought to bear, through the stupidity of some people and the iniquity of others, which would unroll itself fold by fold as certainly as I stand here, if it were properly handled by a competent barrister in one of our courts of law.' And I think that Mr Maguire believed what he was saying, and that he believed, moreover, that he was speaking the truth when he told Mr Walker that the lady had promised to marry him. Men who can succeed in deceiving no one else will succeed at last in deceiving themselves. But the lawyer told him, repeating the fact over and over again, that the thing was impracticable; that there was no means of carrying the matter so far that Sir John Ball should be made to appear in a witness box. Everything that Sir John had done he had done legally; and even at that moment of the discussion between Mr Walker and Mr Maguire, the question of the ownership of the property was being tried before a proper tribunal in London. Mr Maguire still thought Mr Walker to be wrong – thought that his attorney was a weak and ignorant man; but he acknowledged to himself the fact that he in his unhappy position was unable to get any more cunning attorney to take the matter in hand.

But the *Christian Examiner* still remained to him, and that he used with diligence. From week to week there appeared in it articles attacking the lion, stating that the lion was still being watched, that his prey would be snatched from him at last, that the lamb should even yet have her rights, and the like. And as the thing went on, the periodical itself and the writer of the article became courageous by habit, till things were printed which Sir John Ball found it almost impossible to bear. It was declared that he was going to desert the lamb, now that he had taken all the lamb's property; and that the lamb, shorn of all her fleece, was to be condemned to earn her bread as a common nurse in the wards of a common hospital – all which information came readily enough to Mr Maguire by the hands of Miss Colza. The papers containing these articles were always sent to Sir John Ball and to Miss Mackenzie, and the articles were always headed, 'The Lion and the Lamb.' Miss Mackenzie, in accordance with an arrangement made to that purpose, sent the papers as soon as they came to Mr Slow, but Sir John Ball had no such ready way of freeing himself from their burden. He groaned and toiled under them, going to his lawyer with them, and imploring permission to bring an action for libel against Mr Maguire. The venom of the unclean animal's sting had gone so deep into him, that, fond as he was of money, he had told his lawyer that he would not begrudge the expense if he could only punish the man who was hurting him. But the attorney, who understood something of feeling as well as something of money, begged him to be quiet at any rate till the fate of the property should be settled. 'And if you'll take my advice, Sir John, you will not notice him at all. You may be sure that he has not a shilling in the world, and that he wants you to prosecute him. When you have got damages against him, he will be off out of the country.'

'But I shall have stopped his impudent ribaldry,' said Sir John Ball. Then the lawyer tried to explain to him that no one read the ribaldry. It was of no use. Sir John read it himself, and that was enough to make him wretched.

The little fable which made Sir John so unhappy had not, for some months past, appeared in any of the metropolitan newspapers; but when the legal inquiry into the proper disposition of Mr Jonathan Ball's property was over, and when it was known that, as the result of that inquiry, the will in favour of the Mackenzies was to be set aside and the remains of the property handed over to Sir John, then that very influential newspaper, which in the early days of the question had told the story of the Lion and the Lamb, told it all again, tearing, indeed, the Littlebath *Christian Examiner* into shreds for its iniquity, but speaking of the romantic misfortune of the lamb in terms which made Sir John Ball very unhappy. The fame which accrued to him from being so publicly pointed out as a lion, was not fame of which he was proud. And when the writer in this very influential newspaper went on to say that the world was now looking for a termination of this wonderful story, which would make it pleasant to all parties, he was nearly beside himself in his misery. He, a man of fifty, of slow habits, with none of the buoyancy of youth left in him, apt to regard himself as older than his age, who had lived with his father and mother almost on an equality in regard to habits of life, the father of a large family, of which the eldest was now himself a man! Could it be endured that such a one as he should enter upon matrimony amidst the din of public trumpets and under a halo of romance? The idea of it was frightful to him. On the very day on which the result of the legal investigation was officially communicated to him, he sat in the old study at the Cedars with two newspapers before him. In one of these there was a description of his love, which he knew was intended as furtive ridicule, and an assurance to the public that the lamb's misfortunes would all be remedied by the sweet music of the marriage bell. What right had any one to assert publicly that he intended to marry any one? In his wretchedness and anger he would have indicted this newspaper also for a libel, had not his lawyer assured him that, according to law, there was no libel in stating that a man was going to be married. The other paper accused him of rapacity and dishonesty in that he would not marry the lamb, now that he had secured the lamb's fleece; so that, in truth, he had no escape on either side; for Mr Maguire, having at last ascertained that the lamb had, in very truth, lost all her fleece, was no longer desirous of any personal connection, and felt that he could best carry out his pledge by attacking the possessor of the fleece on that side. Under such circumstances, what was such a man as Sir John Ball to do? Could he marry his cousin amidst the trumpets, and the halo, and the doggrel poetry which would abound? Was it right that he should be made a mark for the finger of scorn? Had he done anything to deserve this punishment?

And it must be remembered that from day to day his own mother, who lived with him, who sat with him late every night talking on this one subject, was always instigating him to abandon his cousin. It had been admitted between them that he was no longer bound by his offer. Margaret herself had admitted it – 'does not attempt to deny it,' as Lady Ball repeated over and over again. When he had made his offer he had known nothing of Mr Maguire's offer, nor had Margaret then told him of it. Such reticence on her part of course released him from his bond. So Lady Ball argued, and against this argument her son made no demur. Indeed it was hardly possible that he should comprehend exactly what had taken place between his cousin and Mr Maguire. His mother did not scruple to assure him that she must undoubtedly at one time have accepted the man's proposal. In answer to this John Ball would always assert his entire reliance on his cousin's word.

'She did it without knowing that she did so,' Lady Ball would answer; 'but in some language she must have assented.'

But the mother was never able to extract from the son any intimation of his intention to give up the marriage, though she used threats and tears, ridicule and argument – appeals to his pride and appeals to his pocket. He never said that he certainly would marry her; he never said so at least after that night on which Margaret in her bedroom had told him her story with reference to Mr Maguire; but neither did he ever say that he certainly would not marry her. Lady Ball gathered from all his words a conviction that he would be glad to be released, if he could be released by any act on Margaret's behalf, and therefore she had made her attempt on Margaret. With what success the reader will, I hope, remember. Margaret, when she accepted her cousin's offer, had been specially bidden by him to be firm. This bidding she obeyed, and on that side there was no hope at all for Lady Ball.

I fear there was much of cowardice on Sir John's part. He had, in truth, forgiven Margaret any offence that she had committed in reference to Mr Maguire. She had accepted his offer while another offer was still dragging on an existence after a sort, and she had not herself been the first to tell him of these circumstances. There had been offence to him in this, but that offence he had, in truth, forgiven. Had there been no Littlebath *Christian Examiner*, no tale of the Lion and the Lamb, no publicity and no ridicule, he would quietly have walked off with his cousin to some church, having gone through all preliminary ceremonies in the most silent manner possible for them, and would have quietly got himself married and have carried Margaret home with him. Now that his father was dead and that his uncle Jonathan's money had come to him, his pecuniary cares were comparatively light, and he believed that he could be very happy with Margaret and his children. But then to be pointed at daily as a lion, and to be asked by all his acquaintances after the lamb! It must be owned that he was a coward; but are not most men cowards in such matters as that?

But now the trial was over, the money was his own, Margaret was left without a shilling in the world, and it was quite necessary that he should make up his mind. He had once told his lawyer, in his premature joy, on that very day on which Mr Maguire had come to the Cedars, that everything was to be made smooth by a marriage between himself and the disinherited heiress. He had since told the lawyer that something had occurred which might, perhaps, alter this arrangement. After that the lawyer had asked no question about the marriage; but when he communicated to his client the final intelligence that Jonathan Ball's money was at his client's disposal, he said that it would be well to arrange what should be done on Miss Mackenzie's behalf. Sir John Ball had assumed very plainly a look of vexation when the question was put to him.

'I promised Mr Slow that I would ask you,' said the lawyer. 'Mr Slow is of course anxious for his client.'

'It is my business and not Mr Slow's,' said Sir John Ball, 'and you may tell him that I say so.'

Then there had been a moment's silence, and Sir John had felt himself to be wrong.

'Pray tell him also,' said Sir John, 'that I am very grateful to him for his solicitude about my cousin, and that I fully appreciate his admirable conduct both to her and me throughout all this affair. When I have made up my mind what shall be done, I will let him know at once.'

As he walked down from his lawyer's chambers in Bedford Row to the railway station he thought of all this, and thought also of those words which Mrs Mackenzie had spoken to him in the bazaar. 'You have no right to scold him yet,' she had said to Margaret. Of course he had understood what they meant, and of course Margaret had understood them also. And he had not been at all angry when they were spoken. Margaret had been so prettily dressed, and had looked so fresh and nice, that at that moment he had forgotten all his annoyances in his admiration, and had listened to Mrs Mackenzie's cunning speech, not without confusion, but without any immediate desire to contradict its necessary inference. A moment or two afterwards the harpies had been upon him, and then he had gone off in his anger. Poor Margaret had been unable to distinguish between the effects produced by the speech and by the harpies; but Mrs Mackenzie had been more clever, and had consequently predicted her cousin's speedy promotion in the world's rank.

Sir John, as he went home, made up his mind to one of two alternatives. He would either marry his cousin or halve Jonathan Ball's money with her. He wanted to marry her, and he wanted to keep the money. He wanted to marry her especially since he had seen how nice she looked in black-freckled muslin; but he wanted to marry her in silence, without any clash of absurd trumpets, without ridicule-moving leading articles, and fingers pointed at the triumphant lion. He made up his mind to one of those alternatives, and resolved that he would settle which on that very night. His mind should be made up and told to his mother before he went to bed. Nevertheless, when the girls and Jack were gone, and he was left alone with Lady Ball, his mind had as yet been made up to nothing!

His mother gave him no peace on this subject. It was she who began the conversation on this occasion.

'John,' she said, 'the time has come for me to settle the question of my residence.'

Now the house at Twickenham was the property of the present baronet, but Lady Ball had a jointure of five hundred a year out of her late husband's estate. It had always been intended that the mother should continue to live with her son and grandchildren in the very probable event of her being left a widow; and it was felt by them all that their means were not large enough to permit, with discretion, separate households; but Lady Ball had declared more than once with extreme vehemence that nothing should induce her to live at the Cedars if Margaret Mackenzie should be made mistress of the house.

'Has the time come especially to-day?' he asked in reply.

'I think we may say it has come especially to-day. We know now that you have got this increase to your income, and nothing is any longer in doubt that we cannot ourselves settle. I need not say that my dearest wish is to remain here, but you know my mind upon that subject.'

'I cannot see any possible reason for your going.'

'Nor can I – except the one. I suppose you know yourself what you mean to do about your cousin. Everybody knows what you ought to do after the disgraceful things that have been put into all the newspapers.'

'That has not been Margaret's fault.'

'I am by no means so sure of that. Indeed, I think it has been her fault; and now she has made herself notorious by being at this bazaar, and by having herself called a ridiculous name by everybody. Nothing will make me believe but what she likes it.'

'You are ready to believe any evil of her, mother; and yet it is not two years since you yourself wished me to marry her.'

'Things are very different since that; very different indeed. And I did not know her then as I do now, or I should never have thought of such a thing, let her have had all the money in the world. She had not misbehaved herself then with that horrible curate.'

'She has not misbehaved herself now,' said the son, in an angry voice.

'Yes, she has, John,' said the mother, in a voice still more angry.

'That's a matter for me to judge. She has not misbehaved herself in my eyes. It is a great misfortune – a great misfortune for us both – the conduct of this man; but I won't allow it to be said that it was her fault.'

'Very well. Then I suppose I may arrange to go. I did not think, John, that I should be turned out of your father's house so soon after your father's death. I did not indeed.'

Thereupon Lady Ball got out her handkerchief, and her son perceived that real tears were running down her face.

'Nobody has ever spoken of your going except yourself, mother.'

'I won't live in the house with her.'

'And what would you have me do? Would you wish me to let her go her way and starve by herself?'

'No, John; certainly not. I think you should see that she wants for nothing. She could live with her sister-in-law, and have the interest of the money that the Rubbs took from her. It was your money.'

'I have explained to you over and over again, mother, that that has already been made over to Mrs Tom Mackenzie; and that would not have been at all sufficient. Indeed, I have altogether made up my mind upon that. When the lawyers and all the expenses are paid, there will still be about eight hundred a year. I shall share it with her.'

'John!'

'That is my intention; and therefore if I were to marry her I should get an additional income of four hundred a year for myself and my children.'

'You don't mean it, John?'

'Indeed I do, mother. I'm sure the world would expect me to do as much as that.'

'The world expect you! And are you to rob your children, John, because the world expects it? I never heard of such a thing. Give away four hundred a year merely because you are afraid of those wretched newspapers! I did expect you would have more courage.'

'If I do not do one, mother, I shall do the other certainly.'

'Then I must beg you to tell me which you mean to do. If you gave her half of all that is coming to you, of course I must remain here because you could not live here without me. Your income would be quite insufficient. But you do owe it to me to tell me at once what I am to do.'

To this her son made no immediate answer, but sat with his elbow on the table, and his head upon his hand looking moodily at the fire-place. He did not wish to commit himself if he could possibly avoid it.

'John, I must insist upon an answer,' said his mother. 'I have a right to expect an answer.'

'You must do what you like, mother, independently of me. If you think you can live here on your income, I will go away, and you shall have the place.'

'That's nonsense, John. Of course you want a large house for the children, and I, if I must be alone, shall only want one room for myself. What should I do with the house?' Then there was silence again for a while.

'I will give you a final answer on Saturday,' he said at last. 'I shall see Margaret before Saturday.'

After that he took his candle and went to bed. It was then Tuesday, and Lady Ball was obliged to be contented with the promise thus made to her.

On Wednesday he did nothing. On the Thursday morning he received a letter which nearly drove him mad. It was addressed to him at the office of the Shadrach Fire Insurance Company, and it reached him there. It was as follows –

> 'Littlebath – June, 186–
>
> 'Sir
>
> You are no doubt fully aware of all the efforts which I have made during the last six months to secure from your grasp the fortune which did belong to my dear – my dearest friend, Margaret Mackenzie. For as my dearest friend I shall ever regard her, though she and I have been separated by machinations of the nature of which she, as I am fully sure, has never been aware. I now ascertain that some of the inferior law courts have, under what pressure I know not, set aside the will which was made twenty years ago in favour of the Mackenzie family, and given to you the property which did belong to them. That a superior court would reverse the judgment, I believe there is little doubt; but whether or no the means exist for me to bring the matter before the higher tribunals of the country I am not yet aware. Very probably I may have no such power, and in such case, Margaret Mackenzie is, to-day, through your means, a beggar.
>
> 'Since this matter has been before the public you have ingeniously contrived to mitigate the wrath of public opinion by letting it be supposed that you purposed to marry the lady whose wealth you were seeking to obtain by legal quibbles. You have made your generous intentions very public, and have created a romance that has been, I must say, but little becoming to your age. If all be true that I heard when I last saw Miss Mackenzie at Twickenham, you have gone through some ceremony of proposing to her. But, as I understand, that joke is now thought to have been carried far enough; and as the money is your own, you intend to enjoy yourself as a lion, leaving the lamb to perish in the wilderness.

'Now I call upon you to assert, under your own name and with your own signature, what are your intentions with reference to Margaret Mackenzie. Her property, at any rate for the present, is yours. Do you intend to make her your wife, or do you not? And if such be your intention, when do you purpose that the marriage shall take place, and where?

'I reserve to myself the right to publish this letter and your answer to it; and of course shall publish the fact if your cowardice prevents you from answering it. Indeed nothing shall induce me to rest in this matter till I know that I have been the means of restoring to Margaret Mackenzie the means of decent livelihood.

'I have the honour to be, Sir,

'Your very humble servant,

JEREMIAH MAGUIRE.

'Sir John Ball, Bart., &c., &c.,
'Shadrach Fire Office.'

Sir John, when he had read this, was almost wild with agony and anger. He threw up his hands with dismay as he walked along the passages of the Shadrach Office, and fulminated mental curses against the wasp that was able to sting him so deeply. What should he do to the man? As for answering the letter, that was of course out of the question; but the reptile would carry out his threat of publishing the letter, and then the whole question of his marriage would be discussed in the public prints. An idea came across him that a free press was bad and rotten from the beginning to the end. This creature was doing him a terrible injury, was goading him almost to death, and yet he could not punish him. He was a clergyman, and could not be beaten and kicked, or even fired at with a pistol. As for prosecuting the miscreant, had not his own lawyer told him over and over again that such a prosecution was the very thing which the miscreant desired. And then the additional publicity of such a prosecution, and the twang of false romance which would follow and the horrid alliteration of the story of the two beasts, and all the ridicule of the incidents, crowded upon his mind, and he walked forth from the Shadrach office among the throngs of the city a wretched and almost despairing man.

✵ TWENTY-NINE ✵

A Friend in Need is a Friend Indeed

WHEN THE WORK OF THE BAZAAR WAS finished all the four Mackenzie ladies went home to Mrs Mackenzie's house in Cavendish Square, very tired, eager for tea, and resolved that nothing more should be done that evening. There should be no dressing for dinner, no going out, nothing but idleness, tea, lamb chops, and gossip about the day's work. Mr Mackenzie was down at the House, and there was no occasion for any domestic energy. And thus the evening was passed. How Mrs Chaucer Munro and the loud bevy fared among them, or how old Lady Ware and her daughters, or the poor, dear, bothered duchess or Mr Manfred Smith, or the kings and heroes who had appeared in paint and armour, cannot be told. I fear that the Mackenzie verdict about the bazaar in general was not favourable and that they agreed among themselves to abstain from such enterprises of charity in future. It concerns us now chiefly to know that our Griselda held up her head well throughout that evening, and made herself comfortable and at her ease among her cousins, although it was already known to her that the legal decision had gone against her in the great case of Ball *v*. Mackenzie. But had that decision been altogether in her favour the result would not have been so favourable to her spirits, as had been that little speech made by Mrs Mackenzie as to her having no right as yet to scold Sir John for his extravagance – that little speech made in good humour, and apparently accepted in good humour even by him. But on that evening Mrs Mackenzie was not able to speak to Margaret about her prospects, or to lecture her on the expediency of regarding the nicenesses of her dress in Sir John's presence, because of the two other cousins. The two other cousins, no doubt, knew all the story of the Lion and the Lamb, and talked to their sister-in-law, Clara, of their other cousin, Griselda, behind Griselda's back; and were no doubt very anxious that Griselda should become a baronet's wife; but among so large a party there was no opportunity for confidential advice.

On the next morning Mrs Mackenzie and Margaret were together, and then Mrs Mackenzie began:

'Margaret, my dear,' said she, 'that bonnet I gave you has been worth its weight in gold.'

'It cost nearly as much,' said Margaret, 'for it was very expensive and very light.'

'Or in bank-notes either, because it has shown him and me and everybody else that you needn't be a dowdy unless you please. No man wishes to marry a dowdy, you know.'

'I suppose I was a dowdy when he asked me.'

'I wasn't there, and didn't know you then, and can't say. But I do know that he liked the way you looked yesterday. Now, of course, he'll be coming here before long.'

'I dare say he won't come here again the whole summer.'

'If he did not, I should send for him.'

'Oh, Mrs Mackenzie!'

'And oh, Griselda! Why should I not send for him? You don't suppose

I'm going to let this kind of thing go on from month to month, till that old woman at the Cedars has contrived to carry her point. Certainly not.'

'Now that the matter is settled, of course, I shall not go on staying here.'

'Not after you're married, my dear. We couldn't well take in Sir John and all the children. Besides, we shall be going down to Scotland for the grouse. But I mean you shall be married out of this house. Don't look so astonished. Why not? There's plenty of time before the end of July.'

'I don't think he means anything of the kind; I don't indeed.'

'Then he must be the queerest man that ever I met; and I should say about the falsest and most heartless also. But whether he means to do that or does not, he must mean to do something. You don't suppose he'll take all your fortune away from you, and then leave you without coming to say a word to you about it? If you had disputed the matter, and put him to all manner of expense; if, in short, you had been enemies through it all, that might have been possible. But you have been such a veritable lamb, giving your fleece to the shearer so meekly – such a true Griselda, that if he were to leave you in that way, no one would ever speak to him again.'

'But you forget Lady Ball.'

'No, I don't. He'll have a disagreeable scene with his mother, and I don't pretend to guess what will be the end of that; but when he has done with his mother, he'll come here. He must do it. He has no alternative. And when he does come, I want you to look your best. Believe me, my dear, there would be no muslins in the world and no starch, if it was not intended that people should make themselves look as nice as possible.'

'Young people,' suggested Margaret.

'Young people, as you call them, can look well without muslin and without starch. Such things were intended for just such persons as you and me; and as for me, I make it a rule to take the goods the gods provide me.'

Mrs Mackenzie's philosophy was not without its result, and her prophecy certainly came true. A few days passed by and no lover came, but early on the Friday morning after the bazaar, Margaret, who at the moment was in her own room, was told that Sir John was below in the drawing-room with Mrs Mackenzie. He had already been there some little time, the servant said, and Mrs Mackenzie had sent up with her love to know if Miss Mackenzie would come down. Would she go down? Of course she would go to her cousin. She was no coward. Indeed, a true Griselda can hardly be a coward. So she made up her mind to go to her cousin and hear her fate.

The last four-and-twenty hours had been very bitter with Sir John Ball. What was he to do, walking about with that man's letter in his pocket – with that reptile's venom still curdling through his veins? On that Thursday morning, as he went towards his office, he had made up his mind, as he thought, to go to Margaret and bid her choose her own destiny. She should become his wife, or have half of Jonathan Ball's remaining fortune, as she might herself elect. 'She refused me,' he said to himself, 'when the money was all hers. Why should she wish to come to such a house as mine, to marry a dull husband and undertake the charge of a lot of children? She shall choose herself.' And then he thought of her as he had seen her at the bazaar, and began to flatter himself that, in spite of his dullness and his children, she would choose to become his wife. He was making some scheme as to his mother's life, proposing that two of his girls should live with her, and that she should be near to him, when the letter from Mr Maguire was put into his hands.

How was he to marry his cousin after that? If he were to do so, would not that wretch at Littlebath declare, through all the provincial and metropolitan newspapers, that he had compelled the marriage? That letter would be published in the very column that told of the wedding. But yet he must decide. He must do something. They who read this will probably declare that he was a weak fool to regard anything that such a one as Mr Maguire could say of him. He was not a fool, but he was so far weak and foolish; and in such matters such men are weak and foolish, and often cowardly.

It was, however, absolutely necessary that he should do something. He was as well aware as was Mrs Mackenzie that it was essentially his duty to see his cousin, now that the question of law between them had been settled. Even if he had no thought of again asking her to be his wife, he could not confide to any one else the task of telling her what was to be her fate. Her conduct to him in the matter of the property had been exemplary, and it was incumbent on him to thank her for her generous forbearance. He had pledged himself also to give his mother a final answer on Saturday.

On the Friday morning, therefore, he knocked at the Mackenzies' house door in Cavendish Square, and soon found himself alone with Mrs Mackenzie. I do not know that even then he had come to any fixed purpose. What he would himself have preferred would have been permission to postpone any action as regards his cousin for another six months, and to have been empowered to use that time in crushing Mr Maguire out of existence. But this might not be so, and therefore he went to Cavendish Square that he might there decide his fate.

'You want to see Margaret, no doubt,' said Mrs Mackenzie, 'that you may tell her that her ruin is finally completed;' and as she thus spoke of her cousin's ruin, she smiled her sweetest smile and put on her pleasantest look.

'Yes, I do want to see her presently,' he said.

Mrs Mackenzie had stood up as though she were about to go in quest of her cousin, but had sat down again when the word presently was spoken. She was by no means averse to having a few words of conversation about

Margaret, if Sir John should wish it. Sir John, I fear, had merely used the word through some instinctive idea that he might thereby stave off the difficulty for a while.

'Don't you think she looked very well at the Bazaar?' said Mrs Mackenzie.

'Very well, indeed,' he answered; 'very well. I can't say I liked the place.'

'Nor any of us, I can assure you. Only one must do that sort of thing sometimes, you know. Margaret was very much admired there. So much has been said of this singular story about her fortune, that people have, of course, talked more of her than they would otherwise have done.'

'That has been a great misfortune,' said Sir John, frowning.

'It has been a misfortune, but it has been one of those things that can't be helped. I don't think you have any cause to complain, for Margaret has behaved as no other woman ever did behave, I think. Her conduct has been perfect.'

'I don't complain of her.'

'As for the rest, you must settle that with the world yourself. I don't care for any one beyond her. But, for my part, I think it is the best to let those things die away of themselves. After all, what does it matter as long as one does nothing to be ashamed of oneself? People can't break any bones by their talking.'

'Wouldn't you think it very unpleasant, Mrs Mackenzie, to have your name brought up in the newspapers?'

'Upon my word I don't think I should care about it as long as my husband stood by me. What is it after all? People say that you and Margaret are the Lion and the Lamb. What's the harm of being called a lamb or a lion either? As long as people are not made to believe that you have behaved badly, that you have been false or cruel, I can't see that it comes to much. One does not, of course, wish to have newspaper articles written about one.'

'No, indeed.'

'But they can't break your bones, nor can they make the world think you dishonest, as long as you take care that you are honest. Now, in this matter, I take it for granted that you and Margaret are going to make a match of it –'

'Has she told you so?'

Mrs Mackenzie paused a moment to collect her thoughts before she answered; but it was only for a moment, and Sir John Ball hardly perceived that she had ceased to speak.

'No,' she said; 'she has not told me so. But I have told her that it must be so.'

'And she does not wish it?'

'Do you want me to tell a lady's secret? But in such a case as this the truth is always the best. She does wish it, with all her heart – as much as any woman ever wished for anything. You need have no doubt about her loving you.'

'Of course, Mrs Mackenzie, I should take care in any case that she were provided for amply. If a single life will suit her best, she shall have half of all that she ever thought to be her own.'

'And do you wish it to be so?'

'I have not said that, Mrs Mackenzie. But it may be that I should wish her to have the choice fairly in her own power.'

'Then I can tell you at once which she would choose. Your offer is very generous. It is more than generous. But, Sir John, a single life will not suit her; and my belief is, that were you to offer her the money without your hand, she would not take a farthing of it.'

'She must have some provision.'

'She will take none from you but the one, and you need be under no doubt whatsoever that she will take that without a moment's doubt as to her own future happiness. And, Sir John, I think you would have the best wife that I know anywhere among my acquaintance.' Then she stopped, and he sat silent, making no reply. 'Shall I send to her now?' said Mrs Mackenzie.

'I suppose you might as well,' said Sir John.

Then Mrs Mackenzie got up and left the room, but she did not herself go up to her cousin. She felt that she could not see Margaret without saying something of what had passed between herself and Sir John, and that it would be better that nothing should be said. So she went away to her own room, and dispatched her maid to send the lamb to the lion. Nevertheless, it was not without compunction, some twang of feminine conscience, that Mrs Mackenzie gave up this opportunity of saying some last important word, and perhaps doing some last important little act with regard to those nicenesses of which she thought perhaps too much. Mrs Mackenzie's philosophy was not without its truth; but a man of fifty should not be made to marry a woman by muslin and starch, if he be not prepared to marry her on other considerations.

When the message came, Margaret thought nothing of the muslin and starch. The bonnet that had been worth its weight in gold, and the black-freckled dress, were all forgotten. But she thought of the words which her cousin John had spoken to her as soon as they had got through the little gate into the grounds of the Cedars when they had walked back together from the railway station at Twickenham; and she remembered that she had then pledged herself to be firm. If he alluded to the offer he had then made, and repeated it, she would throw herself into his arms at once, and tell him that she would serve him with all her heart and all her strength as long as God might leave them together. But she was quite as strongly determined to accept from him for herself no other kind of provision. That money which for a short while had been hers was now his; and she could have no claim upon him unless he gave her the claim of a wife. After what had passed between them she would not be the recipient of his charity. Certain words had been written and spoken from which she had gathered the existence, in Mr Slow's mind, of some such plan as this. His client should lose her cause meekly and graciously, and should then have a claim for alms. That had been the idea on which Mr Slow had worked. She had long made up her mind that Mr Slow should be taught to know her better, if the day for such offering of alms should ever come. Perhaps it had come now. She took up a little scarf that she wore ordinarily and folded it tight across her shoulders, quite forgetful of muslin and starch, as she descended to the drawing-room in order that this question might be solved for her.

Sir John met her almost at the door as she entered.

'I'm afraid you've been expecting me to come sooner,' he said.

'No, indeed; I was not quite sure that you would come at all.'

'Oh, yes; I was certain to come. You have hardly received as yet any official notification that your cause has been lost.'

'It was not my cause, John,' she said, smiling, 'and I received no other notification than what I got through Mrs Mackenzie. Indeed, as you know, I have regarded this law business as nonsense all through. Since what you and Mr Slow told me, I have known that the property was yours.'

'But it was quite necessary to have a judgment.'

'I suppose so, and there's an end of it. I, for one, am not in the least disappointed – if it will give you any comfort to know that.'

'I don't believe that any other woman in England would have lost her fortune with the equanimity that you have shown.'

She could not explain to him that, in the first days of dismay caused by that misfortune, he had given her such consolation as to make her forget her loss, and that her subsequent misery had been caused by the withdrawal of that consolation. She could not tell him that the very memory of her money had been, as it were, drowned by other hopes in life – by other hopes and by other despair. But when he praised her for her equanimity, she thought of this. She still smiled as she heard his praise.

'I suppose I ought to return the compliment,' she said, 'and declare that no cousin who had been kept so long out of his own money ever behaved so well as you have done. I can assure you that I have thought of it very often – of the injustice that has been involuntarily done to you.'

'It has been unjust, has it not?' said he, piteously, thinking of his injuries. 'So much of it has gone in that oilcloth business, and all for nothing!'

'I'm glad at any rate that Walter's share did not go.'

He knew that this was not the kind of conversation which he had desired to commence, and that it must be changed before anything could be settled. So he shook himself and began again.

'And now, Margaret, as the lawyers have finished their part of the business, ours must begin.'

She had been standing hitherto and had felt herself to be strong enough to stand, but at the sound of these words her knees had become weak under her, and she found a retreat upon the sofa. Of course she said nothing as he came and stood over her.

'I hope you have understood,' he continued, 'that while all this was going on I could propose no arrangement of any kind.'

'I know you have been very much troubled.'

'Indeed I have. It seems that any blackguard has a right to publish any lies that he likes about any one in any of the newspapers, and that nobody can do anything to protect himself! Sometimes I have thought that it would drive me mad!'

But he again perceived that he was getting out of the right course in thus dwelling upon his own injuries. He had come there to alleviate her misfortunes, not to talk about his own.

'It is no good, however, talking about all that; is it, Margaret?'

'It will cease now, will it not?'

'I cannot say. I fear not. Whichever way I turn, they abuse me for what I do. What business is it of theirs?'

'You mean their absurd story – calling you a lion.'

'Don't talk of it, Margaret.'

Then Margaret was again silent. She by no means wished to talk of the story, if he would only leave it alone.

'And now about you.'

Then he came and sat beside her, and she put her hand back behind the cushion on the sofa so as to save herself from trembling in his presence. She need not have cared much, for, let her tremble ever so much, he had then no capacity for perceiving it.

'Come, Margaret; I want to do what is best for us both. How shall it be?'

'John, you have children, and you should do what is best for them.'

Then there was a pause again, and when he spoke after a while, he was looking down at the floor and poking among the pattern on the carpet with his stick.

'Margaret, when I first asked you to marry me, you refused me.'

'I did,' said she; 'and then all the property was mine.'

'But afterwards you said you would have me.'

'Yes; and when you asked me the second time I had nothing. I know all that.'

'I thought nothing about the money then. I mean that I never thought you refused me because you were rich and took me because you were poor. I was not at all unhappy about that when we were walking round the shrubbery. But when I thought you had cared for that man –'

'I had never cared for him,' said Margaret, withdrawing her hand from behind the pillow in her energy, and fearing no longer that she might tremble. 'I had never cared for him. He is a false man, and told untruths to my aunt.'

'Yes, he is, a liar – a damnable liar. That is true at any rate.'

'He is beneath your notice, John, and beneath mine. I will not speak of him.'

Sir John, however, had an idea that when he felt the wasp's venom through all his blood, the wasp could not be altogether beneath his notice.

'The question is,' said he, speaking between his teeth, and hardly pronouncing his words, 'the question is whether you care for me.'

'I do,' said she turning round upon him; and as she did so our Griselda took both his hands in hers. 'I do, John. I do care for you. I love you better than all the world besides. Whom else have I to love at all? If you choose to think it mean of me, now that I am so poor, I cannot help it. But who was it told me to be firm? Who was it told me? Who was it told me?'

Lady Ball had lost her game, and Mrs Mackenzie had been a true prophet. Mrs Mackenzie had been one of those prophets who knew how to assist the accomplishment of their own prophecies, and Lady Ball had played her game with very indifferent skill. Sir John endeavoured to say a word as to that other alternative that he had to offer, but the lamb was not lamb-like enough to listen to it. I doubt even whether Margaret knew, when at night she thought over the affairs of the day, that any such offer had been made to her. During the rest of the interview she was by far the greatest talker, and she would not rest till she had made him swear that he believed her when she said, that both in rejecting him and accepting him, she had been guided simply by her affection. 'You know, John,' she said, 'a woman can't love a man all at once.'

They had been together for the best part of two hours, when Mrs Mackenzie knocked at the door.

'May I come in?'

'Oh, yes,' said Margaret.

'And may I ask a question?' She knew by the tone of her cousin's voice that no question could come amiss.

'You must ask him,' said Margaret, coming to her and kissing her.

'But, first of all,' said Mrs Mackenzie, shutting the door and assuming a very serious countenance, 'I have news of my own to tell. There is a gentleman downstairs in the dining-room who has sent up word that he wants to see me. He says he is a clergyman.'

Then Sir John Ball ceased to smile, and look foolish, but doubled his fist, and went towards the door.

'Who is it?' said Margaret, whispering.

'I have not heard his name, but from the servant's account of him I have not much doubt myself; I suppose he comes from Littlebath. You can go down to him, if you like, Sir John; but I would not advise it.'

'No,' said Margaret, clinging to his arm, 'you shall not go down. What good can you do? He is beneath you. If you beat him he will have the law of you – and he is a clergyman. If you do not, he will only revile you, and make you wretched.' Thus between the two ladies the baronet was restrained.

It was Mr Maguire. Having learned from his ally, Miss Colza, that Margaret was staying with her cousins in Cavendish Square, he had resolved upon calling on Mrs Mackenzie, and forcing his way, if possible, into Margaret's presence. Things were not going well with him at Littlebath, and in his despair he had thought that the best chance to him of carrying on the fight lay in this direction. Then there was a course of embassies between the dining-room and drawing-room in the Mackenzie mansion. The servant was sent to ask the gentleman his name, and the gentleman sent up to say that he was a clergyman – that his name was not known to Mrs Mackenzie, but that he wanted to see her most particularly for a few minutes on very special business. Then the servant was despatched to ask him whether or no he was the Rev. Jeremiah Maguire, of Littlebath, and under this compulsion he sent back word that such was his designation. He was then told to go. Upon that he wrote a note to Mrs Mackenzie, setting forth that he had a private communication to make, much to the advantage of her cousin, Miss Margaret Mackenzie. He was again told to go; and then told again, that if he did not leave the house at once, the assistance of the police would be obtained. Then he went. 'And it was frightful to behold him,' said the servant, coming up for the tenth time. But the servant no doubt enjoyed the play, and on one occasion presumed to remark that he did not think any reference to the police was necessary. 'Such a game as we've had up!' he said to the coachman that afternoon in the kitchen.

And the game that they had in the drawing-room was not a bad game either. When Mr Maguire would not go, the two women joined in laughing, till at last the tears ran down Mrs Mackenzie's face.

'Only think of our being kept prisoners here by a one-eyed clergyman.'

'He has got two eyes,' said Margaret. 'If he had ten he shan't see us.'

And at last Sir John laughed; and as he laughed he came and stood near Margaret; and once he got his arm round her waist, and Griselda was very happy. At the present moment she was quite indifferent to Mr Maguire and any mode of fighting that he might adopt.

⌘ THIRTY ⌘

Conclusion

THINGS HAD NOT BEEN GOING WELL WITH Mr Maguire when, as a last chance, he attempted to force an entrance into Mrs Mackenzie's drawing-room. Things, indeed, had been going very badly with him. Mr Stumfold at Littlebath had had an interview with the editor of the *Christian Examiner*, and had made that provincial Jupiter understand that he must drop the story of the Lion and the Lamb. There had been more than enough of it, Mr Stumfold thought; and if it were continued, Mr Stumfold would – would make Littlebath too hot to hold the *Christian Examiner*. That was the full meaning of Mr Stumfold's threat; and, as the editor knew Mr Stumfold's power, the editor wisely turned a cold shoulder upon Mr Maguire. When Mr Maguire came to the editor with his letter for publication, the editor declared that he should be happy to insert it – as an advertisement. Then there had been a little scene between Mr Maguire and the editor, and Mr Maguire had left the editorial office shaking the dust from off his feet. But he was a persistent man, and, having ascertained that Miss Colza was possessed of some small share in her brother's business in the city, he thought it expedient to betake himself again to London. He did so, as we have seen; and with some very faint hope of obtaining collateral advantage for himself, and some stronger hope that he might still be able to do an injury to Sir John Ball, he went to the Mackenzies' house in Cavendish Square. There his success was not great; and from that time forward the wasp had no further power of inflicting stings upon the lion whom he had persecuted.

But some further annoyance he did give to Griselda. He managed to induce Mrs Tom Mackenzie to take him in as a lodger in Gower Street, and Margaret very nearly ran into his way in her anxiety to befriend her sister-in-law. Luckily she heard from Mr Rubb that he was there on the very day on which she had intended to visit Gower Street. Poor Mrs Mackenzie got the worst of it; for of course Mr Maguire did not pay for his lodgings. But he did marry Miss Colza, and in some way got himself instituted to a chapel at Islington. There we will leave him, not trusting much in his connubial bliss, but faintly hoping that his teaching may be favourable to the faith and morals of his new flock.

Of Mr Samuel Rubb, junior, we must say a few words. His first acquaintance with our heroine was not made under circumstances favourable to him. In that matter of the loan, he departed very widely from the precept which teaches us that honesty is the best policy. And when I feel that our Margaret was at one time really in danger of becoming Mrs Rubb – that in her ignorance of the world, in the dark gropings of her social philosophy, amidst the difficulties of her solitude, she had not known whether she could do better with herself and her future years, than give herself, and them, and her money to Mr Samuel Rubb, I tremble as I look back upon her danger. It has been said of women that they have an insane desire for matrimony. I believe that the desire, even if it be as general as is here described, is no insanity. But when I see such a woman as Margaret Mackenzie in danger from such a man as Samuel Rubb, junior, I am driven to fear that there may sometimes be a maniacal tendency. But Samuel Rubb was by no means a bad man. He first hankered after the woman's money, but afterwards he had loved the woman; and my female reader, if she agrees with me, will feel that that virtue covers a multitude of sins.

And he was true to the promise that he made about the loan. He did pay the interest of the money regularly to Mrs Mackenzie in Gower Street, and after a while was known in that house as the recognised lover of Mary Jane, the eldest daughter. It this way it came to pass that he occasionally saw the lady to whose hand he had aspired; for Margaret, when she was assured that Mr Maguire and his bride were never likely to be seen in that locality, did not desert her nephews and nieces in Gower Street.

But we must go back to Sir John Ball. As soon as the coast was clear in Cavendish Square, he took his leave of Margaret. Mrs Mackenzie had left the room, desiring to speak a word to him alone as he came down.

'I shall tell my mother to-night,' he said to Margaret. 'You know that all this is not exactly as she wishes it.'

'John,' she said, 'if it is as you wish it, I have no right to think of anything beyond that.'

'It is as I wish it,' said he.

'Then tell my aunt, with my love, that I shall hope that she will receive me as her daughter.'

Then they parted, and Margaret was left alone to congratulate herself over her success.

'Sir John,' said Mrs Mackenzie, calling him into the drawing-room; 'you must hear my congratulations; you must, indeed.'

'Thank you,' said he, looking foolish; 'you are very good.'

'And so is she. She is what you may really call good. She is as good as gold. I know a woman when I see her; and I know that for one like her there are fifty not fit to hold a candle to her. She has nothing mean or little about her – nothing. They may call her a lamb, but she can be a lioness too when there is an occasion.'

'I know that she is steadfast,' said he.

'That she is, and honest, and warm hearted; and – and Oh! Sir John, I am so happy that it is all to be made right, and nice, and comfortable. It would have been very sad if she hadn't gone with the money; would it not?'

'I should not have taken the money – not all of it.'

'And she would not have taken any. She would not have taken a penny of it, though we need not mind that now; need we? But there is one thing I want to say; you must not think I am interfering.'

'I shan't think that after all that you have done.'

'I want her to be married from here. It would be quite proper; wouldn't it? Mr Mackenzie is a little particular about the grouse, because there is to be a large party at Incharrow; but up to the 10th of August you and she should fix any day you like.'

Sir John showed by his countenance that he was somewhat taken aback. The 10th of August, and here they were far advanced into June! When he had left home this morning he had not fully made up his mind whether he meant to marry his cousin or not; and now, within a few hours, he was being confined to weeks and days! Mrs Mackenzie saw what was passing in his mind; but she was not a woman to be driven easily from her purpose.

'You see,' she said, 'there is so much to think of. What is Margaret to do, if we leave her in London when we go down? And it would really be better for her to be married from her cousin's house; it would, indeed. Lady Ball would like it better – I'm sure she would – than if she were to be living alone in the town in lodgings. There is always a way of doing things; isn't there? And Walter's sisters, her own cousins, could be her bridesmaids, you know.'

Sir John said that he would think about it.

'I haven't spoken to her, of course,' said Mrs Mackenzie; 'but I shall now.'

Sir John, as he went eastwards into the city, did think about it; and before he had reached his own house that evening, he had brought himself to regard Mrs Mackenzie's scheme in a favourable light. He was not blind to the advantage of taking his wife from a house in Cavendish Square, instead of from lodgings in Arundel Street; and he was aware that his mother would not be blind to that advantage either. He did not hope to be able to reconcile her to his marriage at once; and perhaps he entertained some faint idea that for the first six months of his new married life the Cedars would be quite as pleasant without his mother as with her; but a final reconciliation would be more easy if he and his wife had the Mackenzies of Incharrow to back them, than it could be without such influence. And as for the London gossip of the thing, the finale to the romance of the Lion and the Lamb, it would be sure to come sooner or later. Let them have their odious joke and have done with it!

'Mother,' he said, as soon as he could find himself alone with Lady Ball that day, not waiting for the midnight conference; 'mother, I may as well tell you at once. I have proposed to Margaret Mackenzie again to-day.'

'Oh! very well.'

'And she has accepted me.'

'Accepted you! of course she has; jumped at the chance, no doubt. What else should a pauper do?'

'Mother, that is ungenerous.'

'She did not accept you when she had got anything.'

'If I can reconcile myself to that, surely you can do so. The matter is settled now, and I think I have done the best in my power for myself and my children.'

'And as for your mother, she may go and die anywhere.'

'Mother, that is unfair. As long as I have a house over my head, you shall share it, if you please to do so. If it suits you to go elsewhere, I will be with you as often as may be possible. I hope, however, you will not leave us.'

'That I shall certainly do.'

'Then I hope you will not go far from me.'

'And when is it to be?' said his mother, after a pause.

'I cannot name any day; but some time before the 10th of August.'

'Before the 10th of August! Why, that is at once. Oh! John; and your father not dead a year!'

'Margaret has a home now with her cousins in Cavendish Square; but she cannot stay there after they go to Scotland. It will be for her welfare that she should be married from their house. And as for my father's death, I know that you do not suspect me of disrespect to his memory.'

And in this way it was settled at the Cedars; and his mother's question about the time drove him to the resolution which he himself had not reached. When next he was in Cavendish Square he asked Margaret whether she could be ready so soon, and she replied that she would be ready on any day that he told her to be ready.

Thus it was settled, and with a moderate amount of nuptial festivity the marriage feast was prepared in Mrs Mackenzie's house. Margaret was surprised to find how many dear friends she had who were interested in her welfare. Miss Baker wrote to her most affectionately; and Miss Todd was warm in her congratulations. But the attention which perhaps surprised her most was a warm letter of sisterly affection from Mrs Stumfold, in which that lady rejoiced with an exceeding joy in that the machinations of a certain wolf in sheep's clothing had been unsuccessful. 'My anxiety that you should not be sacrificed I once before evinced to you,' said Mrs Stumfold; 'and within the last two months Mr Stumfold has been at work to put an end to the scurrilous writings which that wolf in sheep's clothing has been putting into the newspapers.' Then Mrs Stumfold very particularly desired to be remembered to Sir John Ball, and expressed a hope that, at some future time, she might have the honour of being made acquainted with 'the worthy baronet.'

They were married in the first week in August, and our modern

Griselda went through the ceremony with much grace. That there was much grace about Sir John Ball, I cannot say; but gentlemen, when they get married at fifty, are not expected to be graceful.

'There, my Lady Ball,' said Mrs Mackenzie, whispering into her cousin's ear before they left the church; 'now my prophecy has come true; and when we meet in London next spring, you will reward me for all I have done for you by walking out of a room before me.'

But all these honours, and, what was better, all the happiness that came in her way, Lady Ball accepted thankfully, quietly, and with an enduring satisfaction, as it became such a woman to do.

THE END

COUSIN
HENRY

⌘ ONE ⌘

Uncle Indefer

'I HAVE A CONSCIENCE, MY DEAR, ON THIS matter,' said an old gentleman to a young lady, as the two were sitting in the breakfast parlour of a country house which looked down from the cliffs over the sea on the coast of Carmarthenshire.

'And so have I, Uncle Indefer; and as my conscience is backed by my inclination, whereas yours is not –'

'You think that I shall give way?'

'I did not mean that.'

'What then?'

'If I could only make you understand how very strong is my inclination, or disinclination – how impossible to be conquered, then –'

'What next?'

'Then you would know that I could never give way, as you call it, and you would go to work with your own conscience to see whether it be imperative with you or not. You may be sure of this – I shall never say a word to you in opposition to your conscience. If there be a word to be spoken it must come from yourself.'

There was a long pause in the conversation, a silence for an hour, during which the girl went in and out of the room and settled herself down at her work. Then the old man went back abruptly to the subject they had discussed. 'I shall obey my conscience.'

'You ought to do so, Uncle Indefer. What should a man obey but his conscience?'

'Though it will break my heart.'

'No; no, no!'

'And will ruin you.'

'That is a flea's bite. I can brave my ruin easily, but not your broken heart.'

'Why should there be either, Isabel?'

'Nay, sir; have you not said but now, because of our consciences? Not to save your heart from breaking – though I think your heart is dearer to me than anything else in the world – could I marry my cousin Henry. We must die together, both of us, you and I, or live broken-hearted, or what not, sooner than that. Would I not do anything possible at your bidding?'

'I used to think so.'

'But it is impossible for a young woman with a respect for herself such as I have to submit herself to a man that she loathes. Do as your conscience bids you with the old house. Shall I be less tender to you while you live because I shall have to leave the place when you are dead? Shall I accuse you of injustice or unkindness in my heart? Never! All that is only an outside circumstance to me, comparatively of little moment. But to be the wife of a man I despise!' Then she got up and left the room.

A month passed by before the old man returned to the subject, which he did seated in the same room, at the same hour of the day – at about four o'clock, when the dinner things had been removed.

'Isabel,' he said, 'I cannot help myself.'

'As to what, Uncle Indefer?' She knew very well what was the matter in which, as he said, he could not help himself. Had there been anything in which his age had wanted assistance from her youth there would have been no hesitation between them; no daughter was ever more tender; no father was ever more trusting. But on this subject it was necessary that he should speak more plainly before she could reply to him.

'As to your cousin and the property.'

'Then in God's name do not trouble yourself further in looking for help where there is none to be had. You mean that the estate ought to go to a man and not to a woman?'

'It ought to go to a Jones.'

'I am not a Jones, nor likely to become a Jones.'

'You are as near to me as he is – and so much dearer!'

'But not on that account a Jones. My name is Isabel Brodrick. A woman not born to be a Jones may have the luck to become one by marriage, but that will never be the case with me.'

'You should not laugh at that which is to me a duty.'

'Dear, dear uncle!' she said, caressing him, 'if I seemed to laugh' – and she certainly had laughed when she spoke of the luck of becoming a Jones – 'it is only that you may feel how little importance I attach to it all on my own account.'

'But it is important – terribly important!'

'Very well. Then go to work with two things in your mind fixed as fate. One is that you must leave Llanfeare to your nephew Henry Jones, and the other that I will not marry your nephew Henry Jones. When it is all settled it will be just as though the old place were entailed, as it used to be.'

'I wish it were.'

'So do I, if it would save you trouble.'

'But it isn't the same – it can't be the same. In getting back the land your grandfather sold I have spent the money I had saved for you.'

'It shall be all the same to me, and I will take pleasure in thinking that the old family place shall remain as you would have it. I can be proud of the family though I can never bear the name.'

'You do not care a straw for the family.'

'You should not say that, Uncle Indefer. It is not true. I care enough for the family to sympathise with you altogether in what you are doing, but not enough for the property to sacrifice myself in order that I might have a share in it.'

'I do not know why you should think so much evil of Henry.'

'Do you know any reason why I should think well enough of him to become his wife? I do not. In marrying a man a woman should be able to love every little trick belonging to him. The parings of his nails should be a care to her. It should be pleasant to her to serve him in things most menial. Would it be so to me, do you think, with Henry Jones?'

'You are always full of poetry and books.'

'I should be full of something very bad if I were to allow myself to stand at the altar with him. Drop it, Uncle Indefer. Get it out of your mind as a thing quite impossible. It is the one thing I can't and won't do, even for you. It is the one thing that you ought not to ask me to do. Do as you like with the property – as you think right.'

'It is not as I like.'

'As your conscience bids you, then; and I with myself, which is the only little thing that I have in the world, will do as I like, or as my conscience bids me.'

These last words she spoke almost roughly, and as she said them she left him, walking out of the room with an air of offended pride. But in this there was a purpose. If she were hard to him, hard and obstinate in her determination, then would he be enabled to be so also to her in his determination, with less of pain to himself. She felt it to be her duty to teach him that he was justified in doing what he liked with his property, because she intended to do what she liked with herself. Not only would she not say a word towards dissuading him from this change in his old intentions, but she would make the change as little painful to him as possible by teaching him to think that it was justified by her own manner to him.

For there was a change, not only in his mind, but in his declared intentions. Llanfeare had belonged to Indefer Joneses for many generations. When the late Squire had died, now twenty years ago, there had been remaining out of ten children only one, the eldest, to whom the property now belonged. Four or five coming in succession after him had died without issue. Then there had been a Henry Jones, who had gone away and married, had become the father of the Henry Jones above mentioned, and had then also departed. The youngest, a daughter, had married an attorney named Brodrick, and she also had died, having no other child but Isabel. Mr Brodrick had married again, and was now the father of a large family, living at Hereford, where he carried on his business. He was not very 'well-to-do' in the world. The new Mrs Brodrick had preferred her own babies to Isabel, and Isabel when she was fifteen years of age had gone to her bachelor uncle at Llanfeare. There she had lived for the last ten years, making occasional visits to her father at Hereford.

Mr Indefer Jones, who was now between seventy and eighty years old, was a gentleman who through his whole life had been disturbed by reflections, fears, and hopes as to the family property on which he had been born, on which he had always lived, in possession of which he would certainly die, and as to the future disposition of which it was his lot in life to be altogether responsible. It had been entailed upon him before his birth in his grandfather's time, when his father was about to be married. But the entail had not been carried on. There had come no time in which this Indefer Jones had been about to be married, and the former old man having been given to extravagance, and been generally in want of money, had felt it more comfortable to be without an entail. His son had occasionally been induced to join with him in raising money. Thus not only since he had himself owned the estate, but before his father's death, there had been forced upon him reflections as to the destination of Llanfeare. At fifty he had found himself unmarried, and unlikely to marry. His brother Henry was then alive; but Henry had disgraced the family – had run away with a married woman whom he had married after a divorce, had taken to race courses and billiard-rooms, and had been altogether odious to his brother Indefer. Nevertheless the boy which had come from this marriage, a younger Henry, had been educated at his expense, and had occasionally been received at Llanfeare. He had been popular with no one there, having been found to be a sly boy, given to lying, and, as even the servants said about the place, unlike a Jones of Llanfeare. Then had come the time in which Isabel had been brought to Llanfeare. Henry had been sent away from Oxford for some offence not altogether trivial, and the Squire had declared to himself and others that Llanfeare should never fall into his hands.

Isabel had so endeared herself to him that before she had been two years in the house she was the young mistress of the place. Everything that she did was right in his eyes. She might have anything that she would ask, only that she would ask for nothing. At this time the cousin had been taken into an office in London, and had become – so it was said of him – a steady young man of business. But still, when allowed to show himself at Llanfeare, he was unpalatable to them all – unless it might be to the old Squire. It was certainly the case that in his office in London he made himself useful, and it seemed that he had abandoned that practice of running into debt and having the bills sent down to Llanfeare which he had adopted early in his career.

During all this time the old Squire was terribly troubled about the property. His will was always close at hand. Till Isabel was twenty-one this will had always been in Henry's favour – with a clause, however, that a certain sum of money which the Squire possessed should go to her.

Then in his disgust towards his nephew he changed his purpose, and made another will in Isabel's favour. This remained in existence as his last resolution for three years; but they had been three years of misery to him. He had endured but badly the idea that the place should pass away out of what he regarded as the proper male line. To his thinking it was simply an accident that the power of disposing of the property should be in his hands. It was a religion to him that a landed estate in Britain should go from father to eldest son, and in default of a son to the first male heir. Britain would not be ruined because Llanfeare should be allowed to go out of the proper order. But Britain would be ruined if Britons did not do their duty in that sphere of life to which it had pleased God to call them; and in this case his duty was to maintain the old order of things.

And during this time an additional trouble added itself to those existing. Having made up his mind to act in opposition to his own principles, and to indulge his own heart; having declared both to his nephew and to his niece that Isabel should be his heir, there came to him, as a consolation in his misery, the power of repurchasing a certain fragment of the property which his father, with his assistance had sold. The loss of these acres had been always a sore wound to him, not because of his lessened income, but from a feeling that no owner of an estate should allow it to be diminished during his holding of it. He never saw those separated fields estranged from Llanfeare, but he grieved in his heart. That he might get them back again he had saved money since Llanfeare had first become his own. Then had come upon him the necessity of providing for Isabel. But when with many groans he had decided that Isabel should be the heir, the money could be allowed to go for its intended purpose. It had so gone, and then his conscience had become too strong for him, and another will was made.

It will be seen how he had endeavoured to reconcile things. When it was found that Henry Jones was working like a steady man at the London office to which he was attached, that he had sown his wild oats, then Uncle Indefer began to ask himself why all his dearest wishes should not be carried out together by a marriage between the cousins. 'I don't care a bit for his wild oats,' Isabel had said, almost playfully, when the idea had first been mooted to her. 'His oats are too tame for me rather than too wild. Why can't he look any one in the face?' Then her uncle had been angry with her, thinking that she was allowing a foolish idea to interfere with the happiness of them all.

But his anger with her was never enduring; and, indeed, before the time at which our story commenced he had begun to acknowledge to himself that he might rather be afraid of her anger than she of his. There was a courage about her which nothing could dash. She had grown up under his eyes strong, brave, sometimes almost bold, with a dash of humour, but always quite determined in her own ideas of wrong or right.

He had in truth been all but afraid of her when he found himelf compelled to tell her of the decision to which his conscience compelled him. But the will was made – the third, perhaps the fourth or fifth, which had seemed to him to be necessary since his mind had been exercised in this matter. He made this will, which he assured himself should be the last, leaving Llanfeare to his nephew on condition that he should prefix the name of Indefer to that of Jones, and adding certain stipulations as to further entail. Then everything of which he might die possessed, except Llanfeare itself and the furniture in the house, he left to his niece Isabel.

'We must get rid of the horses,' he said to her about a fortnight after the conversation last recorded.

'Why that?'

'My will has been made, and there will be so little now for you, that we must save what we can before I die.'

'Oh, bother me!' said Isabel, laughing.

'Do you suppose it is not dreadful to me to have to reflect how little I can do for you? I may, perhaps, live for two years, and we may save six or seven hundred a year. I have put a charge on the estate for four thousand pounds. The property is only a small thing, after all – not above fifteen hundred a year.'

'I will not hear of the horses being sold, and there is an end of it. You have been taken out about the place every day for the last twenty years, and it would crush me if I were to see a change. You have done the best you can, and now leave it all in God's hands. Pray – pray let there be no more talking about it. If you only knew how welcome he is to it!'

❆ TWO ❆

Isabel Brodrick

WHEN MR INDEFER JONES SPOKE OF LIVING for two years, he spoke more hopefully of himself than the doctor was wont to speak to Isabel. The doctor from Carmarthen visited Llanfeare twice a week, and having become intimate and confidential with Isabel, had told her that the candle had nearly burnt itself down to the socket. There was no special disease, but he was a worn-out old man. It was well that he should allow himself to be driven out about the place every day. It was well that he should be encouraged to get up after breakfast, and to eat his dinner in the middle of the day after his old fashion. It was well to do everything around him as though he were not a confirmed invalid. But the doctor thought that he would not last long. The candle, as the doctor said, had nearly burnt itself out in the socket.

And yet there was no apparent decay in the old man's intellect. He had never been much given to literary pursuits, but that which he had always done he did still. A daily copy of whatever might be the most thoroughly Conservative paper of the day he always read carefully from the beginning to the end; and a weekly copy of the *Guardian* nearly filled up the hours which were devoted to study. On Sunday he read two sermons through, having been forbidden by the doctor to take his place in the church because of the draughts, and thinking, apparently, that it would be mean and wrong to make that an excuse for shirking an onerous duty. An hour a day was devoted by him religiously to the Bible. The rest of his time was occupied by the care of his property. Nothing gratified him so much as the coming in of one of his tenants, all of whom were so intimately known to him that, old as he was, he never forgot the names even of their children. The idea of raising a rent was abominable to him. Around the house there were about two hundred acres which he was supposed to farm. On these some half-dozen worn-out old labourers were maintained in such a manner that no return from the land was ever forthcoming. On this subject he would endure remonstrance from no one – not even from Isabel.

Such as he has been here described, he would have been a happy old man during these last half-dozen years, had not his mind been exercised day by day, and hour by hour, by these cares as to the property which were ever present to him. A more loving heart than his could hardly be found in a human bosom, and all its power of love had been bestowed on Isabel. Nor could any man be subject to a stronger feeling of duty than that which pervaded him; and this feeling of duty induced him to declare to himself that in reference to his property he was bound to do that which was demanded of him by the established custom of his order. In this way he had become an unhappy man, troubled by conflicting feelings, and was now, as he was approaching the hour of his final departure, tormented by the thought that he would leave his niece without sufficient provision for her wants.

But the thing was done. The new will was executed and tied in on the top of the bundle which contained the other wills which he had made. Then, naturally enough, there came back upon him the idea, hardly amounting to a hope, that something might even yet occur to set matters right by a marriage between the cousins. Isabel had spoken to him so strongly on the subject that he did not dare to repeat his request. And yet, he thought, there was no good reason why they two should not become man and wife. Henry, as far as he could learn, had given up his bad courses. The man was not evil to the eye, a somewhat cold-looking man rather than otherwise, tall with well-formed features, with light hair and blue-grey eyes, not subject to be spoken of as being unlike a gentleman, if not noticeable as being like one. That inability of his to look one in the face when he was speaking had not struck the Squire forcibly as it had done

Isabel. He would not have been agreeable to the Squire had there been no bond between them – would still have been the reverse, as he had been formerly, but for that connexion. But, as things were, there was room for an attempt at love; and if for an attempt at love on his part, why not also on Isabel's? But he did not dare to bid Isabel even to try to love this cousin.

'I think I would like to have him down again soon,' he said to his niece.

'By all means. The more the tenants know him the better it will be. I can go to Hereford at any time.'

'Why should you run away from me?'

'Not from you, Uncle Indefer, but from him.'

'And why from him?'

'Because I don't love him.'

'Must you always run away from the people you do not love?'

'Yes, when the people, or person, is a man, and when the man has been told that he ought specially to love me.'

When she said this she looked into her uncle's face, smiling indeed, but still asking a serious question. He dared to make no answer, but by his face he told the truth. He had declared his wishes to his nephew.

'Not that I mean to be in the least afraid of him,' she continued. 'Perhaps it will be better that I should see him, and if he speaks to me have it out with him. How long would he stay?'

'A month, I suppose. He can come for a month.'

'Then I'll stay for the first week. I must go to Hereford before the summer is over. Shall I write to him?' Then it was settled as she had proposed. She wrote all her uncle's letters, even to her cousin Henry, unless there was, by chance, something very special to be communicated. On the present occasion she sent the invitation as follows: –

'Llanfeare, 17th June, 187–, Monday.

'MY DEAR HENRY

Your uncle wants you to come here on the 1st July and stay for a month. The 1st of July will be Monday. Do not travel on a Sunday as you did last time, because he does not like it. I shall be here the first part of the time, and then I shall go to Hereford. It is in the middle of the summer only that I can leave him. Your affectionate cousin,

'ISABEL BRODRICK.'

She had often felt herself compelled to sign herself to him in that way, and it had gone much against the grain with her; but to a cousin it was the ordinary thing, as it is to call any different man 'My dear sir,' though he be not in the least dear. And so she had reconciled herself to the falsehood.

Another incident in Isabel's life must be told to the reader. It was her custom to go to Hereford at least once a year, and there to remain at her father's house for a month. These visits had been made annually since she had lived at Llanfeare, and in this way she had become known to many of the Hereford people. Among others who had thus become her friends there was a young clergyman, William Owen, a minor canon attached to the cathedral, who during her last visit had asked her to be his wife. At that time she had supposed herself to be her uncle's heiress, and looking at herself as the future owner of Llanfeare had considered herself bound to regard such an offer in reference to her future duties and to the obedience which she owed to her uncle. She never told her lover, not did she ever quite tell herself, that she would certainly accept him if bound by no such considerations; but we may tell the reader that it was so. Had she felt herself to be altogether free, she would have given herself to the man who had offered her his love. As it was she answered him anything but hopefully, saying nothing of any passion of her own, speaking of herself as though she were altogether at the disposal of her uncle. 'He has decided now,' she said, 'that when he is gone the property is to be mine.' The minor canon, who had heard nothing of this, drew himself up as though about to declare in his pride that he had not intended to ask for the hand of the lady of Llanfeare. 'That would make no difference in me,' she continued, reading plainly the expression in the young man's face. 'My regard would be swayed neither one way nor the other by any feeling of that kind. But as he has chosen to make me his daughter, I must obey him as his daughter. It is not probable that he will consent to such a marriage.'

Then there had been nothing further between them till Isabel, on her return to Llanfeare, had written to him to say that her uncle had decided against the marriage, and that his decision was final.

Now in all this Isabel had certainly been hardly used, though her ill-usage had in part been due to her own reticence as to her own feelings. When she told the Squire that the offer had been made to her, she did so as if she herself had been almost indifferent.

'William Owen!' the Squire had said, repeating the name; 'his grandfather kept the inn at Pembroke!'

'I believe he did,' said Isabel calmly.

'And you would wish to make him owner of Llanfeare?'

'I did not say so,' rejoined Isabel. 'I have told you what occurred, and have asked you what you thought.'

Then the Squire shook his head, and there was an end of it. The letter was written to the minor canon telling him that the Squire's decision was final.

In all this there had been no allusion to love on the part of Isabel. Had there been, her uncle could hardly have pressed upon her the claims of his nephew. But her manner in regard to the young clergyman had been so cold as to leave upon her uncle an impression that the matter was one of but little moment. To Isabel it was matter of infinite moment. And yet when she was asked again and again to arrange all the difficulties of the family by marrying her cousin, she was forced to carry on the conversation as though no such person existed as her lover at Hereford.

And yet the Squire remembered it all – remembered that when he had thus positively objected to the grandson of the innkeeper, he had done so because he had felt it to be his duty to keep the grandson of an innkeeper out of Llanfeare. That the grandson of old Thomas Owen, of the Pembroke Lion, should reign at Llanfeare in the place of an Indefer Jones had been abominable to him. To prevent that had certainly been within his duties. But it was very different now, when he would leave his girl poorly provided for, without a friend and without a roof of her own over her head! And yet, though her name was Brodrick, she, too, was a Jones; and her father, though an attorney, had come of a family nearly as good as his own. In no case could it be right that she should marry the grandson of old Thomas Owen. Therefore, hitherto, he had never again referred to that proposal of marriage. Should she again have spoken of it his answer might perhaps have been less decided; but neither had she again spoken of the clergyman.

All this was hard upon Isabel, who, if she said nothing, still thought of her lover. And it must be acknowledged also that though she did not speak, still she thought of her future prospects. She had laughed at the idea of being solicitous as to her inheritance. She had done so in order that she might thereby lessen the trouble of her uncle's mind; but she knew as well as did another the difference between the position which had been promised her as owner of Llanfeare, and that to which she would be reduced as the stepdaughter of a stepmother who did not love her. She knew, too, that she had been cold to William Owen, giving him no sort of encouragement, having seemed to declare to him that she had rejected him because she was her uncle's heiress. And she knew also – or thought that she knew – that she was not possessed of those feminine gifts which probably might make a man constant under difficulties. No more had been heard of William Owen during the last nine months. Every now and then a letter would come to her from one of her younger sisters, who now had their own anxieties and their own loves, but not a word was there in one of them of William Owen. Therefore, it may be said that the last charge in her uncle's purpose had fallen upon her with peculiar hardness.

But she never uttered a complaint, or even looked one. As for utterance there was no one to whom she could have spoken it. There had never been many words between her and her own family as to the inheritance. As she had been reticent to her father so had he to her. The idea in the attorney's house at Hereford was that she was stubborn, conceited, and disdainful. It may be that in regard to her stepmother there was something of this, but, let that be as it might, there had been but little confidence between them as to matters at Llanfeare. It was, no doubt, supposed by her father that she was to be her uncle's heir.

Conceited, perhaps, she was as to certain gifts of character. She did believe herself to be strong of purpose and capable of endurance. But in some respects she was humble enough. She gave herself no credit for feminine charms such as the world loves. In appearance she was one calculated to attract attention – somewhat tall, well set on her limbs, active, and of good figure; her brow was broad and fine, her grey eyes were bright and full of intelligence, her nose and mouth were well formed, and there was not a mean feature in her face. But there was withal a certain roughness about her, an absence of feminine softness in her complexion, which, to tell the truth of her, was more conspicuous to her own eyes than to any others. The farmers and their wives about the place would declare that Miss Isabel was the finest young woman in South Wales. With the farmers and their wives she was on excellent terms, knowing all their ways, and anxious as to all their wants. With the gentry around she concerned herself but little. Her uncle's habits were not adapted to the keeping of much company, and to her uncle's habits she had fitted herself altogether. It was on this account that neither did she know the young men around, nor did they know her. And then, because no such intimacies had grown up she told herself that she was unlike other girls – that she was rough, unattractive, and unpopular.

Then the day came for the arrival of Henry Jones, during the approach to which Uncle Indefer had, from day to day, become more and more uneasy. Isabel had ceased to say a word against him. When he had been proposed to her as a lover she had declared that she had loathed him. Now that suggestion had been abandoned, or left in abeyance. Therefore she dealt with his name and with his coming as she might with that of any other guest. She looked to his room, and asked questions as to his comfort. Would it not be well to provide a separate dinner for him, seeing that three o'clock would be regarded as an awkward hour by a man from London? 'If he doesn't like it, he had better go back to London,' said the old Squire in anger. But the anger was not intended against his girl, but against the man who by the mere force of his birth was creating such a sea of troubles.

'I have told you what my intentions are,' the Squire said to his nephew on the evening of his arrival.

'I am sure that I am very much obliged to you, my dear uncle.'

'You need not be in the least obliged to me. I have done what I conceive to be a duty. I can still change it if I find that you do not deserve it. As for Isabel, she deserves everything that can be done for her. Isabel has never given me the slightest cause for displeasure. I doubt whether there is a better creature in the world living than Isabel. She deserves everything. But as you are the male heir, I think it right that you should follow me in the property – unless you show yourself to be unworthy.'

This was certainly a greeting hard to be endured – a speech very difficult to answer. Nevertheless it was satisfactory, if only the old Squire would not again change his mind. The young man had thought much about it, and had come to the resolution that the best way to insure the good things promised him would be to induce Isabel to be his wife.

'I'm sure she is all that you say, Uncle Indefer,' he replied.

Uncle Indefer grunted, and told him that if he wanted any supper, he had better go and get it.

❋ THREE ❋

Cousin Henry

COUSIN HENRY FOUND HIS POSITION TO BE difficult and precarious. That suggestion of his uncle's – or rather assertion – that he could still change his mind was disagreeable. No doubt he could do so, and, as Cousin Henry thought, would be the very man to do it, if angered, thwarted, or even annoyed. He knew that more than one will had already been made and set aside. Cousin Henry had turned the whole matter very much in his mind since he had become cognizant of his uncle's character. However imprudent he might have been in his earlier days, he was now quite alive to the importance of being Squire of Llanfeare. There was nothing that he was not ready to do to please and conciliate his uncle. Llanfeare without Isabel as a burden would no doubt be preferable, but he was quite ready to marry Isabel to-morrow, if Isabel would only accept him. The game he had to play was for Llanfeare. It was to be Llanfeare or nothing. The position offered to him was to come, not from love, but from a sense of duty on the part of the old man. If he could keep the old man firm to that idea, Llanfeare would be his own; but should he be excluded from that inheritance, there would be no lesser prize by which he might reconcile himself to the loss. His uncle would not leave him anything from love. All this he understood thoroughly, and was therefore not unnaturally nervous as to his own conduct at the present crisis.

It was only too manifest to him that his uncle did in fact dislike him. At their very first interview he was made to listen to praises of Isabel and threats against himself. He was quite prepared to put up with both, or with any other disagreeable hardship which might be inflicted upon him, if only he could do so successfully. But he believed that his best course would be to press his suit with Isabel. Should he do so successfully, he would at any rate be safe. Should she be persistent in refusing him, which he believed to be probable, then he would have shown himself desirous of carrying out his uncle's wishes. As to all this he was clear-sighted enough. But he did not quite perceive the state of his uncle's mind in regard to himself. He did not understand how painfully the old man was

668

still vacillating between affection and duty; nor did he fathom the depth of the love which his uncle felt for Isabel. Had he been altogether wise in the matter, he would have kept out of his uncle's presence, and have devoted himself to the tenants and the land; but in lieu of this, he intruded himself as much as possible into his uncle's morning room, often to the exclusion of Isabel. Now it had come to pass that Uncle Indefer was never at his ease unless his niece were with him.

'Nobody can be more attached to another than I am to Isabel,' said the nephew to his uncle on the third morning of his arrival. Whereupon Uncle Indefer grunted. The more he saw of the man, the less he himself liked the idea of sacrificing Isabel to such a husband. 'I shall certainly do my best to carry out your wishes.'

'My wishes have reference solely to her.'

'Exactly, sir; I understand that completely. As she is not to be the heiress, the best thing possible is to be done for her.'

'You think that marrying you would be the best thing possible!' This the uncle said in a tone of scorn which must have been very hard to bear. And it was unjust too, as the unfortunate nephew had certainly not intended to speak of himself personally as being the best thing possible for Isabel.

But this too had to be borne. 'I meant, sir, that if she would accept my hand, she would have pretty nearly as great an interest in the property as I myself.'

'She would have much more,' said Uncle Indefer angrily. 'She knows every man, woman, and child about the place. There is not one of them who does not love her. And so they ought, for she has been their best friend. As far as they are concerned it is almost cruel that they should not be left in her hands.'

'So it will be, sir, if she will consent to do as you and I wish.'

'Wish! Pshaw!' Then he repeated his grunts, turning his shoulder round against his nephew, and affecting to read the newspaper which he had held in his hand during the conversation. It must be acknowledged that the part to be played by the intended heir was very difficult. He could perceive that his uncle hated him, but he could not understand that he might best lessen that hatred by relieving his uncle of his presence. There he sat looking at the empty grate, and pretending now and again to read an old newspaper which was lying on the table, while his uncle fumed and grunted. During every moment that was so passed Uncle Indefer was asking himself whether that British custom as to male heirs was absolutely essential to the welfare of the country. Here were two persons suggested to his mind, one of whom was to be his future successor. One of them was undoubtedly the sweetest human being that had ever crossed his path; the other – as he was inclined to think at the present moment – was the least sweet. And as they were to him, would they not be to the tenants whose welfare was to depend so much on the future owner of the property? The longer that he endured the presence of the man the more desirous did he feel of turning to the drawer which was close at hand, and destroying the topmost of those documents which lay there tied in a bundle together.

But he did not allow himself to be at once driven to a step so unreasonable. The young man had done nothing which ought to offend him – had, indeed, only obeyed him in coming down to South Wales. That custom of the country was good and valid, and wise. If he believed in anything of the world worldly, he believed in primogeniture in respect of land. Though Isabel was ever so sweet, duty was duty. Who was he that he should dare to say to himself that he could break through what he believed to be a law on his conscience without a sin? If he might permit himself to make a special exemption for himself in the indulgence of his own affection, then why might not another, and another, and so on? Did he not know that it would have been better that the whole thing should have been settled for him by an entail? And, if so, how could it be right that he should act in opposition to the spirit of such an entail, merely because he had the power to do so? Thus he argued with himself again and again; but these arguments would never become strong till his nephew had relieved him of his presence.

While he was so arguing, Cousin Henry was trying his hand with Isabel. There had been but a week for him to do it, and three days had already passed away. At the end of the week Isabel was to go to Hereford, and Henry, as far as he knew, was still expected by his uncle to make an offer to his cousin. And, as regarded himself, he was well enough disposed to do so. He was a man with no strong affections, but also with no strong aversions – except that at present he had a strong affection for Llanfeare, and a strong aversion to the monotonous office in which he was wont to earn his daily bread up in London. And he, too, was desirous of doing his duty – as long as the doing of his duty might tend to the desired possession of Llanfeare. He was full of the idea that a great deal was due to Isabel. A great deal was certainly due to Isabel, if only, by admitting so much, his possession of Llanfeare was to be assured.

'So you are going away in two or three days?' he said to her.

'In four days. I am to start on Monday.'

'That is very soon. I am so sorry that you are to leave us! But I suppose it is best that dear Uncle Indefer should not be left alone.'

'I should have gone at this time in any case,' said Isabel, who would not allow it to be supposed that he could fill her place near their uncle.

'Nevertheless I am sorry that you should not have remained while I am here. Of course it cannot be helped.' Then he paused, but she had not a word further to say. She could see by the anxiety displayed in his face, and by a more than usually unnatural tone in his voice, that he was about to make his proposition. She was quite prepared for it, and remained silent, fixed, and attentive. 'Isabel,' he said, 'I suppose Uncle Indefer has told you what he intends?'

'I should say so. I think he always tells me what he intends.'

'About the property I mean.'

'Yes; about the property. I believe he has made a will leaving it to you. I believe he has done this, not because he loves you the best, but because he thinks it ought to go to the male heir. I quite agree with him that these things should not be governed by affection. He is so good that he will certainly do what he believes to be his duty.'

'Nevertheless the effect is the same.'

'Oh yes; as regards you, the effect will be the same. You will have the property, whether it comes from love or duty.'

'And you will lose it.'

'I cannot lose what never was mine,' she said, smiling.

'But why should we not both have it – one as well as the other?'

'No; we can't do that.'

'Yes, we can; if you will do what I wish, and what he wishes also. I love you with all my heart.'

She opened her eyes as though driven to do so by surprise. She knew that she should not have expressed herself in that way, but she could not avoid the temptation.

'I do, indeed, with all my heart. Why should we not – marry, you know? Then the property would belong to both of us.'

'Yes; then it would.'

'Why should we not; eh, Isabel?' Then he approached her as though about to make some ordinary symptom of a lover's passion.

'Sit down there, Henry, and I will tell you why we cannot do that. I do not love you in the least.'

'You might learn to love me.'

'Never; never! That lesson would be impossible to me. Now let there be an end of it. Uncle Indefer has, I dare say, asked you to make this proposition.'

'He wrote a letter, just saying that he would like it.'

'Exactly so. You have found yourself compelled to do his bidding, and you have done it. Then let there be an end of it. I would not marry an angel even to oblige him or to get Llanfeare; and you are not an angel – to my way of thinking.'

'I don't know about angels,' he said, trying still to be good-humoured.

'No, no. That was my nonsense. There is no question of angels. But not for all Llanfeare, not even to oblige him, would I undertake to marry a man even if I were near to loving him. I should have to love him entirely, without reference to Llanfeare. I am not at all near loving you.'

'Why not, Isabel?' he asked foolishly.

'Because – because – because you are odious to me!'

'Isabel!'

'I beg your pardon. I should not have said so. It was very wrong; but, then, why did you ask so foolish a question? Did I not tell you to let there be an end of it? And now will you let me give you one little bit of advice?'

'What is it?' he asked angrily. He was beginning to hate her, though he was anxious to repress his hatred, lest by indulging it he should injure his prospects.

'Do not say a word about me to my uncle. It will be better for you not to tell him that there has been between us any such interview as this. If he did once wish that you and I should become man and wife, I do not think that he wishes it now. Let the thing slide, as they say. He has quite made up his mind in your favour, because it is his duty. Unless you do something to displease him very greatly, he will make no further change. Do not trouble him more than you can help by talking to him on things that are distasteful. Anything in regard to me, coming from you, will be distasteful to him. You had better go about among the farms, and see the tenants, and learn the condition of everything. And then talk to him about that. Whatever you do, never suggest that the money coming from it all is less than it ought to be. That is my advice. And now, if you please, you and I need not talk about it any more.' Then she got up and left the room without waiting for a reply.

When he was alone he resolved upon complying with her advice, at any rate in one respect. He would not renew his offer of marriage; nor would he hold any further special conversation with her. Of course, she was hateful to him, having declared so plainly to him her own opinion regarding himself. He had made the offer, and had thereby done his duty. He had made the offer, and had escaped.

But he did not at all believe in the sincerity of her advice as to their uncle. His heart was throbbing with the desire to secure the inheritance to himself – and so he thought, no doubt, was hers as to herself. It might be that the old man's intention would depend upon his obedience, and if so, it was certainly necessary that the old man should know that he had been obedient. Of course, he would tell the old man what he had done.

But he said not a word till Isabel had gone. He did take her advice about the land and the tenants, but hardly to much effect. If there were a falling roof here or a half-hung door there, he displayed his zeal by telling the Squire of these defaults. But the Squire hated to hear of such defaults. It must be acknowledged that it would have required a man of very great parts to have given satisfaction in the position in which this young man was placed.

But as soon as Isabel was gone he declared his obedience.

'I have asked her, sir, and she has refused me,' he said in a melancholy, low, and sententious voice.

'What did you expect?'

'At any rate, I did as you would have me.'

'Was she to jump down your throat when you asked her?'

'She was very decided – very. Of course, I spoke of your wishes.'

'I have not any wishes.'

'I thought that you desired it.'

'So I did, but I have changed my mind. It would not do at all. I almost wonder how you could have had the courage to ask her. I don't suppose that you have the insight to see that she is different from other girls.'

'Oh, yes; I perceived that.'

'And yet you would go and ask her to be your wife off-hand, just as though you were going to buy a horse! I suppose you told her that it would be a good thing because of the estate?'

'I did mention it,' said the young man, altogether astounded and put beyond himself by his uncle's manner and words.

'Yes; just as if it were a bargain! If you will consent to put up with me as a husband, why, then you can go shares with me in the property. That was the kind of thing, wasn't it? And then you come and tell me that you have done your duty by making the offer!'

The heir expectant was then convinced that it would have been better for him to have followed the advice which Isabel had given him, but yet he could not bring himself to believe that the advice had been disinterested. Why should Isabel have given him disinterested advice in opposition to her own prospects? Must not Isabel's feeling about the property be the same as his own?

✖ FOUR ✖

The Squire's Death

WITH A SORE HEART ISABEL WENT HER way to Hereford – troubled because she saw nothing but sorrow and vexation in store for her uncle.

'I know that I am getting weaker every day,' he said. And yet it was not long since he had spoken of living for two years.

'Shall I stay?' asked Isabel.

'No; that would be wrong. You ought to go to your father. I suppose that I shall live till you come back.'

'Oh, Uncle Indefer!'

'What if I did die? It is not that that troubles me.' Then she kissed him and left him. She knew how vain it was to ask any further questions, understanding thoroughly the nature of his sorrow. The idea that this nephew must be the master of Llanfeare was so bitter to him that he could hardly endure it; and then, added to this, was the vexation of the nephew's presence. That three weeks should be passed alone with the man – three weeks of the little that was left to him of life, seemed to be a cruel addition to the greater sorrow! But Isabel went, and the uncle and nephew were left to do the best they could with each other's company.

Isabel had not seen Mr Owen or heard from him since the writing of that letter in which she had told him of her uncle's decision. Now it would be necessary that she should meet him, and she looked forward to doing so almost with fear and trembling. On one point she had made up her mind, or thought that she had made up her mind. As she had refused him when supposed to be heiress of Llanfeare, she certainly would not accept him, should he feel himself constrained by a sense of honour to renew his offer to her now that her position was so different. She had not accused him in her own heart of having come to her because of her supposed wealth. Thinking well of him in other matters, she thought well of him also in that. But still there was the fact that she had refused him when supposed to be an heiress; and not even to secure her happiness would she allow him to think that she accepted him because of her altered circumstances. And yet she was in love with him, and had now acknowledged to herself that it was so. Her position in this as in all things seemed to be so cruel! Had she been the heiress of Llanfeare she could not have married him, because it would then have been her duty to comply with the wishes of her uncle. No such duty would now be imposed upon her, at any rate after her uncle's death. As simple Isabel Brodrick she might marry whom she would without bringing discredit upon the Indefer Joneses. But that which she had been constrained to do before her uncle had changed his purpose now tied her hands.

It did seem to her cruel; but she told herself that it was peculiarly her duty to bear such cruelty without complaint. Of her uncle's intense love to her she was fully aware, and, loving him as warmly, was prepared to bear everything on his account. His vacillation had been unfortunate for her, but in everything he had done the best according to his lights. Perhaps there was present to her mind something of the pride of a martyr. Perhaps she gloried a little in the hardship of her position. But she was determined to have her glory and her martyrdom all to herself. No human being should ever hear from her lips a word of complaint against her Uncle Indefer.

The day after her arrival her father asked her a few questions as to her uncle's intentions in reference to the property.

'I think it is all settled,' she said. 'I think it has been left to my Cousin Henry.'

'Then he has changed his mind,' said her father angrily. 'He did mean to make you his heiress?'

'Henry is at Llanfeare now, and Henry will be his heir.'

'Why has he changed? Nothing can be more unjust than to make a promise in such a matter and then to break it.'

'Who says that he made a promise? You have never heard anything of the kind from me. Papa, I would so much rather not talk about Llanfeare. Ever since I have known him, Uncle Indefer has been all love to me. I would not allow a thought of mine to be polluted by ingratitude towards him. Whatever he has done, he has done because he has thought it to be the best. Perhaps I ought to tell you that he has made some charge on the property on my behalf, which will prevent my being a burden upon you.'

A week or ten days after this, when she had been nearly a fortnight at Hereford, she was told that William Owen was coming in to drink tea. This communication was made to her by her stepmother, in that serious tone which is always intended to convey a matter of importance. Had any other minor canon or any other gentleman been coming to tea, the fact would have been announced in a different manner.

'I shall be delighted to see him,' said Isabel, suppressing with her usual fortitude any slightest symptom of emotion.

'I hope you will, my dear. I am sure he is very anxious to see you.'

Then Mr Owen came and drank his tea in the midst of the family. Isabel could perceive that he was somewhat confused – not quite able to talk in his usual tone, and that he was especially anxious as to his manner towards her. She took her part in the conversation as though there were nothing peculiar in the meeting. She spoke of Llanfeare, of her uncle's failing health, and of her cousin's visit, taking care to indicate by some apparently chance word, that Henry was received there as the heir. She played her part well, evincing no sign of special feeling but her ear was awake to the slightest tone in his voice after he had received the information she had given him. She knew that his voice was altered, but she did not read the alteration altogether aright.

'I shall call in the morning,' he said, as he gave her his hand at parting. There was no pressure of the hand, but still he had addressed himself especially to her.

Why should he come in the morning? She had made up her mind, at the spur of the moment, that the news which he had heard had settled that matter for ever. But if so, why should he come in the morning? Then she felt, as she sat alone in her room, that she had done him a foul injustice in that spur of the moment. It must be that she had done him an injustice, or he would not have said that he would come. But if he could be generous, so could she. She had refused him when she believed herself to be the heiress of Llanfeare, and she certainly would not accept him now.

On the next morning about eleven o'clock he came. She had become aware that it was the intention of all the family that she should see him alone, and she made no struggle against that intention. As such intention existed, the interview must of course take place, and as well now as later. There was no confidence on the matter between herself and her stepmother – no special confidence between even herself and her half-sisters. But she was aware that they all supposed that Mr Owen was to come there on that morning for the sake of renewing his offer to her. It was soon done when he had come.

'Isabel,' he said, 'I have brought with me that letter which you wrote to me. Will you take it back again?' And he held it out in his hand.

'Nay; why should I take back my own letter?' she answered, smiling.

'Because I hope – I do not say I trust – but I hope that I may receive an altered answer.'

'Why should you hope so?' she asked, foolishly enough.

'Because I love you so dearly. Let me say something very plainly. If it be a long story, forgive me because of its importance to myself. I did think that you were – well, inclined to like me.'

'Like you! I always liked you. I do like you.'

'I hoped more. Perhaps I thought more. Nay, Isabel, do not interrupt me. When they told me that you were to be your uncle's heir, I knew that you ought not to marry me.'

'Why not?'

'Well, I knew that it should not be so. I knew that your uncle would think so.'

'Yes, he thought so.'

'I knew that he would, and I accepted your answer as conveying his decision. I had not intended to ask the heiress of Llanfeare to be my wife.'

'Why not? Why not?'

'I had not intended to ask the heiress of Llanfeare to by my wife,' he said, repeating the words. 'I learned last night that it was not to be so.'

'No; it is not to be so.'

'Then why should not Isabel Brodrick be the wife of William Owen, if she likes him – if only she can bring herself to like him well enough?'

She could not say that she did not like him well enough. She could not force herself to tell such a lie! And yet there was her settled purpose still strong in her mind. Having refused him when she believed herself to be rich, she could not bring herself to take him now that she was poor. She only shook her head mournfully.

'You cannot like me well enough for that?'

'It must not be so.'

'Must not? Why must not?'

'It cannot be so.'

'Then, Isabel, you must say that you do not love me.'

'I need say nothing, Mr Owen.' Again she smiled as she spoke to him. 'It is enough for me to say that it cannot be so. If I ask you not to press me further, I am sure that you will not do so.'

'I shall press you further,' he said, as he left her; 'but I will leave you a week to think of it.'

She took the week to think of it, and from day to day her mind would change as she thought of it. Why should she not marry him, if thus they might both be happy? Why should she cling to a resolution made by her when she was in error as to the truth? She knew now, she was now quite certain, that when he had first come to her he had known nothing of her promised inheritance. He had come then simply because he loved her, and for that reason, and for that reason only, he had now come again. And yet – and yet, there was her resolution! And there was the ground on which she had founded it! Though he might not remember it now, would he not remember hereafter that she had refused him when she was rich and accepted him when she was poor? Where then would be her martyrdom, where her glory, where her pride? Were she to do so, she would only do as would any other girl. Though she would not have been mean, she would seem to have been mean, and would so seem to his eyes. When the week was over she had told herself that she must be true to her resolution.

There had been something said about him in the family, but very little. The stepmother was indeed afraid of Isabel, though she had endeavoured to conquer her own fear of using authority; and her half-sisters, though they loved her, held her in awe. There was so little that was weak about her, so little that was self-indulgent, so little that was like the other girls around them! It was known that Mr Owen was to come again on a certain day at a certain hour, and it was known also for what purpose he was to come; but no one had dared to ask a direct question as to the result of his coming.

He came, and on this occasion her firmness almost deserted her. When he entered the room he seemed to her to be bigger than before, and more like her master. As the idea that he was so fell upon her, she became aware that she loved him better than ever. She began to know that with such a look as he now wore he would be sure to conquer. She did not tell herself that she would yield, but thoughts flitted across her as to what might be the best manner of yielding.

'Isabel,' he said, taking her by the hand, 'Isabel, I have come again, as I told you that I would.'

She could not take her hand from him, nor could she say a word to him in her accustomed manner. As he looked down upon her, she felt that she had already yielded, when suddenly the door was opened, and one of the girls hurried into the room.

'Isabel,' said her sister, 'here is a telegram for you, just come from Carmarthen.'

Of course she opened it instantly with perturbed haste and quivering fingers. The telegram was as follows: – 'Your uncle is very ill, very ill indeed, and wishes you to come back quite immediately.' The telegram was not from her Cousin Henry, but from the doctor.

There was no time then either for giving love or for refusing it. The paper was handed to her lover to read, and then she rushed out of the room as though the train which was to carry her would start instantly.

'You will let me write to you by-and-by?' said Mr Owen as she left him; but she made no answer to him as she rushed out of the room; nor would she make any answer to any of the others as they expressed either hope or consolation. When was the next train? When should she reach Carmarthen? When would she once more be at the old man's bedside? In the course of the afternoon she did leave Hereford, and at about ten o'clock that night she was at Carmarthen. Some one concerned had looked into this matter of the trains, and there at the station was a fly ready to take her to Llanfeare. Before eleven her uncle's hand was in hers, as she stood by his bedside.

Her Cousin Henry was in the room, and so was the housekeeper who had been with him constantly almost ever since she had left him. She had seen at once by the manner of the old servants as she entered the house, from the woeful face of the butler, and from the presence of the cook, who had lived in the family for the last twenty years, that something terrible was expected. It was not thus that she would have been received had not the danger been imminent.

'Dr Powell says, Miss Isabel, that you are to be told that he will be here quite early in the morning.'

This coming from the cook, told her that her uncle was expected to live that night, but that no more was expected.

'Uncle Indefer,' she said, 'how is it with you? Uncle Indefer, speak to me!' He moved his head a little upon the pillow; he turned his face somewhat towards hers; there was some slight return to the grasp of her hand; there was a gleam of loving brightness left in his eye; but he could not then speak a word. When, after an hour, she left his room for a few minutes to get rid of her travelling clothes, and to prepare herself for watching by him through the night, the housekeeper, whom Isabel had known ever since she had been at Llanfeare, declared that in her opinion her uncle would never speak again.

'The doctor, Miss Isabel, thought so, when he left us.'

She hurried down, and at once occupied the place which the old woman had filled for the last three days and nights. Before long she had banished the woman, so that to her might belong the luxury of doing anything, if aught could be done. That her cousin should be there was altogether unnecessary. If the old man could know any one at his deathbed, he certainly would not wish to see the heir whom he had chosen.

'You must go – you must indeed,' said Isabel.

Then the cousin went, and so at last, with some persuasion, did the housekeeper.

She sat there hour after hour, with her hand lying gently upon his.

When she would move it for a moment, though it was to moisten his lips, he would give some sign of impatience. For hours he lay in that way, till the early dawn of the summer morning broke into the room through the chink of the shutters. Then there came from him some sign of a stronger life, and at last, with a low muttered voice, indistinct, but not so indistinct but that the sounds were caught, he whispered a word or two.

'It is all right. It is done.'

Soon afterwards she rang the bell violently, and when the nurse entered the room she declared that her old master was no more. When the doctor arrived at seven, having ridden out from Carmarthen, there was nothing for him further to do but to give a certificate as to the manner of death of Indefer Jones, Esq., late of Llanfeare, in the country of Carmarthen.

✳ FIVE ✳

Preparing for the Funeral

ISABEL, WHEN SHE WAS LEFT ALONE, FELT that a terrible weight of duty was imposed on her. She seemed to be immediately encompassed by a double world of circumstances. There was that world of grief which was so natural, but which would yet be easy, could she only be allowed to sit down and weep. But it was explained to her that until after the funeral, and till the will should have been read, everything about Llanfeare must be done by her and in obedience to her orders. This necessity of action – of action which in her present condition of mind did not seem clear to her – was not at all easy.

The doctor was good to her, and gave her some instruction before he left her. 'Shall I give the keys to my cousin?' she said to him. But even as she said this there was the doubt on her mind what those last words of her uncle had been intended to mean. Though her grief was very bitter, though her sorrow was quite sincere, she could not keep herself from thinking of those words. It was not that she was anxious to get the estate for herself. It was hardly in that way that the matter in these moments presented itself to her. Did the meaning of those words impose on her any duty? Would it be right that she should speak of them, or be silent? Ought she to suppose that they had any meaning, and if so, that they referred to the will?

'I think that you should keep the keys till after the will has been read,' said the doctor.

'Even though he should ask for them?'

'Even though he should ask for them,' said the doctor. 'He will not press such a request if you tell him that I say it ought to be so. If there be any difficulty, send for Mr Apjohn.'

Mr Apjohn was the lawyer; but there had been quite lately some disagreement between her uncle and Mr Apjohn, and this advice was not palatable to her.

'But,' continued Dr Powell, 'you will not find any difficulty of that kind. The funeral had better be on Monday. And the will, I suppose, can be read afterwards. Mr Apjohn will come out and read it. There can be no difficulty about that. I know that Mr Apjohn's feelings are of the kindest towards your uncle and yourself.'

Mr Apjohn had taken upon himself to 'scold' her uncle because of the altered will, the will that had been altered in favour of Cousin Henry. So much the old man had said to Isabel himself. 'If I think it proper, he has no right to scold me,' the old man had said. The 'scolding' had probably been in the guise of that advice which a lawyer so often feels himself justified in giving.

Isabel thought that she had better keep those words to herself, at any rate for the present. She almost resolved that she would keep those words altogether to herself, unless other facts should come out which would explain their meaning and testify to their truths. She would say nothing of them in a way that would seem to imply that she had been led by them to conceive that she expected the property. She did certainly think that they alluded to the property. 'It is all right. It is done.' When her uncle had uttered these words, using the last effort of his mortal strength for the purpose, he no doubt was thinking of the property. He had meant to imply that he had done something to make his last decision 'right' in her favour. She was, she thought, sure of so much. But then she bore in mind the condition of the old man's failing mind – those wandering thoughts which would so naturally endeavour to fix themselves upon her and upon the property in combination with each other. How probable was it that he would dream of something that he would fain do, and then dream that he had done it! And she knew, too, as well as the lawyer would know himself, that the words would go for nothing, though they had been spoken before a dozen witnesses. If a later will was there, the later will would speak for itself. If no later will was there, the words were empty breath.

But above all was she anxious that no one should think that she was desirous of the property – that no one should suppose that she would be hurt by not having it. She was not desirous, and was not hurt. The matter was so important, and had so seriously burdened her uncle's mind, that she could not but feel the weight herself; but as to her own desires, they were limited to a wish that her uncle's will, whatever it might be, should be carried out. Not to have Llanfeare, not to have even a shilling from her uncle's estate, would hurt her but little – would hurt her heart not at all. But to know that it was thought by others that she was disappointed – that would be a grievous burden to her! Therefore she spoke to Dr Powell, and even to her cousin, as though the estate were doubtless now the property of the latter.

Henry Jones at this time – during the days immediately following his uncle's death – seemed to be so much awe-struck by his position, as to be incapable of action. To his Cousin Isabel he was almost servile in his obedience. With bated breath he did suggest that the keys should be surrendered to him, making his proposition simply on the ground that she would thus be saved from trouble; but when she told him that it was her duty to keep them till after the funeral, and that it would be her duty to act as mistress in the house till after that ceremony, he was cringing in his compliance.

'Whatever you think best, Isabel, shall be done. I would not interfere for a moment.'

Then some time afterwards, on the following day, he assured her that whatever might be the nature of the will, she was to regard Llanfeare as her home as long as it would suit her to remain there.

'I shall go back to papa very soon,' she had said, 'as soon, indeed, as I can have my things packed up after the funeral. I have already written to papa to say so.'

'Everything shall be just as you please,' he replied; 'only, pray, believe that if I can do anything for your accommodation it shall be done.'

To this she made some formal answer of courtesy, not, it may be feared, very graciously. She did not believe in his civility; she did not think he was kind to her in heart, and she could not bring herself to make her manner false to her feelings. After that, during the days that remained before the funeral, very little was said between them. Her dislike to him grew in bitterness, though she failed to explain even to herself the cause of her dislike. She did know that her uncle had been in truth as little disposed to love him as herself, and that knowledge seemed to justify her. Those last words had assured her at any rate of that, and though she was quite sure of her own conscience in regard to Llanfeare, though she was certain that she did not covet the possession of the domain, still she was unhappy to think that it should become his. If only for the tenants' sake and the servants, and the old house itself, there were a thousand pities in that. And then the belief would intrude itself upon her that her uncle in the last expression of his wishes had not intended his nephew to be his heir.

Then, in these days reports reached her which seemed to confirm her own belief. It had not been the habit of her life to talk intimately with the servants, even though at Llanfeare there had been no other woman with whom she could talk intimately. There had been about her a sense of personal dignity which had made such freedom distasteful to herself, and had repressed it in them. But now the housekeeper had come to her with a story to which Isabel had found it impossible not to listen. It was reported about the place that the Squire had certainly executed another will a few days after Isabel had left Llanfeare.

'If so,' said Isabel sternly, 'it will be found when Mr Apjohn comes to open the papers.'

But the housekeeper did not seem satisfied with this. Though she believed that some document had been written, Mr Apjohn had not been sent for, as had always been done on former similar occasions. The making of the Squire's will had been a thing always known and well understood at Llanfeare. Mr Apjohn had been sent for on such occasions, and had returned after a day or two, accompanied by two clerks. It was quite understood that the clerks were there to witness the will. The old butler, who would bring in the sherry and biscuits after the operation, was well acquainted with all the testamentary circumstances of the occasions. Nothing of that kind had occurred now; but old Joseph Cantor, who had been a tenant on the property for the last thirty years, and his son, Joseph Cantor the younger, had been called in, and it was supposed that they had performed the duty of witnessing the document. The housekeeper seemed to think that they, when interrogated, had declined to give any information on the subject. She herself had not seen them, but she had seen others of the tenants, and she was certain, she said, that Llanfeare generally believed that the old Squire had executed a will during the absence of his niece.

In answer to all this Isabel simply said that if a new will, which should turn out to be the real will, had actually been made, it would be found among her uncle's papers. She knew well the manner in which those other wills had been tied and deposited in one of the drawers of her uncle's tables. She had been invited to read them all, and had understood from a thousand assurances that he had wished that nothing should be kept secret from her. The key of the very drawer was at this moment in her possession. There was nothing to hinder her from searching, should she wish to search. But she never touched the drawer. The key which locked it she placed in an envelope, and put it apart under another lock and key. Though she listened, though she could not but listen, to the old woman's narrative, yet she rebuked the narrator. 'There should be no talking about such things,' she said. 'It had been,' she said, 'her uncle's intention to make his nephew the owner of Llanfeare, and she believed that he had done so. It was better that there should be no conversation on the matter until the will had been read.'

During these days she did not go beyond the precincts of the garden, and was careful not to encounter any of the tenants, even when they called at the house. Mr Apjohn she did not see, nor Dr Powell again, till the day of the funeral. The lawyer had written to her more than once, and had explained to her exactly the manner in which he intended to proceed. He, with Dr Powell, would be at the house at eleven o'clock; the funeral would be over at half-past twelve; they would lunch at one, and immediately afterwards the will should be 'looked for' and read. The words 'looked for' were underscored in his letter, but no special explanation of the underscoring was given. He went on to say that the tenants would, as a matter of course, attend the funeral, and that he had taken upon himself to invite some few of those who had known the Squire most intimately, to be present at the reading of the will. These he named, and among them were Joseph Cantor the elder, and Joseph Cantor the younger. It immediately occurred to Isabel that the son was not himself a tenant, and that no one else who was not a tenant was included in the list. From this she was sure that Mr Apjohn had heard the story which the housekeeper had told her. During these days there was little or no intercourse between Isabel and her cousin. At dinner they met, but only at dinner, and even then almost nothing was said between them. What he did with himself during the day she did not even know. At Llanfeare there was a so-called book-room, a small apartment, placed between the drawing-room and the parlour, in which were kept the few hundred volumes which constituted the library of Llanfeare. It had not been much used by the late Squire except that from time to time he would enter it for the sake of taking down with his own hands some volume of sermons from the shelves. He himself had for years been accustomed to sit in the parlour, in which he ate his meals, and had hated the ceremony of moving even into the drawing-room. Isabel herself had a sitting-room of her own upstairs, and she, too, had never used the book-room. But here Cousin Henry had now placed himself, and here he remained through the whole day, though it was not believed of him that he was given to much reading. For his breakfast and his supper he went to the parlour alone. At dinner time Isabel came down. But through all the long hours of the day he remained among the books, never once leaving the house till the moment came for receiving Mr Apjohn and Dr Powell before the funeral. The housekeeper would say little words about him, wondering what he was doing in the book-room. To this Isabel would apparently pay no attention, simply remarking that it was natural that at such a time he should remain in seclusion.

'But he does get so very pale, Miss Isabel,' said the housekeeper. 'He wasn't white, not like that when he come first to Llanfeare.' To this Isabel made no reply; but she, too, had remarked how wan, how pallid, and how spiritless he had become.

On the Monday morning, when the men upstairs were at work on their ghastly duty, before the coming of the doctor and the lawyer, she went down to him, to tell him something of the programme for the day. Hitherto he had simply been informed that on that morning the body would be buried under the walls of the old parish church, and that after the funeral the will would be read. Entering the room somewhat suddenly she found him seated, vacant, in a chair, with an open book indeed on the table near him, but so placed that she was sure that he had not been occupied with it. There he was, looking apparently at the book-shelves, and when she entered the room he jumped up to greet her with an air of evident surprise.

'Mr Apjohn and Dr Powell will be here at eleven,' she said.

'Oh, ah; yes,' he replied.

'I thought I would tell you, that you might be ready.'

'Yes; that is very kind. But I am ready. The men came in just now, and put the band on my hat, and laid my gloves there. You will not go, of course?'

'Yes; I shall follow the body. I do not see why I should not go as well as you. A woman may be strong enough at any rate for that. Then they will come back to lunch.'

'Oh, indeed; I did not know that there would be a lunch.'

'Yes; Dr Powell says that it will be proper. I shall not be there, but you, of course, will be present to take the head of the table.'

'If you wish it.'

'Of course; it would be proper. There must be some one to seem at any rate to entertain them. When that is over Mr Apjohn will find the will, and will read it. Richard will lay the lunch here, so that you may go at once into the parlour, where the will will be read. They tell me that I am to be there. I shall do as they bid me, though it will be a sore trouble to me. Dr Powell will be there, and some of the tenants. Mr Apjohn has thought it right to ask them, and therefore I tell you. Those who will be present are as follows – John Griffith, of Coed; William Griffith, who has the home farm; Mr Mortimer Green, of Kidwelly; Samuel Jones, of Llanfeare Grange; and the two Cantors, Joseph Cantor the father, and Joseph the son. I don't know whether you know them by appearance as yet.'

'Yes,' said he, 'I know them.' His face was almost sepulchral as he answered her, and as she looked at him she perceived that a slight quiver came upon his lips as she pronounced with peculiar clearness the two last names on the list.

'I thought it best to tell you all this,' she added. 'If I find it possible, I shall go to Hereford on Wednesday. Most of my things are already packed. It may be that something may occur to stop me, but if it is possible I shall go on Wednesday.'

SIX

Mr Apjohn's Explanation

THE READER NEED NOT BE DETAINED WITH any elaborate account of the funeral. Every tenant and every labourer about the place was there; as also were many of the people from Carmarthen. Llanfeare Church, which stands on a point of a little river just as it runs into a creek of the sea, is not more than four miles distant from the town; but such was the respect in which the old squire was held that a large crowd was present as the body was lowered into the vault. Then the lunch followed, just as Isabel had said. There was Cousin Henry, and there were the doctor and the lawyer, and there were the tenants who had been specially honoured by invitation, and there was Joseph Cantor the younger. The viands were eaten freely, though the occasion was not a happy one. Appetites are good even amidst grief, and the farmers of Llanfeare took their victuals and their wine in funereal silence, but not without enjoyment. Mr Apjohn and Dr Powell also were hungry, and being accustomed, perhaps, to such entertainments, did not allow the good things prepared to go waste. But Cousin Henry, though he made an attempt, could not swallow a morsel. He took a glass of wine, and then a second, helping himself from the bottle as it stood near at hand; but he ate nothing, and spoke hardly a word. At first he made some attempt, but his voice seemed to fail him. Not one of the farmers addressed a syllable to him. He had before the funeral taken each of them by the hand, but even then they had not spoken to him. They were rough of manner, little able to conceal their feelings; and he understood well from their bearing that he was odious to them. Now as he sat at table with them, he determined that as soon as this matter should be settled he would take himself away from Llanfeare, even though Llanfeare should belong to him. While they were at the table both the lawyer and the doctor said a word to him, making a struggle to be courteous, but after the first struggle the attempt ceased also with them. The silence of the man, and even the pallor of his face might be supposed to be excused by the nature of the occasion.

'Now,' said Mr Apjohn, rising from the table when the eating and drinking had ceased, 'I think we might as well go into the next room. Miss Brodrick, who has consented to be present, will probably be waiting for us.'

They passed through the hall into the parlour in a long string, Mr Apjohn leading the way, followed by Cousin Henry. There they found Isabel sitting with the housekeeper beside her. She shook hands in silence with the attorney, the doctor, and all the tenants, and then, as she took her seat, she spoke a word to Mr Apjohn. 'As I have felt it hard to be alone, I have asked Mrs Griffith to remain with me. I hope it is not improper?'

'There can be no reason on earth,' said Mr Apjohn, 'why Mrs Griffith should not hear the will of her master, who respected her so thoroughly.' Mrs Griffith bobbed a curtsey in return for this civility, and then sat down, intently interested in the coming ceremony.

Mr Apjohn took from his pocket the envelope containing the key, and, opening the little packet very slowly, very slowly opened the drawer, and took out from it a bundle of papers tied with red tape. This he undid, and then, sitting with the bundle loosened before him, he examined the document lying at the top. Then, slowly spreading them out, as though pausing over every operation with premeditated delay, he held in his hand that which he had at first taken; but he was in truth thinking of the words which he would have to use at the present moment. He had expected, but had expected with some doubt, that another document would have been found there. Close at his right hand sat Dr Powell. Round the room, in distant chairs, were ranged the six farmers, each with his hat in hand between his knees. On a sofa opposite were Isabel and the housekeeper. Cousin Henry sat alone, not very far from the end of the sofa, almost in the middle of the room. As the operation went on, one of his hands quivered so much that he endeavoured to hold it with the other to keep it from shaking. It was impossible that any one there should not observe his trepidation and too evident discomfort.

The document lying at the top of the bundle was opened out very slowly by the attorney, who smoothed it down with his hand preparatory to reading it. Then he looked at the date to assure himself that it was the last will which he himself had drawn. He knew it well, and was cognizant with its every legal quiddity. He could judiciously have explained every clause of it without reading a word, and might probably have to do so before the occasion was over; but he delayed, looking down upon it and still smoothing it, evidently taking another minute or two to collect his thoughts. This will now under his hand was very objectionable to him, having been made altogether in opposition to his own advice, and having thus created that 'scolding' of which the Squire had complained to Isabel. This will bequeathed the whole of the property to Cousin Henry. It did also affect to leave a certain sum of money to Isabel, but the sum of money had been left simply as a sum of money, and not as a charge on the property. Now, within the last few days, Mr Apjohn had learnt that there were no funds remaining for the payment of such a legacy. The will, therefore, was to him thoroughly distasteful. Should that will in truth be found to be the last will and testament of the old Squire, then it would be his duty to declare that the estate and everything upon it belonged to Cousin Henry, and that there would be, as he feared, no source from which any considerable part of the money nominally left to Miss Brodrick could be defrayed. To his thinking nothing could be more cruel, nothing more unjust, than this.

He had heard tidings which would make it his duty to question the authenticity of this will which was now under his hand; and now had come the moment in which he must explain all this.

'The document which I hold here,' he said, 'purports to be the last will of our old friend. Every will does that as a matter of course. But then there may always be another and a later will.' Here he paused, and looked round the room at the faces of the farmers.

'So there be,' said Joseph Cantor the younger.

'Hold your tongue, Joe, till you be asked,' said the father.

At this little interruption all the other farmers turned their hats in their hands. Cousin Henry gazed round at them, but said never a word. The lawyer looked into the heir's face, and saw the great beads of sweat standing on his brow.

'You hear what young Mr Cantor has said,' continued the lawyer. 'I am glad that he interrupted me, because it will make my task easier.'

'There now, feyther!' said the young man triumphantly.

'You hold your tongue, Joe, till you be asked, or I'll lend ye a cuff.'

'Now I must explain,' continued Mr Apjohn, 'what passed between me and my dear old friend when I received instructions from him in this room as to this document which is now before me. You will excuse me, Mr Jones,' this he said addressing himself especially to Cousin Henry – 'if I say that I did not like this new purpose on the Squire's part. He was proposing an altogether new arrangement as to the disposition of his property; and though there could be no doubt, not a shadow of doubt, as to the sufficiency of his mental powers for the object in view, still I did not think it well that an old man in feeble health should change a purpose to which he had come in his maturer years, after very long deliberation, and on a matter of such vital moment. I expressed my opinion strongly, and he explained his reasons. He told me that he thought it right to keep the property in the direct line of his family. I endeavoured to explain to him that this might be sufficiently done though the property were left to a lady, if the lady were required to take the name, and to confer the name on her husband, should she afterwards marry. You will probably all understand the circumstances.'

'We understand them all,' said John Griffith, of Coed, who was supposed to be the tenant of most importance on the property.

'Well, then, I urged my ideas perhaps too strongly. I am bound to say that I felt them very strongly. Mr Indefer Jones remarked that it was not my business to lecture him on a matter in which his conscience was concerned. In this he was undoubtedly right; but still I thought I had done no more than my duty, and could only be sorry that he was angry with me. I can assure you that I never for a moment entertained a feeling of anger against him. He was altogether in his right, and was actuated simply by a sense of duty.'

'We be quite sure of that,' said Samuel Jones, from 'The Grange,' an old farmer, who was supposed to be a far-away cousin of the family.

'I have said all this,' continued the lawyer, 'to explain why it might be probable that Mr Jones should not have sent for me, if, in his last days, he felt himself called on by duty to alter yet once again the decision to which he had come. You can understand that if he determined in his illness to make yet another will –'

'Which he did,' said the younger Cantor, interrupting him.

'Exactly; we will come to that directly.'

'Joe, ye shall be made to sit out in the kitchen; ye shall,' said Cantor the father.

'You can understand, I say, that he might not like to see me again upon the subject. In such case he would have come back to the opinion which I had advocated; and, though no man in his strong health would have been more ready to acknowledge an error than Indefer Jones, of Llanfeare, we all know that with failing strength comes failing courage. I think that it must have been so with him, and that for this reason he did not avail himself of my services. If there be such another will –'

'There be!' said the irrepressible Joe Cantor the younger. Upon this his father only looked at him. 'Our names is to it,' continued Joe.

'We cannot say that for certain, Mr Cantor,' said the lawyer. 'The old Squire may have made another will, as you say, and may have destroyed it. We must have the will before we can use it. If he left such a will, it will be found among his papers. I have turned over nothing as yet; but as it was here in this drawer and tied in this bundle that Mr Jones was accustomed to keep his will – as the last will which I made is here, as I expected to find it, together with those which he had made before and which he seems never to have wished to destroy, I have had to explain all this to you. It is, I suppose, true, Mr Cantor, that you and your son were called upon by the Squire to witness his signature to a document which he purported to be a will on Monday the 15th of July?'

Then Joseph Cantor the father told all the circumstances as they had occurred. When Mr Henry Jones had been about a fortnight at Llanfeare, and when Miss Isabel had been gone a week, he, Cantor, had happened to come up to see the Squire, as it was his custom to do at least once a week. Then the Squire had told him that his services and those also of his son were needed for the witnessing of a deed. Mr Jones had gone on to explain that this deed was to be his last will. The old farmer, it seemed, had suggested to his landlord that Mr Apjohn should be employed. The Squire then declared that this would be unnecessary; that he himself had copied a former will exactly, and compared it word for word, and reproduced it with no other alteration than that of the date. All that was wanted would be his signature, efficiently witnessed by two persons who should both be present together with the testator. Then the document had been signed by the Squire, and after that by the farmer and his son. It had been written, said Joseph Cantor, not on long, broad paper such as that which had been used for the will now lying on the table before the lawyer, but on a sheet of square paper such as was now found in the Squire's desk. He, Cantor, had not read a word of what had there been set down, but he had been enabled to see that it was written in that peculiarly accurate and laborious handwriting which the Squire was known to use, but not more frequently than he could help.

Thus the story was told – at least, all that there was to tell as yet. The drawer was opened and ransacked, as were also the other drawers belonging to the table. Then a regular search was made by the attorney, accompanied by the doctor, the butler, and the housemaid, and continued through the whole afternoon – in vain. The farmers were dismissed as soon as the explanation had been given as above described. During the remainder of the day Cousin Henry occupied a chair in the parlour, looking on as the search was continued. He offered no help, which was natural enough; nor did he make any remark as to the work in hand, which was, perhaps, also natural. The matter was to him one of such preponderating moment that he could hardly be expected to speak of it. Was he to have Llanfeare and all that belonged to it, or was he to have nothing? And then, though no accusation was made against him, though no one had insinuated that he had been to blame in the matter, still there was apparent among them all a strong feeling against him. Who had made away with this will, as to the existence of which at one time there was no doubt? Of course the idea was present to his mind that they must think that he had done so. In such circumstances it was not singular that he should say nothing and do nothing.

Late in the evening Mr Apjohn, just before he left the house, asked Cousin Henry a question, and received an answer.

'Mrs Griffith tells me, Mr Jones, that you were closeted with your uncle for about an hour immediately after the Cantors had left him on that Tuesday – just after the signatures had been written. Was it so?'

Again the drops of sweat came out and stood thick upon his forehead. But this Mr Apjohn could understand without making an accusation against the man, even in his heart. The unexpressed suspicion was so heavy that a man might well sweat under the burden of it! He paused a moment, and tried to look as though he were thinking. 'Yes,' said he; 'I think I was with my uncle on that morning.'

'And you knew that the Cantors had been with him?'

'Not that I remember. I think I did know that somebody had been there. Yes, I did know it. I had seen their hats in the hall.'

'Did he say anything about them?'

'Not that I remember.'

'Of what was he talking? Can you tell me? I rather fancy that he did not talk much to you.'

'I think it was then that he told me the names of all the tenants. He used to scold me because I did not understand the nature of their leases.'

'Did he scold you then?'

'I think so. He always scolded me. He did not like me. I used to think that I would go away and leave him. I wish that I had never come to Llanfeare. I do – I do.'

There seemed to be a touch of truth about this which almost softened Mr Apjohn's heart to the poor wretch. 'Would you mind answering one more question, Mr Jones?' he said. 'Did he tell you that he had made another will?'

'No.'

'Nor that he intended to do so?'

'No.'

'He never spoke to you about another will – a further will, that should again bestow the estate on your cousin?'

'No,' said Cousin Henry, with the perspiration still on his brow.

Now it seemed to Mr Apjohn certain that, had the old man made such a change in his purpose, he would have informed his nephew of the fact.

✖ SEVEN ✖

Looking for the Will

THE SEARCH WAS CARRIED ON UP TO nine o'clock that evening, and then Mr Apjohn returned to Carmarthen, explaining that he would send out two men to continue the work on the Tuesday, and that he would come out again on the Wednesday to read whatever might then be regarded as the old Squire's will – the last prepared document if it could be found, and the former one should the search have been successful. 'Of course,' said he, in the presence of the two cousins, 'my reading the document will give it no force. Of those found, the last in date will be good – until one later be found. It will be well, however, that some steps should be taken, and nothing can be done till the will has been read.' Then he took his leave and went back to Carmarthen.

Isabel had not shown herself during the whole of the afternoon. When Mr Apjohn's explanation had been given, and the search commenced, she retired and went to her own room. It was impossible for her to take a part in the work that was being done, and almost equally impossible for her to remain without seeming to take too lively an interest in the proceeding. Every point of the affair was clear to her imagination. It could not now be doubted by her that her uncle, doubly actuated by the presence of the man he disliked and the absence of her whom he so dearly loved, had found himself driven to revoke the decision to which he had been brought. As she put it to herself, his love had got the better of his conscience during the weakness of his latter days. It was a pity – a pity that it should have been so! It was to be regretted that there should have been no one near him to comfort him in the misery which had produced such a lamentable result. A will, she thought, should be the outcome of a man's strength, and not of his weakness. Having obeyed his conscience, he should have clung to his conscience. But all that could not affect what had been done. It seemed to be certain to her that this other will had been made and executed. Even though it should have been irregularly executed so as to be null and void, still it must for a time at least have had an existence. Where was it now? Having these thoughts in her mind, it was impossible for her to go about the house among those who were searching. It was impossible for her to encounter the tremulous misery of her cousin. That he should shiver and shake and be covered with beads of perspiration during a period of such intense perturbation did not seem to her to be unnatural. It was not his fault that he had not been endowed with especial manliness. She disliked him in his cowardice almost more than before; but she would not on that account allow herself to suspect him of a crime.

Mr Apjohn, just before he went, had an interview with her in her own room.

'I cannot go without a word,' he said, 'but its only purport will be to tell you that I cannot as yet express any decided opinion in this matter.'

'Do not suppose, Mr Apjohn, that I am anxious for another will,' she said.

'I am – but that has nothing to do with it. That he did make a will, and have it witnessed by these two Cantors, is, I think, certain. That he should afterwards have destroyed the will without telling the witnesses, who would be sure hereafter to think and talk of what they had done, seems to be most unlike the thoughtful consideration of your uncle. But his weakness increased upon him very quickly just at that time. Dr Powell thinks that he was certainly competent on that day to make a will, but he thinks also he may have destroyed it a day or two afterwards when his mind was hardly strong enough to enable him to judge of what he was doing. If, at last, this new will shall not be forthcoming, I think we must be bound to interpret the matter in that way. I tell you this before I go in order that it may assist you perhaps a little in forming your own opinion.' Then he went.

It was impossible but that she should bethink herself at that moment that she knew more than either Dr Powell or Mr Apjohn. The last expression of the old man's thoughts upon that or upon any matter had been made to herself. The last words that he had uttered had been whispered into her ears; 'It is all right. It is done.' Let the light of his failing intellect have been ever so dim, let his strength have faded from him ever so completely, he would not have whispered these words had he himself destroyed that last document. Mr Apjohn had spoken of the opinion which she was to form, and she felt how impossible to her it would be not to have an opinion in the matter. She could not keep her mind vacant even if she would. Mr Apjohn had said that, if the will were not found, he should think that the Squire had in his weakness again changed his mind and destroyed it. She was sure that this was not so. She, and she alone, had heard those last words. Was it or was it not her duty to tell Mr Apjohn that such words had been uttered? Had they referred to the interest of any one but herself, of course it would have been her duty. But now – now she doubted. She did not choose to seem even to put forth a claim on her own account. And of what use would be any revelation as to the uttering of these words? They would be accepted in no court of law as evidence in one direction or another. Upon the whole, she thought she would keep her peace regarding them, even to Mr Apjohn. If it was to be that her cousin should live there as squire and owner of Llanfeare, why should she seek to damage his character by calling in question the will under which he would inherit the property? Thus she determined that she would speak of her uncle's last words to no one.

But what must be her opinion as to the whole transaction? At the present moment she felt herself bound to think that this missing document would be found. That to her seemed to be the only solution which would not be terrible to contemplate. That other solution – of the destruction of the will by her uncle's own hands – she altogether repudiated. If it were not found, then – ! What then? Would it not then be evident that some fraud was being perpetrated? And if so, by whom? As these thoughts forced themselves upon her mind, she could not but think of that pallid face, those shaking hands, and the great drops of sweat which from time to time had forced themselves on to the man's brow. It was natural that he should suffer. It was natural that he should be perturbed under the consciousness of the hostile feeling of all those around him. But yet there had hardly been occasion for all those signs of fear which she had found it impossible not to notice as she had sat there in the parlour while Mr Apjohn was explaining the circumstances of the two wills. Would an innocent man have trembled like that because the circumstances around him were difficult? Could anything but guilt have betrayed itself by such emotions? And then, had the will in truth been made away with by human hands, what other hands could have done it? Who else was interested? Who else was there at Llanfeare not interested in the preservation of a will which would have left the property to her? She did not begrudge him the estate. She had acknowledged the strength of the reasons which had induced the Squire to name him as heir; but she declared to herself that, if that latter document were not found, a deed of hideous darkness would have been perpetrated by him. With these thoughts disturbing her breast she lay awake during the long hours of the night.

When Mr Apjohn had taken his departure, and the servants had gone to their beds, the butler having barred and double-barred the door after his usual manner, Cousin Henry still sat alone in the book-room. After answering those questions from Mr Apjohn, he had spoken to no one, but still sat alone with a single candle burning on the table by his elbow. The butler had gone to him twice, asking him whether he wanted anything, and suggesting to him that he had better go to his bed. But the heir, if he was the heir, had only resented the intrusion, desiring that he might be left alone. Then he was left alone, and there he sat.

His mind at this moment was tormented grievously within him. There was a something which he might do, and a something which he might not do, if he could only make up his mind. 'Honesty is the best policy!' 'Honesty is the best policy!' He repeated the well-known words to himself a thousand times, without, however, moving his lips or forming a sound. There he sat, thinking it all out, trying to think it out. There he sat, still trembling, still in an agony, for hour after hour. At one time he had fully resolved to do that by which he would have proved to himself his conviction that honesty is the best policy, and then he sat doubting again – declaring to himself that honesty itself did not require him to do this meditated deed. 'Let them find it,' he said to himself at last, aloud. 'Let them find it. It is their business: not mine.' But still he sat looking up at the row of books opposite to him.

When it was considerably after midnight, he got up from his chair and began to walk the room. As he did so, he wiped his brow continually as though he were hot with the exertion, but keeping his eye still fixed upon the books. He was urging himself, pressing upon himself the expression of that honesty. Then at last he rushed at one of the shelves, and, picking out a volume of Jeremy Taylor's works, threw it upon the table. It was the volume on which the old Squire had been engaged when he read the last sermon which was to prepare him for a flight to a better world. He opened the book, and there between the leaves was the last will and testament which his uncle had executed.

At that moment he heard a step in the hall and a hand on the door, and as he did so with quick eager motion he hid the document under the book.

'It is near two o'clock, Mr Henry,' said the butler. 'What are you doing up so late?'

'I am only reading,' said the heir.

'It is very late to be reading. You had better go to bed. He never liked people to be a-reading at these contrairy hours. He liked folk to be all a-bed.'

The use of a dead man's authority, employed against him by one who was, so to say, his own servant, struck even him as absurd and improper. He felt that he must assert himself unless he meant to sink lower and lower in the estimation of all those around him. 'I shall stay just as late as I please,' he said. 'Go away, and do not disturb me any more.'

'His will ought to be obeyed, and he not twenty-four hours under the ground,' said the butler.

'I should have stayed up just as long as I had pleased even had he been here,' said Cousin Henry. Then the man with a murmur took his departure and closed the door after him.

For some minutes Cousin Henry sat perfectly motionless, and then he got up very softly, very silently, and tried the door. It was closed, and it was the only door leading into the room. And the windows were barred with shutters. He looked round and satisfied himself that certainly no other eye was there but his own. Then he took the document up from its hiding-place, placed it again exactly between the leaves which had before enclosed it, and carefully restored the book to its place on the shelf.

He had not hidden the will. He had not thus kept it away from the eyes of all those concerned. He had opened no drawer. He had extracted nothing, had concealed nothing. He had merely carried the book from his uncle's table where he had found it, and, in restoring it to its place on the shelves, had found the paper which it contained. So he told himself now, and so he had told himself a thousand times. Was it his duty to produce the evidence of a gross injustice against himself? Who could doubt the injustice who knew that he had been summoned thither from London to take his place at Llanfeare as heir to the property? Would not the ill done against him be much greater than any he would do were he to leave the paper there where he had chanced to find it?

In no moment had it seemed to him that he himself had sinned in the matter, till Mr Apjohn had asked him whether his uncle had told him of this new will. Then he had lied. His uncle had told him of his intention before the will was executed, and had told him again, when the Cantors had gone, that the thing was done. The old man had expressed a thousand regrets, but the young one had remained impassive, sullen, crushed with a feeling of the injury done to him, but still silent. He had not dared to remonstrate, and had found himself unable to complain of the injustice.

There it was in his power. He was quite awake to the strength of his own position – but also to its weakness. Should he resolve to leave the document enclosed within the cover of the book, no one could accuse him of dishonesty. He had not placed it there. He had not hidden it. He had done nothing. The confusion occasioned by the absence of the will would have been due to the carelessness of a worn-out old man who had reached the time of life in which he was unfit to execute such a deed. It seemed to him that all justice, all honesty, all sense of right and wrong, would be best served by the everlasting concealment of such a document. Why should he tell of its hiding-place? Let them who wanted it search for it, and find it if they could. Was he not doing much in the cause of honesty in that he did not destroy it, as would be so easy for him?

But, if left there, would it not certainly be found? Though it should remain week after week, month after month – even should it remain year after year, would it not certainly be found at last, and brought out to prove that Llanfeare was not his own? Of what use to him would be the property – of what service – how would it contribute to his happiness or his welfare, knowing, as he would know, that a casual accident, almost sure to happen sooner or later, might rob him of it for ever? His imagination was strong enough to depict the misery to him which such a state of things would produce. How he would quiver when any stray visitor might enter the room! How terrified he would be at the chance assiduity of a housemaid! How should he act if the religious instincts of some future wife should teach her to follow out that reading which his uncle had cultivated?

He had more than once resolved that he would be mad were he to leave the document where he found it. He must make it known to those who were searching for it – or he must destroy it. His common sense told him that one alternative or the other must be chosen. He could certainly destroy it, and no one would be the wiser. He could reduce it, in the solitude of his chamber, into almost impalpable ashes, and then swallow them. He felt that, let suspicion come as it might into the minds of men, let Apjohn, and Powell, and the farmers – let Isabel herself – think what they might, no one would dare to accuse him of such a deed. Let them accuse him as they might, there would be no tittle of evidence against him.

But he could not do it. The more he thought of it, the more he had to acknowledge that he was incapable of executing such a deed. To burn the morsel of paper – oh, how easy! But yet he knew that his hands would refuse to employ themselves on such a work. He had already given it up in despair; and, having told himself that it was impossible, had resolved to extricate the document and, calling Isabel up from her bed in the middle of the night, to hand it over to her at once. It would have been easy to say he had opened one book after another, and it would, he thought, be a deed grand to do. Then he had been interrupted, and insulted by the butler, and in his anger he had determined that the paper should rest there yet another day.

EIGHT

The Reading of the Will

ON THE WHOLE OF THE NEXT DAY the search was continued. In spite of his late watches, Cousin Henry rose up early, not looking at anything that was being done while the search was continued in other rooms, but still sitting, as he had heretofore sat, among the books. The two men whom Mr Apjohn had sent from his office, together with the butler and Mrs Griffith, began their work in the old man's bed-room, and then carried it on in the parlour. When they came to the book-room, as being the next in turn, Cousin Henry took his hat and went out into the garden. There, as he made short turns upon the gravel path, he endeavoured to force himself away from the close vicinity of the window; but he could not do it. He could not go where he would have been unable to see what was being done. He feared – he trembled in his fear – lest they should come upon the guilty volume. And yet he assured himself again and again that he wished that they might find it. Would it not in every way be better for him that they should find it? He could not bring himself to destroy it, and surely, sooner or later, it would be found.

Every book was taken from its shelf, apparently with the object of looking into the vacant spaces behind them. Through the window he could see all that was done. As it happened, the compartment in which was the fatal shelf – on which was the fatal volume – was the last that they reached. No attempt was made to open the books one by one; but then this volume, with so thick an enclosure to betray it, would certainly open of itself. He himself had gone to the place so often that certainly the enclosure would betray itself. Well, let it betray itself! No one could say that he had had guilty cognizance of its whereabouts! But yet he knew that he would have been unable to speak, would have gasped, and would surely have declared himself to be guilty by his awe-struck silence.

Three by three the books came down, and then were replaced. And now they were at the shelf! Why could he not go away? Why must he stand there fixed at the window? He had done nothing – nothing, nothing; and yet he stood there trembling, immovable, with the perspiration running off his face, unable to keep his eyes for a moment from what they were doing! At last the very three came down, in the centre of which was the volume containing the will. There was a tree against which he leaned, unable to support himself, as he looked into the room. The vacant place was searched, and then the three books were replaced! No attempt was made to examine the volumes. The men who did the work clearly did not know that these very volumes had been in constant use with the old Squire. They were replaced, and then the search, as far as the room was concerned, was over. When they were gone, Cousin Henry returned again to the room, and there he remained during the rest of the day. The search as it was carried on elsewhere had no interest for him.

Whatever harm might be done to others, whoever else might be injured, certainly no one was ill-treated as he had been ill-treated. It was thus he thought of it. Even should the will never be found, how cruel would be the injustice done to him! He had not asked to be made heir to the property! It was not his doing. He had been invited to come in order that he might be received as the heir, and since he had come, every one about the place had misused him. The tenants had treated him with disdain; the very servants had been insolent; his Cousin Isabel, when he had offered to share everything with her, had declared that he was hateful to her; and his uncle himself had heaped insult upon injury, and had aggravated injustice with scorn.

'Yes; I had intended that you should be my heir, and have called you hither for that purpose. Now I find you to be so poor a creature that I have changed my mind.' That in truth was what his uncle had said to him and had done for him. Who, after that, would expect him to go out of his way in search of special magnanimity? Let them find the will if they wanted it! Even though he should resolve himself to have nothing to do with the property, even though he should repudiate any will in his own favour, still he would not tell them where this will might be found. Why should he help them in their difficulty?

Every carpet was taken up, every piece of funiture was moved, every trunk and box in the house was examined, but it occurred to no one that every book should be opened. It was still July, and the day was very long. From six in the morning till nine at night they were at work, and when the night came they declared that every spot about the place had been searched.

'I think, Miss, that the old Squire did destroy it. He was a little wandering at last.' It was thus that Mrs Griffith had expressed her opinion to Isabel.

Isabel was sure that it was not so, but said nothing in reply.

If she could only get away from Llanfeare and have done with it, she would be satisfied. Llanfeare had become odious to her and terrible! She would get away, and wash her hands of it. And yet she was aware how sad would be her condition. Mr Apjohn had already explained to her that the Squire had so managed his affairs as to have left no funds from which could be paid the legacy which had nominally been left to her. She had told her father when at Hereford that her uncle had taken such care of her that she would not become a burden upon him. Now it seemed that she would have to return home without a shilling of her own. For one so utterly penniless to think of marrying a man who had little but his moderate professional income would, she felt, be mean as well as wrong. There must be an end to everything between her and Mr Owen. If her father could not support her, she must become a governess or, failing that, a housemaid. But even the poor-house would be better than Llanfeare, if Lleanfeare were to be the property of Cousin Henry.

Mr Apjohn had told her that she could not now leave the place on the Wednesday as she had intended. On the Wednesday he again came to Llanfeare, and then she saw him before he proceeded to his business. It was his intention now to read the last will which had been found, and to explain to those who heard it that he proposed, as joint executor with Dr Powell, to act upon that as the last will – but still with a proviso that another will might possibly be forthcoming. Though he had in a measure quarrelled with the Squire over the making of that will, nevertheless, he had been appointed in it as the executor, such having been the case in the wills previously made. All this he explained to her up in her room, assenting to her objection to be again present when the will should be read.

'I could not do it,' she said; 'and of what use could it be, as I know everything that is in it? It would be too painful.'

He, remembering the futile legacy which it contained for herself, and the necessity which would be incumbent upon him to explain that there were no funds for paying it, did not again ask her to be present.

'I shall go to-morrow,' she said.

Then he asked her whether she could not remain until the beginning of next week, urging objections to this final surrender of Llanfeare; but she was not to be turned from her purpose. 'Llanfeare will have been surrendered,' she said; 'the house will be his to turn me out of if he pleases.'

'He would not do that.'

'He shall not have the chance. I could not hide it from you if I would. He and I do not love each other. Since he has been here I have kept away from him with disgust. He cannot but hate me, and I will not be a guest in his house. Besides, what can I do?'

'The will will not have been proved, you know.'

'What difference will there be in that? It will be proved at once. Of course he will have the keys, and will be master of everything. There are the keys.' As she said this she handed over to him various bunches. 'You had better give them to him yourself when you have read the will, so that I need have nothing to say to him. There are some books of mine which my uncle gave me. Mrs Griffith will pack them, and send them to me at Hereford – unless he objects. Everything else belonging to me I can take with me. Perhaps you will tell them to send a fly out for me in time for the early train.'

And so it was settled.

Then that will was read – that will which we know not to have been the last will – in the presence of Cousin Henry, of Dr Powell, who had again come out with Mr Apjohn, and of the farmers, who were collected as before.

It was a long, tedious document, in which the testator set forth at length his reasons for the disposition which he made of the property. Having much considered the matter, he had thought the estate should descend to the male heir, even in default of a regular deed of entail. Therefore, although his love for his dearest niece, Isabel Brodrick, was undiminished, and his confidence in her as perfect as ever, still he had thought it right to leave the old family property to his nephew, Henry Jones. Then, with all due circumstances of description, the legacy was made in favour of his nephew. There were other legacies; a small sum of money to Mr Apjohn himself, for the trouble imposed upon him as executor, a year's wages to each of his servants and other matters of the kind. There was also left to Isabel that sum of four thousand pounds of which mention has been made. When the lawyer had completed the reading of the document, he declared that to the best of his knowledge no such money was in existence. The testator had no doubt thought that legacies so made would be paid out of the property, whereas the property could be made subject to no such demand unless it had, by proper instrument to that effect, been charged with the amount.

'But,' he said, 'Mr Henry Jones, when he comes into possession of the estate, will probably feel himself called upon to set that matter right, and to carry out his uncle's wishes.'

Upon this Cousin Henry, who had not as yet spoken a word throughout the ceremony, was profuse in his promises. Should the estate become his, he would certainly see that his uncle's wishes were carried out in regard to his dear cousin. To this Mr Apjohn listened, and then went on to explain what remained to be said. Though this will, which he had now read, would be acted upon as though it were the last will and testament of the deceased – though, in default of that for which futile search had been made, it certainly was what it purported to be – still there existed in full force all those reasons which he had stated on the Monday for supposing that the late Squire had executed another. Here Joseph Cantor, junior, gave very strong symptoms of his inclination to reopen that controversy, but was stopped by the joint efforts of his father and the lawyer. If such a document should ever be found, then that would be the actual will and not the one which he had now read. After that, when all due formalities had been performed, he took his leave, and went back to Carmarthen.

The keys were given up to Cousin Henry, and he found himself to be, in fact, the lord and master of the house, and the owner of everything within it. The butler, Mrs Griffith, and the gardener gave him notice to quit. They would stay, if he wished it, for three months, but they did not think that they could be happy in the house now that the old Squire was dead, and that Miss Isabel was going away. There certainly did not come to him at the present moment any of the pleasures of ownership. He would have been willing – he thought that he would have been willing – to abandon Llanfeare altogether, if only it could have been abandoned without any of the occurrences of the last month. He would have been pleased that there should have been no Llanfeare.

But as it was, he must make up his mind to something. He must hide the paper in some deeper hiding place, or he must destroy it, or he must reveal it. He thought that he could have dropped the book containing the will into the sea, though he could not bring himself to burn the will itself. The book was now his own, and he might do what he liked with it. But it would be madness to leave the paper there!

Then again there came to him the idea that it would be best for him, and for Isabel too, to divide the property. In one way it was his – having become his without any fraudulent doing on his part. So he declared to himself. In another way it was hers – though it could not become hers without some more than magnanimous interference on his part. To divide it would certainly be best. But there was no other way of dividing it but by a marriage. For any other division, such as separating the land or the rents, no excuse could be made, nor would any such separation touch the fatal paper which lay between the leaves of the book. Were she to consent to marry him, then he thought he might find courage to destroy the paper.

It was necessary that he should see her on that afternoon, if only that he might bid her adieu, and tell her that she should certainly have the money that had been left her. If it were possible he would say a word also about that other matter.

'You did not hear the will read,' he said to her.

'No,' she answered abruptly.

'But you have been told its contents?'

'I believe so.'

'About the four thousand pounds?'

'There need be no question about the four thousand pounds. There is not a word to be said about it – at any rate between you and me.'

'I have come to tell you,' said he – not understanding her feeling in the least, and evidently showing by the altered tone of his voice that he thought that his communication would be received with favour – 'I have come to tell you that the legacy shall be paid in full. I will see to that myself as soon as I am able to raise a penny on the property.'

'Pray do not trouble yourself, Cousin Henry.'

'Oh, certainly I shall.'

'Do not trouble yourself. You may be sure of this, that on no earthly consideration would I take a penny from your hands.'

'Why not?'

'We take presents from those whom we love and esteem, not from those we despise.'

'Why should you despise me?' he asked.

'I will leave that to yourself to judge of; but be sure of this, that though I were starving I would take nothing from your hands.'

Then she got up, and, retiring into the inner room, left him alone. It was clear to him then that he could not divide the property with her in the manner that he had suggested to himself.

⚒ NINE ⚒

Alone at Llanfeare

ON THE DAY AFTER THE READING OF the will, Henry Indefer Jones, Esq., of Llanfeare, as he was now to be called, was left alone in his house, his cousin Isabel having taken her departure from the place in the manner proposed by her. And the lawyer was gone, and the doctor, and the tenants did not come near him, and the butler and the housekeeper kept out of his way, and there was probably no man in all South Wales more lonely and desolate than the new Squire of Llanfeare on that morning.

The cruelty of it, the injustice of it, the unprecedented hardness of it all! Such were the ideas which presented themselves to him as hour after hour he sat in the book-room with his eyes fixed on the volume of Jeremy Taylor's sermons. He had done nothing wrong – so he told himself – had not even coveted anything that did not belong to him. It was in accordance with his uncle's expressed desire that he had come to Llanfeare, and been introduced to the tenants as their future landlord, and had taken upon himself the place of the heir. Then the old man had announced to him his change of mind; but had not announced it to others, had not declared his altered purpose to the world at Llanefeare, and had not at once sent him back to his London office. Had he done so, that would have been better. There would have been a gross injustice, but that would have been the end of it, and he would have gone back to his London work unhappy indeed, but with some possibility of life before him. Now it seemed as though any mode of living would be impossible to him. While that fatal paper remained hidden in the fatal volume he could do nothing but sit there and guard it in solitude.

He knew well enough that it behoved him as a man to go out about the estate and the neighbourhood, and to show himself, and to take some part in the life around him, even though he might be miserable and a prey to terror whilst he was doing so. But he could not move from his seat till his mind had been made up as to his future action. He was still in fearful doubt. Through the whole of that first day he declared to himself that his resolution had not yet been made – that he had not yet determined what it would be best that he should do. It was still open to him to say that at any moment he had just found the will. If he could bring himself to do so he might rush off to Carmarthen with the document in his pocket, and still appear before the lawyer as a man triumphant in his own honesty, who at the first moment that it was possible had surrendered all that which was not legally his own, in spite of the foul usage to which he had been subjected. He might still assume the grand air of injured innocence, give back the property to the young woman who had insulted him, and return to his desk in London, leaving behind him in Carmarthenshire a character for magnanimity and honour. Such a line of conduct had charms in his eyes. He was quite alive to the delight of heaping coals of fire on his cousin's head. She had declared that she would receive nothing at his hands, because she despised him. After that there would be a sweetness, the savour of which was not lost upon his imagination, in forcing her to take all from his hands. And it would become known to all men that it was he who had found the will – he who might have destroyed it without the slightest danger of discovery – he who without peril might thus have made himself owner of Llanfeare. There would be a delight to him in the character which he would thus achieve. But then she had scorned him! No bitterer scorn had ever fallen from the lips or flashed from the eyes of a woman. 'We take presents from those we love, not from those we despise!' He had not resented the words at the moment; he had not dared to do so; but not the less had they entered upon his very soul – not the less he hated the woman who had dared so to reply to the generous offer which he had made her.

And then there was an idea present to him through it all that abstract justice, if abstract justice could be reached, would declare that the property should be his. The old man had made his will with all the due paraphernalia of will-making. There had been the lawyer and the witnesses brought by the lawyer; and, above all, there had been the declared reason of the will and its understood purpose. He had been sent for, and all Carmarthenshire had been made to understand why it was to be so. Then, in his sickness, the old man had changed his mind through some fantastic feeling, and almost on his death-bed, with failing powers, in a condition probably altogether unfit for such a duty, had executed a document which the law might respect, but which true justice, if true justice could be invoked, would certainly repudiate. Could the will be abolished, no more than justice would be done. But, though the will were in his own power, it could not be abolished by his own hands.

As to that abolishing he was perfectly conscious of his own weakness. He could not take the will from its hiding-place and with his own hand thrust it into the flames. He had never as yet even suggested to himself that he would do so. His hair stood on end as he thought of the horrors attendant on such a deed as that. To be made to stand in the dock and be gazed at by the angry eyes of all the court, to be written of as the noted criminal of the day, to hear the verdict of guilty, and then the sentence, and to be aware that he was to be shut up and secluded from all comforts throughout his life! And then, and then, the dread hereafter! For such a deed as that would there not be assured damnation? Although he told himself that justice demanded the destruction of the will, justice could not be achieved by his own hand after such fashion as that.

No; he could not himself destroy the document, though it should remain there for years to make his life a burden to him. As to that he had made up his mind, if to nothing else. Though there might be no peril as to this world – though he might certainly do the deed without a chance of detection from human eyes – though there would in truth be no prospect of that angry judge and ready jury and crushing sentence, yet he could not do it. There was something of a conscience within him. Were he to commit a felony, from the moment of the doing of the deed the fear of eternal punishment would be heavy on his soul, only to be removed by confession and retribution – and then by the trial with the judge, and the jury, and the sentence! He could not destroy the document. But if the book could get itself destroyed, what a blessing it would be! The book was his own, or would be in a few days, when the will should have been properly proved. But if he were to take away the book and sink it in a well, or throw it into the sea, or bury it deep beneath the earth, then it would surely reappear by one of those ever-recurring accidents which are always bringing deeds of darkness to the light. Were he to cast the book into the sea, tied with strings or cased in paper, and leaded, that it should surely sink, so that the will should not by untoward chance float out of it, the book tied and bound and leaded would certainly come up in evidence against him. Were he to move the book, the vacant space would lead to suspicion. He would be safe only by leaving the book where it was, by giving no trace that he had ever been conscious of the contents of the book.

And yet, if the document were left there, the book would certainly divulge its dread secret at last. The day would come, might come, ah! so quickly, on which the document would be found, and he would be thrust out, penniless as far as any right to Llanfeare was concerned. Some maid-servant might find it; some religious inmate of his house who might come there in search of godly teaching! If he could only bring himself to do something at once – to declare that it was there, so that he might avoid all these future miseries! But why had she told him that she despised him, and why had the old man treated him with such unexampled cruelty? So it went on with him for three or four days, during which he still kept his place among the books.

There would be great delight in possessing Llanfeare, if he could in very truth possess it. He would not live there. No; certainly not that. Every tenant about the place had shown him that he was despised. Their manner to him before the old Squire's death, their faces as they had sat there during the ceremonies of the will, and the fact that no one had been near him since the reading of the will, had shown him that. He had not dared to go to church during the Sunday; and though no one had spoken to him of his daily life, he felt that tales were being told of him. He was sure that Mrs Griffiths had whispered about the place the fact of his constant residence in one room, and that those who heard it would begin to say among themselves that a practice so strange must be connected with the missing will. No, he would not willingly live at Llanfeare. But if he could let Llanfeare, were it but for a song, and enjoy the rents up in London, how pleasant would that be! But then, had ever any man such a sword of Damocles to hang over his head by a single hair, as would be then hanging over his head were he to let Llanfeare or even to leave the house, while that book with its inclosure was there upon the shelves? It did seem to him, as he thought of it, that life would be impossible to him in any room but that as long as the will remained among the leaves of the volume.

Since the moment in which he had discovered the will he had felt the necessity of dealing with the officials of the office in London at which he had been employed. This was an establishment called the Sick and Healthy Life Assurance Company, in which he held some shares, and at which he was employed as a clerk. It would of course be necessary that he should either resign his place or go back to his duties. That the Squire of Llanfeare should be a clerk at the Sick and Healthy would be an anomaly. Could he really be in possession of his rents, the Sick and Healthy would of course see no more of him; but were he to throw up his position and then to lose Llanfeare, how sad, how terrible, how cruel would be his fate! But yet something must be done. In these circumstances he wrote a letter to the manager, detailing all the circumstances with a near approach to the truth, keeping back only the one little circumstance that he himself was acquainted with the whereabouts of the missing will.

'It may turn up at any moment,' he explained to the manager, 'so that my position as owner of the property is altogether insecure. I feel this so thoroughly that were I forced at the present to choose between the two I should keep my clerkship in the office; but as the condition of things is so extraordinary, perhaps the directors will allow me six months in which to come to a decision, during which I may hold my place, without, of course, drawing any salary.'

Surely, he thought, he could decide on something before the six months should be over. Either he would have destroyed the will, or have sunk the book beneath the waves, or have resolved to do that magnanimous deed which it was still within his power to achieve. The only one thing not possible would be for him to leave Llanfeare and take himself up to the delights of London while the document was yet hidden within the volume.

'I suppose sir, you don't know yet as to what your plans are going to be?' This was said by Mrs Griffith as soon as she made her way into the book-room after a somewhat imperious knocking at the door. Hitherto there had been but little communication between Cousin Henry and his servants since the death of the old Squire. Mrs Griffith had given him warning that she would leave his service, and he had somewhat angrily told her that she might go as soon as it pleased her. Since that she had come to him once daily for his orders, and those orders had certainly been very simple. He had revelled in no luxuries of the table or the cellar since the keys of the house had been committed to his charge. She had been told to provide him with simple food, and with food she had provided him. The condition of his mind had been such that no appetite for the glories of a rich man's table had yet come to him. That accursed book on the opposite shelf had destroyed all his taste for both wine and meat.

'What do you want to know for?' he asked.

'Well, sir; it is customary for the housekeeper to know something, and if there is no mistress she can only go to the master. We always were very quiet here, but Miss Isabel used to tell me something of what was expected.'

'I don't expect anything,' said Cousin Henry.

'Is there anybody to come in my place?' she asked.

'What can that be to you? You can go when you please.'

'The other servants want to go, too. Sally won't stay, nor yet Mrs Bridgeman.' Mrs Bridgeman was the cook. 'They say they don't like to live with a gentleman who never goes out of one room.'

'What is it to them what room I live in? I suppose I may live in what room I please in my own house.' This he said with an affectation of anger, feeling that he was bound to be indignant at such inquiries from his own servant, but with more of fear than wrath in his mind. So they had in truth already begun to inquire why it was that he sat there watching the books!

'Just so, Mr Jones. Of course you can live anywhere you like – in your own house.'

There was an emphasis on the last words which was no doubt intended to be impertinent. Every one around was impertinent to him.

'But so can they, sir – not in their own house. They can look for situations, and I thought it my duty just to tell you, because you wouldn't like to find yourself all alone here, by yourself like.'

'Why is it that everybody turns against me?' he asked suddenly, almost bursting into tears.

At this her woman's heart was a little softened, though she did despise him thoroughly. 'I don't know about turning, Mr Jones, but they have been used to such different ways.'

'Don't they get enough to eat?'

'Yes, sir; there's enough to eat, no doubt. I don't know as you have interfered about that; not but what as master you might. It isn't the victuals.'

'What is it, Mrs Griffith? Why do they want to go away?'

'Well, it is chiefly because of your sitting here alone – never moving, never having your hat on your head, sir. Of course a gentleman can do as he pleases in his own house. There is nothing to make him go out, not even to see his own tenants, nor his own farm, nor nothing else. He's his own master, sir, in course – but it is mysterious. There is nothing goes against them sort of people' – meaning the servants inferior to herself – 'like mysteries.'

Then they already felt that there was a mystery! Oh! what a fool he had been to shut himself up and eat his food there! Of course they would know that this mystery must have some reference to the will. Thus they would so far have traced the truth as to have learnt that the will had a mystery, and that the mystery was located in that room!

There is a pleasant game, requiring much sagacity, in which, by a few answers, one is led closer and closer to a hidden word, till one is enabled to touch it. And as with such a word, so it was with his secret. He must be careful that no eye should once see that his face was turned towards the shelf. At this very moment he shifted his position so as not to look at the shelf, and then thought that she would have observed the movement, and divined the cause.

'Anyways, they begs to say respectful that they wishes you to take a month's warning. As for me, I wouldn't go to inconvenience my old master's heir. I'll stay till you suits yourself, Mr Jones; but the old place isn't to me now what it was.'

'Very well, Mrs Griffith,' said Cousin Henry, trying to fix his eyes upon an open book in his hands.

※ TEN ※

Cousin Henry Dreams a Dream

FROM WHAT HAD PASSED WITH MRS GRIFFITH, it was clear to Cousin Henry that he must go out of the house and be seen about the place. The woman had been right in saying that his seclusion was mysterious. It was peculiarly imperative upon him to avoid all appearance of mystery. He ought to have been aware of this before. He ought to have thought of it, and not to have required to be reminded by a rebuke from the housekeeper. He could now only amend the fault for the future, and endeavour to live down the mystery which had been created. Almost as soon as Mrs Griffith had left him, he prepared to move. But then he bethought himself that he must not seem to have obeyed, quite at the moment, the injunctions of his own servant; so he re-seated himself, resolved to postpone for a day or two his intention of calling upon one of the tenants. He re-seated himself, but turned his back to the shelf, lest the aspect of his countenance should be watched through the window.

On the following morning he was relieved from his immediate difficulty by the arrival of a letter from Mr Apjohn. It was necessary that a declaration as to the will should be made before a certain functionary at Carmarthen, and as the papers necessary for the occasion had been prepared in the lawyer's office, he was summoned into Carmarthen for the purpose. Immediately after that he would be put into full possession of the property. Mr Apjohn also informed him that the deed had been prepared for charging the estate with four thousand pounds on behalf of his Cousin Isabel. By this he would bind himself to pay her two hundred a year for the next two years, and at the end of that period to hand over to her the entire sum. Here was an excuse provided for him to leave the house and travel as far as Carmarthen. There were the horses and the carriage with which his uncle had been accustomed to be taken about the estate, and there was still the old coachman, who had been in the service for the last twenty years. So he gave his orders, and directed that the carriage should be ready soon after two, in order that he might keep the appointment made by the lawyer at three. The order was sent out to the stable through the butler, and as he gave it he felt how unable he was to assume the natural tone of a master to his servants.

'The carriage, sir!' said the butler, as though surprised. Then the owner of Llanfeare found himself compelled to explain to his own man that it was necessary that he should see the lawyer in Carmarthen.

Should he or should he not take the book with him as he went? It was a large volume, and could not well be concealed in his pocket. He might no doubt take a book – any book – with him for his own recreation in the carriage; but were he to do so, the special book which he had selected would be marked to the eyes of the servants. It required but little thought to tell him that the book must certainly be left in its place. He could have taken the will and kept it safe, and certainly unseen, in the pocket of his coat. But then, to take the will from its hiding-place and to have it on his person, unless he did so for the purpose of instant and public revelation, would, as he thought, be in itself a felony. There would be the doing of a deed in the very act of abstracting the document; and his safety lay in the abstaining from any deed. What if a fit should come upon him, or he should fall and hurt himself and the paper be found in his possession? Then there would at once be the intervention of the police, and the cell, and the angry voices of the crowd, and the scowling of the judge, and the quick sentence, and that dwelling among thieves and felons for the entire period of his accursed life! Then would that great command, 'Thou shalt not steal,' be sounding always in his ear! Then would self-condemnation be heavy upon him! Not to tell of the document, not to touch it, not to be responsible in any way for its position there on the shelf – that was not to steal it. Hitherto the word 'felon' had not come home to his soul. But were he to have it in his pocket, unless with that purpose of magnanimity of which he thought so often, then he would be a felon.

Soon after two he left the room, and at the moment was unable not to turn a rapid glance upon the book. There it was, safe in its place. How well he knew the appearance of the volume! On the back near the bottom was a small speck, a spot on the binding, which had been so far disfigured by some accident in use. This seemed to his eyes to make it marked and separate among a thousand. To him it was almost wonderful that a stain so peculiar should not at once betray the volume to the eyes of all. But there it was, such as it was, and he left it amidst its perils. Should they pounce upon it the moment that he had left the room, they could not say that he was guilty because it contained the will.

He went to Carmarthen, and there his courage was subjected to a terrible trial. He was called upon to declare before the official that to the best of his belief the will, which was about to be proved, was the last will and testament of Indefer Jones. Had this been explained to him by the lawyer in his letter, he might probably have abstained from so damning a falsehood. There would have been time then for some resolution. Had Mr Apjohn told him what it was that he was about to be called upon to perform, even then, before the necessity of performance was presented to him, there would have been a moment for consideration, and he might have doubted. Had he hesitated in the presence of the lawyer, all would have been made known. But he was carried before the official not knowing that the lie was to be submitted to him, and before he could collect his thoughts the false declaration had been made!

'You understand, Mr Jones,' said the lawyer in the presence of the official, 'that we still think that a further will may eventually be found?'

'I understand that,' croaked the poor wretch.

'It is well that you should bear it in mind,' said Mr Apjohn severely – 'for your own sake, I mean.'

There was nothing further spoken on the subject, and he was given to understand that Llanfeare was now in truth his own – his own, whatever chance there might be that it should be wrested from him hereafter.

Then followed the business as to the charge upon the property which was to be made on behalf of Isabel. The deeds were prepared, and only required the signature of the new Squire.

'But she has refused to take a penny from me,' said the Squire, hesitating with a pen in his hand. Let us give him his due by declaring that, much as he hated his cousin, he did not doubt as to bestowing the money upon her. As far as he was concerned, she was welcome to the four thousand pounds.

But the lawyer misinterpreted his client's manner. 'I should think, Mr Jones,' he said, with still increased severity, 'that you would have felt that under the peculiar circumstances you were bound to restore to your cousin money which was expended by your uncle under a misconception in purchasing land which will now be yours.'

'What can I do if she will not take it?'

'Not take it? That is an absurdity. In a matter of such importance as this she will of course be guided by her father. It is not a matter requiring gratitude on her part. The money ought to be regarded as her own, and you will only be restoring to her what is in truth her own.'

'I am quite willing. I have made no difficulty, Mr Apjohn. I don't understand why you should speak to me in that way about it, as though I had hesitated about the money.' Nevertheless, the lawyer maintained the severe look, and there was still the severe tone as the poor wretch left the office. In all this there was so great an aggravation of his misery! It was only too manifest that every one suspected him of something. Here he was ready to give away – absolutely anxious to give away out of his own pocket – a very large sum of money to his cousin who had misused and insulted him, by signing the document without a moment's hesitation as soon as it was presented to him, and yet he was rebuked for his demeanour as he did it. Oh, that accursed will! Why had his uncle summoned him away from the comparative comfort of his old London life?

When he returned to the book-room, he made himself sure that the volume had not been moved. There was a slight variation in the positions of that and the two neighbouring books, the centre one having been pushed a quarter of an inch further in; and all this he had marked so accurately that he could not but know whether any hand had been at the shelf. He did not go near to the shelf, but could see the variation as he stood at the table. His eye had become minutely exact as to the book and its position. Then he resolved that he would not look at the book again, would not turn a glance on it unless it might be when he had made up his mind to reveal its contents. His neck became absolutely stiff with the efforts necessary not to look at the book.

That night he wrote a letter to his cousin, which was as follows –

'MY DEAR ISABEL,

'I have been into Carmarthen to-day, and I have signed a document in the presence of Mr Apjohn, by which four thousand pounds is made over to you as a charge upon the property. He stated that you had what might be called a right to that money, and I perfectly agreed with him. I have never doubted about the money since my uncle's will was read. The agent who receives the rents will remit to you one hundred pounds half yearly for the next two years. By that time I shall have been able to raise the money, and you shall then be paid in full.

'I don't want you to take this as any favour from me. I quite understood what you said to me. I think that it was undeserved, and, after all that I have suffered in this matter, cruel on your part. It was not my fault that my uncle changed his mind backwards and forwards. I never asked him for the estate. I came to Llanfeare only because he bade me. I have taken possession of the property only when told to do so by Mr Apjohn. If I could not make myself pleasant to you, it was not my fault. I think you ought to be ashamed of what you said to me – so soon after the old man's death!

'But all that has nothing to do with the money, which, of course, you must take. As for myself, I do not think I shall continue to live here. My uncle has made the place a nest of hornets for me, and all through no fault of my own. Should you like to come and live here as owner, you are welcome to do so on paying me a certain sum out of the rents. I am quite in earnest, and you had better think of it.

'Yours truly,

'HENRY JONES.'

His resolution as to the first portion of the above letter was taken as he returned in the carriage from Carmarthen; but it was not until the pen was in his hand, and the angry paragraph had been written in which he complained of her cruelty, that he thought of making that offer to her as to the residence. The idea flashed across his mind, and then was carried out instantly. Let her come and live there, and let her find the will herself if she pleased. If her mind was given to godly reading, this might be her reward. Such conduct would, at any rate, show them all that he was afraid of nothing. He would, he thought, if this could be arranged, still remain at his office; would give up that empty title of Squire of Llanfeare, and live in such comfort as might come to him from the remittances which would be made to him on account of the rents, till – that paper had been found. Such was his last plan, and the letter proposing it was duly sent to the post office.

On the following day he again acknowledged the necessity of going about the place – so that the feeling of mystery might, if possible, be gradually dissipated – and he went out for a walk. He roamed down towards the cliffs, and there sat in solitude, looking out upon the waters. His mind was still intent upon the book. Oh, if the book could be buried there below the sea – be drowned and no hand of his be necessary for the drowning! As he sat there, feeling himself constrained to remain away from the house for a certain period, he fell asleep by degrees and dreamed. He dreamt that he was out there in a little boat all alone, with the book hidden under the seats, and that he rowed himself out to sea till he was so far distant from the shore that no eye could see him. Then he lifted the book, and was about to rid himself for ever of his burden – when there came by a strong man swimming. The man looked up at him so as to see exactly what he was doing, and the book was not thrown over, and the face of the swimming man was the face of that young Cantor who had been so determined in his assertion that another will had been made.

The dream was still vivid as a reality to his intellect when he was awakened suddenly, whether by a touch or a sound he did not know. He looked up, and there was the young man whom he had seen swimming to him across the sea. The land he was on was a portion of old Cantor's farm, and the presence of the son need not have surprised him had he thought of it; but it was to him as though the comer had read every thought of his mind, and had understood clearly the purport of the dream.

'Be that you, Squire?' said the young man.

'Yes, it is I,' said Cousin Henry, as he lay trembling on the grass.

'I didn't know you was here, sir. I didn't know you ever com'd here. Good morning, sir.' Then the young man passed on, not caring to have any further conversation with a landlord so little to his taste.

After this he returned home almost cowed. But on the following morning he determined to make a still further effort, so that he might, if possible, return to the ways of the world, which were already becoming strange to him from the desolation of the life which he had been leading. He went out, and, taking the road by the church, up the creek, he came at about a distance of two miles from his own house to Coed, the farmstead of John Griffith, the farmer who held the largest number of acres on the property. At the garden gate he found his tenant, whom he was inclined to think somewhat more civil – a little, perhaps, more courteous – than others who had met him.

'Yes, sir,' said John Griffith, 'it's a fine day, and the crops are doing well enough. Would you like to come in and see the missus? She'll take it civil.'

Cousin Henry entered the house and said a few words to the farmer's wife, who was not, however, specially gracious in her demeanour. He had not the gift of saying much to such persons, and was himself aware of his own deficiency. But still he had done something – had shown that he was not afraid to enter a tenant's house. As he was leaving, the farmer followed him to the gate, and began to offer him some advice, apparently in kindness.

'You ought to be doing something, sir, with those paddocks between the shrubberies and the road.'

'I suppose so, Mr Griffith; but I am no farmer.'

'Then let them, sir. William Griffith will be glad enough to have them and pay you rent. The old Squire didn't like that the land he had held himself should go into other hands. But he never did much good with them lately, and it's different now.'

'Yes, it's different now. I don't think I shall live here, Mr Griffith.'

'Not live at Llanfeare?'

'I think not. I'm not quite fitted to the place. It isn't my doing, but among you all, I fear, you don't like me.' As he said this he tried to carry it off with a laugh.

'You'd live down that, Squire, if you did your duty, and was good to the people – and took no more than was your own. But perhaps you don't like a country life.'

'I don't like being where I ain't liked; that's the truth of it, Mr Griffith.'

'Who'll come in your place, if I may be so bold as to ask?'

'Miss Brodrick shall – if she will. It was not I who asked my uncle to bring me here.'

'But she is not to have the property?'

'Not the property – at least I suppose not. But she shall have the house and the grounds, and the land adjacent. And she shall manage it all, dividing the rents with me, or something of that kind. I have offered it to her, but I do not say that she will agree. In the meantime, if you will come up and see me sometimes, I will take it as a kindness. I do not know that I have done any harm, so as to be shunned.'

Then Farmer Griffith readily said that he would go up occasionally and see his landlord.

❈ ELEVEN ❈

Isabel at Hereford

ISABEL HAD NOT BEEN MANY HOURS AT home at Hereford before, as was natural, her father discussed with her the affairs of the property and her own peculiar interest in the will which had at last been accepted. It has to be acknowledged that Isabel was received somewhat as an interloper in the house. She was not wanted there, at any rate by her stepmother – hardly by her brothers and sisters – and was, perhaps, not cordially desired even by her father. She and her stepmother had never been warm friends. Isabel herself was clever and high-minded; but high-spirited also, imperious, and sometimes hard. It may be said of her that she was at all points a gentlewoman. So much could hardly be boasted of the present Mrs Brodrick; and, as was the mother, so were that mother's children. The father was a gentleman, born and bred as such; but in his second marriage he had fallen a little below his station, and, having done so, had accommodated himself to his position. Then there had come many children, and the family had increased quicker than the income. So it had come to pass that the attorney was not a wealthy man. This was the home which Isabel had been invited to leave when, now many years since, she had gone to Llanfeare to become her uncle's darling. There her life had been very different from that of the family at Hereford. She had seen but little of society, but had been made much of, and almost worshipped, by those who were around her. She was to be – was to have been – the Lady of Llanfeare. By every tenant about the place she had been loved and esteemed. With the servants she had been supreme. Even at Carmarthen, when she was seen there, she was regarded as the great lady, the acknowledged heiress, who was to have, at some not very distant time, all Llanfeare in her own hands. It was said of her, and said truly, that she was possessed of many virtues. She was charitable, careful for others, in no way self-indulgent, sedulous in every duty, and, above all things, affectionately attentive to her uncle. But she had become imperious, and inclined to domineer, if not in action, yet in spirit. She had lived much among books, had delighted to sit gazing over the sea with a volume of poetry in her hand, truly enjoying the intellectual gifts which had been given her. But she had, perhaps, learnt too thoroughly her own superiority, and was somewhat apt to look down upon the less refined pleasure of other people. And now her altered position in regard to wealth rather increased than diminished her foibles. Now, in her abject poverty – for she was determined that it should be abject – she would be forced to sustain her superiority solely by her personal gifts. She determined that, should she find herself compelled to live in her father's house, she would do her duty thoroughly by her stepmother and her sisters. She would serve them as far as it might be within her power; but she could not giggle with the girls, nor could she talk little gossip with Mrs Brodrick. While there was work to be done, she would do it, though it should be hard, menial, and revolting; but when her work was done, there would be her books.

It will be understood that, such being her mood and such her character, she would hardly make herself happy in her father's house – or make others happy. And then, added to all this, there was the terrible question of money! When last at Hereford, she had told her father that, though her uncle had revoked his grand intention in her favour, still there would be coming to her enough to prevent her from being a burden on the resources of her family. Now that was all changed. If her father should be unable or unwilling to support her, she would undergo any hardship, any privation; but would certainly not accept bounty from the hands of her cousin. Some deed had been done, she felt assured – some wicked deed, and Cousin Henry had been the doer of it. She and she alone had heard the last words which her uncle had spoken, and she had watched the man's face narrowly when her uncle's will had been discussed in the presence of the tenants. She was quite sure. Let her father say what he might, let her stepmother look at her ever so angrily with her greedy, hungry eyes, she would take no shilling from her Cousin Henry. Though she might have to die in the streets, she would take no bread from her Cousin Henry's hand.

She herself began the question of the money on the day after her arrival. 'Papa,' she said, 'there is to be nothing for me after all.'

Now Mr Apjohn, the lawyer, like a cautious family solicitor as he was, had written to Mr Brodrick, giving him a full account of the whole affair, telling him of the legacy of four thousand pounds, explaining that there was no fund from which payment could be legally exacted, but stating also that the circumstances of the case were of such a nature as to make it almost impossible that the new heir should refuse to render himself liable for the amount. Then had come another letter saying that the new heir had assented to do so.

'Oh, yes, there will, Isabel,' said the father.

Then she felt that the fighting of the battle was incumbent upon her, and she was determined to fight it. 'No, papa, no; not a shilling.'

'Yes, my dear, yes,' he said, smiling. 'I have heard from Mr Apjohn, and understood all about it. The money, no doubt, is not there; but your cousin is quite prepared to charge the estate with the amount. Indeed, it would be almost impossible for him to refuse to do so. No one would speak to him were he to be so base as that. I do not think much of your Cousin Henry, but even Cousin Henry could not be so mean. He has not the courage for such villainy.'

'I have the courage,' said she.

'What do you mean?'

'Oh, papa, do not be angry with me! Nothing – nothing shall induce me to take my Cousin Henry's money.'

'It will be your money – your money by your uncle's will. It is the very sum which he himself has named as intended for you.'

'Yes, papa; but Uncle Indefer had not got the money to give. Neither you nor I should be angry with him; because he intended the best.'

'I am angry with him,' said the attorney in wrath, 'because he deceived you and deceived me about the property.'

'Never; he deceived no one. Uncle Indefer and deceit never went together.'

'There is no question of that now,' said the father. 'He made some slight restitution, and there can, of course, be no question as to your taking it.'

'There is a question, and there must be a question, papa. I will not have it. If my being here would be an expense too great for you, I will go away.'

'Where will you go?'

'I care not where I go. I will earn my bread. If I cannot do that, I would rather live in the poor-house than accept my cousin's money.'

'What has he done?'

'I do not know.'

'As Mr Apjohn very well puts it, there is no question whatsoever as to gratitude, or even of acceptance. It is a matter of course. He would be inexpressibly vile were he not to do this.'

'He is inexpressibly vile.'

'Not in this respect. He is quite willing. You will have nothing to do but to sign a receipt once every half-year till the whole sum shall have been placed to your credit.'

'I will sign nothing on that account; nor will I take anything.'

'But why not? What has he done?'

'I do not know. I do not say that he has done anything. I do not care to speak of him. Pray do not think, papa, that I covet the estate, or that I am unhappy about that. Had he been pleasant to my uncle and good to the tenants, had he seemed even to be like a man, I could have made him heartily welcome to Llanfeare. I think my uncle was right in choosing to have a male heir. I should have done so myself – in his place.'

'He was wrong, wickedly wrong, after his promises.'

'There were no promises made to me: nothing but a suggestion, which he was, of course, at liberty to alter if he pleased. We need not, however, go back to that, papa. There he is, owner of Llanfeare, and from him, as owner of Llanfeare, I will accept nothing. Were I starving in the street I would not take a crust of bread from his fingers.'

Over and over again the conversation was renewed, but always with the same result. Then there was a correspondence between the two attorneys, and Mr Apjohn undertook to ask permission from the Squire to pay the money to the father's receipt without asking any acknowledgement from the daughter. On hearing this, Isabel declared that if this were done she would certainly leave her father's house. She would go out of it, even though she should not know whither she was going. Circumstances should not be made so to prevail upon her as to force her to eat meat purchased by her cousin's money.

Thus it came to pass that Isabel's new home was not made comfortable to her on her first arrival. Her stepmother would hardly speak to her, and the girls knew that she was in disgrace. There was Mr Owen, willing enough, as the stepmother knew, to take Isabel away and relieve them all from this burden, and with the 4000l. Mr Owen would, no doubt, be able at once to provide a home for her. But Mr Owen could hardly do this without some help. And even though Mr Owen should be so generous – and thus justify the name of 'softie' which Mrs Brodrick would sometimes give him in discussing his character with her own daughters – how preferable would it be to have a relation well-provided! To Mrs Brodrick the girl's objection was altogether unintelligible. The more of a Philistine Cousin Henry was, the more satisfaction should there be in fleecing him. To refuse a legacy because it was not formal was, to her thinking, an act of insanity. To have the payment of one refused to her because of informality would have been heart-breaking. But the making of such a difficulty as this she could not stomach. Could she have had her will, she would have been well pleased to whip the girl! Therefore Isabel's new home was not pleasant to her.

At this time Mr Owen was away, having gone for his holiday to the Continent. To all the Brodricks it was a matter of course that he would marry Isabel as soon as he came back. There was no doubt that he was 'a softie.' But then how great is the difference between having a brother-in-law well off, and a relation tightly constrained by closely limited means! To refuse – even to make a show of refusing – those good things was a crime against the husband who was to have them. Such was the light in which Mrs Brodrick looked at it. To Mr Brodrick himself there was an obstinacy in it which was sickening to him. But to Isabel's thinking the matter was very different. She was as firmly resolved that she would not marry Mr Owen as that she would not take her cousin's money – almost as firmly resolved.

Then there came the angry letter from Cousin Henry, containing two points which had to be considered. There was the offer to her to come to Llanfeare, and live there as though she was herself the owner. That, indeed, did not require much consideration. It was altogether out of the question, and only dwelt in her thoughts as showing how quickly the man had contrived to make himself odious to every one about the place. His uncle, he said, had made the place a nest of hornets to him. Isabel declared that she knew why the place was a nest of hornets. There was no one about Llanfeare to whom so unmanly, so cringing, so dishonest a creature would not be odious. She could understand all that.

But then there was the other point, and on that her mind rested long.

'I think you ought to be ashamed of what you said to me – so soon after the old man's death.'

She sat long in silence thinking of it, meditating whether he had been true in that – whether it did behove her to repent her harshness to the man. She remembered well her words – 'We take presents from those we love, not from those we despise.'

They had been hard words – quite unjustifiable unless he had made himself guilty of something worse than conduct that was simply despicable. Not because he had been a poor creature, not because he had tormented the old man's last days by an absence of all generous feeling, not because he had been altogether unlike what, to her thinking, a Squire of Llanfeare should be, had she answered him with those crushing words. It was because at the moment she had believed him to be something infinitely worse than that.

Grounding her aversion on such evidence as she had – on such evidence as she thought she had – she had brought against him her heavy accusation. She could not tell him to his face that he had stolen the will, she could not accuse him of felony, but she had used such quick mode of expression as had come to her for assuring him that he stood as low in her esteem as a felon might stand. And this she had done when he was endeavouring to perform to her that which had been described to him as a duty! And now he had turned upon her and rebuked her – rebuked her as he was again endeavouring to perform the same duty – rebuked her as it was so natural that a man should do who had been subjected to so gross an affront!

She hated him, despised him, and in her heart condemned him. She still believed him to have been guilty. Had he not been guilty, the beads of perspiration would not have stood upon his brow; he would not have become now red, now pale, by sudden starts; he would not have quivered beneath her gaze when she looked into his face. He could not have been utterly mean as he was, had he not been guilty. But yet – and now she saw it with her clear-seeing intellect, now that her passion was in abeyance – she had not been entitled to accuse him to his face. If he were guilty, it was for others to find it out, and for others to accuse him. It had been for her as a lady, and as her uncle's niece, to accept him in her uncle's house as her uncle's heir. No duty could have compelled her to love him, no duty would have required her to accept even his friendship. But she was aware that she had misbehaved herself in insulting him. She was ashamed of herself in that she had not been able to hide her feelings within her own high heart, but had allowed him to suppose that she had been angered because she had been deprived of her uncle's wealth. Having so resolved, she wrote to him as follows –

'MY DEAR HENRY,

'Do not take any further steps about the money, as I am quite determined not to accept it. I hope it will not be sent, as there would only be the trouble of repaying it. I do not think that it would do for me to live at Llanfeare, as I should have no means of supporting myself, let alone the servants. The thing is of course out of the question. You tell me that I ought to be ashamed of myself for certain words that I spoke to you. They should not have been spoken. I am ashamed of myself, and I now send you my apology.

'Yours truly,

'ISABEL BRODRICK.'

The reader may perhaps understand that these words were written by her with extreme anguish; but of that her Cousin Henry understood nothing.

✖ TWELVE ✖

Mr Owen

IN THIS WAY ISABEL SPENT FOUR VERY uncomfortable weeks in her new home before Mr Owen returned to Hereford. Nor was her discomfort much relieved by the prospect of his return. She knew all the details of his circumstances, and told herself that the man would be wrong to marry without any other means than those he at present possessed. Nor did she think of herself that she was well qualified to be the wife of a poor gentleman. She believed that she could starve if it were required of her, and support her sufferings with fortitude. She believed that she could work – work from morning till night, from week to week, from month to month, without complaining; but she did not think that she could make herself sweet as a wife should be sweet to a husband with a threadbare coat, or that she could be tender as a mother should be tender while dividing limited bread among her children. To go and die and have done with it, if that might be possible, was the panacea of her present troubles most commonly present to her mind. Therefore, there was no comfort to her in that promised coming of her lover of which the girls chattered to her continually. She had refused her lover when she held the proud position of the heiress of Llanfeare – refused him, no doubt, in obedience to her uncle's word, and not in accordance with her own feelings; but still she had refused him. Afterwards, when she had believed that there would be a sum of money coming to her from her uncle's will, there had been room for possible doubt. Should the money have proved sufficient to cause her to be a relief rather than a burden to the husband, it might have been her duty to marry him, seeing that she loved him with all her heart – seeing that she was sure of his love. There would have been much against it even then, because she had refused him when she had been a grand lady; but, had the money been forthcoming, there might have been a doubt. Now there could be no doubt. Should she who had denied him her hand because she was her uncle's heiress – on that avowed ground alone – should she, now that she was a pauper, burden him with her presence? He, no doubt, would be generous enough to renew his offer. She was well aware of his nobility. But she, too, could be generous, and, as she thought, noble. Thus it was that her spirit spoke within her, bidding her subject all the sweet affections of her heart to a stubborn pride.

The promised return, therefore, of Mr Owen did not make her very happy.

'He will be here to-morrow,' said her stepmother to her. 'Mrs Richards expects him by the late train to-night. I looked in there yesterday and she told me.' Mrs Richards was the respectable lady with whom Mr Owen lodged.

'I dare say he will,' said Isabel wearily – sorry, too, that Mr Owen's goings and comings should have been investigated.

'Now, Isabel, let me advise you. You cannot be so unjust to Mr Owen as to make him fancy for a moment that you will refuse your uncle's money. Think of his position – about two hundred and fifty a year in all! With your two hundred added it would be positive comfort; without it you would be frightfully poor.'

'Do you think I have not thought of it?'

'I suppose you must. But then you are so odd and so hard, so unlike any other girl I ever saw. I don't see how you could have the face to refuse the money, and then to eat his bread.'

This was an unfortunate speech as coming from Mrs Brodrick, because it fortified Isabel in the reply she was bound to make. Hitherto the stepmother had thought it certain that the marriage would take place in spite of such maiden denials as the girl had made; but now the denial had to be repeated with more than maiden vigour.

'I have thought of it,' said Isabel – 'thought of it very often, till I have told myself that conduct such as that would be inexpressibly base. What! to eat his bread after refusing him mine when it was believed to be so plentiful! I certainly have not face enough to do that – neither face nor courage for that. There are ignoble things which require audacity altogether beyond my reach.'

'Then you must accept the money from your cousin.'

'Certainly not,' said Isabel; 'neither that nor yet the position which Mr Owen will perhaps offer me again.'

'Of course he will offer it to you.'

'Then he must be told that on no consideration can his offer be accepted.'

'This is nonsense. You are both dying for each other.'

'Then we must die. But as for that, I think that neither men nor young women die for love now-a-days. If we love each other, we must do without each other, as people have to learn to do without most of the things that they desire.'

'I never heard of such nonsense, such wickednes! There is the money. Why should you not take it?'

'I can explain to you, mother,' she said sternly, it being her wont to give the appellation but very seldom to her stepmother, 'why I should not take Mr Owen, but I cannot tell you why I cannot take my cousin's money. I can only simply assure you that I will not do so, and that I most certainly shall never marry any man who would accept it.'

'I consider that to be actual wickedness – wickedness against your own father.'

'I have told papa. He knows I will not have the money.'

'Do you mean to say that you will come here into this house as an additional burden, as a weight upon your poor father's shoulder, when you have it in your power to relieve him altogether? Do you not know how pressed he is, and that there are your brothers to be educated?' Isabel, as she listened to this, sat silent, looking upon the ground, and her stepmother went on, understanding nothing of the nature of the mind of her whom she was addressing. 'He had reason to expect, ample reason, that you would never cost him a shilling. He had been told a hundred times that you would be provided for by your uncle. Do you not know that it was so?'

'I do. I told him so myself when I was last here before Uncle Indefer's death.'

'And yet you will do nothing to relieve him? You will refuse this money, though it is your own, when you could be married to Mr Owen to-morrow?' Then she paused, waiting to find what might be the effect of her eloquence.

'I do not acknowledge papa's right or yours to press me to marry any man.'

'But I suppose you acknowledge your right to be as good as your word? Here is the money; you have only got to take it.'

'What you mean is that I ought to acknowledge my obligation to be as good as my word. I do. I told my father that I would not be a burden to him, and I am bound to keep to that. He will have understood that at the present moment I am breaking my promise through a mistake of Uncle Indefer's which I could not have anticipated.'

'You are breaking your promise because you will not accept money that is your own.'

'I am breaking my promise, and that is sufficient. I will go out of the house and will cease to be a burden. If I only knew where I could go, I would begin to-morrow.'

'That is all nonsense,' said Mrs Brodrick, getting up and bursting out of the room in anger. 'There is a man ready to marry you, and there is the money. Anybody can see with half an eye what is your duty.'

Isabel, with all the eyes that she had, could not see what was her duty. That it could not be her duty to take a present of money from the man whom she believed to be robbing her of the estate she felt quite sure. It could not be her duty to bring poverty on a man whom she loved – especially not as she had refused to confer wealth upon him. It was, she thought, clearly her duty not to be a burden upon her father, as she had told him that no such burden should fall upon him. It was her duty, she thought, to earn her own bread, or else to eat none at all. In her present frame of mind she would have gone out of the house on the moment if any one would have accepted her even as a kitchenmaid. But there was no one to accept her. She had questioned her father on the matter, and he had ridiculed her idea of earning her bread. When she had spoken of service, he had become angry with her. It was not thus that he could be relieved. He did not want to see his girl a maid-servant or even a governess. It was not thus that she could relieve him. He simply wanted to drive her into his views, so that she might accept the comfortable income which was at her disposal, and become the wife of a gentleman whom every one esteemed. But she, in her present frame of mind, cared little for any disgrace she might bring on others by menial service. She was told that she was a burden, and she desired to cease to be burdensome.

Thinking it over all that night, she resolved that she would consult Mr Owen himself. It would, she thought, be easy – or if not easy at any rate feasible – to make him understand that there could be no marriage. With him she would be on her own ground. He, at least, had no authority over her, and she knew herself well enough to be confident of her own strength. Her father had a certain right to insist. Even her stepmother had a deputed right. But her lover had none. He should be made to understand that she would not marry him – and then he could advise her as to that project of being governess, housemaid, schoolmistress, or what not.

On the following morning he came, and was soon closeted with her. When he arrived, Isabel was sitting with Mrs Brodrick and her sisters, but they soon packed up their hemmings and sewings, and took themselves off, showing that it was an understood thing that Isabel and Mr Owen were to be left together. The door was no sooner closed than he came up to her, as though to embrace her, as though to put an arm round her waist before she had a moment to retreat, preparing to kiss her as though she were already his own. She saw it all in a moment. It was as though, since her last remembered interview, there had been some other meeting which she had forgotten – some meeting at which she had consented to be his wife. She could not be angry with him. How can a girl be angry with a man whose love is so good, so true? He would not have dreamed of kissing her had she stood there before him the declared heiress of Llanfeare. She felt more than this. She was sure by his manner that he knew that she had determined not to take her cousin's money. She was altogether unaware that there had already been some talking that morning between him and her father; but she was sure that he knew. How could she be angry with him?

But she escaped. 'No, not that,' she said. 'It must not be so, Mr Owen – it must not. It cannot be so.'

'Tell me one thing, Isabel, before we go any further, and tell me truly. Do you love me?'

She was standing about six feet from him, and she looked hard into his face, determined not to blush before his eyes for a moment. But she could hardly make up her mind as to what would be the fitting answer to his demand.

'I know,' said he, 'that you are too proud to tell me a falsehood.'

'I will not tell you a falsehood.'

'Do you love me?' There was still a pause. 'Do you love me as a woman should love the man she means to marry?'

'I do love you!'

'Then, in God's name, why should we not kiss? You are my love and I am yours. Your father and mother are satisfied that it should be so. Seeing that we are so, is it a disgrace to kiss? Having won your heart, may I not have the delight of thinking that you would wish me to be near you?'

'You must know it all,' she said, 'though it may be unwomanly to tell so much.'

'Know what?'

'There has never been a man whose touch has been pleasant to me – but I could revel in yours. Kiss you? I could kiss your feet at this moment, and embrace your knees. Everything belonging to you is dear to me. The things you have touched have been made sacred to me. The Prayer-Book tells the young wife that she should love her husband till death shall part them. I think my love will go further than that.'

'Isabel! Isabel!'

'Keep away from me! I will not even give you my hand to shake till you have promised to be of one mind with me. I will not become your wife.'

'You shall become my wife!'

'Never! Never! I have thought it out, and I know that I am right. Things have been hard with me.'

'Not to me! They will not have been hard to me when I shall have carried my point with you.'

'I was forced to appear before your eyes as the heiress of my uncle.'

'Has that made any difference with me?'

'And I was forced to refuse you in obedience to him who had adopted me.'

'I understand all that very completely.'

'Then he made a new will, and left me some money.'

'Of all that I know, I think, every particular.'

'But the money is not there.' At this he nodded his head as though smiling at her absurdity in going back over circumstances which were so well understood by both of them. 'The money is offered to me by my cousin, but I will not take it.'

'As to that I have nothing to say. It is the one point on which, when we are married, I shall decline to give you any advice.'

'Mr Owen,' and now she came close to him, but still ready to spring back should it be necessary, 'Mr Owen, I will tell you what I have told no one else.'

'Why me?'

'Because I trust you as I trust no one else.'

'Then tell me.'

'There is another will. There was another will rather, and he has destroyed it.'

'Why do you say that? You should not say that. You cannot know it.'

'And, therefore, I say it only to you, as I would to my own heart. The old man told me so – in his last moments. And then there is the look of the man. If you could have seen how his craven spirit cowered beneath my eyes!'

'One should not judge by such indications. One cannot but see them and notice them; but one should not judge.'

'You would have judged had you seen. You could not have helped judging. Nothing, however, can come of it, except this – that not for all the world would I take his money.'

'It may be right, Isabel, that all that should be discussed between you and me – right if you wish it. It will be my delight to think that there shall be no secret between us. But, believe me, dearest, it can have no reference to the question between us.'

'Not that I should be absolutely penniless?'

'Not in the least.'

'But it will, Mr Owen. In that even my father agrees with me.' In this she was no doubt wrong. Her father had simply impressed upon her the necessity of taking the money because of her lover's needs. 'I will not be a burden at any rate to you; and as I cannot go to you without being a burden, I will not go at all. What does it matter whether there be a little more suffering or a little less? What does it matter?'

'It matters a great deal to me.'

'A man gets over that quickly, I think.'

'So does a woman – if she be the proper sort of woman for getting over her difficulties of that kind. I don't think you are.'

'I will try.'

'I won't.' This he said, looking full into her face. 'My philosophy teaches me to despise the grapes which hang too high, but to make the most of those which come within my reach. Now, I look upon you as being within my reach.'

'I am not within your reach.'

'Yes; pardon me for my confidence, but you are. You have confessed that you love me.'

'I do.'

'Then you will not be so wicked as to deny to me that which I have a right to demand? If you love me as a woman should love the man who is to become her husband, you have no right to refuse me. I have made good my claim, unless there be other reasons.'

'There is a reason.'

'None but such as I have to judge of. Had your father objected, that would have been a reason; or when your uncle disapproved because of the property, that was a reason. As to the money, I will never ask you to take it, unless you can plead that you yourself are afraid of the poverty –.' Then he paused, looking at her as though he defied her to say so much on her own behalf. She could not say that, but sat there panting, frightened by his energy.

'Nor am I,' he continued very gently, 'the least in the world. Think of it, and you will find that I am right; and then, when next I come, then, perhaps, you will not refuse to kiss me.' And so he went.

Oh, how she loved him! How sweet would it be to submit her pride, her independence, her maiden reticences to such a man as that! How worthy was he of all worship, of all confidence, of all service! How definitely better was he than any other being that had ever crossed her path! But yet she was quite sure that she would not marry him.

✂ THIRTEEN ✂

The 'Carmarthen Herald'

THERE WAS A GREAT DEAL SAID AT Carmarthen about the old Squire's will. Such scenes as that which had taken place in the house, first when the will was produced, then when the search was made, and afterwards when the will was read, do not pass without comment. There had been many present, and some of them had been much moved by the circumstances. The feeling that the Squire had executed a will subsequent to that which had now been proved was very strong, and the idea suggested by Mr Apjohn that the Squire himself had, in the weakness of his latter moments, destroyed this document, was not generally accepted. Had he done so, something of it would have been known. The ashes of the paper or the tattered fragments would have been seen. Whether Mr Apjohn himself did or did not believe that it had been so, others would not think it. Among the tenants and the servants at Llanfeare there was a general feeling that something wrong had been done. They who were most inclined to be charitable in their judgment, such as John Griffith of Coed, thought that the document was still hidden, and that it might not improbably be brought to light at last. Others were convinced that it had fallen into the hands of the present possessor of the property, and that it had been feloniously but successfully destroyed. No guess at the real truth was made by any one. How should a man have guessed that the false heir should have sat there with the will, as it were, before his eyes, close at his hand, and neither have destroyed nor revealed its existence?

Among those who believed the worst as to Cousin Henry were the two Cantors. When a man has seen a thing done himself he is prone to believe in it – and the more so when he has had a hand in the doing. They had been selected for the important operation of witnessing the will, and did not in the least doubt that the will had been in existence when the old Squire died. It might have been destroyed since. They believed that it had been destroyed. But they could not be brought to understand that so great an injustice should be allowed to remain on the face of the earth without a remedy or without punishment. Would it not be enough for a judge to know that they, two respectable men, had witnessed a new will, and that this new will had certainly been in opposition to the one which had been so fraudulently proved? The younger Cantor especially was loud upon the subject, and got many ears in Carmarthen to listen to him.

The Carmarthen Herald, a newspaper bearing a high character through South Wales, took the matter up very strongly, so that it became a question whether the new Squire would not be driven to defend himself by an action for libel. It was not that the writer declared that Cousin Henry had destroyed the will, but that he published minute accounts of all that had been done at Llanfeare, putting forward in every paper as it came out the reason which existed for supposing that a wrong had been done. That theory that old Indefer Jones had himself destroyed his last will without saying a word of his purpose to any one was torn to tatters. The doctor had been with him from day to day, and must almost certainly have known it had such an intention been in his mind. The housekeeper would have known it. The nephew and professed heir had said not a word to any one of what had passed between himself and his uncle. Could they who had known old Indefer Jones for so many years, and were aware that he had been governed by the highest sense of honour through his entire life, could they bring themselves to believe that he should have altered the will made in his nephew's favour, and then realtered it, going back to his intentions in that nephew's favour, without saying a word to his nephew on the subject? But Henry Jones had been silent as to all that occurred during those last weeks. Henry Jones had not only been silent when the will was being read, when the search was being made, but had sat there still in continued silence. 'We do not say,' continued the writer in the paper, 'that Henry Jones since he became owner of Llanfeare has been afraid to mingle with his brother men. We have no right to say so. But we consider it to be our duty to declare that such has been the fact. Circumstances will from time to time occur in which it becomes necessary on public grounds to inquire into the privacy of individuals, and we think that the circumstances now as to this property are of this nature.' As will be the case in such matters, these expressions became gradually stronger, till it was conceived to be the object of those concerned in making them to drive Henry Jones to seek for legal redress – so that he might be subjected to cross-examination as to the transactions and words of that last fortnight before his uncle's death. It was the opinion of many that if he could be forced into a witness-box, he would be made to confess if there were anything to confess. The cowardice of the man became known – or was rather exaggerated in the minds of those around him. It was told of him how he lived in the one room, how rarely he left the house, how totally he was without occupation. More than the truth was repeated as to his habits, till all Carmarthenshire believed that he was so trammelled by some mysterious consciousness of crime as to be unable to perform any of the duties of life. When men spoke to him he trembled; when men looked at him he turned away.

All his habits were inquired into. It was said of him that the Carmarthen Herald was the only paper that he saw, and declared of him that he spent hour after hour in spelling the terrible accusations which, if not absolutely made against him, were insinuated. It became clear to lawyers, to Mr Apjohn himself, that the man, if honest, should, on behalf of the old family and long-respected name, vindicate himself by prosecuting the owner of the paper for libel. If he were honest in the matter, altogether honest, there could be no reason why he should fear to encounter a hostile lawyer. There were at last two letters from young Joseph Cantor printed in the paper which were undoubtedly libellous – letters which young Cantor himself certainly could not have written – letters which all Carmarthen knew to have been written by some one connected with the newspaper, though signed by the young farmer – in which it was positively declared that the old Squire had left a later will behind him. When it was discussed whether or no he could get a verdict, it was clearly shown that the getting of a verdict should not be the main object of the prosecution. 'He has to show,' said Mr Apjohn, 'that he is not afraid to face a court of justice.'

But he was afraid. When we last parted with him after his visit to Coed he had not seen the beginning of these attacks. On the next day the first paper reached him, and they who were concerned in it did not spare to send him the copies as they were issued. Having read the first, he was not able to refuse to read what followed. In each issue they were carried on, and, as was told of him in Carmarthen, he lingered over every agonizing detail of the venom which was entering into his soul. It was in vain that he tried to hide the paper, or to pretend to be indifferent to its coming. Mrs Griffith knew very well where the paper was, and knew also that every word had been perused. The month's notice which had been accepted from her and the butler in lieu of the three months first offered had now expired. The man had gone, but she remained, as did the two other women. Nothing was said as to the cause of their remaining; but they remained. As for Cousin Henry himself, he was too weak, too frightened, too completely absorbed by the horrors of his situation to ask them why they stayed, or to have asked them why they went.

He understood every word that was written of him with sharp, minute intelligence. Though his spirit was cowed, his mind was still alive to all the dangers of his position. Things were being said of him, charges were insinuated, which he declared to himself to be false. He had not destroyed the will. He had not even hidden it. He had only put a book into its own place, carrying out as he did so his innocent intention when he had first lifted the book. When these searchers had come, doing their work so idly, with such incurious futility, he had not concealed the book. He had left it there on its shelf beneath their hands. Who could say that he had been guilty? If the will were found now, who could reasonably suggest that there had been guilt on his part? If all were known – except that chance glance of his eye which never could be known – no one could say that he was other than innocent! And yet he knew of himself that he would lack strength to stand up in court and endure the sharp questions and angry glances of a keen lawyer. His very knees would fail to carry him through the court. The words would stick in his jaws. He would shake and shiver and faint before the assembled eyes. It would be easier for him to throw himself from the rocks on which he had lain dreaming into the sea than to go into a court of law and there tell his own story as to the will. They could not force him to go. He thought he could perceive as much as that. The action, if action there were to be, must originate with him. There was no evidence on which they could bring a charge of felony or even of fraud against him. They could not drag him into the court. But he knew that all the world would say that if he were an honest man, he himself would appear there, denounce his defamers, and vindicate his own name. As day by day he failed to do so, he would be declaring his own guilt. Yet he knew that he could not do it.

Was there no escape? He was quite sure now that the price at which he held the property was infinitely above its value. Its value! It had no value in his eyes. It was simply a curse of which he would rid himself with the utmost alacrity if only he could rid himself of all that had befallen him in achieving it. But how should he escape? Were he now himself to disclose the document and carry it into Carmarthen, prepared to deliver up the property to his cousin, was there one who would not think that it had been in his possession from before his uncle's death, and that he had now been driven by his fears to surrender it? Was there one who would not believe that he had hidden it with his own hands? How now could he personate that magnanimity which would have been so easy had he brought forth the book and handed it with its enclosure to Mr Apjohn when the lawyer came to read the will?

He looked back with dismay at his folly at having missed an opportunity so glorious. But now there seemed to be no escape. Though he left the room daily, no one found the will. They were welcome to find it if they would, but they did not. That base newspaper lied of him – as he told himself bitterly as he read it – in saying that he did not leave his room. Daily did he roam about the place for an hour or two – speaking, indeed, to no one, looking at no one. There the newspaper had been true enough. But that charge against him of self-imprisonment had been false as far as it referred to days subsequent to the rebuke which his housekeeper had given him. But no one laid a hand upon the book. He almost believed that, were the paper left open on the table, no eye would examine its contents. There it lay still hidden within the folds of the sermon, that weight upon his heart, that incubus on his bosom, that nightmare which robbed him of all his slumbers, and he could not rid himself of its presence. Property, indeed! Oh! if he were only back in London, and his cousin reigning at Llanfeare!

John Griffith, from Coed, had promised to call upon him; but when three weeks had passed by, he had not as yet made his appearance. Now, on one morning he came and found his landlord alone in the book-room. 'This is kind of you, Mr Griffith,' said Cousin Henry, struggling hard to assume the manner of a man with a light heart.

'I have come, Mr Jones,' said the farmer very seriously, 'to say a few words which I think ought to be said.'

'What are they, Mr Griffith?'

'Now, Mr Jones, I am not a man as is given to interfering – especially not with my betters.'

'I am sure you are not.'

'And, above all, not with my own landlord.' Then he paused; but as Cousin Henry could not find an appropriate word either for rebuke or encouragement, he was driven to go on with his story. 'I have been obliged to look at all those things in the Carmarthen Herald.' Then Cousin Henry turned deadly pale. 'We have all been driven to look at them. I have taken the paper these twenty years, but it is sent now to every tenant on the estate, whether they pay or whether they don't. Mrs Griffith, there, in the kitchen has it. I suppose they sent it to you, sir?'

'Yes; it does come,' said Cousin Henry, with the faintest attempt at a smile.

'And you have read what they say?'

'Yes, the most of it.'

'It has been very hard, sir.' At this Cousin Henry could only affect a ghastly smile. 'Very hard,' continued the farmer. 'It has made my flesh creep as I read it. Do you know what it all means, Mr Jones?'

'I suppose I know.'

'It means – that you have stolen – the estates – from your cousin – Miss

Brodrick!' This the man said very solemnly, bringing out each single word by itself. 'I am not saying so, Mr Jones.'

'No, no, no,' gasped the miserable wretch.

'No, indeed. If I thought so, I should not be here to tell you what I thought. It is because I believe that you are injured that I am here.'

'I am injured; I am injured!'

'I think so. I believe so. I cannot tell what the mystery is, if mystery there be; but I do not believe that you have robbed that young lady, your own cousin, by destroying such a deed as your uncle's will.'

'No, no, no.'

'Is there any secret that you can tell?'

Awed, appalled, stricken with utter dismay, Cousin Henry sat silent before his questioner.

'If there be, sir, had you not better confide it to some one? Your uncle knew me well for more than forty years, and trusted me thoroughly, and I would fain, if I could, do something for his nephew. If there be anything to tell, tell it like a man.'

Still Cousin Henry sat silent. He was unable to summon courage at the instant sufficient to deny the existence of the secret, nor could he resolve to take down the book and show the document. He doubted, when the appearance of a doubt was in itself evidence of guilt in the eyes of the man who was watching him. 'Oh, Mr Griffith,' he exclaimed after a while, 'will you be my friend?'

'I will indeed, Mr Jones, if I can – honestly.'

'I have been cruelly used.'

'It has been hard to bear,' said Mr Griffith.

'Terrible, terrible! Cruel, cruel!' Then again he paused, trying to make up his mind, endeavouring to see by what means he could escape from this hell upon earth. If there were any means, he might perhaps achieve it by aid of this man. The man sat silent, watching him, but the way of escape did not appear to him.

'There is no mystery,' he gasped at last.

'None?' said the farmer severely.

'No mystery. What mystery should there be? There was the will. I have destroyed nothing. I have hidden nothing. I have done nothing. Because the old man changed his mind so often, am I to be blamed?'

'Then, Mr Jones, why do you not say all that in a court of law – on your oath?'

'How can I do that?'

'Go to Mr Apjohn, and speak to him like a man. Bid him bring an action in your name for libel against the newspaper. Then there will be an inquiry. Then you will be put into a witness-box, and be able to tell your own story on your oath.'

Cousin Henry, groaning, pale and affrighted, murmured out

something signifying that he would think of it. Then Mr Griffith left him. The farmer, when he entered the room, had believed his landlord to be innocent, but that belief had vanished when he took his leave.

FOURTEEN

An Action for Libel

WHEN THE MAN HAD ASKED HIM THAT question – Is there any secret you can tell? Cousin Henry did, for half a minute, make up his mind to tell the whole story, and reveal everything as it had occurred. Then he remembered the lie which he had told, the lie to which he had signed his name when he had been called upon to prove the will in Carmarthen. Had he not by the unconsidered act of that moment committed some crime for which he could be prosecuted and sent to gaol? Had it not been perjury? From the very beginning he had determined that he would support his possession of the property by no criminal deed. He had not hidden the will in the book. He had not interfered in the search. He had done nothing incompatible with innocence. So it had been with him till he had been called upon, without a moment having been allowed to him for thinking, to sign his name to that declaration. The remembrance of this came to him as he almost made up his mind to rise from his seat and pull the book down from the shelf. And then another thought occurred to him. Could he not tell Mr Griffith that he had discovered the document since he had made that declaration – that he had discovered it only on that morning? But he had felt that a story such as that would receive no belief, and he had feared to estrange his only friend by a palpable lie. He had therefore said that there was no secret – had said so after a pause which had assured Mr Griffith of the existence of a mystery – had said so with a face which of itself had declared the truth.

When the farmer left him he knew well enough that the man doubted him – nay, that the man was assured of his guilt. It had come to be so with all whom he had encountered since he had first reached Llanfeare. His uncle who had sent for him had turned from him; his cousin had scorned him; the tenants had refused to accept him when there certainly had been no cause for their rejection. Mr Apjohn from the first had looked at him with accusing eyes; his servants were spies upon his actions; this newspaper was rending his very vitals; and now this one last friend had deserted him. He thought that if only he could summon courage for the deed, it would be best for him to throw himself from the rocks.

But there was no such courage in him. The one idea remaining to him was to save himself from the horrors of a criminal prosecution. If he did not himself touch the document, or give any sign of his consciousness of its presence, they could not prove that he had known of its whereabouts. If they would only find it and let him go! But they did not find it, and he could not put them on its trace. As to these wicked libels, Mr Griffith had asked him why he did not have recourse to a court of law, and refute them by the courage of his presence. He understood the proposition in all its force. Why did he not show himself able to bear any questions which the ingenuity of a lawyer could put to him? Simply because he was unable to bear them. The truth would be extracted from him in the process. Though he should have fortified himself with strongest resolves, he would be unable to hide his guilty knowledge. He knew that of himself. He would be sure to give testimony against himself, on the strength of which he would be dragged from the witness-box to the dock.

He declared to himself that, let the newspaper say what it would, he would not of his own motion throw himself among the lion's teeth which were prepared for him. But in so resolving he did not know what further external force might be applied to him. When the old tenant had sternly told him that he should go like a man into the witness-box and tell his own story on his oath, that had been hard to bear. But there came worse than that – a power more difficult to resist. On the following morning Mr Apjohn arrived at Llanfeare, having driven himself over from Carmarthen, and was at once shown into the book-room. The lawyer was a man who, by his friends and by his clients in general, was considered to be a pleasant fellow as well as a cautious man of business. He was good at a dinner-table, serviceable with a gun, and always happy on horseback. He could catch a fish, and was known to be partial to a rubber at whist. He certainly was not regarded as a hard or cruel man. But Cousin Henry, in looking at him, had always seen a sternness in his eye, some curve of a frown upon his brow, which had been uncomfortable to him. From the beginning of their intercourse he had been afraid of the lawyer. He had felt that he was looked into and scrutinised, and found to be wanting. Mr Apjohn had, of course, been on Isabel's side. All Carmarthenshire knew that he had done his best to induce the old squire to maintain Isabel as his heiress. Cousin Henry was well aware of that. But still why had this attorney always looked at him with accusing eyes? When he had signed that declaration at Carmarthen, the attorney had shown by his face that he believed the declaration to be false. And now this man was there, and there was nothing for him but to endure his questions.

'Mr Jones,' said the lawyer, 'I have thought it my duty to call upon you in respect to these articles in the Carmarthen Herald.'

'I cannot help what the Carmarthen Herald may say.'

'But you can, Mr Jones. That is just it. There are laws which enable a man to stop libels and to punish them if it be worth his while to do so.' He paused a moment, but Cousin Henry was silent, and he continued, 'For many years I was your uncle's lawyer, as was my father before me. I have never been commissioned by you to regard myself as your lawyer, but as circumstances are at present, I am obliged to occupy the place until you put your business into other hands. In such a position I feel it to be my duty to call upon you in reference to these articles. No doubt they are libellous.'

'They are very cruel; I know that,' said Cousin Henry, whining.

'All such accusations are cruel, if they be false.'

'These are false; damnably false.'

'I take that for granted; and therefore I have come to you to tell you that it is your duty to repudiate with all the strength of your own words the terrible charges which are brought against you.'

'Must I go and be a witness about myself?'

'Yes; it is exactly that. You must go and be a witness about yourself. Who else can tell the truth as to all the matters in question as well as yourself? You should understand, Mr Jones, that you should not take this step with the view of punishing the newspaper.'

'Why, then?'

'In order that you may show yourself willing to place yourself there to be questioned. "Here I am," you would say. "If there be any point in which you wish me to be examined as to this property and this will, here I am to answer you." It is that you may show that you are not afraid of investigation.' But it was exactly this of which Cousin Henry was afraid. 'You cannot but be aware of what is going on in Carmarthen.'

'I know about the newspaper.'

'It is my duty not to blink the matter. Every one, not only in the town but throughout the country, is expressing an opinion that right has not been done.'

'What do they want? I cannot help it if my uncle did not make a will according to their liking.'

'They think that he did make a will according to their liking, and that there has been foul play.'

'Do they accuse me?'

'Practically they do. These articles in the paper are only an echo of the public voice. And that voice is becoming stronger and stronger every day because you take no steps to silence it. Have you seen yesterday's paper?'

'Yes; I saw it,' said Cousin Henry, gasping for breath.

Then Mr Apjohn brought a copy of the newspaper out of his pocket, and began to read a list of questions which the editor was supposed to ask the public generally. Each question was an insult, and Cousin Henry, had he dared, would have bade the reader desist, and have turned him out of the room for his insolence in reading them.

'Has Mr Henry Jones expressed an opinion of his own as to what became of the will which the Messrs Cantor witnessed?'

'Has Mr Henry Jones consulted any friend, legal or otherwise, as to his tenure of the Llanfeare estate?'

'Has Mr Henry Jones any friend to whom he can speak in Carmarthen-shire?'

'Has Mr Henry Jones inquired into the cause of his own isolation?'

'Has Mr Henry Jones any idea why we persecute him in every fresh issue of our newspaper?'

'Has Mr Henry Jones thought of what may possibly be the end of all this?'

'Has Mr Henry Jones any thought of prosecuting us for libel?'

'Has Mr Henry Jones heard of any other case in which an heir has been made so little welcome to his property?'

So the questions went on, an almost endless list, and the lawyer read them one after another, in a low, plain voice, slowly, but with clear accentuation, so that every point intended by the questioner might be understood. Such a martyrdom surely no man was ever doomed to bear before. In every line he was described as a thief. Yet he bore it; and when the lawyer came to an end of the abominable questions, he sat silent, trying to smile. What was he to say?

'Do you mean to put up with that?' asked Mr Apjohn, with the curve of his eyebrow of which Cousin Henry was so much afraid.

'What am I to do?'

'Do! Do anything rather than sit in silence and bear such injurious insult as that. Were there nothing else to do, I would tear the man's tongue from his mouth – or at least his pen from his grasp.'

'How am I to find him? I never did do anything of that rough kind.'

'It is not necessary. I only say what a man would do if there were nothing else to be done. But the step to be taken is easy. Instruct me to go before the magistrates at Carmarthen, and indict the paper for libel. That is what you must do.'

There was an imperiousness in the lawyer's tone which was almost irresistible. Nevertheless Cousin Henry made a faint effort at resisting. 'I should be dragged into a lawsuit.'

'A lawsuit! Of course you would. What lawsuit would not be preferable to that? You must do as I bid you, or you must consent to have it said and have it thought by all the country that you have been guilty of some felony, and have filched your cousin's property.'

'I have committed nothing,' said the poor wretch, as the tears ran down his face.

'Then go and say so before the world,' said the attorney, dashing his fist down violently upon the table. 'Go and say so, and let men hear you, instead of sitting here whining like a woman. Like a woman! What honest woman would ever bear such insult? If you do not, you will convince all the world, you will convince me and every neighbour you have, that you have done something to make away with that will. In that case we will not leave a stone unturned to discover the truth. The editor of that paper is laying himself open purposely to an action in order that he may force you to undergo the cross-questioning of a barrister, and everybody who hears of it says that he is right. You can prove that he is wrong only by accepting the challenge. If you refuse the challenge, as I put it to you now, you will acknowledge that – that you have done this deed of darkness!'

Was there any torment ever so cruel, ever so unjustifiable as this! He was asked to put himself, by his own act, into the thumbscrew, on the rack, in order that the executioner might twist his limbs and tear out his vitals! He was to walk into a court of his own accord that he might be torn by the practised skill of a professional tormentor, that he might be forced to give up the very secrets of his soul in his impotence – or else to live amidst the obloquy of all men. He asked himeslf whether he had deserved it, and in that moment of time he assured himself that he had not deserved such punishment as this. If not altogether innocent, if not white as snow, he had done nothing worthy of such cruel usage.

'Well,' said Mr Apjohn, as though demanding a final answer to his proposition.

'I will think of it,' gasped Cousin Henry.

'There must be no more thinking. The time has gone by for thinking. If you will give me your instructions to commence proceedings against the Carmarthen Herald, I will act as your lawyer. If not, I shall make it known to the town that I have made this proposition to you; and I shall also make known the way in which it has been accepted. There has been more than delay enough.'

He sobbed, and gasped, and struggled with himself as the lawyer sat and looked at him. The one thing on which he had been intent was the avoiding of a court of law. And to this he was now to bring himself by his own act.

'When would it have to be?' he asked.

'I should go before the magistrates to-morrow. Your presence would not be wanted then. No delay would be made by the other side. They would be ready enough to come to trial. The assizes begin here at Carmarthen on the 29th of next month. You might probably be examined on that day, which will be a Friday, or on the Saturday following. You will be called as a witness on your own side to prove the libel. But the questions asked by your own counsel would amount to nothing.'

'Nothing!' exclaimed Cousin Henry.

'You would be there for another purpose,' continued the lawyer. 'When that nothing had been asked, you would be handed over to the other side, in order that the object of the proceedings might be attained.'

'What object?'

'How the barrister employed might put it I cannot say, but he would examine you as to any knowledge you may have as to that missing will.'

Mr Apjohn, as he said this, paused for a full minute, looking his client full in the face. It was as though he himself were carrying on a cross-examination. 'He would ask you whether you have such knowledge.' Then again he paused, but Cousin Henry said nothing. 'If you have no such knowledge, if you have no sin in that matter on your conscience, nothing to make you grow pale before the eyes of a judge, nothing to make you fear the verdict of a jury, no fault heavy on your own soul – then you may answer him with frank courage, then you may look him in the face, and tell him with a clear voice that as far as you are aware your property is your own by as fair a title as any in the country.'

In every word of this there had been condemnation. It was as though Mr Apjohn were devoting him to infernal torture, telling him that his only escape would be by the exercise of some herculean power which was notoriously beyond his reach. It was evident to him that Mr Apjohn had come there under the guise of his advisor and friend, but was in fact leagued with all the others around him to drive him to his ruin. Of that he felt quite sure. The voice, the eyes, the face, every gesture of his unwelcome visitor had told him that it was so. And yet he could not rise in indignation and expel the visitor from his house. There was a cruelty, an inhumanity, in this which to his thinking was infinitely worse than any guilt of his own. 'Well?' said Mr Apjohn.

'I suppose it must be so.'

'I have your instructions, then?'

'Don't you hear me say that I suppose it must be so.'

'Very well. The matter shall be brought in proper course before the magistrates to-morrow, and if, as I do not doubt, an injunction be granted, I will proceed with the matter at once. I will tell you whom we select as our counsel at the assizes, and, as soon as I have learnt, will let you know whom they employ. Let me only implore you not only to tell the truth as to what you know, but to tell all the truth. If you attempt to conceal anything, it will certainly be dragged out of you.'

Having thus comforted his client, Mr Apjohn took his leave.

❈ FIFTEEN ❈

Cousin Henry Makes Another Attempt

WHEN MR APJOHN HAD GONE, COUSIN HENRY sat for an hour, not thinking – men so afflicted have generally lost the power to think – but paralysed by the weight of his sorrow, simply repeating to himself assertions that said no man had ever been used so cruelly. Had he been as other men are, he would have turned the lawyer out of the house at the first expression of an injurious suspicion, but his strength had not sufficed for such action. He confessed to himself his own weakness, though he could not bring himself to confess his own guilt. Why did they not find it and have done with it? Feeling at last how incapable he was of collecting his thoughts while he sat there in the book-room, and aware, at the same time, that he must determine on some course of action, he took his hat and strolled out towards the cliffs.

There was a month remaining to him, just a month before the day named on which he was to put himself into the witness-box. That, at any rate, must be avoided. He did after some fashion resolve that, let the result be what it might, he would not submit himself to a cross-examination. They could not drag him from his bed were he to say that he was ill. They could not send policemen to find him, were he to hide himself in London. Unless he gave evidence against himself as to his own guilty knowledge, they could bring no open charge against him; or if he could but summon courage to throw himself from off the rocks, then, at any rate, he would escape from their hands.

What was it all about? This he asked himself as he sat some way down the cliff, looking out over the sea. What was it all about? If they wanted the property for his Cousin Isabel, they were welcome to take it. He desired nothing but to be allowed to get away from this accursed country, to escape, and never more to be heard of there or to hear of it. Could he not give up the property with the signing of some sufficient deed, and thus put an end to their cruel clamour? He could do it all without any signing, by a simple act of honesty, by taking down the book with the will and giving it at once to the lawyer! It was possible – possible as far as the knowledge of any one but himself was concerned – that such a thing might be done not only with honesty, but with high-minded magnanimity. How would it be if in truth the document were first found by him on this very day? Had it been so, were it so, then his conduct would be honest. And it was still open to him to simulate that it was so. He had taken down the book, let him say, for spiritual comfort in his great trouble, and lo, the will had been found there between the leaves! No one would believe him. He declared to himself that such was already his character in the county that no one would believe him. But what though they disbelieved him? Surely they would accept restitution without further reproach. Then there would be no witness-box, no savage terrier of a barrister to tear him in pieces with his fierce words and fiercer eyes. Whether they believed him or not, they would let him go. It would be told of him, at any rate, that having the will in his hands, he had not destroyed it. Up in London, where men would not know all the details of this last miserable month, some good would be spoken of him. And then there would be time left to him to relieve his conscience by repentance.

But to whom should he deliver up the will, and how should he frame the words? He was conscious of his own impotence in deceit. For such a purpose Mr Apjohn, no doubt, would be the proper person, but there was no one of whom he stood so much in dread as of Mr Apjohn. Were he to carry the book and the paper to the lawyer and attempt to tell his story, the real truth would be drawn out from him in the first minute of their interview. The man's eyes looking at him, the man's brow bent against him, would extract from him instantly the one truth which it was his purpose to hold within his own keeping. He would find no thankfulness, no mercy, not even justice in the lawyer. The lawyer would accept restitution, and would crush him afterwards. Would it not be better to go off to Hereford, without saying a word to any one in Carmarthenshire, and give up the deed to his Cousin Isabel? But then she had scorned him. She had treated him with foul contempt. As he feared Mr Apjohn, so did he hate his Cousin Isabel. The only approach to manliness left in his bosom was a true hatred of his cousin.

The single voice which had been kind to him since he had come to this horrid place had been that of old Farmer Griffith. Even his voice had been stern at last, but yet, with the sternness, there had been something of compassion. He thought that he could tell the tale to Mr Griffith, if to any one. And so thinking, he resolved at once to go to Coed. There was still before him that other means of escape which the rocks and the sea afforded him. As he had made his way on this morning to the spot on whch he was now lying that idea was still present to him. He did not think that he could do a deed of such daring. He was almost sure of himself that the power of doing it would be utterly wanting when the moment came. But still it was present to his mind. The courage might reach him at the instant. Were a sudden impulse to carry him away, he thought the Lord would surely forgive him because of all his sufferings. But now, as he looked at the spot, and saw that he could not reach the placid deep water, he considered it again, and remembered that the Lord would not forgive him a sin as to which there would be no moment for repentance. As he could not escape in that way, he must carry out his purpose with Farmer Griffith.

'So you be here again prowling about on father's lands?'

Cousin Henry knew at once the voice of that bitter enemy of his, young Cantor; and, wretched as he was, he felt also something of the spirit of the landlord in being thus rebuked for trespassing on his ground. 'I suppose I have a right to walk about on my own estate?' said he.

'I know nothing about your own estate,' replied the farmer's son. 'I say nothin' about that. They do be talking about it, but I say nothin'. I has my own opinions, but I say nothin'. Others do be saying a great deal, as I suppose you hear, Mr Jones, but I say nothin'.'

'How dare you be so impudent to your landlord?'

'I know nothin' about landlords. I know father has a lease of this land, and pays his rent, whether you get it or another; and you have no more right, it's my belief, to intrude here nor any other stranger. So, if you please, you'll walk.'

'I shall stay here just as long as it suits me,' said Cousin Henry.

'Oh, very well. Then father will have his action against you for trespass, and so you'll be brought into a court of law. You are bound to go off when you are warned. You ain't no right here because you call yourself landlord. You come up here and I'll thrash you, that's what I will. You wouldn't dare show yourself before a magistrate, that's what you wouldn't.'

The young man stood there for a while waiting, and then walked off with a loud laugh.

Any one might insult him, any one might beat him, and he could seek for no redress because he would not dare to submit himself to the ordeal of a witness-box. All those around him knew that it was so. He was beyond the protection of the law because of the misery of his position. It was clear that he must do something, and as he could not drown himself, there was nothing better than that telling of his tale to Mr Griffith. He would go to Mr Griffith at once. He had not the book and the document with him, but perhaps he could tell the tale better without their immediate presence.

At Coed he found the farmer in his own farmyard.

'I have come to you in great trouble,' said Cousin Henry, beginning his story.

'Well, squire, what is it?' Then the farmer seated himself on a low, movable bar which protected the entrance into an open barn, and Cousin Henry sat beside him.

'That young man Cantor insulted me grossly just now.'

'He shouldn't have done that. Whatever comes of it all, he shouldn't have done that. He was always a forward young puppy.'

'I do think I have been treated very badly among you.'

'As to that, Mr Jones, opinion does run very high about the squire's will. I explained to you all that when I was with you yesterday.'

'Something has occurred since that – something that I was coming on purpose to tell you.'

'What has occurred?' Cousin Henry groaned terribly as the moment for revelation came upon him. And he felt that he had made the moment altogether unfit for revelation by that ill-judged observation as to young Cantor. He should have rushed at his story at once. 'Oh, Mr Griffith, I have found the will!' It should have been told after that fashion. He felt it now – felt that he had allowed the opportunity to slip by him.

'What is it that has occurred, Mr Jones, since I was up at Llanfeare yesterday?'

'I don't think that I could tell you here.'

'Where, then?'

'Not yet to-day. That young man, Cantor, has so put me out that I hardly know what I am saying.'

'Couldn't you speak it out, sir, if it's just something to be said?'

'It's something to be shown too,' replied Cousin Henry, 'and if you wouldn't mind coming up to the house to-morrow, or next day, then I could explain it all.'

'To-morrow it shall be,' said the farmer. 'On the day after I shall be in Carmarthen to market. If eleven o'clock to-morrow morning won't be too early, I shall be there, sir.'

One, or three, or five o'clock would have been better, or the day following better still, so that the evil hour might have been postponed. But Cousin Henry assented to the proposition and took his departure. Now he had committed himself to some revelation, and the revelation must be made. He felt acutely the folly of his own conduct during the last quarter of an hour. If it might have been possible to make the old man believe that the document had only been that morning found, such belief could only have been achieved by an impulsive telling of the story. He was aware that at every step he took he created fresh difficulties by his own folly and want of foresight. How could he now act the sudden emotion of a man startled by surprise? Nevertheless, he must go on with his scheme. There was now nothing before him; but still he might be able to achieve that purpose which he had in view of escaping from Llanfeare and Carmarthenshire.

He sat up late that night thinking of it. For many days past he had not touched the volume, or allowed his eye to rest upon the document. He had declared to himself that it might remain there or be taken away, as it might chance to others. It should no longer be anything to him. For aught that he knew, it might already have been removed. Such had been his resolution during the last fortnight, and in accordance with that he had acted. But now his purpose was again changed. Now he intended to reveal the will with his own hands, and it might be well that he should see that it was there.

He took down the book, and there it was. He opened it out, and carefully read through every word of its complicated details. For it had been arranged and drawn out in a lawyer's office, with all the legal want of punctuation and unintelligible phraseology. It had been copied verbatim by the old Squire, and was no doubt a properly binding and effective will. Never before had he dwelt over it so tediously. He had feared lest a finger-mark, a blot, or a spark might betray his acquaintance with the deed. But now he was about to give it up and let all the world know that it had been in his hands. He felt, therefore, that he was entitled to read it, and that there was no longer ground to fear any accident. Though the women in the house should see him reading it, what matter?

Thrice he read it, sitting there late into the night. Thrice he read the deed which had been prepared with such devilish industry to rob him of the estate which had been promised him! If he had been wicked to conceal it – no, not to conceal it, but only to be silent as to its whereabouts – how much greater had been the sin of that dying old man who had taken so much trouble in robbing him? Now that the time had come, almost the hour in which he had lately so truly loathed, there came again upon him a love of money, a feeling of the privilege which attached to him as an owner of broad acres, and a sudden remembrance that with a little courage, with a little perseverance, with a little power of endurance, he might live down the evils of the present day. When he thought of what it might be to be Squire of Llanfeare in perhaps five years' time, with the rents in his pocket, he became angry at his own feebleness. Let them ask him what questions they would, there could be no evidence against him. If he were to burn the will, there could certainly be no evidence against him. If the will were still hidden, they might, perhaps, extract that secret from him; but no lawyer would be strong enough to make him own that he had thrust the paper between the bars of the fire.

He sat looking at it, gnashing his teeth together, and clenching his fists. If only he dared to do it! If only he could do it! He did during a moment, make up his mind; but had no sooner done so than there rose clearly before his mind's eye the judge and the jury, the paraphernalia of the court, and all the long horrors of a prison life. Even now those prying women might have their eyes turned upon what he was doing. And should there be no women prying, no trial, no conviction, still there would be the damning guilt on his own soul – a guilt which would admit of no repentance except by giving himself up to the hands of the law! No sooner had he resolved to destroy the will than he was unable to destroy it. No sooner had he felt his inability than again he longed to do the deed. When at three o'clock he dragged himself up wearily to his bed, the will was again within the sermon, and the book was at rest upon its old ground.

Punctually at eleven Mr Griffith was with him, and it was evident from his manner that he had thought the matter over, and was determined to be kind and gracious.

'Now, squire,' said he, 'let us hear it; and I do hope it may be something that may make your mind quiet at last. You've had, I fear, a bad time of it since the old squire died.'

'Indeed I have, Mr Griffith.'

'What is it now? Whatever it be, you may be sure of this, I will take it charitable like. I won't take nothing amiss; and if so be I can help you, I will.'

Cousin Henry, as the door had been opened, and as the man's footstep had been heard, had made up his mind that on this occasion he could not reveal the secret. He had disabled himself by that unfortunate manner of his yesterday. He would not even turn his eyes upon the book, but sat looking into the empty grate. 'What is it, Mr Jones?' asked the farmer.

'My uncle did make a will,' said Cousin Henry feebly.

'Of course he made a will. He made a many – one or two more than was wise, I am thinking.'

'He made a will after the last one.'

'After that in your favour?'

'Yes; after that. I know that he did, by what I saw him doing; and so I thought I'd tell you.'

'Is that all?'

'I thought I'd let you know that I was sure of it. What became of it after it was made, that, you know, is quite another question. I do think it must be in the house, and if so, search ought to be made. If they believe there is such a will, why don't they come and search more regularly? I shouldn't hinder them.'

'Is that all you've got to say?'

'As I have been thinking about it so much and as you are so kind to me, I thought I had better tell you.'

'But there was something you were to show me.'

'Oh, yes; I did say so. If you will come upstairs, I'll point out the very spot where the old man sat when he was writing it.'

'There is nothing more than that?'

'Nothing more than that, Mr Griffith.'

'Then good morning, Mr Jones. I am afraid we have not got to the end of the matter yet.'

✂ SIXTEEN ✂

Again at Hereford

SOME OF THE PEOPLE AT CARMARTHEN WERE taking a great deal of trouble about the matter. One copy of the Herald was sent regularly to Mr Brodrick, another to Isabel, and another to Mr Owen. It was determined that they should not be kept in ignorance of what was being done. In the first number issued after Mr Apjohn's last visit to Llanfeare there was a short leading article recapitulating all that was hitherto known of the story. 'Mr Henry Jones,' said the article in its last paragraph, 'has at length been induced to threaten an action for libel against this newspaper. We doubt much whether he will have the courage to go on with it. But if he does, he will have to put himself into a witness-box, and then probably we may learn something of the truth as to the last will and testament made by Mr Indefer Jones.' All this reached Hereford, and was of course deeply considered there by persons whom it concerned.

Mr Owen, for some days after the scene which has been described between him and Isabel, saw her frequently, and generally found means to be alone with her for some moments. She made no effort to avoid him, and would fain have been allowed to treat him simply as her dearest friend. But in all these moments he treated her as though she were engaged to be his wife. There was no embracing, no kiss. Isabel would not permit it. But in all terms of affectionate expression he spoke of her and to her as though she were his own; and would only gently laugh at her when she assured him that it could never be so.

'Of course you can torment me a little,' he said, smiling, 'but the forces arrayed against you are too strong, and you have not a chance on your side. It would be monstrous to suppose that you should go on making me miserable for ever – and yourself too.'

In answer to this she could only say that she cared but little for her own misery, and did not believe in his. 'The question is,' she said, 'whether it be fitting. As I feel that it is not fitting, I certainly shall not do it.' In answer to this he would again smile, and tell her that a month or two at furthest would see her absolutely conquered.

Then the newspapers reached them. When it became clear to him that there existed in Carmarthenshire so strong a doubt as to the validity of the will under which the property was at present held, then Mr Owen's visits to the house became rarer and different in their nature. Then he was willing to be simply the friend of the family, and as such he sought no especial interviews with Isabel. Between him and Isabel no word was spoken as to the contents of the newspaper. But between Mr Brodrick and the clergyman many words were spoken. Mr Brodrick declared at once to his intended son-in-law his belief in the accusations which were implied – which were implied at first, but afterwards made in terms so frightfully clear. When such words as those were said and printed there could, he urged, be no doubt as to what was believed in Carmarthen. And why should it be believed without ground that any man had done so hideous a deed as to destroy a will? The lawyer's hair stood almost on end as he spoke of the atrocity; but yet he believed it. Would a respectable newspaper such as the Carmarthen Herald commit itself to such a course without the strongest assurance? What was it to the Carmarthen Herald? Did not the very continuance of the articles make it clear that the readers of the paper were in accordance with the writer? Would the public of Carmarthen sympathise in such an attack without the strongest ground? He, the attorney, fully believed in Cousin Henry's guilt; but he was not on that account sanguine as to the proof. If, during his sojourn at Llanfeare, either immediately before the old squire's death or after it, but before the funeral, he had been enabled to lay his hand upon the will and destroy it, what hope would there be of evidence of such guilt? As to that idea of forcing the man to tell such a tale against himself by the torment of cross-examination, he did not believe it at all. A man who had been strong enough to destroy a will would be too strong for that. Perhaps he thought that any man would be too strong, not having known Cousin Henry.

Among all the possible chances which occurred to his mind – and his mind at this time was greatly filled with such considerations – nothing like the truth suggested itself to him. His heart was tormented by the idea that the property had been stolen from his child, that the glory of being father-in-law to Llanfeare had been filched from himself, and that no hope for redress remained. He sympathised altogether with the newspaper. He felt grateful to the newspaper. He declared the editor to be a man specially noble and brave in his calling. But he did not believe that the newspaper would do any good either to him or to Isabel.

Mr Owen doubted altogether the righteousness of the proceeding as regarded the newspaper. As far as he could see there was no evidence against Cousin Henry. There seemed to him to be an injustice in accusing a man of a great crime, simply because the crime might have been possible, and would, if committed, have been beneficial to the criminal. That plan of frightening the man into self-accusation by the terrors of cross-examination was distasteful to him. He would not sympathise with the newspaper. But still he found himself compelled to retreat from that affectation of certainty in regard to Isabel which he had assumed when he knew only that the will had been proved, and that Cousin Henry was in possession of the property. He had regarded Isabel and the property as altogether separated from each other. Now he learned that such was not the general opinion in Carmarthenshire. It was not his desire to push forward his suit with the heiress of Llanfeare. He had been rejected on what he had acknowledged to be fitting grounds while that had been her position. When the matter had been altogether settled in Cousin Henry's favour, then he could come forward again.

Isabel was quite sure that the newspaper was right. Did she not remember the dying words with which her uncle had told her that he had again made her his heir? And had she not always clearly in her mind the hang-dog look of that wretched man? She was strong-minded – but yet a woman, with a woman's propensity to follow her feelings rather than either facts or reason. Her lover had told her that her uncle had been very feeble when those words had been spoken, with his mind probably vague and his thoughts wandering. It had, perhaps, been but a dream. Such words did not suffice as evidence on which to believe a man guilty of so great a crime. She knew – so she declared to herself – that the old man's words had not been vague. And as to those hang-dog looks – her lover had told her that she should not allow a man's countenance to go so far in evidence as that! In so judging she would trust much too far to her own power of discernment. She would not contradict him, but she felt sure of her discernment in that respect. She did not in the least doubt the truth of the evidence conveyed by the man's hang-dog face.

She had sworn to herself a thousand times that she would not covet the house and property. When her uncle had first declared to her his purpose of disinheriting her, she had been quite sure of herself that her love for him should not be affected by the change. It had been her pride to think that she could soar above any consideration of money and be sure of her own nobility, even though she should be stricken with absolute poverty. But now she was tempted to long that the newspaper might be found to be right. Was there any man so fitted to be exalted in the world, so sure to fill a high place with honour, as her lover? Though she might not want Llanfeare for herself, was she not bound to want it for his sake? He had told her how certain he was of her heart – how sure he was that sooner or later he would win her hand. She had almost begun to think that it must be so – that her strength would not suffice for her to hold to her purpose. But how sweet would be her triumph if she could turn to him and tell him that now the hour had come in which she would be proud to become his wife! 'I love you well enough to rejoice in giving you something, but too well to have been a burden on you when I could give you nothing.' That would be sweet to her! Then there should be kisses! As for Cousin Henry, there was not even pity in her heart towards him. It would be time to pity him when he should have been made to give up the fruits of his wickedness and to confess his faults.

Mrs Brodrick was not made to understand the newspapers, nor did she care much about the work which they had taken in hand. If Isabel could be made to accept that smaller legacy, so that Mr Owen might marry her out of hand and take her away, that would be enough to satisfy Mrs Brodrick. If Isabel were settled somewhere with Mr Owen, their joint means being sufficient to make it certain that no calls would be made on the paternal resources, that would satisfy Mrs Brodrick's craving in regard to the Welsh property. She was not sure that she was anxious to see the half-sister of her own children altogether removed from their sphere and exalted so high. And then this smaller stroke of good fortune might be so much more easily made certain! A single word from Isabel herself, a word which any girl less endowed with wicked obstinacy would have spoken at once, would make that sure and immediate. Whereas this great inheritance which was to depend upon some almost impossible confession of the man who enjoyed it, seemed to her to be as distant as ever.

'Bother the newspapers,' she said to her eldest daughter; 'why doesn't she write and sign the receipt, and take her income like any one else? She was getting new boots at Jackson's yesterday, and where is the money to come from? If any of you want new boots, papa is sure to tell me of it!'

Her spirit was embittered too by the severity of certain words which her husband had spoken to her. Isabel had appealed to her father when her step-mother had reproached her with being a burden in the house.

'Papa,' she had said, 'let me leave the house and earn something. I can at any rate earn my bread.'

Then Mr Brodrick had been very angry. He too had wished to accelerate the marriage between his daughter and her lover, thinking that she would surely accept the money on her lover's behalf. He too had been annoyed at the persistency of her double refusal. But it had been very far from his purpose to drive his girl from his house, or to subject her to the misery of such reproaches as his wife had cast upon her.

'My dear,' he had said, 'there is no necessity for anything of the kind. I and your mother are only anxious for your welfare. I think that you should take your uncle's money, if not for your own sake, then for the sake of him to whom we all hope that you will soon be married. But putting that aside you are as well entitled to remain here as your sisters, and, until you are married, here will be your home.'

There was comfort in this, some small comfort, but it did not tend to create pleasant intercourse between Isabel and her step-mother. Mrs Brodrick was a woman who submitted herself habitually to her husband, and intended to obey him, but one who nevertheless would not be deterred from her own little purposes. She felt herself to be ill-used by Isabel's presence in the house. Many years ago Isabel had been taken away, and she had been given to understand that Isabel was removed for ever. There was to be no more expense, no more trouble – there should be no more jealousies in regard to Isabel. The old uncle had promised to do everything, and that sore had been removed from her life. Now Isabel had come back again, and insisted on remaining there – so unnecessarily! Now again there were those boots to be bought at Jackson's, and all those other increased expenditures which another back, another head, another mouth, and another pair of feet must create. And then it was so palpable that Hereford thought much of Isabel, but thought little or nothing of her own girls. Such a one as Mrs Brodrick was sure to make herself unpleasant in circumstances such as these.

'Isabel,' she said to her one day, 'I didn't say anything about you being turned out of the house.'

'Who has said that you did, mother?'

'You shouldn't have gone to your father and talked about going out as a housemaid.'

'I told papa that if he thought it right, I would endeavour to earn my bread.'

'You told him that I had complained about you being here.'

'So you did. I had to tell him so, or I could not explain my purpose. Of course I am a burden. Every human being who eats and wears clothes and earns nothing is a burden. And I know that this is thought of the more because it had been felt that I had been – been disposed of.'

'You could be disposed of now, as you call it, if you pleased.'

'But I do not please. That is a matter on which I will listen to no dictation. Therefore it is that I wish that I could go away and earn my own bread. I choose to be independent in that matter, and therefore I ought to suffer for it. It is reasonable enough that I should be felt to be a burden.'

Then the other girls came in, and nothing more was said till, after an hour or two, Mrs Brodrick and Isabel were again alone together.

'I do think it very odd that you cannot take that money; I certainly do,' said Mrs Brodrick.

'What is the use of going on about it? I shall not be made to take it.'

'And all those people at Carmarthen so sure that you are entitled to ever so much more! I say nothing about burdens, but I cannot conceive how you can reconcile it to your conscience when your poor papa has got so many things to pay, and is so little able to pay them.'

Then she paused, but as Isabel would not be enticed into any further declaration of independence, she continued, 'It certainly is a setting up of your own judgment against people who must know better. As for Mr Owen, of course it will drive him to look for some one else. The young man wants a wife, and of course he will find one. Then that chance will be lost.'

In this way Isabel did not pass her time comfortably at Hereford.

❌ SEVENTEEN ❌

Mr Cheekey

A MONTH HAD BEEN LEFT FOR COUSIN HENRY to consider what he would do – a month from the day in which he had been forced to accede to Mr Apjohn's proposal up to that on which he would have to stand before the barrister at Carmarthen, should he be brave enough at last to undergo the ordeal. He had in truth resolved that he would not undergo the ordeal. He was quite sure of himself that nothing short of cart-ropes or of the police would drag him into the witness-box. But still there was the month. There were various thoughts filling his mind. A great expense was being incurred – most uselessly, if he intended to retreat before the day came – and who would pay the money? There was hardly a hope left in his bosom that the property would remain in his hands. His hopes indeed now ran in altogether another direction. In what way might he best get rid of the property? How most readily might he take himself off from Llanfeare and have nothing more to do with the tenants and their rents? But still it was he who would be responsible for this terrible expense. It had been explained to him by the lawyer, that he might either indict the proprietor of the newspaper on a criminal charge or bring a civil action against him for damages. Mr Apjohn had very strongly recommended the former proceeding. It would be cheaper, he had said, and would show that the man who brought it had simply wished to vindicate his own character. It would be cheaper in the long-run – because, as the lawyer explained, it would not be so much his object to get a verdict as to show by his presence in the court that he was afraid of no one. Were he to sue for damages, and, as was probable, not to get them, he must then bear the double expense of the prosecution and defence. Such had been the arguments Mr Apjohn had used; but he had considered also that if he could bind the man to prosecute the newspaper people on a criminal charge, then the poor victim would be less able to retreat. In such case as that, should the victim's courage fail him at the last moment, a policeman could be made to fetch him and force him into the witness-box. But in the conduct of a civil action no such constraint could be put upon him. Knowing all this, Mr Apjohn had eagerly explained the superior attractions of a criminal prosecution, and Cousin Henry had fallen into the trap. He understood it all now, but had not been ready enough to do so when the choice had been within his power. He had now bound himself to prosecute, and certainly would be dragged into Carmarthen, unless he first made known the truth as to the will. If he did that, then he thought that they would surely spare him the trial. Were he to say to them, 'There; I have at last myself found the will. Here, behold it! Take the will and take Llanfeare, and let me escape from my misery,' then surely they would not force him to appear in reference to a matter which would have been already decided in their own favour. He had lost that opportunity of giving up the will through Mr Griffith, but he was still resolved that some other mode must be discovered before the month should have run by. Every day was of moment, and yet the days passed on and nothing was done. His last idea was to send the will to Mr Apjohn with a letter, in which he would simply declare that he had just found it amongst the sermons, and that he was prepared to go away. But as the days flew by the letter was left unwritten, and the will was still among the sermons.

It will be understood that all this was much talked of in Carmarthen. Mr Henry Jones, of Llanfeare, was known to have indicted Mr Gregory Evans, of the Carmarthen Herald, for the publication of various wicked and malicious libels against himself; and it was known also that Mr Apjohn was Mr Jones's attorney in carrying on the prosecution. But not the less was it understood that Mr Apjohn and Mr Evans were not hostile to each other in the matter. Mr Apjohn would be quite honest in what he did. He would do his best to prove the libel – on condition that his client were the honest owner of the property in question. In truth, however, the great object of them all was to get Henry Jones into a witness-box, so that, if possible, the very truth might be extracted from him.

Day by day and week by week since the funeral the idea had grown and become strong in Carmarthen that some wicked deed had been done. It irked the hearts of them all that such a one as Henry Jones should do such a deed and not be discovered. Old Indefer Jones had been respected by his neighbours. Miss Brodrick, though not personally well known in the country, had been spoken well of by all men. The idea that Llanfeare should belong to her had been received with favour. Then had come that altered intention in the old squire's mind, and the neighbours had disapproved. Mr Apjohn had disapproved very strongly, and though he was not without that reticence so essentially necessary to the character of an attorney, his opinion had become known. Then the squire's return to his old purpose was whispered abroad. The Cantors had spoken very freely. Everything done and everything not done at Llanfeare was known in Carmarthen. Mr Griffith had at length spoken, being the last to abandon all hope as to Cousin Henry's honesty.

Every one was convinced that Cousin Henry had simply stolen the property; and was it to be endured that such a deed as that should have been done by such a man and that Carmarthen should not find it out? Mr Apjohn was very much praised for his energy in having forced the man to take his action against Mr Evans, and no one was more inclined to praise him than Mr Evans himself. Those who had seen the man did believe that the truth would be worked out of him; and those who had only heard of him were sure that the trial would be a time of intense interest in the borough. The sale of the newspaper had risen immensely, and Mr Evans was quite the leading man of the hour.

'So you are going to have Mr Balsam against me?' said Mr Evans to Mr Apjohn one day. Now Mr Balsam was a very respectable barrister, who for many years had gone the Welsh circuit, and was chiefly known for the mildness of his behaviour and an accurate knowledge of law – two gifts hardly of much value to an advocate in an assize town.

'Yes, Mr Evans. Mr Balsam, I have no doubt, will do all that we want.'

'I suppose you want to get me into prison?'

'Certainly, if it shall be proved that you have deserved it. The libels are so manifest that it will be only necessary to read them to a jury. Unless you can justify them, I think you will have to go to prison.'

'I suppose so. You will come and see me, I am quite sure, Mr Apjohn.'

'I suppose Mr Cheekey will have something to say on your behalf before it comes to that.'

Now Mr John Cheekey was a gentleman about fifty years of age, who had lately risen to considerable eminence in our criminal courts of law. He was generally called in the profession – and perhaps sometimes outside it – 'Supercilous Jack,' from the manner he had of moving his eyebrows when he was desirous of intimidating a witness. He was a strong, young-looking, and generally good-humoured Irishman, who had a thousand good points. Under no circumstances would he bully a woman – nor would he bully a man, unless, according to his own mode of looking at such cases, the man wanted bullying. But when that time did come – and a reference to the Old Bailey and assize reports in general would show that it came very often – Supercilious Jack would make his teeth felt worse than any terrier. He could pause in his cross-examination, look at a man, projecting his face forward by degrees as he did so, in a manner which would crush any false witness who was not armed with triple courage at his breast – and, alas! not unfrequently a witness who was not false. For unfortunately, though Mr Cheekey intended to confine the process to those who, as he said, wanted bullying, sometimes he made mistakes. He was possessed also of another precious gift – which, if he had not invented, he had brought to perfection – that of bullying the judge also. He had found that by doing so he could lower a judge in the estimation of the jury, and thus diminish the force of a damnatory charge. Mr Cheekey's services had been especially secured for this trial, and all the circumstances had been accurately explained to him. It was felt that a great day would have arrived in Carmarthen when Mr Cheekey should stand up in the court to cross-examine Cousin Henry.

'Yes,' said Mr Evans, chuckling, 'I think that Mr Cheekey will have something to say to it. What will be the result, Mr Apjohn?' he asked abruptly.

'How am I to say? If he can only hold his own like a man, there will, of course, be a verdict of guilty.'

'But can he?' asked he of the newspaper.

'I hope he may with all my heart – if he have done nothing that he ought not to have done. In this matter, Mr Evans, I have altogether a divided sympathy. I dislike the man utterly. I don't care who knows it. No one knows it better than he himself. The idea of his coming here over that young lady's head was from the first abhorrent to me. When I saw him, and heard him, and found out what he was – such a poor, cringing, cowardly wretch – my feeling was of course exacerbated. It was terrible to me that the old squire, whom I had always respected, should have brought such a man among us. But that was the old squire's doing. He certainly did bring him, and as certainly intended to make him his heir. If he did make him his heir, if that will which I read was in truth the last will, then I hope most sincerely that all that Mr Cheekey may do may be of no avail against him. If that be the case, I shall be glad to have an opportunity of calling upon you in your new lodgings.'

'But if there was another will, Mr Apjohn – a later will?'

'Then of course, there is the doubt whether this man be aware of it.'

'But if he be aware of it?'

'Then I hope that Mr Cheekey may tear him limb from limb.'

'But you feel sure that it is so?'

'Ah; I do not know about that. It is very hard to be sure of anything. When I see him I do feel almost sure that he is guilty; but when I think of it afterwards, I again have my doubts. It is not by men of such calibre that great crimes are committed. I can hardly fancy that he should have destroyed a will.'

'Or hidden it?'

'If it were hidden, he would live in agony lest it were discovered. I used to think so when I knew that he passed the whole day sitting in one room. Now he goes out for hours together. Two or three times he has been down with old Griffith at Coed, and twice young Cantor found him lying on the sea cliff. I doubt whether he would have gone so far afield if the will were hidden in the house.'

'Can he have it on his own person?'

'He is not brave enough for that. The presence of it there would reveal itself by the motion of his hands. His fingers would always be on the pocket that contained it. I do not know what to think. And it is because I am in doubt that I have brought him under Mr Cheekey's thumbscrew. It is a case in which I would, if possible, force a man to confess the truth even against himself. And for this reason I have urged him to prosecute you. But as an honest man myself, I am bound to hope that he may succeed if he be the rightful owner of Llanfeare.'

'No one believes it, Mr Apjohn. Not one in all Carmarthen believes it.'

'I will not say what I believe myself. Indeed I do not know. But I do hope that by Mr Cheekey's aid or otherwise we may get at the truth.'

In his own peculiar circle, with Mr Geary the attorney, with Mr Jones the auctioneer, and Mr Powell, the landlord of the Bush Hotel, Mr Evans was much more triumphant. Among them, and indeed, with the gentlemen of Carmarthen generally, he was something of a hero. They did believe it probable that the interloper would be extruded from the property which did not belong to him, and that the doing of this would be due to Mr Evans. 'Apjohn pretends to think that it is very doubtful,' said he to his three friends.

'Apjohn isn't doubtful at all,' said Mr Geary, 'but he is a little cautious as to expressing himself.'

'Apjohn has behaved very well,' remarked the innkeeper. 'If it wasn't for him we should never have got the rascal to come forward at all. He went out in one of my flies, but I won't let them charge for it on a job like that.'

'I suppose you'll charge for bringing Cousin Henry into the court,' said the auctioneer. They had all got to call him Cousin Henry since the idea had got abroad that he had robbed his Cousin Isabel.

'I'd bring him too for nothing, and stand him his lunch into the bargain, rather than that he shouldn't have the pleasure of meeting Mr Cheekey.'

'Cheekey will get it out of him, if there is anything to get,' said Mr Evans.

'My belief is that Mr Cheekey will about strike him dumb. If he has got anything in his bosom to conceal, he will be so awe-struck that he won't be able to open his mouth. He won't be got to say he did it, but he won't be able to say he didn't.' This was Mr Geary's opinion.

'What would that amount to?' asked Mr Powell. 'I'm afraid they couldn't give the place back to the young lady because of that.'

'The jury would acquit Mr Evans. That's about what it would amount to,' said the attorney.

'And Cousin Henry would go back to Llanfeare, and have all his troubles over,' remarked Mr Jones. This they deemed to be a disastrous termination to all the trouble which they were taking, but one which seemed by no means improbable.

They all agreed that even Mr Cheekey would hardly be able to extract from the man an acknowledgment that he had with his own hands destroyed the will. Such a termination as that to a cross-examination had never been known under the hands of the most expert of advocates. That Cousin Henry might be stricken dumb, that he might faint, that he might be committed for contempt of court – all these events were possible, or perhaps, not impossible; but that he should say, 'Yes, I did it, I burnt the will. Yes, I, with my own hands' – that they all declared to be impossible. And, if so, Cousin Henry would go back again to Llanfeare confirmed in his possession of the property.

'He will only laugh at us in his sleeve when it is over,' said the auctioneer.

They little knew the torments which the man was enduring, or how unlikely it was that he should laugh in his sleeve at any one. We are too apt to forget when we think of the sins and faults of men how keen may be their conscience in spite of their sins. While they were thus talking of Cousin Henry, he was vainly endeavouring to console himself with the reflection that he had not committed any great crime, that there was still a road open to him for repentance, that if only he might be allowed to escape and repent in London, he would be too glad to resign Llanfeare and all its glories. The reader will hardly suppose that Cousin Henry will return after the trial to laugh in his sleeve in his own library in his own house.

A few days afterwards Mr Apjohn was up in town and had an interview with Mr Balsam, the barrister. 'This client of mine does not seem to be a nice sort of country gentleman,' said Mr Balsam.

'Anything but that. You will understand, Mr Balsam, that my only object in persuading him to indict the paper has been to put him into a witness-box. I told him so, of course. I explained to him that unless he would appear there, he could never hold up his head.'

'And he took your advice.'

'Very unwillingly. He would have given his right hand to escape. But I gave him no alternative. I so put it before him that he could not refuse to do as I bade him without owning himself to be a rascal. Shall I tell you what I think will come of it?'

'What will come of it?'

'He will not appear. I feel certain that he will not have the courage to show himself in the court. When the day comes, or, perhaps, a day or two before, he will run away.'

'What will you do then?'

'Ah, that's the question. What shall we do then? He is bound to prosecute, and will have to pay the penalty. In such a case as this I think we could have him found and brought into court for the next assizes. But what could we do then? Though we were ever so rough to him in the way of contempt of court and the rest of it, we cannot take the property away. If he has got hold of the will and destroyed it, or hidden it, we can do nothing as to the property as long as he is strong enough to hold his tongue. If he can be made to speak, then I think we shall get at it.'

Mr Balsam shook his head. He was quite willing to believe that his client was as base as Mr Apjohn represented him to be; but he was not willing to believe that Mr Cheekey was as powerful as had been assumed.

✖ EIGHTEEN ✖

Cousin Henry goes to Carmarthen

ON HIS RETURN FROM LONDON MR APJOHN wrote the following letter to his client, and this he sent to Llanfeare by a clerk, who was instructed to wait there for an answer –

'MY DEAR SIR, –

'I have just returned from London, where I saw Mr Balsam, who will be employed on your behalf at the assizes. It is necessary that you should come into my office, so that I may complete the instructions which are to be given to counsel. As I could not very well do this at Llanfeare without considerable inconvenience, I must give you this trouble. My clerk who takes this out to you will bring back your answer, saying whether eleven in the morning to-morrow or three in the afternoon will best suit your arrangements. You can tell him also whether you would wish me to send a fly for you. I believe that you still keep your uncle's carriage, in which case it would perhaps be unnecessary. A message sent by the clerk will suffice, so that you may be saved the trouble of writing.

'Yours truly,
'NICHOLAS APJOHN.'

The clerk had made his way into the bookroom in which Cousin Henry was sitting, and stood there over him while he was reading the letter. He felt sure that it had been arranged by Mr Apjohn that it should be so, in order that he might not have a moment to consider the reply which he would send. Mr Apjohn had calculated, traitor that he was to the cause of his client – so thought Cousin Henry – that the man's presence would rob him of his presence of mind so as to prevent him from sending a refusal.

'I don't see why I should go into Carmarthen at all,' he said.

'Oh, sir, it's quite essential – altogether essential in a case such as this. You are bound to prosecute, and of course you must give your instructions. If Mr Apjohn were to bring everything out here for the purpose, the expense would be tremendous. In going there, it will only be the fly, and it will all be done in five minutes.'

'Who will be there?' asked Cousin Henry after a pause.

'I shall be there,' answered the clerk, not unnaturally putting himself first, 'and Mr Apjohn, and perhaps one of the lads.'

'There won't be any – barrister?' asked Cousin Henry, showing the extent of his fear by his voice and his countenance.

'Oh, dear, no; they won't be here till the assizes. A barrister never sees his own client. You'll go in as a witness, and will have nothing to do with the barristers till you're put up face to face before them in the witness-box. Mr Balsam is a very mild gentleman.'

'He is employed by me?'

'Oh, yes; he's on our side. His own side never matters much to a witness. It's when the other side tackles you!'

'Who is the other side?' asked Cousin Henry.

'Haven't you heard?' The voice in which this was said struck terror to the poor wretch's soul. There was awe in it and pity, and something almost of advice – as though the voice were warning him to prepare against the evil which was threatening him. 'They have got Mr Cheekey!' Here the voice became even more awful. 'I knew they would when I first heard what the case was to be. They've got Mr Cheekey. They don't care much about money when they're going it like that. There are many of them I have known awful enough, but he's the awfullest.'

'He can't eat a fellow,' said Cousin Henry, trying to look like a man with good average courage.

'No; he can't eat a fellow. It isn't that way he does it. I've known some of 'em who looked as though they were going to eat a man; but he looks as though he were going to skin you, and leave you bare for the birds to eat you. He's gentle enough at first, is Mr Cheekey.'

'What is it all to me?' asked Cousin Henry.

'Oh, nothing, sir. To a gentleman like you who knows what he's about it's all nothing. What can Mr Cheekey do to a gentleman who has got nothing to conceal? But when a witness has something to hide – and sometimes there will be something – then it is that Mr Cheekey comes out strong. He looks into a man and sees that it's there, and then he turns him inside out till he gets at it. That's what I call skinning a witness. I saw a poor fellow once so knocked about by Mr Cheekey that they had to carry him down speechless out of the witness-box.'

It was a vivid description of all that Cousin Henry had pictured to himself. And he had actually, by his own act, subjected himself to this process! Had he been staunch in refusing to bring any action against the newspaper, Mr Cheekey would have been powerless in reference to him. And now he was summoned into Carmarthen to prepare himself by minor preliminary pangs for the torture of the auto-da-fé which was to be made of him.

'I don't see why I should go into Carmarthen at all,' he said, having paused a while after the eloquent description of the barrister's powers.

'Not come into Carmarthen! Why, sir, you must complete the instructions.'

'I don't see it at all.'

'Then do you mean to back out of it altogether, Mr Jones? I wouldn't be afeared by Mr Cheekey like that!'

Then it occurred to him that if he did mean to back out of it altogether he could do so better at a later period, when they might hardly be able to catch him by force and bring him as a prisoner before the dreaded tribunal. And as it was his purpose to avoid the trial by giving up the will, which he would pretend to have found at the moment of giving it up, he would ruin his own project – as he had done so many projects before –by his imbecility at the present moment. Cheekey would not be there in Mr Apjohn's office, nor the judge and jury and all the crowd of the court to look at him.

'I don't mean to back out at all,' he said; 'and it's very impertinent of you to say so.'

'I didn't mean impertinence, Mr Jones – only it is necessary you should come into Mr Apjohn's office.'

'Very well; I'll come to-morrow at three.'

'And about the fly, Mr Jones?'

'I can come in my own carriage.'

'Of course. That's what Mr Apjohn said. But if I may make so bold, Mr Jones – wouldn't all the people in Carmarthen know the old Squire's carriage?'

Here was another trouble. Yes; all the people in Carmarthen would know the old Squire's carriage, and after all those passages in the newspapers – believing, as he knew they did, that he had stolen the property – would clamber up on the very wheels to look at him! The clerk had been right in that.

'I don't mean it for any impertinence, Mr Jones; but wouldn't it be better just to come in and to go out quiet in one of Mr Powell's flies?'

'Very well,' said Cousin Henry. 'Let the fly come.'

'I thought it would be best,' said the clerk, taking cowardly advantage of his success over the prostrate wretch. 'What's the use of a gentleman taking his own carriage through the streets on such an occasion as this? They are so prying into everything in Carmarthen. Now, when they see the Bush fly, they won't think as anybody particular is in it.' And so it was settled. The fly should be at Llanfeare by two o'clock on the following day.

Oh, if he could but die! If the house would fall upon him and crush him! There had not been a word spoken by that reptile of a clerk which he had not understood – not an arrow cast at him the sting of which did not enter into his very marrow! 'Oh, nothing, sir, to a gentleman like you.' The man had looked at him as he had uttered the words with a full appreciation of the threat conveyed. 'They've got a rod in pickle for you – for you, who have stolen your cousin's estate! Mr Cheekey is coming for you!' That was what the miscreant of a clerk had said to him. And then, though he had found himself compelled to yield to that hint about the carriage, how terrible was it to have to confess that he was afraid to be driven through Carmarthen in his own carriage!

He must go into Carmarthen and face Mr Apjohn once again. That was clear. He could not now send the will in lieu of himself. Why had he not possessed the presence of mind to say to the clerk at once that no further steps need be taken? 'No further steps need be taken. I have found the will. Here it is. I found it this very morning among the books. Take it to Mr Apjohn, and tell him I have done with Llanfeare and all its concerns.' How excellent would have been the opportunity! And it would not have been difficult for him to act his part amidst the confusion to which the clerk would have been brought by the greatness of the revelation made to him. But he had allowed the chance to pass, and now he must go into Carmarthen!

At half-past two the following day he put himself into the fly. During the morning he had taken the will out of the book, determined to carry it with him to Carmarthen in his pocket. But when he attempted to enclose it in an envelope for the purpose, his mind misgave him and he restored it. Hateful as was the property to him, odious as were the house and all things about it, no sooner did the doing of the act by which he was to release himself from them come within the touch of his fingers, than he abandoned the idea. At such moments the estate would again have charms for him, and he would remember that such a deed, when once done, would admit of no recall.

'I am glad to see you, Mr Jones,' said the attorney as his client entered the inner office. 'There are a few words which must be settled between you and me before the day comes, and no time has to be lost. Sit down, Mr Ricketts, and write the headings of the questions and answers. Then Mr Jones can initial them afterwards.'

Mr Ricketts was the clerk who had come out to Llanfeare. Cousin

Henry sat silent as Mr Ricketts folded his long sheet of folio paper with a double margin. Here was a new terror to him; and as he saw the preparations he almost made up his mind that he would on no account sign his name to anything.

The instructions to be given to Mr Balsam were in fact very simple, and need not here be recapitulated. His uncle had sent for him to Llanfeare, had told him that he was to be the heir, had informed him that a new will had been made in his favour. After his uncle's death and subsequent to the funeral, he had heard a will read, and under that will had inherited the property. As far as he believed, or at any rate as far as he knew, that was his uncle's last will and testament. These were the instructions which, under Mr Apjohn's advice, were to be given to Mr Balsam as to his (Cousin Henry's) direct evidence.

Then Cousin Henry, remembering his last communication to Farmer Griffith, remembering also all that the two Cantors could prove, added something on his own account.

'I saw the old man writing up in his room,' he said, 'copying something which I knew to be a will. I was sure then he was going to make another change and take the property from me.' 'No; I asked him no questions. I thought it very cruel, but it was of no use for me to say anything.' 'No; he didn't tell me what he was about; but I knew it was another will. I wouldn't condescend to ask a question. When the Cantors said that they had witnessed a will, I never doubted them. When you came there to read the will, I supposed it would be found. Like enough it's there now, if proper search were made. I can tell all that to Mr Balsam if he wants to know it.'

'Why didn't you tell me all this before?' said Mr Apjohn.

'It isn't much to tell. It's only what I thought. If what the Cantors said and what you all believed yourselves didn't bring you to the will, nothing I could say would help you. It doesn't amount to more than thinking after all.'

Then Mr Apjohn was again confused and again in doubt. Could it be possible after all that the conduct on the part of the man which had been so prejudicial to him in the eyes of all men had been produced simply by the annoyances to which he had been subjected? It was still possible that the old man had himself destroyed the document which he had been tempted to make, and that they had all of them been most unjust to this poor fellow. He added, however, all the details of this new story to the instructions which were to be given to Mr Balsam, and to which Cousin Henry did attach his signature.

Then came some further conversation about Mr Cheekey, which, however, did not take an official form. What questions Mr Cheekey might ask would be between Mr Cheekey and the other attorney, and formed no part of Mr Apjohn's direct business. He had intended to imbue his client with something of the horror with which his clerk had been before him in creating, believing that the cause of truth would be assisted by reducing the man to the lowest condition of mean terror. But this new story somewhat changed his purpose. If the man were innocent – if there were but some small probability of his innocence – was it not his duty to defend him as a client from ill-usage on the part of Cheekey? That Cheekey must have his way with him was a matter of course – that is, if Cousin Henry appeared at all; but a word or two of warning might be of service.

'You will be examined on the other side by Mr Cheekey,' he said, intending to assume a pleasant voice. At the hearing of the awful name, sweat broke out on Cousin Henry's brow. 'You know what his line will be?'

'I don't know anything about it.'

'He will attempt to prove that another will was made.'

'I do not deny it. Haven't I said that I think another will was made?'

'And that you are either aware of its existence –' here Mr Apjohn paused, having resumed that stern tone of his voice which was so disagreeable to Cousin Henry's ears – 'or that you have destroyed it.'

'What right has he got to say that I have destroyed it? I have destroyed nothing.'

Mr Apjohn marked the words well, and was again all but convinced that his client was not innocent. 'He will endeavour to make a jury believe from words coming out of your own mouth, or possibly by your silence, that you have either destroyed the deed – or have concealed it.'

Cousin Henry thought a moment whether he had concealed the will or not. No! he had not put it within the book. The man who hides a thing is the man who conceals the thing – not a man who fails to tell that he has found it.

'Or – concealed it,' repeated Mr Apjohn with that peculiar voice of his.

'I have not concealed it,' said the victim.

'Nor know where it lies hidden?' Ghastly pale he became – livid, almost blue by degrees. Though he was fully determined to give up the will, he could not yield to the pressure now put upon him. Nor could he withstand it. The question was as terrible to him as though he had entertained no idea of abandoning the property. To acknowledge that he knew all along where it was hidden would be to confess his guilt and to give himself up to the tormentors of the law.

'Nor know where it lies hidden?' repeated Mr Apjohn, in a low voice. 'Go out of the room, Ricketts,' he said. 'Nor know where it lies hidden?' he asked a third time when the clerk had closed the door behind him.

'I know nothing about it,' gasped the poor man.

'You have nothing beyond that to say to me?'

'Nothing.'

'You would rather that it should be left to Mr Cheekey? If there be anything further that you can say, I should be more tender with you than he.'

'Nothing.'

'And here, in this room, there is no public to gaze upon you.'

'Nothing,' he gasped again.

'Very well. So be it. Ricketts, see if the fly be there for Mr Jones.' A few minutes afterwards his confidential clerk was alone with him in the room.

'I have learned so much, Ricketts,' said he. 'The will is still in existence. I am sure of that. And he knows its whereabouts. We shall have Miss Brodrick there before Christmas yet.'

❀ NINETEEN ❀

Mr Apjohn Sends for Assistance

THE LAST WORDS IN THE LAST CHAPTER were spoken by Mr Apjohn to his confidential clerk in a tone of triumph. He had picked up something further, and, conscious that he had done so by his own ingenuity, was for a moment triumphant. But when he came to think over it all alone – and he spent many hours just at present in thinking of this matter – he was less inclined to be self-satisfied. He felt that a great responsibility rested with him, and that this weighed upon him peculiarly at the present moment. He was quite sure not only that a later will had been made, but that it was in existence. It was concealed somewhere, and Cousin Henry knew the secret of its hiding-place. It had existed, at any rate, that morning; but now came the terrible question whether the man, driven to his last gasp in his misery, would not destroy it. Not only had Mr Apjohn discovered the secret, but he was well aware that Cousin Henry was conscious that he had done so, and yet not a word had been spoken between them which, should the will now be destroyed, could be taken as evidence that it had ever existed. Let the paper be once burnt, and Cousin Henry would be safe in possession of the property. Mr Cheekey might torment his victim, but certainly would not extract from him a confession such as that. The hiding of the will, the very place in which it was hidden, might possibly be extracted. It was conceivable that ingenuity on one side and abject terror on the other might lead a poor wretch to betray the secret; but a man who has committed a felony will hardly confess the deed in a court of law. Something of all this would, thought Mr Apjohn, occur to Cousin Henry himself, and by this very addition to his fears he might be driven to destroy the will. The great object now should be to preserve a document which had lived as it were a charmed life through so many dangers. If anything were to be done with this object – anything new – it must be done at once. Even now, while he was thinking of it, Cousin

Henry was being taken slowly home in Mr Powell's fly, and might do the deed as soon as he found himself alone in the book-room. Mr Apjohn was almost sure that the will was concealed somewhere in the book-room. That long-continued sojourn in the chamber, of which the whole country had heard so much, told him that it was so. He was there always, watching the hiding-place. Would it be well that searchers should again be sent out, and that they should be instructed never to leave that room till after Cousin Henry's examination should be over? If so, it would be right that a man should be sent off instantly on horseback, so as to prevent immediate destruction. But then he had no power to take such a step in reference to another man's house. It was a question whether any magistrate would give him such a warrant, seeing that search had already been made, and that, on the failure of such search, that Squire's will had already been proved. A man's house is his castle, let the suspicion against him be what it may, unless there be evidence to support it. Were he to apply to a magistrate, he could only say that the man's own manner and mode of speech had been evidence of his guilt. And yet how much was there hanging, perhaps, on the decision of the moment! Whether the property should go to the hands of her who was entitled to enjoy it, or remain in the possession of a thief such as this, might so probably depend on the action which should be taken, now, at this very instant!

Mr Ricketts, his confidential clerk, was the only person with whom he had fully discussed all the details of the case – the only person to whom he had expressed his own thoughts as they had occurred to him. He had said a word to the clerk in triumph as Cousin Henry left him, but a few minutes afterwards recalled him with an altered tone. 'Ricketts,' he said, 'the man has got that will with him in the book-room at Llanfeare.'

'Or in his pocket, sir,' suggested Ricketts.

'I don't think it. Wherever it be at this moment, he has not placed it there himself. The Squire put it somewhere, and he has found it.'

'The Squire was very weak when he made that will, sir,' said the clerk. 'Just at that time he was only coming down to the dining-room, when the sun shone in just for an hour or two in the day. If he put the will anywhere, it would probably be in his bed-room.'

'The man occupies another chamber?' asked the attorney.

'Yes, sir; the same room he had before his uncle died.'

'It's in the book-room,' repeated Mr Apjohn.

'Then he must have put it there.'

'But he didn't. From his manner, and from a word or two that he spoke, I feel sure that the paper has been placed where it is by other hands.'

'The old man never went into the book-room. I heard every detail of his latter life from Mrs Griffith when the search was going on. He hadn't been there for more than a month. If he wanted anything out of the book-room, after the young lady went away, he sent Mrs Griffith for it.'

'What did he send for?' asked Mr Apjohn.

'He used to read a little sometimes,' said the clerk.

'Sermons?' suggested Mr Apjohn. 'For many years passed he has read sermons to himself whenever he has failed in going to church. I have seen the volumes there on the table in the parlour when I have been with him. Did they search the books?'

'Had every volume off the shelves, sir.'

'And opened every one of them?'

'That I can't tell. I wasn't there.'

'Every volume should have been shaken,' said Mr Apjohn.

'It's not too late yet, sir,' said the clerk.

'But how are we to get in and do it? I have no right to go into his house, or any man's, to search it.'

'He wouldn't dare to hinder you, sir.'

Then there was a pause before anything further was said.

'The step is such a strong one to take,' said the lawyer, 'when one is guided only by one's own inner conviction. I have no tittle of evidence in my favour to prove anything beyond the fact that the old Squire in the latter days of his life did make a will which has not been found. For that we have searched, and, not finding it, have been forced to admit to probate the last will which we ourselves made. Since that nothing has come to my knowledge. Guided partly by the man's ways while he has been at Llanfeare, and partly by his own manner and hesitation, I have come to a conclusion in my own mind; but it is one which I would hardly dare to propose to a magistrate as a ground for action.'

'But if he consented, sir?'

'Still, I should be hardly able to justify myself for such intrusion if nothing were found. We have no right to crush the poor creature because he is so easily crushable. I feel already pricks of conscience because I am bringing down Jack Cheekey upon him. If it all be as I have suggested – that the will is hidden, let us say in some volume of sermons there – what probability is there that he will destroy it now?'

'He would before the trial, I think.'

'But not at once? I think not. He will not allow himself to be driven to the great crime till the last moment. It is quite on the cards that his conscience will even at last be too strong for it.'

'We owe him something, sir, for not destroying it when he first found it.'

'Not a doubt! If we are right in all this, we do owe him something – at any rate, charity enough to suppose that the doing of such a deed must be very distasteful to him. When I think of it I doubt whether he'll do it at all.'

'He asked me why they didn't come and search again.'

'Did he? I shouldn't wonder if the poor devil would be glad enough to be relieved from it all. I'll tell you what I'll do, Ricketts. I'll write to Miss

Brodrick's father, and ask him to come over here before the trial. He is much more concerned in the matter than I am, and should know as well what ought to be done.'

The letter was written urging Mr Brodrick to come at once. 'I have no right to tell you,' Mr Apjohn said in his letter, 'that there is ground for believing that such a document as that I have described is still existing. I might too probably be raising false hope were I to do so. I can only tell you of my own suspicion, explaining to you at the same time on what ground it is founded. I think it would be well that you should come over and consult with me whether further steps should be taken. If so, come at once. The trial is fixed for Friday the 30th.' This was written on Thursday the 22nd. There was, therefore, not much more than a week's interval.

'You will come with me,' said Mr Brodrick to the Rev. William Owen, after showing to him the letter from the attorney at Hereford.

'Why should I go with you?'

'I would wish you to do so – on Isabel's behalf.'

'Isabel and I are nothing to each other.'

'I am sorry to hear you say that. It was but the other day that you declared that she should be your wife in spite of herself.'

'So she shall, if Mr Henry Jones be firmly established at Llanfeare. It was explained to me before why your daughter, as owner of Llanfeare, ought not to marry me, and, as I altogether agreed with the reason given, it would not become me to take any step in this matter. As owner of Llanfeare she will be nothing to me. It cannot therefore be right that I should look after her interests in that direction. On any other subject I would do anything for her.'

The father no doubt felt that the two young people were self-willed, obstinate, and contradictory. His daughter wouldn't marry the clergyman because she had been deprived of her property. The clergyman now refused to marry his daughter because it was presumed that her property might be restored to her. As, however, he could not induce Mr Owen to go with him to Carmarthen, he determined to go alone. He did not give much weight to this new story. It seemed to him certain that the man would destroy the will – or would already have destroyed it – if in the first instance he was wicked enough to conceal it. Still the matter was so great and the question so important to his daughter's interest that he felt himself compelled to do as Mr Apjohn had proposed. But he did not do it altogether as Mr Apjohn had proposed. He allowed other matters to interfere, and postponed his journey till Tuesday the 27th of the month. Late on that evening he reached Carmarthen, and at once went to Mr Apjohn's house.

Cousin Henry's journey into Carmarthen had been made on the previous Thursday, and since that day no new steps had been taken to unravel the mystery – none at least which had reference to Llanfeare. No further search had been made among the books. All that was known in Carmarthen of Cousin Henry during these days was that he remained altogether within the house. Were he so minded, ample time was allowed to him for the destruction of any document. In the town, preparation went on in the usual way for the Assizes, at which the one case of interest was to be the indictment of Mr Evans for defamation of character. It was now supposed by the world at large that Cousin Henry would come into court; and because this was believed of him there was something of a slight turn of public opinion in his favour. It would hardly be the case that the man, if really guilty, would encounter Mr Cheekey.

During the days that had elapsed, even Mr Apjohn himself had lost something of his confidence. If any further step was to be taken, why did not the young lady's father himself come and take it? Why had he been so dilatory in a matter which was of so much greater importance to himself than to any one else? But now the two attorneys were together, and it was necessary that they should decide upon doing something – or nothing.

'I hoped you would have been here last week,' said Mr Apjohn.

'I couldn't get away. There were things I couldn't possibly leave.'

'It is so important,' said Mr Apjohn.

'Of course it is important – of most vital importance – if there be any hope.'

'I have told you exactly what I think and feel.'

'Yes, yes. I know how much more than kind, how honourable you have been in all this matter. You still think that the will is hidden?'

'I did think so.'

'Something has changed your opinion?'

'I can hardly say that either,' said Mr Apjohn. 'There was ground on which to form my opinion, and I do not know that there is any ground for changing it. But in such a matter the mind will vacillate. I did think that he had found the will shut up in a volume of sermons, in a volume which his uncle had been reading during his illness, and that he had left the book in its place upon the shelf. That, you will say, is a conclusion too exact for man to reach without anything in the shape of absolute evidence.'

'I do not say so; but then as yet I hardly know the process by which that belief has been reached.'

'But I say so – I say that is too exact. There is more of imagination in it than of true deduction. I certainly should not recommend another person to proceed far on such reasoning. You see it has been in this way.' Then he explained to his brother attorney the process of little circumstances by which he had arrived at his own opinion – the dislike of the man to leave the house, his clinging to one room, his manifest possession of a secret as evinced by his conversations with Farmer Griffith, his continual dread of something, his very clinging to Llanfeare as a residence which would not have been the case had he destroyed the will, his exaggerated fear of the coming cross-examination, his ready assertion that he had destroyed nothing and hidden nothing – but his failure to reply when he was asked whether he was aware of any such concealment. Then the fact that the books had not been searched themselves, that the old Squire had never personally used the room, but had used a book or one or two books which had been taken from it; that these books had been volumes which had certainly been close to him in those days when the lost will was being written. All these and other little details known to the reader made the process by which Mr Apjohn had arrived at the conclusion which he now endeavoured to explain to Mr Brodrick.

'I grant that the chain is slight,' said Mr Apjohn, 'so slight that a feather may break it. The strongest point in it all was the look on the man's face when I asked him the last question. Now I have told you everything, and you must decide what we ought to do.'

But Mr Brodrick was a man endowed with lesser gifts than those of the other attorney. In such a matter Mr Apjohn was sure to lead. 'What do you think yourself?'

'I would propose that we, you and I, should go together over to Llanfeare to-morrow and ask him to allow us to make what further search we may please about the house. If he permitted this –'

'But would he?'

'I think he would. I am not at all sure but what he would wish to have the will found. If he did, we could begin and go through every book in the library. We would begin with the sermons, and soon know whether it be as I have suggested.'

'But if he refused?'

'Then I think I would make bold to insist on remaining there while you went to a magistrate. I have indeed already prepared Mr Evans of Llancolly, who is the nearest magistrate. I would refuse to leave the room, and you would then return with a search warrant and a policeman. But as for opening the special book or books, I could do that with or without his permission. While you talk to him I will look round the room and see where they are. I don't think much of it all, Mr Brodrick; but when the stake is so high, it is worth playing for. If we fail in this, we can then only wait and see what the redoubtable Mr Cheekey may be able to do for us.'

Thus it was settled that Mr Brodrick and Mr Apjohn should go out to Llanfeare on the following morning.

TWENTY

Doubts

'I KNOW NOTHING ABOUT IT,' COUSIN HENRY had gasped out when asked by Mr Apjohn, when Ricketts, the clerk, had left the room, whether he knew where the will was hidden. Then, when he had declared he had nothing further to say, he was allowed to go away.

As he was carried back in the fly he felt certain that Mr Apjohn knew that there had been a will, knew that the will was still in existence, knew that it had been hidden by some accident, and knew also that he, Henry Jones, was aware of the place of concealment. That the man should have been so expert in reading the secret of his bosom was terrible to him. Had the man suspected him of destroying the will – a deed the doing of which might have been so naturally suspected – that would have been less terrible. He had done nothing, had committed no crime, was simply conscious of the existence of a paper which it was a duty, not of him, but of others to find, and this man, by his fearful ingenuity, had discovered it all! Now it was simply necessary that the place should be indicated, and in order that he himself might be forced to indicate it, Mr Cheekey was to be let loose upon him!

How impossible – how almost impossible had he found it to produce a word in answer to that one little question from Mr Apjohn! 'Nor know where it is hidden?' He had so answered it as to make it manifest that he did know. He was conscious that he had been thus weak, though there had been nothing in Mr Apjohn's manner to appal him. How would it be with him when, hour after hour, question after question should be demanded of him, when that cruel tormentor should stand there glaring at him in presence of all the court? There would be no need of such hour – no need of that prolonged questioning. All that was wanted of him would be revealed at once. The whole secret would be screwed out of him by the first turn of the tormentor's engine.

There was but one thing quite fixed in his mind. Nothing should induce him to face Mr Cheekey, unless he should have made himself compara-tively safe by destroying the will. In that way he almost thought he might be safe. The suffering would be great. The rack and the thumbscrew, the boots and the wheel, would, to the delight of all those present, be allowed to do their work upon him for hours. It would be a day to him terrible to anticipate, terrible to endure, terrible afterwards in his memory; but he thought that not even Mr Cheekey himself would be able to extract from him the admission of such a deed as that.

And then by the deed he would undoubtedly acquire Llanfeare. The place itself was not dear to him, but there was rising in his heart so strong a feeling of hatred against those who were oppressing him that it seemed to him almost a duty to punish them by continued possession of the property. In this way he could triumph over them all. If once he could come down from Mr Cheekey's grasp alive, if he could survive those fearful hours, he would walk forth from the court the undoubted owner of Llanfeare. It would be as though a man should endure some excruciating operation under the hands of a surgeon, with the assured hope that he might enjoy perfect health afterwards for the remainder of his life.

To destroy the will was his only chance of escape. There was nothing else left to him, knowing, as he did, that it was impossible for him to put an end to his own life with his own hands. These little plots of his, which he had planned for the revelation of his secret without the acknowledgment of guilt, had all fallen to pieces as he attempted to execute them. He began to be aware of himself that anything that required skill in the execution was impossible to him. But to burn the will he was capable. He could surely take the paper from its hiding-place and hold it down with the poker when he had thrust it between the bars. Or, as there was no fire provided in these summer months, he could consume it by the light of his candle when the dead hours of the night had come upon him. He had already resolved that, when he had done so, he would swallow the tell-tale ashes. He believed of himself that all that would be within his power, if only he could determine upon the doing of it.

And he thought that the deed when done would give him a new courage. The very danger to which he would have exposed himself would make him brave to avoid it. Having destroyed the will, and certain that no eye had seen him, conscious that his safety depended on his own reticence, he was sure that he would keep his secret even before Mr Cheekey.

'I know nothing of the will,' he would say; 'I have neither seen it, nor hidden it, nor found it, nor destroyed it.'

Knowing what would be the consequences were he to depart from the assertion, he would assuredly cling to it. He would be safer then, much safer than in his present vacillating, half-innocent position.

As he was carried home in the fly, his mind was so intent upon this, he was so anxious to resolve to bring himself to do the deed, that he hardly knew where he was when the fly stopped at his hall door. As he entered his house, he stared about him as though doubtful of his whereabouts, and then, without speaking a word, made his way into the book-room, and seated himself on his accustomed chair. The woman came to him and asked him whether money should not be given to the driver.

'What driver?' said he. 'Let him go to Mr Apjohn. It is Mr Apjohn's business, not mine.' Then he got up and shut the door violently as the woman retreated.

Yes; it was Mr Apjohn's business; and he thought that he could put a spoke into the wheel of Mr Apjohn's business. Mr Apjohn was not only anxious to criminate him now, but had been anxious when such anxiety on his part had been intrusive and impertinent. Mr Apjohn had, from first to last, been his enemy, and by his enmity had created that fatal dislike which his uncle had felt for him. Mr Apjohn was now determined to ruin him. Mr Apjohn had come out to him at Llanfeare, pretending to be his lawyer, his friend, his advisor, and had recommended this treacherous indictment merely that he might be able to subject him to the torments of Mr Cheekey's persecution. Cousin Henry could see it all now! So, at least, Cousin Henry told himself.

'He is a clever fellow, and he thinks that I am a fool. Perhaps he is right, but he will find that the fool has been too many for him.'

It was thus that he communed with himself.

He had his dinner and sat by himself during the whole evening, as had been his practice every day since his uncle's death. But yet this peculiar night seemed to him to be eventful. He felt himself to be lifted into some unwonted eagerness of life, something approaching to activity. There was a deed to be done, and though he was not as yet doing it, though he did not think that he intended to do it that very night, yet the fact that he had made up his mind made him in some sort aware that the dumb spirit which would not speak had been exorcised, and that the crushing dullness of the latter days had passed away from him. No; he could not do it that night; but he was sure that he would do it. He had looked about for a way of escape, and had been as though a dead man while he could not find it. He had lived in terror of Mrs Griffith the housekeeper, of Farmer Griffith, of the two Cantors, of Mr Apjohn, of that tyrant Cheekey, of his own shadow – while he and that will were existing together in the same room. But it should be so no longer. There was one way of escape, and he would take it!

Then he went on thinking of what good things might be in store for him. His spirit had hitherto been so quenched by the vicinity of the will that he had never dared to soar into thoughts of the enjoyment of money. There had been so black a pall over everything that he had not as yet realised what it was that Llanfeare might do for him. Of course he could not live there. Though he should have to leave the house untenanted altogether, it would matter but little. There was no law to make a man live on his own estate. He calculated that he would be able to draw 1500*l.* a year from the property – 1500*l.* a year! That would be clearly his own; on which no one could lay a finger; and what enjoyment could he not buy with 1500*l.* a year?

With a great resolve to destroy the will he went to bed, and slept through the night as best he could. In the dark of his chamber, when the candle was out, and he was not yet protected by his bed, there came a qualm upon him. But the deed was not yet done, and the qualm was kept under, and he slept. He even repeated the Lord's Prayer to himself when he was under the clothes, struggling, however, as he did so, not to bring home to himself that petition as to the leading into temptation and the deliverance from evil.

The next day, the Friday, and the Saturday were passed in the same way. The resolution was still there, but the qualms came every night. And the salve to the qualm was always the same remembrance that the deed had not been done yet. And the prayer was always said, morning and night, with the same persistent rejection of those words which, in his present condition, were so damning to him – rejection from the intelligence though with the whispering voice the words were spoken. But still there was the resolve the same as ever. There was no other way of escape. A stag, when brought to bay, will trample upon the hounds. He would trample upon them. Llanfeare should all be his own. He would not return to his clerk's desk to be the scorn of all men – to have it known that he had fraudulently kept the will hidden, and then revealed it, not of grace, but because he was afraid of Mr Cheekey. His mind was quite made up. But the deed need not be yet done. The fewer nights that he would have to pass in that house, after the doing of the deed, the better.

The trial was to be on the Friday. He would not postpone the deed till the last day, as it might be then that emissaries might come to him, watching him to see that he did not escape. And yet it would be well for him to keep his hands clean from the doing of it up to the last moment. He was quite resolved. There was no other escape. And yet – yet – yet, who would say what might not happen? Till the deed should have been done, there would yet be a path open to the sweet easiness of innocence. When it should have been done, there would be a final adieu to innocence. There would be no return to the white way, no possibility of repentance! How could a man repent while he was still holding the guilty prize which he had won? Or how could he give up the prize without delivering himself as a criminal to the law? But, nevertheless, he was resolved, and he determined that the deed should be done on the Tuesday night.

During the whole Tuesday he was thinking of it. Could he bring himself to believe that all that story of a soul tormented for its wickedness in everlasting fire was but an old woman's tale? If he could but bring himself to believe that! If he could do that, then could he master his qualms. And why not? Religious thoughts had hitherto but little troubled his life. The Church and her services had been nothing to him. He had lived neither with the fear nor with the love of God at his heart. He knew that, and was but little disposed to think that a line of conduct which had never been hitherto adopted by him would be embraced in his later life. He could not think of himself as being even desirous to be religious. Why, then, should qualms afflict him?

That prayer which he was accustomed to repeat to himself as he went to rest was but a trick of his youth. It had come down to him from old, innocent days; and though it was seldom omitted, without a shiver, nevertheless it was repeated with contempt. In broad daylight, or when boon companions had been with him round the candles, blasphemy had never frightened him. But now – now in his troubles, he remembered that there was a hell. He could not shake from himself the idea. For unrepented sin there was an eternity of torment which would last for ever! Such sin as this which he premeditated must remain unrepented, and there would be torment for him for ever. Nevertheless, he must do it. And, after all, did not many of the wise ones of the earth justify him in thinking that that threat was but an old woman's tale?

Tuesday night came – the late hours of Tuesday night – the midnight hour at which he was sure that the women were in bed, and the will was taken out from its hiding-place. He had already trimmed the wick and placed the candle on an outspread newspaper, so that no fragment of the ash should fall where it might not be collected. He had walked round the room to make himself sure that no aperture might possibly be open. He put out the candle so as to see that no gleam of light from any source was making its way into the room, and then relighted it. The moment had come for the destruction of the document.

He read it all through yet again – why he knew not, but in truth craving some excuse for further delay. With what care the dying old man had written every word and completed every letter! He sat there contemplating the old man's work, telling himself that it was for him to destroy it utterly by just a motion of his wrist. He turned round and trimmed the candle again, and still sat there with the paper in his hand. Could it be that so great a result could come from so short an act? The damning of his own soul! Would it in truth be the giving up of his own soul to eternal punishment? God would know that he had not meant to steal the property! God would know that he did not wish to steal it now! God would know that he was doing this as the only means of escape from misery which others were plotting for him! God would know how cruelly he had been used! God would know the injustice with which the old man had treated him! Then came moments in which he almost taught himself to believe that in destroying the will he would be doing no more than an act of rough justice, and that God would certainly condemn no one to eternal punishment for a just act. But still, whenever he would turn round to the candle, his hand would refuse to raise the paper to the flame. When done, it could not be undone! And whether those eternal flames should or should not get possession of him, there would be before him a life agonised by the dread of them. What could Mr Cheekey do worse for him than that?

The Wednesday would at any rate do as well. Why rob himself of the comfort of one day during which his soul would not be irretrievably condemned? Now he might sleep. For this night, at any rate, he might sleep. He doubted whether he would ever sleep again after the doing of the deed. To be commonly wicked was nothing to him – nothing to break through all those ordinary rules of life which parents teach their children and pastors their flocks, but as to which the world is so careless. To covet other men's goods, to speak evil of his neighbours, to run after his neighbour's wife if she came in his path, to steal a little in the ordinary way – such as selling a lame horse or looking over an adversary's hand at whist, to swear to a lie, or to ridicule the memory of his parents – these peccadillos had never oppressed his soul. That not telling of the will had been burdensome to him only because of the danger of discovery. But to burn a will, and thereby clearly to steal 1500*l.* a year from his cousin! To commit felony! To do that for which he might be confined at Dartmoor all his life, with his hair cut, and dirty prison clothes, and hard food, and work to do! He thought it would be well to have another day of life in which he had not done the deed. He therefore put the will back into the book and went to his bed.

※ TWENTY-ONE ※

Mr Apjohn's Success

EARLY ON THE WEDNESDAY MORNING MR APJOHN and Mr Brodrick were on foot, and preparing for the performance of their very disagreeable day's work. Mr Brodrick did not believe at all in the day's work, and in discussing the matter with Mr Apjohn, after they had determined upon their line of action, made his mind known very clearly. To him it was simply apparent that if the will had fallen into the power of a dishonest person, and if the dishonest man could achieve his purpose by destroying it, the will would be destroyed. Of Cousin Henry he knew nothing. Cousin Henry might or might not be ordinarily honest, as are other ordinary people. There might be no such will as that spoken of, or there might be a will accidentally hidden – or the will might have been found and destroyed. But that they should be able to find a will, the hiding-place of which should be known to Cousin Henry, was to his thinking out of the question. The subtler intellect of the other lawyer appreciating the intricacies of a weak man's mind saw more than his companion. When he found that Mr Brodrick did not agree with him, and perceived that the other attorney's mind was not speculative in such a matter as this, he ceased to try to persuade, and simply said that it was the duty of both of them to leave no stone unturned. And so they started.

'I'll take you about half a mile out of our way to show you Mr Evans's gate,' Mr Apjohn said, after they had started. 'His house is not above twenty minutes from Llanfeare, and should it be necessary to ask his assistance, he will know all about it. You will find a policeman there ready to come back with you. But my impression is that Cousin Henry will not attempt to prevent any search which we may endeavour to make.'

It was about ten when they reached the house, and, on being shown into the book-room, they found Cousin Henry at his breakfast. The front door was opened for them by Mrs Griffith, the housekeeper; and when Mr Apjohn expressed his desire to see Mr Jones, she made no difficulty in admitting him at once. It was a part of the misery of Cousin Henry's position that everybody around him and near to him was against him. Mrs Griffith was aware that it was the purpose of Mr Apjohn to turn her present master out of Llanfeare if possible, and she was quite willing to aid him by any means in her power. Therefore, she gave her master no notice of the arrival of the two strangers, but ushered them into the room at once.

Cousin Henry's breakfast was frugal. All his meals had been frugal since he had become owner of Llanfeare. It was not that he did not like nice eating as well as another, but that he was too much afraid of his own servants to make known his own tastes. And then the general discomforts of his position had been too great to admit of relief from delicate dishes. There was the tea-pot on the table, and the solitary cup, and the bread and butter, and the nearly naked bone of a cold joint of mutton. And the things were not set after the fashion of a well-to-do gentleman's table, but were put on as they might be in a third-rate London lodging, with a tumbled tablecloth, and dishes, plates, and cups all unlike each other.

'Mr Jones,' said the attorney from Carmarthen, 'this is your uncle, Mr Brodrick, from Hereford.' Then the two men who were so nearly connected, but had never known each other, shook hands. 'Of course, this matter,' continued Mr Apjohn, 'is of great moment, and Mr Brodrick has come over to look after his daughter's interests.'

'I am very glad to see my uncle,' said Cousin Henry, turning his eye involuntarily towards the shelf on which the volume of sermons was resting. 'I am afraid I can't offer you much in the way of breakfast.'

'We breakfasted before we left Carmarthen,' said Mr Apjohn. 'If you do not mind going on, we will talk to you whilst you are eating.' Cousin Henry said that he did not mind going on, but found it impossible to eat a morsel. That which he did, and that which he endured during that interview, he had to do and had to endure fasting. 'I had better tell you at once,' continued Mr Apjohn, 'what we want to do now.'

'What is it you want to do now? I suppose I have got to go into the assizes all the same on Friday?'

'That depends. It is just possible that it should turn out to be unneccessary.'

As he said this, he looked into Cousin Henry's face, and thought that he discerned something of satisfaction. When he made the suggestion, he understood well how great was the temptation offered in the prospect of not having to encounter Mr Cheekey.

'Both Mr Brodrick and I think it probable that your uncle's last will may yet be concealed somewhere in the house.' Cousin Henry's eye, as this was said, again glanced up at the fatal shelf.

'When Mr Apjohn says that in my name,' said Mr Brodrick, opening his mouth for the first time, 'you must understand that I personally know nothing of the circumstances. I am guided in my opinion only by what he tells me.'

'Exactly,' said Mr Apjohn. 'As the father of the young lady who would be the heiress of Llanfeare if you were not the heir, I have of course told him everything – even down to the most secret surmises of my mind.'

'All right,' said Cousin Henry.

'My position,' continued Mr Apjohn, 'is painful and very peculiar; but I find myself specially bound to act as the lawyer of the deceased, and to carry out whatever was in truth his last will and testament.'

'I thought that was proved at Carmarthen,' said Cousin Henry.

'No doubt. A will was proved – a will that was very genuine if no subsequent will be found. But, as you have been told repeatedly, the proving of that will amounts to nothing if a subsequent one be forthcoming. The great question is this; Does a subsequent will exist?'

'How am I to know anything about it?'

'Nobody says you do.'

'I suppose you wouldn't come here and bring my uncle Brodrick down on me – giving me no notice, but coming into my house just when I am at breakfast, without saying a word to any one – unless you thought so. I don't see what right you have to be here at all!'

He was trying to pluck up his spirit in order that he might get rid of them. Why, oh! why had he not destroyed that document when, on the previous night, it had been brought out from its hiding-place, purposely in order that it might be burned?

'It is common, Mr Jones, for one gentleman to call upon another when there is business to be done,' said Mr Apjohn.

'But not common to come to a gentleman's house and accuse him of making away with a will.'

'Nobody has done that,' said Mr Brodrick.

'It is very like it.'

'Will you allow us to search again? Two of my clerks will be here just now, and will go through the house with us, if you will permit it.'

Cousin Henry sat staring at them. Not long ago he had himself asked one of Mr Apjohn's clerks why they did not search again. But then the framing of his thoughts had been different. At that moment he had been desirous of surrendering Llanfeare altogether, so that he might also get rid of Mr Cheekey. Now he had reached a bolder purpose. Now he was resolved to destroy the will, enjoy the property, and face the barrister. An idea came across his mind that they would hardly insist upon searching instantly if he refused. A petition to that effect had already been made, and a petition implies the power of refusal on the part of him petitioned.

'Where do you want to look?' he asked.

Upon this Mr Brodrick allowed his eyes to wander round the room. And Cousin Henry's eyes followed those of his uncle, which seemed to him to settle themselves exactly upon the one shelf.

'To search the house generally; your uncle's bed-room, for instance,' said Mr Apjohn.

'Oh, yes; you can go there.' This he said with an ill-formed, crude idea which sprang to his mind at the moment. If they would ascend to the bed-room, then he could seize the will when left alone and destroy it instantly – eat it bit by bit if it were necessary – go with it out of the house and reduce it utterly to nothing before he returned. He was still a free agent, and could go and come as he pleased. 'Oh, yes; you can go there.'

But this was not at all the scheme which had really formed itself in Mr Apjohn's brain. 'Or perhaps we might begin here,' he said. 'There are my two clerks just arrived in the fly.'

Cousin Henry became first red and then pale, and he endeavoured to see in what direction Mr Brodrick had fixed his eye. Mr Apjohn himself had not as yet looked anywhere round the books. He had sat close at the table, with his gaze fixed on Cousin Henry's face, as Cousin Henry had been well aware. If they began to search in the room, they would certainly find the document. Of that he was quite sure. Not a book would be left without having been made to disclose all that it might contain between its leaves. If there was any chance left to him, it must be seized now – now at this very moment. Suddenly the possession of Llanfeare was endeared to him by a thousand charms. Suddenly all fear of eternal punishment passed away from his thoughts. Suddenly he was permeated by a feeling of contrition for his own weakness in having left the document unharmed. Suddenly he was brave against Mr Cheekey, as would be a tiger against a lion. Suddenly there arose in his breast a great desire to save the will even yet from the hands of these Philistines.

'This is my private room,' he said. 'When I am eating my breakfast I cannot let you disturb me like that.'

'In a matter such as this you wouldn't think of your own comfort!' said Mr Apjohn severely. 'Comfort, indeed! What comfort can you have while the idea is present to you that this house in which you live may possibly be the property of your cousin?'

'It's very little comfort you've left me among you.'

'Face it out, then, like a man; and when you have allowed us to do all that we can on her behalf, then enjoy your own, and talk of comfort. Shall I have the men in and go on with the search as I propose?'

If they were to find it – as certainly they would – then surely they would not accuse him of having hidden it! He would be enabled to act some show of surprise, and they would not dare to contradict him, even should they feel sure in their hearts that he had been aware of the concealment! There would be great relief! There would be an end of so many troubles! But then how weak he would have been – to have had the prize altogether within his grasp and to have lost it! A burst of foul courage swelled in his heart, changing the very colour of his character for a time as he resolved that it should not be so. The men could not search there – so he told himself – without further authority than that which Mr Apjohn could give them. 'I won't be treated in this way!' he said.

'In what way do you mean, Mr Jones?'

'I won't have my house searched as though I were a swindler and a thief. Can you go into any man's house and search it just as you please, merely because you are an attorney?'

'You told my man the other day,' said Mr Apjohn, 'that we might renew the search if we pleased.'

'So you may; but you must get an order first from somebody. You are nobody.'

'You are quite right,' said Mr Apjohn, who was not at all disposed to be angry in regard to any observation offered personally to himself. 'But surely it would be better for you that this should be done privately. Of course we can have a search-warrant if it be necessary; but then there must be a policeman to carry it out.'

'What do I care for policemen?' said Cousin Henry. 'It is you who have treated me badly from first to last. I will do nothing further at your bidding.'

Mr Apjohn looked at Mr Brodrick, and Mr Brodrick looked at Mr Apjohn. The strange attorney would do nothing without directions from the other, and the attorney who was more at home was for a few moments a little in doubt. He got up from his chair, and walked about the room, while Cousin Henry, standing also, watched every movement which he made. Cousin Henry took his place at the further end of the table from the fire, about six feet from the spot on which all his thoughts were intent. There he stood, ready for action while the attorney walked up and down the room meditating what it would be best that he should do next. As he walked he seemed to carry his nose in the air, with a gait different from what was usual to him. Cousin Henry had already learned something of the man's ways, and was aware that his manner was at present strange. Mr Apjohn was in truth looking along the rows of the books. In old days he had often been in that room, and had read many of the titles as given on the backs. He knew the nature of many of the books collected there, and was aware that but very few of them had ever been moved from their places in the old Squire's time for any purpose of use. He did not wish to stand and inspect them – not as yet. He walked on as though collecting his thoughts, and as he walked he endeavoured to fix on some long set of sermons. He had in his mind some glimmering of remembrance that there was such a set of books in the room. 'You might as well let us do as we propose,' he said.

'Certainly not. To tell you the truth, I wish you would go away, and leave me.'

'Mr Cheekey will hear all about it, and how will you be able to answer Mr Cheekey?'

'I don't care about Mr Cheekey. Who is to tell Mr Cheekey? Will you tell him?'

'I cannot take your part, you know, if you behave like this.'

As he spoke, Mr Apjohn had stopped his walk, and was standing with his back close to the book-shelves, with the back of his head almost touching the set of Jeremy Taylor's works. There were ten volumes of them, and he was standing exactly in front of them. Cousin Henry was just in front of him, doubting whether his enemy's position had not been chosen altogether by accident, but still trembling at the near approach. He was prepared for a spring if it was necessary. Anything should be hazarded now, so that discovery might be avoided. Mr Brodrick was still seated in the chair which he had at first occupied, waiting till that order should be given to him to go for the magistrate's warrant.

Mr Apjohn's eye had caught the author's name on the back of the book, and he remembered at once that he had seen the volume – a volume with Jeremy Taylor's name on the back of it – lying on the old man's table. 'Jeremey Taylor's Works. Sermons.' He remembered the volume. That had been a long time ago – six months ago; but the old man might probably take a long time over so heavy a book. 'You will let me look at some of these,' he said, pointing with his thumb over his back.

'You shall not touch a book without a regular order,' said Cousin Henry.

Mr Apjohn fixed the man's eye for a moment. He was the smaller man of the two, and much the elder; but he was wiry, well set, and strong. The other was soft, and unused to much bodily exercise. There could be no doubt as to which would have the best of it in a personal struggle. Very quickly he turned round and got his hand on one of the set, but not on the right one. Cousin Henry dashed at him, and in the struggle the book fell to the ground. Then the attorney seized him by the throat, and dragged him forcibly back to the table. 'Take them all out one by one, and shake them,' he said to the other attorney – 'that set like the one on the floor. I'll hold him while you do it.'

Mr Brodrick did as he was told, and, one by one, beginning from the last volume, he shook them all till he came to volume 4. Out of that fell the document.

'Is it the will?' shouted Mr Apjohn, with hardly breath enough to utter the words.

Mr Brodrick, with a lawyer's cautious hands, undid the folds, and examined the document. 'It certainly is a will,' he said – 'and is signed by my brother-in-law.'

❋ TWENTY-TWO ❋

How Cousin Henry was let off Easily

IT WAS A MOMENT OF GREAT TRIUMPH and of utter dismay – of triumph to Mr Apjohn, and of dismay to Cousin Henry. The two men at this moment – as Mr Brodrick was looking at the papers – were struggling together upon the ground. Cousin Henry, in his last frantic efforts, had striven to escape from the grasp of his enemy so as to seize the will, not remembering that by seizing it now he could retrieve nothing. Mr Apjohn had been equally determined that ample time should be allowed to Mr Brodrick to secure any document that might be found, and, with the pugnacity which the state of fighting always produces, had held on to his prey with a firm grip. Now for the one man there remained nothing but dismay; for the other was the full enjoyment of the triumph produced by his own sagacity. 'Here is the date,' said Mr Brodrick, who had retreated with the paper to the furthest corner of the room. 'It is undoubtedly my brother-in-law's last will and testament, and, as far as I can see at a glance, it is altogether regular.'

'You dog!' exclaimed Mr Apjohn, spurning Cousin Henry away from him. 'You wretched, thieving miscreant!' Then he got up on to his legs and began to adjust himself, setting his cravat right, and smoothing his hair with his hands. 'The brute has knocked the breath out of me,' he said. 'But only to think that we should catch him after such a fashion as this!' There was a note of triumph in his voice which he found it impossible to repress. He was thoroughly proud of his achievement. It was a grand thing to him that Isabel Brodrick should at last get the property which he had so long been anxious to secure for her; but at the present moment it was a grander thing to have hit the exact spot in which the document had been hidden by sheer force of intelligence.

What little power of fighting there had ever been in Cousin Henry had now been altogether knocked out of him. He attempted no further struggle, uttered no denial, nor did he make any answer to the words of abuse which Mr Apjohn had heaped on his head. He too raised himself from the floor, slowly collecting his limbs together, and seated himself in the chair nearest at hand, hiding his face with his hand.

'That is the most wonderful thing that ever came within my experience,' said Mr Brodrick.

'That the man should have hidden the will?' asked Mr Apjohn.

'Why do you say I hid it?' moaned Cousin Henry.

'You reptile!' exclaimed Mr Apjohn.

'Not that he should have hidden it,' said the Hereford attorney, 'but that you should have found it, and found it without any search; – that you should have traced it down to the very book in which the old man must have left it!'

'Yes,' said Cousin Henry. 'He left it there. I did not hide it.'

'Do you mean,' said Mr Apjohn, turning upon him with all the severity of which he was capable, 'do you mean to say that during all this time you have not known that the will was there?' The wretched man opened his mouth and essayed to speak, but not a word came. 'Do you mean to tell us that when you refused us just now permission to search this room, though you were willing enough that we should search elsewhere, you were not acquainted with the hiding-place? When I asked you in my office the other day whether you knew where the will was hidden, and you wouldn't answer me for very fear, though you were glib enough in swearing that you had not hidden it yourself, then you knew nothing about the book and its enclosure? When you told Mr Griffith down at Coed that you had something to divulge, were you not then almost driven to tell the truth by your dastardly cowardice as to this threatened trial? And did you not fail again because you were afraid? You mean poltroon! Will you dare to say before us, now, that when we entered the room this morning you did not know what the book contained?' Cousin Henry once more opened his mouth, but no word came. 'Answer me, sir, if you wish to escape any part of the punishment which you have deserved.'

'You should not ask him to criminate himself,' said Mr Brodrick.

'No!' shrieked Cousin Henry; 'no! he shouldn't ask a fellow to tell against himself. It isn't fair; is it, Uncle Brodrick?'

'If I hadn't made you tell against yourself one way or another,' said Mr Apjohn, 'the will would have been there still, and we should all have been in the dark. There are occasions in which the truth must be screwed out of a man. We have screwed it out of you, you miserable creature! Brodrick, let us look at the paper. I suppose it is all right.' He was so elated by the ecstasy of his success that he hardly knew how to contain himself. There was no prospect to him of any profit in all this. It might, indeed, well be that all the expenses incurred, including the handsome honorarium which would still have to be paid to Mr Cheekey, must come out of his own pocket. But the glory of the thing was too great to admit of any considerations such as those. For the last month his mind had been exercised with the question of this will, whether there was such a will or not, and, if so, where was its hiding-place? Now he had brought his month's labour, his month's speculation, and his month's anxiety to a supreme success. In his present frame of mind it was nothing to him who might pay the bill. 'As far as I can see,' said Mr Brodrick, 'it is altogether in order.'

'Let us look at it.' Then Mr Apjohn, stretching out his hand, took the document, and, seating himself in Cousin Henry's own chair at the breakfast-table, read it through carefully from beginning to end. It was wonderful – the exactness with which the old Squire had copied, not only every word, but every stop and every want of a stop in the preceding will. 'It is my own work, every morsel of it,' said Mr Apjohn, with thorough satisfaction. 'Why on earth did he not burn the intermediate one which he made in this rascal's favour' – then he indicated the rascal by a motion of his head – 'and make it all straight in that way?'

'There are men who think that a will once made should never be destroyed,' suggested Mr Brodrick.

'I suppose it was something of that kind. He was a fine old fellow, but as obstinate as a mule. Well, what are we to do now?'

'My nephew will have to consult his lawyer whether he will wish to dispute this document or not.'

'I do not want to dispute anything,' said Cousin Henry, whining.

'Of course he will be allowed time to think of it,' said Mr Apjohn. 'He is in possession now, and will have plenty of time. He will have to answer some rather difficult questions from Mr Cheekey on Friday.'

'Oh, no!' shouted the victim.

'I am afraid it must be "oh, yes," Mr Jones! How are you to get out of it; eh? You are bound over to prosecute Mr Evans, of the Herald, for defamation of character. Of course it will come out at the trial that we have found this document. Indeed, I shall be at no trouble to conceal that fact – nor, I suppose, will be Mr Brodrick. Why should we?'

'I thought you were acting as my lawyer.'

'So I was – and so I am – and so I will. While you were supposed to be an honest man – or, rather, while it was possible that it might be so supposed – I told you what, as an honest man, you were bound to do. The Carmarthen Herald knew that you were not honest – and said so. If you are prepared to go into the court and swear that you knew nothing of the existence of this document, that you were not aware that it was concealed in that book, that you did nothing to prevent us from looking for it this morning, I will carry on the case for you. If I am called into the witness-box against you, of course I must give my evidence for what it is worth – and Mr Brodrick must do the same.'

'But it won't go on?' he asked.

'Not if you are prepared to admit that there was no libel in all that the newspaper said. If you agree that it was all true, then you will have to pay the costs on both sides, and the indictment can be quashed. It will be a serious admission to make, but perhaps that won't signify, seeing what your position as to character will be.'

'I think you are almost too hard upon him,' said Mr Brodrick.

'Am I? Can one be too hard on a man who has acted as he has done?'

'He is hard – isn't he, Mr Brodrick?'

'Hard! Why, yes – I should think I am. I mean to be hard. I mean to go on trampling you to pieces till I see your cousin, Miss Brodrick, put into full possession of this estate. I don't mean to leave you a loop-hole of escape by any mercy. At the present moment you are Henry Jones, Esq., of Llanfeare, and will be so till you are put out by the hard hand of the law. You may turn round for anything I know, and say that this document is a forgery.'

'No, no!'

'That Mr Brodrick and I brought it here with us and put it in the book.'

'I sha'n't say anything of the kind.'

'Who did put it there?' Cousin Henry sobbed and groaned, but said nothing. 'Who did put it there? If you want to soften our hearts to you in any degree, if you wish us to contrive some mode of escape for you, tell the truth. Who put the will into that book?'

'How am I to know?'

'You do know! Who put it there?'

'I suppose it was Uncle Indefer.'

'And you had seen it there?' Again Cousin Henry sobbed and groaned.

'You should hardly ask him that,' said Mr Brodrick.

'Yes! If any good can be done for him, it must be by making him feel that he must help us by making our case easy for us. You had seen it there? Speak the word, and we will do all we can to let you off easily.'

'Just by an accident,' said he.

'You did see it, then?'

'Yes – I chanced to see it.'

'Yes; of course you did. And then the Devil went to work with you and prompted you to destroy it?' He paused as though asking a question, but to this question Cousin Henry found it impossible to make any answer. 'But the Devil had not quite hold enough over you to make you do that? It was so – was it not? There was a conscience with you?'

'Oh, yes.'

'But the conscience was not strong enough to force you to give it up when you found it?' Cousin Henry now burst out into open tears. 'That was about it, I suppose? If you can bring yourself to make a clean breast of it, it will be easier for you.'

'May I go back to London at once?' he asked.

'Well; as to that, I think we had better take some little time for consideration. But I think I may say that, if you will make our way easy for us, we will endeavour to make yours easy for you. You acknowledge this to be your uncle's will as far as you know?'

'Oh, yes.'

'You acknowledge that Mr Brodrick found it in this book which I now hold in my hand?'

'I acknowledge that.'

'This is all that I ask you to sign your name to. As for the rest, it is sufficient that you have confessed the truth to your uncle and to me. I will just write a few lines that you shall sign, and then we will go back to Carmarthen and do the best we can to prevent the trial for next Friday.' Thereupon Mr Apjohn rang the bell, and asked Mrs Griffith to bring him paper and ink. With these he wrote a letter addressed to himself, which he invited Cousin Henry to sign as soon as he had read it aloud to him and to Mr Brodrick. The letter contained simply the two admissions above stated, and then went on to authorise Mr Apjohn, as the writer's attorney, to withdraw the indictment against the proprietor of the Carmarthen Herald, 'in consequence,' as the letter said, 'of the question as to the possession of Llanfeare having been settled now in an unexpected manner.'

When the letter was completed, the two lawyers went away, and Cousin Henry was left to his own meditation. He sat there for a while, so astounded by the transaction of the morning as to be unable to collect his thoughts. All this that had agitated him so profoundly for the last month had been set at rest by the finding of the will. There was no longer any question as to what must be done. Everything had been done. He was again a London clerk, with a small sum of money besides his clerkship, and the security of lowliness into which to fall back! If only they would be silent – if only it might be thought by his fellow-clerks in London that the will had been found by them without any knowledge on his part – then he would be satisfied. A terrible catastrophe had fallen upon him, but one which would not be without consolation if with the estate might be made to pass away from him all responsibilities and all accusations as to the estate. That terrible man had almost promised him that a way of retreat should be made easy to him. At any rate, he would not be cross-examined by Mr Cheekey. At any rate, he would not be brought to trial. There was almost a promise, too, that as little should be said as possible. There must, he supposed, be some legal form of abdication on his part, but he was willing to execute that as quickly as possible on the simple condition that he should be allowed to depart without being forced to speak further on the matter to any one in Wales. Not to have to see the tenants, not to have to say even a word of farewell to the servants, not to be carried into Carmarthen – above all, not to face Mr Cheekey and the Court – this was all he asked now from a kind Fate.

At about two Mrs Griffith came into the room, ostensibly to take away the breakfast things. She had seen the triumphant face of Mr Apjohn, and knew that some victory had been gained. But when she saw that the breakfast had not been touched, her heart became soft. The way to melt the heart of a Mrs Griffith is to eat nothing. 'Laws, Mr Jones, you have not had a mouthful. Shall I do you a broil?' He assented to the broil, and ate it, when it was cooked, with a better appetite than he had enjoyed since his uncle's death. Gradually he came to feel that a great load had been taken from off his shoulders. The will was no longer hidden in the book. Nothing had been done of which he could not repent. There was no prospect of a life before him made horrid by one great sin. He could not be Squire of Llanfeare; nor would he be a felon – a felon always in his own esteem. Upon the whole, though he hardly admitted as much to himself, the man's condition had been improved by the transactions of the morning.

'You don't quite agree with all that I have done this morning,' said Mr Apjohn, as soon as the two lawyers were in the fly together.

'I am lost in admiration at the clearness of your insight.'

'Ah! that comes of giving one's undivided thoughts to a matter. I have been turning it over in my mind till I have been able to see it all. It was odd, wasn't it, that I should have foretold to you all that happened, almost to the volume?'

'Quite to the volume!'

'Well, yes; to the volume of sermons. Your brother-in-law read nothing but sermons. But you thought I shouldn't have asked those questions.'

'I don't like making a man criminate himself,' said Mr Brodrick.

'Nor do I – if I mean to criminate him too. My object is to let him off. But to enable us to do that we must know exactly what he knew and what he had done. Shall I tell you what occurred to me when you shook the will out of the book? How would it be if he declared that we had brought it with us? If he had been sharp enough for that, the very fact of our having gone to the book at once would have been evidence against us.'

'He was not up to it.'

'No, poor devil! I am inclined to think that he has got as bad as he deserves. He might have been so much worse. We owe him ever so much for not destroying the will. His cousin will have to give him the 4000*l*. which he was to have given her.'

'Certainly, certainly.'

'He has been hardly used, you know, by his uncle; and, upon my word, he has had a bad time of it for the last month. I wouldn't have been hated and insulted as he has been by those people up there – not for all Llanfeare twice over. I think we've quenched him now, so that he'll run smooth. If so, we'll let him off easily. If I had treated him less hardly just now, he might have gathered courage and turned upon us. Then it would have been necessary to crush him altogether. I was thinking all through how we might let him off easiest.'

TWENTY-THREE

Isabel's Petition

THE NEWS WAS SOON ALL ABOUT CARMARTHEN. A new will had been found, in accordance with which Miss Brodrick was to become owner of Llanfeare, and – which was of more importance to Carmarthen at the present moment – there was to be no trial! The story, as told publicly, was as follows – Mr Apjohn, by his sagacity, had found the will. It had been concealed in a volume of sermons, and Mr Apjohn, remembering suddenly that the old man had been reading these sermons shortly before his death, had gone at once to the book. There the will had been discovered, which had at once been admitted to be a true and formal document by the unhappy pseudo-proprietor. Henry Jones had acknowledged his cousin to be the heiress, and under these circumstances had conceived it to be useless to go on with the trial. Such was the story told, and Mr Apjohn, fully aware that the story went very lame on one leg, did his best to remedy the default by explaining that it would be unreasonable to expect that a man should come into court and undergo an examination by Mr Cheekey just when he had lost a fine property.

'Of course I know all that,' said Mr Apjohn when the editor of the paper remarked to him that the libel, if a libel, would be just as much a libel whether Mr Henry Jones were or were not the owner of Llanfeare. 'Of course I know all that; but you are hardly to expect that a man is to come and assert himself amidst a cloud of difficulties when he has just undergone such a misfortune as that! You have had your fling, and are not to be punished for it. That ought to satisfy you.'

'And who'll pay all the expenses?' asked Mr Evans.

'Well,' said Mr Apjohn, scratching his head; 'you, of course, will have to pay nothing. Geary will settle all that with me. That poor devil at Llanfeare ought to pay.'

'He won't have the money.'

'I, at any rate, will make it all right with Geary; so that needn't trouble you.'

This question as to the expense was much discussed by others in Carmarthen. Who in truth would pay the complicated lawyers' bill which must have been occasioned, including all these flys out to Llanfeare? In spite of Mr Apjohn's good-natured explanations, the public of Carmarthen was quite convinced that Henry Jones had in truth hidden the will. If so, he ought not only to be made to pay for everything, but be sent to prison also and tried for felony. The opinion concerning Cousin Henry in Carmarthen on the Thursday and Friday was very severe indeed. Had he shown himself in the town, he would almost have been pulled in pieces. To kill him and to sell his carcase for what it might fetch towards lessening the expenses which he had incurred would not be too bad for him. Mr Apjohn was, of course, the hero of the hour, and, as far as Carmarthen could see, Mr Apjohn would have to pay the bill. All this, spoken as it was by many mouths, reached Mr Brodrick's ears, and induced him to say a word or two to Mr Apjohn.

'This affair,' said he, 'will of course become a charge upon the property?'

'What affair?'

'This trial which is not to take place, and the rest of it.'

'The trial will have nothing to do with the estate,' said Mr Apjohn.

'It has everything to do with it. I only mention it now to let you know that, as Isabel's father, I shall make it my business to look after that.'

'The truth is, Brodrick,' said the Carmarthen attorney, with that gleam of triumph in his eye which had been so often seen there since the will had tumbled out of the volume of sermons in the book-room, 'the whole of this matter has been such a pleasure to me that I don't care a straw about the costs. If I paid for it all from beginning to end out of my own pocket, I should have had my whack for my money. Perhaps Miss Isabel will recompense me by letting me make her will some day.'

Such were the feelings and such were the words spoken at Carmarthen; and it need only be said further, in regard to Carmarthen, that the operations necessary for proving the later will and annulling the former one, for dispossessing Cousin Henry and for putting Isabel into the full fruition of all her honours, went on as quickly as it could be effected by the concentrated energy of Mr Apjohn and all his clerks.

Cousin Henry, to whom we may be now allowed to bid farewell, was permitted to remain within the seclusion of the house at Llanfeare till his signature had been obtained to the last necessary document. No one spoke a word to him; no one came to see him. If there were intruders about the place anxious to catch a glimpse of the pseudo-Squire, they were disappointed.

Mrs Griffith, under the attorney's instructions, was more courteous to him than she had been when he was her master. She endeavoured to get him things nice to eat, trying to console him by titbits. None of the tenants appeared before him, nor was there a rough word spoken to him, even by young Cantor.

In all this Cousin Henry did feel some consolation, and was greatly comforted when he heard from the office in London that his stool at the desk was still kept open for him.

The Carmarthen Herald, in its final allusion to the state of things at

Llanfeare, simply declared that the proper will had been found at last, and that Miss Isabel Brodrick was to be restored to her rights. Guided by this statement, the directors in London were contented to regard their clerk as having been unfortunate rather than guilty.

For the man himself, the reader, it is hoped, will feel some compassion. He had been dragged away from London by false hopes. After so great an injury as that inflicted on him by the last change in the Squire's purpose it was hardly unnatural that the idea of retaliation should present itself to him when the opportunity came in his way. Not to do that which justice demands is so much easier to the conscience than to commit a deed which is palpably fraudulent! At the last his conscience saved him, and Mr Apjohn will perhaps be thought to have been right in declaring that much was due to him in that he had not destroyed the will. His forbearance was recompensed fully.

As soon as the money could be raised on the property, the full sum of 4000l. was paid to him, that having been the amount with which the Squire had intended to burden the property on behalf of his niece when he was minded to put her out of the inheritance.

It may be added that, notorious as the whole affair was at Carmarthen, but little of Cousin Henry's wicked doings were known up in London.

We must now go back to Hereford. By agreement between the two lawyers, no tidings of her good fortune were at once sent to Isabel. 'There is so many a slip 'twixt the cup and the lip,' said Mr Apjohn to her father. But early in the following week Mr Brodrick himself took the news home with him.

'My dear,' he said to her as soon as he found himself alone with her – having given her intimation that an announcement of great importance was to be made to her – 'it turns out that after all your Uncle Indefer did make another will.'

'I was always quite sure of that, papa.'

'How were you sure?'

'He told me so, papa.'

'He told you so! I never heard that before.'

'He did – when he was dying. What was the use of talking of it? But has it been found?'

'It was concealed within a book in the library. As soon as the necessary deeds can be executed Llanfeare will be your own. It is precisely word for word the same as that which he had made before he sent for your cousin Henry.'

'Then Henry has not destroyed it?'

'No, he did not destroy it.'

'Nor hid it where we could not find it?'

'Nor did he hide it.'

'Oh, how I have wronged him – how I have injured him!'

'About that we need say nothing, Isabel. You have not injured him. But we may let all that pass away. The fact remains that you are the heiress of Llanfeare.'

Of course he did by degrees explain to her all the circumstances – how the will had been found and not revealed, and how far Cousin Henry had sinned in the matter; but it was agreed between them that no further evil should be said in the family as to their unfortunate relative. The great injury which he might have done to them he had abstained from doing.

'Papa,' she said to her father when they were again together alone that same evening, 'you must tell all this to Mr Owen. You must tell him everything, just as you have told me.'

'Certainly, my dear, if you wish it.'

'I do wish it.'

'Why should you not have the pleasure of telling him yourself?'

'It would not be a pleasure, and therefore I will get you to do it. My pleasure, if there be any pleasure in it, must come afterwards. I want him to know it before I see him myself.'

'He will be sure to have some stupid notion,' said her father, smiling.

'I want him to have his notion, whether it be stupid or otherwise, before I see him. If you do not mind, papa, going to him as soon as possible, I shall be obliged to you.'

Isabel, when she found herself alone, had her triumph also. She was far from being dead to the delights of her inheritance. There had been a period in her life in which she had regarded it as her certain destiny to be the possessor of Llanfeare, and she had been proud of the promised position. The tenants had known her as the future owner of the acres which they cultivated, and had entertained for her and shown to her much genuine love. She had made herself acquainted with every homestead, landmark, and field about the place. She had learnt the wants of the poor, and the requirements of the little school. Everything at Llanfeare had had an interest for her. Then had come that sudden change in her uncle's feelings – that new idea of duty – and she had borne it like a heroine. Not only had she never said a word of reproach to him, but she had sworn to herself that even in her own heart she would throw no blame upon him. A great blow had come upon her, but she had taken it as though it had come from the hand of the Almighty – as it might have been had she lost her eyesight, or been struck with palsy. She promised herself that it should be so, and she had had strength to be as good as her word. She had roused herself instantly from the effect of the blow, and, after a day of consideration, had been as capable as ever to do the work of her life. Then had come her uncle's last sickness, those spoken but doubtful words, her uncle's death, and that conviction that her cousin was a felon. Then she had been unhappy, and had found it difficult to stand up bravely against misfortune. Added to this had been her stepmother's taunts and her father's distress at the resolution she had taken. The home to which she had returned had been thoroughly unhappy to her. And there had been her stern purpose not to give her hand to the man who loved her and whom she so dearly loved! She was sure of her purpose, and yet she was altogether discontented with herself. She was sure that she would hold by her purpose, and yet she feared that her purpose was wrong. She had refused the man when she was rich, and her pride would not let her go to him now that she was poor. She was sure of her purpose – but yet she almost knew that her pride was wrong.

But now there would be a triumph. Her eyes gleamed brightly as she thought of the way in which she would achieve her triumph. Her eyes gleamed very brightly as she felt sure within her own bosom that she would succeed. Yes: he would, no doubt, have some stupid notion, as her father said. But she would overcome his stupidity. She, as a woman, could be stronger than he as a man. He had almost ridiculed her obstinacy, swearing that he would certainly overcome it. There should be no ridicule on her part, but she would certainly overcome his obstinacy.

For a day or two Mr Owen was not seen. She heard from her father that the tidings had been told to her lover, but she heard no more. Mr Owen did not show himself at the house; and she, indeed, hardly expected that he should do so. Her stepmother suddenly became gracious – having no difficulty in explaining that she did so because of the altered position of things.

'My dearest Isabel, it does make such a difference!' she said; 'you will be a rich lady, and will never have to think about the price of shoes.' The sisters were equally plain-spoken, and were almost awe-struck in their admiration.

Three or four days after the return of Mr Brodrick, Isabel took her bonnet and shawl, and walked away all alone to Mr Owen's lodgings. She knew his habits, and was aware that he was generally to be found at home for an hour before his dinner. It was no time, she said to herself, to stand upon little punctilios. There had been too much between them to let there be any question of a girl going after her lover. She was going after her lover, and she didn't care who knew it. Nevertheless, there was a blush beneath her veil as she asked at the door whether Mr Owen was at home. Mr Owen was at home, and she was shown at once into his parlour.

'William,' she said – throughout their intimacy she had never called him William before – 'you have heard my news?'

'Yes,' he said, 'I have heard it' – very seriously, with none of that provoking smile with which he had hitherto responded to all her assertions.

'And you have not come to congratulate me?'

'I should have done so. I do own that I have been wrong.'

'Wrong – very wrong! How was I to have any of the enjoyment of my restored rights unless you came to enjoy them with me?'

'They can be nothing to me, Isabel.'

'They shall be everything to you, sir.'

'No, my dear.'

'They are to be everything to me, and they can be nothing to me without you. You know that, I suppose?' Then she waited for his reply. 'You know that, do you not? You know what I feel about that, I say. Why do you not tell me? Have you any doubt?'

'Things have been unkind to us, Isabel, and have separated us.'

'Nothing shall separate us.' Then she paused for a moment. She had thought of it all, and now had to pause before she could execute her purpose. She had got her plan ready, but it required some courage, some steadying of herself to the work before she could do it. Then she came close to him – close up to him, looking into his face as he stood over her, not moving his feet, but almost retreating with his body from her close presence. 'William,' she said, 'take me in your arms and kiss me. How often have you asked me during the last month! Now I have come for it.'

He paused a moment as though it were possible to refuse, as though his collected thoughts and settled courage might enable him so to outrage her in her petition. Then he broke down, and took her in his arms, and pressed her to his bosom, and kissed her lips, and her forehead, and her cheeks – while she, having once achieved her purpose, attempted in vain to escape from his long embrace.

'Now I shall be your wife,' she said at last, when her breath had returned to her.

'It should not be so.'

'Not after that? Will you dare to say so to me – after that? You could never hold up your head again. Say that you are happy? Tell me that you are happy. Do you think that I can be happy unless you are happy with me?' Of course he gave her all the assurances that were needed, and made it quite unnecessary that she should renew her prayer.

'And I beg, Mr Owen, that for the future you will come to me, and not make me come to you.' This she said as she was taking her leave. 'It was very disagreeable, and very wrong, and will be talked about ever so much. Nothing but my determination to have my own way could have made me do it.' Of course he promised her that there should be no occasion for her again to put herself to the same inconvenience.

❌ TWENTY-FOUR ❌

Conclusion

Isabel spent one pleasant week with her lover at Hereford, and then was summoned into Carmarthenshire. Mr Apjohn came over at her father's invitation, and insisted on taking her back to Llanfeare.

'There are a thousand things to be done,' he said, 'and the sooner you begin to do them the better. Of course you must live at the old house, and you had better take up your habitation there for a while before this other change is made.' The other change was of course the coming marriage, with the circumstances of which the lawyer had been made acquainted.

Then there arose other questions. Should her father go with her or should her lover? It was, however, at last decided that she should go alone as regarded her family, but under the care of Mr Apjohn. It was she who had been known in the house, and she who had better now be seen there as her uncle's representative.

'You will have to be called Miss Jones,' said the lawyer, 'Miss Indefer Jones. There will be a form, for which we shall have to pay, I am afraid; but we had better take the name at once. You will have to undergo a variety of changes in signing your name. You will become first Miss Isabel Brodrick Indefer Jones, then Mrs William Owen, then, when he shall have gone through the proper changes, Mrs William Owen Indefer Jones. As such I hope you may remain till you shall be known as the oldest inhabitant of Carmarthenshire.'

Mr Apjohn took her to Carmarthen, and hence on to Llanfeare. At the station there, were many to meet her, so that her triumph, as she got into the carriage, was almost painful to her. When she heard the bells ring from the towers of the parish churches, she could hardly believe that the peals were intended to welcome her back to her old home. She was taken somewhat out of her way round by the creek and Coed, so that the little tinkling of her own parish church might not be lost upon her. If this return of hers to the estate was so important to others as to justify these signs, what must it be to her and how deep must be the convictions as to her own duties?

At the gate of Coed farmyard the carriage stopped, and the old farmer came out to say a few words to her.

'God bless you, Miss Isabel; this is a happy sight to see.'

'This is so kind of you, Mr Griffith.'

'We've had a bad time of it, Miss Isabel – not that we wished to quarrel with your dear uncle's judgment, or that we had a right to say much against the poor gentleman who has gone – but we expected you, and it went against the grain with us to have our expectations disappointed. We shall always look up to you, miss; but, at the same time, I wish you joy with all my heart of the new landlord you're going to set over us. Of course that was to be expected, but you'll be here with us all the time.' Isabel, while the tears ran down her cheeks, could only press the old man's hand at parting.

'Now, my dear,' said Mr Apjohn, as they went on to the house, 'he has only said just what we've all been feeling. Of course it has been stronger with the tenants and servants than with others. But all round the country it has been the same. A man, if an estate belong to himself personally, can do what he likes with it, as he can with the half-crowns in his pocket; but where land is concerned, feelings grow up which should not be treated rudely. In one sense Llanfeare belonged to your uncle to do what he liked with it, but in another sense he shared it only with those around him; and when he was induced by a theory which he did not himself quite understand to bring your cousin Henry down among these people, he outraged their best convictions.'

'He meant to do his duty, Mr Apjohn.'

'Certainly; but he mistook it. He did not understand the root of that idea of a male heir. The object has been to keep the old family, and the old adherences, and the old acres together. England owes much to the manner in which this has been done, and the custom as to a male heir has availed much in the doing of it. But in this case, in sticking to the custom, he would have lost the spirit, and, as far as he was concerned, would have gone against the practice which he wished to perpetuate. There, my dear, is a sermon for you, of which, I dare say, you do not understand a word.'

'I understand every syllable of it, Mr Apjohn,' she answered.

They soon arrived at the house, and there they found not only Mrs Griffith and the old cook, who had never left the premises, but the old butler also, who had taken himself off in disgust at Cousin Henry's character, but had now returned as though there had been no break in his continuous service. They received her with triumphant clamours of welcome. To them the coming of Cousin Henry, and the death of the old Squire, and then the departure of their young mistress, had been as though the whole world had come to an end for them. To serve was their only ambition – to serve and to be made comfortable while they were serving; but to serve Cousin Henry was to them altogether ignominious. The old Squire had done something which, though they acknowledged it to be no worse on his part than a mistake, had to them been cruelly severe. Suddenly to be told that they were servants to such a one as Cousin Henry – servants to such a man without any contract or agreement on their part – to be handed over like the chairs and tables to a disreputable clerk from London, whom in their hearts they regarded as very much inferior to themselves! And they, too, like Mr Griffith and the tenants, had been taught to look for the future reign of Queen Isabel as a thing of course. In that there would have been an implied contract – an understanding on their part that they had been consulted and had agreed to this destination of themselves. But Cousin Henry! Now this gross evil to themselves and to all around them had been remedied, and justice was done. They had all been strongly convinced that the Squire had made and had left behind him another will. The butler had been quite certain that this had been destroyed by Cousin Henry, and had sworn that he would not stand behind the chair of a felon. The gardener had been equally violent, and had declined even to cut a cabbage for Cousin Henry's use. The women in the house had only suspected. They had felt sure that something was wrong, but had doubted between various theories. But now everything was right; now the proper owner had come; now the great troubles had been vanquished, and Llanfeare would once again be a fitting home for them.

'Oh, Miss Isabel! oh, Miss Isabel!' said Mrs Griffith, absolutely sobbing at her young mistress's feet up in her bed-room; 'I did say that it could never go on like that. I did use to think that the Lord Almighty would never let it go on like that! It couldn't be that Mr Henry Jones was to remain always landlord of Llanfeare.'

When she came downstairs and took her seat, as she did by chance, in the old arm-chair which her uncle had been used to occupy, Mr Apjohn preached to her another sermon, or rather sang a loud pæan of irrepressible delight.

'Now, my dear, I must go and leave you – happily in your own house. You can hardly realise how great a joy this has been to me – how great a joy it is.'

'I know well how much we owe you.'

'From the first moment in which he intimated to me his wish to make a change in his will, I became so unhappy about it as almost to lose my rest. I knew that I went beyond what I ought to have done in the things that I said to him, and he bore it kindly.'

'He was always kind.'

'But I couldn't turn him. I told him what I told you to-day on the road, but it had no effect on him. Well, I had nothing to do but to obey his orders. This I did most grudgingly. It was a heartbreak to me, not only because of you, my dear, but for the sake of the property, and because I had heard something of your cousin. Then came the rumour of this last will. He must have set about it as soon as you had left the house.'

'He never told me that he was going to do it.'

'He never told any one; that is quite certain. But it shows how his mind must have been at work. Perhaps what I said may have had some effect at last. Then I heard from the Cantors what they had been asked to do. I need not tell you all that I felt then. It would have been better for him to send for me.'

'Oh, yes.'

'So much better for that poor young man's sake.' The poor young man was of course Cousin Henry. 'But I could not interfere. I could only hear what I did hear – and wait. Then the dear old man died!'

'I knew then that he had made it.'

'You knew that he had thought that he had done it; but how is one to be sure of the vacillating mind of an old dying man? When we searched for the one will and read the other, I was very sure that the Cantors had been called upon to witness his signature. Who could doubt as to that? But he who had so privately drawn out the deed might as privately destroy it. By degrees there grew upon me the conviction that he had not destroyed it; that it still existed – or that your cousin had destroyed it. The latter I never quite believed. He was not the man to do it – neither brave enough nor bad enough.'

'I think not bad enough.'

'Too small in his way altogether. And yet it was clear as the sun at noonday that he was troubled in his conscience. He shut himself up in his misery, not knowing how strong a tale his own unhappiness told against him. Why did he not rejoice in the glory of his position? Then I said to myself that he was conscious of insecurity.'

'His condition must have been pitiable.'

'Indeed, yes. I pitied him from the bottom of my heart. The contumely with which he was treated by all went to my heart even after I knew that he was misbehaving. I knew that he was misbehaving – but how? It could only be by hiding the will, or by being conscious that it was hidden. Though he was a knave, he was not cunning. He failed utterly before the slightest cunning on the part of others. When I asked him whether he knew where it was hidden, he told a weak lie, but told the truth openly by the look of his eyes. He was like a little girl who pauses and blushes and confesses all the truth before she half murmurs her naughty fib. Who can be really angry with the child who lies after that unwilling fashion? I had to be severe upon him till all was made clear; but I pitied him from the bottom of my heart.'

'You have been good to all of us.'

'At last it became clear to me that your uncle had put it somewhere himself. Then came a chance remembrance of the sermons he used to read, and by degrees the hiding-place was suggested to me. When at last he welcomed us to go and search in his uncle's bed-room, but forbade us to touch anything in the book-room – then I was convinced. I had but to look along the shelves till I found the set, and I almost knew that we had got the prize. Your father has told you how he flew at me when I attempted to lift my hand to the books. The agony of the last chance gave him a moment of courage. Then your father shook the document out from among the leaves.'

'That must have been a moment of triumph to you,'

'Yes – it was. I did feel a little proud of my success. And I am proud as I see you sitting there, and feel that justice has been done.'

'By your means!'

'That justice has been done, and that every one has his own again. I own to all the litigious pugnacity of a lawyer. I live by such fighting, and I like it. But a case in which I do not believe crushes me. To have an injustice to get the better of, and then to trample it well under foot – that is the triumph that I desire. It does not happen to a lawyer to have had such a chance as this, and I fancy that it could not have come in the way of a man who would have enjoyed it more than I do.' Then at last, after lingering about the house, he bade her farewell. 'God bless you, and make you happy here – you and your husband. If you will take my advice you will entail the property. You, no doubt, will have children, and will take care that in due course it shall go to the eldest boy. There can be no doubt as to the wisdom of that. But you see what terrible misery may be occasioned by not allowing those who are to come after you to know what it is they are to expect.'

For a few weeks Isabel remained alone at Llanfeare, during which all the tenants came to call upon her, as did many of the neighbouring gentry.

'I know'd it,' said young Cantor, clenching his fist almost in her face. 'I was that sure of it I couldn't hardly hold myself. To think of his leaving it in a book of sermons!'

Then, after the days were past during which it was thought well that she should remain at Llanfeare to give orders, and sign papers, and make herself by very contact with her own property its mistress and owner, her father came for her and took her back to Hereford. Then she had incumbent upon her the other duty of surrendering herself and all that she possessed to another. As any little interest which this tale may possess has come rather from the heroine's material interests than from her love – as it has not been, so to say, a love story – the reader need not follow the happy pair absolutely to the altar. But it may be said, in anticipation of the future, that in due time an eldest son was born, that Llanfeare was entailed upon him and his son, and that he was so christened as to have his somewhat grandiloquent name inscribed as William Apjohn Owen Indefer Jones.

THE END